THREE STALWARTS

Walter D. Edmonds
THREE STALWARTS

Drums Along the Mohawk
Rome Haul
Erie Water

[COMPLETE NOVELS]

BOSTON
LITTLE, BROWN AND COMPANY

DRUMS
ALONG
THE
MOHAWK

*To my son and daughter
and to the descendants
in their generation
of these men and women
of the Mohawk Valley*

AUTHOR'S NOTE

To those readers who may have felt some curiosity about the actual occurrences in the Mohawk Valley during the Revolution, I should like to say here that I have been as faithful to the scene and time and place as study and affection could help me to be. A novelist, if he chooses, has a greater opportunity for faithful presentation of a bygone time than an historian, for the historian is compelled to a presentation of cause and effect and feels, as a rule, that he must present them through the lives and characters of "famous" or "historical" figures. My concern, however, has been with life as it was; as you or I, our mothers or our wives, our brothers and husbands and uncles, might have experienced it. To do that I have attempted to be as accurate in the minutiæ of living as in the broader historical features. Food, crops, game, and weather played an important and ever-active part in the Mohawk Valley. As far as possible I have checked them through old journals, histories, and dispatches, so that, before I was well embarked in the writing of the book, I knew when snow was falling, and how deep it was; how high the river came, and when there was a rain. Naturally, for spaces of time, no data were available, and there I had to rely on my own knowledge of our climate. In those cases, however, the action usually concerned the purely imagined characters of the book.

How few these imagined people are may be another point of interest. Let me list them. Gilbert Martin, Lana Martin, Joe Boleo, Sarah Mc-Klennar, John Weaver, Mary Reall, Mrs. Demooth, Jurry McLonis, Nancy Schuyler, Gahota, Owigo, Sonojowauga, Mr. Collyer, and the paymaster. All other characters named played actual parts. As I learned more about them, it astonished me to see how a simple narration of their experiences carried the book along with only slight liberties with the truth. Even so, I found it necessary to alter the facts of very few of their lives. One case was that of John Wolff. He must have had Tory inclinations, but he was never arrested or tried. But the grafted episode in the novel is taken from the experience of a very similar man whose story may be encountered in the Clinton papers. Only the similar man, with far less evidence against him, was taken out and shot.

Of the other actual characters with the circumstances of whose lives I have tampered, I shall name George Weaver, Reall, Captain Demooth, Mrs. Reall, Adam Helmer, and Jacob Small. For one reason or another I altered the numbers of their families, or the characters of their relations. But in so far as they act for themselves in the pages of the novel, anyone with little pains may check their histories. Women and children, of course, are the bane of the student. Often they are listed without names given. "Dependants over 16, dependants under 16." When confronted by that wall, the novelist must see through as far as his conscience will permit.

The description of Newgate Prison at Simsbury Mines is strictly according to facts—most of them offered by the patriotic party, at that. It was, however, no worse than British prisons, and the prisoners, I suspect, had infinitely more to eat.

In the book, I have not set out to belittle the efforts of Congress and the Continental command so much as to show their almost light-hearted disregard of actual conditions. The maintenance at vast expense of Fort Stanwix is a case in point. I cannot but believe that the reactions of the valley people, who have been vilified for years, were justified by those conditions. Some of the letters which appear in the novel are proof sufficient.

All of these quoted documents may be read in the records, with one exception—Mr. Collyer's summary of his report to General Clinton of the seizure of the grain by the starving populace. But as the General used Mr. Collyer's argument in his own report on the matter, no doubt the inspector, whoever he was, used very similar words.

I owe several debts which I should like to acknowledge. First to two helpful booksellers: Mr. Lou D. MacWethy of St. Johnsville, and Mrs. James C. Howgate of Albany. To Mr. Howard Swiggett for his suggestive study, *War Out of Niagara.* To the older historians, Benton, Stone, Jones, and the inimitable Simms. And to that invaluable listing of the military rolls, *New York in the Revolution,* compiled under the direction of Comptroller James A. Roberts. A complete bibliography would be out of place in a novel, perhaps, but I must add the names of Morgan and Beauchamp, whose Indian studies first roused my interest in the Iroquois. There, I suspect, I shall find the kernel of many controversies. Finally, for those who would like to understand what valley life was really like before the actual hostilities commenced, when the fear of the Indians was first maturing, I suggest an hour spent with the *Minute Book of the Committee of Safety* of Tryon County, printed in 1905 by Dodd, Mead, and Company.

To those who may feel that here is a great to-do about a bygone life, I have one last word to say. It does not seem to me a bygone life at all. The parallel is too close to our own. Those people of the valley were confronted by a reckless Congress and ebullient finance, with their inevitable repercussions of poverty and practical starvation. The steps followed with automatic regularity. The applications for relief, the failure of relief, and then the final realization that a man must stand up to live. They had won at Oriskany, without help, the first decisive battle of a dismal conflict; Burgoyne was helpless once the Mohawk Valley had been made safe from the British possession. They suffered the paralysis of abject dependence on a central government totally unfitted to comprehend a local problem. And finally, though they had lost two thirds of their fighting strength, these people took hold of their courage and struck out for themselves. Outnumbered by trained troops, well equipped, these farmers won the final battle of the long war, preserved their homes, and laid the foundations of a great and strong community.

WALTER D. EDMONDS

One

THE MILITIA

1

GILBERT MARTIN AND WIFE, MAGDELANA (1776)

IT was the second day of their journey to their first home. Lana, in the cart, looked back to see how her husband was making out with the cow. He had bought it from the Domine for a wedding present to her. He had hesitated a long while between the cow and the clock; and she had been disappointed when he finally decided on the cow, even though it cost three dollars more; but now she admitted that it would be a fine thing to have a cow to milk. As he said, it would give her companionship when he was working in the woods.

Privately she had thought at the time that she would show him that she could manage their first house and help him with the fields also. She was a good strong girl, eighteen years old the day she married, and she thought that if they both worked hard, in a few years they would have money enough to pay thirteen dollars for a clock if they really wanted it. There were only two cows anyway at Deerfield Settlement, and she might make money with the extra butter.

The cow had given a good deal of trouble yesterday, leaving its own village, but this morning it seemed to be anxious to keep up with the cart. Lana supposed the land looked strange to the poor beast, and that now the cart and the small brown mare were the only things it felt at home with.

Gilbert smiled when she looked back, and raised the hand in which he carried the birch switch. He had taken off his jacket, for the weather was warm, and his shirt was open at the neck. She thought, "He's handsome," and waved back cheerfully. Anyway, the Reverend Mr. Gros made two clocks a year which he tried to sell to any couple he was marrying, and no doubt a year or two from now there would be one to pick out if they ever came back so far.

The Domine had wedded Magdelana Borst to Gilbert Martin in the Palatine Church at Fox's Mills two days ago. There had been just her family in the little stone structure, Mr. and Mrs. Gros, and a couple of Indians, half drunk, who had heard of the ceremony and happened over from Indian Castle in hopes of getting invited to the breakfast. Lana's father had given them a York shilling to get rid of them and they had gone down to Jones's tavern to buy rum, saying "Amen" very gravely in English.

It was a pleasant breakfast in the Dutch-like kitchen with its red and black beams. They had had glasses of the hard cider saved over from last fall, and sausage and cornbread, and then Gilbert had gone out to get the cart and cow and Mother had slipped tearfully upstairs and come down again with the air of a surprise and given Lana the Bible for a departing present.

It was a beautiful book, bound in calfskin, with a gilded clasp. She had taken it to the Domine for him to write in, and he had put her name very elegantly on the flyleaf, Magdelana Martin, and then very solemnly he had turned to the empty pages at the back and had written there:—

> July 10, 1776—married this day *Gilbert Martin,* of Deerfield Settlement, Tryon County, the State of New York, North America, to *Magdelana Borst,* of Fox's, Tryon County, by Reverend Daniel Gros.

They had all thought it was very impressive, seeing "the State of New York," and Mother had looked tearful again for a moment or two, because, as she said, there was no telling what kind of country it was now, with its name changed, and all the troubles of the war in Canada.

But that had passed over quickly. It had been too late then to bring up the old argument about the Indian menace, by which for a week they had tried to persuade Gilbert to settle on their own farm. His place seemed so far away—it would take two days to get to—it was more than thirty miles.

But Gilbert had been unshakable. He had paid for the land in Hazenclever's Patent beyond Cosby's Manor. He said that it was good land. He had worked there all fall and got his house up and cleared some ground already, and would have a crop of Indian corn, on part of it. It was something no one in his right senses could abandon. And he was capable of looking after Lana as well as any man.

She remembered how he and her father had talked together, and that talk had impressed her father. "He has paid for his land," he said, "and he has built his house alone so that he could buy himself a yoke of oxen, with the money saved."

"But, Henry," said her mother, "Lana knows nobody up there. It is so far away."

"Gilbert has friends and neighbors," he said. "I think Lana will get along all right," and he had smiled at her. "You can't keep all your daughters to yourself, you know, Mummschen. What would the poor young men do, if all the mothers in the world did that? Where would I have been, if your mother had done that to you? I ask you." He had even laughed about it, while Gilbert, for some reason, looked embarrassed, maybe because Lana's sisters were looking at him so admiringly. It seemed a wonderful thing to them for a girl to start off to a strange place with a man like Gilbert, whom she had seen not more than half a dozen times before in her life.

That first time she had seen him seemed long ago now, though it was still less than a year. Ten months and four days, to-day, Lana said to herself, shaking the reins over the mare's back. She and her sisters had been drying flax over the pit on the hillside. They had been playing at kentecoying, and perhaps they had become careless, for they had not noticed the young man coming along the road. And when they had at last seen him just below them, looking up at Lana and smiling, Lana had stepped back inadvertently onto the poles on which the flax was spread, and the poles had come loose from the hillside, throwing her and the flax at once into the pit of coals. The flax instantly burst into flame, but with the quickness of lightning, the sisters said, the young man had flung down his pack, run up the hill, and jumped down into the pit. Lana's heavy linsey petticoat had not caught fire; but by the time he had hoisted her out, her calico short gown was burning; and with great presence of mind he had lifted her petticoat over her head, wrapping the upper half of her body in it and so smothering the flames.

If he had not saved her daughter's life, Mrs. Borst told him half an hour later, he had certainly saved her from being badly scarred. She called it a noble action and asked him to stay the night. He had accepted. At supper he had told them that he was going west. He had no family, but he had enough money to buy some land with.

Little did Mrs. Borst or Lana herself guess how it would turn out. But when he left he caught her alone outside the door and whispered that he would return some day, if she were willing he should. Lana could not answer, beyond nodding; but that had seemed enough for him; and he went away with big strides while her father said behind her, "That's a fine young man."

Lana had dreamed about him during the winter. Often she thought he would not come back. But in the end of the winter, just when the sugaring was beginning, he had arrived one afternoon. He told them about his experiences in the westward. Up there they didn't hear much of the political doings of the lower valley. They knew that Guy Johnson and the Butlers had gone west, of course, and Mr. Weaver, Gil's neighbor, attended Committee meetings from time to time, which gave them some news. But Mr. Kirkland, the missionary, had made the Oneida Indians so friendly that one did not have the same feeling about the possibility of an Indian war. And besides, when people were clearing land they were too busy all day and too tired at night to think much about other things.

Gilbert himself had started clearing his first five acres. He had boarded during the winter with the Weavers, who had been very nice to him, paying for his food by helping George Weaver one day a week. He had got his cabin walls laid up and a good chimney in. The cabin was set right at the turn the road made for the Mohawk River ford. One could look from the door south across the marsh to the river itself, a fine prospect. Behind the house there was a natural spring.

Though he told the family about these things, Lana, in her heart, knew he was telling them to her alone. She was afraid, after supper, to go out, knowing that he would follow her. But nothing she could do could keep her from offering to step down to Jones's for her father's beer. And as she knew he would, the young man offered to go with her to carry the jug.

On the way down he had told her still more about the place. It sounded like the most wonderful place she had ever seen. He was going to buy a plough and also get a yoke of oxen this summer. There was some natural pasture along the river on his place. The loam was deep. He expected it was four feet deep in places. He had built the cabin with an extra high roof, which made the sleeping loft quite airy. He had never slept better in his life than he had slept in that loft. In March he had bought two window sashes from Wolff's store in Cosby's Manor, glass sashes, so that the kitchen seemed as light as a church. He wished Lana could see it.

Though Lana wished so herself, they had by that time come to Jones's, and she had had to go in after the beer. When she came out again, the young man had been quite silent. Even when she had asked him a shy question or two, he had hardly answered. It was only as they came in sight of the lighted windows of the Borst house that he asked her suddenly whether she would come and look at it as his wife.

"Yes," said Lana. Though she had expected the question all along, and though she knew what her answer was going to be, the word put her into a panic. "You'll have to ask Father," she added.

He had done so, much more calmly than he had asked her; and after their talk together, her father had also said "Yes." And then Gilbert had arranged to come back for her when his first rush of spring work was ended, so long as he should not be called out on militia duty.

Now they were on the Kingsroad. It ran from the ford at Schenectady the length of the Mohawk Valley; passing the Johnson land, Guy Park and Fort Johnson, Caughnawaga, Spraker's, Fox's, Nellis's, Klock's, and on to the carrying place at the falls. Then past the Eldridge Settlement, which was on the north side of the river opposite German Flats, and so to the settlement at the West Canada Creek crossing. From that settlement it continued into the woods through Schuyler, to Cosby's Manor, and then to Deerfield, where it crossed the river. West of there it was a barely passable track into the Indian camp at Oriska on Oriskany Creek. It ended at Fort Stanwix, which some people were saying would be repaired this summer by the Continental government.

From her high perch on the cart, Lana had looked out over the Mohawk all day. Last evening they had climbed the steep ascent beside the falls. A little before that, Gilbert had come alongside the cart to point out to her the fine red brick house of Colonel Herkimer with its gambrel roof, higher than any roof she had ever seen. But once past the falls they had burrowed into a stretch of woods, and for a way the land seemed wild. There was only one house, a small one, glimpsed through an opening in the trees. Then, almost at dark, they had emerged on the broad intervale lands that marked the beginning of German Flats. A little tavern stood beside the road, and they put up in it.

Lana thought of their arrival with swelling pride. The landlord, a Mr. Billy Rose, was smoking an after-supper pipe in the door. He was in his shirt, with a leather apron, and had bidden her "Good evening," quite politely.

Gil came up, harrying the cow. He walked directly to the innkeeper and asked for a night's lodging. "Two shilling for you and the missis," said the innkeeper, "and one for the mare. You can turn the cow in by the apple tree."

"We'll want a room to ourselves then," said Gil.

"You can have the top room," said Mr. Rose. "I can't guarantee not to have to stick in someone else, though."

Gil never so much as batted his eye. He held his purse open in one hand and put his fingers in. "Would two fips be worth a guarantee, Mr. Rose?"

"Seeing it's the top room," said Mr. Rose, "I'll guarantee it." He took the two fips and slipped them into a pocket under his apron; and after that he became most obliging, addressing Lana continually as "Mrs. Martin" and calling Gil "Mister," and once even "Esquire."

Lana fixed her hair in the back shed with Mrs. Rose's glass, shook the dust from her dress with a whisk of twigs, and came back to Gil. They had supper at a table for themselves in the tap, as quietly as any well-wedded couple in the world. There was only one other man there and he hardly noticed them. He was a one-eyed man, a stranger, Mr. Rose said, on his way up from Albany.

They had had some blood sausage with pig greens, sauerkraut, and smoked trout, and Gil had insisted on her taking a small glass of gin with him. "Seeing it's to-night," he managed to whisper. "Just especial." The whole affair seemed to Lana ruinously expensive, but after the drink she found herself flooded with a feeling of utter irresponsibility. She even enjoyed it when a small stout man named Captain Small, with a couple of friends, dropped down from Eldridge's and started talking in loud voices about Sir John Johnson's having broken his parole and taken off the Highlanders to Canada. One side said that that was a good thing, getting the Scotch out of the valley; and the other said that it meant there would be nothing to hold back the Tories. But Mr. Rose reminded them that it had happened two months ago, nearly to the day, and there had been no change in the war.

Lana felt herself very mature to be sitting in a taproom listening to men, and she tried to understand what they were saying about the army's being driven back out of Canada. Small said, "Georgie Helmer come back last month. He was with Montgomery's regiment. He said it all went fine till the last day of last year when they didn't take Quee-bec. Then he said everything went to pieces. Arnold got hurt and since then the smallpox has got into the army. He had it. He said he bought an inoculation off a Dr. Barker for fifteen cents cash money. And he was the first man in his company to get it. Everybody that bought inoculations off Barker got the disease. They thought it was because his hands was dirty and he didn't clean his nail, which he scratched them with. Then they found out he'd been all through the army and everybody he touched got it. Ain't that an awful way to fight, though?"

Everybody nodded. Lana watched the shadow of Mr. Rose's queue nodding up and down along the neck of a bottle. When she looked at him, he was still nodding, and the eelskin his hair was clubbed in glistened a greenish gray.

"The trouble is," he said, "there ain't anybody up there worth two cents except Arnold, and Captain Brown."

"Brown says Arnold is no better than the rest."

"John Brown's a good man."

They argued. The one-eyed man in the corner, who hadn't said anything, now raised his voice. He had a pursy mouth and spoke softly.

"The trouble with the American army is your Continental Congress," he said.

"What do you mean?" It was Gil who asked, and the truculence in his voice thrilled Lana. All the others were looking from him to the stranger.

But the stranger said calmly, "I mean what I said. It's no better than a cesspool. What good there is in it is hid by the scum that keeps getting on top."

Captain Small said, "I guess you mean Adams and that Yankee bunch."

The one-eyed man nodded, looking at Gil. The patch over his eye gave his face an oddly sinister expression.

"They're a bunch of failures and they talk loud to keep themselves in power. I wouldn't put the dependence in them I'd put in a bedbug. They all bite when you're asleep. Why, if I lived up here, I wouldn't take chances playing with them."

"Wouldn't you?" said Gil. "Why not?"

"Because they only play politics with the army. How many regulars do they send up here? None. Why not? Because you don't count to them for votes. You can't bring pressure on them. And I hear there's seven hundred British troops moving up to Oswego this fall. But that won't bother them, safe in Philadelphia. Why, anybody could see this war would have to be won up north."

"Say, what's your business up here?"

"My business is to see what's going on," the man said equably, "and my name's Caldwell." He got up from his corner and moved towards Billy Rose. "How about my tally?" he asked.

Nobody said anything as he paid across the plank bar. But when he stopped in the door to ask how far it was to Shoemaker's, they told him it was eight miles.

"He's a queer-acting cuss," observed Small.

Rose said, "There's a lot of queer people in the valley, now. Did he mean the Indians was coming down?"

"I think," said Gil, "that there's a lot of foolish talk about this Indian business. Just because it happened in the French war, don't mean it will now."

"Listen, young man," said Captain Small. "How would you feel if you'd been drove out of your land and house? If you was a mean man naturally?"

"You mean the Butlers and Johnsons?"

"Them," said Small. "Them and all their bunch."

"But that don't mean they'll bring the Indians."

"Listen, Mr. Martin. The Mohawks went west with them. They've got to feed them, hain't they? They plain can't do that in Niagara. Ten to one they get them foraging down here."

"Well," said Gil, "I guess we can look after them all right."

"I guess we'll have to, young man."

Gil rose and, feeling his hand on her arm, Lana rose with him. As she saw the others watching her, she went suddenly pink. She felt she was blushing all over while they said good-night. Mr. Rose picked up his Betty lamp and took them to the stairs.

"Have a good sleep," he said.

"Good night," they said.

Gil went first. When Lana climbed through the trapdoor into the small stuffy room with its cord bed in the middle, like a fortress in a little clearing, he was facing her.

"You didn't get scared with what they said?" he asked anxiously. "You hear that kind of talk all over the place."

She was still faintly tingling from the unaccustomed drink. And she looked at him, so straight and tall, with his good features and his blue eyes, and lean broad shoulders, remembering the way he had picked her out of the flax kiln. She felt proud and reckless and gay.

"Not of Indians," she said.

Then her eyes dropped and she couldn't look at him again as they undressed.

It was odd that in the morning she felt fidgety under Mr. Rose's eyes as they prepared to leave the inn. Mr. Rose brought a small book of blank paper and a pen. He said apologetically, "The way George Herkimer's rangers check up on a man he has to keep record of whoever stays in his place. Would you just sign your name, Mr. Martin?"

Gil complied. He took the pen and filled in beside the date, "Gilbert Martin and wife, Magdelana."

Watching round his arm, Lana thought it marked the beginning of a life. She wondered whether she had pleased him, and now she was thinking, whatever came, it would be her duty to please him, and she swore a small oath to herself that she would always be a good wife to him.

The mare went slowly and the cow kept up to the cart without trouble. They passed through the German Flats where the new fort was being built. It was called Dayton, after the colonel in charge. Peeled logs were being skidded down from the spruce-covered hills behind the village; and soldiers, militia, and hired farmers were working together at setting the stockade.

Gil must have seen her watching it as they went past, for shortly after they had left the settlement behind, he came up beside the cart. He had been silent all morning, and now as she looked down into his face he seemed to her to be troubled.

"How are you?" he said, fetching a grin.

She smiled back timidly, wanting to ask him what was worrying him. "Just fine."

He said, "It isn't so far now. It's not above fifteen miles." He looked at her again. "We ought to get there before dark, Lana."

"That will be nice," she said.

She looked so pretty and young to him, high up on the cart, with her feet in their cloth shoes demurely side by side. Her face was shaded by a calico bonnet to match her short gown. Her hair curved away under the wide brim; it was almost black. When she met his look, she flushed a little, and her brown eyes grew solemn. He thought of her gay light-heartedness, and he looked ahead to where the road entered the woods towards the Schuyler settlement. But instead of saying what was on his mind, he described the place to her.

"They've got nice bottom land. And they've built big framed houses. You'll like it, Lana, I think."

She said, "The country's nice."

They lunched before they came to Schuyler, by a little stream in a patch of hemlocks, eating bread and cheese side by side on the carpet of short brown needles and tossing crumbs to the chipmunks. It was cool there, for the trees held the sunlight far above them. In front of them the mare drowsed in the shafts and the cow found a cud to chew.

Looking at the cart, Lana imagined placing her things in the cabin before dark.

"Will we set the bed up downstairs," she said, "or put it in the loft?" He looked at her. "I've heard Mother say that in the cabins when she first came to Klock's they sometimes had the bed set up in the kitchen."

If he was worrying about her, she would show him that she was prepared.

"You're not scared coming west so far with me, like this?"

She shook her head.

"It'll be different from living in a house." He poked the needles with a stick. "It seemed so fine to me, because I built it, that I didn't think it might look different to a girl who was raised in a big house like yours."

He was trying to prepare her.

"Mother started the same way," she said. "In a few years we'll have all those things. But beginning this way, Gil, we'll like them better when we get them." She glanced sidewise. "I've always thought it would be nice living in a cabin. It'll be handy to look after if it's small."

He said, "It ain't much cleared."

"We won't have to buy much now," she added. "Mother was awfully good to me."

He touched her hand.

Quite unexpectedly they came out on Schuyler. The open land, well cleared and cultivated, with men mowing hay along the river, and broad-framed houses, was like a release after the woods. Lana knew, as she looked about her, that their place was only a few miles farther on. It would not seem so far out of the world, now that she had seen these healthy farms.

Some people came to the fences to watch them by. They greeted Gil by name and looked curiously towards Lana. They asked for news, and when Gil said he hadn't heard any worth telling, they smiled and said, "You've brought along quite a piece of news of your own, though."

They were half an hour traversing Schuyler. Then once more the woods closed in on the road and river, great elms, and willows and hemlock along the brooks. Now and then through swampy pieces the cart lurched and tottered over corduroy, and the mare had to set her feet carefully.

When they reached Cosby's Manor, it seemed to Lana a queer lost place. There was a fine house by the river, and a store built of logs, and a tenant's house. But all had a forgotten aspect.

A woman came to the door of the store, shading her eyes with her hand. She did not seem like a live and healthy person. She seemed like someone in a trance. And she did not call to them, but met Lana's shy nod with a dull stare.

Gil came hurrying up beside the cart.

"Never mind her, Lana. She's queer. They're Johnson people here, and they haven't got friends."

"Who is she?"

"It's Wolff's wife. I get along with Wolff all right, but people here don't speak to them much. I guess she gets lonely."

He lifted his voice to call good-day to her.

"Hello," she said, flatly, and turned as if to reënter the store.

"You all alone, Mrs. Wolff?" Gil asked.

"John's round somewhere," she replied over her shoulder. "You want him?"

"No. I only thought the place looked lonely."

"Thompsons left last Thursday," she said.

"Left?"

"Yeah. They went for Oswego. They say the Congress is going to fix the fort at Stanwix, and that means trouble. I wanted John to go, but he said he couldn't afford to. You can't leave if you ain't got cash money to live on up there, he says." She tilted her head to the northwest, stared at them, and then went into the store.

Gil and Lana looked after her. Then he turned to the house. "They've boarded the windows," he said. That explained the blankness. "I guess they've taken their cattle, too."

In spite of herself, Lana shivered.

"Do just she and Mr. Wolff live here?"

"I guess so. He's got a daughter married to Dr. Petry. But Doc's a Committee member, and I guess he don't let her come up here any more."

"It's a terrible thing," whispered Lana.

Gil glanced quickly at her.

"It don't have to bother us," he said. "We're all the right party."

Lana did not answer. They were in the woods again now, and the road had become both narrower and rougher. Their pace was reduced to a mere crawl under the hazy slanting bars of sunlight, yet for the first time every step the mare took seemed to Lana to be drawing her an irrecoverable distance from her home. She told herself, "But we're going home." But it didn't mean the same thing any more.

The light through the leaves softened, became more golden. Off on a hill to the right a cock grouse began drumming, starting with slow beats, and gradually gathering pace.

A great mess of flies collected round the mare's head, like sparks in the sunlight, deer flies, and horseflies an inch long, that drew blood when they bit. The mare kept shaking herself. She stopped to bite at them, and kicked and snorted, and then went on with a sullen resignation. Lana could have cried. She looked back at Gil and saw that he was switching the cow with a branch of maple; and the cow had moved up close behind the wagon.

"Are they always like this, Gil?" Lana asked.

"There's always flies in the real woods," he said shortly. "It must be going to rain, though, the way they take hold."

He had a lump on his forehead, with a red trickle issuing from it. She said, "They never are so thick at home."

"You'll have to get used to it then. Here, take this and slap them off her."

He gave her the branch and stopped to cut himself another. Lana kept switching the mare, and after a moment she was glad of the occupation. There had been no driving for her to do for some time, for the mare had to have her head in getting over the rough spots. Lana became so absorbed in batting off the flies that she did not notice the small side road turning off to the left, or the clearing through a narrow fringe of trees. It was only when Gil said, in a pleasanter voice, "That was Demooth's place," that she realized she had missed something.

"Where?"

"We've passed it. But Weaver's is just ahead."

She raised her eyes to see the leaves thinning at last. The sun was just ahead, nearing the horizon, and putting fiery edges on some overtaking slate-gray clouds.

While she watched, the clouds overlapped the sun, and at the same moment a fresh east wind struck the road, dispersing the flies, and they emerged into the clearing with the rain.

Lana saw Weaver's, dimly, through the slanting spear-like fall of rain. A square cabin, with a small wing added on, in which the logs were unweathered, a roof of bark, and a chimney sending up smoke. It stood in the midst of the clearing, surrounded on three sides by Indian corn through which the stumps, blackened by their burning, still showed. In front of the house, like a showpiece, was a three-acre patch of wheat in well-worked ground. A track ran through it toward a low log barn, and just in front of the cabin door two hollyhock plants, one red, one yellow, stood together with a small border of pinks.

Nowhere was there any sign of people. But on the edge of the woods a new road ran off, making a Y, which Gil told her led to Reall's on the creek.

"We're straight ahead," he said.

The Kingsroad burrowed into the woods again, but they ended shortly, and Lana looked out over a long swamp of alder. Half a mile to the left lay the river, sluggish and dark. Beyond, behind a fringe of old willow trees, the ground rose again. Suddenly the road turned left down to the alders, going straight through to the ford.

The mare stopped there, and Gil came alongside with the cow. His face was streaming wet, but he smiled at her.

"Well," he said, "we're here at last."

"Where?" asked Lana, dully.

"Home."

He looked at her.

"Giddap," he said roughly to the mare.

She turned off the road onto a winding pair of wheel tracks. Then Lana saw.

A small new cabin standing on the higher ground. Beyond, a muddy brook flowed widely through some scattered alders. On the far side the land widened out in swamp grass for perhaps two acres. She saw, almost without seeing these things.

Her heart was in her throat. "You mustn't cry," she said to herself, over and over, "you mustn't start crying."

It seemed to her so utterly forlorn. Behind the cabin were the marks of Gil's first struggle with the land: the stumps, half burnt, surrounded by corn of all heights, the most uneven patch she ever saw. All round the cabin the earth was bared to the rain and fast turning into mud. Beyond was a low shed to shelter the horse and cow.

Then Gil cried out, "Look, there's smoke!"

She saw it feebly beginning to rise from the chimney. Somehow it made the rain seem drearier than ever. She wanted to say, "Oh, let's go home." But then, in a saving moment, she took hold of herself. For better or worse she had married him, she was out of reach of home; it would have to be her business to change the looks of the place.

They came up to the door, the cart creaking in the rain. The door opened. A raw-boned gray-haired woman, in a faded, dirty calico dress that had been blue once upon a time, was holding a basket with two pinks in it. She looked completely taken aback.

"Why, Gil," she said. "You surely did surprise me. I was figuring to get the place ready for you. I'd only lit the fire and was going to set these pinks out by the door."

Gil held out his hands to help Lana down.

"You go inside," he said. "I'll unload. This is Mrs. Weaver, Lana."

The woman opened her arms and clasped Lana, without letting go the pinks.

"My God," she said. "I'm surely glad to see you. I've heard enough about you, Lord He knows it. But you're even prettier than Gil let on!"

2

DEERFIELD (1776)

1. The Peacock's Feather

A SMALL haystack stood beside the shed. That was one of the great advantages of the Martins' place—the fact that part of it was already open land and covered with swamp grass. Most people, opening new land, had to let their cattle browse for what they could find in winter, having barely enough corn leaves to subsist their horses on. "We could keep two teams on the natural grass in that old beaver fly," Gil said more than once, "if we could afford to buy that many horses." They had harvested the hay together, Gil mowing and Lana raking, and both pitching it onto the cart through a week of dry breezy weather. Her father had taught her a little about thatching and she had put in two days' work on the stack. Though it looked to her a bungling kind of job compared to the work her father did, Gil swore that there was no better-looking stack between Schenectady and the Indian country.

But everything she did seemed to please him. The way she had fixed the cabin over, arranged their scanty furniture to make the place look, he said, as if they'd lived in it for years. The way she sanded the floor every morning; and the little cotton curtains she made for the two windows, stringing them on cord. It had been exciting, after that first gloomy day of their arrival, to unpack the two trunks and the boxes from the cart. Gil had had no idea of all the things in them. "You brought a complete outfit," he said. She felt a little shy, replying, "I told Mother there wasn't any sense in me bringing a lot of clothes, and such things. I told her I'd rather have the money spent in house things."

The cabin lost its dreariness when they had the dresser set up against the wall beside the fireplace, with its dishes laid out on the shelves. It was one her father had made of pine in his young married days, with scalloped mouldings, but it had been put by upstairs years before when he brought home the maple cupboard he bought in Caughnawaga. It had seemed like an old and clumsy piece. When Lana asked for it, her mother had been glad to let it go. But now, in its new place, the dresser looked impressively handsome. It gave Lana a comforting feeling to see it there, and to think that her father and mother must have admired it together in their first house.

On its shelves she placed her brown earthenware plates, the baking dish, and the six glasses from Albany. On the top shelf out of harm's way she put the Bible and the white china teapot that had been her Grandmother Lana's, and the peacock's feather that her mother had given her out of the cluster of six, so that she should have a reminder of home always in sight. War on sea or land could not affect its fantastical colors.

When Mrs. Weaver saw it first, she held up both her hands and marveled stridently.

"It's like the feather off an angel's wing. You say it come from an actual bird?"

"Oh, yes," said Lana.

"What might such a bird be called?"

"A peacock, Mrs. Weaver."

"Think of that!" exclaimed Mrs. Weaver. "I wonder what he looks like."

"I couldn't say."

"Would they be wing feathers, do you suppose?"

"My mother had an uncle who went to sea," said Lana modestly. "He said it was off the peacock's tail. Mother inherited them. She has five at home."

"You certainly know a lot," Mrs. Weaver said admiringly.

Mrs. Weaver made Lana feel very proud. She examined all the other fixings of the cabin with a new respect; she went upstairs into the loft and sat upon the bed, bouncing a little.

"That's a dandy bed," she said.

"Mother made it for me. It's all genuine white goose."

"God! Imagine! I ain't seen a genuine white goose since I come up here. Your Ma must have been a knowing person, Mrs. Martin."

She tried the spinning wheel, saying it ran nice but felt a little light for a woman like herself. "I'll bet, though, that a dancey body like yourself would get a first-rate tone out of it."

But what inevitably attracted her was the peacock's feather. She stopped again before it, holding her hands before her petticoat, tight down against her legs. Her curving nose looked rigid with the wonder of it. Her kindly mouth was hushed. Her gray eyes shone. Beside her Lana looked small and young and frail.

"My," said Mrs. Weaver. "I'll have to tell George about it right away."

As a result, George Weaver came at noon, a bulky, square-faced man, with solid wrists and a deliberate way of talking. He stood before the feather, breathing loudly through his nose, for quite a while, before he turned to Lana and Gil.

"A man could hardly paint a thing like that," he said, pointing to the heart-shape in the eye. He shook his head. "No, sir, not hardly. You've married yourself quite a girl, Gil."

His slow, good-humored eyes fixed themselves on Lana with respect. "Would you mind showing that thing to John and Cobus sometime, ma'am?"

"Why, I'd be glad," said Lana.

"I'll send them over sometime, then," he said.

"You ought to tell Demooth," Mrs. Weaver said. "I'd like to have his Missis look at that. Maybe she won't feel so fine and mighty."

"Now Emmy," said her husband in his slow fashion. "She ain't so bad. It's just the way she talks."

Mrs. Weaver snorted.

"Anyways," she said, "if you stand there admiring all day you won't get any dinner to eat."

They went outside, Gil and Lana following them to the door.

"You come over anytime you're mind to," Mrs. Weaver said to Lana.

"Thank you, Mrs. Weaver. I'm pretty busy right now, but I'd like to later on."

"Everybody's busy settling a new house," Mrs. Weaver nodded.

The two Martins watched their neighbors move off down the cart track: the faded calico hanging limp down the woman's straight, vigorous back; the man's woolen shirt drawn tight over his round shoulders.

"They're nice people, Gil," said Lana.

He agreed.

"They're plain," he said, "but they're good neighbors."

Word of the peacock's feather got round Deerfield in a day. First John and Cobus Weaver came to see it. Gil was finishing his last hoeing of the corn and Lana was boiling clothes in the iron kettle at the outdoor fireplace. They stared at her curiously, rather as if they expected to see the feather sprouting on her.

John, fourteen years old, was spokesman for the pair.

"Are you Mrs. Martin?" he asked.

Lana nodded cheerfully. Their freckled faces were very sober. They examined her from head to toe. Cobus, who gave promise of his father's beamy build, rubbed the calves of his scratched, bitten legs together; but John stood upright on both feet, his hands behind his back, his shirt and trousers parting company to show his belly button, and stared frankly.

"Pa said you had a feather you'd be willing to show us."

"Yes, if you want to see it. Come inside."

She wrung the water from her hands and led them in. They did not say a word, but stood side by side, and stared, but when they left they thanked her with gravity and marched solemnly down the cart track to the woods. Just as they reached the brush she heard them yell, and looking up she saw them running home with all their might.

The Realls came over in a mass: Mrs. Reall, a talkative woman, dressed in a French red short gown, though her face was almost colorless and her hair light faded brown; and Mr. Reall, a sly-looking meaching man, if ever Lana had seen one, carrying the youngest child in his arms. The other seven trailed behind in a gradation of age and size to the three-year-old, who was barely able to keep up. They had a rascally look about them, and they swarmed all over the cabin, chattering back and forth as if the Martins had never been.

The children wished to take the feather down, but Gil was good-humoredly firm about that. "They might break it," he said, "even without meaning to."

"That's the truth," Mrs. Reall said tolerantly to Lana. "There ain't a thing they won't break or destroy some way, if they get a-hold of it. You know the way children act."

The youngest child, on Christian Reall's lap, began to bawl, and she snatched it from him, opened up her blouse, and started nursing it. Throughout the rest of the visit, the child continued nursing, puffing and sucking away, even when Mrs. Reall went upstairs to examine the bed.

"My, my," she said, surreptitiously lifting the coverlet to feel the blankets, "you surely have nice things. I used to myself, before I got to bearing children." She shifted the baby to the other breast and led the way downstairs. "You and Gilly will have to come on over to our place next Sunday," she invited. "Most generally Kitty reads us Bible Sundays. Weavers come, and sometimes Mark Demooth. Missis come once, but the children seemed to bother her. She ain't been in two years." She whispered significantly, "Kitty, he's a great reader. Reads as loud as any parson. You'd be surprised, the meaching kind of a man he looks."

They went away like a tailing swarm of bees, or like a bunch of rabbits, as Gil said. "Reall's religious," he said to Lana. "But they're just like rabbits, all of them, the way they breed, and run around."

"Nobody seems to like Mrs. Demooth," Lana said. "What's she like?"

"She's all right, I guess," said Gil. "But he married her somewhere down near Schenectady. Her folks had money. I guess she don't like it up here much. And Mark being a captain in the militia, she likes to tend her place."

Mrs. Demooth did not arrive for several days. When she did come for her call,—she emphasized the fact that she was calling,—Lana had been helping Gil clear brush.

Mrs. Demooth made her feel conscious of her heat and soiledness. The woman carried a parasol against the sun, a faded thing, ridiculous to see in the woods, and she wore a white cap on her hair. She bent her head when Lana invited her in from the heat and perched herself on their one chair, beside the hearth, while Lana sat on a low stool across from her.

"It's real nice of you to come and see me," Lana said, anxious to be polite.

"Don't say so," said Mrs. Demooth. She dabbed her face with a small handkerchief. "I meant to come much sooner. I would surely have come. But you know how it is. I have to watch that hired girl of mine during wash days. I declare sometimes I think it's more work having hired help than doing the work yourself."

Lana, who was tired and hot, and cross with herself, felt like saying, "Oh, indeed, Mrs. Demooth." But she nodded instead.

"That's a real nice teapot, isn't it?" said Mrs. Demooth. "What is it, Wedgwood?"

"I don't know," said Lana. "It's white chinaware, I think."

And it was Mrs. Demooth who said, "Oh, indeed." Her voice made Lana bristle; she flushed all the way to her eyes and bit her lip.

Mrs. Demooth was looking round her.

"You've got one of those feathers, I see," she said, pointing at the peacock's feather with her parasol. "We used to have a bunch of them at home, but it was terrible the way they collected the dust."

Lana only stared at her, and after a moment more Mrs. Demooth rose.

"You're tired," she said kindly. "Do you like it up here, Mrs. Martin?"

"Yes; why?"

"I suppose one's bound to when one's just married. But it was dreary for me, coming here. These cabins. We've lined ours with boards, anyway. That helps. But one gets so tired of the woods; first they're so still you hear yourself breathing; then at night there's all the noise—the frogs, the bugs. It's terrible." Her voice broke for an instant, and her thin and sullen face puckered so childishly that for an instant Lana could feel sorry for her. "And now there's this awful war. My folks were King's people. I don't understand what everything's about. And now Mark's a downright Whig, on the Committee, captain of the militia. He ought to know, I suppose. But I feel so terrible when he's away. He says there's chance of the army coming down against us from the west. He talks about our moving down to Herkimer. Of course Mr. Butler wouldn't do anything to me, but the Indians—you can't ever tell about what they'll do. Every time Mark goes to a meeting, I'm left alone. . . ."

Her voice trailed off.

"Yes," said Lana, finally. "It must be lonesome. But I guess there's nothing a woman can do about it." She tried to shift the woman's thoughts. "Nobody's got a right to be taxed," she said, "without their say-so."

"Probably not," said Mrs. Demooth. "I don't know, I'm sure. It don't seem right—the price of tea, I mean."

She halted in the door.

"I'm sure," she said over her shoulder, "that some real tea would be a tonic to you. You must come and visit with me and have some. You must really, Mrs. Martin. It's such a pleasure to me to have found one woman up here I can talk to."

"Thank you," said Lana in a muffled voice.

"And, my dear girl," continued Mrs. Demooth. "You shouldn't work so hard in the fields. That's a man's job. They bring us here and shut us up here. And I say they ought to do their own work. You're overtired. Overwrought. Remember. Come and see me."

She went out.

When Gil came in to see why Lana had not returned, he found her hunched upon her knees and sobbing.

"What's the matter?" he asked irresolutely from the door. "Did she turn nasty on you?"

Lana looked up at him with wet eyes.

"She said I hadn't ought to work with you. She said I got too tired."

"Maybe she's right," he said doubtfully. "If you wasn't tired you wouldn't be crying now." He looked defensive. "I said you hadn't ought to come out with me to-day. Brushing's the hardest work there is."

"I don't care," said Lana. "I'm strong. I want to work. I want to be out with you. It's all there is to do." She looked round her contemptuously. "This place," she said scornfully, "why, a little girl could mind it in half a morning." Her eyes traveled over Gil's uneasy face and fell upon the feather. "Oh, Gil. She said it was an awful thing for collecting dust!"

In a vague way, Gil understood. He clumsily put his arm over her shoulders and kissed her.

"Gil!" she said. "I could have *bitten* her. I like it here. I love being here with you. I'm not afraid when I've got work to do."

"Why," he said, "what's there to be afraid of anyway? I'm looking out for you, ain't I?"

"I don't know, Gil. Not Indians. I don't know."

Their eyes met, and they smiled.

"I guess I am just mad, Gil. I thought it was so fine in here till she came in." She wiped her nose. "I can't imagine. I ain't been homesick hardly at all. I been busy trying to be useful."

"You've helped fine. I guess it was that woman. No doubt Mark's told her muster day will be next week."

He stared through the window at the green, shadowed edge of the woods.

"Muster day?" asked Lana.

"Yes. The four of us has to go down and drill with our company at Schuyler. I never thought of it before."

"You have to go?"

"Yes," he said. "The fine's five shilling if you don't turn up. I can't afford to pay that. I guess I'll go down and see the captain to-morrow about it."

2. Captain Demooth

Next morning Gilbert Martin walked down to see Demooth. Though they had no children, the Demooths lived in a double cabin. It was big enough to have the air of a house, perhaps because they had let in so many glass sashes, even in the gable ends of the loft. Inside, also, it was boarded with pine. A kitchen on the ground floor, and a sitting room, where the captain had his desk of mahogany wood; a hall between that joined the two halves of the cabin—it seemed like a manor in the woods.

A small separate cabin housed his farm hand, Clem Coppernol, a cantankerous elderly man, who lived by himself.

"Where's Demooth?" asked Gil, meeting Coppernol in the cornfield. Coppernol raised up from feeling of a squash and pointed his thumb. "Writing letters in the office," he said.

Gil went to the house.

Mrs. Demooth had not yet appeared, and Nancy, the hired girl, with a long braid down her back and big stupid blue eyes, was clearing the breakfast dishes.

"Morning, Mr. Martin," she said, rolling her eyes towards Gil, and then immediately rolling them away. "You want *him?* He's inside."

Gil thanked her and crossed the big kitchen with its bricked-in hearth, went down the short hall that connected the two halves of the house, where he saw with envy Demooth's rifle and shotgun hung on deerhorns, each with its powder flask and shot pouch, and tapped on the door of the sitting room.

"Come in."

Gil opened the door.

Captain Demooth was a small, slight-built man, in his middle thirties, with dark hair and eyes. He was sitting before the mahogany desk that was one of the marvels of Deerfield. It had taken three men to get it into the cabin.

"Hello, Gil," he said. "What can I do for you?"

Gil prevaricated.

"I came down to make sure when muster day was."

"It's Wednesday. You knew that."

"Yes, I did," said Gil.

"What's on your mind?"

Gil looked down at the floor.

"I never stopped to think of it before, Mr. Demooth. But do you think we ought all of us to go?"

Captain Demooth smiled.

"It makes a difference being married, eh?" He leaned back in his chair and stretched out his legs. He wore lightweight, fitted boots. He had small feet and hands, about which his wife often made satisfied remarks, and in which he himself seemed to find his own satisfaction. Gil looked at him again and thought that he must be going down valley, for he had on a blue coat and a lace stock over his linen shirt.

"Yes," said Gil. "I guess it does."

"Your wife's nervous?"

"She don't say so."

Captain Demooth sighed.

"I hope she's got more nerve than Sara. By the way, Sara told me she'd called on Mrs. Martin. Says she's a mighty nice-appearing girl. Congratulations."

"Thanks," said Gil, wondering if that was what he ought to say and trying not to flush. Then it occurred to him to wonder if that was what Mrs. Demooth had actually said.

Captain Demooth smiled a little, watching him. "Yes, Gil. I think we ought to go. We've got to do our part. With Wolff in between us and Schuyler, it don't hurt to have him see us going down in arms to muster. And it don't hurt some people between Schuyler and Herkimer to see our muster day."

"Who would that be, sir?"

Captain Demooth glanced at him sharply.

"Who is there, do you suppose?"

"Why, there's Shoemaker's tavern." Gil paused. "But I thought he was on the Committee."

"Yes, he is. There are a lot of people on the Committee. But some of them used to be King's men a couple of years ago. Shoemaker was King's justice. He was a Butler man, too. That's more to the point. When it comes to war, if it does, it won't be King and Congress up here, Gil, as much as us against the Butlers and Johnsons. They don't give a damn about Congress, and I don't know that I do about the King. But they do hate our people as having settled on the best land in the Mohawk Valley. That's what makes them mad." He tapped the table with his finger. "Sit down, Gil."

Gil sat down.

He said, "Yes, sir. I guess that's so. But ain't it all the more reason for leaving somebody to look out after the women?"

"It might be." Captain Demooth thoughtfully stared between the white curtains at the surrounding woods. "But what good could you do if we left you? One man. Look at that."

"Yes, sir." He looked down at his fists. "What right have we got to leave them here?"

"None. If you look at it that way. I know we don't do much at muster day. But we have a good time, that's something."

"Well, I've got to go. I can't afford to pay a fine, Mr. Demooth. But I don't see what right anybody has to make me pay it if I don't want to. Ain't that what we're fighting a war about? About paying up without our say-so?"

"Officially. Up here, Gil, we're going to fight, if we have to fight, to save our necks."

"Then why don't we stay home and look after ourselves?" He felt belligerent; he thought that Captain Demooth was baiting him in some way he could not understand. "I don't care who's running things so long as I'm let alone. I've got to clear my land. I've got a wife to support. And I don't want to leave her where a parcel of Indians can come in and bother her without anybody to stop them."

Captain Demooth looked at him gravely.

"Listen, Gil. Do you think I'd leave my wife here if I thought anything was going to happen?"

"No, sir. I don't suppose so." He met the captain's eye. "But how do you know?"

"It's my business to. I'll tell you. Everybody knows there's queer people going up and down the valley. Running news. In this kind of war there's bound to be some people making money every way they can. Some of those people run news for both sides. They have stations like Shoemaker's. You can believe them if you want to. A lot of them draw pay in Niagara as well as Albany. Well, we have a few people we can believe in. It's my business to collect news from the west and sift out what's likely to be true. Spencer's one of our men."

"The Oneida?"

"Yes. He's somewhere out at Oswego. Another's Jim Dean. He's near Montreal somewhere. I check our other men against what those two say. Right here on this table I've got a better idea of what's happening than they've probably got in Albany this minute. I know that Carleton's building a fleet on Champlain, and anybody can see that he'll drive our side back to Ticonderoga. That means that our frontier isn't going to be Canada any more. It means as sure as shooting that the British will try to take Albany next summer. And it means before they can do that they'll have to get hold of the Mohawk Valley."

Gil said, "Yes, sir."

"I'm telling you this, Gil, to ease your mind. You can keep your mouth shut. Now listen. All along they've been telling us we'd better come around before the Indians come down on us. But the Indians haven't come. There's been a little trouble round Schoharie, but nobody's been damaged much. There hasn't been any up here. The nearer we are to Canada the less there's been. Have you stopped to think why?"

Gil shook his head.

"It's more than a year since Guy Johnson had his Indian council down at Cosby's. That happened just before you got here. They sat around one day and then moved up to Stanwix. They had chiefs from every nation there. But nothing happened, even though it's known Guy Johnson and Daniel Claus and maybe Sir John wanted the Indians turned loose. The hitch was Butler, according to Spencer. He was Sir William Johnson's man. He knows that the Indians are good for just about one big fight. Once he started letting them loose in parties he'd never get them together again. And he's been holding them off until he can get an army to come with them. That's my idea. You can say John Butler don't want to start an Indian war. But I don't think any Butler has that much decent feeling where a German's concerned. He would like to lick the pants off of us. But he's got enough sense to know that in a country like ours he can't accomplish anything by just picking off one farm here and another there. It's the whole hog against the brisket. He'll go for the whole hog any day. That's the Irish of it, too."

Gil drew his breath.

"Then you think there ain't anything going to happen this year, but next year we'll have a bad time."

"Just so," said the captain. "The bigger army they can send down here the more they figure to take away from any army defending Ticonderoga." He smiled wryly. "The one thing they don't figure on, though, is that those people down in Albany aren't going to take any chances, any more than the ones in Philadelphia or New England are, of weakening themselves. Do you know what they call us, Gil? Anything west of Schenectady is called 'bush-German' country."

"Then we've got to look out for ourselves."

"Oh yes. They write us about patriotism. And the great cause. And tell us to look after ourselves and not cry for help. They won't send us troops. The damned Yankees don't want to leave home. They hear that the likker's poor west of Albany. They won't send us powder even. Not even lead. Right now Herkimer's making out an order to take sash weights out of any window that has them between Schenectady and my house. No, boy, we'll have to look out for ourselves. Then if we win the war we'll see if we can get representation in our Congress. It won't be easy, I expect. You see the Yankee merchants started this business because they couldn't make a 12 per cent profit any more. They used the Stamp Tax just to make the country people mad. Who gives a damn for the Stamp Tax, come to think of it? How much money have you paid out to it yourself?"

"That's so," said Gil, wonderingly. "It ain't bothered me." He looked up at the captain. "Why do we have to go and fight the British at all?"

"Because, now the war's started, people like the Butlers and Johnsons will be in power if they win and they'll take it out of our hides, the cost of it."

Gil said, "Yes." As far as he could see, though, they were just about where they had started. Captain Demooth had risen and there seemed to be nothing more to say. He felt the captain take his arm as he went towards the door.

"Don't get scared," the captain said. "And don't let your wife get nervy, either. I've got people of my own, patrolling west and north of here. You know Blue Back, don't you?"

"The old Indian who traps the Canadas in winter?"

"Yes. Mr. Kirkland's guaranteed him. He's got the northern beat, and if there's any trouble this year, I imagine it would come from there."

3. *The Farm*

When he reached his own place, Gil Martin found that Mrs. Reall had come over to borrow some soft soap. "I don't know how I come to be out of it." She had the baby under one arm. "I don't know what a person can do anyway with a family like mine."

"Make some of your own and quit borrowing everything all your life," was what Gil wanted to say. Instead he stood beside the door frowning down at the frowsy woman and gloomily watched Lana measuring out some soap in a chipped cup.

"Gil's just been down to Mr. Demooth's," Lana said brightly, in an effort to make them all easy. She knew that Gil did not approve of her lending so many things to Mrs. Reall.

Mrs. Reall perked up at once.

"It's a pity," she remarked, "that a nice man like Mark Demooth hasn't got a decent woman to look out for him."

"Did you see Mr. Demooth, Gil?" Lana asked hurriedly.

"Yes," he said. "He's getting ready to go down valley this morning. He said muster day was Wednesday."

Mrs. Reall looked surprised.

"Why didn't you step over to our place? It's shorter, and Kitty would have told you. He keeps all such things wrote down in a book. He's such a methody man."

Gil was nettled.

"I knew when it was. I wanted to see him about something else."

"Well, that wasn't what you said first," said Mrs. Reall with perfect good humor. "Of course you needn't tell me what you did go down for. I don't mind." But she made no move to get up.

Gil knew that she was likely to stay till noon if the humor seized her. With strained facetiousness, he said, "I went down to see if he didn't think we had ought to leave a bodyguard for all you women."

Mrs. Reall laughed heartily.

"My, my," she said, dabbing the baby's nose with the front of her blouse. "Bodyguard! Why, I'm always that relieved when Kitty goes to muster! I figure he's safe enough for one day. If he don't break his legs coming home drunk the way he does. It's one strange thing about a God-fearing man like Kitty, the way he gets drunk muster days. But then, as he says, war is war, and religion is religion, and both is pretty well concerned with hell."

"What did Mr. Demooth say, Gil?" asked Lana.

"He said we ought to go down. He didn't think there was any trouble coming for a while."

Gil wheeled and went out through the door. Mrs. Reall rose and said, "Thank you for the soap, Lana dearie. I'll return you some the next time I get around to making it."

Lana watched her go, then started after Gil. Gil had begun work on clearing a three-acre strip along the creek behind the place. He was felling the trees in windrows widthwise of the land, preparatory to the autumn burning. The sound of his axe in the heavy August air had no ring, but when she found him he was laying savagely into a tree, sinking half the blade at every stroke.

She watched him awhile, her dark eyes anxious.

"Gil," she said.

He stopped, leaving the axe driven, and turned round. His head and neck were covered with sweat and sweat drops ran slowly down his arms. The sun beating down on the newly uncovered ground brought forth a suffocating, tindery smell, as if it might start the firing of itself at any minute.

He stood for a moment looking out on his work. With what he already had cleared, he could see in his mind's eye the first beginnings of a farm taking shape. Next year his present patch of corn would go to wheat. Two years from now, he ought to have eight acres sown to wheat. Once a farm could produce a hundred bushel of wheat the farmer had got past the dangerous years. He could begin to count on a yearly income of around two hundred dollars. He could then consider building him a barn. From where he stood, Gil saw where he would build his barn against the slope. A sidehill barn. It was going to be a great place to pasture stock in. Later they would plan on building a framed house.

But women, he knew, put stock in board walls and a board floor. And Lana deserved a house. When he had married her, he hadn't considered such things, or the fact that she would have to be left here on muster day. There were a lot of things to being married he hadn't considered at all.

She said again, "Gil!" quite sharply.

In her work clothes, with her slim legs bare and her dark hair in a braid down her back, she looked light enough for him to raise her with one hand around her waist, like a daisy stem.

She stamped her foot and the dust powdered her ankle.

"Speak to me! Don't stand there staring like a crazy man gone deaf! What's on your mind?"

"I was just thinking how the place would look, in five years from now."

He looked so sheepish that she laughed. "I'll bet you were thinking about a barn and the cows in it."

"Horses. And I was thinking how long it would seem to you before it would be right for me to build you a decent house."

"What's the matter with the cabin? Don't it look nice?"

"It does. But I thought you'd probably be hankering for a house."

"Well," said Lana, "I probably will. But that doesn't mean you've got to moon about it so. When I get discontented I'll let you know it fast enough." She sat against the bevel of a stump. "What did Mr. Demooth actually say?"

"Just about what I told her. He said I ought to go down. I told him I wanted to stay. It does seem kind of hard." He repeated everything the captain had said.

"Who's this Blue Back?" she asked.

"He's an old Indian. Once in a while he stops with me."

"It's a funny name."

"Yes, it is. If he ever comes round when I'm out, you treat him nice, Lana."

"Of course," she said. "Why wouldn't I?"

"Well, you know how Indians is."

"You mean drunk."

"No, he don't drink much. For an Indian."

He glanced at her.

"You won't be scared, being left here?"

"No."

"You could pass the time with Mrs. Weaver."

"Maybe I will or go to Reall's. But I'll get back to have your supper."

"You wait for me at Weaver's. No telling when we get back," he said. "If I got time, maybe I'll fetch you something from the store."

She laughed.

"Me. I don't need anything. Lord! You're kind of silly about me still, aren't you?"

"I'm just about crazy," he said, grinning.

"This isn't time to start that kind of business," she said. "What do you want me to do, now?"

"If you mean work, you could drag the lopped branches so the tops lay on the logs."

She set to work. The tree trunks lay where they had fallen almost end to end, sometimes overlapping. She dragged the lopped branches so that they lay over the trunks, the tops all pointing eastward to favor the prevailing west winds of fall, when the burning would take place.

They didn't talk. The dust and the heat choked them both. But as her brain dulled with the labor she kept wondering whether a man would continue to feel like Gil when his girl began to lose her looks. After a while, she even began to forget that. There was just the work.

They stopped at noon, and ate, and came out again into the heat, the flies following them from the cabin and then going in again, but a new swarm met them in the lot. The leaves were already wilting on the cut branches.

It was like that, day after day. At sunset Lana stopped to hunt the cow and milk her. She had dropped off in her milk and only gave a quart at night.

Then Lana started their supper. She gathered a few green ears from the cornfield, stripped the kernels out, crushed them in a bowl, and cooked them in the milk. The milk tasted of cherry and wild onion. All the time, as she worked in the kitchen, she could hear the strokes of Gil's axe.

He came in at dark all soaked with sweat and they went down to the creek together where a pool was, and stripped and washed side by side.

Each night, to Lana, that marked the beginning of life again. She felt tired afterwards, her back ached, but she was clean; and while she ate, the natural uses of her body gradually returned. And the sight of Gil naked, knee deep in the slow flow of the creek, was still the one exciting thing she had to see. Even when she looked up at the peacock's feather in the dark, his lean white shape came between it and her eyes. One did not see the burned hands and face in the dark, only the whiteness.

They could begin to talk a little. They talked about a certain tree that had been hard in falling, or the way the mare was swelling in her neck from the flies. Gil would then go out with some of their precious salt in a cup and mix it with water and swab the mare's shoulder, while Lana was clearing up. When he came in again, they would be wordless, and would wait only for a term of decency before going up to bed.

All day, her place to him might be taken by anything with hands and arms and the knowledge to cook. When they lay down together, she was Lana Martin, who had been Lana Borst, once, long ago.

4.   Muster Day

When he came in from work on Tuesday evening, Gil took his rifle down from the pegs over the door.

"Where's the sweet oil?" he said to Lana.

"Sweet oil? You'd better look on that shelf in the woodshed. Maybe I stuck it up there somewhere. It started to smell bad."

Without a word he went out to the shed, where she could hear him stirring round with a heavy hand and muttering to himself. But he came back after a moment, carrying the earthenware saucer.

"It does smell kind of bad," he said, and sat down near her, with the saucer on the hearth between his feet and a filthy bit of woolen rag in his hand. "George Weaver's a particular man on muster. You wouldn't think he was, to look at him. You wouldn't think," he went on, glancing at her slyly, "looking at him and me, that he was a sargint over me, would you?"

Lana refused to meet his eye. But she said, "I think George Weaver would make a better sergeant than you, Gil. You get up your mad too easy. The way you was getting ready to because I'd moved out your smelly old oil."

"Mad! Listen, Lana, you just ought to hear him curse and swear on muster day."

"He wouldn't do that to me."

"Who's talking about you anyway?" He had run the scourer down the barrel with the rag wrapped round it, and now he was examining the result with the rag held close to his nose. There wasn't any rust. He let the ramrod fall and patted her head.

"Don't do that," cried Lana, wriggling off from him. "You'll have me smelling just like a gun."

But he had taken to wiping the barrel. "I wouldn't mind it if you did."

"Gil!" she cried. "You wouldn't talk that way to me before we married!"

"You wouldn't have been dragging out my sweet oil on me, before we got married. Ain't it a dandy rifle, though?" He held it in his hands. "I bought the barrel from Wolff. He ordered it from Albany." He turned the gun over and looked at the scroll behind the trigger guard. "It was made in Peekskill. G. Merritt, Peekskill. Come and look at it, Lana."

She felt suddenly jealous of the gun, which she had seen ever since she came to Deerfield, hanging in place over the cabin door. It had been just a thing till now; but when Gil put his hands on it, it seemed to have acquired the power of life. However, a queer little sense of wisdom compelled her to obey, and she looked down over his shoulder at the nicely etched name. She wondered if the man who put it there could have any idea that the barrel would come so far westward and have the power there to make a woman jealous.

But though she looked at the name, she would not praise it. "That's nice wood," she said, tapping the stock.

Gil blushed all over.

"I carved that out myself last winter. It's a piece of black walnut Mark Demooth gave me. I spent pretty near every night all winter working on that stock."

He put the gun back on its pegs, replaced the ramrod in the slot, and again looked round the cabin.

"Do you remember where I kept my hatchet?"

"What do you want with it?"

"I've got to have it to-morrow. You have to have an Indian axe or a bayonet."

"Oh," she said. "Well now, you listen to me, Mr. Martin. You just sit here till you've had your supper. After that I'll hunt up everything you want."

However, he found the axe for himself. Then he greased his boots; and after supper, all there was for Lana to do was to get down his hunting shirt.

"It's filthy dirty," she said.

"That don't matter. So long as your gun's clean and you've got your four flints and your pound of powder, nobody cares."

"I care. As long as you've got to go, you'll go looking decent. What would they say about me if they saw you had the same shirt on and it hadn't been washed since last muster?"

She held it up under her nose, as he had held up the scourer under his, and made a face at him. Then she stuffed it into the iron kettle and put some more sticks on the fire and set about boiling the shirt. It came out finally, looking rather pale.

It was made of heavy linen, dyed butternut brown, with long fringes or thrums round the shoulders and down the sleeves. Ironing it out was a hard job. By the time she had finished, Lana was flushed and heated and the whole cabin smelled steamily of soft soap.

She felt out of sorts until her eye fell on Gil laboriously turning up the brim of his hat, by tacking the edge to the crown in three places.

"What you doing?" she demanded.

"Well," he said, "you're fixing the rest of me so fine I thought I'd ought to make my hat look smart."

"You ought to have a cockade on it then, Gil."

"That would look fine. But aren't you tired?"

"No, I'll make you a cockade. What do you want?"

"Something red," he said. "Red's the color of our party. George Herkimer's company's got a solid red flag. It's handsome."

Lana went upstairs to her trunk with a candle and found a piece of French red calimanco. They sat quite peacefully together while she gathered pleats in it and sewed it on. The light of the candle flashed on her white teeth biting the thread.

"Put it on," she ordered.

He sheepishly did so.

She thought he looked even handsomer the next morning, starting off down the track. She had promised to visit with Mrs. Weaver as soon as she had got the dishes cleared, but halfway down the clearing he wheeled to remind her of it.

"I will," she called.

He waved his hand and went off with long strides. She leaned against the door. The early morning sun was just beginning to reach down under the level of the treetops, making islands of light in the clearing, and showing the glitter of the night's dew. Gil's feet had left a dark track through it.

"But I'll bet he won't think about me once all day," she thought.

He had reached the Kingsroad by now. Christian Reall was waiting for him there on the edge of the underbrush. They saluted each other stiff as two dogs meeting at the corner of the fence. Then they moved off side by side into the woods.

On muster day, Christian Reall was a different man from the meaching Bible reader his wife professed to admire. Gil had never been able to understand why in his family he should pretend to such devoutness if he wished to be such a rip hell once he got loose from them. His very walk was different. He cocked on his toes at each step, instead of flat-footedly shuffling the dust, and as soon as they were safely in the woods he clapped Gil on the shoulder and told him he looked like a God-damned gentleman.

"You don't look so bad yourself," Gil said good-humoredly.

Walking with a swing of his outthrust elbows, Reall preened himself like a jay bird.

"Not too bad," he admitted, "but by Jesus it takes more than clothes to get the girls to look at you. You got to have something. Like a gentleman. Not just lace around your neck or a handkerchief to blow your nose in. *You* know."

"I can't say I do."

"Well, you could. You've got it. Look at the girl you got to marry you! Lana's prettier than the nigh side of a peach. But that ain't what I mean. Who actually wants to marry? Gentry do and gentry don't, but they always have a trot with the girls notwithstanding." He shouldered his rust-pitted Spanish musket and jerked his flopping hat brim over his eyes. "The stories I used to hear when I was down in Caughnawaga was a caution. The way the young gentry went around the country. Just like a bunch of stallions. Why, a girl of fourteen couldn't hardly dast get up a sweat without fearing one of those gentry would be tagging on her heels like a breed bull. Young Sir John, and they say young Walter Butler. And Claus and Guy Johnson. And young Cosby. The whole lot. They rutted the year round. Mostly they hung around the Indian camps or went up into the Sacandaga bush clearings."

"I've heard some of those stories," Gil said. "But I don't believe the half of them."

"You don't? You're a fool then. Everybody knows Sir John had Clare Putnam living in sin in the Fort with him when he got married to Miss Watts. Even Sir William Johnson kind of dabbled in such things. He didn't marry the Weisenberg woman till she was ready to die. He bought her for his bed the way a man would buy new sheeting. Then he had two Indians. One afore Brant's sister. And God knows how many he happened against. All you've got to do is look at all the Jacksons there was in the Lower Castle. It was a joke he had. He let all the papooses born in the house get called Johnson. All outside he called Jackson. Otherwise, he said he'd be feeding half the Mohawk nation. By God, he ought to know, too."

"Well, he was a great man," said Gil. "I'll bet if he was alive he wouldn't have run off to Canada."

"Well, maybe he was. But he surely could rip hell around."

"It's just the fashion with gentry."

"*Fashion*, that's the word I tried to remember." Christian Reall licked his lips. "Wish to God I had some of it myself."

Gil laughed out loud.

They passed Cosby's Manor about when Wolff and his wife must have been having breakfast in the store, for smoke was still trailing out of the chimney. There was no sign of the storekeeper or the woman, but a couple of Indians, like two sleepy cats, sat in the woodshed in a patch of sunlight.

"What's them?" whispered Reall.

"I don't know," Gil answered. "I never seen them."

"They've shaved fresh, look at their heads."

"Yes."

"Do you expect they're painted?"

"I don't know. Not on their faces anyways."

Gil took a good look at them. They didn't seem as stocky as the Mohawks he had seen. But they weren't Oneidas. They were too dark, he was sure, to belong to either tribe. They were thin, almost starved-looking. As they sat under their blankets, they made him think of snakes.

"Morning," he said to them, walking by.

They said good-morning with their mouths. But their heads did not move. Nothing about them moved but their brown eyes, which were small and bright and followed the two militiamen slowly across the front of the woodshed.

A moment later, in the woods once more, Reall said, with a quick backward glance, "Who do you think they was, Gil?"

"I don't know. I think they might be Cayugas. Or more likely Senecas. But I don't know."

Reall drew a shuddering deep breath.

"My God," he said, "the way they stared at me. I've heard the Senecas and the Erie tribes eat human meat."

Reall quickened his pace. "We ought to tell Demooth right off there's a couple of Senecas at Wolff's. God knows what they're up to. They must be from Niagara. Niagara's where John Butler is. Oh, my Jesus, Gil. Maybe he's down here too. Wolff's looked shut up pretty tight."

"It always does," said Gil. "That don't mean anything."

"Wolff's always been a King's man. Always said so." He looked round again. "We ought to tell them the first thing." He had that fixed in his mind.

The men of Demooth's company of the fourth regiment of Tryon County militia were gathered along the barnside fence in Kast's field, opposite the ford. There were twenty-five of them. They had the half-uneasy look of men who have been caught loafing on the job. When one happened to laugh, two or three would join him explosively. Then they would spit and look away from each other and eye George Weaver, who was standing a little down the fence.

He said, "Captain hain't here to-day. I ain't got a watch. Anybody know what time it is?"

"It ain't time yet."

"Must be past ten," said Weaver. "I'm to fine anybody's late."

"There comes Martin and Reall now. There ain't anybody else missing except them that have a lawful excuse."

At that moment Kast came out of his house in a brown coat. "It's two minutes to ten," he said. "By the clock."

Somebody laughed.

"Time's always by that clock of his, when Kast's around."

Martin and Reall walked up.

Reall cried out immediately, "George."

"Yes," said Weaver.

"There's a couple of Seneca Indians up to Wolff's. They're shaved. Reckon they're going to paint. Maybe Butler or somebody's hanging around there."

"How do you know they're Senecas?" Weaver asked sourly. He didn't want anything to interfere with the muster. With Captain Demooth away, the whole responsibility devolved on him.

"Ain't I telling you, George?"

Just then, tardily, Kast's clock wound itself up and struck seven. The notes came feebly metallic to the waiting men.

"That's ten," cried Kast. "She hurt her inwards somehow coming up here, and the bell's never caught up to the time since."

Weaver took his tobacco from his mouth and cradled it behind him in his hand while with the other he held a paper before his eyes and rattled off the names.

"Adam Hartman."

"Here."

"Jeams MacNod."

"Here."

On down the list. Now and then a man answered, "He can't come. He's gone to the Flats getting flour." . . . "Perry's home. Doc Petry told him his wife might most likely freshen this morning." . . . "He cut his foot grubbing brush in the stump lot."

Obedient to the prescribed ritual, Weaver turned round to face the absent captain.

"All present or accounted for."

It brought the plug in his hand into view. He recovered too late. Restoring it to his mouth, he roared thickly, "Shoulder arms."

The line raggedly shouldered their guns, some to the right, some to the left. They faced Weaver with the gravity of cornstooks. No two of them were dressed alike. Some had coats, of homespun or black cloth; some, like Gil, wore hunting shirts.

Weaver stared at them as if he were hypnotized. Without the captain he couldn't think what should be done next.

Someone said, "Can't we have the inspection and get it over with? It's damned hot standing here."

"Sure," said Weaver.

He went down the line. Now and then he took a rifle and looked it over closely. Once he made a man lift his shoes.

"You got to get new soles on them. I ought to fine you, Marcy."

"I got paper in their inside," said Marcy.

"Law says shoes equipped for a month's march."

"I couldn't walk that far if I had the shoes."

"It's law." He came to Reall. He looked at him for a long minute. "Give me your gun."

Reall handed it over.

"It's clean, sergeant," he said. "I cleaned it yesterday myself."

"Give me your ramrod."

"It's in the gun," said Reall, with a wink.

"No it ain't."

"God, one of the kids had it, I guess."

"Give me yours, Martin."

He took Gil's ramrod and dropped it down the barrel. It sank less than halfway. Weaver took it out, then tipped the gun nose down and whacked the stock with the palm of his hand. An assortment of bean seeds dropped out. Somebody started laughing. Reall stared.

"Them boys been playing bean game," he said. "I couldn't find the seeds. They said they threw them out. Ain't that a place to hide them!"

Weaver handed back the gun.

"Private Reall, dirty gun, one shilling."

The inspection was finished.

"Fall out."

The men drifted apart.

"Say," said someone. "How about eating early? Then we can go home. I got my two-acre patch to finish to-night."

"That's a good idea."

"Maybe it ain't legal," said George.

"We ought to do something."

"Let's eat first."

They had a meal cooked for them by Mrs. Kast. She and her two daughters scurried and finished the cooking of it and brought it out with six jugs of beer. The men lay around on the stubble of the hayfield and drank and ate and got up a company pool on the time of arrival of the expected Perry baby. Sixpence a ticket. Reall took two. That made twelve shilling. Two for the baby and ten for the winner.

After the beer was finished some of the more serious-minded thought they ought to try keeping step once around the field. Everybody thought that was a good idea. They wrestled up and got their guns. They formed threes and did their best. They were all blown when they got back to the barn. It was the best muster they had had in a long while. They felt like celebrating.

Jeams MacNod said seriously, "I bet we could lick the whole British army, marching that good."

Weaver admitted they had done well. He had seen them coming round the corner. They were all in step but Reall, but he was the odd man at the rear and didn't count.

Reall came up now, briskly, his eyes a little bloodshot, saying, "How about them Seneca Indians up to Wolff's? Why don't we march up there and see what they're a-doing?"

Weaver thought they might as well. They could dismiss at Wolff's and he and Reall and Gil wouldn't have to walk home so far. He gave the order.

As they marched past Mrs. Kast they took off their hats to her.

5. *Arrest*

The company went up the Kingsroad in two ragged files, each taking a rut. There was a good bit of laughing, and some talk. They hadn't much idea of what they were going to do when they got to Wolff's store; it seemed like a kind of joke. Most of them had been there only one or two times in their lives. "Does he keep any likker?" they wanted to know.

"I don't think so," Weaver said. "Cosby didn't like him having too much on hand, with the Indians coming round all the time. Only in spring when they brought in their peltry."

He plodded along, hunched forward, as if he had a plough in front of him. By nature he was an abstemious man and the beer had gone to his head, what with the heat, and the responsibilities of running the muster; and nearly all the way he kept trying to think what he ought to do when they got to Cosby's. As it turned out, it was Jeams MacNod, the school-teacher, who had the great idea.

He said, "If them Indians ain't there, what are we going to do?"

Nobody had thought of that. Jeams said, "Suppose Thompson has some men around, he might get nasty."

"Thompson cleared out a month ago," Reall said.

A kind of deliberate sunrise of intelligence dawned in the school-teacher's narrow, befuddled face. He was a poor man, and he led a hard and thankless life. He wiped the sweat out of his eyes with the cuff of his coat sleeve and said, "Why don't we take a look around the manor then?"

"Ain't that thieving?" asked Gil.

MacNod shook his head. "No, it ain't. Not when there's war. That's what they're a-doing down the valley. They done it in Johnson Hall when Sir John cleared out. There was some of the Flats people in Colonel Dayton's regiment. They went right over the place. They didn't steal nothing. Captain Ross, he said it was confiscated property and he went around with them showing what he wanted retained for himself. Retaining ain't like robbery."

The suggestion gave them the feeling of being on military service. They were doing what regular army troops had done in command of a regular army officer, and they were doing it of their own initiative. By the time they came to Cosby's they were, as Kast said afterwards, looking sober enough to eat hay. They wouldn't have seen the British army, perhaps, if it had been drawn up in squares round the big house, but they saw Mrs. Wolff all right. She was just coming in from the corn patch with a squash in her arms, like a baby.

When her eyes first fell on them, entering the clearing, she started instinctively to run. A woman of forty-five or fifty, her bleached hair half fallen to her shoulders, the bone pins clinging here and there, loosely, like oversized white lice.

Then she caught hold of herself and stood still.

"Mrs. Wolff," said Weaver, when the company had drawn up behind him, "where's your husband?"

"What do you want with John?"

Weaver said heavily, "We're militia on duty. Where's John?"

"We hain't done nothing," she said in her dull voice. "John, he's out in the lot."

"You call him in," said Weaver.

She stared at them for a moment more. When her eyes met his, Gil felt vaguely ashamed. But she didn't say anything as she turned for the log store. She went onto the porch ahead of them and took a small hand bell and swung it slowly.

They all waited for John Wolff.

He came in a moment with a dead pipe in his hand. A little charred corn silk sticking over the bowl showed that he must be out of tobacco. He was a year or so older than his wife, but he had a healthier color, and a set stubborn jaw.

"What do you want?" he demanded. He didn't try being friendly. Every-

body knew which way he stood. He thought they were damned fools.
"Where's them two Seneca Indians was around here this morning?"
"There wasn't any Senecas around here."
Reall's voice piped up from the back of the line.
"Yes there was. Me and Gil saw them. Setting in the woodshed."
"Oh, them. They wasn't Senecas. I don't know who they was."
"What were they doing here?"
"They come in last night. Hungry. I let them bed in the barn and give
them something to eat. I never saw them before."
"You admit they wasn't Oneidas or Fort Hunter Mohawks."
"I don't admit anything. I gave them something to eat. What the hell
business is it of yours, Weaver?"
"John." His wife breathlessly touched his arm. "Don't get angry, John."
"Shut up," he said. "What right have these Dutch punks got coming onto
my land?"
"We're on duty. We got to keep track of people without business in
these parts."
"Why don't you ask them what their business was, then? I don't know."
"Where are they?"
"Go and find out. They left here at nine o'clock."
Weaver stood uncertainly on the porch. Jeams MacNod went up to him
and whispered. Weaver put his finger in his ear.
"Yes," he said. "You stay in the store. Both of you. We've got to in-
vestigate the grounds."
Wolff said, "Suit yourself. But you can't do anything to me."
"I'll just go through your place first," said Weaver. He called for Gil
and MacNod and Kast to come with him. The rest were to surround the
store and wait till he came out.

The inside of the store was a long room with a fireplace at the end and
a bed in the corner. There were rough shelves along one wall and storage
chests along the other. There were two benches set end to end down the
middle of the floor. The benches were made of split basswood logs with
hickory legs let into them. Two windows allowed some sunlight to filter
through the fly specks.
There wasn't anything an Indian could hide behind. Weaver went into
the woodshed. He found about a month's supply of wood stacked sloppily,
two pairs of snowshoes, an axe, a wedge, and a maul. "No one out there,"
he said, and helped the other three lift aside some axe helves, a keg of lamp
oil, and a couple of rum kegs. The oil keg had four inches of oil. The other
kegs were empty.
They stood looking round. It was so still inside the store that they could
hear the men outside talking softly through the buzzing of the flies.
Jeams MacNod tried to lift the lid of a chest.
"It's locked," he said.
Weaver turned on Wolff.
"Give us the keys, John."
"Like hell I will."
"Then we'll have to take an axe to the chests and bust them in."
"All right," Wolff grinned thinly. "You'll find it's a hot job."

"Get the axe, Kast. It's in the woodshed."

Kast returned with the axe.

Wolff said, "You spoil them chests and you'll hear of it. I'll make a complaint to Captain Demooth." He drew his hand over his thin mouth. "I and Demooth had a talk. He said I could stay here as long as I didn't do nothing. I ain't been looking for trouble. He said he'd look out for me. You touch them chests and you look out."

Weaver had begun to get mad.

"Go ahead, Kast. Bust the lock if you can."

Kast swung the axe like a hammer.

"You stop that. There ain't nothing in them," said Mrs. Wolff. "Don't you spoil them."

"Let them do it," said Wolff.

"No, I won't. There ain't anything in them. I'll give them the keys."

"You do that and there won't be any bother," said Weaver.

Wolff stared at his wife, but said nothing. She gave them the keys to open the chests. They found some blankets for the Indian trade. Some cheap knives. Some flour. Some salt beef. There were two bales of skins in the last. When they opened the lid a rank smell came out. "Shut it," said Weaver. Kast started to obey, but MacNod, who was a curious man, pulled up the bales. "Look here," he said.

Two twenty-pound bags of powder lay in the bottom of the chest.

"That's my powder," said Wolff. "I've had it a long while."

"We'll have to take it. I'll give you a paper. It's more powder than we've got for the company."

"You leave me a couple of pounds, anyway."

"What do you need it for?"

"It'll save you wasting it on your damn muster days, anyways."

"All storekeepers been asked to turn their powder in and make a statement of it."

"That's my business."

"You set down," said Kast. He leaned towards Wolff.

"Set down, John. Please." Mrs. Wolff touched him timidly. He threw her hand off his sleeve. After a minute he sat down, though.

Mrs. Wolff turned to Gil.

"You can't take it all. We hain't got fresh meat. We need some." She looked frightened. "Make them leave us a little."

"I'm sorry," said Gil, flushing. "George is in charge. He's sergeant." A little breath went out of the woman. She sat down beside her husband.

Weaver listened to MacNod. He nodded his head.

"You stay here, Wolff. We've got to look over Thompson's house."

"That's illegal entry," said Wolff.

"You mind your business and we'll mind ours."

Probably Gil and Weaver were the only two among the company who had ever been inside of Thompson's house, and neither of them had been beyond the little office to the right of the door. They had found Mr. Thompson a decent neighbor, but the big house had overawed them with its black slaves who seemed to feel contempt for any white man who didn't own people like themselves, its sounds of voices from the parlor doors, and the tinkle of a spinet coming down from upstairs. To them it had been the expression of all the possessions they vaguely hoped to have come to them in their time. Weaver had been there twice to see about the loan of a yoke of oxen in the early days. Gil had come to sell a large buck he had shot once when some gentlemen had been stopping there.

Standing on the wide verandah that fronted the river, they now felt the same awe in the face of the closed shutters. Most of the men with them caught the feeling. Only Jeams MacNod, who had some education and a fanatical contempt for all success other than his own, was ready to break down the door. He threw his weight against it, but the heavy pine panels had no thought of yielding to a Scottish scholar.

His gesture, however, had been enough to renew their appetite. There had been nothing exciting at Wolff's; they had come a long way, and the wearing off of the effect of beer had left them spoiling for action. When Jeams pointed out a heavy pole lying on the dock by the river shore, half a dozen of them ran down for it. They swung it against the door together. But the bars held solid. The sound of the blow was like the tap on a gigantic drum, sounding hollowly throughout the house.

It stopped them for an instant; then they shouted. They swung the pole again; and again they got no more than the hollow crash, as if the whole house joined in one derisive shout.

To Gil, however, the empty sound was upsetting.

"It'll take too long to break it down," he said. "Why don't we open a window?"

The others let the pole drop.

"That's right," said Weaver. "There ain't no sense in spoiling a good door."

They swarmed against a window together, hacking round the shutter bolts with their hatchets. In a few minutes they had the bolts cut out, the boards pried off, and Reall had thrown his hatchet through a pane. The glass tinkled chillingly into the dark room. They lifted the sash and climbed in, one after the other.

The room was the office, with Mr. Thompson's desk and chairs, and little else beyond the ashes of paper on the hearth where wind in the chimney had stirred them from the grate.

"Hell," said Kast. "There ain't anything in here. Let's look around."

There was a short commotion at the door, before one man at last stepped into the hall. As soon as he had crossed the threshold, the others trooped after him.

The size and darkness of the hall were impressive. The wide boards under their boots creaked a little to their shifting feet, but for the instant it sounded more as if some ghostly person were descending the staircase. While they stood still to listen, chipmunks behind one of the walls took sudden fright.

The sound of panic reassured them. The men broke apart, going from room to room. Gil and Weaver, remaining in the hall, listened to the stamp of boots overhead and back in the kitchen. When men walked overhead a thin dust sifted from the cornices.

"I can't find the cellar stairs," shouted Kast.

"Where are you?"

"In the pantry."

"Try the closet off the dining room," said Reall.

Weaver turned to Gil.

"I don't rightly know what we're doing here, Gil."

"I don't either," Gil said.

"Maybe we'd better go around and see they don't get too rough with things."

"All right, I'll go upstairs."

Gil wanted to get away from the big downstairs rooms. The fine black-cherry dining room table and the delicate chairs worried him; for they were things he would have liked Lana to have. But seeing them against the papered wall, dark though the room was, made him realize that a person could not merely own them.

The holland cupboard in the hall, with its wax figures, half like persons in spite of their small size, the soft feeling of the green carpet under his boots, gave him the same uneasiness. It was not until he stepped onto the bare wood of the stair treads that he felt remotely like himself.

But even on the stairs, the voices of the militia had an alien sound, as if by their entry they had done more than violate a house. They had put an end to a life. The house, shut up, could have fallen to ruin in dignity.

On the second floor, however, seeing the bedrooms opening from the hall, with the big beds unmade, as they had been left by the Thompsons, Gil felt a kind of unreasoning anger. By abandoning it, the people, apparently, had thought no more of the house than the militia had in forcing an entrance. And those that were abovestairs felt no compunctions.

One was holding up a flimsy dressing gown.

"Would a man or woman wear this?" he was asking.

The lace that edged the sleeves hung limply, and his calloused fingertips rasped on the silk.

"You can't tell what they wear," said a muffled voice. Christian Reall came backing from under the bed dragging a piece of crockery. "Look at this, Van Slyck. It's got gilt on it."

Van Slyck glanced down with lukewarm interest. "Yes, it's a nice article," he said politely. He dropped the dressing gown. "I wish I could get me one of these good and warm."

Reall crouched over the chamber pot. "It would be a handy thing. My wife gets chilblains horrible in winter."

They were as conscienceless as men inspecting a line of goods in a store. Gil wandered into the next room. There was less in it to interest one, perhaps, for there was only a narrow bed and a great closet of dark wood standing in the corner. He was curious to see what might be inside the closet.

He found it empty of everything except, lying in a corner, a piece of silk that might have been used as a head wrapping. It was bright green with little white birds printed on it. He picked it up almost mechanically, thinking suddenly how well it would look on Lana's dark hair. Glancing round, he saw that he was alone. It made him feel like a thief, but he comforted himself with thinking that it had no real value. And he had meant to bring Lana something. He had not been so long away from her since they were married. Inevitably it went into his pocket.

Then he looked round him. He felt that he ought to do something, to show his zealous sense of duty.

In the corner of the room behind the door a ladder leaned against the wall. He had not noticed it at first. He would not have noticed it now except that in the pale light creeping through the shutters the dust on the rungs looked disturbed.

At first Gil thought that there might be rats in the house; but he did not see why rats should be climbing to the attic. He decided to have a look. He had to lift a trapdoor.

The attic seemed no darker than the rest of the house, and he could see quite plainly. The two central chimneys came up side by side out of the floor and continued at a slight outward angle like the trunks of a double tree. Between them was a bed.

There was nothing else in the attic. Gil stared a long time to make sure before he hoisted himself through.

He kept well away from the chimneys until he had circled both of them. On their outside edges the dust lay thick and unmarked, but sometime recently a man had come through the trap and gone to bed. Even if it had not been for the tracks, Gil would have noticed the faint tobacco smell.

He sniffed at the blankets. It hadn't been an Indian. The bed would have had the sickish sweet smell, a little greasy, that Indians had. It had been a white man. Gil sat down on the bed.

Whoever it was, the man must have cooked downstairs, or have got food from Wolff's, for the bed had the appearance of being used often. But the man could not have used the fireplaces except at night or the smoke would have given him away.

Without being quite sure of what he looked for, Gil began poking round. He couldn't find anything except the old dottles of pipes and some small bits of paper. They didn't have writing on them. He got up and began a circuit of the attic. Coming back, he noticed that when the chimneys began to slope towards the roof the bricks were laid in tiers, making small shelves. He went back to the bed and stood on it. On one of the chimneys he found a piece of black cloth. He could just reach it.

For a minute he could not tell what it was. But as he held it in his fingers, his mind went back, for some strange reason, to his wedding day. He remembered how they had left Fox's Mills and how he had hardly been able to take his eyes off Lana, and how pretty and bashful she had seemed when they came to Billy Rose's tavern. They had had the place to themselves except for the one-eyed man who had talked so brashly against the Continental Congress.

Gil caught his breath. It was the patch for a blind eye.

George Weaver's voice came through the trap rather plaintively.

"You up there, Gil?"

"Come up here, George."

George grunted and the ladder shook as he climbed. He took a slow look round him, and listened to what Gil had to tell.

"You're right, Gil."

"The man's name was Caldwell."

"Well, he ain't here now."

Jeams MacNod, the curious man, appeared on the ladder. Immediately he had ideas.

"No doubt he's one of them spies that George Herkimer's rangers keep chasing after all the while. There's a great leakage of news." He took the patch in his hand. "No doubt he ain't blind at all."

"What's he wear this for?"

"So a person will know what he is without having to ask. There's been men with bad eyes, and a man with a lame hand. Herkimer's never been able to catch one of them."

George Weaver said, "I don't know about it. Where's the rest of you?"

"Reall's down in the cellar. They've broke it in. They've got some good gin and they're bringing it up to the dining room. They had to use a chair or two breaking in the door." He lifted the patch. "What are you going to do about this?"

"I don't know. They hadn't ought to be breaking things. I'll get into trouble."

"Listen," said MacNod. "We'll all get into trouble. There ain't a man here hasn't got something out of the house unless it's you and me and Gil." Gil had his own doubts about what MacNod had taken. The man looked too satisfied. "But," continued the schoolmaster, "this here shows that there've been unlawful people using this house."

Weaver said, "I got to get down before the boys do too much damage."

Gil said, "He must have boarded with Wolff," before he meant to. He didn't want to get into trouble.

"How do you mean?" asked MacNod sharply.

"He couldn't use the fireplaces here daytimes."

"No," said the schoolmaster. "He must have gone to Wolff. We can tell easy, looking at the fireplaces. Look here, George. You don't have to worry what the boys do now. You've got proof of unlawful doings. If you find he ain't used the house to cook in, you can arrest Wolff. That'll get you out of trouble."

Weaver said, "I don't want to get John into trouble."

"Man," said MacNod, "ain't he a traitor?"

"I don't know about that."

"Well, you better do it to keep yourself out of trouble."

Downstairs they found that the fireplaces had not been used. In the dining room the men had started building a fire of the broken chairs. They were drinking gin out of blue china cups which they handled carefully.

Weaver broke in on them.

"You boys'll have to step out smart. We're going to arrest John Wolff."

"What for?" they wanted to know.

"Hiding King's people."

"Oh hell, leave him alone."

"Get up!" said Weaver. "You can bring the gin along."

He got them out with arguments and cajolery and finally had them lined up on the porch. From where they stood they could see Wolff's backhouse. Mr. and Mrs. Wolff were coming back quickly from the door.

"My God," said Weaver. "I never thought to look there."

He broke into a run, and the rest streamed after him, Reall at the end, carrying his chamber pot in both hands so as not to spill the gin.

Mrs. Wolff gave a little cry, but her husband only looked sullen and stood his ground.

"Who'd you have hiding there?" demanded Weaver.

"Nobody. My wife felt sick. I went out with her."

"You swear to that?"

"My God," said Wolff, turning away.

"John Wolff," said Weaver, fumbling for the proper words, "I'm going to arrest you."

"Oh, my Jesus, John," said Mrs. Wolff.

Weaver had to go back with the company, but he dismissed Gil and Reall. Reall had a little trouble on the way home, and lost the gin. But he said at parting that it was the best muster he ever attended.

Gil stopped at Weaver's to pick up Lana and to tell Mrs. Weaver that George had had to take Wolff down to Herkimer.

Emma Weaver was not disturbed by the news. "Likely he'll get back after dark," she said. "I'm sorry, though, to hear about John Wolff. What'll they do to him, Gil?"

"I don't know, Mrs. Weaver. Where's Lana?"

"She went home about an hour ago to get your supper ready."

Gil was annoyed. "I told her to stay till I fetched her."

"Now don't get cross with her, Gil. She said you'd be tired and didn't ought to have to wait. She's a real good girl."

"I don't like having her alone."

Mrs. Weaver smiled.

"You men all think a woman can't take care of herself, don't you? Well, we ain't so frail. You think she's so slim, and so pretty, and just about like a stem of grass when you lay hold of her, and you hate the idea of her being in that there cabin where anyone can get at her? Listen, mister, a lot more women get worked to death by their husbands than is killed by other men."

It seemed a long way to his own turn-off. He was almost running when he came in sight of the cabin. He seemed for the first time to see how lonely the place looked. The small cabin, and the stump lot, and the ragged corn, and the swale out beyond.

6. *Blue Back*

When he opened the door, Lana was in front of the hearth, on which the fire had caught briskly. She started up at his entrance, smiling, her welcome in her eyes.

"Oh, Gil, I'm so glad you're home."

"Miss me?"

"Some."

"Come here."

She still held the spoon, covered with batter.

"You're going to scold me, ain't you?"

"Come here."

She obeyed meekly.

He fished the green silk out of his pocket and put it round her neck.

"I ought to take you out back of the woodshed and shingle you proper."

"Isn't it beautiful? Oh, Gil, where did you get it?"

"The company marched up to Cosby's. We had to break into Thompson's house. Somebody had thrown this down when they was clearing out, as if they didn't want it." He felt shamefaced to tell her. "It's hardly a real present. Only when I saw it I thought how pretty it would look on you."

"Imagine leaving a thing like that. I wouldn't; not if I was being driven out naked to the north pole. Oh, it's lovely, Gil."

She had no compunctions about wearing the thing.

"Look at those birds, those little white ones. Oh, look! Do you know what they are?"

"No."

"They're peacocks."

"No!" exclaimed Gil. It made him feel better about the whole business. He put up his gun over the door and loosened his hatchet.

"You got supper ready?"

"Pretty near. I bet you're hungry. You set down there on the stool and tell me what you did."

He told her the whole business, seeing the Indians on the way down, mustering, the return, finding the place in the attic, and the discarded patch for a blind eye.

Lana turned white at the recital.

"Oh, Gil, supposing he'd been there! He might have killed you."

"He wouldn't dast shoot with all the rest downstairs. And I didn't give him a chance to get hold of me."

"I was afraid of that man in the tavern. He didn't have a nice face. It wasn't just the eye. It was all of him."

Gil became serious.

"Suppose you'd found him here when you came home alone, Lana."

"Him? What do you mean? What would he want here?"

"I don't know, exactly. But this is the house furthest west in the valley except at Fort Stanwix." He said very seriously, "You see, Lana, that's what I meant about you waiting at Weaver's."

"I never thought. I will next time, Gil. It's awful." She returned to her cooking, speaking to him over her shoulder. Gil sat down and watched her. Even though they had been married more than a month now, she seemed like such a young girl. And for the moment he could see that she was afraid. "A man like him might be out in the woods this minute and you and I couldn't tell it. Not till they came right to the door. And then there wouldn't be anything we could do at all."

"Lord," he said. "You mustn't get scared, Lana. Just because we arrested a man."

"What will they do to him?"

"I don't know."

"I feel sorry for his wife. Maybe she felt the same way about you, the way I'd feel about that man."

"I didn't think of that. I guess she did. She looked scared."

"And the Thompson people. They'd be mad if they found out who broke into their house. They'd be mad at us if they saw me now wearing this silk."

"You don't need to wear it, Lana."

"I will, though. I don't care. You thought of me when you saw it and I'd made up my mind you wouldn't think about me all day."

She smiled a little furtive sidelong smile, and rose from her crouch with the quick lithe movement Gil liked to see. "You can put the forks and spoons on the table, mister."

They ate, sitting across from each other, Lana with her back to the door. They were nearly through their supper when Gil rose quietly and went round the table. He stood in the door, with his hand against the jamb, over his head, looking out.

"What is it, Gil?"

"Somebody's coming."

It was the mare, at the far end of the swale, that had caught his eye. She had thrown her head up. She was tossing it now, and snorting, though she was too far off for him to hear her. Then on the edge of the bushes near the river he saw a man. It was impossible to tell who or what he was, for he ducked back out of sight almost immediately. But the mare's nose, swinging like a needle to a magnet, showed the man's course. He was following the edge of the swale towards the house.

Lana crept up behind Gil.

"Who is it?"

"The mare acts like it was an Indian."

"How do you mean?"

"See her stomp her hoof? She don't like their smell."

"Ain't you going to shut the door, Gil?"

"No."

"But you ain't going to stand there in plain sight like that?"

"What's got into you? You didn't mind coming here alone, did you?" She shook her head.

"I hadn't thought."

"Well, you needn't act like a scared bitch just because a horse has seen a man."

He didn't turn around, and Lana stood stock-still, her hand halfway raised to her mouth, staring at him. After a moment she backed quietly to her place at the table and sat down with her face between her hands. She didn't say anything. But her eyes seemed to have enlarged.

Neither did Gil say anything. He kept his eyes on the swale and the edge of the creek bed, and he kept his hand over his head, within reach of the rifle. The only sound in the cabin was the everlasting low buzz of the flies.

To Lana the wait seemed unending. But she could not force herself to look at him. "He's got no right to say such a thing to me. I wasn't scared only for myself. If I was near home, he wouldn't do it. I could go home if he did. But he knows I can't up here."

She showed no sign of tears. But her jaw set tight, and her eyes narrowed.

As for Gil, he didn't think at all. All his energy was in his eyes, which he kept unwaveringly on the clearing.

He saw the man the instant the battered felt hat came up over the creek bank, only half a shot from the cabin door. As soon as he saw the crown of that hat, he relaxed. He said over his shoulder, "It's Blue Back, Lana," and stepped outdoors. "Hello there, Mr. Blue Back."

The Indian climbed out of the creek bed and walked forward slowly with a grin on his broad face. He was obviously an old man, and he liked to go slow.

"How!" he gave Gil greeting. "You fine? I'm fine." He shook hands with satisfaction.

"I haven't seen you for a long time," said Gil. "I've got married since I saw you last."

"Yes?" said the Indian. "Got good woman?"

"Come and sit down inside and see her."

"That's fine," said the Indian. He followed Gil through the cabin door.

Lana forced herself to get up and face him. She saw a brown wrinkled face with dark eyes on which the lids seemed shrunk, a broad, rather flat nose, a simple grinning mouth.

Gil was standing at the Indian's shoulder.

"Mr. Blue Back," he said, "meet Mrs. Martin. Lana, this is Blue Back." Just as if he were a white man.

The Indian had a paunch. He seemed to be pushing it out like a turkey cock. His face did not change, but he said, with great sincerity, "Fine."

"How do you do?"

Lana bowed her head slightly. The man's smell had already taken possession of the room. It was sweetish and greasy. If water had ever touched him, she thought, it had only been when wading the creek; and his moccasins showed how the dirt stuck to them afterwards.

He wore leggings, he had a battered skirt arrangement of deerskin with a few beads on the edge, and a weathered hunting shirt, which, if it had ever had a color, was now so greasy that it was impossible to tell. On his head was the felt hat, with a hole in the pointed crown through which the stem of a basswood leaf was sticking. He also carried a brown musket, a knife, and a hatchet.

"Fine," he said again and sat down on the bench Lana had just risen from.

"Is there any milk left?" Gil asked her. "We haven't any rum, but Blue Back likes milk fine. Don't you?"

"Fine," said the Indian, grinning and slapping his hand on his stomach. "Yes, fine."

Lana threw Gil a glance, she didn't care what he thought of it. The Indian's feet were making muddy pools on her clean floor. And her stomach felt queasy. Then without a word she went out to the spring for their jug of milk. She brought it in and set it on the table.

"Get two cups," said Gil. "And pour him some."

Lana said, "You can pour it yourself."

After one look at her scarlet face, Gil silently did so. He said nothing to her as she went up the ladder to the loft. Blue Back, apparently, took no notice, but fixed his brown eyes on the peacock's feather. He obviously admired it, but said nothing. He accepted the cup of milk.

When he had finished drinking it, Gil asked, "What are you doing this way, Blue Back?"

It always amused him that the stout stodgy Indian had been named for the noisy blue jay.

"Looking for deer." In his broken English, interspersed with innumerable "fines," the Indian explained that he had been hunting over the Hazenclever hill. He had shot a doe which he had left in a tree down by the river to take home. He had a haunch there for Gil if Gil wanted it. But it had taken a long time.

He had found the tracks of two Seneca Indians. He thought they must have come from Cosby's Manor. They had had a small fire and lain around on top of the hill all day. Then they had been joined by a man with shoes on. They had taken the trail for Oswego, he thought. He was going to take the doe home and then he was going up north and west for a scout. He wanted to tell Gil that if he saw two fires on the hill at night, he had better look out. Gil could tell Captain Demooth. Blue Back, in explanation, went on to say that he had heard that the Senecas had sent word to the Oneidas that a party might come down to the head of the valley soon and the Oneidas were to mind their business.

"Thanks for letting me know," Gil said.

Blue Back said it was all right. "Like you. Fine friends. Me, you. Fine." He finished his second cup and got up.

"I'll come for that deer meat," said Gil.

He accompanied the Indian down to the river where the doe had been hung in a willow crotch. The Indian butchered off a hind leg and then turned aside and after some search selected a willow switch. This he peeled and handed to Gil.

"Got fine woman. You young man. You use this on her. Indian don't need it. English man do. I know. I old man. You lick her. She fine woman."

He beamed at this indication of his own sophistication in the matter of white man's culture, shouldered the carcass of the doe and took to the ford.

Feeling very foolish, Gil wiggled the switch and watched him cross the river. It was annoying that Lana had had the poor taste to get up a mad before a guest, even if he was an Indian. Perhaps the greasy old fellow was right, and she needed discipline to take her mind off herself. It made Gil unhappy that he should have noticed.

7.   Talk at Night

Gil walked round the outside of his cabin, taking a piece of flannel from the woodshed on his way. He wrapped the haunch of venison in this and hung it from a branch over the spring where it was cool. He thought he heard Lana in the kitchen, but if she was she was working in the dark. At any rate, when he returned, she was not downstairs.

He saw that she had cleaned up the supper things and washed the two cups he and Blue Back had used. She must have gone back up to bed.

He sat down in the dark by the table, wondering what he ought to say to her. He was half angry, half nettled; and yet he felt sorry for her, too. It was the first time he had wished that they lived close to neighbors, for he would have liked to be able to get the advice of George Weaver, or even of Emma. He did not know what a man ought to do.

Whatever was the matter with her, she had no business talking and acting the way she had before anyone he chose to bring into his house. But on the other hand she had been frightened just before, and a frightened woman could not rightly be held responsible for much, he supposed.

It seemed very serious to Gil. To him it was the kind of thing that shouldn't be let pass. He should not just go up to bed without having it out, and discovering, if he could, what was wrong in her mind. Their whole future life might hinge on what he did. And then it occurred to him what a silly business it was, and he got up angrily from the table.

He didn't light the tallow dip. He took his shoes off in the dark and felt his way upstairs.

The loft was like ink, with the window in the gable showing only a pale gray set of squares. The air smelled faintly of Lana and of spruce wood. Standing beside the trap, Gil stripped to his undershirt.

The boards gave springily as he walked slowly to the bed. His hand touched the foot and then guided him round to his side. He sat down on the edge and said "Lana."

She did not answer. He held his breath and could not hear her breathing. He put his hand out cautiously and felt her hip under the blanket. She was lying with her back to him, and she must be holding her breath.

They were both holding their breath.

"Lana!" He spoke explosively.

She rolled over on her back and said in a very low, calm, forced voice, "Yes, Gil."

"You going to listen to me?"

"Yes, of course, if you want to stay awake."

Dutiful as damnation.

"You didn't have no right acting the way you did."

"What way?" she asked with such deliberate sweetness that he wished he could see her face.

"The way you did in front of Blue Back."

"I brought you what you asked me, didn't I?"

"You could have poured his glass, couldn't you?"

"I didn't know my marriage contract called for waiting on the heathen."

"He ain't a heathen. He's one of Reverend Kirkland's Indians." Gil swallowed. "I bet he's a better Christian than either one of us, for that matter. And even if he wasn't you or me could go into his house and they'd offer us anything there was in it."

"It's too bad you didn't marry an Indian girl."

"It don't matter what you think, Lana. You've got no right to shame me in front of a visitor."

"You've got no right bringing any muck out of the woods into my house, using my things; and I won't stand for it."

"You won't? What will you do?"

She said furiously, "I'll take them and myself back out of here."

"You won't either. As long as we're talking this way you might just as well understand you couldn't do that if you wanted to. There ain't a thing you own here under the law. Now, you listen to me. You behave decently and I won't talk about it. But you can't act like this and expect me to allow it."

He heard her draw a deep breath.

Then she cried out, "You can't stop me. I don't care what the law is. And I don't care what there is in here, either. You can have it. But you can't talk to me that way." She breathed again. "I'll just walk out of here, that's all. You won't know anything of it."

"Now, Lana." Gil tried to talk calmly. "We didn't marry to act this way."

"I don't care what we married for. I won't stand it. I don't mind living here alone. I didn't as long as you was here. I didn't mind working my share outdoors. I didn't let myself get scared. I done everything I thought you'd like. I tried to be good to you. And then you call me a bitch."

"Bitch?" He didn't understand. "I never called you a bitch."

"Yes, you did. When you told me to shut my mouth and not act like a scared bitch."

"And you got mad because of that?" He reached for her hand in the dark. "I didn't think what I was saying. I didn't mean it. Honest, Lana. I wouldn't call you that. I was scared myself, and I didn't want you scaring me worse."

He had sense enough not to try to hold her hand. He felt her shaking. But he got into the bed and lay on his back.

"I never thought that things could begin to work up here the way they are. I don't know what I ought to do."

He waited in the dark. He felt beside him the trembling lengthen into jerks. Suddenly she rolled over against his side. The way she cried was almost brutal.

"Oh, Gil. I hadn't ought to've done so. Only he smelled so bad. I couldn't think he was nice. Oh, Gil!" She put her face against his undershirt. "You were right to call me so. I did act like a bitch."

He didn't say anything, for he felt as if all nature had upheaved inside his chest. He let her go on crying until she had quieted.

Then, when he was just dropping off to sleep himself, damned if she didn't start poking him.

"Gil!"

"Yes."

"You awake?"

"Yes."

"Gil, I better tell you sometime, and I've been trying to all day."

"Tell me what?"

"You and me are going to have a baby."

8. *Trial*

The trial of John Wolff for treason was set for the twenty-fifth of August, Sunday, so that witnesses against the prisoner would not be discommoded in traveling down to Herkimer. It would make no difference to the prisoner; he was already there. They had kept him under guard in the new fort; but the trial, though handled by the military, would take place in the office of Dr. William Petry, son-in-law of the accused man, and a member of the Tryon Committee for German Flats.

The office, which adjoined Dr. Petry's framed house, had originally been a small log barn. One end of it was the general store, the other and smaller section, the dispensary. A sort of counter ran across the room with a removable leaf in the middle, so that doctor and patient were continually within view of those who were buying or who were waiting their turn with the doctor. In that way, a very suggestive and doubled-ended atmosphere was maintained. People waiting would be prompted to buy—groceries or goods; and store customers would be reminded of the fact that their children needed sulphur, or rhubarb and soda, or be encouraged to show the doctor the thumb they had sprained the week before and that had somehow never got just right since.

The doctor was a choleric, tall, and heavy man, invariably dressed in a black coat and a shirt with no cravat. He served both sorts of customers simultaneously, naming prices as he looked down a patient's throat; or, leaving the gut and needle in a cut, he lifted the counter and took down a bolt of calico.

On the day of the trial he was leaning back in a chair under the diploma from the Electoral Palatine Medical Assembly at Mannheim which announced in no uncertain terms that William Petry had successfully answered all questions as to *wounds, in general, contusions, tumors, fractures, luxations,* and *anatomical* and *surgical operations.* The fact that the fort was still noisy with carpenters and joiners had led him to suggest that his store be used as the largest available room in the settlement, the fact of the recent arrival of a shipment of French cloth goods having, naturally, no bearing.

When Lana entered with Gil, the room already seemed unpleasantly crowded. People had lined the counters, until there was hardly passageway up the middle of the floor. They sat wherever they could find a perch, on the grindstones, on the kegs of oil, applejack, and molasses and rum. Even on the road outside people were gathered between the houses: farmers in their best homespun coats, with their wives on their arms, carrying prayer books in their hands, and still with the chilled damp look of churching on their faces.

Someone pointed out herself and Gil as new settlers up under Hazenclever's hill; Gil as the man who had uncovered the evidence. As soon as he helped Lana down from her place behind him on the mare, they gave way readily, offering little encouraging half-words of praise that made her realize that Gil had made a mark in the community and become a person of importance. It was even more impressive as they entered the store. At the door a soldier in a brown coat asked Gil who he was, and when Gil gave his name bawled out in a high, untuneful nasal voice: "Witness for the United States."

A little lane opened for them. Lana would have stayed in the background, but Gil still held her hand, and perforce she had to move forward towards the counter or make a scene. There, at what was now the bar of justice, he let her go and she shrank against the wall, holding her small chintz pocket in both hands.

A terrific smell of snuff causing her to look to her left, she met the quizzical eyes, under shaggy black brows, of the doctor himself. He stared at her with such frank curiosity that the blood flowed to her head and she wondered dizzily whether an educated doctor could tell from merely looking at a girl in a bonnet if she was pregnant.

Gil was standing at the edge of the transverse counter beside George Weaver. Beyond them, sitting down, the lean bright face of Captain Demooth was turned a little away from her, as he talked to the lieutenant from the garrison at the fort who was to preside. Then the lieutenant looked at Gil, and nodded, and met Lana's eye. He pulled out his cuffs very slowly. Lana looked away. When she glanced back again, Captain Demooth was talking over his shoulder and the lieutenant was staring her way, and as their eyes met he smiled.

He must be a young man,—about Gil's age, she thought,—but when he was serious he looked older, less impulsive, and rather lonesome. He had a narrow Yankee face with a snubbed nose and an oddly thin wry mouth that was a little sad. He looked like gentry to Lana, for all his homely face.

Gil was reaching up his right hand to scratch the top of his head as Captain Demooth talked to him. Just in the nick of time, he remembered how carefully he had oiled and combed his hair, and his hand hovered, as if he couldn't think how to disguise the gesture; and the back of his neck got bright red.

Lana's heart swelled. That little piece of defeat on his part showed her how much she loved him. She let her eyes close under the shade of the bonnet and locked her fingers round the pocket strings, and prayed.

"Oh, God, let Gil show up well before the gentry."

The Committee of Safety had committed various disaffected people remaining in German Flats before this. But in a case like Wolff's, in which the suspect was believed to have harbored spies, they had preferred to turn the matter over to the regular army. Lieutenant Biddle had been appointed by Colonel Dayton to handle the business. The colonel was busy with arrangements for the repairing of Fort Stanwix before fall and, as he said, "These damn valley Dutch seem to think the army ought to send up a general for their housecleaning."

"Do you know anything about the case, sir?"

"No. I don't want to. All I want is to get Stanwix decently fixed, but I can hardly get a team out of these people. If I had my say we'd fall back on Fort Hunter and let them take their medicine."

"Yes, sir." The lieutenant swallowed. "But what ought I to do? What line should I take, sir?"

"Please youself, Mr. Biddle. It doesn't matter a hang to us one way or the other. We'll be the butts any way we do it. I'll stand behind you."

Lieutenant John Biddle looked at Gilbert Martin, and he knew that both of them must have the same unhappy feeling on their breakfasts. He wished to God the sergeant would bring in the poor devil and get it over. All about him the German faces kept staring at him. They weren't easy people to get acquainted with. They distrusted soldiers of any rank. The girls were as standoffish as unbroke fillies.

He glanced towards the door again, meeting Lana's eye on the way. He thought, "There's one girl that looks as if she had a heart in her. But Demooth says she's married to the witness, and just as God-saving as the rest of them."

The people outside the door were moving left and right. There sounded the clicking walk of men in step. The sergeant pushed his face through the door, with his hand still wiping his lips, saluted, and announced the prisoner.

"Bring him in," directed the lieutenant. He sighed and took a last look at Lana. The old turkey cock of a doctor was stretching his neck at the girl.

The sergeant drew a paper out of his pocket, and announced: "The prisoner, John Wolff, of Cosby's Manor. Accused of harboring the King's spies and trafficking with treasonable persons."

John Wolff entered. Lana saw his face, stubborn, rather pale, the eyes fixed on the lieutenant. There was another stir at the door and Mrs. Wolff squeezed through. "I got the right," she was saying in a subdued, desperate voice. "I'm his wife. I got the right, ain't I?"

The lieutenant rapped his pistol butt on the counter, and some capsules collapsed in a bottle.

"Order, please."

There was a silence.

"You are John Wolff of Cosby's Manor, as represented?"

"Yes, I am."

"You can stand over against the counter," the lieutenant said.

"Easy on the jug," said the doctor. "It's got acid in it."

Captain Demooth, as a member of the Committee, and the commanding officer of the company of militia which had made the arrest, read the indictment. It caused no titillation. Everyone knew what was in it.

Lana thought, "He'll call on Gil now."

But George Weaver had to give his evidence. . . .

"What were you doing downstairs, Sergeant Weaver?"

"I was kind of keeping my eye on the boys."

"What were they doing?"

"Most of them was looking for Thompson's cellar."

"Did they find it?"

"Yes, they did."

"Did they break in?"

"Yes, sir."

"What were they looking for?"

"I don't know. But they found gin, anyway."

"In other words, they were just looting?"

George hawed a little.

"I guess you could call it that," he admitted.

"Were they all so employed?"

"No. Gil Martin, there. He was looking up in the attic."

"He was sober, I take it."

"You could of fed him hay," said George.

"How did you know he was there?"

"I went to see where he was. I got upstairs and hollered. He said for me to come up. I went up in the attic. We found where there had been people sleeping. We found evidence that there had been a man named Caldwell there. A blind man."

"What is the matter with this man Caldwell?"

"The Committee says he is a spy. George Herkimer's been looking for him."

"Thank you," said Lieutenant Biddle. He wondered where all this was getting him. There was no proof at all about Wolff's harboring spies.

"Gilbert Martin."

Gil was sworn to tell the truth. He spoke in a clear hard voice. It didn't sound quite like his voice, even to himself.

"You are acquainted with the prisoner Wolff?"

"Yes, sir."

"Have you ever to your personal knowledge known him to be associated with treasonable characters?"

"I know he's always stood out for the King's side. Mr. Thompson went after the Johnsons this summer. John's always said the way he stood on things."

"He is known for a Loyalist?"

"Yes, sir."

The lieutenant considered. Then he asked Gil to tell what he had found in the attic, and Gil did so. He further described the man he and Lana had seen at Billy Rose's tavern. He was asked for and gave his deductions. He did so plainly and simply.

"Why hadn't you arrested Wolff when you first caught him in the store?"

"We didn't have nothing on him. Only the powder."

"Were you drunk when you got to the clearing?"

"Some of us was a little lit up, sir."

"That will do," said the lieutenant. Lana felt the doctor touch her leg. "Your boy's done all right," he whispered. "He was fair enough to John, too."

Gil had stepped back. He stood quite still, perspiring. People murmured and nodded. It was all how you looked at the matter. Nine tenths of them thought that there was reasonable cause to judge the prisoner guilty. But there wasn't much proof, not the way the lieutenant was asking questions. Only that business about the eye patch.

The lieutenant turned to Captain Demooth. He asked if there were any other witnesses against the prisoner. There were.

Story Grebb was called. He said he lived the west side of Fall Hill, beyond Bellinger's. He testified that three days before the arrest he had been awakened by his negro man, Hans. He had shut the negro out because the negro had been in the habit of sneaking down to the Herkimer place where they had a black wench named Frailty, and Esquire Herkimer was being annoyed. Hans was frightened because he said there was two Indians on the road. They was asking the way to John Wolff's store. He yelled to them to keep on moving, and he let in Hans and tied him up in the pantry and gave him a hiding.

The following witness made the greatest impression. He was a heavy-handed oldish man, with a white moustache stained at the ends and edges. He said his name was Hon Yerry Dorsch. He lived just west of Eldridge Patent. He testified that on the evening of July 14 he came home from settling a paper with Isaac Paris. That he had taken all day to the trip back, and in the evening when he got to James Jones's house there was a man with a lame left hand sitting in it. That he had on a speckled under jacket, a brown surtout coat, blue woolen stockings and strings in his shoes. . . .

Lana caught her breath as Dorsch continued with circumstantial relish.

That the said man was lame in his left hand: that Dorsch asked him, Jones, where the man came from, and that Jones said he did not know; that the man stood him, Dorsch, a drink, and that then the three of them set out along the Kingsroad in company; that as they went he asked the lame-handed man what his name was, but he would not tell him, but told him that he came up from Albany; that Dorsch was sure the lame-handed man was carrying a bundle of letters, because he stumbled against him once and felt them crackle inside the man's shirt; that the lame-handed man said he was meeting a man with a blind eye, and did Dorsch know such a person, which Dorsch said he did not and would take oath to same now before the lieutenant if need be.

Lieutenant Biddle, listening to the tortuous slow testimony, became aware of the excitement in the audience. The stupid Dorsch had brought with him a peculiar nervous tension. The prisoner Wolff stood against the counter, apparently not hearing a word. The woman who had said she was the prisoner's wife had her hand to her mouth. The pretty girl beside the doctor looked a little better now that her husband had testified, though the stuffiness of the store seemed to be getting on her nerves.

Dorsch droned on in his monotone:—

That they had had to spend the night in the woods, but that in the morning they had come to Billy Rose's tavern and he, Rose, had asked them to come in and sign their names to the Committee Register, and that he, Dorsch, had done so, but that Jones and the lame-handed man had gone out and sat under the apple tree in Rose's yard.

Next witness, William Rose, tavern keeper, corroborated the occurrence, as also Martin's testimony about the man Caldwell. Further said, when he went out into the yard with the register, the lame-handed man had gone, but that Jones was sitting there with Jacobus Seeney.

The lieutenant felt sorry for the prisoner, who had to bear all this on his feet.

"Any more, Captain Demooth?"

There was some similar testimony that took fifteen minutes. It began to seem as if the whole United States had been converging on Cosby's Manor, but Captain Demooth made the point that nobody ever knew the business of any of these people; that it stood to reason from what was reported that many of them were hostile to the United States; and that indubitably some of them had stopped with John Wolff.

A little murmur went out of the room and into the group of people outdoors.

"John Wolff, have you heard the testimony of the witnesses?"

Wolff's mouth twisted sarcastically.

"Some of it."

He met the lieutenant's eye. He saw that the lieutenant looked friendly. But he had lost his own temper listening to all these insinuations.

"John Wolff, have you ever assisted King's people?"

"Yes, I have," he replied in a loud voice. His face was a little pale and his jaw was set. His wife stifled an "Oh, John!" The lieutenant did not notice. His voice went on quietly, with a queer sort of encouragement.

"How did you assist them?"

"If they came to my place without grub, I gave them something."

"When they couldn't pay?"

"Sometimes they paid."

"You haven't a permit under the Committee of the County to run a public house."

"Hell, no. But I don't sell likker over the counter."

"Did you sell them any?"

"In jugs if they could pay for it. Store purchase."

His jaw snapped. His voice was beginning to sound ugly.

"Have you done so lately?"

"I haven't any more to sell," said John Wolff.

"Would you if you had?"

"Yes, I would. I got to make a living."

"Did you feed the two Seneca Indians referred to?"

"Yes."

"Did they pay?"

"No."

"You gave them the food?"

"They was hungry."

"Did you do so willingly?"

He was giving the prisoner every chance to crawl out. But John Wolff was raw. He was sick of the business.

"Yes."

"Why?"

"I couldn't turn them out, could I? They behaved decent. Didn't break in nor nothing like those God-damned drunken Dutch!"

The lieutenant hammered his pistol butt on the counter.

"Talk decent, Wolff."

"Nobody else has."

"Would you have assisted these people on their illegal King's business if you had known?"

"I knew they was on King's business. I didn't know what it was. Why, mister? I didn't ask. I minded my own business, see?"

The lieutenant patiently overlooked it. He could see how the man felt.

"Would you willingly assist the King in his oppression of the United States?"

"If he'd promise to exterminate these damned Dutch I would."

"Is that all you have to say for yourself?"

"Do you want more?"

"If you can't justify yourself under the law you'd better not say anything."

"There ain't any law I know of. Except the King's law. I ain't busted that."

"That will be all."

Lieutenant Biddle looked down at his hands on the counter. He hoped he hadn't marred his pistol hammering with it. As far as he could see, the prisoner was only suspected. Suspected persons, however, were not wanted here. It was his business to call him guilty.

He thought, "Guilty of what?"

"John Wolff," he said, "you have been heard before this court, with the witnesses against you. You have produced no witnesses in your own cause. In the opinion of this court sufficient testimony has been given to prove reasonably that you have entertained people whose business is hostile to this country. You have not denied your entertainment of them, and you have not shown that you have not shared in their business. I therefore find you guilty as charged of being a Loyalist. Therefore, according to regulations, you shall be taken back to Fort Dayton and there imprisoned until such time as you shall be taken out by a squad and shot. The court is now adjourned."

A little murmur again flowed out of the room. Outside people said, "They're going to shoot him."

Lana saw Mrs. Wolff standing like a post, a peeled post, white and brittle.

Gil Martin's jaw dropped open. George Weaver went white and red. The man was a neighbor. The lieutenant got up and signaled to the sergeant. The men took the prisoner by the arms and walked him out the length of the store. Then the lieutenant followed them.

9.   *Fate of Wolff*

Clumping along on his old horse, George Weaver overtook the brown mare just outside of Schuyler. The mare was moving at a walk for the comfort of Lana, who sat sidewise behind Gil. She asked, as if George had happened into the midst of an argument, "Are they really going to shoot him, Mr. Weaver?"

"They are, according to law, I guess."

"But why *shoot* him? I can't see that he's done any real harm."

"Why," said George, "I don't know that he has, either."

"Then, *why?*"

Gil spoke from the encirclement of her arms, crossly, so that she thought she felt the words rise through his body.

"That's what she's been asking me till I'm just about ready to get sick."

Lana lifted her chin and stared at George.

"What did you really arrest him for, Mr. Weaver?"

George uncomfortably scratched his head. Lana's dark eyes had a sort of seeking-after-truth look that made him want to get the rights of it in his own dim way.

"I don't know, Lana. It was Jeams MacNod's idea it would keep me out of trouble for letting the lads into Thompson's house. I didn't have no idea John Wolff would get killed for it." He colored. "Honest, Lana."

"Of course," she said. "I know you wouldn't want to hurt anybody, Mr. Weaver."

"What makes it real bad," continued George, "is that it didn't do no good anyhow. I got a regular tongue roasting off the lieutenant. Why, you'd have thought I was a thief, the way he talked. Mark Demooth stood up for us, though. He said it wasn't a cobbler's patch on the way the Yankees have been stripping women and girls down in Albany County."

"I know, I know. But this is terrible. We ain't Yankees."

"Yes," said George. "I expect it really is. I asked the lieutenant. Mister, I says, are you going to shoot poor John *dead*? And he said, well, what do *you* expect? As if I was responsible."

"What's ever going to become of Mrs. Wolff?"

"I don't know. She's a sour kind of person. Doc Petry offered her a place in his house (she's his wife's stepmother), but she said she'd go back to Cosby's and starve afore she'd do that."

"I don't blame her."

"Doc ain't so bad," George replied earnestly. "He's the only doc hereabouts, but he takes care of anybody he can get to, whether they pay or not. He don't press you. It took us a year to pay for Cobus. Eggs and a sucking pig. Me and Emma made our minds up to pay for Cobus afore he got weaned, and we did."

"I thought he looked cruel."

"Oh, I guess he'll get John's life saved. He's got influence. He's gentry."

"I don't believe it."

Gil broke in, "Oh, hush your noise, Lana. It couldn't be helped. The King's people didn't think anything of beating the tar out of unarmed men while they had the strength. Look at the way they licked Jake Sammons when they raised the liberty pole in Caughnawaga, last year."

Lana was silent. She could tell that the business was preying on Gil's mind. She made up her own mind to see if she could do anything about it. She thought, maybe, she could get Mrs. Demooth to interest the captain.

Next day, while Gil was away at Christian Reall's, helping the little man clear logs off a piece, she went down to Demooth's. When she came into the clearing she saw Clem Coppernol leading the captain's horse round to the barn. She went herself to the kitchen.

"Is Mrs. Demooth inside?" she asked the hired girl.

"God!" said Nancy, dropping a platter. "I don't know."

She stared with petrified blue eyes at Lana. But the crash had brought in Mrs. Demooth.

"Nancy!" she said in a hard voice. "If you've broke it I'll have Clem put his belt on you this time."

"It ain't broke, Mrs. Demooth." Nancy began to blubber. "Honest it ain't, only a piece. I'll fix it. I got startled so."

Mrs. Demooth then saw Lana. The swing of her skirts stilled and she became calm all in a gesture.

"How do you do, Mrs. Martin? It's nice you came down. Come into the sitting room with me."

The incongruity of polished dark wood furniture, of fine chairs, and board floors with carpet on them, all within log walls, made Lana feel shy. She sat down straight and silent and did not look at Mrs. Demooth. Overhead she could hear the quick steps of the captain moving back and forth.

"Captain Demooth's just got back," explained Mrs. Demooth. "Will you move out of the sunlight or shall I draw the curtain for you?"

"Please don't trouble. I like the sun," said Lana, not without a momentary malicious pleasure as she looked at Mrs. Demooth's carefully powdered face. "Mrs. Demooth, I came down to see you. To see if you would speak to Captain Demooth. About John Wolff."

"Oh," said Mrs. Demooth, who had sat down beside an embroidery frame. "Oh. You don't mean the man that got arrested in Cosby's Manor?"

"Yes."

"Is he a friend of yours? I understand Mr. Martin was one of the men who arrested him. He found the evidence of that awful blind man's being in Thompson's house. I never had much of an opinion of the Thompsons," she ended with satisfaction.

"Gil was there," said Lana slowly.

"Yes, Mark said some very complimentary things about your husband."

"I know. Gil was trying to do what he ought." Lana had a momentary thought of the silk piece, but let it go. "But he feels bad about Wolff's being shot."

"Oh, that!" Mrs. Demooth gave a brittle little laugh. "Do you think it matters much?"

Lana said slowly, "Yes, it does. Gil wouldn't say anything. But I don't want him to have an awful thing like that on his conscience."

"My dear," said Mrs. Demooth, "what can women do? It's men's business. Killing each other. I believe personally that the man must be guilty."

"Not to be killed," said Lana.

"I try to keep things peaceful here. It's hard enough to make life pleasant. Mark gets so fretted. I'm sure you'll understand."

Lana's small dark face became almost grim.

"I'm bound and determined to do something. What I can. I can't sleep myself, thinking of Mrs. Wolff." She stopped. She had seen Mrs. Demooth look up. Now an automatic brightness came over her face.

"Oh, there you are, Mark. Have you met Mrs. Martin? She's been so obliging as to call on me."

Captain Demooth stepped into the room.

"Good morning, Mrs. Martin."

Lana rose and curtsied, hardly knowing how to look at him. Nor did she know how to judge a man like Demooth. The doctor may have been gentry, as Weaver maintained, but he had none of the captain's air of self-containment. By his very politeness in bowing to her he put her definitely outside of his life.

"It's so nice to have you back, Demooth," his wife said. "Are you going to favor me for any time?"

"A day or so," he said, looking straight at Lana. But when he spoke it was to his wife. "My dear, I didn't mean to eavesdrop, but I heard you and Mrs. Martin talking about John Wolff." He helped himself to a little snuff, flicked himself, and sniffed. Lana thought he did it like any other man, except more quietly. Then he looked at Lana and his smile was quite pleasant. "What is it you want of me?"

Lana took hold of her courage.

"Are they going to shoot Mr. Wolff?"

"I'm not sure. You don't want it to happen?"

"No," said Lana passionately.

"Neither do I. For the same reason."

Lana discovered that she and Captain Demooth could talk quite frankly. She was afraid to look at his wife. She knew that if she did, she could not go on talking, even though he sounded so impersonal.

"For Gil," she said with a little nod.

"For the whole company. They were just lit. And they tried to find an excuse."

"Gil didn't!"

"No, he was just doing his duty. He took orders. That Jeams MacNod is the whole trouble. School-teachers ought to get more pay. They sometimes have brains. Then they get discontented. I'm afraid Jeams MacNod is going to make trouble."

"I don't know him."

"He's honestly patriotic. To me patriotism doesn't mean a great deal. So are the Butlers, you see. I wish they weren't."

Slapping his boot, he walked over to the window. He saw a hundred yards of worked ground, a split rail fence, then the rising waves of treetops, all the way up the Hazenclever hill to the sky line. No break, but the running water, all the way to Canada. The split rail fence was a frail dam against the wilderness.

He turned so that his face was in shadow against the clean panes. "I tried to get John Wolff off. The best I could do was to get a stay of one week. Dr. Petry went down to see Colonel Herkimer. He was willing to back the petition in confidence, but he could not put his name to it. It's essential that we get him appointed general of our militia because he's the only man that could pull the valley together in war. Otherwise it would be easy to get Wolff off."

Lana said "Yes," but her righteous anger was aroused. Now Wolff would die because a man wished to become a general. She raised hot eyes to the captain, and she was surprised to see him smile.

"Mrs. Martin," he said, "believe me, Herkimer doesn't like this. We advised him to keep out of it. We had to. But Petry will have to get other names and he's blistering mad about it. I was trying to keep him calm enough to write to Schuyler. We'll get John Wolff off, though. I promise." He paused. "And I understand your feeling, and I think you're dead right."

Lana could not think of anything to say.

He turned to Mrs. Demooth.

"Sara, don't you thing we might have a glass of sack?"

"Yes, of course. Mrs. Martin ought to have something against the walk home." Mrs. Demooth's voice was smoothly acid. But she left the room. The captain said quietly, "You'll understand, Mrs. Martin, that I think John Wolff has been working against us. That he was a dangerous man to have around?"

"I know," she said. "I guess so. But what's going to happen to him, sir?"
"Well, if he does get off, he'll have to go to jail anyway. A lot of people have already been sent for less offense than his."
"Where will they send him?"
"Simsbury, I suppose. The mines." He let the matter drop. Lana understood that she was supposed to do the same. She took the slender stemmed glass and drank the sack without tasting it.

Dr. William Petry was boiling with rage. He marched through the front door and out on the verandah that faced the river. He stopped there, thinking of some of the things he might have said to Nicholas Herkimer. It would be beneath his dignity to go back and stick his head inside the door like a fishwife; but if he waited a moment or two Nicholas Herkimer might come out to see why. Then he would tell him.

The Herkimer place was the finest farm west of Johnstown. A lot of people thought that the high brick house, painted a bright red, was as impressive to look at as Sir William Johnson's fancy hall. Certainly the wheat and corn were as good as any you could see in the valley; and the herd of mares in the willow pasture along the river bank were the kind that most men only dreamed of.

The mere sight of them served to enrage the doctor more. When Herkimer obliged him by coming out and saying, "Well, Bill," Dr. Petry started swearing, without even turning his head.

"Now, Bill," said Herkimer.

But the doctor had remembered something.

"I forgot you don't speak English decent," he said, and repeated his remarks in German. His translation was free, fluent, and forceful. German was a good language to curse in.

They stood in the sunlight—the doctor at the edge of the steps, red-faced, twitching his black eyebrows, standing very erect in his rusty black coat, and fixing with his eye the astonished little black negro who was holding the old gray saddle horse. Behind him Nicholas Herkimer came barely to his shoulder blades. He had round shoulders and a big head with an unkempt mop of grizzled hair. His eyes were coal black, passionate, and very sharp. But just now, like the long upper lip of his loose mouth, they showed amusement. He looked more like a farmhand than the owner of this opulent farm.

As the doctor caught breath, he said quietly in his heavy accent, "All right, Bill. If you say so. But it don't make any difference. I won't do it. You can get Wolff off all right; but I can't. If I make a move for Wolff there is a lot of people who will say I'm interested in the other side—with my brother in Canada."

"You don't have to give a damn," exploded the doctor.

"No I don't," Herkimer said. He flushed slowly. "But I've got to listen. There's nobody else could get our own militia out. You know that."

But the doctor, whose passion was still up, refused to see sense.

"All right, general," he said. "Go your own way. Be a general if you like. If you want to hang a man to be one. But if you get hurt with your damn war, don't come to me to get your arm fixed." He snorted. "By God, though, I'd like to do one operation on you."

He stamped down the steps, snatched the old horse's reins from the hand of the negro, and humped himself goutily up into the saddle.

"Bill," called Herkimer, "you write to General Schuyler."

"I'll do what I like," roared the doctor. He kicked the old horse's side and headed him for the river. Herkimer sat down on the steps. He grinned a little. Bill Petry had forgotten that you had to ferry over the river there. He waited until the doctor had turned back from the bank.

"Hello, Bill," he said. "What is it?"

The doctor cursed.

Herkimer turned to the negro.

"Trip," he said, "take the doctor over."

"Yassah, Cunnel," said the negro, and rushed to the scow.

Herkimer got up and went into his house.

"Frailty," he shouted. "Bring some beer in the blue mug."

He went into his office and sat down at his desk. A slim negress, with high shoulder bones showing through her print dress, brought in the beer. Then his wife entered.

"Hon," she said quietly, using his old name, "there's another Indian out there."

"Bring him in."

His wife ushered in a young Indian buck. He was without blanket or shirt. Sweat made beads on his greased, yellowish-brown hide. His kilt twitched over his knees to his deep breathing. He handed Herkimer a letter tied to a stick.

Herkimer opened it.

The Reverend Mr. Kirkland was writing from the Oneida town. He had had word from Spencer that a party had set out from Oswego towards the east. They had not touched Oneida Lake, therefore they must be going through the woods to the north.

The little man's big head nodded. Hazenclever's and the upper part of the West Canada Kill should be watched. Up above Schell's blockhouse. He forgot about Bill and John Wolff.

"Frailty," he shouted. She came in on her broad feet.

"The men are busy," Herkimer said, over his shoulder, as he wrote in his crabbed laborious way: "Tell George to send oud ten men nord of Schell's to find a party of eight peeble. Pass the word to Demuth to look out at Deerfield also."

He said to the negress, "You can run pretty fast?"

"Yassah, pretty good, Cunnel."

"You run like the devil to Mr. Dygert's and give him this."

"Yassah, Cunnel."

He looked at her sharply.

"Frailty, you feeling all right?"

"Yassah, Cunnel. Good enough."

"Has Mrs. Herkimer spoke to you?"

"Yassah. She say I can have de baby in de house again dis time ef'n I pass my promise not to have no more on her."

"Whose is it this time?"

"I guess hit's from dat Hans of Mr. Grebb's, Cunnel. He de pesteringest nigger. I jus' couldn' think of no other way to get rid of him. Dat's de truth, Cunnel."

"You run," he said.

As she went out, his eyes came back to the Indian, who had been standing immovably through this conversation, with his brown eyes seeing everything, but showing nothing.

"Come on," said Herkimer, "I'll get you one drink."

The Indian nodded intelligently.

Dr. Petry had been framing in his mind the letter he was going to write to General Schuyler. But at the turn-off he recollected that Mrs. Small was expecting and that he had promised to attend her. He thought he would look in and see how she was coming on with it.

He stopped off at the blockhouse the settlement was erecting, and found that the stockade had been completed. Jacob Small was not there, but one of the Helmer boys was putting the spy loft roof on. He called down, "Yes, Doc, Cap'n got word from his house to go down there. He ain't come out since. I know. I can see pretty near everything in the country from up here."

The doctor grunted. He could foretell what he would find. The woman, after going through ten years of married life as barren as a bedpost, had now started labor two weeks ahead of time. She was thirty-one years old and Jake was sixty-five, and he had told the red-haired hussy at the time that she had no business marrying a man that old. He didn't like this way of men of fifty taking girls to bed. Better look around for a widow their own age. It irritated him; and the girl had laughed in his face.

She was a sharp-spoken girl, officious, pushing, pert, and he had a feeling she must have known he might drop in and have planned the labor just to catch him when he had other things to do. It would take a long time. She was built like a trout, with no pelvic bone worth the name, and she was old enough anyway to have a bad time. The business was going to be hell for everybody, and especially for her. Well, it might be a good experience for her to go through. A good lesson.

That thought eased him as he swung himself grumpily off the horse and took the saddlebags off his withers. He knocked on the door and found himself effusively welcomed by Captain Small.

"By God, Doc, the Lord must have brought you. I sent Joe Casler after you two hours ago. How'd you get here so soon?"

Doc explained. "How long's Betsey been at it?"

"Commenced just after breakfast. She let herself go at some griddle cakes and they seemed to settle right down in her."

"Five hours," grunted the doctor. "Where'd you bed her?"

"She's back in the bedroom. We didn't have time to carry the bed in here. Jake, she says, Jake, just let me get right down on a bed. And don't you touch me, Jake. My God, Doc, it's a hell of a thing for a man my age to come up against."

"Pains bad?"

"Terrible. You ought to hear the way she takes on."

"She always made a lot of noise," said the doctor. "She's a fresh girl.

You needn't act like a run sheep, Jake. I bet you hurt your Ma just as bad. That's the only sensible way to look at it."

"You think so, Doc? Crimus, once or twicet I felt like laying down dead myself."

"Have a drink. Got anything in the house?"

"I got some distilled apple juice."

"Get some, but bring it to me first. Who's with her?"

"She wouldn't let me send for anybody. Said she didn't want them mussing up her house."

The doctor glanced round the immaculate kitchen, with its shining brass pans and the copper kettle and the dishes in the dresser. Somehow it made him think of Betsey herself, pert, and spicy. She'd told him off before. Now she'd have to eat pie. People never thought of that when they spoke their piece to the doctor.

"You go and get in a woman."

"There ain't nobody handy but Mrs. Helmer. Betsey can't stand her."

"Good," said the doctor. "She's just the person. Fetch her right off. But bring me that apple juice first."

He walked into the bedroom with a heavy tread. It was a nice bedroom, with a good, solid, four-post bed. The white curtains drawn over the window moved gently with a stir of air and took the curse off the smell of pigs from the yard out back. The floor had a crocheted round rug on it and there was a good chest under the window.

"Well," said the doctor, "you're damn well married at last, ain't you, Betsey?"

He carried along a stool with his foot and sat down beside the bed. The woman lying on the bleached sheet seemed younger than her age. Her waving red hair was a tangled wet mop on the pillow. The pins had fallen out and lay all over the bed. Her face was thin, quite white, especially about the mouth. The eyes staring at him were blue and looked feverish. Her body under the rumpled coverlet was shaped like a sixteen-year-old's.

She didn't answer. She was holding onto the coverlet with clenched, thin, and slightly freckled fists, and the doctor said nothing as he watched the progress of a pain. But he pulled out his watch and laid it on the bed and then put his hands in hers and let her have something to clinch on.

When the pain was over, she raised her eyes to his and drew a tremendous long breath.

"Hello, Doc," she said. "You've been a long time getting here."

"So have you, Betsey."

Her lips drew back over her teeth. They were uneven, but strong and white. They and her natural smile were, for him, her saving grace.

"Where you been?" she asked.

He told her. "And now you've got to start this when I'm trying to get John Wolff out of trouble. You always were a contrary devil of a girl."

She closed her eyes and said, "God damn," under her breath, and the doctor glanced at his watch. The husband came in carrying a jug and two glasses. He poured one sloppily for the doctor and set it down. "I just can't drink, Doc," he said. "I got to run."

He bolted out of the house after Mrs. Helmer.

"Where's Jake gone?"

"After Mrs. Helmer."

"I don't want her."

"I've got to have a woman. Jake's no good. And you're down now, and you can't do anything. Nobody can help you but the Lord, unless it's me. You'll just have to lay down and take what's coming. See?"

"Damn you, Doc," she said. She grinned. "It's a hell of a business."

"Swearing won't help," the doctor said with gravity.

She laughed in his face, and he felt better.

"I'm going to take your clothes off," he said.

"Why can't you wait for Mrs. Helmer?"

"You'll feel better. And I'll have to take a look at you anyway."

"All right," she said.

She sighed, after he had undressed her and tightened the sheet. He went out into the kitchen, built up the fire, and put on a couple of kettles. When he came back, he sat down beside her.

He said, "When you married Jake you thought he was too old to corner you like this, didn't you?"

She nodded.

"Well," he said, "it serves you right."

She said, "My mother died when I was born."

"Yes, I remember. I did the best I could."

"It's just a curse with us, I expect."

"You ain't built right."

"I know." She turned her eyes to his and said, "There's one thing, Doc. You won't believe it, but I'll tell you anyway. I loved Jake and I still do. We had a lot of fun."

"I'll bet," said the doctor dryly.

"You troubled about John Wolff?"

"He's a mean sort of cuss," said the doctor. "I never liked him. But he's Kate's Pa. I've got to do something."

She nodded.

"It's all a mess," she said brightly, and then caught hold.

When Jake returned with Mrs. Helmer, both breathing hard, the doctor drank his apple juice and let the woman attend Betsey. Mrs. Helmer was a stout German *Frau*. She had had twelve children of her own and she probably knew as much about it as he did. She looked at Mrs. Small's bare body with a critical eye and then went out to see how the water was coming.

Jake Small gulped at his glass and looked away from his naked wife. He felt that the world had turned immodest. He couldn't control it; but it didn't seem right for a human being to be handled that way. It was his doing, too; and to think that he had been quite delighted at first! It was one of those surprises that happen to a man after a long life. It just went to show.

"It's a terrible thing for a man my age, Doc."

"Now, Jake. Don't say that again."

"All right, Doc." He paused and fumbled the glass with his hands. He was looking for a nice outside topic. "You think they're going to shoot Wolff?" he inquired.

"I don't know," said the doctor. "I can't get help from Herkimer. And Colonel Dayton won't see me. He's all twittered on account of not being able to get teams to haul stuff out to Stanwix. Schuyler wants the fort finished before spring. He's got some crazy notion of the British coming down on sleds or something."

"My God!" said Small. "You don't say?"

"Everybody's got crazy ideas about this country."

A motion on the bed made him look at his watch again and Jake went over to the window and leaned out. Mrs. Helmer came bustling in from the kitchen and bent over the footboard. But Betsey shook her head. "No, thanks, Mrs. Helmer." Her voice held no gratitude for the woman. "Listen, Doc. If Dayton feels that way and you can get him four or five teams, maybe he would get John Wolff off. Jake would send ours, I guess."

"Sure," said Jake, explosively. "Casler owes me work too. You fix her up, Doc, and I'll promise you two teams, maybe three, for a couple of weeks."

Dr. Petry got up and leaned over the bed with admiration on his homely face.

"Betsey, you're quite a girl."

She stuck her tongue out, bit it, and shrieked.

"Get out of here, Jake," said the doctor. He took Betsey's hand. "I'll fix you up all right, Betsey, if it's the last job I ever do."

Her lips drew back. Jake took one look at her and fled.

Dr. Petry arrived at Fort Dayton after dark. He had a job getting in to see Colonel Dayton, but when he did he came right to the point.

"How many teams do you need?"

"Do you know of any, doctor?"

"How many?"

"How many can you promise?"

"Would four teams be any use?"

"I'd shoot my grandmother for that many."

"You needn't shoot any. You can have those teams if you let John Wolff off."

"What the devil . . ."

"I don't care what you do to him. I mean I don't want him shot. I married his daughter, see? I reckon you can fix it."

"I'll have to send him to jail for the duration of the war; I can't do better than that."

"That's all right with me. I just don't want the poor fool killed."

The colonel got up and shook hands.

The doctor went home and routed his wife out of bed.

"They ain't going to shoot John," he said flatly.

She came out of the bedroom in her nightdress and stared at him with her pale face that so resembled Wolff's.

"Oh, Bill," she said. They stared at each other. Then she asked, "Where've you been all day?"

"Getting John off," he said crossly. "And attending a case."

"You must be tired," she said. "You coming to bed?"

Her voice invited him. She was making up for the way she had acted since her father's arrest, as if that had been his fault. He couldn't really blame her. He supposed you got fond of your father sometimes, even if he was John Wolff. But he shook his head. He went down to the kitchen and stirred up the fire and got some rum from the store. He was thinking about Betsey Small. He wouldn't have believed it was possible to have got a baby out of a body like that, and have both live.

Dayton had said that Herkimer had had word of trouble to be expected on the West Canada or at Hazenclever's. Some of the rangers had gone up the Kill before dark. They had sent word to Demooth.

When he finally changed his mind and went into his bedroom his wife found him difficult. She couldn't understand why he should act so, but she accepted her lot like a martyr.

Two mornings after the birth of Jacob and Betsey Small's first child, John Wolff was prodded on his blankets by the muzzle of the sergeant's musket. It was close after sunrise and the fort was yet quiet.

"Get up," said the sergeant. "Your wife wants to see you."

He said, "My wife."

"Yes, she wants to say good-bye to you."

John Wolff sat dumbly on the edge of the blankets, with his hands round his knees, his dull eyes staring at the soldier's Yankee face.

"They ain't going to shoot you," the sergeant said with contemptuous kindness. "They're sending you down to Albany." He walked out of the door, holding it open behind him. Through it Wolff heard his wife sobbing. It seemed to him the last unnecessary jab of fate that he should have to put up with his wife's weeping before breakfast. But he knew that he had a duty to perform. "Come in," he said. "And quit that crying."

"Oh, John. They ain't going to kill you."

"No," he said dazedly.

"Where are they taking you to?"

"I don't know," he said.

She had sat down beside him on the blanket. She was sniffling her sobs back into her nose. Her clothes were put on which-way and her hair was still braided.

"How long will you be away, John?"

"I don't know," he said. He began to feel more kindly. "Listen, dear." (He hadn't called her *dear* for a good many years; she was a fool woman, always scared to death of something. She got on his nerves; but he had to admit she was loyal, if she was weak-minded.) "Listen," he said, "what are you going to do?"

"I don't know."

He said bitterly, "There's fourteen dollars hid in the store. But that won't last so long. Maybe you could live with Kate."

"She asked me, but I said I'd rather die than stay in his house."

"I don't blame you. But it's the only thing."

"I'll get the money. I'll board with somebody. Maybe I can get work somewheres. Maybe I'd move down to where they're taking you, if we knew where it was."

"People look at me here," she added plaintively. "How long will they keep you away, John?"

"They can't keep me after the army comes down. That won't be long. Maybe next spring. Then I'll get back here."

"Oh, John!"

He put his arm round her shoulder and kissed her.

"You look out for yourself," he said.

He stood uncertainly as the sergeant waited for him. He couldn't understand how you could get fond of a person without ever knowing you were. Then he handed her what silver he had on him.

"It's only just over a pound," he whispered. "I won't need it. If you could get to Canada, you could see Mr. Thompson or Mr. Butler. Walter Butler, he's helped people. He helped Witmore a couple of years ago with his land. But I guess you can't get there." He faced the sergeant. "Where are you taking me to?"

"Albany."

"Well, good-bye, Ally."

"Good-bye, John."

They put him in a wagon with two soldiers and drove out through the settlement towards the Kill ford. There was still morning mist over the creek, and as the team hauled out on the Kingsroad on the far side, they surprised a doe drinking.

The afternoon of the third day, the sergeant delivered John Wolff to the keeper of the Albany jail. He was put in a room with four other men, and the room was so small that they could not all lie down in it.

Two days later they were all five ferried over the river and put into the hands of a teamster named Bush, who was getting five dollars for taking them to Simsbury with two sheriff's officers as guards. They traveled by the way of Canaan and they were two days making the trip—the longest John Wolff had ever made, for he had been born and spent his life in Tryon County.

He did not feel sociable, either, with the other prisoners. He kept thinking of Ally all the time, of the way he had never managed decently to appreciate what a good woman she was, whine or no whine. It preyed upon him. It was the worst part of going to jail. Even when he was informed that two of the other men were Mr. Abraham Cuyler, the former mayor of Albany, and Mr. Stephen DeLancey of the great family that ranked with Schuylers, Johnsons, Van Rensselaers, and Livingstons, it made no difference to him. He answered their request by telling who he was, and what had happened to him; but he listened to their furious indignations like a person outside himself.

When they reached Simsbury, the heel of the moon was over the barracks on the high hill. The horses climbed the road painfully and walked through the gate. An officer in underdrawers and a black coat and hat took them inside. He led them through a door into the face of the hill. They found themselves in a room with no windows. It was the guardroom. The officer kicked one of the soldiers, who got up and started a small forge working in one corner.

The officer said, "You can have new irons for twenty shilling apiece. Or

you can take rusty ones." One of the five, a tailor, with an instinct for
getting on the right side, purchased new ones.

John Wolff watched the dexterous soldier hammer on the manacles.
They were joined together by a chain of long links, which in turn was
linked by two chains to the anklets. The whole affair weighed over forty
pounds. The heated iron burned his wrists, but he hardly felt it at all. He
seemed dazed. Mr. DeLancey gave his name for him when the officer
checked the list the sheriff's officers had handed him.

Then the blacksmith opened a trap in the floor.

"That's where you're going," said the officer. "If you don't make trouble,
I won't trouble you. You can come up every other day, when your name's
called. You'll get your meals lowered down like the rest."

He watched them with apathetic eyes. The two gentlemen went down
the ladder first. They did not even look at the officer. The tailor shuddered
at the dank smell of stale water. The fourth man, like John Wolff, seemed
to be dazed. He was being sent down for beating up a soldier who had
molested his wife. John Wolff went last.

They found themselves twelve feet down in the mine, in a small sentry
room. There were a couple of soldiers there with a lantern and a pack of
cards. As the prisoners descended, one of these opened another trap and
said, grinning, that there was another flight.

He held the lantern over the hole for them to see. Far down below they
saw men lying on a patch of damp sand. The men yelled when they saw the
light. "Company's coming," the soldier roared, and laughed. He dropped
the trap over John Wolff's head, barely missing his hands.

John Wolff went slowly down a slimy iron ladder, which had been
grouted into the stone. It was hard work; the irons were heavy to handle,
and the chains clashed on the rungs. The air grew damper and cooler.
He began to shiver. His eyes were lustreless when he reached the bottom
at last. A bearded man in the remains of a cravat and broadcloth clothes
took him by the hand.

"You'll get used to the cold," he said. "It never gets colder, even in
winter. It just stays about the same temperature as that."

He pointed at the water. Now John Wolff saw that it was like an underground pond at one end of which he stood. Directly overhead, the walls
rose into obscurity. "It's seventy feet to open air," said one of the men.
"They've iron bars over it." John Wolff lowered his eyes to the water again.
It filled two passages of the mine; and all around the trickle and drip of
water sounded unceasingly from every wall.

"You can't get out," the man explained. It was obvious.

Mr. DeLancey asked through chattering teeth, "What are those for?"
He pointed to three braziers.

"Charcoal. We burn them or we suffocate. If we make trouble they
threaten us by keeping back the charcoal. It's all very simple." He smiled.
"I've been here over a year now. I got taken by the Committee. I come
from Virginia. My name's Francis Henry."

There were thirty men or more, lying on the sand. They didn't get up.
They didn't speak. They lay there like half-dead beasts.

Mr. Henry said, "It's the custom for new arrivals to attend to the
braziers. You can settle it between yourselves."

John Wolff spoke for the first time that day.

"I'll look after them. I want to get warm."

Mr. Henry showed him the charcoal box.

"Don't fall asleep," he said. He pointed to the dark water. "We've a rule. Anybody who goes to sleep tending fire gets thrown in there. It takes you a week to dry out."

"I won't," said Wolff. Then he looked up. "Mister, do they let you write letters?"

"It's against the rules. But one of the guards can be bought. It costs a pound."

John Wolff sat down. He watched Mr. Henry return to his dirty blanket. Then he watched the braziers, and the smoke from them curling up to the ceiling. It went straight up, but when it reached the ceiling, seventy feet above, it started slowly seeping back down the walls and slowly licked away into the shafts of the mine. It seemed to be floating on the water like canoes.

One pound. He wondered whether Ally had gone back to Cosby's Manor yet. He wondered if she would be as scary by herself as she was when he was round to be complained at.

10. *Nancy Brings a Note*

About a week later, Lana was alone in the cabin. Gil was working out time against the fall logging and burning he expected to do, when he would want George Weaver and Christian Reall and Clem Coppernol for two or three days. He was paying off Captain Demooth in grass from the swale. The trees were mostly girdled, and already had dried out on the lower branches, the leaves turning brown, with only tufts of green at the tops. From the window Lana could see in a vague way how the new land would lie, straight to the west of the cabin.

She felt listless and dull-headed. There was no doubt in her mind now that there was a baby on the way, and though she could have wished that there might have been a year or so without one, Gil was pleased. A man could clear his land well enough, but when he began to work crops he needed help; and there was only one way to get help in the back country, and that was to lay up children against the time. She wondered whether he would be displeased if the child were a girl. Girls weren't much use around a farm. But the main thing for a successful wife was to prove herself fertile. The sex of her offspring was generally ascribed either to an act of God or to the male parent, according to the reaction of the man himself. She thought, in any case, she wouldn't have to be afraid of Gil.

He had recently bought a fleece from Kast, in Schuyler, and he had told her that in his absence she had better not try to keep on with piling brush. It would be better if she stayed indoors and carded and cleaned the fleece. She forced herself to the task, now, for she had been putting it off all day, on the pretext that the cabin needed a doing over. She had cleaned and sanded the floor and swept out the loft. All the pans had been taken down to the brook, where it was cool, for scouring. But there was no other thing to do after that and she had finally forced herself to come back to the hot kitchen.

The wool had a greasy smell; it put oil on her fingers; it was matted and torn from grazing on the edge of the woods; and the leg fleece had clay dried hard as shot that must be carefully removed. It was too precious to waste a hair of it.

From where she sat, Lana could look up from time to time at the peacock's feather on the dresser. Sight of it made her think of home. By now they would be finishing the wheat harvest; her sisters would be binding sheaves, laughing with the reapers. With the team hitched to the crib wagon, her father would be driving down to them. Her mother, standing in the door, would shade her eyes against the sun and stare after him, westward over the field, westward; perhaps thinking of Lana, trying to see her.

During the past week she had had a feeling of her mother's solicitude, when she herself sat down alone with her thoughts, when she took to dreaming with the peacock's feather.

She resolutely set to work. It made her feel better when she got down to it and could see the time of spinning coming nearer. Spinning was the next best thing to music: the vibration of the wheel entered your body; its humming got into the heart; the thread mounted on the spindle, like dreams come true when you were a girl, or hope fulfilled when you got older, or like the memory of life itself. When a woman spun, she had her destiny in her own hands to make. A man had no place in spinning.

Lately she had noticed a queer thing in herself—that though her mind might wander, and her body lose awareness, senses like sleeping dogs awoke and walked. It was so now. She had heard nothing. Her hands were occupied with the comb and wool. She was not thinking any more of her girlhood home or her home with Gil. If she had been thinking at all, it had been of herself as a being past herself, growing without her own volition, like a lone plant in the woods.

Yet long before she heard a thing, before her mind wakened her senses to the approach of anyone, she knew that some person was coming near the cabin. When she finally did react it was to start up in a cold sweat with the greasy fleece clutched in both hands like an apron over her knees.

She faced the door, slender and dark, her eyes clouded like damp glass, completely defenseless.

The person stopped before her in the door, hesitantly, awkwardly, half frightened.

"It's me," she was saying. "It's just me. Nancy. I've got a letter for you, Mrs. Marting."

"A letter?" Lana said mechanically.

Nancy looked into her face and swallowed noisily.

"Yes, Mrs. Marting, from Mr. Demooth. Capting, I mean." She thrust a folded piece of paper out at arm's length. "I don't aim to stay. I'll just give it and get along."

Lana came to herself.

"Oh, no, Nancy." The girl's foolish face and wide blue eyes looked pitifully afraid of her. "Come in, Nancy."

"Oh no, Mrs. Marting. I couldn't set in with you. Missis is always after me, reminding me I'm just a hired help. I've got no place inside your house. I know it. Only sometimes I forget it."

"Of course you have. I'm glad to have company. Come in."

Nancy put a tentative foot across the threshold. It was shod in an old blue cloth shoe of Mrs. Demooth's, too small, and slit to let the toes out. As she took the letter, Lana felt like weeping, to think how nearly she had deprived the girl of a great excitement.

Nancy was got up with care. In spite of the heat, she was wearing a blue camlet cloak over her dress, which was a calico, also obviously handed down. She had a string of beads round her neck, of blue and red glass, and a red ribbon in her yellow hair. The hair, too, had been brushed with thought and elaborately braided round her head.

Now she came in and sat down on a stool, denying herself the backed chair. Her china-blue eyes made one rapid revolution of the room.

"My," she said, with an unconscious imitation of Mrs. Demooth's inflection, "you have a nice place, Mrs. Marting."

"Do you like it, Nancy? I'm glad."

"You haven't any picters. But that feather's prettier than a picter, I believe."

"I'm fond of it."

"We hain't got feathers in the big house."

Lana read the letter.

DEAR MRS. MARTIN,

I am writing you this to let you know that John Wolff has been sent to Simsbury Gaol instead of shot. I know you will be glad to hear that, as I am. He will be out of harm's way there and we need have nothing on our consciences. But I wish we all could feel as impartially on both sides as you do.

Respectfully,
MARK DEMOOTH

P.S. I understand that Mrs. Wolff has returned to her house at Cosby's. If so, she must be there alone. I shall try and drop in and see her.

Lana's eyes filled with tears.

"What is it, Mrs. Marting?"

"I think Captain Demooth must be a very good man, Nancy."

"Yes, he's a nice man. Sometimes Missis is hard on me. But she says I'm stupid and I guess I am. I think Mr. Demooth likes me. He said so once. He said, 'Nancy, you're a pretty girl.' Then he got on his horse and went to town."

Lana, surprised, looked at Nancy.

"Why, you are," she said.

It was quite true. When any rational emotion showed behind the doll-like eyes, Nancy was pretty. She was a large girl, with strong square shoulders. Under the dress her breasts showed firm and high. She was long-legged and she moved with an unconscious sleepy grace when she was walking. She reminded Lana somehow of a well-bred filly, in her body, now that she tried to see her with a man's eyes.

"What's your name, Nancy?"

"Schuyler. Nancy Schuyler." A trained sort of pride entered her voice. "My mother was Elisabeth Herkimer. She's sister of the colonel. I do hear he has a fine place. I been there once, only I don't remember it very well, only the nice horses and the cherry trees. They was in bloom, not bearing. Do you like cherries, Mrs. Marting?"

"Yes, I do. Have you any brothers or sisters?"

"I've got two brothers, Mrs. Marting. Hon Yost. He gave me these beads. He won them off an Indian down at Canajoharie. Nicholas, he's younger, and black-complected, not like me and Hon."

"Do you have to work?"

"Pa's dead. Ma put me out to work with Captain Demooth and the Missis for four years. She gets three pounds a year in English money for me. I was sixteen then. Unless I want to get married after I'm nineteen. I'll be nineteen next month. Did you want to get married?"

"Yes," said Lana, with a smile.

"I wonder what it's like."

"You've never wanted to?"

"I don't know. Old Clem Coppernol, he's always bothering me to come sleep in his cabin. It's dirty there. I don't think I'd want to. And Missis puts me in my room every night anyway and locks me up. I wouldn't mind sleeping with Captain if he told me to. But that ain't marrying, is it?"

"It isn't quite the same," said Lana, gravely.

"That's what Hon Yost told me. He said you and me ain't got much brains, Nancy, but we've got looks to beat all. You make a feller to marry you if he wants anything. Don't you trust a feller, he says. I think Hon Yost has got some brains, don't you, Mrs. Marting?"

Nancy leaned forward on her knees. Her back was straight. She had a kind of animal strength that was invigorating to see, in spite of her foolish eyes.

"You'll stay and have some milk with me?" Lana suggested.

"Oh no, I couldn't."

"Yes, please."

The girl beamed.

The milk tasted a little bitter from cherry browse. But it was cool from the spring. And Nancy chattered happily. Her brother had gone off to Canada. He was making money in the army. She supposed she wouldn't see him for a spell, but maybe he might come next year.

"How do you know?" asked Lana with a tightening of her breath.

"He sent word down to Nicholas. He sent word to me he'd try to fetch me an officer, too. I wouldn't mind it if the army was to come down here, would you, Mrs. Marting?"

She finished her milk and rose.

"I'll clean the things," she said. "It's getting late."

"No, I'll do them."

"I wouldn't feel easy, Mrs. Marting. Missis might scold about it. It's nice you letting me set with you this way, but I'd feel better if I could."

She looked so anxious, Lana let her wash the cups. Afterwards she repeated Lana's message of thanks to the captain.

"He'll like that. It's real nice to say it so. I'll tell him after supper when he comes to clean his rifle in the kitchen."

She went away.

11. *Blue Back Hunts a Buck*

The old Indian, Blue Back, had crossed the Hazenclever hill and gone down the north slopes for the valley of the West Canada Creek. He had kept on the west shore northward towards the big falls, and there, on the edge of the chasm, in a small forest swale he had come on the bed of a deer. He moused around in the grass like an old hound dog until he picked up the track, which he followed through all the deer's morning manœuvres.

They led Blue Back to where the deer had watered, dunged, drunk, and browsed. A little later, a couple of miles to the northwest, they brought him to a pond in which the deer had pulled lilies. By then the Indian knew that he was dealing with a heavy buck. He didn't want a big deer, now that he had come so far from home; he wouldn't be able to carry the half of it back to Oriska. What he was supposed to be after was a nice young doe or a grown fawn. His young wife, Mary, recently baptized by Mr. Kirkland, had asked him to get her a nice doeskin for a kirtle she wished to make for herself.

But Blue Back couldn't let the deer go. He wanted to see the horns. He was what Joe Boleo, the trapper, called meat hungry. Every autumn, when the nights grew frostier and the trees began to get a tinge of color on the ridges, Blue Back began to feel an urge to get hold of big meat. Big horns. Something big in the way of a deer, to start the hunting; something that, when you ate the meat of it, didn't digest so easy as a fawn, but kept the belly tight for a long time.

Last night, sitting in the door of his hut at Oriska, and hearing the creek flowing towards the Mohawk River with a misty sound in the dark, it had come into his mind that he ought to take a hunt north just to keep track of things the way he had promised Captain Demooth. When his wife said she wanted a doeskin, he said all right, he would get one. But he knew he wasn't going to look for does.

He had started in the hour before dawn, fording the Mohawk and going down towards the Martin clearing. He thought of stopping in on the Martins, but he wanted to get well north early. In the swale he roused out the foolish brown mare and watched her kick her heels through the mist and thought it was a pity, the way she was getting fat, that she belonged to his friend Martin. Otherwise he could slip over any time with a bow and arrow and do some neat night work on her. Horse meat was good meat, and very handy.

But Martin was his good friend, and the squaw was getting pleasanter. He let the horse go. It was well past noon when he came to the big buck's bed.

With the patience and phlegm of a shadow he trailed the buck through the afternoon until he found that the animal was circling. Then he left the tracks and struck out across country for where the deer had bedded the night before. He trotted steadily, his kilt of deerskin flapping up and down on his knees, the fingers of his leggings jumping and shaking. The sweat came out on his hunting shirt, staining it where the grease would let it through. Sweat made a dark ring round the band of the disreputable felt hat. As he went, he gnawed at a small loaf of pressed dried meat and blueberries, got himself a mouthful, sucked till the juices enlivened the meat, and chewed it. It was all the food he had with him; but he was not troubled by that. It was good to get hungry before you killed a big deer. You wanted to bring it home when you were on the point of famishment. Then you would throw it down in the house and lie down on your bed, and watch your young wife cut it up and put it in the kettle. Now and then you would tell her to hurry. It was pleasant to see her hurried and anxious, to smell the steam from the cook kettle, and to lie with your hands on your belly.

The air had a bluish thickness of smoke. It lay all along the horizon. That smoke was another sign of the autumn. It enlarged the trees and made the land look flat when you came out of the woods. You saw a deer on a day like this and it was a deer worth seeing.

Blue Back got back to the swale a little before sunset and made a long examination of the weather. There was no wind, and there would be none till moonrise. Then it would draw from the southeast for an hour or two. But by then the buck would have come to bed, to graze a little before he lay down. At half an hour before dawn, the wind would rise from the southeast again; later it would probably turn to the west.

Blue Back took his post a half-dozen rods from the edge of the swale on a knoll where big hemlocks were standing. He lay down on the needles, with his head on a root and his musket by his hand, pulled the unspeakable hat over his wet face, and went to sleep.

He woke at dusk, looked out into the swale, but saw no sign of the buck. Grunting, he rolled back on the ground. He was a good Indian, so he said a prayer before he went to sleep again.

"Our Father God, I am hungry, I want a good buck, I have been a good man, I will sell the horns to Demooth for a drink of rum, but I will give Kirkland a piece off the shoulder. But if it has twelve points I will give Kirkland a piece off the leg and not take his tobacco for a week. I am a good man. For ever and ever, Amen." A Christian prayer that was. Then just for safety he repeated in his mind, without moving his lips, a prayer he used to say.

He woke once more to hear the buck come through the woods from the northwest, against the wind, just as he had expected, and realized that the Lord was taking an interest. He put his hand under his cheek and slept without snoring.

A squirrel twitched its red tail on a stub of a branch twenty feet up the purple trunk of the hemlock. "Be still, little robber," Blue Back said in his mind, and the squirrel cocked his head. He was still. But he went from tree to tree, forty feet above the forest floor, in the wake of the wet, greasy, crawling old Indian.

A kind of twilight, like a left-over of the day before, hung in the swale. The high gray-green grass was topped by mist. There was yet no sign of the sun, but flying birds were astir in the upper air. Their voices came down in double sweetness through the mist.

Blue Back lay down behind a fallen tree on the edge of the grass. With great caution he found a rest for his gun and pointed it to where the deer's bed was. He himself was stretched out behind the butt of the musket so that Indian and gun made one brownness on the brown ground.

As soon as the mist began to rise, a slightly tenser quiet oversettled the quiet already in the old man. His eye came into the notch of the rear sight. It was beautiful to fit so well together—gun, sights, man's eye, man's finger on the trigger, God in Heaven and the birds in the mist. All that was lacking was the buck.

The buck rose and lifted its beautiful head. Twelve points anyway, thought Blue Back. By damn God, he was meat hungry now. He let his finger tighten as if the will of God were in it. A flat, belly-filling roar of the musket sent swirls through the mist after the round heavy ball. The birds above broke into a cacophonous twitter. The deer leaped straight up, snapped down its tail, leaped again, keeled over. The black powder smoke, rank as rot, came in a wreath over Blue Back's broad brown face. It filtered off, showing the face wreathed in a wide grin. The old Indian, rather like a bear, was humping through the grass. He bent over the dead buck, cut the throat with his long knife, turned the deer over, slit the belly to the ribs, and plunged his arms, sleeves and all, into the vent. The hot steamy smell of the buck's entrails was all about, seeming to blow his belly full of wind. He hauled the entrails out and then went to look at the deer's head. Fourteen points. God was surely working.

He grinned; he hadn't agreed with God about any fourteen-point buck. But maybe he would give Kirkland a rib or two at that.

With true Indian carelessness he had not bothered to reload the old musket. Now, in the silence that had succeeded the shot, he heard a couple of men coming out of the woods. He looked up in time to see them pointing rifles at him. There was nothing he could do but lift his hand in greeting, blood and knife and all.

The first man blew on a little silver whistle. The note was sharp, carrying, and peremptory. He was answered by a shout behind Blue Back.

"I've got his muskit, captain."

The man with the whistle then lowered his own gun and advanced through the waist-deep grass.

"Hello, there."

Blue Back went on with the business of cutting up the deer. He waited till the man was standing by his hand. The man was wearing moccasins. He had on Indian leggings, but his shirt was green, and had a kind of strap arrangement over it to hold his powder flask and shot pouch.

Blue Back looked up still further to meet the cool gray eyes above the thick nose and pursy mouth, and gave greeting.

"That's quite a deer," said the man in a friendly enough way.

Blue Back agreed.

"You alone?"

"Yes," said Blue Back.

"Hunting alone?"

Blue Back ran his knife down just before the short ribs. He nodded.
"What are you? Oneida? Onondaga?"
"Oneida. Turtle Clan. My name's Blue Back."
The man with the whistle held out his hand. He said, "My name's Caldwell."
Blue Back gravely shook.
Several other men had come through the grass. Eight white men, he counted; they were dressed in moccasins and leggings like the first. But they weren't trappers. Trappers, white men, couldn't stand each other's company. Then on the edge of the swale a couple of Indians stood out of the mist with the sudden quiet of ghosts.
Blue Back took one look at them with his glistening brown eyes and saw that they were Senecas. They had paint on. Vermilion stripes across the cheeks. One had a blue turtle on his chest. That was all right. He could claim clans even though the Seneca nation had been sending deputations to find out why the Oneidas hadn't joined Guy Johnson and Butler at Niagara.
"Got one good fine buck," he observed. "You want meat?"
"Thanks, Blue Back," said the man named Caldwell. "We'll take what you can't carry."
Blue Back put his arm around the deer, as a man might put his arm around the waist of a girl, just below the cut he had made. He braced his stocky body and heaved suddenly, breaking the backbone. Then he took his axe and cut off the horns.
He pointed to the front half of the carcass.
"Thanks," said Caldwell, again.
"Now I go home," said Blue Back.
"Where do you live?"
"Oriska."
"Listen, Blue Back. Do you know where the Deerfield Settlement is?"
"Yes, at the big bend of the big road."
"Yes. But where is it from here?"
"You going there?" Blue Back asked, raising his brown eyes.
"Yes. But we come by the north, and these Indians," he pointed to the Senecas, "got mixed. Is that the Canada Creek over there?"
"Yes."
"Is there any short cut?"
"Yes."
"Who's living there now?"
"Demooth, Reall, Weaver, and Martin. You want to see them?"
"Thought I'd like to see Mr. Demooth. Is he there now, hey?"
"Yes," said Blue Back.
"Where's this short cut?"
Blue Back got up slowly. He called to the Senecas. They were dark thin men. He talked to them in Indian. He explained the route. They nodded. It was quite clear. They would surely find the way now.
Blue Back smiled. He nodded, too. It was four miles longer than his own route would be.
"You'll come and eat with us?" suggested Caldwell.
Blue Back would. He needed some food. He took up his half of the

buck and went to their camp, half a mile back in the woods. On the way one of the Senecas told him that he had been making an early cast round the camp and had found Blue Back's tracks. They had sent out a scout.

The camp was a fire in an opening on a knoll. There were three bark shanties set up. There were also four more Indians. All of them looked as if they had come a long way, for their moccasins were worn thin.

Blue Back listened while he sat with the Senecas and ate boiled stump-ground cornmeal. The party had run out of salt and their tempers were not good. They looked tired and a little feverish, some of them. When he had finished, he shouldered the hind quarters and took his musket in his hand. He thanked them. They were breaking camp when he left.

Blue Back went slowly at first, making a cast to the west. He stopped on the first ridge and waited for five minutes, till he was sure he wasn't being tailed. He wouldn't leave the deer meat yet. But he started a steady plodding trot to the southeast.

When he came to the top of Hazenclever hill, he hung the deer meat in a tree, wrapped in his shirt, the legs through the arms, and set off for Deerfield.

12. *Logrolling*

To Gilbert Martin, that began as a great day. When he woke up, he got straight out of bed and sprang across to the window. Lana watched him from the pillow. His brown hair needed cutting; it was tangled as a crow's nest.

"What are you looking at, Gil?"

He turned from the window as if her voice had broken a spell. But his eyes still shone.

"Oh, just the land," he said.

"The land?"

"Our place." He came back to the bed and looked down at her.

"What's happened to it?"

"My Jesus!" he said. "You ain't forgot, have you? We're rolling logs to-day."

Lana felt immensely shamed.

"I guess I'm not all the way awake yet," she said apologetically.

"I guess you aren't." He laughed, tousled her hair with both hands. "Get up, Lana. You'll be busy cooking for those men."

"I will, I will, Gil. I'm getting up now. Leave go my hair."

He started putting on his clothes, saying half to himself, "We'll roll towards the creek. The boys can begin burning on the far side." He glanced at the window again. "That's right. Wind's southerly. It'll be a fine day. And the wood's dried out fine."

There were ten acres to log and burn. Two days from now, his farm would look like a farm in fact. He would have to think about getting his own yoke of oxen.

He never considered the heat, and the dirt, and the labor. He would see the fashioning of his own place; the cutting he had worked a year on would be laid bare to the eye. His opinion would be deferred to; every minute of the day would be his own—both those he spent himself, and those of the other men.

"Hurry," he said to Lana, and went down the loft ladder with a clatter. By the time she got downstairs he was in with the milk. He had milked for her this morning. It made him grin. "I had to do something." He looked down at the pail. "She surely is a fine cow to have bought off a minister."

Everything pleased him.

At six-thirty, about an hour after sunrise, Gil, from the slashing, saw Demooth's fine red oxen turning up from the road. The heavy-shouldered beasts with their great jointed knees, fashioned as if to hold still the earth, came slowly towards him.

"Hey, Clem!"

Clem Coppernol glanced at him with an unfavorable eye.

"Hello, Martin."

His voice was dry, but Gil could take no heed of that.

"It surely is kind of Demooth to send his oxen over."

"Well, maybe. I'd consider it was kind of him to throw me in. But it's easy being kind when another man has got to work it out for you."

He sat himself on a stump while the oxen stood with lowered heads and drowsy eyes.

Five minutes later, George Weaver appeared with his own yoke. They were smaller than Demooth's good Johnson cattle. A black and a red-and-white, rough-coated, narrow-shouldered, they did not have the pulling power, but they were quicker on their feet, as well as twice as hard to handle. But taken together, the two yokes made an ideal combination to log a piece of land.

George Weaver said, "Sorry I'm late, Gil. The boys tried to sneak off and fish the spawn beds up above Reall's. I had to get them back. They'll be right along now, though."

"That's all right."

"You going to wait for Reall?" Clem asked hopefully.

"No," said Gil.

"Hain't no sense in that," agreed Weaver. "That man never got on time to anything except a drink. How do you want to start?"

In a few words, a little self-consciously, Gil outlined his idea. He felt relieved when both men nodded.

"We hadn't ought to start the burning till we get that mass of boys. Emma's coming up with them," said George. "She'll be handy helping Lana, or working out here."

"It'll burn fast," said Clem.

He pricked his nigh ox with the goad and swung the yoke for the heavy beech logs, up against the woods, that Gil had not been able to fell into windrows. The beasts moved off at their lethargic tread, the hoofs spreading with deliberate consideration of their weight and power, the heavy chain, like an iron snake, weaving along the dirt behind them.

By the timber, Clem wheeled them. They moved like smooth, slow-going, well-greased wheels, presenting their rumps to the end of the log. The sour old Dutchman hooked the chain round a butt and spoke in Dutch, and the chins of the beasts lifted a little, their necks went out, the chain straightened its links, and the thirty-foot stick began to slide like taffy, inch by inch and foot by foot.

Before they had delivered it to Gil at the edge of the creek, Weaver had arrived with his smaller stick, and started back. But Gil had no eye for anything but Demooth's fine yoke. Power like theirs was dignified by slowness.

He helped the Dutchman roll the log in place along the brush that crumpled under its weight. He had no thought of the fine tree that had drawn its life through that stick. He thought of the land the felling of its top had opened. Beech trees killed the soil. It made him glad to know there were so few on his place.

Weaver's boys came sullenly. They stood in their unaccustomed boots, put on against the burning, and looked enviously at the nearly naked Realls. All the children but the sucking baby had accompanied their father, who walked behind them with the downcast look of an unsuccessful Sunday-school teacher.

Gil felt a moment's hesitation at putting them under Reall's command. He thought that with a shiftless man like that the fire might get out of hand. But he himself wanted to attend to the burning of the big logs. It was important to burn them clean as could be.

He had not, however, taken into account the childish streak in Christian Reall. The little man led the chase to the hut to get the first brand. His entry, with the flood of children after him, nearly submerged Lana, who was thrust against one wall and had to watch the spoliation of her fire with mingled amusement and annoyance. Every child wanted some fire. But Reall, using his Bible voice, squelched them.

"No one sets to burning but me!" he roared. "You get yourselves some branches to beat with."

He marshaled them along the first windrow.

"All right, Gil?" he shouted, but he did not look for Gil's raised hand. He thrust the brand into the dried twigs and watched the first small flames take hold. They seized the points of the twigs, the curled leaves, making innumerable tiny contoured shapes, each in its own entity. The flames ran together. They grew and swelled and merged under the rush. The sputtering subsided in a long deep draught of sound, and the first big flame came up, like a pointed heart.

The children screeched at sight of it. Reall stood with the brand on his hip watching it. Then he sprang down the windrow, crablike, all head and arms, and set another section afire.

In half an hour the whole windrow was burning. The fire, making fast from the inside, filled the early autumn air with the voice of its increase.

Gil, on the creek bank, piling logs and drawing brush across them, felt the smoke in his lungs. White acrid clouds of it drew past him; ashes and swirling sparks, light with the instinct to leap up, came against his sweating skin. It seemed to him that he smelled the burning of the shadow of

the forest, the fungus growths, the decay, the gloomy things. The yelling
of the children and Reall was hardly to be heard above the noise of burning.

Punctually to their times, one yoke or other of the oxen would appear
with a new log to place, coming through the smoke with heads kept low,
Weaver or Coppernol walking beside them.

At first they had a word to say.

"She's burning clean."

"The logs are taking hold real active."

"It's going to make a pretty piece for wheat."

"You've got deep soil here, Gil."

The windrows now were all ablaze. The smoke appeared to run from
the tops of them like lines of fleeing rats. Only when it had drawn over
the creek, above Gil's head, it lost its first mad impetus and rose on the
gentle wind. When he turned, Gil could see it, a great cloud, filtering
through the branches and slowly mounting the hillside. Its immensity filled
his heart. He hardly heard Clem Coppernol, "I'll have to drag to the next
windrow, Martin. Fire's getting too clost for the beasts."

They were working fast now, the burning, the heat, the smoke, half
smothering them all. Each log stirred up a cloud of ashes as it was dragged.

Lana appeared with a kettle of water. Drinking it, Gil seemed to feel
the coolness flooding all his system, rising to the skin, as if after the fire
the touch of water could make him new. He grinned when she stared with
horror at his singed hair and crusted face. But he waved his arm for her
to see the accomplishments of the fire.

They stood for a moment, looking together at the raging holocaust that
once had been green trees.

"Oh, Gil!" she cried. "It's beautiful!"

Her lips left a heart-shaped print of freshness on his cheek.

Whether they wanted to or not, they had to leave off at noon. The fire
had mastered all the slash. The great logs were being eaten, and they discharged sounds like shots. All sat outdoors, watching what they had started.
Grimy, singed, parched—food tasted like ashes in their mouths.

It was Emma, shading her eyes, who said suddenly, "Who's that?"

They saw a shape at the far edge of the burning, running towards them
through the smoke. Then one of the trees along the creek caught fire, making a torch that for the moment seemed to take all blue out of the sky and
turn it black. The suction of the flame drew off the smoke, and all of them
saw the Indian, stripped to the waist, trotting towards them with his old
felt hat drawn low over his eyes.

13. *Catastrophe*

Lana stood dully in the box of the cart, stowing away what things Gil
and Blue Back handed up to her. There had been no time to pack properly.
Their clothes, the two trunks, the chinaware, the axe and gun and knives
and scythe and hoes, the churn, all these things were jumbled up like Lana's
thoughts.

One moment they had all been sitting there before the door, watching the emergence to reality of their plans; the next the old greasy Indian had arrived. Ten minutes after not a soul was on the place but themselves. George Weaver had said, "We've got no time to lose. Bluc Back says an hour, maybe they'll come quicker."

"Where'll we go?" asked Reall.

"We'll head for Schuyler and the Little Stone Arabia Stockade. Clem, you'd better hit right off for Demooth's."

The sour old Dutchman shook his head.

"*Nein,*" he said. "I will not leave mine oxen."

"Turn them into the woods," said Weaver. "We'll find them when we come back with the militia."

"I will take them with me," said Clem. "They are good beasts. I have a place to hide them there."

"Then get going now, you fool. Blue Back said the Senecas told him they'd be left to themselves. There ain't no Indians worse than Senecas. I went with Johnson against Fort William Henry. I know. But, my Jesus, then they was on our side."

As Coppernol set off, Weaver turned to his fourteen-year-old son. "John, you run to Captain Demooth's. Tell him what we've heard. Remember, eight whites and six Indians. Blue Back says they're Senecas, and they're painted."

"Yes, Pa."

"Run like God Almighty, John."

"Can I leave my shoes off? I can't run in them so good."

"Yes, Cobus will fetch them home. Now git."

Cobus took the shoes from John. He asked, "Can I take mine off too, Pa?"

"Stop asking questions," bellowed Weaver, but Emma Weaver nodded at the little boy. "Reall, you'd better light out right away. Don't try to bring anything heavy. You'll have a little time to hide stuff in the woods. But not over twenty minutes. Meet us at my place, but we won't wait for you."

"We'll be along."

Reall was amazingly unperturbed. He gathered his children as a man might herd his calves, started them off up the path, cut himself a stick, and flogged on the laggers.

Weaver turned to Gil and Lana.

"You got the longest way to travel. You'd better get to work."

Gil was already striding off to catch the brown mare. His face was set. Lana said, "Do you think they'll do harm?"

"God knows," said Weaver, catching Cobus by the hand. "We just don't dast to chance it. They want Demooth."

"Poor dearie," said Emma, glancing back at the burning. That day she had been reminded of her own bare start.

"Emma!" shouted George from down the track.

Lana realized that she was alone with the greasy old Indian. He was still puffing a little, but his brown eyes looked at her kindly.

"You pack your load," he suggested. "I'll help."

Lana felt dizzy. She hardly knew where to begin. The smell of the Indian, when he followed her inside, suffocated thought, but now it roused no animosity. He looked at her a moment, pushed his hat back on his head, and picked up her spinning wheel.

"You go up, get blankets," he suggested.

Lana went.

Gil came with the mare. They piled what had already been gathered into the cart. Then he and Blue Back brought the bed downstairs and took it bodily out into the woods above the spring. After they set it down among the hemlock thicket, they came back for the dresser. To Lana they seemed to act like the confused half-drunken figures one meets in dreams.

Gil shook Blue Back's hand.

"Thanks." His voice was tight and dry. "You're a good friend, Blue Back."

The Indian nodded.

"Oh sure," he said. "Fine friends."

"Maybe we'll be seeing you again."

"Oh sure. But you go way now. Men come pretty fast soon."

"Did you know any of them?"

"One man with a whistle was named Caldwell."

"Caldwell!"

He struck the mare. Lana caught herself against the lurch of the cart. They both looked backward as they rolled down the track. They saw the slash still sending clouds of smoke against the hill; but the flames were lower. On the other side of the cabin the corn stirred its leaves in the slight breeze. The Indian had vanished and the place already looked forlorn.

Gil said roughly, "Don't look at it, Lana."

Obediently she turned her face away. But her eyes filled with slow tears. She had hated the cabin at first. She still hated it on certain days. And yet to leave it was like leaving a part of herself, and a part of Gil.

Through the window glass, Blue Back watched them go. They were fine friends. It was too bad.

When they had turned the corner into the Kingsroad, he stopped looking through the glass and carefully began to take it out of the frame. He had always wanted a glass window. He did not have much time to waste; he had a feeling that the man Caldwell wouldn't be a friendly person to anybody when he found the settlers gone. He took the glass under one arm, and laid hold of his musket with his free hand. He trotted out past the burning and slid down the creek bank. He waded in the creek until he came to the river. There he stood in deeper water, with his eyes just over the level of the bank. He waited perhaps fifteen minutes before he saw the hooped headdress of the Seneca rise over the grass on the far edge of the swale.

The dark, painted face was still as an image. It made no move at all. From the look of it, the man behind it might be using his nose, the way a good dog would.

Then the Indian raised his hand. Another appeared by his shoulder, so like him that together they lost all human aspect. They were like two foxes you might see together, two weasels, two cats.

"Cats!" thought Blue Back, with contempt. The Indians began to move through the swale, but unless you had seen them first you would not have known they were there. Blue Back followed their progress anxiously. He hoped they would not strike the creek bank where he had come down.

But they missed the place. They lay against the bank for half a minute looking at the cabin. Then they rose up. One waved. A whistle blew on the far side of the burning and the rest of the party came bursting through the smoke. They thronged together at the door, they rushed inside, they poured out again and stood in a group before the door.

Suddenly the six Indians slid away and began working over the ground like foxes hunting mice. They went to the edge of the burning, returned, went up the path towards Reall's, reappeared in the edge of the woods, and knelt at the wagon track.

A little apart from the rest the man Caldwell watched them. Now they ran up to report to him. Even at that distance Blue Back saw his face flush up; and unluckily for her, at that moment Martin's cow came out of the underbrush and looked at all the visitors. One of the Indians pointed at her, and Caldwell nodded.

It was over in an instant. The cow raised her tail, but before she could whirl out of reach, the Indian had leaped beside her and drawn his knife across her throat. Plunging away down the track after the cart, she seemed to go blind, suddenly, crashing head on into a tree. As she bounced off, she bellowed once so that the whole hill made an echo. Then, until she fell, she stood in silence, head out, pouring blood.

In the meantime one of the white men had seized a stick from the burning brush. He ran into the cabin with it, and laughed as he came out at Caldwell's whistle.

All the men ran straight down the wagon track for the Kingsroad. Blue Back straightened himself as the last man turned the corner. At the first puff of smoke in the doorway of the cabin, his hand went under his deerskin kilt and emerged holding the peacock's feather. He put it through two holes of his hat, so that the eye end dangled in front of his face as he walked, where he could see it all the time. Blue Back had coveted that feather ever since he had first laid eyes on it. But it was too bad about the cow. He had thought to come back and use that cow himself, if Gil Martin left it behind. To go back for it now, though, would be unwise.

Besides, he had to retrieve the hind half of the deer from the top of the Hazenclever hill. His wife would be annoyed with him for shooting a buck, but he would pacify her with the feather.

14. *Little Stone Arabia Stockade*

Gil lashed the brown mare with the reins and Lana had to hold on hard. The wheels bucketed, the box creaked and strained and banged, and the jumbled load in it clattered deafeningly.

"You didn't do much of a job packing," he said savagely.

Lana did not answer. The jolting made her sick; each bounce was like a fist delivered in her back, her abdomen. She remembered something about not riding in a cart when you were pregnant; she wouldn't have thought it would have made a difference so early. For her body was like a dead weight on the seat. She had to fight herself to keep from being sick, to keep from crying, to keep from falling off. It was a pain to get a breath.

Gil took one look at her and lashed the mare again. He hadn't yet begun to feel. But he drove in a blind resentment against fate.

The road reëchoed to the noise of flight. At Weaver's the cart picked up Reall's wagon. Reall was driving a superannuated black and weedy stallion. He had bought it for next to nothing with the idea of getting rich on stud fees; but nobody had seemed to fancy that particular horse as sire of a colt. He looked like a doubtful proposition anyway.

Mrs. Reall sat on the seat beside him with an anxious face. She felt obliged to carry the baby, but neither did she dare to trust her new possession to the children's care. So she had wedged the baby into Thompson's chamber pot and thus held both together.

The children perched in the body of the wagon wherever they could find room, and stared behind them, hoping to see Indians. They shouted shrilly as the brown mare galloped past.

The Weavers came last. Both George and Emma looked grim. He waved once to Gil; then he handed the reins to Emma and climbed back into the cart and took his rifle from Cobus. He shook the priming out, refreshed the pan, and leaned himself against the rack. It was a comforting feeling, to know he was watching the rear.

At Demooth's they found John waiting for them, a small white-faced figure under the trees. He said that the captain had taken Mrs. Demooth in the light wagon and driven straight off for Schuyler to gather the militia.

Clem Coppernol had hidden the oxen in the woods, and he and Nancy were now somewhere ahead with the odd horse.

The mare was laboring when Gil swung her into Cosby's Manor. Reall's ancient stallion was going weak in the knees. Lana struggled in the respite to regain her senses. She felt half dead, and after the first blessed relief she felt more pain in standing still than in the fury of travel on the jolting road.

Gil handed her the lines. "I've got to tell Mrs. Wolff, if she's here."

He jumped off and ran onto the porch of the store. The building looked as deserted as Thompson's house; but when he knocked, Mrs. Wolff opened the door.

"What do you want?"

Her white face stared at him as if he were someone she had never seen. He said, "We've had warning of a party of British and Indians up above our place. Lana and I can give you room in our cart."

"Thanks."

"You'll have to hurry, though. They can't be far back."

She still stared at him.

"I'd rather trust to Indians than you people," she said.

The Weavers came into the clearing and drove up beside the Martins' cart.

"You'd better come with us," George said.

"I'll stay here." She raised her voice. "I told John I'd stay here and wait for him. I don't want help from you. You put him there. You tried to get him killed, George Weaver." She gave a little unnatural laugh. "I've been praying lately, Weaver. And I guess the Lord, He's heard me."

They all followed her look to the westward. When they saw the fresh smoke, they knew it wasn't from the Martin place. More likely Weaver's.

George Weaver turned back to his wagon, walking heavily. "Get back into the wagon," he roared to John. His boot just missed the terrified boy. He hauled himself up after and said to Emma, "Start the horse. If she wants to be fried by Indians, let her. I won't feel sorry."

The three wagons were halfway to Schuyler when they heard the bell begin to ring. It was a small sound at first, hardly to be heard over the crash of wheels and rattle of harness. But when one of the Reall children called attention to it they all heard the sound quite plainly, even Lana.

As they proceeded she felt the slow harsh clamor growing in her. It beat with the hammering of her heart; now with the dinning of this bell through all her being, it seemed to her that she would never clear herself of the sound.

She hardly heard Gil shouting at her. He had to yell into her ear to make her hear, and she had to fight herself upward into consciousness, like a drowning person.

"What's the matter with you?"

She wrenched the words free: "I can't stand it any more."

"You've got to."

He grabbed her as she started to slide away; and all the rest of the way he had to hold her on the seat.

The three horses were all played out when they broke out of the woods at Schuyler and found the level road at last. Now the bell was clear in the open air.

They saw the sky, the fields, the fences, houses that looked secure. The cattle that had gathered in the pastures to listen to the bell turned curious uneasy eyes to their passage. Women hovered in their doorways, staring across the river to the fort. Beyond the ford was Demooth's light wagon, towards which men were running.

As he saw the scene, the power to think returned to Gil. He let the brown mare splash through the river and drew her up beside Demooth's wagon. The captain had already got down and was examining his rifle.

He said, "All here?"

"All but Nancy and Coppernol."

"They've gone into the fort. You'd better leave your own things there. We're going right back now."

Emma Weaver said, "You go along, Gil. I'll look after Lana."

The stockade made an irregular square, the twelve-foot posts following the level of the ground around a well. In the width of the valley it seemed a puny resource against the chances of Providence. Even the blockhouse, projecting its second story five feet higher than the palisade, made but a tiny show against the autumn sky.

Inside, the place seemed smaller yet. Along the four sides of the stockade, low sheds, whose roofs served for rifle platforms, crowded the enclosure, and the slope of the roofs brought the eaves so low to earth that Lana had to stoop as Mrs. Weaver helped her in.

You would have thought that Emma Weaver had lived there all her life. She showed neither dismay nor impatience. She made the two boys bring her blankets for Lana's bed, and then sent them out to find fresh hay to make a pallet. As Nancy appeared, she ordered her to get her water and build a fire against any need. When Mrs. Demooth demanded Nancy's services, Emma strode out and confronted her.

"You ought to be ashamed," she said, her strident voice filling the entire place. "Nobody's asked you to do a thing, yourself. But Mrs. Martin's bad sick and you'll let Christian-hearted people help her, or you'll get outside."

Mrs. Demooth made a frightened defense: "I'll have to tell the captain."

"Go ahead. Just go ahead," said Emma grimly. "And if he doesn't put a strap to you the way he ought, I will. For my own sake, if not for yours, Mrs. Demooth."

But Lana was neither conscious of this bicker nor aware of the straggling arrival of the women and children of the settlement. Under the guidance of a few old men and younger boys, everyone clustered in the fort. The arrival of the Deerfield people brought the number to over fifty souls. They bestowed their bedding and their more easily fetched belongings where they could. The boys then scrambled onto the shed roof; the old men went to the blockhouse where Clem Coppernol with Grandfather Kast was watching from the spy loft, in which at last the alarm bell ceased its tolling.

The Schuyler folk were not alarmed particularly. But they were eager to hear the story of the raid. It was the first occurrence of the kind in the western end of the Mohawk Valley, though in Schoharie there had been some trouble.

The women crowded the entrance of the shed where Lana lay like a beast upon her bed of hay. Their thronging faces watched every move of Emma's.

"She going to lose it?" they wanted to know.

They suggested remedies. One said, "You'd ought to lean a board against the wall and lay her with her head down on it."

It was, in Emma's opinion, the first sensible idea.

"Who said that?"

"Me," said an elderly, wrinkled woman. "I've see it work once when I lived in Rensselaer Manor. They did it to a nigger woman. But I don't know will it work here."

"Well, find a board."

There wasn't one to be found in the stockade. One of the boys volunteered to go out and look for one across the river at Kast's, the nearest place. But it was then getting dark and his mother refused to let him go. So four women held Lana in her struggle.

It was like a corner of hell. The darkness that the Betty lamps made yellow firefly glows in, the silhouetted figures of the women under the shed roof, the restless boys on the roofs, trying to see what was going on. The hushed female voices and the guttural tones of the old men in the blockhouse punctuated with silences each articulation of the sufferer.

After the first half hour, Lana was only fitfully conscious of her own part in it. She knew that the bell had stopped, but her own pains had taken its place. At moments she was conscious of unfamiliar hands. . . .

When she awoke in the black of the night, the stockade all dark but for one low mass of coals and the small flame of the lamp quivering in a draft of air, she found herself alone with Emma.

The raw-boned woman was sitting at her feet and staring into the dark.

"What happened, Emma?"

"Poor dearie." Emma turned. "You feeling better now?"

"Only sore. And kind of sick. What happened?"

Emma's eyes filled slowly with tears. The unaccustomed compassion in her face made it ugly.

"Don't you fret." She smoothed the dark damp hair. "Poor pretty thing."

Lana lay still for hours it seemed. Finally thought and words coincided in her tired brain.

"Did I lose it?"

Emma nodded.

The militia bivouacking at Demooth's burnt house and barn slept on the ground like tired dogs. Only Gil and George Weaver, who had asked for the duty of keeping watch, were awake. Faint glows in the sky to west and north told them that all the places were destroyed.

They sat together now, beyond the rim of firelight, not speaking. Demooth's wheat had been fired and trampled. There was nothing left. They knew that nothing would be left of their own crops.

Gil said, "What do you plan to do, George?"

"I hain't had time to think. We haven't any money. You don't get a chance to save money up here."

"I'd saved enough to buy some oxen with," said Gil. "But it won't last long, unless I can find work. Lana's having a baby, too."

George nodded. "Work for money's going to be hard to find."

Gil said, "A man could join the army, maybe."

"I'd thought of that. But now, I don't know. If people all join the army, who's going to look out for this country?"

"I didn't really believe it till now," Gil said. "It don't seem possible for a man to work as hard as I did, just for nothing."

There was nothing left west of Cosby's Manor. Houses, barns, Reall's mill, even, that had no stones, were burned. The militia, at Martin's place, found Gil's cow in the road, untouched, but dead. Somehow that raised their anger more than any other thing, even as they skinned a quarter and cut off steaks for their lunch.

They did find Demooth's oxen and one of Weaver's yoke and drove them back on the slow march home. They ate at Wolff's store.

Of Mrs. Wolff there was no sign. The building, as well as Thompson's house, was deserted. Footprints showed that Caldwell's party had come so far. Whether the woman had gone off to Canada of her own free will, been taken, or been destroyed somewhere in the woods, they could not tell. There was no sense in following the trail with the start the destructives had had, and there was no telling what they might have done. The whole raid seemed such an ugly senseless thing to happen.

For the first time they began to realize that there was no protection for them except in themselves. An unpredictable force had been born in the Mohawk Valley, with potential destructiveness as devastating as the old French rapes. It seemed a pitiful remonstrance when, in spite of Demooth's wishes, Jeams MacNod led on the company to burn down Thompson's and Wolff's store.

When Gil came back with the company that night to Little Stone Arabia Stockade, he found Lana speechless with pain and shame. She tried to meet his eyes, then burst out crying. Emma unexpectedly kissed him before going out of the shed.

He sat down on the earth beside Lana's bed and held her hand. He could not say, "Never mind." He could not think of what Reall had said in breaking the news: "It's too bad, Martin. But there'll be plenty more." He merely held her hand, because it was all he could think of to do.

15. *Winter*

The house Gilbert and Lana Martin had rented for the winter—it was no more than a shack, with one room, for all it had plank walls instead of logs, and a small, poorly drawing fireplace—stood opposite the old ford in German Flats, and close to the river bank. From it, the West Canada Creek could be seen across the river, coming straight out of the woods. The house had belonged to Mrs. Schuyler, Nancy's mother, but now that one son was working for himself, that the daughter was in service to the Mark Demooths, and the other son working out, Nicholas Herkimer had good-naturedly offered his sister a room in his house below the high falls.

It was Nancy, who had developed a great admiration for Lana since the day of the call with the captain's letter, who suggested it. They had been able to rent the place for one dollar a month, and in October they had brought their effects from Little Stone Arabia Stockade and moved in.

Lana had been cooped up there all winter. Every morning Gil went upriver to a farm, which Demooth had repossessed when the Herters went down to Schenectady, and worked with Clem Coppernol. He returned after dark, restless and irritable, for he felt that Captain Demooth had given him work out of charity. Even an old man like Coppernol could have handled the cattle and horses single-handed during the winter.

Lana had tried to persuade Gil to take her back to her father's place. There was plenty of room for them there, and plenty of work for him to do. Her family would have been glad to have them. It was better, as long as he felt the way he did, to depend on one's family than on one's neighbors.

But he would not listen. Her mother, he said, had been doubtful about his taking Lana westward. He would not go back now, within a year, to let them get an unjust satisfaction out of it. When Lana tried other persuasion, he talked so harshly that she dropped the matter for good.

At first she had been afraid, living alone in the little house. Though they were within sight of Fort Herkimer, she felt more lonely than she had even in Deerfield. Nancy Schuyler came once a month, for her afternoon out had become a regular institution when the captain learned where she spent it, but the simple-minded girl, for all her natural cheerfulness, depressed Lana; and it was Nancy who first brought to Lana's notice the disappearance of the peacock's feather.

"You hain't hung up that feather of yourn anywhere," she said on her first call. "I should think you would. It would make the place seem homey to you."

At the moment, Lana was pleased. She said, "I'll get it out right away." But it could not be found. She and Nancy turned over all the pitifully few belongings in vain.

"I packed it," Lana said. "I remember taking it off the dresser when I went to get the white china pot."

"You must have put it somewheres. Or maybe Mr. Marting did."

That night she asked Gil, but he swore he had not seen it. "You ought know where it is, Lana. You did the packing."

She left the subject, listlessly, continuing the preparation of his supper. It was nothing but stewed corn mush. They put water on it, having no milk except when Nancy kept a little out of the Demooths' supply and sent it down with Gil, and salt was so dear that they used it only once a week. She put his bowl before him and stayed crouched down on the hearth herself.

"You'd better eat," he said.

"I don't want anything."

"Doc said you ought to eat." He glanced down at her. Her face was pale and thin, it seemed to have lengthened, and there were unnatural shadows under her eyes. She still looked young; but she looked as if she had been hurt. "You know why," he said, roughly.

"I know," she said. "But I don't dare."

"You ought to."

"Who wants a baby now? Living like this. We haven't any chance of getting started again this year. If ever."

"We'll get back in the spring, maybe. That's why I want to stay up here."

"Go back there? To Deerfield?"

"Where did you think I meant?"

"It's so far away, Gil."

"It's no further than it used to be."

She did not answer. She did not even look at him. She heard him finish his supper and drop the spoon back in the bowl. He got up and walked across the cabin, got his rifle down.

"What you want with that?"

He said, "To-morrow's Sunday. I'll go up in the woods and see if there's any deer come down."

He cleaned the rifle in silence.

She said, "Isn't the snow too deep?"

"Adam Helmer's lent me a pair of snowshoes. Maybe he'll come with me."

Adam Helmer was a new friend of Gil's. He was a young man, very tall and heavy, almost a giant. He had blond hair and a thin blond beard, and strangely bright gray eyes. Women admired him, for his strength and his good looks. But he had never married. If he married, he often said, he would have to go to work. As it was, any girl was glad to give him supper. Lana had not been glad. She felt that he was taking Gil away the only days that he might have stayed at home.

Helmer shot a thin doe that Sunday, but Gil missed three. They split the deer and parted in the village below Fort Dayton. When he noticed the light burning in Dr. Petry's office store, instead of heading for the house across the river, Gil went to see him. He found the doctor alone.

"Well," said Dr. Petry, raising his heavy brows, "what do you want?" Gil handed him a steak he had cut off.

"Here's some deer meat, Doc. I guess you don't remember me. My name's Martin. My wife was taken sick in Little Stone Arabia last September. You came up to see her."

"Yes, I remember her, and you too. It's too bad she had a miscarriage. She's a fine girl. But you paid me for that visit."

"Yes."

"How is she now?"

"That's what I want to ask you about. She don't seem healthy. She don't eat hardly anything. She just moons around the house all day."

"She ought to be getting over it by now. Maybe I ought to see her again. Fetch her up."

"It wouldn't do any good. She's afraid of you, anyway. She's afraid of everything." Gil blushed suddenly and looked at a bottle on the wall marked *Sal. Ammon.* Like a girl's name.

"What's the trouble, Martin?"

"She's scared to death of having another baby, Doc. She's so scared of me, I just have to leave her alone. I don't know what to do."

The doctor grunted and looked at him.

"Do you think I ought, Doc? It gets hard on me. But I can't stand to see her scared."

"Women get notions," observed Dr. Petry. "But she seemed like a sensible girl to me."

"Why, she always used to be. She's a damn good wife. She was."

"Was she scared about the first?"

"Hell, no, Doc. That's what beats me so. She was about all a man could expect to handle. She made jokes about it. Not but what she's modest. She's a decent girl."

"Yes, I understand that."

"But sometimes I wonder, Doc, if she wouldn't be better off if I treated her different."

Dr. Petry drew a long breath and let it out again. He remembered Martin's wife—a pretty girl, he had thought then, sensible, and full of feeling. He didn't know the first damn thing about this young man's problem. No man could. Take Jacob Small's wife. Since she had successfully had a baby she was crazy for another, though he had warned her and Small that it was just about likely to kill her. And this Mrs. Martin, who was equipped to have a dozen or fourteen and had probably started out with every intention of having them, was scared to death.

He wondered if the girls of his mother's and grandmother's times had been so unpredictable. But he couldn't tell. He had trained for an army surgeon, and then he had come over to this country. He had located here in German Flats fourteen years ago, and he had delivered probably a hundred women, or women a hundred times, and yet when this young man asked him a perfectly simple question, he couldn't possibly answer him.

He would like to help him, too. Help them both. Dr. Petry, having married no beauty himself, felt a cranky tenderness for all pretty young women; but he was going to have to admit to Martin that he didn't know the answer, any answer.

Watching the doctor's red, heavy, Bavarian face, Gil began to feel frightened.

"Doc," he said, "you don't think there's anything gone wrong with her? Inside, I mean."

The doctor exploded with a solid German curse.

"No, I don't. She just had the devil shaken out of her at a bad time. Three weeks later, maybe, and she'd have been all right. That girl's able to have all the brats you can get. Baskets of them. Oh, I know she's small; but not when you look at her with my eye, boy."

Gil felt weak.

"Her mother said that to me. She said all Borst women had babies easy. But I got wondering. And now . . ."

"Yes," said the doctor, "and now . . ." His eyes swelled as he looked over at Gil. "I don't know. Do you see? I don't know."

Gil nodded. "I guess it's hard to tell."

"You feel as if I'd let you fall down," growled the doctor. "But I can't help that. I can set bones. I can sew up cuts. I can deliver a baby." Suddenly he fell back on religion. "But God's supposed to look out for the soul. You can't expect me to know everything."

"I shouldn't have asked. Only I didn't want to make a mistake."

The doctor got up with him and shook hands.

"You're a good man, Martin. But there's some things we have to trust to luck about. Or God. Or whatever. I guess this is just one. I wish to God I could answer you. I can't. I'm tired. You better go have a drink and get to supper."

Gil picked the half of the doe up off the floor and started out.

"But listen," the doctor said after him. "It's awful easy to get impatient. See? You've been patient. It won't hurt waiting a while."

Gil went down to the river and crossed on the ice. He wanted to leave a cut of the meat at Demooth's. When he got to the house, there was nobody home but Nancy. She told him, smiling, that Captain and Missis had gone down to Herkimer's place and were spending the night. Coppernol was out. She held the door open for him to enter, the candlelight making ripples on her yellow hair when she moved her head.

"You better set down and get warm," she said, taking the cut from him. "I'll put this away, Mr. Marting, and fetch you some cordial. Captain would want for you to have it."

The kitchen was warm. There was a deep fire on the hearth. Gil couldn't resist the cheerful heat, the wide comfort that the slate-gray walls enclosed. He was tired from the long cold hunt, and the heat seemed to go all through him. He sat drowsily, waiting Nancy's return, listening to her footsteps in the storage pantry and then in a back room. She took quite a while. When she came in she carried a glass for him. As he took it, he saw that she had put a red ribbon round her head.

The ribbon made him look at her.

"Sit down here with me, where it's warm," he said.

She giggled a little and sat down on the settle between him and the fire.

"You're real pretty, Nance," he said.

She flushed up to her ears and turned her slow blue eyes on him.

"Oh, Mr. Marting!"

He sat quite still, watching her struggle in her mind for something to say. The stupidity on her face made no impression on her prettiness. He kept thinking of Lana's listless paleness, and comparing it to Nancy's full smooth pink skin. She seemed so incredibly warm and bursting with health.

"Here," he said, extending the glass. "You've got to have your share."

"Oh, Mr. Marting, Missis said I wasn't ever to drink, with my head."

"Nonsense. It ain't going to hurt you. I don't get much fun any more."

"Mrs. Marting's so poorly," she said.

"Yes. It's not her fault. Go on." His voice hardened.

She sipped from the glass, her eyes wide on his. She choked a little, laughed, and had another sip.

He watched her face. The liquor fixed her flush. But her eyes became almost animated. She sat up for a moment, with a queer animal expectancy. Her voice sounded quite bright. "Oh, Mr. Marting!"

Gil threw his arm round her waist and pulled her to him. He felt her waist swell under his hand. While he kissed her the sheer force in her seemed to lift him. Then she let herself sag into his arm and lie like a dead weight, her head thrown back on his shoulder, the full round of her throat bare to the light, and one hand ineffectually pulling at the laces between her breasts. But her quiescence let her hand slip down again to her side. Her mouth slowly relaxed, the lips shakily finding their normal shape. Almost the only sign of life in her was the formation of sweat beads on her forehead and her upper lip.

He stared down at her a moment and saw the mouth form itself for words. *Oh, Mr. Marting!* He knew she would say it. And it made him feel sick. He shoved her back into her corner of the settle and got up.

The night was piercing cold, the air clear as ice, the wind like the edge of a knife. Gil, with the deer on his back and his rifle freezing to the palm of his mitten, walked home along the snowy road.

Across the river, the lights of the old Palatine settlement were contracted to points. The fort was a dark square on the snow-buried knoll. Along the road small houses and barns stood like little empty boxes. Further down the valley the earthworks and the low palisade atop them of Fort Herkimer, with the two blockhouses and the old stone church raising their roofs among the stars, were hushed in dormance by the frosty night. The only sound was the steady rapid squeak of his snowshoes.

Gil did not even hear them. He did not see the valley. He walked in a

blind rage, Nancy, Lana, himself, and human decency like fumes in his
tired brain. He hardly saw the Schuyler shack and the single pitiful light
its window made against the river ice.

Lana was waiting with his supper when he flung open the door.

"Here," he said, "Adam shot a doe. Let's throw the mush out and fry a
steak."

He sat unmoving on the stool, staring at her slow and listless obedience
before the hearth, smelling his own sweat rising through the steam of his
clothes, feeling contempt for the tiny room with its leaky walls, rage against
himself and her and Petry. Petry didn't really know; he had said as much.

As Lana put the steak on the table, he caught hold of her wrist.

"Sit down and eat some."

"I don't want it, Gil."

"Sit down and eat some, I said."

She said, "I've had my supper."

"I said sit down and eat some."

She sat down.

"Get a plate. You can't eat off the table."

She got a plate, mutely accepted the helping, sat staring at it.

"I can't, Gil." Her eyes filled with tears. He watched them come out beside her nose and follow down her cheeks with ugly slowness.

"You're going to, though. And you're going to quit this business of
treating me like this. You're going to start to-night, see?"

He watched her struggle with the meat. He thought she was going to
be sick. But she wasn't. She got through it somehow. But when she looked
up at him, as a dog might for a kind word of praise, he saw that she
understood what was in him. Her face turned deathly white and her eyes
showed fear as tangible as tears. She never said a word.

They didn't speak to each other next morning. They went several weeks
without any words but absolutely necessary ones. Gil kept trying to tell
himself that he was doing better than having to do with Demooth's hired
girl, but when he looked at Lana he had to check himself from fleeing
the house. She was completely compliant now. Yet her compliance had the
fearful quality of a misused dog's.

On Christmas Day he broke down. He had brought her, from the store,
a piece of ribbon, which he could not well afford, and as he watched her
mechanically putting it in her hair, with mechanical gestures of pleasure,
like a travesty in female flesh and blood, he cried out, "For God's sake
throw it away."

Her hands stopped at her hair, and for a long while she stared at him.
Then when he sprang up to get out of the house, she stepped before the
door.

"Gil."

Her face was so white that he was afraid of her. Then his hand raised
and clenched. And suddenly he broke down.

"It was all wrong, Lana. I was all wrong."

After his words the silence between them in the shack was as complete
as the silence of winter beyond the door. He could hear his own heart
beating, and then, with amazement, he heard her breathing.

"Maybe it wasn't," she said.

"You're like a dead person." He felt the words rush from his heart. "As if I'd killed you."

"I don't know, Gil." Her face for all its pallor became thoughtful. It hadn't the quick responsiveness any more. Looking at it, he felt that that had gone forever. "It wasn't you altogether, Gil. It was me, too."

While they stood there, they heard the bell of the old church, which had been taken out of the belfry to make room for the alarm gun and hung over the barrack door, send its slow notes over the snow.

Gil saw the pathetic question in her eyes.

"Let's," he said.

They went to church across the snow. They had no joy in the service or in the Reverend Mr. Rozencrantz's ponderable sermon on God's nearness in the wilderness or his prayer for the continued fruitfulness of God's earth. The water in the flat pans between the pews, placed there to draw the frost from the stone walls, the white icy light that filtered through the panes, the slow measured encroachment of the damp chill air to their very bones, were all beyond their senses. They sat side by side, untouching, yet close.

3

ORISKANY (1777)

1. *Council Fire*

To the west of Deerfield, where the Mohawk River made the great bend from north to east, the wooden ramparts of Fort Stanwix, striped with new palisades to patch the old, rose on their embankment above the swampy, snow-filled clearing. Beyond the cleared land the woods looked contracted in the frosty air. Sentries on the walks looked out at them through clouds of their own breathing, lethargically, for there was nothing, as there had been nothing since November, for them to see. Not even the river, which ran under ice; no movement about the two small deserted farms lying under the protection of the fort. Nothing at all but the snowshoe tracks of the five Oneida Indians who that morning had approached the glacis from the west and been admitted through the sally port.

Now they were in the commandant's quarters, a low frame building, of the shape of a cattle shed, set against the north wall. The smoke from the end chimney rose in a blue, thin, transparent tape against the gray sky.

The commandant's office was also the officers' messroom, walled with hand-hewn boards, furnished with tables of milled plank, and heavy chairs, the product of the garrison. There was not one in which a man could be comfortable. At the end of the big table, Colonel Elmore, of the New

York line, sat in his shirt sleeves, his back to the roaring fire, with his coat hung over his chair. Down the table before him four of the Indians huddled in their blankets, sweating, putting their odor in the room, staring with eyes that missed nothing while they seemed to be unseeing. The fifth Indian stood at the end of the table opposite the commandant.

This Indian was an old man, but his bearing was like a young brave's. His thin, tan, hawk-featured face was turned steadily toward Colonel Elmore. He spoke in a slow deep voice that rose and fell rhythmically, while one of the officers of the garrison, at another table, scratched down his own translation with a squeaky goose quill.

"We are sent here by the Oneidas in conjunction with the Onondagas. They arrived at our village yesterday. They gave us the melancholy news that the grand council fire at Onondaga has been extinguished. . . ." His voice was raised for a moment. "However, we are determined to use our feeble endeavors to support peace through the confederate nations. But let this be kept in mind, that the council fire is extinguished. *Brother, attend:* It is of importance to our well-being that this be immediately told to General Schuyler. In order to effect this, we deposit this belt with Tekeyanedonhotte, Colonel Elmore, commander at Fort Stanwix, who is sent here by General Schuyler to transact all matters relative to peace. We therefore request him to forward this intelligence in the first place to General Herkimer. . . . *Brother, attend:* let the belt be forwarded to General Schuyler, that he may know that our council fire is extinguished, and can no longer burn. . . ."

Joe Boleo, the news runner, was a thin man whose joints seemed always on the point of coming loose. He used snowshoes of the Algonquin shape, with spurs at the back, that left prints in the snow like the hind finger of a heron's foot. He went out from the fort while the Indians were still working their jaws on the salt pork Colonel Elmore had served them. He did not take the road along the south bank. He followed the river, where the snow was packed hard on the ice by the wind.

At noon the old Indian, Blue Back, sticking his nose outside the door of his bark shanty at the mouth of the Oriskany, saw the runner and looked long at the bent lank figure, shuffling past beneath the big coonskin cap, at a steady four miles an hour.

"By damn it," he said to his wife. "Joe Boleo's in a hurry."

"Why don't you holler for him to come in?" she said, gathering spit to work into the doeskin.

"It's too cold to holler," Blue Back said, shutting the door. "Besides, he always knows if there's any rum."

"We haven't got any," she said.

Blue Back sat down and put his hand on his stomach.

"No," he admitted, "but when I smelled Joe Boleo I'd want some myself."

He lay back on the bed and looked from the peacock's feather over his head to his young wife. She was growing a belly. The sight of it filled Blue Back with conflicting emotions. It was gratifying at his age to be able to show the tribe a legitimate offspring; but at his age, too, it was going to be hard work hunting for three people.

Joe Boleo had seen the group of Indian shanties and his squirrel-like, round, small black eyes had noticed the closing chink in Blue Back's door.

"God damn," he thought, "that old timber beast has got some likker and he's afraid I might turn round and visit with it."

He glanced up two hours later to see what was left of Martin's cabin at Deerfield. A corner of the log wall, charred away in sloping angles, thrust broken black teeth through the snow. The sight meant nothing to Joe. If anything it made him feel pleased to think that the settlers for a few years would be held back from the trapping country.

Joe Boleo hadn't many convictions in life, beyond the fact that he was the best shot in the Mohawk Valley; that women couldn't get along without him—not in their right minds, they couldn't; and that if rum wasn't a very good substitute for whiskey, whiskey was a first-rate substitute for rum. He was also annoyed at the British efforts for regulating the Indian trade and price of peltry. If it hadn't been for that he might as well have tailed along to Canada with the Johnsons. But if you couldn't cheat an Indian, who in the name of God could you cheat in this Godforsaken country?

Men were coming in from barns and cattle sheds when he passed Schuyler Settlement, and the setting sun drew Joe's shadow long before him on the crust. It put a spark of red on the lip of the alarm bell in Little Stone Arabia Stockade. The farmers were hurrying so that the milk would not freeze in the pails. Farming, Joe considered, was a hell of a life. You milked and milked at a cow for half a year, and just about as soon as you got her dry, the animal would get herself a fresh supply. But when he saw the warm vapor left in the evening air by the closing doors, it seemed to him there were advantages. A farmer in winter could sit at home and order his womenfolks around, while a scout might have to be running thirty miles to tell General Herkimer that a fire in an Indian lodge had gone out.

Joe wondered whether that had been an accident, or whether the old women watching it had gone to sleep, or whether the God-damn thing had been put out a-purpose. The Indians said the fire had been lit in the early life of mankind, and the Iroquois had kept it alive ever since. Even when they moved they had carried it around with them in a stone pot.

An hour after black dark he slogged his way up to Fort Dayton, handed in the news, and asked for a sleigh to take him down to the falls. The commandant got him the sleigh and a driver and packed him off with a pan of rum in his inside and called in the members of the Committee, Demooth, and Petry, and Peter Tygert, and gave them the news in front of the fire in his own quarters.

Their faces animated, even at the bad news, for having a new thing to talk about. The commandant said, "I'm from Massachusetts, but maybe I'm wooden-headed. What difference does it make?"

Demooth answered him soberly.

"It means that the Six Nations can't act together any more without the fire to confer around. That means that the Senecas and the Mohawks and the Cayugas and anyone else are free agents. While the fire was lit, no single tribe could go to war unless the other five were in agreement."

Herkimer, who had been appointed Brigadier General of the Tryon County militia in September, wrote a letter in his crabbed English to Schuyler and then had Eisenlord the clerk translate it and transcribe it while he and Joe Boleo did a little sober drinking.

Herkimer wanted Joe's opinions.

The scout, sprawling at the table in the white-paneled room whose windows looked out on the river and towards the falls, rinsed the liquor slowly round what teeth he still had claim to.

"If you want to know what I think," he said, "it just ain't safe hanging onto Stanwix. The wall's rotten. They've spiked in enough pickets to keep the others from falling down. If a man's got a cold he dassn't do sentry work there, for fear he'll sneeze and level the whole shebang. Poor old Dayton done a lot of complaining, but that ain't never stopped a leaky roof so far's I know."

Herkimer said he hadn't seen the fort.

"You needn't," said Joe. "Because I'm telling you about it. It would take a regiment four months to fix that place. And it don't do nobody any good way up there. It might have been a pertection for John Roof while he was living there, but he's come down here to your farm, since Deerfield got burnt. If the British was to come that way they could march right round with their pants off."

Herkimer said, "Maybe they won't think of that. Not if they send an army officer. An army officer has got to keep his line of communications open."

"My God!" exclaimed Joe. "What's that?"

"Well, he don't want anybody cutting in on his back trail."

Joe scratched his head.

"Oh, you mean he wants to know which way he's going when he has to run home. I thought it was a bowel complaint. But you could cut off his communications if you had a decent garrison at Dayton and Herkimer. They're a whole lot better forts, and they're handy for us to get to if we have to help them out. Take Stanwix, now: it's way the hell off from nobody's business. It stands to reason that it ain't sense making two armies in a war walk a long ways just to kill each other. Somebody ought to have some comfort."

Herkimer was looking older than his fifty years. It wasn't the liquor. His face was grim; the firelight showed it cut all in angles, the big nose, the heated black eyes, the long lips closed.

"I guess our militia ought to have one good fight in them, anyways. *Verdammt!* If they get in deep enough." He looked at Joe. "Have you heard from Joseph Brant? Any news anywhere?"

"We ain't had any word of him," Joe Boleo said. "What's on your mind, Honnikol?" He gave Herkimer his old name, the one he had had when they went hunting together as boys, before Herkimer got to be a successful man, a landholder, second only in wealth to Johnson. It was queer how the young lads diverged as they grew up, he thought—look at Honnikol, a brigadier general; and look at Joe Boleo, a plain scout. Just the same, Joe bet he could outshoot Honnikol nine times out of ten at a hundred yards.

2. *Mrs. McKlennar*

"Listen, Gil," said Captain Demooth, "you're a fool even to think of going back to Deerfield. You've seen George Weaver, haven't you? And Reall?"

"Yes."

"They aren't going, are they?"

"No."

"Well, I'm not. I'm going to stay down here until it's over. Even if we all went up we wouldn't have a chance when they turn the Indians loose."

"Do you think they will?"

"Everything goes to show so. Schuyler believes it. Herkimer believes it. You'd be as good as murdering your wife to take her up there. If you've got to go, leave her down here."

"I can't afford that, Mr. Demooth." Gil stood beside the table, touching it with his hands. He wanted to lean on something, but he didn't know whether it would look polite. His face had thinned during the winter. The lines beside his mouth had deepened, and under his eyes. His eyes had a misery in them. "When I think about my land," he said. "All the work I put in it. Burning off the new piece. And letting it just go back to woods."

"I know," said the captain. "I feel like that. But look here, Gil, the militia's bound to be turned out. You'll have to come. You'll have to bring Lana down with you then."

"Oh, damn the militia!"

"That don't do you any good."

"I've got to live. I'd made a good start. We were real happy up there. There's no land for me to work around here, and there's no real work for me on your place, you know that."

"Well, now look here, Gil." The captain crossed his legs and tapped the table with his fingers. "I don't suppose it's any good if that's how you feel, but I'd been thinking about you. I just heard that Mrs. McKlennar's man has left her. No doubt he's run off to Canada. Ever since they started rounding up the disaffected people down the valley, others have been leaving here." Gil knew about that. The Albany Committee had taken charge of four hundred wives and children of departed Tories. The idea was to hold them as a kind of hostage. "Mrs. McKlennar asked me about a man to work her place. I said I'd speak to you."

Gil frowned. "I don't want to work for a woman."

"Think it over. She's a decent woman, and she's able to do well in the world, Gil. She's got a temper, but that's because she's Irish. And listen, things have changed. There's going to be real war. Now Carleton has driven Arnold off the Champlain Lake, the British are bound to make a try for this country. There's already action starting at Oswego. Spencer writes that Butler's moving out of Niagara in May. They'll surely bring an army down this way, and if they do, Deerfield's right in the track of it. Now if you take a job with Mrs. McKlennar for a year or two, you'll know your wife's handy to a decent fort. Eldridge Blockhouse is close by, and she could also get to Herkimer or Dayton, if you were off on militia duty. It's a small farm, but it's good."

"I don't want to work for a woman," Gil repeated.

The captain was exasperated.

"It won't hurt you to go and talk to her, will it?"

He spoke so sharply that Gil looked at him.

"No," he said slowly.

That was what Lana said to him after he had told her about the captain's suggestion. Her face was sweet and comforting. Even though it was subdued, though her mouth had a downward bend, he could rely on her eyes, the honesty in them. The winter had been like a nightmare to Gil; it must have been to her; he thought it was time they moved out of this shack, and there was nowhere else to go, if they did not go back to her family. He didn't want to use that argument even to himself, but she helped him by reminding him.

"We won't have to go back to Fox's Mills," she said. "If we like the place we can stay, and maybe we can save up for what we'll need when we go back to Deerfield."

They walked down to Mrs. McKlennar's farm on a Sunday. The river had opened, spring was in the air. That spring of 1777 had come with a rush. One night when Gil and Lana were going to bed they had seen mist over the river ice. And before moonset in the early morning, they had been awakened by the breaking of the ice. It had cracked first in one long traveling report that carried eastward nearly to the falls.

In the morning the whole valley had changed. The air had been soft and moist; and the rising sun, a red ball on the misty hills, already warm. But the wonder, after the long silence of the snow, had been the sound of water. Water was everywhere. It was flowing in its accustomed channel of the river, dark and soiled against the white banks, but catching a red glitter on the rift below the ford. It came across the low land with a steady seeping sound, overflowing the frozen marshes and putting long lakes in the sleigh ruts. And everywhere on the dark slopes of the hills arched yellow falls burst downward.

Gil and Lana dressed themselves carefully, he in his good black jersey coat, and she in her striped blue and white short gown and striped petticoat. She wore her shawl over her head, but she had a white cap on her black hair, and to Gil she seemed unexpectedly dainty as she walked beside him, for all her muddy feet, and carried her chintz pocket before her, almost with demureness. He kept looking down at her, as if in the soft air he had rediscovered the girl in her body, and she looked to him too fine and gentle for a hired help.

In Lana must have run some inheritance from the old Palatine persecutions. The history of her race was one of oppression and of the struggle to survive against it. It was that which made the Palatines strong—through suffering they had preserved their personal independence.

So now, instead of arguing with Gil, she let him take his own way, contenting herself with the presence of spring, the steady drip of trees, the shimmer of the water, the scent of earth unfettered of the snow, and the

clear infinity of the April sky. It was good to be walking so, beside Gil.
It was the first time all winter, except when they had gone to church.
Through her own contentedness she softened his resentment, and they
were walking almost peaceably when they first saw the McKlennar farm.

The land lay prettily for a small farm, bordering both sides of the Kingsroad, its back against the sudden rise of river hills, its front upon the
river. At a single glance the eye could comprehend the system of the land.
The pasture went along the river on a long low round that carried above
flood water. Enough willows grew there to give shade. The great trees
spread wider, and their branches to-day lifted their upthrusting twigs like
brassy arrows against the violet shadows on the southern hills.

Behind the pasture the fields lay level to the plough, rich black bottom
land. In spite of himself, Gil felt his heart swelling when he saw them,
with an ache for Deerfield. This land had been worked for many years.
And there was a good hay bottom, with bluejoint in the wet and a sod that
looked like English grass in the higher portions. He could see that the
fences had been well set up.

Gil found himself eagerly searching out the farm buildings. What he
saw was even better than he had supposed. The house he let pass; it was a
stone-walled house, with a piazza facing the road. Behind it in a slope of
ground was a farm barn of hewn logs, laid up with plaster joints and a
pine shingle roof. The very look of it was warm.

But Lana was looking past the barn to the small house that stood to the
right of the springhouse. It also was built of hewn logs, but she could
tell by the way it sat above the ground that it had a board floor laid on actual
sills. And in front of the door, in the sunny place, were reddish-orange
fowls busily prospecting in the dirt.

"Gil!" she cried. "They keep poultry."

Now she began to be afraid that Gil would shy off from the place, that
he wouldn't like the woman of the place, or that the woman of the place
would not like them. She closed her lips tight, and she said a small prayer
in her heart, and she dared not look ahead.

When she did look up again, it was because a woman's voice had
roused her.

"Good morning. Is your name Martin?"

"Yes, ma'am," Gil was saying.

"I'm glad you've come," said Mrs. McKlennar.

From her appearance there, Lana would never have supposed that she
was gentry. Her boots were muddy, the tops of them showing plainly underneath her petticoat, which Mrs. McKlennar had pinned up all around,
nearly to her knees. Her hair she wore clubbed up at the back of her head
in a string net that looked as if some birds had put it together in a hurry.
She looked hot and she smelled of her stable.

"Yes," she said, suddenly meeting Lana's gaze. "I'm hot and I smell and
I look like the devil and I'm mad as well. Every time I lift a fork of cow
manure I am reminded of that damn man of mine. He sneaked out of here
without so much as a word. The first I knew of it was the freshened heifer
bellowing in the barn. I thought he was drunk and I went down to haul
him out of bed. I don't mind a man having his likker, Martin, but if he

doesn't do his work he can go somewhere else. The quicker the better, for him."

She snorted like a bell mare and stamped her feet as she went up the steps.

"Come inside."

She led them into the kitchen of her house, a lovely place, to Lana's eyes. The stone walls had been sheathed in wide pine paneling and painted a snuff brown. Overhead the beams were painted black with bright red undersides. Mrs. McKlennar sat on one settle. She pointed to the other, and Gil and Lana sat down side by side.

"Now," said Mrs. McKlennar, "you're here on business. Let's get down to it. I want a man. Demooth says you need a job. Is that so?"

"Yes, ma'am."

"You're a passable farmer?"

"I had my own place."

"I heard about it being burned. Too bad. Well, it's an ill wind. And it's neither here nor there. Mark wouldn't have sent you here if you hadn't known something about it. I don't do much farming. Just keep up the meadows and feed my stock. I'm a widow woman. My husband was Captain Barnabas McKlennar. He was with Abercrombie. I may as well say I've had army life all my life, and I expect to get an order obeyed when I give it. Whether you like it or not. Is that understood?"

Gil flushed. "If I take your pay, I'll do the best I can."

"Well, I don't want you coming around afterwards and complaining. How much do you want?"

"I've never worked for anyone else," Gil said. "What did you expect to pay?"

"Well, I asked Mr. Demooth and he suggested forty-five pounds a year, with the house, with the wood, and with the food. It's not a big wage, but if you work well you'll have a good home here. Besides, if your wife can sew, I'll pay her for sewing for me. Can you sew, what's your name?"

"Lana."

"That's a nickname. Magdelana, I suppose."

Lana nodded, blushing.

"Well," said Mrs. McKlennar tartly, "can you sew, Magdelana?"

"Yes," said Lana.

"Would you do sewing for me?"

"I'd like to," Lana said shyly.

"That's understood. I hate to sew. I hate housework, so I do the barn myself and let Daisy, my nigger, do the cooking. I took care of my husband, but now he's gone I'll do as I like. I've got a long nose, Martin, and I poke it where I like. You may think I'm a nuisance."

"Yes, ma'am," said Gil, at a loss for what to say.

"A nuisance?" she said sharply.

Gil flushed.

"I hadn't meant it." Then, meeting the glitter in her eye, he couldn't help but grin. "But I guess I'll think so if you do."

Lana's heart contracted. She looked quickly towards Mrs. McKlennar and was surprised to find the woman's bold stare fixed upon herself. For a moment the face seemed more horselike than ever. Then the weathered cheeks twitched a little, Mrs. McKlennar put a large hand to Lana's hair and gave it a pat, as she would have patted a dog's head.

However, her voice was uncompromising.

"Your thoughts are your own property, Martin. But keep them to yourself when they arise. And don't presume on your good looks."

"No, ma'am," said Gil.

Lana sighed. She could tell that Gil was amused, that he had made up his mind.

"Perhaps," said Mrs. McKlennar, "you'd like to see your house?" She glanced at Lana and lifted her voice. "Would you, Magdelana?"

Lana bestirred her senses. "Yes," she said timidly.

Mrs. McKlennar snorted, rose, and led them out the back door. As she did so, she said, "I'll expect you to use the back door when you want to ask me for anything. I don't want muck tracked through my kitchen. I track enough myself."

A stout negress in a bright bandana watched them from the woodshed. But Mrs. McKlennar ignored her, and walked with hard-heeled strides towards the little house.

"It's a mess. McLonis never cleared out. A single man. You'll have a sight of work here, Magdelana. But there's water running through a puncheon, a good spring. Have you got bedding?"

"Most of our things were burned," said Gil.

"Well, I'll help you out with a bed." She opened the door. "It's a good chimney, and it's a dry house."

The inside surfaces of the logs were mellowed. Mrs. McKlennar stalked to the middle of the floor and stood there. "You've got a good-sized bedroom upstairs. It's light and airy. It's the original house. Barney was possessed to build the stone one, but I always fancied this house. I lived here a good many years."

Lana looked round her. It was a good chimney, the kind that would be easy to cook at. It had an oven. It made her think of her mother's oven. She turned to look at Gil.

"It's a nice house," she said softly.

"I'm glad you've sense enough to see it. Well, as for me, you can consider the job yours. It's up to you, now, Martin." She paused. "Maybe you'd like to ask some questions."

Gil said, "Yes. I'm in Mr. Demooth's company. If the militia gets called, and I go out with it, will I get paid my wages?"

"Fortunes of war." Mrs. McKlennar nodded. "I'll expect Mrs. Martin to do the milking."

"I will," Lana said eagerly.

"There's another thing." Gil spoke hesitantly.

"Yes?" Mrs. McKlennar was gruff.

"I'd have to know if you were in the right party."

"A woman hasn't got political opinions. I run my farm. And I'll shoot the daylights out of anybody, British or American, that thinks he can come here monkeying with my business. Does that satisfy you?"

Gil said, "Yes," quite seriously.

"Then maybe you'd like to talk it over."

"That ain't necessary, Mrs. McKlennar. We'll do the best we can for you. I like the farm. And you'll find my wife useful, I guess."

Mrs. McKlennar grinned.

"That's fine." She held her hand out like a man. "When can you move in?"

"To-morrow. I've got a mare."

"You can keep her here."

Lana said, "Would it be all right for me to mind the chickens, ma'am?"

"Chickens?"

"Yes. I used to mind them at home. I missed them up in the woods."

The widow snorted.

3. A Prayer

The people had sat down. Now they bowed themselves forward. The pews stopped creaking. Inside Herkimer Church, there was no sound at all but the sudden cracking of the Reverend Mr. Rozencrantz's knees as he got down from his chair, buttoned his coat, and folded his hands in front of him; and through the open windows the tread of military boots upon the sentry walk of the surrounding fort sounded like the impersonal slow laborious ticking of a clock.

Mr. Rozencrantz was a well-advised man, who knew as well as anyone did that to hold his congregation a preacher must give them something to talk about on their way home. Hell and damnation didn't get far when followed by a Sunday dinner.

In the forefront of the church, high up, in the shadow of the sounding board, he knelt—his white hair hanging to the collar of his shirt, his thin face, his high arched nose, his eyelids stretching tight over his eyeballs as he closed his eyes, the easy mobility of his colorless lips forming themselves for the first word:—

"*O Almighty God,* Father of our Lord Jesus Christ, hear us, we beseech Thee, answer our prayers and bring succor and guidance and consolation according to the needs of those we are about to bring to Thy divine notice."

The domine's stertorous breathing punctuated the pause. He gathered himself visibly, raised up his voice again, and then let it get to business.

"*O Almighty God,* we are thinking right now of Mary Marte Wolla-ber. She is just fifteen years old, but she is going with one of the soldiers at Fort Dayton. He is a Massachusetts man, *O God,* and it has come to my attention that he is married in the town of Hingham. I have had her father and mother talk to her, I have talked to her my-self, but she won't pay attention. We ask Thy help, *God Almighty,* in bringing her back to the path of virtue, from which, we believe, she has strayed pretty far.

"*O Almighty God,* You have brought us an early spring, keep off the frosts until the fruit is set. O Lord, the English codlin Nicholas Herkimer has grafted onto his Indian apple tree has bloomed this year.

May it bear fruit. It is a wonderful example of Thy ways, and worth our going to see, and Nicholas Herkimer will show it to anybody. Also, *God Almighty,* our *Heavenly Father,* we return thanks for the good lambing we have had this year, particularly Joe Bellinger, who has had eleven couples lambed from his twelve ewes, which is a record in this county.

"*O Almighty God,* we ask Thy compassion and aid for all of us who are in sickness. We ask it for Petey Paris, who got the flux real bad on Saturday. His Uncle Isaac Paris sent the news up to us and asks our prayers and says that he has got in a new supply of calicos, French reds, broadcloths, Russias, fancy hank'chers, some new hats and heavy boots, scythes and grindstones.

"*O Almighty God,* give comfort to the following women, both expecting mighty quick, especially Hilda Fox, who is only sixteen next July and getting close to her time. It is her first. And also for Josina Casler, who is due the end of this month."

The domine halted once more, let go a strong breath, and resumed:—

"*O Almighty and most merciful God, Lord Jehovah,* who is also God of Battles, come to our aid, we beseech Thee, hear the prayers of Thy people, gathered here before Thee, bring them aid against the British. It surely looks like war was coming on us directly. There is activity, *O God,* at Crown Point, and they say General Burgoyne is bringing an army of 10,000 men, with Russians and Indians, against Ticonderoga. St. Clair is in charge there, so help him, God. And we thank *Thee, O God,* for sending up the Third New York to Fort Stanwix. We have faith in them, let it not be displaced. For Spencer sends us word that Butler and Guy Johnson and Daniel Claus are meeting at Oswego, and they are hard men, as we know. They aim to bring the savages. It certainly looks like war.

"*O God Almighty,* our own Colonel Peter Bellinger wants the fourth company to muster at Dayton to-morrow, June sixteenth. He is marching them to Canajoharie to meet up there with Herkimer, and they are going to try to see Joseph Brant, the chief of the Mohawk savages, who has been making trouble down to Unadilla. May all the militia be punctual to assemble and let them come back in time to defend this settlement if Butler comes quicker than we do expect him. O Lord, we ask only to be allowed to lead our lives here in peace and fruitful cultivation of our land.

"The muster will be at eight o'clock sharp on Monday morning.

"For Christ's sake, Amen."

Gilbert Martin, bowing behind the back of Mrs. McKlennar, who sat by herself in her own pew, looking stiffly elegant in her black silk dress and smelling violently of a rose scent, felt Lana's hand come quickly into his. He did not move; he did not look at her; he felt the same surprise that the whole congregation, by their utter stillness, showed. It was the first time that the realization of the imminence of war had been brought home to them.

In the stillness, the cracking of the Reverend Mr. Rozencrantz's knees could be distinctly heard as he got to his feet.

4. *Unadilla*

The militia had no uniform. Demooth's company came nearest to it, with the red cockades they had adopted. They marched better because of them; nearly half the company were keeping step. The Massachusetts garrison of Fort Dayton, lined up in front of the palisade, gave them a cheer, the derisiveness of which was entirely lost on George Weaver. *"Hup,"* he said, *"hup, hup, hup."*

Half the women of the valley were there to see them off, and while he watched the shrill adieus, Gil Martin felt glad that Lana had not come to say good-bye to him. He had persuaded her not to, saying that she would see him pass Mrs. McKlennar's anyway. And Mrs. McKlennar had backed him up, with one of her snorts.

"Mush," she had said. "I remember when Barney went off on Abercrombie's expedition. He kissed me in bed and gave me a wallop behind and he said, 'You stay here, Sally, old girl, and keep it warm against the time I get back.' He couldn't stand anything sentimental, you see."

But when she heard the ragged tapping of the militia drums coming along the Kingsroad, she went stamping down to the fence behind Lana like an old warhorse, to wave at the officers and clap her hands like any girl.

The colonel's mare went past, blasting air in her excitement at the drums behind her tail, while astride her Colonel Bellinger himself tried to look as if he were unconscious of her failing, as well as of Christian Reall's bawling that it was too bad they didn't have a trumpet for the mare to blow on.

The two women stayed by the fence, watching the familiar faces of the men, with the red flag of the regiment flapping at its head against the green river hills, and the slant of their rifles, until they saw Gil walking towards them between George Weaver and the angular Jeams MacNod. Gil looked so dark and tall between them, and his face was so set, that Lana's throat grew tight. She was grateful for the squeeze of Mrs. McKlennar's large hand on her arm.

"He's a handsome man," she said. "God save him."

The German Flats company was five days marching down to Unadilla. At the evening of the first day they encamped at Palatine Church, above Fox's Mills, where on the following morning a detachment of the Palatine company joined them under Colonel Jacob Klock. The two companies together, nearly two hundred men, continued east, and reached the rendezvous at Canajoharie at noon. There they pitched camp again, between the Canajoharie company and a company of regulars from the First New York Line sent up from Albany under Colonel Van Schaick. The presence of the regular troops in their uniform blue campaign coats was inspiriting, particularly on the following morning when the drums beat them to parade. The regular troops had three-foot deep drums with a resonance beyond compare, finer than the militia drums. All that day, the militia marched south from the Mohawk behind the drums. Again and again they found themselves keeping step as they went up through the hills.

But at Cherry Valley, Colonel Van Schaick halted his men and announced to General Herkimer that he could go no farther as he had to wait for his provisions. However, he would be ready to back up the general if the Indians got out of hand.

Herkimer, on his old white horse, sat moodily staring away from the colonel towards the palisade that enclosed the Campbell farm and made the only fort for the protection of the settlement. He listened without comment, his black eyes staring on the landscape, the green field set in a saucer of the hills. Since winter a foreboding sense of gloom had come over the little German, and now it seemed to him it was fulfilled.

He touched the cocked brim of his hat to the army colonel and swung the old horse to the road. Waiting for him, Colonel John Harper stood at the head of a small company of rangers, and the sight of him and his men seemed to brighten Herkimer. He asked him whether Brant were still at Oghkwaga, and when Harper nodded asked him if his company, knowing the land, would act as scouts. Harper agreed. Herkimer gave the word.

The militia started forward like the disjointed parts of a snake. Twenty minutes later, the head of the little army of three hundred men was past the settlement on the path to Otsego Lake. In half an hour they had all disappeared into the woods.

On the twentieth they pitched camp on the south shore of the Susquehanna, three miles below its junction with the Unadilla. A runner was sent out that afternoon to Oghkwaga to announce to Brant that Herkimer was waiting to see him and talk as neighbor to neighbor.

The militia had no tents, except the general's. They peeled hemlocks and laid the bark on poles, facing the north, for the weather was hot. The next morning, under orders, they set up a bark shed, fifty feet long, on a knoll a quarter of a mile below, in an irregular growth of apple trees, some of which were still in bloom.

During the course of the morning the runner returned from Oghkwaga and went at once to Herkimer's tent. The general was sitting alone in his shirt sleeves, a field desk on his knees and a quill pen in his fist. He never felt like writing, and writing this way made it pretty near impossible.

Joe Boleo sat down.

"I seen him."

"Will he come talk with me?"

"Oh, sure, in a few days, he says."

"Did you get a look around, hey?"

"Not much last night. But I looked around pretty good this morning. He ain't got so many Injuns there."

They looked at each other.

"Honnikol," said Joe Boleo earnestly, "you want to tie up this twerp, don't you?"

"Yes. But if I go after him now and don't catch him it's an act of war."

"He ain't got two hundred with him."

"Yes, but Congress still thinks they're going to get the Indians on their side. A bunch of them went down last year and called John Hancock a great tree, or something."

"Is that all they called him?" asked Joe Boleo. "My God, they missed their chance."

"Yes, I'm to get Brant to agree to keep neutral. But, by God, I'd like to shut him up somewhere."

"Why don't you grab him when he comes over?"

The militia lay around for seven steaming days and didn't do a thing. Then, on the morning of the twenty-seventh, the scouts fell in towards camp with the news that Brant was coming up four miles below. At noon an Indian walked into camp and asked for General Herkimer.

He stood like a post under his blanket, his small dark eyes flickering here and there over the camp. General Herkimer emerged from his tent, pulling on his coat as he came.

The Indian asked, "What do you want to talk to Brant about?" in English as good as Herkimer's.

"I want to talk with him as an old neighbor."

"That's fine," said the Indian. "I tell him all these men be his old neighbors too?"

He did not look amused, but Herkimer grinned.

"Yes, tell him that."

The Indian turned. In half an hour he was back suggesting that the already erected shed would do as a meeting place if Herkimer came with fifty unarmed men, which Brant also agreed to do on his part. The shed was out of shot from the surrounding woods, and the bare approach to it was a guarantee against any treachery.

A little after noon, Herkimer walked up the hill and sat down in the shade of the shed roof. He took with him Colonels Cox, Harper, Klock, and Bellinger, and each colonel brought a squad from his own company. Gil was in Bellinger's squad.

They sat around on the benches for ten minutes before Brant appeared at the edge of the woods.

It was the first time Gil had ever seen the man whose name since winter had come to be on everybody's tongue. He was under six feet, but he walked like a taller man. His clothes were made in the Indian fashion, but, except for the deerskin moccasins, they were made of English cloth, and instead of the traditional headdress he wore a cocked black hat bedizened with gold lace. His blanket was a vivid blue, turned back from the shoulders to show the scarlet lining.

Behind him his companions were dressed like shabby replicas. There were five of them, in front of the warriors. A white man in deerskins, whom Brant introduced as Captain Bull, and who smirked a little as he bowed; a half-breed Indian who turned out to be Sir William Johnson's bastard son by Brant's sister, a dark-skinned fellow with an Irish face; a Mohawk chief whose name Gil didn't catch; and a half-breed, negro-Indian, whom Brant didn't bother about.

Brant smiled a little as he looked down at Herkimer and shook him by the hand. His features were straight, well shaped, and full of animation. He kept looking round on the militia as if to see what their reactions were.

But their reactions to himself, not to the situation. It took but one look at him to see that he was vain.

Though he was pure-bred Mohawk, Joseph Brant could easily have been mistaken for a white man, and he talked more educated English than old Herkimer could have mastered had he been thrice reborn and three times sent to college. He had a great dignity of behavior, too, that made the militia look like simple men; but it was not the natural dignity of a plain Indian. It had the manners of a white man who has been to a royal court. It was filled with pride, which even so meaching-minded a man as Christian Reall could see was an unnatural thing.

Joe Boleo, watching his back, grunted to George Weaver, "Brant used to be a nice lad, too. But now he wants the world to know he's a nice man."

Joe Boleo had put his finger on Brant's weakness. He wanted to be admired, by both Indians and whites, gentlemen and farmers. He wanted to be a great man, by both standards, with whatever person he was at the moment engaged. It was an attitude that later would account for his irrational kindnesses and friendships, as well as his cruelties and hates. The mistake he always made was his utter inability to understand that forthright people like Boleo or Herkimer or Gil could see straight through him. Vainer people, he enraged.

Brant's complaints had been that the Mohawks who had stayed at the Indian town in friendliness to the colonies were held as virtual prisoners, together with their minister, Mr. Stuart; that Butler's wife and children were kept as hostages, and that forts were being erected on Indian property.

Herkimer had asked if the Indians would remain neutral if these complaints were met, to which Brant replied that the Six Nations had always been allied with the King of England, that they still were. Beyond that he could not go. Herkimer then asked him whether he would talk again to-morrow, and Brant agreed. But as he turned to go, he said quietly, "I've got five hundred men. If you start trouble, they'll be ready."

That night Herkimer talked with Joe Boleo and another man named Wagner, and George and Abraham Herkimer. "It's no use at all," he said. "Brant's made his mind up. And there isn't a damn thing we can do about it. He's got five hundred men, and if he wants he can wipe us out."

"I could draw a bead on him," Joe Boleo suggested.

Herkimer shook his head.

"Shucks," said Joe. "We can lick them Indians. If we get Brant the rest of them will run like rabbits."

"I can't take the chance. I've got to get these men back to the Mohawk. We're going to need them all."

His nephew George said, "What if he starts trouble to-morrow?"

"That's what I want to see you about. If he does you're to shoot him. You can lay behind the top of the hill. They won't see you if you go before sunrise. Lay in those ferns. But don't you start anything."

Nothing happened on the next day. Brant greeted Herkimer blandly with the announcement that the Indians under no circumstances would break their allegiance to the King. Herkimer shrugged.

"All right, Joseph," he said. "There's no sense in talking any more."

That was all there was to it. Three hundred men had marched southward ninety miles; they would march ninety miles back.

"No sense," Brant agreed. "It was nice to have the visit." The sarcasm was barely veiled. "Seeing you're old neighbors, all of you, we'll let you go home. And we won't bother this country now. As a matter of fact, I've got to go to Oswego to meet Colonel Butler."

Herkimer nodded, stood up, shook hands, and watched Brant calmly walking down the knoll towards the woods with his fifty men behind him. As if he had half a mind to signal to Joe Boleo and Wagner, he kept his hands clenched in his trousers' pockets. He did not move until the last Indian had stepped into the underbrush.

Then he said, "Call up the men."

The militia, held under arms, came quickly up the hill and formed companies. At the same moment, a wild yelling burst from the woods; the brush suddenly disgorged a band of Indians. As they came into the open, they brandished their muskets, tossed up their tomahawks, and yelled again.

"Don't anybody notice them."

Herkimer's voice was calm and contained. He had lit his pipe and now he stood in front of the militia, puffing it and staring up at the sky.

"God damn," he said. "I didn't see that storm coming up. But I guess we'll all get wet anyway. Let's break camp and go home."

The Indians were still yelling and prancing at the woods' edge. But now they too heard the thunder. The clouds suddenly engulfed the sun, a still sultry light came over the rolling valley, and then the rain, in large drops, like a volley from heaven, struck the land. The Indians dove back into the woods and the militia were left alone in the falling rain.

Then they too broke for their own camp. They heard the Indians popping off their rifles through the woods, but the sound was like play in the noise of wind and thunder.

When the last man got into camp, the general's tent was struck and he was hunched on the back of his miserable old white horse. Joe Boleo said, "They've all skedaddled."

Herkimer grinned. "They're touchy as women about their paint when they've just put it on."

"It was war paint," said Cox.

"Yes, I saw it." He was unruffled. "It's time we got back home." He raised his voice above the rain. "This trip ain't altogether a waste. We've learned to march together and get along without scrapping between ourselves." He grinned and rubbed the rain off his mouth. "Boys, it looks like a bad time was coming. But you've seen painted Indians, now, so you'll know what to shoot at."

Plenty of the men had been wondering what the expedition had been for. But as they listened to the little German talking to them through the rain, they realized that they had a man who could take them into the woods, and who wasn't scared of Indians, and they felt that when the time came he could set his teeth in a situation and hang on. "Boys," he said, "go back and get your haying done as early as you can. Peter," he called to Colonel Bellinger, "I'm going back the way we came by. We have food waiting for us at Cherry Valley if the Conti   als ain't ate it all. But I give you enough extra so you can take a sno   Follow up Butternut Creek. If these Indians ever make a shy at German Flats they'll come that way. You ought to see the country. Joe Boleo'll show you how to go."

So the German Flats company crossed the Susquehanna at the ford above the Unadilla and headed home straight north without more than an Indian trail to follow the course of the Creek.

It was wild land. Gil, floundering through a swamp, found Adam Helmer, whom he had hunted with during the winter, beside him. "It's great hunting country," Helmer said. "I've hunted it for years. I know it like my fist and I'd like to see the Indian who could catch me in it. Or that I couldn't catch."

When they came out at Andrustown Helmer asked permission to leave the ranks. He wanted to visit one of Bower's girls. When he got permission he dropped back to Gil's side. "Why don't you stop off? Polly's got a sister that can give you fun."

Gil grinned and said, "I'm a hired man, Adam. I got to get back to work. You heard what Herkimer said about hurrying the crops."

"You mean you're married." Helmer shook his big blond head. "But you're kind of behind with your sowing, mister." He laughed, stepped out of line, and entered the woods. All girls were does to Adam, and some had to be still-hunted.

The company tramped through the little cluster of eight farms while the women and children ran to the fences. For the Indian trail turned suddenly into a road that ran straight to Fort Herkimer.

That evening, on the second day of their march, the company disbanded. By dark, Gil had got home. There was no light in his house, so he went to the stone one. Looking through the door, he saw Lana and Mrs. McKlennar and Daisy, her negress, sitting together.

They all made much of him, and Mrs. McKlennar went down cellar for some sack, which all three white people drank. She snorted a good deal at his description. "It sounds just like rioters trying to get up their nerve. What we need is regular troops."

"Herkimer has nerve enough," said Gil.

"I don't doubt it, when he gets pinched. But you don't win wars by pinching." She snorted, sipped, and grinned, showing her teeth. "But we're glad to have you back, my lad. Ain't we, Magdelana?"

Lana seemed subdued, and at the question she dropped her eyes to her sewing and flushed.

"Hup, hup," said Mrs. McKlennar. "Leave that and go to bed. That's where he ought to have found you, anyway. Go on."

Gil hardly felt Lana's light touch on his arm. She was looking up with tenderness in her eyes. "I'm glad you're back, Gil." And then, "Gil, are you glad? Because I'm real glad."

"Yes," he said. "But I'm hungry as sin, too."

5. Proclamation

The summer was like any other summer in the upper Mohawk Valley, except for the heat. No one remembered such heat as came in that July.

Day after day of it, that even dried the woods so that ranging cattle returned early to their barns. The air was sultry, and there was a dusty smell in it, as if a spark dropped anywhere could set the whole world blazing.

Men swinging their scythes through standing grass could feel the brittle dryness of it through the snathe from blade edge to palm; and the women, at work with the rakes, found the hay cured almost as fast as they could handle it.

In German Flats, people, starting the haying, found it hard to believe that war was going on in other places. The plain farmer, thinking of his hay and wheat, had no real idea of what the war was about. In the evenings, reverting to the subject listlessly, all he recalled was the early days of 1775, when the Butlers and the Johnsons and their sheriff, Alexander White, had ridden the length of the valley to chop down the liberty pole in front of Herkimer Church, as they had done at Caughnawaga. But now they were all skyhooted off to Canada for these two years.

It seemed they couldn't take account of the messengers riding horseback up and down the Kingsroad. Men who went at a gallop and didn't stop to drink. All they thought of it was that you couldn't find day labor any more for love or money. Congress was paying men to work up in the woods around Fort Stanwix, a crazy notion for a crazy place—as crazy as the heat.

Up at Fort Stanwix two men had taken charge. One was an apple-faced young Dutchman with a chin as sullen as a growing boy's and very bright blue eyes. His name was Peter Gansevoort, he wore a colonel's epaulets, and was so gentrified about his linen that one soldier, whose wife (by courtesy) had come along, was doubling the family pay. The other was the second in command, Lieutenant Colonel Marinus Willett, a man who looked like a farmer, with a lantern-like face of rusty red all over, and a nose like a grubbing hoe. When he first appeared the settlers said the very smell of him was Yankee; but he came from New York, and he was able to laugh and enjoy himself.

The five hundred men in the garrison considered that their commanding officers were slave drivers. Not only did they start rebuilding the entire cheval-de-frise, they burnt John Roof's place to the ground, they cleared the scrub laurel from the clearing, and worse than that they sent two squads out every day to fell trees across Wood Creek. To the local labor, that didn't make sense. What was the use of repairing the fort if, at the same time, you made it impossible for the British to get there?

Then like a thunderclap, on the seventh of July, word came up the valley that Fort Ticonderoga had been taken by Burgoyne. Though half the people did not know where Ticonderoga lay, the very sound of the sentence had the ominous ring of calamity.

All at once, George Herkimer's company of militia was mustered and turned into squads of rangers. They blocked the roads to the four points of the compass—west at Schuyler, east at Frank's tavern beside Little Falls, south at Andrustown, and north at Snydersbush. Rumor said that the Butlers and the Johnsons were returning to the valley, bringing their Indians and the wild Highlanders of whom the Germans were as fearful as they were of the Senecas themselves.

Reports came in of men in the woods at Schoharie, and at Jerseyfield. Overnight the little town of Fairfield was deserted. A man named Suffrenes Casselman had led the Tory villagers westward. The word was brought down by a settler on Black Creek, who described them: twenty men, women and children with them, carrying what they could.

As they finished the haying, the people of German Flats were aware of the rebirth of their old racial fears. The Committee of Safety began enforcing their new laws. A negro was shot for being out after dark without permission. Communities began repairing the old stockades. The hammering at Eldridge Blockhouse came up the valley on those still days, so that Gil Martin, struggling with Lana to get the last of the hay under the barrack roof, heard it plainly.

That evening Jacob Small rode down from Eldridge. He said, "We've got a cannon set up in the tower," as proudly as though Betsey Small had borne another son. "If you hear it go off, it's Injuns. If she shoots twice, don't try to fetch anything, but run like sixty. If she shoots three times, try to get across the river. It means they've got so close you couldn't get inside the fort."

After supper Gil got down the Merritt rifle. And seeing him clean it, Mrs. McKlennar, who had dropped by in the dark, nodded her head from the door.

"Don't look so scared, though, Magdelana. They haven't got here yet."

A canoe came down the river in the dark, cutting an arrow through the moon. In the bow a big-shouldered man stroked steadily. In the stern, Joe Boleo was paddling with his usual appearance of exhaustion.

They ran the bow aground above the falls and took the path down the hill by Warner Dygert's. They found Nicholas Herkimer sitting on his porch.

"Who's that?"

"It's Spencer, Honnikol."

Herkimer got up. The big man shook hands.

"Where you from, Tom?"

Spencer said, "Onondaga."

"What's up?"

"The Indians are at Oswego. Both the Butlers. Sir John Johnson."

"How many all together?"

"They've got four hundred regular soldiers. The Eighth Regiment and the Thirty-fourth. There's about six hundred Tories. They're wearing green uniforms. All the Senecas are there. Brant and his Mohawks. The Cayugas and some Onondagas. A thousand, maybe."

Herkimer grunted.

"Who's in command?"

"A man named Sillinger." (Spencer gave the local contraction of Colonel Barry St. Leger's name.) "He has a big tent and five servants."

"I never heard of him," said Herkimer. "Is he an army man, Tom?"

The Indian blacksmith said, "I don't know. He wears a red coat with gold strings."

"Thank God for that," said Herkimer. He yelled for a negro.
"Go get Mr. Eisenlord. He's at Frank's. Go quick." He turned to Joe. "I can't write this myself. It's too damned hot to-night."
Eisenlord's neat hand made English of the general's dictation:—

> Whereas it appears certain that the enemy, of about 2000 strong, *Christians* and *savages,* are arrived at Oswego, with the intention to invade our frontiers, I think it proper and most necessary for the defense of our country, and it shall be ordered by me as soon as the enemy approaches, that every male person, being in health, from 16 to 60 years of age, in this our country, shall, as in duty bound, repair immediately, with arms and accoutrements, to the place to be appointed in my orders; and will then march to oppose the enemy with vigor, as true patriots, for the just defense of their country. And those that are above 60 years, or really unwell, and incapable to march, shall then assemble, also armed, at their respective places, where women and children will be gathered together, in order for defense against the enemy, if attacked, as much as lies in their power. . . .

Spencer had already started back to the woods to watch Wood Creek for the first arrival of St. Leger's advance guard.

Eisenlord had been ferried over the river with copies of his proclamation to be distributed through the county. There was nobody left but Joe Boleo. As he said to himself, he was dry enough to make a hen quack; but old Honnikol sat so grim and still in the darkness that he couldn't bring himself to make any suggestion. He tried to think of a funny story, but the only one he remembered was the one about Lobelia Jackson and the hired man, and Honnikol had never taken much to dirty stories.

So in the kindness of his heart Joe Boleo set himself to thinking about a draft of beer. He thought about it in steins, and in a blue glass, and a pewter mug; and by and by he got so thirsty with his thoughts that he thought of beer in a keg, with the bung open and his mouth the same and the beer establishing a connection.

Herkimer shook himself. "Yah," he said. "You're thirsty, Joe."

"How'd you guess that, Honnikol? I didn't say nothing."

For a moment the little German's voice was deep with amusement.

"Yah," he said. "That's how."

"Well," Joe admitted, "if you come to mention it."

"Maria," called the general.

His wife came out on the stoop. She was a young, plump, serene woman, who might have been the general's daughter. She came to the steps and he reached out and put his arm round her knees.

"Maria, Joe Boleo's thirsty. And I think I am. Bring us both beer. In the two big mugs."

"All right, Nicholas."

He said apologetically, "I don't want the niggers round just now."

"I know," she said.

It seemed to Joe she was a long time coming back. But she came. Her husband made her sit down beside him and held her in his arm.

"Well, Joe"—holding up his mug.

Joe almost made his usual reply about a catamount's biological neces-
sities; he restrained himself in time.

"Here's to you both, Mister and Missis."

The beer was cool from the cellar. The night was dark. The moon was
low upon the falls and the rapids were a living shine. The sound of broken
water reached dimly towards the house.

"I'm getting to be old," Herkimer said quietly. "Maria's young." His
arm tightened. "When my wife died I never thought I'd marry her niece."

"All in the family." Joe was trying to ease the general's voice.

"Yes," said the general gravely. "That's how it is here—too. Schuyler
won't send help. He writes I ought to be ashamed to ask it. He says I had
no right to agree to anything with Joseph Brant. And now Cox and Fisscher
and some others are blaming me because I did not shoot Brant, because
I don't get troops from Albany. They will send some Massachusetts people
up to Dayton, that's all. But everything else I do is wrong."

"Hell, Honnikol, all the people are back of you. The dirt farmers and
timber beasts like me."

"That's good. We'll have one damn fight anyway. All in the family, Joe.
Our side and Johnson's. There won't be any soldiers at all. You could say
it's got nothing to do with a war at all."

6. *Muster*

FORT STANWIX
July 28, 1777

SIR:

We have received accounts which may be relied on that Sir John
Johnson has sent orders to Colonel Butler to send a number of Indians
to cut off the communications between this place and German Flats
who are to set out from Oswego in five days from this, perhaps
sooner, and that Sir John is to follow them with 1000 troops consist-
ing of regular Tories and Vagabone Canadians with all the Indians
they can muster. I hope this will not discourage you, but that your
people will rise up unanimously to chastize these miscreants and depend upon it we will not fail to do our part.

I am, Sir, etc.,

MARINUS WILLETT

When General Herkimer received this he blew through his lips and put
on his best coat. He rode right up to Fort Dayton and walked in to speak
to Colonel Weston.

Colonel Weston was a man of sense—the first Massachusetts soldier that
had managed to grasp just what the German settlers faced. He didn't like
Germans, particularly, but he liked still less anything that smacked of British aristocracy; and he agreed at once to send up provisions from his com-
missariat and two hundred men under Colonel Mellon, as soon as he could
get them ready.

On the twenty-ninth, Tom Spencer sent down a message to Herkimer. It was the first definite assurance of the friendly stand of the Oneida nation in the face of war.

> At a meeting of the chiefs, they tell me that there is but four days remaining of the time set for the King's troops to come to Fort Stanwix and they think it likely they will be here sooner.
>
> The chiefs desire the commanding officers at Fort Stanwix not to make a Ticonderoga of it; but they hope they will be courageous.
>
> They desire General Schuyler may have this with speed and send a good army here, there is nothing to do at New York, we think there is men to be spared, we expect the road is stopped to the inhabitants by a party through the woods, we shall be surrounded as soon as they come. This may be our last advice. . . .

There was one thing left to do. Before night, Herkimer sent men down the valley as far as Johnstown to muster the militia on the third of August at Fort Dayton.

It gave Gil a strange feeling, on that Sunday morning, to hear the church bell ringing across the river at Herkimer; to look out from his doorway and see the farm peaceful in the still hot August air, the blue river, and the wooded hills beyond. Children, playing outside the ramparts of the fort, were stilled by the ringing bell and began their reluctant straggling into church.

The sight brought back the bitterness he had felt when his own place was burnt; it made him think of the winter and of the happiness he and Lana had had together before that time. It had seemed to him, lately, that she was slowly regaining her old ways. But since Adam Helmer, now become a ranger, had brought the muster word, she had grown quiet again. She was so quiet now, working in the kitchen, that he wondered what she was doing. When at last he turned back, he found that she was sewing a new cockade on his hat, while the tears dropped slowly down her cheeks. Her bowed shoulders and her silent crying made him tender.

"You mustn't be like that, Lana."

"I know," she said. "I hadn't ought." She did not look up in replying. "But the last two days, Gil, I've been remembering. I've been feeling different. And now I wonder if it isn't going to be too late."

"Too late?" He tried to understand. "Oh. You mean I might get killed. . . . I won't get killed, Lana."

"No, no, no. Not that. I wondered if it was too late for you to love me again."

"I do," he said.

"I know. No girl ever had a better man, Gil. I want you to know that." She got up swiftly, her hand like a head under the hat. She smiled and wiped the tears away with the back of her hand. "Put it on."

He obeyed, standing in front of her the way he had before that first muster down in Schuyler. But it was different now. They both felt it.

"Lana. You'll be all right. You stick to Mrs. McKlennar." He paused. "If anything goes wrong . . ."

"Yes, Gil."

Mrs. McKlennar strode down the path from her house.

"Still here?" she asked. "I'm glad. I wanted Gil to have this."

She held out a small flask fastened to a loop of rawhide.

"It's brandy," she said. "Brandy's the next best thing to powder in a fight."

Lana said politely, "Isn't it a pretty flask?"

"It used to be Barney's." There seemed to be some kind of stoppage in the widow's long nose. "It's no good to me, now," she said briskly. "I thought it might come handy to you."

Gil thanked her.

They stood a moment awkwardly. Then Mrs. McKlennar's head lifted. "Drums," she said.

The steady rattle of the drums came up the Kingsroad. Gil stepped to the door. His voice lifted a little.

"That's Klock and the Palatine regiment," he said. "I've got to go."

He turned to kiss Lana, but Mrs. McKlennar stepped between.

"I'm going to kiss you, Gilbert Martin. I'd better do it now. You don't want to go off tasting a widow on your mouth."

She took his face and kissed him firmly.

"Good-bye, lad."

She stepped through the door with a snap of skirts.

Bright crimson, Gil stooped down to his wife.

"Good-bye, dear."

Lana lifted her lips. Her eyes closed suddenly. He saw the tears welling at the roots of her dark lashes.

"Good-bye," he said again. "We'll make out all right. The both of us."

He caught the rifle up and tossed the blanket roll across his shoulder. He tramped down to the fence. He turned there, waved his arm, and stepped over into the road, not a hundred yards beyond the oncoming Palatines.

Lana could only stand and watch. He was walking along the road behind the railings, rifle on his shoulder, the long barrel like a finger pointing back towards home. Then for a moment the ragged rattle of the drums submerged her senses.

She felt an arm round her waist, and Mrs. McKlennar was breathing harshly beside her ear.

"It's hard on a woman," said the widow. "Many a time I've seen Barney go off just the same way. Good-bye. And he's off. Maybe he waves, but he ain't seeing you. He's thinking about the men, you see. All the men together."

The arm tightened.

"It's bad enough when he's your son, or even your father." Her stoppage seemed to trouble her again. "A man can't help it if he's your son—and almost any man can be a father. But there are so damn few good husbands in a woman's life."

Gil was by the turn of the road now; he hadn't looked backward again. In his place the uneven files of Palatine farmers trudged along the road, bent over in their walk, as if they followed a plough. Men and officers were indistinguishable—except the colonel, who sat like a sack of meal on the thumping black mare he used to draw manure with.

7. *March*

The men made an uneasy, sprawling mass throughout the little settlement. On the edge of the knoll the fort had been built on, Nicholas Herkimer straddled his old white horse, leaning his hands heavily on the somnolent withers.

He was using his deep voice to good effect, now giving orders in English to an officer, locating the muster ground of each company, now checking the list of supplies that trundled past in carts drawn either by oxen or by horses, now hailing in Low German some neighbor or acquaintance.

When Gil preceded the Palatine company into the village, he saw the general in the same position, in his worn blue campaign coat, warm enough in the stifling heat to keep the sweat steadily rolling down his cheeks. He was listening to the bombastic voice of Colonel Cox.

"All right, colonel," he said finally. "If you want to push ahead to-night, you can. But don't go beyond Staring's Brook. And don't go until your whole regiment's here, either. Leyp's and Dievendorf's companies haven't showed up yet."

Cox, flushed with heat and drink, said loudly that they were wasting time, he'd undertake to lick the Tories with his own company, and he could look out for his company, too, without being told.

"Those are orders," Herkimer said, tartly, for once. "I make Colonel Weston witness, if you don't like them."

The commandant of the Dayton garrison nodded brusquely, met the embattled colonel's eye with a Yankee gleam in his own, and said, "I've noticed them already."

"Where's Bellinger's regiment?" asked Gil.

"Beyond Doc's house," replied a delighted farmer from Snydersbush. "Cox had to haul his tail down that time." He grinned. "He used to hunt around and raise hell with young Johnson, and now he thinks he's drawn title to being a gentleman."

But Gil noticed what the Snyders man had not, that several of the other officers were looking after Cox with sympathetic eyes. Like him they rode good horses, with English-made saddles and polished riding boots. In their company, Herkimer's faded outfit, horse and coat, looked like a shabby imitation. No doubt they thought him one.

George Weaver greeted him. "You're only just in time, Gil. How's Lana? We ain't seen her in a month, now."

"She's fine," said Gil. "How's Emma?"

"Just the same. She's been considering going down to visit Lana to get a quilting pattern off her. She said she might go down while I was away."

"That's fine," said Gil.

Finding the company mustered took him back more clearly than ever to the time before his house was burnt. Reall, with his gun clean for once, was there; and Jeams MacNod, looking a little pallid at the thought of war; and Clem Coppernol.

Gil said, "I thought you were over sixty."

The white-haired Dutchman said, "Too old? By Jesus, a Dutchman ain't ever too old to take a pot at the British."

Weaver said, "We're to camp along the road to-night, right here. We've got to wait for Fisscher's Mohawk company, and Campbell's Minutemen."

"I thought they'd have to stay, with Brant around there."

"Brant's cut back west again," said Weaver. "He's at Stanwix now."

A man gaped. He said, "That Indian can move through the woods faster than you get the news of him."

"He'd better look out where he shows his head," said Reall in a boisterous voice, raising his gun and aiming at a cabbage in the doctor's garden.

George Weaver smacked the barrel down, roaring:—

"Do you want to kill somebody?"

That evening it looked as if the drought might break. Slate-colored clouds with traveling veils of white lifted their heads over the southern hills. There was a distant rumble of thunder, but no rain came. Fires broke out beside the ox carts. Eatables were unloaded. Pork and bacon frying made an odor through the village. Men sat together, grumbling because they had been kept out of decent beds—men like Fred Kast who couldn't see the sense of walking east seven miles one day to walk back seven miles the next, merely for the sake of sleeping in a blanket on the ground.

"I ain't complaining of your company," he explained. "It's just the idea."

"You ought to have brought your bed along," a man said.

"Yes, with Katy in it," said Christian Reall.

Kast laughed.

"I thought of that, and then I thought I couldn't find no room in it, with all you ground pigs trying too."

George Weaver looked down the slope of ground to the river, where Peter Tygert's house was. Herkimer was staying there. Few noticed the late arrival of the Mohawk regiment until they saw Colonel Frederick Fisscher, dapper and dandy for all his gray hair, go cantering down to Tygert's.

"Well, they got here," Weaver said. "I'm going to bed."

He rolled over in his blanket. Reall said, "You'd better pull your feet out of the road, though."

Demooth came round at breakfast time, wearing the homespun coat he used around the farm. The men were pleased to see him. They had got sick of the handsomely outfitted officers of the other regiments. It made them feel too much like the plain bush Germans the others claimed they were.

"All present?" he said to Weaver.

"Yes. There's nobody missing."

"That's fine." His dark face, lean, alert, quick-eyed, looked them over.

"Boys," he said, "Herkimer was going to put us in front. But the way feeling is, he had to let Cox go up ahead. Bellinger's regiment and Klock's are going to be the main guard. Fisscher's so tired he'll just naturally have to come behind. You can fall in when you hear them cheering Herkimer off from the fort. When he goes by, you just drop in behind him. I've got to send Cox off now, but I'll join you up the road."

"Yes, captain," said George.

They both grinned.

It took them all one day to get to Staring's Brook. Ten miles. The companies straggled along the road, taking it easy in the heat. Up ahead, Cox led the Canajoharie men, festering all the time in his wounded vanity. Then, after a long gap, came Herkimer, musing on the old white horse who picked his footing with such caution. With Herkimer rode half a dozen officers, Colonels Fisscher, Veeder, Klock, and Campbell, and Paymaster Isaac Paris, talking volubly on how a campaign of this sort should be conducted, making a bright patch of blue coats, like out-of-season gentians in the woods; and then the German Flats regiment and the Palatine, perhaps five hundred men. Then another gap, and the long line of ox carts jolting on the road, making their painful crawl, beasts and drivers choking in their own dust, stung by horse and deer flies. And after another gap, the Mohawk regiment, taking its ease along the way.

The total force of the army was eight hundred men. The number weighed heavily on Herkimer's mind that morning. He knew that St. Leger had four hundred regulars, that he had six hundred Tories, men just as good or better than his own straggling militia, and in addition almost a thousand Indians.

At Fort Stanwix, Gansevoort had seven hundred men under arms, but Gansevoort couldn't be expected to send them all out. His duty was to hold the fort. But if it were put up to him in time, he might be willing to spare a couple of hundred of them for a diversion.

The advance guard crossed Staring's Brook early in the afternoon. It took three hours for the train of carts and wagons and the rear guard to arrive. The army pitched camp wherever they could find room along the road, a scattering, unorganized mess of men, nearly two miles long. The fires were like glowworms in the big timber—the men lying beside them, talking softly, hugging close to get in the smoke, cursing the flies, and wondering how things were going at home.

In the morning camp was broken at ten and the troops set out at a good pace. A little before noon, Gil and Weaver, marching side by side along the road, came out in Deerfield, on their own land.

It was incredible how quickly the land had become overgrown, as if the mere fact that men had moved away had emboldened the weeds. The burnt acres on Gil's place already had a scrub of blueberries, and tall clumps of fireweed were flourishing among the charred stumps where corn by now should be beginning to tassel out. The houses were no more. Only the black lines of dead coals marked the squared outlines where the walls had stood.

"It don't do any good to look at it, Gil."

Weaver turned his face towards the alder bottom, through which, deeprutted by the army carts that had passed that way last fall, the road headed straight to the river.

In the ford, a mile away, Cox's regiment was stirring up the mud.

"Thank God the water's low," said Captain Demooth. "All these wagons going through at once are going to cut the bottom out of the river."

The passage of two hundred men had softened the bottom. By the time Klock's and Bellinger's regiments had waded over, the mud was getting pulpy.

Klock and Bellinger halted their companies on the bank and ordered them to stack arms and take their pants off. But with the way the mosquitoes were taking hold, the men preferred wet leggings and shoes to bites, and raucously refused.

They had to wait an hour before the horns of the first yoke of oxen appeared at the bend of the Kingsroad. The animals came on, snuffing the corduroy and planting each hoof as if they wished the things to grow there. When they reached the riverbank, they came down willingly enough, then stopped and drank.

The teamster swung his bull whip on them, but they refused to stir. Behind the tailboard yoke after yoke was halted, until the train filled all the alder swamp, a dozing mass of beasts, with switching tails. Other teamsters came forward and applied their lashes to the first yoke. The cracking of the whips banged like musketry. There was no room to bring another yoke around the first cart. The whole army was held up by a pair of lousy steers.

Even Colonel Fisscher had time to overtake them. He came storming and swearing along the edge of the road on his bay horse and stared and said loud enough for all the men to hear, "You'd think they were a couple of brigadier generals to look at them."

The men looked up. This militia business, with its high-toned colonels all over the lot, was new to them. They couldn't think what to say. But Bellinger had also heard him. He jumped off his horse and waded into the ford.

"Just what did you say, Fisscher?"

"I said they were like brigadiers, the way they take their time."

"Perhaps they wanted to see whether you'd catch up," said Bellinger.

The Palatine and German Flats outfits guffawed. But the teamster, who was embittered by the whole concern, turned the situation off. "It's got me beat," he said, helplessly. "The buggers don't even want to move their bowels."

Fisscher splashed his horse through the water to find Colonel Cox.

"Can't you do anything?" Bellinger asked the teamster.

"I've licked them. I've twisted their tails. I bit the off one by the ear. It's got me beat."

Old Coppernol crossed the ford. He said, "I've cut me an ox gad. If you bush twerps will make two lines and look like fences, these critters might mind a sensible man."

People laughed. But Demooth called to Bellinger, "Clem knows oxen. Let him try."

Clem said, "You see, these animals have got intelligence. They wasn't born for Baptists and they have to be convinced. Besides, they're kind of bored with all the colonels around."

"Meaning me?"

Clem looked at Bellinger.

"Hell, no. You ain't even a brigadier's nephew. You only married his niece."

In the laughter, Bellinger said good-humoredly, "All right, Clem. Try a hand."

The men waded into the ford and formed two lines, like fences for a lane, but Clem Coppernol acted as if he didn't see them. He talked to the oxen, patted them behind their horns, and then he walked the length of the ford and back, between the lines of men. He said to the oxen, "If an old man like me can do it, you two God A'mightys ought to."

Then he pricked the off ox with the stick and said, "Hup."

The oxen, miraculously, blew their breaths out, lowered their heads, and lifted their knobbed knees. The cart creaked, sank into the mud, but did not stop. The beasts had got to work again.

Clem bawled, "The others will come now, but don't let one get stuck. If it starts to stop, lay hold of the spokes and pull like God A'mighty."

To the admiring teamster he said tolerantly, "You can fetch my muskit for me. Somebody's got to show these twerps the way."

He went ahead as unconcernedly as the slow brown beasts, talking to them happily, as if for the first time since the muster he had found something he could do.

That night the head of the straggling column got as far as the Oriskany Creek. Colonel Cox picked his camp site on the eastern bank, opposite the little hamlet of Oneida huts. But the huts were empty, and Joe Boleo explained that the Oneidas had cleared out the same day the British Indians left Oswego.

Along the road the rest of the army bivouacked as they had the night before, wherever there was room. It was nearly dark when Demooth's company were finally fed and ready to lie down in their smudges. But as they sat on the ground, quietly in the dark, with the firelight streaking the boles of the trees, and a white mist creeping towards them from the river flats, a man floundered down the line, calling over and over, "Captain Mark Demooth. Captain Mark Demooth."

"This way," Demooth answered for himself. "What is it?"

"Herkimer wants to see you in his tent."

"Who are you?"

"Adam Helmer. Do you know where Joe Boleo is?"

"Right here," said Joe. "Has Herkimer got any likker on him?"

Herkimer's tent was pitched in a natural clearing a little behind the Canajoharie militia. His old white horse, ghostly and gray in the mist, was grazing stodgily beside it. They could hear the steady crunching of his teeth, and the small tearing sound of the parting roots. There was no sentry. Nobody hailed them. Even the horse didn't trouble to prick his ears.

Joe pulled the flap open and asked, "What's bothering you, Honnikol?"

"Come in, Joe."

Seated on his blanket, the little German was thoughtfully smoking his pipe. "Sit down," he said when they had entered. "Spencer's bringing Skenandoa."

The low tent was rank with the tobacco, but none of them noticed that.

Even Joe Boleo, when he saw the general's troubled face, forgot the liquor question.

"Those bug-tits been dripping again?" he asked.

"If you mean Cox and Fisscher and Paris," the general said quietly. "Yah." He pushed the tobacco down in the pipe bowl with a calloused thumb. "It ain't them bothers me."

But they could tell by his voice that the officers were getting under his skin.

"It ain't them," he said. "Spencer says Skenandoa thinks that Butler has moved out of camp and that he's waiting for us." He cocked his head towards the west and for a minute all four men were so still that the flowing of Oriskany Creek on its rift in the mist was audible in the tent. And queer mingling sounds come with it: the clink of a halter link on a tied horse; the raised voice of a distant man; the hooting of a small owl back in the hemlocks; the grumble of a frog by the waterside.

"Spencer's bringing Skenandoa." Herkimer stopped again. "That must be them outside."

The two Indians had come quietly. Turning, the four white men saw Spencer's blacksmith hand pull back the flap. Then the old chief of the Oneidas stepped in. He bent his head with dignity. He was wrapped around in his blanket, and he scarcely seemed to crease it as he squatted down in the door, so that they saw his dark-skinned wrinkled face, and the red head covering against the fire on the ground.

Spencer said above him, "Skenandoa's young men have come back."

Herkimer said nothing. After a minute more, Skenandoa nodded his head. "They say Butler and Brant have moved the Indians down the road from the camp. They are doing it now. The white men are coming along soon."

Herkimer thanked him quietly.

"That's all?"

"Yes."

"Have you Oneidas made up your minds?"

The chief seemed to have withdrawn inside his own old thoughts. When he replied, his voice was low. "The Mohawks and the Senecas have sent threats. Mr. Kirkland is my good friend. Some of us will go."

"Thanks."

The two Indians departed, almost as quietly as they had come.

"You see," said Herkimer. "It's what we would expect. But these military gentlemen, they want to ride right through, banging on drums. Cox says it is disgraceful we ain't got trumpets!"

"What do you want us to do, Honnikol?"

"I've been thinking, all day. I think if we could get Gansevoort to send out men against their camp, eh?"

Demooth nodded.

"You, Joe, and you, Adam, you know these woods. Do you think you could get into the fort? With the Indians coming this way, you could go round and get inside?"

Helmer laughed.

"Sure," he said offhand.

"I can't let Bellinger or Klock go. Mark, will you? You're the only other officer that knows these woods and Indians."

"What'll we tell him?" Demooth asked.

"Send out men if he can, and fire three cannon to let us know." He got up and walked to the door. "It's misty. You'll have good cover." The pipe smoke mingled with the mist. "You better get going now."

In the morning, Herkimer sent out a call for all commanding officers to come to his tent. While the men were cooking breakfast they arrived. They made a knot of uniforms, bright, lighthearted, against the dark hemlock boughs. Cox with his bellicose flushed face and staring eyes; Bellinger, raw-boned, simple, honest, looking worried; Klock, stodgy, chewing snuff and still smelling faintly of manure and already sweating; Campbell's gray face freshly shaved; Fisscher, dapper and dandy in his tailor-made coat and new cocked hat; and the black-coated, clerkly, calculating Mr. Paris. Behind them assorted captains and majors waited, watching.

Cox had the first word, as he always did.

"Well, Herkimer. Going to give us marching orders?"

"Pretty soon."

"Why not now? The sooner we get going, the sooner we'll have Sillinger making tracks for home."

"Listen, the Oneidas told me last night that Brant and Butler have got the Indians somewhere up the road. They moved down after dark. Johnson's troops ought to be there by now."

"Fine," Cox said boisterously. "We can lick the Tories and then we can tend to the regulars. Like eggs and bacon for breakfast."

Herkimer looked thoughtfully from face to face, looking for support, perhaps, or perhaps just looking for what was there. Only Bellinger was attentive—and maybe Klock.

"We won't break camp for a while," Herkimer said. "I've sent Demooth and two men up to the fort. They'll send a party out and shoot off three cannon when they do. We'll move when we hear the guns."

For a moment no one said a word. But they all looked at Herkimer in the sunshine, while the morning birds cheeped in the surrounding trees.

"You mean we've got to sit here on our arses?" demanded Cox.

"If you like to wait like that," said Herkimer. "I do not mind."

"Personally," said Fisscher, "I'm getting sick of waiting."

Herkimer said nothing.

"It's a good idea," Bellinger said loyally.

"You getting scared too?" said Paris.

Herkimer held up his hand with the pipe in it.

"There's no sense fighting among ourselves."

"What's the matter? We'll outnumber them. The whites. We can handle the Indians on the side."

"You've never seen an Indian ambush," said Herkimer.

"Oh, my God," cried Cox, "this isn't 1757! Can't you get that through your thick German head?"

Rumor had gone down the road that the gentry were having words. The men abandoned their fires to hear the fun. Many of them left their guns behind. They pushed off the road, surrounding the clearing, till the little German seated before his tent was the focal point of over a hundred pairs of eyes.

Gil Martin, coming with the rest, listened among strangers. For over an hour the silly fatuous remarks went on. Some said you could not hear a cannon that far; some said that the three men would surely get captured; some said that probably they'd never gone to the fort at all. That was Paris's voice.

Herkimer sat in their midst with the voices flinging back and forth above his head; his shirt was still unbuttoned, showing his stained woolen undershirt. Now and then he took his pipe from his lips to answer some remark that had a rudiment of sense behind it; but the rest of the time he kept his head turned to the west, listening. Apparently he was unheeding; but the men close to him could see his cheeks flexing from time to time and the slow even reddening of his skin.

It was Cox who finally touched the match.

"By Jesus Christ," he shouted in his roaring voice, "it's plain enough. Either he's scared, or else he's got interest with the British. I didn't bring my regiment this far to set and knit like girls." He looked round with his staring eyes. "Who's coming along?"

Fisscher cried, "I am."

Suddenly all the officers were shouting; and the men, following their voices, filled the woods with shouts.

It seemed to Gil that nobody was looking at Herkimer but himself. He saw the old man sitting there, his face pained, his eyes worried. He saw him knock the pipe out on his hand, blow out his breath, and lift his head.

"Listen to me, you damned fools." He used German. He was getting on his feet and yanking his coat over his arms. But his voice was enough to stop them. "Listen," he went on in English. "You don't know what you're doing, you Fisscher, Cox, the bunch of you. But if you want to fight so bad, by God Almighty, I'll take you to it."

He climbed aboard the old white horse and sat there, looking down on them for a change.

"God knows what's going to happen. But I'll tell you one thing," he said bitterly. "The ones that have been yelling so much here will be the first to pull foot if we get jumped."

For a moment they gaped up at him.

"*Vorwaerts!*" he shouted, and put the horse toward the creek. Some of them were still standing there when he splashed through and waited on the other side. Then the officers were running to their companies, yelling, "Fall in. Fall in."

The men went scrambling through the brush to find their guns and blankets.

"March! March!" The word was in all the woods where the abandoned breakfast fires still sent up their stems of smoke among the tree trunks. Up ahead at the ford, a drummer gave the double tap of the flam. It was like the first nervous beating of a drummer partridge. It was too early for such a sound, but there it was.

Then the whips began their rapid fire along the wagon train. The cartwheels screeched in starting. The still heat in the woods was overflowed with shouts, stamping hoofs, the rattle and slam of carts along the corduroy, the treading feet. The dust rose over the column. All at once it was jerking, getting started, moving.

At the head of the army, Cox moved his big horse beside Herkimer's. His face was triumphant, almost good-humored once more, because he had planted his will on the column. He felt half sorry for the little German farmer. But he would help the little bugger out.

The rough road went nearly straight along the level ground of the Mohawk Valley's edge, following the course of the low hill. Now and then it dipped down sharply to get over a brook. But the bottom was solidly corduroyed. The wagons didn't get stuck. They had even moved up a little on the marching men.

Blue jays squawked and fluttered off, cool spots of angry blue against the leaves. Squirrels, chattering, raced from limb to limb. A porcupine took hold of a tree and climbed it halfway, and turned his head to see the thronging, jumbled mass that heaved and started, checked, and went again along the narrow road.

The men marched in two lines, one for either rut, their rifles on their shoulders, their hats in their hands. When they came to a brook, the thirsty fell out and drank. Nobody stopped them. When they were through they wiped their mouths and looked up, startled, to see their company replaced by another. They got out of the way of other thirsty men and floundered in the bushes to catch up. There was no room left on the road to pass.

Even George Herkimer's company of rangers, who were supposed to act as scouts, would stop at a spring. And when they went ahead they crashed in the undergrowth like wild cattle. There was nobody to stop them. There were no tracks. The woods were dusty. Branches, whipping on hot faces, stung like salt. The heat grew. Not a breath of air in the branches anywhere, not a cloud in the bits of sky high overhead, nothing but leaves, nothing in all the woods but their own uproarious, bursting, unstemmable progress on the narrow road.

Gil, pushed on from behind, pushing on George Weaver just ahead of him, heard the birds singing in the dark swamp ahead. The ground fell steeply to a quiet flowing brook with a cool moss bottom. He felt his own step quicken with the instinct to drink and cool himself. Looking over George Weaver's thick round shoulders, he had a glimpse of the road turning into a causeway of logs across the stream; of George Herkimer's rangers crowding down on the crossing to make it dry-shod; of the Canajoharie regiment floundering in the swamp and drinking face down by the brook; of Cox turning his red sweaty face to Herkimer and bawling, "Where did you say Butler was?"; of the two banks, precipitous and thickly clothed with a young stand of hemlocks, so soft and cool and damp and dark that it made one wish to lie down there and rest. Now he felt the ground falling under his feet, and the resistless push at his back thrusting him out on the causeway. They had passed half of Cox's regiment and were plugging up the other side. The stamp of Klock's regiment came down the bank at their backs. Behind in the woods the jangle and rattle of the carts, steady cracking of whips, and little futile *rattle-tats* of Fisscher's drummers. All in the moment: "I meant to get a drink of water," Reall's voice was saying at his shoulder. "So did I," said Gil. "My God," said Weaver, "what was that?"

At the top of the hemlocks a little stab of orange was mushroomed out by a black coil of smoke. They heard the crack. Cox's voice, caught short in another remark, lifted beyond reason. His big body swayed suddenly against his horse's neck. The horse reared, screamed, and, as Cox slid sack-like off his back, crashed completely over.

A shrill silver whistle sounded. Three short blasts. The young hemlocks disgorged a solid mass of fire that made a single impact on the ear. Gil felt George Weaver slam against his chest, knocking him sidewise on top of Reall. A horse screamed again and went leaping into the scrub. As he got up, Gil saw the beast fall over on his head. It was Herkimer's old white horse, galvanized into senseless vigor. He felt his arm caught and Bellinger was shouting, "Give me a hand with the old man." The old man was sitting on the causeway, holding onto his knee with both hands. His face was gray and shining and his lips moved in it.

But the voice was lost.

Gil stood before him with his back to the slope and stared down into the ravine. The militia were milling along the brook, flung down along the bank, like sticks thrown up by a freshet, kneeling, lying on their bellies, resting their rifles on the bellies of dead men. They were oddly silent. But the air around them was swept by the dull endless crash of muskets and a weird high swell of yelling from the woods.

Then beyond them he saw the Indians in the trees, adder-like, streaked with vermilion, and black, and white. From the head of the rise the first orderly discharge went over his head with a compelling, even shearing of the air, as if a hand had swung an enormous scythe. He saw the green coats on men firing at him; but he bent down and grasped the general by the knees and heaved him on up the bank while Bellinger lugged him by the armpits.

The colonel was swearing in a strange way. He wiped his mouth on his sleeve and said, "By God, Fisscher has pulled foot!"

East of the causeway, where the rear guard had been, a dwindling tide of yells and firing fled backward into the woods. They dumped the general down behind a log and fell beside him. Gil put his rifle over the log and pulled the trigger on the first green coat that filled the sights. The butt bucked against his cheek. He yanked the rifle back and tilted his powder flask to the muzzle. He saw the man he had fired at lean forward slowly in the bushes, buckle at the hips, and thump face down. He felt his insides retract, and suddenly had a queer realization that they had just returned to their proper places; and he thought with wonder at himself, "that's the first shot I've fired."

"Peter."

"Yes, Honnikol."

"It looks as if the Indians was mostly chasing after Fisscher. You'd better try and fetch the boys up here."

The little German's voice was calm.

8. Battle

There was no sense at first in any of it. The opening volley had been fired at ten o'clock. For the next half hour the militia lay where they had dropped, shooting up against the bank whenever they saw a flash. Their line extended roughly along the road, beginning with the disrupted welter of the wagon train, and ending at the west, just over the rise of ground, where a mixed group of Canajoharie men, and Demooth's company of the German Flats regiment, and what was left of Herkimer's rangers, made a spearhead by hugging the dirt with their bellies and doing nothing to draw attention to themselves. If the Indians had stayed put or if Fisscher had not run away, the entire army would have been destroyed.

But the Indians could not resist the temptation of chasing the terrified Fisscher. More than half of them had followed his men as far as Oriskany Creek before they gave over the attempt. And a large proportion of the rest, seeing easy scalps ready for the taking, started sneaking down out of the timber. When, at last, Bellinger began to rally the men and get them up the slope, the Indians made no attempt to follow them, for they had discovered that killing horses was an intoxicating business.

The ascent of the slope was the first orderly movement of the battle. It also revealed the initial mistake of the British side. Their flanks made no connection with the Indians, and they had to retire from the edge of the ravine to the bigger timber. It gave the Americans a foothold. They pushed to right and left along the ravine and forward with their centre, until their line made a semicircle backed on the ravine.

No single company remained intact. It was impossible to give intelligent orders, or, if that had been possible, to get them carried out. The men took to trees and fired at the flashes in front of them. And this new disposition of the battle, which remained in force till nearly eleven, was the salvation of the militia. They began to see that they could hold their own. Also it was borne in on them that to go backward across the valley would be sheer destruction.

The general, by his own orders, had been carried still farther up the slope until he could sit on the level ground under a beech tree, and see out through the tall timber. His saddle had been brought up for him to sit on, and Dr. Petry sent for. While the doctor was binding up his shattered knee, Herkimer worked with his tinder box to get a light for his pipe. Then, finally established, he looked the battle over and gave his second order of the day.

"Have the boys get two behind each tree. One hold his fire and get the Indian when he comes in."

It was an axiomatic precaution that none of the militia would have thought of for themselves. Gil, moved up behind a fallen tree, heard a crash of feet behind him, turned his head to see a black-bearded, heavy-shouldered man plunge up to him carrying an Indian spear in one hand and a musket in the other.

"You got a good place here," said the man.

He drove the butt of the spear into the ground.

"It may come handy."

"Where'd you get it?"

"Off an Indian." He turned his head. "Back there. They're scalping the dead ones. There's one of the bastards now."

He pushed his gun across the log and fired.

"Christ! I missed him. You'd better do the long shots, Bub. You've got a rifle there. I ain't a hand at this stuff."

Gil had found a loophole in the roots. He poked his gun through and waited for a sign. While he waited he said, "My name's Martin."

"Gardinier," said the bearded man. "Captain in Fisscher's regiment. Don't ask me why. We didn't have the sense to run when he did. There's fifty of us left, but I don't know where they are. Old Herkimer told me to get up in front. He said he wanted to see us run away next time."

Gardinier cursed. Gil saw a shoulder, naked, and glistening with sweat, stick out on the side of a tree. He pressed the trigger, easily. The Indian yelped. They didn't see him, but they saw the underbrush thresh madly.

"Pretty, pretty," said Gardinier. "We ought to make a partnership. You take my musket and I'll load for you. Jesus, you ain't a Mason, are you?"

"No," said Gil.

"You ought to be." He touched Gil's shoulder with the rifle barrel. "Here's your rifle, Bub."

Gil caught a spot of red over a low-lying bough. A headdress. It was a pot shot, but he let it go. The Indian whooped and the next moment he was coming in long buck jumps straight for the log. He was a thin fellow, dark-skinned like a Seneca, and stark naked except for the paint on face and chest.

Gil felt his inside tighten and rolled over to see what had become of Gardinier. But the heavy Frenchman was grinning, showing white teeth through his beard.

He had set down his musket and taken the spear. The Indian bounded high to clear the log and Gardinier braced the spear under him as he came down. The hatchet spun out of the Indian's hand. A human surprise reformed his painted face. The spear went in through his lower abdomen and just broke the skin between his shoulders. He screamed once. But the Frenchman lifted him, spear and all, and shoved him back over the log.

"Hell," he said. "No sense in wasting powder."

Gil turned back to face the woods. The Indian, with the spear still sticking out of him, was trying to crawl under some cover. The odd thing was that he wasn't bleeding. But he kept falling down against the spear, as if his wrists had lost their strength.

"For God's sake shoot him."

The Frenchman stuck his head over the log.

"Jesus!" he remarked. He made no motion.

The Indian heaved himself up. He half turned toward the log. Then his mouth opened, and, as if a well had been tapped by the spear, and all the time had been necessary for the blood to find its level, it poured through the open mouth, down the painted chest, turning the front of his body wet and red.

Gil yelled, jumped up, and fired straight down into the pouring face.

The Indian jerked back and flopped, raising the needles with his hands. Gardinier said, "You hadn't ought to have done that. Wasting ball that way."

"For God's sake kill the next one, then."

"All right, all right. You don't need to get mad." But after a moment, he muttered. "I wish to God I'd pulled that spear out first, though. It was a handy tool."

All a man could see was the section of woods in front of him. The woods were dark with a green gloom, made by the high tops of the hemlocks, through which the sun came feebly. The heat was stifling. There was no movement of air. Only the bullets ripped passionate sounds out of the heat.

The ravine behind the militia had long since quieted with the death of the last horse. But now and then a solitary war whoop lifted in the trees to right or left; and the answering shot was like a period marking off the time.

In the American line, out of the disruption, figures began to grow into command that had no bearing on their rank. A man who shot better than his neighbors began to give orders. Jacob Sammons on the left began the first outward movement by taking twenty men in a quick charge against the Indian flank and halting them on a low knoll of beech trees. They started a cross fire against the white troops in front, and the militia in the centre, finding the woods cleared for a space, moved forward. Gil went with them. Gardinier stood up and scouted.

"There's a first-class maple up in front," he said.

They took it in a rush. Then they had a breathing space in which they could look back. They were surprised to find that this new view disclosed men lying on the intervening ground.

Back at the edge of the ravine, old Herkimer was still smoking his pipe. He had taken his hat off and his grizzled head showed plainly from where Gil and Gardinier had taken stand.

Gardinier laughed out loud.

"Look at the old pup," he said. "I wish Fisscher was here."

Both of them realized that they had one man they could depend on, though there was nothing one man could do for them. But it was a feeling all the same.

The lull did not endure.

In the woods ahead they heard a whistle shrilling. The firing had stopped, except for sporadic outbursts way to right and left, where a few Indians still persisted.

Then Herkimer's voice came to them surprisingly loud.

"Get out your hatchets, boys. They're going to try bayonets."

To Gil it seemed as though the fight had begun all over again. Lying behind a tree was one thing. Standing up in the open was something he had not thought of.

But Gardinier suddenly found something he could understand. He heaved his great bulk up and asked, "What you got, Bub?" When Gil merely stared, "Hatchet or bagnet, son?"

Gil reached for the hatchet at his belt with stiff fingers.

"All right. You give them one shot with your rifle. I've got a bagnet." He was fixing it to the muzzle of his army musket. He wheeled back and roared, "Come on."

He seemed surprised when some of his own company came round the trees behind.

Gil saw them coming. They all saw them, in the green gloom under the trees which covered their faces with a pale shine. They were like water coming toward the militia, flowing round the tree trunks, bending down the brush, an uneven line that formed in places and broke with the shape of the ground and formed.

There was a moment of silence on both sides as the militia rose up confronting them. It was almost as if the militia were surprised. Herkimer's warning had suggested to them that regular troops were going to attack. Instead they saw only the green coats they knew belonged to Johnson's company of Tories, and men in hunting shirts and homespun like themselves.

As the line came nearer, they saw that some of these men were the Scotch from Johnstown who had fled with Sir John. They weren't Sillinger's army at all. They were the men who had passed threats of gutting the valley wide open. For a moment the militia could hardly believe what they were seeing.

Then it seemed as if the senseless glut of war would overflow. Men fired and flung their muskets down and went for each other with their hands. The American flanks turned in, leaving the Indians where they were. The woods filled suddenly with men swaying together, clubbing rifle barrels, swinging hatchets, yelling like the Indians themselves. There were no shots. Even the yelling stopped after the first joining of the lines, and men began to go down.

The immediate silence of the woods was broken afresh. Gil, jostled and flung forward, saw a face in front of him met by a musket stock. The face seemed to burst. He swung his hatchet feebly against the arm that clubbed the musket and felt the axe ripped from his fingers. The man he had struck cried out, a small clear sound as if enunciated in a great stillness. Then Gil's ears cleared and he heard a man crying and he stepped on a body and felt it wince under his boot. The wince threw him, and he hit the dirt with his knees, and at the same time a gun exploded in front of him and he thought his whole arm had been torn away.

The boughs of the hemlocks heeled away from him, and the back of his head struck the ground and a man walked over him, three steps, down the length of his body, and he felt sick and then he forgot entirely everything but the fact that he was dying.

He did not feel any more. He was lying on the ground. It seemed to him that every needle leaf and twig on the ground stood up with painful clearness beyond any plausible dimension. A little way off someone kept yelling, "For God's sake, oh, for God's sake." He thought that if he could look he could see what the sound was, but he could not look.

Then the forest darkened. There was a blinding flash. He felt a man's hands taking hold of his shoulders. He felt himself moving backward while his legs trailed behind him. He was jerked up and put on his feet, and he knew that it was raining. He thought, "The drought's broken."

Peal after peal of thunder shook the hemlocks. The rain fell directly down, hissing on the dry ground, and raising mist in the trees. There was no sound left but the pouring rain and the continuous devastating thunder. You couldn't see when you opened your eyes. Only the tree trunks rising close to you, shining black with wet and the falling rain and the distortion of the lightning glares that lit up crooked alleys in the woods and shut them off again.

He felt himself being shaken, and a voice was saying, "Can you walk, Bub?"

He tried to walk, but his feet were overcome with a preposterous weariness.

"Put them down, Bub, put them down. Flat on your feet and stand up. Have a drink; you're all right."

He opened his eyes again and saw the beard of Gardinier matted with rain, and the wild white teeth and staring eyes of the Frenchman.

"Brandy makes the world go round," said the Frenchman. "It makes the girl handy, it makes for boys and girls, Bub. It'll fix you. Hell, you ain't only creased in one arm, and me, I've lost an ear."

The side of his face was streaming blood into his collar.

"They've quit, Bub. They're all to hell and gone. We've licked the pus clean out of them. Come on. Doc will fix you."

He sat Gil down on a mound, and then Dr. Petry's big fleshy face, muttering, looking enraged and tired, bent down. The Doc was splashing alcohol of some sort on his arm. He was being bandaged. The stinging revived him, and he looked up and saw just above him old Herkimer, white in the face now, but still puffing at his pipe, which he held in his mouth inverted against the rain.

"They'll come back," Herkimer was saying. "They're bound to. But we'll rest while it rains."

A little way off a man was eating on a log. The rest were standing, lying on the ground, steaming in the rain. Everyone looked tired, a little sick, and ugly, as if there had been a tremendous drunk a while before.

Nobody was keeping watch. They merely stood there in the rain.

The rain passed as suddenly as it had broken. The men got up and kicked other men to get up, and picked up their rifles. They drew the priming and reprimed, or loaded entirely fresh.

Gil got to his feet shakily, surprised to find his rifle still in his hand. It seemed a long time since the rain. The woods had changed so that he did not know where west lay, or east, or any direction.

Then he saw that Herkimer had moved the position so that the militia were in the centre of the level ground between the first ravine and a smaller, shallower watercourse. Any new attack would have to take them on a narrow flank, or directly up the new slope on top of which their line was formed.

The first shots came scatteringly. The Indians were firing from long range. They seemed to have lost their taste for war. They were being very careful now. Everybody was being careful. The militia stood their ground, but kept to cover.

In a line running north and south through the new position, a broken mass of men lay on the ground, like an uneven windrow of some preposterous corn. They seemed almost equally made up of militia and the green-coated troops that had come through the hemlocks. They lay in queer positions, on their arms, grasping knife or hatchet or musket, the purpose still on the blank face like an overlying plaster; or else they lay on their backs, their empty hands flung out as if to catch the rain.

The militia stepped over this line impersonally. There was an Indian transfixed to a tree by a bayonet, waist high, with his legs dangling lifelessly against the ground. But he kept his eyes open and the eyes seemed to Gil to turn as he went by.

A little way along a face struck him as familiar. He looked at it again. The possessor of the face had fallen with his chin over a log so that the face was tilted up. Gil looked at it curiously before he recognized it for Christian Reall's face. He had been scalped. The top of his head looked flat and red; and the circumcision of the crown had allowed the muscles to give way so that his cheeks hung down in jowls, tugging his eyes open and showing enormous bloody underlids.

The two armies merely sniped at each other for an hour. Then the second attack by the enemy developed from the southwest along the level ground. At first the militia mistook them for reënforcements from the fort. The direction they came from and the fact that they had pinned up their hat brims to look like the tricorn hats of Continental soldiers were deceptive.

The militia broke cover, cheering, and rushed forward to shake hands, and the enemy let them come. There was no firing. It was only at the last moment that the sun came through the wet trees, dazzling all the ground and showing the bright green of the approaching company.

Gil was not in the direct contact of the two companies. From where he stood he seemed divorced from the whole proceeding.

But another company of green coats was coming round the first in his direction, with the same quiet march, and the same bright glitter on their advanced bayonets.

He became aware of the instinct to run away. It suddenly occurred to him that he was hungry. Not merely hungry as one is at supper or breakfast; but a persisting, all-consuming gnawing in his intestines that moved and hurt. He felt that it was not worth staying for. He was too tired. And the oncoming men looked tired. And it seemed to take forever for them to make a contact. But they came like people who couldn't stop themselves, while he himself could not make his feet move to carry him away.

They made less noise. The rainstorm which had broken the drought had not had power to take the dryness from their throats. They seemed to strike each other with preposterous slow weary blows, which they were too slow to dodge, and they fell down under them preposterously.

It couldn't last.

Gil found himself standing alone in the militia. There were a few men near him, but there was no one whose face he recognized. They kept looking at each other as if they would have liked to speak.

On the flank, the firing continued where the Indians still skirmished. But that, too, broke off except for stray shots, the last survivors of all the holocaust of firing.

The Indians were calling in the woods. A high barbaric word, over and over. "*Oo*nah, *Oo*nah, *Oo*nah." Suddenly a man shouted, "They've pulled foot!"

At first they thought another thunderstorm had started. Then they realized that what they had heard, with such surprising force, had been three successive cannon shots.

The messengers had reached the fort, and the garrison was making a diversion.

A deliberate understanding gradually dawned on all their faces. They leaned on their rifles and looked round. The woods were empty, but for themselves, for their dead, and for the enemy dead. The living enemy had run away.

Those that could walk began a retrograde movement to the knoll on which Herkimer was sitting under his tree. The old man was looking at them; his black eyes, yet ardent, passing feverishly from face to face, and then turning slowly to the lines of dead.

One of the officers spoke fatuously, "Do we go on to the fort now, Honnikol?" He paused, swallowed, and said, as if to excuse himself, "We know they know we're here."

The little German swung his eyes to the speaker. The eyes filled and he put his hand over them.

Peter Bellinger and Peter Tygert came up to him and touched his shoulder. They said to the officer, "We can't move forward."

They picked Herkimer up by the arms.

"I can't walk, boys." He swallowed his tears noisily. "There's still Sillinger up there. With the British regulars there ain't enough of us. I think we'd better go home."

He asked first that the live men be assembled and counted. It was a slow business, getting them to their feet and lining them up under the trees. The earth was still steaming from the rain. There was a sick smell of blood from the ravine.

The naming of men took too long. The officers went along the wavering lines, cutting notches in sticks for every ten men. They figured that after Fisscher pulled foot with the Mohawk company there had been about six hundred and fifty concerned in the ambush and battle. Out of them about two hundred were judged able to walk. There were forty more who were not dead. How many had been killed and how many taken prisoner no one could say.

Stretchers were made of coats and poles, and the worst wounded were piled onto them. Those who were not acting as bearers dully reprimed or loaded their guns. They started east.

It seemed a long way to the ravine where the battle had started. It seemed a long time, longer than they could remember, since they had seen it last. It was sunset by the time they reached Oriskany Creek. From there men were sent ahead to order boats rowed up the Mohawk, to meet the wounded at the ford. The whole army lay down when they reached the ford. They lay in the darkness, along the edge of the sluggish river, until the boats came up. They were apathetic.

Only when the boats arrived did they get onto their feet and help put the wounded men in. Several of them afterwards remembered Herkimer's face in the light of the fire. He had stopped smoking, though the pipe was still fast in his teeth. He wasn't saying anything. He sat still, holding onto his knee.

At the time they had just stood around watching him being loaded aboard the boat and laid out in the bottom. Then they had been told to march through the ford, and along the road. They went wearily, too exhausted to talk, even to think. And tired as they were, they were forced to do the same march they had taken three days to make on the way up.

They did not look at the terrified white faces of the people when they came to the settlement. They were too exhausted to see. The word had already gone down the river. People were expecting the appearance of the enemy.

It was a calamity. The army had looked so big going west that nobody had thought they would not get through to the fort. Now they were back; they looked licked, and they acted licked, and they had not even met the regulars. It was pointless to think that the enemy had left the scene of battle before they had.

An officer, some said afterwards that it was Major Clyde, yelled from the foot of the fort stockade that they were dismissed. They were to go home and try to rest while they could. They should expect another summons very soon.

But the men did not stop to listen to him. Ever since they had come out of the woods at Schuyler they had been dropping from the ranks. The instinct to get home was irresistible. They weren't an army any more, and they knew it better than anyone could have told them.

4

STANWIX (1777)

1. *The Women*

MRS. MCKLENNAR simply would not hear of removing to a fort. "What's the use of women being left behind in a war, if they can't stay home and do the man's work?"

"Yes, ma'am."

Captain Jacob Small, who had been placed in command of Eldridge

Blockhouse, shifted his feet on the kitchen floor, turned his hat over twice in his hands, and looked anxiously towards the fireplace. "It's orders, though. 'Where women and children shall be gathered together,' it says. And me and other men over sixty and under sixteen is to collect with them and protect them."

"Pshaw, Captain Small, don't you think I can look after myself?"

"Yes, ma'am." Captain Small was uneasy. "But them's the orders. You're rightly in my district. But if you don't want to come to Eldridge, you can go over the river to Herkimer, I guess. Only we've been keeping the corner space in the shed for you."

"Shed!" snorted Mrs. McKlennar. "Do I look like the kind of woman at my time of life who'd go live in a shed? Herded up like a freshened heifer. With everybody else, eh?"

"Yes, ma'am." Captain Jacob looked appalled. "I mean, no, ma'am."

"Well, look at me, damn it, man. Can't I take care of myself?"

"Yes, ma'am." Captain Small raised his eyes and turned them abruptly away again towards the fireplace.

"If you want to spit," said Mrs. McKlennar, "for God's sake, spit, and get it over with." There was an almost piercing look about her long nose as he availed himself of the ashes. "I suppose it's nice of you to come down here to make a damn-fool woman see some sense. The trouble is my idea of sense just doesn't coincide with yours."

The captain said, "Well, I only tried to be neighborly. But if you change your mind we'll have the corner space ready for you. Phil Helmer has got his cows in it now, but we'll move them right out any time."

"Thank you, captain."

Captain Small hawked a little, as he reached the door. He looked over his spit at Fort Herkimer beyond the river.

"See there," he said significantly. "Ma'am, there's some women coming to the fort now."

A line of teetering carts, overloaded with goods and women and children, dragged across the flats from the southern hills.

Mrs. McKlennar blew out her breath.

"I've been seeing them for two days. I'm sick of the sight. Scared as rabbits."

Mrs. McKlennar watched him trudge away down the road. Then she stamped over the porch and down the steps and went towards the barn. "Indians!" she said to herself.

She saw Lana coming down from the springhouse with a crock of butter in her arms. "How much did it make?" called Mrs. McKlennar.

"About three pounds," Lana replied. She looked cool and pink, but her eyes seemed to darken. "Was that Captain Small, Mrs. McKlennar?"

"Yes, it was."

"Did he have any news?"

"He was down to try to persuade us to move into his blockhouse. He's got a stall ready for us. There's some cows in it now, but he was cordial enough to suggest he would prefer us."

Lana smiled slightly. She was getting used to the widow's way of talking.

Mrs. McKlennar said, "And then he pointed out some women going in to Fort Herkimer. And he said a lot more about the way Indians handled women." She paused and looked keenly at Lana. "What do you think about it, Magdelana? Getting scared?"

Lana said, "No," quietly. She wasn't looking at Mrs. McKlennar; with the crock still hugged up in her arms, she was staring westward. "Gil expected I'd stay here, unless we got news things had gone wrong out west. When he comes back, he'll probably expect to find me here."

"Good for you," said Mrs. McKlennar. She tramped away to the barn to curry the horses. It was a job she fancied just then. She didn't have the faintest idea of what might happen, but in any case she had no intention of living like a pig in a sty and having all the farm women constantly peering at her to see what kind of underclothes she wore. . . .

On her way from the stone house to her own kitchen, Lana heard the widow hissing like a whole stableful of grooms. She stopped again in the doorway to look out over the valley.

Two days—and they had had no news. The valley was still and hot; the earth was dry; the river, shallow and slow. Whenever she looked across it, Lana had a feeling of the hills drawing together. She felt the presence of the woods behind her back, as if, on the north bluff, the wilderness crept close and watched her movements through the day with an invisible intelligence.

At the departure of Gil, life as it was known on the farm seemed to have departed too. The three women, in spite of Mrs. McKlennar's noisiness, were imprisoned in a green silence. There was nothing to hear but the crows at evening, or the sounds of their own voices. There were not even any wagons on the Kingsroad, now. No boats on the river. It was as if the valley held its breath; as if the going of the militia drained it of all the things that made for life. One stopped one's talk suddenly for no reason except an unexpected instinct to listen. Listen for what? Lana did not know. But her breast ached.

A thought lived in her with the beating of her heart. He would surely die. Sometimes it occurred to her that since last fall both of them had been dead. Even in the little Schuyler hut she had had that feeling, though they had felt crowded there, so near that they withdrew from each other, as though to avoid physical encounter. Later, in the early summer, life had seemed easier. Work had been good for Gil. He was the kind of man who needed to be tired. But on Lana's part, living had been merely a slow regulation of the breath. What they did, what they said, had lost all personal significance.

Then had come the first muster and Gil's departure for the Unadilla. And then he had come home, and her first quickening had come and gone like a moth's temptation. She was healthier. But she had not been able to regain her vanished impulse towards happiness.

Gil seemed unaware, detached, and baffled. Often Lana had heard women say of other women that they "got along" with their husbands. She wondered whether that was how she was living with Gil. She submitted to him as she had submitted to the fact of the destruction of their farm, wordlessly, blindly. Blindly until she had seen him making the turn in the road to Fort Dayton, with the erratic flamadiddles of the Palatine drums passing after him. When it was too late she had had the choking thought that he would surely die.

As she looked westward she could see the Schuyler house. The little shack stood by the river, shuttered and forlorn; but it seemed to her that she was again lying on the narrow bunk bed, exhausted, still, cold, pressed down entirely by the bleak terror and her sense of outrage. She struggled against the memory. Her mind worked vaguely with the words with which she must try to tell him they were not themselves then. That she had got past that time. That it was neither his fault nor hers, but that they both had been forced by something which was neither of their making nor of their understanding. Her effort to find words and reasons was pathetically inadequate. She wrenched herself away from the sight, turning into her own kitchen, with an awareness that when two people acted so against each other it was beyond the power of their minds ever to retract the moment.

It was Mrs. McKlennar who first heard Gil coming home. The night before, she and Daisy and Lana had been roused by the noise of Fisscher's fleeing rabble. She had come down to the farmhouse and knocked on the door.

Lana went down the stairs in her nightdress to open it. Mrs. McKlennar was standing in the moonlight, her hair stringily fringing the edge of her white cap.

"Did you hear them, Magdelana?"

"Yes."

"Something's gone wrong with them," said the widow. "I'm going down to the road and see if I can find out how bad it is. Give me something dark to throw over this and go up and make sure Daisy don't scuttle off somewhere."

"I'd like to go with you," said Lana.

"Well, you can't. No telling who they are. They sound almighty like licked militia to me. But if there's anybody chasing them, a pretty girl has got no business hanging around in a nightgown."

Lana fetched her shawl.

"Will you be all right?"

Mrs. McKlennar grunted.

"Don't be silly!"

But as she went down to the road, Mrs. McKlennar almost wished she didn't feel so safe. She remembered how Barney once said to her, "Now don't you go traipsing round the militia camp at night. You can't tell about militia. And, begod, in the dark you've got a figger would make a lion out of a rabbit."

But that was long ago, when he liked her in a green silk nightgown, to go with her red hair. Now her body had taken after her face, with angles and joints, and no waist that Barney used to try to enclose in his two big hands. All that was left of those days was the fact that the militia were an unpredictable force.

She stood by the rail fence until she saw a man drop beside the road to take off his shoes, and she moved over behind him and prodded him with her forefinger.

He jumped and yelled and swung his gun round.

"I'm only a woman," said Mrs. McKlennar, "and I'm too old to bite."

"Oh, my Jesus," he said. "I thought the Indians were still after us."

"What happened?"

He cast a look down the road after his comrades, a dark disorderly shadow hurrying on the white dust.

"God! I got to get going."

"Is the army licked?"

"I don't know. I guess so. We was in back and then they started shooting out of the woods. You couldn't see. Fisscher came back and yelled the army was licked. That's all I know. We ain't seen anybody since. Only we heard them yelling after us in the woods. And I seen some. All painted. To look like devils."

He was already down the road. Edging off from her, breaking into a weary shuffling run.

Mrs. McKlennar sniffed and turned back towards the house. There was no use waiting for more, the way those men had gone.

She walked into the kitchen, getting an "Oh, my Gawd, Mis'," from Daisy, shut the door and dropped the bar.

"We'd better stay here to-night. You too, Magdelana. And I think we'd better not light a candle." She made her way through the moonlight from the window to the settle and sat down. "Stop your jibbering, you black baboon." When she had sat down she repeated what the militiaman had said.

"Fisscher's run away. And I guess they've surrounded the rest of the army. John Butler always was a clever devil."

Lana's voice surprised herself. She said quite calmly, "They'll be killed."

"Some of them. Magdelana dear, that's the business of war."

"Gil will be killed," Lana said.

Mrs. McKlennar pulled her shawl tighter.

"Go ahead and think so if it does you any good. I used to be just a baby myself when Barney was away. But there's no sense in it." She straightened herself with a slight shake. "I think we'd just better sit quiet here until morning. Then we'll see what's actually happened. I'll even move to a fort if necessary. Hush your noise, Daisy."

"I was only saying de Praise-God-from-whom."

The widow would not even let them light a fire until she had come back from the road. She went down, dressed, soon after sunrise, and held up a horseman with her brandy flask. He turned out to be a dispatch rider from Fort Dayton, starting down to General Schuyler's camp somewhere below Fort Edward. But you couldn't expect a soldier to disoblige a lady with a flask.

"No, ma'am, we don't know what's happened to the army. We've just got word they had an action up the river. They've sent for boats to fetch down Herkimer. He's bad hurt. But they say the British left the field."

"God bless you," said Mrs. McKlennar. "Take the flask with you."

The rider accepted it, touched his hat with it, and spurred his horse. Mrs. McKlennar watched him go with a small swelling of her heart. A nice-looking lad, a poor soldier—God knew what would happen to this country if a regular army ever came against them. She was humming a dim alto to something or other as she came back to the stone house.

"There's been a fight. They've stood the British off. I don't see why we should move yet. Magdelana, get some sleep. You look a sight. I'm going to wash and eat and lie down myself. Daisy can milk this morning."

Lana was upstairs in her house. She had prayed for Gil. It seemed futile to pray, now that the battle was over, but it was the only thing she could think of to do.

She was still on her knees, her elbows deep in the bedtick, her head in her hands, when Mrs. McKlennar shouted from the yard.

"Magdelana, Magdelana! Here he is!"

For one breath Lana was like ice. Then she got on her feet and went down. She went out into the yard, where, in the hot sunlight, she saw him kneeling at the horse trough, drinking, while Mrs. McKlennar stood at his side and splashed cold water on his head with her hand.

All Lana could think of was how dirty he looked. His face was dirty, almost black with grime; his hair was matted with sweat and hemlock needles. His shirt was torn and his trousers looked as if he had been lost in a briar patch.

He raised his face at her across the trough, and she thought he looked indescribably old. Then, as if he had seen enough of her, he put his lips to the cold surface of the water and drank.

Mrs. McKlennar nodded.

"Come here, he's had plenty. We must get him to bed."

Lana went to his other side. His shirt sleeve had been torn off and there was a dirty rag round the upper part of his arm. The rag was stiff with a brown clot.

"Gil," she said softly.

But Mrs. McKlennar was abrupt.

"Up, lad!"

He got up. The two women bolstered him on either side as he made slowly for the farmhouse.

"We'll get him some brandy," said Mrs. McKlennar. "It'll put him to sleep like a poleaxe, the way he is. We can look after him when he's sleeping."

"Don't you think we ought to fetch the doctor?"

"Doctor?" Mrs. McKlennar stared. "Anything that old fool Petry can do, I can do. And this arm is nothing. He walked home, didn't he? All he needs is a little sleep."

"Yes," said Gil, unsteadily. "I'm tired."

2. *Gil*

He had gone to sleep, as Mrs. McKlennar had foretold, within ten minutes of swallowing the brandy. Mrs. McKlennar had taken charge in a way that allowed Lana no protest. As soon as Gil's eyes had closed, she started cutting free the bandage with her sewing scissors. She held the dirty rag by the tips of the scissors and took hearty sniffs of it. "It isn't mortified," she said. "But anyway we'll swab it out." She dipped the chewed birch twig that was her toothbrush in the brandy and swabbed it through the bullet furrow. To Lana it looked like a brutal operation. "Nonsense," said Mrs.

McKlennar. "So long as he don't feel it we might as well be thorough."

"He might wake up."

"Don't be a fool. I don't know whether you've ever seen him drunk before. But he couldn't be any drunker if he was lying in a ditch."

She bandaged the arm deftly.

"Now," she announced, "I'll help you bathe him. You get his clothes off while I fetch some warm water."

While she was gone, Lana worked quickly. Gil lay like a log. She found that he would not wake no matter how she shoved and heaved, and for some reason she was glad to have him stripped and a blanket over him by the time Mrs. McKlennar returned with towels and a pail.

"Pull back the blanket," ordered the widow.

"Thanks," said Lana. "I can do the rest myself."

Suddenly Mrs. McKlennar laughed.

"Don't you think I ever saw a naked man, Magdelana? And I old enough to be his mother, or his grandmother, too. Heaven help me! Oh, come on!"

Her decisive hand laid hold of the blanket and peeled it back, and she looked down on Gil's straight brown body with frank curiosity. Then she raised her eyes to Lana's.

"Don't look so shamefaced, girl. He's nothing to be ashamed of. Why, damn it, you ought to feel proud!"

But Lana could not feel that way. It seemed unrighteous for her and the widow woman to be working over Gil like that. But she said nothing, only dried the parts of him that Mrs. McKlennar had done washing.

The widow, to do her justice, wasted no time.

"There," she said. "He ought to have one blanket. He's tired. But no more, or he'll wake up with a head like a punkin."

She picked up the pail and the soiled towels and said, "I'm going now."

"Thank you, Mrs. McKlennar."

The widow snorted.

"Thanks, my foot. You're just wondering when the old fool's ever going to take herself off." She stamped deliberately down the stairs.

Gil slept all the through the day. He was still asleep when the sun set. But as darkness came he had a spell of restlessness. In the first dusk, while Lana was getting a bite of supper, she heard him muttering overhead, and stole swiftly up to him. He was saying over and over, "I won't run. Oh, God, I won't run." She put her hand on his forehead and he flung round in the bed and shouted, "For God's sake, kill the next one." She shuddered. His face had not changed, but his voice frightened her.

His forehead was slightly feverish, and she went down again to get cool water, with which she bathed his head until his muttering stopped. Then she fetched the Betty lamp, lit it, and sat down where she could watch him on the bed.

Now that he was quiet again, the look of age went gradually out of his face. He had turned on his side with the complete rest of a boy.

As the night crept over the valley, she heard the widow finish milking and turn the cattle into the yard. A little later the light in the window of the stone house went out. There was no further sound except the last sleepy clucks of the hens settling on their roosts. All the farm was dark but for the light in their own room. It brought her a queer feeling of the world withdrawing, leaving them together, just they two. And as she watched his face, hour after hour, she lost all track of time.

A breath of air stirred in the room, flickering the lamp. Looking up from her hands, Lana saw Gil's eyes upon her.

She got up from her chair and went to the bed.

His eyes followed her. His hands lay on the blanket in front of him.

"It seems a long time, Lana."

"It does to me, too."

"You didn't see me."

"I didn't see you wake up."

"I was watching you. You made me think about the way you were when you were burning flax. In Fox's Mills. Do you remember? On the side of the hill?"

Her voice had a small catch. "I was thinking of it too."

"Were you?"

Suddenly she put out her hand to touch his. At the touch he turned his hand over and grasped her wrist.

"Have you been sitting up with me?"

"Yes."

"How long was I asleep?"

"I don't know. I don't know what time it is."

He did not comment. But he began increasing his pressure on her wrist. It frightened her, and she had to force herself to look at his face. She made herself relax until his grip was so strong that her fingers spread apart and stiffened.

He let go.

"I'm sorry. I didn't mean to do that."

"It didn't hurt."

"It must have."

"A little," she admitted.

"I'm sorry."

"Do you want to do it again?" she asked suddenly.

"Do you want me to?"

"I don't know."

She felt that a spell had come upon her. Whether it was the darkness or his hand upon her wrist, or both, the fatigue of her long watch was transmuted. She was no longer afraid of him, and yet she was afraid. In that moment when he had taken hold of her wrist his dark eyes had lost uncertainty.

"Sit down."

His hand guided her so that she sat beside him. She could feel herself trembling; but if he felt it, he did not mention it.

"What are you looking at?"

"There's a light," she said. "Up beyond the fort, on the hill to the west."

A pale tongue of flame was lifting from the hilltop. He hoisted himself, without letting go her wrist, and looked at it. While he watched, it mounted rapidly, and sank again.

"That's Indian fire."

"What does it mean?"

"I don't know. It makes you realize we've got no way of telling if the fort surrenders. They might come down any day."

"Yes."

"Are you afraid?"

The fire dropped, before she could answer. In a moment it was gone. They were just they two again, in the low-ceilinged room, with the wide bed and its swelling feather mattress.

"Tired?"

"I was."

He was watching the small oval of her face, with its dark hair. As she spoke her lids closed and the curves of her lips softened and filled. She sat beside him as if entranced.

She could not stir for the swelling blood; she felt it in her helpless quiet through all her body, breasts, thighs, and arms. Suddenly he let go her wrist, and she raised both hands to her temples, pushing the hair back. She turned her face to him.

He saw that she was tremulous, half shrinking.

"Lana."

"Yes, Gil."

"When I was up there, I kept thinking about you."

"Did you?"

"About what it would be like coming home."

The pause drew out. Her heart started beating.

He said quietly, "Are you coming?"

"If you want."

"Yes."

She got up slowly from the bed. Her fingers had a feeling of fullness as she took the laces of her short gown. She met his eyes and flushed painfully, and slowly. It was no use to think that he was her husband. He was a strange person who had acquired a right; and she felt completely without power or desire to thwart him. But her instinct made her turn from him towards the far corner of the room.

She did not recognize his voice.

"Don't go away."

She hesitated.

"Turn around."

Again she obeyed. Then her hands went to her hair.

"No," he said. He was smiling now. His eyes were deliberate. "Leave it for last," he said.

She felt the last drop of strength going out of her. It almost made her cry out as she surrendered. She pulled away the laces of the short gown, put it back over her shoulders, and let it drop from her bare arms.

The lamp put a soft shine on her skin as she bent her neck and undid her petticoat. It fell round her ankles. For an instant she stood so, half bent, in its encircling rough folds. Then she stepped from it, timidly, and for a brief moment encountered his eyes, her hands raised tentatively to undo her hair. She had no will of her own under his deliberate and amorous dominance; and she seemed held for an eternity in her submissive pose.

His nod released her. Her fingers flew to the pins, loosening them and letting her hair fall of its own weight down her back. Her breath came out of her breast with a shudder, and the pins dropped from her hair with a little sprinkle of sound on the broad planks. She stood quite still with her hands hanging limply at her sides, the palms turned childishly forward.

For a moment more Gil watched her. Then he smiled slowly, stretched out his hand, and pressed it down over the small flame of the Betty lamp.

3. At Herkimer Fort

The same evening, across the river in Fort Herkimer, Emma Weaver sat on the hearth considering all the things on her mind. What chiefly troubled her was the effect this garrison life was having on her oldest son. John had turned fifteen during the winter and grown fast. Already he was almost as tall as his mother, and since he had been issued an old French musket and appointed to regular sentry go, he considered himself a man.

It wasn't that he was undutiful to her; but she could tell that in the last few days he no longer acknowledged her authority in his personal affairs. She had only to look up from her shed against the stockade wall and see him passing, lanky and rawboned, with stiff strides back and forth upon the walk, to know that John had passed beyond her reach. And when he came in from his duty and sat down to supper she saw the impatience in his face to be through with the meal and get off to the blockhouse on the east, where the squad of soldiers bunked and where he could listen to what he now considered man's talk. The rough laughter, in the evenings, would pass heavily across the enclosure.

Emma didn't mind man's talk. Men together were entitled to their own ways of fun; but John was too young yet. Careless ideas took hold too hard. And with the way the place was crowded, so that there was no privacy, she was afraid that John would get entangled with some girl she herself could not like. There were plenty of them, and there were plenty of times when she had seen John, with the exhibitionism of the first impulse of manhood, stretching himself out in the sun before the blockhouse. He would take off his shirt, like the other men, baring his skinny torso, and drawing deep arching breaths with his chest, while he pretended to doze.

So far, she thought, he had not made a shine at any particular girl. It was just the idea of manhood getting at him now. But there were one or two girls her maternal eye had noticed watching John. Young Mary Reall for one, the Realls' oldest. She had no special urge against the girl, except that the Realls were idle, shiftless, loose-thoughted people, and if John were to marry early he ought to marry a girl with a settled way of seeing things. She wished George would come back so she could put the matter in his hands. George was sure to stamp on any nonsense. For all his easy-going temper, George had an instinct for righteousness that would put a curb on the boy, as it had curbed her own quick temper in their first married days.

The Realls, two partitions down, all reveled in the life. There was no steady work to do. They had no cattle to look after. Mrs. Reall eased about all day, letting the brats run wild. Peebles, the baby, had been weaned, and scurried like a puppy all over the parade ground on his hands and knees. In the evening he had to be hunted up and brought to bed, but Mary had taken on that duty. Mary was doing all their cooking, and it was also Mary who swept out their eight-foot square of space when she could borrow a broom, shook up the hemlock bedding, and saw that one of the boys carried their night's pail of slops to the dumping ground outside the stockade. It was a comfort to have a child at last grow up, and Mrs. Reall let herself luxuriate. She had another baby on the way and it did her good to be idle.

Mary Reall was fourteen now, a colorless girl, with light brown unbraided hair down her back. She had her father's rather pointed and effeminate features, but in her narrow face they were appropriate. On the rare occasions when excitement or heat or worry brought color to her face, it startled one who knew it, seeming beautiful. Not until the gradual cramped settling down of all the people had she noticed the lads being handed out guns. There were thirty boys, and only seven guns, and looking at them while she leaned idly against the wall of the shed, her eyes had singled out John Weaver.

Like the other boys he looked excited and tense. It would be an honor to be given a musket by the army sergeant—a man who knew war and men and guns. He was a grizzled old fellow with a swollen red nose and a lewd mouth and sharp eyes, and he lined the lads up before him and learned their names and looked at them. John Weaver, standing with the others, tried to keep his eyes on the sergeant, but he also felt that people were watching his back. He sent a sidelong estimating glance round the stockade, and met Mary Reall's gaze. He did not show that he recognized her. He let his eye run past, quickly faced front, and colored to his hair. It had surprised him to see how she had grown. Her faded cotton short gown was tight over her breast and her long slender legs looked less slatty.

"You first," said the sergeant, and tapped John with the point of his forefinger. John turned quite white and weak and unbelievingly stepped forward to accept the musket. Though some of the boys were older, he had been singled out the first. He felt the envious stares of the other boys on his back, as surprised as himself, then, following the sergeant's nod, went forward into the door of the blockhouse, walking a little stiffly like a young dog, into the company of men.

Mary Reall did not change her position for several moments, but leaned where she was, thinking about how often she used to meet John Weaver up in Deerfield and how he had seemed to her just any dirty boy. But now she saw how tall he had become, how his shoulders had begun to fill at the back like a man's; and it came to her with a sense of awe that she had been brought up almost next door to him, so that in a sense she shared the honor of his first promotion.

When she went inside their hut, she was ashamed to see that supper had not yet been started. Mrs. Reall snickered when the fact was pointed out. "What difference?" she wished to know. "What difference?" Mary could not say rightly even to herself. But there was a dim apprehension that if John could do a man's part it was time for her to think of a woman's. She set to work at supper, and then cleaned out all the magpie mess of their inhabiting, picking up the children's shirts where they had been trodden into the dusty earth of the floor, shaking them and hanging them up, and borrowing a broom from the next shed to sweep with. "I declare," said Mrs. Reall. "You've made it look real homey."

Mary felt proud and tired, but also ashamed when she was through and, looking up, beheld John, for the first time, marching back and forth across the opposite sentry walk. His beat took him behind the church, so that she saw him first at one end, then the other. She could have cried because they had not even a tallow dip that she could light, for him to see her work, and herself sitting in the entrance. Instead she had to move over to another door and stand there, trying to be noticed by him while at the same time she kept out of sight of the people whose light she had unobtrusively borrowed.

It was there that Emma first noticed her, and it was there also that John saw her again, for he was paying as much attention to the interesting interior of the stockade as he was to the outside and faceless night.

And on being relieved he went back to the blockhouse the long way, passing the hut, and finding her still there.

"Why, hello," he said carelessly, "ain't that you, Mary Reall?"

"Hello," she said, with an effort at surprise. "I hadn't seen you before, John. How are you?"

"You didn't?" he couldn't help contradicting her. "I thought you was watching when they passed the muskets out."

"Well, I was," she said. "But I didn't notice anyone particular."

He was huffed. But he didn't like to say he was the first selection. So he said, "I hope you're all well."

"Nicely," she said. "And you?"

"We're fine," he said. "It's funny you didn't see us, though. We came in this morning."

"It's so crowded," Mary said. "You know how it is."

"Yes," he said. "We're awful crowded."

He paused a moment, then shouldered his musket awkwardly.

"Well, I got to report to Sergeant," he said, and stalked off. "See you again, maybe."

Mary watched him go. Then she hurried back to her own space and crept in over the sleeping bodies of her family. She lay down in the corner space reserved for her, glad that there was no candle now. For she was crying, and wondering what in the world had made her talk the way she had.

The fort was a stifling place. The twelve-foot pointed logs of the palisade cut off what air might move. The bark-sheathed roofs of the sheds, only a foot over the people's heads, were their only shelter against the sun, which burned through the heavy air with the intensity of a burning glass. Even in the church, whose stone walls kept it relatively cool, the air grew so stale that people left it for the outdoor heat.

The life was enervating; there was no chance to exercise, except to walk round the fields in sight of the stockade, keeping a safe distance from the woods or fields of standing corn that might give cover to an Indian. They dared go only to the nearest farms, since the garrison could offer them no protection beyond the walls. And after their first few morning chores were performed, the pails emptied in the ditch, the sheds brushed out, and the water drawn, there was nothing left to do but get their meals and talk.

Even the talking petered out. There was not a family who didn't have a father or brother or son in the army that had gone west with Herkimer. Once the first conjectures had been interchanged and the family news caught up with, nothing remained to be talked about except the heat.

They had no news from the army. They had no news from Fort Stanwix. They had no news from the east. All they could do was to listen and wait, and watch with a growing concern for the first possible appearance of the enemy.

Only the squad of Massachusetts soldiers in the blockhouse kept up a kind of conversation in their nasal Yankee voices; but they kept their talk to themselves. They feared and disliked the Palatines as much as the Palatines disliked them. Most of the time their captain, who commanded at the fort, went over the river to pass the time with Colonel Weston, at Fort Dayton, returning after supper in the dusk, giving the countersign outside the gate, marching through in his rust-colored coat and cocked hat, looking neither to left nor to right, as if he held his breath against a troublesome smell, until he reached the blockhouse. He passed through the guardroom with a curt good-night and mounted to his quarters in the upper room. The people could see his shadow there at times, drinking brandy by himself—or sometimes he leaned from the window, smoking a last pipe.

It was queer how quickly all these things became familiar parts of their existence, as if they had spent long lives already in a confined space. It made them apathetic, resigned, and fearful, and the soldiers spoke contemptuously about the German race.

In the midst of it, Mary and John continued their gradual approach in a kind of hushed expectancy. They moved their separate lives through the crowdedness and the dirt and the hostility as if they made a mist in which they apprehended each other's shapes, dimly. Yet the meetings had poignance that only two such beginners could be aware of.

The time when Mary, rising in the middle of the night, heard the sentry steps halt overhead and recognized them for his, and realized that he must have heard her stirring, was mysterious and intimate; and the next morning when she encountered him at the well and they said good-morning to each other with formal politeness, they saw in each other's face that both had shared it.

In spite of Emma Weaver's doubts, that was as far as either of them had got till the night of the sixth, when, long past sunset, a boat was rowed across from Fort Dayton and the news of the retreat delivered.

Then, three hours later, the first bateaux had arrived with General Herkimer. The fort had been hailed. The gate opened, and the general was carried in past the waiting silent people, holding torches here and there, to the church. After the gates were closed the people moved up to the church windows and talked softly to those who had their beds inside, and learned that the general was wounded in the leg. The men who had brought him lay down in the western blockhouse and would not answer any question. They slept like animals.

In the next few hours other boats arrived. One of the first brought George Weaver home, and John was one of the garrison sent to help him to the fort. As he entered with his father, he saw Mary standing beside the gate, her eyes searching the faces of the new arrivals, and it came to him that alone of all her family she had the interest to look for her father.

He helped put his father down on the hemlock bed and stood back while his mother unwrapped the bandage from his chest.

His father said, "Hello, John."

"Hello," said John.

Emma said, "I'll tend to Pa. You'd better get back where you belong. Cobus can fetch me things."

"I will," said John. He looked down on his father's big body hesitantly. "Where'd you get the gun, son?"

Emma said, not without pride, "He's one of the watch."

"You'd better get along." His father lay back and groaned as Emma ruthlessly pulled away the cotton. Then he opened his eyes and met John's. "What's on your mind, son?"

"Did Christian Reall . . . ?"

He saw his mother's back stiffen.

"I don't know. I didn't see him. But Jeams MacNod's outside. He'll know." George closed his eyes. Without opening them he said almost apologetically, "I got this at the first beginning, son."

John left them with a sudden realization that they might like to be alone. He returned to the gate where the schoolmaster sat in his tattered black coat, hatless and unshaven, a venomous kind of terror still printed on his face.

He looked up at John's question.

"Kitty Reall?" he said. "You want to know where Kitty Reall is? Well, I can tell you. He's laying with his face over a log. He's scalped. But he ain't half of what there is to see. . . "

John said savagely, "You know he's dead?"

"I'm telling you. . . . What do you think? They ain't satisfied with just killing. I never saw Indians before. It ain't war. My God!"

Turning away, John saw Mary Reall standing by the corner of the church. She was watching him still, her thin pale face a little lowered, looking out from her brows.

A wave of sick pity went over John and he walked up to her, taking her arm without a word. She didn't protest, but went with him quietly. As he walked her forward he kept searching for a place they could be private in. But there was no unoccupied corner within the stockade, till it occurred to him to look up at the sentry walk.

All the men were round by the gate, looking down over the points of the palisades at the river.

"Come up with me," said John, and climbed the ladder. They could stand in the angle of the walk made by the palisade and the blockhouse wall. No one could see them from below.

John waited for her, with his eyes on the faceless night beyond the stockade. She came up quietly beside him on her bare feet and leaned with him against the pointed upright logs.

It was the nearest to him she had been since he had first become aware

of who she really was. Her dress touched his side, and through the dress
he could feel the slim round hardness of her body. Her hair had a faint
smell of its own, like spice over the body scent.

She waited for him to speak. She had not yet said a word on her own
part. But she leaned beside him against the stockade, taking one point between her breasts like a spear, and when he turned his head she did not
turn hers.

"Mary," he said.

"Yes." She waited again; but when he could not go on she asked quietly,
"Did you hear anything about Father, from that man?"

"Yes."

It seemed an awful thing to say. As if he were killing Christian Reall
with his own words.

"He's dead, isn't he?"

She was making it easy for him.

"Yes, Mary."

She did not cry or do anything that he might have expected. But she
turned suddenly to him, so that he saw her face oval against the peeled logs
of the blockhouse.

"It was kind of you, John, to find out. I wouldn't have known how to
ask."

"It's nothing. I wanted to help."

"I'm grateful to you."

He felt himself grow stiff and his voice tightened.

"It's awful. But, Mary, I'll always be willing to help you. Whatever there
is you need, you'll let me know. I think you're the finest girl in German
Flats."

It wasn't what he had set out to say, but he meant it. And she was standing just as stiff as he. "You've been so good," she was saying. "I'll always
remember how good you've been, John."

"I wanted to tell you myself," he said. Then suddenly he leaned forward over his musket. She bent a little towards him and they kissed each
other, briefly.

He pulled back quickly, and then, as she looked at him, held out his
hand. She put her own in it and they held hands for a moment. Then he
said, "I ought to get back to the gate."

"Yes, John."

"You'd better go down here, and I'll go down the walk." They stood
silent for a moment and he added, "It would look better."

"Yes, John."

She went down under his eyes, shy and swift, and he turned round the
sentry walk, marching openly with his musket on his arm.

It was a wonderful thing to have a girl like Mary Reall. It made him
feel protective, as if the musket really meant something. As if Sergeant had
picked him out for the very purpose. And it was a wonderful thing to have
someone accept your opinions the way Mary did. It was a wonderful thing
to be betrothed, he thought.

4. *Marinus Willett*

As the wounded were brought into the stockades, and the last of the Palatine and Canajoharie companies departed for their own precincts, a pall of terror settled on German Flats. Even the garrisons in the two forts became irascible and bitterly sarcastic about the German race. Everyone thought it was only a matter of days before the Tories and Indians would be among them.

Word got round that among the wounded at Dr. Petry's house was a man who had been scalped, and many people were moved by a morbid curiosity to see him. He turned out to be George Walter, a stout German farmer living below Fall Hill, well known for his good humor. It had not deserted him now. He was entirely willing that people should come and look at him and offer him drinks behind the doctor's back.

"Ja, ja," he would say. "I was lying behind a tree, und the Indian comes und shoots me, und then he comes with his liddle axe und hits me und takes the top off mine head, und he goes away mit it. He thought I was dead." He would pause to grin, and say, "I thought I was dead too," as if that were a peculiarly funny coincidence.

It was that grin that was described around the settlements. They said his face had lost all its fatness and the features seemed on the point of running out of his chin, and that when he grinned all his features seemed to get together there, down below his face. He did it so much that the stitches tore out and the doctor had to work on him all over and lock him up on the top floor. But even so, small boys climbed the maple tree across the road to look at him through the window.

Other sufferers, less picturesque than Walter, had circumstantial stories of Tories recognized in the opposing side. People began to repeat from them how Ritter had been dragged off by two Indians and how the Indians had been driven off by Ritter's former neighbor, Casselman, who had then cut Ritter's throat with his own hand. There were stories of some Scotch Highlanders in Sir John Johnson's regiment scalping the militia just as if they were Indians themselves.

A few people made feeble efforts to the effect of combating these horrors. Domine Rozencrantz read in church from the Ninety-first Psalm:—

> "He shall cover thee with his feathers, and under his wings shall thou trust: his truth shall be thy shield and buckler.
> "Thou shalt not be afraid for the terror by night; nor for the arrow that flieth by day."

But the Lord's presence was not an active thing like John Butler's before Fort Stanwix. People in the stockades began to talk about how he used to be Sir William Johnson's right-hand man when the Indians were taken care of, bribed and pampered, so that any man might take up land in safety, and Joseph Brant was just a neighbor. More than one man began to shake his head and think that he had been a fool, and wish for the old safe days back again.

The members of the Committee of Safety in German Flats were well aware of the swing of popular feeling. On the ninth of August, Peter Tygert wrote the Albany Committee as spokesman for his district by virtue of his own survival.

Demooth and Helmer and Joe Boleo had left Fort Stanwix on the night of the sixth, and it had taken them three days of circuitous traveling to elude the Indian scouting parties. They brought news to German Flats of the increasing shortage of provisions and ammunition. Colonel Gansevoort had put the garrison on a single daily ration. The one bright spot was the account of a sortie led by Lieutenant Colonel Willett against the Tory camp on the day of the battle. It was a daring raid and it resulted in the removal to the fort of all the munitions and food the enemy's camp contained, together with Butler's and Johnson's papers and half a dozen flags. They spoke with admiration of Willett's conduct. They said he was a cool, unhurried man. But they also said that the fort could not hold out indefinitely, that the Indians and the regulars were keeping a tight network of lines round the fort. They said that in Butler's papers they had found endorsements for scalps taken, at eight dollars per scalp. When they got through, the sortie seemed a drop of victory that was ironical.

Tygert, writing these things down, continued with the battle itself:—

> Gen. Herkimer is wounded; Col. Cox seemingly killed; and a great many officers are among the slain. We are surrounded by Tories, a party of 100 of whom are now on their march through the woods. . . .
>
> Gentlemen, we pray you will send us succour. By the death of most of our committee members, the field officers, and Gen. Herkimer being wounded, everything is out of order; the people entirely dispirited; our county at Esopus unrepresented, that we cannot hope to stand it any longer without your aid; we will not mention the shocking aspect our fields do show. Faithful to our country we remain,
>
> Your sorrowful bretheren,
> THE FEW MEMBERS OF THIS COMMITTEE

But two days after this letter had been dispatched by Helmer, a scout escorted two men into Fort Dayton. One of these was a young lieutenant named Stockwell; the other was Lieutenant Colonel Marinus Willett. As soon as they arrived they were taken to Colonel Weston's quarters, and he in turn immediately sent for Tygert, Demooth, and Dr. Petry.

These three took comfort from the very look of Colonel Willett. He was standing before the fireplace, and at their entrance withdrew his hooked nose from the glass in his hand, a drop hanging from the tip of it, and eyed them with unwavering hard blue eyes. As he was being introduced to the three Committee members, the drop fell to his waistcoat. He said to them bluntly, "Gentlemen, I've had you sent for to know what you've written to Schuyler."

He nodded again when Tygert had repeated the gist of his letter to the Albany Committee.

"You put it to them pretty strong. But they'll send the letter on to General Schuyler. I'm going to see him myself." He smiled at them. "Somebody needs to raise a stink, and Gansevoort seemed to think I could do it."

His big nose seemed to arch.

"Just how bad are things up at Stanwix?" asked Dr. Petry.

"Bad enough. We've got food enough for a while, but we're low on shot. Right now St. Leger's busy writing letters about what he's going to do to us and to you people if we don't surrender. But the troops are taking them right. We made a flag on the new Continental pattern and flew it over the flags we took in the sortie, and that tickled them. And then I thought to read them the passage in the Book of Joel." His blue eyes twinkled close on either side of his high nose as he solemnly quoted:—

" 'But I will remove far off from you the northern army, and will drive him into a land barren and desolate, with his face toward the east sea, and his hinder part toward the utmost sea; and his stink shall come up.' "

There was a commotion in the parade yard, and an orderly looked in to announce a dispatch rider. He entered with his papers in his hand.

"Colonel Weston?"

"Yes."

"Papers from General Schuyler."

Weston did not ask to be excused. He immediately opened his letter. Then he looked up.

"Schuyler's sending up General Arnold and Learned. He hopes to add the First New York Line."

There was a silence in the room through which the panting of the dispatch rider's horse came heavily. They all looked at one another. Then Willett wiped his mouth. "Maybe you ought to give this lad a drink," he suggested.

"Yes, yes," said Weston, and filled his own glass. He turned to Willett. "Do you think you'll have to go down to headquarters, now?"

"By God, yes. I want to be damned sure they don't waste any time. Is that decent horse you spoke of ready yet?"

"He's outside."

They all went to the door, then walked to the gate after he mounted. He paused there, gathering up the reins.

"Who do I have to pay if I spoil this horse?"

He grinned and kicked the horse into a canter before he was answered. They watched him down the road towards the creek ford. He sat straight in the saddle, like an electrified ploughman; but as they saw his square shoulders disappearing under the low maple branches they remembered the hardness of the blue eyes, and the big nose in the long face. He wasn't the kind of man who would return without what he was after.

"They'll hear him even if they hold their fingers in their ears," the doctor said. "What was that flag he was talking about, Mark? Did you see it?"

Mark Demooth nodded.

"Yes. It's got thirteen stripes, red and white ones, and a blue box in the upper corner, with thirteen white stars in a ring. They made it out of ammunition shirts, and a blue cloak, and a woman's red petticoat." He grinned thinly. "She's got to be a heroine with the men up there. They say it's the first time she ever took the petticoat off in an honest cause."

Tygert looked solemn.

"I hadn't heard of it before. It sounds like a fancy pattern for a flag, though."

5. Nancy Schuyler

The party of one hundred Tories that Mr. Tygert had mentioned in his letter to the Albany Committee materialized in the form of a party of fifteen who turned up on the thirteenth at Rudolph Shoemaker's house.

Shoemaker was an anomalous person. Before hostilities commenced he had been a Justice of the Peace under the King. In '75 he had signed the Loyalist manifesto against sedition and treason. But he had not chosen to move west with the Butlers and Johnsons later that spring. Instead, relying on his kinship to Nicholas Herkimer, he had joined the German Flats Committee of Safety. Since then his public house had become a sort of neutral ground, and it caused no particular surprise when the news went through the valley that the hostile party had taken up quarters there.

Captain Demooth first heard of it when he asked Nancy at suppertime where Clem Coppernol was. She flushed, as she always did when the captain asked her a direct question.

"He said he was going up to Shoemaker's."

"What's he doing there, do you know, Nancy?"

"He said there was some people from the westward."

Captain Demooth frowned, and Nancy, looking down on his dark head, saw his neat hands hesitate as they put the pudding on his plate. He hurried to finish his supper and then went out again. He said to his wife, "I ought to ask Weston about this, Sara. He may have heard something."

Mrs. Demooth was petulant; but Nancy hardly noticed her. It never occurred to her that this news, more than any other news, could have any importance in her life. She cleared away the dishes, washed them, wiped the table, and fetched Mrs. Demooth's lamp, and then retired to her own corner of the room.

Nancy Schuyler had not been happy in German Flats, though she had expected to be. She had thought the life would be exciting there, with the soldiers in the two forts and the young men on the farms. In such a place she had supposed there would be unmarried men who might be interested in her.

But such men seemed not to exist for Nancy, and, if there had been, Mrs. Demooth kept her so closely under watch that she would have had no opportunity. Her one moment of excitement had been that night in early winter when Gilbert Martin had stopped in with the deer meat and she had felt so sorry for him. Whenever she thought of that night, she felt a shiver take her. She thought that she must have been in love with Gilbert Martin on that night; at the time she had thought that he was in love with her. As she had sat in his arms, she had felt her very being swim into a high kind of happiness. And then abruptly, for no reason she had ever discovered, he had left her and gone home.

Later she had recalled how her brother Hon Yost used to warn her against married men. He had said a girl should never put dependence in a married man. She supposed that must be Gilbert Martin's trouble. Sometimes she wished that she could talk to Hon, who was the one member of her family who had ever understood her. Perhaps that was because, as he said himself, he was light-headed too.

Nancy's mother had made a visit at the end of the preceding year, coming, as she said, to see what kind of girl Nancy had grown into, and also to collect her daughter's pay for the year, and Nancy had glowed with pride to see her mother in her black shaw facing up so well to the captain's wife.

"I hope Nancy's satisfactory to you, Mrs. Demooth."

"Oh yes, Nancy means very well." Mrs. Demooth used her chilly, lady voice; but it had no effect on Mrs. Schuyler's dark dominant Herkimer eyes.

"She's never been lazy," said her mother. "I'm sure she earns every penny of her wages. Now, if you'll kindly settle the account, Mrs. Demooth, I'll get back to my brother, the general."

"Will you fetch my pocket, Nancy?" Though Mrs. Demooth had not apparently noticed what Mrs. Schuyler said, Nancy was aware that she was impressed. She fetched the pocket and Mrs. Demooth took out three paper bills, saying, "Captain Demooth left the money in case you called."

Mrs. Schuyler looked at the bills.

"Why," she said, "these aren't pound notes."

"Oh, no," said Mrs. Demooth. "They're Continental dollars. They're five-dollar bills."

"They are pretty with those harps drawn on them," Mrs. Schuyler said, "but I'd rather have the money in English if you don't mind."

"I'm sorry, but it's all I have in the house. Of course, if you like, I'll speak to Captain Demooth about it. But he says these are just as good."

"The contract called for three pounds a year," Mrs. Schuyler objected. "I'm not used to these new dollars."

"They'll buy just the same, Mrs. Schuyler. As a matter of fact Captain Demooth said you were getting more than three pounds' worth, but as we did not have the change and Nancy had been a good girl he said you might give her the change as a present if you did not want to take more."

That was what her mother wished to know.

"Thank you," she said. "Maybe I'll buy her something with it. But, you know, I think she's better without money of her own."

The two women bowed to each other, and then Nancy walked out with her mother to the corner of the road.

There they had parted.

"Mrs. Demooth speaks highly of you, Nancy," her mother had said with satisfaction. "I am pleased. Your uncle will be pleased. Be a good girl."

"Yes, Mother."

"You don't get homesick, do you?"

"Oh no," said Nancy.

"Well, good-bye, daughter."

That was the way her mother always said good-bye. Calling Nancy "daughter," as if the word were a gad she pricked her own heart with. But it was a relationship that had no meaning. Her mother did not really belong to her. She was the general's sister. All her talk was about the general, or his big house and the figure he now made in the nation. She never mentioned Nancy's father. That was a mistake the general wished to have forgotten, since the man was dead. Nancy and her brother Hon were the only reminders of their mother's indiscretion, for the other brother, Nicholas, was black-complexioned and quite steady. Mrs. Schuyler never talked about Hon any more than she did of her dead husband.

Sometimes, sitting by herself in the corner of the room, Nancy could feel her heart swell with her own loneliness, and then she would pray that Hon might come down to German Flats as he had promised a year ago. She wished that he could write and she could read, so he might tell her what he was doing. He was such a light-hearted man that Nancy felt that it would do her good just to hear what he was up to.

Now, as she stitched away on her piece of handkerchief linen, she amused herself with remembering all the things she could about Hon Yost. She knew, for instance, that he had joined a regiment of regular troops. She even remembered the name of it—the Eighth King's Regiment. And she remembered his last message. She had once repeated it to Mrs. Martin when they were in Deerfield. The very words came back to her. "He said he'd try to fetch me an officer, too."

Her mouth curved over her sewing, and Mrs. Demooth, looking across the room, thought petulantly how easy it was for a simple-witted woman like Nancy Schuyler to be happy.

It startled both Mrs. Demooth and Nancy when they heard the captain's voice outside hailing Clem.

"Where've you been, Clem?"

"Up to Shoemaker's."

"What did you go up there for?" The captain sounded stern.

Clem answered gruffly.

"I heard there was some British there. I thought it wouldn't do no harm to hear what was going on."

"What were they doing?"

"Nothing much."

"Look here, Clem, if you don't tell me what I want to know, I'll have to take you to the guardhouse in the fort."

"Why don't you ride over there yourself?" the Dutchman said sourly.

"Stop your impudence."

"They ain't doing nothing but set around and drink. Ensign Butler has a paper he's reading out of."

"Butler?"

"What I said."

"John Butler! No, he's a colonel."

"No, this is a young man. Nice-spoken, too. He's Ensign Walter Butler of the Eighth King's Regiment, he says. Wears a red coat. They all do, barring the Indians."

"How many are there?"

"Ten or a dozen. I didn't count. They was reading this paper saying how anybody going over to their side will be pertected. And anybody not will be cut up by the Indians. There was only four Indians, so I didn't put stock in that part."

The Eighth King's. That was Hon's regiment. In spite of Mrs. Demooth's
"Nancy!" she went out to the two men.

"Clem," she said breathlessly. "Did you see Hon?"

"Hon?" Both men turned. Then Clem guffawed in the midst of his aura
of rum. "Yes, by God! I did see him. Why?"

But Nancy had stepped back into the house. Already she had made up
her mind to do a desperate thing. She would go up and see Hon herself.
It might not be safe for him to come so near the fort, so she would go to
him at Shoemaker's, no matter what Mrs. Demooth would surely say. She
wouldn't even let them know.

As she sat down on her stool her heart beat so fast that she was unable
to thread the needle. She tried again and again, knowing that Mrs. Demooth's unsympathetic eyes were watching her. Finally, in desperation, she
merely pretended that she had succeeded. She made the motion of drawing
the thread through the eye and with the empty needle began to take fine
stitches in the handkerchief seam.

The color glowed in her soft cheeks. She realized that she had fooled
Mrs. Demooth. She had never been clever like that before. It seemed like
a good omen. Outside of the house the night was uninterrupted. Clem
had gone off tipsily to his bed in the barn. The captain had hurried back
to the fort. All through the grass crickets were singing. The rhythm of their
united notes swung into the beat of Nancy's heart, bringing the darkness
close to her.

All she need do was wait until Mrs. Demooth should go to bed, and
Mrs. Demooth was already yawning.

6.   *Tories at Shoemaker's*

It was nearly a two-mile walk to Shoemaker's. Nancy followed the road
as fast as she could, but though she knew her direction, and had traveled
the distance before, the darkness handicapped her. Now and then on a
good patch of the road the ruts failed to guide her and she found herself
walking in the rough grass at the side.

There was neither moon nor stars. No sign of life showed anywhere
except the light of two torches that appeared in the main gate of Fort
Dayton. But they were too far behind Nancy to look like more than
sparks, and shortly after she had first noticed them, they vanished. With
their going the intensity of blackness became deathly. Even the crickets
were still, as if they felt the imminence of storm.

In her secretiveness she had pulled a dark shawl over her head, so that
with her plain dress she was nearly invisible. A man rising suddenly in the
darkness on the other side of the road never saw her at all, and she had
time to shrink into the grass with the timid stillness of a deer.

He was coming away from Shoemaker's, and like herself he seemed
in a hurry and anxious not to be noticed. She could not tell who he was,
but she smelled the rankness of tobacco in his clothes and a strong breath
of rum was left behind him after he had gone.

Nancy waited until his footsteps had faded out before resuming her own
way. She was not frightened, but she did not wish to be seen by anyone

who might know her, lest the word of her adventure might get back to
Mrs. Demooth. She was too absorbed in her desire to see Hon to feel afraid.

It took her half an hour to reach Shoemaker's house. As she approached
it she encountered more men coming away; and one or two men overtook
her, going in her own direction. The queer thing about them was that
none of the men spoke. They moved furtively, and they seemed anxious
even to avoid each other. Since her first encounter she had traveled more
cautiously, listening for every footfall on the road, so that she had time
enough to step out of the way, sometimes standing by the side of the road,
and sometimes finding one of the old river willows near enough to hide
behind.

Shoemaker's house stood back a little from the road. When Nancy
reached it, it was merely a darker square against the sky. The shutters
were closed over the windows, so that the frames were barely indicated
by threads of light. The only sign of life was the recurrent faint mumble
of voices.

Nancy stood on the far side of the road, pressing herself against Shoemaker's pasture fence. Now that she had come so far, doubts overcame
her and she felt suddenly shy of Hon. It seemed to her that the business
the men were conducting must be very important, and her original plan
of walking up to the door and asking for Hon, if he were not outside,
was quite impossible. She did not want to do anything that might embarrass
him in front of so many people. Not that she thought that Hon would be
annoyed with her; but all her life she had been made to realize her un-
importance before people.

With the opening of the front door, she suddenly discovered herself
full in the light. She had one glimpse of the interior of the house. It was
full of farmers, standing along the walls. They did not appear to be saying
anything. Their faces looked stupid in the tobacco smoke. They were all
staring through the door into Shoemaker's taproom.

Nancy could see through the door also, but only enough to have a
flashing glimpse of a scarlet coat or two, and, beyond, the face of one
man, pale, young, and dark-haired. He was addressing the gathering in
a high, decisive voice.

Then the men who had come out on the stoop closed the door, and
the darkness was returned. As the men stepped off the stoop, Nancy felt
herself seized from both sides. She was taken by the arms and hauled
stiffly erect. She started to cry out, but a hand put over her mouth checked
the cry. The men who held her did not move until the men leaving the house
were well away down the road.

Then a voice said, "You come now."

She was led quickly towards the house, but not to the front door. They
turned the corner to the left towards the kitchen porch. Nancy stumbled a
little on the steps.

She was not afraid now, only surprised, and bitterly ashamed that she
should have been discovered and have been brought to Hon's attention in
so humiliating a fashion after she had tried to be so careful. She could not
understand how the men had got so close to her. She had not seen them
even when the door was open. And now on the porch boards their feet made
hardly a sound.

One spoke to the other, and she felt him taking hold of her with both hands, and as the other moved towards the door her nostrils were filled with a strong sweet greasy odor and she knew that the two men must be Indians. As the door opened she looked up at the man who held her.

He was a powerful thickset man. He wore a red cloth headdress, with a single eagle feather hanging down over his left ear. From the waist up he was naked, his hairless chest beaded through the grease with tiny drops of sweat, so that the light shimmered on his skin with a bronze sheen. He was looking curiously down at her, the eyes a strange parody of intelligence behind the red and yellow painting of his face.

"You be good," he said, and relaxed the pressure of his hands slightly; but he did not let go of her.

The door opened again, showing her the second Indian and a soldier in a scarlet coat.

"You can let her go," the soldier said to the second Indian.

He looked down at her. His coat was unbuttoned. Between the flaps Nancy saw that his shirt was wringing wet. He blew out his breath. "God, it's good to get some fresh air. It smells like a Dutch funeral in there. Well, Missy, what do you want here?"

Nancy flushed within the protection of her shawl. She tried to find words.

"All right, Missy," the soldier said. "Nobody's going to hurt you."

"I know," Nancy replied. At the sound of her fresh young voice the soldier looked at her more closely. "I didn't mean to make a bother," Nancy went on. "I just heard my brother, Hon, was here and I haven't seen him for two years and I wanted to say something to him."

The soldier said kindly, "You've got a brother with us?"

Nancy nodded.

"What did you say his name was?"

"Hon Yost."

"We ain't got anybody named that with us. What's your name?"

"Nancy Schuyler."

"Nancy is a nice name." He hesitated, still looking at her. Then, as if he couldn't help himself, he took his hands from his belt and put the shawl back from her face. She stood in the light, hesitant and flushed, looking up at him with large eyes. Her full lips trembled a little.

He seemed to miss the simpleness in her eyes. He kept looking at her face, her lovely mouth, her heavy yellow hair, and the long soft curves of her body showing through the thin dress.

"Is your brother Jack Schuyler? He looks a little like you. Not really, you know. Jesus!" He drew his breath. "I haven't seen a pretty girl since I left Montreal, last April." He seemed to recollect himself with an effort. "Jack's got yellow hair like you. Do you think he'd be your brother?"

Nancy was staring in a trance. But her eyes were on the glittering sergeant's stripes, on the red coat, and the white breeches, now stained from his passage through the woods. She did not see at all the eagerness of his face, the almost feverish brilliance of his eyes.

"I don't know," she said timidly. "He had yellow hair. But I always called him Hon."

"That's Dutch for John. The Eighth is supposed to be all English. I'll fetch him out, anyway. I'd do a lot for you, Missy." He smiled deliberately at her. "You just stay here." He put his hand on her shoulder, letting it slide down her arm as he turned away to the door.

"Where's that half-wit Schuyler?" she heard him ask another red-coated man.

"What do you want him for?"

"His sister's outside. She wants to see him."

"His sister?" The man laughed out loud.

He disappeared in the throng and one of the Indians closed the door, leaving Nancy and themselves in darkness. She heard their catlike tread moving past her along the porch, and presently she made out their heads, shadowy silhouettes, staring east together from the steps.

She had to wait quite a while before the door opened again. But it was not Hon Yost; it was the soldier who had gone to look for him.

"Jack can't get out right now," he said.

She asked timidly, "Did you tell him I was here, Mister?"

"Yes. He said for you to wait. I told him I'd look after you." He leaned himself against the wall of the house and stared at her. He had left the door open a crack, so that the light shone on her, but when she moved he put his hand out.

"Don't move. Please. You don't know how it is, in the woods. So long. You get half crazy with the heat, and the flies, and there's nothing to see but men like yourself. You don't know what it is for a man just to look at a pretty girl."

Nancy stood still. She couldn't see his face now—only his brown hair over his ear in the edge of the light; but she could see where his eyes were.

He said, "I used to live down here. Down beyond Fort Dayton. On the other side of the Canada Creek. I worked for an old woman named Mc-Klennar. It's funny I never heard of you."

Nancy could not think of anything to say. She was listening and looking for Hon. But the soldier's voice sounded so unhappy that she turned her face a little towards him and smiled her slow smile, with its meaningless warmth.

He said, "My name's Jurry McLonis."

"Yes, Mr. McLonis."

She smiled again and he was silent for a time. Through the door the same decisive voice she had heard before came with the stilted precision of a man reading:—

> ". . . For which reasons, the Indians declare, that if they do not surrender the garrison without further opposition, they will put every soul to death—not only the garrison, but the whole country—without regard to age, sex, or friends; for which reason it is become your indispensable duty, as you must answer the consequences, to send a deputation to your principal people, to oblige them immediately to what, in a very little time, they must be forced—the surrender of the garrison; in which case we will engage on the faith of Christians, to protect you from the violence of the Indians.
>
> "Surrounded as you are by victorious armies, one half (if not the greater part) of the inhabitants friends to government, without any resource, surely you cannot hesitate a moment to accept the terms proposed to you by friends and well-wishers to the country.

"It's signed by John Johnson, D. W. Claus, and my father John Butler. It's plain honest sense, and the last chance you people will have to save your necks. I'm going back day after to-morrow. Every man who goes with me gets a uniform coat, a musket if he needs it, pay in good English money, and a land bounty when this war's over."

Again the silence, and again the low mumbling of voices.

"God, I'm sick of hearing all that, Nancy. The same thing over and over for two days." Jurry McLonis touched her arm. "Jack can't come out a while. Let's go out where it's quiet and dark." Her eyes turned to him, large and questioning and hesitant and foolish. "He told me to look out for you, you know."

"Yes, Mister. I don't mind. While Hon's busy."

The steady sound of Butler's voice had muddled her head. McLonis's arm round her waist was comfortable to lean against. The Indians moved over on the steps and glanced at them, and moved back.

McLonis led her out, his arm tightening round her as she found the footing uncertain in the darkness. He took her behind Shoemaker's barn. There he let her go and leaned against the log wall. But Nancy did not move away. She stood where he had left her, within reach of his arm, quite still, thinking that it was a long time to have to wait for Hon, but glad to be away from the house and the Indians. She could hear his steady breathing just beside her.

Suddenly she was caught again in his arm and swung in front of him. His free hand came behind her back, forcing her against him so hard she thought she could almost feel the logs through his body. She felt his face feeling for hers, his chin scraped across her shoulder in the opening of her dress, moved over her cheek, and his mouth fastened upon hers. For an instant, startled and dizzy, she was inert against his chest. Then under the pressure of his arms her strength came to life. She put her arms around him, pulling herself even closer to him, and lifted her face.

She was silent as an animal. When suddenly he let her go, she stood before him trembling and still; but when he put his hands out again, she moved hard into his embrace. Her hands pressing into the small part of his back became clumsy. Her breath came out with a little moan at the end and her breast arched. She had no recollection of Hon left, only of herself and the man in her arms. He kept saying, "You . . ." without finding any other word to add to it.

Nancy lay in the long grass. The soldier was standing up, like a tower in the darkness rising from her feet. For an instant he was motionless. Then without as much as saying good-bye, he broke into a run away from the barn. Not towards the house, but back up the hill from the river. For an instant her disordered senses followed his crashing progress through the underbrush. Abruptly, the sound ceased, and Nancy, coming to herself at last, knew that something had gone wrong at Shoemaker's.

She heard men shouting, and feet stamping on the other side of the barn as men ran past. She sat up in the grass, fumbling for her shawl. Her hair was snarled and full of grass. Panic swept over her, and without thinking of Hon, only of the instinct to get hidden at home, she found the shawl and started running towards the road.

As she scrambled over the yard fence a man shouted, "There goes one!"

A musket roared behind her head, but she was too close to hear the bullet. She ran frantically, sobbing, and yanking at her skirt. For a moment she heard men pursuing, then she was out down the road and going for her life.

She did not stop until she was nearly home, and she stopped then only because she could not run another step. She veered from the road like a hurt deer and fell full length. She kept drawing her breath in great sobbing gasps.

She was still there when she heard the men tramping towards her down the road. Her first instinct was for renewed flight, but immediately afterwards she drew down into the sheltering brush like a hare in its form, to stare with horrified eyes at the approaching group.

Several of the men were carrying torches, and under the smoky light their bodies made a dark throng in the road, with the willow limbs like arms lifted above them.

They came without talking, in open files, their muskets on their shoulders, soldiers from the garrison at Fort Dayton, with the prisoners between them.

With them, at the head of the procession, Nancy's appalled eyes recognized Captain Demooth, and Gilbert Martin, his arm still bandaged, and one of the officers from the fort, a Colonel Brooks, who had sometimes come to supper at the Herter house. But as the files passed her she took her eyes from them and stared into the prisoners' faces. The first was the man who had been reading in Shoemaker's house, the man she had heard addressed as Ensign Butler. It was her first sight of Walter Butler, with his whittled attorney's face, black hair cut short, and black eyes. His mouth reminded her a little of McLonis's, long and thin-lipped, but, unlike McLonis's, tipped with a passion of contempt.

He was dressed in a scarlet coat with an ensign's tabs on the shoulders, and the men who followed him between the tramping files of Massachusetts soldiers were of the same regiment. She kept looking for McLonis, but he was not with them. He must have escaped. Her heart rose, even in her fright, until, as the last of the white prisoners passed, she saw her brother.

Even in the uncertain light Hon Yost looked as she remembered him, his yellow hair reaching to his shoulders, his straight features and red cheeks, and the blue eyes, irresponsible. He walked jauntily, as if he hadn't a fear in the world; but watching the faces of the garrison, Nancy sank down still lower in the brush, and bit her hand to keep from crying aloud. Before she could think what she should do, the tail of the procession was going by with the last torch shining on four captured Mohawk Indians.

The light flashed over their painted cheeks, picked out a wolf's head on the chest of the first, a drooping eagle's feather in his headdress. The light made a dark shine on their oiled skins.

It was not till long after they had gone, until she had seen the torchlights reflected in the water of the ford, that Nancy stumbled to her feet.

The Herter place was dark when she reached it, but, though she was still sobbing softly, she moved as quietly as she could round the corner of the barn. She had crossed halfway to the house when Clem Coppernol rose up in front of her, surrounding them both with his fog of rum.

"Who's that?" he asked unsteadily. As she tried to elude him, he stum-

bled forward and caught her skirt. He used it to help himself off his knees.
"'S a pullet anyways," he mumbled. "'S you Nancy, ain't it?"

"Yes," she whispered.

"Been out. I seen you going. I seen you. You can't lie." He nodded
against her shoulder. "Been to Shoemaker's. See Hon?"

She shivered and the tears gathered under her lids.

"No. No. I want to go to bed."

"Saw somebody. You tell me and I'll let you go," he said slyly.

"Yes. I saw a soldier."

He chuckled.

"Nice girl. So awful nice with me, ain't you? Bet a dollar you got laid."

"No," she said frantically.

"Did, though. Or you wouldn't act this way. Where's Hon?"

Her sobs started again.

"They caught him. They've taken him to the fort. What are they going
to do, Clem?"

"That's good. Good business." He scratched his head with his free hand.
"Probably they'll hang him. Hang the bunch. Yes, sir."

Nancy managed to whisper, "Please let me go."

"Maybe I will, and maybe I won't. You got to be nice to me now, or
I'll tell."

"I'll be nice."

"I'm still kind of drunk."

"Yes."

"But I ain't real drunk, neither." He paused to wipe his mouth. "You're
a good girl just the same, Nance. I'll stand up for you. If you've got
fixed, I'll marry you if you want."

Nancy sprang out of his grasp and fled for the house. He made no
move to chase her. He was open-mouthed in the darkness, trying to recollect what he had just said. Long after she had crept inside the house,
he remembered.

"By God!" he said aloud. "I am drunk."

7.   Death of a Brigadier

The unexpectedness of Butler's capture and the ease with which it had
been accomplished did much to hearten the Committee members of German Flats. It had had an immediate effect upon the people, checking all
danger of wholesale desertion to St. Leger's camp. Word got out about
when the prisoners were permitted to exercise and curious people went to
look at them in their regimental coats, walking up and down the small
parade space in the middle of the fort.

It seemed a wonder to them. The last time they remembered Walter
Butler was on that day in the spring two years before when he had ridden
up the valley with Sheriff White to cut down the liberty pole in front of
Herkimer Church. Then he had been a man to fear, as all the Johnsons
and Butlers were, with the law in his fist. Now they saw that he was a slight
man of nervous action, who took his exercise deliberately, making ten
circles of the parade,—they counted them, always ten,—looking neither

right nor left, his pale face inclined slightly forward. His soldiers might stop and chat with the guard or with the Palatines themselves; Hon Yost sometimes greeted former acquaintances and asked about his family; but Walter Butler seemed unaware of his surroundings. To the spectators he was more like the four Indians who always kept apart by themselves, not even speaking to each other.

Gilbert Martin, like the others, stopped one morning to watch, and afterwards went on to speak to Captain Demooth. He found the captain at the Herter house and asked, "When will those men be tried?"

"They're under military law. They'll have to be court-martialed, Gil. And Weston wants to wait for General Arnold. Technically he's under Arnold now, you see."

Gil said, "I should think it was better to get it over with. Some people there at Shoemaker's will lose their nerve."

The captain smiled a little.

"There are plenty of witnesses who won't. You, for one. That's why I sent for you the other night." His face grew serious. "And personally, Gil, I'm just as glad to have it put into the army's hands. I used to know the Butlers. They've got powerful friends. Some of our Committee would be afraid to convict him if the responsibility was on our shoulders."

"What will they do to him?"

"He'll be tried for a spy," Captain Demooth said dryly.

"How about the others?"

"I don't know about them. They were under orders. Prison, I guess. Except Hon Yost Schuyler. He's a deserter. He's on the rolls of the Third Company of Tryon militia. We can't let him off light."

"Has Nancy seen him? I've heard she was very fond of him."

"Mrs. Demooth's been having trouble with Nancy. She was hysterical when she heard about it. We thought it was better for her not to see her brother. Her mother thought so, too."

"He's just a half-wit," said Gil. "I don't see why he should be shot."

"It's not in our hands, Gil. And as I said before, I'm glad it isn't. How's your arm?"

"It's doing fine. But I can't use it much yet for work. That's one reason I came to see you. Mrs. McKlennar wants to know where she can hire a man. Our wheat's begun dropping."

"So has everybody's. If it isn't reaped inside the next two weeks we'll lose more than half the crop." He shook his head. "I don't know where you can find a man. There are plenty doing nothing in the forts. But they don't want to work. They don't want to do anything until Arnold gets here."

Gil said, "Yes." He hesitated. "Mrs. McKlennar wanted to know if you'd heard how General Herkimer was. She thought she might be able to rent one of his slaves for a week."

"I haven't heard from Herkimer for several days. His leg got mortified. And Petry can't get down to see it, so we don't know much."

"Do you think it would be all right if I went down to see him?"

"Why, yes. He'll probably be glad to have some news. You can tell him from me we've heard the First New York has got as far as Klock's."

Gil went down on the brown mare next morning. It was the first time he had ever been at Herkimer's house, and the size of it, together with the well-kept fields, impressed him.

A full-breasted negress met him at the door and said, "Gener'l ain' seein' nobody," in an impressive voice. Gil was ready to turn away when the right-hand door opened into the hall and Mrs. Herkimer came out.

"What is it, Frailty?"

"Dish yer man he's askin' fo' de Gener'l," Frailty said contemptuously.

Gil removed his hat.

"I'm from Mrs. McKlennar, ma'am. She wanted me to come down and find out if you could rent her a slave for a few days to get her wheat in. I work for her myself, but my arm's no good, now."

She glanced at the arm.

"Were you at the battle?"

"Yes," said Gil.

The pained look in her eyes increased. But she stepped back through the door.

"Come in. Honnikol's always glad to see anyone who was with him up there."

The general's big bed had been set up in the northwest room with its head to the fireplace so that he could look through the windows towards the river. Herkimer was wearing a flannel nightshirt open at the throat, showing the black hair on his chest, and to Gil, seeing him against the pillows, his shoulders looked heavier than he remembered them.

Herkimer's face was drawn, the mouth set, and it was obvious that he suffered a good deal of pain. But the black eyes stared keenly at Gil as he said, "Good morning."

His wife came over to the bed with a lighted candle for his pipe and he sucked on the stem without turning his eyes from Gil's.

"You want to see me about a nigger, ja? I heard you. How's Mrs. McKlennar? They keep me cooped up here, and I don't hear anything, not even how my neighbors are. I'm done with—old Herkimer—he lost his army. . . . Look! Aren't you the lad who picked me up mit Peter Bellinger and histed me up the hill?"

Gil turned brick red. It seemed to him a miracle that Herkimer, badly wounded, in the midst of that confusion, should remember a strange face. He nodded.

Herkimer said nothing either. Then he held his hand out. His grip was still strong.

"Sure," he said suddenly in a deep voice, "you can have a nigger." He looked across at his wife, who had sat down again in a corner, looking on with swimming eyes. "Tell Trip he's to go back with—what's your name, young man?"

"Gilbert Martin."

"Tell him with Mr. Martin, Maria. Tell him if he don't work hard I'll lick him myself when I get on my two feet." He made a gesture with his hand, as if he brushed the business aside, and at the same time he lifted his eyes to Gil's.

His eyes were tired and sad and, in a queer way, very shy.

"Will you be honest with an old man?" As Mrs. Herkimer made a cluck of protest, he shook his head. "I know. I'm only fifty-one, Maria, and young women don't like their husbands to say how old they feel." His smile made Gil feel the sadness more. "But it makes me feel old, nobody coming down here, nobody telling me anything. The army gets licked and I am brought down here in a boat and left here, *ja*. Tell me, Martin, what they're saying about me."

Gil did not know what to say, but the general did not help him out. "Tell the truth or don't say anything."

"They're saying nothing."

"And what do they think?"

"I don't know," said Gil miserably. Then he remembered the knoll before the second charge. "But, by God, there are plenty who were up there who wish you were back and kicking, Mr. Herkimer."

"Kicking." He looked down at his leg. He looked up again and sucked on his pipe. "I let myself get into a mess. I didn't have the insides to stand up to all those downriver gentlemens. This house, it was a mistake to build a big house just because I could. They did not like it." He came back to the point suddenly. "It was a good fight, though, once the fools was killed or run away."

The room was silent.

Finally, Herkimer asked from the pillows, "What's the news? What are they going to do with Butler?"

"They're waiting for General Arnold, sir."

"Benedict Arnold. He got up to Quebec, and then he didn't take it. I heard he was coming. Trip heard it in Frank's across the river," he added bitterly.

His wife spoke. "Honnikol, people don't think the way you think they do."

"No? Hardly anybody comes here. Only Warner und Peter. Und John Roof, because he's staying with me here." He shifted his shoulders. "When's Arnold coming?"

"Captain Demooth said to tell you the First New York was at Klock's last night. They ought to come by here this morning."

Herkimer's eyes brightened.

"That's good," he said. "*Ja*. Maria, open the window, so I can hear them when they come."

His depression lifted and for a while he talked to Gil about the early days in the valley. He talked about Oriskany and the men and what he had seen during the fight. It was surprising how many men and how many individual acts he had seen, until Gil remembered how he had sat up on his saddle throughout the whole six hours, in plain sight of everything.

He was still talking when they heard the first sound of the troops. At the moment it was like the distant ruffle of a drummer partridge in the still air. Then, suddenly, all three people in the room recognized the beat of drums. They heard the slap of bare feet running round the corner of the house from the slave cabins; a boy's voice shouting down at the dock.

"I can see them." The voice was shrill. Some of the negro children took it up. "*I can see them. I can see them.*"

Inside the room the three people stared at each other. For a moment all the yelling had obscured the sound of the drums. Mrs. Herkimer moved towards the window.

"*Nein,* Maria. Let them make a noise. I feel the same way also." He put his pipe down carefully. "But I can't see them."

Maria Herkimer's eyes filled again. Then she looked at Gil. "Do you think we could drag his bed to the window?"

"No," said Herkimer. "Call in the men. Trip, Joseph. Martin's got a bad arm."

Gil understood her silent pleading. She couldn't bear to have anyone else in the room. "Sure we can drag him." It took all their strength, he with his bad arm, she a slight woman, but they got the bed beside the window, and Herkimer heaved up on his elbow.

The drums, even from across the river, had now mastered the raised voices of the children. "It's the *flam,*" said Herkimer. The staccato double tap brought the shivers to Gil's spine. These drums hadn't the rattletrap sound of the militia. He felt courage as the flam was repeated, three times, a pulse between each beat. And then the drums with a crash banged out the opening bar of "Roslyn Castle."

With the pronouncement of the rhythm a sigh issued from the negroes' throats. Herkimer's fingers started picking at the blanket. "Fifes," he said suddenly. "*Ach Gott!* It is the army."

Through the beating of the drums the squealing of the fifes swept over the river like a cold wind, and close on the heels of the sound, made small by the distance, but clear against the dull green hillside, the troops came marching up the Kingsroad.

They made a compact blue stream above the fence rails, keeping close ranks, their rifles slanting rays of wood and iron on their shoulders, their cocked hats in rows for the eye to see. They marched like men who were accustomed to covering the ground, with a long stride, their faces stretched forward against the pull of the blanket rolls. They reached along the straight stretch of the road, two hundred and fifty men behind the drums, and slowly covered the great bend westward for the falls.

A break came in the line, and wagons passed to the same pace, the teamsters alert, keeping their horses up to the mark. Another break and two light cannon bounced on their light carriages. Behind them rode a group of officers, their horses' heads on the edge of the white powdery rise of dust. Then the rear guard. Fifty men.

Already the drums had passed from sight behind the river willows. But the fife sound floated behind. Long after it was still and gone, Gil thought he could hear the sound of them. He turned suddenly to Herkimer's voice.

"*Ach Gott.* One gompany. If they had only sent me up one gompany." His face did not change. He didn't hear the quiet crying of his wife.

Gil helped to move the bed back to its first place so nothing showed that it had been moved but the scrapes of its feet on the wide boards. Then he left. He did not say good-bye to the general, for it was obvious that the general could not talk. But Maria Herkimer followed him into the hall. "Trip will go back with you, Mr. Martin. God bless you." She reached up both her hands and took his face and kissed him.

Outside, Gil looked round him for the negro. He was surprised to see him coming from the ferry with an officer he had just rowed over, a fresh-faced young man in blue regimentals carrying a bag. He asked Gil, "Is this the Herkimer house?"

Gil nodded, and Mrs. Herkimer came out again to the hall.

"I'm Maria Herkimer, sir."

"General Arnold's compliments. I had instructions to stop in at General Herkimer's and see whether I might do anything to help him." He took his hat off, bowing. "Robert Johnson, ma'am. Surgeon, *pro tem*, First Regiment, the New York Line."

Waiting for Trip to reappear with his belongings, Gil overheard their voices.

"Come in, doctor. *Ja*. You can look at my leg."

A pause.

"Is Arnold far behind?"

"Ought to come by to-night, sir. He's been in a tearing hurry."

"It was kind of him to send you here."

"He was particular. Said something about you being too good to lose. Said it must have been a great piece of fighting."

Herkimer's voice deepened.

"*Ja*. He should have been there." Another silence. The doctor, saying in his fresh young voice, "I see. I see."

"You think it should come off? Petry said I should keep it. But he iss hurt und can't come down."

"Off? By gad, sir, it ought to have been off a week ago! With all respect. But these back-country surgeons sometimes . . ."

"Petry's a stubborn cuss. Don't get sick, Maria. It's no good to me anyway. I want some rum und my pipe. The one with the big bowl on it. *Ja*."

Gil realized that Trip was standing beside him. The negro's eyes rolled round to his.

"Yassah."

Without a word, Gil went down to the ferry.

It was all over in the northwest room. The surgeon, hat in hand, was saying good-bye. "I have to report to-night at Dayton."

Herkimer looked at him calmly with his black eyes. The room was full of smoke. The negress Frailty was gingerly carrying out the bloody sheet they had used to cover the table. Mrs. Herkimer, pale face swollen, swayed a little as she waited.

"Goot luck, doctor. Thank General Arnold for me."

"Thank you, sir."

"Tell me something. Did you ever cut off a leg before?"

The surgeon blushed.

"No, sir."

"Don't pe ashamed. A man has to start somewhere. I remember the first deer I shot." His face brightened suddenly. "Maria, have one of the poys find out if Boleo's at Warner's." He set down his pipe in the candlestick. His eye fell on the bundle in the corner.

"Give it to Johnny Roof to bury. It should please a poy to do that."

He sank back and closed his eyes. Nobody had heard him make a sound

beyond the grinding of his teeth. Now his breathing was like a blow repeated and repeated against the walls of the room.

While he slept, two boys took the severed leg and walked with it in the
orchard. They did not know where a good place would be until one thought
of the ox-heart cherry tree the general was so fond of. They dug the hole
and filled it.

While he slept, one of the negro lads went up to Warner Dygert's tavern
and gave the news of the amputation. Joe Boleo started getting sober then.
"My Jesus, what did they do that for?" He picked his rifle from the corner
and ambled unsteadily in the negro's wake. Already it was getting dark.

There was no light in the northwest room while Herkimer slept, for
Maria, from exhaustion, had fallen asleep herself in the chair by the hearth.
She was awakened by Joe Boleo's hand on hers. "It's Joe."

"Oh, Joe," she whispered back.

"They took his leg off?"

"Yes."

"I thought the nigger was lying."

She stirred softly under his hand and left the chair and went into the
dim light of the hall. She fetched a candle back. Together she and the
gangling trapper leaned over the bed.

"Poor old Honnikol. He never could get round very fast, anyways."

She gasped. She wasn't pointing at the white face in which the nose
seemed to have grown overlarge. Her finger pointed at the blanket.

Joe looked at the drench of blood and swore. He went right out himself
and woke the entire lot of negroes.

"Get up to Fort Dayton," he ordered. "Get Petry. Doc Petry. Bring
him down in a canoe if he can't ride. Tell him a fool army man cut off
Honnikol's leg and it's still bleeding."

He returned to the house.

"Hello, Honnikol."

"Joe?"

"Shut up," said Joe. He helped Maria Herkimer twist a tourniquet on
above the bloody stump. "We'd better leave the bandage on. It might clot
yet."

"I don't think so." Herkimer spoke quietly. "Get me my pipe, Maria,
and one for Joe, and beer for both of us. We both need beer. Me, I'm
thirsty. How about you, Joe?"

"Oh, my Jesus, Honnikol. I ain't drank in two weeks."

They smoked and drank through long hours, while Herkimer talked fitfully about old hunting trips. They didn't mention war. "Remember the
trout above Schell's riff?"

"Sure," said Joe. "Sure, Honnikol."

"I don't know what's become of all the fishing, Joe."

When Herkimer finally went to sleep, Joe left the room, wandering hopelessly to the river side. There was nothing to see. They couldn't bring
Petry down before morning. And the bleeding did not stop.

Making a restless circuit of the house, he met Johnny Roof and the other
lad standing in the orchard with two spades. "What you doing?" Joe asked
sourly. They said they'd heard the general was dying. They were wondering

about digging up his leg. "What for?" They said to bury with him. He merely cursed them. He walked around for an hour in the dark, leaving Honnikol to his wife. It was what a woman expected.

In the morning, Herkimer was not talking. Even when Colonel Willett came over the river and reported that General Arnold was passing on the north shore, Herkimer did no more than stare.

About nine, however, he rallied and asked for his pipe. When he had been smoking a little while he asked for his Bible, opened at the Thirty-eighth Psalm. He started to read aloud in a strong voice, but as he went on the voice started to fail. He did not appear to be aware of it, but read on, moving his lips slowly, and only now and then achieving utterance, so that his wife and the lank, uneasy woodsman, who leaned against the sunny window frame, heard only snatches:—

" 'O Lord, rebuke me not in thy wrath. . . .' "

8. *Arrival of a Major General*

The death of Herkimer shook the people. He had been the squire, the man with the money who had built a great house that rivaled Sir William Johnson's Hall. Now they remembered that he had been one of themselves, a quiet man, who came to dinner in his shirt, likely as not. They missed his steadfastness. The men who had been with him at Oriskany battle re-called how he had lit his pipe. Now that he was gone they had no one to depend on.

For three days. On the morning of the twentieth, officers on good mounts, wearing the blue coats of the regular army, rode the length of German Flats reading a proclamation.

> *By the Hon.* BENEDICT ARNOLD, *Esq., Major-General and Com-mander-in-chief of the army of the United States of America on the Mohawk River.*
>
> WHEREAS a certain Barry St. Leger, a Brigadier-general in the serv-ice of George of Great Britain, at the head of a banditti of robbers, murderers, and traitors, composed of savages of America, and more savage Britons (among whom is the noted Sir John Johnson, John Butler, and Daniel Claus), have lately appeared in the frontiers of this state . . .

It was not what the proclamation said that roused the people. There were too few Tories left in German Flats to make the promised amnesty applicable to themselves. It was rather the choice of words. Here was a man who put down what he said as if he meant it, who wasn't afraid of calling scoundrels by their proper names.

Militiamen who hadn't thought of heading west again began to talk of going along with Arnold's army. He was the man who had taken troops overland through Maine and would have conquered Quebec and all Can-ada but for one unlucky bullet that got him in the knee. In the knee, like Herkimer; the coincidence was striking. They listened to his invitation to all able-bodied men, militia or exempts, to join him in a victorious march against St. Leger's camp. But they waited awhile to see what he would do.

He did a lot. He made an inspection of the forts round German Flats. In each he made another speech about his expedition. He also urged the people out to take care of the wheat.

"This valley's not only got to feed you; it's got to feed General Washington's army. And the army will pay you high. Right now it's buying unmilled wheat at seven shilling." They listened to him, watching him—a black-visaged, hawk-like man, with arrogant round eyes and an opulent mouth. "You've got more than your families to look out for here. You've got the bread of the army in your care. That's what St. Leger's after. And that's what Gansevoort's saving by hanging out in Stanwix, and that's what we're going to save Gansevoort for." His face was flushed high; his voice had a queer habit of sliding up the scale; but they liked the way he walked up and down, light on his feet, like a man who knew the woods.

"Listen to me. Over in Bennington, Vermont, Colonel Stark and a bunch of minutemen captured and licked and manhandled five hundred Hessian cavalry. Do you know why the Hessians went over there? Because Burgoyne's getting pinched for food. General Schuyler has him bottled up. His murdering Indians have gone home, they can't find any more girls to kill, like Jenny McRae. He's just sitting still and praying for St. Leger, and that's what we're here to stop. Lick St. Leger and you lick Burgoyne. You people can do it. You damn near did. I'm here to help you take another whack at it, and both of us together can win this war, right here."

He had Learned's artillery manœuvre in Petry's field, and the men went from all the forts and stockades to look at cannon dragged on wheels. The soldiers lined one up and fired it down the river, and the awed people saw the heavy ball send up a tower of spray three hundred yards downstream. They thought of what that would have done to the Indians at Oriskany, and Arnold had a battery.

"By Jesus," said Joe Boleo, making his first emergence from his gloom, "I calculate I'll go along and see one of them balls let loose after Sillinger myself."

Arnold's next step was to court-martial Walter Butler. He appointed Willett Judge Advocate, which made men shake their heads and say conviction would be pretty near conclusive, with that arrangement. When they found that the trial was open to any and all spectators, they so crowded Dr. Petry's store that a guard had to be thrown round it to keep out late comers.

It gave them a strange thrill to see one of the men who had run the valley standing up before an officer. Butler was self-contained but scornful. He argued in his clear attorney's voice that he had come with a flag to parley with the inhabitants of German Flats. He did not know anything of this new law, he only knew the King's law. He did not consider it necessary to report to Colonel Weston, for he did not know of any Colonel Weston or of any Fort Dayton. The natural pallor of his face was not accentuated when he was brought back into court and sentenced to the pain and penalty of death. The new law he had scorned, as administered by Willett and Arnold, had ground him down. It gave all men pause for thought.

By contrast the succeeding trial of Hon Yost Schuyler as a deserter from the Tryon County militia was an anticlimax. But it showed that General Arnold was not missing any tricks at all; and some of the spectators were reminded how nearly they might have found themselves in Schuyler's shoes, guilty, and sentenced to a hundred lashes.

Arnold had no authority for court-martialing Butler. Both Gates and Schuyler had sent definite orders that the captured men be removed to Albany. But he and Willett had been putting on a show to divert attention from their unavoidable delay. The militia were not coming in as they had expected, and the commissary train as usual was lagging no one knew quite where.

That night while he and Willett sat together in headquarters tent trying to think up some new game and wondering whether they dared disobey instructions and execute Butler anyway, the guard announced two women to see the general. The women were Mrs. Schuyler and her daughter, Nancy.

Both officers were men to whom directness invariably appealed. Mrs. Schuyler wasted no time in pleading her own shame, she only mentioned that she was Herkimer's sister, they could see her position for themselves. She had brought a proposition from her son. If Arnold let him off, he guaranteed to go to Sillinger's camp and, pretending he had escaped from the American army, to put the fear of death into the Indians. He volunteered the information that when he left with Ensign Butler, the Indians were already getting restless. He believed that if the Indians left, the Tories, and maybe Sillinger himself, would lose their nerve.

It was the kind of notion to appeal to men like Arnold and Willett. They admitted it. But Arnold said, "What guarantee can you give us of your son's good faith?"

"I've brought my daughter with me," said Mrs. Schuyler. "You can keep her for a hostage."

Arnold studied Mrs. Schuyler and then glanced at Nancy's face. Nancy was pale and her eyes were wide with emotion. As she met the general's eye her lips parted. She had made the suggestion herself to her mother, and she was ready, if anything happened to Hon, to take his punishment.

Arnold smiled grimly.

"Mrs. Schuyler, you're too intelligent to think I could accept a girl for a hostage. What would people think of me if I ordered my sergeant to give a girl a hundred lashes on her bare back?"

Mrs. Schuyler sighed.

"I thought so. Very well, my son Nicholas has agreed to put himself in your hands till Hon returns."

Nancy's face flushed darkly, then it went pale again. And she stood there shivering. The two officers smiled sympathetically. It seemed quite natural; they admired her heroism. Her mother said, "Be still."

Nancy did not move or speak.

9. *Relief of Stanwix*

On the twenty-first of August, militiamen began to appear at Fort Dayton. They came from as far east as Klock's, and with the arrival of the first groups the men of German Flats started to turn out. By nightfall the count had reached three hundred, and Arnold called Willett and all local militia officers into his tent for a council of war.

"Gentlemen, we start to-morrow."

His eyes swept over the circle of faces, and fastened on the hesitant ones. Peter Tygert murmured, "Give us another day and maybe we can get another hundred rifles out for you."

"In another day," said Arnold, "Colonel Gansevoort may have to cut his way out of Fort Stanwix. It's my opinion we could be more useful there than here. You can fetch the other hundred along to-morrow." His eyes protruded at them. "This country's rotten with its hemstitch policies. It's time somebody acted. I'm going to. How about those militia? Are they decently organized?"

Captain Demooth said quietly, "They're pretty disorganized. A lot of the officers got shot or captured. Most of these men were in the first two companies."

Arnold nodded.

"Very well. I suggest that they be turned over to the surviving officers and made into an irregular brigade. Bring them along in the rear. They ought to shake down as we march. We march to-morrow after sunrise."

It was a still morning, a little cooler than usual. The river lay like glass between the rifts, not stirring the reflection of a leaf.

At dawn, so still was the air that from Little Stone Arabia Fort to El-dridge Blockhouse people heard the muster rolling of the army drums. Gil Martin, reporting, was appointed temporary sergeant of those of the Schuyler company whom he could get together. Of twenty-five he found eleven. Reall was dead, Weaver wounded, Kast wounded; of the other eleven men one was known to be dead, two taken prisoner, three wounded, and the rest disappeared.

Survivors of other companies even more unfortunate, Joe Boleo and Adam Helmer among them, asked to be attached to Demooth's company. They made a compact knot of men when Demooth himself rode up to count them. "Good work, Martin," he said, and wheeled his horse to let General Arnold pass on the narrow road.

But the general reined his horse.

"Is this your company, Captain?"

"Yes, sir."

"They aren't all sound."

"Sound enough, I think," said Captain Demooth.

Arnold smiled suddenly.

"By God, then, let them come. Do they know the woods? Good. I suggest they act as an advance guard." He turned to Gil. "Keep a quarter mile ahead of us."

The way he said it made Gil feel inordinately proud.

"Yes, sir." Then he asked, "How far will this day's march go, sir?"

"Just as far as we can get." Arnold grinned again. "You do a thorough job of combing the woods and I reckon we'll keep up."

They took the road, with the rolling of the drums recommencing behind them. It prickled their scalps to hear the fifes break out.

The woods covered them with their green silence and they went swiftly westward. In Gil there was a lifting of the heart. He nodded when Helmer said, "This beats the militia. Being our own men and eating nobody's dust." As soon as they had passed Schuyler, Joe Boleo and Helmer took over the direction of the company, but Joe Boleo was tactful about it.

"You ain't timber beasts like me and Helmer, Martin. The two of us can find out a whole lot more of what's going on if we don't have you to keep track of. The rest of you keep on the road and go a little slow. We'll let you know fast enough if we find anything. Wait at the ford until we pick you up, though."

The two men broke away and trotted forward into the woods, one on each side of the road. Their moccasined feet made no sound. Gil and the others continued along the road.

They could still see traces of the first march towards Stanwix; deep ruts off the road where an ox cart had bogged down, a rotting blanket, a dropped bayonet. But already the growth of the woods was beginning its work of hiding them. The ferns had straightened round the edges and grass was growing through a hole in the blanket. A deer runway crossing the road had blotted out the wheel tracks.

Well before noon they passed Deerfield and turned toward the river. There, where the oxen had balked, they sat down on the bank and ate.

They were still eating their food when Gil heard a hail from the woods across the river. Helmer appeared with his hand raised. A moment more and he had splashed over the ford. One look at his big handsome face told that he carried good news.

"Joe's got a squad of Gansevoort's men up the road. They say Sillinger's pulled foot."

"Pulled foot?"

"Yes, pulled foot. Bag and baggage. The Indians lit out yesterday. The whole mess of them, and Sillinger pulling his foot with the rest. They've left everything they've got behind." He burst out laughing.

The other men suddenly joined in.

"By Jesus!" A British brigadier galloping hell for leather down the Indian track towards Oneida. They could see it themselves. Bed, tent, writing desk, and chest of likker, cooking pots and silver forks, sword, spurs, epaulets, and oaths. They saw the whole shebang. "Pulled foot." It was a joke.

They fell silent after a few minutes and started looking at each other. "Where'd you find them?" Gil asked.

"About where Honnikol camped, at the crick."

"What are they doing there?"

"Eating," said Adam. "Eating their lunch. When Joe walked in on them they asked him to set down and eat."

Inexplicably they all burst out laughing again.

The rest of the march went swiftly. As soon as Arnold was notified he let his baggage and artillery come on at their own pace and pushed ahead with the troops alone. The army crossed the Mohawk early the next morning. Two hours later they had reached and forded Oriskany Creek.

Gil and his small company marched at the head of the column. As they went on they began to recognize the lay of the land and their talking gradually stopped.

It was Joe Boleo who first began sniffing. He stopped his shambling stride and lifted his face, and the others crowded up behind them.

"What's the matter, Joe?" Gil asked.

"Smell for yourself, lad."

He started forward again. The road was familiar now, running in the gloom of hemlocks above the river bottom. And as they proceeded they began to pick up more strongly the odor of decay that the woodsman had spotted long before.

It became an overpowering stench. It rose up in their faces, like a wall, through which they felt they could hardly pass. They found themselves suddenly on the edge of the ravine, staring down at the causeway. They all stopped again. Then Helmer said, "God! Come on," and they went down the incline and out along the corduroy.

Some of the men looked curiously right and left, but Gil, after one glance, kept his eyes to the track. And even then more than once he had to step carefully round the disintegration of the dead.

They lay, not as they had fallen, but as the foxes and wolves and Indian dogs had left them. The grass or ferns were trodden down around each body, impartially, horse or man, Indian or white; and the half-opened skeletons were like white roots of a miasmal wilderness.

Along the rising bank the corpses thinned out, the air seemed to lighten, and the men could hear each other breathing. Then on the plateau the frequency of dead was resumed, always thicker till they reached the edge of the gulch of the farther side; and here they lay so close together that the preying animals had not disturbed them all—postured as they had fallen, in the attitudes of fighting, or grasping the earth with swollen hands.

As they saw the end of the battleground ahead, the little knot of living men began to quicken pace. They were running when they finally rose on the far side of the gulch.

Presently, while they waited, they heard the sounds of the marching army far behind across the blanketing silence of those bodies. The tramp of feet coming down on the corduroy, the rattle of harness, and the jolt and clatter of the munition carts. There was a momentary disorder and halt, and Joe Boleo's sardonic voice inquired at large, "I wonder what Mr. Benedict Arnold makes of that?"

It was the first word any one of them had spoken. They looked in each other's faces, seeing them sallow and wet.

But then the first bluecoats were visible along the road. They came in two columns, their white breeches and the white facings on the buttoned-back skirts of their coats swinging steadily, as their solid boots trod heavily on the rough ground. They were marching at attention, eyes to the front, muskets at right shoulder. Above the heads of the first company, the shoulders and flushed face of Benedict Arnold rose to the extended branches of the trees, and his lips moved as if he talked to himself. His eyes looked blazing mad. Demooth's company of militia turned, all twenty-five as one, and took up the march again towards the fort.

At three o'clock the advance companies came out on the vlei land at the great bend of the Mohawk. Half a mile ahead, the walls of the fort stood square and brown above the grass, surrounding the low roofs of its four buildings. The sun, westering, picked out the sticks of the stockade along the south wall facing the army and shadowed the sally port.

But above this shadow, on the main or northeast flagstaff, the new flag hung in its bright colors. Even at that distance the men were able to make out the red and white stripes and the blue field. The air was too still to move it.

Men were moving across the fields outside the gate; a wagon was crawling towards the sally port from some abandoned tents on the high ground to the north; nowhere was there any sign of war.

The gathering resonance of the deep army drums reached onward past Gil's moving head. He saw a man spring up on the sentry walk and the men in the field scramble to their feet. The wagon halted momentarily. The horses turned their heads. The banging of the drums grew stronger, putting a lift in the tramping feet. The sun over the fort glanced in two sparks from the shoulders of an officer. Man after man appeared behind the points of the stockade. They seemed to stand in a frozen silence. Then, suddenly, hats were scaled in the air. Four cannon on the southeast station let loose orange bursts of flame and the entire side of the fort was engulfed in a black cloud of smoke. The thudding roars beat down the sound of drums; but they swelled again triumphantly. At a signal, the fifers licked their fifes and filled their cheeks. The shrill notes leaped upward, piercing the valley.

As he walked, Gil watched the black smoke from the cannon rising over the stockade until it obscured even the flagstaff. Then it began to drift gradually towards the north. When it had vanished he saw the flag as it had been, limp against the flagpole. But now it brought him a strange sensation that it was his and that it hung in victory and peace.

10.   Dr. Petry Sees Two Patients

The mid-October sun was already low over the southwest hills as Dr. Petry rode his old gray horse homeward past Herkimer Church. The fort looked almost deserted. Only George Weaver's family and the Realls were living in it now, besides the small remaining garrison; and George Weaver no longer needed his services. He was just as glad, for Emma Weaver had become so concerned about her son John and one of the Reall girls that she was unpleasant company. The jealousy of an ambitious mother: Emma, for all her homely face, had strong passions for all her menfolks. And then, he was tired.

He was so tired that if it hadn't been for Bell's abominable hen squawking in the sack behind the cantle, Dr. Petry would have been dozing in comfort.

He had long ago caught the trick of sleeping in the saddle. The old gray horse had a steadfast sort of ambling gait; his back was flat and broad enough to lay a table on, and he knew every road, bridge, ford, and footpath in the western half of Tryon County. People said that he knew every patient as well, and what was wrong with him, and what the prescription ought to be.

Now the doctor took off his hat and banged it behind him against the sack, causing an unexpected fluttering commotion. The silence was grateful and complete. He put his hat back on his head, tilting it well forward, and closed his eyes under the brim. Well, when he got home, he'd take his boots off and sit down and have a drink before the fire. A fire would feel good. The cold was getting more pronounced and he thought they were not far off from frost. He could feel admonitory twinges in his wounded foot. It was a good thing people were getting in the last of the corn. They had got it all in at Andrustown; they were going to have a bee there next week for the husking and had asked the doctor to spread the word of it.

"God damn that God-damn hen." She was making a little moaning in her nose, or bill, or wherever it was. He hadn't wanted her. He was sick of poultry round the house, but George Bell swore she was a layer, and an egg in his rum, now . . . Well, a man oughn't to complain. It was all Bell had to pay with. It was all the pay he had collected for his thirty-mile ride. He had started at four o'clock that morning, and here it was past five in the afternoon.

But a man ought not to complain. The crops were in and they were good this year. The price of wheat was soaring. Bill Petry ought to collect on a few back accounts this winter. It surely looked as if the war were over, now that St. Leger had skedaddled back to Canada, frightened off by the simple lies of Hon Yost Schuyler. Hon himself, the hero of the day, seemed to have returned to his American allegiance. Fort Stanwix was in first-rate order, with that unswerving, stolid Dutchman, Gansevoort, returned to the command. And best news of all, a battle had been fought with Burgoyne at a place called Freeman's Farm, three weeks ago, and it had been a stand-off. But they said the American army had swelled to twenty thousand men (that ought to make an earful for the King of England) and Burgoyne couldn't even run away. They had him, and they ought to lick him any day. There wasn't any question that Great Britain would have to give in and recognize American Independence. . . .

Let the damn hen squawk. The doctor grinned a little and the old horse pricked his ears and turned for the ford. They were home in half an hour; the horse amiably waiting while Doc uncreaked his weary legs and got them off, and then taking his own way to the barn. The doctor let him go. He entered his kitchen, carrying the bag, and sniffed at the pot on the fire. "What is it?" he asked the negro woman. "Dat's rabbit stew"—with turnips and cider vinegar and flour gravy thickening in the pan to a dark, rich, voluptuous brown.

"Bring me a glass of the Kingston rum," said the doctor, "and here's a hen for you to mind."

The negress, eager for something new, made little soothing sounds as she cautiously opened the sack.

"You ain't been 'busin' her, has you, Doc? She lay so daid. My Lawd, de messin'es' bird. My Lawd! Oh, de poor perty . . . Watch out! You make any of dem desperate messes in mah kitchen and you's gwine to fin' yo'se'f de makin's of de gravy, chickun!" Her black hand had the pullet by the neck.

The doctor chuckled, and went to the store to enter a note in his ledger against the government. He was writing it down in his careful hand:—

> 1777, October 14, George Bell, to one stab wound in thigh, and scalped. Dressed scalp twice a day. Under my steady care six weeks and this day visited and dismissed, cured . . . £16.0.0.

A knock on the store door startled him. The evening was already growing dark, but he could hear a timid hand fiddling with the latchstring. "Come in," he called.

The door opened and closed quickly at the farther end of the store, and the doctor said heavily, "I don't see people this time of day."

The woman stopped short, timidly. He peered at her. But she wore her shawl all the way over her head.

"Who the devil are you?" he demanded.

"I'm Nancy Schuyler." Her voice was hushed and breathless. "I know it ain't the time to come and see you; but Captain had to go to the fort after supper and Missis went with him; she wanted the air."

"Well, girl, what's that got to do with it?"

"I didn't want them to know I was here."

"Oh," he said. He began grumbling half aloud, something about the old business, and a man having supper, and he supposed he ought to look. "Well, what's the matter?" he asked aloud.

Nancy was flushing inside her shawl so painfully she thought something in her would burst. But at his question she turned white.

"I don't know," she said. "I've been being sick. Sometimes I can't hardly get to do my work in the mornings. But I don't know."

The doctor groaned and heaved himself out of his chair. He went to the windows one by one, closing the shutters, and then pulled in the latchstring. Then he took a sulphur wick and went out into the kitchen and lit it at the fire, and came back and lit the lamp on the counter. He cleared away some blankets, a jar of bear grease, a pot of bean seeds, and some Indian beads.

"Well," he said roughly, "get up on it."

Nancy was trembling so badly that she hardly had the strength to get up on the counter and lie down. When he touched her she shivered convulsively.

"That's all," said the doctor, going behind the counter to a pail and basin and starting to wash his hands, giving her time to get down and straighten herself out. "When did it happen?"

"In August," said Nancy in a hushed voice.

"*When*, I said?"

"I don't know. It was the day they arrested Hon."

"Was it one of them?"

She nodded. He glared down at her through his frowning long-haired brows. She was so damn good-looking and there were times when she almost looked intelligent. As now, when she was worried; the way she lifted her chin at him, chewing at her lip. "How in God's name did he get at you at Demooth's?"

"I went up to Shoemaker's that night."

"Where were you when we got there?"

"Out back of the barn."

"I bet."

Nancy didn't notice.

"He got away, they never heard him, but they chased me."

"Then you were the fellow they chased down over the fields? They shot at you?" Nancy nodded, and the doctor breathed through his nose. "They said it was a heavy man, about six foot tall, with long black hair! You must have run like blind destruction."

"I was scared."

"What are you going to do about this, Nancy?"

She was silent.

"You want that I should straighten it out, hey? Well, who was the fellow did it?"

"Jurry McLonis," she said in a hushed voice.

The doctor swore.

"That black-complected Mick, eh?"

"He was nice to me," Nancy said.

"He seems to have been. Well, there's no way I can get hold of him that I can see. He's probably in Niagara, Oswego at the nearest. I guess you'll have to button up and made the best kind of a job you can. I'll see Captain Demooth, if you like. You went up to find Hon, of course, and then this fellow took advantage of you." He was sarcastic.

Her eyes filled with tears.

"I did. But he didn't, doctor. It just was."

"You'd like to marry him if I can get hold of him?"

"Yes, doctor."

"Well, I'll see what I can do. Now get out. I want some rest. I've ridden thirty miles to-day." He put his hand on her shoulder, marching her to the door.

"But, doctor?"

"Well . . ."

"You didn't say was I going to have a baby?"

"What do you think I was talking to you about? Yes. Yes. Yes!"

"Thank you, doctor. When will it?"

"It takes nine months." He counted his fingers savagely just in front of her face. "May."

"It wouldn't be sooner?" she asked eagerly.

"Hell, no. The insides of a girl like you are just like a clock. Say May thirteenth at half-past twelve at night." He pushed her through the door, slammed it after her, and went back to his chair and called to Chloe. "Chloe, bring that rum here and then get me another glass ready. I'll drink the second one in there."

"Yes, suh!"

Chloe came sweeping in behind her bosom, the little finger of the hand that carried the glass cocked doggily. "Missis say supper's ready when you is." God help all doctors.

"Yes, Chloe. I want to sit down first. Here. And then by the fire. I want to edge up to eating."

"Yes, *suh!*" Chloe whipped her huge bulk away with her uncanny nimbleness. The doctor sipped his glass. The door was tapped.

"Who's that?" roared the doctor.

A woman answered. He didn't recognize the voice. "Go away," he shouted. Then he was ashamed. If he hadn't been so tired he could have sent her away, but being so tired he couldn't defend himself. He would work himself to death.

"Wait a minute," he shouted, and closed the door into the house. Then he opened the store door.

"I didn't mean to disturb you, doctor."

He peered into the darkness. "Who is it?"

"Magdelana Martin, doctor."

His face cleared suddenly. Of course, Martin's pretty wife. A bright girl. It would be fun having her after that half-animal half-wit. "Come in, Mrs. Martin. You mustn't mind my growls. Did you want to see me about yourself?"

"Yes, doctor. But it won't take long."

"Well, come and sit down. Do you like egg and rum? Never tried it? Where were you brought up? Taste some of my glass."

Lana obligingly bent forward towards his hand. It pleased him to hold something to her lips. She took it like a bird. He began to feel sentimental.

"Like it?"

Lana nodded.

"Chloe. Bring that second glass."

"Oh no, thanks, doctor."

"Do you good."

"I oughn't to now. That's what I came to see you about." She looked at him frankly. "I'm pregnant, doctor, and I want to find out if after—after that time, I ought to be especially careful about anything."

"Lord, no. You're all right. If you want it."

"Yes, I do."

"That's fine. I'm eternally glad, I tell you. I was sorry about you. It's the best thing. It's woman's natural function, Mrs. Martin, and you're a fine healthy girl. When do you expect it?"

Lana, remembering, colored slightly; but she smiled at the same time. "Sometime after the first week in May."

The doctor didn't even swear. He just popped out his eyes and stared. He looked so funny that Lana started laughing.

"I must be kind of a ghost."

"Oh, no. No, indeed." He cleared his throat. "It just happens another girl is expecting almost the identical time. She was in just before you and I'm beginning to wonder what's been going on with my patients." He glanced at her. "Will you be round this district, then?"

"Yes. Gil said we'd stay till the baby was born. He seems so pleased." Her lips trembled. "Oh, doctor, I feel as if I'd just begun living again."

"Yes, yes." Chloe knocking, he called her in. "Give that to Mrs. Martin. Drink it, girl. It's a good thing to celebrate with. Here's to Gilly or Magdelana second. Or both!" He laughed.

Lana laughed and drank with him.

"Afterwards, Gil talks about our moving back to Deerfield. He thinks we might get back in time to get our spring corn in. The Weavers will go with us."

"Fine," he said. "Fine. How's your husband, by the way? Arm troubling him any?"

"Not a bit. He came down to meet Captain Demooth at the fort. We thought it might be about their taking Burgoyne, and I walked along hoping I'd see you here."

"We ought to be having news."

He showed her out and sat down again. A fine girl. He was feeling better. He was going to have a busy spring, though. Very busy. Well, he might as well get in to supper.

He went in and kissed his wife dutifully and Chloe served them. He was just starting on the rabbit stew when Demooth appeared.

"Doc," he said. "Can you come down to Ellis's at the falls? Right now. I said I'd drive you down."

"What's the matter, Mark?"

"There's been trouble in Jerseyfield. You know that man George Mount who wouldn't move down when St. Leger was at Oriskany?"

Petry nodded and stuffed his mouth full.

"Well, I saw him in Ellis's a few days ago. He'd brought his wife down to buy some things at Paris's. They were gone from home a week, and they'd left the two boys there with his nigger. Well, he went back. He found his place burned and the two lads scalped. One of them was still alive and he brought him out with the nigger. They hadn't touched the nigger. The boy's only seven and they say he can't live, but Mount wondered whether you'd come down."

The doctor dropped a morsel of rabbit.

He stared like a fish.

Then he wiped his mouth, and spoke slowly, "It isn't over, then."

Demooth's face was drawn and bitter.

"It was two Indians that used to stay with Mount. Caderoque and Hess. The nigger recognized them. There were some white men in the same party. They didn't do any scalping. They only shot the first boy."

"Did the nigger recognize any of them?"

"He recognized Suffrenes Casselman. And he said the head man was called Caldwell."

5

JOHN WOLFF'S JOURNEY (1777)

1. *The Cavern*

JOHN WOLFF had been in Newgate Prison for over a year, but he wasn't sure himself how long it was. He seemed to have lost the sense of time.

There were days when he couldn't have said offhand whether it was *to-day,* or *yesterday;* they were days beyond track.

Sometimes he would catch himself saying the days of the week, *"Monday, Tuesday, Wednesday . . ."* Or the months of the year. There were many things he used to say. *"Lucy Locket, lost her pocket . . ."* Sometimes he would wake up some of the near-by prisoners and they would throw odd pieces of rock at his bed and yell. It was awful when the men yelled. It started the echoes whirling in the high air shaft, seventy feet high. It was fifty feet across at the bottom, they said, though you couldn't find that out by pacing because the water lapped against the far side. But at the top the shaft was four feet across with an iron grating fixed into the stone; and what with the smoke from the charcoal braziers one could hardly tell where the sun was in the sky, except at noon. A little before and a little after summer solstice, you could see the sun itself upon the grating if you waded out into the water far enough. You could even imagine a faint warmth from it on your head. John Wolff had felt it, and the next man, walking out, felt it also, but he started a convulsion, and they had to haul him out of the water for fear he would drown.

But when the men started yelling and got the echoes going, it used to make John Wolff feel sick. The voices would start picking each other up, catching and passing each other, and coming up and down, until the echoes managed to acquire individual personality of their own, having echoes of their own, and the echoes had echoes, and it went on and on, a bedlam that wouldn't die even when the trapdoor opened above the iron ladder and the guard looked down and yelled back furiously. Then the men would work on the echoes and a queer singsong rise and fall would be worked out that, even after everyone was tired, kept the echoes working endlessly.

It was like the eternal drip of water magnified. The drip of water had the same effect, when everyone was silent. At first you would notice it on the wall right beside you. Drip, and a pause; drip, and a pause. Gradually this soft impingement of a single drop would lead you to listen for drops farther away, and soon your ears would become attuned to drops much farther off. Then you would begin to be aware of the graduation of loudness that distance made, and all at once the drop you had first noticed would have the regular clang of a ringing bell. You couldn't then put it back into its proper equivalent in the sound of sense.

Sometimes a man would get up from his wet straw and work at the bare rock for hours to change the direction of an individual drip, so that its sound would be altered and thus restored to a sane proportion.

But one night when the men were making their singsong, it happened that the guard was drunk. Maybe the guard went a little crazy himself. Anyway, he opened the trap and fired his musket. They could all see him, fifty feet above their heads in the lighted square of the trap, his furious red face, and the musket pointing down like the finger of wrathful retribution. The bullet striking made no sound through the yelling voices and they yelled twice as loud. Even John Wolff yelled that night. And the guard lost his head entirely. He fired again and again, and finally a ball ricocheted and killed one of the prisoners. He was the man who had come in with John Wolff, the man who had beaten a soldier for molesting his wife.

But they did not notice he had died till it was time for them to go up the next day.

They had to haul him up with a rope and carry him to the smithy so that his irons could be taken off. Then he had been buried, and the commandant, Captain Viets, in a fury, had had half a dozen men flogged, choosing the ones the outraged guard who had committed the murder pointed out, and one man, who owed the guard three shillings, was hung by his heels for an hour and a half. Nobody had had any food for two days, but the guard did well instead, for it was necessary for the prison to consume its full ration of beef if the commandant were to receive his regular allowance.

It was odd, after that, to think of the dead man. He was buried in the prison yard. And yet he was sixty feet above any of his fellow prisoners. He was decomposing somewhere underground, but they were still more underground than he. Waiting for him to come down, one man said: "to come down in drops of water." He embarked on an intricate calculation of how long it would take the first drop to come down to their level. John Wolff started watching the drops on the stone beside his bed.

Now and then long firey discussions would start up over the progress of the British army. They all knew one was on the way. But the guard would give them no news. The guard struck a man if he asked. They gathered from that that the army was making progress. But one night the commandant himself opened the trap and they saw his bare legs squatting under his nightshirt as he yelled down, Did they want to hear about General Burgoyne? They let the drops answer. But Captain Viets wasn't to be stopped. "He's surrendered his entire army. Seven thousand men," he bawled. "And the Hessians have been licked at Bennington, Vermont, and Sillinger has been driven off from Fort Stanwix by Benedict Arnold. How do you like that? Hey?"

Purely from habit they started their singsong and he had to slam the door shut. They kept the singsong up all night. They knew now that all hope of their being rescued from the caverns must be deferred. In fact it was a question now if they ever would get out. People didn't even know where they were, a lot of them. They didn't really know themselves. They were conscious only of the vast formation of rock that was above them. Black tons of it, they thought. A person wouldn't think of looking for a man so deep down in the rock.

For a week afterwards they beguiled themselves by saying what they thought of General Burgoyne. They imagined General Burgoyne if he were put down among them. They wondered if he would be. But people like General Burgoyne, who made war and brought Indians and wore epaulets and carried his private whiskey with him, weren't ever put in places like this. Only a person who preached in the pulpit for the King, or who said he was a Loyalist, or who owed a new Yankee judge some money, or who hit a soldier who was raping his wife—only that man was an atrocious villain.

2. *The Drainage Level*

Most of them thought John Wolff was going crazy. He was not aware of it himself. Only he liked to repeat things he knew. And he also dictated to himself letters to his wife every week, though he hadn't money to smuggle them out if he had been able to write them. He would ask her to write what she was doing and then he would say what had happened in the prison. The letters sounded pretty much alike even to himself. He got tired of them. The day after the captain delivered the news of Burgoyne's surrender, he wrote Ally about it; but then he could think of nothing to add. The Mr. Henry who had first welcomed him to the caverns asked what the trouble was. "I'm writing my wife, Alice," explained John Wolff, "but I can't think of anything new to tell her."

"Have you described this lovely home of ours?" said Mr. Henry.

"No, I haven't."

"Why don't you? Take a look around and see what there is to see."

Several men laughed, but John Wolff did not mind. It was an idea. He began looking round and made up his letter, about the air shaft and the beds and the queer beach of sand and the water. "The water is queer," he said, "the water keeps dropping down off the walls all the while and the water don't never get higher nor lower." He realized that he was saying something nobody had noticed.

Suddenly John Wolff came out of his daze and he had a long fit of the shakes. But they were not the damp shakes that everybody had. He was shaking with excitement. He went and looked at the water.

He said, "Has anybody ever tried to wade out there?"

"It's too deep," one of the men said.

"Has anybody tried to swim?" asked John Wolff.

A roar of laughter went up. One of the men reached out and rattled the chains connecting his ankle and wrist fetters. "Try and swim with forty pounds," he suggested. John Wolff stood in their midst looking at their faces, gaunt and filthy with rock dust and charcoal smoke and unwashed beards. It came to him that he must look like that himself. His hand went to his beard. He had never had a beard before. He had always shaved.

Then his eyes grew cunning. He felt them growing so and closed the lids lest the other men should see it, and he went and lay down. They were still making jokes about him when the guard opened the door and shouted at them to "Heave up!" for their exercise.

From his bed, John Wolff watched them clambering toilsomely up the ladder, their chains clashing against the iron rungs, as they fought upward with one hand and carried the night buckets with the other. The smoke from the braziers drew into the guardroom and the guard stepped away from the door. John Wolff lay there till they had all gone up.

"Hey, you!" the guard yelled. "What's your name, Wolff!"

John Wolff didn't answer.

"Come up."

John Wolff remembered all the filth he had ever heard and sent it up to the guard. The guard laughed. "All right," he said. "Stay down. Stay down for a week." Wolff was a harmless man, not worth coming down for and lugging up and flogging. He slammed the trap shut.

John Wolff got up. He clanked slowly down to the beach, looking at the water. Then he started rummaging in the straw beds. Some of the prisoners had bought pieces of plank from the guard, to put under the straw. He hadn't any himself because they cost a shilling a foot. Moving with the slow, half-hopping motion the irons forced him to use, he took down planks and put them in the water. They floated soggily. He got more. He laid them on top of each other, side by side. Then he waded out and straddled them and tentatively pulled up his feet. The planks sank under him and he rummaged for more. He finally had enough to float him and he tied them together with strips torn from his blanket.

He straddled the raft and pushed it out with his feet. He paddled with his hands. The weight of the irons made his hands splash no matter how careful he was. But he had only a little way to go to get out of the brazier lights.

John Wolff had thought a long time about which shaft to choose. But as he could not make up his mind he chose the farthest. When he entered it, the noise of his splashing diminished. The light behind him was circumscribed by the low ceiling of the shaft and the flat level of the water. Looking back, it seemed to him that he had come a great distance. He could not see far ahead, because the shaft made a turn. He paddled slowly round that, and then in the darkness that instantly became complete he felt the front of his raft strike the rock. The blow was very slight, but it almost knocked him forward off balance. He barely saved himself by lifting his hands and bracing himself against the rock wall. He realized that the drift was filled to the ceiling, and that there was no way out. He felt all round the water level to make sure and then tried to turn his raft.

There was not room to turn it in the darkness, and he had to back out. It was a laborious and painful process. His arms dragged and his legs had gone cold and numb, except for the ache the cold made in his ankle scars.

When he came back into view of the sand beach and the smouldering braziers and the mussed straw of the beds he had despoiled of planks, he was sobbing with exhaustion. He lay forward along the boards, eyes shut. From a vague sense of habit he started dictating a letter to Ally. "The right drift is full of water so I can't get out that way. I shall have to try the other one. It is so hard to paddle."

Then it occurred to him that he could not wait another day. It would take almost as long to get fifty feet back to shore as to paddle into the next drift. In either case he would not have time to put the planks back under the straw. They ducked men who monkeyed with the beds of others. It took two weeks to get dry.

John decided to paddle into the next drift.

Again the splashing he made seemed to crash against the upward walls of the air shaft. But again the noise was shut off when he finally entered the second drift.

He had been working for an hour to cover his hundred feet or so of progress and the men should be coming down soon. He forced himself to keep at it until the last reflected light of the water was left behind. Then he came to a slight curve and continued round that, and then he stopped.

He had a sudden new sensation. The sweat was pouring out of his skin. It was the first time he had sweated for months. It made him feel weak, as if the whole energy of his body had been put to work at the process of creating sweat in him; but at the same time he felt an access of courage because he was able to sweat.

It gave his hands power to paddle on. Behind, and far away, shut off by the rock wall, he heard the muffled clanking as the men started coming down the ladder. He kept on.

It was dark now, and he was scraping the side of the drift. But he kept paddling. When he heard his name called behind him, the sound was dim and the echoes that entered the drift were mere whispers of his name,— *John Wolff, John Wolff,*—like voices for a person departing this world.

His arms lifted and fell and lifted. He had gone a long way. He was not completely conscious any more of what he was doing. He was quite unprepared when the raft struck a projection of the wall, dumping him sideways off the board into the water. His last flurry broke the wrappings of the raft and the boards came apart. He thought he would drown. Then he struck bottom. He stood up and his head came out of water. Against his wet face, in the dark, he felt an icy draft of air.

He started wading. The bottom was quite smooth, but the water deepened. It reached his chin. He knew that he was going in the right direction, because the air still drew against his forehead.

The boards were now out of his reach and it was too dark to see anything, anyway. John Wolff stood still in the water, thinking aloud: "Dear Ally, the water is up to my mouth. It is getting deeper. But there is surely air coming along this drift and I can't get back and I figure to go ahead. It is better to drown than to stand still in water. It is not very cold water, but it makes me shake some. Otherwise I am well and hoping you are the same. . . ." He drew a deep breath and took a full stride forward.

The water fell away from his chin, from his throat. He felt the cold air against his wishbone. He drew another breath and took still another step and the water dropped halfway to his waist. He shouted.

It was thin sound and it was drowned by his sudden threshing in the water. All at once he was reaching down, holding tight the chains to his ankles and floundering knee-deep along a narrow stream. The air was cold all over him. He went on for half a dozen yards and shouted again. There was light on the right-hand wall. Faint, but actual light. Daylight. He turned the corner to the left and saw the dazzle on the water which now ran downhill quite fast through a small tunnel that seemed to narrow to the dimension of a large culvert. He had to bend and get on his knees. He took another turn as he dragged himself in the water, and he saw ahead of him the gray of woods in October.

But between him and the woods was a wooden grille.

It shocked and amazed him to find that grille after so long and baffling a distance. It seemed to him a malicious manifestation of the godlessness in man. In its way it seemed to him infinitely more wicked than the trial which had sent him to prison in the first place.

He dragged himself up to it and put his hands against the lower bar and rested his head on his hands. The shakes were getting hold of him again. He closed his eyes, and let go of his body.

He felt the grille shaking as he shook and opened his eyes. It came to him that the wood was old and the joints the crossbars made with the frame were very rotten. He braced his feet against a stone and threw his weight against the grille.

The whole business gave way, tumbling out under him down the steep hillside. He fell with it, with a last clank of his irons, rolled over down the slope, and came to rest with his face upward, seeing the breast of the hill against the sky. He lay still, weeping.

A cold rain was falling steadily.

3. *The Hammer*

In two hours, he had covered a mile and a half through the woods. He had got beyond caring about the noise he made. Just after sunset he struck a path that led him into a pasture.

The pasture sloped toward a valley through which a road ran. On the road were a small house, with a barn attached to it by a woodshed, and a building that had a chimney and looked like a forge. The wet bricks shone faintly in the light from the house window.

He stopped with the rain beating down on him, and stared at the lighted fire visible through the kitchen window. The whole world smelled wet and cold.

Presently a man came out of the house and went to the barn. John Wolff could hardly credit this good luck as he saw the man lead out a horse and take it to the front door. The man waited there while a woman came out, shawling herself against the rain, and let the man help her onto the pillion. He then mounted in front of her and yelled to someone in the house to bar the door till they came back.

John Wolff could hear the answer in a negro voice. It sounded like a woman's. The man said they would return in two hours. He kicked the horse to a trot down the road in the rain.

As soon as he was gone, John Wolff started down the hill. He went first to the building he thought might be a smithy and opened the door. There was enough light in the banked fire to show him the anvil and the hammers and files.

He was like a man obsessed. He made no effort to be quiet, but picked up one of the hammers and started striking on the seams of his wrist bands. It was hard to get a good swing. His aim was clumsy from the cold and the hammer head kept rolling off the iron onto his arm. But the seam cracked finally and he pulled the iron loose. For a minute he stood looking at the rusty imprint on his wrist. Then he slowly flexed his arm and raised it over his head. He felt as if his fist could strike high heaven.

He broke the other fetter handily enough and began to work on the anklets. These were harder to break, for it was almost impossible to keep his leg on the anvil within striking distance of his arm and yet get a free swing with the hammer. Finally he thought of tipping the anvil over.

It took all his strength to do it, and the anvil teetered a long time before he could overbalance it. It fell with a terrific crash, but John Wolff did not seem to notice the noise until the screaming of the negro woman in the house broke in on his hearing. He lifted his chin and automatically started to join her—as if it were the singsong starting back in the cavern.

Then he remembered what he was doing and held his ankle against the anvil and swung the hammer with both hands. The seam smashed all to pieces. He broke the second at the first blow.

The negress was still shrieking over in the house, and John Wolff listened to her, cocking his head a little, while a queer look of cunning came into his eyes. The hand which held the hammer began to swing with little jerks. Suddenly he became aware of the motion of his hand and stopped it. He stood quite still with a growing excitement on his face and his breath coming and going sharply.

At his first step he nearly toppled over on his face. He recovered himself, went out through the door, and closed it behind him with great care. He stopped for a moment more, turning his head towards the house as if he tasted the fear in the black woman's shrieks. The hand holding the hammer twitched again. He started for the house.

Habit forced his legs into the queer hobbling gait the shackles had trained them to; but the release from the weight deprived them of all sense of balance. He kept lurching forward; and on the second hop he measured his length in the mud of the yard. He scrambled up and forced himself to move more slowly until he had got onto the porch. He knocked on the door. At the first blow the woman stopped screaming.

He forced his hand to knock gently again: this started the woman off on her shrieks and he listened with his ear to the panel. When she stopped, the house was quiet as death, with only the sound of the rain dripping from the eaves.

The drip distracted him until he heard the woman moan inside the house, and then the sound of her feet sneaking towards the back.

It infuriated him. He raised the hammer with both hands and smashed it against the door. It was an eight-pound hammer and he broke in a panel in half a dozen blows. He became intoxicated with the destruction he was making of the door and forgot all about the woman. He knocked in the panels one by one and hammered at the bar behind them until the bar fell away, brackets and all. Then he opened the door and walked into the warm lighted room.

A fire was burning on the hearth and a kettle was steaming. He had not seen a kettle with a spout for more than a year. The hammer dropped out of his hand, clanked on the hearthstones, but he let it lie.

He thought he was standing steady, but he was weaving on his feet. He had forgotten all about the woman; even when she stole down the stairs to see what had become of him he did not hear her. She stood there watching him with her round eyes rolling the whites in her black face and her lips hanging flabbily open.

She saw a man so thin he hardly seemed like a man at all, with a mess of light brown hair showing white streaks and hanging down on his shoulders, and a matted beard and a torn shirt, and rotten wet trousers and bare feet. The feet were bleeding. She saw the blood on the hearthstones. And then she saw the fetter scars on his ankles and wrists.

"Lan' sakes," she breathed. "You ain' no booger, is you?" His chin lifted, but his glazed eyes did not shift from the kettle. "If I could have a cup of tea . . ." He sat down weakly. The negress was a young wench. Her curiosity and sympathy were powerfully aroused. "You one of de prison people," she announced. She nodded as he did not contradict her. "Soon as I lay my eyes on you, I say, 'Leeza, dat am one of de prison people. He got put in jes' like ol' Massa. Dat's what he did.' " She came forward. "Co'se you can have some tea. And I'll jes' bring along some eatables wid it." She flurried about her job, chattering, "Dey takes away de hones' people. Dey takes me away f'um 'em. Mistah Phelps he join de Committee of Safety and he get to be a powerful big man and he get me when dey lock up my ol' fambly. He's gone to de Committee to-night. He used to go by hisse'f, but since he tuk to fallin' off de horse, Missis she jest obliged to go wid um. Lot of de wimmen folks has to now. Dey have their party and de man they have theirs."

John Wolff shivered with the tea. It scalded him, but the taste was so penetrating that he could not stop drinking. Warmth flooded him. The negress stood beside him, offering a collop of cold pork and a slice of heavy bread. She watched him with a kind of pride.

"Whar you gwine?" she asked softly. "You cain' stay here."

"No," said John Wolff. "No, I'm going to Canada."

"You cain' go dat way." Her courage made her swell herself. "Here," she said. "I'll fix you fo' de trip. I use' to shave old Massa."

John Wolff was content just to sit still. He let the black wench work on him. She shaved him with her master's razor and she hacked his hair short. Then she went upstairs and rummaged an old pair of shoes, and a coat and a pair of trousers.

"Dey're kind of monst'us-lookin' on you," she said, "but you got to cover up dem iron marks."

Her face was proud over her handiwork. She was a clean-looking wench, quite young.

"Thanks," said John Wolff. "Maybe I better be going."

"You take me wid you?" she suggested, making eyes at him.

He said, "I've got to find Ally."

"I he'p you."

"No," he said. "It's too far. I'm going out to Niagara."

He felt strength coming back to him. He hadn't thought of going there, before. But it occurred to him now that he might be able to find someone who had heard of Ally at that place.

The negress sighed.

"I guess you wouldn't take me along nohow. I guess I'll have to stay here."

She watched him sidelong.

"I'll jes' have to chase myself out into de rain," she went on, as he made no sign of having heard her. "Less'n you bash me wid de hammer a couple of times."

He shivered.

"No."

"Den I got to say you bus' in here and took dese things. Oh, Mr.

Phelps, he'll lay into me. But he ain' so smart. Ain' none of dese folks is so smart."

John Wolff took his eyes from the hammer. He turned and went out into the rain. The negress called after him shrilly:—

"You take de lef' branch, Massa. Dat bring you into Canaan bimeby."

He went along without a word.

4. *Niagara*

It was late in November. A light snow had begun early in the afternoon. It drifted down without noticeable wind. But a heavy gathering of clouds in the northwest promised a storm to come.

The walls of the fort looked brown and close to the earth. Even the stone mess house and its two flanking towers seemed to huddle between the parallel expanses of lake and sky. The river and the flat of the land were gray with cold. The smoke from the barracks and the officers' mess rose thinly against the falling flakes and mingled with the smoke from the small Indian camp and the huts of trappers, traders, and independent rangers that made a struggling kind of village beyond the gate.

The people moving down desultorily to the shore seemed pinched. They talked a little and they stared with a kind of deferred eagerness at the small sloop that was approaching the dock. The freeze was due on the lake any day; and the sloop was the last boat expected till next April.

In their scarlet coats a squad of soldiers from the fort marched down among the Indians and whites and took their station at the head of the makeshift dock, grounding their muskets and standing at a chilled attention. The dock could not bear the weight of many people. At the last boat's arrival it had been swamped and the outer end broken off. But nobody was expecting much of this boat. . . .

John Wolff, staring from the foredeck, watched the low land creeping towards the boat. His eyes wandered slowly over the crowd. He had been six weeks reaching Niagara. He was gaunt and footsore. But his pallor was disappearing.

He had crossed the Hudson at the mouth of the Hoosic and made his way to Ballston village, and there, by chance, he had picked up two men named Kennedy and Miller who had come down from Saint John's to visit their families. They had used their leaves to cross Champlain and tramp sixty miles of enemy country, and the day John Wolff arrived they were planning to return. They took him with them. At Saint John's he learned that Major John Butler was in garrison at Niagara. There was talk that Butler was recruiting a regiment of his own. Nobody knew very much about it, but John Butler was a good man to serve under. If you liked frontier service.

As the boat drew in, people began calling out to the sloop from the shore, and the deck hands yelled back. Nobody said anything in particular. There was nothing to say.

The boat warped alongside the dock and the business of unloading began at once without ceremony, for the master wanted to get back across the lake before the freeze.

He moved up beside John Wolff now, smoking his short pipe, the tail of his red knitted cap hanging down beside his cheek.

He said, "Here's where you get off." His voice was sarcastic in spite of his joke.

John Wolff said, "Maybe I can get to see Mr. Butler and he'll lend me the money."

The master spat over the side.

"I'll collect it next spring. Ain't no hurry." He sucked his pipestem free and stared westward across the river. "That's where you'll live, I reckon."

"Over there? I thought that was the fort."

" 'Tis. But that's where they're building the barracks. They ain't got any nails. I just as soon not see Major Butler till I got some nails to bring him. Maybe I'll have them next spring."

John Wolff looked west. Well back from the river shore a low line of log buildings raised bark roofs against the sky. They looked even more bleak, even more huddled under the snow, than the fort.

"God," said the master. "I don't see how folks can stand to live here. They must be crazy. Ain't more than eighty women in the whole place, barring the Indians. And what I've seen of most of them, they wouldn't raise the hackles of a six weeks' rabbit." He looked companionably at John Wolff. "You said you'd lost your wife, didn't you?"

"Yes."

"That's how it is," nodded the master. "You lose them, or something." He gestured with the pipe. "But out here you can't even find them. I don't see why you came out here."

He cocked his head.

"By God," he said, "hear the falls. When they sound that way I begin to expect ice. Well, you might as well get off. I ain't spoiling my time here much longer."

The dock was now loaded with boxes and barrels—shoes, flour, rum, powder kegs, pork, salt beef, blankets.

"I wish there was some nails, though," said the master. He shook hands. "There's a couple of the new rangers coming down. Maybe it's Butler. Guess I'll get below."

Wolff saw three men in green coats coming down to the opposite shore. They got into a skiff and rowed over the river. In the stern sat a short gray-haired man with a red face and black eyes and a long Irish lip to his mouth.

"Grange!" he shouted. "Mr. Grange. Did you bring me any nails?"

"No, I didn't."

The master stuck his knitted cap out of the cabin.

"Why didn't you?"

"I couldn't get them. That's why!"

"Did you hand over my requisition?"

"Yes, I did!"

Major Butler's face was black with suppressed rage.

"Didn't they say anything?"

"They said nails was scarce."

"That's a lie."

"I ain't saying it ain't, am I?"

"What did they say?"

"They said, 'Jesus Christ, you'd think the old bastard was going to win the war with a kag of nails.' "

The major drew in his breath. Then he seemed to collapse back into himself and his eyes became helpless. But he started to grin.

"Why couldn't you tell me that in the first place?"

The master grinned back.

"Well, I didn't just want to crucify you, Major." In his relief, he prodded John Wolff to the side. "Here's a man wants to jine on with you, Major. Come all the way from Simsbury Prison in Connecticut. I thought he might kind of take the place of a kag of nails. He's kind of built like a nail, ain't he?"

John Wolff flinched at the major's direct stare. Then he drew in his breath and stared back.

Butler lowered his voice.

"What's your name?"

"John Wolff."

"Wolff? Wolff? I seem to remember the name."

"I kept store at Cosby's Manor."

"Oh, I remember you now. You want to join Butler's Rangers?" His voice had a kind of pride at the name. As if the organization were something tangible, like hand work.

"Yes, sir."

"And you've been in jail?"

"Yes, sir. I was arrested a year ago last August."

"That's a long time." The red face quieted. "Get into the boat, man, and come back with us. This is Sergeant McLonis. He came from your part of the valley. You may know him?"

John Wolff shook hands with the young man as he got into the boat. He felt shy. He thought he might feel better when he had a good warm uniform coat like McLonis's. He studied the uniform. Green coat, with crossed buff breast straps. The lining of the coat was scarlet. The hat was a skullcap of black leather, with a leather cockade over the left ear and a brass plate over the forehead. The waistcoat was of heavy green woolen, and the full-length leggings of Indian tanned deerskin. It was a good uniform, Wolff thought, fixed for use in the woods.

"Sit down," said Major Butler. "We'll row back, lads. I don't want to see Bolton to-day." He turned to Wolff. "I hear that Thompson's house and your store were burnt by the rebels, Wolff. It's too bad. It's going to be a long while before you can get back, I guess. With the mess St. Leger and Burgoyne made of it. We can't get any government support for a full-sized campaign. By God, we can't even get nails from them."

The skiff smacked over the slight ripple. The drip from the oars had an icy sound. The air was raw and piercing.

"We'll have to do the best we can ourselves," said Butler. "How old are you, Wolff?"

"Fifty-odd."

He was holding his breath to ask. He couldn't seem to get the question out, he wished so desperately to ask.

"That's not too old if you're in sound health. But it's hard work, campaigning through the woods. If you don't feel up to it, I can give you work round here."

"Thank you, sir. I ain't so strong now. But I'll be all right. I used to have good health."

The other men kept watching him. Then he saw that Major Butler was looking too. He saw that his sleeves had drawn back showing the iron scars.

"You've had a hard time," said Butler. "Maybe you can't forget it, but it's better to try to, Wolff." He raised himself stiffly as the boat landed on the shore. "They've kept my wife and children down there. I can't get them exchanged."

"Yes, sir." Wolff's face started to work. He blurted out, "Do any women come here from the valley, sir?"

"Some got through." He was brief. "Why?"

"You haven't seen my wife—Alice Wolff? Ally, she's called. Kind of a pale woman? A little younger than me?"

Butler shook his head and glanced away. The men shook their heads too. McLonis said, "It would be known if she was here. It would be bound to." His voice was gentle with sympathy.

"Can you send letters down there, ever?"

Butler said, "I can send one under a flag, when a flag goes. But a letter's not likely to reach her unless you know where she is."

John Wolff, walking behind him towards the low log barracks, said, "Yes. I'd forgot. The store got burned, didn't it?"

The snow began to drive a little before the first breath of the wind.

Two

THE DESTRUCTIVES

6

GERMAN FLATS (1777–1778)

1. *Paid Off*

THOUGH there had been several light falls at German Flats early in November, the snow had not lasted. But now, as Lana looked out from the kitchen window of Mrs. McKlennar's house, it seemed to her that snow must surely come soon. She had prayed for snow, as all the valley had prayed for it since the murder of the Mount boys in Jerseyfield. Deep snow alone, in the woods between themselves and Canada, could ensure their safety. Until it came, no family living beyond easy reach of the forts could feel secure; and many of them had once more moved into German Flats. At Mrs. McKlennar's, Gil and Lana had moved into the stone house, while their own log house had been turned over to Joe Boleo and Adam Helmer. Both were homeless men, but Gil said that in the event of a raid, he and they together could hold a stone house like McKlennar's safe as a castle.

For two days long lines of steely clouds had been moving out of the northwest. People in the valley could feel no wind; there was no visible sign of it except the clouds, or the sudden bending of the trees on one of the higher hills.

As Lana looked through the window she saw Joe Boleo emerge from the farmhouse, drawing on his foul pipe and studying the sky. She herself was impelled to join him in the yard.

"Do you think it's going to snow?" she asked.

He held his position, eyes aloft, the sparse hair on his half-bald head shivering as if with cold. "Women are the devil," he replied at large.

"Why, Mr. Boleo! I only asked a question."

He turned a sober face on her.

"That's so," he said in obvious surprise.

Lana flushed, then laughed. Her cheeks were bright, against the gray background of the winter trees; her eyes shone. She enjoyed this shambling, indolent, gangling man for all his musky smell that reminded her of pelts. Now she made her voice sound humble: "Well, is it going to snow, do you think, please, Mr. Boleo?"

Joe kept grinning to himself. He wasn't like Adam Helmer, who hated the sight of a pretty girl carrying a baby in her inside because it seemed to take the point out of her good looks. Joe liked any pretty face, and he had grown especially fond of Lana's.

"Sure," he replied. "It's going to snow hard. There's a real storm coming. Feel the cold. No, you can't feel it on your skin. You've got to feel it in your nose. You can smell a big snow before it comes. And look there!" He pointed his long finger at a gap in the tumbling rollers of the clouds. "Just watch there a minute."

As Lana came close to sight along his finger, Joe's eyes slid sidewise. He thought she looked happy to-day. She was a real nice girl, he thought, the way she brought him and Adam things to eat and cleaned their house out for them. "You keep watching." He moved his shoulder so that it touched hers and he could feel the round soft solid curve through her dress. He even felt her draw her breath.

"Oh, the geese?"

"Geese," he nodded. "They've been going by all day. Higher than hell and straight south."

She saw them come and go, leaving the clouds in their wake, a rippling line.

"And there's another thing," said Joe. "Keep still. Don't even breathe." He liked to see her when she held her breath.

"You mean that singing sound? What is it?"

"That's high wind. You can hear it that way in the westward country where the land lies flat. Down here we get it when the wind blows high." Her lips were parted, quick and red to breathe the cold.

"Now you'd better get inside," he said. "A girl in your shape has got responsibilities. And anyways, Gil will be hungry for his dinner. He'll want to get started right after."

"Oh yes," she exclaimed. "The paymaster's coming to-day."

"Yes," said Joe. "We're going to draw militia pay. By God, we ought to be rich. Rich enough so I can buy you a present maybe." He eyed her with sly eyes.

"Oh, thank you, Mr. Boleo. But you ought to save your money."

"I ain't a hand at saving. Why, sometimes I've made thirty pounds and spent it all in a couple of throws in Albany."

"Throws?"

"Well, maybe I got tossed around by the girls a little." He spoke with a kind of boastfulness. "Down there the girls get at a man like me. He can't hardly help it." His wrinkled face expanded. "God," he said, "the things that have happened to me, though!"

"Why, Mr. Boleo!" Lana was bubbling with delight.

"Well, I hadn't ought to talk this way to you."

"I'm sure a girl wouldn't rob you. Not up here."

His eyes became lugubrious.

"That's the trouble. Women are the devil."

Gil and Adam came in at noon. Gil with the cart piled high with firewood to add to the corded tiers already in the woodshed, and Adam carrying the hog-dressed carcass of a buck on his broad shoulders. The three men hung up the deer in the woodshed, and all came up to the stone house for dinner, sitting down at the table with Mrs. McKlennar, who derived a monstrous satisfaction from all Joe's stories. She was delighted also with Adam Helmer. Any big man could put a flutter under her ribs, and Adam, with his coarse, good-featured face and long yellow hair, pricked her mettle.

The kitchen reeked of their tobacco-tainted clothes, and there was a wet bloodstain on the shoulders of Adam's deerskin shirt. Beside the two, Lana always noticed Gil's cleanliness with pride. But to-day he was as excited and noisy as they. All three men were bursting with the prospect of ready money coming in. They hadn't decided what to do with it, but Gil had earlier said to Lana that they would need the money. What little cash he had had dwindled away to nothing, and he would not receive his year's salary of a hundred and twelve dollars until April. Militia money would be handy to buy some necessary stuff for clothes, shoes, and store flannel, out of which Lana could work things for the baby during the winter. Besides, their powder was getting short (and the price was high).

Lana and the negress, Daisy, served them with samp and pork, and slices of dried squash fried in lard and flour, and apples baked in maple sugar. In the midst of dessert, Mrs. McKlennar got up suddenly and fetched a bottle of sack from the cellar, pouring them each a glass.

"My husband always celebrated on pay day," she explained. "I ought to start you boys off right."

Joe Boleo rolled the liquor on his tongue.

"I'd like to have met your husband, ma'am. He must have had some right good notions," he said politely. But as they went out of the door, he whispered to Adam, "I'll bet that horny Irishman got him a good stiff drink of rum to wash it out with."

Mrs. McKlennar watched them go. "Look," she said to Lana, "it's started snowing."

Fine white flakes were driving down upon the valley. Already they had made a thin dusting over the earth and the three men tramping abreast towards Fort Dayton left muddy footprints in it.

"Lord," said the widow, "they're three fine boys." Then she flung her arm round Lana's shoulders and her horselike face softened. "Come upstairs," she said. "I was in the attic before dinner and I found some things I thought you might use for the baby."

Lana wondered what Mrs. McKlennar could possibly have that would be useful to a baby.

The house grew warmer as they went up the stairs. Then when they passed through the trap into the attic, the air was cold again. It was darker too, with the snow falling outside the one small gable window. The loose boards clattered under the widow's tread. She bent down suddenly.

"I got these out," she said.

Lana looked down. She saw a cradle and blankets, a miniature plate, and a silver spoon.

The widow breathed harshly through her nose. Two bright spots had flushed her gaunt cheeks.

"One of Barney's soldiers made the cradle, and Barney got the other things and showed them to me on our wedding night for a joke. I remember how we both laughed. But we never used them. I don't know why. We tried the best we knew, too."

Lana said softly, "I think it's awful nice of you to let me have them."

"Nonsense," snorted Mrs. McKlennar. "Don't get sentimental."

She rubbed her nose.

"Take them down to your room. No, I'll carry them; you better not lift such heavy stuff."

The snow was driving hard against their faces when the three men forded West Canada Creek and came in sight of the fort. The number of footprints on the road made Adam laugh.

"I bet the militia never turned out as good before."

Joe Boleo grinned.

"How much do you think the pay amounts to?" Gil asked.

"Plenty," Adam replied. "I don't know how they figure it, but we commenced in June, going down to Unadilla, and we was pretty busy right along till Arnold went home. It's pretty near three months, up here. Down east the campaign was longer. Maybe they'll pay us for the whole campaign."

They encountered George Weaver going through the gate. He was looking so solemn and embarrassed that they asked him what was bothering him.

"Why," he said, "Mrs. Reall wanted to come along to collect what was due on Kitty's pay. She asked if she could come with me. And Emma didn't like it much on account of John and Mary Reall. But I said it wouldn't be neighborly not to take her. She's just ahead."

Mrs. Reall, looking surprisingly cheerful, turned back to greet them. She had her daughter Mary with her. Mary, Gil thought, was growing into a nice girl. There was a still, brown earnestness in her eyes he didn't expect to see in any Reall. And she looked a little appalled by all the men round her and her mother, a little ashamed that her mother should have come, perhaps. Gil held his hand out, introducing his two companions to the Realls.

Adam smiled at the girl and said to the mother, "You come with us, ma'am. We'll all go in together."

The soldiers' mess had been turned into the paymaster's office for the afternoon, and a couple of the garrison were assigned to guard duty at the door. When Adam worked a lane for his companions through the crowd, the soldiers barred the entrance.

"When does this paying start?" Adam demanded.

"When he gives us the say-so." One of the soldiers jerked his head back toward the door.

They stopped and chatted with the men round them. Some people eyed Mrs. Reall and Mary curiously, but nobody took notice of them more than to say "How do you do."

Then a pompous voice cried sharply from the messroom, "All right, lads." One of the soldiers turned and bawled, "Do I let in the whole she-bang, mister?"

"No! Let in twenty or so, that's all the room will hold comfortably; and then close the door until they're paid off. Then let in another lot. We can't freeze, you know."

With Adam's broad shoulders clearing a path, Gil and Weaver and Joe and the Reall women were among the first to enter.

The room seemed dark after the swirling whiteness of the snow outside. And the snow itself, when one looked out at it, seemed to lend to the darkness. A log on the hearth was disintegrating into a mountain range of coals. With his back to it, in a black coat, red waistcoat, and soiled white tie, sat the paymaster, come up from Poughkeepsie at Colonel Bellinger's request. He had the roll of the regiment before him and the colonel's muster sheets, and these he was comparing and checking against each other. He finished as the men crowded in and barked a little in his throat. "Line up," he said. "Line up down the table. I can't handle you all at a time."

As he stepped up to the table, Gil noticed that Colonel Bellinger was in the room. The colonel looked grim. Gil could not understand why.

"Hey, there," said the paymaster. "What's that woman doing in here?"

Mrs. Reall, who was third in the line of men, stepped out of it and drew herself up before the paymaster.

"I came to collect my husband's pay."

"*Hak, hak, hak,*" went the little man. "No women allowed in here, ma'am."

"But I said why I came."

"What's his name? Why isn't he here himself?"

"His name is Christian Reall," said Mrs. Reall. "He's dead."

The little man examined his list.

"He ain't marked so. Now, ma'am, will you kindly get out?"

"Just a minute." Colonel Bellinger came forward. "I don't know why Christian Reall isn't marked on the list as dead. But he was killed and scalped. I saw him myself. I think his widow is entitled to his pay."

The little man looked angrily at the colonel.

"I'm sorry," he said. He seemed to swell with the importance of his position. "I'm appointed to pay militia wages. I don't pay dead men." He gave his little barking cough.

"But where do I get his pay? I'm entitled to it. I'm his lawful wedded widow," said Mrs. Reall.

"Claim against the state. Swear it to a justice. File the claim. *Hak, hak.*"

"But I ain't got any money. I need it. I've got children, mister."

"They're no business of mine."

"Look here," said the colonel. "Surely he earned his money as well as any man could. I'll swear to the time of his death and to Mrs. Reall's being his wife. Can't you pay her for his time up to then?"

"My dear sir," said the paymaster. "We don't do things that way. I've explained the procedure. The claim will be filed before the auditor-general and passed by an act of Congress."

"Jesus Christ, listen to the bug-tit."

Adam Helmer's voice was heavy with admiration.

"Sir?"

No one answered.

Colonel Bellinger took Mrs. Reall's arm. "I'll see you get it, and I'll see you have something on account." He led her to the door.

The men turned back to the paymaster, who was clearing his throat. "Give your names," he said. "I've got the money sorted for you."

A man named Hess and a man named Stoofnagle drew pay. Then it was Gil's turn.

"Gilbert Martin."

"Company?"

"Mark Demooth's."

"Oh yes, Captain Demooth's. Here you are. The account's different from the other companies. You get no pay for the five days' service with General Arnold. You were requested to act as scouts for Continental troops. Therefore your expenses will be due you from the United States Congress. You will receive it in due course. That makes your pay $4.27 instead of $5.52, which is the regular private's pay for last summer's militia service in this regiment."

A stunned silence fell upon the room. The two men who had already received pay began counting it. Gil looked down at the money in his hands. Four dollars and twenty-seven cents. Suddenly his throat swelled. He thought of Oriskany. He didn't feel like waiting for the others to be paid. He went towards the door.

Perhaps the little man felt uneasy, for he started coughing again as Joe Boleo gave his name. The gangling woodsman slouched over him.

"Thanks," he said. "It sure is fun to lick the British."

The little man coughed.

"It's the regular pay according to the regulations of the New York Congress. Militia serving in its own precincts draws pay only for actual duty. In your case, expedition to Unadilla—fourteen days. You were then discharged. Expedition to relieve Fort Stanwix, unsuccessful—five days. You were again discharged. Expedition under General Arnold, successful—five days. Twenty-four days at twenty-three cents a day is five dollars and fifty-two cents. It seems plain to me."

"You said the word, bug-tit."

Joe followed Gil out into the snow. The roofs of the buildings were whitened. The stockade looked black against it. The air was getting colder; soldiers blowing into their hands on sentry walks made clouds of steam that whipped rapidly away among the swirling flakes.

Adam Helmer overtook them. He was laughing loudly. "I ought to have brought my purse along."

Gil had nothing to say. He went out through the fort gate and turned left for home. The snow was making fast.

The other two men walked in his footprints, Joe at the tail end, muttering to himself.

"What you talking about?" Adam demanded.

"I was wondering how in hell those buggers got to be that way."

"How in the hell what buggers got to be what way, Joe?"

"Those Congresses."

2. *The Snow*

The snow lay two feet deep when the storm cleared. The weather remained cold. Winter, thought Emma, had come to stay; and she walked along on her husband's bear-paw shoes with a feeling of complete security. She hadn't told any of her menfolk where she was headed for. She had merely announced at dinner that she was feeling housebound and that a romp in the snow would do her good. The cabin seemed awfully small for four large people: herself, and George, a solid man, and John, nearly a man; and now Cobus was catching up to John. All three had looked at her from over their plates; all three had said, "All right, Ma," grinning their boys' grins. She was proud of her menfolk, and as she left the house she had a comforting assurance that they were proud of her. Even John was, preoccupied though he had been these past months with the Reall girl. She felt sure that he had no idea that she was going to Fort Herkimer, with the deliberate intention of talking to Mary Reall.

She had not seen the girl since they left Fort Herkimer to live in the cabin on Peter Weaver's place, where George had agreed to give his time and the boys' for a third share in the farm produce. She had had no intention of ever seeing the girl; when George announced that he was going to take Mrs. Reall to the pay-off, Emma had been hurt, as if by doing this George were taking John's and Mary's side against herself. But as soon as he told her how the paymaster had treated Mrs. Reall, all Emma's natural wrath had risen blazing.

"I wish I'd been along," she said; and "I wish you had, Emma," said George. "The girl seemed to take it hard, ashamed to see her Ma put down, and all."

"It's a wonder you men didn't stand up for them."

"There wasn't nothing we could do. Bellinger was there. He couldn't and he's the colonel, too."

She let it drop. But the idea came to her, now that she felt the Realls had been put upon, that maybe Mary could be talked into a state of sense. It was just as important for the girl, after all, as for Emma's John, not to hasten to a wedding.

As the blood started flowing through her body, she pulled the shawl back from her gray hair, drawn uncompromisingly to its honest knot. The cold whipped up the color in her cheeks. Her stride was masculine; the weight of the snowshoes made her swing her feet. She ought to have been wearing trousers. She kept kicking the loose snow from the webs. It was powdery and it glittered when she flung it off. She trod down hard to hear the squeak, putting her weight forward over her knees.

God hadn't granted it to Emma to have a pretty face; but she had a fine, well-working body. Walking by herself made her conscious of its strength and vigor, feeling herself in every part; yet to tramp this way, for the sheer muscular delight, was an expression of her underlying femininity. Where pretty women who had looking-glasses might have examined their naked selves, Emma, instead, renewed acquaintance with herself by means of what she called her romps.

To Mary Reall, who saw her swing through the gate, Emma's hearty good health was an expression of ruthlessness. The girl was afraid of her. She knew instinctively, even as Emma asked to see Mrs. Reall, that John's mother had come down to talk to her.

They had a corner of the northwest blockhouse, which they shared with two of the Andrustown families. Mary's mother was lying on one of the bunks originally built for a garrison. A fire in the centre of the floor gave all their heat to the three families. The smoke had blackened the rafters and the ceiling boards. It found its way upwards through the trap and out of the spy loft when the wind allowed. It was a miserable place.

"It's surely nice of you to call, Emma!" said Mrs. Reall.

"I was just out for a walk." Emma looked round her. No chance in here to talk to Mary. "How are you making out?"

Mrs. Reall explained that Colonel Bellinger had lent her money out of his private purse. He was such a nice man. So gentrified.

"Yes," said Emma, forcing herself to be agreeable. "But you can't live like that forever. What will you do next year?"

Mrs. Reall was not disturbed.

"I've sent in the claim for damages that Kit made out before he got killed. I guess I ought to hear of it pretty soon. I showed it to Mr. Rebus White, and he said it ought to be honored by the state." She used the words with importance.

"Who's this Mr. White?" demanded Emma.

"He's the corporal here. He comes from Massachusetts. He's a real nice man, Emma, and thinks maybe he'll settle here. He's talked about my keeping house for him."

Emma gave a neutral grunt. "George talks about making a claim. How much did yours mount up to?"

Mrs. Reall began to shuffle among her bedding. "I've got it somewhere. The copy, I mean. Oh yes, here it is. It comes to two hundred seventy-one pounds and fifteen shilling."

"Two hundred pounds! How on earth did you figure it out that way?"

"Jeams MacNod wrote it out for Kitty. One dwelling house, a hundred pounds. One grist mill, twenty-five; one bedstet, fourteen pounds; one hollan' cupboard, seven pounds." She rattled off the items, having them by heart.

Emma's jaw fell open.

"But that ain't so. They never was worth that much in hard money. That bed. And that hollan' cupboard—you never had one."

Mrs. Reall was not disturbed.

"I've always wanted one. Mr. MacNod said it was best to put down everything, because sometimes they cut down on the list."

Emma stared.

"Well," she said suddenly, "it's not my business." Her eyes swung round to Mary. The girl was watching her. Her thin face was dark red. "My Lord!" thought Emma. "She's ashamed."

"You see," continued Mrs. Reall, "we got our government now, we ought to use it for ourselves. That's what Mr. White says, too."

"It's how you look at it, I guess." Privately Emma considered it stealing;

she never had trusted the Realls. But she must not show her thoughts too plainly. "How are you fixed for the winter?"

Mrs. Reall laughed.

"I guess we'll make out all right. They're sending food to us, and we all share in here. It's hard on the little ones, not having shoes. They've started chilblains early this year. But there's always Providence."

There always was for people like the Realls. Out of her sense of shame, Emma said, "There's some shoes Cobus has outgrown. I'll send them down." She got up and said good-bye. She was glad she had two miles to walk home, to get some fresh air into her.

"Good-bye," called Mrs. Reall.

Emma halted outside the door to put on her snowshoes.

"Can I help you, Mrs. Weaver?"

Mary had come out with her.

Emma said, "I guess I'm still young enough to put them on myself."

The girl drew back as if she had been slapped. Her thin face was quite white. It made her eyes seem larger.

"Mrs. Weaver," she said quietly. But her voice had the tenseness of a child's. She looked like a child in her ragged, poorly sewn petticoat. Even in her rough home-knitted stockings her legs were thin. Emma felt like pitying her as she would pity any miserable object, man or beast.

She got up on her snowshoes and stamped her feet to settle them in the laces.

"What is it, Mary?"

She looked at the child's face. She wasn't getting enough to eat. She didn't look half strong enough for her age; why, at her age Emma had had a breast and shoulders, whatever her face looked like. The girl drew a shuddering breath.

"You mustn't think too bad about Ma. She doesn't think that's stealing. It's just the way she thinks."

Emma said heartily, "I know. She can't help it."

Then she was caught by the girl's level gaze. Whatever else you could say about her, the girl was brave. She was scared to death, but she was standing up to it. Emma liked that.

"What you mean is we're all the same, don't you? You think so because John and I are in love with each other."

"In love." The words bounced from Emma's lips. "What do you two children know about love?"

"What did you, Mrs. Weaver, when you were fifteen?"

"Nothing," said Emma, staunchly.

"But you got married, didn't you?"

The girl had spunk. Her forehead looked too big for her face, thin the way it was. And her underlip was shaky. But she looked straight at Emma, and Emma, instead of getting angry, found herself liking it, to her surprise.

"Have you ever been sorry?"

"Not more than most women, Mary."

"Has Mr. Weaver?"

Emma suddenly smiled. "He hasn't said so." She drew a deep breath. "Will you walk to the gate with me?"

The girl came. The snow seemed to pinch the calves of her legs as she stood beside Emma outside the palisade. She held her hands in front of her and waited for Emma to speak.

Emma thought for several moments before she did speak.

"Do you and John see each other often?"

"He comes down when he can." Mary's narrow face was wistful. "It's not often, though."

"John's a good boy." Lord knows how they make love here in this place, Emma thought.

"Mary, I don't mean to be hard on you. Or on John. But you don't know anything about getting married."

Again the small half-smile.

"I know," said Emma hastily. "A girl has to begin. I'm thinking of you, too. How do you know you love John? How do you know John loves you? I'd hate for either of you to be unhappy."

"We ain't scared to try, Mrs. Weaver."

"I know. I know. You're never scared at your age. Or at least not much. Do you think you could make a good wife? Look at it that way."

Mary's eyes were downcast.

"I don't know. I'd try. I never had much chance to learn things."

"I should think you hadn't!" Emma's contempt got the best of her. "Not but what your Ma means well, though—in her own way."

She saw the girl taking another deep breath. Again the eyes met hers in the same level regard.

"I wanted to tell you, Mrs. Weaver, that John and I are in love and we aim to get married. If he wants to keep on we'll do it anyway." Her color rose. "You couldn't stop me without killing me, Mrs. Weaver."

"Look here," Emma said. "I'm not going to stand in your way, Mary. But I want you both to be sure. Will you promise me not to get married for a year?" And meeting the eyes again, "Or not to get married without talking to me first?" Her mouth twisted. "After all, it wouldn't be easy to do that up here, without banns, you know."

The girl gulped.

"We won't."

Emma believed her. "Don't start crying," she said abruptly.

She swung away for home, making her best pace. She didn't look round; but kept at her work. She felt her blood restored to its racing beat that she enjoyed so much. She was flushed and breathless when she got back to the cabin, barely in time to start the evening meal.

She looked at John's face. "You can't guess where I've been," she said, laughing at him. "No you can't. I've been to Fort Herkimer seeing the Realls."

John blushed.

"I thought it would be nice for John to go down for me with some shoes of Cobus's I promised. I thought while he was there, he might ask Mary to come up here for Christmas dinner."

John had turned brick red to his eyes. George merely looked at Emma. He was used to her, but there were times when he felt quite confounded. Her and her romps in the snow!

3. *March Thaw*

The winter in German Flats passed uneventfully enough. The cold continued and the snow lay deep. Unmilled wheat was fetching seven shilling a bushel at Little Falls, where Ellis's Mills were grinding for the army. Almost every week the mills shipped flour to Albany. When men heard stories of how the Continental army was starving at a town called Valley Forge, they found it hard to believe. They wondered where the flour was going to.

Occasional sleds that passed along the Kingsroad, Lilliputian in the still white world of snow, reminded the inhabitants that men were yet in garrison westward at Fort Stanwix. The sleds stopped the night at Fort Dayton and in the morning put out for the upper fort. They followed the river—hauling on the ice, a natural road. They went without a guard. The army, evidently, had no apprehensions. It made the people feel secure. Some even came to regard the murder of the Mount boys as the trick of drunken Indians; nobody could tell what to expect from a drunken Indian, least of all the Indian himself. It made them discount the story of the presence of white men. That depended entirely on a nigger boy's say-so.

Up at McKlennar's, the further the winter drew along, the more Joe Boleo expressed misgivings. When he and Adam and Gil were off hunting in the woods, Joe would keep tracking along the ridges spying across country, and he never came to a creek bottom without following it for half a mile or so. "Indians always hang to water," he said. Gil and Adam Helmer often laughed between themselves at the figure he made, bent over on his snowshoes, his long neck outstretched, among the snow-loaded balsams. "You can laugh, you twerps," he would say. "But wait till the snow starts going down." Then he would strike off and bring them to a deer yard, and he and Adam would begin killing deer.

Adam was inclined to be jealous of Joe's shooting. In his own overflowing strength, Adam liked to strike cross-country, running on his shoes for miles on end. But it was generally Joe, mousing along quietly, who found the deer. Then he would squat with his narrow tail just over the snow and wait for the other two to come back to him. He would sit there, looking at the deer, who always herded to the far side of the yard and stared back at him with their queerly lambent, soft eyes. Joe would be saying, "Poor pretty, poor pretty," in a sorry sort of way, like an old woman sort of woodpecker, according to Adam, and then when Adam came he would begin shooting. Sometimes the two of them would shoot three or four deer, picking out the marks, calling the shots, pacing off the distance from the wall of the yard, before Gil stopped their senseless killing.

"Hell," said Joe, "we got to keep our eye in."

"Shoot at a tree," suggested Gil.

Adam would be scornful.

"You can't waste powder and ball on a tree."

Then they would select a doe that looked fairly plump and kill her and leave the rest lying in the yard. They kept not only McKlennar's well supplied with meat, but carried deer after deer to the forts and the settlement, sometimes selling the meat, sometimes giving it away. It depended on how they felt.

In the evenings they would light a great fire in the farmhouse fireplace and lie in front of it, drinking rum and molasses; and Gil generally went down to sit with them. Up at the stone house the women took to sewing things, making things for the baby, spinning. Mrs. McKlennar liked to spin with her big wheel, working the treadle with her vigorous foot, and making a hum come out of the whirling wheel like a voice against the cold. They talked about things, the three women together. Daisy, the negress, sitting in a corner, made a rug for the baby with a wooden crochet hook and strips of rags. Daisy couldn't sew and she was unhappy till the widow suggested that she make the rug. She embarked upon a five-foot project, though what good a five-foot rug could do a baby nobody ever figured out, unless it was Daisy herself. Sometimes she had a run on a color, like red; sometimes she spent two nights with brown, as if that were the color of her thoughts. It was no place for a man.

In the farmhouse atmosphere, with the two woodsmen sprawled on the floor before the fire, telling each other tales or passing off the gleanings of the valley news, a man could be at ease.

Joe liked to have the news from Herkimer's house. There was talk of raising a monument that had been voted down in Albany, on the other side of the house from the well. Five hundred dollars had been mentioned. Joe went down one day to see how it would look. He returned still wondering.

In February there was some talk that the Massachusetts garrisons of Dayton and Herkimer were returning to their homes, having completed their service. It was said that they would leave in March. No provision was made for their replacement. Demooth and Bellinger had been down to Colonel Klock in Palatine to organize a protest. All three men were trying to have Fort Stanwix abandoned and the German Flats forts strengthened. But Congress would not listen to their arguments. Congress held that Stanwix was the strategic defense of the valley. It was intimated that they might send some troops to Cherry Valley, but that was all.

Joe shook his head about it.

"They might just as well have nobody at all. You wait till the snow leaves. You'll see."

"See what?" asked Gil.

Joe grunted. "Indians."

Adam Helmer said skeptically:—

"They got their medicine up there at Oriskany."

"That's the trouble. If they hadn't been whipped so bad, they might wait to come along with the next army. But the way it is they won't wait. They'll want to get their face back. They'll be after scalps. They won't care whose. They'll feel they've got to. Hell, boy, I've lived with the Senecas, and I know."

"You lived with them, Joe?" asked Gil.

The gangling trapper stretched himself on the hearth to kick over a log with his heel. The fire blazed upward, pouring a ruddy light across his sweating body. The room reeked of the men's smell, tobacco, and rum. It was stifling hot, making them all drowsy, and Joe's voice was pitched low.

"Oh yes, when I was young, like you lads. I used to trap up the Chinisee.

I got along real good with the Senecas. I had a wife out there. She was a real nice girl, too." He stirred himself lazily. "They ain't as light as the Mohawk girls, but they're thinner."

He drank a little rum and turned his eyes thoughtfully on Gil and Adam. Outside the wind had died down with the coming of darkness, and the burning of the fire was even and fierce.

"I never knew you was married, Joe."

"Sure," said Joe. "I stayed there with her four years, without ever coming out." His reminiscent grin made his face unbelievably homely. "My God, that girl was set on me!"

Adam was crouched in front of Joe. The firelight made his big face scarlet and threw lights in his long yellow hair. He held his glass in both hands, his hands passed over his knees. The shadow of his broad shoulders filled all the opposite wall. Now he turned a facetious eye on Gil. Gil grinned.

But Joe knew what was going on in their minds. He said seriously, "You ought to have been along with me, Adam. You'd have liked it. Gil, now, he's a settled kind of man." He drew his breath, slowly, and belched. "Along in those days, a white man was just about the finest thing that could happen to an Indian girl. It made her important in her town. When I first went out there, the Indians treated any white man like he was one of their sachems. Like a big bug, see, come visiting. They gave him a house in the town and then they sent in all the best-looking girls so he could take his pick and feel comfortable while he was staying. It was a good idea. Only it wasn't so easy making your pick. Some of them girls was pretty nice." He poured himself another drink and stirred the molasses in with his finger. "Some trappers got the idea of staying and then going off for a day and coming back and beginning over. There wasn't any harm in that. It don't matter what a girl did till she got married, see? But it didn't happen that way to me. I got to the Chinisee Castle, the one they call Little Beard's town now, and they sent in eighteen hand-picked ones. But right away I knew the one I wanted. I knew she'd suit me fine. I was young-and-coming, see, and I suited her too. Don't laugh, you timber beast. It's truth. She stood with the rest of them looking on the ground, the way they all done, but as soon as she made out all the rest was looking down, she just took one look at me and it fixed me. Boy, she could throw her eyes at you!"

"I believe you," Adam said.

"Go to hell. I reached out at her and I said, 'You, you me fine!' I hadn't learned the language then. But she understood all right. The others went out, leaving just her. And as soon as they'd gone she just looked up at me, kind of scared and shy. I was pretty young, I guess, but it made me feel big.

"She didn't come only to my shoulder and she had braids reaching down to the middle of her thighs. She wasn't only medium dark, too, and she was pretty in her best clothes. She had on a kind of red overdress, what they call Ah-de-a-da-we-sa, and a blue skirt with beadwork on it. She was a great hand with beadwork. It was what made her come high in marriage. And her pant things was doeskin with more beading on the foot."

"She come high?"

"I didn't know how I could pay her Ma," Joe said seriously. "I didn't have only a bare stake. No beads for trading. I needed everything I had, see? The girl's Ma was something big. One of the chief's lines. They keep their family on the female side. The way the girls act up they've got to if they're going to keep the children anywhere near straight. . . . But I've got away from me and the girl. Soon as we was alone she signed for me to set down by the fire and take off my shirt. She took a bone comb out of her belt and started combing my hair. She greased it and picked out the ticks and took pains where it was curled. She liked them curls. I had fine curly hair, you know."

Even though Joe looked so serious, they had to laugh. They stared at the shiny expanses of bare scalp between the remnants of his past beauty. Joe rolled over and turned his back and lifted his shirt to let the heat strike against the rum in his belly.

"Lord," he said over his shoulder. "When I went to bed with her it was pretty dark. But I didn't have to see her to know she was good-looking. I told her in the morning I'd like to marry her."

"I thought you said you couldn't speak the language."

Joe looked hurt. "You don't have to when you've done that to a girl. I just said so, and she caught on all right. She colored some. Most Indians don't show color, but that was one of the things about her. That and teaching her to kiss. The way she caught on. You can fool around with all the heifers between here and Albany if you want to, but you won't know just what teaching a wild Indian to kiss is like. Well, she said she'd like to fine, so I said fine, and she said what did I have to buy her with? Well, I opened my pack, and she went through it like a dog after a rabbit. She shook her head. She made it plain there wasn't anything good enough. I felt bad, and she looked sorry. Then she clapped her hands."

"Yes," said Adam, "she clapped her hands."

"God damn you, Adam. She did." Joe began to look embarrassed. "I'd been getting dressed and she come up to me and put her hands on my waist and made the motions I was to take my drawers off. I had red flannel drawers."

The two young men guffawed.

"Honest to God," said Joe. "I told the chief how I felt, and I got him to take them round to the old lady and she went near crazy over them. Later I heard she'd gone right in and tried them on. They was some tight, but they stretched enough. Though she had to rig a kind of tassel in front when she wore them in the turtle dance. She made a little bark box for them and hung them over her bed. They were still in good shape four years later when the old lady led the Okewa for Lou."

"What's that, Joe?"

"It's the woman's all-night Dead Song."

"Your girl died?"

"Yes," said Joe. He blew smoke against the logs and watched the flame snatch it up the chimney. "After we got married, I and Lou went up the Chinisee. I built us a hunting cabin up there. It was good beaver country and a wonderful range for fisher. And she was a first-rate woman for a man. Knew how to take care of me. She was the only woman I ever had around that didn't get on a man's nerves. When I felt like laughing, she was ready to bust with it herself. Never saw anybody so always happy. She wouldn't call me Joe. Just Boleo, only she couldn't ever say the B. She called it Do-le-o." Joe's face was deeply concentrated. "And when the trap lines weren't bearing so good, she didn't make a lot of talk—what a white woman would call distracting you. She minded her business. I knew she was around, that's all. She was good to have around. And she never got lonesome. Seemed as if I was good enough for her. Of course we'd go down to the Castle every once or twice a year. I had to trade my fur pack, see? . . . It was a good life. And healthy. The way she kept me healthy. Used to make me hemlock tea to keep my skin open. Her cooking was Indian cooking, but she learned a few things, to please me. I told you she learned kissing. But is was a funny thing, she never got to be like a white woman. She was always shy about the way she acted with me. She wouldn't wash with me in the crick. Sometimes it got me mad. I never saw her naked in plain light. A bear kilt her while she was berrying." Joe drank and drew a breath. "The queer thing was we never had no children."

"What's queer about that?" Gil asked.

"Why, those girls could have children easy as letting go a crock of lard. John O'Beal now. He come out there and traded; he bought my furs. He married a girl too, and had a mess of children. One of them's got to be a chief. His name's Cornplanter."

"You said John O'Beal?" Adam asked.

"Sure, he was quite a lad, too. But he soured on it. He came back here and lives down the valley somewhere."

"Near Fort Plain?" suggested Adam.

"Sure, that's the man. I ain't seen him in some time."

Joe Boleo lay full length on his back, draining his glass.

Gil asked, "What did you say her name was, Joe?"

"Well, her Indian name was Gahano. Means something like Hanging Flower. But I told you I called her Lou. You ought to have been out there in those days, Adam. You'd have got along good. But now they ain't so friendly about white men. You can marry all right. But they don't trot the girls out for you any more. I quit myself when Lou died. . . .

"But that was the way for a trapper to live. All you had to do was run your lines, and you had a nice cabin to come back to, and your dinner cooked, and a woman to mend your clothes. You just lay around, and got up warm in the morning. It didn't cost you a cent." He looked at them again. "Most trappers came home in summer. They cleared out with the furs and spent their money, and the woman took care of herself while they was gone. Some kept two families going. But those buffaloes never spent the summer the way I did. We'd take trips, her and me, and lay around fishing. We'd go off where there wasn't anybody, not even the tracks of anybody but ourselves, for three months. We'd build a summer shanty and she'd plant corn. Yes, sir. You'd just lay around listening to a big fish jump and wondering if it was worth the bother putting the worm in the water. Lou worked all the time we was on our vacation, readying hides and putting up quitcheraw against the winter. I whittled her a little press for making the cakes in, which tickled her a lot. And then she'd go berrying to make pemmican. That was when the bear got at her. An old she-one with a couple of cubs. I spent a while tracking them and I killed the lot—" Joe paused and spat. "But, hell," he went on, "that's not what I set out to tell you. Indians ain't no good. This country would be a whole lot better off without any Indians. We'd be better off right now, I tell you. And I wouldn't be setting here listening to that drip off the roof."

Adam Helmer stirred himself. Adam had been wishing he had been born in a good time of civilization so he could have gone out to the Indian country. His full lips were compressed and wet just thinking of it. A little lithe hard girl like Joe's Lou, right now, would suit him fine. "Drip?" he asked.

"Yes," said Joe with scorn. "Drip. The thaw's commencing."

Gil got to his feet. He went to the door of the cabin, opened it, and stood there, leaning out.

The wind had turned to the south. He felt it damp against his face; he could feel it even with the outrush of overheated air from the kitchen. "You're right, Joe," he said over his shoulder. "It's the thaw beginning. Sugaring ought to start early this year."

"Shut that door!" yelled Joe. "Do you want to freeze us?"

4. *Fairfield*

Towards the end of the month, when the sugaring was in full progress and the smoke from the sugar bushes made pale blue wavering ribbons against the hillsides, a horseman left the Snydersbush stockade and rode full gallop the eight miles south to the falls, turned west along the Kingsroad, and flogged his way through the slushy ruts as fast as his blowing horse could lay foot to the ground.

The spattery thudding of his hoofs was audible in Mrs. McKlennar's sugar bush, high though it was above the road. They were boiling for the fourth day and some of the Eldridge people, the Smalls and the Caslers and the Helmers,—Adam's cousins, Phil, his wife Catherine, and son George,—were attending. The women were knitting by the fire, minding the kettle. Adam, on his own initiative, was bringing the wood for the fire and hanging round the women as much as possible. He was wearing a new hunting shirt, colored after the pattern Morgan's Riflemen were supposed to wear. It was of heavy white linen with long green thumbs along the sleeves, the double capes, and the bottom hem. He looked inordinately handsome in it; his yellow hair was carefully combed, and he had shaved.

Gil and Captain Jacob Small and George Helmer were hauling in the sap on hand sledges from the trees where the boys gathered it from the small pails. It was a sunny, windless day, warm enough to make sitting in the open pleasant. The steady drip in the pails was like the ticking of a clock, as if the trees together combined to mark the passage of the time. The distance one could hear a drop fall in a bucket was surprising; it was audible even above the women's voices.

Of all the men, only Captain Small, and Adam and Joe Boleo, had brought their guns. Adam and Small had left theirs in the little bark shanty before the kettle. But Joe was prowling the woods. They did not know that he was making a cast three or four miles to the north and west. They would have laughed if they had known. The snow still lay more than five feet deep in the woods. Even with snowshoes it made heavy going.

When they heard the horseman coming up the road, Gil and Captain

Small left their sledges and walked to the edge of the bluff. From there they could look down on him. The horse was floundering, but the man's arm rose and fell with pitiless fatigue. Jacob Small took one look.

"That's Cobus Mabee. He looks scared." He took his hat off and rubbed his grizzled head and stared incredulously at Gil.

Adam, seeing them move to the edge of the bush, left the women and joined them.

"What's going on?" he asked.

Small said, "Cobus Mabee just went up to Dayton."

Adam laughed.

"Maybe he's after Doc."

"He didn't look to me like that. Did he to you, Gil?"

"He was spoiling his horse," said Gil.

Adam's face sobered.

"That's serious."

They looked at each other.

"Do you think we ought to move down out of the woods?"

Adam said, "No. Joe's back there in the woods."

Small said, "One of us ought to find out what's happened. Gil, there's George Helmer on the edge. You send him down and let him ride your mare up. No sense scaring the womenfolks. It's the first party of the year."

Adam went back to the shanty. He got his gun. "I'm going to see if I can get a partridge," he explained. "You ladies have got wood enough?"

"Oh yes, Adam." They smiled at him. They went on with their talk. All except Lana. Suddenly Gil found her staring at him. He forced himself to smile. But she wasn't deceived. And he shook his head and put his finger to his lips.

His heart was like something shrunk inside himself as he watched her face. He thought, "What's it going to do to her?" Her face went deathly white. Then suddenly her chin went up and she said something in a quick high voice to Mrs. Small that made the latter laugh and pat her red hair. Mrs. McKlennar nodded, looked at Gil and smiled. Mrs. McKlennar had the instinct for such things. He guessed that she had caught on even before Lana.

He made himself go back to his sledge and haul it to the kettle. Nobody had missed George Helmer. The sugaring continued. But he and Captain Small managed to bring the children to trees closer to the fire without anyone's noticing, and themselves kept a watch on the woods. They would hear Adam shoot if anything went wrong, and he would hear Joe. Now the drip of the sap seemed startlingly loud.

Two hours passed before George Helmer returned. He came quietly without fuss, and without fuss Small and Gil joined him at his trees. He told them at once.

"The destructives have been in Fairfield. Indians and Tories. The whites was all the Fairfield people who went off before last August. Suffrenes Casselman, and Countryman, and the Empies. They killed little John Mabee and they took everybody else prisoner but Polly. She got away from the Indians. But she seen the rest. They've burnt every house and barn in the town. There ain't a thing left."

George Helmer was an earnest young man, and he was scared.

Captain Small said, "Did anybody see which way they went?"

"They went out on the Jerseyfield road," said George. "Cobus Mabee had it all planned to move down to his uncle's place in Indian Castle. He's moved his wife and the baby down and he was going back to get Polly and John and the cow. He stopped for dinner in Snyder's. When he got up to Fairfield the houses was still burning. Hadn't nobody known a thing about it, anywheres else." He caught his breath sharply and looked over at the shanty. "Do you plan to stay here, Jake?"

Jacob Small said, "Yes. Ain't no sense in moving till Joe or Adam comes in. Don't you go acting scared, George. We got to make sugar. We got to make enough for next winter, same as we'll have to do our planting."

"My God, Jake!" The young man's face was pale. "How can a man go out and plough and plant with *them* in the woods?"

"I don't know," Small replied. "But either you got to die hungry or you got to raise food."

George said unsteadily, "That's right." But his eyes kept rolling towards the woods. It was he who spied Joe and Adam coming in abreast. Joe was wringing wet with sweat and snow. He came over to Gil and Small and rested the rifle butt on the toe of one of his snowshoes.

"Where's George been to?" he asked, and pointed to the horse lather on the inside of George's pant legs.

They told him.

"That's good," said Joe.

"Good?" cried George Helmer.

"That's what I said. If they hadn't gone there, they'd've come right down here. They had an open camp six miles back. I guess they wanted to make sure of Fairfield before they hit so near a fort." His eyes were owlish. "There was about twenty of them, nine Indians. They struck out some time yesterday for the northeast."

The five men stood together a moment.

Joe asked, "How much more boiling have you got to do?"

"We could finish in a couple of hours."

"I guess you might as well finish," said Joe.

"You don't think they'll come back?"

Joe pursed his thin lips.

"Not that particular bunch, maybe. Maybe nobody right off, either. I've took quite a circle and there weren't no signs. This time of year, jays holler easy."

5. At Demooth's

Nancy was inside the house when the news of Fairfield was brought to the captain by a soldier from the fort. She had just finished clearing up after dinner, and in the silence she heard the captain go out into the warm sunshine and she heard every word the man told him. When the captain came in she saw that he was worried. He looked almost frightened to her.

"Where are you going?" he asked sharply.

"I'm going to give this to the pigs, sir."

She held a plate of food scraps, and she stared at him with wondering blue eyes.

"Pretty good food for pigs," he said irritably, but Nancy forgave him that. With the doctor, the captain had stood up for her against Mrs. Demooth. She couldn't have borne it otherwise. All day long Mrs. Demooth was after her with stinging, small remarks. Mostly low, unladylike things about her shape, how big her belly was, and how bastard children always showed more—things Nancy would never have believed Mrs. Demooth capable of saying.

"Men are fools," Mrs. Demooth said. "If I had my way you'd be turned out. Girls like you ought to be whipped before the town. But your own mother wouldn't have you round—I don't blame her—and the men say you couldn't starve. Men all take a sneaking pleasure in it. They always do if the girl's young. Get out of here. Get out of my room, anyway, if you won't get out of my house."

Nancy knew she was big, but it had seemed natural at first. The soldier had been a big man, and she was a big girl, and sometimes she thought the child would be big even if he was lawful. But as time went on and the captain seemed to notice her more, the sight seemed to make him irritable with her, and she began to think that what Missis said must be true.

Hon Yost laughed about it. Hon Yost would pat her belly as if he were patting the child itself.

"I'll bet it's going to be a dinger of a boy. Just like you and me, Nancy. But we get fun out of life."

Hon Yost had had a wonderful time the first half of the winter. He had never done less work in his life. For a long time everybody seemed glad to talk to Hon. Men slapped him on the back wherever he went and stood him drinks. He had been a regular public hero and generally drunk. But he was a harmless drunkard and came home every night to the barn, where he shared the stall with Mr. Demooth's horse. Nancy took him out what scraps of food she could steal. That was the plate's destination now.

But lately nobody paid much attention to Hon. At first he had been unhappy about it; disbelievingly, he would stick his face into Shoemaker's tavern, or the place across the river, and say hello. Once he even started the story of how he licked Sillinger with his wonderful account of Arnold's army. He got to where he said to the Indians, "Can you count the leaves on the trees?" Meaning, of course, that Arnold's army was as big as creation. But they kicked him out of the tap. He hardly ever got a drink. He once thought that if he enrolled in the militia he would get popular again, and saw Captain Demooth about it. But the militia were disorganized. Captain Demooth said Colonel Bellinger was trying to have new companies organized. New officers were needed. Over half the old ones had been killed.

Captain Demooth was sorry. He said that he appreciated Hon's patriotic sense and that as soon as the new organization was complete he would be proud to have Hon on his own company's roster.

At first Nancy was happy about it. While Hon had been a public figure she hardly ever saw him, but now that nobody else would talk to him, he hung around the Herter place. He seemed to like to talk to her. He was pleased when she asked shy questions about McLonis. McLonis was

quite a man. The Butlers thought high of McLonis. Some people thought
it likely McLonis would get to be a commissioned officer some day.

"Yes, Hon. But what is he like?" asked Nancy.

Hon poked her.

"Gee, *you* ought to know!" He burst out laughing, flinging himself back
in the straw so that his long hair gathered chaff. Hon had a nice voice,
for all he was dim-witted like herself. She loved to hear him laugh, and
she smiled a little herself. Sitting in the cool light of the barn window that
day, Nancy looked like a goddess of fecundity. With her yellow hair down
her back and the lids of her eyes full and her lips half parted in the remnant of the smile, she might have been the original mother. Hon always
made her feel that her accident was a distinction.

But now that he was on the subject of McLonis he liked showing his
familiarity.

"Jurry," he said, "he's a fine, ruthless man. That's quite a word. I heard
Major Butler call him that. I was right close to Major. It was the night we
camped at the Royal Blockhouse coming down here."

"Do you think we'll ever see him?"

"I will," said Hon.

"But I've got to see him, you know."

"Well, maybe you will."

"Do you think he'd like me now?"

"Say," said Hon. "If you ever got to Niagara you'd be just about the
queen of the company there, Nance."

"What do you mean?" She was breathless.

"Why, there's not a white woman there looks half of you."

"Oh. Then he might marry me out there."

Hon suddenly was silent.

"Mightn't he, Hon?"

"Well," Hon shook his head wisely. "If he gets to be an officer, maybe
he wouldn't."

"But you said he would."

"That's when he was a corporal."

"Yes, but I'm me, aren't I?"

"Yes," said Hon. Hon did have a few ideas. He had seen enough to
know that an ambitious man would not marry a girl like his sister. The
trouble with Nancy was that she had been happened on by an ambitious
man. He liked Jurry and he wanted to keep friends with him. And it didn't
seem important.

"But I've got to get married," Nancy said urgently. "Mrs. Demooth says
I am the living sin."

"Old Clem said he'd marry you."

Nancy shuddered. "I couldn't marry Clem. He always smells so sour
every morning."

"Listen, Nancy. I used to say for you to marry. But now I don't know.
Out there at Niagara lots of the women ain't married. They're nice women
too. Some of them in the officer barracks. Maybe you could get in the
officer barracks."

"Couldn't you take me out there, Hon?" she pleaded.

Again he slapped her belly.

"With a load like that, Nance?"

"I can walk all right."

"If you had it on your back, maybe." Hon laughed at his own joke. But Nancy looked as if she were going to cry.

"Sometimes I get scared you'll leave me here."

"Why shouldn't I?"

"I get so scared, Hon. *She* keeps talking at me some days. She says it makes girls awful sick. She says sometimes they die—bad girls do. It ain't like having honest children."

For the moment Hon was troubled. He was fond of Nance, in a way. After a minute or two he said, "I don't believe you'll die."

She was called to the house by the tinkle of the captain's bell, to Hon's immense relief. She was the devil to reason with. He took himself away from the barn before she could return.

Nancy had thought of late that Hon was getting restless. As the snow softened towards the end of March, and mists rose in the valley, he had been acting more and more uneasy. He kept making excursions into the woods. At last he spent a night away. Nance was terrified. But he had come back the evening after; he was in the barn at supper time when she carried out his plate of left-overs. He was sitting on some straw he had raked out of the mare's stall, whetting his hunting knife on his boot sole. She thought he looked excited.

"I found tracks where a party had been across West Canada Crick," he said. "Three or four days ago."

"A party?"

"About twenty. I guess they was some of ours."

"Ours, Hon?"

He was impatient with her. "Sure. What do you think? From Niagara, maybe?"

"Oh, Hon! You don't want to go with them?"

Immediately he was sly.

"How could I go with them? They're way the hell off by now. I wish I knew where they went to, though."

In her relief she wanted to please him, and she repeated everything the soldier had told Demooth. But as soon as she was done, she saw that she must have been dim-witted. Hon didn't say anything at all. He reared up like a dog and looked through the open door towards the woods.

"Please don't go, Hon. Not till I'm through."

When he didn't answer, she sneaked back to the house. She thought if Hon went she would surely die.

He was gone in the morning. Clem told her. Clem was feeling pretty grand; he had thought for some months that things were bound to come his way. With that damn fool out of reach, maybe he could work on Nancy.

The way she drooped in the soft morning sunlight, there in front of him at the barn door, he felt lustful. He didn't want to be a lustful man, particularly, but he thought what a damn fool he had been to be drunk that night when Hon was captured. Any sober man could have horned in on the game.

"Don't cry, Nance. You've always got me to look out for you."

She just looked wilted.

"Do you know he's gone, Clem?"

"Yes, he told me to tell you good-bye." Seeing her frantic glance at the woods, he laughed. "He didn't go north. He went by Unadilla. He'll need to get food in the Indian villages. Him and Indians get on good. He'll be all right."

"That's why he didn't ask me for any." Nancy gave a small miserable nod.

Clem said harshly, "You needn't figure on catching up with him. He'll be going like a wild hog. You couldn't ever keep up with him, girl."

"Why?" she said like a child.

"He don't want anybody catching up with him." Clem thought it might be just as well to give her a little plain sense. "Hon may be a half-wit, but he knows what'll happen to him if they catch him another time."

6. *Mrs. Demooth*

Only a little over a week later a second attack was made on Snydersbush. Word came to German Flats on the fifth of April. This time the information was complete. The enemy were over fifty strong, half white, half Indian. They had left the stockade alone. The people inside the stockade possessed a swivel they had let loose when the enemy first appeared in the road. The roar of it had kept them from the fort. They sashayed up the road instead.

They took Garter at his mill and burned the mill in plain sight of the fort. At Windecker's they cut off a threshing party, four men and two boys, and took them prisoner. They sent Indian scouts ahead to pick up the four settlers on the edge of the town and took them all: Cypher, Helmer, Uher, and Attle. They moved with great swiftness and discipline. They burned the farms, houses, barns, barracks, even Attle's brand-new backhouse. They killed all the horses and cows in their way. They headed for Salisbury; and swept that settlement at dusk. There they captured only three men, for the other inhabitants had moved into the Mohawk Valley down around Klock's and Fox's Mills and hadn't yet returned. But the destructives razed the town. Then they headed out along the old Jerseyfield road, northwest, past Mount's, the scene of their first irruption.

The leader of the party had attracted a good deal of attention in Snydersbush because of his uniform. It was a strange one; nobody had seen anything like it. A green coat, it was said, and deerskin breeches, and a black leather hat like a skullcap with a brass badge on the front of it. He roused a great deal of morbid speculation. Some of the old settlers said it reminded them of the uniform worn by the French commander, Beletre, back in '58. It was over a month before a report from James Dean, outside Niagara, informed them of Butler's Rangers. With his usual precision in detail he included a description of the new uniform.

The conviction gradually took root that John Butler was making an attempt to cut off German Flats. They knew that he had always hated Germans; and he had always been jealous of their rich soil. . . . They pointed to the fact that the number of each party had been just adapted to the strength of the place struck. Each party had burst out of the woods unheralded, had burned and killed and taken prisoner, and then hightailed it back for Canada. There was no point in even calling out the militia, let alone chasing them. They had the whole northwestern wilderness to make cover in.

Mrs. Demooth was terrified. Mark would not take her away, he would not even send her. She stayed in the house all day, but she was always listening. She had nothing to distract her, no one to help her in the house but that miserable wench, whose mere presence was an insult to a decent woman—first with her constant sickness, now with her swollen belly and her great blue stupid staring eyes. Whenever Mrs. Demooth saw Nancy she had something to say to her; whenever she sent Nancy out of her sight, she began to think of sayings that would give her pain.

Mrs. Demooth was not consciously torturing a half-wit. Far from it. Having, like a dutiful wife, been forced to violate the nicer feelings, in her own household, she told herself that she was merely trying to make Nancy understand the enormity of her fornication. At first she had started her tongue lashings in the captain's presence, but he had not liked it, and now she never spoke to the girl until he had left the house.

He was away nearly all day now. He was down at Palatine, seeing Colonel Jacob Klock. Mrs. Demooth could always tell when he had been to Klock's because he smelled of manure. It made her think that the Klocks must keep the cows in their kitchen.

The men were trying to reorganize the militia and above all to get regular troops sent up from Albany. Demooth even went to Albany to confer with General Stark in person. But all the great hero of Bennington would say was that he needed every man he had to defend the Hampshire grants, and the Hudson Valley north and south. He refused to consider the opinion that these raids were parts of a larger plan. He called them mere riotous excursions. He cursed about the useless militia and said that if German Flats and the Mohawk Valley could not take care of themselves like other frontiers they might as well lie down and die. Even Philip Schuyler spoke in the same vein. The security of Albany made all of them sound patriotic. Schuyler showed Demooth General Washington's reply to his reports of Klock's demands for troops. Washington said the same thing exactly. Let them take care of themselves like the other frontiers: the New York militia had been the least effective of any state's. The logic seemed thin to Demooth. He pointed out that troops were being sent to the Virginia frontier.

He returned, worn-out and hopeless. By the end of the month, the sum total of encouragement was the announcement that Alden's company of Massachusetts troops would be sent to Cherry Valley as a base from which they could operate against any important incursions of the enemy. It made one want to laugh.

At the end of the month the hamlet at Ephratah, to the north of Stone Arabia, was struck. This time the invaders were a small party, entirely of Indians, according to first reports. They burned the Hart house, killed Conrad Hart, took his son prisoner, and murdered a four-year-old boy. But a day later, the word reached German Flats that the man who had killed the boy had been seen by Mrs. Rechtor to have blue eyes, and when he raised his sleeves to rinse his hands, his wrists showed white skin.

Colonel Bellinger, sitting with Demooth and Petry in the Herter kitchen, nodded.

"It was bound to start some day. That's not a regular raid. But there'll be plenty more like them now they've seen how easy it is."

Dr. Petry also nodded. "They'll start picking off all the little places. They'll start hanging round the field fences. And it's time planting began. Already they're ploughing at Weaver's."

Demooth said bitterly, "Schuyler told me the Indians had never been effective in battle. He said we'd demonstrated that ourselves at Oriskany. Couldn't we act like men?"

"If we had wings," said the doctor in his heavy voice. "But my feet weigh too much."

Nobody even grinned, it was too true. No one could be expected to rush off after raiders leaving his own place undefended. They couldn't make anybody realize that the valley was ninety miles long, that the Tories had the whole of the wilderness to hide in, but that everything the militia might do would be plain to see. It was as if the leaves of the trees had eyes.

"There's one thing we can do," said the doctor. "Everybody out of reach of the forts should be told to move in. If they want to work their farms from the forts, they do it by themselves."

They all agreed.

Demooth made another suggestion.

"We ought to have a company of rangers of our own. Somebody to watch the trails. Mostly to the south. Any big force will have to come at us from Unadilla or Tioga."

"What can they do?" demanded the doctor.

"Give us warning. If we can get inside the forts we can hold them off, barring cannon, no matter how many of them come. It's a long way to bring cannon. And men like Adam Helmer or Joe Boleo could make it risky for their scouts." He paused. "They might be able to pick up a few of these murdering parties, too."

"How'll you pay them?"

"Militia money. We'll list them in different companies and work out 'service' for them."

"It's not regular. They're good at making smells in Congress."

"I'm responsible," said Bellinger. "I can stand some smells."

The doctor got up. "While I'm here I might talk to that Nancy. How is she?"

"All right. You'll probably find her out in back."

Dr. Petry stamped heavily into the small back room. He found Nancy sitting white-faced, very upright, on a chair. Her hands were on her knees.

As he saw her, the doctor's brows gathered.

"What's the matter?" he asked in his harsh voice.

Nancy's lip quivered.

"Doctor, what does the fornication look like?"

"What!" he exclaimed.

"She said the fornication would be my death."

Dr. Petry started a German curse.

"She? That woman. She's crazy." He was exasperated and confused.

They were all crazy. He turned on Nancy. "Don't talk blasted nonsense at me."

Nancy began to blubber.

"I don't want to die."

"You won't die," shouted the doctor. "I tell you. Listen to me. You won't die."

Nancy was appalled at the way the doctor looked down at her with the breath-making noises in his nose.

"Did Mrs. Demooth say that?"

Nancy nodded.

Without another word he turned and stamped out. He had his own war to wage and he laid down the law to Demooth. Nancy heard it all. Her terror increased. She was afraid that Mrs. Demooth would want to kill her. In her heart she had the unavoidable conviction that Mrs. Demooth knew better than the shouting doctor. She wanted to find somebody, Hon, McLonis, any friendly person, before she died. . . .

The doctor had reduced Mrs. Demooth to tears. He not only dressed her down, he told the captain what he thought of him for letting his wife behave so to a poor, defenseless girl. His whole big face was flushed and his eyes stared at them as if they would burst out of their sockets. Nothing could stop him until Mrs. Demooth began to laugh. She went off into peals of screaming laughter, one after the other, drowning all other sound.

The doctor took one look at her, stepped to the pantry, where he found the water bucket, and doused the woman with the entire bucketful. He slammed the bucket on the floor, swore once, and told her to go and dry her face. Then he stormed out of the house to his horse.

After the doctor had left, Nancy listened to Captain Demooth leading his wife to her room. She sat where she was, not getting supper, not even moving, but listening to the continued sobbing in the bedroom. Over and over, Mrs. Demooth kept saying, "I'm so frightened, Mark. I've been so frightened. I can't sleep. I don't see how you can sleep. I dream about them. I dream about Indians. They won't let me even sleep. . . ." The sun set. Twilight came into the small room, cool, with a wet smell from the sopping land. The snow was nearly gone. Only here and there stretches of it left in the folds of the land made shimmers in the dusk.

The house gradually quieted. A long time after, the captain came into the kitchen. Nancy could hear him moving there. She saw the light come on in the crack under the door. She tried to stir herself, and she got as far as the door.

Her own face was swollen from crying. Her eyes felt as though they were filled with blood. When she opened the door the captain was standing by the table.

He turned his face.

"Yes, Nancy."

"Do you want me to get some supper?"

He looked at her gravely.

"No, thanks."

Nancy forced herself to speak.

"How about *her?*"

"I don't think she needs anything. I think you'd better not go to see her. I think she's sleeping."

Nancy swallowed. Her contracted throat gulped with the effort.

"I'm sorry, sir."

The captain's face was not kind. It was not unkind either. It frightened her. She would rather have had him swear at her the way the doctor had.

"You'd better stay in your own room, Nancy. I may have to move you somewhere else for a while. But I'll take care of you till your child's born."

"Yes, sir."

"I've got to go over to the fort for half an hour. I think she'll be all right. She's sleeping."

Nancy's eyes widened as she saw him go through the door. She knew better. She knew that *she* wasn't asleep. It was just a pretense to get him to go. To get him to leave Nancy alone. As the door closed after him, Nancy gave a little moan. She couldn't cry to him to come back. Her voice wouldn't work. She wrestled with her brain to make her voice work, but it would not. The bedroom door had opened.

"Don't you dare to make a sound."

Mrs. Demooth was standing in the door. Her hair was bunched about her head in wild damp masses, but her eyes, which stared at Nancy, were dry and brilliant inside the red lids. Crying had made her voice hoarse and nasal.

Totally unable to stir, Nancy watched her in horror; but Mrs. Demooth stayed in the door. Both listened to the diminishing sound of the captain's footsteps along the muddy road. It was a full minute after they had died away before either woman spoke.

"He said I wasn't to leave the room."

She did not raise her voice; but for a moment her eyes wavered, as if even yet she feared that the captain might hear her. For a moment she was silent. There was no sound at all but the rapid beating of Nancy's heart. Then Mrs. Demooth lifted her chin.

"I never hired you. He hired you and then he told me. I didn't want you to begin with."

Suddenly Nancy started shuddering. The shudders brought little repercussions of sound out of her throat, a hushed animal whimpering. Her mouth began to open. "Stop it." Mrs. Demooth's voice was raised a note; it was still hoarse. Nancy closed her mouth and swallowed, and wiped her mouth with her hand and wiped her hand on her apron.

"You're nasty," said Mrs. Demooth, watching her. "You're not only a whore, you're nasty." She nodded. "Don't you move. He said I mustn't leave my room. I was younger than you when he married me. I used to live in a fine house in Schenectady. Our servants weren't idiots. There weren't any Indians. There was a wall round the town. I came with him. I went into those awful woods and lived in a log cabin. I never said No to anything he wanted. And he hired you. Do you know I've always hated you? Do you know how I've wanted to kill you? Answer me. Answer me, will you?"

Nancy could barely nod. The motion opened her lips.

"You're nasty. Nasty. But you can't move. Neither of us can move. Do you understand? It's what he wanted. It's his orders. It's the will of God.

You can't move. I have to stay here. He made me promise. I never said No to him. But I'm going to kill you, Nancy. I'm going to kill you, do you understand? I know *I'll* be killed soon. The Indians are coming to kill me. But I'll kill you first. The Lord will let me live long enough for that. To kill you and that abomination inside your body. Don't move. You can't move." She laughed deep in her throat. No one had ever heard her make a sound like that. She laughed again, listening, herself fascinated. "God has made me an instrument in His hand. He removes all unclean things from His earth. He comes and walks the earth to do it Himself, or else He makes instruments like me. He walks the earth. Do you hear me, you?"

Nancy's eyes were dull. Suddenly she put her hands to her abdomen, taking hold of herself.

Mrs. Demooth began to laugh.

"It knows. It is dying. I told you I would kill it."

Nancy screamed.

"You know I hated you, but you didn't go. You couldn't. He wouldn't let you, because he wanted me to kill you. Now He comes walking. To see you die. You and what's dying in you now."

Nancy's knees buckled. She seemed to collapse over herself onto her face.

Mrs. Demooth watched her. There was no tremor to the open flame of the lamp. There was no tremor in Nancy's body. Mrs. Demooth smiled. She looked right and left, listening. Her smile deepened. Her face seemed even paler. Little bunches of flesh swelled beside her nostrils. Slowly she took a step over the threshold of her room and stopped. She looked right left again and listened. Then she walked over to where the girl lay and bent down and lifted her shoulder. Nancy rolled partly on her side, and lay limp, bent slightly at the hips, preserving the position. Mrs. Demooth let go the shoulder and straightened up. Then deliberately she kicked Nancy.

She returned to her room and paused for a moment to look back at the prone figure with exalted eyes. She raised her eyes slightly, closed the door, and went to bed.

The evening mist drifting into the shadows drew across Nancy's face. Her lids fluttered. Gradually she opened her eyes. There was no sound. Her eyes rolled slowly towards the bedroom door and found it closed. Tears came into her eyes and rolled down over her face.

Suddenly she blenched. She put her hand to her belly and pressed against herself. Her face was contorted with the effort to rise soundlessly. Her long legs moved with infinite care. She took off her shoes and tiptoed to her room. There the horror overwhelmed her completely. No longer trying to be quiet, she gathered her belongings in a panic,—her dress, her comb, her nightgown, and her cloth shoes,—and twisted them into her shawl. She came back through the kitchen, bent slightly forward, keeping her eyes from the door, and went out into the darkness. She ran heavily.

On Captain Demooth's return he found his wife rigid on her bed, with a slight froth drying at the corners of her mouth. He could not waken her and called for Nancy. When she did not answer, he went into the kitchen and rang the bell. Then he went to her room and found that she had gone.

He took the lamp into the yard, shouting for Clem, and with the old Dutchman searched the yard. By the fence they found Nancy's fresh tracks. She had climbed the rails and crossed the meadow towards the south. They managed to follow her tracks as far as the woods. But there they had to stop.

"There's no use in looking any more."

Clem shook his head: "Only an Indian could foller her through that brush."

"Didn't you hear anything at all?"

"I was sleeping pretty hard. I was tired."

"I'll have to get back to my wife."

"Anything wrong with her?"

"She's had a fit, I think. Her mother told me she used to have them when she was little. Will you go fetch Doc, Clem?"

Clem said, "*Tschk, tschk,*" in his best manner.

"Hurry up, Clem. I feel as if I was going crazy myself. We just had an express from Albany. Walter Butler's escaped."

"God help us," exclaimed Clem; but he was thinking about fording the river. The water was high, now.

7. *The Indian*

When, a few hours later, Nancy broke free of the woods, she found herself on one of the bare, hillside pastures. Looking back, she saw the mist lying below her in the valley. She had come a long way.

Her shawl was a sodden bundle hanging from her clinched fingers. Her short gown was torn over one shoulder. Her petticoat clung wetly to her legs. She felt like a flogged person; she was reeking with sweat and wet from the whipping branches. Her hair hung round her face. A little stream of blood trickled from a cut cheek.

She fought hard to gain her breath, turning her back on the valley and fixing her eyes on the stars. Gradually against their distant patterns she made out the dark shoulder of the hill. When she saw it, she started once more at her heavy walk. Her body was like a dead weight precariously balanced on the arch that joined her legs.

Somewhere under the mist behind her, a dog rushed out of an invisible house. She could hear his furious barks traveling back and forth. All at once the dog's voice deepened, fixed, and she realized that it had picked up her scent.

But at the same moment a long whistle pierced the mist. It was followed by a man's incensed shouting. "Prince! Come back here, Prince!" Nancy heard the name quite plainly. The dog stopped barking and then, a moment later, yelped; and the night became still. A long shuddering breath went out of Nancy. She set herself with a desperate deliberation against the hill.

A half hour later she stopped on top of the hill in a scattered grove of maples to draw deep breaths. Though she knew that she was out of reach of pursuit, she did not dare stop for long. She was convinced that what Mrs. Demooth had told her would surely take place. The pain she had carried out of the house had died, but she was sure that it would come to life again. Even now she could feel its premonitory stirrings.

She tramped nearly all night. The general slope of the ground was downward, but at times she was brought up against sharp rises that took interminable climbing. A little before dawn she lost her sense of direction. She could no longer see the stars; the sky had turned to a dull gray with neither light nor shadow. The ravine in which she floundered was gray, like the sky, and the wet touch of branches on her cheeks or breast was cold.

She stumbled into a small stream without seeing it and came at last to a halt in water that pushed icily against her knees. She put her hand down and lifted a little water to her mouth. Her lips felt swollen to her hand's touch. She could not drink.

After a minute she gave up and wearily forced her way out of the water. Her knees would not lift her feet the height necessary to climb out on the bank, and she struggled futilely, feeling the cold earth against her thighs. She splashed heavily, though she did not hear it, and fell face down on the thick dead sodden grass, and lay there.

It was then that the pains returned. Nancy lifted her swollen, pale, and tear-streaked face and cried out. Her voice was not loud, it was utterly forlorn. It made the Indian think of a rabbit in a faulty snare.

The Indian had been scouting down towards the flats when the dog scented him and barked. His first intention had been to sneak up beside the corner of the barn to see whether he could pick up an easy scalp. He wanted to save up for a new gun; his old French trade musket that he had inherited from his father shot very badly. For hunting he even had to carry his bow. He had picked up two scalps that month, one down at Ephratah, and one of a lone trapper between Edmeston and the little lakes. The one he had got at Ephratah had not come off well and he was not sure whether he would be able to get the eight-dollar bounty for it at Niagara. He ought to take another to be sure.

But the dog had so obviously spotted him that the Indian decided to give up that chance, and he legged it up the hill with the dog chasing him. The man had called in the dog; and the Indian had nothing to show. But then he had heard somebody floundering in the wet way above him. When he reached the pasture, whoever it was had disappeared, but the Indian found plain tracks and a tatter of cloth together beside a juniper. He could not understand it; it was too dark to see the tracks, but just on the chance he had started following. In the dark, that was slow and painful work. As soon as it got lighter, however, he made the surprising discovery that the footprints had been left by a woman. He fingered the pouch under his belt in which he carried his *Oki,* the skin of a red-headed woodpecker, and realized that at last it was bringing him a little luck. You got eight dollars for any scalp regardless of sex. This ought to be an easy eight dollars. The woman was alone.

He went at a trot, for the trail was easy to follow, and a little past dawn he broke out on the edge of a steep ravine and looked down on her. She had fallen forward on the bank of a small stream.

The Indian ran down the bank, jumped the stream in a single leap, and stood beside her, fingering his hatchet. He had several ideas. He might shoot her—he hadn't shot anything with his musket this trip—or he could bang her on the head and save the powder. He was still considering when Nancy looked up at him and screamed again, and he realized that she had not seen him at all or heard him either until that instant. Then he saw that she no longer saw him. She was unconscious. He caught her by the arm and hauled her out of the water and looked at her. He found out that she was in the act of giving birth.

He was very much puzzled. To find a woman like her there alone in such a case was extraordinary. It made him uneasy. He decided that he had better think things over before he killed her, so he dragged her over the ground to a clump of hemlock and built a fire. He left her on a slight incline, with her legs downward, and sat down himself with his back to her.

The light increased gradually while he sat before the fire. Birds moved in the branches. He heard their voices all through the woods and the smooth musical sliding of the water over a sunk log. While he watched the birds he took out of a pouch a piece of pemmican and began sucking and gnawing at it. He considered that his wife had died that winter and that he had no children and that he might get eight dollars for the torn scalp anyway. But he was not sure.

He seemed oblivious of the event taking place behind him. But suddenly his dark eyes were attracted by the flashing passage of a woodpecker. Black and white, and the red head like a traveling spark. A great twittering and fluttering broke out in a tree, and a moment later the woodpecker returned in hot pursuit of a female. The Indian grunted, relaxed, and went ahead with his chewing. He decided that she was a strong girl, or she would not have journeyed so far. And her light long hair and her blue eyes interested him; he was different from most Indians in his own town. He liked to live solitary and had a small log house on the outskirts of Deodesote village. He had never been markedly successful on a warpath. Two scalps and this woman prisoner might make him some reputation. If, now, he decided to marry her, it wouldn't be necessary to give presents, either.

He waited complacently for the woman to finish the business.

When some poor order emerged from the flux of Nancy's consciousness and she opened her eyes to the world before her, she saw the Indian sitting in sunlight before his fire with his blanket drawn over his shoulders. The musket was leaning against the stub of a dead hemlock branch and the bow and quiver were hung beside it.

The sides of the Indian's poll were shaved and the scalplock was braided like some queer kind of handle to his head. One battered feather hung from it. He looked comical to her lightheaded fancy, and she felt sorry for him, he was so dark and ugly. When she tried to speak, and he turned, she almost laughed at the way his face looked with smeared paint, white and vermilion, in stripes. She even remembered how it had terrified her when she saw it on the bank of the stream; then it had appeared like the arrival of the abomination itself. But now Nancy knew that she was alive.

To her awakening senses came the sound of the water in the stream, the birds' voices, and the smell of smoke from the Indian's fire. Her body felt

torn and sore and exhausted, but it was alive. She met the Indian's expressionless eyes with a slight smile; then struggled to sit up.

As she did so he rose to his feet and moved away from her. He went
down the ravine to a piece of dry raised ground and started peeling sheaths
of bark from a big hemlock. He used his hatchet and scalping knife together.

For a while Nancy watched him erecting a tiny bark shanty. Then she
made her eyes look down at herself and at the small, soiled, male shape
to which she had given birth. For a moment she was chilled by the old
fear; but her movement upset the child so that it rolled over and bumped
against her knee; and suddenly it opened its infinitely small mouth and
gave a flat bawling wail.

It was alive. Nancy laughed. Then she picked up the baby and moved
it into the sun and went down to the stream with unsteady steps and washed
herself as well as she was able. While she was there she found her bundle,
and, bringing it back, unwrapped it and took out the nightgown, which was
of worn flannel. In the dryest piece of this she could tear out, she wrapped
the baby, after first wiping its body with the other portions.

When she was done, the Indian came back to her and said something she
could not understand. He was a squat, slightly bow-legged man who did
not quite come to her shoulder. He pointed to the shed he had made.

"Oh yes. Thank you very much."

Nancy smiled wanly and managed to follow him. He did not offer to
help her with the child or her belongings, but he put down his blanket for
her.

He tapped himself on the chest.

"Gahota," he said. "Gahota."

Then he poked Nancy's breast with his forefinger and stared at her. She
giggled slightly. He poked again. Finally she understood.

"Oh, my name's Nancy."

He repeated it. Then he said, "Gahota."

"Gahota," said Nancy. The Indian smiled. Some of the paint cracked
on his cheek. He watched her sit down on his blanket, put some more
wood on the fire, took his bow, quiver, and musket, and disappeared into
the woods.

Nancy sat still for a long time, holding the baby in her lap. Finally she
lay down with it and slept.

It was nearly dusk when she smelled cookery and woke again. The Indian was squatting before the fire. He had fashioned a bark dish in which
he was boiling some meat. Every now and then with a small ladle of birch
bark he would skim off a wet mass of feathers. But as soon as he saw that
Nancy was awake, he moved over and gave her the ladle, signing to her
that it was time she assumed the woman's job.

The two partridges boiling away in the soup smelled strong, for they had
been immersed, feathers, entrails, and all; but Nancy was hungry. She
skimmed with good will. When the two carcasses fell apart she took the
bark dish off the stones it rested on and set it between herself and Gahota.
As she started to dip her ladle, the Indian took it from her hand.

He ate slowly and steadily until the soup was half gone. Then he shoved
the vessel towards her and tossed the ladle in. Nancy was ravenous. While
she was eating the baby began to cry. But she did not heed it until she had

finished the soup. Twice she saw the Indian stare at the child, and the third time she reached for it and set it on her lap.

A little later in the evening she felt the milk filling her breasts. Clumsily she lifted the child. She caught Gahota's eye. He looked contented now, indifferent. He had removed his shirt and was slowly rubbing his belly.

Nancy felt a great friendliness for this kind man.

"Will you help me find my brother?" she asked.

He did not turn his head, nor answer.

"My brother, Hon? Hon Yost Schuyler."

He did not answer.

"I must find him," said Nancy, with a slight panic. But the Indian continued to ignore her. She dropped the subject, for she thought obviously the poor heathen did not understand the English language. Besides she felt warm and soothed and preoccupied with the tugging at her breast. Almost as an afterthought she said companionably, "He lives at Niagara, you know."

Gahota, whose name meant Log-in-the-Water, had been politely ignoring her bad manners in addressing him. But now he grunted.

"Deodesote," he said flatly.

He did not look at Nancy. But Nancy nodded behind his funny back. She was contented for the first time in many months. Quite happy.

"Deodesote," she repeated in a dutiful voice.

They started just at daybreak.

8. *Smoke*

As the days of May went by, the settlers in German Flats became increasingly aware of the gradual closing in of the destructives. Captain Demooth was asking for volunteers to add to the Ranger service. He had been able to find only ten men willing to spend all their time in the woods. There had been thirty at first, but as the sun grew daily warmer, and the earth dried, many of them returned to work in their fields.

Gil was one of these. He knew that Mrs. McKlennar would have willingly found another man and taken care of Lana into the bargain; but the farm was on his mind. He had to see to the planting of the corn himself. When he was out with Joe and Adam, he found himself uneasy, after the first two days, to see how the wheat was growing.

"He ain't nothing but a farming man," Joe would say, disgustedly. They had set up a tiny lodge a few miles north of Edmeston, which was still inhabited by several Tory families. From the hillside, as he lay on his belly in the leaves, Gil could look down on the clearings and watch the small ploughings; the women putting in the hills of corn and squash and beans; the children fetching the cattle at dusk and dawn.

The children were the only people they had to be careful of. Sometimes the cattle strayed near the shanty and had to be driven off, though once or twice, before he did so, Gil took their kettle and filled it with fresh milk.

The other two would never allow Gil to make one of the weekly solitary scouts to the southward. They said he had no sense in the woods; he would get killed surely. An Indian squaw could hear him coming half a mile. They made him stay at the lodge, and when they thought they had any news, he had to run up the back trail fifteen miles to the next station. There a man was always waiting to relay the word.

Gil was not as bad in the woods as they made him out to be. He became quieter as time went on, and they admitted that he was turning into a good runner—not in Adam's class, of course, but better than middling. But he had no eye for things. He couldn't tell what a crow or jay or kingfisher was chattering of. They said tolerantly that he would never learn.

There were odd times when he felt the lazy contentment creeping into him. When for days they just lay round on a hilltop, when the sun was hot and the sky dry, watching the tops of the trees to the south and particularly the east.

Once old Blue Back came into the camp. He had taken his wife on a spring tour to Unadilla to visit a Tuscarora family as soon as she had her planting done. He had left her there and struck north to give them the news.

They saw him sauntering up the hill, shifting his eyes left and right, looking everywhere but in their direction. Joe muttered, "The old twerp seen us a hundred yards back. He looked me right in the eye. Now he's going to act surprised."

He did.

He beamed all over and said "How" to all of them, shaking hands and holding his hat up to each in turn. He had not shaved his head. He looked greasy and brown and dirty and he smelled of fish. He said they had been curing bullheads for three days in his friend's cabin. They had all the windows and doors closed to keep the smoke in the cabin. He said it got pretty hot, sometimes, so he came up to see how Joe Boleo was, and his friend, Gil Martin. He said an Indian couldn't get any drink in Unadilla or Oghkwaga either. The white men laid hold of all of it. He thought somebody up north might have a drink. He had a twitching in his right leg when he went without it too long himself. Did Joe ever have that?

Joe resignedly handed him a small swallow of rum and Blue Back sat down. He said he needed a new hat.

"Go to hell," said Joe. "You can't have mine."

"Too big," agreed Blue Back. "Yours too big." He pointed at Helmer. "What you going to do about that, Gil?"

Gil grinned and said he needed his own hat himself.

"Me make trade," suggested Blue Back.

"No, thanks," said Gil.

"What's on your mind?" asked Joe.

The old Oneida sighed and said that Joseph Brant was in Unadilla. He was gathering the Indians. There were already about fifty whites under Captain Caldwell there, and quite a lot of runaway negroes. He hadn't talked to Captain Caldwell himself, because he thought they might not be friends. But Captain Caldwell drank a great deal. All the white men drank a great deal. Sometimes it seemed to Blue Back that they were sick or afraid of the woods.

"Brant still there?"

Brant, said Blue Back, had gathered together about two hundred and taken the party eastward. But he was due to return soon. He had to meet with John Butler at Unadilla in the end of June.

Boleo whistled under his breath.

"Adam," he said, "you better take a cut through Springfield and pass out a warning. They won't pay no attention, though."

"No," said the Indian. He had been that way himself. People just kicked him out. He hadn't even had a drink. He had only managed to steal a couple of young pigs.

"What did you do with them?" asked Adam hopefully.

It appeared that they were eaten.

Joe said, "When did Brant move out of Unadilla?"

A week ago, said Blue Back.

Joe swore. "Why didn't you come here right away, you old timber beast?"

"No good."

He's right, thought Gil. The people wouldn't move, now that crops were in the earth, and there were no troops to send to them. He looked at Joe. Joe was standing up and staring eastward.

"By God," he said, "Brant's on the loose already!"

Gil could not see the smoke for a long time. It was such a pale, frail, insubstantial thing, a mere mist in the sky.

"You better pull foot for home, Gil. Tell 'em Brant's burning Springfield way. Me and Adam will make a scout, and Adam will come back here and I'll report at Herkimer."

They had their own path marked out. They did not use the old Iroquois trail. Their route lay along the ridges, above it, following deer runs.

Gil hit a steady pace. He was going all the way through to the forts. On such long running—even on this one, when he knew that the destructives were loose he had a singular feeling of freedom. Often he thought that if he were making such a run with Adam, he would quite easily break off with the easy-going giant to a party with the Bowers girls. Adam had pestered him about it more than once when they were lying before their fire at night.

The sunset was fading when Gil came out on the top of Shoemaker hill. He paused for a moment to get his breath for the last miles down to the river.

The sky was like a great silken sheet over all the world, misty in the north, but edged with sunset to the west. Under it, on a level with Gil's eyes, the wilderness rolled northward—mile upon mile, ridge upon ridge, until the mountains lifted against the sky. The color of it in the late spring was like water, gray-green, with darker shades where the evergreens marked out the long pine ridges or the balsam swamps, and with occasional frothy streaks of white of the wild cherries in bloom. As the light waned, the whole panorama conveyed a sense of motion; the ridges rolling higher and higher, as the hollows of the balsam swamps were deepened.

The valley itself was like a crystal under his feet through which he could look down on a picture painted in miniature. The bright line of the river was still tinged with the sunset; the two forts—from this elevation they looked close together—were geometrical shapes in the irregular varicolored fields; the fences between the fields were like small stitches painstakingly made to patch the surface of the flats. But the houses and barns alone in the farther clearings were infinitesimal blocks in the crooked fingers of the wilderness.

As he started down the bald slope of the hill, Gil's eyes searched across the river, picking up the line of the Kingsroad and following it towards McKlennar's. He could see house and barn, and the stone house behind the blooming apple tree. The sunset made the windows blind burning eyes in the stone face. But the rest of the place was clear, even to young John Weaver turning the cows into the yard. Lana, of course, would not be milking. She was two weeks overdue. Gil trotted downward.

Then he saw a familiar figure moving along the road. He knew at once who it was. It moved into a lighted stretch, showing the gray horse and the heavy, upright, black-clad rider. He was going out from German Flats. He was approaching McKlennar's. Now he turned in, and John Weaver's small dog rushed out barking to meet him.

It was Dr. Petry. For some reason, Gil remembered what Mrs. Mc-Klennar had once called the doctor, when she saw him riding his gray horse along the road. "Like death on a pale horse," she had said.

9.   Night on the Farm

Young John Weaver tingled with excitement, curiosity, and dread. He could tell by Daisy's voice that things had started in the stone house. He had just finished the milking; it had taken longer with the spotted cow freshened, as she had that morning; one hind quarter of her bag had shown a sign of caking and he had to work on her. The negress stuck her calico-wrapped head in the barn door and called, "You, boy!" He knew it then, but he didn't like being called "You, boy," by a nigger, even though he was hired help; and he didn't answer. Daisy peered in and said, "Oh, white boy!"

"What is it?" John asked gruffly.

Immediately Daisy put on her importance.

"You got to fotch me mo' wood."

"I took it in before I went after the cows."

"Dat trash! I want birch. I want a lot of it. Fust thing dey'll holler fo' hot water, and whar Daisy den? W'en ol' Miss wants something she wants it first off, immeedjut, and now. I got to have birch split fine to fotch de bilin' wid de fust bref. Here, give me dat milk and get on de mare and go tell Doc Petry. And don' you spare de hickory stick on'r."

John wrenched the halter off the mare, bridled her, and mounted bare-back. He rode hard, hunching himself over the withers, and wondering, "Will I be in time?" He drew up at the doctor's and called in through the window.

"They just told me to fetch you."

With agonized eyes he watched the doctor pop in a tart of preserved currants and wipe his mouth. "I thought it might start to-night," said Doc. "Well, well. You might unhitch my horse—he's all saddled—and bring him round here."

John flung off the reeking mare and got the doctor's horse, lugging him by main force. He waited till the doctor came out and mounted. "Hup," said Dr. Petry. It was like winding a piece of clockwork: the spring seemed jammed for a minute; then the insides of the gray animal whirred and rumbled and his legs started to gesticulate, and all of a sudden you realized that he was actually walking away. John clambered onto the mare and caught up. The mare was hot and full of fettle.

"Excuse me, sir," he said to Doc. "I think I'd better get on back. They want me to split some more wood."

The doctor, who had got the hiccoughs from starting out on a new-filled stomach, put his hand to his mouth, and then turned his staring eyes on John.

"Oh, yes," he said. "Split wood. Just what we need. Half a cord."

But the mare was already helling away up the road like the backsides of forty rabbits. John rushed her into her stall and yanked his axe out of the shed and got to work on the wood. As soon as he had three or four armfuls he delivered them to the kitchen. He could hear Mrs. McKlennar moving round the front room and talking. Daisy bustled in. "Dat's enough in here," she said. But John still stood there. He wasn't sure. Yes, it was —her voice! Mrs. Martin was talking! Thank God she was still alive!

He went back to the woodpile and chopped and split enough wood to boil water for all the babies this side of China. But he was thinking, wouldn't this be an awful time to have the destructives strike the flats? Of course the scouts were out. Of course there would be some warning. But to move her! Move her now! It was too late. Why hadn't she moved into a house close to the fort? When the doctor came there would be two of them, though. John left off chopping and got down his musket and re-primed it. He wished that Gil was back. He felt a tremendous responsibility. But he wished now that the doctor would hurry up. Then he remembered that he hadn't turned the cows out, so he did that. And then the doctor arrived.

"Chopped the wood?" he inquired gravely as John took his horse.

"Yes, sir," said John.

The doctor went into the house. When John came back to the porch and sat down with the musket on his knees, he could hear the doctor's heavy voice rumbling away to Mrs. McKlennar, a pause, laughter, and then Lana's voice joining in.

Young John felt the blood rush all through him. He positively burned with the thought, "By God, women were brave!"

He thought what it would be like when he and Mary got married. What it would be like, being in there, watching her, seeing her go through it. It seemed awful. Mary was even slimmer than Mrs. Martin was. But it had to be. A man couldn't get away from facing it. It was right, too. It was what you expected.

He heard silence fall heavily in the room. Then he heard Mrs. Martin give a gasp and the doctor say with unction, "They're picking up, aren't they?"

"Well, for God's sake, John Weaver!"

He turned to see the widow looking at him. Her horse face was flushed high with excitement. But she appeared to struggle with something in her own inside.

"What on earth are you doing, John?"

He tried to explain. But Mrs. McKlennar seemed to understand. "Very good idea," she said. "Yes indeed. But I think you ought to patrol the place. You better keep marching round the buildings. Suppose an Indian should be coming up from the back?"

John wasn't a fool. He blushed. He knew that she meant he wasn't to sit there right outside the window. He couldn't imagine how he had come to do it.

"Yes, ma'am."

Now he was marching round the yard. Now he was down on the road, looking to see if anybody were coming. He leaned against the fence rails, and thought, "Even if we get able to marry this summer, that couldn't happen for quite a while."

For he and Mary had it all settled. They had realized last winter that John's mother still didn't want them to get married, and that she had asked Mary up just for John to see how little Mary knew. But Mary had been apt at picking things up, and Mrs. Weaver hadn't liked that. She had stopped asking the girl in March.

George Weaver had taken it pretty much to heart. He had said to his son, "That's how your Ma is. You've got to take her the way she is, John. I've done it, and she's been an almighty good wife. She's been a good mother, too. If times were different I could give you something to get married on. As it is, you'll have to work for yourselves. When you get enough, you'll have my agreement, and I'm not going to take your pay, as I might otherwise. You go ahead, and you work it out when you can, and you get married. Mary's a fine girl, and your Ma's just notional now. Once you've gone and done it, she'll come round."

It was the longest talk he had ever had with his father. He had gone down to see Mary about it the next week. That was the day when Mrs. Reall had announced that she was going to go back to Massachusetts with Corporal Rebus White. Mrs. Reall was taking her family, but Mary had refused to go. She was ashamed. She broke down with John and explained that Mrs. Reall would not marry Mr. White until the state had paid her widow's claim. It was shameful.

Mary had stayed. She had, through March and April, eked out enough, by working for the garrisons, to feed herself. But it had seemed pretty desperate to them both. At first John could not get work. Then when the spring came there was plenty of work to do for widow women, but there was no cash money involved. There was almost no money left that people were willing to lay out in hired help.

But at the end of April they had had a great stroke of luck. Captain Demooth's hired girl had run away and the captain had been willing to let Mary go there and try the job. And then Gilbert Martin had joined the Rangers, which took him away part of the time, and while he was gone he paid John half a shilling a day to look after the McKlennar place. They realized they were getting along. For a while they even talked of getting married right away, until it occurred to Mary that it might interfere with her job; so they decided to wait a few months longer and save maybe twelve or fifteen dollars.

John had wanted to join the Rangers, but they said he was too young. They did promise to enroll him in the militia, though, when the companies were reorganized. He told Mary about it.

His mother never spoke about Mary. Every time John returned to see his family, she cooked some dish she knew he would like, but she froze all over if he mentioned the girl. She seemed bitter and unhappy. And now John, thinking of what one day Mary would surely have to go through, never considered that his mother had been through the same process to bring him into the world.

All he thought of was Mary. Since she got her job, she had taken to winding her braids round her head. Her neck showed slim and pliant. There were moments when she greeted him with a dignity and fondness through which her slim ardency emerged as a thing so surprising that it took the breath of them both. It gave John a queer feeling that her visible maturing, instead of giving her defenses against himself, was putting her in his power. She was so anxious to improve herself, she was so conscious of the fact that she had come between him and his mother, that she wanted to do everything to please him.

Even John did not think she was pretty, except in the way any girl that wasn't too fat was pretty. He didn't know why it was he had fallen in love with her. She was long-legged and she had an abrupt way of moving; but every now and then, when she looked at him, she seemed struck in a moment with grace.

He tried to figure it all out. She was never malicious, and she was always honest; and yet she was shy. He realized vaguely that she was fine, but it was hard to understand that, with her parents and her upbringing. That was what he called her to himself. She was fine.

It was quite a beautiful discovery for a boy so young as John to have made.

He tried to imagine how it would be when they were married, what kind of room they would have, and what Mary would have on. He wondered whether he would be shaving by then. Mary had once said she hoped he would never let his beard grow. He thought of her lying slim and snug under the blankets, and himself shaving over the slop basin.

Young John shouldered his musket and marched back to the road with his little brown dog trotting before him like a fox. He wondered how long the dog had been with him; he had not noticed; he had not even noticed that he had strayed away from the road. With surprise he saw that it had become dark. A still, black night, in which sounds carried long distances. He could hear a whippoorwill in the cornfield as plain as though it were in the road beside him. The peepers down by the river began to whimper into their night singing. John shivered, and looked back up the slope towards the stone house.

The windows of the bedroom were lighted. Against the curtains he saw the silhouettes of the doctor, bent over like a grubbing bear, and the dragoon-like figure of the widow.

"God," thought John. "It's happening now."

The sweat came pouring out of him. Then there was one uncontrollable welling of sound that he would never have taken for Mrs. Martin's voice. The doctor ducked down. Mrs. McKlennar bent forward. They were like people smitten out of the power of life.

And then the doctor straightened up, and John suddenly relaxed weakly against the fence. He had forgotten all about destructives, Indians, war, Mary, his mother, himself. It was over. But John stayed still and struggled with himself, to make himself go up, to find out what had happened.

Then the little brown dog started growling.

"Shut your mouth," said John savagely. He aimed a cuff at the beast, but the dog eluded him and spun off down the road barking high and shrill. Then John heard a man running towards him.

"Hello, hello. That you, John?"

"Is it Mr. Martin?"

"Yes. I saw Dr. Petry coming up when I was on the hill. What's happened?"

John said with a strangely controlled voice:—

"The baby's just got born."

"Is everything all right?"

"I was just going up to see," said John, "when I heard you coming."

They turned towards the house. They saw the door open and a path of light shoot towards them down the slope. Mrs. McKlennar was standing there with a bundle.

"John! John Weaver!"

"Yes, ma'am."

"It's all right. I thought you'd like to know."

John's throat filled.

"Yes, ma'am. Here's Mr. Martin. He just got back."

He felt Gil take hold of his arm. They ran that way, full tilt up to the porch. Mrs. McKlennar stood waiting for them, grinning wide, but with tears sliding bumpily down beside her nose. She was snorting and sniffing like a dog with a breathful of smoke.

Gil shoved right past her and went into the room; and John couldn't help peering through behind him. Dr. Petry was in the act of covering up Mrs. Martin. But the thing that surprised John was that Mrs. Martin had her eyes open. She gave Gil a small smile.

The doctor grunted.

"Everything went off first rate, young man."

There it was. There in Mrs. McKlennar's arms. She pulled back the wrapping and showed John the red small face with its intimations of humanity quite plainly to be seen already.

John breathed hard.

"It's a perfectly beautiful boy," said Mrs. McKlennar.

10. *Andrustown*

Whatever she might be doing, Mrs. McKlennar beamed like the rising sun. She would not hear of Lana's working more than to wash the baby and change its diaper cloths. One day when Lana was bathing herself and the baby started to yell, Lana asked Mrs. McKlennar whether she would change the cloths for her. Mrs. McKlennar did. "Nasty, nasty," she said. "He's just like a man already, the way he don't care how he musses." That afternoon, when John showed up to say good-bye, she gave him the brightest shilling she had in the house. "Don't you put it away," she said to him. "You go down to Petry's and buy your girl a hair ribbon with it." John was amazed. He looked at the shilling in his soiled palm and he looked at Mrs. McKlennar. Her horselike face was still beaming because she had been asked to change the baby's dirty cloths.

John went down to the hay piece to see Mr. Martin. He had already been paid; he had nearly three dollars in his pocket, but he thought he ought to say good-bye again. And he hated to leave the farm. Somehow it had become associated in his mind with the life he and Mary were going to start as soon as they were able. He had lately imagined themselves in such a place.

Gil was mowing some of the corners along the bottom land and he rested his scythe on the point of the snathe when he saw John coming and began to whet the blade. The stone against the steel gave ringing notes in the still heat.

"Well, John. You're going?"

"Yes, Mr. Martin."

"I hate to let you go."

"I kind of hate to go myself, Mr. Martin."

"I'd keep you here if I could afford to. The hay's standing heavy and I'm going to have a lot of work with it, now my wife can't help on the cart."

They accepted this gravely. But Gil was obviously proud and pleased that he was going to have to do extra work.

"Yes, sir," said John.

"You've got another job, John?"

"I promised Mr. Leppard I'd make a trip over to Andrustown with him and help him get in some of his hay."

Gil was thoughtful. "I hope it's all right."

"They only figure on staying a couple of nights. There's been no news in, has there?"

"Not that I know of," said Gil. "But it's pretty far off."

"I guess we'll be all right."

"Joe Boleo's down towards Edmeston, right now. Who's going?"

John said, "Mr. Leppard said him and both the Bells, and Hawyer and Staring, and then young Bell's wife and Mrs. Hawyer and Mrs. Staring. They're coming to rake and to cook for us."

"They oughtn't to take the women."

"I guess it'll be all right," John said again.

"Well, good luck, John."

John raised his hand. "You've treated me real well," he said. "When I come back I'll come around here. Maybe I can give you a couple of days if I haven't got other work."

Leaning on his scythe, Gil watched the lad go. John was a good worker and it would have been fine to keep him round the farm. If it hadn't been for having to pay Dr. Petry's fee, Gil would have hired John out of his own pocket, just for the sake of the place. Another hoeing wouldn't hurt the corn, with all the wet there had been; there would be a big hay crop;

and the wheat looked absolutely clean. It looked pretty close to a record harvest all along the line.

But Gil couldn't lay half a dozen sweeps of hay without having to look up towards the house. And then he would naturally swing his eyes across the valley, taking in the sky line from Eldridge Blockhouse to Fort Dayton. Then he would look back to the house again.

The house was always the same. He could see Mrs. McKlennar and Daisy doing their jobs, and nowadays he could see Lana doing fine work on the verandah—Mrs. McKlennar wouldn't hear of their moving back into the farmhouse, any more than she would consider moving down to one of the forts herself. "What's the sense of your staying in that hot cabin?" she would demand. "You ought to keep the baby cool nights like these." And she was right about the forts, too. They were overcrowded. Since the word had come, at the end of last week, of Butler's attack on Wyoming, the people in Schuyler had moved down. Little Stone Arabia Stockade could not contain all of the local families. Now, with the people from up the Creek Valley and from south, by Andrustown, the forts were jammed. "Me live in a fort!" Mrs. McKlennar's voice was raucous. "Have you *smelled* them? Have you seen the flies? I'd rather be scalped!" But the people wouldn't live outside—even some people with near-by houses came into the fort at night, since they had heard of Wyoming. There had been Wyoming Tories in Butler's brigade. They had been the ones who had searched out fugitives. They hadn't hurt the women and children to speak of; they had just driven them into a swamp without food, to make their own way to safety as well as they were able. There weren't any berries ripe at that season for them to live on; many of those who were lost starved to death. Of those who managed to reach the settlement of Wilkes-Barre, more than half were naked and so stung with flies and infected with ague that it wasn't expected they would survive. Blue Back, who had got the story from his Tuscarora friend in Unadilla, said the swamp was named by the Indians "The Shades of Death." It didn't seem possible that civilized man could allow such things even in war.

A dog was barking over the river to the eastward. Gil's scythe stopped. Now all he could hear was the high screech of the locusts in the woods and he cursed them silently because they obliterated any distant sound. Looking over the river, he saw that men at work in their fields had also stopped. A few were moving slowly to the places where they had left their rifles. The whole valley seemed to have become still. It had happened that way again and again, all the men Gil could see, stopping, and looking in the same direction. He glanced back at the house. That was all right. Up there the baby was squalling about something or other and they had not even noticed.

Then the dog's barking picked up and made a fluent ascent of the hillside woods and everybody knew that he must be running a rabbit; yip-yapping for hell and gone as if the one object of creation were a rabbit and a dog to chase him. Mechanically Gil's scythe sheared again through the standing stems of grass.

Up at the house, Lana opened her dress for the baby's second feeding of the day. She had never felt so much contentment since her first wedded days. In her heart she felt that it was even better than that time. She no longer worried about herself and Gil. The baby was a tangible expression of their success together in the world, while at the same time he was a defense against the world and Gil. She took no thought for the future, except vaguely, thinking of the boy as a man; she was too full of love and the sense of her own easement in feeding her son to feel beyond the moment. It made her proud to know that she could feed him; small as she was, she had a splendid flow of milk; and he was a big demanding child, moreover, who had weighed ten pounds on the doctor's estimate, a child many a larger woman would have envied having.

Mrs. McKlennar often noticed Lana's passionate preoccupation at feeding time. She did not, like many women, take it as a chore; her whole day seemed governed by the expectation that led up to the appointed time. She was a natural mother, Mrs. McKlennar thought, and knew that she herself, supposing she had had a child, would never have felt like that. From now on, Gil would have to walk behind the family cart. He would no longer be the girl's husband, but the father of her family. It was the patriarchal instinct from her Palatine blood. Some of those girls were wonderful things to see before they married; then they became great mothers. "She'll shut him out of both their lives until she wants him." It seemed queer to an Irishwoman.

And yet it was not altogether so. Lana always greeted Gil with happiness and anxiety for his comfort. He was to be pleased, to have just what he wanted. But there it was again; he was the father. Mrs. McKlennar wondered how Gil would stand up under this attitude.

Three mornings later, Joe Boleo appeared at the house for breakfast. He had reached the valley late the night before, sleeping in Demooth's barn. Now he said he wanted a good meal, a wash and shave, and a bed with feathers in it. Nothing was up in the south that he had seen. There was no news. He must admit that he preferred Daisy's cornbread to Adam Helmer's idea of nocake.

After feeding he dropped down to the hay meadow to pass a few minutes with Gil.

"The boy's a dinger," Joe said gravely. "He's growed since I was here before."

Gil grinned.

"He gets lots of nourishment."

"By God," said Joe heartily.

"Who's down in the lodge?" Gil asked.

"Hain't nobody," said Joe. "I got sick of being by myself, but Adam's due back there to-morrow."

"Where's Adam?"

"He's picking up John Butler's trail back to Niagara. There weren't no point in staying down. They've all gone from Unadilla."

"Listen, Joe. Did you see any of the Andrustown people?"

"No, I didn't. I didn't come through Andrustown. I took a swing west of there. Why?"

"There's a party gone there to cut hay."

Joe swore. "Why didn't they tell me?"

"They supposed you were down south."

"Well, I can't stay there all the time. I hain't been out of the woods for two weeks. Everybody's so busy cutting hay they don't think of a poor timber beast like me. Dingman wasn't at the second lodge, either." He leaned against the fence. "Hell, nothing's going to happen."

"Dingman's haying for Mrs. Ritter. They spent last night there."

"No," said Joe.

"They've took their women with them."

Joe gawped. "What do they think they're doing?" he demanded.

"Cutting hay. Like me. Like anybody else. They thought the Rangers were out."

"Now listen," said Joe. "Everybody's cutting hay and nobody spells me and Adam. We got to get some time off, ain't we? Look here."

Gil said, "We better see Demooth. I think you and me had better go after them." He hooked his arm through his scythe snathe and picked up his rifle.

Joe stared.

"By God, you are an earnest man, Gil."

Gil did not answer.

They reported to Demooth and set out before seven o'clock. They kept to the road. The tracks of the two wagons were plain in the road. Joe pointed to them scornfully. "What do they think it is, a frolic?"

"What do you mean?"

"All of them riding in the wagons. Probably singing songs. I hope they took along some cider for the girls."

Gil thought grimly that they probably weren't singing, anyway. But it was true that they hadn't sent a man ahead. There wasn't a sign of a human foot anywhere. But there wasn't a hostile sign along the road, either. The woods were still and close with the July heat. Only the locusts made a sound. Nothing moved but the two men trotting along the road.

It was eight miles south to Andrustown by the road. They had left the Mohawk Valley and were cutting through the hills when Joe pulled up sharp. "Listen." Gil stopped beside him. He himself had thought it sounded like a shot. Now, after a short interval, they knew. Half a dozen shots were made in quick succession.

"God," said Joe. "I wonder if they got him."

"Got him?" Gil's brain was dazed.

"Yes." Joe was irascible. "That was firing after somebody running. Probably trying to reach the woods. They must have been lined up." He started running. "Run," he said.

It was surprising how his shambling stride covered the ground. He ran like a dog, with his head up, as if he took scent out of the wind. Now that he was started he seemed perfectly calm. He even jerked some talk over his shoulder to Gil.

"So long as they're shooting they'll all be watching the houses," he said. "Must have got them inside the houses."

Twenty minutes later, Joe slowed down. There had been two more shots, but since then there had been not a sound. He and Gil had covered a little over three miles.

"No sense in running right into their laps," he said. "Your wind is licked anyway. You couldn't hit a standing barn." He himself was breathing deep but easily. The only sign of his running was the sweat on his forehead, which stood out in big drops. "We'll kind of edge up and see what they're doing."

He circled to the west in order to get up on the slope of the hill. If you were going to be spotted and chased, it was good to begin running halfway up a hill. That meant that the man chasing you would put on his first spurt, nine times out of ten, the full length of the hill, so you had him licked before he could ever get in shooting distance.

He and Gil circled round till they could look through a slash in the trees down onto the little settlement. It was a small place—just the seven cabins and five small log barns, and the barracks under which the crops were stored. It was familiar enough to them both, except that about four acres of hay had been mowed and half of it cocked. But the two men were not looking at the hay.

What they were looking at was the group of people on the road. There were about sixty Indians, painted for the most part. The hot sunlight glistened on their greased hides and the feathered tufts of hair on their heads. They were standing around a cabin which they had just set on fire. The flames ran along the bark on the logs. The flames were dull red and yellow and tipped with thick smoke. The smoke went up against the trees and rolled into the sky. The bark roof caught with a gush of sound, and suddenly the whole cabin seemed to be enfolded with fire. It was unbelievable that a house could burn so fast.

Joe said suddenly under his breath, "There's somebody in that house."

"How do you know?"

"They wouldn't be bothered to watch it otherwise. Look, they've got everything they could out of the other houses."

It was an effort for Gil to take his eyes from the burning cabin. Now he looked carefully at the crowd of Indians. He saw the three women standing among them. They were not making any demonstration. They stood perfectly still, watching the cabin with a dull kind of fascination. The way sheep will look at something dreadful. They stood like that until the roof fell in. If there were a man inside he made no sound. "Killed himself if he had sense," Joe said. "Look, they got somebody there."

Gil saw for the first time the body hanging on the fence. It was old Bell. He was caught with one leg through the rails up to the crotch and both arms hanging over the top rail; his head tilted to one side, against his shoulder. He had been scalped. The top of his head was like a red gape against the sunlight, with a little halo of flies.

Joe started moving from tree to tree, to get a fresh view, while Gil followed him. When they had moved far enough to look past the other side of the burning cabin, they saw two men lying on their faces in the road. One was young Bell, in front of his own door; the other they thought must be Staring's son, but they could not be sure from that distance. Joe began to swear.

Gil had a crazy impulse to take a shot at one of the Indians, any one, to put a shot into the midst of the whole bunch; but Joe, who seemed aware of it, whispered, "Don't shoot. We can't do anything. I don't see Leppard or Hawyer or young Weaver anywhere. Maybe they got away."

His rifle muzzle twitched up in his hands. "They ain't all Indians either, Gil. Look there."

A man in a green coat with a black skullcap on his head had come out of the Leppard cabin. He seemed unconcerned. He went over to the Indians and watched the burning cabin with them. Then he said something that started them picking up burning sticks.

"That's one of Butler's Rangers," said Joe. "Do you suppose Leppard or Weaver would have the sense to get back to the fort?"

Gil did not know. He was too fascinated by what was happening to think of anything except that this was how his own place must have looked with the Indians burning it.

Butler's man turned round to the women and his face was towards Gil.

"Joe!"

"Don't talk so loud," said Joe.

"That's Caldwell!"

He remembered him as plain as if his wedding night had happened only a week ago. Even without the patch over the eye the man's face looked the same.

He acted perfectly quiet, as if he knew just what he was doing. He motioned the women to walk north along the road. He kept saying something to them. The women looked back at him almost stupidly, and he jabbed the air with his hand. The women turned and started walking along the road. Every now and then they turned their heads to see the Indians setting fire to another cabin or barn. The Indians were swarming all round the settlement now. A couple of them were even going through the hayfield touching off the cocks.

One of the women began to run and the other two brokenly took their pace from hers. As if the Indians had heard their quickened footfalls, half a dozen of them broke away from the burning and yelled. The women started to run hard. They looked ineffectual scurrying up the road. They ran with their heads back, stiff above the hips, their legs working furiously and twice too hard under the heavy petticoats. The rest of the Indians, hearing the yell, threw down their sticks and yelled themselves and poured out on the road.

Gil was trembling like a dog. He felt sick and cold. Even his hands seemed to feel nausea. He started shouting at Joe. "We got to do something."

Joe whirled on him and struck his face with his open hand.

"Shut up. God damn you, shut up." He turned back to watch. His eyes had a glittering kind of interest in the proceeding. The women did not bother him. There were plenty of women. He wanted to see. But he kept saying over and over to quiet Gil, "We can't stop them. Not even if we shot."

Gil saw that he was right. The Indians were overtaking the women easily. They weren't even hurried about it, but the women were too terrified to realize that. They still ran along the road, erect and desperate, with the funny skittering motion that a woman has when she tries to run. The Indians let them get almost to the beginning of the woods, then they yelled again with the piercing high note that an Indian can make and surrounded the three women.

Six or seven bucks caught the women by the shoulders and threw them down on the road and fell on top of them. The rest of the Indians crowded round. They were still yelling, but some of them were laughing.

Joe said suddenly, "I guess they ain't going to kill them."

Gil saw that the white officer was standing in the road looking after the Indians. He was making no motion to stop the proceedings. Even from that distance he looked almost amused by it. Then he turned his back and started systematically to feed the fires where they were not doing their job.

Gil looked back at the women and Indians. The crowd had given back a little. Now there was a shrill whoop and one of the Indians bent down and straightened up waving a petticoat. All the Indians whooped. Then another bent down and came up with a short gown. In a moment a couple of dozen of them were waving pieces of the women's clothing. Then they all backed away so that the two men on the hill were able to see the three naked bodies of the women lying in the road.

The Indians looked down at them for a while, shaking their clothes at them, until the man in the green coat put a whistle to his mouth and blew a shrill blast. The Indians answered it stragglingly. They left the women.

The women lay where they were, beaten and stupefied, until the Indians were quite a way off, when one by one they got up slowly. They stood naked looking back at their burning homes, at the Indians, and the three dead men. Then they stampeded for the woods. The Indians sent a few whoops after them, and at each yell the women seemed to buck up in the air and come down running harder. They weren't like women any more without their clothes. They were like some kind of animal, and they went a great deal faster than they had before.

Joe whispered to Gil, "Come on, we got to head them off."

He led Gil at a rapid rate back through the woods until they got to the road. The women heard them coming and ran like fury, but Gil and Joe did not dare call to them. The women were too scared to look back. They had to run them down. It was only when two of them fell that the white men were able to overtake them.

The women were Mrs. Leppard and Mrs. Hawyer and young Bell's wife. The oldest woman, Mrs. Leppard, was the first one to recover her wits. She said the Indians had come up just before the men went out to hay it. They had got Bell and had shot old Bell when he was going to get a horse. Young Crim, who had decided to join their party at the last minute, got into his house and would not come out, so the Indians burned his house with him in it. The three men in the hayfield had made the woods. John Weaver had been down by the spring and had got away too.

Joe helped up Mrs. Staring, who was a pretty girl, quite young, and urged all three off the road. While they were still talking, young Weaver, unarmed, came down the hill to them. His face was white and he looked terribly scared. But he had stuck around. He said he thought something might turn up for him to do.

Joe grinned at him.

"Did you see Leppard and the others?"

"They went for the fort."

"You take the women back and tell them I and Gil are going to camp on their trail for a while."

The men gave the women their hunting shirts and started them off for

Fort Herkimer with John. Then Joe and Gil returned to the edge of the clearing and watched the Indians burning the rest of the settlement. It took them about an hour more before the white officer was satisfied. Then they picked up their loot and made packs of it. They had a queer collection of odds and ends, which Indians were apt to value, like small mirrors and a china bowl; but the men with the women's clothes were the ones that seemed the most envied. Some of them tied the clothes round their heads. They rounded up the two horses that had brought in the carts, which had already been burnt, and took off south down the road, a compact mass of men, moving, now that they had finally got started, quite fast. They made Gil think of wild dogs which had been running sheep. They kept no order in their march, but stuck together with the instinct for killing.

11. *Adam Helmer's Run*

The destruction of Andrustown was something that Adam Helmer had missed: he had made a long swing to the west with old Blue Back, following John Butler and his thousand men on their trip back from Wyoming. He had gone all the way to Chemung behind the army. Butler had left off some of the men at Tioga, but he himself was indubitably headed for Niagara. Helmer and the Oneida had struck back cross-country with the news that Brant had met Butler at Chemung and had gone back to Tioga to pick up the Rangers left there, and his own Indians at Unadilla. There was some talk of attacking Cherry Valley, apparently; but Helmer believed, and so did Blue Back, that Brant would strike at German Flats.

At the news of Andrustown the first impulse had been to chase the raiders down to Unadilla. Conrad Franck had immediately set out with twenty volunteers on the understanding that Colonel Klock, whom Congress had appointed chief of the militia battalions, should bring up the Palatine companies to join Bellinger and back them up. But Jacob Klock got no farther than the sight of Andrustown; while he was still apprehensively eyeing that smoking ruin, a runner came from Little Stone Arabia Stockade to report a new irruption by the enemy. They had burned houses in Schuyler and taken two men prisoners, one of them George Weaver, and killed four. That was enough for Jacob Klock. He would not listen to Bellinger's protests. He gave orders for Bellinger to return to Fort Herkimer while he himself took his companies overland to the falls, and as soon as he was home he sat right down and wrote a letter to Governor Clinton.

The puffy old colonel was so disturbed that he got his sequence of events completely muddled; he even dated his letter June 22, instead of July 22. He wrote:—

> Sir, Tryon County has once more experienced the Cruelty of a restless Enemy. Springfield, Andrewtown, and the Settlements on Lacke Osego were at once attacked and destroyed last Saturday. House, Barns, and even Waggons, ploughs and the Hay Cocks in the Meadows were laid in Ashes. . . . As soon as the news came, I ordered immediately the Militia to March to stop the progress of the Enemy. The same Instant I received a Letter from Coll. Peter Bellinger

of the German Flats, that the Enemy was burning Houses within four Miles of the Flats praying for Assistance. I did order up five Companies of the Palatine and Cona Johary Battallion; The rest I marched straight to Andrewtown; ordering Coll. Bellinger to join me in order to intercept if possible the Enemy. But on my March thiter I learnt that he the Enemy was gone; and nothing was left, as to scour the woods, as I got information, that still a strong part of the Enemy was left to do mischief. As soon as the Flats Militia was on their March in the woods, the Enemy fell out at the Flats and toock two prisoners. . . . We are informed that Brandt boasted openly that he will be joined at Unatelly by Butler, and that within eight days he will return and lay the whole County waste. . . . Harvest time is at Hand & no prospect of a speedy Assistence. . . . Last Sunday Morning I dispatched an Express to general Ten Broeck, and desired the recommendation of the Situation of our County to your Excellency & to gen Starcks, but did not receive an Answer. Your Excellency, the common father of the good People of this State, upon whose fatherly Exertions the People of this County relieth, and which keepeth the many poor, the numerous widows and the fatherless still in hopes, will, we fervently pray, grant us such speedy relief, as your Ex'llcy in your wisdom shall see meet; & In case it chould be an impossibility; to afford us any Assistance with Batteaus, to bring off wifes and Children, that they might not be prey to a Cruel Enemy. Having tacken the Liberty to macke your Excellency aquainted with the Situation and Sentiments of the people I remain as in duty Bound Sir Your most obedient and most humble Servant

JACOB KLOCK

While Jacob Klock was busying himself with this effort and Colonel Peter Bellinger was crossing the hills north again as fast as his men could set down their feet, Conrad Franck and his thirty volunteers were sitting on their tails round Joe Boleo's lodge on the hill above the Edmeston settlement. They were waiting there for Bellinger and Klock. Gil and Joe had intercepted them on the road barely in time to keep them from being run over by Brant's main gang, which was returning from the little lakes. Brant and Caldwell had joined just above Edmeston, making an army of three hundred men, and the thirty farmers from German Flats lay up in the witch hobble and sumac, a quarter of a mile off, and looked down on the fringe of the army. It was apparent to them that Caldwell was but an offshoot of Brant's main army, and it might well have been that the whole three hundred would have turned that afternoon. Instead, however, they bore off south into the woods, passing Edmeston. They made a motley army: Indians for the most part, Cayugas, Senecas, and Mohawks in their paint and feathers, Eries with strange headdresses made of the dried heads of animals, greencoat soldiers, with their black caps and leather gaiters, a few scattered remains of the old Highland guard of Fort Johnson, dark limber men, wearing tartan kilts and knee-length leggings of deerskin and carrying long-barreled, smooth-bore rifles and Indian war clubs. They came down the trail with the long loose stride of woodsmen, their tread light on the ground, but their voices were upraised in talk as if there were no other living thing in all the woods. They shouted back and forth, calling each other's

names, lifting the fresh scalps from their belts,—those that had them,—
roaring to know whether the bounty still held at eight dollars in Niagara.

Gil and Joe Boleo and Conrad Franck, lying well beyond the line of
their men, plainly saw Caldwell and Brant meet and report to each other.
The dour unemotional white man was nearly a head taller than the Indian.
Watching the latter's temperamental face, Gil could not help but remember
how Brant had towered over Herkimer that day at Unadilla thirteen
months ago. Herkimer was dead; Herkimer must have known what would
happen with Brant loose in the woods with armed men to manage. Even to
Gil, who knew little of the general strategy of war, it seemed that Brant was
the leading actor in the gradual encircling of the flats. He wondered for an
instant whether it would be worth while to shoot Brant where he stood. A
fair mark, with his red blanket over his shoulder and cocked hat with
yellow lace and the silver gorget on his chest that a man could hold his
sights just under. But even as the thought occurred to him, Joe Boleo
touched his hand and shook his head. "There ain't no Indian worth getting
killed for," he whispered. Before Gil could think it out in his own mind,
the army was on the move.

They disappeared as quickly down the road as they had come. A few of
the Senecas deployed in front; a few of the Mohawks spread out in the rear,
loitering along until the main body was well ahead. One man came within
a hundred yards of where Gil lay. He was close enough for Gil to see
the lines of his face under the paint, the broad nose, slightly hooked, with
the deep nostrils; the little silver socket that held the eagle's feather over his
right ear; the notches on the handle of his tomahawk.

The thirty men stayed where they were for over an hour, but when no
one else came from the east or north, they withdrew to Boleo's lodge to
take council. They waited for Bellinger and Klock until sundown. Gil found
that several, like himself, had felt the itch to draw a bead on Brant. But
having seen Brant's army, they felt less anxious to open battle on them.

There was nothing thirty men could do. It was obvious that they ought
to go home. But the men were spoiling for something now they were out,
and it was Joe who calmly mentioned Young's settlement two miles east of
Edmeston, on a branch of Butternut Creek. The inhabitants were all out-
spoken King's men.

Nobody had any arguments. As soon as it was dark, they moved across
the trail. Within an hour they came out on the creek shore and found the
wagon ruts that led to Young's; an hour more and their work was done.
Behind them the small clearings were alight with the burning farms; three
of them, belonging to Young, Bollyer, and a man named Betty. The men
from the flats had found only women and children, but that fact—that Tories
felt it safe to leave their families unprotected in the woods—served only to
infuriate them. They hauled the women out of bed and drove them and the
children down the trail. Then they burned every standing wall, killing cattle
and horses and even shooting the pigs that ran squealing round the firelight.
They stripped one of the women, who returned to save three pounds in
hard money, and laughed at her, dividing the money among themselves,
and telling her to talk to Captain Caldwell.

Adam Helmer had missed all these events while he was traversing a
hundred and fifty miles of wilderness, and he felt bitter at having missed

the fun. For a month and a half nothing happened. Every time he returned to the flats, Demooth or Bellinger sent him out again at once. He had hardly had time for more than a couple of visits with Polly Bowers; he hadn't been back to McKlennar's for a good meal at all. He hadn't seen Gil; Gil was too busy getting in his wheat. But the wheat would all be in now; and the next trip down they might be able to get up a decent crowd. Joe Boleo was covering the west since the raid on Schuyler in which George Weaver had been taken prisoner. Helmer alone was responsible for the Unadilla trail, unless he included the three men who were supposed to be watching the trail with him. Most likely they were sitting together throwing dice.

Adam combed his hair as he lay in the green filtered sunlight. The woods were dim with the September haze. The August heat was continuing; but it was better to be hot than to lie out in the rain.

His first sight of the Indians came so abruptly that he knew it would be impossible to warn the men beyond him. There were forty Indians, he judged, Mohawks too, coming up the trail at a dogtrot. That many meant surely that there were flankers out. He heard them now. Whatever force it might be, it was coming fast.

At last what everyone had feared had come to pass, and Adam had allowed himself to get caught like a fifteen-year-old boy on his first scout. He knew that there was only one chance of those three fools getting away; and he knew also that someone would have to get away if German Flats were to be warned in time. Adam did not hesitate. He rolled over on his knee and took the leading Indian a clean shot right under the wishbone. Then, while they milled, he charged straight down the slope and over the trail and up the opposite bank. He made it so fast that the first shots the Indians had at him he was dodging through the scrub.

The musket fire crackled like dry sticks, and the stink of black powder reached out in the still air so that he smelled it as he ran. But he paid no attention to the shooting and yelling on the trail. He dodged into some heavier timber, and wheeled down the bank again. He had judged his course exactly. He hit the trail three hundred yards ahead of his first crossing, just beyond a bend.

He ran lightly, listening to the surge of voices behind him. Up at the lodge a sudden feeble burst of three shots sounded, then more yells. The damned fools hadn't had the sense to cut and run when he gave them the diversion. He knew as sure as he knew which end of himself he ate with that the three men were dead. It left him alone to carry the warning into German Flats.

German Flats lay twenty-four miles to north and he knew he had probably the pick of Brant's Indians on his trail, men who could run eighty miles through the woods between sunrise and noon. But Adam knew that he could run himself, and he knew that he would have to run on an open trail and that once the Indians discovered that, they would know he would stick to it. They wouldn't have to be bothered with tracking.

He eased up slightly, listening behind him. The first surge of yelling had overshot the eastern ridge; now it returned. It would be only a minute before they brought his tracks down to the trail. He began to put on a little pressure to make the next bend; but just before he rounded it he heard the war whoop slide up to its unhuman pitch and a wild shot cut the air high over his head.

His wind had come back from that first foolish burst up and down the ridge. He lengthened his stride. His yellow hair, fresh-combed and beautiful, whipped up and down on his shoulders like a short flapping blanket. His mouth opened as he reached his full pace and he took the slight grade with the bursting rush of a running buck deer.

The Indians had stopped yelling. At the end of the next straight stretch Adam flung a look over his shoulder and saw the first brave running bent over, going smooth and quick and soundless. The Indian knew that Helmer had seen him, but he didn't lift his gun. He wasn't carrying a gun. He had only his tomahawk, which was a great deal more deadly if he could pull up within forty feet.

The Indian must have been gaining, Adam thought, or else he was the leader of a group, following the old Mohawk dodge of sprinting to made the fugitive travel at top speed. The others would take a steadier pace; but as soon as the leader tired another man would sprint up. By keeping pressure on the fugitive in this way they could run down any man in four or five hours plain going. Adam would not only have to keep ahead of the press, he would have to run the heart completely out of them.

He sprinted himself now; not blindly, but picking his next easing point beforehand; he knew the trail, every stone and root of it, from Edmeston to German Flats, as well as he knew Polly Bowers. His easing point would be the ford over Licking Brook. A half mile.

At any time it was worth while to see Adam run. He was the biggest man in the flats, six feet five in his moccasins. With his mass of yellow hair he seemed yet taller. He weighed close to two hundred pounds, without an ounce of fat on him.

He began to draw away from the Indian as soon as he started to sprint. Glancing back again, he saw that the Indian had straightened up a little. He got the feeling that the Indian's face was surprised. Probably the Indian fancied himself as quite a runner. Maybe he was champion of some lousy set of lodges somewhere. Adam could have laughed if he had not needed his wind, but the laughter went on in his inside, sending the blood into his hands. His head felt fine and clear. He figured he had gained thirty yards on the Indian when he hit the brook.

He jumped the ford. It was too early to risk wetting his feet and going sore. But as he cleared the water, he threw his rifle from him. It splashed into the pool below the ford and sank. Now that his hands were free, Adam began unlacing his hunting shirt. He got it off. By the time he came to the big butternut tree, he had wrapped his powder flask and bullet pouch in it, and he threw it over a small clump of witch hobble. Then he tightened his belt and stuck his hatchet into the back of his belt where the handle would not keep smacking against his legs.

He was now naked from the waist up. The wind of his running felt good on his chest, cooling the sweat as it trickled down through the short golden mane. He was a wonderful man to see; his skin white as a woman's except for his hands and face, which were deeply tanned. He was feeling fine and going well. He felt so fine he thought he might almost let the leading Indian pull up and maybe chance a throw at him with his tomahawk. He eased a little, enough to see the Indian. When the buck appeared behind him, Adam saw that he was a new man. He was taller, and his face was painted black and white instead of red and yellow as the other's had been. He did not come quite so fast, but Adam's trained eye saw that he had better staying power. Adam decided then and there that he would put all ideas of a quick fight out of his mind. The Indians meant real business.

For the next four miles the chase continued with only a slight variation of the pace, Adam adapting himself to the man behind. He was beginning to feel the pressure, but he was running with greater canniness. He kept his eyes glued to the trail now. He did not dare risk a blind step. His ankles wouldn't hold up as well if he lit on a rolling stone or a slippery root. He had the feeling very definitely that the race was reaching a climax, and though he ran strongly, strong enough to lick any man in the flats at a hundred yards straightaway this minute, he knew that these Indians were good.

His breathing was still excellent. He had no fear of giving out; he could run till sundown, he thought; and then it came upon him that it would be a fact, if he managed to clear the Indians, that he would hit the flats just about sundown. Even while he ran, he reasoned it out that Brant must have figured on reaching the valley at dark and striking in the morning. Adam wondered what would happen when Brant knew that the word had gone ahead of him. He doubted whether Brant could get up his main body anyway much before sunset. But it didn't matter much. The only thing in the world Adam could do was to reach the flats. If he got there first some people could get into the forts.

His eyes kept checking in his landmarks and he realized that Andrustown was only a mile, or a little more, ahead. He must have outdistanced most of even the first pursuit. He expected there would not be more than half a dozen who could have held on as long as this, and if that were so they would have to be sending up another man pretty soon. And they would all begin bearing down at the same time.

Adam figured that if he could get through Andrustown clearing he might better take to the woods, for he would have gained as much time as anyone could on the main body.

As he chanced a backward glance, he saw that the Indians were going to try to run him down now. The new man was there and it was evident that he was their best man. He was not tall. He was thickset and had thick short legs. He was entirely naked except for ankle moccasins and breech clout and he was oiled and painted and rather light-colored. He looked like a Mohawk. He wore three feathers. It seemed impossible that he could have kept up with the rest, just to see him at first, for he had a belly that showed out in front. But his belly did not bounce at all. After a minute Adam thought it must be an enlarged place where he kept his wind.

The Indian's legs moved with incredible rapidity. He had already taken his tomahawk from his belt as if he were confident of being able to haul up on the white man. That gesture gave Adam the incentive he needed. He was enraged, and he took his rage out in his running. When the Indian entered the clearing, Adam was already down past the black ruins of the houses and going away with every stride. It was the greatest running the Indian had ever looked at. He knew he was licked, and he started slowing up very gradually. By the time Adam hit the woods, the Indian had stopped and sat down by the roadside.

When Adam looked back from the woods the Indian wasn't even looking at him. He was all alone in the clearing and he was futilely banging the ground between his legs with his tomahawk. Adam knew he had made it. He did not stop, nor even let down quickly on his pace. All he had to race now was time. He would have laughed if he could have got the breath for it. Time? Time, hell!

They saw the runner coming down the long hill, his body glistening with sweat and reflecting red from the low-lying ball of the sun. He was coming hard. The sentry in the spy loft of Fort Herkimer saw men come out of houses as the runner passed. Then the men ran back into the houses. Before the runner was out halfway over the flat land, the family of the first house he had passed had their horse hitched to the family cart in front of the door and were piling their belongings and children into it.

The sentry let out a yell.

"It's Helmer!"

In the yard an officer stopped on his way out.

"Helmer?"

"Yes, Adam Helmer. He's running hard. He ain't got his gun. He ain't got his shirt on." He paused, looked out again, and then bawled down once more. "He looks pretty near played out." His voice flattened. "I reckon it's Brant."

"What makes you think so?"

"The people are coming in after him."

Without another word the officer went round the corner of the blockhouse on the run for the church. It was Colonel Bellinger. The sentry heard the whang of his feet on the rungs of the belfry ladder.

Bellinger was now in the steeple. He was yanking the canvas off the swivel. The brass barrel glinted in the sunset. Bellinger stood back, waving the match.

The gun roared. One shot.

All over the valley it brought people outdoors to stare at the church steeple. Before dark they were thronging towards the forts by road and river. Those who had already reached Fort Herkimer stood in front of the church and stared at Helmer's naked chest. It was whipped with branches, the white skin welted and bloody. But Helmer was breathing easily again. He had never, he thought, felt finer in his life.

12. *A Night—and a Morning*

Mrs. McKlennar's barn was a comfortable place to milk in. It was cool and dusky. There were no windows—only the walls of logs and the log ceiling overhead. The four cows stood in a row on rough plank. The whole place was filled with dust and the dry earthy smell, mingled with dung, from the walk behind the cows. It was quiet with the soft breathing of the cows, and the hiss of milk striking its own froth in the pails. Mrs. McKlennar, gray bare head butting one cow's flank, and Gil, face turned to look through the open door, were milking together. They were not making any conversation. They were tired from lashing down the wooden barrack roofs over the wheat stacks. And they were both conscious of the finish of the harvest, a good harvest, one they were both proud of—Mrs. McKlennar because the farm belonged to her, and Gil because she had dropped the remark that it was the best yield they had ever had from the land. He knew that it was he himself who had made that best yield a fact. They were thus contented, balanced on the one-legged stools, when the flat impact of the swivel's roar fell on their ears.

In the first breath, they could hardly believe what they had heard. Then Daisy's voice lifted in a falsetto screech from the house. "Oh, Mis' McKlennar! Hit's de cannon gun over de foht. I seen it going off! Oh, Mis'!"

The widow rose with Gil. Her long face was set. She saw how white he was.

"It's the alarm gun," he said. "It's a raid."

"One gun." Her lips compressed; she nodded.

"We've got to move to the fort."

She nodded again. They were out of the barn now, striding towards the stone house. "Don't run," said Mrs. McKlennar. "We won't get there by running. And *she's* all right."

But Gil had to see Lana. Lana would have been feeding young Gil—christened Gilbert McKlennar Martin, with the widow as sponsor.

Lana was sitting in the kitchen, with Gilly at her breast. Her eyes met Gil's, questioning, terror-stricken, but full of enforced quiet. Thank God, he thought, she hasn't lost her nerve, yet.

"Now, Gil, where do you think we'd better go?"

"We can get to Dayton by the road. But I'd rather cross the river to Herkimer. It's quicker. We can take the cart down to the river."

Mrs. McKlennar nodded.

"We won't try to take much. I'll get my money and some brandy. Daisy, you take the pail from Gil and fill a stone jug. Milk is handy sometimes. And that fresh baking of bread and the two hams. And don't scream. They don't pay for nigger scalps."

"Yas'm."

Gil was surprised to find that he was still carrying the pail. He got the rifle down from the pegs between the beams, and then started through the house, closing and barring the shutters. Mrs. McKlennar collected her money and the brandy and her own clothes and Lana's. She made bundles of the clothes on the kitchen floor and wrapped the brandy and money in them. Daisy brought the food in a basket. "I fetched de new currant preserve and de side of fresh pohk," she said proudly. "That preserve and pohk tas' good together."

Gil was already out of the house. He chased the pigs into the woods, drove out the cows after taking off their bells, and then hitched the mare to the cart. As soon as he brought it to the door, Mrs. McKlennar tossed their belongings in. Lana buttoned her short gown. She met Gil's eyes with a pale face, saying, "I thought I'd let Gilly finish his feed. I thought he'd be quieter."

"Good girl," said Mrs. McKlennar.

He helped Lana into the cart. Daisy and Mrs. McKlennar scrambled over the tailboard. Gil closed the door and poked the latchstring in. They had done all they could. He took the mare by the head and led her down to the road. As they turned into it, they heard the express rider coming along from Dayton. He passed them at full gallop, leaning forward in his saddle. He did not appear to notice them.

The alarm gun at Eldridge Blockhouse made a single dull thud.

"They haven't reached the valley yet," Gil thought. He opened the bars on the far side of the highway and led the mare into the wheatfield. They went at a walk over the stubble towards the river.

Though the darkness was already a shadow in the east, and a mist had begun to hover on the water where brooks entered the river, a hazy after-sunset light reached from beneath a dark bank of clouds rising in the west. Through this dim haze the four adults in the cart could see people moving across the flat land on the far side of the river. The creak of the cart, even the tread of the horses on the opposite road, reached them with startling clearness, but the absence of all talk gave to the approaching night a singular effect of silence.

They themselves got out of the cart without a word when Gil stopped the mare on the riverbank. He drew the bow of the boat on shore and helped the widow into the stern. Then, standing in the water, he passed the baby from Lana's arms to Mrs. McKlennar's lap. The child lay still as a mouse. It seemed to them that it must be aware of what was going on, it lay so still, looking straight up at the unaccustomed sky with wakeful eyes. Lana got in next and helped to stow away the basket and bundles. Daisy nearly upset the boat in her anxiety. Her fat hams filled the bow, her striped petticoat swelling over the gunwales. She sat motionless, holding her treasure, a framed small picture of Christ, close to her bosom. Her face was gray under her bright calico kerchief.

Gil climbed up the bank again and unharnessed the mare. After a moment's hesitation he backed the cart down the bank into the river and threw the harness into it. It would be hard to burn a cart in the river. Then he slapped the mare's rump, slid down to the water side, and shoved the boat out.

It was overloaded. He had to row slowly. He pulled out into the middle of the quiet river and paused for a last look at the mare. She had stopped a little way from the bank to look after them. She kept pricking her ears nervously.

"Hadn't we better start?" Mrs. McKlennar suggested quietly.

Gil pulled upstream. The reflections of the willow trees were fading into the general darkness of the water. The valley was yet quiet. There was no sound anywhere, except the passage of carts along the road, until the Casler family, also rowing up the river, overtook them.

Jacob Casler said softly over the water, "You folks all right?"

"Yes. You?"

"We brought all we could. I ain't got any gunpowder, though."

"They have some in the fort."

Mrs. Casler said with a slight shrillness in her voice, "We got plenty of bullets. Jake made a lot this spring."

They then rowed steadily ahead without further conversation.

The clouds, without rain, gradually filled the sky, and pitch-dark night had fallen by the time the two boats reached Fort Herkimer. Though the gates were still open, there was little noise from inside. Gil got his family on shore and hauled the boat out of the water. Lana carried the baby, and Mrs. McKlennar, Daisy, and he carried everything else. They passed through the gates into the crowded square.

Every inch of space was taken by people standing together in groups, by carts yet unloaded, horses nervous but still. Gil asked for the news and for the first time learned of Helmer's race and the fact that Brant at last was on the way.

He found a place for his family on the north wall in a corner shed which they had to share with Mrs. Weaver and Cobus. Directly across the square from them they saw Captain Demooth arranging his wife's bed with Mary Reall's help.

Mrs. Weaver said "Hello" to them in a dull voice. She had grown gaunt. She kept watching Mary Reall's quiet attendance on the captain's wife. There was great unhappiness in her face. She made no move as John went over to see Mary before coming across the yard to find his mother. Gil drew young Cobus aside and asked in a whisper whether anyone had heard of George Weaver. Cobus shook his head.

"We don't reckon he was killed."

Emma Weaver lifted her voice.

"We don't know. They pay the same for scalps they pay for prisoners." She turned away from John. "We're all right. Cobus looked out for me."

Gil saw that Lana was settled in the corner with Mrs. McKlennar beside her. He bent down and kissed her cheek. "I've got to talk to Bellinger or Demooth," he said.

The yard was now alive with the hushed murmur of people straightening themselves out. Suddenly Colonel Bellinger lifted his voice.

"We've got to get the horses out of here." He caught sight of Gil. "You, Martin. You get them out. All of them, and the carts. Right away."

"I want to keep my horse," a man protested. "The Indians stole my cow."

"All of them, I said. We can't have the yard cluttered up. We haven't room for horses. If they get scared and get kicking they'll damage somebody. Get them out. All the women . . ." he raised his voice so that it carried throughout the fort . . . "I want all the women to stay in the sheds or the church until we get the yard clear. If any shooting starts, all the women and children must get into the church. Keep the north pews for a hospital. All men with guns, who haven't been assigned posts on the stockade, report to Captain Demooth on the east blockhouse." As the subdued movement of disentanglement commenced, Bellinger moved over to the central fire, watching them. There was disorder, but it was quiet disorder, as if the people were accustoming themselves to a dark room; and Bellinger was patient. The horses and carts were being quickly taken out into the blackness beyond the gates, unharnessed, and the horses loosed. The banging of dropped shafts was a loud sound. In fifteen minutes Gil returned to report all horses outside the stockade. Bellinger raised his voice again. "One more thing." He waited till everyone's attention was fixed on him as he stood in the firelight. "We don't know where the Indians are. It's a black night and a fog is rising off the river. We can only listen for them. So as soon as you're settled you'll have to be quiet. No talking anywhere. If a baby cries, and you can't hush him, take him into the church and cover him up."

He turned to meet Demooth. He seemed quite calm. His long dark face and broad shoulders made a comforting bulk in the firelight. Gil remembered him at Oriskany, lugging Herkimer up the slope.

He said to Demooth: "Martin here has cleared out all the horses. Have you got all your men up, Mark?"

Demooth's voice was tightly strained, though the strain did not show in his face.

"Yes, I have."

"How much longer do you think we ought to let the fire burn?"

"It ought to be put out now. Nobody's come in for the past ten minutes. We can't check everybody. Some of the people may go to Fort Dayton. We don't expect anybody from Eldridge."

Bellinger said, "I'll put out all lights in ten minutes. I'll have to give the people warning."

He was shouting the warning as Gil climbed up on the west sentry walk. Gil passed young John Weaver, looking white and set in the face. "Hello, John," he said. "Hello, Mr. Martin," said John.

Down in the yard, Bellinger and Demooth had moved to the gates. They were closing them now, with two men helping. The gates squealed and ground on their straps. The three bars fell heavily into place. The shutting off of light from inside the enclosure also shut off the eyes of the horses outside. The animals had gathered in a small herd to look in at the gate. Now they whinnied in the darkness. The familiar sound, for some reason, was fearful.

Gil found that his position was next to Adam Helmer. They shook hands. Helmer laughed softly. "Did you hear about me running away from those Mohawks?" he wanted to know.

He was bursting with pride. He was wearing a shirt too small for him— there wasn't a shirt in German Flats that would have made a decent fit for him. He leaned easily against the picket points, with a borrowed rifle propped handy to his hand. He talked softly about the run, becoming dramatic as he told about outdistancing each Indian. He made quite a story about the heavy-set fellow who had just sat down and banged the ground with his tomahawk. "He looked like he was crying," said Helmer. "I don't blame him. I've got quite a scalp, by God." He shook his head, tossing his yellow hair, and laughed.

"When the fire's put out, nobody's to talk," shouted Bellinger. "I mean that. Anybody that can't keep their mouth shut had better plan to get outside."

A couple of men had lugged a great kettle to the fire. They emptied it over the flames. The light seemed to burst and spread with the steam. At the hissing, and the steam smell, and the added darkness, the horses whinnied again. Then they stampeded.

In the fort the darkness was black and voiceless. Lana felt as if the people she had been watching were all dead. She felt alone in the world with Gilly, until Mrs. McKlennar put her hand out. The two women held hands.

Cobus whispered to his mother, "I don't see why they won't let me have a musket up there."

"Hush. Hush your mouth." His mother's voice was savage. Then almost inaudibly she began to pray for George. George had taken a trip up to Schuyler on that fatal day to see about some work he had heard of. He had wanted to get the job as a surprise for John.

Mrs. Demooth was quite docile. She lay on her back on the blankets with her hands folded on her breast. She had a queer notion that her husband had tied her hands after she had kicked Nancy. She thought they were still tied. She would not even dress, or feed herself. Mary had to take complete care of her; but she was nice to Mary. She wasn't afraid any more. She lay there singing under her breath. She sang snatches of a hymn, of which only now and then, by leaning close, could Mary hear a phrase. "A mighty fortress is our God . . ." Mary remembered how her father liked to sing it; he sang it always in German, rolling it out with his surprising deep voice. Her tears came close to her eyes as the woman's colorless voice went on with the hymn. And then, after a silence, the voice sang thinly—it was like the voice of an insect, it was so small—a little light sad tune.

> "Twixt the water and the willow tree,
>   There stood I,
>   When I spied my gallant gentleman
>   Riding by . . ."

It went on, so plaintively that Mary hugged her knees tight and tried to see John up on the sentry walk. But since the fire had gone out, she could see nothing. Her heart was sad, thinking of him and herself. It was impossible for him to find work anywhere that paid money. He had worked through most of the harvest for nothing but food and keep. He always seemed to be cheerful when he came to see her, and he was happy that she should be doing so well. It made her feel very humble that she should be earning money while he wasn't.

> "Oh, my Lord, why did you pass me
>   In the time gone by,
>   That only now you speak of love
>   When death rides nigh?
>   For I'll never love another
>   Though the stream run dry,
>   Though the willow leaf be withered
>   And my heart doth die."

Listening to the thin voice, Mary felt her love for John well up in her. She said a prayer for him, addressing God as a literal person who could, if He would, take care of John.

She put out her thin hand to the woman's forehead, in the dark, and began to stroke her face, very gently. The singing stopped after a while, and a little later Mary's hand felt wet.

In the darkness by the eastern blockhouse Bellinger and Demooth talked in low voices. They tried to feel confident that the fort could hold off Brant and the Indians. They had eighty-seven armed men. Fort Dayton should have sixty-odd. The most dangerous place was Little Stone Arabia Stockade with only twenty, but they believed that the raid would be confined to the flats. Altogether there were one hundred and forty families in the flats—that figure included the Eldridge Settlement, which contained eight families and fourteen men. Men were any male persons over fifteen. They did not know how big Brant's force was. They had no way of telling. All their scouts but Joe Boleo were inside the fort; and the scouts were the nucleus of any real defense. They could not afford to send one out. Boleo, they decided, must have been cut off and have gone over to Dayton.

They had a fair supply of powder, enough for a week, though the often demanded supply had not been sent up from Albany. There was plenty of shot. They knew that an express had been sent down to Cherry Valley, where the Massachusetts Regiment of Colonel Alden had gone into garrison; but they did not expect any succor from him for two days— if indeed any ever came at all. They had to rely on themselves. Their greatest hope lay in the fact that Indians never cared to face fire from behind a stockade.

When they stopped speaking, the fort was still and black about them. Not a light showed anywhere. There were not even any stars to give an outline to the palisade. Nothing moved but the mist eddying damply against their faces in a vagrant draft.

Demooth climbed the nearest ladder to make a round of the sentry walk. All the men were wakeful. Each one whispered as Demooth passed that he had heard no hostile sound. Demooth paused from time to time to listen for himself.

The only sound he heard was the slow tread of a grazing horse. It seemed to be quite near, but the horse was totally invisible.

The faceless night dragged on interminably. As near as Gil could figure, it was getting on to dawn when his ears were first attracted by the soft blowing of a horse's breath. He nudged Helmer. But Helmer had already heard it.

He whispered, "If that was an Indian the horse would have run."

They waited for several minutes. Then they heard a man whistle.

Adam stiffened. He whistled back on the same note. The answer returned.

"It's Joe," he murmured. "He's edging up to the sally port."

Helmer dropped off the sentry walk, lighting on his feet as gently as a cat. He went quickly towards the gate where he found Bellinger and told him that Joe Boleo was coming in. Together they opened the sally port, and Joe Boleo stepped through like an embodiment of the darkness itself.

"What have you been up to?" Adam asked.

"That you, Adam? I been sleeping with your grandma's aunt. Where's Bellinger?"

"He's right alongside of me." Adam grinned in the darkness. "Did you hear about me running off from the Mohawks?"

"No," said Joe. He turned to Bellinger as the latter demanded what news he had.

"Brant's up at Shoemaker's. He's got a big army. Mostly whites, too, that's the funny part. I couldn't figure out how many—about five hundred all together. They camped there the first part of the night, but two hours ago they commenced moving out over the valley. I thought maybe I'd better come back and get some sleep."

Bellinger asked, "Are they moving all in one bunch?"

"Naw. They've broke up in parties."

"Then I guess they won't attack the fort."

"I ain't guessing," said Joe.

"Well, Helmer. You get back on the walk."

"Come with me, Joe," said Helmer. "I want to tell you . . ."

"Go to hell," said Joe. "Where can I get a drink of water?"

Joe's news was passed from man to man. The whisper traveled the circumference of the stockade like the flitting of an owl through the dark. The women and children could hear the shuffle of feet passing over their heads, as each man moved to his neighbor, whispered, and moved back. But no one bothered to tell the women. They had to stay in their dark and airless sheds, listening and waiting and unwarned.

Lana felt Gilly wake up in her lap. First the slight stiffening of his hard little back, then the bump as he slung his head down against her thigh. He would begin to cry for his feed. He was an early feeder—voracious and demanding, a regular rooster. She whispered to Mrs. McKlennar, as she dandled Gilly, and Mrs. McKlennar leaned away from Lana's shoulder. When Gilly opened his mouth for his first bawl, he found the breast popped in. The smack of his mouth as it closed in surprise was almost like the clap of two hands. He gave a little grunt and, applying himself directly, sucked with noisy gusto. Mrs. McKlennar gave a positive snort of delight.

"The little warrior!"

Lana eased her back, which ached from the long hours of sitting in the darkness, and let him feed. She was glad of the distraction. It was the first thing that had happened all night, and her brain was worn out with her unceasing effort to listen.

A cock crowed.

The bird's voice was so familiar in its accents that more than one person imagined it at his own farm. But as the bird crowed again, the voice became isolated and infinitely distant in the mist. Presently another bird answered, and then a third took it up.

Listening to the birds crowing here and there throughout the valley, Demooth felt that something was out of place. He drew out his watch and read the face by the light of the gunner's match kept going in the church. The watch told him that it was 4.25, almost an hour and a half before dawn.

He climbed up into the belfry to get a higher view. As he went up the ladder into inky darkness, he heard a dog start barking far up the valley.

Standing beside the swivel, under the beam that used to carry the bell, Demooth looked out. He could not hear a human sound. Only the frantic furious barking of the dog persisted. But suddenly the dog yelped and went away yelping through the fog.

At that instant, Demooth lost his illusion. Red glows of light swelled in the fog to the west, and, refracted in the moist air, they took spherical shape. Even as he located their position, new globes of light swelled behind them; then with the unexpectedness of a blow they started springing up on the right and left, north and south of the fort, and finally to the east, so that the fort was surrounded as if by a phantasmal manifestation.

He was so absorbed in the sight that for the moment he was not aware of the stirring on the sentry walks below him. But as the voices of men reached upwards, he was brought sharply to his senses.

"That's Ritter's barn, see."

"Which one?"

"That one, the little one, just to the right of the other and a little back of it."

The globes were dispelled and became bonfires. They seemed to have aroused a wind, for suddenly it began drawing from the west, slowly driving the mist past the fort and appearing to build a wall with it over Little Falls. Looking down again, Demooth found that he could see the sentry walk quite plainly, picked out by the firelight, and encircling the darker well of the yard. But even this darker place had come to life. Hearing the men's voices, the women had stolen out of the sheds. They were standing now with their faces lifted skyward. To Demooth they looked pale and swimming with a queer pained realization of disaster, though as yet they had not been. Then they started moving for the ladders and began to climb up on the sentry walks. They kept shifting, as if they sorted themselves out, to stand with their menfolk, and all together, men and women, they stared out at the burning valley.

The whole valley was alight. Trees stood out against the darkness, distinct and black and two-dimensional. Houses and barns assumed their accustomed shapes with suddenness in a bed of rising fire, then seemed to sink and vanish as the flames went up. The watchers in the fort had ceased talking. Their voices, however, continued; a guttural sort of punctuation of helplessness that swelled inarticulately as they got their first sight of the destructives.

The Indians were plainly silhouetted, darting into the zones of firelight, with their crested heads and their naked shoulders shining. The white men were darker shapes, more governed in their motions. They ran before the fires, or stopped momentarily to watch, before running on. There was as yet no sound of shooting.

Now and then a band of destructives could be traced through the darkness by the burning sticks they carried. They followed the roads as though they were illuminating a map.

On the sentry walk a man shouted, "My God, they've set fire to my wheat!"—he strained out over the picket points, his eyes were incredulous. Beside him a woman stood stiff as a spear, with her face turned outward and her eyes closed, as if she could see the roaring burst of flame against the back of her eyelids. The man stopped muttering to himself, and gradually the entire fort became so still that the noise of the nearer fires became distinctly audible. The Indians were too preoccupied to pay attention to the fort, but the first attempt at a sally, the first shooting, would have drawn the entire mob of them. There was nothing that men could do but stand and watch the swift destruction of their homes.

Gil had been keeping watch on the opposite side of the river. Fires already had broken out as far east as Eldridge Settlement, and the small squat tower of the blockhouse was sharply etched against them. But not until an hour had passed did he see the first small fire start at Mrs. McKlennar's place.

He watched for a moment, identified the barn, then the log house, then the two wheat stacks. They burned so fiercely that after a minute or two they seemed to merge in one tremendous conflagration. In ten minutes half a dozen men had managed to destroy the entire results of his year's work—the best yield the farm had ever had. He felt that if he watched longer he might burst out crying like a baby.

A volley of musket shots distracted him. The shots came from Fort Dayton, where already there had been considerable burning done in the cluster of the village. It was impossible to tell what had happened, whether the Indians had attacked the fort, or whether the garrison had made a sortie. Joe Boleo lifted his thin face like a fox into the wind and listened to the shots. "Look," he said after three or four minutes. "That's a runner. There's some more coming after him. I reckon they chased some of them away from Dayton."

The men on the sentry walk saw the band coming through the ford. They made a dark blot on the water. The water was an almost pearly gray. "By Jesus Christ, it's daylight!" said Helmer.

None of them had noticed the rising sun. It poured a rosy light through the valley, tinting the stray remnants of the mist that hung on the brooks or the edges of the river. The last line of the bank of rainless clouds that all night long had passed from west to east caught fire along its lower edge, burned crimson for a while, and slowly sank away. A flight of plover, riding high against the sunrise, came down West Canada Creek with their soft intermittent calling back and forth.

The runner was passing due south in the direction of the Herter place. As the men followed him with their eyes, they saw that a large group of the destructives stood in the yard. One man kept slightly aloof, in his Indian blanket, with the sunrise catching a faint shine in the gold lace covering his cocked hat. A whisper went the rounds again. "That's Brant."

The runner spoke to him, and the following group of men came up to merge with those that waited. Brant called out several men, who raised their rifles and fired a volley skyward. They loaded, fired again. Once more they repeated it. Then, round the smouldering coals of the Herter barn, they sat down, cooked, and ate their breakfast.

The people in Fort Herkimer did not move. All of them watched the destructives eating breakfast. None of them thought of cooking breakfast for themselves. They were unable, even for a minute, to tear their eyes away. Indians were herding the cattle from the woods. The Indians ran like active dogs, uttering yapping cries; and the cows, confused by the smoke and fire, went in a blind panic-stricken flight before them. Such bands came from all over the valley, apparently erratic, but always con-

verging on the spot where the men were eating. As they approached, the
men got to their feet and made ready to mill them.

Other men, white men, were rounding up horses, riding them in singly,
or leading a string of them, or driving them hitched in their carts. The
process seemed endless.

In reality it took only three hours. The rounding up of the cattle had
been thoroughly organized. By ten o'clock the entire herd, inextricably
mixed together but moving steadily in their ordained direction to the south,
began to stretch out over the flats. They followed the road towards Andrustown. Long after they had disappeared, the bellowing of the cows
came back to Fort Herkimer from the hills.

In the fort the people leaned against the pickets in exhaustion, staring
with bloodshot eyes at the place they had been accustomed to live in. The
wind had died and the fires burned low, but the smoke rose steadily as
far as the eye could see in bars against the limitless blue sky.

Gradually the people stirred. Their movements were halting, their voices
fumbled at words and gave over the attempt to speak. They looked into
each other's blank faces and looked away. Someone had started a fire in
the yard and women gathered round it to cook. They did it mechanically,
apathetically, silently, as if they sought comfort in the routine of regular
existence.

When he came down, Gil found Lana among the other women. She
was bending in front of the fire with the same burdened apathy, but when
he touched her she lifted her face. Neither of them spoke for several
seconds.

Then he said, "The stone house didn't burn."

Lana nodded.

"We were lucky," he said.

She was looking at him.

"The corn's standing," he said.

"And there's the potatoes," she said gravely.

13. *Brief Activities of the Military*

The express rider who had taken the news to Cherry Valley returned
late in the afternoon with a message that Colonel Alden could spare one
hundred and eighty men and was sending them under Major Whiting across
country north of the Little Lakes, in the hope of cutting off the enemy.
Half an hour later, Bellinger, with two hundred men, recruited during
the day from the two forts, Eldridge's and the Palatine companies, set out
on Brant's trail.

They knew that they could not expect to give battle to Brant's army;
they went with a sense of futility. It was more for something to take their
minds off the destruction of the valley. They did not hope to consummate
a rendezvous with Alden's troops—if that had been Alden's intention, it
was a delusion that any man, they supposed, was entitled to. They had not
even bothered to ask for soldiers from Fort Stanwix, where Major Cochran commanded two hundred and fifty line troops in garrison. They knew

that his orders from headquarters were definite to hold that fort and let
the valley go hang.

They spent two days on Brant's trail without getting anywhere near him.
They would have liked to find and kill some stragglers from the army;
but the only men they found were the three dead scouts on the hill over
Edmeston. They buried the scouts. The people of Edmeston had fled behind Brant, taking their livestock with them.

The militia half-heartedly set fire to their dwellings and turned back towards home with twenty or thirty cows and horses which had eluded the
Indian herders. They brought the animals to the forts and tethered them.

It took the people more than a week to figure out the extent of the
damage. A few men returning to the ashes of their barns and houses found
a cow or a horse waiting uncertainly near by. A few flocks of sheep still
remained, but these were being harried by the dogs, which, homeless now,
had taken to the woods like wolves, and at night could be heard howling
over the hills.

Colonel Bellinger's tabulation, which he sent to General Stark in Albany,
offered the following figures:—

> To buildings burned:
> Houses 63
> Barns 57
> Grist-mills 3
> Barracks of wheat 62
> Hay stacks 87
> To stock taken and carried away:
> Horses 235
> Horned-cattle 229
> Sheep 269
> Oxen 93

Those figures made an impression on even the dogged wits of the hero
of Bennington. He began casting round for something he could do, something to balance the German Flats accounts when he sent in his report
to headquarters. In this foggy process of thought he remembered that in
August Governor Clinton had persuaded him to send in a regiment of
Pennsylvania riflemen to the Schoharie Valley. Stark, in a pique, had ordered the commanding officer, Colonel William Butler, to act only defensively, in the only district of Tryon County that was not seriously
threatened. Now that he remembered where they were, he dispatched an
express ordering Colonel Butler to destroy the Tory base at Unadilla.

For three weeks the regiment had been expecting a shipment of shoes.
They continued to wait for three weeks more. Finally they marched without them; but by that time all the hostile Indians and Tories had fled south
to Cookoze on the Delaware, where they did some unmolested depredating.
The riflemen, however, performed a brilliant march, half barefoot as
they were. When at last they reached the Unadilla towns, they found only
four or five Oneida and Tuscarora families, who had remained because
they were friendly to the American cause.

But Colonel William Butler had come to make war. His orders were to
wipe out the Indian towns, so he wiped out the friendly Indians in them,

men and women. His riflemen were hard-bitten Morgan men and they had been bored in the Schoharie Valley: they made a spree of the process. Consequently Colonel Butler did not mention the Indians killed in his report. He wrote instead:—

> I am well convinced that it has sufficiently secured these Frontiers from any further disturbances from the savages, at least this winter.

General Stark, feeling that at last he had done something, piously echoed the conviction. He considered James Dean's reports that Walter Butler had left Niagara with a hundred and fifty Rangers and fifty regulars, ostensibly to defend Tioga and possibly to make an attack on the Mohawk Valley, were sheer delusions. Anyway they were not headed for the Hampshire Grants. And shortly thereafter he resigned his portfolio to Brigadier General Hand.

Edward Hand found that there were several reports from spies in the west, all predicting the same raid, and there seemed to be a general trend of agreement that the raid would strike Cherry Valley. Being an earnest man, General Hand decided he would visit Cherry Valley himself in November. He found the fort short of bread and powder and returned to rectify the mistake. He also sent copies of his reports to Colonel Klock and ordered him to collect militia and hold them ready to march to Cherry Valley should occasion arise. He directed Colonel Butler at Schoharie to keep a watch in the same direction. He stopped in to see Colonel Van Schaick, commanding line troops at Johnstown, and said the same thing to him. Then, apparently, General Hand settled himself in for the winter at Albany.

14. *Prospects*

By the end of October two clusters of log cabins had been erected round the two forts in German Flats. Even to the men who had rolled up the walls, they looked small and pathetic. They had had to work too fast to hew the logs. They were the same as the cabin a man would erect for himself when he first went into the wilderness. To some of the old ones in the community, they restored memories of German Flats when it was known as Burnetsfield—just after the French raid of '57. Though the fields were, perhaps, ten times as wide as the cleared land of those days, they lay as desolate under the thin sifting of the snow. The black jagged lumps that once were barns and houses looked just the same to the old men, except that there were more of them now. The river ran dark and swift and cold in its white banks; and at night the northwest wind howled down West Canada Creek. The expectation of winter confronted everyone.

In the noon sunlight, under the slow downward drift of flakes, children laboriously puddled clay that was stiff with frost, and women were sealing the cracks between the logs. Men worked with adzes on planks for the doors. The few horses and oxen remaining to the community were all at work drawing in firewood and the cornstalks from the outlying farms. Boys were guarding the stooks set up among the cabins. Browse was already scarce in the woods and the cows anxiously tailed the carts in from the fields and had to be driven away.

Men had not felt like building again out of reach of the forts, though it meant that they must travel back and forth to work, next spring. Since the September raid several families who had gone back had been taken up by marauding parties; and as the autumn waned the Indians took fewer prisoners and more scalps. It was difficult to feed prisoners on a two-hundred-mile march through a snowy wilderness.

The surprising thing was that so many people stayed at all. A dozen or so of men who had relatives to the east had left the flats with their wives and children and what remained of their possessions; and a few had gone in the dubious hope of finding work. But most of them felt that they could not afford to leave. With the destruction of their wheat, their only source of income had been obliterated. Besides, many of them did not want to move. They had brought the land from wilderness to farm. In the past two years they had been tasting their first prosperity. To abandon their homes would be, it seemed to them, to give up the human right to hope.

On November first, a train of seven wagons hauled slowly up the Kingsroad. As it passed McKlennar's, Gil came out of the stone house and hailed the driver of the leading wagon. The driver pulled in his steaming team and yelled back.

"We're hauling to Fort Stanwix."

"What have you got?"

"Mostly flour and salt beef."

"You've got a lot of wagons."

"Yes," said the driver. "We're the last train for this year. I ain't sorry, either."

"Haven't you got an escort?"

"We will have. They're sending down a company from the fort. We've got to wait this side of Dayton till they get to us."

"Why this side?" asked Gil. "We haven't heard of any Indians."

The driver laughed. He was a red-faced, lantern-jawed man, a Continental teamster, in a battered campaign coat.

"They ain't afraid of Indians," he said. "They're afraid some of you people will get together and steal one of our wagons."

He spat between the rumps of his wheelers and swung his arms to warm his hands. He added, with a drawled tolerance, "I guess they need wheat up there, too."

"I guess they do," Gil said grimly.

"Ain't you pretty far off, living here?"

"There's always two men, here," Gil said. "There won't be any big parties down now, I guess, with the snow coming."

"I guess not," said the driver jovially. "I guess you've got a pretty comfortable place there. Didn't the destructives burn it?"

They tried to. They burned the barn and the log house."

"I thought it looked different somehow." His red face shifted and admiration came into his eyes. Behind his wagon the other teamsters had begun to yell. He motioned with his arm for them to haul past. "I'm having a talk with my friend," he bawled. "You go ahead."

Lana had come out beside Gil. She looked small and bright-cheeked in the cold, but there was a queer kind of speculation in her eyes as she stared at the wheat wagon. Now she raised them to look at the driver and smiled.

"Good morning," she said. "Did you come up the valley?"

He said with a sort of gallantry, "From Ellis's Mills, ma'am."

"Oh," she said. "I thought you might have come from Schenectady."

"No. Why?"

"I was wondering how things looked like in Fox's Mills."

"I was through there last month. Hauled down to Johnstown with wheat for Van Schaick's regiment."

"How was it in Fox's Mills?"

"It looked just the same as any place. Why? Do you know folks down there?"

"My family lives there," said Lana. "I haven't heard from them in two years now."

"Well, they ain't been much troubled with destructives. Only at the outside farms, some."

Lana's sigh made a little cloud before her face.

"I ought to be starting, I guess," said the driver. His voice was vaguely suggestive. He looked down at the lines in his mittens.

"Say, mister."

"Yes."

"Ellis will sell you wheat all right, or flour. He's asking nine shilling English money, or old York, if it's silver."

"Nine shilling?" It was incredible.

"It's a good bargain."

"He knows we can't get flour. Our mills are burned."

"I guess so."

Gil said bitterly, "The damned Scotchman."

"I don't like the Scotch so good myself," said the driver. "Look here. I'm a neighborly man. Would you like a sack out of this wagon? I'll sell it for five shillings hard cash."

"No!" said Gil, suddenly.

"It's the best price you'll get this winter. But it's got to be hard money. I don't deal with Continental money, generally," he went on as Gil turned, "but I'll let you have the sack for $6.25 in notes if you like. Seeing it's you, mister."

Gil turned back and stared.

"That's five to one," he said incredulously. "Money'd dropped to four to one the last I heard."

"Oh, no," said the driver. "I was in Schenectady last month. It's down to eight to one now. You'll get a real good bargain, see."

"Go to hell!" said Gil.

"You needn't act like that to a favor."

"Get out of here."

"It's a highway."

"Get out of here before I drag you off your wagon, by God."

The driver stared a moment and then spoke to his horses. "My Jesus," he said. "I never seen such a crazy fool."

Adam Helmer came round the house with his rifle. He had been listening, apparently, for he said to Gil, "Shall I shoot the bug-tit? We could drag his wagon down the road and make it look like destructives. We'd burn the wagon." He lifted his rifle suggestively. "I could scalp him. I ain't very good at it, but I could get it off all right. Then we could give an alarm."

The driver took one look at Adam's great bulk and started to flog his horses.

Going back to the house, Gil said bitterly over his shoulder:—

"Save your powder for something we can eat."

But Adam could not resist putting a ball through the canvas top. The rifle made a roar in the snowy sunshine and as the powder smoke drifted gently away from Adam's big red face he gave a whole-souled grin. The wagon was careening round the bend of the road; the four horses bucking up their rear ends like unanimous rabbits while the driver screeched and flogged them with all his might.

Gil had turned back at the shot.

"You damn fool. Now he'll probably report on you and come back with a squad."

"No!" said Adam. "I hadn't thought of that." And he beamed all over.

Gil had worked hard. He and Adam had rigged up a small log shelter for the horse and the sole remaining cow. It was a great streak of luck that had let the Indians find the other three and leave the freshened cow; but she was already feeling the pinch of light rations and was falling off in her bag. She gave only about a quart at each milking, and Gil figured gloomily that by January she would be giving less than a quart a day. The quality of the milk, too, had changed. It had turned whiter and thinner and it had a peculiar pungent, barky taste that the baby still gagged over.

That did not trouble Lana, who said that she could take care of the baby, whatever happened. She was sure of it, too. It was a kind of inward confidence that made her seem to bloom, even on the day they came back to the farm and saw the familiar sights obliterated—the barn, the log house, even the fence rails leading from the barn, had been burned up. But Gil was not sure in his own mind of Lana's ability to nurse the baby. He felt that they would have meat enough with Adam around most of the time. Joe Boleo was expected to come back also. But Gil doubted whether Lana's milk would hold up on a meat diet.

He cursed himself now for persuading Mrs. McKlennar to let him put practically all the ploughed land into wheat. They had been banking on the rising market of course. But he wished to God he had put more in corn.

The corn was all gathered, the husks braided, and the ears hung by them along the red and black rafters of the kitchen in long rows of gold and maroon. But considered in terms of six adult people, it looked like a small supply.

Occasionally he found Mrs. McKlennar watching him when she thought he wasn't noticing her. She herself was quite happy now that she had got back to her own house. She continually breathed defiance and war at the thought of ever leaving it again, vowing she would rather lose her scalp a dozen times than go away. But she was worried about Gil and spoke to Lana about him.

"He lies around too much," she said. "You ought to get him out. Working. Doing something."

Lana lifted her dark eyes.

"What can I get him to do?"

"It doesn't matter," said Mrs. McKlennar. "Anything."

"But he's done all he can. Now the little stable's finished and he's got the wood cut. Adam doesn't do anything, and he's all right. I guess Gil is."

The widow snorted.

"Adam's not the same. He's just a bear, a big brainless yellow-haired bear. Bears naturally lie up in winter. They lie around and scratch their bellies." She smiled to herself. "I like Adam."

"Gil will be all right," Lana said confidently.

"Well, you're his wife. You think I'm a stuff-budget. All young people think old people are, girls worse than boys. Nobody pays any attention to an old woman like me."

Lana smiled and held up the baby to Mrs. McKlennar.

"Here's two do, anyway. After all you've done for us."

"Go on!" But Mrs. McKlennar smiled and took the baby in her arms, and the baby confidently began to bounce. "The warrior," she muttered. "Lord!" Then she looked across him at Lana. "You're so pretty. And you've got your baby. And Gil loves you. And you aren't afraid. I hope you never will be."

Later she said to Gil, "Why wouldn't it be a good idea to start work on the new barn? We'll need it next year."

"I can't build a barn till the frost's out of the ground."

Mrs. McKlennar controlled her impatience.

"You could cut the logs, couldn't you?"

"Yes," said Gil, doubtfully. "But what's the use? It'll soon be too deep in snow to skid them out." He turned away from her and added, "It would probably get burned next year, anyway."

Mrs. McKlennar allowed herself to be tart.

"Nothing will ever get built again if you think that way."

As he lay before the fire, watching Daisy's broad shape bending down to place a pone on the coals, he wondered where Adam was. Adam had returned to McKlennar's for a purpose. With the Bowers girls at Fort Dayton, he couldn't carry on his commerce if he lived in the community of cabins. It was not private enough. He knew that if he were so handy to Polly he would soon give himself away. Besides that, he had a new distraction in Jake Small's wife over at Eldridge. He hadn't made much progress, he admitted to Gil, but give him a little time. He knew her well enough by now to know that she was crazy for another baby, and that she was beginning to lose faith in poor old Jake.

"I don't say nothing against Jake's powers," Adam maintained honorably, "but I just hang around so she can look at us both at once. She's quite a girl." He combed his hair. "No doubt she'll get the idea."

Gil thought of that and thought of Betsey Small, red-haired, quicktongued, and thin and tight-looking. For a moment he didn't catch on to what Daisy was saying about Mrs. McKlennar. Then he cursed and told

told her to keep a civil tongue. He wrenched himself off the floor, got his axe, and presently all the people in the house could hear its clear hard cracks as it bit into a spruce.

At supper time he felt better than he had in weeks. He was tired; but he had felled and cut to lengths twenty logs. He said to Mrs. McKlennar, "I think I'll make the new barn sixteen wide."

Immediately she got up an argument for a narrow barn, delighted to see him get his teeth into conversation. But finally she succumbed. "You probably know better, Gil."

He replied good-naturedly, "Well, you see I've done farming all my life."

He left her in the kitchen and went to find Lana. It was cold in the bedroom, so cold that they saw their breaths between them and the baby. Lana tucked it in, while Gil got undressed, and covered the whole cradle with a thick quilt, making an airless tent.

He watched her slight start when she discovered that he was already in bed. She glanced at the cradle sidewise, looked at him from under her lashes, and, smiling slightly, took her comb from the top of the chest.

He lay still and straight in the deep trough of the feather bed, watching her. He loved to watch her comb her hair when she was in this quiet and contented mood: the way she undid the braids; the way she flung the hair forward over her shoulder and combed it in front of her, head down, looking out at him over it, quiet, refreshed, as if the touch of the comb on a single strand of her hair might soothe them both; the way she lifted it behind her head and combed it from beneath, in long arm-length strokes that were slow, almost languid, with sensation. Her strokes were so deliberate that it seemed as if the thick mantle of black hair to her waist must keep her warm. The comb crackled very faintly as it passed through her hair; and the sound of it made Gil conscious of his own tired ease and the increasing warmth beneath the covers.

"Hurry up, Lana."

She smiled at him in the bed, deliberately going on with the combing. Her voice was soft, and she watched him through the motions of her hands with sleepy, humorous eyes.

"Mrs. McKlennar was worrying about you," she said. "But I wasn't worried about you."

"What about?" His voice was sharp at her irrelevance.

"About you lying around and not doing anything."

"I've started getting logs for the new barn." He stopped himself and said sternly, "What's that got to do with things?"

"Nothing, only I said I wasn't worried."

He grinned.

"You weren't worried a bit?"

"Not a bit," she said. . . .

Captain Demooth walked with Dr. Petry to the latter's store. The doctor had been over to the cabin to see Mrs. Demooth. But the men had not been able to talk; there was no place in the cabin where one might talk without everyone hearing you.

"Come inside, Mark," said the doctor. "I'll get you a drink."

"I don't want a drink."

"Well, I want one. And you better join me."

The doctor went to his office and faced the shelves. He stood for a minute looking at the rows of bottles; then he said: "It was a dispensation of Providence they didn't burn this office. This town could a whole sight better spare a church than those bottles." He reached for one marked *Tarta Emetic* and took two glasses, and poured out a yellow liquid with affection. "Don't get nervy, Mark. It's good Kingston. The last I have. I put it there to make sure it don't get misapplied. Now if it was Tartar Emetic in a rum bottle, that would be something."

He drank and watched Demooth drink.

"How long have you been married?"

Demooth started. He met the doctor's eyes.

"Why . . ." Then suddenly he caught on—the drink, the question. Demooth swallowed and said in the same tone, "Twelve years, Doc."

Dr. Petry grunted, held out the bottle, and poured two more glasses. He closed his eyes as he drank; then he said, "Twelve years is a long time, for some people, and short for others. I've been married only ten, myself. Well, Mark, I might as well tell you . . ." He drew a deep breath.

"You needn't, Doc. I've thought so for some time myself."

"Yes, it went to her head."

"It wasn't the raid, you know," said Demooth. "It was waiting for it to happen. She was scared."

"Weak head, weak head. She was one of the prettiest women, when I first saw her, I ever saw," said Dr. Petry.

"How long do you think she'll live?"

"A week, a month, maybe till next spring. She's strong in some ways. But she doesn't want to hang on."

Demooth turned to the window.

"I think the thing for me to do is to take her to Schenectady. She never got used to living up here. When I see her in that hut, I remember the way she used to look at me when we first settled in Deerfield, before the house was finished. I used to laugh at her then."

"Some people never get over being scared, Mark. There's nothing you can do about it. Yes, I'd move the poor lady down. It might make her happy. It might give her a new lease. But if she dies, don't take it too much to heart, Mark. Try not to. It doesn't pay to get brooding. Not up here. Not now."

Demooth ignored what he said.

"I can take her down to Little Falls in one of those wheat wagons that went up to Fort Stanwix yesterday. They ought to be back by the end of the week. Ellis will lend me his sleigh."

"The sooner the better," nodded the doctor. "Before it gets too cold. She won't stand much cold. Will you stay down there?"

Demooth hesitated.

"Yes."

"Will you come back next spring?"

Again he hesitated.

Finally he said again, "Yes."

"Good thing," said the doctor. "You'll probably be needed. While you're down, try and get me some stuff. I've got a list. I haven't been able to get anything sent up from the army hospital. Good luck, Mark."

They shook hands.

. . . "What will we do, John?"

She wasn't crying, but her eyes were helpless and tragic.

"Won't he take you?"

"He says he can't. He says he'll have to take Ellis's sleigh and there'd be no room for me. He told me, too, that I'd done Mrs. Demooth as much good as anyone could have done. He was very nice, and he gave me a month's wages, too. I didn't want to take them, but he made me. Do you think that was all right?"

"I guess so," said John. "As long as he said so."

They were walking out along the Kingsroad, because they had no other place to be alone. It was snowing a little; there was no sunlight; the sky was gray, and even the snow looked lifeless, as if it died in falling.

Walking through it, both Mary and John looked thin and small and cold. Mary was cold. She was wearing moccasins she had made herself, stretched over rough knitted stockings. Whenever she had to answer him, she drew a deep breath so that her teeth would not chatter. She was afraid he would see how cold she was and make her turn back. But he was too preoccupied to notice her. He walked bent over, watching his own feet in the snow, a frown on his face. The frown made him seem older; she liked him when he frowned, knowing he did so on account of her. Ordinarily it gave her confidence in him. But now she thought, what could even John do in such a situation?

He suddenly blurted out, "If I could get work anywhere . . ."

It was to her a confession of his hopelessness. There was no work—she knew that as well as he and she knew also how he felt about his mother. Now that his father had been taken by the enemy he felt a natural responsibility for her welfare and for Cobus's. Cobus wasn't yet old enough to be solely responsible. He was a stout strong lad, but he was too young to hunt. Moreover, the Weavers had less corn than almost any other family; and almost no money at all.

"John," she said, "how much money have you got?"

She knew already, but he answered again, glad of something to say, that he had given the money to his mother.

She said, "With what Mr. Demooth has given me, I've got ten dollars, now."

She had not told him before how much. Ten dollars. Ten dollars. He looked at her. The sum automatically reminded him how six months ago they had thought they could get married when they had that much saved up.

"What is it in?" John asked.

"Mr. Demooth always paid me in hard money. He said that was what he had made the offer in and he would stick to it."

John said, "Then you've got—let's see—you've got eighty dollars in American money."

Suddenly they were awed by the miracles of Congressional finance. Just by the word of it, apparently, Congress had made them incredibly wealthy.

Eighty dollars—why, some people who were respectable had lived and died with less than that. They started smiling at each other.

Seeing him so pleased, Mary relaxed, and immediately the shivers got the best of her, and because John was looking at her he noticed them at last.

"You're cold."

She only nodded.

"You ought to have told me."

She kept her teeth clinched, but she pleaded to him with her eyes. And he could not scold her. He knew how she looked forward to going out with him.

The wind had begun to blow also, and it seemed to him that he could see it cutting through her threadbare jacket and shawl. Her face was pinched now with cold, and her brown eyes very large. The freckles stood out startlingly on her face.

John was frightened. He cast a wild look around and spotted Mrs. Mc-Klennar's stone house.

"We can get warm in there," he said. "Come on, Mary."

He grabbed her arm and began lugging her towards the house.

It was midafternoon and they found only the women at home.

"For Lord's sake!" said Mrs. McKlennar. "What have you two children been up to?"

"It's my fault. I brought her walking. She got cold. I didn't notice how cold it was. Do you think she'll get sick?"

John was breathless and white. He couldn't get his eyes off Mary, and now that the shakes had taken hold of her she could not have stopped them with the whole world looking on. They both started as Mrs. McKlennar cried, "Sick! Pshaw! I'll give her some sack. Daisy! Fetch the sack. Now sit down by the fire. John hasn't introduced you, but I know all about you, Mary Reall. John's a good boy and his mother thinks you're lucky, but you're not half as lucky as he is. I can see that." Mrs. McKlennar meant what she said. The girl was already cocking her chin, and Mrs. McKlennar liked any girl who could cock her chin. She gave her some sherry and had some herself and motioned the two young people to sit down on one settle.

She sat down opposite them.

"What on earth brought you two so far—just talking?"

To John, troubled as he was, Mrs. McKlennar's long and horsy face, seen against the ears of corn, and the strings of dried apple and squash, in her large and comfortable kitchen, wore a kind and powerful beneficence. His young mind had been troubled too long with his and Mary's burdens. Before he remembered that Mrs. Martin and the negress were still in the room he had started to tell Mrs. McKlennar everything.

"You see," he concluded, "now Pa's gone, I've kind of got to look out for Ma. And she won't let Mary in the house. It ain't as if we hadn't waited quite a while, and we aren't so terrible young. And then I don't know where Mary's going to live. She can't live alone."

"Can't she stay in Demooth's cabin?"

John flushed.

"He said Clem Coppernol was going to stay there."

"Then of course she can't," said Mrs. McKlennar. "Do you know what I'd do, John?"

She was sitting very straight on the settle and looking down her nose at the two of them. As John replied, "No, ma'am," the end of her nose quivered visibly.

"I'd marry the girl before some man with more brains than yourself snatched her from under your nose." Her deferred snort was quite deafening.

John's eyes shone. Then they sobered again. He had thought of it so many times. "It ain't possible, Mrs. McKlennar. It wouldn't be right to Ma. Taking Mary into her house. And I can't build us another now. I couldn't keep the two in wood. Cobus ain't much yet. Somebody's got to look out for Ma."

Mrs. McKlennar said, "No, I don't think you ought to abandon your mother, and I'm not telling you to. Now listen, John Weaver. What house are you living in?"

"In the cabin at the end of the row near the fort," he said wonderingly.

Mrs. McKlennar snorted once more. "You *are* a stupid boy, John— maybe you shouldn't get married after all. Now I've got to tell you all the things Mary could tell you but has been too sensible to tell you. What I meant was, who built the cabin?"

"I did," said John.

"Item one. You did. How much money of your father's has your mother got? How much of yours?"

"She's got five dollars of Pa's and seven dollars I earned."

"Item two, you are mostly supporting her and your brother. Item three, how much money has Mary got saved?"

"Ten dollars," Mary said softly, but with pride. She couldn't help it. Her voice made Mrs. McKlennar swing her eye round, and a sly little smile pulled the corner of her mouth.

"Then," said Mrs. McKlennar, "marry the girl, take her to the cabin, and tell your mother that you've brought your wife home to your own house, and that Mary has said that she will be very glad and proud to have your mother stay with her." Mrs. McKlennar's grin had infinite relish. "She hasn't another place to live in so she'll have to put up."

"We haven't much corn. Pa was trying to get his money back in wheat. We haven't much to live on."

Mrs. McKlennar tossed her head.

"Mary's money will take care of her as well when she's married as when she's single, and she won't eat more. To look at her I'd say she'd gladly go without food every other day for the sake of being married to you. Shame on you, John Weaver. You're trying to be too respectable. Respectability never made a saint. Saints most always start their careers with some good honest sinning. If you're going to starve, you might as well all starve together. And that reminds me. There's no stores where I can buy Mary a wedding present. So you'll have to use your ingenuity to find yourself something. I shall give you a pound, Mary."

John and Mary both stared at her. Then John looked at Mary and flushed painfully. But she did not flush at all. She merely looked at him.

The voice of Mrs. McKlennar went on almost like the voice of a higher power. Lana had told her the whole story; and long ago the widow had thought something ought to be done about it.

"John," said Mrs. McKlennar, "I'll tell you something you don't prob- ably know. Reverend Sam Kirkland's over in Fort Herkimer, and he sent word by an Indian he'd be down this afternoon to spend the night here. He always stops on his way out from the Oneida towns each fall. He won't mind marrying you without banns when I tell him about you. Now—would you like to wait and get it over with here and now? You, John Weaver, would you?"

John glanced at Mary. He looked positively shamefaced. Then he faced Mrs. McKlennar again and gulped.

"Yes, ma'am," he said.

"And you, Mary, would you?"

"Yes," said Mary. Her voice was very low, but very steady.

"Oh, Lord," thought Mrs. McKlennar. "See what I've done now! They're nothing but children. The girl's just a child." But Lana was smiling at her, and black fat Daisy was muttering, " 'Clare to gracious, ain' dey sweet?"; and she went on thinking, "God, what nasty sentimental things women are, and God knows why either. Likely as not he'll beat her or something, and she'll be miserable with her mother-in-law, and the two of them will hate me all their lives." But suddenly she began chuckling, and when they all looked at her, she said, "Anyway, Mary's lost her chill."

Now that it was done, it seemed hardly possible. It had taken so short a time. First Reverend Mr. Kirkland had come, and both John and Mary had been impressed with his kindness, and a little awed to think that he was the man who had kept the Oneidas on the American side of the war. He was a tall lean man, dressed like any other man, except for his black hat. He had straight thin features and a gentle mouth, and his eyes seemed com- pletely detached from all the world. But the solemn, nasal tones of his voice as he repeated the service yet rang in Mary's ears.

She felt humble and uplifted together. It was odd, too, walking home, though the daylight had waned, that she did not feel cold. She took John's arm just as they reached the outskirts of the settlement. The feeble lights of tallow dips coming through the paper windowpanes of the cabins were like solemn light brown eyes. Her thin hands were strong on his arm, helping him to walk to the cabin where they would now live together with his mother.

"John," she said. "Are you unhappy?"

He said, "No." But she knew that he was worried.

"I'll always be anything you want me to be, John. I'll always love you, no matter what."

He squeezed her hand against his side without speaking. But he looked into her face as they went under the first window and saw it brave, and patient, and adoring, and so young that he felt frightened to think that she was now his own.

Frightened, and excited, and glad that they would not have to sit through supper. Mrs. McKlennar had given them a supper before leaving. It was a marvelous meal—the bone end of the last ham, some heated chocolate in china cups, a pone with jelly, and apple sauce. It now occurred to him that he and Mary would have to find themselves a place to sleep together. He would take Cobus's bed for themselves, as it was in the corner—though farthest from the fire, it would be more private. They had nothing but two deerskins to make curtains of—he hoped it would not turn so cold these would be needed for bed covers. He felt himself prickling all over; and then with a rush of elated confidence he knew that Mary had felt his elation, and that suddenly she had lost all her courage, and was afraid of him. When he opened the door, the light shone softly on her face, her eyes on his, and the color rushing into her cheeks.

He turned to the room, "Hello, Ma."

Emma Weaver said, "We saved you some supper."

"I've had it," said John. He closed the door behind him and swallowed hard.

"Ma, I've brought Mary home."

Emma turned her head. Her homely face, grown more gaunt, became animate. Anger, doubt, conviction, and fear passed over it.

"John," she said softly, "you mean?"

John managed to nod.

"Mary's staying. We got married this afternoon. Reverend Kirkland married us at Mrs. McKlennar's."

Cobus, who was whittling an ash stick for snowshoes, became all eyes. He turned from Mary to stare apprehensively at his mother. Emma said, "Do you want me and your brother to move out?"

"No, Ma. You know that we wouldn't want that."

Emma said, "I heard Captain Demooth would not take Mary to Schenectady. I didn't know you'd do this." All at once tears, big helpless ones, poured out of her eyes, and trickled unevenly down her lined face.

Mary's breath caught.

"Don't, Mrs. Weaver. Please don't cry. I want to help you, John and me both do. And we can, please, if you'll let us."

She had stepped forward and bent slightly down towards Emma. Now, to her astonishment, and to the two boys', Mrs. Weaver lifted her wet face. "I'm so tired," she said. "You don't know how tired I have got since George got took." The sobs rose in her breast. She hid her face, and, as Mary touched her, leaned against the girl's knees. John thought that he was going to cry himself. He had never seen his mother licked before; she seemed physically beaten, as if he himself had laid a stick across her shoulders.

They got her to bed on the floor before the fire, where she lay sobbing quietly. John ordered Cobus to bed and then he and Mary moved the chest as he had planned and hung the deerskin up. They blew the tallow dip out and crept under the blankets, dressed as they were, for warmth. They could see the soft glow of the firelight pulsing over the bark on the log walls. The fire burned without sound.

Over in the other corner, in John's old bed, fat Cobus lay like a hare, unmoving, holding breath, soundless, and all ears. Emma's sobbing continued softly. The deerskin, not completely cured, had a faint tangy rankness that seemed to grow as the fire sank to coals. . . .

In one of the cellar cells, in the very wall of the old fortress at Chamblée, George Weaver was wondering whether German Flats had managed to get through the summer and autumn without suffering the raid everyone had been afraid was coming. He did not know. There were nine other men distributed around the walls of the small cell. They had no window to see each other by. Their faces must be remembered from the brief flashes that the jailer's torch made when he came to bring them their food. Since they had entered the cell they had not been allowed out of their irons; and their irons were fastened to heavy rings in the stone walls.

It had taken George two months to get there. First three weeks of following his Indian captor through the wilderness to a Seneca town, where they had made him run the gantlet. It was his plodding patient strength that had brought him through that, though George would have said it was the fact that they could not beat him off his feet. His captor had become a celebrity on the strength of George's performance and told George in broken English that he had never seen a man take so slow a pace and survive.

George had stayed two weeks in the Indian town before being led on to Niagara, where he was traded for the customary eight dollars to a beefy British major. They had kept him at the fort for eight days before shipping him with some other prisoners on a small sloop to Montreal. All the prisoners hoped they would be kept in Montreal, and most of them were. But George, with two other men who had been captured near Cobleskill, was shipped on to Chamblée.

When he saw the immense square walls of the old fortress, he had thought that it would be a hard place to get out of; but he had had no idea that men treated prisoners the way he was treated. A man could stand up, and he could sit down, and he could lie down if he got in a particular position parallel to the wall. That was bad, but worse was the fact that since the ten men had entered the cell they had not been allowed loose for even long enough to clean the filth out. The place had an unbelievable stench. Some of the men had periods of raving, and others never said anything. George was managing to get used to the stench. It was becoming part of him, like an integral function of his own skin. The only thing that bothered him was his belief that the man in the corner behind the door had been dead for four days. He had not touched food for that period nor said anything nor rattled his chains, and the jailer's light never reached into that corner, except to touch the unused food, which was left lying there. There was quite a heap of it now on the board the man used to use as a plate. But no one else could reach it.

To keep himself from thinking about it, George used to try to think about his family. It came easier to-night because the jailer had said it was snowing outside. George thought what a nice thing it would be for his family if he could write them a letter saying that he was not dead.

15. *By Cherry Valley*

The same snow that the jailer at Chamblée told George Weaver was falling over the valley of the Richelieu River, in the woods south and west of Cherry Valley took the form of sleet. The scout of twelve men and a

sergeant ten miles out on the Beaver Dam road decided that there was no
sense in running a scout at all on such a night. The sergeant was sure that
he was getting up the beginnings of a chill. He had never been able to
stand being in the woods anyhow; and when darkness began to filter
through the sleet, he gave orders to halt on the next dry spot, or drier spot,
or spot less wet was what he meant, and light one hell of a big fire.

Only one man asked if it was wise to light a fire near the road; the rest
laughed or cursed, according to how wet they felt, and began breaking
off dead spruce limbs. But the sergeant thought that he ought to take cog-
nizance of such a remark. He set about explaining to the private that they
had had rumors all fall of a raid on Cherry Valley, and it hadn't come,
had it? What if Colonel Ichabod Alden had sent them out; he had to do
something, hadn't he? But he wasn't worried, was he? He was sleeping
in the Wells house, four hundred yards from the fort, wasn't he? Him and
Colonel Stacia and Major Whiting—and if the private thought that that
looked as if the officers expected a raid, he was entitled to think so or to
drain himself in the creek, or to kiss the sergeant's great-aunt if he liked.
The private responded that to him it didn't matter a damn if the whole
General Continental Staff slept in the Wells house so long as Mr. Wells
raised no objections; the officers always slept in the houses where there were
pretty girls, didn't they? Well, said the sergeant, he wasn't himself going
to stand under an eternal and universal piddle while Colonel Ike lay in a
feather bed, and not build a fire anyway, and to hell. He sneezed.

In ten minutes they had a great fire going, shooting the sparks up
through the drizzle-soaked boughs, and they stood around it, dripping and
steaming and feeling sorry for themselves, with the light red on their
faces, and their guns stacked under a near-by hemlock tree.

All the Indians under the advance scout of Ranger Captain Adam Crysler had to do was to give a couple of yelps and step in and pick the guns
up. The Continental scout of Massachusetts men never offered to leave the
fire. They stared and gawped. These were the first Indians many of them
had ever seen, painted Senecas with their heads bare to the wet and
their blankets sopping dismally about their sides. They looked bulky and
stuffed out under their deerskin shirts, but for all that they looked damned
ugly, too. The ugliest thing they did was to herd the prisoners away from
their own fire and take their places.

The first the Continental scout knew of a hostile British army was when
a distant whooping answered the Indians who had captured them. Then
for a long time there was not a sound except the crackle of spruce on the
fire, the muttering of the Indians, and the everlasting drip and piddle from
the branches. Then more Indians came through the woods, more Indians
than these Massachusetts men believed existed. They seemed like a thousand. There were five hundred of them. They gathered round and started
building new fires. Soon the little valley glowed with light, like a hillside
in a dripping sort of hell. Into this infernal glow penetrated the steady beat
of shod men marching.

The marching soldiers followed a slender man, swarthy as an Indian,
without paint, whose lank hair clung to the back of his neck in wisps. He
looked drawn and cold and tired. Behind him came one hundred and fifty
men in green campaign coats and black leather skullcaps. Behind them

marched fifty British regulars in red. Some of the regulars were even keeping step. All at once the woods had overflowed with living men. It seemed a miracle that they were there.

It was almost a miracle. On the Chemung River the Rangers had been watching the movements of the Eleventh Pennsylvania Regiment. The Continentals had penetrated nearly to Tioga before turning back to garrison Wyoming. Then Walter Butler, young, headstrong, and consumed with his ambition, decided to make a late fall march on Cherry Valley, All year the Canadian command had been making useless plans for taking Cherry Valley, one of the military depots for the Continental army, a frontier fort, and a menace to their own base at Unadilla. It was late in the year to make a start. He had insufficient supplies for his troops, and he had only two hundred men. But he put it up to them and they answered by offering to start next day.

They started late in October, through the cold rainy days, following down the Chemung, then turning up the Susquehanna, on which they met Brant returning towards Canada.

John Wolff would never forget that meeting on the banks of the river, filled with floating sodden leaves and driftwood: Brant at the head of his five hundred Indians, Butler with his two hundred men, showing an order from Haldimand that gave him sole command of any expedition undertaken against Cherry Valley and requested aid from all and any British officers. Brant demanded the command as senior captain. Butler curtly refused. There was a long argument before Brant, bitter and silent, turned his Indians to the northeast ahead of the white troops, and the long march was continued.

A hundred and fifty miles through swamps and along riverbanks and over hills, up the Susquehanna to Otsego Lake, thence overland to strike this road. There was little talking in the company of Rangers. They marched with a dogged, damp, and dreary sullenness. But they never stopped, for always they had the indomitable nervous figure of Butler ahead of them.

The Indians were unfriendly as Brant himself. They did not know why they had to come. They hated the rain. They wanted to go home. Many of the Senecas had been out all summer. The Indian scouts all said it was impossible to take Cherry Valley. There were two hundred and fifty men in garrison; there were three hundred more at Schoharie and nearly five hundred at Johnstown. Better to make a raid in the upper, unprotected valley.

But Butler was stubbornly setting his heart on Cherry Valley; his winter in prison seemed to have given him a bitter power. He drove the Indians on; even Brant, wrapped in his blanket, his gold-lace hat a sodden scarecrow mockery of himself, no longer argued.

John Wolff, marching in the last squad of the Ranger company, had fits of nervous fear when he saw the Indians all around them. He and some of his company thought it likely that the Indians might turn on them. Once a scalp was taken off a head, you couldn't tell whose head it had come off of. The white men were so much easy money for the Indians, if they chose; and stories went round that that had happened in a small way with St. Leger's retreating army, and that Bolton in Niagara had paid eight dollars for more than one member of the Eighth King's Regiment.

It was a nightmare march, with insufficient food. War had driven the deer far off the trails, and the wolves had begun running. They heard them at night in the hills above Unadilla as they came by.

November eighth and ninth and tenth they came through the Tryon country. It was on the tenth that they rounded up the twelve scouts with the sergeant and learned that the officers were at the Wells house. The scouts were willing to talk. Any man would have been willing with all those predatory Senecas squatting round him in the rain. They crowded close to Butler and answered questions.

Wolff heard the order to march as if it were part of a dream. Darkness no longer had any bearing on his thoughts. He shouldered his gun and took his place, and presently his feet began to take him forward through the rain. They had gone a mile when the rain gave up for a breath. The night seemed suddenly to clear and the marching feet left a dark track in the dark, and the mud felt cold and brittle. "It's freezing," said the man next to Wolff. "I hope to God my shoes hold out." Then from the north a flake drifted down, and another flake. The ground whitened under the trees. A luminous imitation of light was counterfeited in the woods.

At twelve o'clock they halted, filed off the road, and entered a swamp. Through the trees on the edge of the swamp they saw white hills dimly rising against the sky, one a steep cone, like a sugarloaf. The word came down the line, "No fires to-night." The men stood crowded close together for what warmth their clothes could give off. The sleeve of Wolff's coat stiffened with frost.

"We'll be lucky if half this army gets back to Niagara."

The man beside Wolff was talking. Wolff did not hear him. He was so cold that even his brain was numb. He did not even think.

At daylight the snow unexpectedly turned to warm rain from the south. A mist that was more like steam rose over the snow and hid the valley. Low orders were given: Eighty men with Captain Crysler to cut off the Wells house and take the officers; the rest to charge the fort, Butler leading the main group; the Indians to circle the fort and rake the palisade from the far side. Brant appeared and disappeared. A whistle sounded and the army moved.

At seven o'clock they heard a challenge on the road, and the sudden frantic galloping of a horse. The army moved behind it at the double. Wolff's squad followed the main force for the gate of the fort. They passed houses. People were stupidly looking out of their doors. The file of eighty men swung off towards the Wells house. Then in the fog ahead of Wolff the palisade loomed like a dark mass, and he saw the closing gate. Musket shots made little orange blobs. A lieutenant cried, "Lie down." Wolff fell in the slush and felt its cold soak through his coat. He started firing. At the same instant the cannon of the fort discharged over their heads. Behind where the town lay, he heard the wild shrill screeching of the Seneca war cry.

Just ahead of him Captain Butler raised up on one arm to look back. His face was bitter and hopeless. He said distinctly, "Oh, my God. Brant's taken all the Indians into the town." There was no firing from the other side of the fort. Every man there knew—both inside and outside the palisade—that the fort was safe. But they fired at each other for three hours, until the burning houses began to show up the Rangers' position. Whistles shrilled along the line of prostrate, slush-sodden men, and a slow crawling retreat was effected. The men rose up behind the first houses they came to and stayed there in the heat of the burning walls. It was the first warmth they had experienced in forty-eight hours. They began fishing in their wallets for scraps of smoked meat and chewed hungrily. It took them several minutes to realize that the houses burning in front of them must contain better food. And at the same time their numbed consciousness made them aware that the Indians were running amok.

The weary Rangers were mustered and sent to protect the burning houses, but it was then too late. The whooping and firing had receded into the edges of the woods. Only a few inhabitants were discovered unharmed. All through the settlement were signs of the Indian work, women lying beyond their doors indecently soaked even in their deadness, a child, an old man.

Butler was traversing the road like a madman. He gathered up an old man and his daughter and sent them to the fort with a flag and passed them in. Brant saw them enter too late to stop them. He confronted Butler with the warning that the Senecas demanded that the other prisoners be reserved. He said he could do nothing. He pointed out that if the Senecas were roused, they could and likely would annihilate the little army of whites. His face was expressionless, his voice as casual as if he talked of driving rabbits.

Butler withdrew his Rangers to the woods behind the Wells house, where they found Captain Crysler and his men surrounding forty shivering men and women and children. One of these, a man in a nightshirt, turned out to be Colonel Stacia, second in command of the fort. He reported that Colonel Alden had been killed, and surrendered himself to Butler.

The women huddled together like sheep. They did not move except to turn their heads when Indians whooped in the woods. When the mist began to clear and a colorless November sunlight fell upon them, they still looked cold. The ragged, soaking Rangers regarded them without interest.

After a while the army withdrew to a hillside and made a camp and lit fires. They rounded up some cattle and killed a dozen cows and skinned them and threw the meat in pots as fast as it could be dissected.

The Indians, suddenly returning, took the remainder of the cattle and killed them for themselves. They lay around all day watching the burning settlement and the palisade of the fort with all the firing platforms alertly manned. Butler kept by himself. A little way off Brant camped with a few Mohawks and watched Butler. John Wolff lay on his back with his comrades and digested food. He was too weary to do more.

They stayed all day, and at night they made windbreaks of bark, and brush, keeping the prisoners in the middle of the white encampment. The mist came up again from the snow, smelling of wet earth and charred wood and rotting leaves.

Early in the morning they skirmished the fort for an hour or two; but the business was half-hearted. They withdrew to their camp, and then orders were passed for the long retreat to Canada. Nothing had happened except the destruction of the houses and the murder of twenty-five noncombatants.

The weather was turning colder and a little after noon the snow began again. Butler unexpectedly sent back thirty-eight of the prisoners under guard and waited till the escort had returned. By then it was too late for the Indians to object. Three hundred miles confronted them, cold days, colder nights, and the steady and inexorable increase of snow, and, yet more bitter, the loneliness of the woods and the consciousness of failure. Only the Indians who had scalps at their belts took any comfort. The rest, Indians and white troops, marched on with the touch of snowflakes on their faces, in dogged silence.

7

ONONDAGA (1779)

1. *March 1779*

IN the opinion of some people, the winter had been providentially mild; but in another way it had been hard, for after the beginning of February the snow had so far decreased in the woods that the deer no longer yarded. With the steady hunting round German Flats, they had also become wild; and by March most of them seemed to have moved south to the grass flies on the Unadilla tributaries. It often meant a two days' hunt for even good woodsmen like Joe Boleo and Adam Helmer to pick up one deer.

But to Gil Martin, the problem was more than one of food. He had worked hard and had his logs all cut and ready to roll for the new barn. Now, as the snow went down in the valley, bringing up to the eye the lay of the soil again, he wondered where he would find seed for his fields. There had been no wheat to plant last fall. He would have to find oats and barley. He had none left. During the first months Mrs. McKlennar had bought oats, and wheat and barley flour, not only for herself, but to help the neighborhood. There was no question of her paying Gil's wages. Such things as wages and money belonged to a former time. But her supply of cash was nearly spent.

It was in Gil's mind this Monday, the fifteenth of March, to go down to Fort Dayton. He wished that Captain Demooth were back from Schenectady; but failing him, Gil thought he had better talk to Colonel Bellinger.

He stood outside the shed, looking up at the sky. The blue was softer than it had been all winter, and a white cottony tier of cloud hung over the southern hills. Some of the brooks already had opened, loosening a smell of earth.

He said through the open door, "I'm going down to Dayton. I don't know when I'll be back. You'll be here, Adam?"

"Till five o'clock," said Adam. "I've got an errand over to Eldridge's."

Lana smiled over his head and Mrs. McKlennar tossed hers. They all knew that Adam was making his play at Mrs. Small. "Her and her red hair," Adam would say. "And just wasting her time with Jake." So far he had made no progress.

"I'll be back," said Gil.

Whenever he went to Fort Dayton, Gil realized how lucky they were at McKlennar's. The stamp of hunger was bitten deep into all the people's faces. You could see it at McKlennar's, and you could feel it too, in the sharp answers they gave one another. But many of these people looked apathetic, or their eyes were like the eyes of ghosts.

Even Bellinger's eyes were unnatural. He opened the door of his cabin to confront Gil. He was a big man, and rangy, with a great coarse-cut head on his stooped shoulders. He looked tired.

"Oh, it's you, Martin. Come in. I've company." His voice was dry. "But he's about through here. Come in, will you?"

Gil entered.

A man in a brown coat was sitting at Bellinger's plank table. He had a rather studious face and mild eyes. He didn't look like a farmer or a soldier; but by the way he folded the papers before him, it seemed to Gil that the man's soul was filled with a love of writing. For the papers were covered with neat, pointed script, precisely ruled.

Bellinger said tiredly, "Mr. Martin, let me acquaint you with Mr. Francis Collyer. Mr. Collyer has been sent up by the Governor at the request of General Clinton."

Mr. Collyer made a slight bow. He took no interest in Gil, but addressed himself to Bellinger.

"Thank you, Colonel. You've given me everything. I'm sorry that I shall be compelled to report as I have told you."

"That's all right, sir. It's your business."

"Of course, Colonel, I have no idea what action Congress will take in the matter. I merely report. I am leaving you a copy of my summation. You know the figures anyway, as you've obligingly supplied them yourself."

"I don't give a damn what Congress does," Bellinger said suddenly. "You can tell the Governor so. Put it in your report, sir."

Mr. Collyer wisely said no more. He took his leave politely and walked to the fort, where his horse waited for him. Bellinger closed the door on his back. He leaned against it for a moment, staring at Gil. Then he began slowly and wearily to swear.

"I've had that gentleman on my hands for a day and a half, Martin. He's made me feel sick to my stomach. It's queer how sick to your stomach you can feel when you're half empty. Oh, he was very polite. A nice quiet gentleman. Mr. Collyer. Sent by Congress! Think of it!" He wiped his mouth and stepped to a stool and sat down. "Listen, you know I took things into my own hands in January and started signing requisitions for food from the army depot at the falls. But, by God, somebody had to do something! I signed the requisitions as on Congress. People had to have flour. I had to keep them. If I hadn't done it they would have been forced to leave. It was the only wheat in this part of the country. Thank God I got a double requisition yesterday! Just in time."

He stopped.

Gil asked, "What's Mr. Collyer?"

"That's it. What is he? He's a damned accountant sent up from Albany to look into all my requisitions of wheat. We were very patient together. We visited people. He heard their stories. Then he made a report. There's the summation. Read it! Read it, will you!"

What Gil read in the precise writing was this:—

Copy of the summation of my report to Governor George Clinton, March 15, at German Flats, Tryon County, State of New York, U. S. A.

(Re requisitions on Army depot at Ellis's Mills by Col. Peter Bellinger, 4th Company Militia, for wheat for the inhabitants.)

Having thus collected all evidence and made due personal investigations thereof, with the aid of said Col. Bellinger, who was in every way obliging and whom I may say I believe to have acted in the best faith, it is my finding that undue employment of his power has been made by said Col. Bellinger and that from my investigation it is plain that most of the inhabitants drawing said rations were not sufficiently destitute to warrant the use of *Continental Army* supplies. Respectfully submitted.

FRANCIS COLLYER

Bellinger was regarding Gil with deep-set angry eyes. "I suppose we ought to have been dead to warrant using army food. My God! Can't they realize that if we don't stay here, the frontier will automatically drop back to Caughnawaga? Can't they realize anything?"

Gil had nothing to say.

"I don't care what they do to me. I've pilfered, stolen, robbed the damned Continental army of enough to see us through till April. They can't hurt me, now. I'll resign my blasted commission. It won't make any difference if I do."

He stared hard at Gil.

"What did you want to see me for?" he asked belligerently. "You aren't out of food, are you? You haven't been on rations yet." Suddenly Bellinger smiled. "Come on. I won't kill you. Though I'd like to, too."

Gil felt better.

"Maybe this will kill you, sir. I came down to see where I could get twenty bushels of oats or barley for seed."

"Oh, my God!" Bellinger burst out laughing. The little cabin rang with his deep voice. "That's good." He slapped Gil's shoulder. "And I'd clean forgot about seed! Christ, what a man!"

"What can we do now?" asked Gil.

Bellinger got up.

"We'll take some wagons down to the mills. We'll beat the conscientious Mr. Collyer, who's going to leave an order with Ellis not to issue any grain except for Continental use. And we'll take along enough men to make the Continental guard surrender it, too, by God."

It took them two hours to round up men and wagons, and then the half-starved horses went so slowly through the pawsh of snow that they did not reach the mills until late afternoon. Mr. Collyer had already been there. The sergeant in charge of the mills forbade the entrance of the German Flats men. But the sergeant wasn't armed, and neither were the guard. They were sitting in the miller's loft playing a chilly game of cards and drinking beer. Bellinger simply locked them in.

The sergeant watched them with grim eyes.

"What do you dumb-blocks think you're doing?"

"We're going to help ourselves to a little oats and barley," said Colonel Bellinger, returning from the loft. "If we can find any."

"You'll catch it plenty if you do," threatened the sergeant. "I'll name the bunch of you by name in my report."

"You'd better explain how you came to be caught like this. Garrison! As your superior officer I ought to have the lot of you court-martialed."

"Superior bug-buttocks," said the sergeant.

Bellinger's shoulders suddenly hunched towards the man.

"What kind of buttocks did you say?"

The sergeant was furious with himself as well as the world for having been caught without a single guard on duty.

"I didn't name no bug."

"No? Why not?"

"I wouldn't insult no bug," said the sergeant.

The men had forgotten all about the grain and were now crowding the space between the bins to watch. It was too close quarters for them really to see. But even over the roar of the falls and the empty clack of the wheel ratchets, the impact of Bellinger's fist against the sergeant's middle was a solemn sound. The man's wind shot out all beery in the floury atmosphere. His hands went to his middle and his jaw came forward and his eyes swelled directly at Bellinger's fist. The fist traveled beautifully to meet the jaw. The sergeant straightened, went over backwards flat on his back, bursting a sack of flour in the process, so that a white cloud engulfed him. He lay there, dead to the world. The men yelled suddenly as Bellinger breathed on his knuckles. He turned on them. "Get to work," he bawled. "And don't waste any." He waited till they started to the bins. Then he sat down beside the prostrate sergeant and studied the gradual discoloration of his face until the wagons were loaded.

Gil found him still sitting there when he came to report that they had barreled and sacked almost a hundred and fifty bushels of oats, and thirty bushels of barley, and about ninety of wheat they could store for next fall's planting.

"Good," said Bellinger. "We'd better start." He took from his pocket a written requisition he had prepared before leaving the flats, and with a sharpened bullet filled in "150" and "30" in two blank spaces of his badly formed writing. At the foot of the paper he added: "P.S. 90 Bushels wheat too. PB, Col." He bent over to slip the sheet into the front of the sergeant's coat and dusted his hands as he rose. "You know, Martin, I kind of like that fellow now," he said. "Well, we better get going."

As they emerged from the door into the late afternoon air, all misty with the spray from the falls and vibrant with the thundering water, they found Mr. Ellis, the miller, anxiously regarding the five wagons.

"The boys tell me you've taken oats and barley and some wheat for seed, Peter," he yelled.

"We took only ninety bushels of wheat," Bellinger yelled back over the noise of water.

"Where's the guard?"

"They're locked up in the loft. I don't know whether they finished their card game. The sergeant's busted a bag of flour. But he's got my receipt."

"How'd he do that?"

"With his head, Alec."

The men burst out laughing, but the roar of the falls swallowed their laughter. Ellis's jaw dropped.

"You did that, Peter?"

"Sure we did. By the way, where did all those oats come from?"

"It was shipped in last week from Stone Arabia, Klock's, and Fox's Mills," bawled the miller. "I was going to mill the wheat to-morrow." He shook his head as though to clear it of the roar of water. "You'd better take it back, Peter. Honest you'd better. I can fix the sergeant so he won't say anything."

"Like hell I'll take it back."

"Listen. Don't be a fool, Peter. Don't you know they're collecting supplies all over the valley? They say Clinton will muster the line regiments up here inside of six weeks." He watched Bellinger swing onto his starved horse, which had been nudging up to the tail of the nearest wagon and snuffing with exalted shivers of its slatty sides. "Listen, Peter. That grain's for them."

Bellinger leaned out of his saddle, and stared at Ellis, then wiped spray from his eyes. "Where's the army heading for?" he shouted.

"I don't know for sure. Some say they're going to wipe out the Indians."

"What Indians?" yelled Bellinger, as the men crowded up to listen.

"The Iroquois."

"By God," shouted Bellinger. "How?"

"I don't know. But you take that wheat back, anyway. There's going to be five regiments. Maybe a thousand men. You'll get into bad trouble, Pete."

A lull in the wind made his words startlingly loud as the roar of the falls was swept north. Bellinger was leaning on the withers of his horse. He seemed to be thinking with his whole body. He looked tired again. All his men, including Gil, watched him. Bellinger lifted his reins. His voice was as resonant as it had been at Oriskany. They all heard it.

"Like hell I'll take anything back. They can do what they like, Alec. It's worth it to get seed into the ground." He moved his horse to the front, regardless of his yelling men.

The men went at the horses with their whips. The wagons lurched and groaned inaudibly and gathered a semblance of speed against the foot of the hill. The miller, watching them leave, thought they looked like animated scarecrows. Not very animated, either. He lifted his hand.

2. *Drums*

Scattered bits of news that filtered in to German Flats during the next two weeks seemed to confirm the miller's words. The First New York had gone into garrison at Fort Stanwix and Colonel Van Schaick himself had ridden through to take command. And on Captain Demooth's return from Schenectady in the first days of April, they learned that a great many bateaux were being built in that town for army use. Demooth said it was no secret that Congress intended an expedition, though where and when it would start, nobody knew.

The people listened to the rumors without much heart. Nothing had ever happened before to lend credulity to such reports. More pressing things occupied them—the spring ploughing and the sowing of the stolen seed. Bellinger was anxious to have it in the ground before a company was sent to reclaim it. He himself waited for court-martial papers to be served on him with a kind of grim fatality, and in the meantime thought of ways to hide the seed until it could be sown. He never was court-martialed. He never found out why not. Probably no one knew.

On the sixth of April, Gil went down with the mare and cart to secure his allotment of seed. He had already had a talk with Bellinger and De-mooth, and both officers agreed that he should stay on the McKlennar place. It was the one farm that had a stone house standing that could be defended, and the soil was of the best. The other people had marked off temporary land around the forts, each man with his field to cultivate, to raise communal food. "You'll understand we'll expect you to bring your grain into common stock next winter if it's necessary," said Bellinger.

On the seventh and eighth of April, Gil sowed the oats. The earth had dried fast and worked easily. All day he marched back and forth over the soft loam while the mare on the other side of the fence watched him wist-fully. Poor beast, she had been worked to death on insufficient pasturage, hauling the plough and then the drag, until she could hardly stand. Gil had got Adam down to help, and one or the other had hauled with the mare. At that they were better off than some people who hauled their drags with-out beasts. Now Adam Helmer was resting on the sunny porch, and the women were down by the river gathering the early marigold leaves for their first green food in months. The baby lay on a shawl in the grass at a corner of the field where Gil could keep his eye on him. The boy looked thin, lately, and seemed dull, for they had been feeding him on meat broth since Lana's milk had given out, and the cow would not freshen until June. They borrowed a little milk from time to time—enough, Gil thought, to keep the baby from getting too sick. But he was worried that it cried so seldom.

Lana did not seem worried. She was carrying another child; they thought it would be born in August. But she looked older. She had a queer look of frailness above the waist, while her hips and thighs had grown inordi-nately heavy. She took no interest in anything but food. But Gil hoped that, when they were getting plenty to eat again, she would brighten up.

He was glad that Demooth was back, for that meant that John Weaver could get work. Though his wife had died, Demooth was fixing up the Herter house, of which the stone walls yet stood, and he needed a younger man than Clem Coppernol now to work what farm he had left. The old Dutchman had not wintered well. He had always been a heavy eater and the thin winter had left him sour and difficult and given to unpredictable and dangerous flights of passion. He had nearly killed a horse that had lain down with him from exhaustion. They said he would have beaten it to death if he himself had not collapsed from the exertion of swinging the fence rail.

All these things had bothered Gil like a buzzing in his head, like the sound of bees outside a window on a hot afternoon. A good many others complained of the same buzzing of the head. They thought it might be weakness that made it, or the unaccustomed warmth.

Gil himself did not put much stock in the rumors of a Continental offensive against the Indians and Tories to the west. Not even when he saw an unusually large munition train hauling west to Fort Stanwix on the sixth. But on the seventh he had forgotten about them. He had started sowing at dawn. At first he had cast badly and unsteadily. Later the old accustomed rhythm had returned to his tired arm. This morning at last he had felt like himself and the seed fell in even sweeps, and by afternoon, with only four bushels of barley left to sow, he had felt his confidence rise.

The women came back with baskets of green leaves, Lana, Mrs. McKlennar, and the negress, walking through the still evening air. He thought Lana looked better. She picked up the baby, slinging it on her hip, and stopped before him.

"Come back," she said. "You've sowed enough to-day."

"Don't walk on the seeding," he said. "I've only a little left to do."

She obediently stepped off the seeding and let him pass. Her eyes brightened to watch the even swing of his arm, hand from the bag, over and round and back, making a sort of figure eight that the grain traced wide in the air and spread, in touching earth, to make an even sheet. To watch it soothed her. It was a familiar gesture, elemental in faith and hope.

She said, "I wonder how they're fixed for seed at Fox's Mills."

"I guess all right," he said, turning and coming back towards her. "How's Gilly?"

"I think the sun's doing him good. I wish he had more flesh on his legs."

"Where's Joe, to-day?"

"He was back of the house in the sumacs. He had a spade. I don't know what he was doing."

They let Joe Boleo's activities drop. Then Lana went on to the house. She said over her shoulder, "Daisy's going to bake a spinach pie with the greens."

Gil was finishing the last row of the field, at the river-side fence. He thought the buzzing was coming back to his head, but he was tired. He stopped to let his ears clear, letting the last grain trickle through his fingers. After a moment, he turned the bag inside out and shook it. He could not waste a single seed. The field lay square before him, traversed in parallels by his own footprints.

A still clear light lay all across the sky, and a flock of crows traversing the valley from north to south caught rusty flashes from it on their wings. Gil watched them turn their heads to look at the field and wondered whether they felt hungry enough to steal his oats.

Joe Boleo came down the field and said, "Gil. Your wife wants you to come home and rest."

"I'm resting right here."

"I figured so. But a woman don't think a man can rest unless he's where she can talk at him."

Winter had not upset Joe. He looked the same—gaunt, stooped, wrinkled, lackadaisical.

"I can't get the buzzing out of my head, Joe."

"What buzzing?" Joe was never bothered by buzzings.

"It's so loud I'd think you could hear it," said Gil.

Joe pretended to listen.

Suddenly his face tilted.

"By Jesus," he said soberly, "I do." He waited a moment. Then he climbed onto the fence and turned his face southeast, across the river. "It ain't buzzing, Gil," he said excitedly. "It's drums. They're coming up from the falls across the river. Hear them now."

Gil's head cleared. He too heard them. He climbed up beside Joe and stared with him through the infinite clearness of the evening air.

"There they come," said Joe. A file of blue was marching up the road. They saw them, but it was hard to believe.

"They're going to camp," said Joe. "They're falling out in that five-acre lot of Freddy Getman's."

Gil could see the drummers with their deep drums drumming beside the single black stud that was all that remained of Getman's house. Behind them lay the lot. Into it were wheeling a company in blue campaign coats, their muskets all on shoulder. They began to stack arms.

"What are they doing?"

"Taking the fences apart for firewood, I guess."

Another company with white showing through the blue, white gaiters and white vests, followed the first. Then came a swinging company of men in grayish hunting shirts.

The drums were now a stirring resonance throughout the valley. Adam came loping down the field. He asked excitedly what Joe had made out. "Let's go over," he said.

"Sure," said Joe. "You coming, Gil?"

Gil said he would go home. He didn't want to leave the place alone. He was tired, too.

The two woodsmen were like two boys. "We'll come right back and tell you," they shouted, and piled down to where the boat was fastened. Adam rowed, forcing shiny swirls with the oars, and Joe jerked his fur cap in the stern.

Supper was nearly over when the two men returned, but Daisy had kept a plate hot for each of them. They talked together like boys, both at once, both contradicting.

"There's a hundred and fifty soldiers," said Adam. "Two companies. The Fourth New York."

"No, it's the Fourth Pennsylvania. The New York Regiment's the fifth."

"You're crazy."

"Who gives a dang? You ought to've gone over, Gil. Their wagons come in right behind them. Remember how we had to wait for our wagons going up to Oriskany? These bezabors were sore as boils because they had to wait for fifteen minutes for the wagons."

"That ain't nothing. Do you know what they had for supper?" Joe Boleo's small eyes blinked.

"No," said Mrs. McKlennar. "How could we know, you crazy fool?"

"He's just like a bedbug," said Adam. "He gets ideas from humins, but they go to his belly. They had fresh pork. Yessir, Mrs. McKlennar. Fresh pork. I et some. And they had white bread. Soft bread. God, this country's getting luxuries now the army has soft bread."

"You big blond-headed bug-tit," said Joe Boleo. "Anybody could have guessed that. What they had, Mrs. McKlennar, ma'am, was white sugar in their tea!" He pursed his lips. "They offered me some tea, and I said yes. And they said how much sugar in it? And I said, well, about two and a half inches of it, with a spoonful of tea. And the son of a gun gave it to me! I brought it home in my shirt." Chuckling, he drew the cup from inside his shirt and handed it to Mrs. McKlennar.

Mrs. McKlennar began to sniff. She tried twice to speak, and then she said, "Thank you, Joe. I wish we had tea to go with it. But we'll have it in water. Daisy, boil some water."

"Yas'm, sholy does. It's ready bilin'."

Daisy in her ragged dress fluttered round the table laying the cups. She poured the water from the kettle. With great care Mrs. McKlennar put two teaspoonfuls in each cup. Nobody spoke as they stirred. They all watched her till she lifted her cup. Then they sipped together.

"It surely is a treat," said Mrs. McKlennar.

Lana suddenly got to her feet.

"I'm going to see if Gilly likes it," she said. She brought him to the table and sat him on her lap while he stupidly nodded his big head and rubbed his sleepy eyes. They all held their breaths when she put the spoon to his mouth, carefully cooled by her own blowing. He made a face, feebly, then stiffened and was very still. Then he started to cry. Their disappointment was intense.

Lana said defensively, "He's never tasted any sugar."

"Don't be silly," cried Mrs. McKlennar. "All he wants is more."

When Lana lifted the spoon again the child opened his mouth eagerly. "See!" cried Mrs. McKlennar. "I told you."

Everybody felt jubilantly happy.

"Did you find out where they were going?"

"Stanwix," said Joe and Adam together.

"Just there? There's two hundred men there already."

"That's what they said," said Adam.

"It's my idea they're going to make some kind of pass against Oswego," said Joe.

"What would they send Rangers for against a fort?" Adam was scornful.

Gil said, "Do you suppose they're going to go against the Onondagas?"

"By God!" said Joe.

They all remembered what Ellis had said. The Iroquois.

"They'll need scouts, I'll bet," said Adam. Joe met his eye.

"It would be fun going with an army like that and wiping out some Indians," said Joe quietly. "I always wanted to do some destruction against them."

He turned to Gil. "If they do, will you come along with us?"

Gil shook his head. Adam said, "You got your planting done, ain't you? Come on."

"The womenfolks will be safe enough with an army that size flogging around the woods. You ought to see them. They ain't like those Massachusetts boys."

"We ain't been asked," said Gil.

"Shucks," said Joe, blushing, because he had thought of something else to say and barely saved it before women. "You come along. I fixed something for the women in case they should get cut off. It's a hide-hole. I been working on it for three days."

"Really?" Mrs. McKlennar was interested. "What is it?"

"Come out," said Joe. "No, damn it, it's dark. I'll show you to-morrow."

"What's that, Gil?" Lana had risen.

Adam said soothingly, "That's just the taptoo, Lana."

They all went out on the porch with the tattoo of the drums thudding faintly across the valley towards them. It was pitch-dark, but the regularly spaced fires seemed very near.

They stood a long time watching them, in the damp coolness of the night. They saw the sentry figures small and silhouetted. They could even see the stacked rifles.

"They been a long time coming," said Joe.

Back in the house there was a scraping of silver against china as black Daisy scraped the cups for her own taste of sugar. She was humming softly.

3. *At Fort Stanwix*

Half an hour after sunrise, young John Weaver galloped into the McKlennar yard, waving a letter for Gil. It was a hasty scrawl from Colonel Bellinger asking Gil, Adam, and Joe to report to him immediately at Fort Dayton. While Gil was reading it, the calling of the robins was hushed by a long roll from the drums across the river. Gil ran round the house. He found Adam and Joe watching the camp. They could see the men breaking away from the fires and rolling their blankets.

"It's the general," said Joe. "I've heard it before." He answered Adam's question scornfully. "Not General Washington, you dumbhead. It just means the army's going to march."

Gil gave them Demooth's orders and the men went into the house together to get their rifles.

Lana confronted them in the doorway.

"Gil!"

"Don't get worried," he said.

"Where are you going?"

"Bellinger wants to see us. That's all."

"You're going with the army," she said accusingly.

Adam interposed awkwardly, "Aw, now, Lana. Nothing can happen to Gil with me and Joe along."

She looked white and stiff and her arms hung straight at her sides. Gil said to Mrs. McKlennar, "If we do have to go I'll send John Weaver back. He'll let you know if you ought to move to the fort."

Mrs. McKlennar nodded her gray head.

Joe slapped himself. "Lord, ma'am, I'd forgotten clean about it."

"What, Joe?"

"That hide-hole I made. It'll only take a minute to show it to you. Come along."

He led them quickly out into the sunlight and up through the sumac scrub. "You want to come this way, so you won't leave tracks."

He stopped a hundred yards up the slope.

"There it is," he said modestly.

He pointed to a fallen tree whose roots had lifted a great slab of earth.

"I don't see anything," said the widow.

Joe beamed. "That's it. You don't see nothing. Come here."

He led the two women to the roots of the tree, round to the trunk, and pointed. There was a small hole in the ground. "Don't walk out there," he cautioned them. "That's just poles laid over with dirt. There's room inside for the bunch of you. You can drop right down. I made it soft."

Mrs. McKlennar said, "Thank you, Joe."

Joe said, "You want to remember the way up here. Go over it in your heads so you could do it at night. I don't reckon you'll have to use it, though."

"I don't think so."

"It's a good thing to have handy, though."

He went back down the hillside and found Adam and Gil ready and John Weaver mounted. Lana came, still as death, behind Mrs. McKlennar. The men went down to the road and turned and waved. The widow waved back. Then Lana lifted her hand. Her arm looked frail and white in the morning sunlight.

She began to cry.

"He might have said good-bye to the baby," she sobbed.

Mrs. McKlennar put her arm over Lana's shoulders.

"Don't say that. He didn't want to go any more than you wanted him to. That's why he acted like that."

Over the river the drums beat out the assembly and the troops began to mass along the fence. A moment later the "march" sounded, and the two women saw the lines gather themselves like a single organism and start moving out on the road. They saw what they had not seen last night, that there was a flag in the middle of the line. They had never seen the flag before. The sight of it, clean and bright, with its stripes and circle of stars, for some reason made them feel like crying.

It appeared that Colonel Van Schaick had requested three guides from Bellinger.

"I don't know why he won't take Indians with the Oneidas so close and willing to go. He wanted three white men, he said. I thought of you. He says it will be only three weeks at most."

"Where does he want us to take him?" Joe asked.

"I don't know," said Bellinger. "You'd better start right away. Martin, did you plan for your women to come down here?"

"I think it would be better."

"It may not be necessary. I'll have young Weaver stay out there. But I'll keep an eye on them." He paused. "Van Schaick's got the woods covered to the west and I'll cover the south. And the Oneidas are out. I don't think there's any danger with the size army that's coming." He shook hands with the three in turn. "You'd better go."

The three men reached Fort Stanwix the same day, coming out on the bend of the river just before sunset. While they were yet approaching the fort, a small swivel was discharged and the flag fluttered down from the pole over the gate. It was a beautiful flag, silky and shining against the setting sun; but Gil felt that no matter how often he saw this American flag, he would only see the one that had flown from the same pole two years ago, with its botched stripes of uneven thickness, and its peculiarly shaped stars. Then it had stood for something besides the Continental army.

They trotted up to the sally port and announced themselves to the guard as three scouts from Colonel Bellinger. They were at once admitted and taken directly to the officers' mess. There they found Colonel Goose Van Schaick and his second in command, Major Cochran. The major was well, almost meticulously uniformed; but the colonel was a heavy man with coarse hair turning gray and small calculating eyes, and his collar rode high on his thick neck. He accepted Bellinger's letter and eyed the three Rangers.

"I don't want to be asked questions," he said belligerently. "You'll stay here, you'll live with the noncommissioned officers. Now, does any one of you know the woods west of Oneida Lake?" His eyes had unerringly picked Joe, who was leaning his tail against the table and gazing into the fireplace as if it were a wonder of the world. Now he nodded his head.

"Sure," he said. "I do."

"How about you two?"

Joe answered: "Gil ain't a timber beast, but the young lad's not going to get lost as long as I tell him where to go."

Adam opened his mouth to roar, but he met the colonel's eye in time. There was something about the colonel's eye which quelled him.

The colonel said, "You big ox, if you start fighting around here I'll have you flogged before the fort. I don't want to be bothered with yelling louts like you. And just so you'll know what it would be like, you can go out on the parade to-morrow morning and see what happens when a man gets flogged."

He turned back to Joe. "Listen you, what's your name? Boleo. You're to stay ready to march. You're to report to me an hour before the first troops start. I'll tell you where we're going. Then you'll pick the route, though I imagine there's just one way to get there."

"Sure." Joe was looking out of the window. "Down Wood Crick and across the lake. You land on the southwest shore, march over to Onondaga Lake, cross the arm—you can wade it. It's not over four feet deep. Then hit Onondaga Crick and go up. That will bring you to the first town. Jesus, Colonel, I used to play around there as a young lad. You ought to have been out there then."

The major's Irish face was a study, but the colonel wasn't taking the same pleasure in Joe.

"How did you figure that out?" he asked in a steady hard voice.

"Why," said Joe, innocently, "I ain't a complete fool or I wouldn't have been sent here, mister."

"Did you get that from somebody else?"

"No, we figured it out coming up."

The colonel grunted. "Keep your mouths shut. You're sure you can wade over the arm of the lake?"

"If you don't mind getting wet."

The colonel stared very hard at Joe. Then he said in cold, level tones, "That's all. If you want to eat you'd better hurry."

As they came out onto the parade, the garrison were filing into the mess, and the three men followed them dubiously. These soldiers didn't look quite natural somehow. They seemed to keep step with a kind of instinct. A corporal came out of the shadow of the officers' mess and touched Gil's arm. "You the three scouts?"

They said they were.

"My name's Zach Harris. You're to eat with us." He led them into the mess to a table at which sergeants and corporals ate together. They were greeted friendlily enough and sat down to heaped wooden bowls of beef stew cooked with turnips, tea and sugar, a slab of white bread, and a piece of cheese. The way they ate made the soldiers regard them with curiosity.

"What's the matter, ain't you fed all day?"

Adam replied, "We ain't had a feed like this since last September, Bubby. Does the old man always feed you like this?"

"He's a dinger to get provisions. But he bears down pretty hard on the discipline. Ever since that Dutchman Steuben came around last year, old Goose has been cock-eyed over discipline. But he can act real nice sometimes."

"He looks to me as if he could act just about as nice as a wolverine with the bilious complaint," remarked Adam.

The table roared and the word, going clean round the mess hall, set all the men to laughing. But Corporal Harris's was a dry grin. "I guess I see why the old man wanted you to watch a flogging, mister."

The flogging took place an hour after sunrise and just before breakfast. It was one of the colonel's theories that it made more impression on an empty stomach.

The three Rangers were routed out of bed by Corporal Harris and told to appear on the parade in five minutes. Before they were dressed they heard the drums beating a muster, and as they stepped out into the soft April morning the tap of a single drum came from the guardhouse.

Corporal Harris led them to a position in front of his own company. The entire garrison had been lined up in a hollow square. Set up on the bare beaten earth in the middle of the square was a single post about a foot thick. It made a long shadow towards the guardhouse, and now the tapping of the single drum marked the approach of the culprit along this shadow. He came between two sergeants. He was naked to the waist. He looked neither right nor left, but kept his eyes on the post.

Joe Boleo looked on with an abstracted kind of interest. Adam stood straight. The faces of the soldiers were expressionless as the culprit was taken by the arms, his hands lifted, and two nooses of fine rope passed over the wrists. The rope was then hauled up over a groove in the top of the post until the arms were stretched over the man's head, and his shoulder blades stood out sharp and his toes barely touched the ground.

The two sergeants then stepped back. The sergeant major of the garrison stepped out from the ranks and the drums beat a short roll. The sergeant general read from a paper:—

"Private Hugh Deyo, Captain Varick's Company, tried before court-martial and found guilty of stealing a shirt. Sentenced to fifty lashes with the hide whip. April 9th, 1779. To be administered before the entire garrison on parade, by order of Colonel Goose Van Schaick."

He shifted the paper to read the back. "Captain Wandle's company." "All present or accounted for." "Captain Gregg's company." In turn each company was called and answered.

The sergeant major of Varick's company then stepped forward to the left of the post. He unwrapped the six-foot hide whip from his arm, on which it had beeen coiled like an inanimate snake, and tossed out the folds in the dust so that they lay flat behind him.

The drums rolled.

"Sergeant, do your duty."

Adam looked up to see the colonel standing grimly with the officers in the opening through which the prisoner had come.

The whip sang forward and snapped with a preliminary report to one side of the culprit. It snapped a second time and cracked solidly across his back. It made a small puff of dust as it snapped. The man's body seemed to leap inside itself. A diagonal welt was marked on the skin, with a break between the shoulder blades, but the man made no sound.

The whip cracked again, and the sergeant said aloud, "Two."

It was beautiful whipping, the second welt appearing a half inch below the first. The welts went down the man's back in parallels. The man still made no sound. At the count of ten the stripes began to climb again and the first overlay occurred. A little spurt of blood was drawn and trickled slowly into the hollow of his back, which looked tight and cupped, to receive it. It went down inside his pants.

Gil could not take his eyes off the man. He saw him duck his head against his arm and bite it. He still made no sound. But at the fifteenth stripe he gave way and yelled for the first time. Then with a pathetic stiffening of the back he kept silent for three more strokes, and then he broke down, and at last Gil managed to tear his eyes away.

He could hear only the whip stroke, the yell, and the stolid counting of the sergeant's voice. When finally it was over the man hung against the post, quite still, but with a palpable throbbing all along his back, which now had puffed and dripped slowly all along the line of his belt.

The flies, which had been buzzing round and round the post throughout the punishment, darted in several times, and then lit delicately. The drums beat. It was over. The companies filed in to breakfast.

As they went the sentry hailed from the gate, and it was opened to admit four Indians. But Gil did not look at them. If he had, he would have recognized two—the sachem, Skenandoa, the old man who had been Herkimer's friend and who had come to the American camp before Oriskany, and Blue Back.

Blue Back was feeling pretty big these days, for he had succeeded to a sachemship with the title Kahnyadaghshayen, which, in English, meant "Easy Throat." But he still continued his enlightened habits of thought, for he did not wear a blanket like the other three Indians. Instead, he wore a British campaign coat. If the gold braid was somewhat tarnished, the scarlet was redeemingly bright. It was much too tight across the back, which made it uncomfortable to wear, because it bound under the arms and made the lice go down into his leggings. But it did look well with the peacock's feather, which he wore over his right eye. His wife had made a tricorn of his old hat, and as far as Blue Back could see, he was just as handsome as a major general. As he entered the fort, he was convinced that Colonel Van Schaick would hire him to guide the expedition, wherever it might be going, for forty cents a day, though he had made up his mind to accept twenty, so long as he was offered a full rum ration.

It gave him a genuine shock to see Gil Martin. For one frenzied instant he planned to run back through the gate; but as soon as he observed that Gil had not seen him, he took the feather surreptitiously out of his hat and hid it inside his coat. He didn't feel quite so important, but he felt a lot safer. With the other three Indians, he stopped for a moment to stare at the flogged soldier, wondering inwardly why they had not burned him also.

A sergeant came up to lead them into the colonel's office, where they all sat down on benches and accepted tobacco, while Skenandoa announced their names; and none of them looked at the colonel. None of them knew what to make of the colonel: he wasn't like Gansevoort or Willett, and they were a little afraid of him. He had a patience like their own; but it was cold patience in which they felt no courtesy.

Finally Skenandoa remarked that his young men had seen a big army coming west through Dayton. Was it so? Or had their eyes been deceived?

It was so, said Colonel Van Schaick.

So many men must be going on an expedition.

As to that, the colonel did not know. There were no orders. It would probably mean no more than a change of garrison.

Skenandoa looked crafty. That was too bad, because his young men had all come to the fort to offer themselves as guides and scouts. He had sixty young men and three sachems to keep them in order.

The colonel allowed that it was too bad. There was nothing for them to do unless they made an expedition of their own. He wished he had someone to send to Oswegatchie. He would pay five kegs of rum for the destruction of that place. But he had no men of his own to send.

Skenandoa still looked crafty. His men were very young. Maybe the colonel could send two officers to show them how to act.

Colonel Van Schaick thought for a moment. Very well, he had two. When would the Oneidas want to start?

In a week.

Very well, it would be seen to. The great Lieutenant McClellan and the Ensign Hardenberg would go. He called in the two young officers and introduced them and ordered them to report to Skenandoa in the Oneida camp on the seventeenth, equipped for a three weeks' march. The Indians grunted and ceremoniously departed.

"Sorry," said the colonel to the two young officers. "We've got to get them out of here before they get the wind up about the expedition. I'm telling you in confidence, we're to wipe out the Onondagas. If they knew it, the Oneidas might give it away."

Blue Back, passing through the parade, saw his three white acquaintances emerge from the mess. "How?" he said to Martin, and "How?" to each of the others.

Joe said, "You're looking fine, Blue Back."

"I fine," said Blue Back grinning. "How?" He beamed.

"We're fine."

"Fine," said Blue Back.

"Come and have a drink."

Blue Back hesitated. His fat face was sorrowful.

"Neah," he said. "No drink. Go home. Go make expedition." That was a new word. Sadly he went out through the gate after his companions.

4. Blue Back's Troubled Mind

When Blue Back got home to his new house in Oneida Castle, he lay down on his skins on the floor. His wife found him there when she came in bearing a heavy faggot of firewood. His wife was still pretty and young-looking, though she was big with an expected addition to the family, which now, to old Blue Back's continuing amazement, already amounted to two children. The eldest he had driven out to play with the other neighboring children. The youngest, still on her board, he had hung on the peg beside the door. So when his wife returned, she knew at once that Blue Back was engrossed either in sorrow or in deep thought.

She immediately brought up the fire and put on a dish of stew. And then she did what he always adored—stripped him and began picking him over for bugs.

Old Blue Back liked to feel her hard cool fingers going over his stout body. He liked the way her braids fell over her shoulders and tickled along the temple of his upstanding belly. She was infinitely proud of him and proud too of the way he was proving fertile. She even boasted about him to the women. Where was another man of her husband's age that could get two children like that? And now another coming ten months after the second! She knew young warriors from their first successful warpath that didn't produce as masterfully as that. It must be his belly, they said. Other old men lost their bellies, or they became round and hard like a walnut with shriveled meat, and rattled continually; but Blue Back had a stomach like Ganadadele, the steep hill. Truly, thought his wife, it was a wonderful thing, and her pride and duty to keep it so. She left him for the moment to fetch the meat, wishing that it might be autumn so that she could fill him with new beans.

When the two officers appeared in the Indian town, they brought a keg of rum, which restored some of Blue Back's confidence and made the other sachems feel quite sure that what the officers said was true. Apparently, the new troops under Colonel Willett were to take over the fort, but for the time being both armies were remaining in garrison. The weather had turned cold, said the officers, and there was no point in marching back down the valley in cold weather. One could even see snowflakes falling beyond the door of the house. It was so.

However, being active men, they themselves were eager to join their Oneida brothers on a warpath. And the next morning, since the sun shone again, the sachems called up the young men. There were sixty of them, painted for war. Dressed in their best beadings, they made an imposing array among the small houses and lodges, and they set up a great yelling as they marched off into the woods, with the Indian wives following at the proper distance.

Inside the first woods, the men all took off their best clothes, leaving them in bundles for the women to take back. They painted a couple of trees, and set out. Blue Back left his red coat and put on his greasy old hunting shirt. He did not feel much like marching through the dripping April countryside; he felt vaguely uneasy. As he sobered, it occurred to him that Colonel Van Schaick was an artful man. Suddenly he did not believe anything of all the things that had been said. He decided that he would drop off by himself and see whether the troops were actually remaining in garrison.

He came out on the vale in which Fort Stanwix stood on the evening of the eighteenth, and beheld a sight that confirmed his suspicions.

Large squashy flakes of snow, falling steadily, made it hard for him to see what the soldiers were hauling west from the fort into the woods. Blue Back scouted round through the tamaracks and lay down beside the road St. Leger had constructed two years ago. One of the wagons came groaning by close enough for him to see that it carried two bateaux. After it had passed, he followed it all the way to the shore of Wood Creek.

There he found thirty soldiers encamped as guards for a great number of boats tied up to trees. He listened to the men's conversation, but they made so much noise that he could understand little of it. Mostly it seemed to have to do with women and the new rum, which they did not think highly of.

After a while, Blue Back withdrew into the woods and built himself a bark shed and lit a small fire. He stayed there all that night. In the morning he went back to the fort and saw the troops marshaling outside the glacis, and a couple of wagons hauling food towards Wood Creek.

Blue Back's round face grew rounder with thought. If the army were really going to travel, they would normally have been glad of Indian guides. If they had elaborately sent off the Indians towards Oswegatchie and paid rum in advance, it meant that they did not wish Indians. If they did not wish Indians, it was because they did not wish Indians to know what they were going to do. Even Blue Back knew enough to realize that there was just one objective against which such an army would move—the Onondaga towns.

Though the Onondagas had claimed to be neutrals, Blue Back was aware that the Americans thought the Onondagas had done some raiding of their own. He knew himself that they had taken Caldwell down against Little

Stone Arabia. Skenandoa had remonstrated with them about it. They had refused to take warning. They were having all the fun of raiding with little risk of retaliation. Now they were going to be raided by the Continentals.

Blue Back didn't care about that; but what he did care about was the indubitable fact that the Onondagas would claim that the Oneidas had told on them, and would therefore still more indubitably bring the hostile western nations down on the Oneidas. He decided that there was just one thing for him to do, and without wasting another minute he started jogging west towards Wood Creek.

His belly bounced a little at first, but gradually he got the wind out of himself and by the time he reached the shore of the creek he was making good time.

He circled the landing, taking note that no bateaux had yet started, and set off along the bank. He was relieved to see how full of drift the creek was. Bateaux drew so much water that the men would take a full day getting them down to the lake. By that time he himself should have found a canoe and got far across the lake.

He found a small canoe well hidden in a growth of young balsam, turned it over, and found two paddles in it. He picked it up easily and carried it to the water. He sighed with satisfaction when he got in and picked up a paddle and shot off with the roily current.

He looked enormous in the canoe, like some kind of brown frog, corpulent with May flies. But his arms were strong and the canoe handled like a leaf under his earnest paddling. The sweat came out on his brown face, and he took his hat off, showing his braided lock held in shape with a red, lady's shoelace. Before midafternoon he came out into Oneida Lake to meet a rising west wind, and he skirted the southern shore. He paddled all afternoon and evening, making heavy weather of it, and having to land every hour or so to drain the canoe.

Along towards midnight, however, having been compelled to go ashore for the second time in an hour, he decided that he had enough of a lead on the army, and he lay down under his canoe and slept. The snow formed a white backbone on his canoe and dripped off on either side of him as he lay, but neither the cold nor the wet disturbed him.

He was awakened at dawn by the screaming of gulls. The wind was still in the west, but lighter; and the waves had a brittle slap along the sand. It was a clear day with a mild sun that only intermittently could be felt through the wind. The lake was a cool dark blue, and the sky, still shadowed in the west, had a rim of brightness all round the horizon. It looked to Blue Back like a regular rain-making day. He turned his attention to the gulls, which were streaming past him in groups of two and three, great white birds, with the sunlight golden on their underwings. Off to the east a flock of them had collected and were wheeling and rising and swooping like enormous snowflakes.

For some time Blue Back studied them. He stood on the beach, the wind flapping the edges of his hunting shirt, his hat tilted back on his head and his belly feeling as empty as the windy sky. Slowly an expression of the purest surprise came over his brown face. He put his hand to his mouth, then took it away and plodded back up the shore for his canoe. It was sodden and heavy with snow, but he swung it over his head in his haste as if it were a brand-new one. His bowlegs trotted under it; he gave a grunt and heaved it off his shoulders and tossed it into the water, sprang in, and made two strokes standing—still looking back towards the east. Then he sat down and paddled, striking out across the bay called Prosser's, and heading straight into the wind for the Onondaga landing.

He could scarcely believe what he had seen, though he knew his eyes were good. They were unmistakably bateaux, about thirty of them, he thought. They would be carrying about five hundred men. Even at that distance he had been able to make out the blue coats in some of them. And the boats were all close together, though they must have rowed all night to have come so far. Who had ever heard of an army of that size traveling so quickly?

Blue Back felt a little quiver far under his fat at the root of his backbone. Those soldiers weren't going to do anything to the Oneidas, but it made him uneasy to think that they could move about the country with that speed. He kept the bow of his canoe straight in the wind and paddled hard, hoping that he had not been seen. He knew that he could paddle away from them. But he had figured on having a day or two to break the news.

A couple of gulls started following him and squalling, but luckily the main flock were too interested in the flotilla to be attracted to him, and little by little the canoe drew ahead until it was safely out of sight.

Blue Back did not land at the landing, but a half mile to the east of it. He hid his canoe a good hundred yards up the shore, before starting his stout trot for the Onondaga Castle.

He reached it, fairly tired out, before dark, and helped himself to a good meal before he delivered his news. The largest part of the Onondaga fighting force was in the west, supposedly to meet Colonel John Butler somewhere beyond the Genesee. There were only a few men left in any of the villages, he was informed, and they were mostly older men, or boys. When he told the men that there were five hundred soldiers coming against them, they decided that they must move at once, and started sending out runners to the surrounding villages. They planned to move in the morning. They appeared to feel perfectly friendly towards Blue Back and offered him a bed in one of the best houses.

He was glad to accept, and slept heavily all night; but next day his uneasiness recurred to him. The approaching invasion had nothing directly to do with him; it was rather the sight of all these people starting out into the west that troubled his mind. They were very quiet. Even the multitudinous dogs did not bark. The main town, in which he was, boasted fourteen horses, and these were all loaded to the limit of their capacity until their half-starved, beaten bodies were almost lost to view. The women carried their babies, their seeds, and bundles of their finery, as much as they could manage. Even the little girls were given each a bundle or basket. And nobody said good-bye to Blue Back. They moved off in single file into the southwest to strike the Iroquois trail, a hundred souls of them, without a house to go to.

When he started looking into the empty houses, it made him sad to see how much they had been forced to leave. Green pelts, the larger household dishes—unexpectedly his probing finger found a pouch of wampum beads.

His face looked singularly thoughtful as he transferred the pouch from its hiding place to his belt. But there were so many things left. In the council houses were a lot of oldish muskets which Blue Back carefully went over to see whether there was one better than his.

It was well on in the morning before he gave up his investigation of the deserted town and wandered off into the woods. He stopped for an instant to look back on the empty silent houses, most of them with bark roofs, some beautifully rounded in the old Iroquois fashion that the fathers used to know, all scattered any which way in the woods, with the long council house standing alone.

In that council house had burned once the council fire that made the Six Nations a great and undivided race. "Onenh wakalighwakayonne. Now it has become old; now there is nothing but wilderness. You are in your graves; you who established it." The words entered Blue Back's mind, the beginning of the great hymn. He had not thought of them for a long time. They went through his brain like a lost bird crossing the sky. He lifted his eyes and beheld rain clouds driving down from the northwest.

The old Indian, in his dirty shirt and his dirty moccasins and his limp, leaf-stained hat, shuffled indolently into the underbrush. A patch of blood-root bloomed like the whitest snow, and among them his feet made no sound.

So, suddenly, he heard to the southeast the report of several rifles, irregular, distinct, but tiny thuds of sound.

5. The Expedition

It had been Blue Back's plan to return to his home before the troops arrived; but now he realized that they must have marched overland from Oneida Lake with far greater rapidity than he had counted on. They were already cutting into the outlying villages, between him and the home trail.

He drifted uneasily up on a low hill from which he could see out over the forest tops. The drizzle had already begun, driving through the stems of the trees and striking him in waves of wet. Four miles south and east a vast cloud of dark smoke was tumbling skyward. Blue Back wondered whether the people had moved away in time. A great curiosity laid hold of him to find out how the army would act. There had been shooting.

He hesitated for only a few minutes; then, like a fat brown shadow in the gray spring woods, he began to move towards the smoke. And in half an hour he had picked up the bluecoat company, led by a detachment of Rangers, coming towards him among the trees.

It was Blue Back's first sight of the Morgan Rangers. He did not like their looks. He could tell by their faces that they would pot an Indian as quick as a rabbit. They would not be troubled to find out what nation he belonged to. He sank down into the scrub, watching them pass with beady eyes. . . .

For two days, Blue Back dogged the army in the rain, watching everything they did. He saw them burn the old towns, loot the houses, taking very little. He saw them casting muskets into the hottest fire. He saw the store of Indian gunpowder exploded in the main town and the council house curl apart, hissing under the raindrops, and fall in a mass of sparks. He saw a lone returning dog, a white dog, looking for food, shot in the head and swung into the fire by its tail. He saw squads of men sticking pigs with their bayonets and roasting them in the ashes of the burning houses.

The troops did everything systematically and quietly. It was not like an Indian raid. It was done with a cold-blooded calculation that overlooked no ear of corn.

On the morning of the second day, Blue Back picked up a small detachment that had surprised the one village in which Indians yet remained. They had rounded up fifteen women and brought them as prisoners, a silent, sullen, hopeless group, wet, shivering, mishandled. Later he found the remains of the village; and here he came upon signs that the discipline had not been observed. There were a few men lying about the open ground, unscalped for the most part. And there were women, some of them half naked. He was not much interested in the dead women until he happened to notice one in the bushes beyond the town. She was lying under a low-growing hemlock, on the soft needles, where it was yet quite dry. She had been hit on the head and was dying. She was quite naked. She was a young woman. Her tangled hair was long and black. She made no sound at all and did not move except for the very slow and painful heaving of her breast.

The old Indian did not let her see him; but he waited near by, dog-like, until she was dead. Then he beat around the town looking at the other dead women. Almost all of them were young.

The army camped that night on the site of the old town with great roaring fires. The officers had a long lean-to set up on a rise of ground. Blue Back, who hung on the outside of the pickets, could see everything they did. He recognized Colonel Van Schaick entering notes in a small book with the feather of a bird and receiving reports from the other officers. He also recognized Colonel Marinus Willett by his huge nose and slab-sided ruddy cheeks. He saw Joe Boleo and Adam Helmer come into the light of the officers' fire to be questioned. He understood enough of what they said to realize that all the towns had been burned and that the army would start its return march on the next morning.

One by one, captains and lieutenants made their reports. When the last one had spoken, Colonel Van Schaick turned to Colonel Willett.

"We've not lost a man," he said with satisfaction. "How's that for a record? Ninety-odd miles into the Indian country, a nation destroyed, no casualties. By the Lord, I'm proud of you all!"

Everyone seemed pleased. Only Willett spoke through his great nose.

"I'd like to know where all the Indians went to, Goose. I'd like to know who warned them. Somebody did, you know."

"I'm just as glad," said Van Schaick. "We've given them a lesson and we've committed no atrocities. I'm proud of you all. It ought to have the effect we hoped for."

"What effect, Goose?"

"Why, it practically guarantees safety to the western settlements."

Next morning Blue Back stayed only long enough to make sure that the army had started back towards their bateaux on Oneida Lake before cutting off on his own path to find his canoe. He was well ahead of the army when he reached the lake, and he launched his canoe without being noticed by the boat guard.

Two days later he was back in his own house, talking to Skenandoa and eating a hot meal. The ancient sachem was as upset as Blue Back himself. He said he would have liked to protest to Van Schaick at once over the expedition, but to do that would be to acknowledge that the Onondagas had been warned by one of the Oneidas. When they considered everything that Blue Back had seen, they decided it would be dangerous to let the colonel know. They felt singularly helpless. They decided to wait until the news became general and then to demand army protection against the western nations and the British.

After Skenandoa had left, Blue Back's wife combed out his hair and pampered him in his favorite ways. She was immensely proud of him; but at the same time she was disturbed by his persistent staring at her. She did not know that he was wondering whether a white man would consider her young enough, or pretty enough. He felt that he no longer comprehended white men.

6. *Destruction of the Long House*

Colonel Van Schaick was doing the talking. He stood up before the three men, now that he had shaken their hands in turn—Joe Boleo, Adam Helmer, and Gil. On one side Major Cochran looked on with obvious pleasure. On the other Colonel Willett was preternaturally solemn. But when Adam's restless eye met his, the yellow-haired giant felt like laughing out loud. Willett's right eyelid was perceptibly fluttering.

"I am obliged to you three men," said Colonel Van Schaick. "You have done a splendid job for me. For the whole army. I flatter myself the whole army has done a splendid job, but it would have been impossible without such sure guides. You will now return to your homes, and you will kindly convey to Colonel Bellinger my gratitude for having sent me three such excellent men. Tell him I shall write him personally as soon as pressure of duty permits. Here's your pay. I thank you."

To each man he handed a slip of white paper neatly inscribed, except where his own pigeon-track writing wandered through the letters of his name. The two woodsmen, neither of whom could read, were too dumbfounded to speak. They held the papers in their big hands gingerly and merely stared. Gil tugged them by the sleeves. They followed him out, heads bare.

Joe muttered, "It's like church."

"Shut up," said Gil. Adam burst out laughing. Then they heard a chuckle behind them and found that Marinus Willett had come after them. "You did a good job, boys," he said. "I want to remember you." He shook hands, the way Van Schaick had, but he seemed like somebody a man could talk back to. His big erect shoulders had none of this new drill-masterish stiffness. "I don't know how much good the expedition did, but we did all there was to do."

Joe looked sober. "Those Onondagas will holler like cats with their tails in traps."

Willett nodded.

"I hope they'll only howl."

He nodded his head to them and went away to his own quarters. The three men walked out through the gate. As soon as they were out of hearing, Adam demanded, "What's this paper anyway? It ain't money."

"I'll read you mine," said Gil. "They're all the same."

By Goose Van Schaick, Esquire, Colonel, the First Regiment, the New York Line.

To Gilbert Martin & Greeting—

You are hereby authorized to impress for your own use as a return for your services in this regiment in the service of the United States, 3 bushels of wheat from any Person whom Col. Peter Bellinger, Esquire, shall deem can conveniently spare the same & whose name shall by him be endorsed on this warrant.

Given under my hand at Fort Stanwix this twenty-fifth day of April 1779

Goose Van Schaick, Col.

"Well, for God's sake!" said Adam. "Who's got three bushel of wheat in German Flats anyway?"

"Shut up, can't you? Always yelling. Look, Gil, does mine say, 'Joe Boleo and Greeting' on it?"

"Yes, it does."

"Show me where."

Gil showed him.

"Well, I'll be God damned. Boleo and Greeting."

"Yes, but what good's this thing to me?" demanded Adam. "It ain't money, it ain't likker, and there isn't any wheat."

"Oh, give it to your girl for dinner," growled Joe, lengthening his stride to pull ahead of them.

"Listen, Gil. Maybe you'd like to buy my paper, hey?"

"I haven't any money," Gil said, with a laugh.

"Well, how am I going to get paid, then?"

"I don't know. You can ask Bellinger."

The road wound out of the grass into the woods. Joe Boleo shambled along in the lead. He didn't act anxious for company. He was bent way over, his lean shoulders hanging and his wrinkled face absorbed. When the other two got in hearing of him, he was muttering, "Joe Boleo and Greeting. By God! Joe Boleo and Greeting. . . ."

The three reported to Bellinger at Fort Dayton and were given supper there. Men crowded round Bellinger's cabin to hear the news of the expedition, and to many of them it seemed—now that Congress had decided to act—that the end of the war could not be far away. They started discussing the feasibility of rebuilding on the sites of their old farms. Some regretted that they had sown their spring seed in borrowed land.

Bellinger told Gil that the women had remained at McKlennar's, for there had not been a single alarm throughout the valley. It was now generally admitted that a powerful campaign was going to be carried on against the Iroquois that summer. Quartermasters were scouring the valley for supplies. In Schenectady they were constructing numberless bateaux. It was believed that one wing of the army would muster at Canajoharie within six weeks. James Clinton was the brigadier appointed to command it— fifteen hundred men. But that was only the wing. The main army would muster in Pennsylvania and come up the Susquehanna. The expedition Gil had just returned from was no more than a preliminary demonstration.

As he walked down the road from the fort after dark, Gil felt a strange sense of peace. The air had turned warm on a southerly wind. It was damp, and it felt like more rain; but a rain from the south would be a growing rain. He was walking alone, for Joe had accepted an invitation to drink, and Adam, having caught sight of Polly Bowers at the corner of the fort, had been overwhelmed with the desire to describe the Indian country to her. Gil was glad to be alone, just then.

The house was quite dark. Either they had gone to bed or they had closed the blinds. He thought that perhaps in a few months it would be safe for people to burn candles in their houses once more, without darkening the windows.

He was startled when a dog rushed barking down the slope. Then he realized that John Weaver must be staying at the farm and he whistled to the dog. The dog recognized him and jumped about his legs, and the next moment the door opened and Lana was pushing her way past John. "It's Gil. I know it's Gil. Let me out," she was saying.

He jumped up the porch steps and put his arms round her. She was whispering, "I was sure you were coming home to-night. I knew it, Gil, but they wouldn't believe me."

He pulled her through the door and they walked together into the kitchen, where Daisy was holding a splinter to the coals and blowing through her thick lips at it. It took only a moment to get the light. It was good to be home, to see women's faces, people he loved. He shook John's hand. John said, "We heard you'd gone against the Indians."

"Yes," said Gil, "we burned the towns. We took some prisoners, but the men were mostly away. It wasn't much but marching."

John's face colored.

"Now you're back," he said, "maybe it would be all right for me to get on home."

"Yes, yes, go ahead, John. And thank you for all you've done." Mrs. McKlennar grinned at his retreating back. "I keep forgetting John's a married man."

They sat down together while John whistled to his dog and set out for Fort Dayton.

"You look healthy," observed Mrs. McKlennar.

"I'm fine," said Gil. He felt Lana pressing his hand under cover of her petticoat. "How have you all been? How's Gilly?"

"Everything's been fine."

"How's the cow?"

"She freshened day before yesterday. She's in good shape," said Mrs. McKlennar.

"What was it?"

Lana smiled.

"A heifer. A nice one. Brown and white."

"That's fine." It was better than fine. It would have been tragic if the cow had dropped a bull calf. With the few remaining cows in German Flats one bull was enough for service for the entire district.

The next evening at sundown the army came from the west, a long line of bateaux rowing steadily down the river. They camped on Getman's farm, and in the morning they continued for the east. Two days later their munition wagons hauled through with a company for escort. The commanding officer brought an order to Colonel Bellinger demanding levies to fill out one squad, and the militia was mustered and lots drawn.

Gil was miserable with the dread of having to leave the farm again; but he did not draw a long straw; and he was able then to feel sorry that young John Weaver was one of the unlucky ones. He could see Mary's face, thin and tragic; and he thought of how Lana would have looked if John's bad luck had happened to him. He tried to cheer John, telling him that he would draw pay for the three months and get a campaign coat, but John only nodded. He had almost an hour to see if he could buy himself off, but having no money to trade with, he was unable to interest anyone else.

He went to see Demooth about it. The captain said he would get Mary for his housekeeper, so that at least she should be taken care of. John marched at sunrise.

In May, having planted his corn and squash and pumpkins, Gil finished the barn roof. It was a great day on the farm. Mrs. McKlennar got out a bottle of Madeira, the last she had, and they drank it together.

Then in June the news came that the army was mustering at Canajoharie. They would have been slow to believe it had not Mary Weaver had a letter from John. She brought it up to McKlennar's to have it read, and Mrs. McKlennar read it aloud to them all. John wrote badly, but his letter was confirmation of the report.

> Dear wife Mary I am now at CONJHARY I am in Col Willets regiment Cap bleeckers comp. Hav a new blew cote am well Nothing remarkabel has happened we have 1500 men, & Pars rifle comp, They say we will merch for Springfeld nex Satday the 19 i think I think of you Mary & wonder if you have found out you are to have a baby yet I send my love with this and also beg you will give love to ma and Cobus
>
> Your husband, recpectfully,
> JOHN WEAVER

There was a silence in the kitchen after Mrs. McKlennar finished. They could hear outside a man far away whetting his scythe, and across the river Casler shouting to his team as he brought in logs for his cabin. Casler was rebuilding.

"It's a good, manly letter, Mary," said Mrs. McKlennar.

"Yes," the girl gave a sort of gasp. She reached out for the letter and folded it over and over and stuck it inside her dress. She seemed to be ready to cry. Gil went outdoors. It was no place for a man. He drove down to the hayfield with the mare and cart.

When the bumping and creaking had died away, Mary looked up at Mrs. McKlennar and blushed painfully.

"Colonel Bellinger said he had to send an express down to-morrow and I could send a letter, but I can't write."

"Would you like me to write for you?"

"Yes. Please. John's mother can't write either, and I couldn't ask anyone else."

Mrs. McKlennar snorted softly as she fetched her desk and ink. She sat down again opposite Mary with the desk on her knees, and dipped the quill.

"Now what would you like to tell him? You just say it and I'll write it down."

"Dear husband John—" and then, appalled, she listened to the scratching of the quill and saw Mrs. McKlennar's capable wrist arching along the paper, and she burst into a flood of tears.

"Now, now, child. You mustn't act like that. Remember that he's probably homesick and wants this letter more than anything in the world."

"I can't do it. I can't. I don't know how," wailed Mary.

"Well, what do you want to tell him? He's anxious, you know."

"Yes, he was worried about it. About me having a baby. He didn't know how we could buy flannel for it. His mother doesn't think I could ever be a good breast feeder and we've got no cow."

"Well, dear, are you going to have a baby?"

Mary shook her head. Her face crimsoned, and suddenly she covered it with her hands.

"Then tell him." Mrs. McKlennar drew herself up, without being aware of it, and looked formidable. "Just imagine I'm John and say it to me."

With an effort Mary governed herself. "I'll try."

And Mrs. McKlennar wrote:—

> DEAR HUSBAND JOHN,
> I am well and I hope you are really well. I am not going to have the baby now but will surely some day. I am sure I could feed a baby even though your mother thinks not. She is well and so is Cobus. I am keeping house for Capt Demooth and he is nice to me but it is not nice to cook for him like cooking for you. I think of you every night and do you think of me? It is my hope to see you home safe soon. I pray for you, and that is my prayer.
>
> Your loving wife . . .

"Would you say 'Mary Weaver,' or just 'Mary'?"

Her breast was rising and falling as if she had run.

"I would say just 'Mary,' I think, myself, though the other is dignified."

"I think John would like 'Mary Weaver' best."

Mrs. McKlennar wrote "Mary Weaver."

They did not hear from John again, except through general news of the movement of the army. On the twenty-third the word came by an express to Colonel Van Schaick at Fort Stanwix that the army was not to march west through the Mohawk Valley, as many people hoped, but to join Major

General Sullivan's huge corps at Tioga. Clinton had already started his first troops south from Canajoharie and was hauling bateaux overland to the head of Otsego Lake.

The same express coming east again the following day reported to Colonel Bellinger that Oneida Indians had brought news to Fort Stanwix that John Butler was taking an army up the Genesee, planning to cross above the Indian Lakes and mobilize the Indians at Tioga. That John Butler not only knew of the American rendezvous but knew the names of all regiments and the numbers of men contained in them. As proof, the Indian named what he could remember, and his figures were correct. That was how Peter Bellinger was first informed of the numbers and personnel of the southern army, and that was how the people of German Flats first heard of it—information supplied by their own spies from observations of the British.

Five thousand men would move against the Iroquois, with cannon and Morgan's rifle regiment, and four states supplying the infantry. It was an impressive thing to think of. To people like Demooth, and Gil Martin, and Bellinger, came the first realization that there was a power in their own country, the country that had been made theirs. A power beyond the unlimited muddleheadedness of Yankee politicians.

They felt that now they would be safe from the Indians as long as that army was campaigning in the wilderness. The whole settlement breathed easier. The women went out on the haying parties, and the last of the hay was brought in with a rush. Gil Martin abandoned his first plan of stacking his hay in small lots hidden in the near-by woodland and stacked it all against the barn. The sight of the new barn, and the high mound of hay which Lana had thatched, working in the cool of the late afternoon, was an emblem of their new security.

Towards the middle of July, Joe Boleo and Adam Helmer returned from a scout to the southeast and reported having been all the way to Otsego Lake to see the army.

"We got down beyond Butternuts and there was a lot of Indian signs heading east, and we figured they was watching the army, so we thought we might as well get a look at it ourselves."

Adam bubbled over with descriptions of the tents, the boats. "They've dammed up the entire lake," he said. "And when they start they'll bust the dam and have four foot of water to float their boats downriver." They had seen the execution of two Tory spies and listened to a sermon by the Reverend Mr. Kirkland and had a drink with Marinus Willett, who wanted them to serve with him as scouts. "Joe figured the rum wouldn't hold out as far as Chinisee," Adam explained, "so we didn't go."

"I wanted to see what fifteen hundred men looked like, all together," Joe said. "I didn't want to make it bigger than it was, though. Somebody would have had to go without his rations."

Bellinger was thankful that they hadn't gone. He gave them each a present of liquor and a little cash, and after Adam had spent one more fruitless day with Betsey Small, he and Joe went into the woods again.

Then people heard that the army had set off. They heard it in the prayer of Reverend Rozencrantz, who gave credit to Rimer Van Sickler, who had returned from Otsego. He was one of the levies taken at the same time as

John Weaver. He turned up in church and listened to himself being quoted by the domine, and explained to his friends that he had come back to finish his barn. He figured that the army under Clinton could do just about as well with one less man, but that he himself couldn't get along without a barn next winter. And all it needed was the roofing of one bent, if a log barn could be said to have a bent. It would take him only three days. He said the army had made him lame in the left foot. On Monday he got cheerfully to work. On Tuesday he had finished the roof. He told Bellinger that even if he was a deserter and got taken for it, it was worth more than the regular thirty-dollar fine to roof his barn.

On the night of the twenty-fourth, Lana was restless. She was suffering continually from pains in her legs, and therefore she heard the gallop along the road in time to wake Gil. They sat up side by side in the dark, hearing the furious thudding swell towards them through the night, pass, and die rapidly away.

They got up and went out onto the porch, searching the night instinctively for fires. Mrs. McKlennar woke and came out to join them with an old red coat drawn over her nightdress. They held their breath to listen, but heard nothing except the whimper of the whippoorwills in the wheatfield.

For a while they thought it must have been an ordinary express, though expresses seldom went by at night. But before they had decided to get back to bed, the sound of galloping again was born in the west and swept towards them.

As the horse came round the bend in the road, the rider began shouting, "McKlennar's! McKlennar's!"

"Hello!" shouted Gil.

"That you, Mr. Martin?"

"Yes, who's that?"

They could see him now, the hoofbeats stilling as the horse pulled up, a shadow on the vague pale ribbon of the road.

"Fred Kast. Bellinger says for you to come to the fort. The Onondagas are out! They killed some soldiers up to Stanwix this afternoon."

Lana gave a choked cry, but Mrs. McKlennar said, "Get the baby. I'll close and bolt the shutters."

The horse was stamping. "I've got to get to Eldridge's," yelled Kast. He was off again.

As he hitched the mare to the cart, Gil had a dull feeling that nothing was any use. The destructives would be there. They would burn his new barn. He couldn't turn the cow out either, because of the calf. Better to leave them in the barn than chance a bear's getting the calf. He set down a pail of water for the cow and dragged in some forkfuls of hay.

It was just like the start for Fort Herkimer almost a year ago, except that this time they would go all the way in a cart. Thank God the wheat wasn't yet quite ripe enough to burn!

They were two thirds of the way to the fort when Kast overtook them. Eldridge's was warned. "They've only got powder for about twelve rounds," he said. "Jake Small ain't been able to get any anywhere."

At Dayton the squad of regular soldiers with whom Van Schaick had garrisoned the fort assigned them to a space along the barrack wall and told them to keep out of the way. The night continued clear, warm, and uneventful, except for an outraged screech owl, and the myriad mosquitoes.

But late the next afternoon they were informed that reënforcements would be with them in twenty-four hours. The army had not yet left Otsego. About three hundred men were marching under Gansevoort.

Everyone breathed easier, except Van Sickler.

Towards sunset of the following day the drums were heard approaching, and within the hour the little army was encamped outside the fort. Gansevoort rode in with his pink Dutch face delighted at having made the swiftest march the valley had ever seen—two days from the foot of Otsego Lake to German Flats. He promised to wait until the Rangers came in, and in the meantime he arrested and court-martialed Van Sickler for desertion.

But Gansevoort was so pleased with himself that he let Van Sickler off with a fine of thirty-one dollars, and, since the man could not possibly pay it, announced that he would have to be on fatigue for the rest of the campaign.

Van Sickler himself was dubious about it all. At first he figured he had lost sixty-one dollars; but later he decided that he had got his barn roofed for a dollar, and that was a bargain.

As soon as the information was brought in that the Onondagas had passed to the south of Springfield, Gansevoort departed. His troops moved fast, their three light wagons keeping close up, their drums banging a quickstep.

The people watched them go and, long after they had disappeared, listened for the last faint mutter of the drums. That sound, hauntingly faint, was the last sound of war in the valley until the same detachment appeared, surprisingly, from the west in September.

In the meantime, it seemed as if the great army had disappeared from the face of the earth. They heard no news at all of it, but what it might be doing, whether it had met the army under John Butler,—Rangers, Greens, British, Tories, Senecas, and Mohawks,—whether it would reach Niagara, or even the Seneca towns, was the one thing men talked about in the settlement.

Gil thought little of it. During the last week in August Lana's labor started, and they lived for three days with Dr. Petry in the house. Mrs. McKlennar, and Daisy, and Betsey Small, who had come down to help from Eldridge's, were all worn-out and haggard.

To Gil it seemed as if the thing would never finish. Now and then, even in the wheatfield, he thought he heard her crying. Dr. Petry seemed helpless. He blamed it on the lack of food, on the drain that nursing the first baby had put on her. "Last winter took about everything out of her. And this is a big baby. I don't see how she got to have such a big one."

"Can't you help her some way?" demanded Mrs. McKlennar.

"How can I help her? It's part of a woman's job—that's all. We can't do anything but wait."

"But it's unnatural!" Mrs. McKlennar's voice grew harsh. "It's terrible."

Betsey Small remembered her own painful childbed, but that had been full of violence, and quickly over. Once when Petry was alone with her, he said, "Do you still want another one?" He tilted his head towards the room in which Lana lay.

Though Betsey's eyes were shadowed, her mouth shaped itself impudently. "It's part of a woman's job—that's all. I wonder whether a man or a woman said that first."

"Don't talk to me like that," he growled. "I hear tales about you and the fool Adam Helmer."

"Well, you needn't believe them! I'm fond of Jakey." Her eyes brightened. "But I would like some more, if you want to know. Plenty of them. Poor Jake." She turned her eyes away.

The doctor grunted.

"Will she die?" asked Betsey.

"I don't think so. But you might."

"Not with you looking after me, Bill."

"Oh hell," he said.

Mrs. McKlennar was beckoning him to the door.

The baby was born at noon on the fourth day, a huge and handsome boy. It looked so big to Gil that Lana's body seemed to him completely caved in after the birth. She did not speak to him, but lay inert, eyes closed.

"She's all right," said Dr. Petry. "You needn't whisper. She wouldn't hear the trump right now. She won't be good for much for quite a spell, though. No, don't thank me. I didn't do anything. I just sat here to earn some money."

He growled, and wearily mounted his old horse, and rode away.

"Bill's aging lately," Mrs. McKlennar said.

Betsey Small was dandling the child and calling it her lusty man.

"I'm just as glad Adam's not around," thought Mrs. McKlennar, watching her.

7. The Hard Winter

Throughout the summer and fall their feeling of security was strengthened. After each scout Joe and Adam reported the same emptiness of the woods. Maybe a lone Indian: if they followed his tracks up, they found he was an Oneida or Tuscarora going fishing. Or sometimes they saw the tracks of several Indians; but these parties always included squaws. They weren't war parties. They were Indians looking for the blueberries. "They say it's going to be a hard winter. They're doing a lot of berrying."

It got so that the two men hated to go out. Especially Joe; for Adam generally dropped off a scout and came back to spend a while with Betsey Small, and, when he got sick of getting nothing from that red-haired woman, to make a night excursion somewhere with Polly Bowers. But with the latter he went out just enough to keep his own inside track with her. Betsey Small had infatuated him. It got so that he would pick her a bunch of flowers, maybe, besides bringing her in a good fish or two, or some venison, or a couple of prime partridge. Once he asked her whether she would think any more of him if he brought her a couple of scalps.

"Senecas?" she asked.

"Sure," he said. "Senecas, or a couple of them Tories. If you ever want anybody's scalp, you let me know."

She smiled, veiling her eyes and looking insolent and badgering, studying all his magnificent body as he sprawled on the bench with his back against the table and his chest bare to the fire.

"You like me an awful lot, don't you, Adam?"

He tossed his yellow hair back and grinned.

"Don't you ever get tired waiting around here?"

He kept on grinning.

"If it wasn't for Jake, I'd have had you a long while ago. But I like Jake."

He looked puzzled, as she repeated, "Yes, if it wasn't for Jake."

Jake Small came in. He was getting bald and looked fatter.

"Hello, Adam," he said. "You back for a while?"

"Yes, I'm back. I just stopped by on my way home. How are you, Jake?"

"Fine, boy, fine."

He reached for an apple off the shelf.

"Have one, Adam?"

"No, thanks," said Adam.

"Well, I will," Jake said, biting into it. "I've always had the awfulest hankering for apples, Adam."

He put his arm round Betsey when she came up to kiss him. It was the damnedest thing Adam ever had to look at—the happy way she looked when she kissed him back. He got himself lazily onto his feet and picked up his rifle and went out of the house.

Though Lana was getting about again, she had not much strength. She worked because there was a great deal to be done. Gil was threshing in between days of picking the ripened corn, and he needed help in sifting the chaff. He wanted to get his oats all threshed and safely stored before the fall was over. The steady thump of the flail on the barn boards was like the drumming of a partridge, hour after hour.

The air was cold and very clear, as if frost were in the offing. Lana sniffed it in the yard and looked up the valley. The sky to the west had a greenish glassy tinge. One could almost think that the sky was reflecting the shine from the river. The tips of balsams seemed more sharply pointed, needlelike, and made of iron. The low sun looked like a thin coin. In its light, Lana seemed pale and full of stillness; her black hair was heavy and without lustre. As she stood beside the shed door, the evening found in her the same hushed intentness it found in the darkening woods. Only the front of her short gown moved with her light breathing, showing her full and heavy breasts.

Joe Boleo, stepping quietly in the shed for an extra log of wood, watched her for a moment. He thought she had not heard him, any more than she seemed to have heard the thudding of Gil's flail. But she said suddenly, "Joe, what's that bird?"

"Which bird?"

"There on the bottom branch of the maple. I never saw one like it."

She seemed to have a sixth sense for spotting anything alive. The bird had neither moved nor made a sound.

He said, "That's a Canada Jack. It's early to see one of them—and so close to a house, too. Most generally it means a hard winter."

They both stayed still, and the bird on its limb was still, staring back at them. Then the calf bawled flatly in the barn, and they heard the blatant answer of the cow homing through the woods.

In the kitchen, Daisy rattled her pans.

At sunset the two companies of soldiers swung down the road from Fort Stanwix. They were lean and tired. Their ragged uniforms gave them at first sight a kind of ghostliness. Their long strides brought them swiftly and with an odd effect of silence, for half of them wore moccasins, to replace the shoes they had used up. And the drums of the two drummers were headless.

John Weaver returned with them. He did not look at all like the boy who had started out. He was like a stranger to Mary. She felt even younger than on her bridal night; and when they went to bed in the Herter house, she was shy and half frightened. He seemed so much stronger—even in his happiness with her she was aware that he had been with men and become a man. Though she had never thought of him otherwise, she knew that the John she had married was a boy; and proud as she was of him, now, his touch conveyed to her a strange sense of warning that she would never be as close to him again in all their lives.

Gansevoort had given him his discharge, and paid him in a wheat warrant, so that he felt quite comfortable about feeding his mother and Cobus during the winter. For themselves, he and Mary would stay on with Demooth.

He was glad to get home. The next morning, when the conch horns sent their dim invading wail over the valley, they lay under the blankets close together and heard the cannon fired from the fort as a salute to the departing soldiers. The rising sun, entering the low window, touched the shoulders of his campaign coat, stained, frayed, and faded. . . .

"John, was it awful out there?"

"It was the finest farming country I ever saw. But we got so we were sick of it. Every time we saw a cornfield we were sick. They made us cut it down—all of it. We cut down the apple trees. They had peaches, even. We cut them down. We did at first; but there was so many we just girdled the last orchards. We burned every house. Some of them had nice houses, framed ones, with glass windows. Nicer than this house, Mary."

"It must have been hard work."

"I don't know how much we burned. Captain Bleecker figured it out that the army had destroyed one hundred and sixty thousand bushel of corn. The Indians all went west to Niagara."

"Was there any battles?"

"Only one. It was short. There was five thousand of us and only fifteen hundred of them, more than half Indians. Afterwards they cornered a scouting party. Twenty men. They caught two of them and burned them in Little Beard's town. Chinisee Castle."

He stopped suddenly.

"Poor John," she whispered.

"It was mostly just walking," he said. "Walking every day and sometimes at night. Or burning. Or cutting corn with your bayonet. We got short of food and had to eat our horses. We wished we hadn't burned everything, coming home."

"The Indians will never come again," she said.

"No. They've gone to Niagara. I don't know."

"Were the burned men anyone we knew?"

"No, a Lieutenant Boyd. And a sergeant. His name was Parker. I didn't know either of them. I don't want to talk about them. I been dreaming of the way they looked. It makes me afraid sometimes. I don't want to go to war again, Mary."

She tried to hush him.

"You won't need to."

"I never was scared of the Indians before. But they did things to those men."

"Don't talk." She lifted up her lips. But he didn't kiss her. He lay close beside her, with his face hidden in the hollow of her shoulder. He didn't move.

Gil and Joe Boleo and Adam made a trip up to Fort Dayton to talk to Rimer Van Sickler. The squat, overmuscled Dutchman sat in his cabin among his fourteen children, with his second wife cooking him an apple pie. Her thin face, prematurely aged from bearing children and too much heavy work, was exalted with the social eminence her returned hero had brought the family. Why, only yesterday, Colonel Bellinger and Captain Demooth had spent the whole afternoon listening to her Rimer tell about his western expedition. Here in her own cabin. She had had to send the children over to Mrs. Wormwood's out of politeness, seeing they were gentry, but she herself had stayed. And now here was Mr. Martin and Joe Boleo and that worthless Helmer, who had thought he was a hero himself when he outran the Indians.

Rimer yelled a "Come in" to the men. He was obviously tickled to have them come to see him. Timber beasts.

"Get out some rum for my vriendts," he yelled. "You voman: Py Godt, I think I haf to put my belt across you und learn you again who is boss, hey!" He turned to the three. "I had to do it pefore, I can do it again, *ja!*" He had her almost in tears. The light went out of her face as in obedience she fetched the jug and set it down before him.

He was sitting in front of the fire on a deerskin, whittling calluses on the balls of his feet. "Efry time I cut a piece off I say to mineself, 'Rimer, you old timber beast, dot is t'ree miles from Kandesago to Kanandaque.'"

Joe said dryly, "I always figured that fifteen miles, myself."

"Ach, *ja.* You peen out dere. I haf forget it. You're right, Joe. But, py Godt, dot big hunk over there, dot is twenty-seven und a half we marched Candaya to Appletown. In te afternoon. Py Godt! Efry shtep I feel dot punion grow, like a horn. Dot vas de day mine boots broke through, too."

"Did you kill many Indians, Pa?"

"Don't talk. No, de Indians vas alvays de trees behind, or de hill behind, or de shwamp across. Only once we haf a battle, dunder, shmoke de cannons, und de Indians run right off. Old Pa Rimer couldn't run so fast as Indians. *Ja.*"

They had to listen to the full details of the campaign as witnessed, memorized, and amplified by the aggrandized imagination of Van Sickler; but finally he came to Boyd's capture, telling how the army found the ambush and marched the next day to the Genesee, forded it, and entered the great town.

How, in the open space before the council house they saw the two stakes. Even Van Sickler forgot himself as he described it. Those Senecas, what they could think of! The two corpses half consumed from the waist down before the fires burned out, eviscerated; the nails removed from the toes and fingers, the fingers disjointed or cut off at various lengths. "Ve found two thumbs, so ve knew de nails vas pulled. Dere vas clam shells dey had cut de fingers off mit." The eyes had been pushed out and the nostrils slit, the cheeks pierced, the lips skinned off, the tongues pulled out, and all over the chest slabs of hide removed.

The children listened with popping eyes and a dull apathetic horror came over the woman's face as she stared at her husband, though whether at the torture or at the man, describing each detail with bestial accuracy, she hardly knew herself. "Dey cut de heads off. But de last thing vas de heart." His small eyes glittered as he told it. "Cut out between de ribs, und stuck de mouth into. Only dere vasn't any lips, joost de teeth. *Ja!* It vas a sunny day."

The winter came early, and it turned piercing cold. By the first of October the hills were white in the north, and the leaves fell with the snow. The snow never went down. By November, before the blizzard, it was more than a foot deep on the ground. But after the sixth day of the snowstorm it was four feet deep. It mounted up against the sides of house and cabin and barn until the paths to the door were like inclined chutes, holes in the earth. No one had ever felt such cold or known such snow.

Few people went visiting. Lana, who had thought of trying to see her parents during the slack season in December, gave up the notion. Provisions coming up to Stanwix took two days even on the river ice. More than once horses broke down and froze where they had fallen.

At McKlennar's, Gil was thankful that he had stacked his hay beside the barn. He could never have found it in the woods, once the big snow came.

All day he and Lana and Mrs. McKlennar and the babies hugged the fireside. The negress suffered a strange change in her complexion. It was as if her skin had turned gray with dark brown blotches underneath. She could hardly walk for her chilblains. Joe Boleo never left the place. The idea of raiding parties coming in that cold was simply preposterous. But he took great satisfaction in his idleness. "I can't get them Senecas out of my mind," he said. "They ain't got any food. I bet they're dying every which way." It was a comforting thought to them all.

The only thing that troubled him was having to help Gil get wood. They cut great logs and skidded them in the front door and set the butt ends in the fire. Every hour or so they would pry the log forward into the coals. They kept it going all night, taking turns at watching.

Even so it was so cold in the kitchen that Lana's fingers were too numb to spin, except occasionally when the sun shone at noon. They became silent for long periods. And Mrs. McKlennar seemed to age during the winter, and sat more and more, close to the fire. Finally she succumbed to Lana's suggestion of having her bed moved into the kitchen.

Only Adam went about at all, visiting occasionally at Eldridge's or paying a dutiful visit to Dayton. The cold did not affect him as it did the others. He did all the hunting alone. But hunting was poor, and the deer, when he got one, were terribly thin. The meat was tasteless as old leather.

The wind seemed never to stop blowing. It had a high note on the crust. At night, when it came from the north, they could hear the howling and threshing of the pines on the high ridges half a mile away. But on the few quiet nights, the cracking of frosted trees in the icy darkness was worse to listen to.

In the barn Gil had built a kind of wall around the cow and heifer and mare, banking it every day with the manure that was dropped overnight, but that was always frozen. The three animals kept close together. Their coats were shaggy as sheep's wool. To milk the cow was an ordeal; his bare hands received no warmth from the teats; and the milk froze before he could get it to the house.

But the knowledge of their security was one comforting thing; and when the weather finally broke towards the end of February, they waited uneasily for a week, hoping for more snow. It came at last, heavy, without wind, a deep, protecting blanket between them and Niagara.

Though it came in time to save them, it did not come in time to save the Oneida Indians. On the last day of February, the entire fighting strength of the Onondaga nation, with a few white men and a party of Cayugas and Senecas, fell upon Oneida Castle. In German Flats they never learned the rights of it; all they knew was that a mass of half-frozen Indians,—men, women, and children,—and a few starved dogs, appeared at Fort Dayton and asked for food and shelter. They crowded the fort for two days, making dangerous inroads on the supplies, before Bellinger was able to get them started for Schenectady. The town had been utterly destroyed, but the raiders, they said, had gone back to Canada.

When Adam went down to see them, he found old Blue Back, his fat cheeks mottled with the cold, squatting in his blankets and watching his wife make a sort of hot mash of whole oats. The two larger children huddled against him, and the baby on the squaw's back was wrinkled like a nut, with two enormous eyes. The old Indian accepted tobacco wordlessly.

"They'll take care of you all in Schenectady," Adam said in an attempt to cheer him up.

"Sure. Fine." But the old man obviously did not think so. He smoked, looking past Adam along the soiled snow of the parade. "You watch'm woods close," he said. "They come some more. They mad."

"I wish you was going to be around, Blue Back. It'd be handy having you scouting with us."

"Maybe." He went on puffing. Then he said, "You going back to Martin?"

"Yes."

Blue Back reached a dirty hand inside his shirt, and felt of something. "You fetch'm this. No luck," he was going to say; but as he touched the peacock's feather it occurred to him that in a white man's town it might be lucky after all.

His eyes grew blank. He shook his head.

"You watch'm woods," he muttered dully.

Adam told Bellinger what Blue Back had said that afternoon, and Bellinger wrote letters to the Governor, and to General Clinton, and to Schuyler. Three weeks passed before he got a reply. All three sounded upset and indignant. The army last fall had been organized to wipe out the Indian towns. It had done so. The Indians were bound to be crippled for years to come. The menace had been removed at a vast expense; no other single campaign of the war could compare to it in cost. Over a million of dollars had been expended, purely for the benefit of the frontier. There was some mention of common gratitude. And let him be reminded that such continual fears and apprehensions and baseless alarms would have deleterious effects upon the inhabitants. It was felt in Albany that the time had come for the frontier settlements to stand on their own defense.

In German Flats, the settlers began to look for spring.

8

McKLENNAR'S (1780)

1.   *Jacob Casler's Tax Problem*

GIL was getting some hay into the barn. There wasn't much left. He had been feeding the three animals one good forkful between them. They showed it. The mare was gaunt, and, as Joe said, the hip bones of the cow and heifer stood out sharp enough to hang the milk pails on them.

He heard a man's boots squash through the wet snow in the yard, and then the door opened to let Casler come in. "You in there, Martin?"

"Yes. I'm just feeding the stock. Walk in."

Casler closed the door behind him and walked up to Gil. The light in the barn was a dim, dusty twilight gray, in which the animals looked even more meagre than they were.

"How are you all?" asked Gil.

"We're in pretty good health. How're you, Martin?"

"All right." Gil leaned on his fork and looked at his neighbor. Casler was a good neighbor to have, even though Gil did not see a great deal of him. He was a thin, earnest-looking man, with a slow way of speech, and a hard worker. He had rebuilt on the site of his old house across the river —a tiny cabin, in which he had wintered his wife, his two young daughters, and his three-year-old son.

"It's getting bad footing," he remarked, picking up a straw to chew. "It looks to me as if the snow was going pretty quick now."

"I've been thinking so myself."

They considered that fact in silence for a few minutes, before Casler asked, "You folks going back to the fort soon?"

"I hadn't planned. Mrs. McKlennar is against it till we have to."

Casler nodded slowly.

"She's a stout-hearted woman, ain't she?"

"Yes. I hate to move her, too. She's been poorly, off and on."

"Yes. I hate to move, myself. I was figuring on getting pretty near all my ground working again this season. Now I don't know."

Gil had the feeling that Casler had only got round to part of what was in his mind.

"Listen," he said, "if anything happens, why don't you folks plan to come over to this place? We could hold that house against quite a lot of them. It's as good as Klock's fort."

"That's right," said Casler. "How about her? Would she mind?"

"Mrs. McKlennar, you mean? No."

"I don't allow that anything's going to happen somehow. I ain't really bothering about that, Martin. How about her? Has she got one of these tax papers?"

"Tax papers?" repeated Gil. "I hadn't heard of any tax papers."

"Then they ain't got down this side of the river yet. They've been around Herkimer and they got down to my place this noon. They served them on me. It's that tax law they passed in Albany. It's got to collect eighty thousand dollars out of Tryon County. They said what German Flats had to pay, but I forgot. I know what I got to pay," he finished grimly.

"How much do you?"

"A hundred and seventy-seven dollars and forty-eight cents!" Casler's mouth closed suddenly and he stared at Gil.

"Did you say a hundred and seventy-seven dollars, Casler?"

"And forty-eight cents. What in God's name is that forty-eight cents for?"

"But you can't pay that!"

"You don't need to tell me, Martin. I ain't got the forty-eight cents, even."

"They can't make you pay it."

"The paper says if I don't pay it in cash and half down in two months' time, it will be collected from me. They'll take my stock—I ain't got only the cow and she's dry now. And they'll forfeit my land for taxes."

Gil said again, "They can't do that, Casler!"

Casler nodded slowly.

"The man told me it's on account of all the cost of that army last year. He said we got the benefits of it, but he said our rates wasn't as high as other parts of the state. But I can't pay it. I want to do what's right, but I can't pay that." His voice began to rise. "I'll do my share; I ain't never missed muster; but if they take my land I can't feed my folks. I thought the reason them Boston people started this war was so we wouldn't have to pay taxes."

Gil tried to comfort him. He tried to show that nobody else could pay more than a small share of such a tax in German Flats. Most of them couldn't pay a cent, any more than Casler could. Even Congress couldn't wipe out a whole community. There was something wrong about it.

"There ain't nothing wrong in what I told you, Martin. It's all wrote out. I'll bet you'll get one yourself for the land you had in Deerfield. You wait. There ain't any money in my house. I got to buy some seed potatoes, as it is, this spring. I got twenty-five cents."

"I'll let you have some seed potatoes and welcome, too. I got more'n enough, Casler. Did yours get froze?"

Casler explained that he hadn't had time to dig himself a cellar last fall. They had sacked the seed potatoes against the chimney, but they had frozen even there.

As Casler turned to the barn door, Gil added, "You remember what I said about coming over here."

"Thanks," said Casler. "That's kind. But I ain't really figuring the Indians will come this spring."

Gil stood in the door and watched him trudge down through the wet snow to the river. The tracks he had made coming showed on the river and up the far bank and across the flats. In the damp air they collected violet shadows for every footprint, over the fields, all the way to the tiny cabin from whose stick chimney a thread of smoke trailed uncertainly.

Gil had Casler and his tax on his mind all the rest of the day. Before supper he told Mrs. McKlennar about it. Adam was out, probably hunting up a girl of his,—the spring unease had hit him a month ahead of time,— but Joe Boleo was there, squatting down in the corner and watching Lana suckle the baby. At first he had been a good deal embarrassed, when the cold forced Lana into the kitchen to feed her child; and he had offered to leave. But Mrs. McKlennar said that was ridiculous, Joe must have played the same game himself, once.

The process, as Lana and the young boy carried it out, took hold of Joe's imagination; and he made up all sorts of reasons why he ought to get back to the house about feeding time. There was something in the full white springiness of the breast and the way the child mishandled it that softened Joe's ideas, so that he seemed to get drowsy with the baby; and he would sit there on the floor, nodding his bare cranium and trying to figure what it must have been like when he used to be doing a similar business.

Sitting on the settle, with her feet wrapped in an old blanket, Mrs. Mc-Klennar held Gilly on her lap. Somebody had to hold Gilly to keep him from getting one of his jealous fits of screaming. He hated cow's milk so, and, though he was only two years old, Mrs. McKlennar maintained that he had all the passions of a grown-up man.

The negress stumped from fire to table, preparing the adult food—the last of the hominy, part of a dark loaf, and some salt pork. Now and then, if she moved unexpectedly, she would give a kind of singsong moan that was an echo of her winter's chilblains.

The sound of Gil stamping his feet in the shed was the signal for all of them to hurry. Lana looked down at her breast and saw the baby's mouth languorous round the nipple and pushed it away.

"He's had plenty," said Mrs. McKlennar. "He's greedy as all get out. He'd wear you to the bone if you let him."

Gil watched from the doorway, his dark face sharp and quiet, while Lana took the baby away to its cradle. Gilly slid down from the widow's lap and started crawling after his mother and had to be fetched back by Daisy, who dandled him and whispered "Honey boy" in his ear. Joe looked up sheephishly and said, "Evening, Gil. What's the news?"

"I was talking to Casler."

Briefly he told them about Casler's tax papers. He turned to Mrs. Mc-Klennar. "If they tax Casler that much they'll try to get three hundred dollars for this place."

Mrs. McKlennar let out a snort that sounded like old times.

"I wouldn't pay it, Gil. I can't, for one thing. And for another, I'll be damned if I do."

Joe let out a shrill "Hurraw!" causing the widow to look down her nose at him.

"What do you mean by that?"

Joe grinned like an old half-rabid wolf.

"I was thinking it would be fun to be around here if they tried to put you off this place."

Mrs. McKlennar snorted again.

"I don't know what I'd do if they did that. I've used up almost all the money Barney left to me. I used to think it was enough to put me in my coffin, till Congress started printing this new-fashioned currency."

Joe said quickly, "I guess you won't have to move."

"I suppose they'd send soldiers. I couldn't do anything if they did that."

"That's why I said it would be fun to be around. I was thinking of me and Adam. I guess it would be quite a lot of fun."

"You're a fool, Joe Boleo," and her long face softened. "Just a gawking lazy fool."

"Yes, ma'am." Joe grinned.

She hitched her shawl up on her shoulders and got up to move to the table. It was a little pathetic to see her walk, when one remembered her former vigor, but there was plenty of snap left in her eyes.

She sat down in front of her bowl of samp and bent her head. "For all we are about to receive, O Lord, make us thankful, in Christ's name." She giggled. "You know, Joe, I think it might be quite a party, you and Adam and a squad of Continentals."

"Amen," said Joe, who enjoyed the formalities. "It sure would."

"I feel sorry for that poor man, though. He's probably just miserable."

Joe pulled his spoon out of his mouth.

"Casler always was an honest kind of a fool," he observed. He dipped his spoon, heaped it, and blew on it daintily, while Gilly watched him with disturbed eyes.

In the course of the ensuing week, a man served Mrs. McKlennar with her tax assessment. The paper was a thoroughly impressive document. It listed one stone house; one log house, floored, in excellent repair; one springhouse; one log barn; three cows; two horses; forty acres tillable land, prime soil; sixty acres woodland; one stand of King's spar spruce, twenty acres. Mrs. McKlennar read it in front of the man, whom she kept standing before her in a state of extreme embarrassment. "Melchior

Foltz," she said. "Have you really got the nerve to come down here and serve this paper on me? Asking me to pay you four hundred dollars tax?"

"Yes, ma'am," Foltz said dubiously.

"Then," said Mrs. McKlennar, "I think you are a bigger fool than Absalom's ass. Tell me, where's my barn? Where's my log house in good repair? Eh?"

"That ain't any business of mine," mumbled Foltz. "I'm just hired to serve the papers. I ain't collecting it now."

"You better not," said Mrs. McKlennar, "or you'll get kicked where Absalom's ass ought to have been." A faint color touched her leathery cheek. She peered hard at Foltz and then, in the silence, snorted.

"Yes, ma'am. I guess I'd better leave now. I got to go to Eldridge's." He was wiping his forehead as he came out.

"That woman just about had me worried," he confessed to Gil. "I ain't doing this because I want to. I get off some of my taxes for doing it."

"Oh, you do?"

"Well, I got to do something, ain't I?"

"There's one thing you better hadn't. That's come around here again. If Adam Helmer was here, he'd probably take a branch of thorn apple at you."

"I don't want no trouble with Adam Helmer. I ain't collecting the bachelor tax."

"Is there a tax on orphans and lost pigs?" inquired Joe Boleo.

Foltz took a look at Joe and started down the yard to his horse. The two men watched him ride slowly down to the Kingsroad. They went into the house.

"You know what I bet they're doing," said Mrs. McKlennar. "I bet they got hold of the old King's tax list." She threw the paper into the fire.

"For God's sake!" said Joe, sincerely.

Casler came over the river one morning and heard that Mrs. McKlennar had thrown her tax paper into the fire. It heartened him a little; but then he shook his head. "She's gentry," he said. "She knows how to hire law." Gil couldn't think of any way of reassuring him. He tried to talk to him about sugaring. But Casler was not interested beyond admitting that the sap was on the rise and that he planned to sugar next week.

"You'd better sugar over in our bush," said Gil.

"It's too far," said Casler.

He went away a little before noon. He walked like a defeated and embittered man.

That afternoon the weather turned warm and clear. The snow seemed to be falling in on itself. The boles of the river willows stood out thick and dark against it, and their upper twigs gleamed in the sun like brassy spears. The warmth and the sunlight and the lack of wind made Joe so lazy that he refused to try to get a trout through the ice.

Instead, he was plaiting cords of elm bark with which Gil patched the mare's harness. Behind them the house sounded as drowsy as they themselves felt. One of the babies was making a whining to itself, and Lana and Daisy were washing.

"Right now," Joe remarked, passing over a completed cord of bark, "I bet that Adam he's just laying on his back in Betsey Small's kitchen doing nothing at all. That's a shot, Gil!"

Gil looked up.

"Did you make out where?"

"I wasn't paying attention."

Neither of them moved. "I think it was across the river," said Joe. He carefully laid down the elm bark; Gil held the harness on his knees. The valley was hushed; the ice on the river beyond the willows looked sodden and rotten, near to breaking. The only thing they saw was the smoke on the hillside beyond Fort Herkimer, where a party, with most of the garrison to guard them, were sugaring.

Slowly their eyes came down the valley and turned eastward. Nothing there to see but the roof of Casler's new cabin. The walls of the building were mostly hidden by a grove of trees and a growth of brush; but one corner of it showed up in the sunlight. A path went round that corner through the snow to the well.

Now, along that path, they saw someone moving. It was Casler's oldest girl. They could tell who she was because of her two tow-colored braids. She was carrying a bucket, and she was running. She was floundering slightly in the soft snow, and she was not looking back, and the bucket kept slopping little glittering waves of water. Something in the child's attitude brought the two men to their feet. As they rose, they heard, very faintly, almost like a whisper, somebody shouting.

The little girl suddenly turned her head, dropped the bucket, and tucked up her elbows. Her legs looked thin and long under her short petticoat and the two braids lifted behind her back. At the instant of her leap, another shot cracked with complete finality.

The child's body fell away from it, struck the corner of the cabin, bounced, and dropped in a huddle against the snowbank. For an instant it lay there; then slowly rolled over on its back and slid down into the path.

Powder smoke puffed out all through the bushes, rose, and merged into a thin level line, and a volley of reports succeeded it. Then, distantly, men yelled.

"Indians," said Joe. "Get inside. Close the shutters, Gil, and get the guns down. I'll stay here and see how many there are."

In the kitchen, the washing had stopped and the women rested over the tub, black arms and white, their faces turned together. The baby had stopped whining. Mrs. McKlennar rose from the settle, and, as Gil went to the blinds, reached down the guns.

"Where is it, Gil?"

"Casler's. Fetch the children in here, Lana, and keep them on the floor, near the fireplace. They ain't near us, yet. Joe's outside, watching."

In the house the firing was the faintest tapping of the air. A woodpecker would have made more noise.

Joe came in silent and quick.

"There's about twenty-five or six of them. Indians. Three whites."

"Aren't you going to help the Caslers?"

"There's too many of them. It wouldn't do any good my going to the fort, either. Put the fire out. Maybe they ain't noticed our smoke. Maybe they'll forget about this house. No, don't use water. Get some manure out of the barn, and bury it. Don't look like that, Lana. They aren't any of them over here, I'm pretty sure. By the time I went to the fort for help, them destructives will have done all the killing possible down there. The thing we want is not to be noticed by them. I'm calculating they'll hear the racket over to Eldridge's. Mrs. McKlennar?"

"Yes, Joe."

"Can you load guns?"

"Yes, Joe."

"I know Lana can. You two will have to load. Ain't I seen two pistols somewheres round here?"

"My husband's. I'll fetch them. If they get close enough I can shoot them better than either of you. I used to practise." Her face colored and her lips set.

"I bet," said Joe. "Gil! You cover that fire with the manure and then bank the edges with the ashes. That way you won't get smoke. Pack it right down. How much water have we got in here?"

"There's the washtubs."

"By God, what luck! Having a raid on wash day!" He chuckled. "I'll just take another look outside and see what's doing and fetch in a couple pails of water to drink. I don't think they'll come over this way, but we're pretty well fixed if they do."

He slipped out of the front door. Gil finished banking the fire. For a minute all the people in the room were quite still. In their silence, like a faint far patting of the air, another burst of shooting sounded. Lana's face seemed to draw in on itself and her eyes grew dark and still. She sat down suddenly on the floor and caught the two children onto her lap and looked up at her husband. It came to Gil that it was all a dream, a nightmare, and pretty soon he would wake up and find the three years' dreaming was only the space between cockcrow and milking. He went out on the porch to cover Joe's return from the well.

Joe was standing in the open, a bucket in each hand. He heard Gil come out and said, without turning his head, "Take in these buckets." As Gil relieved him he picked up his rifle. But he kept watching all the time across the river. When Gil returned, Joe's speech followed the crack of a rifle.

"I know that feller. He shoots left-handed. The skinny one, see. He sticks his head out forward after he shoots and drops his left shoulder."

"Who is he, Joe?"

"Suffrenes Casselman. I've heard him swear before he quit Fairfield that he'd get his uppings back out of German Flats."

It was no dream.

The Fairfield Scotch had always bitterly resented the fact that the Palatines held all the rich river flat land.

It was easy to follow all that was taking place across the river. There were at least two dozen Indians surrounding Casler's, and though they kept under cover from the house some of them were in open view of anyone at McKlennar's. They kept firing at the window. The paper panes were already torn away by bullets. But now and then from a chink in the logs a dull yellow-red stab pricked out and the valiant roar of Casler's old musket sounded over the other guns. As soon as it had fired, the Indians crept up nearer to the house. They were quite close already. Their bodies left long winding uneven trenches in the wet snow.

Under the firing the body of the little girl retained its motionless, crumpled posture.

Suddenly a couple of Indians sprang up to the corner of the cabin with two bundles of dry brush and laid them against the logs. They leaped back at once, but one of them stumbled, and the roar of the old musket showed that Casler had managed to find one bull's-eye. They saw the Indian behind the brush hopping around and around holding onto his arm. All the Indians yelled, and three of them rushed up to the brush, carrying lighted splinters. They ducked down immediately and ran back to the cover.

Gil turned his eyes towards Eldridge Blockhouse. It seemed incredible to him that no one had yet heard the firing. Joe said, "The air's drawing straight from the south." When Gil looked back to the cabin, the brush was smoking. A small flame ran up several twigs, zigzag, and leaped out into the air. Then all the brush caught and blazed. It was like a picture of fire. The Indians whooped again; their shrill voices, that seemed hardly human to a white man's ear, were like birds' voices.

"The cabin's caught. I didn't think it would be so dry." Joe was leaning on his rifle, resting his chin on his left wrist. "I wonder will they stick it out. Or make a break for it."

The rising force of the fire tossed large loose flames up against the eaves, and suddenly they laid hold of the bark roof. The sheaths curled up, revealing the rafter poles, and the fire swept up to the rooftree and strained into space. The encircling group of Indians drew in on the cabin.

At the same instant the dull thud of the swivel in Eldridge Blockhouse struck the valley, and a heavy somnambulant cloud of black smoke hung in the window of the spy loft. A moment later the thud was repeated from Herkimer Fort; and then, almost at once, but louder, from one of the three-pounders on Fort Dayton.

The Indians in view of the two men at McKlennar's wheeled to stare towards the forts. Then they lifted their muskets and yelled.

"Herkimer can't send any men till the sugaring party gets back," said Joe. "If they send any out from Dayton, they'll come down this side."

Gil found himself shaking. He remembered how he had felt watching the Indians chase the three women at Andrustown, but this time his conviction of horror could not escape fulfillment.

The end happened abruptly. For some moments there had been no shooting from the house. Now, suddenly, he and Joe saw Casler jumping out round the corner of the house. He had his musket held in front of him and he fired as soon as he stopped. It was impossible to tell whether he had hit anyone. Things happened too fast. As soon as he had fired he ran straight at the concealed Indians, who knelt with leveled guns. They let him get just to the bushes before shooting him. Immediately they swarmed all over him. It was impossible to see him under the pile of Indians. Then the Indians drew apart and one of them gave a loud yell and raised his hand.

At the same time, in the snowy field behind the trees, Mrs. Casler appeared, running clumsily with the baby in her arms, while her younger daughter clung to the back of her petticoat. About a hundred yards behind the child five or six Indians, dark lean shapes, ran easily in the path beaten down by the woman and the child. They overtook them without haste. The first one caught the little girl by the back of the neck and raised his hatchet. The woman kept running. The Indian who was now leading leaped clear of the snow and landed hard on her back. They went down together almost buried by the snow. The Indian was like a dog worrying a sheep. He rose up on all fours and got to his feet and held up his hand. The sunlight caught his hand, reflecting on the inside of the scalp. The woman's long hair surrounded his arm.

In the sunset the militia marched down both sides of the river. The Dayton men stopped at the McKlennar house, but Joe and Gil had already crossed to join those from Herkimer.

They had seen the destructives band beyond the house and take a straight path to the hills, striking for Springfield. Joe led forty men on their beaten trail, but there was no chance of catching them with the half hour's start they had. The Indians could outrun militia any day.

Gil stayed long enough to help gather the bodies. They buried them near the house, where the earth was thawed—Mrs. Casler and the two little girls and Casler, all scalped, all with the same lost faces that scalped people had. Only the baby had not been scalped; he had no hair at all.

2. Deodesote

Like all the other Seneca towns east of the Genesee River, Deodesote had been razed by the American army in September of the preceding year. Only one house remained, and that because it was not near the town, but down the Hemlock Lake Outlet, at the northwest corner of the widewater pond. The pond was all shored with high hemlock timber hiding Gahota's cabin, which was on the low ridge. Behind the cabin, where the evergreens gave way to leaf trees, the small field that his wife worked was open to the sun, a hidden place, warm and well-drained.

The squaw had finished planting the corn. The hills stood in rows of patted mounds. She gathered up her basket and her wooden hoe and stared happily at the work she had done. Her own field: her own corn would soon pierce the brown earth; her own squash and pumpkin vines invade the soil between, lacing the whole together; her own beans climb the growing cornstalks. Beans, corn, and squash—the three sisters, Gahota called them.

Though the time of terror and famine had gone by, no other Indians had returned to Deodesote. Gahota said they would not return. The heavy passage of the army had rolled them irretrievably into the west. But Gahota and Nancy, and the baby, Jerry Log-in-the-Water, and the baby to be born, could all live where they were.

Nancy straightened her back proudly: Gahota would hunt them meat and fish them fish; but it was she who would earn them their indispensable provender of grain. The field was a large one and well hoed. Gahota had grunted and stopped to look at it when he passed it yesterday, and Nancy had been able to tell from his brown lined face that he was satisfied with her.

Her back had rounded slightly, and there was a pad of fleshy muscle across her shoulders. In her doeskin clothes she looked larger than she used to. But her face was as pink and white, her eyes as blue, and her yellow hair fell in two thick braids to the joints of her hips. She left her field like a goddess of earth, placidly secure in her awareness of fruition.

When she reached the cabin, Gahota was sitting beside the door coiling his fish line, with four trout on a pile of ferns before him.

"What big ones!" Nancy said.

Gahota grunted. She passed into the cabin. It had no chimney, only the circular fireplace of stones on the earth floor, and the small opening in the roof above it. All the ceiling was blackened, shiny, and offering a faint bitter smell of soot. In the corner, where she and Gahota slept, the baby was poking his fingers through the eyeholes of the bearskin, laughing the while with long, soft, rich gurgles. He shouted when he saw his mother, rose up on his unsteady legs, and followed his stomach towards her.

She took him by the hand to lead him out and, gathering up the four trout, went down to the lake to clean them for dinner. Gahota found himself a sunny spot against a tree bole and stretched out.

Squatting at the water's edge, Nancy opened the fish with deft slices of her knife, while her son, imitating her, sat suddenly in the shallow water. The splash and the chill made him raise furious wails to the four winds; but Nancy laughed, and let him yell.

A hail across the lake caused her to lift her eyes. She saw at first only the surrounding hemlock trees, with their breathless reflections an inverted forest, and the clear sheet where the Onehda entered the wide water in the south. Beside this stream early azaleas coming into bloom gave a first hint of their clear pink, so ineffably soft that even the untouched crystal of the lake had failed to capture it.

Waist-deep in the azaleas, some men were standing.

"Gahota. Come." Nancy's voice was quiet, untroubled.

She heard her husband's feet pad down behind her. He stood over her, his shadow falling across her bent back, shading his eyes.

"Nundawaono," he said. He lifted his arm and called.

"Who is that?"

"Gahota. You come."

The men disappeared back into the woods. Nancy finished cleaning the four trout and followed Gahota back to the cabin, the baby tumbling along behind like a hungry puppy.

"Nine come," Gahota said to her. He got his pipe and tobacco and sat down at the threshold, leaving her to gather wood and start the pot cooking. Luckily there were three rabbits and the quarter of the fawn.

Outside the door she heard the men arrive and squat and talk in the Indian language. But they did not say much for a while, and what they did say failed to interest her.

When she had finished the stew she carried the pot outdoors and set it down before the men. There were nine of them, as Gahota had said, six Senecas, three white men. One of the white men wore a brown coat and battered pants. He had a lean jutting throat from which his small head pointed like a turkey cock's. Nancy hardly noticed him. She glanced at the other two.

One of them wore Indian clothes. His face was painted with remnants of vermilion and black, and his hair had been awkwardly stained. As she looked at him, he lifted his eyes from the steaming pot, and stared.

"Nancy!"

It was Hon.

Nancy could not speak for several moments. Neither she nor Hon could find words. But the struck silence of their attitudes made the others look at them. Gahota grunted impatiently. A woman's place was not here. Obediently Nancy turned to go.

"It's my sister, Nancy," Hon said. "Don't you remember me telling you about her?"

"Her, who?" The third man licked his fingers.

"The girl you had at Shoemaker's."

"By God." Jurry McLonis looked up. "I never noticed her."

Gahota was watching them with small inexpressive eyes. Nancy had just passed into the shadowed interior of the cabin, but there she turned and her white skin and blonde braids made a ghost of her, as if glimpsed in a twilight.

McLonis rose.

"It's true," he said. "What's she doing here?"

"Set down, you fool," growled the third white man. "Can't you see the Indian's took her for a squaw?"

"That ain't right, Casselman," exclaimed McLonis. "It's bad business —Indians taking white women. Butler's afraid of it at Niagara."

"Butler!" Suffrenes Casselman's lean face became contemptuous. "Who talks about Butler now? The Indians won't go with him any more since Sullivan licked them. Johnson don't have anything to do with him. Let the Indians alone. It's hard enough to get them to go with us."

"Maybe," said McLonis. "But this girl's Hon's sister."

"Yes," said Hon. "She's my sister—Nancy."

Casselman snarled at them both. "Sit down." He leaned forward and said in a lower voice: "Listen, you dumbheads. These buggers we got with us ain't feeling any too good about us. They didn't get no loot out of that house we burned, and the four scalps wasn't enough to go round. You'd better not give them the chance to get mad at us."

The ever-present mistrust of Indians that most of the Tories felt, the knowledge that their scalps, delivered at Niagara, would look the same and fetch as much as any rebel's, made even McLonis pull in his horns. He sat down in his faded green Ranger coat and stared back at the Indians. Their host was still watching him. Now he said something in Seneca over his shoulder and Nancy obediently closed the door. McLonis dropped his eyes and resumed his eating. It was not that he cared where she was, or who she was: it was just that the sight of her, her handsome pink-cheeked face and yellow hair and vacuous blue eyes, had reminded him of that hour behind Shoemaker's barn; and he had been away in the woods now for eight weeks.

Suffrenes Casselman explained to their host that Hon was his squaw's brother, and had not seen her for two years. The Indian nodded understandingly. Such encounters were surprising to a man; he looked more closely at Hon. He realized that Hon was like Nancy, slightly touched.

"You see your sister," he suggested. "Yes?"

Hon nodded.

McLonis whispered to him, "Fetch her out. I'll drop back in the woods. We can take her with us, whatever Casselman thinks. If he don't like it he can go by himself."

Before Hon moved, McLonis rose and wandered off into the woods. He went with studied aimlessness and the Indians paid no attention to him. Some men always went into the woods after a hearty meal.

McLonis found a fallen tree and sat down on the trunk. The more he thought about her, the more fun he thought it would be to take her to Niagara. A lieutenant up from the ranks had to content himself with Indian girls. If anything better than Nancy came his way he could always hand her over to the privates. There'd be plenty of men anxious for a girl, with her looks, whatever her brain was like. He thought that they could kill a few days on the march back to Niagara. There was no hurry. They had to collect ammunition and round up another gang since the one they had taken east in March had fallen apart. Suffrenes wanted fifty men. He meant to wipe out Eldridge's and the other outlying small forts, and if one of the promised expeditions materialized, he would plan to join it. A little fun before a campaign like that would hurt no man.

McLonis sat on the fallen tree and cleaned his nails and thought he would buy her a dollar's worth of dress goods. It would seem like a fortune to her after a year in that cabin. He had smelled it through the open door. It had the Indian reek. But she looked clean and healthy. She had a kind of perfection, he remembered, a kind of ripe apple roundness to her. It made him realize how eternally tired he was, how lonesome he was, month after month in the woods, with the inevitable return to the barracks and the Indian town and the long uncompromising level of the lake with its level shores, with the everlasting dinning of the falls. Leg-weary and heart-weary.

Hon's arrival startled McLonis.

"Where's Nancy?" he asked.

Hon scuffed the hemlock needles with a moccasin toe.

"She's talking to Gahota," he said. He looked ashamed.

"What did you say to her?"

"I told her you wanted her to come with us. I said you would take her back to Niagara."

McLonis nodded. "Sure. Where is she?"

"I said she was talking to Gahota."

"You mean he won't let her come?"

"I don't know," Hon mumbled.

McLonis got to his feet.

"I'm going to talk to her myself. You've made a mess of it."

"I wouldn't," Hon said. He began following McLonis, then thought better of it and branched off to join Casselman.

McLonis walked straight towards the cabin. Before he reached it he saw Nancy emerging from it behind Gahota. They turned towards him. McLonis halted.

Nancy came straight up to him, stopping before him, with her hands clasped in front of her. She stared into his face now with a curious insistence.

"Gahota says you want to talk to me. He says I better talk to you."

The Indian beamed at her shoulders.

"Yes talk. Yes talk." He turned away and left them.

McLonis found himself swallowing as he looked at her. She looked so indescribably appealing, big though she was, in her soft doeskin costume, with her clear eyes and her clear skin with the whiteness of winter still on it. She looked cool as snow, the kind of snow that sometimes fell at the end of April, a few flakes suddenly, in a day of heat. And she stood there waiting for him to speak.

"Don't you remember Shoemaker's, Nancy?"

"Yes."

"Don't you want to come with me? I'll take you to Niagara."

"No, I don't want to come."

Her eyes had dropped and she spoke hesitantly.

He said, "But you don't want to stay in a place like this. It's not right. It's not decent, Nancy."

"I don't want to go," she said, after a moment.

"You needn't be scared of him. I'll look out for you. Hon will be along."

As she did not answer, his speech went on, more quickly, almost desperately. "But I'll take you to Niagara. Don't you remember how it was? You said you'd—you said you loved me. I loved you. I never forgot you, Nancy. Honest. I said I'd marry you, don't you remember? You can't stay here. I'll marry you when we get to Niagara."

She raised her eyes then to his.

"I am married," she said. "I don't want to go. Thank you," she added softly, and turned back to the cabin.

He stood where he was for a long minute, half minded to overtake her; then he noticed Gahota a little way off, leaning against a tree and idly swinging his casse-tête by its thong. From the waterside Casselman and Hon were yelling to him to hurry up.

3. In the Valley

Days were to come in which Lana would find herself wondering if she were herself, or some fear-deadened creature existing in human flesh. The mounting tide of dread gained impetus with each express that came through German Flats from the east. In April and May they heard successively of smaller settlements cut off, their few inhabitants killed and scalped. The Sacandaga bush, Harperfield, Fox's Creek, in Schoharie, Getman's, Stamford, Cherry Valley for the second time, and isolated homesteads, one by one, to which families had returned in their eagerness once more to work their farms. The Indian parties did their work and vanished before rescuers could so much as start from the nearest fort. A puff of smoke against the warm May sky; the faint sounds of firing; another name crossed off the militia list; and who knew who was with him at the place. His wife? His children? Sometimes later it was learned that he was there alone.

The Indians were not taking many prisoners, for they were not returning all the way to Niagara after every raid. They burrowed off into the woods like dogs, circling, lying hidden till all threat of a pursuit was by, and then entering a new district. Five times that month of May the men at McKlennar's had been called for the militia. Five times they had marched into the woods. And five times they had found only the burning ruins of the homestead cabin and stayed only long enough to bury such dead as they found.

The militia were positive that white men led the raids. Twice, following up the tracks of the destructives, Adam and Joe had found women at the site of their first camp. In each case it was obvious how they had been treated before being scalped.

Whenever the militia were called, Lana and Mrs. McKlennar had moved down to one of the forts. Once Adam had been sent to fetch them in when Joe and Gil were both on duty. He had taken them to Eldridge Blockhouse, where thirty people were crowded inside a stockade fifty feet by forty. They had spent seven days there, with no news of what was happening.

Jacob Small or Dingman or Robhold Ough was always on watch in the spy loft and from time to time he called down what he saw. Once it was an express riding along the Kingsroad, full gallop into the west. Another time it was a wagon train, presumably for Fort Stanwix, since it was escorted by sixty soldiers. Again, in the middle of one night, the watcher saw fire to the south and west, far up the valley, beyond Shoemaker hill.

It was so still in the darkness that even at that distance a brief session of firing could be heard. Lana and Mrs. McKlennar, sharing a shed with Betsey Small and her four-year-old boy, talked together in low voices, trying to imagine what was happening to keep the militia out so long. As soon as he had brought them safe inside, Adam Helmer had departed to run a single-handed scout, he said, to the northward. But he had been gone six days.

Betsey spoke tenderly of him as she lay on her back and stared at the square roof of the blockhouse against the stars. There in the spy loft Jacob was keeping the second watch.

"I'd miss Adam," she said. "I'd hate to have anything happen to him. He's such a crazy fool."

"He's crazy about you," said Mrs. McKlennar.

"I know he is." She added, after a minute, "I'm fond of Jake."

One of the children turned on his straw bed with the noise a mouse might make in a barn. In the pitch-dark across the stockade another child began to cry. Instantly Jake's voice came down from the spy loft. "Stop that noise." The mother's fierce whispering could be heard. Then again the silence.

The small stockade cut a segment out of the sky through which stars traced the passage of the night.

"The last express said they expected Sir John Johnson would be down; do you think that's it?"

"It might be."

One of the four cows kept in the stockade began to moo; and Jake's instinctive call for silence brought a smothered laugh from a boy. You couldn't tell a cow to hush its mouth. Then, as the cow continued its bawling, the ridiculousness changed to terror. They could see Jake leaning over the sill of the spy-loft window. His voice was thick with passion.

"Take a club to her! My God, are you all idiots down there?"

Betsey whispered, "Jake feels mad. We'd better quit talking."

There were only five grown men in the stockade, to protect the twenty-odd women and children. Both the Snells who had survived Oriskany—seven of that family had been killed there—and the Forbush men and the two younger Borsts had been called up to Dayton. A solider man than Jacob Small would have been frightened by the responsibility. Eldridge's was too far away from any other fort to expect any reënforcement if they should be attacked.

Their only hope lay in keeping a strict silence during the night, and hoping during the day that any marauding party coming their way would be small enough for five men to handle. He thought he could frighten off any bunch of Indians with the swivel. But supposing the Indians were brought by some Tory renegade—like Casselman, for instance; he would know that a swivel mounted that high was next to useless.

The alarm guns at Herkimer and Dayton both sounded three times. That meant that there was a large party of Indians. Jacob wished he knew how large. They must have burned the Moyer place during the night—that would be the fire he had seen. The Moyers, three families of them, had set out to build that spring, he had heard.

The worst time of watching was in the hour before dawn, when light was just beginning and there were no stars. The valley, then, became like a gray blanket, without shape or distance. It was harder for a man to see than during the darker hours, and no sound was reliable.

It was at this hour that Adam Helmer returned. He was crossing the highland on a dead run. Jacob heard him come over the edge and down the slope to the lesser incline on which the stockade was situated.

"Eldridge," he was calling. "Helmer."

"That you, Adam?"

"Let me in, Jake."

Small bawled down the word to open the gate and Helmer came in, his wide shoulders filling the narrow gap. He stood in the yard, breathing deep, while Small leaned out of the spy-loft window to hear his news.

"The Indians are out again, Jake."

"Where?"

"I almost ran into them. They were coming from West Canada Crick. They'd crossed below Schell's and they're headed this way."

"How many?"

"About sixty, I guess. I ran around them, after they'd gone by. I had to climb a tree and they went right under me. Mostly Senecas, and about ten white men. Casselman. Empie. McDonald. I heard their names."

"How far back of you?"

"They'll be here in about two hours."

Small swore.

"That's after sunrise. They'll see us plain."

"They've got the militia after them. But they figured the militia would chase up the crick, I guess. They'll find out pretty quick what happened if Joe's with them."

"We only got five men here, Adam. Six, with you."

There was a silence. All the women and the older children had come out of their sheds. Now they looked up at the spy loft, making a pond of white, strained, frightened faces. They were all depending on him, and he had no more idea than any of them what to do.

In the midst of that silence Mrs. McKlennar's snort was a challenging blast.

"There's fifteen grown women here," she said. "We'll rig up to look like men. If we show up along the rifle platforms, they can't see we're women. They'll go by."

They found a few extra hats and some old shirts. The five men passed their hats out. Betsey put on her husband's; Lana borrowed Adam's. They stuffed their hair inside. Three of the women, having no hats, hacked off each other's hair with a razor. They put on shirts and coats and armed themselves with broomsticks and pitchfork handles. For a moment they stared at each other in the yard, then, hiking their skirts up, they climbed the ladders to the rifle platform.

"Don't hold those sticks so plain," admonished Small from the spy loft. "Just hold onto them as if they was guns, but don't try to show them. If they come while it's still misty you'll look all right. And if any shooting commences, duck."

He pulled his head out of sight, then stuck it forth again for a last word.

"And don't talk. A woman's got no idea how far a woman's voice will carry."

It was so still now, in the misty pre-dawn, that they heard the splashing of Small's brook under the alders a hundred yards away. It was cooler than it had been during the night. Even Jacob Small, twenty feet above them, saw nothing; and he did not hear the padding feet as soon as they did.

The footfalls came along the way that Adam had taken, over the crest of the highland and down the slope, at a run. But before they reached the wheatfield they slowed down and faded out of hearing. For a long time Lana tried to hear them again. She kept staring toward where they had last been audible, away on her left.

She never knew what sound had caused her to turn her eyes straight out from the stockade, but when she did she nearly screamed. An Indian was standing there, vaguely defined in the pale light. She knew it was an Indian. She could see the feather over his ear and the scarlet on his face and chest and the blanket hanging from his shoulder. Her courage seemed to drain out at her feet. She could only stare as a bird would at a snake. She felt her heart beating so hard that she could scarcely fetch her breath; the blood pounded in her ears, stopped suddenly, and the painted figure of the Indian began to sway in her eyes. She thought she was going to faint.

Then Mrs. McKlennar caught sight of her and reached out and poked Adam. He glanced at Lana, slipped over to her, and followed the direction of her gaze. His rifle crept out noiselessly between the points of the sticks.

The smell of his sweat beside her brought Lana to her senses. "Don't move," he muttered. She did not dare move. Out of the tail of her eye, she saw his thick finger bending on the trigger. She could not help herself from looking back to the Indian. As she did so the rifle roared in her ears and the smoke flushed up in her face, choking her. But before it did, she saw the Indian spin on his heels and fall, head towards her, on his back.

"Hell," said Adam. "I must have got him to one side."

The tear of his teeth on the cartridge paper, the cold slither of the ramrod whanging home the bullet, and he was gone back to his post. She found that she was panting.

"Get him?" Jacob called down.

"Got him," Adam answered.

The shot brought on the main body of the destructives. They could be heard on the highland, then coming down the hill. Then their progress faded out. But the mist was thinning, and here and there the vague shapes of them were visible.

A musket flashed from the spot at which the Indian had been killed. The ball whipped over the women's heads with a sharp tearing sound. "Down, you," shouted Jacob.

For a minute there was no other shot. Then a yelling broke out. They loosed a volley at the palisade and the bullets broke splinters off along the points. And then a shrill whistle called out of the mist.

Jacob called down, "They're pulling off. It did the trick. They seen you." He waited a moment. "I think the militia's coming. I heard a conk-shell horn."

Lana turned her back to the palisade and sat down. She also had heard the deep dismal wailing of the conch shell.

"Hey," bawled Jacob. "They're a-going! They're going down the road."

They were trotting down the road in Indian file. Lana, getting to her feet, watched them with the others. About sixty of them, Adam counted, perhaps a dozen white men. They plodded along at a steady pace, not looking back. They carried blankets on their shoulders, and rifles and muskets trailing from their hands. They all looked brown in the thinning mist, dark and dirty and implacable. There were enough of them to have stormed the stockade in five minutes if they had not mistaken the women for men. . . .

An hour later the militia came over the edge of the highland behind Joe Boleo. They came at a trot, also, but the gait was not like the smooth Indian tread. The militia plodded like farmers, stubbornly setting down their feet, forty weary men.

Joe Boleo drew a little ahead of them.

"You all right?" he yelled.

"Yes."

"How long ago did they go by here?"

"An hour."

Joe gave a groan. "All night long I been kicking these twerps to make them run and all we do is get farther behind."

"You're lucky at that. There was sixty."

"They burnt out the Moyers. We got Dolly Moyer, scelpt but not kilt. They'd started to carry her off, but we come up too quick. We was right on them there."

The militiamen fell out of rank any which way and lay down on the grass bank before the stockade. Joe eyed them disgustedly. "Say, is Adam in there?"

Adam was already pushing the gate open.

"Hello, you bug-tit," he said to Joe. "Want to go after them?"

"Yeah. I want to see them out of the valley. Come on."

Lana issued from the fort with the other women, looking for Gil. He was sitting on the bank with his back against the stockade. He looked back at her without smiling.

"Have you got any food?" he asked. "I'm hungry. Young John here's just about played out."

"I'll cook up some wheat right away. There's no flour."

In one corner of the fort was an old burned-out stump, an Indian mill, they called it, in which they crushed their wheat grains to a kind of rough meal. Lana threw some of this in water and borrowed a pinch of salt.

While she was tending it, Gil brought John Weaver in with him and sat down in the shed.

"Are we going home with you?" Lana asked with a nod towards the children.

"Yes. It's over, I guess. Sir John has headed north."

"Sir John? North?"

"I forgot you wouldn't know," he muttered. "Sir John brought five hundred men across the Sacandaga flows. He's struck the valley by Johnstown. They say he's burned down every house in Caughnawaga. He's killed fifty or sixty people. Old Fonda that used to be his neighbor, eighty years old, scalped on his front door. They crucified a man at Tribes hill, they say. There was three hundred Indians. Everything burnt. They say a hundred or more men went off with Sir John. They took their families with them. And the families of Tories that got left behind four years ago." His voice became uncertain. "Bellinger got orders to muster us in case they came this way. But yesterday afternoon we heard they'd headed north. The soldiers hadn't even started after him from Schenectady when the express left there. They'd been called back there until they knew that town and Albany was safe. We were just coming home when we got the word that there was burning up at Moyer's. We started out after them. . . ."

"Don't talk," said Lana. "Stop. Eat something. It's all ready."

Outside the upright sticks at their backs a woman cried, "Tom! Tom! You come back here! You mind your Ma."

A surly voice answered back, "We was just playing Indian, Ma. We was trying to scalp him."

In the sunlit field two little boys with wooden knives were squatting beside the dead Indian.

4. Terror by Night

No man, all summer long, had gone to his field alone. The haying had been done by armed parties, of thirty or more, sent out from the forts. The people in Fort Herkimer attended to the south side of the river, those in Dayton to the north. At the end of July twenty men were sent to help out with the Eldridge haying. The hay was all stored in small stacks within sight of the stockades, but out of shooting range, so that they could offer no cover to the enemy. At the same time, they could be watched and sallies made to protect them against any small force.

The destructives had hung in the woods through June and July. The scouts sent out left and entered the forts under cover of darkness. In July a mob of sixty Indians almost surprised three hay wagons, chasing them right under the Dayton stockade.

Lana had heard the warning gun go off on the southeast rampart of the fort and gathered her children and run them through the gate. She did not know whether Gil was on that particular hay party, but she was not allowed on the rifle platform to see. She had to remain under it, out of the way, with the other women, listening—first to the shooting out across the valley; then to the rumble of the wheels and the squeaks of the racks as the heavy loads swayed in and out of ruts at their mad gallop. Then the thudding of the horses' hoofs and the racket of harness; the screech of the gates swinging open; the yelling of the Indians close behind; and at last the thunder of the wagons rolling into the parade. As the gates screeched shut again a volley from the rifle platforms seemed to split the fort apart, and four swivels went off with sullen booms, and the yelling outside stopped.

Holding the two children to her, she crowded out with the other women, to see the men sliding down off the loads and running to join the sortie forming at the gate. She saw Gil looking over his shoulder at the line of women's faces. His eyes met hers. He did not raise his hand or smile, no more than she. In the next moment he had passed with the others through the opening gates to drive the Indians away from the cabins and haystacks outside the wall.

That was the nearest any party of savages came to the forts that summer. Most of the time they lay in the woods, trying to pick up berrying parties, and burning all the new outlying cabins one by one. The valley now was as desolate as it had been after Brant's raid. Most of the remaining cattle had been killed and eaten by the destructives. The scouts reported that the pigs, left to run loose in the woods, were getting to be as cute as the deer.

Though the women still cooked in the cabins, most families slept inside the forts; for, towards the end of July, Brant had appeared below Stanwix with eight hundred Indians. They had actually seen his army from Fort Herkimer, crossing the valley to the south. He made no demonstration against the forts, however. Instead, two weeks later he turned up at Canajoharie at the site of his old place, and desolated six miles of the Mohawk. Men, women, and children were killed and taken prisoner, one hundred houses were burned, mills and churches. Wagons were destroyed, ploughs and harrows broken. They said that opposite Frey's you could see human bodies in the water.

After the second burning of the Herter house, Captain Demooth had moved into Fort Dayton. John Weaver, however, was sent across the river to Herkimer. Since he had served with the Continentals under Sullivan, he was now classed as an experienced soldier and was appointed by Bellinger a sergeant of the garrison.

The promotion made Mary proud, and thankful, also, that his duties kept him entirely in the fort. They lived on the second story of the northwest blockhouse, sharing space with Sergeants Stale and Smith and their wives and Stale's two children. They had no room for privacy between themselves, but they all felt that it was better, airier, and quieter than living in one of the sheds.

It had been dry and very hot. The green had been slow in returning to the mown hayfields. The river ran very shallow. But since August there had been few alarms.

On the north side of the river Mary and John could see through the loophole next their bunk the stone McKlennar house with its shuttered windows. The survival of that house, the last left standing but Shoemaker's, was one of the mysteries they often talked about, together, for they liked to look at it and plan on having a house of their own some day resembling it.

The other women, hearing them, would sometimes smile, half bitterly, that people could still be so young. But Mary ignored them. She understood how these two women felt, having lost everything that belonged to them. She did not try to answer when Mrs. Smith told her to wait until she had had a child and seen it sicken from lack of food and die from cold. Mrs. Smith had taken her child to bed with her during the past winter, but it had caught a malignant quinsy of the throat. "Doc Petry couldn't do nothing. He said it needed milk." Her toneless voice went on: "My own milk gave out. I ain't like some people. I got to have food myself to breast feed a child. I'm the hearty-eating kind of woman. I've got another in me now. What's going to become of it?" She glanced at Mary's figure. "You're lucky. You ain't never had one. You talk about stone houses. Well, all I want to think about is a log house of my own again, and dried punkin and corn ears and hams on the rafters. Just to set down and look at them and know they're all mine."

Mary knew how lucky she was without being told. She was growing up. She would be eighteen before long, and John told her that she was getting prettier every day. Her breasts were filling out, and she had more flesh on her shoulders, and her cheeks were rounder. Her legs were still the slim hard legs of a girl; but John liked them, even though he used to tease her about how long they were. "When the war's over," he said one day, "I'm going to buy you a print dress. I'm going to get it made. With a long skirt. Right to your toes. Your legs won't show, and you'll be beautiful."

"I'll powder my hair," she said. "There'll be flour then."

Imagine it, flour enough to use it on your hair.

"I'll ride you over on a pillion saddle. You'll look like a lady, Mary. With your bonnet tied with bows."

These thoughts seemed so possible and real when they looked at the McKlennar house. As if the house might be their own, waiting for them to ride across the river and enter it.

The time would surely come. She did not tell John how she hoped he would look in a new blue coat and snuff-colored pants and polished boots, perhaps, and certainly a cocked hat. She felt too shy; his talking about her like that always made her remember with humility the way he had first noticed her in this same fort, the way he had talked to her and they had got engaged to one another. She was a little skinny brat then, with one braid down her back and one plain petticoat to her name; and he had stood out before his mother for her, and kept on loving her, and finally they had got married. Now he was getting to be a great man. He had been noticed and had started upwards. She had no doubt that the war would be won with people such as John in power. They would make it a fine free country afterwards, and maybe it was not too much to think of owning a black house servant.

Down in the yard there would be a shout for the changing of the sentries and John would have to get up and pull his boots on and go down and stand his watch. The square black room would become blacker after his going down. Mary would huddle herself against the wall and listen to the sounds of changing watch: the sound of men clambering onto the rifle platforms; the thump of Smith's or Stale's feet on the blockhouse ladder; his boots dropped on the floor; his little grunt as he stooped to take his pants off; one of the women, whichever wife it was, murmuring querulously in the hot darkness as she made room on the straw bed. Mary would lie straight and narrow, trying to shut out the sounds from her ears. The grossness of these men compared to John was sickening to her.

The militia reaped the wheat systematically along the valley from west to east and the McKlennar fields were, consequently, the last to be visited. As the farm was so far from Fort Dayton, both Bellinger and Demooth agreed with Gil that it would be simpler to move down ten or fifteen men to the house and let them camp there while the grain was harvested. But Mrs. McKlennar would not hear of a herd of men let loose in her home unless she went along.

"It's my house," she said, looking the colonel in the eye.

Bellinger sighed.

"Besides," pursued the widow, "with a couple of women looking after their food they'll do the work a whole lot quicker."

Lana was delighted that they were allowed to go. It seemed quite safe with all those men close by. The last scout had reported the Indians moving west towards Tioga. The frequency and magnitude of the earlier raids led people to suppose that nothing much more could be expected to happen that fall.

As the first wagon turned off the road and drew up to the porch, the mystery of the immunity of Mrs. McKlennar's house was explained. Just above the front steps a horse's skull lay on the porch floor.

The men noticed it at once, and one asked suspiciously, "How'd that get there?"

"I put it there myself," said Mrs. McKlennar proudly.

"It's a Tory sign," the man said.

"Of course it is; that's why I put it there."

"It's a Tory sign," he repeated, eyeing her.

"Where'd you get that skull?" another asked her.

Mrs. McKlennar snorted.

"It's the skull of my own mare. I found it this spring when I was strawberrying. She was killed two years ago."

The fact that the skull could be identified seemed to make them feel better about it. One man laughed; it was a joke on the destructives; and they all began to lug in their bedding and spread it on the porch.

But when Mrs. McKlennar went into the house she found that someone had been making free with it. Men apparently had cooked at the fireplace, for the hearthstones were greasy. They found a bit of bloody bandage on the floor. Some of the destructives must have used the place, keeping it securely shuttered and lighting a fire with no fear of detection. Mrs. McKlennar grinned wryly. "I guess I didn't have my whole joke to myself, Lana, and I'll bet these men have left their bugs in here." The women opened all the windows to let in the sun and clear away the mustiness, and then, while Lana mopped the floor, Mrs. McKlennar attacked the sooty cobwebs.

She was in a fine temper by the time they had the kitchen habitable. "I'll not leave this house alone again," she said. "I'd rather lose my scalp than go through this again."

Gil had brought wood and Daisy was cooking before her fireplace once more, muttering to herself, as she had to clean one pot after another, "Dear, dear, dear, dear," with a clucking noise like an offended hen. But she had the men's food ready by sundown and they came up from the wheatfield to eat it on the porch, where they sat admiring the swathe they had cut through the grain and eyeing the full moon that rose through a shelf of mist upon the hills by Little Falls.

They spent a week at bringing the wheat up to the barn, and the second week they started threshing. Some of the men had returned to their cabins, a new lot succeeding them, and as fast as the grain was threshed it was barreled and carted to Fort Dayton.

The women worked longer hours than the men. The cooking and washing were far more than Daisy, the negress, could handle alone, and before the wheat had been threshed Gil began pulling ears from the corn and expected Lana to help him. Mrs. McKlennar therefore had to assist the negress.

But they all enjoyed it, even the cow, which had been led down from the fort when it was decided to thresh at the farm. The feeling that they were in a house, that they had a place to themselves, made up for all their labor.

Gil decided to talk to Bellinger about their staying. His first argument was that if the destructives had actually been using the house for a hideout, it was better either to burn it to the ground or else to have a guard upon it. His second argument had more effect. The McKlennar wheatfields were among the best in the valley. It would be of advantage to the whole community if Gil were allowed to plough them in the fall. He thought if he could have six men on hand continually that he could safely keep on at the house. In case of any large raid, naturally, the family would withdraw again to one of the forts. If Bellinger realized that Gil's principal idea was to keep his fields in order, it only agreed with his own passionate conviction that the one hope for the settlers was to hold their land and feed themselves. He agreed. And though the tiny garrison changed personnel every day or so, there were always six men working with Gil at the ploughing or helping Lana to gather the apples which were just beginning to fall.

The leaves were turning and the nights growing colder. Though there had been no frost as yet in the valley, it had touched the hills, and the maples were already scarlet and crimson and flaming orange. The after-noons were hazy and full of silence and without wind.

The two children began to put on flesh, eating the new wheat in mushes and samp from the new corn. It was a quiet time. Though Daisy fell ill of a queer fever and was sent to Dr. Petry to be treated for several days, and Lana had to do all the work, she felt a sense of peace take root in her own being, and now and then she caught herself looking forward. It was something she had not done with happiness for several years.

Mrs. McKlennar spoke of it to her one day. "I can see you're planning things. About you and Gil and the two boys, ain't it?"

Lana nodded.

"There's one thing I want you to know. You needn't tell Gil now. But when I die I want you two to have this place."

The widow's face reminded Lana of that March morning when she and Gil had come to interview her, perhaps in the way Mrs. McKlennar drew her breath. There was a sharpness in her eye as if she dared Lana to answer her back.

"In some ways," she continued, "I've been happier than I've been since my husband died. That's because you two have been like children to me. I've appreciated it."

Lana said softly, "It's nothing to what you've been to us."

"Nonsense. I've just told you. Let's forget it." Then she said sharply, "Maybe, though, you'll want to go back to Deerfield if this mess ever gets done with."

Lana shook her head. "I can't tell. I don't know what Gil thinks—he's never spoken of it."

"Well," said Mrs. McKlennar, "it's up to you. The place is yours to leave or take."

As she went out of the kitchen Lana thought, as she had more than once of late, that Mrs. McKlennar seemed a little frail.

Gustin Schimmel was a little man who could only be described as burly. He walked as if he weighed two hundred pounds, with a hunch to his shoulders, and his solemn face belligerently outthrust. He was a very serious person and he took his duty at McKlennar's very hard.

Two days ago a lone Tuscarora Indian had come in to report to Bellinger a huge army of men moving east of Unadilla. He was so emphatic about the numbers of this army, whose trail he had happened on, that Bellinger wanted a scout sent out. He had summoned Gil to join Helmer and Boleo, and had sent word to Gustin Schimmel that on no account was any man to leave McKlennar's until specific orders were received or others arrived to relieve them. It put Gustin in a very serious position, for it was his first command.

He came into the kitchen that evening to assure himself that all the shutters were bolted and the back door barred. With the colder nights, the men were sleeping in the front rooms of the house and the women and children occupied the kitchen.

"I tended to them myself, Gustin," said Mrs. McKlennar.

"Yes, ma'am. But I got to see *myself*. I'm responsible."

His eyes did not allow him to see Lana hastily veiling herself in a blanket, or to observe the widow pushing the chamber pot hastily under the bed. He wondered how such embarrassments could conceivably be avoided.

Having finished his inspection, he addressed the floor.

"I hope you sleep good, ma'am."

"Good night," said Mrs. McKlennar without hope.

"Good night, ma'am." He backed himself out, closing the door. "You ain't to bolt this door," he said from the other side.

"There isn't any bolt," said Mrs. McKlennar.

"Thank you, ma'am."

They had a good night as he had wished them, except for one interruption: the sound of a horse coming from the falls. The clear chop of his hoofs on the hard road past the farm—increase, diminishment, and silence. Before they went to sleep again, a light rain started to fall. In the men's room the snoring continued on its heavy course; then they heard one man stirring in the hall and the half-stifled breathing of Gustin Schimmel deep in his perplexities beyond their door. He breathed there for some time before he finally once more retired.

The morning showed them the last of the rain. A west wind had begun to blow, to clear after the rain, so powerful in its deep gusts that it was like moving silver on the hills.

The wind blew all day.

Gustin Schimmel stood on the porch from time to time, facing it. He wanted to know what that express had carried. He wished mightily that Gilbert Martin would return and relieve him of this new habit of thought he was acquiring. The unaccustomed involutions of his brain had affected his appetite. Laboriously that afternoon he wrote on the piece of paper on which he had decided to keep a journal of his command.

Thirsdey, Oct. 19. It raind some. it clerd this morning. Express went by last nit Today nothing remarkabel.

He stared awhile at the paper. For the seventeenth he had inscribed in his burly hand, "Warm to-day noboddy on the road. Skvash py for super." Squash pie as an entry disturbed him somewhat, for it did not seem very military. He had put it down to fill out the line, since he could think of nothing else. Ultimately he decided to let it stand, folded the paper, and breathed in the widow's direction.

"If you'll excuse me, ma'am," he apologized, "I think I'll just go down to the road and see if I can see anybody."

Mrs. McKlennar fixed him with a marble eye.

"I shall miss you, Gustin Schimmel."

"I could send in one of the boys to keep you company," said Gustin.

"No, thanks, since you can't stay with us, I think we'd rather be alone."

"That's what I thought, ma'am. I want to see if I can find out about that express."

Mrs. McKlennar looked at Lana.

"Do I seem like somebody who's going crazy?"

"No," said Lana smilingly.

"I am, though. Raving crazy. He's making me." She smiled in turn and went on, "Why don't you take the children out? It would do all three of you good."

"Won't you come with us?"

"No, I'd like to just lie here and rest. You stay out till the cow comes in for milking. There's no cooking to do with those four pans of beans all baked."

Lana saw that she wanted to be alone, so she put Gilly's deerskin jacket on him, which made him think he looked like his father, and wrapped a blanket round the baby. The baby had thriven for all the moving they had done that summer. He lay like a great fat lump on her arms, as much as she could carry. He hadn't been christened till the spring when, one day, Domine Rozencrantz had come by McKlennar's; and they had named him Joseph Phillip, with Joe Boleo for a sponsor. Young Gilbert, however, had never seemed to make such flesh, and Lana thought it was due to a combination of the hard winter after Brant's raid and her own milk's giving out when he was still so young. The last was due no doubt to the prompt occupancy of herself by Joey; and at the time it had seemed to her a strange and unjust manifestation of Providence that she should lose her milk. But now that Gilly was becoming so hardy she found it easier to accept the ways of God.

For Gilly was a tough little nugget, active as a young squirrel, and for all that he was only two and a half he was able to walk for quite a little way. And he seemed to take great satisfaction in going into the woods, which, of course, meant the sumacs behind the barn.

Lana took the two children a little way up the slope, perhaps a hundred yards, to an open patch she had found one day, where the earth was smooth enough for the baby to tumble about unwatched. The patch was on the brow of the upland, and, there being no trees round about, the sumac leaves, all gold with bloody crimson tips, and the dark red tassels, seemed to touch the blue of the windy heavens overhead.

The earth was fairly dry, even after the night's rain. The sweep of the wind hushed everything. Sitting there, Lana found herself growing drowsy, and after a while she glanced round to make sure that the children were close by and then stretched out upon her back. The house was so near that she could hear any sound that might rise from below, and yet, for all that could be seen of it, it might be under the moon.

Lana wondered briefly whether Mrs. McKlennar were having a decent rest. Then her eyelids slowly closed. The voice of the booming wind lulled her. Her face was almost girlish as she lay there, the pink whipped up in her cheeks by the wind, and her hair pulled forward under her cheek so that her mouth seemed in a nest.

A few minutes later, Gilly lifted his sharp little face. He acted as if he had heard a sound—a hail from the Kingsroad, perhaps. His mother had stirred in her sleep and the little boy walked up to her and stared down gravely. He glanced at his brother, but his brother wasn't much good at covering the ground, so Gilly, after another moment, walked unsteadily down the slope and into the forest of sumacs. . . .

The hail he had heard had been young Fesser Cox riding his first dispatch from Fort Dayton. Colonel Klock had sent up word from Schenectady that Sir John Johnson had struck the Schoharie Valley with fifteen hundred men. The seventeenth he had laid waste eight miles of the Schoharie. On the eighteenth he had entered the Mohawk and turned west, burning both sides of the river. All people were warned to enter the forts. The militia at Stone Arabia were to stand before the ravaging army. General Robert Van Rensselaer was bringing the Albany militia up the valley to take him in the rear.

Bellinger sent orders to the detail at McKlennar's. It was at once to proceed to Ellis's Mills at the falls and reënforce the garrison there. Fifty militia were about to march from Dayton and Herkimer to back up Colonel Brown at Stone Arabia or join Colonel Klock. A detail would be sent out in an hour to pick up the women at McKlennar's and carry them to Eldridge's, where the men would amplify the garrison of the blockhouse.

Gustin Schimmel did not like it. But he believed in orders. He woke Mrs. McKlennar out of a sound nap and explained that the second detail was on the way and that they would be taken to Eldridge. He himself hated to leave Mrs. McKlennar like that, but it would not be for long. He would prefer to wait until the others arrived or take them himself to Eldridge's, but there it was, plain orders.

"Godsake, man!" cried the widow. "Get along." ("And thank God it's the last of you," she thought, realizing that her cap was caught in the pins over one ear.)

She had been having her first good nap in a long time, but when she awakened she realized suddenly how old she had become. She did not feel like getting up at all, and she thought she would stay where she was until Lana came in. Lana would be down in a moment and could help her with her things. It was hard to have to move again, when a woman began to feel old and tired. Hard to leave the house she had been happy in, so wildly happy sometimes.

She thought of Barney. Barney in his dragoon coat. Barney coming home from the Masonic meeting where he and his friends had been pooling the scandal and news of the valley, Barney coming home slightly tipsy, though he might have ridden fifteen miles, and singing his favorite song— they said he sang it whenever the rum began to seep around a little in his enormous barrel. The words came back to Mrs. McKlennar with her memory of his flushed, handsome face.

> Oh, I love spice,
> I love things nice,
> And I love sugar-candy.
> I like my life
> With my dear wife,
> Unless the girls are handy.

The rascal! He would tumble her hair all out of its cap, her red hair it was, and look as full of sin as the devil himself, and all the time he was as chaste and simple as the brooks he was forever fishing. She remembered the way they dined on warm summer evenings when Sir William once came, with his son,—plain John then,—or John Butler, or Varick, or one of the Schuylers. The gentlemen took off their boots and put their pumps on in her bedroom, and they ate on the porch, with the white table napkin and the candles slobbering with moths, and the hill, the valley, the stars in the sky and in the river, like the finest French paper in the world. The gentlemen seldom brought their ladies, and for that Sally was just as glad, for she had the gift of making men treat her as equals and could crack as hard a joke as anyone if occasion required, and she liked her half bottle of port in the old days, and, *tsk, tsk, tsk*—what a waggery of scandal that would have started if a woman had the telling of it back in Albany. . . . They had planted the orchard together and they had planted a flower garden, but somehow neither of them had had the patience for gardening, or felt the need of being fashionable. It was better to straddle the mare for a gallop to Klock's than to fork the roots of a bleeding heart. It was a pity he should die so long before her, and yet she was glad, for she could not imagine what Barney would have done in these days. He never was much of a man to think things out, poor dear, with his handsome useless head —Lord knew how he could have managed to hold court as Justice of the Peace if the courtroom hadn't been the pub; he could always give both sides a drink and tell them one of his stories if the judgment was beyond him, and then sell them a cock or a foal at the end of it. And come home at night and tell her about it with great rib-swelling roars that tossed her beside him in the bed like being in a storm at sea. And the nice way he liked things, and on the minute—the linen spotless, his shaving water with the crystal salt in it, and the small lace stitched to his good shirts before they were put back in the drawer. Once when she hadn't done it and he had looked in the wrong drawer for a pocket handkerchief, she had really believed he would lift the skin of her back for a minute. But instead he had sat down and explained it to her, the way a grandfather would to his youngest daughter's little daughter, great stupid hand that he was, good only for handling guns or cursing men into level files. Oh, Barney, Barney. . . .

She was not conscious of the minutes passing, or of the time it was, for the whole house had bloomed before her tired eyes and become beautiful and sweet once more. She did not hear the men marching down to the road, and half an hour later she did not hear the detail going by—the detail that should have stopped and taken them. She did not think of Lana, nor why the girl was not yet back with her two children, though it was getting shadowy in the sky across the east window. She had just remembered something that she had not thought of for years, showing how familiarity and custom makes one forget.

This bed she was now lying in so contentedly was the bed that she had been a bride in. (At the tavern in Albany. The best in the house, the landlord had taken his oath, and it was a decent-looking bed for a tavern, though no great piece of furniture in a private house. Just honest maple wood; but in the morning Barney had waked up and looked at her and sat up with the bedclothes over his knees,—and a cold draft pouring down inside her nightgown,—and he had sworn that he would never sleep in another bed unless he had to. He had rung the landlord up then and there. "Good morning," said the landlord. "Your Honor had a good night?" Impertinent, sly-tongued devil: Sarah had sat up beside Barney and flushed furiously in his face; but she hadn't made him change expression. Barney laughed, till he coughed, and swore. "I want to buy your bed, landlord. How much is your asking price?" The man was so confounded that he named three guineas.

"I'll give you four and not a penny less," shouted Barney, "and bring me a bottle of the lobo pale for my breakfast. Oh, and I forgot, what will you have, Sarah, my dear?" She said she would have a glass of his bottle. "You will not. If there's one thing I can't stand it's a wife always cornering in on her husband's drink. Two bottles, landlord, and in twenty-three minutes to the second. Get out and good morning.")

What a thing it was, this delicious revival in her mind of all those early days. Sleighing down the frozen river to the barracks by Hudson Village. Or driving out to the flats at sundown. . . . No, no, it was better to remember coming to this place and building the house together, and Barney being dumbfounded because a chimney could not be laid up in a day. . . .

She did not hear the muffled tramp of the German Flats militia going along the Kingsroad—sixty frightened men with orders to proceed as far as the falls for the night and wait there with a scout out to the north in case Sir John's Indian forces broke loose from his army.

She was thinking of Indians though, and the way Barney would not let them in the house, because they smelled so beasty it spoiled his taste for claret for three days. . . . He could even taste it in the cottage cheese the evening one had slept beside the kitchen fire. . . .

That reminded Mrs. McKlennar that the past was not hers to recapture. She realized that she was sleeping in the kitchen and that the house was bare of people and that she was alone, and it was dark.

No, not alone. Somebody was walking in the next room. Somebody being very cautious. Somebody carrying a firebrand. Two people, she could tell it now, carrying torches. The pine smoke scent came in to her, aromatic, bitter, clearing her head. The light was coming down the hall. Suddenly it occurred to her that the detail Gustin Schimmel had apologized about had never turned up. These could not be they. The detail must long since have got to Eldridge's. Sir John was in the valley.

The door opened slowly and an Indian wobbled into the room. He was slightly tipsy, having just found and emptied a brandy flask, but not so tipsy as his companion. He held the torch over his head with one hand, and clutched a mass of clothing and blankets and a green glass bottle in the other, and the light flared down on his shaven head with its startled scalp-lock dangling a broken feather. His face was painted black with liverish yellow spots and a white stripe that went down his nose and over his mouth and chin, as though his face had been put together by an inexperienced cabinetmaker. He was very hot, and he smelled not only of himself, but of the bear grease all over him that had turned rancid in the heat and wet. And he stared at the old lady in her bed as if she were the great snake demon of Niagara Falls.

"What do you mean by coming into my house?" demanded Mrs. Mc-Klennar.

She had sat up very straight in the bed with her wool jacket over her shoulders and her cap awry. Her long nose was sniffing. She was thinking of the cottage cheese. Barney.

The Indian's jaw dropped. He was not used to being talked at so. And though he did not understand English, his companion said he did.

"Owigo," he said softly. "Come quick."

Owigo was a squattish individual with white circles painted round his eyes. He hit the doorjamb with his shoulder and dropped both muskets and spun round till he was facing the bed.

"Speak English," grunted the first Indian.

"Bellyache bad," were the first words Owigo thought of, and he said them.

"Something worse than that will happen to you, my lad," Mrs. McKlennar said grimly. "You talk English. Well, what have you got to say for yourself? Coming into my house like this!"

Owigo teetered into what he thought was dignified politeness.

"How," he said after a pause.

"What are you doing in my house?" repeated Mrs. McKlennar, drawing herself a little more rigidly erect.

Enlightenment traced a devious course through the Indian's fuddled brain.

"Ho. Set house on fire. Burn quick. All burning there." He waved his hand, a wide gesture that embraced the universe.

For a moment Mrs. McKlennar stared at the two. It was true. She could hear the fire now, she could see the faint light on the floor beyond the open door. These drunken, beastly, good-for-nothing, stinking fools! All the Irish in her blazed.

Her lips parted to a stream of invective that might have silenced even Barney. It certainly silenced the Indians. They were appalled. They recognized virtuous outrage when they saw it, and they did not know what to do.

"Burning my own house with me in it!" cried Mrs. McKlennar. "You ought to be whipped. If my husband were here he'd have the hides off your backs clean down to your heels."

"Yes, yes," apologized Owigo anxiously. "You get out quick, you catch on fire."

It was true enough. The very door smelled hot. Already little fingers of flame pointed round the edge and were withdrawn.

But Mrs. McKlennar would not move.

"I'll not," she said. "I'm not a well woman. I can't sleep outdoors on a cold night like this."

The slowly seeping intelligence in Owigo's eyes was transmuted into words. He explained to his puzzled companion what the white lady had said. The companion looked worried. He replied in Seneca.

"Friend Sonojowauga say," explained Owigo, "you get'm out quick. Burn bad. Burn very bad."

Mrs. McKlennar said then, "If I'm to get out of this house, you'll have to move my bed out for me." She tapped the bed and pointed to the door. Sonojowauga understood the gesture while Owigo was still trying to get the sentence translated in his mind.

He grunted. Then Owigo said, "Yes. Fetch it out. Sure, fine."

"Don't look at me while I get up," said Mrs. McKlennar, mastering a slight shiver. She rose and donned a coat.

"Now," she said severely, "you hurry up."

Willingly they caught up the bed and ran it to the door.

"On its side," said Mrs. McKlennar, "like this. And don't scratch it, you careless lazy beast."

"Make quick," panted Owigo.

They blundered through the door and set the bed up in the yard beside the barn, and hurried back for the bedclothes; by then the kitchen was ablaze. Mrs. McKlennar shrieked at them.

"Don't touch my sheets with your filthy hands; I'll carry them myself." They escorted her, nonetheless, and watched her with mystified faces while she made the bed. Then she got into it.

"Go away, now," she said. "And don't ever come near me again." Owigo smiled ingratiatingly. "Burn fine."

"Get away," said Mrs. McKlennar. "Quick. I don't like you two. You are very bad."

Owigo looked dismayed. He had done everything. His face was sorrowful. Seeing his friend so, Sonojowauga made his face look sorrowful too.

"We go," said Owigo. They gathered up their muskets and trooped off into the woods, one behind the other, feeling very bad, and still a little drunk.

Mrs. McKlennar looked after them, then she returned her gaze to the house, and watched it burn. The red light covered her in the maple bed, showing her long face very quiet. Her eyelids blinked against the light as she sat there, backed against the pillows, and after a few minutes, slow, heavy, silent tears began to drop over her lined cheeks. She lay down in the bed, with her back to the house, but she could not keep the light away. She did not then think of Lana. Her heart was breaking with the destruction of her house. For three years it had escaped the destructives. Now at last two drunken Indians had set it off.

An hour after she had lain down, Lana had wakened, and after a single glance around her had sprung up in terror. The baby lay sound asleep, but Gilly was gone. She called, but as she started down through the sumacs she had a view across the valley.

In the late afternoon sunlight, for one instant, between two groves of trees, she saw a party of men, proceeding at a trot that was unmistakable. Indians were in the valley.

She stopped with Gilly's name frozen on her lips, overwhelmed with the bitter knowledge of her own criminal foolishness. It was well that she did. Following the fences along the Kingsroad she saw two Indians, painted on chest and face, one red, one black, and Lana realized that they could not have missed the house. They were turning up to it. Utterly helpless, she watched them pad softly onto the porch and nose their way inside like two inquisitive dogs. It was too late to see what had happened in the house. No shooting had greeted the Indians. The six men must have gone.

Not only must they have deserted her for some incredible reason; they must have taken Mrs. McKlennar with them. There was just one thing Lana could think of to do. To hide the baby first in Joe Boleo's hide-hole, then to search out Gilly without calling.

It took her several moments to find the hide-hole from this new direction; but as soon as she did, she lowered the baby into it and wrapped him in her coat. He slept like an angel. Lana pulled herself out of the hole, leaving the baby in darkness on the hemlock twigs, praying that he would continue to sleep. Her heart fluttered as she stole out on hands and knees, listening for any tread that might be heard among the sumacs. There was none.

The valley was quiet save for the western wind that drew across the hill with its inevitable booming force.

Carefully and furtively Lana began creeping down towards the house. She kept her head low to the ground, seeking through the stems of the sumacs for a sign of Gilly. She understood now how much like forest trees those stems must look to a baby. She went all along the lower edge of the sumac growth, hoping to intercept him if there were yet time, stopping every little way to listen for a hostile sound, forcing her terror to be calm, her eyes to search through every opening in the brush.

The Indians in the house, if they still were there, were being remarkably quiet. She had now covered all the lower part of the slope and begun to crawl upward once more. She wondered if she could risk a call. She was torn with the desire to stand up and shout to Gilly and anxiety for what was happening to the baby in the hide-hole. If he woke up now and screamed he would be heard, even over the wind, far beyond the house.

The sticky branches of the sumac catching in her hair dragged it loose from the pins. It fell forward over her face, impeding her sight. It was hard enough to see anyway, for the sun was well down. The sky, when she glanced up at it, looked as if it promised cold. She began to fear the night now, almost as much as the Indians. If she did not find Gilly before darkness came, she felt that she would never find him.

The desire to weep was one more thing to struggle against; she felt that if she could lie down on her face and sob and make a noise she would find help. But she did not dare to. Even as the tears streamed helplessly from her eyes, she put her hands and knees out to feel for dry sticks, moving them out of her path with the instinct that hunted creatures have of destruction beyond every leaf. . . .

Her heart was bitter, even bitter against Gil for having left her so. If he loved her truly, he would surely know that she was in trouble. He would come to find her. But she knew that Gil would not come, and that the trouble she was in was entirely of her own making. She started to pray as she went on and on with her nearly insensate patience, forcing her eyes to search ahead through the increasing darkness. And then she heard it. The thin voice. For one dreadful moment she listened—afraid that it was Joey.

But it came more clearly.

"Ma, Ma." He had learned to say "Ma" that summer. He said it so distinctly.

She governed her tired senses, compelling them to a sane judgment of the direction of the voice. Yes, up the slope. Near the little cleared space where they had sat down. He had found his way back to it.

She risked a cry, soft and urgent and clear, "Ma's coming. Hush." It was so dark now that it didn't matter. She stood up and ran, blundering through the bushes, scratched and whipped, to see his little dark shape standing up all alone in the exact centre of the open space.

She caught him in her arms.

"Ma's boy," she whispered. "Hush, hush."

He whimpered a little and settled himself snugly against her breast, and she began to feel her way in the direction of the hide-hole and was surprised at the ease with which she located it. She perched the boy on the edge of the hole and lowered herself cautiously in case the baby had moved. Then she stretched up her hands and took the boy down. She sat down with a child in either arm. She did not cry. She kept dry-eyed, alert, in the dark little hole, straining for any sound that might mean danger.

The glow against the sumac leaves visible through the hole first told her that the McKlennar house was burning. She risked one glance above the hole, standing up and peering over the tree trunk. The wind was tearing flames in banners from the roof. She had a glimpse of the two Indians carrying the bed and then Mrs. McKlennar following with the bedding. She could not understand it.

She lingered till the bed had been set down and the old lady ensconced. She saw the Indians depart. And she wondered if she could go down and tell Mrs. McKlennar to come back to the hide-hole. But the babies kept her. Joey was beginning to whine. He would wake up and want his food. Gilly was hungry too. Lana's head swam. What on earth had happened?

Mrs. McKlennar had lain down in the bed. Was she sick? Too sick to move? But she had followed the bed out there.

Suddenly her eyes were caught by the shape of a man, stooping down among the sumacs, well away to her right. She dropped inside the hide-hole. At the same moment Joey let out his first bawl. He had a voice like a calf when he was hungry. She fumbled frantically in the dark for his mouth and pressed her hand on it. She felt his instantaneous convulsion of protest, arms flying, legs kicking, as he tried to get his breath. Gilly started to whimper. "Hush," she whispered. With her free hand she tore at her short gown, ripping it in two, baring her breasts. "Oh God. If my milk doesn't come now!" She huddled Joey up to her and withdrew her hand and pressed his little face towards her. She felt him start to yell, then his surprised jaws clamped on her breast so hard she almost cried out. And then the reassuring pressure beginning.

Gilly was starting softly to cry now. Cold and hungry as he was the smell of milk was too much for him. He would not hush. She pulled him towards her too and let his face rest against the free breast and left it to him whether he would accept it. They had worked so hard to wean him. But when, fumblingly, he touched the breast, her heart welled over.

The man in the sumacs was Joe Boleo. He and Adam and Gil had returned from their scout reporting that an Oneida Indian had seen the army of hostiles strike the Schoharie. When they had reached Fort Dayton, Bellinger had ordered them to take a detachment of men with Mark Demooth to the south. An express had said that Van Rensselaer's army was fighting Sir John above Klock's, and that the Tories were breaking over the river. If possible Demooth was to capture Johnson or John Butler or some of the leaders.

Gil had asked at once for his family and Bellinger had explained what he had done. "You've got to go, you three. You're the only scouts to find them after dark in those hills. I can't spare one of you." He looked gaunt and haggard and determined. "Your women are all right," he said.

Gil hurried off to report himself to Demooth. Joe Boleo, however, didn't give a damn for Bellinger or General Washington himself, if it had come to that, or army discipline or cause or justice. He remembered that he had a godson in McKlennar's and he was going to make damn sure he was all right. If he felt like it afterwards, he could circle and still catch up with Demooth.

He reached McKlennar's in time to see the roof fall in and the widow lying on her bed. The old woodsman took one look, then bolted down to her. He was sure he had heard stray shots at Eldridge's. More of the destructives were on the way; running the woods like driven wolves, they would snap at anything that crossed their path.

He snatched up the bedclothes and pulled Mrs. McKlennar to her feet. He didn't ask her why she had not used his hide-hole. He ran her up the slope and shoved her in. As he did so he felt the presence of terror in the pit and called, "Lana, is that you in there?" Then he added, "It's Joe."

"Yes." He could hardly hear the word through her release of breath.

"Here's Mrs. McKlennar. You keep quiet and you'll be all right. I ain't coming in. But I'll stay close."

He was right about more Indians. Three of them came to the burning house and started nosing round. They picked up footprints at the edge of the sumacs and began to work up the slope. The women heard their footfalls gradually approaching the hide-hole. Then they stopped. Suddenly a man whooped, a terrible ear-piercing sound. Then he was still, waiting for the frightened stir that should point out his victim.

There was a clean, sharp crack. The two others yelled, and at the same time the women heard Joe Boleo shout. The sumacs crashed overhead with the sounds of pursuit and flight, and in only a minute the wind again was audible.

Mrs. McKlennar leaned against Lana and wept.

The clear October dawn woke them—unbelievable as it seemed to wake, to have fallen asleep at all. The babies began to cry.

"It's all right," Joe's voice reassured them from above. When Lana looked out she found him on the fallen tree, cleaning his long rifle. His hatchet and knife were polished at his side. "Three of them," he nodded at her. He helped haul out the babies. "I did a perty on the one that yelled. Twenty rod, right through the head. He's down there."

Lana would not look, but Mrs. McKlennar stared curiously at the dead painted body. "Jurry," she said suddenly. "Jurry McLonis!"

"Deader'n fish," nodded Joe. "Come on. I'll lead you back to the fort." He picked up the baby. "I'll lug Joey," he said.

The threads of news were slowly gathered during the day. The Tory army had disappeared to the west. But they had burned the whole of Schoharie and both sides of the Mohawk from Canajoharie and Caughnawaga to the fording place above Klock's. They had not been caught as they might have been. They had killed forty men at Stone Arabia who had tried to stop their march; and the Indians and destructives as usual had dropped away from the main army in their uncontrollable desire to hurry.

Then the detail that had gone to Eldridge reported that Jacob Small had been caught by the first appearance of the Indians before Fesser Cox had given the alarm. He had gone out to gather apples. He had always liked apples and there was a tree a few rods from the blockhouse, behind some woods, whose apples he particularly fancied. He had been shot and scalped and left where he was in the branches. They found an apple in his hand, with one bite out of it.

Towards dark, Adam and Gil returned with two thirds of their force. They had been surprised. Demooth and eight men had been captured by Johnson's Greens and Butler's Rangers.

As darkness came that night, the still-booming great west wind brought clouds and the first early fall of snow.

9

WEST CANADA CREEK (1781)

1. *The May Flood*

THE rain as it started on the fifth of May looked like an ordinary spring shower, clouding over a little after noon, and the first cold drops slanting out of the northwest. The river was already high between Dayton and Herkimer. In the falling rain it flowed with a smooth force, which covered the fording place without a riffle.

Lana and Mrs. McKlennar kept the fire going and listened to the steady patter on the bark sheaths of the roof. It was damp in the small cabin that Gil, with Joe and Adam to help him, had laid up after the McKlennar house had burned, though it stood on the high ground north of the fort. Mary Weaver said that her place, which was the next below Petry's store, had a stream running through one corner. Cobus had been trying unsuccessfully to dam it out with clay all afternoon.

After Mary left them, Mrs. McKlennar turned on the negress, who as usual hugged the hearth.

"Can't you stop that chattering?"

"Fo' God I can't, Mis'. Hit's de way dey is, dat's all."

Daisy felt the damp since her fever of last fall. She claimed she felt it on all the bones in her "skelington." "If you could des' leave me have a little drap of rum, Mis'."

"Rum!" snorted the widow. "If I had it I'd drink it myself. Even Dr. Petry hasn't any."

Lana began to prepare supper. They had a small cut of deer meat and a little milk for the children; there was no flour in the place.

Her face had a new quality of transparentness. She was very thin; even her hips that had grown so heavy a year ago were now fined down like a young girl's. She was dressed, as were Mrs. McKlennar and the negress, in a strange collection of odds and ends; her petticoats, raveled out almost to her knees, seemed ready to fall apart with the rottenness of age. She wore clumsy homemade moccasins on her feet and a deerskin jacket poorly tanned over a shrunken woolen shirt of Gil's.

As she set the iron kettle on the logs to boil, she tried not to think of her family; but for months her mind had been conjecturing about their fate. Expresses coming up the valley in November had said that Fox's Mills was one of the settlements entirely wiped out by Sir John's Tory army. Most of the people were believed to have been killed. But there was no way in which Lana, in German Flats, could find out. All that she had been able to discover was that her second sister had been married the year before to a man from Johnstown. Her informant could not say who the man was; it was something he had heard in Klock's. Lana thought that her sister would now be twenty years old. Lana herself was twenty-three; but she felt that she must look much older than that.

Her thoughts went round and round, making no connected sense. When she heard Gil's footsteps hastily squelching through the mud outside, she had to force her face into a smile. She wanted to smile; the instinct lifted her out of the day's listlessness whenever she heard him coming home. But to make her lips respond was an effort of translation which she was always conscious of.

As the door opened to let him in, she turned her head and saw the rain sheeting down in the dusk beyond him, and Joe Boleo standing at his side, dripping in damp deerskins.

"I brought home Joe to see his godson," Gil cried.

"I'm glad," said Lana. The children were always glad when Joe or Adam came to visit. She thought, "I'll have plenty. I'm not hungry myself."

"Come in and sit close," Mrs. McKlennar said. "You poor boys certainly look wet."

"It's quinsy weather all right," said Joe, grinning at them all and hanging his rifle, muzzle down, on a peg through the trigger guard. The two boys came up to him.

"Did you bring us anything, Uncle Joe?" they asked.

"I got a piece of soft pine in my pocket," he said. "What'll I make you?"

They disputed for a moment between a buck deer and a tomahawk. But the vote finally settled on the buck. A buck with twelve points, Gilly specified. Joe looked a little blank. He could whittle pretty well, but a buck deer was a large order for a man with a hunting knife. Then a thought crossed his mind and made him smile, and he set to work manfully on the rear quarters.

"It's quite a rain," said the widow. "Where've you been, Joe?"

"I was over the river to Herkimer seeing Adam."

"We haven't seen Adam much, lately."

"No; he's sitting on Betsey Small's tail, just about. She won't have him less'n he marries her, and seeing she's the first woman ever stood him off it seems like he just can't stand to come away from her."

"I thought Adam had another girl," said Lana.

"Polly Bowers? Sure, but now she's having a baby, Adam ain't interested in her."

"Sinner," exclaimed Mrs. McKlennar, but she did not say it with the proper moral indignation at all. She was too fond of the hulking, handsome, yellow-haired brute.

"Has anyone talked to the girl?"

"Oh, I did, some. I kind of got the idea she was willing to peddle it out to any father, though she had the belief it was one of them Continentals was in garrison here last year for a spell."

"Well, my land," cried Mrs. McKlennar, "doesn't she know?"

"She said she hoped it was the corporal," Joe replied; "but she's trying to lay it onto Adam and I guess that's why he's hanging on after the Small woman. You know how it is with a man like Adam when he finds a woman has acted inconsiderate like that."

"Uncle Joe," cried Gilly, "it ain't got no head on it yet."

"I know. I'm coming to it when I get to it," said Joe. "Even the Lord had to begin somewhere on a buck. I just ain't so quick. This here's quite a rain. Last Wednesday I was up to Stanwix and the water was getting up close to the sally port. Yes, ma'am, I figure it's going to rain real hard. How long? Three or four days. It'll be a flood."

"How can you tell?"

"Wind's passing through the north. You can hear it on the north side of the roof now."

His Adam's apple bobbled a little as he lifted his lean face.

"When the wind passes through the north to southeast you get a real storm."

"Ain't it de troof," Daisy said dismally.

Lana lifted the steaming kettle from the fire and the rich soup smell was a momentary beneficence in the cabin. They hitched up to the plank that served for a table, Joe last.

"There's your buck," he said to Gilly.

"That ain't a buck," cried the boy.

"Yes it is. It's a good twelve-pointer."

"It ain't. It ain't got no horns at all, Uncle Joe."

Gilly's underlip began to twitch.

"'Tis so a buck," said Joe Boleo. "Ain't you got any sense? Who ever seen a buck with horns this time of year?"

Gilly set the crudely carved animal in front of his plate. He still sniffled to himself, thinking it looked almightily like a sheep; but he ate his soup down. And pretty soon he piped up, "It is a buck, Uncle Joe. I can see now."

Joe looked embarrassed. But Lana smiled and caught Mrs. McKlennar's eye. The two women had small helpings; now they watched the men eat. Four men, Lana thought, sentimentally. Four boys, thought Mrs. Mc-Klennar.

The spatter against the north side of the house swelled to a driving gust, reducing everyone to silence. Then it stopped abruptly, and for an instant everyone listened to the eaves drip outside. But in a moment the wind began again, stronger and steadier, and the rain seemed to come all the way across the valley and strike the cabin like the flat of an enormous hand against the south and east.

"She's beginning now," said Joe. "This valley's going to be a wet place to-morrow, when the river gets hold of it."

Listening to the fall of rain all night, like a voice in the dark that would not hush, Gil wondered whether there would be any seed left in the riverside meadows, supposing the river got as high as Joe thought it would. His ears stretched for a sound of the river; but there was no sound beyond the rain.

Lana, with that strange awareness of things beyond her senses that sometimes came to her, thought of all the places down the valley, tracing the brown swelling course of the river, and thinking how desolate Fox's Mills must look, with its close-gathered houses, now burned. It would be hard on older people like her parents to camp out this way. As hard as it was on Mrs. McKlennar.

Sarah McKlennar managed to keep up her spirits during the day. She was the kind of woman that always reacted well to an audience, and instinctively played her part. But when night came and the babies dropped off and the light faded down on the hearth, she began to think of her house. She hadn't many years left to live, she knew, so it did not matter to her as it did to Lana and Gil, who should have inherited the house along with the place. And it didn't even matter to them as much as it did to the house itself. She imagined it now, the scorched stone walls, blackened and split, under the cold rain, streaking the soot marks—no matter if it was rebuilt the house would always wear scars.

Joe Boleo didn't think at all. He knew enough to sleep, when he had food in his inwards and a warm bed. His snores went up and down as evenly as a pendulum.

The rain fell in a continuous grayness over the valley. In the morning the stockade of the fort, only a couple of hundred yards away, was a brown shadow, indistinct, and without visible life. Lana threw a piece of horse blanket over her head and shoulders and went out with Gil and Joe to look at the valley. As soon as they stepped through the door their ears were greeted by the roar of the West Canada Creek away on their left. The sound was nothing like the usual roar of the rapids that came down through the hills. It was more a deep-toned humming, as though gigantic harpstrings had been stretched from bank to bank. Joe said, "The rocks are covered." He thanked them for his supper and went away to the fort. Gil and Lana proceeded until they could see out across the flat land towards the river.

The Mohawk was as smooth as glass, but the color was changed from gray to a roily brown, and the shape of it was unfamiliar, reaching back in spots well south across the fields.

There was nothing on earth a man might do now, except gather firewood and wonder how far the water had risen.

No one had ever seen such a rain. When, on the third day, the wind changed to the southwest and the sky opened towards noon, and the first small space of blue appeared like a vision on the top of Shoemaker hill, they saw the flats half covered by a brown and fluid waste. The hillside streams arched out from the hills and stood like carved dark yellow columns clear in the air. Where the West Canada Creek met the Mohawk was a boiling pot of waters, in which a spruce tree, entire, from tip to roots, revolved with a kind of gigantic dismay.

People felt queerly disturbed to see the sunset reflected where they had planted wheat. Men stood in futile groups along the edge of the flood, tossing out sticks and trying to estimate the force of the current and the effect it would have on the topsoil.

Towards dusk a bateau with five soldiers shot down the main current from the west. The four men at the oars swung it into the quieter water and rowed steadily towards Fort Dayton. They were men from Fort Stanwix, carrying dispatches. The woods, they said, were impassable, but coming by river they had covered the whole distance during the afternoon.

The east and north and south walls of Fort Stanwix had been practically leveled by the flood. The parade was under two feet of water, and there were really no defenses left except the pickets on the outer glacis. If an army could have crossed the woods against them now, the garrison would have had to defend itself in the open. It was obvious that the garrison could not repair the damage.

While the men ate, Bellinger read the letter from Cochran, which confirmed the men's story and added that the officers unanimously recommended the transfer of the Stanwix garrison to Forts Herkimer and Dayton. He did not, however, feel sure that the Albany command would receive this recommendation with any more favor than in the past, and suggested that Bellinger write a letter to the Governor endorsing the transfer.

The bare possibility of a suitable garrison of regular troops in German Flats roused a hope in Bellinger that he had not felt since the beginning of the war. He wrote a long letter to the Governor promising local labor for the erection of suitable barracks and for any other work the army officers might require.

But when the boatload of soldiers departed on the following morning Bellinger felt less confident. He had become painfully aware of Albany's fixed habits of thought about the western settlements.

That afternoon, however, any other possibility was put out of the question by the complete destruction of the remaining fortifications at Stanwix by fire. How it had started no one ever told; why, in the saturated condition of the fort, it had not been got under control, no one ever explained.

2. Return of Marinus Willett

The hope and confidence inspired at German Flats by the arrival of the garrison from Fort Stanwix were short-lived. The Albany command had conceded the necessity of their removal in May; before the first week of June they had withdrawn two companies for the defense of the Hudson Valley. At Fort Dayton were left only a few squads and at Fort Herkimer a Captain Moody with his artillery company of twenty men, and two light field pieces which were mounted on the walls.

Bellinger grimly supervised the spring planting with armed guards of militia. The small group of Rangers were no longer permitted to make long scouts, but were stationed close along the hills. It was not necessary any more to have long warning of a raid. The women and children were kept huddled to the forts, and the farming parties were instantly convertible to armed companies that might either cut their way back to the forts without assistance or, if the raid proved numerically small, attack the destructives in the open.

There was nothing left to destroy; and the parties that turned up early in June were only looking for stray scalps. More than half of the planting of wheat had been buried or washed out by the spring flood, and the spring planting of grain came up in serried patches of buckwheat, barley, and oats, put in as seed had been procured.

Gil Martin had made no attempt this spring to work the McKlennar farm. Most of his wheat had been washed out. The gutted walls of the stone house, the sashless windows, like lipless mouths, were good only to house stray hedgehogs. The empty barn, which had survived the burning of the house, was burned towards the middle of the month. The fire was seen from the two forts during the night, burning sullenly, with a small party of men surrounding it, but no one suggested going out against them.

Then, towards the end of June, as he came back to Fort Dayton from scout duty with Adam Helmer and John Weaver, Gil saw ten mounted Continentals riding east along the Kingsroad. Adam and John remained outside the fort to watch them, but Gil went in to make his report to Colonel Bellinger. While he was yet talking to Bellinger he heard the horses enter the stockade, and a moment later a sentry stuck his head in the door to announce the arrival of Lieutenant Colonel Willett.

It was a still hot evening, and the smoke from the cooking fires drew in through the windows, filling the small room. But Gil saw Bellinger's dark eyes brighten as he got up from the table, and he himself felt a quickening of his heart. Both of them remembered Willett's first arrival at the fort while St. Leger was investing Stanwix four years ago. Willett had come through the Indian lines; and Willett had ridden straight on to Albany to hurry up Benedict Arnold. They had forgotten Arnold in German Flats until the news had come last winter of his attempted betrayal of West Point. But for some reason no one had forgotten Marinus Willett.

"That's all, Martin," Bellinger said. "You can go now."

"There's no need of that, is there?" said the nasal voice from the door. "It's his business as much as yours and mine, Bellinger."

Marinus Willett looked just as they remembered him. The hard small twinkling blue eyes, close above the huge hooked nose, the red face, the square uncompromising shoulders, filled the doorway. As he came up to Bellinger he looked even taller, for Bellinger had the regular farmer's stoop. His large nose sniffed while he shook hands, and he said, "I hope you've got enough extra to feed us, Bellinger."

"I guess we can scrape up something."

"I'm glad to know it. There's lots of places down the valley that can't do that. Even at my headquarters in Fort Plain we haven't anything to drink."

"We've had no liquor up here since last October, Colonel." Bellinger stopped himself short. "Your headquarters?" he asked. "What do you mean?"

The blue eyes twinkled.

"They've merged the five New York Continental companies into two, and George Clinton came around and pestered me to come up here and command the Mohawk levies. He said I was going to be my own man and would have a regiment to work with and a couple of companies of regulars now in garrison. With that and the militia—me and you—we're supposed to make this frontier safe." Willett sat down and stared humorously along his nose. "I thought, with that, by God, I could do a lot more than anyone has done so far and I said I'd come. I've been up the valley for two weeks. I've reckoned up the men." He didn't look humorous now, his flat cheeks hardened. "I found Stark had drawn off the two companies: now the British won't buy Vermont, he's scared they'll come and take it for nothing. God damn him."

"God damn all Yankees," Bellinger said fervently.

"God damn the whole shebang. I've got a sore tail. Man, I've been to every stockade and fort between Schenectady and this place like a God-damned census taker, checking the militia list Clinton gave me before I set out. That was the '77 list, Bellinger. There were twenty-five hundred enrolled men. Do you know how many of you there's left?"

"I know that we've lost nearly half of our men in this district," Bellinger said grimly.

Willett nodded his big head.

"There were twenty-five hundred in 1777. Now the total, including yours, is less than eight hundred." He stared at Bellinger and Gil. "That's why I said it was this man's business as much as ours. God, it's a mess. Besides the militia I've got one hundred and thirty levies, in good shape. But I'm responsible for Catskill and Ballston as well as this valley. And I'm sending most of them to those two places and the middle fort in Schoharie. I'll leave Moody and his twenty men in Herkimer. For the rest of the valley I'd rather depend on the militia." Suddenly he grinned widely, showing his large yellow teeth. "Clinton's landed me on you, and, by the Lord, I'm not going to run off now. There's nobody outside the forts, and I can get hold of men fast. We'll do the job, one way or the other. Have you got a pipe around anywhere?"

Bellinger produced a clay, which Willett filled from his own pouch. "I've got a few exempts and a few levies not listed and I'll keep them as my own garrison in Fort Plain and as the centre of any army I get together. This section, though, I'm going to leave to you. I'm not going to call you out, either, to go down the valley, but I want you to keep your men handy to join me if I ever come this way."

Bellinger nodded with his usual sombreness. But for the first time in a long while there was a gleam in his eye. "We'll be around. Can you get us a little powder?"

"I've got the Governor's ear. By God, I ought to, after taking on this job! I'll guarantee powder. Food's hard to come by. There's plenty of it in Albany, but the Congress has impounded it for the regular army. Even Heath can't get it for his garrison at West Point. Lord knows what's up. But there's one satisfaction in it—the destructives won't find much to eat when they come this way."

3. The First Rumor

One of Willett's first acts was to impound the best horses at the various forts along the valley for use by his expresses. It had an immensely heartening effect on German Flats to realize that there was someone in the valley who was keeping close touch with them; and the first express to arrive brought news of an irruption in Currietown and Willett's gathering of the militia, his quick pursuit, and total rout of the destructives at Dorlach. For the first time a band of the destructives had actually been caught and licked.

The harvest of their mixed crops in August, after that, was comparatively undisturbed, though there were occasional brushes in the woods when stray Indians attacked the berry pickers.

Another effect of the expresses was the bringing of news from the rest of the country. Willett always included in his dispatches to Bellinger whatever word had come to him. Men began to talk about the war in the south as if it were in some way allied to their own difficulties.

It was strange how that simple illusion had restored their courage. They were not aware of it themselves. They did not know that Willett was raising heaven and earth that fall to get even one company of well-equipped regulars sent up to him. To Governor Clinton he wrote how "the prospect of this suffering country hurts me." He even went over General Clinton's head to General Washington, describing the valley as he had first seen it, and as it stood now. But Washington was meditating his march into the south to join Greene and Lafayette against Cornwallis, and he would not spare a man.

In the Mohawk Valley the fall was early, arriving with a long stretch of northwest weather, small cold showers that pebbled the surface of the river, and day after day of rolling clouds. The roads became heavy, and the expresses, when they traveled, were coated with mud to their thighs.

The corn was stacked about the stockades and the threshing went on in the barns close to the forts, and the winnowed grain was carried into the magazines and stored. Joe Boleo predicted a cold winter that would break early. He did not know why he thought so, when John Weaver tried to cross-examine him; but he had no doubt of it.

They were standing guard on top of the Shoemaker hill, bare to the wind, with the clouds passing over their heads, and occasional showers, which they could see entire from their height, leaving wet trails across the tossing wilderness. The trees were mostly bare, and the forests filled the air with the wintry smell of mouldering leaves. Now and then they saw small flights of duck scudding before the rain.

"Winter's coming," said Joe. "It's getting cold. They hain't ever bothered us none after October, only when Butler went to Cherry Valley."

John was glad to believe him. All day he had been keeping scarcely half a watch. He had hardly felt the cold as he crouched down behind the windbreak Joe had constructed. It seemed to him that his whole being was filled with what Mary had told him that morning about being sure that she was going to have a baby.

He thought he would never forget her; she acted so proud.

"Do you think I should tell your mother, John?"

But he said, "Wait till I come home." He wanted to have time to think. His mother hadn't been herself for two years now. She kept very quiet. Sometimes it seemed to him as though a half of her mind had deserted her when George got taken; for while she did her share of work, she had fits of talking vaguely. She never wept any more as she had at first. Though she was convinced that since they had never heard a word of George he must be dead, it was plain that she could not reconcile herself. Sometimes John used to have the feeling that she was only keeping herself alive until she was sure. Now, he wondered what effect this news would have on her. Rarely, she would have flagrant bursts of temper, when she would try to take a strap to him or Cobus as if they were still children. He didn't want to have her start a thing like that with Mary.

But when John reached the top of the hill and the wind surrounded him, he forgot about his mother and thought only of his wife. He had felt a month before that Mary had something on her mind—apparently she had known then, but she had wanted to be sure. She was sure now. Her face shone with her tidings. She had stood with him outside the door in the cold October sunlight, proud and straight, tilting her thin face to speak over the wind, her eyes beaming on him—he could not tell that at last Mary felt that she had raised herself to his level, nor could he ever know the love and gratitude and pride she had in him.

Instead, with the silent Joe on the hilltop, he had been wondering all day, remembering that time when Mrs. Martin's boy was born: how he had been frightened, how slow the hours had gone by, how dark the night had been. He knew that Mary would laugh at him if she ever suspected how he dreaded it. Her face had been gallant and taut like a flag in the wind when she told him.

It made him think of the first time he had noticed her, in Fort Herkimer: the same thin eagerness in her face, the same anxiety to know what he was thinking. It used to make him feel foolish to think how often he had played with her in Deerfield without being aware. He might so easily never have discovered her at all.

Her face stayed before his eyes so vividly all day; she still seemed so young to him. He thought of her now at different times transformed by the same eagerness: that first time in the fort; and again in the fort when he had taken her up on the sentry walk to break the news of her father's death at Oriskany; and again the cold day when they had walked towards Mc-Klennar's and been married, when Mrs. McKlennar put it up to them both; and again when he had gone away to join the expedition against the Iroquois, and when he had come home; and the day that Bellinger had made him corporal in the Herkimer garrison; and once there in the blockhouse when they were planning their own stone house like the McKlennar house.

Sometimes she had been anxious, sometimes sorrowful, and sometimes overflowing with joy; but always in every part of her he felt her love, her eagerness for their life together, and her pride in him. It made him wonder whether Gilbert Martin, for instance, felt the same way about Mrs. Martin, or whether, like most men, he took his wife for granted. At times John thought there must be something unmanly in feeling the way he did about Mary. He would try to be short with her and resolve not to answer her questions, but on those occasions Mary invariably was quiet. She was a quiet girl anyway. He had no chance to act like other men; and he always found out that he had no wish to once he was with her.

He knew that the coming winter would probably bring more months of short rations, and he did not think that Mary was the sort of woman who could nurse a child. A child needed a lot of food in cold weather. Suppose that it was born in March. But Joe Boleo had just told him that the winter would break early. Suddenly he decided to believe Joe. It would have to be a short winter.

John felt that divine Providence had taken a hand in all his life. His eyes were so rapt that the old woodsman hesitated momentarily before touching his elbow.

"Express coming in from the falls," he said.

John saw the rider driving his horse to a sluggish trot through the sticky going. It was growing dark.

"Come on," said Joe. "We might as well go down."

Mary met him at the door.

"Come in, John. I've got supper ready for you."

She kissed him, putting her thin arms hard about his shoulders, but her eyes were tender and calm. He supposed that women acted that way.

"I've told Mother," she said softly. "I thought it was best. There may not be much time."

She had closed the door behind them and was leaning against it with her hands clasping the latch. He now saw that she was pale and was watching him with that level regard that invariably stirred him so, as if she were hoarding him up like a treasure.

"Time, Mary?"

He heard his mother rise from the hearth. Emma's gaunt face showed that she had been crying.

"I'm glad she did, John. It's made me happy. I ain't been so happy since when . . . I can't think, hardly. I wish your Pa knew of it. Maybe he does."

The door swung open, putting Mary aside, and Cobus entered with some wood.

"I wish they'd let me go too. Can't you make 'em, John? You're a corporal."

"What are you talking about?"

"Gil Martin was here just a short spell ago. He said for you to come up to the fort. Butler's this side of Johnstown heading this way."

It was hard to take it in. Even Joe Boleo had thought that the raiding must be over for the year. John stood for a moment staring from one to the other.

"I guess I'd better go up there," he said.

"Can I go with you, John?"

John turned to his brother.

"You stay here, Cobus. I want to know somebody's looking after Ma and Mary."

Cobus looked down at his feet.

"All right, John."

Emma came up to John and put her arms round him. "We'll look after her while you're away, John. Don't you worry. But come back here before you leave, if they'll let you."

"I will," John promised.

He looked at Mary as he picked up his musket, and she went to the door ahead of him. It had begun to snow. He could see the flakes snared in her hair against the light from the small window.

For a moment neither of them spoke.

Then Mary said, "I told her we'd call the baby after your Pa, John. Do you mind? It made her happy."

"I don't mind." He answered without thinking, mechanically. He was thinking of the long marches through the woods with Sullivan's army, in the Indian country. He suddenly shook himself out of it. They wouldn't be going into Indian country. "I think it's fine," he said. "Did she ask you?"

"Oh, no. I just thought of it, when I started telling her."

Mary was silent again.

When she lifted her face her eyes were clear.

"You'd better go up now, John."

She hated for him to go. But she didn't want men thinking John behindhand, now he was corporal.

"Yes," he said. "Good-bye, Mary. I'll try to come back before we leave. But take care of yourself."

"Don't worry about me." She made herself smile, not thinking how dark it was. "I'm tougher than I look. You ought to know that, John."

He leaned over her quickly, kissing her, and turned away towards the dark wall of the fort.

The wind was going down. Already, under the falling snow, a heaped bonfire in the centre of the parade was putting light on the inner walls of the blockhouses. The points of the stockade stood out needlelike and black. John saw men moving in through the snow, carrying their guns under their arms, the muzzles pointed down. The dark tracks they left on the whitening ground were like the gathering of a web towards the open gate.

There was no noise inside the fort, except the crackling of the fire and the mutter of men's voices. When John entered, he found them lining up in companies along the four sides of the parade. They went to their own companies; Demooth's (Demooth was gone, but young Lieutenant Tygert was in command of it) had only twelve men left. John, the corporal, Gil Martin, Boleo and Helmer, the Rangers. Clem Coppernol was not fit for a march. And a few men who used to live in Schuyler; Spankrable and the two Kasts. John moved over to join them, asking Martin in a low voice whether he had heard the news.

"The express came in just a little while before you did. The British have burned Warrensbush and crossed the river to Johnstown. They had six hundred men. Willett chased them. He licked them outside of Johnstown. But they got away. They headed west, north of Stone Arabia. Willett was at Stone Arabia when he sent the express up. He's waiting to find out which way they're headed and he wants us ready to cut them off."

"Willett licked them?"

"Yes, with four hundred."

Gil's thin face looked set and red against the leaping firelight.

Before the fire Bellinger was checking in the militia as they entered the fort. The sentries on the rifle platform stood up over him, half lighted against the snowing night, watching the parade inside as much as the surrounding darkness.

Every now and then a man came forward to the fire with an armful of logs and threw them on the flames. Ten minutes later, after another freshening of the fire, Bellinger closed his book.

The men fell silent. He stood, with his rounded shoulders, staring back at them. He did not seem to speak loudly, but everyone heard him plainly.

"I guess you know what's happened. Butler's in the valley. Butler and Ross with six hundred men. They ain't just Indians. They're Tories and regulars, trained soldiers. But Willett's licked them with four hundred militia."

The silence continued. But Bellinger did not look as if he expected a cheer or anything like that. He was thinking about things, the way all of them were thinking.

"We've had our farms wiped out. It's been four years. We've had the Butlers down here and we had John Johnson last year, and we've never had a real crack at them since Oriskany. We had Nicholas Herkimer then, and we've got Willett now. And we licked them then."

He was looking at the ground, watching the snow melt back from the fire.

"Willett wants the whole bunch of you ready when he gives the word. I don't know when that's going to be. But last June I promised him we'd have ninety men when he asked for them. I want you all to make sure you got powder and ball. If you ain't filled up, get it to the magazines. I guess we all feel just about the same. Go back to bed when you get done. If I want you to-night I'll let off the gun." He raised his face towards the swivel on the southeast corner. "Bring a blanket with you and the warmest shirt you've got. Herkimer men better stay here in the fort."

He turned his back on them and trudged into his room.

So they weren't to go yet. John drew a deep breath. He had powder enough and ball; he had filled his flask that morning. He heard Gil ask Joe Boleo if he wouldn't come back to the Martin cabin, so he himself asked Adam Helmer to the Weavers'. Adam thanked him, but declined.

Adam had figured that he could perfectly well get over to Herkimer and tell Betsey Small what was going to happen. If the gun went off he could run back long before any body of men could leave the fort.

As he slipped out of the gate he saw Doc Petry stumping back to his office in which he now lived, ate, dispensed, and slept.

Adam trotted down to the river crossing and hopped into a boat and rowed himself over. In thirty minutes he was inside the Herkimer stockade. Five minutes later he had got Betsey out and told her.

They stood in the lee of the church wall.

"Listen, Betsey," he said, "Butler's coming up the valley."

"Yes, Adam," she said quietly. "But what are you doing over here?"

"Oh hell," he said, "can't I do anything to suit you?"

Her voice was slow with the same quiet amusement she always showed towards him.

"A lot of things you do suit me fine. But what do you expect me to do? Cry? Laugh? Kiss you, I expect."

"Kissing's better than nothing."

You could have cut his head off with a feather when she said quietly:—

"All right. Where are you?"

She put her arms around his neck, and Adam locked her in his arms. He gave it to her, but he couldn't even make her gasp. And he had been saving up two years just to give it to her. Beside her, Polly Bowers was like putty. It made him mad, and he started casting his eyes round for a place they could get away to, under cover. You couldn't take a girl out in the snow, somehow; but while he was thinking about it, she had slipped out of his arms.

"There. That ought to suit you."

Adam felt suddenly hurt.

"Betsey!"

"What is it?" She sounded so kind, God damn her, she was probably laughing at him.

"I thought we was just beginning," he muttered. "I was just thinking where we could go."

"I'm not one of your girls, Adam." She laughed softly. "Can't you tell the difference?"

"I can," he said glumly. "What do you want me to do, marry you?"

"You've never asked me."

Adam knew he was a fool to say it.

"All right. Will you marry me?"

"You sound as if you was swearing, Adam. But I will. When you leave me to go horning round the country, I want the law."

As she laughed again, he caught hold of her.

"Come on, where can we go?"

"I'll tell you after we're wedded."

"But we can't get married now."

"Well, then, we can't go anywhere. I'm not taking chances, Adam."

He swore at her, cajoled, pleaded with her; but nothing could shake her amused silence.

"By God. I'll wake the domine."

That jolted her. "You can't do that. You'll make a scandal."

"For God's sake, what do you want me to do?"

He stood like a muddled bear, confronting the snow and darkness. She laid her long hand on his arm. "Poor Adam," she said. Her voice grew sober. "You've promised me, ain't you?"

"Yes."

"You'll marry me when you come back? You'll swear it?"

"I'll swear it. Cross my heart. Honest to God, Betsey."

"I want banns read. I want the whole business. So everybody will know I've got you." She gave a low, delicious laugh.

He didn't answer her with words. He knew now that she was acting like a skittish mare, all along. But he knew that she would hold him to his word. He didn't care. As he reached out for her she put aside his hands. "Come with me."

She led him to the door of the northwest blockhouse. Captain Moody's men were quartered in the other. There was no one here but Moody himself, and he slept on the bottom floor.

She put her hand on Adam's lips. Her fingers felt cold as rifle iron, so cold that he had a sense of heat beneath the icy skin.

"He's deaf," she whispered. "But be quiet."

They stole past the captain's bunk and up the stairs to the loft. The paneless window frames were faintly marked by snow upon the sills. The place was empty and bare and smelled of cold; but when Adam followed her up through the loft she met him quietly. There was a sureness in the way she came to him in the dark. He might have known. And then when he had her she went all soft, shaking as if her soul had gone away from her.

4. The Last Muster

The dawn of October 28 was windless and cold. When Gil got out of bed to start the fire up, the valley was white with snow and all the trees metallic from the frozen mist. The sky was so clear, just before sunrise, that it looked colorless.

There had been no sound from the fort. Lana dressed and moved furtively about the cabin as the first sticks caught.

"Do you think you'll have to go to-day, dear?"

"I don't know," he whispered. "We're waiting to hear from Willett."

After that they were silent. The children, Joe Boleo, Mrs. McKlennar, and the negress lay like logs of wood under their blankets, heads covered for warmth. The paleness of the light dimly entering the paper panes increased the sense of cold and made them look as if they would sleep forever. Crouching down before the tiny fire, side by side, Lana and Gil had this waking moment to themselves, and though they could not talk, they were conscious of each other's nearness. In their unspoken thoughts affection served as well as speech. When, without looking from the fire, Gil put out his hand, Lana's was ready to meet it. They stayed so, watching the fire grow, watching the vapor of their breaths diminish, for several minutes, until the first thin warmth made itself felt beyond the confines of the hearth.

Gil stepped outside for more wood, and then took the bucket and his axe down to the nearest spring. When he had gone, Lana's tears welled up. For an instant she let them come in the sheer luxury of her love; then she wiped them away to smile and take the icy bucket from Gil's red cold fist, and fill the kettle for their morning mush. Again they stayed together till the first faint tinkles of the heating water roused the negress, as any sound of warmth invariably did. Probably she had been awake all along, but fire sounds meant nothing to Daisy unless they were hot enough to cook with. Gil and Lana relinquished each other for the day.

The men left the cabin after breakfast. They found the Herkimer militia already cooking at the fort and Bellinger sorting provisions in the magazine. No word had come in from the east. None came all morning.

But in the afternoon a man who stood watch beyond the Canada Creek ford let off his musket. The men mounted the rifle platforms to look out. During the day the frost had melted from the trees and the limbs were black and wet against the sky and the soft gray indistinctness of the hills. The wind, which had returned more gently towards noon, was carrying a high scud of cloud, shadowing the valley. The universe looked cold and smelled of coming snow.

Underneath, along the straight road, they saw the line of men in double files marching towards them. They walked like tired men. They hunched themselves against the wind which picked at their nondescript clothes, and kept the locks of their muskets under their arms, the barrels pointing forward and down. But their pace kept them moving with a dogged steadiness that had the teams on the three provision wagons reeking to keep up in the half-frozen muddy ruts.

Bellinger let off no cannon salute. There was no powder to spare for salutes, and he knew that Willett wasn't the kind of man that wanted one. The arrival of the weary downriver militia and the entrance to the fort were accomplished in a silence as grim as the gray passing of the day.

Willett went straight to Bellinger's room and called him in. He had discarded his long campaign coat for a woolen hunting shirt and high fur cap; except for his square shoulders he looked like any farmer of militia. But under his fatigue was the inevitable twinkle of the small blue eyes. He wiped the drop from his nose and shook hands.

"I hear you licked them," Bellinger said.

Willett grinned.

"We didn't actually whip them. They ran away. It was too dark for me to chase them." He glanced away from Bellinger. "*We* ran away once. But Rowley took their flank, and, by God, we came back again."

He let himself down on his chair.

"I followed them to Stone Arabia, but they'd struck north of there. I sent a scout after them to see if they were heading for Oneida Lake or straight for Buck's Island through the woods. The scout's to send an express as soon as they find out. So I marched up here. It was hard going. Have you got your ninety men?"

"They're waiting."

"Fine. Got any boys who really know the woods north of here?"

"Yes. Bolco and Helmer do."

"Good. I've got about fifty Oneida Indians under a fat old fool called Blue Back. They turned up after the fighting was over. But I don't want to trust them for scouts."

"Blue Back knows every leaf on the West Canada that's fallen in the last forty years. It's his private hunting ground."

"I'm glad to know it. I'll use him with your two men."

"Do you want me to keep the men belonging to this fort inside? The Herkimer men are staying here."

"Let your men go home. We won't start now before to-morrow. Can you help me out with five days' rations for four hundred men? I've brought along about three hundred, including the Indians."

"I think so."

"One thing more. You're to stay here."

"That's not fair," said Bellinger.

Willett grinned wearily in his face.

"I'm not going to argue. They're orders. Look here, Bellinger. You've got to. If anything goes wrong we've got to leave one man here who knows how to hold onto this land. You've had more practice than me."

Bellinger glowered. "It's a dirty trick, Willett."

"If you think you're going to lose credit, you needn't worry. Nobody's going to get credit going with me. I'm supposed to be turning up at Ballston to protect Albany from Ross and Butler."

"I don't give a damn about the credit, Willett. I just want to get at them once and see some of them knowing they're licked."

"I know," said Willett quietly. "I wish I had a drink."

"Verdammt! You'll have it then, for not stealing my medical supply."

Both men turned round to confront Dr. Petry, who held a small keg in both arms as a man might hold a baby on his chest. He peered at them for a moment through his bushy eyebrows, then advanced to set the keg on the table in front of Willett.

" 'For wounds and surgical needs,' " he read the label. "Well, I'm prescribing now. A little glass apiece—and one for the doctor, Peter. I'd get a hemorrhage watching you drink if I didn't have some too."

John had gone home again—the second time after he had said good-bye —and he felt foolish about it. He was beginning to think that maybe after all the army would not march. But the way Mary's face lit up when he came through the door dispelled all his uneasiness.

He told them at supper the extraordinary news that Willett had brought with him, that General Washington had taken his army south to confront Cornwallis in Virginia. They had no idea, any of them, what it could mean; but Gil Martin had heard Willett telling Bellinger in a very excited way, as if it were a tremendous thing for Washington to have done.

Cobus's eyes glistened.

"Next year I'm going to 'list with the army," he said.

John laughed.

"Enlist for what? A drummer boy?"

Cobus's face was still a round one, and now the sullenness of it on top of his skinny body made even Emma smile.

She said to him, "Don't you mind John. I'll let you go, next year, if you want to. But come along with me now."

"Where?"

"I want to visit with Mrs. Volmer."

"I don't want to go. What do I have to for, anyway?"

Mrs. Weaver took him firmly by the hand. "You come along." She said from the door, "We'll be down there for a couple of hours."

As she closed the door, John smiled at Mary. Both of them realized that Emma had never been a special friend of Widow Volmer.

"Ma's making up," John said. "She'll go on making up to you now all her life. You'll see."

Mary said loyally, "She's been good to me ever since we got married, John."

It made him deeply happy.

The wind was not strong enough to make the cabin cold when the fire drew so well. They were like an old married couple sitting side by side upon the hearth, John thought, and he said, "You ought to have some fleece to spin."

Mary smiled. She had been thinking the same thing. She would not need much wool.

"You with a pipe and reading out of a book to me."

"I never read very good," John said.

"You would if you practised at it. My Pa used to read real fine. I think he read better than Mr. Rozencrantz. . . ."

Her face stilled with her voice. But even memory of Christian Reall's death at Oriskany could not deprive them of their contentment at having the cabin to themselves. All that was long ago; and John had a queer sense of the three of them sitting there.

"Suppose it's a girl, how can we name it after Pa?"

Mary said, "I knew a woman named Georgina once."

"Why, yes," said John.

The fire popped and sparked and they watched the exploded coal gradually glimmer out on the damp dirt floor.

"Do you suppose that battle down in Johnstown means this war is getting over, John?"

"I don't know. It's only a little battle the way they think of things, I guess. Not like Burgoyne's army. Nor not like General Washington's in Virginia. I guess down there they don't think it's much."

"I mean, would it end the war up here, John?"

"I don't know. I guess not."

She said, "It would be nice, wouldn't it? We could live in our own cabin. Have you figured where it would be, John?"

"Why, I guess we'd go back to Deerfield on Pa's place."

"I'd like that. It used to be nice there."

"Yes," he said.

She lifted her face and looked across at him. She smiled with her eyes. She felt so still, watching his intent face studying the fire. It didn't matter in a moment like this what you said, so long as you talked softly. . . .

The express from Stone Arabia arrived in the darkness before dawn; the horse dead lame and the man's hands so cold he could hardly let loose the bridle reins.

He brought the scout's dispatch. Butler and Ross had taken a circle straight north. The scout thought they must have got lost. Now they were heading west so far above the valley he thought they surely must be striking towards Buck's Island.

Willett and Bellinger, shivering in their drawers, read it in the light of the coals.

"Where would they hit the Creek?" Willett asked.

"I guess about twenty miles north. Blue Back could probably tell you, or Joe Boleo, but Joe's sleeping out."

"Let's get Blue Back."

A sentry routed out the Indian, bringing him in, blinking his sleepy eyes and hugging himself with his blanket. "How," he said to Bellinger, and then to Willett, "How? I fine."

Immediately he squatted in front of the fire where the heat drew an unholy smell from him, and lighted the greasy rounds of his brown cheeks with shiny moons.

Bellinger explained while Blue Back slowly rubbed his belly underneath his shirt and fetched up silent belches one by one.

"Where do you think they'd cross, Blue Back?"

"Indians lost," said Blue Back. "Senecas, Mohawks, no damn good. Get lost. White men go for Fairfield. Make find Jerseyfield road."

"I think he's right," Bellinger said.

"Sure," said Blue Back. "Ask Joe Boleo."

"How far north is that?" Willett asked.

"One day."

"How many miles?"

"One day," Blue Back repeated with firm politeness.

Willett gave up.

"Do you think we can find the army up there?"

"Sure yes," said Blue Back. "Like rum. Like drink."

"I haven't any likker."

"Sorry," said Blue Back. "Walking bad. More snow."

"What time is it?"

Bellinger replied.

"About five."

"We'll have daylight enough in about an hour. You'd better get your men."

As Bellinger went towards the door, Blue Back asked anxiously, "Shoot cannon?"

Bellinger grinned stiffly, nodded, and went out. He felt the cold against his empty belly.

Willett said, "You better get back to your boys and cook breakfast."

"Stay here," said Blue Back quietly. He drew his blanket over head and hat and crouched beneath it, motionless as a dormant toad beneath a basswood leaf.

When the swivel thudded, he gave one convulsive flop, but he did not emerge until he heard Bellinger shouting in the parade. Then he poked out his head and eyed Willett dubiously.

"You take cannon?"

Willett shook his head impatiently.

"Fine," said Blue Back, standing up. "I go too."

The muster was as silent a business as the arrival on the afternoon before. The men entering the fort from the surrounding cabins were told to return for their breakfasts and report in half an hour. The men cooking over the open fires in the parade had little to say. The feeling of winter hung in the air. The sky was lustreless. The wind drew steadily from the north, and though they did not feel it in the shelter of Fort Dayton, they could hear its voice in the woods.

Gil and Joe Boleo ate together with Lana and Daisy waiting on them, and the two little boys, staring like owls, pressed close together across the hearth where they had been told to stay. Their fascinated eyes had watched their father and Uncle Joe oiling their rifles; they had seen the yet more wonderful operation of Joe whetting his knife and Indian hatchet on a stone, sinking the edges into the board table when he was satisfied. He ate between these implements, knife to right and tomahawk to left. The hinges of his jaw worked visibly and audibly in the thin leather above his cheeks. Only occasionally his eye slid round toward the children's solemn faces.

There was a hush in the cabin; partly from the belly-shrinking cold, partly from the thinness of the dawn light, which made one wish to yawn; partly from the anxiety in Lana's eyes that seemed to have affected Mrs. McKlennar as well as Daisy. The widow lay on her low hemlock bed with her coat still thrown over her blankets. Her long pale face was tilted forward awkwardly by her hands behind her head. She had not even a snort this morning, nor a single caustic word to relieve her feelings. But when Gil and Joe got up she said, "Come kiss me, Gil."

Gil got down on his knees on the floor to kiss her and she took one hand from behind her head. Her fingers seemed fleshed with ivory.

"Good-bye, lad," she said. Then, "Good-bye, Joe."

Joe took off the hat he had just put on and said, "Good-bye, ma'am." He turned to Daisy. "When I get back I want one of them hot poncs."

Then the two men at last came to the two boys, and Gil kissed them and Joe tossed them once in the air.

They went out through the door with Lana following them, huddling her clothes about her against the cold. The door closed for a moment, then Gilly yelled, "Uncle Joe!" He had been watching that knife and tomahawk all along. When Joe put in his head and saw them, he said, "How'd I come to do that?" He closed the door behind him and put them in his sheath and belt and said to Gilly, "I ought to have you along with me to look after me."

He hesitated with his hand on the doorlatch and met Mrs. McKlennar's eye.

"You've got a good heart, Joe."

Joe blushed brick red and bolted.

The men marched off over the thin snow side by side. Lana, her face all pinched against the cold, watched their bodies merge among the tree trunks, and then pass round the corner of the fort. She put her hand to her mouth. It felt frosty where Gil had kissed her. A few snowflakes, hard as shot, drove scatteringly after them.

The muster in the parade was performed quietly. Willett and Bellinger stood side by side. Once Willett shouted, "I want no dead pans. Keep your priming covered." The men formed lines, holding their rifles under their arms. They kept shifting from foot to foot with the cold. The dim light and the snow ran the assorted faded colors of their clothes into one indistinguishable muddy brown.

Bellinger said, "Every man carries his own rations."

The rations were passed out and folded inside the blankets and the blankets strapped to the backs.

"We're going to march fast," Willett said quietly. "No straggling. Any man we leave behind will have to look out for himself."

For one cold moment more he spoke to Bellinger. Then he called for Demooth's company.

Young Lieutenant Tygert stepped forward, followed by the twelve men. Willett looked them over.

"You boys are to be our advance. I want Helmer, Boleo, and Martin to step forward." They did so. For an instant Willett eyed Helmer's huge bulk; what he thought of him was impossible to tell. "Better have one more. Name one," he said to Martin.

Gil never knew why he called for John. He had not seen him; perhaps it was because John and Mary had been on his mind. As John stepped forward, Willett said, "You look pretty young."

John saluted, and Bellinger said over Willett's shoulder, "Corporal Weaver served with General Sullivan."

"You'll do," Willett said without changing expression. "I want you four men to scout ahead. I'm telling you before the army that Ross and Butler are running away. We're going to try and head them. They've still got more men than we are, but they're running. Blue Back, the Indian, says they'll head for Fairfield."

Joe, characteristically holding his rifle by the muzzle and resting his chin on his hands, nodded. "They'll head for the Jerseyfield road and pass Mount's mill. That takes them on the upper trail across the West Canada, to strike the Black River. Where do you want to hit them, General?"

Willett did not bat an eye.

"I leave it to you where. I want to hit them, that's all."

"We'd better cross the Crick this side of Schell's Bush, by the shallow ford, and then we'll hit for Jerseyfield. Better pick up their trail than take a chance they'll get lost again."

"It's up to you," said Willett. "Strike your own pace, but make it a fast one. We'll keep up. Good-bye, Bellinger."

He shook hands, picked up his rifle, and followed Demooth's company through the gates. Outside they were joined by the fifty Oneidas. These, it was arranged, should screen the flanks, but Blue Back, beaming and saying, "How!" joined the four men at the head. He trotted along with a paunchy jounce, covering the ground as fast as Adam and going as quietly as Joe. Gil and John found themselves pressed to keep up.

They rapidly drew away from the main force, along the Schell's Bush road, and for fifteen minutes held the pace. Then Joe lifted his hand. They jogged more comfortably. The first burst had warmed them, and they thought that the men behind would be a long time getting warm. There was not enough snow to keep the frost from getting at your feet.

"We won't spread out till after we've got over the ford," said Joe.

They jogged along in single file. First Joe, making pace, then Blue Back padding in his tracks, then Gil, then John. Adam, hitching up his blanket, came easily in the rear, swinging his big shoulders and humming to himself.

5. The Two Camps in Jerseyfield

The West Canada Creek rolled down through the hills, opaque and brown and swift, a thigh-deep flood even on the shallow ford. It thrust against them icily as they worked their way across holding each other with their left hands, their right hands keeping their rifles over their heads. Adam stemmed the current for them, surefooted, solid as a rock.

The five men jogged into the woods to make a short circle. Finding all clear, Joe brought them back to the ford. A few moments after their return they saw Lieutenant Tygert lead the advance down to the water's edge. "Tell him they better cut poles and march across in squads," Joe said to Adam. Adam lifted his stentorian voice just as Willett's long red face appeared. In a moment, unheard across the rushing water, they saw the men take hatchets to the nearest maple saplings.

The snow was thickening, falling with a steady slant into the current of the stream as if it urged it onward. On the pointed hills, the pines were swaying their boughs against the sky.

Joe sniffed the air.

"It's making up," he said. "We'd better not get too far ahead." He turned to the Indian. "How about it, Blue Back?"

Blue Back, the only one of them who had not started shivering, grunted. He said his Indians would keep track of them, and pointed. Already two groups of Indians were trotting down from the flanks and taking to the water one behind the other.

"All right," said Joe.

He trotted off, keeping along the eastern shore of the creek, following a trail that was little more than a deer run. He kept Gil and John with him and sent Adam and Blue Back out to right and left.

All morning they trotted into the blinding snow, winding back and forth to find the easier going, but always going north.

At noon they halted briefly to build a fire and soften some salt beef in Joe's small kettle, fishing out the meat with sticks, swallowing the hot lumps whole and feeling them in their bellies, and taking turns at the resulting broth. The Indian and Adam drifted in through the snow while the three were finishing, and Adam cooked his own food. The Indian huddled in his blanket and gnawed a piece of quitcheraw, but accepted a drink or two from the kettle afterwards. While they were still at it, Joe sent John up a tree to see out over the woods, and he reported smoke visible in the south.

"They're keeping close just like Willett promised. That man has got the makings of a regular timber beast." Joe tilted his face and yelled, "Look north!"

They watched John edge around the tree trunk, but after a minute he shouted down that he could not see anything against the snow.

"They wouldn't be this far south," Joe said. "Come down, John."

They left their little fire to be put out by the snow, which was now beginning to drift. The going became heavier, and they dropped to a much slower pace. By four o'clock they were coming out on the black moss country that stretched from above Fairfield to the Mount's Creek Valley.

The wind swept over these uplands unhindered except by small stands of poplar. As the men stood with their shoulders to the storm, the snow appeared to drive horizontally past their eyes. They had to shout when they wanted to make themselves heard.

"We can't find them to-night," Adam shouted.

Blue Back shook his head, and Joe said, "This snow would cover their tracks in twenty minutes the way it's drifting."

The wind was hitting the flats so hard that it lifted the fallen snow in clouds that disappeared in the air like blown dust. The shirts of the men were already stiff and white with it.

Gil and John, less hardened to woods running than the other three, stood side by side, fighting for their breath. Gil thought the boy looked cold. "All right?" he said close to his ear.

John turned his head. The snow had whitened his eyebrows and lashes. His thin pale cheeks suddenly shot up spots of color.

"Yes," he yelled, and once more turned his face into the wind. Gil looked north. It was getting dark—not dark exactly. He had not been conscious of the fading of light. Instead the whiteness of the storm appeared to increase, draw closer, causing an illusion of emptiness in the land beyond it.

But now as he looked with John he had a glimpse of the conical tops of hills, revealed for a moment between the snowstorm and the sky. Blue Back also saw them.

"Mount's Creek up there," he said.

Then the hills were shut off from view.

Joe yelled, "I think we'd better go back. We'll catch Willett in that stand of spruce. It's the only good place to camp."

As they turned, Gil thought he heard voices. They came from the northwest, very faintly. For an instant they sounded to him like lost men calling for help. Then the wind raised itself against his hearing, and there was only that and the hiss of drifting snow, which was a part of it.

But the old Indian was standing still with his flat nose to the north.

"What's up, you dumb fool?" Joe asked.

"Wolves."

"You heard wolves?"

"Hear 'em plenty."

Joe said, "Come on. We can tell Willett we've found Butler."

As he went over the edge of the flats, and the wind leaped off into space above their heads, he said, "Wolves like that must be tagging the army."

He plunged down the slope, knee-deep in the loose snow. John followed him, walking very erect, and the rest kept to their tracks.

They discovered the militia, a brown attenuated streak against the whiteness, slowly pressing towards them. The Indians had fallen in close on either flank.

Joe found Willett marching near the rear guard.

"You better camp, General."

"Why?"

"Can't camp on the flats. No shelter. There's a good spruce stand off on your left. It's out of the wind. We've found Butler up ahead."

"Found him? How far?"

"We don't know exactly where. But we'll let you know before morning." He paused. "You can't tackle an army in a storm like this, mister. Hell, you'd be shooting yourselves half the time."

"All right," said Willett. "Go ahead."

Joe lead the way to the spruce woods, where the militia set to breaking off dead limbs. The fires burnt hot under the dark trees, first dull spots of red against the white sheen of snow; then, as they reached upward, creating their own light, and forcing back the storm. The men cut saplings, and piled on lengths of wood while others started sticking up spruce-limb shanties. A little brook served them for water. They lay around on the snow under their shanties, watching the snow melt away round the fires, listening to the hiss, and the crackle of burning. Beyond the confines of the woods they could yet see in the last daylight the driving passage of the snow; but in the woods the flakes descended easily, making a watchful pattern against the darkness, or occasionally a burst came down directly, swishing over the fir branches, leaving in its wake released boughs waving, oddly black.

As soon as he had eaten, Joe Boleo rounded up Blue Back and a couple of Oneidas. The four went over to the shanty under which Willett sat wrapped in his blanket—only his fur cap showing. Joe prodded him.

"General."

Willett's long red face emerged.

"We're starting now," said Joe. "We'll find out where they be and what they look like. We ought to be back before midnight."

"Good luck."

The four figures disappeared beyond the firelight with complete suddenness, as if they had walked through a blank wall. As soon as they were out of sight, Blue Back took the lead. Even Joe admitted that the old fellow knew this country better than any other man alive. Having heard those wolves, he would be able to walk straight to where they had been.

They climbed out of the spruce hollow and got the wind in their faces on the barren flats. It was too dark to see whether the storm were slacking, but the loose-blown snow stung them, and they took a slow hunching pace.

They went perfectly straight for more than two miles through the darkness, seeing nothing, hearing nothing, not even each other, not even themselves. The wind was piercing cold.

Joe had a general idea of where they would come out, and as soon as they entered the woods he realized that Blue Back had struck the Black Creek Valley. They dropped down a long slope of rough going with the snow in places well over their knees, crossed the creek on a huge fallen ash. It was uncanny the way Blue Back had come out within a hundred yards of that ash bridge.

The woods were heavier on the far side, and the wind was a lofty sound in a higher sky. Under it they heard the wolves following the hills to the north. Blue Back stood still for a long time listening to them. Then he turned his direction a little westward and went on.

Joe knew exactly where he was when they broke into the next shallow valley. The creek ran out of the woods on his right, broken over rapids, a quick-running black rough water. They crossed it on the remains of a dam. On the far side they caught their feet on square timbers under the snow.

"Mount's mill," grunted the Indian.

A little way beyond was where the barn had stood in which Mount's two youngsters had been scalped so soon after Oriskany.

Blue Back trotted into the woods above the place and then swung down the valley, due west. The howling of the wolves was now closer and above them.

Suddenly Blue Back halted. He stood still as a post. Behind him the woodsman and the two Indians were motionless. Barely discernible, two shapes broke clear of the darkness, themselves embodiments of it, and slipped away.

"Jesus, they're getting bold," thought Joe.

Ten minutes more of cautious feeling forward showed them the first campfires.

No one was standing sentry in the storm. The fires made a long line through the woods, and the men lay close to them, sprawled out; many of them had lain still so long that their blankets were whitened by the snow. In the largest part of the camp, three or four horses huddled together, lifting their heads and snorting at the scent of wolves. But the men paid no attention to them.

The whole place, but for the horses, seemed to sleep. It was a sleep like death, as if the snow that fell on them were a drug they had had too much of.

But while the three Indians and Joe watched, they saw a man stir in one of the shelters, shake off the snow from his blanket, and rise. His face was haggard. His green and black, stained uniform and his leather skullcap on his unclubbed black hair identified him to Joe. He could have picked him off then, and got safe away without trouble, but Willett wanted to hit the army, not Butler.

The man's eyes passed over where the four scouts stood, swept the camp. They saw his lips move. He walked to the edge of the firelight and bent down and prodded a snow-covered shape with his sword. The man lurched over, rose, and lifted his hand, and Butler struck him with the flat of the sword and drove him out to his sentry post.

The man was a Highlander. The knees under the kilt were black as chilled beef. He looked pathetic and wild, shivering, with the icy musket in his hand, confronting the woods, the wind, and the wild voices of the wolves.

He was within a hundred yards of Joe, but he saw neither Joe nor the Indians. What he saw, no one could tell. His eyes were opened inward on his own thoughts.

For a few moments more the four watched Butler go down the camp, beating out the delinquent sentries, indomitably, patiently, wearily, forcing them to posts. Then the scout backed slowly off. The two younger Indians followed reluctantly. There was easy scalping material around that camp. They knew it—as the wolves knew it.

Blue Back took a straight overland course directly to Willett's camp, where Joe roused the colonel.

"Come in here," said Willett. "It's warmer."

Joe sat down beside the colonel and made his report. "They're only three miles north and they look played out. I couldn't see that they carried much food, General."

"Eating their horses as they go along," commented Willett. "We'll go for them before sunrise to-morrow. You've done fine, Major."

Joe grinned.

"I seen Butler," he said. "He was the only man with gimp to put the sentries out."

Willett nodded.

"I told him once he was going to be hung," he said. "After Oriskany. We've been far apart since then."

"I could of killed him easy."

6. John Weaver

The militia camp began to come to life at the dusk hour before dawn. The low fires were replenished. The men moved stiffly, semi-animate, with the cold in their bones. It was still dark in the spruce woods. They ate briefly of boiled beef thickened with cornmeal. Then Willett called them together.

"The enemy's three miles in the northwest. We'll follow our same formation till we hit them. The levies will follow me to the centre. The rear guard break along their south flank. They'll probably try for the West Canada. We want to turn them into the woods."

Helmer, Boleo, Blue Back, Gil, and John Weaver found themselves again in the advance. When they came outside the spruces, they found that the snow for the time being had stopped falling. But the heavy leaden clouds were still in labor over the shadowless land. The cold felt damper with the snow withheld. The breaths of the advancing brown militia crossing the white upland clung to their faces white as cotton. Behind them the beaten path of their feet stretched to the edge of the valley from which they had risen.

It took them an hour to reach the camp site of the enemy; but the enemy had moved as early as themselves. The trail they had broken was like a wide road through the woods. Ahead along the hills the wolves still howled, marking their place.

Willett jogged up to the front.

He formed parties. The Indians split again and went ahead wide on either flank, two horns to the main body of the militia. Like eyes before the head, the same scouts were advanced for contact.

"We've got a beaten path," said Willett. "I want you boys to take their rear guard as quick as you can. We'll be right after you."

The march was now a steady run in the beaten track of the army. Even so it was an hour before the scouts first came up with the enemy's rear.

John Weaver found himself on the right, with old Blue Back half a dozen yards beyond him. In spite of the hard going and the fast pace, he did not feel quite warm. He could not get his mind on the business properly. The white woods seemed to blur before his eyes, trees swimming together, and his mind kept turning to home.

His first awareness of the enemy was a loud yell from Blue Back. He lifted his head dully to see the Indian flop on his belly in the snow, and, looking over him, he saw half a dozen men in red plaid kilts trot out of a clump of trees. He could not realize what it meant for a moment. His head was full of wonder. He had just thought how it would be if George Weaver were not dead after all, if he were to come home and find a grandson named after him. It was the last thought John ever had. One of the Highlanders had heard the old Indian's warning yell. He turned, sighted the standing boy, lifted his rifle, and fired. The ball struck John square in the chest. He jumped straight up, like a deer, clear of the ground.

As he heard the rifle shot, Gil whirled towards it and broke out of the underbrush to see John pitch upon his face. Blue Back fired at the same instant. The belly-filling roar of the brown musket brought a snow load down from the nearest tree. Two clouds of black smoke wavered a little way apart. But the Highlander was not dead. He lay on a doubled leg. His comrades were like a pack boring into the woods.

As Gil stopped beside John, Blue Back humped forward through the snow. The scalp yell broke from his old throat with an unaccustomed quaver. Gil knelt down beside John. But John was dead as he lay, full pitch in the snow, covering his own blood. At the same instant the cry of the Highlander was drowned by a deep roar behind them all. The militia came through the woods in a brown wave. They passed on the dead run, without much order. And after that first yell they were silent. The battle had begun. Gil was picked up by the mass of men and carried forward, leaving John where he was. He had a glimpse of Blue Back beside the dead Highlander, sticking the wet scalp in his belt and lurching into his fat waddle. Then they were in the woods and taking running shots at the army ahead.

The hostile army never stopped. When a man fell he was pushed aside. Feet trod him into the snow. The rear guard of Highlanders was picked up by the militia and surrounded and disarmed, but the main force continued as if they had heard nothing.

They trotted in two files, making for the creek. A little before the valley was reached, the snow began again. And on the near side of the West Canada, Walter Butler rallied the Rangers. They made a stand. It held long enough to let the army get across. The Rangers plunged in, swimming and being carried down where the two units of Oneidas waited hanging over both banks with their hatchets ready.

But the militia were not to be stopped. They surged down the bank and into the water just as Butler lifted his exhausted horse on the far bank. In a volley of shots he was seen to pitch. The horse flung out on the shore, shook him off, and went galloping after the army, raising wet clots of snow. A couple of Indians coming up the bank found Butler, scalped him where he lay, and passed after the horse.

The snow came thicker. The militia, who had crossed, broke into the woods. All morning they followed the fleeing army, picking them off like driven hares. None of them stopped except to fling their blankets off, then their guns. Finally it seemed as if half the British were running unarmed, west and north, on their blind trail towards the Black River Valley.

It was a little after noon that Willett finally worked to the head of the militia and stopped them fifteen miles beyond the Canada Creek. They stopped from exhaustion as much as from obedience, leaning on their guns in the falling snow and staring westward past the colonel over the wintry wilderness where the disrupted path of the beaten army still bore witness to their panic. Slowly a grin passed from Willett to the men.

The job was done at last. They had not captured the army, but everyone seemed to know that Butler was killed; and everyone knew what would happen to a foodless army in full rout, half armed, in eighty miles of pathless woods.

They turned slowly back, not talking, not keeping ranks, trudging for home. Along the way they saw the Oneidas reaping a harvest of scalps that was beyond the dreams and legends of all Indian history. They left them to their bloody work.

The militia reached West Canada Creek again a little before dark and pushed forward for four miles more on the back track. During the evening, Gil tried to find John Weaver's body. But it was not until Blue Back joined him that they found it. It had not been touched, for the wolves had passed on ahead at the first shooting and were now waiting the completion of the Oneidas' work. Gil found stones and brush to build around the body before it became dark.

The march home went quickly. They came over the ford at Schell's a little before sunset and reached Fort Dayton just at dark. Willett let them fire a full round of shots; and then for the first time they cheered. They saw the women rushing out. They saw the torches waving. And then, with unexampled extravagance, Bellinger let off a salute of four cannon. It nearly graveled poor old Blue Back, until he remembered that he had taken scalps himself. He twisted the hair round the muzzle of the ancient musket and started a crazy screeching which his Indians imitated. But they were hardly heard.

They streamed together into the fort, past the women and children, who began sobbing and crying with them, and rushing into the marching men to join their husbands.

Bellinger stood beside the gates. He kept yelling something. Yelling and yelling. Nobody heard for a while. Then Willett entered and met him. They talked for an instant. Willett's face blazed and went white. He jumped up on the blockhouse ladder and set off a swivel over their heads.

For an instant silence settled with the smoke. Through it his nasal voice came down.

"General Washington's taken Cornwallis in Virginia!"

It came to them all slowly. So slowly that Gil, with Lana under his arm, for an instant forgot. Then he saw Mary Weaver passing from group to group, her eyes searching every face with a stilled panic. He said something to Lana, and both of them moved after Mary.

She lay on her bed without crying. It was Emma who cried. The night was still at last. And the snow fell over the Mohawk without wind. Gil, Lana, and Joe Boleo stayed with them, helpless and wordless.

At his table in Bellinger's room in the fort, Willett was wearily writing his dispatch. He had got through with it. The invasion of Warrensbush, the fight at Johnstown, the loss of the enemy's trail, the sally north from

German Flats, the chase through the woods, the bloody crossing of the Creek, Butler's death, only one American killed. He ought to say something to show why he did not capture the army.

He rested his long face on his left hand and finally wrote:—

> In this situation, to the compassion of a starving wilderness, we left them. . . .

10

LANA (1784)

LANA brought the stool to the kitchen door for ten minutes' rest. With Gil away she had so much work to do in caring for the farm that these few minutes before the boys brought the cows in for milking were like a gift from God. The baby was asleep in the cradle with a rag over her to keep the flies off. It was a bad season for flies. So much wet, and then the midsummer heat that had brought the wheat on very fast. Too fast, Gil believed; he was afraid of rust. But the corn had thriven as they had never seen corn thrive before.

When they had returned to Deerfield a year ago, their hearts sank at the way berry vines and scrub brush had encroached on their cleared acres. Yet they had ploughed easily. In one season, Gil had restored all the land they had originally worked, and this summer it was under crops, with the corn in a brand-new lot.

The new cabin stood on the site of the old. It looked like the old cabin from the road, but the end that pointed towards the spring had an extra section in which Gil and Lana and the baby slept, while the two boys occupied the loft over the kitchen. The barn also was larger, for they had two cows and two calves; and instead of the old brown mare, which they had had to kill for food the year after the West Canada Creek battle, they now had a yoke of oxen. The oxen had seemed to them the first material evidence of their future prosperity—even to Lana, who longed for a boughten bed with cords and a feather mattress. She no longer slept as easily as she used to. Her back was apt to pain her after a full day's work from four to nine, as when she had to help get in the hay before a rain and leave her household work till after dark. But the boys helped now, raking, and fetching down the baby at her feeding hours, and saving their mother the walk back to the cabin. The oxen had cost Gil seventy dollars and the big cart thirty dollars more. He had had to borrow from Mark Demooth to make up half the price, so that they had a mortgage on the place; but that would be taken care of partially by back militia pay and the indemnity for the first burning of their farm when Congress started meeting claims. It was hard for them to have to wait so long when down in Ulster and New York claims were already being settled; but Mr.

Yates had explained to Gil that it was a question of votes and that when the new western county became politically important they would be paid surely. It was a matter of being patient.

It was hard for Gil to be patient. If he had had that pay, he could have bought the black girl Klock offered to sell him the week he went after the oxen. Klock's asking price was only a hundred and fifty dollars. To-day, Lana was inclined to share Gil's bitterness. With a girl to do the cooking and help with the cheese, she would have felt quite fresh for to-night's milking.

She did not resent Gil's absence. She had urged him to it. It was the fulfillment of a long-standing promise to take Mary Weaver into the woods and find John's grave. Lana loved Gil for being willing to take time off. They had left four days ago with old Blue Back, who swore he could go straight to the spot. . . .

The Weavers had returned to Deerfield at the same time as Mark Demooth. George and Demooth had been released from prison a year ago, and though George's ankles had been so burned from fetter sores that he was not able to do heavy field work, the Weavers, due to young Cobus's labors, had done as well as the Martins had. Of course, neither family could afford hired help like Demooth. He employed a young man and his wife, in Clem Coppernol's place, and the woman's sister, a pretty girl, whom Emma Weaver thought Demooth might marry even though she was not in his class.

"A durn sight better wife than the first, she'd make," said Emma.

Emma worked like a man. Though her bodily vigor seemed to have increased since George's return, she had become a fussy woman. Fussy over George, and yet more fussy over Mary and John's daughter, Georgina. At times it got on Mary's nerves, the way Emma interfered to spoil the child. But Mary was grateful for the kindness. She had grown into a fine, full-bosomed woman, whom Lana wished John might once see again—it was so unexpected. And it seemed tragic to her that those two should have had each other and been parted before the arrival of Mary's late beauty.

Just before she set out with Gil and the smelly old Indian, who was again pestering their farms as he had in the old days, with four black-eyed little brats trailing him into idle mischief, Mary had heard from her mother that she and her new husband, Rebus White (they had been married as soon as Mrs. Reall drew her indemnity from Congress), were planning to come west to the old Reall place and rebuild the mill. Deerfield would seem then as if it had never been destroyed.

It had not been hard for Gil and Lana to make up their minds to this return to Deerfield; there had been no other place for them to go to. Both Lana's parents had been killed in the wiping out of Fox's Mills. Only her married sister was left alive of her whole family.

As to the McKlennar farm, they had discovered, when Mrs. McKlennar died in the spring of '82, that her will must have burned in the house. So they had no legal title to the place. When they filed a claim, they were informed that the farm was forfeited for unpaid taxes and that their claim would be considered along with others. The man who succeeded in acquiring McKlennar's was a man from Springfield, Massachusetts, a Mr. Jonathan Allen, a decent man, they were told, though they had never seen

him. For when Gil was informed that his claim had been refused in favor
of an army veteran for unpaid service to his country, he had packed up
his family and come straight to Deerfield. As it was, it had been a hard
struggle to meet the taxes. Lana had shared Gil's bitterness then; but soon
she had got over it. Here there were no pushing Yankees to remind you
that the organized army and the New England states had seized the reins
of government. Here she could be reminded of her first arrival as a bride,
how she had been afraid of its dreariness and emptiness. Now it seemed
sweet to her in the rare moments when she found leisure to look out at it.

She lifted her head to listen for the two cowbells up Hazenclever hill.
But there was no sound yet, and she realized how cows hid themselves
away in swampy places on these hot days. She rested her head against the
doorsill, without fear of Gilly's getting lost. He was uncanny in his knowledge of the place. She felt quite safe about him and Joey.

The late afternoon sun poured over her. She was not disturbed by its
heat. She loved it, when she could be still in it. It seemed as though her
body never could get enough warmth after those last cold winters. How
the children had survived those damp cabins she never knew.

As she rested her head, her hair, brushed back above her ears to the
big low knot behind her head, showed silver wings. But her face was still
young, in spite of the lines that marked her cheeks, and her mouth retained
its tenderness. Only the lids of her closed eyes were thinner, and faintly
brushed with a brown shadow like a stain. . . .

In the complete stillness of the afternoon a hammering to the south broke
out like the sound of a woodpecker on a tree. But Lana did not lift her
head. She let the comforting sound drift into her. She knew what it was.
People were building over the Mohawk River beyond the fording place.
Several people. She had not met them yet, though Gil had gone over one
Sunday with Demooth and reported that they were Connecticut men.
But he liked one of them, a sensible, law-abiding man named Hugh
White. There would be a town there pretty soon, Gil thought, and they
would have neighbors.

Now she heard the cowbells coming down through the woods, and after
a while she saw the cows, one behind the other, plod into Reall's brook
to dip their muzzles. The two little boys splashed in after them and whacked
the water with their maple wands. Lana rose.

In a few minutes she was milking in the stuffy darkness of the barn
while Gilly explained how long it had taken to find the cows and complained about how he had had to wait for Joey.

"Joey's not so old as you," Lana said quietly. "He gets tired quicker."

"I didn't get tired," Joey mumbled.

"Go fetch the bucket from the spring then," Gilly said.

"I can't," said Joey. "I want to set here."

"If you ain't tired," said Gilly, "you had ought to get it to help Ma."

"You go and get it, Gilly."

She milked on. The cows were holding up well in spite of the heat.

"Didn't we have a horse?" Gilly asked when he came back from the
spring.

"Yes," said Lana.

"I said so. Joey wouldn't believe me."

"I didn't say we didn't."

"What happened to the horse?" Gilly asked.

"We ate it," Lana said.

"Why did we eat it, Ma?"

"Because there wasn't any food left in the fort."

"Did I eat some too?"

"Yes."

"I don't remember it."

Lana tried to forget the time. It was the summer after West Canada Creek. When everyone believed the war was over, when it *was* over everywhere else in the country, Brant had suddenly appeared with five hundred Indians and a few Tories to harry German Flats. It was only the mercy of God that Adam Helmer and old Gustin Schimmel had happened on them. Adam had brought the warning in time; but the Indians had caught Gustin.

Brant had surrounded Fort Dayton for four days, and the food had got so low that every living thing inside was killed that would serve for meat. On the last day, in an effort to draw the men out of the fort, Brant had had Gustin Schimmel burned to death on the open land towards the river.

The Indians had burned him slowly with small fires, so that he would live for a long time, but they had planted the stake out of shot. Not so far away, however, that the poor old German's screams could not be heard in every cranny of the fort. He had started giving out at sunset, but even after that the sixty defenders on the rifle platforms could see the fire, and the slowly charring shape, and hear the cries continuing with a faint insistence.

Then Brant had vanished into the night and the next day Colonel Willett had arrived from Fort Plain. It was the last time they had been visited by the destructives.

"Come up to supper, boys," she said. As they walked before her, she thought of how she had tried to keep the pleading disembodied voice away from them. She shivered violently at the recollection. She had stretched a blanket over their heads and lain down under it with them. To keep them under it she had pretended they were all three Indians. . . .

After supper was over and they had gone to bed, Lana heated water enough to wash out some of the baby's things, worked for an hour in the steamy kitchen, and then picked up her daughter, who had begun to whimper for her evening feed.

Though night had fallen, Lana blew out her candle and nursed the baby in the dark. It rested her to do so. She needed no candle to see the child's soft hair, which was so light. It seemed perfect to Lana that her daughter should be fair—she remembered how jealous she had been of her sister's yellow hair, like her mother's. She wanted the girl to be a beauty, "tall and fair," like the old song.

The child nursed more gently than the boys had done. Lana smiled at her own conceit. It was like having a woman in the house. Elizabeth Borst. Gil had agreed to the name. He said, when the child was born, that she looked like any little German girl. But he was pleased with her, though he tried not to show it.

Lana still smiled. The cowbells clinked away beyond the brook. The baby's head dropped from the nipple and Lana rose to put her to bed. She had her in her cradle when she heard the man rap on the door.

For an instant all the panics of years past rushed on her heart.

"Hello," the man was calling softly. "Hey! Is there anybody in there?"

Lana forced herself to go to the door.

"Who is it?" she called.

"It's John Wolff. Does Martins live here?"

"I am Lana Martin; what do you want?"

"Please let me in, Mrs. Martin."

Lana knew that he could get in if he wanted to. So she lit her candle at the fire and got down the musket Gil had bought for her when she was alone. She lifted the latch and stepped quickly behind the table.

But the man entered diffidently. He had no gun, and when he saw her he said, "I ain't going to do you harm."

As soon as she saw him Lana lost her fear. He was an old man, with thin white hair and a sad hopeless sort of face.

He said, "Don't you remember me? I used to keep the store at Cosby's Manor."

"Oh yes," she said. "Yes."

"I got sent to prison," he went on, "but I got away. I always wanted to come back. I left my wife here, see? She never turned up anywhere in Canada. Did you see her after that?"

"No," said Lana, quietly setting down the musket.

"Her name was Ally," said Wolff. "I never knew what a good woman she was till I had to leave her. I wanted to come back and find her if she was here. But they chased me out down there. They took my gun away. A big feller named Helmer swore he'd kill me, but some other folks helped me get away. They told me he'd killed three Indians that had come around since. I didn't want to harm nobody. I was looking for Ally."

"No," said Lana, "we never heard from her. They thought she went away."

"I've got a little place near Niagara now. I run the store on Squire Butler's place. I wanted to take Ally to it."

"I'm sorry." Lana could not feel hatred for him now that she was no longer afraid. "Won't you have something to eat?"

"No, thanks. I'll just be getting back."

"Back?"

"Home. To Niagara." He tried to smile. "It's quite a ways."

"You haven't any gun."

"I've got a little food. There's berries now."

"You take this musket," Lana said impulsively. "I don't need it. There's not much powder and ball for it."

"I couldn't do that."

"Oh yes. I expect my husband will be home to-night. Please."

He stared at her with his weak eyes.

"You're kind," he said. "You're the first kind person I've seen. And you know about me, too. But I never did nothing to get sent to jail for."

"I know; I believe you."

"She never turned up, you know. She was good to me that last day when I was into the fort, Mrs. Martin. They wouldn't let me write to her, except I paid them money. I didn't have enough."

She thought he was going to cry. But he did not. He left in a little while, and she closed the door once more. Overhead she heard the boys steal back to their bed, but she did not scold them. She was glad Wolff had gone before Helmer found him. Helmer would kill any Tory or hostile that came into the valley if he could. They said he had killed Suffrenes Casselman. But no one knew that really, unless maybe his wife. Betsey was a strange woman in some ways. Gossip had it that she made Helmer swear an oath to bring her scalps before he got in bed with her, and that he brought her the scalps.

Lana did not go to bed. She had the feeling that what she had told Wolff was so and that Gil would return to-night. When he was away she felt only half alive. Everything she had in her, everything she had done or would do, every thought and every hope, was part of him. And yet sometimes he seemed less close to her. She did not know. As long as he stayed with her, came back to her, it did not matter how little time of his life he gave to her, so long as she could see him, feel him, hear him. She thought of that poor hopeless man, John Wolff, returning to his store in the new settled land, somewhere in the west.

When she heard Gil, he was walking with the Indian. She opened the door and called them to come in. But Blue Back was saying, "No, fine. Fine," and backing into the darkness.

Gil chuckled as he closed the door.

"Blue Back won't come in. He wants me to give you this. He says he'll come round some day after you've had a chance to get your mad off."

"What on earth?"

Gil held out to her a peacock's feather, broken, stripped of half its herl, but still showing enough color in the eye to identify it.

For some reason, to touch it took all the strength from Lana's legs. She plumped down on the stool and leaned against the table. The hand that held the feather started to shake. It was silly of her. She did not understand it herself. And to keep Gil from noticing, she asked him whether they had found the place.

"Oh yes. Blue Back found it. The stones were still there. Nothing had got at him."

He was taking off his wet and dirty shoes.

"How was Mary?"

"She cried some," he said. "But after a while I think she felt better. She borrowed old Blue Back's knife and dug up some posies and stuck them around the place. She didn't take long."

"I'm glad you took her," Lana said. "She wanted to go so much."

"Well, I'm glad too. I'd promised long enough."

He was watching her now, over his shoulder. "What's the matter with you, Lana? Did anything happen?"

"Gil, do you remember that John Wolff? He got arrested on that muster day?"

"John Wolff, by God. The man that kept the store. I testified against him."

"He was here before you came back. They'd driven him out of German Flats and he came up here to see you."

"What did he want?" Gil's face hardened. "If he wants to come back to settle, he better not try."

"Oh no, he was looking for some news of his wife. She never turned up in Canada."

"I remember. After they took him to Albany she went back to the store. But she'd gone from there when the militia went up—you remember, after we went to Little Stone Arabia Stockade."

It seemed they couldn't get away from it. Again and again, day after day, the years came back to them. Lana wasn't thinking of the Wolff woman then—she was thinking of the winter night in the Schuyler hut when Gil brought home the half of a thin doe. All at once she realized that it wasn't herself who had been responsible for that long dread between them, nor Gil. She wasn't like that. She wished he had kissed her when he came in. She lifted her face and looked at him. He wasn't looking at her.

Lana's eyes filled suddenly with tears. Those years, they had entered not only herself, and Gil, and through them the children, they had become part of the land, even on this place, remote as it had been throughout the war—the birds of the air, she thought, the beasts of the field. "Man's days are as grass." Herself, Gil.

"Is Dad come back, Ma?"

Gilly's narrow dark little face peering through the trap from the loft. . . . Joey still snoring on like a half-stifled little hedgepig.

"Yes, son. It's Dad. Get back to bed. Me and your Ma are going now."

He laid his arm round Lana in the dark, leading her to the room they slept in. The baby was snuffling her breath in and out. As Lana started to unlace her short gown, she discovered the peacock's feather still in her hand. She fumbled for the shelf beside the window and laid the feather on it.

She heard Gil getting down on the bed; the rustle of straw beneath the blankets. Beyond the window the faintly clinking cowbells moved along the brook.

"We've got this place," she thought. "We've got the children. We've got each other. Nobody can take those things away. Not any more."

ROME
HAUL

To
CHARLES TOWNSEND COPELAND
with
the writer's
admiration, affection, and gratitude

THE author has made use of two songs taken from *The American Songbag:* "The E-ri-e" (page 429) and "The Erie Canal" (page 430). For permission to reproduce this material he wishes to thank Mr. Carl Sandburg and Harcourt, Brace and Company.

1

THE PEDDLER

IN 1850, the road to Boonville wound out of the Tug Hill country through long stretches of soft wood. On the steady downward slopes it curved back and forth through the balsams and scrubby pine; only on the occasional small ascents it ran straight; so that whoever traveled the road saw fellow travelers at a distance below him, or not at all—until he came upon them in the shadow of a bend.

Along the road a young man was walking. He strode easily, his feet meeting the ground as if they were used to earth. He was tall in spite of the stoop that took inches from his stature. His shoulders were broad and sloped. There was a cleanliness about his face and straight short hair suggesting inexperience of men.

The road, in his hours of walking, had laid a film of grey dust on his cowhide boots and had coated his trousers halfway to his knees. He wore a battered faded green hat with a narrow brim, a blue shirt open at the neck, and a brown homespun coat which puckered under his arms. In his right hand he carried a small carpetbag, ornamented on one side with a design of flowers, which he held turned inward against his leg.

The road brought him to the top of a long easy hill, and as he walked over the lip he heard the creak of a wagon round a bend ahead of him.

It was an odd-looking turnout. Both horse and wagon were of grey antiquity and capable only of slow and cautious movement. The horse leaned gingerly upon his breeching. It was not in him to hurry up hill or down. He footed the road slowly with a shambling sensitiveness and wove from side to side to lighten the effect of the grade. With the lines hanging loose on the dashboard, his head had free play so that he was able to combine his scientific descent of the hill with the demands of his appetite.

On the box, a man was reading a book. His eyes ran from side to side of the page as though he was hurrying to finish a chapter. After a moment he marked his place with a piece of string and closed the book smartly.

"Whoa!" he shouted, catching up the reins and throwing his weight backward.

The horse pricked his ears at a tuft of grass and made for it.

"Dammit!" exclaimed the man. "Have a lift?"

He did not appear to notice that the walker moved with twice the speed of his horse.

"Where're you goin'?"

"Boonville is my destination," replied the driver, dropping the reins. "Will you climb on?"

"Thanks."

The walker jumped over the nigh front wheel and took his seat.

"My name's Jacob Turnesa," said the driver. "Peddler, I am. Peddles clothes and dress goods and jewelry. It's a good business. What's yours?"

"Ain't got any now."

"Name."

"Dan'l Harrow."

"Pleased to know you. Shake hands."

He grasped Harrow's hand with long thin fingers. His eyes over his hooked nose had drooping underlids which showed startlingly red in the pallor of his face. They surveyed Harrow appraisingly before he shifted them to his horse.

He pulled a clay pipe from his pocket and pointed it.

"There's a horse," he said.

"Yeanh."

"There's a horse," he repeated.

"I seen him."

"Ahhh! He's a great one to go, he is."

Harrow nodded.

"He is at that, though. After you get him started where there's grass along the road, there ain't no stopping him."

He nodded, ruminatively spat, and began filling his pipe from a pouch of grey buckskin.

"Look at him now," the peddler continued. The old horse had reached the bottom of the slope, where a small brook stole under the bridge and balsams made the air sweet; and he quickened his pace on the upward grade. "Funny horse. Has notions in his head like a human. Goes slow downhill 'cause he hates to think of the updrag beyont. And when he hits the updrag he perks up his ears, thinking of the downhill he's going to find on the other side. If he was a man, you'd call him a philosopher."

"I wouldn't," said Harrow, dubiously looking at his fists.

"No," agreed the peddler, his thin mouth grinning behind his whiskers, "you'd call him a damn fool."

He struck a match on the iron brace of the dashboard and put it to the bowl of his pipe. A puff of rank sweet smoke popped out of the charred bowl like a recoil and swept into Dan's face.

"Where you come from?" Turnesa asked, flipping the dead match at the rump of the horse, who switched his grizzled tail with irritation.

"Tug Hill way."

"That's lonely country. Leave yer family?"

"They're dead."

"Ahhh."

"Pa, he died. The man that bought the place didn't want no help. I was plannin' to go anyhow. There ain't nothing to that land."

"Like horses?"

"Horses and hogs pretty good. Mostly I admire cows."

They came out on a level piece of road where the trees opened on either side into meadow and pasture, with here and there a house.

"It ain't very far to Boonville, now," remarked the peddler. "That's a nice town."

Men were working in the fields, mowing oats. As the wagon passed a yellow house under big elms, a woman came out of the door. She wore a pink sunbonnet and carried a bucket in her hand. The squeak of the wheels attracted her attention and she looked up and recognized the peddler.

"Hullo, Mr. Turnesa," she called. "Have some root beer?"

"Afternoon, Mrs. Sullivan. Thanks."

He picked up the reins and yanked them. The woman pressed close to the off front wheel and lifted her bucket, in which a dipper lay, mysterious in the brown drink. Turnesa held down his beard with his left hand and brought the dipper, brimming, sidewise to his lips. He drank noisily.

"Won't your friend?" suggested the woman, nodding out from under her bonnet. She had a plump, red, pleasant face, blue eyes, and a mouth suggesting capability. Harrow thanked her and drank eagerly. The beer was cool and very good.

"Done any peddling down the canal?" she asked.

"Only down the feeder. I don't go below Rome any more. That railroad spreads my line of goods too quick through the main line."

"Awful things, them railroads. Some say it'll kill the boating in time."

"Maybe," said the peddler. "But I don't think it will. It ain't got the traction. Mules have, and the railroads can't use mules. I say let the railroads take all the people that's fools enough to risk 'em. Packet boats was a nuisance anyhow."

"That's right," said Mrs. Sullivan. "Lord help me, though, I wouldn't ride in one of them trains. They go too fast."

"Yeanh."

"Any news Rome way?"

"They say Mary Runkle's trial'll come up next month."

"Who's she? Oh, I remember! It was she choked her husband to death while they was in bed together. It don't seem true."

"You can't tell," said Turnesa thoughtfully. "She had the strength."

"Say," exclaimed Mrs. Sullivan, "Drake Gallup was up from Boonville last night. He says all the folks down there is turble brustled up about there being a criminal loose on the canal."

"I wonder who it is?"

"Don't know for sure, but they think he's the man's been pulling these holdups on the canal. Stopped Drake."

"Did Drake get a look at him?"

"No. The man wore a handkerchief over his face. He rode a big grey horse and was dressed like a spark, pipe hat and all. They call him Gentleman Joe Calash. He don't seem to hang in one place any length of time."

"He will one day."

Mrs. Sullivan laughed.

Young Harrow had been listening attentively with a gleam coming into his eyes.

"Excuse me, mam. What do they want him for?"

Mrs. Sullivan smiled at him.

"Plenty. The posters is made out, 'Dead or alive.' "

"Yeanh," said the peddler. "I guess he's a bad one, all right. Say, I'll have to get on. Thanks for the drink. Geddup!"

He struck the horse with the ends of the reins and leaned back on the seat. Mrs. Sullivan nodded to Harrow.

"Good-bye. Young man going to Boonville?"

"Yeanh," said Harrow, diffidently. "Aim to get work there on the canal. Thanks."

The horse walked.

"So you're going on the canal?" said the peddler.

"Yeanh."

"Who with, if I might ask?"

"Pa said once that Hector Berry might give me a job."

"That's right, he needs a driver. He's here now—Boonville, I mean. He's boating one of Uberfrau's fleet. Guess he'll take you on."

He puffed his pipe in tune to the click and creak of the wagon.

"It'll be a new start for you."

He glanced at his companion. Harrow sat leaning forward on the seat, elbows on knees, staring at his large-jointed hands, a kind of hesitation in his blue-green eyes. He did not look stupid. He had been hatched by solitude, which nourishes men on musing, not on thought. But as he glanced up in answer to a question the peddler saw a native shrewdness lurking in the corners of his eyes.

"Well, I hope you'll like it. The Erie is a swarming hive. Boats coming and going, passing you all the while. You can hear their horns blowing all day long. As like as not there's a fight at every lock. There's all kinds of people there, and they're all going all the while. It ain't got the finish and style as when the packet boats was running, but you'll find fancy folk in the big ports. It's better without the packet boats; let the railroads take the passengers. It leaves the pace steady for growing. There's freight going west and raw food east, all on the canal; there's people going west, New Englanders, Germans, and all them furrin folk, and there's people coming east that've quit. But the canawlers keep a-moving."

The peddler folded his hands over his knee.

"Water-level trade route, they call it, and it is. By grab, it's the bowels of the nation! It's the whole shebang of life."

He glanced at his companion. Harrow was staring over the old horse's ears. The cool of evening was born in the air, and shadows began to take a longer shape. Behind them Tug Hill and the sun were sinking together.

"A man can't tell what's coming to him," said the peddler after a while. "The Constitution of these here States says we're all born alike, and I guess maybe that's right. But something takes hold of us different after that. Some people goes after money, and some after women, and some just drinks. I don't know but what they're right; but me, I've set on a wagon all my life, so I don't rightly know. You're a-going out after something."

"I'm wondering where the road will fetch me out," he added after a moment.

"Yeanh."

"Geddup," the peddler said to the horse, but the old beast switched his grizzled tail and snatched at a morsel.

The peddler glanced at Harrow from under his tufted brows.

"What'll you do if you don't like the canal?"

"I ain't thought."

"Thought only how he'd like it," the peddler said to himself.

"Well," he said aloud, "you're to rub around with a queer lot. If I was you I'd stick to Berry. He's all right, I guess. I hope you'll like it down there."

"Reckon I will."

"Ever do any reading?" the peddler asked, after a pause.

"Some. Pa learnt me. I went to school by Turin for a spell."

"Well, then, here's something to take with you."

The peddler felt about under his hams and presently produced the volume he had been thumbing when he greeted Harrow.

"It's a good thing to have a book if you're tied by alone for the night."

Harrow took the book hesitatingly and weighed it in his hand. Then he looked at the title.

"Say, we had a book like that to home. Said 'Shakespeare' onto the back of it. I never read out of it, though."

"Maybe you'll like it," said the peddler. "It's a funny thing. Books is all right—stories, I mean—when there's people around. But when you're so by yourself you keep thinking about it, a play is better. There's people talking all the while, and coming in and going out, and it seems right you should be sitting where you be to see 'em. But in a book you can't go around with anybody without knowing all the while you're setting by yourself."

Harrow did not understand, but later he found that it was so.

The wheels of the wagon began to spin suddenly at a fair rate of speed that seemed miraculous after the lethargic manner of their former revolutions. Both looked up to see the old horse bestirring himself.

"Durned if we ain't almost there," said the peddler.

Harrow saw a neat village street growing out of the road directly in front of him. Large trees sprang on either side, and the sunset behind sent the shadow of the horse's head before them into the town.

"Boonville," said the peddler.

The horse trotted on past an open triangular space of trees and grass and swung into an alley beside a three-story building of grey limestone with pillars running all the way up the front to support three tiers of porches. HURLBURT HOUSE read the black-and-white sign.

They stopped in a large yard, with wagon sheds opening on two sides and the doors of a great stable on the third. A heavy man with a black beard and unpleasantly light blue eyes was sitting on a bucket in one of the open doors watching a cricket, which was persistent in its efforts to enter the barn. Whenever the insect reached the boarding, the man spat unerringly and counted. "Five!" he shouted for the benefit of someone in the stable. Then, seeing the cricket turn away, "Buttoned him up that time, too," he said. Hearing the creak of the peddler's ancient wagon, he glanced up.

"Got your usual truck of junk, ain't you?" he asked. He rose from the bucket, spat on the horse's legs, stuck his hands in his pockets, and started out to the street.

"That's Jotham Klore. He's pretty near the bully of the canal." The peddler grunted. "But some day he's going to get whipped—and it'll be bad."

He watched Harrow put the volume of Shakespeare into his carpetbag; then they got off the wagon and faced each other.

"Reckon I'll move on," said Harrow. "Thanks for the ride and the book."

"Nothing at all, son; see you again sometime. You'll find Berry's boat at Uberfrau's dock; it's the Ella-Romeyn. It's got a red stripe around the cabin roof. You go out on the street and turn left and go on till you get to the basin, and then follow that to the right, and you'll get there."

They shook hands. The peddler began to unhitch.

Harrow walked out into the street.

2

THE HAUL TO ROME

The Man on the Docks

IT was growing dark. The windows of the Hurlburt House threw rectangles of light across the stone porch floor and out on the plank sidewalk. For a while Dan Harrow lingered by them, listening to the clatter of knives and forks and crockery, and drinking in the smells of roasting pork and boiled turnips. The sky was fleeced with small clouds which the moon had just begun to touch, and the streets were quiet.

A lull in the noises from the dining room of the hotel caused him to glance toward the door, and his eyes fell upon a sheet of paper tacked in a conspicuous position beside the frame. He walked over to it and began to read.

$2000.00 REWARD

FOR INFORMATION LEADING TO THE CAPTURE,
DEAD OR ALIVE, OF JOSEPH P. CALASH

"Desperate criminal," remarked a high voice at Dan's shoulder.

Turning, Dan saw a stoutish man dressed entirely in brown, with a black pot hat on his head and a green tie loose round his neck, who stood with his legs wide apart and his hands thrust into his hip pockets. The man regarded him out of shiny brown eyes, almost hidden between puckered lids, and pursed his lips in a silent whistle.

"Not that they've got a great chance of catching him," he went on, "giving such a innocuous likeness."

"Yeanh?"

"Yeanh, my boy. What does it say? Six feet, thin, dresses like a gentleman. Hell! They'll get information about half the county."

"What's he wanted for?" Dan asked.

"Plenty," said the man. "Dead or alive! Two thousand dollars!"

He pulled a cigar out of his waistcoat pocket.

"Have one?"

"No."

The man stuck it into his mouth and began rolling it from side to side, while Dan turned back to his inspection of the poster.

"Last seen in Utica. Riding a grey horse. Sixteen hands."

"That's what interests me," explained the stranger. "I'm a horse trader by profession—I might say by nature. I had a horse like that taken out of my string in Utica. That was a loss! I'm looking for that animal."

"That's hard," said Dan.

"Sour! Prettiest horse you ever see. Sixteen hands and dappled grey. White mane and tail. Gent's horse." He sighed gustily. "Well, it's a hard business. Here to-day, there to-morrow. A man can't find an honest man outside of himself in a horse trade—and if he's honest himself, he's either a fool or a damn sight cleverer than the other feller."

"Yeanh," said Dan. "I guess that's right."

"You ain't seen him?" the man asked hopefully.

"No," said Dan. "Have you got any notion who took him?"

"Stableman said he was a thin, tall man. Couldn't see his face."

"You'd ought to watch out for him," said Dan.

"That's what I'm doing."

"Sounds like this feller," said Dan, pointing his thumb at the notice.

"Think so myself," said the man. "Say, son, if you was to see that horse, I'd call it an almighty favor if you'd notify me where. You can write to the Odd Fellow's Lodge, James Street, Rome. Sam Henderson's the name, care Alva Mudge, Esquire. Here it is wrote out."

He scribbled the address on a slip of paper and handed it to Dan, who read it over, folded it, and put it in his shirt pocket.

"What's your name, son?"

"Dan'l Harrow."

"Pleased to meet you," said Mr. Henderson, holding forth his hand. Dan took it dubiously.

"It's worth fifty dollars to you, if you find that horse. Best I ever got my hands on!"

He sighed.

"Yeanh," said Dan. "I guess he was. They most generally be."

He stepped into the street. Once he glanced back to see Mr. Henderson staring after him, framing a whistle with his lips—and the cigar for a note.

Figures were running in Dan's head.

"Fifty," he said to himself; then, "Two thousand dollars."

He walked on.

"The dirty twerp!"

Following the peddler's directions, he went down a street marked SCHUY-LER high up on a limestone house, where nobody in the world could be expected to see it, and where nobody was expected to. Perhaps a hundred yards, with a slight incline at the end, brought him to the basin, a long, rectangular strip of water, with the feed canal flowing in round the base of a hill opposite, the Watertown Branch flowing out on the left, and far away to the right the Rome Canal winding out of sight between low hills.

Warehouses with big stupid windowless fronts ran along the shore, and stubby quays jutted into the water from their sides. Dan went down to the waterfront and walked along a planked run wide enough for a wagon, with turnouts on the wharves. There were no boats near him, but a little down the basin he saw one of the docks outlined by a lighted window cut into an indistinguishable shape, very low upon the water.

A slight breeze tickled his forehead. The night was cool and the air thick with the odor of grain. He stopped to listen to the slap of the ripple against the piles.

He was to ask Hector Berry, whom he had never seen, for a job; but first he would eat a supper he had in his bag. So he sat down on the planks of the dock with his back to a warehouse, in the thickest of the shadow, and ate slowly two great sandwiches of salty butter and ham, and a piece of green-apple pie.

As he finished the last bit and wiped his hands along his trouser legs, he became aware of a horse walking slowly along the dock. He sat still.

Suddenly the horse stopped, and low voices broke out round the corner of the building. With slow ease Dan rose to his feet and stepped noiselessly to the corner. The moonlight fell at a slant between the high walls, upon a tall dappled grey horse with high raking withers and straight hind legs the very look of which spelled speed. He stood quietly with his head at the shoulder of a man whose back was turned to Dan, but whose pipe hat shone grey in the white light and threw a long zigzagged shadow angle-wise against the clapboards. Facing him was a big man with a long-visored cap, who leaned against the wall and talked in a hoarse harsh voice. The moon fell on his face and brought his black beard into vivid contrast with the pallor of his eyes. As he talked, he punctuated his sentences with long squirts of tobacco juice. In the action Dan recognized the man he had seen in the stable yard.

It took Dan a moment to accustom his ears to their low voices. Even then he was able to hear only occasional snatches of their talk. "Two thousand dollars," from the bearded man. "Better not get me riled and helping them . . . They've got a Department man after you . . . Half and half . . . Nothing to you . . ." And the man in the pipe hat, "Go ahead . . . Watch out if you do . . . No marshal . . . If there is, he's scared . . . One dead . . . Jotham Klore . . ." And Klore again, "Bitch, Calash . . . I will . . . Marshal . . . Damn right . . ."

Suddenly Dan thought of the poster and the fat man and the grey horse. Then he saw the tall man's left hand stealing to the saddle holster, saw the moon trace the revolver barrel and Klore turn round to face the wall, while the tall man walked up behind him and raised the barrel and brought it down. Klore dropped to his knees and the tall man hit him again, and Klore stretched out on his belly. It all happened without a sound for Dan to hear, only the men and their shadows in a corner of the moonlight. Then the horse dropped his head and shook himself, jingling the stirrup irons, and let out a long breath through blubbering lips.

After watching Klore for a second or two, the tall man backed to his horse, mounted quickly, and galloped off up the canal. Dan stared at Klore, lying beside the warehouse and snoring heavily.

"Calash," he said, to himself. "Gentleman Joe. Jeepers!"

He wondered whether he should go for help; but it seemed to him that

Klore was only stunned. "Buttoned up," he said to himself. His sympathy was all with the hunted man, a stranger, like himself, to the canal. He felt a secret kinship between them, roused, perhaps, as much by the beauty of the man's horse as by the man. There lay no temptation for him in the reward.

He gazed up the canal. He wished that he might have seen the man's face. Stepping back round the corner, he picked up his bag and walked on down the dock to the lighted window.

The Ella-Romeyn

A few steps more, and he found himself staring through the lighted window in the cabin of a boat which had been tied up to the dock, stern on to the bank. The name of the boat was cut in two by the tiller shaft, rising stubbily above the roof of the cabin to the ponderous sweep. The name, which had once been dressed in gilt, still carried enough of its paint to be legible. Though Dan spelled out the frank capitals—ELLA-ROMEYN— he scarcely noticed them, for his eyes had been caught by the dark band above the windows. Brown in the lamplight, it would look red to the sun.

He stood back a pace and looked the boat over carefully. Freighted to the gunwales with early potatoes, the Ella-Romeyn squatted on the water with the pregnant massiveness of a farrowing sow. Now and then her timbers grunted under the new load as she shifted against the tie-ropes.

Through the window and the geranium leaves that made a fringe along the sill, Dan caught a diagonal view of the cabin. The cookstove stood against the forward wall with the dish cabinets on each side of the stovepipe and the iron ventilators up above the heating shelf. To the right, under the windows, was a small sewing table, with a shelf over it bearing a ball-dialed clock on a shaft of imitation crystal. And on either side of the clock were cast the shadows of the occupants of the room, themselves invisible from the window.

Using the shelf for a table, and oblivious of the clock, these shadows were playing a comedy at cards. There were three of them: a stoutish man, with his back to the light, who played cautiously, putting his cards on the table with deliberate motions of his invisible hands; a very small man, his right hand to the light, with an egg-shaped head drawn out ridiculously by the angle of the wall; and opposite him an enormously fat woman, gesturing her paddle-like shadow hands with irrepressible flair. The two men were solemn in their game, though the little man was nimble in putting down his cards, in motions which the light carried clean across the shelf to the end of the fat woman's nose. And she, with indefatigable good humor, leaned forward to meet the thrusts, and then leaned back, with chuckles that reached all the way to her bonnet, until the ribbons quivered in grotesque parody of her Gargantuan heaving. He was infected with the fat woman's sense of humor, ridiculous in its parodied motions on the wall; he wanted to see her in the flesh, to mix with her kind, to be accepted as one of kindred joviality. As the comedy proceeded, he chuckled to himself and went aboard the boat. The unfamiliar feel of the gangway beneath his feet brought back the timidity he concealed under his slouch; yet he felt his way aft to the steersman's position, where sufficient light escaped under the cabin door to show him the steps down.

The fat woman's laughter echoed against the panels.

"Mix me another of them rum noggins," she said, "and put in lots of lemon, and don't forget the sugar like you did last time. Dealing makes me dry. What's your bid, Sol?"

"Two hundred!" exclaimed a cracked voice in high determination.

"It's by me," said the third player mournfully.

"I got two suits stopped right here," said the fat woman, "so I'll say two-twenty."

"Two twenty-five," said Sol, with returning caution.

"Thirty," bid the fat woman.

"Five," said Sol, grimly hanging on.

"Take it," said the fat woman, after the figure had reached three hundred and forty-five.

They must have looked at the "kitty."

"Oh, my God," wailed Sol's voice. "Three hearts and two of them nines, and me with one hundred and fifty in spades and diamonds, lacking only queen and jack."

"Them's the suits I got stopped with my double pinochle!" shrieked the fat woman. "Three hundred points, not counting them hundred aces. Look! Look!"

"My God, Hector, let's quit!" cried Sol.

Hector! Dan knocked.

"Come in," cried all three beyond the door.

Dan opened it and stepped into the room.

"Hello. Is Mr. Hector Berry here?"

He took off his hat in deference to the fat woman. About the table, which had not appeared in the shadow pantomime, sat the three players, and, facing the door, the medium-sized man stared at Dan over square spectacles, a look of bewilderment on his plump pink features.

"That's my name, young man," he said. "My name's Hector Berry. Now what do you want? You needn't be afraid to speak to me, young man."

"No," said Dan, slowly. "I ain't."

He glanced at the fat woman. The chuckle he had heard still lingered in her snapping grey eyes.

"The young man ain't afraid to speak to Hector Berry," she whispered to the little man.

"Not a mite," agreed Sol.

"Desperit character," said the fat woman, shaking her head seriously. And she burst into a fit of laughter, till the ribbons of her black silk bonnet appeared to topple for their balance, and the leaden yellow cherries rattled like dice. Her face became redder and redder; her cheeks bulged explosively; and the red-centred paisley shawl on her shoulders worked up the back of her neck to her high knot of red hair.

Berry rubbed his hands nervously and compared his watch with the clock.

"Now," he said irritably to Dan, "what did you say you wanted?"

Dan looked again at the fat woman.

"Set down," she suggested, pointing to a chair.

"Thank you, mam."

"Looking for a job?" asked Sol, with impetuous inspiration.

"Yeanh. I wanted to see if Mr. Berry would take me on as a driver."

"What's your name?"

"Dan Harrow."

"You ain't kin to Cap'n Henry Harrow, be you? He was captain of the packet boat Golden City. He made the smartest run, Schenectady to Buffalo, of any captain on the Erie—three days, eleven hours, and thirty-seven minutes. Three hundred and forty-six miles." Hector Berry clasped his hands over his belly and sighed. "Figger it out for yourself—it's a danged sight better than four miles the hour. Them was the days! Speed? You've got no notion how them boats could travel! Son, you ought to have been there then."

"Well, he wasn't," said the fat woman, "so why not give him a chance to answer what you asked?"

"What was it?"

He cast a reproachful look at her.

"Be you kin to Henry Harrow?" she asked Dan.

"Pa's name was Henry Harrow. I didn't know the rest."

The little man glanced up.

"Where'd he go? I always wondered where he went to."

He nodded his head briskly and put his feet on the rungs of his chair.

"Had a farm up Tug Hill," said Dan.

"Just think of it," exclaimed the fat woman. "Way up there, and him so fancy-dandy in his ways!"

"How is he?" Sol asked.

"He's dead."

"My, my," sighed the fat woman, pushing her hand up to her heart. "We all suffer. Give the young man some rum noggin, Hector. I'll have another glass."

The canal folk looked at each other.

"My, my," they said.

"Good with horses?" asked Berry after an appropriate interval of silence.

"Yeanh," said Dan, looking into his hat.

"Well, the man that drives for me's to Rome. I'll take you on that far; I'm pulling out to-morrow. I'll pay you a dollar for driving me to Rome."

"Thanks."

Berry handed out glasses all round.

"Now, then," remarked the fat woman, when they had all sipped for the taste, "make the young man to home, Hector. Introduce us."

Hector blushed.

"I'd clean forgot. Beg pardon, folks." He cleared his throat, turned to Dan, and began, a trifle pompously, "Young Harrow, this lady, which I want you to meet, is Mrs. Lucy Gurget—Mrs. Gurget, this here's young Harrow. Mrs. Gurget cooks for this gentleman, Mr. Solomon Tinkle. I'm Hector Berry—you know it; and I'm real sorry my wife, Mrs. Penelope Berry, ain't with us now."

"She ain't dead, be she?" Dan asked commiseratingly.

"No chance—" began Berry; then hastily, "No, she's a-visiting with some of her folks to Westernville. We'll pick her up off the towpath when we get through the Lansing Kill."

"You don't play pinochle, do you?" Mrs. Gurget asked hopefully.

"No," said Dan. "I ain't a very good hand at cards."

"That's a shame. Now we might have had another game if you was. But I guess Sol, here, he's too sick of my skillful playing anyhow."

"Skill!" snorted the little man, slapping his hat on. "It's time you went to bed, talking that way, Lucy." . . .

Left alone with Hector Berry, Dan found the time dragging. He was sleepy under his long walk; and the warmth of the fire and the rum noggin in his insides started him nodding. The kettle purred, the clock ticked, and Hector talked.

He was excusing himself for not offering Dan a longer job. But then he was a poor man, and his wife would probably object anyway. . . . This man Calash made him think of old days. Two thousand dollars reward! He'd like to get it. Perhaps he would. He wondered where the man had come from. . . . Now in the old days such doings weren't unusual. There were a bunch of them. They used to hang out at Joshua Ricket's place in the Montezumy swamp. Dan's pa used to be a light in those days. Snabbest packet on the Erie. Great hand to race. Full of dodges as a rabbit's hind legs.

Hector looked at Dan, and Dan looked back sleepily. He had been barely listening, catching the drift but not the words. Hector suggested bed, showed him a bunk forward beside the two horse stalls. The blankets smelled a little sour from lack of washing, but the bunk had a good straw pallet. Dan glanced at the rumps of the horses as he passed—a big black team.

He blew out the lantern after Hector had left, listening to the breathing of the horses and the insistent slapping of the ripple below his ear, and breathing in the sweet smell of new timothy. One of the horses grunted; and Dan turned to the wall and slept.

Early Morning

Dan might have been sleeping in the lonely house on Tug Hill in which he and his father had lived by themselves ever since he could remember. He lay straight out upon his right side, never moving, while the first white bar of light tunneled the dusty air of the stable. A fly buzzed in along a beam, and its wings, brushing Dan's cheeks, woke him.

It was a cold morning, with a smell of frost in the air. The horses were on their feet stepping from side to side in their narrow stalls, nosing their mangers.

Mechanically, Dan heaved his feet to the floor and began pulling on his trousers and lacing his boots. Pans rattled in the kitchen aft, heralding an early breakfast. He brushed the horses down. The off one, which had white stockings on its hind legs, fidgeted; but his quiet words and the unhesitating movements of his hands seemed to reassure it; and it stood easily, leaning against the brush, skin twitching with enjoyment. Dan looked up from finishing the white stockings to see Berry in the door.

"Say, Mr. Berry, how much do you grain 'em?"

An expression of amazement lengthened Hector's usually round face.

"You are pretty good with horses. Say, that off horse, he won't let my driver touch his heels."

Dan was embarrassed.

"Why," said Hector after a moment, "give each one this measure level full."

"Them's their regular harness?"

"Yeanh. Come to breakfast when you're done."

Dan harnessed the horses and fed them. In five minutes he was walking back along the left-hand gangway. The eighty-foot boat looked older by daylight. Her timbers were scarred along the edge of the pit, and the rail was worn smooth, to the detriment of a coat of white paint, now weathered as grey as the wood. But the cabin walls, with the small square curtained window and the blue vein of smoke coiling from the hooded stovepipe, gave her a comfortable hominess.

Berry appeared in the cabin door.

"Come on, Dan. Ain't got no time for daddling. We want to be the first two down-boats into the gorge."

Dan went down the short steps into the kitchen. Sunlight streamed into the small windows and shone on the varnished maple walls. On the table, covered with yellow oilcloth, stood two plates, bearing three fried eggs, bacon rare, and a piece of chocolate cake. Beside them Berry placed two cups brimming with black boiled tea.

They ate silently, until Dan reached for the sugar bowl. It was empty.

"By Cripus!" exclaimed Hector. "Nell said she'd filled it."

He got up and went over to the sink, lifted the gingham curtain, pulled out the garbage tin, and filled the bowl.

"We plop scraps out there," he explained, pointing to a little sliding door in a corner of the wall. "Every man scrapes his own plate. It all goes down to N' York anyways; and the tin is real useful for sugar."

He sat down again.

"You see, we pick up rats every time we stop to a port. They travels into the country by our boats—five years and they'll be the only packet passengers left to the canal. You pick up lots in Albany, and if you goes to New York you'll fill your pit up with 'em enough to give your boat the itch. And they're masterful fond of sweet."

He grew melancholy.

"Every time we hit the Erie by Rome, Nell she'll up and moan for me to drive out the rats."

"Whyn't you get a cat?"

"Jeepers! A cat wouldn't stand no show at all. Them rats're that savage they'd drink the sweat off a man's back."

Footsteps suddenly banged on the deck, clattered on the stairs, and, turning, Dan beheld Mrs. Gurget.

"Morning, mam."

The fat woman was dressed in a red flannel petticoat and a yellow blouse. But on her head she wore the same bonnet. It was becomingly rakish, and under it, with her vivid eyes and sturdy carriage, Mrs. Gurget assumed a kind of unflinching handsomeness.

"Say!" she cried. "Somebody laid out Jotham Klore last night with a bang on the head. Young Uberfrau found him around back of the Butterfield warehouse, dead for all. But he come to after a while. And he claims it was this Joe Calash. Gentleman Joe done it, he says, and took twenty dollars off him. Ain't it awful!"

"I'd say it was a good job," said Hector.

"Well, you boys'll have to step smart. Sol, he's harnessing his mules, and he aims to start as soon as you're ready."

"We'll be ready right off. I'll show young Harrow here how to get out the towrope. He's good with horses; brushed that off black of mine clear down to the heels. That shows he's good with horses, sure's my name's Hector Berry."

"Sure," said the fat woman, giving Dan a smile that set him blushing to his hair. "I could see that right off. All animals like him."

She shooed them to the door with her hands.

"Now, then, hustle along. I'll give the dishes a rinse while you're getting ready."

"You get the team out, Dan," said Berry, after they had run the rope out to the towpath and hooked it to the heavy elm evener. "Lift the hatch they're facing and leave 'em be."

Dan went into the stable and bridled the team, then swung up the hatch, which raised half the wall of the boat with it, and watched the team pick their way off the boat and over to the whiffletrees as nonchalantly as if they were leaving a two-story barn.

"Last link of the traces!" shouted Hector, standing by the gangplank. The fat woman came down and hurried ahead to Solomon Tinkle's boat. There was amazing elasticity in her step.

"Thank the Lord!" she sighed gustily to Dan. "I declare to gracious I'm glad we're leaving this town."

She ran aboard the other boat and swung in the plank just as Solomon started his mules. Then, running to the sweep, she bore it to the left, and the boat nosed out into the water round the bows of the Ella-Romeyn and swung into line with the towpath. Little ripples jerked round the corners of the blunt bow, and evened into lines that grew and grew until they touched either shore. The fat woman swung the rudder away from shore to keep the nose of the boat in midstream. She sat down in a rocking-chair with an abbreviated back, to miss the low bridges. She reached down with her left hand into a box beside her chair, drew out a glass and a long-necked bottle, from which she dexterously poured a measure of whiskey.

"Bridge!" called Solomon from the towpath, his bowlegs trotting nimbly beside the mules.

"Bridge!" roared the fat woman.

As the boat passed under the Main Street Bridge of Boonville, Dan saw Mrs. Gurget tilt her head until the cherries on her bonnet hung as on their native branch, and she downed the whiskey in a single gulp.

"Here's going down to Rome!"

The full light of the early sun followed her broad back under the timbers; the two stern windows of the boat glistened like eyes; and under them Dan read the name, NANCY HASKINS, *Utica*.

"Well, we might as well get a-going," cried Hector.

Looking over his shoulder, Dan saw him standing spraddle-legged behind the cabin, the rudder sweep grasped in both hands, a low black flat-crowned hat upon his head, a huge cigar, tip-tilted, filling his lips to capacity. His was a mouth made for nestling a cigar.

The team picked up a smart pace. They were fast walkers and would quickly overtake Tinkle's mules.

Dan felt the shadows of the Main Street Bridge over him.

"Bridge!" he shouted in imitation of Solomon Tinkle.

"Bridge!" replied Berry with an approving grin, adding, "Better hop up. Going with this flow even with a load on ain't nothing for a good team. It's a five-mile current."

He pointed, and Dan, looking ahead, saw the little man straddling his off mule. Dan looped the reins over the hames of his off horse and vaulted to his back. Evidently it was a customary thing to do, for the animal merely shook his head and grunted once. Dan hooked one knee over the hames and sat sidewise, facing the canal. The swift walk of the blacks had brought him opposite the stern of the Nancy Haskins; but there, they took their stride from the mules and kept pace so evenly that the two boats might have been hitched together.

Once it had left the town, the feeder wound away due south between raw banks, in the cuts of which grass was just getting a foothold. The canal had been opened only the year before. It was the principal feeder of the Mohawk section of the Erie Canal, but it also opened all the Black River country, as far as Watertown, to trade.

The shadows in the wooded bends still held a taint of frost, and out of them the sun drew wraiths of mist that trailed away among the trees, leaving a dank touch lingering on the passer's cheeks. A sadness came into Dan's eyes. It might have been the sight of the open cuts through the meadows, or the scars left by the diggers in the woods, neither offering promise of the future beauty of the dark water which would in a few years reflect banks green with nature's healing, but which now moved sombrely like a soul laid bare.

He started to hear the fat woman clearing her throat. She had been studying him for some time with a sort of smile tugging at the corners of her mouth. When she caught his eye, the smile broke into a grin, like a man's, and he felt an answering grin on his lips. She was amusing in her bright clothes, with all that substantial liveliness of hers.

"Boonville," she said, "will sure grow, now this ditch's been opened up."

"Yeanh."

"Ain't you never had no ma?" she asked after a time.

"Not to recollect it."

She shivered.

"It must have been lonely up there on Tug Hill."

"Yeanh."

"Awful lonely."

"Yeanh."

"Me—I could never have stood it so long."

"No. There weren't pasture to keep good cattle there. Just little cross-bred dinkeys.

"Holsteins," he went on, slowly, "is all right if you can keep big, blooded ones. Or red cattle. But them little dinkeys,"—he glanced at his hands,—"a man can't hardly fetch a-holt of their teats."

"When did your pa die?"

"Two months ago."

"I used to know him, once."

"Yeanh?"

"Everybody knew him on the canal. He was a fine big man. I was just a gal then."

Before them the pasture land narrowed in the hills, and the road came in to the towpath; and way ahead the sky came down upon the level fields.

"The Lansing Kill," Mrs. Gurget said to Dan. . . .

The white beams of lock gates stood out against the autumn green, and as they came closer Dan saw a small square house beside the towpath, and, farther on below, more locks, and next to each another house. He saw that they were entering a narrow deep gorge. On his left the Lansing Kill plunged eighty feet into a foaming cauldron and then roared downward over a long series of rapids. It had cut away a wide amphitheatre where it came first on the soft limestone, and the water fell in a broad curtain. An overflow from the canal shot another, more broken fall into the whirlpool of water. Between the two falls, on a small island, the froth feathering its roots, a white ash grew by itself, its smooth trunk glistening and its leaves trembling with the spray.

On the right side of the gorge, the road and canal went down together; the road in sharp curves and a steady descent, the canal following a straighter course, stairlike in its series of locks, so that to go down it made the boater feel as though he rose and fell. For at times the road ran high over his head, and at times it would lie below him, halfway to the valley floor, while his boat crept into the series of locks with its reflection in the reflection of the sky. . . .

There were no farms in the Lansing Kill Gorge; there were the forest, the stream, the canal, the road, and the lock-tenders living alone. Only the boats and the shadows of clouds went up or down the long defile. A commissioner had called it "a link in transportation." "The Lansing Kill," Mrs. Gurget said to Dan. But Solomon Tinkle, after a backward glance at the upland river country with its rolling hills from which they had just come, called to Dan, "Seventy locks in five miles. Regular stairs, I'd call it. Jeepers! It's the stairways to the Erie!"

"Yeanh," said Mrs. Gurget, "so it be. There's life down there, Dan."

"Yeanh," said Hector Berry. "That's right."

In the Kill Gorge

As if he were an outpost there to hail them, they saw a man sitting his horse in the shadow of the bridge. Both boats stopped.

"Hey, there!" he shouted.

Far down the Kill Gorge they heard, in the instant following, another cry, faintly, "Hey, there!"

The man glanced over his shoulder suddenly, as if he were not sure it was an echo. There was a pastiness about his cheeks which might have come from a bilious constitution or nervousness, or both. While he talked to the boaters, his eyes, which were set flush with his cheeks, kept covering the road and the towpath ahead of him; and he held his right hand inside the flap of his coat resting near his left hip.

Mrs. Gurget had brought the Nancy in close to the towpath, and now she leaned forward toward Dan and said in a low voice, "It's Nick Spinning —he's sheriff to Rome."

Solomon Tinkle engaged the sheriff in conversation. The little man had climbed down off the back of his mule and now stood leaning against it, his head resting on the animal's flank. They had finished exchanging views on the weather.

"What're you doing up this way, Spinning?"

Spinning glanced round him again.

"You've heard of this feller, Calash? Well,"—he opened a small saddle bag and pulled out a sheaf of bills,—"I'm going up to Boonville to set these up."

Dan went over to him. "Two thousand dollars reward," he read, "for information leading to the capture, dead or alive, of Joseph P. Calash."

"Sheriff Jones told me to set these up here. I don't see as there's any point in it. They say there's a special marshal, Department of Justice man, working on the job—regular hound for trailing. But he ain't reported to us yet. Those marshals are rated too damned high. But there ain't any point in hanging up these papers in Boonville."

"No," said Dan. "That's right. There's some posted there already."

"Who done that?" exclaimed the sheriff, open-mouthed with astonishment.

"The marshal, maybe," said Dan.

Spinning swore.

"I'll bet that's right. Jeepers Cripus! How can they expect us to help a marshal if he don't let us know who he is? It ain't right in the first place, their sending him in here to pick up the money."

"Well, there's your chance, Spinning," said Solomon. "Calash is up there now. He laid out Klore last night on Uberfrau's dock. You'd ought to catch him coming out."

"I'd like to see him," said the sheriff. "Just once."

"Damned if I would," said Hector Berry.

"I mean the marshal. I want to know who he is. You don't know who he is?" he asked Dan.

"No," said Dan slowly, "I guess not."

He was thinking of the fat man, Henderson, who claimed he had lost a horse.

"Sol!" cried Mrs. Gurget. "Move them mules along. You'll have the towline tangled!"

The boats had crept on with the current until they were opposite the teams. Now the mules took the weight of the boat upon the towline again and forged ahead until they came abreast of the gate beams of the lock.

"The Five Combines," said Mrs. Gurget.

As if he liked their company, Spinning let his horse follow the boats.

Mrs. Gurget glanced at him and said in a low voice to Dan, "Spinning's scared. There's no doubt of it."

After feeling under her chair, she straightened up, a long brass horn at her lips. Her bonnet rose as she drew in her breath, and then it sank behind a long-drawn braying that moaned in echoes on the wooded hills.

"My God!" chattered Hector. "Don't do it again! It chips my teeth to hear it. Wait, I'll ring my bell."

"Shucks!" she mocked Hector. "Ben can't hear your bell. The Angel Gabriel will have to punch him on the nose come Judgment Day to make him hear."

Again she blew an unearthly blast, until the vein stood out between her eyes.

Solomon ducked his head and screamed.

"Cripus, Lucy! Stop it! Here he comes."

Up from below the level of the lock they heard in the fallen quietness a hoarse voice singing out of key:—

> "Oh God! that I Jerusalem
>   With speed may go behold!
> For why? the pleasures there abound
>   Which cannot here be told.
> Thy turrents and thy pinnacles
>   With carbuncles do shine,
> With jasper, pearls, and chrysolite,
>   Surpassing pure and fine.

> "There be the prudent prophets all,
>   Th' apostles, six and six,
> The glorious martyrs in a row,
>   Confessors in betwixt.
> There doth the crew of righteous men
>   And nations all consist;
> Young men and maids that here on earth
>   Their pleasures did resist!"

The singer was an old man with a white beard falling to his waist, hiding his red flannels (for he wore no shirt), and white hair hanging on his shoulders. He came forward with a swinging, rugged stride, head back and shoulders squared, a six-foot knotty staff in his hand, and his blue eyes peered at Mrs. Gurget like those of a hermit, who has seen no woman since his youth.

Mrs. Gurget cupped her hands to her mouth and shouted, "Two boats going down to Rome!"

"Happy New Year," said the old man.

"Merry Christmas yourself," said Solomon Tinkle. "We've got to get through this lock."

"Course it ain't really a happy new year," observed the old man mildly. "That was just season's greetin's."

He moved over to the sluice levers.

"First boat in," he ordered.

The Nancy Haskins was already nosing in under the skillful direction of

Mrs. Gurget. On one side Solomon and on the other Ben leaned on the balance beams and trod them round to close the gates. Then Ben pushed on the sluice lever at the lower end of the lock, a rush of water hissed through the sluice, and rapidly Mrs. Gurget's bonnet sank from view between the limestone walls. Solomon had unhooked the team, so they poled the boat into the second of the five locks, which went down one after the other like a set of steps.

As soon as the gates had shut behind the Nancy, Ben came back and opened the sluice of the first lock to fill it, and then he and Dan opened the upper gates and closed them behind the Ella-Romeyn. So the boats went down a lock apart, each taking two minutes to a lock, while old Ben ran from sluice to sluice, bending his back as he ran and swinging his staff, with the sweat springing out on his cheeks and a gleam in his eyes like the gleam in the eyes of Elisha the prophet.

As the Nancy came out of the lowest of the five locks, they all heard a horn braying round the bend before them. By the time the last gates opened in front of the Ella, they heard another horn sounding. Then a boat came in view, hauled by three mules, almost on their knees under the heavy load they had to move against the current. Behind them walked a man who was very tall. He appeared to be making knots and patterns with his bull-snake whip over the backs of his mules. They cowered at each report and lunged in their collars, as if generally the patterns were marked upon their backs. And when they came closer Dan saw signs of it.

But the driver knew that a mule works best when he is afraid of being hurt, not when he is hurt.

"They're beasts of extraordinary imaginations," Solomon explained to Dan.

The man who steered the upstream boat kept throwing glances back over his shoulder.

"Hurry up, George," he shouted. "Jason's just cleared the last lock."

"By grab," exclaimed Hector Berry, as Dan passed him to fetch down the two teams to the foot of the five combines, "by Grab, they must be line boats! If the second boat gets up afore the other commences to lock through they'll fight for it."

The shadow of the sheriff's head moved onto the deck. "Danged if I'll let 'em," he said.

Beyond the bend, volleys of profanity burst at them and a team of mules came round on a trot, followed by a great bear of a man who heaved upon the towline at their heels and goaded them with a spike in the end of the whip handle. He made no articulate comment, but rumbled to himself, until he saw the leading boat still waiting at the lock.

"Put her in, put her in!" he shouted to the steersman, and as the boat came into the bank he ran back, caught the rope flung to him, snubbed it round a pose, and before the steersman could jump ashore, had started for the lock at a lumbering run.

"By Jeepers, George," cried the steersman on the first boat, "there ain't no ways out of it now! You've got to stand up to him."

"That's the first honest-to-God thing you ever said." The driver of the second boat stood facing them on thick bowlegs, his arms half raised, his flat heavy hands half clenched, his pig's eyes jumping from one to the other.

"You cheated me out of place down below, George, but you'll have to hold it now or let me through."

The tall man looked a bit scared, but he wanted the place. The first boat through would lead into Boonville.

"Go wipe yourself," he said.

The sheriff rode down to them.

"I'm sheriff of Rome," he announced. "Quit it!"

"Horse to you!"

The steersman of the first boat heaved on the sheriff's right leg, and as he came down over the other side of his horse the steersman of the second boat caught him by the neck and thumped him on his back, and then they both sat on his belly, side by side, and threw pebbles at his horse until it trotted off.

Spinning swore furiously, so the one nearest his head dropped sand into his mouth.

"No sense in you and me arguing," said the second steersman.

"No," said the other, reaching into his hip pocket, "have a chaw."

"Surely."

He helped himself from the bag, chewed, and waited politely for the other to spit.

"Go ahead," they said to the drivers.

The drivers walked up to the level space beside the upper lock. There they faced off, the man George head and shoulders taller than the other, with four inches more of reach. But there was a solidity about the second driver, that grew upon the onlookers.

"He can't be hurt," said the second steersman.

The crews of the down boats stopped where they were. "I guess we can spare the time," said Hector.

"I wouldn't miss it for a keg of real Jamaicy," said Mrs. Gurget. She wiggled her shoulders and settled herself comfortably in her chair.

Solomon Tinkle squatted down beside his mules, and Dan drew in his breath and waited.

Between the drivers and beyond them they could see old Ben leaning on his staff with the sun shining over his shoulder. Below the locks the roar of the Kill falls came upon their ears and filled their heads and took their hearing from them, so that they saw Jason lower his head and rush upon the tall man and take two hard right smashes on his face and turn with his mouth wide open; and there was no sound at all. But they could see his cry.

"All he has to do," explained his steersman, "is to hit him once; then he'll mow him down and set him up in shocks."

"I guess that's right," the other agreed affably. "George isn't no hand for punishment."

They spat together.

Up above them Jason rushed again and again on his deceptively clumsy legs, but each time the other's longer reach helped him to dodge and get in a blow. At first he smiled confidently; but after a time his wind shortened and his hands grew sore, and the other's rushes missed him more narrowly.

Dan had never watched a prolonged fight between two men. He stepped over to Solomon Tinkle and sat down beside him. The sun caught the face of the man Jason as he rushed, and the cheeks showed red and puffed like overripe tomatoes, ready to burst at the pat of a small stick. The two piglike eyes gleamed from the close lids in a controlled frenzy. Then the head sank again and the man bored in.

The sudden glimpse of color flopped something inside of Dan, and he swallowed convulsively.

The tall man landed again, left and right, and the blood came out upon his hands and touched the cuffs of his shirt.

Dan cried aloud. And the tall man grinned.

"Now look!" cried Solomon, hunching forward.

For the grin on the tall man had suddenly become frozen, and it hardened and set and became a leer, and all at once his mouth sprang open; but they heard no scream.

"No doubt it was low," said Solomon. "We might as well pull out."

He spoke to his mules and they took up the slack in the rope. Dan kept on staring.

The bearlike Jason was standing close in on the tall man, his legs spraddly and his back arched, and his hands drove straight in from the waist. The tall man looked over his head, and it seemed to Dan that he was looking straight at him. His fist jumped out at the other's face, but fell aside, as though there were weights hung from his elbows. He gave no sign of moving any more; but he grinned.

"Come on, Dan," cried Hector. "We've got to get along."

Dan started the team, and as they went round the bend he looked back once more. The bearlike man stood in the same position, but old Ben's arms were stretched above his head and he stared at the tall man on the ground at his feet.

Mrs. Gurget glanced at Dan and saw that he was still a bit queasy from the fight. "Pore old man," she said, as the trees shut off their view of the lock-tender. "I reckon he's got religion bad."

"Yeanh?"

"Yes, I guess he has. He used to take tolls at the weighlock to Utica; but one day he bumped his head and went twirly."

"All lock-tenders is twirly," Hector said sententiously from the rear. "I reckon that's why they're lock-tenders."

A few hundred yards farther on, they came upon another lock, with a tender's house standing close beside it, and again Mrs. Gurget woke the echoes with her horn. A small black-haired man with a twisted shoulder stepped out of the door.

"That's Ethan Allen McCarthy," Mrs. Gurget said to Dan. "He's got ideas against God, and him and Ben don't speak any more."

"Hullo, Ethan," she called. "How be you?"

"Morning, morning," he said.

And then, as he walked over to the gate beams, "George Marble just went through with Jason Brown pushing him close."

"They just had it out at the Five Combines. George got a beating."

"Glad to hear it. I'll bet old Ben took a frenzy watching them."

"No, nothing to notice."

"He will, he will. He'll have to think out the sin of it first. He don't mean harm, but he's crazy as a hot bitch with his religion."

He locked them through.

"Do you believe in God?" he asked Dan.

"Well, I ain't thought."

"Don't, young man. Don't do it. You can't get anywhere doing it. Eat your vittles and thank God you ain't got religion to raise a gas on a good meal."

A wind had begun to pick its way down the pass; by eleven o'clock it was blowing strong from the northwest, and tumbled cold grey clouds showed over the northern hills.

Still they wound on with the tops of the trees close to their feet; and again and again they sank between the limestone walls. The canal had come to life; behind them now they heard, in eddies of the wind, the horns of other boats, long-drawn and broken by echoes. And they met boats coming up, hauled by sweating teams, the drivers cracking their bull whips as they walked with long slow strides, and the steersmen stiff beside their rudders at the stern. When they passed, Dan learned to trip his rope by holding back the horses while Hector steered the boat to the far side of the canal, so that the slack of the towline sank into the water as the boat came abreast, and the upstream craft, horse and boat, passed over it.

They locked through number thirty-nine and hauled out onto a stretch a mile and a half long, and for a way the hills were high above them and the roar of the Lansing Kill close at hand. The road stayed up on the hillsides, appearing here and there between the trees.

In a cove where the canal set back, they saw a shanty boat, a hovel on a platform with a porch facing the stern. Tethered by the towpath, an old mule cropped up grass with short, tobacco-brown teeth. He did not look up at them, but one long white ear followed the sound of their passing. On the porch of the boat, a man with a white beard sat smoking a corncob pipe. Dan could see the smoke pop from his lips and hover under the roof before the wind snatched it away. A line between two posts on the roof held a snapping string of clean clothes to the wind. Inside, a woman was singing softly.

"Queer place for a shanty boater," said Mrs. Gurget.

"They come and go," said Hector Berry.

The singing ceased, and the woman came out to stand beside the old man and watch the boats passing. She looked very young and slender and dark. Mrs. Gurget waved to her, but her eyes followed Dan and she did not reply. The old man turned his head to speak to her, and she went in.

"Queer folk," Mrs. Gurget said to herself.

The old man took another puff on his pipe, and the wind carried the smoke away; and a moment after, the boats turned a bend.

Mrs. Gurget's glance fell upon Dan. She did not wonder the girl had looked at him. There was a light in his eyes as he walked. He kept his gaze far ahead to the outlet of the gorge. He was handsome, she decided. He had good features, and the wind had brought a color into his lean high cheeks.

"Seeing things," said Mrs. Gurget. "Young."

She heaved a sigh and caught the tiller in against her side with her right elbow that she might pat smooth her hair and settle her bonnet.

She smiled at him.

"Dan!" she called softly. He did not hear her.

She sighed again, and put her hand to her heart. Presently she felt for the bottle under her chair.

Dan had seen the young woman on the shanty boat. Over the water she had seemed very pretty. He had flushed. . . .

"It must be lonesome living on a shanty boat," he said to Mrs. Gurget. The fat woman smacked her lips against the rim of her tumbler.

"I guess so—but they're queer folk."

"It must be hard on a girl."

"I don't know," said Mrs. Gurget, "perhaps it is."

"It must get lonesome for her, alone with her father."

"Good land!" exclaimed the fat woman. "I guess it would be lonesome."

"Jeepers!" said Dan. "He's too old for her to marry." He looked at her accusingly; but Mrs. Gurget, with considerable delicacy, was taking another drink.

At noon they tied up to the bank. After they had grained the teams, Hector and Solomon and Dan sat on the deck of the Nancy, while Mrs. Gurget cooked dinner. They leaned their backs against the low wall of the cabin to be out of the wind, and the iron ventilators, just over their heads, exhaled the smell of coffee and of frying chops. The clouds had swept full across the sky, and there was a keenness in the wind suggesting snow. Far up the valley a small shower was crossing the hills. A hawk circled dizzily back and forth, his wings on an almost vertical plane when he crossed the force of the wind. Now and then his piercing whistle reached their ears.

All at once Solomon tilted his head.

"What's that?"

They turned their faces to the wind. The road ran along the hillside on their left, and through an opening in the trees almost opposite the Nancy a section of it which had been freshly planked shone white.

In a gust of the wind, from up the valley, they heard clearly a thunder on the wood, and all at once, in the opening, they had a clear view of a tall man riding a grey horse hard.

A spatter of rain struck their faces.

"Jeepers, he was traveling," said Solomon.

Dan had recognized the horse. There was no doubt in his mind that he had seen Calash for the second time.

"Dinner's ready," called Mrs. Gurget as they went into the cabin. "What's the matter with you?"

Solomon told her about the horse they had just seen.

She served them with a platter of pork chops and a round pan of fried potatoes. The smell of her coffee was forewarning of heaven.

"Them chops," she remarked, "is A-1. I guarantee 'em. They raise first-rate hogs to Boonville. Now set down and eat."

She gave them a good example.

"I wonder what that man's hurry was?" said Hector, swishing his coffee round and round in his cup.

"Grey horse?" asked Mrs. Gurget.

"Yeanh."

"Tall man riding him?"

"Pretty tall."

"Well, my gracious! Didn't you read a poster this morning, Sol?"

"By grab! I'll bet it is!"

"What?" asked Hector.

"Gentleman Joe."

"Gol," said Hector.

Hector's Sad Case

There was a pause while Mrs. Gurget brought on an apple pie.

"We ought to pick up Nell by four o'clock," said Solomon.

"Yeanh," said Hector. He turned to Dan. "That's Penelope Berry, my wife."

"We ought to get going pretty quick," said Mrs. Gurget. "She don't like to be kept waiting."

"That's true," said Hector. "She's a remarkable woman, Dan. You'll be pleased to know her. But if you ever get married, make sure she's got no moral sense—either way."

They pulled out shortly afterwards. The wind had died down, but the clouds still hung in the sky.

The locks they came to were spaced farther apart, and at last they reached the lowest three combines, from the top of which they looked down on the village of Northwestern. Before them the hills sloped away and the canal ran again through level farming country.

Three boats were tied up to the Northwestern dock in front of Han Yerry's Saloon, and laughing voices reached out to them from the windows under the long porch. An old man sat with his back against a cleat and fished for sunfish and bass.

"Pushing on?" he asked.

"Yes, sir. We aim to reach Delta to-night."

"That ain't far."

He pulled a paper bag from his pocket, licked his forefinger, thrust it in, and rubbed the snuff that stuck to it back and forth along his gums.

The two teams plodded ahead steadily. The sun came out from under the clouds to the west and shone upon the meadows with brown and yellow tints.

"We ought to pick up Nell Berry pretty soon now. She's staying at a farm behind those trees over there. Some of her kin."

The fat woman pointed out a grove of trees to Dan.

"Poor Hector," she sighed. "If he'd up and lace her once or twice, he'd work some of the cat poison out of her liver. She's a good enough body, too, but he's let her boss him until she's got unhealthy notions.

"Now you wouldn't think it," she went on, smiling, "but Sol, he won't take any nonsense. No, sir. But Hector, he was like one of them Bible men and courted her five years before she said she'd take him. And then on the day of the wedding, when the minister came early, she said there'd be no marrying, but he might as well stay to the wedding dinner that had been cooked anyhow. She told Hector the same thing—he'd ought to've dragged and kicked her to the marrying state, but she was like an old mare that hadn't been harness-broke, and she balked. He asked when; and she made it one year. They ate the dinner and married the next year without it, her pa saying that a woman hadn't ought to have more than one dinner to a wedding. And on the night of the wedding she told him she'd be damned if she'd sleep with him—and I guess she hasn't yet. But that ain't so bad— it wouldn't be no privilege."

The fat woman tossed her head.

"Hector! Hector!"

The cry was shrilly imperative. A little woman with a grizzled knot of hair pushing her straw-colored bonnet over her eyes, and a big carpetbag in her left hand, ran down to the towpath.

"That you, Nell?" said Hector mildly.

"That me? I should guess it was, waiting here for you with this bag in my hand for all of half an hour. What made you so late?"

"I had 'em all into the Nancy for dinner," explained Mrs. Gurget. "I made 'em come, and we killed a little time."

"Who gave you leave to boss my husband?" shrilled the little woman. "If Hector wasn't so mild-mannered, people wouldn't impose on him and keep me waiting like this. Now put that boat against the bank, Hector. Think I'm going to jump eight foot of water?"

Hector swung the Ella in obediently and put out a plank to the towpath. The little woman started up, then stopped and backed off, raising her wizened face to glare at Dan.

"Who's that man, Hector? I never seen him. I won't sleep on board that boat if that strange man is going to be on it."

"Well, this is just Dan Harrow who's driving to Rome for me. That's all."

"I don't care who he is. A good woman can't afford to take risks. Either that strange young man will stay ashore, Hector, or I will. Do you hear?"

"Not you," Hector answered ingratiatingly, and winking at Dan until the tip of his cigar was almost screwed into his eye.

"That's all right," said the fat woman. "He can come aboard with us. I'll give him a good piece of pie for supper."

"No better than what he'd get here if he wasn't a strange man, Lucy Gurget!"

"Bigger, though," said Mrs. Gurget with a broad grin.

"Lucy, you shut up!" said Solomon, coming back from his team. "If you two get arguing, we won't never get to Delta House. Now then, Mrs. Berry," he soothed the little woman, "better get on."

Mrs. Berry put one foot on the plank, and then drew it off as if it had scorched her.

"Hector, you throw that nasty-smelling cigar overboard, you hear me?"

Her husband complied with one last wistful and tremendous puff that left the smoke trailing from his nostrils for a good minute.

This point gained, Mrs. Berry trotted up to the gang-rail, where she stopped stock-still.

"Hector, them rats? Are there any left? Either there are rats, and I won't go, or there ain't—which?"

But Solomon, with a triumphant chuckle, had seized the shore end of the plank and with a strong heave yanked it from under her. She pitched forward with an angry scream and disappeared from sight. Then he ran to the blacks and switched their rumps with his hat. They jumped ahead, and Hector swung the boat away from the bank.

"Gid-ap! Gid-ap! Lift a hoof, by Cripus, or I'll stomp on your innards!" yelled Solomon at his mules.

Both boats gathered way.

"Mercy, Sol," gasped Mrs. Gurget after a volcanic eruption of laughter. "You oughtn't to have done that. You might have hurt the poor woman. Hector!"

"Eh?"

"Nell ain't hurt, is she?"

"I guess not. She lit on some potatoes that was kind of soft."

Black shadows lowered over the canal. The setting sun had left a twilight of pale green; and the wind had begun to rise again, with a piercing note among the trees. Dan walked on the off side of the team, for there was only an occasional white gleam on the water to mark the edge of the towpath. The outlines of the woodlands blurred, and farm buildings merged with their shadows. Here and there they saw a light across the fields. It was quite dark when they came to the Delta House and tied by for the night.

Rome

There was still a star or two way down in the west when they started ahead in the morning. The dark hulk of the Delta House, in which they had heard men laughing and singing the night before, loomed silent beside the dock. The ghost of the night's fires rose in a thin line from the centre chimney. The thump of the horses' hoofs on wood echoed against the walls. But when they had cleared the dock the boats moved into stillness, except for an occasional whimpering of water round the bows.

The hush of morning was all about them; in it small sounds grew suddenly. As they passed a herd of cows, standing at ease in their night pasture, they became aware of their deep rhythmical breathing; and they heard the thin suck of mud about their feet. They could see united clouds hovering above their horses, and the flat green gleam of their eyes; but the cows stood so quiet there was no voice of bells.

With a loud rustling a muskrat ran out of the grass on the side of the towpath and slipped into the canal so smoothly that they barely saw the ring he made; but the slop of his belly against the water came to their ears like a report.

On the stern of the Nancy Mrs. Gurget sat, a mountain of wraps and shawls, with only her face visible. Now and then she would raise a hand to her lips and blow a cloud of steam over it.

"Early morning travel when it's warm is the best there is," she said to Dan; "but this late in the year it's so cold it gives a body the flesh-creep."

It was cold. Both Dan and Solomon stamped their feet as they walked, and, by the rudder of the Ella-Romeyn, Hector Berry was whipping his arms round his middle and puffing and blowing from the exercise. The lights in the cabin windows, where Mrs. Berry was moving about in comfort, shone behind misted glass.

The low hills to the east began to assume clearer outlines; far behind them a white light was growing; but before the sun rose wraiths of mist began to play upon the water, and gradually merged and thickened, until without warning the boats were traveling in a dense white that glistened like hoarfrost on the decks and turned the worn leather on the teams into handsome harnesses. A rich earth smell of potatoes issued from the pits of the boats and followed them along; and though they could not see, and though sound had dimmed and lost its frosty music, the boaters became aware of the smell of barns when they passed them, and the stinging scent of barnyards.

For an hour and a half they pushed on through the mist, feeling their way blindly, as if they were approaching birth. Dan walked behind the black team, his eyes following eagerly the line of the towpath. The grey shapes of Solomon Tinkle and the mules were barely visible a hundred feet ahead. With each stride into the dim whiteness, progress seemed more futile; and distance became an immeasurable quantity. And yet after a time the wetness on Dan's face felt less chilly, and he became aware of something stirring ahead of him.

At first it sounded no louder than the breathing of the herd they had passed earlier in the morning; then it turned into a steady drone, thin, like the awakening of bees; and it gained volume as they approached it, and the mist wavered now and then, so that at moments he saw Solomon quite clearly, and there were articulate sounds in it, and a long *trahn-ahn-uhn-uhn*, repeated over and over like a melody in music. Suddenly Mrs. Gurget sat forward in her chair.

"Listen. There's the horns. Hear 'em, Dan? Them's horns! They're blowing on the Erie Canal."

All at once they heard a cart rattling along a wooden street, the sound of a bell; and the mist lifted without noticeable motion, and they saw upon their right the outline of a town.

And then they felt the sun warm upon them, and a burst of color came upon the buildings; rising smokes, shot with gold, were pulling away to the westward; windowpanes gleamed reflected light; carts and wagons and the voices of men moving rose about them with increasing vigor; and the two boats came round a bend into a long line of docks and warehouses, reflected in the water of a long basin. And everywhere Dan looked upon the water there were boats, of all colors and of many shapes, with men and women moving on their decks. Boats coming in and hauling out, both east and west, the drawn-out wailing of their horns a sound behind the stirring sound of the town.

Solomon stopped the mules upon the dock, and the Nancy swung in close with the Ella-Romeyn at her rudder, and Mrs. Gurget and Hector tossed tie-ropes ashore and came down the gangs.

The fat woman was laughing.

"By Nahum, Dan! What do you think of Rome?"

3

ERIE CANAL

Port of Rome

Mrs. Gurget walked over to Dan, who was hitching the Ella's tie-rope round a post.

"Dan, Sol and me are going to push on for Syracuse right off. It'll have to be good-bye for now."

"Yeanh," said Solomon, trotting up behind her. "Hullo, good-bye; that's the way it is on the Erie."

"We like you a lot, Dan," Mrs. Gurget went on. "Sol and I, we talked about you last night after we went to bed. We'd like to give you a job, but we figger we couldn't pay you as much as you'd get somewhere's else."

"That's right, Dan, we're kind of slow folk."

"No, we ain't. How can you look at me, Sol, and say that?"

"Well, we take our hauling slow. We don't get into no competition for speed. He wouldn't see so much going along with us."

"No, he wouldn't. So we're going to say good-bye. Ain't we, Sol?"

"Yeanh. We'd better." He took hold of her fat hand. "You give it to him," he said in a low voice.

"Well, good-bye, Dan. Good luck."

He shook hands energetically.

"Keep your eye open for that rapscallion, Calash. You can't tell when you mightn't see him and make a penny. It's always a good idee to keep your eye open, Dan; though it's handy not to tell everything you see."

He shook hands once more and trotted off to his mules.

"Hurry, now, Lucy," he called.

Dan noticed him busy unhitching the tie-ropes, but keeping an eye on them over his shoulder.

"What do you aim to do, Dan?" Mrs. Gurget asked.

"I guess I'll get a job."

"Well, it oughtn't to be hard nowadays."

She hesitated a moment and poked at a wisp of her dyed red hair.

"Me and Sol was thinking maybe you ought to have a little extry in your pocket, Dan. Maybe you won't need it. If you don't, you'll want to give it to some gal maybe when you're lonely. Good-bye, Dan. If you get bad off, come and find us. We're apt to be somewhere anywhere."

She caught him suddenly to her with her right hand, and he had the feeling of being smothered against her breast. She kissed him loudly close to his ear and turned away. He watched her hustle over to the Nancy, settling her bonnet as she went. He put his hand in his coat pocket and drew out some bills she had put there. A couple of men, coming along the dock, jostled against him. When he recovered his balance, the Nancy was under

way, Solomon cracking his whip over the mules and keeping his face to
the path, and Mrs. Gurget steering on the stern. He felt a sudden weakness
in his legs, and his eyes blurred. Then a boat cut in behind the Nancy and
he had one view of Mrs. Gurget waving a pudgy arm before she disappeared up the canal to the west.

Dan counted the money in his hand—five dollars and twenty-five cents;
it was a handsome gift.

As he returned it to his pocket, someone took hold of his other arm.

"I'm real sorry," Hector Berry was saying. "Real sorry. This here's my
regular driver. Mr. George Williams, meet Dan Harrow. A man can't have
but one driver to his boat, can he—if he ain't working for one of the line
companies?"

"That's right," said Dan in an embarrassed voice. "A man can't."

He wondered what the fuss was about.

"Well," said Hector, "here's your pay."

He took a dollar out of his pigskin wallet. Dan mechanically pocketed it.

"Well, good-bye," said Hector, making a motion to go.

"Luck," grunted Mr. George Williams. "Pleased to meet yer any time."
And he went aboard the Ella.

Immediately Hector took Dan by the arm again and began to speak
hurriedly in an undertone.

"I'd keep you with me, Dan. Honest to hunkus I would, I like you, for a
fact, and he's no good"—he pointed a thumb over his shoulder in the
direction of Mr. George Williams. "Men that drinks like him is no good,
Dan, and mind I said so. Oh, I don't mean a swaller on a cold day is going
to rumple your innards for the rest of your life—not me. But when a man
drinks so long the likker commences running over at his eyes, there ain't no
chance left for connection of thought. By dang, I'd fire him to-morrow."

He raised his fist.

"By dang, I would, by holy dang. When I say a thing, by dang, I mean
it. But he's Nell's nephey, and she's took a notion against you. Regular snarl
she gets into when I say, 'I guess I'll hire Dan Harrow—he's good with
horses.' I mean what I say, 'Good with horses.' You're a good boy, Dan; I
like you."

He wrung Dan's hand.

"Your pa done me a turn once. Any time you need anything you come
and see me."

"Hec-tor! Hec-tor!"

"Coming!" bawled Hector. "Luck to you, Dan."

He turned round and went hurriedly aboard. Dan saw Penelope Berry's
wizened face thrust from the cabin door under a mammoth pink night
bonnet, her grey hair full of skewers over her forehead, and curl-papers
dangling to her shoulders. He grunted.

"The danged old coot."

But his eyes watched her until the turning of the boat cut off his view
of the door, and then he stared after Hector's plump, spraddle-legged figure
on the poop of the Ella-Romeyn, until the glare of the sun on the canal
brought the water to his eyes. At least they were familiar. . . .

It was all strange to him. The boats, more than he could count, coming
in and going out, many passing through without a stop, each with a man

steering and a man walking behind the towing team, moving at a slow pace, but giving an impression of an intense, suppressed desire for speed. The line boats, recognizable for the hard faces of their captains, largely Irishers, brought in gangs when the great work of the canal was coming to a close; they had an air about them of men aware of physical well-being. Boats bearing emigrants out to the West, Germans, an old man on one with a mug in his hand and a long china pipe to his mouth and a nightcap on his head, stiffly promenading the deck in his stocking feet; and tow-haired children on another. A New Englander going by, driving a boat, a cold-faced bearded man who spoke in a nasal tight voice ordinary words to his horses more impressive than oaths; a boy steering, his young face grimly serious. Two boats of tall, light-haired folk,—"Hunkers" said a man at Dan's back, and his companion answered, "Damn fool Swedes,"—but they had a light in their blue eyes.

Boats of all colors—greys, greens, blues, reds, muddy magentas, and many white, floating on their reflections, many bearing strange folk, entering a strange country, the look of whom made Dan uneasy, so that he found comfort in the figures of the boaters, who rolled their r's in swearing, and who walked as if they knew what their hands were doing. They wore no uniform to tell them by; they were careless in their dress, but their clothes suited them individually—small high felt hats, and broad-brimmed hats with flat crowns, and caps with ear flaps turned up; and some wore coats, and some suits of homespun, and some heavy woolen shirts of dark blue or brown; and one old captain went by wearing a peajacket, and he had a conch at his lips, and his face was red with blowing, and the sound of it swallowed the sounds of the people round him so that he could not hear their laughter, but stood with his pegleg braced in an augur hole; and perhaps he felt the ocean.

The words of the old peddler Turnesa, on his wagon, occurred to Dan: "The bowels of the nation . . . the whole shebang of life." He could see it in the hurry and a certain breathlessness above the easy noise; he could smell it in the boats coming from the West, the raw foods, the suffocating odor of grain, the scent of meat, of pork, the homely smell of potatoes, to be digested in the East and produce growth. It mystified him, though he seemed to understand it, and it stirred a great affection in him for living, for the people round him, and the clean light of the sun.

His hand went to his face and lingered there. A missionary, who had been observing him for several moments, came up behind him and laid a kindly hand upon his shoulder. "What is it, my boy?" he asked, perceiving an opportunity to assist in the regeneration of a soul. "It's a hard life you've had to live, but there's help for every man here." He opened a small bag he carried in his left hand and selected a tract, which he held out to Dan. It was titled, *Esau; or the Ruinous Bargain.*

Dan stared at him vacantly, and the missioner smiled reassuringly.

"Come with me," he said. "Perhaps I can help you."

He was dressed in black clothes, and wore a rather soiled white tie.

"Thanks," Dan mumbled.

The missioner's long face brightened.

"You see the way ahead of you," he said encouragingly. "You're puzzled now; but I'll help you find it if you'll come with me."

Dan's face cleared, as if he understood.

"Yeanh," he said. "That's right. I was wondering where there was a barber."

Perhaps it had been a bad morning for the missioner, or perhaps the work was new to him, for he sighed and told Dan he didn't know and went on down the dock.

Dan picked up his bag and faced the row of warehouses. A couple of teams pulling heavy lumber wagons thumped past him.

"Looking for something?"

A middle-aged man, well dressed in a black coat and black satin waistcoat, grey trousers, and a pipe hat, regarded Dan out of cool grey eyes. He had lean, fine features, a thin mouth sufficiently curving not to be cruel, and his head was set handsomely on his neck. He was of a type new to Dan's experience; there was the clever fit of his clothes, for one thing.

"Yeanh," said Dan. "I was looking for a barber."

"Well, you go up that right-hand street, two blocks, and turn left down the second street, about five houses down. What's your name, if I may ask?"

"Dan'l Harrow."

"Was your father Henry Harrow? He was? I thought I recognized something in your face. I knew him well. Where's he been all these years?"

"Tug Hill way. He's dead."

"I'm sorry. I knew him well. So did all the Erie folks. His name and his boat stood out in the great days of packet traveling. What are you doing in Rome?"

"I aim to get a job," said Dan.

"Located yet?"

"No. I aim to look around some."

"It's a good idea to find out what you want. If you'd like to, I can offer you a job. Come round next week. Butterfield's warehouse. My name's John Butterfield. I'd like to help you any way I can. Your father was a fine man."

He shook hands cordially and went on his way, walking sturdily erect.

M. Pantoulenzo, Barber

Following Mr. Butterfield's directions, after three minutes' walking Dan found himself in a street of wooden houses, some with fancy work on the porches, but for the most part severely plain and painted in quiet colors. Over a second-story window of one of these his wandering eye fell upon a sign bearing the name M. PANTOULENZO, ornately scrolled, with the explanatory legend underneath:—

HAIR TRIMMED. EASY SHAVE.
BLOOD LET.
Teeth drawn at Regular Prices.

A door opening on a pitch-dark flight of stairs advertised M. Pantoulenzo again with a card and the words, "One flight up."

Dan entered and, after a moment's groping, found himself on a small landing with a door on the left-hand side. A small pane of glass was let into one of the panels, affording a view of the shop.

Directly before the window stood a barber chair, gorgeous in crimson plush, and at the moment harboring a tall, very thin man with an abstracted expression on his face. He was sitting up straight, with his hands on his knees, his head bent painfully to one side in the manner of the conscientious and anxiously obliging customer. The towel in which he was enveloped had evidently been manufactured by the barber himself, for it reached just below the tall man's waistcoat and formed a chute down which the shorn hair slid to his trousers. Of the barber himself Dan could see no more than the half of a red face, a glancing black eye, and a pair of thin hands stretching spasmodically for the hair above them.

The attitudes of both men suggested so forcibly a precarious equilibrium of mind and body that Dan fingered the latch and opened the door as quietly as he could.

"Goo' morning," said the barber. "Set down, mister. I'm through in half a mo'."

The tall man did not look up.

The little barber was parting his customer's hair. Then he whipped away the towel, scattering the loose hair broadcast. The tall man leisurely climbed out of the chair and pulled out a billfold.

"Here you be, Francey."

The barber nodded his head and put the bill in his pocket. The tall man picked a broad-brimmed hat from a peg and said, "Morning," and went out of the room with an easy swagger of his shoulders.

"Next!" cried the barber.

Dan looked round.

"You, mister; you're next, I reckon."

Dan took his seat in the chair, and the barber deftly slipped the towel over him and pinned it round his neck.

"What'll you have?"

"Shave."

The sunlight shining through the windows and lighting on his neck made him drowsy, his eyes lazily surveying the varnished board walls, a colored lithograph of the battle of Oriskany their only decoration, the white shelf with its rows of lotions, its two razors and their strops, the worn old mug with a cap of lather gradually settling back into its rimy interior, the kettle of hot water purring on the little corner stove, and all about his feet the shorn hair of former customers lying in heaps like little cords of wood.

The barber set about whipping up a lather. He was a small man, but in spite of his outlandish name there was nothing particularly foreign-looking about him. His pointed face held an expression of keenness, and there was a precocious cock to his head. As he worked, he kept popping questions at Dan.

"Getting warmer?"

"Yeanh."

"I thought maybe it would. We don't get much real cold here till November."

He applied a great deal of lather and then began to strop his razor. He did it with a flourish.

"Stranger?" asked the barber.

"Yeanh."

The barber worked for an instant in silence.

"Well," he said, "you've come to a good place to find work. Rome, New York, is due to become one of the great metropolises." He turned up the left side of Dan's face. "And look where it stands. On the confluence of two canals. Oneida County has just commenced to grow. Look at the timber. Finest white pine in the state. Cribs of timber coming down every spring faster than the locks'll take them. It's right on the trade route to the West. The highroad, the railroad, and the canal right among the streets. You looking for a job on the canal?"

"That's right."

"Well, I wished I'd knowed that. The feller that was in here was looking for a driver. Operates a line boat on the Troy to Michigan Six Day Line."

Dan took an interest. "What's his name?"

"Julius W. Wilson. A celebrated character, now a Roman. Used to belong to Flame and Furnas, the famous knife-throwing team of the American Museum in New York City. Corner of Ann Street and Broadway. If you ever go there, don't miss it. It's one of the wonders of this continent, and if there are any others most likely they're all in it. Every afternoon from four to four-thirty Flame and Furnas did their show. (Flame was Wilson's bill name.) Furnas held the knives and did the talking and Wilson done the throwing. It was a great sight—a cold chill for a thousand people every ten seconds. They had a nine-year-old boy for a target."

"You know a lot about him."

"Why wouldn't I? I'm his regular barber. Most any day he'll tell me all about it; tell me just how close he'd come. Ankle, knee, hip, waist, shoulder (armhole by particular request), neck. Couldn't beat him. It ain't strange, it's the artist temperament."

Dan grunted.

"True as preaching. I've shaved a whole minstrel show; they're all the same.

"Yes, sir," the barber went on, "if you want a job, you go round to Hennessy's Saloon—just round the corner—when you're shaved and ask for Wilson. Probably he'll take you on. He's hauling to Albany."

"I guess I will."

M. Pantoulenzo flourished his razor under Dan's nose and shaved the lip.

"M. Pantoulenzo—quite a name, eh?"

"Yeanh," said Dan.

"A good trade name's a great thing in business. Now, looking at that name, you'd never guess I was born in London, would you?"

"No."

"That's why I picked on it. Real name is Smiggs. That might go in England. Smiggs, barber. But it wouldn't go an inch in this land. Americans are that way. They've got extravagant notions of business and work which makes 'em serious in their notions of pleasure or getting their hair cut, or going to the dentist. My Crikey, 'ow these people do shine to a dentist! If I wasn't a barber, I'd go in for teeth altogether. You can tear out a whole jawful of teeth with them and set up false ones and they'll call it progress."

He reached for a damp towel with which to remove the edges of lather left from the shave, and then, grunting, swung the chair into an upright position.

Dan paid him and made his way slowly down the stairs.

In Hennessy's Saloon

The sun had come out warm, and the air was so sparkling and clear that he stepped out sturdily. Women were going by on their way to market, their baskets on their arms. A carriage crossed the end of the street, and a fast trotter in front of a varnished surrey caught Dan's eye.

Overhead in the cloudless sky he could see a great flock of crows flapping over the town, so high above him that their cawing sounded thin.

There could be no mistaking Hennessy's Saloon; it was so obviously one. Its flashy green doors hooked open, it stood well out toward the roadway; and its two broad glass windows gave it an appearance of extreme open-handedness and sincerity.

Inside the bar, the keep was reading that week's copy of the *Roman Citizen*. There was no one else in the room. He looked up at Dan's entrance, cocking one eye over the edge of the paper.

"What's yours?"

"Is Mr. Wilson here?"

"Come in five minutes ago. He's out back talking to Hennessy. You can see him when he comes out. What's yours?"

"I don't know," said Dan. "I hadn't thought."

"You'll want a bit of a swallow," said the keep. "Julius W. and old Hennessy talk quite a while once they get going. Have a black strap?"

"Surely."

The keep mixed a glassful, drawing first the molasses and then the rum directly from the kegs. There was a great row of them behind the bar, which ran the whole length of the room, and over them, on shelves, rows of bottles obliquely picked out the sunny doorway. The keep covered the glass with another and shook the mixture. His hands worked with great rapidity, and when he set the glass before Dan there was a thin cap of brown foam upon it.

"Four cents."

Dan slapped down the pennies and started to sip the heavy sweet drink. It was cool in the barroom, and the shadow was grateful to his eyes after the sunlight in the street. Gradually he became drowsy; the two preceding days had been hard ones. The keep grinned to see him nod and almost lose his hold on the glass.

"Kind of sleepy, eh? Well, Wilson won't be out for an hour, most likely, and if you want to lie down in the back room I'll call you when he comes out."

He pointed his thumb to a door at the back of the bar. Dan thanked him and picked up his bag.

After he had closed the door behind him, it took Dan a minute to accustom his eyes to the darkness. The one window in the room was boarded over, but enough light crept through the cracks to show him four stout posts, two feet or more in diameter, rising from floor to ceiling. About each post a circular platform had been constructed with a mattress to fit, so that as many as twelve men could sleep about a single upright, their feet to the post and their bodies radiating outward like the spokes of an immense wheel.

Dan stretched himself out with his hands folded behind his head. He must have dozed for a minute, for he suddenly became conscious of three voices speaking beyond the door to the bar; and that strange sense which bridges the gap between sleeping and waking informed him that they had been speaking for some time. In an instant he had recognized the bartender's voice; and it occurred to him that he had heard both of the other voices. And then he caught the names, and placed them—Spinning, the sheriff of Rome, and Mr. Henderson, who called himself a horse dealer. Spinning was talking in his loud voice.

". . . danged near cornered him up by Potato Hill. He'd got himself put up at the Morris place. Old man Morris didn't have no idea about who he was. But he described the horse to me. He can't see very well, and the feller wore his hat in the house, a wide-brimmed one, so it was hard to see his face. Calash had only stayed there overnight. But the horse sounds like the one you lost. Yes, sir, I've no doubt it's the same. Give us a little more time, Mr. Henderson, and we'll have him back for you."

"I don't doubt it." Henderson's voice was harder to follow. "When did he come down this way?"

"That afternoon. We're not such fools. We had a couple of people on the lookout. And I know reliable he's headed for Syracuse. Nothing more I can do for the moment. I'm going to have some rest. We'll get him, though, won't we, Luke? You know me."

"Sure," said the bartender. "Question of time. You'll have him, though."

"They're sending a Department of Justice man up here," the sheriff growled. "But do you think they'd tell me his name? No, they won't. I'm to keep on on my own line and help him if he comes to me. Like as not when we've got Calash he'll join in on the reward."

"It's hard," said Mr. Henderson.

"Sure," said the bartender sympathetically.

The voices of the sheriff and Henderson dimmed, as if they had moved to another part of the room. Then Dan heard a new voice, a woman's this time, asking for Mr. Klore.

"Said he'd be back in half an hour," replied the barkeep.

The young woman's voice replied that she would wait. Quick, light steps came through the half door in the bar to the door of the circular-bed chamber. Dan heard a whisper and the bartender's voice huskily replying, "Just a young lad."

The door opened and Dan sat up and put his feet on the floor.

The young woman was tall and strapping, so much he could see while she paused against the light of the barroom. She wore a red dress and a red hat, from under which a few wisps of light brown hair escaped as though protesting against an unaccustomed confinement. She presented a rather blowsy-looking figure, unaccountably attractive in its blowsiness, with something fresh about it.

When she made out Dan's position, the young woman closed the door behind her and came forward in the unnatural darkness.

"I hope you'll pardon me disturbing you," she said in a strong, clear voice.

Dan felt stuffy and uncomfortable, and wished she had not closed the door.

"You see," she went on, sitting on the circular bed beside him, "I've got to wait for my boater, and I don't like to wait in the bar; and Luke said you was a quiet-looking man, so I come in here."

"I don't mind," said Dan awkwardly. "My name's Dan'l Harrow."

"Pleased to meet you. I'm Molly Larkins."

"Pleased, mam."

A knothole in the boards over the window sent a finger of light against her cheek, so that her profile was outlined to Dan in warm sunlight. She had a wide mouth, with full, decisive lips pressed firmly together, and an expressive chin, well rounded. She had compelling hands, long-fingered, which squeezed the handle of a long bag she held on her knees until they took on the shape of a capable pair of fists. Altogether, she did not belong in the musty darkness of the saloon; even there it seemed the daylight had stolen in to mark her. She should have been handling a rudder sweep instead of her little bag, or swinging a scythe.

"It's a weary place to wait in," she remarked.

"Yeanh," said Dan, trying to guess her age. He had instantly taken a liking to her, for her straightforward manner had put him at ease.

"Be you a-working on the canal, Mr. Harrow?"

It was the first time anyone had put "mister" in front of his name, and he involuntarily checked the "mam" on his tongue.

"No," he replied. "I'm waiting for Mr. Wilson, to get a job with."

She nodded.

"Yes. I know him. Julius W. Hauling for the Troy–Michigan Six Day."

"He's hauling down to Albany," said Dan. "I'd like to get a job with him."

"Well, I wouldn't want to go there."

"Why not?"

"I don't know. I don't like it."

"You been on the canal long?" Dan asked, after a short silence.

She turned her head toward him, and as the light traveled over her eyes Dan saw that they were deep blue.

"Gracious, yes! I was born on a boat. Dad was a captain for the Old Utica Long and Short Haul Line. After I was thirteen I done the cooking for him. He died when I was fifteen and since then I've been working mostly on the canal. I ain't got no recollection of Ma. Once a missioner society got a-hold of me and I took a job working in the ladies' ward of the State Asylum. It's pretty slow work for me and I quit on them. I guess Dad left a bit of Hell in me. He was a big man and never licked. I remember when he fought the Buffalo Bully in Rochester Arcade and licked him after one hour. There was so many people watching I couldn't see till a man let me

stand on his shoulders. Pa give me a hiding afterwards for yelling when
he got knocked down. He said it wasn't right for a lady."

She glanced down at her hands.

"I learned to take care of myself pretty good. So I get along. If I don't
like the man I hire out with I just quit him and get myself another job
through Lucy Cashdollar's agency."

"Yeanh?"

"Yeanh, hers is best. Bentley's Bar. In Utica. Guess I'll spend a time
with her next week."

"Sick of your job?" asked Dan, suddenly.

"Kind of. He's a sort of bully. I don't have much rest from him. He's
hard to handle. But he's an easy spender and he's got good innards for
fighting," she added, a note of pride in her voice.

"I seen him in Boonville, if it's Jotham Klore."

"Yeanh. Did you come down ahead of us?"

"Yeanh. I used to live up above Boonville."

"Is that right?"

Dan began trying to guess her age again; the subject attracted him singularly. Back in Tug Hill country he was considered ahead of his years in
figuring a horse's age, and A-1 in the cow line. Yes, he could judge a cow
into the right year nine times out of ten. But this was something else, trying to figure a girl's age; there was less to go by; you could not use your
hands, for one thing.

He could not see much of her except her outline in that dark room;
coloring could not help him there. But she had walked with a straight back;
there was no sag in her. And she had good solid curves in her figure, and
as she sat by him her tight dress showed no softness. He could not see her
feet, either, and that was a point he always liked to go by. He put a lot of
stock in feet. But she walked like a filly, plenty of lift, and her weight well
under her, no forward splurge at the knees. She was tight in front; she
looked sound. He called her twenty-two.

"Well," said Molly Larkins suddenly, "now you're done, what do you
make of me?"

"Fair, pretty fair," Dan said, still in his professional mood, "a good buy
if the price was right."

She burst out laughing, tilting her head and looking out at him from
half-closed eyes. She had a good whole-souled laugh, pitched low, with no
hoarseness.

"Well," she said, "the price is twelve dollars a month, in case you want
to know."

"Fair enough," Dan said. "If I ever get a boat I'll remember that."

She gave him a quick, square glance; and then smiled slowly.

"You haven't looked at my teeth, you know. How old did you make me
out?"

"Nineteen," he replied, giving her laugh the benefit of one less year,
and her vanity, in a moment of inspiration, the benefit of two.

"Eighteen," she said.

"Jeepers!" he said, ruefully. "I need practice in your line."

Molly laughed again.

"Now I'll guess yours."

"Yeanh?"

"You're nineteen. What's more, you're new on a canal."

He gazed at her admiringly.

"You're pretty good, ain't you?"

"It's a thing you get to learn, in my trade. It's a part of the job."

They sat together without speaking for a while, listening to the voices beyond the door, and to the angry buzz of a bluebottle fly against the windowpanes.

"Are you planning to keep on driving?" she asked Dan.

"Yeanh. For a while, I reckon. I'd like to have my own boat."

"Who would you haul for?"

"I guess you can pick up hauling."

"Probably could," said Molly; "but still, you ain't any idea how many people is working on the Erie. Last year they figgered there was twenty-five thousand—men and women and driver boys working on the main ditch."

"Jeepers!" breathed Dan.

"It probably seems a queer place," Molly said, "until you get used to it. People live by different notions there. They're law-abiding by state law; but they've got their own ideas on how to live. The missioners call 'em bad, but I guess a moral is a kind of figure for personal ciphering. Canawlers would say the missioner was unhealthy; he's letting his mind get rid of what his body should get rid of according to nature."

"Who told you that?" Dan asked.

"Friend of mine. An old feller. He used to be a minister himself, and he goes in for ministering now to make money to live with when he needs it."

More people had entered the barroom. The voices of Mr. Henderson and the sheriff were no longer distinguishable. Then a loud hoarse voice sounded close to the panel; the man was addressing the bartender. "Seen my cook, Luke?" "Inside," said the keep. And a hand fell on the door handle. Molly Larkins suddenly stood up. "He's feeling hostile," she said to Dan in a low voice. "Don't mind his talk."

The door swung open and banged shut behind Jotham Klore. For an instant he stood with his back to it, his pale eyes peering into the gloom of the room.

"Come along, Moll," he said, "we ain't any time to lose."

He stopped speaking and came forward a step or two, and saw Dan.

"Say! How long've you been here, Moll?"

"You kept me waiting a good half hour, Jotham," she said, coolly. "So you needn't talk nasty."

"I'll talk as I damn please. He'd better pick up his bag and get out of here. If he wants to argue, I'm a pretty good hand myself. I won't have no man monkeying with my cook."

"It's none of your business, anyway."

"What do you think I'm paying you for?"

"I'm no slave. I'll do as I please. I don't have to look hard to get a job."

"You shut up!"

He came over and grabbed Dan by the collar of his shirt.

"Are you going to get out?"

Dan's right hand shot up and his arm straightened; he heard a sudden crack, and felt a shoot of pain run into his hand and wrist. Klore's knees sagged, and his hand fell away from Dan's collar. Molly gave a low cry, deep-toned, with a note of pleasure.

"Quick! Hit him again."

But Dan stood back upon his heels; he hadn't thought of hitting him at all; he was completely surprised.

"Quick!" cried Molly, as Klore sucked in his breath whistlingly, his teeth showing white in his black beard.

"Oh, shucks!" she said, and turned away, as if to avoid an unpleasant sight.

"All right," growled Klore. "Try and do it again."

All at once, Dan remembered the grin on the face of the boater in the Lansing Kill, and he felt weak. He wanted to say he would go, but he couldn't force the words past his teeth; and he knew anyway that it wouldn't have done any good. Then he heard an exclamation from Molly.

At the same instant he became aware of a fourth person in the room, he heard a thud, and Jotham Klore's hands leaped past his face and he fell forward limp into Dan's arms.

"Look at the door, both of you."

A man, holding a revolver in his right hand, was standing with his back to the faint stripe of light that came through the window boarding; but a menacing coldness in his tone made Dan fix his gaze on the door. Out of the corner of his eye, he could see that the girl stared as rigidly as he.

"He was set to butter and fry you, young man," said the stranger, almost friendly; then his voice harshened.

"Who was in the bar?" he asked Molly.

"The sheriff," she said, "and Luke and another man. I think his name was Henderson."

"Him!" The man grunted.

"Listen," he said to Dan. "I've just done you a turn; now you can do me one. Go out and get that man Henderson out of the bar for a minute. I've got to get out of here and he's watching out the back window."

"What'll I tell him?"

"Figure it out for yourself. Only don't start anything funny. I'm watching through the back door of this room; I'll be able to see clean into the bar."

"I'll tell him I seen you coming down the Lansing Kill."

"How do you know that?"

"I can make a guess who you are."

"Don't try. I'm getting out of this room. How about you, young woman? Will you keep shut five minutes?"

"Surely," Molly said. "I'll keep a conversation going with Jotham."

"All right."

They heard him leaving the room, and a gentle draft told them that he had opened the back door. They dragged Klore to one side, out of sight of the door.

"He must've been in here all the while," said Molly in a low voice.

"I guess that's right."

"Are you going to do what he said?"

"I guess so," said Dan. "I guess it's the right thing to do this time."

"If you raised a holler now you'd have enough to buy your boat with, and more besides."

"Yeanh," said Dan, "maybe I would."

"He couldn't stop you now."

"I guess he ought to have a chance."

"All right. If you ain't going to say nothing, I won't. You'd better be going out. Good-bye, Mr. Harrow."

She held out her hand. When he took it he found it hard and warm, filling his palm.

"Pleased to have met you," he said awkwardly, and he went into the bar, closing the door behind him.

Several men stood at the bar, and over in a corner the sheriff was sitting with the horse dealer, Henderson. Dan walked over to them. Both looked up.

"Cripus!" exclaimed the fat man. "It's the lad I saw in Boonville."

"Yeanh," said Dan. "I wanted to tell you something about your horse, Mr. Henderson."

Henderson drew his cigar from his lips and they followed it out, pursing themselves in their silent whistle. He glanced round him quickly.

"Say!" he exclaimed. "We might as well step outside."

"Yeanh," said the sheriff.

The three of them went out into the street.

"What is it, young man?"

"I seen a horse just like yourn coming down through the Lansing Kill yesterday noon."

"Who was you with?"

"Solomon Tinkle and Hector Berry."

Sheriff Spinning nodded his head. "That's right. I seen you at the Five Combines."

"We knew he'd come down. You didn't get a good sight of him?" asked Henderson.

"No," said Dan. "He was quite a ways off."

"Shucks. That ain't no news. I can't do nothing till I know what he looks like," the sheriff complained. "He might be any long-legged feller I hadn't seen before. Why, he could be right here in Hennessy's for all I'd know."

"Thanks, anyhow," Henderson said to Dan. "Let me know, or Spinning here, if you see him again."

"All right," said Dan.

He walked back into the saloon with them. As he entered, he saw Julius Wilson approaching him.

"That's the young man," said the bartender.

"What do you want?" asked Wilson.

"I heard you was looking for a driver."

"I am. What's your name?"

"Dan Harrow."

"Done any driving?"

"Some."

"Who with?"

"Mr. Hector Berry."

"That seedless raisin?"

"Yeanh," said Dan, with a grin.

"Well, I'll give eleven a month driver's wages. But I'll only hire you in to Albany. I'll give you one-fifty for the trip."

"It's right by me."

"Come along with me," said Mr. Wilson.

The Line Boat, Xerxes

Julius W. Wilson walked with a long stride.

"You're lucky to get a job with me here," he remarked to Dan. "Line boats generally go straight through, and the Michigan Six Day don't hire a captain that's late. But this trip Wendell, on the western end, shoved a short-haul job on to me, to Rome, so I had to stop over."

He nodded to a boater—and then, with a fine gesture, swept off his wide felt hat to a sharp-faced woman with an outthrust jaw who came striding along the street toward them.

"How d'ye do, Mrs. Quackenbush," he said politely. "How are you this handsome day?"

She swung round at him, and as her skirt lifted a trifle from the swirl Dan noticed that she wore a man's cowhide boots.

"Hullo, Julius, how be you?"

"You're looking good," observed Mr. Wilson.

"Good yourself! Don't try none of your dandiness on me!"

"Here's a young man come down from Boonville with your sister, Nell Berry," said Mr. Wilson, indicating Dan with a wave of his hand.

"Pleased to meet you. My name's Quackenbush."

She grasped Dan's hand, and her palm felt calloused against his.

"Dan Harrow," he said.

"How is the old hen?" she asked good-humoredly.

"Good."

"She always is. The first time she's sick she'll be underground. Well, I've got to get going. Please to've seen you boys."

"There's a character," observed Mr. Wilson, when she was out of hearing. "You don't know it, Harrow, but you've shook hands with the woman that's pumped the canal dry three times."

Dan stared.

"Oh, I ain't guffing you none. You can ask any boater. She married old Idwall Quackenbush two days afore he died. I reckon she shocked the lights clean out of him. And when she'd seen him buried she took up his boat and she's run it ever since. The danged crate leaks so she's got to keep pumping it; you're apt to see it tied up anywhere with the water tossing out in squirts. Ben Rae, he's my steersman, he figgered one night she'd pumped enough water to fill the Erie three times over."

He laughed.

"It don't faze her. And she makes money. She's raising quite a family, too. Got three boys."

They came down to the docks and walked west along them until they came to a lumber yard.

"There's the old Xerxes," said Mr. Wilson. He pointed out a yellow boat, trimmed green, tied up a little way ahead. "We're waiting here for some matched boarding to take down to the Oriskany Mills. Then we pick up a load in Utica from the Ashery for Little Falls—a shipment for West-feldt's soap. It's dirty to handle, but we'll have to clean on the way down to Albany. I'm running down empty from Little Falls."

Just as they came abreast of the boat, an immense old Jew thrust his head from the cabin door, came up the steps, and stood beside the rudder sweep, where he stretched his arms over his head and yawned.

"Hello, Ben," said Mr. Wilson. "Got that boarding on yet?"

The Jew turned toward them slowly. He had a great white beard, like the beard of Moses, and when he spoke the end of it jumped away from him in little jerks.

"No," he said. "There was a big line waiting at the yard. We're just due now; we'll get loaded by noon."

Wilson grunted.

"Time enough, I guess. We can get in to Utica by tomorrow evening."

"Sure, that's right. Whyn't you go see the missis and meet up with us at 'Riskany? It won't cost you more'n a dollar."

"I might, at that. Say, Ben, here's a lad I took on as driver as far as Albany. Name's Dan'l Harrow. Ben Rae."

The Jew wrinkled his long nose and grinned.

"It's a pleasure. Come aboard."

"Ben's in charge," Wilson said. "Well, I guess I'll shove along. It ain't often I get a chance to see Aurelia for a night during summer. She won't travel the canal," he explained to Dan, "and she's quite right. It's degrading for a delicate woman. She used to be the loveliest singer on the New York stage. An artist of the first water. Lovely still, but melancholy."

"No blame to her," said Rae, "living by herself so much."

Mr. Wilson waved an arm and walked rapidly away down the dock.

"Come on down," the Jew said to Dan. "William's cooking dinner."

He led the way into the cabin.

The Xerxes had been built to carry twenty passengers as well as the crew. The cabin took up most of the stern half of the boat; freight space lay forward. There was no stable for the horses, as the line companies had their own service stables the whole length of the canal. They handled only the rush freight, and, in spite of the growing power of the railroads, they did big business in carrying emigrants westward.

Under the windows a row of iron-frame bunks, on which canvas was stretched, were hinged against the walls. To the right of the steps a cur-tain marked the entrance to the crew's bunks, which were built into a cuddy, five feet high, directly under the steersman's deck. In the corner to the left of the steps stood a good-sized stove, at which crew and passen-gers could take turns.

When Dan and Benjamin Rae entered, a man was peering into the oven.

"Here's a lad Julius W. got for driver as far as Albany," said Rae.

The man turned a pair of mild brown eyes toward them and pushed his hand rapidly the wrong way through his hair.

"Hullo," he said.

He was middle-aged and had a lean, thoughtful face.

"Biscuits coming good?" asked Rae.

"Fair," said the man.

"This lad's Dan Harrow," said the Jew. "Meet William Wampy."

"Hullo," said Wampy again.

He turned back to the stove. A coffeepot spouted fragrant steam, and potatoes and bacon, frying together, sizzled when he turned them with a broad knife.

"Put your bag back there," said the Jew, pointing to the sleeping cuddy. "I'll set out the dishes."

They ate leisurely, and the food was good.

"William's studying to be a cook," Rae said to Dan, as he poured syrup over his biscuits. "He's a pretty slick hand, I'd say."

Wampy flushed with pleasure.

"He's a great hand for a fiddle," said Rae. "He sleeps hearty. And he can work when we make him. But mostly he cooks and eats what he cooks."

Wampy raised his dark eyes to Dan's.

"Eating's fun," he said.

Men stamped on deck. Presently they heard them loading the boarding into the pit forward. Rae shoved back his chair and sighed.

"Reckon I'd better go and get a team."

He went out.

Dan started to follow him.

"No need of you going out," said William Wampy. "We're paid to run this boat, not to fill it full of lumber."

He helped himself to more biscuits.

"It ain't a bad job, if you use your privileges," he observed.

Dan sat down again and watched him eat. He ate long and silently. Once in a while he smacked his lips.

"I married once," said Wampy. "For four years I didn't have no good food.

"Well," he added, after a while, "Benjy'll be coming back pretty quick. We'll have to clear up. Will you wipe or will you wash?"

"I don't care," said Dan.

"I'll dry then. We'll let the cups drccn."

When they had finished, Dan went on deck. The last boards were being handed up on to the boat. The Jew was coming along the dock behind a pair of mules. A man, who had been overseeing the lading, went up to him.

"Fifteen thousand," he said. "You'll sign for Wilson."

"Surely," said the Jew.

He signed the bill, and the men who had been loading got off the boat.

"You drive," he called to Dan.

Dan hooked the evener to the towline and threw the tie-ropes on deck. The mules took up the slack and heaved; the Xerxes groaned against the dock, inched slowly out, and they started down the Erie. As they passed other boats tied up, a man on deck would catch the towrope and pass it across the boat. In fifteen minutes they had cleared the basin, and the mules came out upon the towpath. A hundred yards ahead three other boats crept in the same direction.

"No point hurrying," said the Jew; so Dan allowed the mules to take their own pace, until a little after four o'clock they entered the village of Oriskany and tied up beside the woolen mills.

In the gathering dusk of the cabin William Wampy was fondling notes from his fiddle, making a melody from "The Wind that Shakes the Barley." "He's got kind of a pretty softness on the strings," said the Jew.

Dan rested his forehead on his arms and closed his eyes. The whirr of the mill machinery and the clack of the looms dimmed as the notes of the fiddle felt their way toward a tune. Boats that passed seemed a long way off. Dan repeated Molly Larkins's name to himself and all at once saw her again, sitting beside him in her red dress in the darkness in Hennessy's Saloon, while the light from the knothole picked out bits of color here and there. Only now they left the saloon together and went down to the docks. . . .

The Jew glanced down at him and smiled in his white beard. "Tired," he said to himself. He pulled a pipe out of his pocket and filled it and put it in his mouth and leaned back against the cabin. But he forgot to light it. And after a while his head bent forward toward his up-drawn knees.

A Sermon by Request

Sunday-morning breakfast they ate at a comfortable late hour. A little after ten o'clock, Julius Wilson appeared beside the boat. He had been given a lift by Mr. Butterfield, who was driving down to Utica.

"Dandiest pair of trotters I've ever sat back of," he said.

He came aboard briskly.

"We'd better start off now; you get the mules out, Dan, but William'll do the first stretch of driving."

Traffic was lighter than it had been on the preceding day. Almost all the boats they met were company boats.

They drifted along placidly, the mules and William Wampy taking a leisurely pace on the towpath. Dan drowsed on the cabin roof and Mr. Wilson steered. The Jew was busy with his Sunday washing. He had a tub just forward of the cabin, over which he bent, dousing his underwear. His long white beard was tied up in a towel to keep it dry.

After they had traveled for a little over an hour, Dan suddenly became aware of a faint sound of people shouting. Far ahead on the right shore stood a small group of houses; nearer at hand a small barn, by itself, with GEORGE HENRY, FEED STORES, UTICA painted in white letters on the end.

Mr. Wilson and the Jew had also heard the noise, for they were looking ahead with their hands over their eyes. William Wampy trudged on behind the mules, and paid no attention.

"He can sleep walking," said the Jew. "He does it so he won't get tired."

The clamor increased rapidly. A bunch of perhaps twenty people were running along the towpath toward them—one man well ahead, then more men, some women and children.

"Wonder what's up?" said Mr. Wilson.

"Some kind of ruckus."

"Wonder what they're a-chasing him for?"

It was obviously a chase. As it neared them they made out the pursued man clearly. He was running in great strides, his long spindly legs stretching out well ahead of him. In one hand he carried a small satchel, in the other a floppy grey felt hat.

"Knee action a mite too high for speed," observed Mr. Wilson, "but he sure is working for it."

They could see the man's face, as red as his scarlet waistcoat. His head was thrown back; his mouth was open; and his long thin moustaches whipped back against his cheeks at every bound. He was holding his own, but no more.

It could be seen now, also, that the pursuers were got up in their Sunday best. Now and then, when he spied a stone in his path, a man would pick it up and hurl it after the fleeing man. Most shots went wide, but occasionally one found its mark, and the skinny man would spring into the air and gain a foot when he came down.

He and the Xerxes reached the barn at almost the same moment, but he paid no heed to the boat. The doors were open, and with a new burst of speed he rushed through them. In a few seconds all of the yelling pursuers had swept in after him, except a small boy who approached at a much slower pace and carried carefully a basket of eggs in his right hand. He had an intelligent face.

Mr. Wilson bawled to William Wampy to stop the mules.

"We might as well tie up and see what's going on."

The barn was well filled with hay, the air drowsy with motes. A small window to the east let in a shaft of sunlight on the head of a ladder leaning against the mow and glittered on the tines of a pitchfork. The boy who had carried the basket was tossing eggs high up over the edge of hay. One popped flatly, and the man in the mow swore in a strangling voice. The congregation at the foot of the ladder gathered the hubbub of their voices into a deep hollow of delight.

Mr. Wilson took a man by the elbow.

"Excuse me breaking in, but what's going on?"

"Why," replied the man, "there ain't enough of us round Maynar's Corners to have a regular church, there being only Hoofman's store and six farms round; but when this feathered snake come in, saying we'd ought to hire a preacher and that he was a good one, we hired him for six sermons at four dollars per and give him free board. We paid him last night, he having give five of them, but whiles he was waiting for service this morning one of the boys seen him sneaking out the back door with his bag in his hand—ready to cut and run, by Jeepers Cripus!"

He was still red-faced from his running, and he breathed loudly through his nose. A little woman in a stiff black dress, black knitted wristers, and upright small bonnet ran over to him.

"Ain't any of you men going to climb that ladder, Nat Wattles?"

"I don't want to run my stummick on a pitchfork, Annie; not me nor any other man."

"Well, by holy, if you men is all scared, the *womenfolk* will climb that ladder. I'd just like to set my hands on that sermonizing Judas man!"

She started elbowing the men aside.

"Come on, girls!"

There was savagery in her shrill cry and the echoing shout of the women crowding behind her. The man Wattles shifted his feet.

"He's to blame for it," he said nervously.

But the man on the mow, who had been lying so coolly behind his pitchfork, heard the cry and got to his feet. He raised his hand into the bar of sunlight, commanding attention. Suddenly, out of nowhere, an egg broke against his palm, and a quiver shot through him while the brown yolk wriggled slowly to his wrist. But he held his posture.

Little by little the people fell silent. The men stared, and the women stopped struggling at the foot of the ladder. Dan noticed one man with the red, crisp-skinned nose and dull eyes of a drunkard, standing mouth agape in a corner. He looked suddenly afraid.

Rage had brought the color back into the preacher's face; and he cried out, hoarsely, "All right! If you want your sermon that bad, by Holy Jesus; I'll give it to you!"

He shook the pitchfork downward.

"Set down!"

His voice thundered along the rafters.

Dan heard Mr. Wilson whispering to the Jew.

"He's a master hand at acting a part, the old renegade."

A thin sighing rose from the people; even the boy who had thrown the egg so accurately set down his basket. There was a gentle rustling of the hay upon the floor as the congregation settled themselves.

In the quiet, the skinny man on the mow picked up a handful of the hay and wiped his hand, back, palm, between the fingers. He did it deliberately; the gesture was a symbol.

Then he knelt, and folded his hands, and prayed: "O Lord God in Heaven, strengthen me, I pray Thee; visit my tongue with fire, I pray Thee, that I may smite these people with it, for I know there is no good in them. Amen."

He rose slowly to his feet, a small Bible open in his hand; and in a fine, resonant voice he read them the text of his sermon:—

"Hell and destruction are before the Lord."

He closed the book and gazed sombrely down upon his congregation. With his white hair, pink cheeks, black moustache, and scarlet waistcoat showing through his old blue coat, he made a glowing patch of color against the brown dusk of the rafters. The sunlight picked out his white hand as it rose again and suddenly jabbed a long forefinger at the people.

At the motion, the red-nosed drunkard closed his mouth; his face went white, and he gulped.

"Hell and destruction are before the Lord," the preacher repeated.

The little woman in the stiff black dress nodded her head.

"Hell is never full," he reminded them grimly.

Again he paused. About Dan the breathing of the people sounded deeper. Suddenly the drunkard groaned. There was sweat on his face.

The preacher moved his left hand slightly, so that the sunlight traced gleaming spots along the tines of the pitchfork.

"Have you ever stopped to figure out what the pains of Hell were like?" he asked them in a lowered voice.

"Have you ever scalded a hog? You could rub the hair off with one wipe. . . .

"You know how fat stinks and starts to roar when it catches fire. There'll
be fires built on your innards down in Hell. . . .

"Think of the red flames gnawing at your feet. . . . Think of the black
smoke crawling out your mouths and ears. . . . Think of the boiling water
and the tar. . . .

"You've dropped bullheads into a fry-pan for breakfast and watched
'em curl and hop. What'll your poor thin naked souls do when the Devil
lays them on a red-hot iron skillet? . . ."

The drunkard choked a cry with his hands and hid his face. Even Dan
and the crew of the Xerxes stirred restlessly. Out of their own experience
he was painting Hell for them until each sense leaped at the word; and then
he brought it home to the villagers personally.

"Who can escape the damnation of Hell?"

He lifted a menacing hand.

"Who do you find in Hell?" His voice rose to the question. "Judas Is-
cariot burns in Hell.

> *"Iscariot sold*
> *His God for gold. . . .*

"What man of you told the preacher he'd give him three dollars a sermon when you all know you'd give him by a subscription twenty-four
dollars to pay the preacher who took the job? Six into twenty-four goes
four times. Four times six is twenty-four. He tried to make a profit of six
dollars on his own religion. I see him. I see him. But God has seen him a
long time. 'The boldness of his face shall be changed.' Look and see!"

The man Wattles drew in his breath, and his face went red and white.
But the others did not look at him; they were afraid of their own damnation. Only a grim look came into the eyes of the little woman in the stiff
black dress.

The preacher's hand shot out again.

"Who uses doctored scales in Maynar's Corners? 'False weights are an
abomination unto the Lord!'

"Potiphar's wife is burning down in Hell. What woman meets a man in
Phileo's sugar bush on Saturday nights, or oftener? 'Thou hast polluted the
earth with thy wickedness!' Can ye escape the damnation of Hell?"

One by one he fastened on them the stigma of village gossip, until they
huddled under the gleam of his eyes.

Through the shadow, through the drowsy smell of summer's hay, the
gold-moted shaft of light searched out the preacher's vibrant body, so that
in the duskiness he alone showed clear. His white hair glanced as he spoke,
and his words, coming down on their heads, were truly the words of God.

He talked of evil, and the methods of evil, and its reward among men,
and he talked as if he knew. He spoke of Judgment Day, and he brought
them lame and afoot to the Throne. . . . But no mercy lay there for them.
"Which of you can claim blessing in the sight of God?" he cried. With a
sure dramatic sense he opened the Book again and read, in stirring, measured tones, the Beatitudes.

" 'Blessed are the poor in spirit: for theirs is the Kingdom of Heaven.'
You are all set up in envy. You needn't make a claim. God knows your
spirit; He has searched them out.

" 'Blessed are they that mourn: for they shall be comforted.' No mourners here. When you do, it'll be too late. 'And they mourn at the last, when thy flesh and body shall be consumed.'

" 'Blessed are the meek; for they shall inherit the earth.' Woe to the crown of pride! You women folk who gossip—'Thy damnation slumbereth not!'

" 'Blessed are they which do hunger and thirst after righteousness: for they shall be filled.' It's your bellies you take care to fill, and I ain't seen any man here's thirst taking him to righteousness. Two kegs of rum drunk up last week in Hoofman's store. Who lay on the sidewalk yesterday? 'Strong drink shall be bitter.' O God, how true!

" 'Blessed are the merciful: for they shall obtain mercy.' Who threw stones? Who threw eggs? Who reviled with foul language? What woman wanted to set her hands on me—the preacher?"

His hand rose over his head, and clenched.

" 'Blessed are the pure in heart. . . .' "

His voice tolled on solemnly, irrevocably, truthfully. The evidence was his.

Men and women bowed above their knees. A faint moaning rose with their uneven breathing. The power of the preacher's voice brought their sins upon them; and they saw them all clearly, and knew that they stood clearly before their neighbors, and the women cried, and a weakness came upon them all, as if they had been purged.

The preacher's voice fell silent; the fingers that grasped the Book loosened their hold and let it fall. He stood quite still with his arms at his sides. His face was raised to the bar of sunlight; his Adam's apple worked up and down in his scrawny neck. Even Dan, squatting behind the rest with the crew of the Xerxes at his side, could see the trembling of his lips.

"O God," he said, his voice barely above a whisper, "We are all sinners here, and there is no health in us. Humble our hearts, O God, and let us pray: 'Our Father, Who art in Heaven, Hallowed by Thy name . . .' "

Whisperingly, at first, other voices, one by one, fell in with his.

" 'Thy Kingdom come. Thy will be done on earth, as it is in Heaven. Give us this day our daily bread. And forgive us our trespasses, as we forgive those who trespass against us . . .' "

And the barn was filled to the roof with the slow sentences.

" '. . . Lead us not into temptation, but deliver us from evil. For thine is the Kingdom, and the Power, and the Glory, for ever and ever. Amen.' "

He knelt a moment in silence, the people kneeling with him. Then he rose and stretched his hands out over them, and his voice was husky.

"Let us repent and go."

He held his pose until the people began to file slowly through the doors. They went haltingly, and the sunlight outside brought water to their eyes. After the long siege in the barn, some of them stumbled.

The preacher put his Bible back in the small satchel, wiped his hand again with hay, sniffed at it covertly. Then he put on his hat and began to come down the ladder, his narrow quarters thrusting out between the tails of his coat. Wattles and one or two of the others waited for him to reach the floor. They shook his hand solemnly.

"That was as fine a sermon as I ever heard," said Wattles.

"I am glad to hear you say so," replied the preacher. "It encourages me." His black eyes smiled at them out of a maze of tiny wrinkles.

"Now don't you think you'd better get home? It does a man good to meditate once in a while. And after this,"—the resonance returned to his voice,—"when you repeat what I've said about your neighbors, remember there was a word said also about yourself. All our hope is in the Lord."

He took off his hat as he said it, and the men as solemnly removed theirs, and then filed out. The barn was empty but for the crew of the Xerxes and the drunkard, who had fallen asleep in the corner.

Wilson came up to the preacher and shook him energetically by the hand.

"By grab, that was a show! That was a sermon! If P. T. Barnum could have heard you, he'd have signed you on for his museum and your fortune would be made. Yes, sir!" He raised his right knee and thumped it down. "Thousands of dollars!"

The preacher looked at him slyly.

"Is that a fact?"

"Granpap's gospel—every word. I mean it."

The preacher considered it for a moment. Then he shook his head.

"I'm afraid it wouldn't last. That's the first original one I ever preached. Oh, I've learned sermons. I've got five in this," lifting his satchel, "but I bit off more'n I could chaw here. The contract called for six."

"Well, I'd never've guessed it," said Mr. Wilson.

"I wouldn't 've myself. That's why I was cutting away. There's just four things'll make a man preach hard. A lot of money; being religion-crazy; believing just the opposite of what he's preaching; or being gosh-a'mighty blue scared, like I was."

He chuckled, a sudden musical gurgle in his throat.

"There's a lot in that fact," observed the Jew. "The most powerful evangel I ever listened to started drinking Monday and got the sights by Saturday and woke up Sunday with preachings in his head of the most convincing agony I ever listened to. I danged near changed my faith hearing that man rinse his soul."

He grinned at the preacher and held out his enormous hand.

"My name's Benjamin Rae."

"I'm Julius Wilson. This here's young Harrow. And there's William Wampy."

The preacher smiled round at them as though he felt relieved to be among them.

"My name's Fortune Friendly," he said. "Which way are you folks hauling?"

"Utica."

"Could I go along with you that far?"

"Proud to have you," said Wilson. "Come along."

They walked out of the barn. The mules had found some grass to their liking and were cropping it peacefully. Wampy sighed and went over to them and kicked them in the belly. "Go on," he said.

The others went aboard the boat. The Jew resumed his washing. Mr. Wilson steered. Dan and Fortune Friendly sat down on the cabin roof.

"You look troubled, lad," said Friendly, laying his hand on Dan's shoulder. "Don't let what I say bother you."

Dan stared at him as if he did not understand.

"Don't believe a word of it. I just gave them people what they was looking for. You go along and have a good time. Eat, drink. As long as you ain't dishonest, it don't matter. That's my weakness—but it ain't no robbery from folk like them." He pointed his thumb at Maynar's Corners. "There's a lot of catch-talk in the Bible. But there's one or two things that're mortal true. Here's one for you to get a-hold of: 'And also that every man should eat and drink, and enjoy the good of all his labour, it is the gift of God.' "

He lay down on his back and folded his hands behind his head, and crossed one skinny leg over the other. He turned his head to grin at Dan, and suddenly Dan grinned back. There was something likable about the gnomelike black eyes in the man's pink face, and the unexplainable white hair and maze of fine lines about his eyes and the wrinkles in his scrawny neck.

"Got a good cigar on to you, brother?" he asked Mr. Wilson.

Wilson grinned.

"Sure. Catch it."

He tossed it to Friendly, who caught it, bit off the end, and lit up almost in the same motion.

"I reckon I've heard tell about you," said Wilson. "You're sort of a renegade, ain't you?"

Friendly winked.

"Sure. I was trained for an Episcopal minister. Yale College, by holy. I learned all the confabulations there is in books. But I didn't find it fit."

Wilson's eyes lighted.

"Come here, Dan. You might as well steer. How about a game of pinochle? You're about through, ain't you, Ben?"

"Surely."

"Say," grinned Friendly, "I'm seventy years old, but my luck at cards is good, always good. I figured that was one of the reasons I wasn't cut out to be a minister."

He jumped to his feet and clicked his heels together.

"Don't come no religion on us if you lose," said the Jew.

"Religion is a compound of the passions," said the old man seriously; "that's why it puzzles people like you."

Dan took hold of the rudder.

It was straight steering for the most part, and after swinging wide on the first two turns he began to get the knack of the boat. He leaned against the sweep with just enough weight to keep the bows headed straight. And the Xerxes crept ahead.

Down in the cabin he could hear exclamations of disgust from the two boaters, and Friendly's musical chuckles.

Sunday Afternoon in Chancellor Square

Fortune Friendly shook hands with them all.

"Any time you want to make up a hand of pinochle," he said, "you just send out for me."

Rae and Wilson laughed good-naturedly.

"All right, we'll do that."

The old fellow slapped on his hat and picked up his satchel. When his white hair was covered, he looked but little over thirty.

"I've been livin' too strict these past six weeks," he said. "I've got to limber me up. I need a little corn juice for my inwards."

He walked down the plank and waved his hand to them from the dock.

The Xerxes had been tied up at the west end of the basin. Boats lay before them in a long double line. From some of the screw docks they could see smoke rising from the cabin stovepipes. The city basked in its Sunday quiet. The thump of a boater's heels walking over the dock accentuated the stillness.

Wilson came up to Dan.

"Me and Ben's going ashore," he said. "William will stay on the boat. You can come along with us if you like, or stay here, or do what you want. We'll pick up those ashes in the morning about four o'clock, so I guess you'd better be aboard to-night."

"I guess I'll walk round a spell," Dan said. "I'd like to look at some of the streets."

"Go ahead," said Wilson. "Me and Ben'll be at Bentley's most like after six. It's on Liberty Street. Any boater'll tell you where."

They went down the plank.

In the cabin William Wampy had cooked some lunch for himself. He made no comment when Dan sat down across the table, but helped him to food. Dan did not try to talk; neither he nor William wanted to talk; there was no point in it. The flies of the city had found their way into the newly arrived boat; their buzzing was as much as conversation.

Dan went ashore and walked eastward along the course of the canal. Every once in a while he crossed a low bridge under which the canal let into the screw docks by the sides of warehouses. The boats looked deserted for the most part, though now and then he saw two or three women out on deck hobnobbing while they sewed.

He walked as far as the Genesee Street bridge and there turned to the right and went up into the city. The streets, too, were quiet. A couple of gentlemen in high black hats, black coats, and velvet waistcoats and grey trousers, swinging silver-headed canes; a lady ribboned and faintly scented, entering a smart brougham, drawn by a nervous pair of bays, and handsome in basket paneling. He wandered up one street and down another. In the residential district elms grew and the houses stood back behind their brownstone steps. It was quiet there, not with a noonday hush, but with habitual quiet. He tried to visualize the people behind the half-shaded windows, but he saw them only as the two men walking and the lady entering her carriage.

He came to a square which was shady and cool and which had boarded walks running under the trees. There were benches. And all round the square the houses stood on lawns, and the branches of trees showed beyond the corners of their walls, and some smelled faintly of manure spread out in orchards. Dan sat down on one of the benches, where he could drink in the smell, a homesickness in his eyes—not for the meagre Tug Hill meadows, but for a place which, in a way, he could imagine for himself. Now and then a man develops from his labor on his barren land, not an envy of the valley farmer, but an admiration of rich soil.

So Dan's imagined farm was vague in its outlines. But he could see himself feeling of the bags of his cows, hauling his manure, ploughing in the fall, and, when he was done, polishing his plough. He did not see the house, but he had a vague notion of a hip-roofed barn, like one he had seen outside of Rome. . . . And then he started to hear faintly a horn blowing to the north, and he realized that a boat was sounding for a lock.

He was working on the canal. He had left the land. Before him was a product of the life he was to lead. These many fine houses were made possible by the canal. . . .

He was aware of someone walking past him, and then of a catch in the person's breathing, and he glanced up and saw Molly Larkins. She looked very fresh and pretty with the sunlight spilling through the shade on her red dress. And there was a light of genuine pleasure in her dark blue eyes that brought Dan eagerly to his feet.

"Why, Mr. Harrow," she exclaimed in her low voice, "I didn't think to see you here."

He blushed as though he had been caught at some offense.

"I've been walking round the city," he explained. "I've been walking quite a while. So I set down here for a while."

"Well," she said, "I come here once in a while, too. I like to see the people that live here." She gave a little laugh, not self-conscious, but with an undertone of irritation in it. "I'm notional this way, I guess."

They sat down together.

"I didn't think to see you here," said Dan, after a moment.

"I didn't expect to stop here, myself."

She seemed a little depressed.

"Have you quit Klore?" he asked.

"Yeanh. Yes, I quit him. I didn't want to work for him any more. I didn't like him."

"He looks mean."

"He is mean. But not like you say it. He spends easy and he's a fine powerful man. He's a good man taking a girl round. I had a lot of fun with him."

"What did you quit him for?"

"You remember he said he'd lace me when he come into Hennessy's?"

Her eyes grew dark.

"Yeanh," said Dan.

"He done it."

His face slowly reddened and his hands shook.

She went on quietly, her voice cold.

"He didn't say anything when he come to. He didn't say anything about the other man. But he said no cook who took his pay could be another man's"—she hesitated and looked at Dan and her eyes held his honestly—"whore and not get a lacing till she learned better or left. I told him he was crazy and to mind his own business. But he grabbed my arm and walked with me down to his boat and took a strap and give it to me."

She moved her shoulders away from the back of the bench. "He's a strong man. He give it to me. I can feel it."

Dan clenched his hands.

"It ain't right," he said.

"Course it ain't. No man can treat a woman that way without she's married to him."

Her eyes snapped.

"I quit him dead in Utica last night."

"It ain't right," he repeated harshly.

She glanced at him. He certainly looked big and strong, and he'd knocked Klore dizzy, but she remembered his expression when Klore came in on him.

"Well," she said dryly, "what're you going to do about it, then?"

He stared down uncomfortably at his fists.

"I don't know."

"Well," she said. "I wouldn't try to do anything."

He was nothing but a country lump anyway; he didn't know a hotel from a hall. She had seen that in Hennessy's, and had stood up for him.

"Don't worry about me," she said. "I can look out for myself. A girl gets the habit living on the Erie."

"Where is he now?"

"I don't know. He generally winds up his likker in Bentley's."

They fell silent. Out beyond the trees they heard the brisk trotting of a pair of horses, and a carriage drew up in front of a house. A gentleman and two ladies got out and went up to the front door. Molly drew in her breath ecstatically and pointed out particular things about the women's clothes.

Dan hardly noticed. To him she seemed as pretty in her plain red dress. It brought out the flush in her smooth cheeks and matched her bright mouth. Her position, leaning back on the bench, moulded her figure under her clothes; and sitting there in the quiet shade with her, with fine houses and strange people about them, gave him a sense of intimacy. His inarticulate anger against Klore was swallowed by a growing excitement.

"What're you going to do next?" he asked.

"I don't know. Get another job, maybe. I got some money saved; maybe I won't do anything for a little while."

She regarded him with a sidewise glance. He was staring at the toes of his dusty cowhide boots; and his attitude brought out the muscles in his neck, the swell of his shoulders. His hands were heavily boned; she knew he was strong; and his thin face seen in profile with the curved nose and high cheek bones, and the short straight hair on the back of his neck, was attractive.

"I'll wait a couple of weeks," she said, almost as if it were a promise. "I'll see what turns up."

He stared out across the square, above the roofs of the houses. Sparrows were circling there in flocks, all jerking as one in their flight, all atwitter. Her eyes softened.

"What're you planning to do, Mr. Harrow?"

"I don't know," he said. "I'd scarcely thought. I guess I'll go on down with Julius W. as far's Albany. Then I don't know who I'll come back with."

He looked round at her suddenly.

"But I aim to get a boat some day soon."

"You'll find it hard unless you're awful lucky."

"Maybe. Maybe I could get Mr. Butterfield to help me."

"Maybe you might."

"Listen," he said, "if I got a boat of my own? . . ."

"Yeanh."

"Would you—I'd need a cook," he said.

"That's right," she said, puckering the corners of her eyes. "You'd need a cook and a pair of mules and a driver."

"Yeanh," he said, swallowing.

She laughed, putting out her chin at him a little.

"And you'd like for me to be your cook?"

"Yeanh," he said. "That's right."

"Well," she said, "when you come and ask me, I'll let you know."

"Where'll you be?"

"If I ain't otherwise taken, I'll be at Lucy Cashdollar's Agency. That's over Bentley's."

He leaned back heavily against the bench.

"Mr. Harrow—"

"Yeanh?"

He glanced up; but she was looking at her lap, where her fingers were opening and closing her reticule.

"If you'd ask me, I'd say I'd like to cook for you a lot."

His breath caught. After a while he managed to say, "I aim to ask you, Molly."

They did not speak, but watched the shadows come in under the trees and lights spring up in the windows over the front doors of the houses. A couple walked past them without noticing them. And a flock of sparrows took possession of a tree near them for the night.

"My land!" exclaimed Molly. "It's time I was getting back to supper."

Bentley's

On Genesee Street Molly left him. He walked slowly down the hill to the canal. The moon was still low in the eastern bowl of the great valley, and it sent an uneven thread along the course of the canal. Through the city, the warehouses cast black shadows far into the stream, at times cutting off the thread of moonlight; but every here and there night lanterns hung in the bows of boats pierced the blackness and traced the ripple. A wind was rising out of the northwest, and rumpled clouds were bearing down upon the moon.

Dan paused for a time on the bridge. It was very still there. Close at hand was Bagg's Hotel; but it was quiet—whatever noise issued from its windows was hidden by the slap of the ripple on the piles. He stared away to the east and thought of Molly. "By grab," he said under his breath, "if I had a boat I could have her. She said pretty near that much." But there was small chance of his getting a boat. He could ask Mr. Butterfield for a job, maybe, and make more money than he was making now; but he would be asking in his father's name, and he did not want to do that.

"There ain't much chance," he said to himself. "I guess I'll find Bentley's."

But as he turned to take his course along the canal there was still a glow in him. "Like to cook for you a lot," she had said.

Coming along the dock were two men, one a stockily built boater, the other a mild-looking clerk. They both stopped when Dan asked them where to find Bentley's.

"Keep on how you're headed," said the boater. "Turn into Liberty Street after you pass Gridley's warehouse. Walk a block to your right, and if you can't detect it by the noise, ask a man and he'll do it for you."

"It would be simpler—" began the clerk.

"Now you shut up," said the boater. "Don't listen to him. It's folks educated like him lead people off the track."

Dan went along slowly. The city down by the docks seemed to have come to life. There were few lights, and the warehouses loomed high and dark. But in the streets round them there was a pulsation of indistinguishable sound. When he passed a corner, he sometimes heard voices in loud talk, or a fiddle playing high and fast, or someone singing a snatch—a snatch of "Hoosen Johnny," and other voices coming into the chorus:—

> *"Long time ago, long time ago.*
> *The little black bull came down the meadow.*
> *Oh, a long time ago."*

He stopped to listen to it. While he stood there, a man passed him, smoking a cigar. The wind brightened the ash, and, dimly lit as they were, Dan recognized the bulging eyes and pursed mouth of the fat man, Henderson, who claimed to be a horse trader. He was walking along slowly, his gaze on the upper windows of the warehouses.

Dan went on, turned into Liberty Street as he had been directed. A little way down, an alley branched off on the right, and from the end of it sounded voices singing, men's voices, with a swing and bellow that filled the air. It was a canal song.

> *"We were loaded down with barley,*
> *We were chuck up full with rye;*
> *And the captain he looked down at me*
> *With his goddam wicked eye.*

> *"Oh the E-ri-e was a-rising,*
> *The strap was getting low,*
> *And I scarcely think*
> *We'll get a drink*
> *Till we get to Buffalo,*
> *Till we get to Buffalo."*

The swing of it took hold of him and drew him towards the door. He did not need to be told it was Bentley's. It was a three-story building with an eaveless roof, standing stiff as a box at the end of the alley. Bentley's Bar, a boaters' hangout; it hadn't had "Oyster Booth" put into the name then.

Dan pushed his way through the door, and his eyes blinked. The air was thick with tobacco, the sharp-smelling heat of oil lamps, the heavy sound of men talking in a close room.

"Well, well! Look what just come in! And on Sunday, too!"

Someone guffawed.

Dan paid no attention, but let the door swing to behind him. Running down the length of the room on his left was the bar. Four keeps were working behind it in their shirt sleeves; they worked hard.

Dan wedged into an opening in the line before it.

"What's yours?" asked the nearest keep.

"Whiskey."

The glass slid up to his hand. He paid and made his way to a table in a corner of the room.

He drank his whiskey slowly, and its sting brought water to his eyes. Two boaters at the next table were grumbling over low wages. "Good solid rates, heavy trade, where does the money go?" said one. "We don't see it." The other nodded. He wore a cap tilted back on his head and blew his nose often into a red handkerchief. His forehead bulged like a philosopher's. "The coat and pants does all the work," he observed, "but the weskit gets the gravy."

Dan looked round for Wilson and the Jew; but they were not in sight. As he drank, he lost interest in them, and thought of Molly instead, in her red dress. With the surge of talk about him, the laughter, the stamp of men's feet, the clinking at the bar, he felt the push of the canal behind him. . . .

There was a lift to the floor when he got to his feet and went over to the bar for another glass. But the act of walking gave him a feeling of increased strength, and he leaned his elbow on the bar and glanced round him. It was pleasant for him to stand there, not to feel nervous when a man jostled him.

"Beg pardon," said a man when his heel slipped and he lurched against Dan.

"Surely," said Dan, making to steady him with his hand. He was getting a gauge of his own strength. "I'd like to see Klore now," he said to himself, thinking of what Molly had told him. "I'd like to see him now."

Down the room someone was stamping on the floor. "Song! Song!"

A man lurched to his feet and a tumbler smashed.

"Abel Marsters going to sing."

Dan's glass came sliding back, and he gazed over the rim at a tall boater who was standing by himself beside the great round stove, and pulling his moustache away from his mouth. Then he lifted his chin a trifle and half closed his eyes and took one hand in the other. He had a fine, moving tenor.

> "Drop a tear for big-foot Sal,
> The best damn cook on the Erie Canal;
> She aimed for Heaven but she went to Hell—
> Fifteen years on the Erie Canal.

The missioner said she died in sin;
Hennery said it was too much gin:
There weren't no bar where she hadn't been,
From Albany to Buffalo."

The heave, the pull, the plod of the towpath, the people, the men about Dan; all were in the song, all joining the refrain:—

"Low bridge! Everybody down!
Low bridge! We're coming to a town!
You'll always know your neighbor, you'll always know your pal,
If you've ever navigated on the Erie Canal.

"Low bridge! . . ."

The long drag, the meadows, the marshes, the woods and the hills and the rivers, and the canal going through, with the boats, slowly, slowly, one step after another, slow, slow, and the mules' ears flop, and the snake whips crack, and the dust in your throat, and . . .

. . . "we're coming to a town."

And here they were, after the long week's plodding at three miles an hour, on Sunday night, letting off energy to ease themselves.

Then, as Dan watched, a light sprang to the eyes of an old Irishman, red still in his hair, sitting alone in the corner; and, looking toward the door, he saw the white head of Benjamin Rae over the crowd, and the swaggering shoulders of Julius Wilson, and William Wampy with his fiddle. A cry of "William! William Wampy!" and William was hoisted to a table, and the Irishman called for a jig.

Dimly through the swaying smoke Dan saw William seat himself, and tables and chairs rasped over the floor to clear a space. The lantern over him shed yellow light on his bald head and mild brown eyes as he cuddled the fiddle and talked it into tune. Then his hand and the bow awoke, his shoulders swayed to the left, came up, held still, and the bow flashed. . . . And the old man who had called for a jig was doing it, earnestly, concentrating on his feet, for a moment, till the fiddle gave them the rhythm; and the "Irishman's Shanty" was in full swing. . . . The great Jew slapping his hands on his knees in time. Julius grinning and shouting "Hye!" Men shuffling their feet. . . . Another Irishman on the floor, a young man, springing like a buck deer, a shrill cry from the old man, and an old step of his feet, forgotten, a double tap, a roar of delight. . . . William Wampy shaking the sweat from his face, mild-eyed. . . . The barkeeps snatching a moment's rest. . . . Dan looked on, the blood pounding in his head, singing like the fiddle, an itch in his feet. . . .

The tune stops. William Wampy tears open his shirt, bends over, another rush of notes, quick, shrill—"Jamesville on a Drunk," high laughter, men dance together. . . .

Dan stood at the bar, near the end, staring, half seeing the faces come and go, some old, some young, bearded, smooth, laughing, or serious in liquor . . . and then a face materialized in front of him—a black beard, and pale grey eyes, with white spots made by the lamps beside the pupils —that held him stiff against the bar. He was conscious of his right foot feeling its way from the rail to join his left upon the floor, and he braced himself. Still the faces swept by, back and forth, dimly now behind Jotham Klore's; but the fiddle had a rowdy shrillness in his ears.

Jotham Klore was saying something; Dan could see the words coming through his beard, but they sounded vague, without syllables. Suddenly his face stung where Klore had hit him with his open hand, and then the other side. Dan hit out. His balance wavered, he caught it, but the action brought courage to his fists. He struck again, saw Klore's head snap in toward his chest, and hit his ear, and knew that he had landed twice. Then Klore was close to him, and dull pain entered his stomach, but he found he could hit and land as often as he liked. The pain continued; it did not hurt as badly as he had thought, but for some strange reason it made him drowsy, and shook something in his head. . . .

He was aware of Wilson grabbing Klore's collar, of a roar of voices, and Wilson had vanished. Over a mass of faces he saw the great hands and white head of the Jew coming toward him. But Klore was in again, his teeth showing in his beard, and a bit of blood at his mouth gumming the hair. He pounded back, but the purchase was leaving his toes, and the hands came in against his stomach, one two, one two. The faces behind Klore swept in; he saw the Jew's hands reach forward; but the beat and hammer in his head carried him back. . . . A man grabbed his shoulders, he felt his legs dragging on the floor, the lights swam in the smoke, the roar closed in upon him. . . . The feet of one of the keeps vaulting over him, a big cool man, using a bung starter. . . . The cold, the darkness, and faintly the voice of the fiddle, a soothing tune, "The Little Stack of Barley." . . .

"Sick?"

The sound of water lapping against the piles. He was looking down along a tall man's side. The black water of the canal, and over it a plank as thin as a thread, and boards under his back. The deck of the boat. . . .

"Feel better pretty quick."

He was rolled on his stomach, head over the side, a sharp slap over the kidneys and a pain in his stomach. . . . The water, the black water. . . .

"That sort of evens us up."

The voice was familiar. He recognized dimly. He had heard it always in the dark.

"Got a taste of the canal," said the voice. "You'll feel better now."

He struggled to sit up and saw a man bending over him, back to the faint light of the moon; a wide hat—Gentleman Joe. Suddenly the man cocked his head alertly.

"Working for Wilson?"

Dan managed to nod.

"It's his boat. I've got to cut out of here."

The man moved down the plank and disappeared into the shadows along the warehouses.

Dan sat with his back to the rudder post, the sweep curving out over his head. He felt sore and still sick; but it was not as bad as he had thought it would be. He wasn't afraid. He had tasted the canal; he had become part of it.

He heard a faint whistling moving along the docks, and a man came opposite the Xerxes and paused long enough for Dan to recognize the fat man, Henderson, and then moved on.

Dan got to his feet and went down to the cabin and felt his way to his bunk.

Utica Weighlock

When he woke, Benjamin Rae's hand was on his shoulder, shaking him. "Hustle up, Dan. We're loading in half an hour."

He helped Dan sit up.

"Belly sore?" The Jew grinned.

"Yeanh."

"Klore sure set out to rangdangle you. What happened to you?"

"I haven't much of a notion."

"I don't blame you."

He passed out through the curtains.

Dan heaved his feet to the floor; his shoes were still on. The bunks swam dizzily from right to left, and he grabbed his head. But in a moment things came steady.

Through the curtain he could hear the others eating, blowing on the coffee and gulping it.

"Come on out if you want to eat," Wilson called.

Dan stepped into the cabin a bit unsteadily. It was still dark, and a lamp was giving a feeble light over the table. Wilson looked up.

"Who brought you back, Dan?"

"Why, I sort of come to on the boat," said Dan.

"Fill him some coffee, William. You took a lot round the stomach—something hot'll help unlimber you."

"It won't hurt you," said Benjamin Rae. "The best fighter never really fit until he'd got licked once or twicet."

The coffee eased Dan considerably, and cleared his head, but he still felt sore when he went on deck.

A heavy fog misted the Basin; and when Benjamin Rae went down the plank after the mules his broad shoulders were swallowed up in it before he had passed the bow.

"You get the towline ashore," said Wilson.

In a few minutes Dan heard the Jew returning, the sharp thump of hoofs on the dock, and then the heads of the mules came out of the fog. He hooked the towline to the evener and the mules relaxed their off hips and let their ears flop back against their necks.

There was a roll of wood on wood, and two men appeared rolling barrels across the dock. Another man with a short barrel track jumped into the pit, and the barrels began rolling down. Wilson stood on the edge of the pit, watching, occasionally blowing into his hands.

"We'll be first out of Utica at the weighlock," the Jew said to Dan. "But if there's an upstream line we'll have to wait for them to come through."

Wilson signed the bill of lading and Dan tossed off the tie-ropes. The loading hands jumped back to the dock, grabbed poles, and pushed the

Xerxcs out into the current. Wilson passed the towline over the bow standard, so that it would clear boats against the dock, and Ben Rae shortened
it at the eveners to avoid the deep sag.

They went ahead. Some of the boats were coming to life, with sounds of
crockery in the cabins and smell of smoke from the stoves. But the Xerxes
seemed the only boat astir. Ahead of her a black tunnel loomed in the fog.
And then boats began issuing on the other side of the canal, the teams'
nodding heads visible an instant as they passed.

Lanterns bobbed ahead, crossing and recrossing the tunnel. As they came
closer, Dan saw the weighlock, a boat lying in it, heard a muffled voice
calling, "Seventy-one, -two, -three, seventy-three-nine eighty-five."

From a lighted office on the other side of the narrow roofed slip a voice
answered, "Seventy-three tons, nine hundred."

The boat lay in an empty trough on a ribbed rack, with arms fore and
aft extending under the office. At the last words the tender slammed down
a lever, water came sucking in, and the boat rose to canal level. The gates
opened, the mules took up the slack, and the boat slid through.

Beyond the door, the toll-taker spoke to the captain: "Class of freight?"

"Merchandise. Misc."

The upper lock gates closed, the lower opened, and the tender bawled,
"Next!"

Already a boat was sliding in. A man on the bow with a pole to keep it
from fending the side. The mules passed on a narrow runway.

"By grab, come slower, Marcy. You're always running in too fast. You'll
take off them gates some day."

The tender snatched up a pole and pushed back against the bow of the
boat, which was moving with a dangerous momentum. It came up against
the upper gates with a heavy thud.

"Gorl!" breathed the tender, running to close the lower gates. "By
Cripus," he cried to the driver, "the next time you come in like that, I'll
be danged if I'll let you drive into this lock! What do you think it is, a
rubber extension?"

The driver spat into the lock and sat down.

"Oh, go pull up your pants, Buscerk."

Inside the office the toll-taker was making change. "What you got, general merchandise, George?" The captain of the line boat which had passed
snorted.

"Swiss! They've brought the hull damn works with 'em. Ploughs! You
ort to see 'em. Regular teaspoon trinkets! Every dang little thing. Pitch-
forks. They've set up a clock in the cabin with a funny set of works.
Dangdest racket. And their talk! High jabber, high jabber, jabber-jabber,
jabber-jabber-jabber. God! I don't get no rest at all. Jabber! There ain't no
sense into it. Jabber this. Yes, mam, it's a mule. No, boy, it's a calf. Jabber
that. No, mam, mules don't have any. Jabber! Jesus!"

He stamped out after the line boat.

The muffled voice was calling again: "Fifty-one, -two, fifty-two, even."

"Sold!" cried the clerk, under his oil lamp. "Boat number, name, and
cargo."

"Number 1793. Freedom's Flower. Albany. Four bales of 'baccer.
Printing press for Rochester, special valuation. All the rest is merchandise

for St. Louis. Boots and shoes from Lowell, Mass. Two crates of hats. Haberdashery to clothe the pioneer." He chuckled.

Already another boat was coming in.

"How many boats out there?" the Jew shouted across at the tender, pointing his thumb at the misty entrance to the lock, where the headlights of the boats made feeble smears.

"Expect about forty. Next!"

But the boat was coming in already, deftly, under the guidance of a one-armed man. "Whoa!" he yelled as the bows came into the gates and the boat slid in without a rub and drifted to a stop, dead centre.

"That's Jason Jukes. Handiest man with a boat I ever see."

"Hullo, Ben!" His quick smile showed a flash of gold teeth. "Number 3991. Tammany Hall, Rome. Carrying rope."

He went inside, reappeared, and the mist swallowed him and the faint light of his boat on the far side.

Sitting side by side on the runway, the crew of the Xerxes watched the boats come in. The fog formed drops on their faces and ran down their necks. Boat after boat. Manufactured goods. "Stoves," said Wilson. "Fancy furniture; did you ever see such articles?"

"That's forty-three of them," cried the lock-tender. "Next!"

He waited a second.

"Next!"

He waved his arm at Wilson.

"East-bound boats! Hurry up, there."

Wilson leaped up and ran back and jumped aboard. "Geddup!" said the Jew to the mules. "Whoa!" cried Wilson, and the mules stopped. The Jew jumped aboard on one side as Wilson jumped off on the other and stepped into the office. "Number 1613," he said. "Xerxes short-hauling the Michigan Six Day. Ashes to Schenectady. Fifty bar'l."

"Damn it," said the toll-taker. "What do they got to bother us for with that trash?"

The gates opened. "Geddup," the Jew bawled at the mules. Dan started after them. As soon as the Xerxes cleared the lock they stopped and waited for Wilson. He took a running jump from the towpath and made the deck. Dan heard the scrape and thump of his feet as he scrambled up. "Go on. Lay into them, Dan! We're hurrying now."

The city seemed dead as they passed out of the warehouses into the open country. The mules were nervous in the fog, and kept their heads low to the towpath, snorting now and then. They were a young pair and kept a fast pace. Dan felt the stiffness going out of him as he kept up.

"Don't let 'em burn themselves out," said the Jew. "They're green young."

"All right," said Dan. He slowed them a trifle.

"You can always tell a green young mule by the way he handles his ears," said the Jew. "Look at the fancy twirl they're a-putting on. Now an old mule'll either prick 'em or let 'em dangle plain. He knows he's got enough to do just keeping the boat moving."

A boat passed on the other side of the canal; and the puff of the horses, and the oily snap of the snake whip, the sound of the wash meeting their own, the smell of wood smoke; and the boat had passed. More went by.

Little by little, Dan could distinguish their shadows against the mist. There lurked in it now a restless feeling of motion.

Suddenly it thinned, dropped, and for a few seconds he and the mules were wading in it knee-deep, and he saw the canal marked by teams coming up, and men standing in it steering. The sun was red far down the valley, and a wind began to draw over the hills to the south. Then the mist was all about him for twenty minutes, and but for the momentary droop of it he might have thought himself alone with the mules, pulling mysteriously on a rope. But it lifted again as the wind knifed under, wavered, and went away. And the sunlight swept up the valley, glistening on all things.

They started unloading at Westfeldt's soap factory at one o'clock. By two they had eaten a late dinner and were pushing on, the empty Xerxes light upon the mules. All day, passing Fall Hill and the ancient Mohawk Castle, the East Canada Creek, where the devil Butler had his head chopped off by two Oneida Indians, and Fort Plain, with the sunset red upon it. They changed teams at Canajoharie, and went on in the dark, with thunder overhead and hard rain drumming on the deck. White lights marked the locks, and dozing tenders put them through in silence. When the rain cleared, a stillness came upon them. Farms near the canal brooded unseen, recognizable only by the pungent odor of their barnyards. Once a white hound mourned as they went by, and Dan heard the clink of his chain.

The night swallowed them again. They passed Schenectady in the morning, with the canal once more astir with boats. They went through the cut of the Young Engineer and the Wat Hoix Gap, with the Mohawk roaring through the heavy rapids on their right, and the White Horse tossing his mane of spray.

Then over the long aqueduct and down the locks; early in the afternoon they floated out into the basin, and by six o'clock saw Albany rising on a hill to their right. . . .

4

THE SARSEY SAL

Morning, Albany

Two days later Dan watched the Xerxes pulling away towards Troy. He was standing on the outer bank of the great basin, the Hudson at his back. The basin and the canal beyond it were thronged with boats. Dan could scarcely have believed so many boats existed. Albany was the eddy in the long current of trade that swept from New York—from Europe, for that matter—to the farthest reaches of the West. Here the long tows of barges came up the Hudson to dump their freight into the canal boats. Steamers towing queues of canal boats nosed into the basin embankment; Dan counted one line of ninety-eight. Men jumped ashore and went after their horses, left in the great round stable off the north end of State Street; or they brought their horses off the boats, stiff-legged from their long ride, the land uneasy to their hoofs, but rested and fat. Agents for the steamboat lines ran about with ledgers under their arms signing up captains for a queue on the Ronan line or the Swiftsure, or any one of ten. They quarreled among themselves, crying down the other company, fighting sometimes, while the boater grinned as he looked on and signed with a third man. The blare of voices rose in a long murmur under the city smoke; the hiss of steam slid into it here and there from the river, making white cotton-wool patches against the towering black boat-stacks.

On one side the city rose in tiers of brown-housed streets, its smokes pulling away westward, a buzzing hive, its crown of white state buildings aloof above the noise. But, down below, the frayed ends of life were gathered up and loosely knotted. Here came a line of coal barges from the Delaware and Hudson; even the washed clothes snapping in the river wind were grey from the open cargoes of coal. A passenger train was sliding down the hill from the west, the drivers of the engine aglitter with speed; and a stately white steamboat far down the river, stretching on the water its clean white lines, its stacks rolling forth black clouds, sent its long wail between the hills. Its passengers crowded the forward decks, their gaze on the city ahead, with no eyes for the murk their passage left on the blue river.

Men jostled Dan, men of all tongues, arguing for passage money to the West, while their women stayed back with the baggage and held their wide-eyed children hard by the hand. It was bewildering to watch, the urge for hurry begetting confusion which begot again the urge for haste. All the wide tumult of men who had to be on time, who learned its value, talked of it in fractions and measured it anxiously,—clerks getting off their shipments, emigrants seeking passage that they might be settled for the spring sowing, trains scurrying on their narrow rails to fulfill their tables, boat captains sounding whistles for their start,—and all had forgotten that time had no measure, that it had no passage, that it was an image of their own creation, built out of minutes and seconds and purchased with dollars and cents. On Sundays their ministers called it God. By unconscious irony they had come to call the daily transcript of their lives a "press."

Far up the canal, beyond the crowded boats, Dan caught again a glimpse of the Jew's white beard and saw him raise his hand. Then the bustle and confusion swallowed him, and Dan was alone, bewildered. The meagre Tug Hill farm, set between the pointed balsams, had given him no standard by which he could grasp the great restless haste about him and make it his own.

He shoved his way among the people until he stood by the waterside. There he sat down on a short pile, his long legs dangling. All along the wharf, for the better part of a mile, boats had been tied up. They moved slightly, muttering, with the motion of the water, the noon sun washing their decks and whittling the men and women small with its hot light. Directly before him an old brown boat squatted, its cabin windows on a level with his eyes. A woman was washing clothes on deck. She was heavily built and bent only slightly in reaching into the tub; and when she straightened up she breathed hard and squeezed the suds angrily from her reddened hands.

After a while she caught sight of Dan and fell into conversation with him.

"Hullo, young man," she said.

"Morning, mam," said Dan.

She jerked a man's shirt from the tub and wrung it and shook it and hung it on a line between the cabin and the stable. It shuddered in the wind limply, then tossed out its arms and danced.

"It's a very pleasant day," observed the washerwoman, going on with her rubbing.

"Yeanh," said Dan.

The noise of the wharves tumbled about them, but the woman's voice was clear and pleasant; she did not raise it, but she talked to Dan with no thought of the people bustling by, so that it was easy for him to hear.

"The sun is a pleasant thing, to be sure," she went on.

"Yeanh," said Dan.

"Where do you come from?"

"Tug Hill," said Dan.

"Where is that?"

"Fifteen miles north of Rome."

"That's a long way to be from."

"Yeanh."

She bent to her work.

"A house is a fine thing," she said, straightening up again to wring out a nightgown. "The boat comes and goes. It's always stopping, but it never stays."

"No."

"I married a man once, honey, and had a house and a patch of praties and a fine man to come in for his dinner."

She finished her washing and dumped the grey water of the tub with a slosh into the canal. She stopped for a moment, with one hand taking hold of her hip.

"Are ye working on the canal, honey?"

"No," said Dan, "not now."

"Are ye looking for a job?"

"Yeanh."

She sighed.

"It's a hard thing to find with the years mounting up in a body's bones. But you'd not have much trouble. You're a handsome young man."

Dan blushed.

"I must put on a bit of my best, honey, and go off to my marketing."

She went below, leaving Dan in the midst of the noise, sitting there idly, his eyes on the blue water, thinking of Molly Larkins, and wishing one of all the many boats might be his own.

The Chase Begins

It was with a start that Dan became aware of two men going aboard the boat. The first walked heavily with his chin drawn in, his eyes on the ground. In the second, Dan recognized the man Henderson, who called himself a horse trader.

They went down into the cabin. After a minute Dan began to pick out their voices above the hum round him. The curtains were drawn over the windows, so that they could not see him.

"I've tracked him down here, Samson," said Henderson.

"Where's he now?" the boater asked.

"That's what I wanted to find out from you. Do you know where he'd be likely to hang out?"

"Probably one of the canawl houses—Jason Grew's, or Ficha Thrall's, or in the Bent Window Hotel."

"I'll look into them," said Henderson.

"Bad actor, eh?"

"On the records. I was sent out from the Central Office. I'm not in no hurry to lay my hands on him. I've got his description, and I've seen him once, not to see his face. I got on his trail in Black Rock."

"Going to snatch him here?"

"Bad place, Samson. If he got away he'd beat me to New York. Of course, I'd get word through first, but New York's an easy place to miss him, and then he could cut out for Europe if he had to. That'd be too bad."

"Surely," said the boater. "That would be bad."

"I've been tracking him for two months. He isn't going to break loose here; he wants to hide out and wait for things to cool off. Probably he was born in this part of the country. No, Samson, I aim to wait till he's in the middle of the state afore I put out my hands at him."

"Maybe you'll get him," Samson said. "I hope you do."

"Sure, I ought to get him. I'm good at these things. He don't know who I am. All he knows is we know where he is. That comes in the posting for him. I had that done to keep the people excited after him. They're beginning to wake up now. When I'm ready to get after him he'll be easier to track. Yes. I know some of his hide-outs in the ports now. If he heads to a port, I won't have to lose time looking. He don't know who I am. Thinks the sheriffs are doing the posting. It's a hot day, Samson."

"That's right, Sam—real hot; kind of sweaty."

"Makes a man feel dry," said Henderson.

"Yeanh."

There was a moment's silence.

"How about a rum noggin, Sam?"

Henderson cleared his throat.

"Now you say it, Samson, I think it would go pretty good."

Dan heard the boater moving about the cabin.

"Great place for a man to hide out, the canal is," Henderson observed. "There's so danged many boats and so danged many people working on 'em or going through West. The boaters ain't like settled people. They don't keep track of any one place. The only people on the canal I can get anything from is the bank walkers. They've got their patrols to make. But most of them are deef."

"That's probably why he tracked into here," said the boater.

"I guess so. This noggin's pretty good, Samson."

"Yeanh. It's grateful to a man's innards. The lemon makes it kind of blend the stummick, Sam."

"It does, at that."

"Ain't going to make a nab at this Calash here, then?"

"No. Not any chance of getting him. I don't know where he is this minute. I got to learn his habits. Maybe I won't get him till next year. It takes a long time, this underneath working. But it's generally the best way. The bills was marked. But he ain't using them here. He's too neat to do a thing like that. But most likely he'll have to begin using them next year."

"What do you want him for?"

"He's got a list against him other states. He come foul of us last year. Had a gang in Indiana. Once I get on the go, though, I'll have him.—I'll have to be getting along, Samson. Thanks for the noggin. Keep on the watch for him. Anything you see let me know."

"Sure. I'll let you know."

Henderson came on deck and walked off onto the dock. Dan kept his head lowered and the man moved away, shiny brown eyes searching the crowd.

Cholera Rumor

"Well, if it ain't Andy! What're you doing, Andy?"

"Hello, Stark."

"What're you doing now? Balancing the sheet?"

"I'm too old for that, Stark. No, when a man gets old, he leaves the fancy ways of youth. He gets a job in the street department."

"Well, you ain't cleaning a street. What're all them figgers on that paper for? Can't tell me I don't know a figger when I see one."

The other pushed his grey hair from his eyes.

"That's the first four lines of a poem, Stark. It's going to be a ballad."

"What's that?"

"Why, I guess you'd call it a song about something horrid, better spoke than sung."

"Well, it sure looks neat, Andy."

"It's pretty good," said the writer modestly.

He raised his thin face and looked at the newcomer out of bright, dry blue eyes. His face had an unhealthy pallor, his clothes smelt, not too pleasantly, of his daily work in the streets.

Dan had come into Ficha Thrall's Bankside Saloon after dark. He had not found a job; he was lonely. There were men all about him drinking and talking. Sometimes they dropped a remark to him, but he knew none of them. It was hard for him to mix with them. The old man studying his blank sheet of paper had attracted his attention. In all the clatter he was so absorbed by his work that he scarcely stopped to taste the glass at his elbow.

"That's Andy Hikes," a boater told Dan. "He's got education, though you wouldn't guess it by half. He studies things once in a while and writes poetry. I ain't no judge," said the boater, swigging down a noisy swallow of rum, "I wasn't brung up to understand such notions. But it's got a good hammer into it when he reads it out."

"Yeanh."

The old man ran a hand over his eyes and looked back at his paper. He handled it delicately with the tips of his thin fingers.

"What's it about?" asked the boater.

"It's about the capture of Schenectady. I'll read you the first verse. It goes this way." He cleared his throat and read it out in a fine voice. The man who had spoken to Dan thumped out the rhythm on his knee.

> "God prosper long our King and Queen,
> Our lives and safeties all;
> A sad misfortune once there did
> Schenectady befall."

"Listen to that, will you?" exclaimed the man next to Dan. "Didn't I tell you? You could hammer it out with a go-devil!"

"What're you bringing in the King and Queen for? This is a free country."

"I don't mean nothing by it, Stark," said the old man. "The editor up to the *Journal* said he'd give me three dollars for a poem out of history—something folks could get a-hold of and say it happened in their grandpa's time. So I bring the King and Queen into the first line to make the time look proper; and God's a help anywhere."

"What's the safeties for?" asked Stark.

"That's just to show people was scared. It kind of makes the man reading figure there's something uneasy going on. There's lots of tricks to this business; and this here's a neat specimen, if I say it myself. There ain't such a lot of poets could put Schenectady into a poem under its own name."

"Why not?"

"You just try."

"Cripus! I could make it rhyme."

"How?" asked the old man, looking up eagerly.

"Well how about Uticy for a rhyme?"

> "Schenectady, Schenectady,
> Is halfway up to Uticy."

"That ain't the truth. There wasn't any Utica when this poem is being wrote."

"Who gives a dang?"

"Well, a reader likes to have the truth."

"Not if they read poetry. A man that's reading poetry's lost his principles."

"You got to fool them."

"It's a poor notion, reading poetry is. Reading rots the mind."

"Well, I got to get ahead with this," said the old man. He bent over his paper once more, and the boater left him.

Conversation broke out gustily. One man was trying to sell a mule to another. "Five years, sound as a sand-hill potato, see her yourself." "You don't mean that grey one, George?" "That's the one. Handsome article. That cute she can get by a lock without driving." "Then she ain't safe. I don't like a mule with independent ideas. I had a cook had 'em. She walked out on me with fifteen dollars." "Well, this mule won't. You got a tow-line on to her, anyways, ain't you? What's more, she's cheap. Sixty dollars for a five-year-old is cheap." "That's your mule, Andy?" asked a third man. "Sure, you know her. Ain't sixty dollars cheap for a five-year-old mule as kind as she?" "Sure. I know her. That mule's been five-year-old three times." "That ain't the one." "Named Andrew Jackson in full?" "Yeanh." "What for, if it wasn't for his first in-aw-geration?" "That was her ma." "With the same broke knees?" "Just like 'em. It runs in them grey mules. They're just like a breed."

Dan listened and drank. His face was a little pale and he handled his glass with serious care. . . . He was getting very drunk. He kept his hands on the table as though they alone could keep him in touch with the room. A small, ratty-looking pair of men, at the other side of the room, were watching him. . . . The old street-cleaner glanced up from his paper; his face was sweaty; his mouth trembled. "Hey, Stark!" he shouted. "Hey, Stark, come here. I've finished it." All the boaters turned their heads as if they had been waiting for him. "Read it out, Andy," said the man Stark. The old fellow took a stiff swallow and pushed back his chair and stretched out his legs under the table.

"I'm just going to call it 'A Ballad.' Good honest title. But I've put down a foreword—"

"What's that?"

"That's the front end," said a boater. "It's like the cowcatcher on to a engine. It's to clear the track, but it don't do nothing but make the engine longer."

"It's old style," said Andrew, "just to give the notion that this here's a fact. It says:—

> "In which is set forth the horrid cruelties practised by the French and Indians, on the night of February eight last; which I composed last night and am now writing this morning Friday, June twelve, 1690."

"Wait a minute, Andy. That's good and written fine. Them long words go good there. But you ain't said how long it took to do. If it's actual, then people want to know how long it took. People always want to know how long a thing takes to do. Why don't you put in 'Wrote in one hour's time'? That looks as if you knew all about it and only had to figure the rhymes."

"That's a good idea," said the old man, making an insertion.

Then he began to read:—

"God prosper long our King and Queen,
Our lives and safeties all;
A sad misfortune once there did
Schenectady befall."

The boater next to Dan began beating the rhythm on his knee, a smile of admiration on his hot red face.

"From forth the woods of Canady
The Frenchmen took their way,
The people of Schenectady
To captivate and slay."

"He rhymed it!" Stark exclaimed. "He done a regular rhyme on Schenectady! Can-ady: Schenec-tady. What do you know about that?"

"They marched for two and twenty days,
And through the deepest snow;
And on a dismal winter night
They struck the horrid blow.

"The lightsome sun that rules all day
Had sunk into the west,
And all the drowsy villageers
Had sought and found their rest.

"They thought they were in safety all,
And dreamt not of the foe;
But at midnight they all awoke,
In wonderment and woe."

Between stanzas, the old man would take another drink from his glass, —which Stark was careful to keep filled,—shake back his hair, run the back of his hand across his lips, and fling it out in a gesture. He was unsteady on his feet; his white hair swayed dizzily to Dan's eyes;

"For they were in their pleasant beds,
And soundly sleeping, when
Each door was sudden open broke
By six or seven men. . . ."

The doors to the street banged open and swung shut; and a man stood suddenly in the strong yellow light of the bar lamps. His hand was raised halfway to his mouth to remove the quid, but he began talking before it was out and his tongue stuttered under it.

"There's a case of cholera up above the combines."

They swung round on him like one man.

"Where?"

"Up above the combines."

"Who was it?"

"Henry Hindkopfer. Him and his cook and a driver-boy."

In the stillness they became momentarily aware of old Andy's voice sonorously repeating his poem.

> ". . . They then were murdered in their beds,
> Without shame or remorse;
> And soon the floors and streets were strewed
> With many a bloody corpse.

> "Oh, Christie! In the still night air
> It sounded dismally. . . ."

"God!" cried the man Stark. "Asiatic?"

"Bad," said the man. "All three of them deader'n turnips."

"I knew him," said Ficha Thrall from behind the bar. "He owes the house four-sixty-three. You can see it wrote there on the board."

"It's going to be another plague. I don't remember it good. I was a lad then."

"I do."

"I don't believe it is cholera at all. It must be the dyree."

"They give 'em green strawberry leaves, but it didn't do no good," said the man, shaking his head. "The doctor said it was a clear case."

"We've been having hot weather, and a lot of rain."

Dan lifted his head to stare at the men's set faces. He had heard stories of the Great Plague of '32. How the cholera came down Champlain to Albany, and traveled to New York along the Hudson, and found its way up the Erie as far as Rome. There had been great fog that summer, and men were struck as they steered their boats to a landing; or as they walked behind their mules they fell without a sound, letting the boat go by, to be found dead when the next team shied. It had been a time of terror; fog— it had been foggy.

The voice of the old man rang out again:—

> ". . . But some ran off to Albany,
> And told the awful tale;
> Yet, though we gave our cheerful aid,
> It did not much avail.

> And we were horridly afraid,
> And shook with terror, when . . ."

"I'll tell you one thing right off," said the man who had disbelieved the news. "I ain't starting west to-morrow, nor the day after, neither. I'm going to see what's going to happen first. I'm going to stay right here."

> ". . . The news came on the Sabbath morn,
> Just at the break of day. . . ."

"Me neither," said another boater.

"It generally comes quick to the cities," said a third. "I'm danged glad I'll be starting for New York on the Ronan's."

"Cripus! It hit New York worst of all in thirty-two. Better'n a hundred people a day!"

"I'm going to get back to the boat and tell the old woman. It'll tickle her anyway. She thought she wasn't going to have no chance to get her a new hat."

"Guess I'd better move along."

"Me too."

The man who had brought the news whirled and ran out. They stamped after him, the clatter of their quick talking fading down the street. A few remained: the two ratty-looking men who were watching Dan, Stark, Ficha Thrall, at the bar, one or two others, old Andy, staggering, but finishing his piece.

> ". . . And here I end this long ballad,
> The which you just have read;
> I wish that it may stay on earth
> Long after I am dead."

The glass dropped from his fingers; it smashed on the floor with a bright glitter; Thrall moved to the board and made a mark; Dan started drunkenly; the old man slumped down on his chair. . . .

"It's all right," he said in a low voice. "It's good. It's pretty damn good, Andy. I liked it a lot."

Andy dropped his face on his loosely folded arms and went to sleep.

"Sure," said Stark. "Surely."

He shook Andy by the shoulder.

"Better leave him be," said Thrall. "When he wakes up I'll kick him out."

All but the ratty-looking men, Stark, and Dan left.

"I'll take his paper up to the *Journal*," Stark said. "It's worth three dollars to any man. Don't he write a pretty hand?"

"Come on, you," Thrall said to Dan. "Get out. I'm shutting up."

Dan stared at him without appearing to hear.

"Come on, you," Thrall said. "Get out of here."

One of the ratty-looking men touched his arm.

"All right, brother. Leave him be. Me and Frank here'll take him home. Me and Frank knows him. Don't we, Frank?"

"Sure," said the other. "We know him."

"Sure, we know where he lives. We'll take him back. Poor feller, he comes from our town; he's new on the canal. He's drunk."

"Sure," said Frank. "He's drunk. We'll take him back."

Each took hold of one of Dan's arms.

"Come along, Will," they said to Dan.

"My name ain't—"

"Come on," they said. "We'll take you back."

"My name ain't Will," said Dan. "My name's Dan."

"Sure, William Daniel."

"Just Dan."

"All right, Dan."

"Thank you," said Dan.

"He's drunk," Thrall said.

"Sure," said Frank. "He's drunk. We'll take him home. Poor kid."

"I ain't drunk, neither; I'm sleepy. Just kind of sleepy."

"That's it," said Frank soothingly, "just sleepy."

"Thanks," said Dan. "Pleased to meet you."

They walked him through the door. Behind them they heard the bolt bang in.

It was cool and still. At the end of the alley a light mist trembled on the canal. The feet of the three of them beat oddly along the board walk. Up over the city a bit of moonlight showed them a roof here and there, glistening as though there were frost.

"Where'll we fix him, Jack?" asked Frank.

"We'll take him over the lock. There might be somebody coming for him here."

"That's a good idea. Come along, you. Lift your feet and set 'em down ahead. That's the way a man makes progress walking."

"They ain't your feet," Dan mumbled. "How can you tell?"

"Snub him," said Jack.

They yanked him off his balance. Dan stumbled, his feet trying to catch up. They knew how to handle him.

The great basin opened before them. The boats showed vaguely in the mist, here and there a blob of light from a night lantern. The air was fresh. The river lapped softly against the lower gates of the lock.

"Hullo," said the keeper, coming out of his office, a pipe in his hand giving out heavy, sweet smoke that made Dan gag. "Taking sonny home to momma?"

"Just about," said Frank.

They ran him across to the embankment.

"You're good fellers," said Dan. "I'm pleased to meet you."

"Sure," said Frank.

"How about here?" asked Jack.

"Back of the ear, Jack."

"Take his hat off."

Frank took it off. Dan grabbed for it unsteadily.

"Say . . ."

A dull *tunk*. Frank eased Dan down.

"He's heavier'n you'd think."

Let's see what he's got."

Frank bent over him.

"Try the pants pocket."

"Ain't much." He fumbled a couple of bills. "Not over two dollars."

"Well, come along. We might pick up another."

"Not much chance. This damn cholera."

"Come along."

"Wait a minute. I'll put his hat on. He might catch cold."

"Oh, come along."

Their feet moved off quietly through the mist.

Hired On

"Hey there, you!"

A big man stood in bare feet on the deck of the old brown boat in the early dawn and stared at Dan.

Dan's fingers caught at the planks, and he hitched himself forward, and then lay still.

"Well," said the boater. "That's a good thing. He ain't dead. Hey there, you!"

Dan lifted his head and stared sleepily.

"Hey there! Wake up! What's the matter?"

Dan rolled over and sat up and then suddenly caught hold of his head.

"What's the matter?"

Dan groaned.

"I guess I got hit on the head."

"Well, there's worse places to get hit."

"I must've got drunk last night."

"I shouldn't wonder. I did myself."

"I feel sick."

"Go put your head in the canal."

"No," Dan said. "I don't want to do that."

"Well, it's a good thing to do."

Dan let go of his head, shook it once or twice, and looked round.

"Feel better?"

"Yeanh."

It had fallen cool during the night. The dawn wind was lean and fresh. Dan climbed awkwardly to his feet. An idea occurred to him. He felt in his pockets.

"Jeepers," he said. "Jeepers Cripus!"

"Cleaned out, eh?"

"Yeanh."

"You showed the signs."

The boater fished in his pockets.

"Have a chaw?"

"No. I don't want it."

"Well, I find it's good like this. Gives a man to set his teeth again." He bit off a chew, got his jaw going, spat onto the dock. "Well, now you're down to hardpan, what you going to do? Got a job?"

"No."

"Want to hire on to my boat?"

"Maybe."

"Regular wages. Twelve dollars."

"All right. I guess I will."

"She's old, but she's a good boat. I got the best cook on the canal down in the cabin. I'm pulling right out," said the boater. "I've three pair of millstones and mill machinery for Butterfield to Rome, and I've got to get 'em through quick. Cholera or no cholera. I never was scared of no disease. What's your name?"

"Dan Harrow."

"Me, I'm Samson Weaver," the boater said, and held out his hand. "Come aboard. We'd ought to make good time. There won't be many boats till the scare's gone. We ought to get through quick. I ain't scared of cholera."

He turned to the cabin door.

"Annie!" he bellowed. "Hey there! Annie!"

There was no answer.

"Hey, there! Annie! Wake up."

"She's a good cook, but she does sleep hard," Weaver said to Dan. "I'll have to shake her out."

He clattered down the steps shouting, "Annie! Hey, there!"

Dan heard him stamp back to the bunks. Then Weaver swore.

"She's cleared out. She's cleared out clean. Run a regular rig on me. I didn't notice last night, coming aboard drunk like I was. And I got right out this morning without looking. Well, we'll have to get along without no cook. Come on down."

The cabin was large for an ordinary freighter; it was nicely fitted out with two comfortable rocking-chairs and an almost new stove, well blacked. Weaver was slamming wood into the stove when Dan entered.

"The old puddery punk!" he growled. "Well, she stocked up anyhow yesterday."

He poured a handful of coffee into the kettle and put the frying pan over to heat, and cut bacon. The fire caught with a roar and snapped briskly. A bit of sunlight found a bright nasturtium on the wallpaper. Weaver bent over to pull on a pair of socks.

"What do you know about that!" he exclaimed. "She went and darned my sock afore she left!"

He stared at it in wonder, rubbing the back of his head.

"Maybe she was scared of the cholera," Dan suggested.

"The hell she was. I seen she'd took a notion to a tug captain on the Swiftsure. But I never thought to beat it out of her. Well, women are kind of like that. They'll fool you every chance they get, and if you catch 'em, why, gol! they'll fool you into thinking they wasn't fooling."

He laced his boots and went back to his cooking.

"Got any bag?" he asked.

"Yeanh. I left it at the Michigan Six Day offices."

"Well, we can pick it up when we go by. I'm posting through to Utica on their line this time. My team needs a rest, anyway. And I can make quicker time that way. The haul on to Rome won't take no time."

He broke two eggs into the pan and slammed the shells into the coffee kettle.

"She made the best coffee I ever got into my mouth," he said.

In a few minutes they sat down to their breakfast at the table hinged against the wall, with the smell of coffee and bacon filling the cabin, and the sunlight finding another window.

"Listen," said Weaver.

Dan held his cup against his mouth.

"Ain't hardly a sound," Weaver said. "There won't be such a lot of boats pulling out to-day. They're scared. It's funny how people'll think they're better off with a few boards round 'em, hiding the sky. Me, I never was scared of cholera or any damn disease; but I wouldn't want to wait for it to come in a door."

He ate and drank hurriedly. And every now and then he lifted his head, as if he were listening, his square red face, with its night's stubble, hard.

But when they got up to do the dishes his mind came back to the cook.

"If I had the time, I'd go after her," said Weaver. "But she's probably laying low. The Sarsey Sal was a fine boat with Annie on to it."

When he went on deck, Dan recognized other boats; and he realized that Weaver was the man he had overheard Henderson talking to, and that the absent Annie must be the Irishwoman who had been washing clothes on the deck and who had wished for a house and a man to come in for his dinner; and, glancing at Weaver's back and sturdy shoulders, all at once Dan felt sorry for him.

The Burning Boat

At the Troy relay on the Michigan Six Day, they had trouble in getting a driver to take them up to the next change. But Weaver had paid for through horse-and-driver service, and he insisted loudly that he get the full service or have his money back.

He pulled a paper from his pocket and waved it an inch from the man's nose.

"Here's the bill—horse-and-driver service through to Utica. Where's the clerk?"

"I act as such," said the hostler. "There ain't a driver here'll go. Wait a minute, though." He turned and shouted a question into the barn. A voice whined back at him. "Roy's upstairs. Roy's in liquor. He might go if you was to offer him an extra dollar."

"Call him down."

"Roy!" yelled the hostler. "Hey, Roy!"

After a minute a seedy individual, wearing a hat which had lost its crown, appeared in the door, and languidly leaned against it.

"Roy," said the hostler. "This feller wants to go on up. You drive him?"

"Cholera?" asked Roy in a faint voice.

"There ain't much chance," said the hostler. "He's going to give you a dollar extry."

Roy took off his hat and looked into it, as if he used it to keep his thoughts in. Then he spat through the hole.

"A dollar don't show up every day," he said in his thin lazy voice. "So I got to feel it in my pants pocket first."

Weaver snorted.

"That's a hell of a notion. Why, how do I know you can walk that far?"

Roy lifted his eyes mournfully at him, then pointed to the waiting team.

"The off mule's got a tail, ain't she?"

"Yeanh."

"I can hold on to it, can't I?"

"Yeanh. I guess you can do that."

"All right." He reached in the door for his snake whip. "Where's the dollar, mister?"

Weaver gave it to him.

"We make good time with Roy driving," said Roy. "A mule can stand to be licked, but she can't stand to have a man pinching her tail."

Weaver jumped aboard and Dan heaved in the plank.

"You steer first lick," Weaver said to him. "I've got to find where things are. A woman keeps a boat looking neat, but they haven't no sense at all where they put things. A man can't hardly find a thing where a neat woman lives."

He went below, and from time to time as they went on Dan could hear him grumbling to himself.

The boat hauled heavily. But the mules kept up a fair pace, and the walking seemed to be having a good effect on the driver. After the first two miles he was able to get along without holding to the mule's tail; and the animal showed her pleasure by switching it for several minutes with extraordinary rapidity and complication.

At the combines, Weaver came up again.

"Where's the boat?" he asked the lock-keeper.

"Which one?" said the keeper.

"The cholera one."

"Oh. Why, it's half a mile up on the left. You know the Wat cove, set back, where the towpath crosses on a bridge. They took up the bridge and drawed it into there. The doctor said it was best off the canal."

"Disease ain't a thing to be scared of," Samson remarked after a time. "I never had no notions about disease."

"No sense in it."

"No sense at all. Annie used to laugh at it."

"Sure," said Dan.

"I had a cold once into my chest. Regular constricter, but she minded me real handy. She was a queer gal some ways. Knowed a lot. Used to say she thought the Lord loved a drunken man. She said a drunken man never died of no disease. Maybe that's why Roy come along—maybe he knew that."

"Maybe."

"I just had me a good stiff ration of rum. Figure the cholera won't touch a man that's well washed up with liquor."

"Yeanh. I've heard that."

"You better go down and get a drink, Dan."

"Guess I won't just yet. I guess I'll hold off it for a day."

"All right. We ought to be coming up to Wat's cove pretty quick." They rounded a bend.

"There it is," exclaimed Weaver. "Right there where them people are standing on the bridge. You can see the boat over against them balsams, right there where that cloud shows in the water, see? What in nation are they a-doing?"

"Seems like that man was setting fire to it," Dan said.

"That's right, that's right. Setting fire to it. Good idee. He's got some rags he's putting a light to. Oiled rags by that yeller smoke. They've soaked the deck. See it ketch, Dan?"

A queer, white-faced silence hung over the little group of four men on the towpath as their companion jumped into a rowboat and pushed away. Their eyes followed the heavy smoke upward. Blue-and-yellow flame licked delicately at the planking, ate in, and then caught hotly.

"Hey there!" Weaver yelled at the driver. "What're you stopping for? Lay into them mules there! We've got to get on."

The men on the towpath paid no heed to the passing boat.

"See them three boxes?" Weaver caught Dan's elbow. "Reckon they're burning 'em right on the boat. Ain't that an awful way to have to be buried?"

Another bend; but they could see the flames spouting up against sombre dark balsams. A little farther, and they saw only the smoke mounting up, a bright cinder or two in the midst of it.

"Gol," said Weaver gustily. "Gol, Dan. I'm going to get me another drink."

Poor Samson Weaver

All during the day Samson continued to drink. He would come on deck red-faced and sweaty and bothered with a new worry.

"Dan, I've drank down a terrible lot," he would say. "I've drank more'n a man can to keep sober. But it don't do a thing outside of making me sweat. It ain't right, Dan."

At night Dan could hear him tossing in his bunk. Once he lay still for quite a while, talking to himself, telling Annie about the burning boat. Two things kept eating at him, his fear of the cholera and his lonesomeness. When the cook left, the Sarsey Sal had become a strange boat to him. His continual drinking made even the familiar sights beyond the towpath vague and unreal. Quite suddenly his thoughts had been turned in upon himself, unnerving him.

Halfway through his third turn at steering, he stamped for Dan to come up. His eyes shone feverishly.

"What's the trouble?" Dan asked.

Weaver passed his left hand over his eyes and down his nose.

"Dan," he said, "I like you. That's a fact. There's something wrong with me, Dan. I'm kind of nervous. It ain't like I was scared of being sick. I ain't never been sick, only for that chest-cold I told you about. But it don't seem like I see very good."

"Well, that's too bad."

"Set down, set down," Weaver said irritably. "With you standing up there cutting into my sight, I get nervous.—Dan, I wanted to speak to you. I aim to raise your pay, Dan. You're a good lad. You and me ought to get along good. You're satisfied, ain't you?"

"Sure."

Weaver let out a long breath.

"That's good. Just the same I aim to raise your pay. You're doing a steersman's work. I'll give you twenty a month, for this trip, anyhow. Only I got to get you to spell me more. I don't breathe very easy, Dan. If Annie hadn't 've cut along like she did, she could spell you."

"Surely, that's all right, Mister Weaver."

"Just Samson, Dan. Just Samson, to my friends. Plain Samson Weaver. You don't mind taking on for a spell now, do you, Dan?"

"No," said Dan. "I don't mind any."

"All right. I'll go get some sleep."

It was a still night, cold, close to freezing. The stars were mere glittering points. The moon had not yet risen.

The old Sarsey Sal stretched out ahead of Dan in the light of the night lantern, blunt-ended, moving beside the towpath with a faint sibilant whisper against the water. The thin thread of the towline curved on ahead to the mules, plodding patiently with nodding ears, now and then visible over the skyline. A little way behind them walked the driver, his hands in his pockets.

Dan did not call Samson till the sun was up. He was no better; his hands were getting jumpy.

"I dreamed," he said. "I didn't get no sleep at all. Things kept coming in the door."

Dan went forward to tend the team, a thin pair of bays. They were enjoying their vacation and they nuzzled at Dan's hands. He slapped them hearty whacks, and swore at them, though they made all kinds of room for him as he took in their oats. It was good to feel them under his hand, to shove them over with his shoulder when he cleaned the stalls.

When he had finished fixing the horses, he went back to the cabin to cook breakfast, ate it, spelled the driver to let him eat; and then went to his bunk to sleep.

But after an hour Samson, stamping on deck, woke him.

His face and neck were covered with sweat.

"I just seen Annie setting there on the cabin," he said. "I ain't notional, Dan. But she set there just as plain. She was darning the same sock I got on my foot, and I cussed her, and she said, 'What an old roarer you be, Sammy!'—just like she always did. I ain't notional, Dan, but it don't seem right. I need sleep. Would you mind spelling me a bit?"

"No," said Dan. "I guess not."

"I'd lie by for a while, only Butterfield's in such a hurry for his damned machinery. I've got to get it through."

"Sure."

Weaver stared at him with a worried expression, sighed, and went down. But he came up again after lunch and managed to fill out nearly four hours at the rudder. Dan slept like a log.

"I reckon I'll be able to last out most of the night," he said.

There was a stiff frost that night, and the tread of the mules sounded tight and clear. More boats were upon the water than there had been on the two preceding days; but few of them moved after dark.

Down below, in the cabin of the Sarsey Sal, Samson Weaver continued his conversation between himself and the departed Annie; his voice higher than usual, talking fast; then silent while he waited for her to answer. Listening, Dan would feel a stir in the hackles on his neck, and his hand kept straying there to put them down.

Two miles from the relay station between Little Falls and Utica, one of the company mules went dead lame. The driver flogged him ahead for a quarter of a mile and then yelled to Dan to put the boat in shore. He came back, caught the tie-ropes, and snubbed them to posts.

"When a mule can't think of anything else to do, it lames himself," he said. "What would a man want to invent such an animal for is out of my knowledge. Just to see 'em you can tell it's against nature. It spoils a man's stomach."

Grumbling, he climbed on to the sound mule.

"I'll be back with a new pair in maybe an hour."

Dan sat down on the deck. The moon was coming up behind him, and for a long way his eyes followed the small figures of the mules along the black ridge of the towpath, the driver sitting sideways on the leader. Directly under him the voice of Samson Weaver broke out in streaks of muttering. Shadows grew and changed with the mysterious swiftness that is theirs by night. There were no boats visible, no farm lights showing against the hills; only the pocket of yellow glimmer cast by the night lantern of the Sarsey Sal.

Then, far back on the towpath and coming forward in the still gleam of the moon, Dan heard the rapid tapping of a galloping horse. Behind him the canal bent round a wide curve, with trees on either bank. Their shadows clung to the water; and suddenly in the heart of them the hammer of the horse's hoofs echoed sharp and clear.

He broke into the moonlight, his grey coat stained with sweat, running hard with a fine drive, a sparkle of silver snatching his bit; the rider hunched forward on his withers, a black shape, as if he had dropped out of the shadows before the horse burst free.

Dan's quick ears caught the clink of a loose shoe as the horse came on; and just as he reached the stern of the boat he cast it. It dropped in a short silver arc, spun for an instant on the towpath, and splashed into the water beside a clump of arrowhead.

Dan jumped to his feet, and waved his arm.

"Say!" he shouted. "Say, mister. You've dropped a shoe."

He stepped ashore, climbed down to the water's edge, and fished it out, a plate shoe, with light bar calks, as smooth as polished silver.

The rider had drawn in his horse and was returning at a walk.

"Did you get it?"

"Yeanh," said Dan. "I seen it go in by that arrerhead."

"Thanks."

Dan handed it up, looking for the man's face, but all he could see under the wide brim of his hat was a smooth chin and the glitter of two eyes. The man pocketed the shoe.

"Lucky you seen it," he said. "I'd have had to wait too long to have another made. Them shoes were cut special."

"They're handy-looking," said Dan admiringly.

"Ain't I seen you before?"

"Once," said Dan. "That was in Hennessy's saloon. I've seen you twice. Once in Boonville and once in Albany."

"I didn't see you those times."

"No, you didn't."

"Well, we did each other a favor in Hennessy's," said the man.

"Yeanh."

"Well, I've got to get on. I want to get to Rome tomorrow."

"Close after you?"

"I shook 'em in Albany," said the man.

"You seen a horse trader? Calls himself Henderson?"

"Yes. He's the man I got you to get out of Hennessy's with Spinning."

"You better watch for him," said Dan. "He's Department of Justice."

"I'd guessed it."

The man laughed.

"I don't have to worry about a fat twerk like him."

"He was right behind you in Albany."

The man leaned forward and stroked his horse's neck, and the horse pricked his ears. Dan petted his nose and the horse nuzzled him, blowing clouds of steam against his shirt.

"He likes you," said the man suddenly. Then he laughed again. "I can handle a better man than Henderson. There's no use worrying about him. I've got to get on. What's your name, son?"

"Dan Harrow."

"Harrow," repeated the man. "I'll remember that. Thanks for spotting that shoe."

He wheeled the horse and went off at a lope. The horse showed no limp.

"Gol," Dan said to himself. "See him nurse that horse! He can ride."

Hoarfrost was forming on the deck when he got aboard the Sarsey Sal. He looked up the canal once more, but Gentleman Joe and the grey horse had passed from sight. The canal was still.

In the bunk cuddy, he heard Weaver muttering. Suddenly his voice became articulate.

"Dan!" he called. "Dan, Dan! Come here, quick!"

Dan ran down. The curtains to the cuddy were pulled back and the brass lamp sent its light directly into the bunks.

Weaver was lying on his back, stiff under the blankets. His face was still very red. When he saw Dan, he lifted his head for an instant, but immediately it fell back on the pillow, and he glared straight up at the planks above him.

"There's something on deck, Dan. What is it on deck?"

"There ain't nothing on deck," Dan said. "I've just come down."

Dan filled the empty glass with rum. He wondered that Samson had not noticed the stopping of the boat, or heard his meeting with Calash.

The boater swallowed noisily.

"Got to keep myself washed out," he said. "Only way to fool this damn disease. I wish Annie was here. You're a good lad, Dan."

He lay still a moment. Then he tossed his head to one side.

"I'm queer, Dan. I'm feeling mortal queer."

"Kind of bad?"

"Bad. I want to see a doctor, Dan. You won't go off leaving me to Utica, will you?"

"No."

"You're a good lad, Dan. We'll get there to-morrow?"

"Yeanh. I guess so."

"Fetch me a doctor, Dan. First off."

"All right."

"You're an honest lad, Dan. You'll need money to fetch a doctor. Doctors look at your tongue, but they like the color of your money better. It's nature, Dan. It don't mean nothing."

"No."

"I got quite a lot of money on the boat, Dan. Banks go bust, so I put mine right into the boat. It's in the beam, Dan. There's a piece lifts out. I ain't got any kin, Dan, nor nobody to look out after me, now Annie's gone. Only you, Dan. You'll let me see a doctor when we get to Utica?"

"First off."

Weaver closed his eyes, and for a few moments he seemed asleep. Then the lids quivered and jumped up, and he was staring wildly at the roof again.

"It's come back onto the deck. It hadn't ought to be there. Chase it off, Dan. For God's sake, chase it off. I didn't do nothing. I didn't do a thing. It's back there. Go and look."

His voice trailed off into incoherent sentences. "Get on back, Annie. . . . Pa said for you to get the cows, Joe. . . . I always did like buttermilk. . . ."

Dan got up. The cuddy was hot and stuffy, but Samson could not bear to have a window opened. Dan saw to the fire, his mind on Calash, riding ahead of his pursuer. He would never be caught.

Samson's voice followed him.

"It's back again. I can hear it. Chase it off, Dan."

He went on deck. Sam Henderson was sitting with his back to the rudder post, smoking a cigar. The night lantern shone over his plump shoulders, leaving his face in darkness, except for the faint red glow of the cigar end, which was mirrored in his eyes.

"Well," he said, "well, well. Ain't I seen you before, young man?"

"Yeanh, Mr. Henderson."

"Why, sure, that's right. I saw you in Boonville and in Rome. You wanted to tell me about a horse I'd lost, which was nice of you, though Spinning didn't seem to think so. He said this Joe Calash was in the saloon and got out while you was talking to us. But you couldn't know that."

"No."

Henderson grunted.

"What're you doing here?"

Dan glanced out to the towpath where a brown horse stood hitched to one of the tie-ropes.

"Working," he said.

"Yeanh? Who owns this boat?"

"Samson Weaver."

Again Henderson grunted.

"What's that?" he asked suddenly, staring down between his knees.

"That's Samson," Dan said. "He's been that way most of the trip up from Albany."

"Does he do it a lot?"

"He's been that way most of the trip up from Albany," Dan repeated.

Under them Samson shouted.

"Chase it off, Dan! Chase it away!"

The horse snorted and jerked back on the rope.

"Whoa!" Henderson shouted. "I don't blame him, though. I feel that way myself. Poor Samson. He always was a hard drinker. He's got a weak heart. This cholera must have give him a scare. He always was scared of a disease. It's funny thing, a big man like him."

"Dan!" yelled Samson. "Dan!"

"Maybe I'd better go down," Dan said.

"No," said Henderson. "Has there been anybody along the towpath tonight?"

"Not many boats just now," said Dan.

"Listen here, young man. I guess I might as well tell you. See this. I'm a Department of Justice man. I'm after this Calash, called Gentleman Joe. I'm kind of suspicious of you, but I ain't going to do anything if you don't try to head me wrong. Has there been anybody along the towpath to-night?" Dan gazed at the toes of his shoes.

"Yeanh," he said, after a moment. "Yeanh. He was coming fast."

"Well, I can't catch him now. I'll get into Utica in the morning. He ought to be there. Charley Mack, the bank walker, he'll have heard him go by if he ain't seen him."

"Dan! Dan! Dan!"

"I better go down, maybe," said Dan.

"No," said Henderson. "I'll go down. He's an old friend. He'll be glad to see me. Poor Samson Weaver."

He went down the narrow stairs nimbly for so stout a man.

There was the sound of a striking match, and the sharp sour smell of brimstone came up to Dan on deck, and a harsh scream. The horse jumped again and wrenched against his fastening. "Easy," said Dan. "Easy, boy."

"It's only me, Samson," he heard Henderson saying, quietly. "It's only Samuel."

There was no further sound, until all at once Dan could hear Henderson breathing sharply.

The stout man came up again. His face was covered with sweat and his round eyes were glassy.

"He's took a kind of fit," he said. "He's stiff as a cherry post. He must've thought I was somebody else. Poor Samson."

He took off his hat and wiped his handkerchief over his bald head.

"I've got to get along, young man. If you see anything of this man Calash, write to me. I give you the address."

He went down to the horse and lit a fresh cigar; his hands shook a trifle; but, with the cigar once filling his mouth, he steadied himself and mounted, raised his hand to Dan, and galloped off. The horse seemed eager. . . .

Dan sat by himself. The first grey of dawn and the returning driver appeared together, the mules ambling along the towpath at a good pace.

Dan got up and went down into the cabin. The candle on the stove burned feebly in the grey light, but Dan took it up and went back to the bunks. Samson was lying on his side, his knees drawn up and his head back. His eyes were wide-open, his smooth cheeks a dark, unnatural red.

Dan put his hand down against his side. Then he went on deck.

The driver had cast off the tie-ropes and hitched his mules.

"I took longer than I figured."

"Longer than I figured," said Dan.

"Well, we'd better get going. How's the old—?"

He pointed his thumb at the cabin and twirled it between his eyes.

"He's lying quiet," Dan said.

"It's a good thing," said the driver.

The mules heaved up into the collars, took up the slack, heaved, and the Sarsey Sal groaned a bit and moved sluggishly ahead, with the dawn wind against its bows, and the water muttering on the rudder.

Ten-Dollar Corpse

While they waited outside the weighlock in Utica, Dan searched Samson's clothes for money. He felt that it would take him too long to find the beam which the boater had made his bank. But in the trousers Samson still wore he found four dollars, and in the wallet in his Sunday coat he found five more—enough to see them past the weighlock.

When the Sarsey Sal had been passed through, and Dan had paid his toll, the driver asked him where he wanted to tie up.

"Anywhere'll do," Dan said. "We're hauling out for Rome to-morrow."

"That's funny," said the driver. "A short haul like that. I'd think you'd want to go right on."

"Weaver wants to see a doctor."

"Yeanh? Well, a doctor's a good thing when a man's going to die. He can write the certificate, anyway."

"I hadn't thought of that," said Dan.

"Damndest thing you ever see. A man can't marry a woman without getting a certificate—unless he takes a cook on to the canal. And then people'll have to say, 'My, My!' He can't get born respectable without a man writing a document about him. No, sir, the poor lobster can't even pull in his head to die unless somebody says it's O. K."

"That's right, at that."

"Yeanh. It makes life a tough proposition, all right.—Well, I guess I could take you up to Wheaden's wharf. It ain't in use and it's just above the Six Day. Suit you?"

"Surely," said Dan.

"Ged-dup!" The driver cracked his whip at the mules. "*You* ain't got no certificates. I'll leather the tar out of you."

They tied up. Dan went into the cabin to get his coat, and when he left he locked the door after him. Utica again. Though he had been there only once before, the basin had a pleasantly familiar feel.

He walked with the driver behind the mules as far as the Michigan Six Day office, where he signed a receipt for service rendered.

"You ain't the man that paid for this," remarked the clerk, comparing signatures.

"That's all right," the driver said, contemptuously. "Weaver's sick. How the hell could he sign?"

"Then you'd ought to put 'per—whatever your initials is,' " said the clerk. "Anybody'd ought to know that."

"Aw, spit over your chin," said the driver, and he led Dan out, shook hands, and disappeared into the stables.

Dan idly watched the loading and unloading boats, and the boats passing through, the din of voices like a mist beyond his ears. He wondered what he ought to do. He did not know anybody in Utica to whom to go for advice.

After a while he started walking up into the city, eyeing shop fronts as he passed. He did not stop until, in one of the poorer quarters, he came to a store with black curtains at the windows, and a neat sign, white letters on black:—

Lester Cushman

Funeral Director

Dan jerked the bell pull and heard, way back in the house, a single soft bell like the stroke of a clock. In a moment the door was opened, and he was confronted by a tall pale man wearing a sober black coat and black cotton gloves and carrying a clean handkerchief in his right hand.

"Step in," said the man, in a cool, soft voice.

Dan found himself in a dark hall, with stairs leading up from the back and a door on either side. On one of the doors was printed in white letters:—

Bereavement Parlor

"Walk into the parlor," the man in black said quietly. "No, not there, young gentleman,—not yet,—the door across the hall, if you please."

He held open the door. Dan walked stiffly into the room, which was fitted out with grey curtains and black haircloth furniture.

"Sit down," said the man in black, and he took a chair himself, carefully pulling his coat tails over his knees as he did so. Dan sat down and placed his hat beside his feet and took out his handkerchief to wipe his face.

"Too bad," said the man in black, scarcely above a whisper. "High and low, it finds us all; better so, perhaps."

"I guess that's right," said Dan. "I'd like to see Mr. Cushman."

The man in black made a slight, stiff bow.

"I am Mr. Cushman, at your service, Mister—?"

"Harrow," said Dan. "Dan Harrow."

"Thank you, Mr. Harrow. I shall do my best for you. I have a very creditable name in this city, I assure you."

"I guess that's right," said Dan, swallowing.

"Too bad. Just tell me where and I shall take everything off your hands. Details are hard to mind in a case such as this is."

"Yeanh," said Dan. "That's what I come to you for."

"Yes, yes, Mr. Harrow, and that is what I am here for, to relieve sorrow of its burdens."

"I'm afraid," Dan began.

"Certainly, certainly, I shall be glad to suit your needs. Something economical, simple, but dignified. Plain pine, perhaps. Pine, stained, looks very well. And is inexpensive, relatively speaking. Not cheap. At such a time we do not want cheapness, do we? I can show you some very nice coffins if you would care to see them—about twenty-five dollars, say, lined nicely in white satin?"

"No," said Dan. "It wouldn't do."

Mr. Cushman regarded him for an instant out of cold, fortified eyes.

"No," he agreed. "Such things are trying. Sister, might I ask?"

"No," said Dan. "It's a man."

"Dear me, a friend. Very hard."

"Well, I've known him four days," said Dan, "but he was all right." He looked down at his shoes, his cheeks flushed.

"Mr. Cushman, I come in to get advice. He's a boater, name of Samson Weaver, who I hired on to in Albany and he died just outside of Utica. He's down on the basin on his boat, and he ain't got any kin, and I ain't got any money, and I come to see what I ought to do about it, and I thought maybe you could tell me, and I guess that's the whole of it."

Mr. Cushman coughed and took off his gloves.

"What did he die of?" he asked.

"I wouldn't say. He was scared of cholera. There's been a scare."

"Sure," said Mr. Cushman. "I heard about it."

Dan gave him the details.

Mr. Cushman took off his coat and hung it over a chair. His sleeves were rolled up, showing strong forearms, light-colored from indoor work. He unbuttoned a pair of cuffs.

"Hmmm," he said. "Hmmm. It sure wasn't cholera. So you don't know what to do, eh?"

"No," said Dan. "That's what I come in here for. I can't pay for no funeral, but I'd ought to get a certificate of death."

"That might be arranged."

He glanced sideways at Dan.

"You and I might do a dicker on him. He wasn't a close friend, you say."

"No, I wouldn't say he was; but there wasn't anything I had against him."

"Well, I know a doctor that might want to take him. Sometimes I've been able to supply him with a specimen. Suppose I saw to the certificate, et cetera, and took him off your hands, would ten dollars do?"

"I ain't got even that much."

"Ten dollars paid to you," said Mr. Cushman.

"Why, I don't know that that's right," said Dan.

"Why not? He won't know anything about it."

"I guess that's right."

"He'll be serving a useful end of science."

"Surely."

"Then he goes on the books as buried in the public grounds. It's all very proper when you look at it correctly. Where's the boat?"

"Wheaden's wharf. It's the Sarsey Sal, a brown one."

Mr. Cushman rubbed his hands dryly together.

"Well, you can look out for me about eight." . . .

Dan stopped in at a waterside bar and had a drink. There were no familiar faces there, so he walked back to the boat. Once in the cabin, he began to worry about Samson Weaver. The boater's presence was about him, vaguely. The tobacco box, and the charred clay pipe on the shelf with the clock; the clock itself, black marble, a prized possession of Weaver's, with a small silver horse prancing on the top. Once, at the beginning of the haul from Albany, he had said to Dan, "When I hear the tickin' it sounds like he was galloping out the time; and when it strikes, then I think he's crossed a bridge." But the most bothersome thing was his suit of Sunday clothes. Dan could see one elbow of the coat between the cur-

tain and the wall, a dark green cloth with a red hair stripe, if you looked
at it closely.

A fly buzzed along one of the windowpanes. Dan watched it idly. He
wanted something to smooth him down; he looked at the pipe and tobacco,
Warnick and Brown Tobacco, made for boaters. He had smoked some
once, heavy, sweet, soothing stuff. He got up suddenly and filled the pipe
and lighted it. It tasted good. A blue cloud of it floated up to the wall and
the fly came buzzing through it to dart for the other side of the cabin.

But the Sunday coat kept catching Dan's eye, and little by little the
smoke began to lose its flavor.

"Cripus!" he exclaimed after a while. "It ain't right."

He got up, knocked out the pipe, and went into the sleeping cuddy. When
he returned to the cabin it was so dark that he had to light the lamp.
The clock struck six.

He sat down again under the lamp and pulled the boater's Bible from
its shelf. For an hour he thumbed the pages, reading here and there, but
the Book did not hold his interest. The cabin hemmed him in. On the
wharf outside, sounds of passers-by became less frequent. A boat passed
occasionally, but the voice of the driver was dim.

Dan replaced the Bible and went into the sleeping cuddy and fumbled in
his bag. When he returned, he had the volume of Shakespeare's plays the
peddler had given him on the road from Tug Hill.

He opened it haphazard and began to read, "'A made a finer end and
went away an it had been any christom child. 'A parted even just between
twelve and one. . . ." He did not understand it all; but the old man lay
before him, plucking the sheets and calling, "God, God, God!" and he
knew at once that it was real. . . .

It seemed no time at all before he heard a man thumping on the deck.

"Gol," he said, and sighed, and shut the book.

Mr. Cushman came in, dressed in a pair of overalls and a flannel shirt,
and accompanied by a sharp-faced little man with red hair.

"Evening, Harrow. This is my friend, Mr. Nidds. Where's the body?"

Dan pointed his thumb.

They went in. "All curled up," said Nidds. "The doctor likes 'em
straight."

"We only promise delivery," Cushman reminded him. "Wrap him up."
He came out to Dan. "Here's the money, Harrow. All right?"

"Yeanh," said Dan, fumbling the bills.

"All right, then. Any fuss, refer them to Lester Cushman. Ready, Nidds?"

"Sure. He weighs like cement. What's he all dressed up for?"

Dan mumbled.

"Well, they're too big for me, anyways," said Nidds.

They pushed their way up the stairs, the sack between them scraping
on the steps and bunting the sides. As they dropped it on deck to catch
their breaths, there was a click of breaking clay.

"Must've been a pipe on him somewheres," said Nidds. "That's too
bad. I needed a pipe."

Dan put out the lamp and followed them.

"Get along," said Cushman.

They carried it out to the dock and heaved it into the back of a light wagon. There was no one to notice them. The watchman was way down the wharf under a door lamp, whittling a toothpick.

"See you again some day, maybe," Cushman said good-naturedly to Dan. Dan raised his hand. The wagon clattered ahead and turned down a street. When it disappeared, Dan drew in his breath. The air was freer now that Samson had gone to see the doctor.

The Cooks' Agency

Later in the same evening Dan walked through the doors of Bentley's Bar. The big room was full of boaters sitting at the tables, the hubbub of their voices striking his ear heavily. But he had no intention of drinking.

"How do I get to see Mrs. Cashdollar?" he asked one of the keeps.

The keep pointed to a door at the end of the bar.

"Right through there, mister. Turn right down the hall and go up one flight. It's the door right opposite the stairs."

"Thanks," said Dan.

He followed the keep's directions. The hall was lighted only by a small lamp set on a corner shelf halfway up the stairs. The boards under his feet creaked; there was a smell of oldness in the walls; and as he climbed Dan could hear the whisper and stir of rats behind the lathes. An old spotted tomcat, who was watching a hole in the corner of one of the treads, glanced up at him with a harassed expression.

At the top of the stairs, a door opened into the front wall. A card was tacked to the centre panel. It was smudged by fingers which had traced the painstaking printing.

MRS. LUCY CASHDOLLAR

COOKS AGENCY

FOR BACHELLOR BOATERS

KNOCK

Dan took off his hat and knocked.

"Come right in," said a woman's voice beyond the door.

Dan found himself in a large bedroom, colorfully got up in wallpaper patchings of red and blue, yellow curtains at the window, and green rag rugs on the floor. On his left stood a monumental walnut bed, with medallions of fruit in high relief on the head and foot boards; on his right was a Franklin stove bearing a copper kettle which purred lazily, a glass with a spoon in it, and half a lemon. The air smelled sharply of the lemon and heavily of rum. Before the snapping fire a plump woman, rather pretty, in a scarlet Mother Hubbard and a bright yellow wig, stretched scarlet stocking feet to the warmth. She was smoking a large meerschaum pipe, the stem of which lay along her breast, and blowing smoke rings at the toe of her right foot, which was curled back through a hole in the stocking.

"Set down, young man," she said, motioning to another chair beside the stove.

Dan sat down, holding his hat with both hands. The warmth of the fire beat upon his face and showed it flushed. The plump woman gazed at him with a quiet smile. Her face was high-colored, and the edges of her broad nostrils were red, as though rum noggins were a habit.

"Well," she said, "what can I do for you, young man?"

"I come to see if Molly Larkins was here," Dan said.

"What's your name?"

"Dan Harrow."

"So you're the lad! Well, I ain't surprised," she said, looking him over carefully. "You're a well-set-up young man. If I was as young as I used to be, I might want a job with you myself."

Dan felt the blood in his face.

"She said she'd be with you if she was in Utica," he mumbled.

"That's right, Mr. Harrow. She's staying here."

"She ain't gone?"

"No. But she ain't in now. She will be later."

Dan's hands squeezed his hat, and a slow smile came over his face. The corners of Mrs. Cashdollar's eyes crinkled; she smiled back at him.

"Feeling strong about her?"

"Kind of," said Dan.

"I don't blame you. I can't say as I blame you at all. She's real pretty. I made two good commissions on to her. Fat ones."

Dan looked puzzled.

"Oh, you won't have to pay none. She's been expecting you. She was going to stay another week. I'd hate to charge you any, anyhow. It ain't often I can fix up such a pair. When I can, most generally I charges light— for old time's sake."

She settled her wig on with both hands and sighed.

"Yes. Old times. I was as pretty as she was, once; not so long ago, at that. Yeller hair and a tidy figure. Men would look around on the street when I laughed. Oh, well, the world goes by a person and they get left after a while."

"I wouldn't say that, mam."

"You're a nice young man, and you're a lucky young man, too, to get such a pretty cook. You'll make a smart-looking pair if she takes care of you right. She's a good gal, a good cook. She's willing and kind and honest; but there's times when she's hard to hold. I know her right through. I've took special care with her. Yes, sir, I've turned down bids when a man wanted to get her, by telling she had a job already. Jotham Klore turned out a kind of error. But he's a good man, in a way, a fine free spender, and he gives a girl a good time, and Molly'd took an affection to him. There's times, young man, when you'll have to bear right down on her and make her mind. That's the kind she is. She's got to feel a bit all the while."

She leaned forward, her Mother Hubbard wrinkling tight behind her arms, and took a coal out of the fire with a little pair of tongs. When she had her pipe drawing again, she asked Dan how he was fixed. He told her about the boat and Samson's death.

"Poor Samson Weaver," said Mrs. Cashdollar. "He was a nice man. I made quite a bit of money through him, but Annie always was that way. Lucky I don't guarantee my gals'll stay, unless I get a wife proposition. There was an old feller came in a year ago. He had a farm up by Steuben.

Used to be a boater and he come down to me to get him a cook. He
wanted a young gal, so I give him one and told him the gal wouldn't stand
for it. Well, she was gone in a week. Back she come, and back come the
old feller. White was his name. He was all cut up. He wanted another,
when I told him the gal wouldn't go back. So I let him have another. He
tried three. The last time he come in I says to him, 'Mr. White, you don't
want a gal that's pretty,' I said. 'You want a woman that knows that sowing
means reaping.' Oh, I talked to him right like a mother. 'I got a woman
here—she's the best cook in Utica,' I said. 'She ain't pretty; she's forty. But
she's about ready to tie up,' I said. Well, even then he didn't want only a
gal. He thought he was a boater still. So off he went and I called up the
woman, and I told her, 'Hermy, there goes old man White. He's a good
man, but he's notional. He's got a good farm. You get ahead of him and get
a good meal. I'll loan you the money to get there—five per cent profit. If you
can't get there and stick, you ain't the woman I think you are, with your
powers for food. That man don't know it, but he's fonder of his insides
than a hen is of corn. That's the way a man gets when he gets old; with
a gal the trouble comes outside.' So off she went, and she beat him back and
had his supper frying for him; and two weeks later, when it was time to
pay up, I was sitting here one night thinking she might pop in, and getting
ready to tell her she needn't hang round my agency if she hadn't settled
down, when in comes White. He fishes the money I'd give her right out of
his pocket, with the per cent with it, and he says, 'Mrs. Cashdollar, here's
your money, and thank you,' he says. I counted and told him it was right.
'Yeanh,' he says, 'my wife give me the account.' Well, she'd knowed where
she stood all right; they're real happy. I got her off my hands and made a
profit. It was good all round."

"Yeanh," said Dan.

"That kind of a woman won't give you no bother," Mrs. Cashdollar
said. "Give her a little honey-love once a day, and she's fixed. But a gal
like Molly Larkins has got to be rode steady. She's notional."

"Yeanh," said Dan. "Thanks."

"Course you ain't paying a bit of attention to what an old woman tells
you. Well," she sighed again, "I was that way once."

"When'll Molly be back?" Dan asked.

"Pretty late. Shall I tell her you're waiting for her?"

"Yeanh," said Dan. "Please."

"All right, where's the boat?"

"Wheaden's wharf. It's the Sarsey Sal."

"All right. You're certain you want her? I've got a pretty, dark-complected girl here, just in from the country, if you're taken that way."

"No, thanks," Dan said, getting to his feet awkwardly. "I think I'd better
be getting on back."

"All right, young man, good luck to you. If you don't have it, come
back here and I'll see what I can do for you. I'd enjoy having your trade."

"All right. Good night, mam."

"Good night," said Mrs. Cashdollar.

He walked slowly down the stairs. The spotted cat was still at the same
hole; and it looked up at him with a disgruntled air at the sound of his
heavy tread.

Dan did not notice the cat. He went out through the bar and into the street and headed back for the Sarsey Sal. There was an odd feeling of suffocation in him as he went along the docks. Under a light he passed the watchman he had seen earlier in the evening, twirling a toothpick back and forth across his lower lip. The lapping of the water came upon his ears with a clear insistence; the wind was sharper; and the tread of his heels over the planks rang hard. Above him the stars clustered in a clear sky.

In the cabin he lit the lamp, and looked round him. His blue-green eyes shone and his tanned cheeks were flushed. He changed triflingly the position of the two chairs and pushed a stool back into the corner. Then he went into the cuddy. As in some of the older boats, it had a partition dividing the double bunk from the single. On the walls hung odds and ends of Samson Weaver's clothes—a pair of overalls, deeply kneed; an old hat, the brim of which was pulling away from the crown in front; a pair of boots hung on a nail by their laces, the mark of the boater's feet evident in their worn leather. Dan gathered them up and took them forward to the stable. The horses were lying down, but they turned their heads toward him, their eyes glowing warmly in the light of his lantern.

He dropped the clothes in a corner and grinned at the team.

"You old devils, you," he said to them, his voice thick, "what're you thinking about?"

They did not get up; but as he went out again one of them nickered whisperingly.

In the cabin once more he sat down; and then got up to put another stick in the stove; and then sat down with his book on his knee. But his eyes could not follow the letters through the short lines. It was warm in the cabin; the kettle was purring, hiding the mutter of the water outside; the air was dozy with the smell of past cargoes, of sweet apples, the choking smell of grain, the clinging, solemn smell of potatoes. A mist was closing on the windowpanes, shutting in the lights. A horn blew flatly far out along the water. Forward, one of the horses shifted its weight. . . .

Dan heard light footsteps on the dock, on the plank, on the deck of the boat just over him. He sat still for an instant, his hands gripping the arms of the rocker. The steps started down the stairs; the door opened; Molly Larkins came in, in her red dress and hat, carrying a carpetbag.

"Hullo, Dan."

Her face was a bit flushed; but her dark blue eyes were cool. He got up slowly to take her bag.

"I'll just drop it inside," she said, and she carried it into the sleeping cuddy. His eyes followed her in and out again. She stood close before him, taking off her hat, her skirts lifting a little at the sides of her ankles.

"Hello, Molly."

She gave him a wide smile.

"Just to think of you getting a boat so soon."

"It ain't actually mine."

"Mrs. Cashdollar says it's as good as yourn. She'd know."

"I ain't got any money yet. I won't be able to get a driver for a spell."

"Well, I guess I can steer, Dan."

He glanced approvingly at her strong hands.

"I'd ought to get trade from Butterfield," he said.

"Sure," she said. Her blowzy bright hair hung down in a loose coil over one ear. She poked at it.

"My gracious, I can't never make it stay respectable!"

She laughed and shook her head, and the coil slipped out to fall forward over her breast. Dan drew his breath and looked away suddenly.

"Samson said he had money hid on the boat, into one of the beams."

"Goodness," she exclaimed, her eyes shining. "We'll have to look to-morrow."

"I think we'd better wait till I've seen Mr. Butterfield, Molly."

"I don't see why."

"If he says it's our boat," he said almost shyly, "it'll be like looking for our own money."

"It'd be fun to look to-morrow. Why, we might even find it to-night."

He glanced down at his hands and shook his head.

"No, I don't think we'd want to."

She laughed again, low and clear.

"It don't make much difference."

She got up suddenly.

"I've got to nose round," she said. "I always was nosey getting into a new boat."

His eyes followed her here and there as she opened the cupboards and poked into corners, giving little exclamations, or wrinkling her nose as she found dust.

"I'll have to clean up good right away," she said. "My heavens, you could tell just two men had been living on this boat."

He grinned with a warm feeling of pride in him. When she bent over, the loose strand of hair would brush her chin and she would catch it back with a pleasant sharp snatch; but it always curled forward again across her shoulder.

The clock whirred and rapidly beat out the hour.

"Goodness," she exclaimed, looking from it to him. "I'd scarcely noticed it! Ain't it a cute pretty horse prancing like that?"

The lamplight picked out the muscles in the arched neck of the little animal. He looked alive.

"It'll be nice to have him there prancing with his feet," she said. "There won't be no drag in the time."

"Molly," he said.

"Yeanh?"

"Molly," he said.

She came to him and stood by the arm of the chair.

He wanted to speak, but the word snagged in his throat.

Suddenly she reached down for his hand and pulled his arm round her waist. Her eyes were bright and large and a little misty, and there lurked in the long corners enough of the devil to make them sweet, and a dimple poked into her left cheek.

"Gracious me," she said. "Ain't a man a silly thing!"

She spun away from him suddenly, her skirt lifting about her knees, and laughed and went into the cuddy and drew the curtain.

Dan sat by himself a while, listening to the soft stirring beyond the curtain. The fire lulled in the stove; the kettle ceased its talk with a few light tinkles of the dying steam; the lapping sound of the ripple closed in round the boat. The clock struck the half hour.

Dan got up suddenly and turned to the cuddy.

"Land!" said Molly, a low, soft kindness in her voice. "Ain't a man silly? You've forgot to blow out the lamp."

Rome Haul

When Dan woke, he heard Molly moving round the cabin. He could hear the stove roaring and the fat hopping in the pan, and the warmth and the fry smells were already coming in to the bunk. The early morning sunlight, shining against the curtains, traced the barred frame of the cabin window. Dan stretched and yawned silently, and lay still with lazy content-ment. His hand could still feel the warmth in the blankets beside him.

Overnight a new atmosphere had stolen into the Sarsey Sal. As he lay there, Dan could feel it all round him. On the wall to the right of the curtain three print dresses hung, and beside them a cotton bag out of the top of which poked a bit of the collar of Molly's red best dress. Her hat lay on the shelf above the nails; two pairs of shoes sat side by side in the corner. And Molly herself was humming a little tune in the kitchen, over and over, in snatches as she went about her work. Like many women whose speaking voice is strong and low, she sang in a small voice, almost shyly: —

> "Down in the valley,
> The valley so low,
> Hang your head over,
> Hear the wind blow."

Dan swallowed hard, as if he would have liked to cry, and sat up sud-denly. Molly came to the curtain and put her head through. Her hair hung forward on her shoulder in a big loose braid, making her look ri-diculously young. She was wearing a thin green print that brought out the bright flush in her cheeks; and her blue eyes, seeing his tousled hair and the patient, bewildered pleasure in his face, grew dark with tenderness.

"Get up, lazy Dan. Come and get your breakfast."

She tossed his trousers onto the bed and went back to her work.

> "Hear the wind blow, dear,
> Hear the wind blow,
> Hang your head over
> And hear the wind blow."

He pulled on his trousers and laced his boots; his fingers were clumsy. Then he went on deck and drew himself a bucket of water, washed, and went to the stable. The horses were up and eager for their feed. He got them a bucket of water from the butt and stood by their heads watching them drink. The offhorse lifted its head when it had drunk and brushed the back of his neck with its cool damp muzzle. Dan swore and thumped it with his fist, and the horse laid back its ears and pretended to nip him. Dan laughed at it and slapped its neck; and the horse pricked its ears suddenly and stamped. The other, impatient of the byplay, whickered into the belly of the manger for oats.

Dan brushed them down and grained them. They were a fairly good team, a little lighter than he liked a horse; but they were fattening from their week of rest. He put on their collars and adjusted the hames and went back to the cabin.

Molly had let down the table from the wall, and now she sat at one end, the coffeepot before her. The sunlight coming through the window caught in the edges of her hair.

"Good morning," she said, her eyes on the high color the cold water had whipped up in his cheeks.

"Morning," said Dan. He went over to the sink, felt for the comb behind the mirror, and ran it through his hair.

Molly laughed.

"It don't do a bit of good to do that."

"No," he said. "I guess it don't."

"Come and set down, then. Here's your coffee," she said, pouring him a cup. "Whatever woman was on to this boat before you men tried to run things certainly knowed coffee. She stocked up good. There's enough of everything to last us till we get ready to leave Rome, except for eggs and butter and milk."

"Yeanh," said Dan, starting in on his bacon and potatoes with relish.

She eyed him dubiously.

"I haven't had time to make a pie," she said. "But I'll whip up something to-night."

"This is good enough for me," Dan said, looking her over with a broad grin.

Her eyes smiled to watch him eating.

"It's an old boat," she said. "But it's real nice. It's fixed out about the most comfortable of any boat I've lived on to. The china's pretty, too, white and red like this. Just my color. But I'd like to clean it out good."

"We can when we quit Rome."

"It ain't that it's so awful dirty," she went on. "But I don't like to live in it with the old man dead the way he is, and not clean up all round."

She wrinkled her nose.

"He was all right," Dan said. "Samson Weaver was a good man."

"I don't doubt he was all right. It's just a feeling."

"Mrs. Cashdollar said you was notional."

"What did she say?" Molly asked quickly.

Dan grinned.

"Please tell me."

"No, I guess I'd better not."

"It must've been bad."

"No, I wouldn't say it was bad. She seemed to like you all right."

"She's been nice to me," Molly said. "She's a pretty nice old woman."

"I like her a lot."

"She is nice. It's too bad she's getting so fat. She has to wear a wig, too."

"I didn't guess it."

"It is. It's a pity, too. She looks awful with it off her."

"Well, it looks all right on."

"Men don't notice. I'd rather lose my teeth than my hair."

"You've got enough to last a while, if it's real."

"You'd ought to know it was real. I had to pull it out from under you a dozen times."

"It's pretty, such a lot of it," he said, his eyes shining. The dimple stole into her cheek.

"I wish it was yellow."

"I like it just how it is," said Dan, seriously.

She smiled to herself.

"When do you want to start?"

"Just so soon as you're ready."

"I want to hang the blankets outside anyway to-day."

"All right. I'll rig a line while you're washing dishes."

He felt as if he could sit there for hours just watching her, as she bent forward, her elbows on the table, her chin cupped in her hands. There was no denying she was pretty, when you looked at her fresh coloring and the feathery curl of her light brown hair. The sunlight dusted her skin with a luminous bloom and picked out a shadow between her shoulders.

"Dan," she said suddenly.

"Yeanh."

"Could I get a bigger mirror? I can't hardly see to do my hair in this one."

"Why, yes, I guess I could, after Butterfield pays me off."

She sighed, as if relieved.

He pushed back his chair.

"I reckon we'd ought to get ready. I'll hang out them blankets."

"There's some pins in that bag hanging on the door. I found them this morning."

Dan stretched a line between the cabin roof and that of the stable. There were two notched uprights already cleated in place within easy reach of the left runway, as though Annie had superintended the operation. The iron-tipped boat pole, one end against the bottom of the pit, could be used as a brace.

It was a bright windy morning, with white clouds tumbling high up. The blankets wipped and shivered. When he had hung them, Dan raised the half hatch of the stable and laid the gangway for the horses.

In the cabin Molly was drying the dishes, her hands and wrists red from the water. Dan took the dishpan out to empty it.

"It's kind of cold," he said, when he came in again. "You'd better dress up warm."

She nodded, her mouth full of pins as she began twisting the braid round and round her head. It made a heavy coil. When she had finished, she gave her head a little tentative shake.

"Have you got something warm I could use, Dan?"

"Yeanh. There's a blue shirt in my bag."

"I'll get it," she said. "You'd better get the horses out."

The team came down the gang eagerly, but rather stiff from their long ride in the stable. He rubbed down their legs with his hands, while they drew trembling long breaths and bent their knees as he finished.

Molly came on deck. The tails of his blue shirt flapped loosely over her hips.

"All right," she said, swinging the rudder out.

He let down the stable hatch, drew in the gang, tossed off the tie-ropes, and spoke to the team. They settled down willingly under their collars. Dan saw that he would not need to use the reins or Samson's heavy whip.

They were a good pair, active walkers, but too light and quick to do much hauling without another pair to relieve them. Dan decided that he would want another team, and, if he got another team, that he would buy a good one.

The Sarsey Sal swung out from the wharf into the basin. They cleared it quickly and came into the open canal. A cold wind snapped across the water when they passed the last street; looking over his shoulder, Dan saw it drawing Molly's skirt snug about her legs, fluttering it behind her. She stood with her weight on the hip nearest the rudder, both hands on the sweep, her face turned sidewise to meet the wind. A strand of hair whipped her lips, and she caught it suddenly with her white teeth and grinned ahead at Dan while she held it.

He warmed to see her there, on his boat, wearing his own shirt, a heavy woolen one with the collar standing up against the back of her hair. The awkwardness of its fit made it curiously becoming to her. His boat—the water cuddling the clumsy old bows; his cook; his heart rose in him and he turned his head into the wind to feel it beating on his skin, and he smiled to himself.

There were not many boats heading west that morning. The press of the emigrant season was over. Most of the west-bound boats were freighters like the Sarsey Sal, heavy-laden. But there was the autumn push of crops coming east. Grain from the lakes, boat after boat; and potatoes coming down to the cities all along the line; and apples, with their sharp sweet smell. Every few minutes a boat passed him.

At noon he put the horses on board for an hour to feed and rest. Molly got a quick lunch of potatoes and eggs and tea; and she begged some apples from a boater as he passed. He tossed them onto the Sarsey Sal and took off his hat to Molly; and, standing beside her, Dan flushed with pride. His boat, his cook; forward in the stable his team munching their oats; he belonged to the canal.

"Maybe we'll go down to New York next spring," he said to her in the cabin.

She caught her breath.

"I'd like to."

"Ever been down?"

"No. But I'd like to see it. It's a great city, and the streets full all the while. And theatres and museums."

All at once Dan felt a little afraid of it, so many people. He had not liked Albany, and Albany was a small place alongside of New York, by all accounts.

"You can see boats from four canals, there, all to once," Molly said.

He watched her biting out of her apple.

"Seen anything of Klore?" he asked after a while.

She took another bite without looking at him.

"Yeanh," she said, with the apple against her mouth. "He's out hauling to Buffalo."

"Yeanh."

"He come around to Mrs. Cashdollar a dozen times looking for me," she said.

"Yeanh."

"I wouldn't have nothing to do with him. Not any more."

"I'm glad he's away."

"He's looking out for you, Mrs. Cashdollar said. He's mad about you and me."

"I don't want to fight him."

"You'll have to sometime."

"I probably will," Dan said seriously.

"You ain't scared of him?" she asked with a quick sidelong look.

"I don't want to fight him."

"You'll have to lick him if I stay with you. It's got to come," she said, with a definite cold prescience in her tone. "I can see it."

"Yeanh," he said, moodily.

She gave him a long frank look.

"Any kind of a man can get a-hold of something, Dan; but it's keeping it that counts."

They went on after the meal. For an hour Molly walked with the horses and Dan steered.

"Keep 'em slowed down!" he shouted to her.

She nodded her head. She had a free, swinging stride which he liked to watch. He could see that the horses liked her; and that was a good thing, he said to himself; you could trust a horse or cow's opinion better than a man's or a dog's.

She came nimbly up the boat ladder when he swung it in to the tow-path, and he caught her when she came over the side and held her in his arm. She was flushed from her exercise, and he could feel her drawing herself in hard against him.

"Get ashore, lazy Dan," she said, kissing him.

He gave her a squeeze.

"Dan!" she gasped. "Lord! You can lick Klore any time, if you have a mind to!"

For a while he felt as though he could.

"What a thing it'll be to watch!" she said to herself, looking ahead at him where he walked beside the horses, his heavy shoulders bent. "He needs to be stiffened, but it's got to come."

They hauled into Rome at four o'clock, and tied up at the Butterfield dock.

Samson's End

Mr. Butterfield rose from behind the cherrywood desk that faced the door.

"Good afternoon. What can I—"

His grey eyes brightened.

"Why, it's young Harrow, isn't it? I'm glad to see you. Come in and sit down."

He stepped forward, smiling, and shook hands.

Dan put his hat on the desk and looked down at his fists. It was cool in the room. The chairs were black-leather-seated, and a dark green rug lay on the floor. Two small windows high up on the left wall let in the afternoon sun to fall in two squares on the varnished sealing of the opposite wall. Facing Dan, Mr. Butterfield sat erect in his well-fitting black coat, the tips of his fingers touching across his lap, a kindly look in his grey eyes.

"I come to ask you something," Dan said somewhat diffidently.

"I'll give you the best advice I can, Harrow."

Dan swallowed. Even in the office there were traces of the dust of the new grain, with its sweet, musty smell.

"Where have you been since I saw you?" Mr. Butterfield asked.

"Utica and Albany and back to Utica," said Dan.

"Who did you come in with?"

"I come in on the Sarsey Sal."

"Why, that's Weaver's boat. Did you bring up my machinery?"

"Yeanh."

"I'm glad it's here. I expected it yesterday. Did Weaver come into the office with you?"

"No, that's why I come to see you, Mr. Butterfield. Samson's dead."

"Good Lord! What happened to him?"

"I reckon he was scared of the cholera."

"Yes, I heard there was a case. Strange at this time of year, but we'd had a good deal of hot foggy weather. Tell me how he died."

Dan told him how he had signed on in Albany, how they had passed the cholera boat burning, how Samson had been worrying, how Henderson came aboard.

"It must have been his heart," said Mr. Butterfield. "It was a hard trip for you, Harrow. I think you did well to come through so quickly. What did you do with the poor fellow?"

"That's partly what I come to see you about." And Dan told him in detail of his deal with the undertaker.

"I didn't know rightly what I ought to do," he said apologetically. "I hadn't had no experience. When Pa died Mr. Breezy done the job."

"Well, Samson Weaver was a good man. I wouldn't want him to go that way."

"It didn't seem right," said Dan. "But I had to have some money. And I didn't know nobody in Utica to borrow from."

"You ought to have written up to me."

"Weaver said you wanted the machinery right away."

"That's true enough. Still, I don't want to leave him as he is."

"It don't seem right," Dan agreed, wiping the sweat from his forehead with the back of his hand.

"I guess I know the doctor the undertaker was taking him to. He's a first-rate surgeon, and I suppose he has to have a study once in a while. I won't mention his name. There's a good deal of prejudice against the practice, though I don't see anything wrong in it. But we ought to consider Samson. I don't think he would have liked it, Harrow."

"I guess that's right, Mr. Butterfield. He had a kind of horror."

"Well, then, suppose I look up this surgeon; I've got to go to Utica tomorrow anyway; and I'll have the body buried decently and have a stone put up. Don't you think yourself that would be best?"

"Yeanh," said Dan, "it didn't seem right letting him go to the doctor that way—seeing as how I wasn't in Samson's family."

Mr. Butterfield looked grave.

"Yes. I agree with you, Harrow. Seeing he hasn't any family, it's a sort of double obligation to us to see he's treated decently. He was a very decent man."

"Yeanh."

"I'll be glad to pay for the headstone, but maybe you'd like to contribute something, Harrow."

"Yeanh. That's what I come to see you about, Mr. Butterfield."

"How about ten dollars?"

Dan drew a breath of relief.

"That's just what I'd ought to give, I think."

He took the ten dollars Cushman had given him from his pocket and pushed them across the desk. Mr. Butterfield put them in his wallet, took a cigar out of a drawer, lit it, and leaned back.

"What are your plans now, Harrow?"

"That's what I come to see you about, Mr. Butterfield. I wanted to see you about the Sarsey Sal. Samson said he didn't have any folks. I was wondering if you'd know if anybody else had an interest in the boat."

"I happen to know that nobody has."

"I was wondering who'd own the boat then, Mr. Butterfield."

Mr. Butterfield examined the end of his cigar.

"I should think you had as good a claim as anybody, Harrow. You took good care of Weaver on the haul up."

"I didn't have much time to take care of him. I didn't feel right about letting the doctor have him."

"We've straightened that out. I shouldn't worry about it. I don't see why you shouldn't go on with the boat, Harrow, just where Samson Weaver left off. He was very fond of that old boat. He said to me once, 'I'll bet she'll keep on moving as long as there's water to rub her belly on.' I think he'd like to think of the Sal still going along. I had his boat and him working for me regularly. Would you like to sign up with me?"

"Yeanh."

"I want to send a load of corn and oats up to Ney's in Carthage tomorrow. Will that suit you?"

"Yeanh."

"How are you fixed for horses?"

"There's a pair on the boat, bays—six and eight, I'd judge. They're good walkers, but kind of light to suit me. I don't think they're a lot over twenty-three hundred."

"Well, you won't have much more hauling to do this fall. But next spring you'll need a second pair."

"Yeanh, I'd thought so."

"There's going to be a fair on the second of November at Whitesboro. Horses will be cheap in the fall. If I were you, I'd buy them and hire them out during the winter. I send grain and supplies in to the Goldbrook camps in winter. I'd be glad to hire a couple of teams and a pair of drivers. You could tie up at Utica for the winter."

"That would be fine," Dan said.

"All right, then. I'll see to changing the Sal's registration at the Rome lock to-night. How about a driver?"

"I hadn't thought to get one this fall. I've got a cook with me; she's sort of a nice girl," Dan said shyly.

Mr. Butterfield looked at him a moment as if he were about to say something, but evidently changed his mind.

"If she's young and strong she can help you out. I won't ask any rush hauling from you this fall."

"She's real willing to help out."

"That's a good sign. Now let's see your bill of lading."

Dan handed it across.

"I'll have it checked to-morrow morning when we unload. But I know it's all right, so I'll pay you now—Weaver's terms, naturally."

"They suit me," Dan said. "They'll suit me right along."

"All right."

Mr. Butterfield went to a door in the wall, unlocked it, and with a second key unlocked the safe inside.

"Eighty-five dollars?"

"That's right," said Dan.

"Here's the receipt," said Mr. Butterfield, handing him a pen.

Dan signed.

Mr. Butterfield held out his hand.

"You've made a lucky beginning, Harrow. I'm glad of it. I think you deserve it."

He shook hands. Dan went out of the office and crossed the wharf. The Sarsey Sal lay squat and heavy on its brown reflection. Boats passed just beyond it, but Dan had eyes only for its brown hulk. It was his boat.

5

THE CLOSING SEASON

Fortune Friendly

WHEN he boarded the Sarsey Sal, Dan found it empty. For an instant a fear that Molly might have cleared out gnawed at his insides. Her hat and red dress were gone, and her narrow shoes. It was only when he noticed her comb and brush sticking out from behind the mirror that he took comfort. She wouldn't have gone off without them, he told himself; her hair gave her too much bother for her to leave them behind.

So he went up on deck and sat down to wait for her. He listened to the horses munching forward with a sense of pleasure; they were his horses. But he was anxious for the time when he could get the team he wanted. Maybe he could pick them up singly; match up a team, and save money that way. If he bought at all, he would buy good ones.

The long basin was a-crawl with boats. Round from the Boonville feeder a chain of them came one after another, stacked high with firewood—twelve-inch lengths for stoves. It was the first tangible sign of winter. There were times when the canal froze early in December—two years ago it had frozen in the first week, catching many boats. Dan was anxious to get going. The Carthage trip would take better than a week. A great flock of crows which flapped across the valley sounded as if they were talking snow.

Clerks were coming out of the warehouses at the end of the day's work. The docks were crowded. Men from the granaries moved past him, spanking the flour mist from their trouser legs with whitened hands.

A man was standing opposite the bow of the old boat. He wore a wide grey felt hat and a black coat, and his narrow trousers were strapped under his shoes. There was something familiar to Dan in his attitude, and when he pulled a watch from his waistcoat pocket to read the time, Dan recognized the flaming red front. At the same moment the man looked up and met his eye.

"Why, hello, young man," he said, coming forward with a grin wrinkling the corners of his eyes. "Weren't you on Julius Wilson's boat that I went to Utica on after preaching a sermon at them hellions in Maynar's Corners?"

"Yeanh," said Dan. "You're Mr. Friendly, ain't you?"

"I am, but I've forgotten your name."

"I'm Dan Harrow."

"Harrow! That's right. How's Wilson and that old Jew? Have they learned to play pinochle any better?"

"I don't know," said Dan. "Won't you come aboard?"

Mr. Friendly glanced again at his watch.

"I don't know but what I might as well. Thank you."

"We'll step down in the cabin," said Dan, very much tickled at the presence of his first guest.

He poked up the fire and motioned the ex-preacher to the rocking-chair.

"Who's the boater?" Fortune asked.

"Me," said Dan.

"You?"

"Yeanh. Boater, owner, driver, the hull works, all but the cook. Want a job?" he asked, making a poke at a joke.

Fortune laughed; then he sobered down, and a frown appeared on his smooth, child's forehead.

"Serious?"

"It's a gospel fact," said Dan. "This boat's mine and I'm going to haul for Butterfield."

"Where's your next haul?"

"Carthage."

"When you hauling?"

"To-morrow morning first thing."

"Got a cook?"

"A-1."

"Sold!" said Fortune, holding out his hand. "It's the first time I ever hired on to a regular job. What am I going to do?"

"Drive and steer."

"How much do I get?"

Dan scratched the back of his head and looked serious. He began to realize that the ex-preacher was not joking. He would have to be careful now, and hire the man on as cheap as he could.

"You ain't done any driving before, have you?"

"Not to speak of," said Fortune.

"Well, a driver-boy ought to get ten a month, by rights, but I'll give you eleven. How'd that be?"

"Surely. That'd be all right with me, Dan."

The old man hooked his feet in the rungs of the chair and rocked comfortably.

"I don't mind telling you, Dan, I was broke again. Busted bare. It wasn't my fault. I'd done a good haul on the Rome sheriff playing euchre. There was a lot he didn't know about that game. So when he was cleaned out he got sore, took my money and his'n, and said I was cheating and if I was in town next morning he'd lock me up for a public nuisance. You'd think I'm old enough to've known better than play cards with a sheriff."

"Was you cheating?" Dan asked.

"It depends how you look at it, Dan."

The ex-preacher ran his hand down over his smooth face. "How'd you come to get the boat, Dan?"

Dan told him the story. When he had finished Samson Weaver's death, Fortune Friendly clucked his tongue.

"Poor devil."

"He was scared all right," said Dan, and he told about the undertaker and his interview with Mr. Butterfield. Friendly snorted.

"Undertakers! I'd call 'em overtakers. They've got everybody buttoned right into their gloves, and they know there's nobody dares say no to 'em. And when the time comes to themselves, they get a good discount for a trade courtesy!"

"I believe it," said Dan.

"Who's your cook?"

"Why, I got her in Utica. She ought to be back pretty quick."

Dan lifted his head.

"That's her coming along the dock. I can tell her walk. She's kind of a pretty nice girl."

Molly Larkins came into the cabin, carrying a market basket and several packages.

"Hello, Dan. I didn't expect to be so long."

"That's all right, Molly. This here's a driver coming along with us. Mr. Fortune Friendly."

Molly poked her head over a bunch of carrot greens and gave him a bright smile.

"Why, Mr. Friendly. When did you go in for boating?"

"Just fifteen minutes ago, Molly. Lord, girl, you look pretty! What's come over you?"

Her color deepened, and Friendly drew in his breath.

"Well, I don't rightly wonder," he said softly, his black eyes moving from one to the other. "I knew I was going to like driving for this boat, even if it was steady work for a man like me, but I didn't know how much."

He settled back in the chair and smiled happily.

"I'll be a sort of un-hindering pa," he said. "So I'm going to say right off I'm hungry for my dinner."

Molly laid down her purchases.

"I've bought a regular outfit of food. Turnips, 'tatoes, eggs, butter, and lard. We didn't need sugar and salt and pepper. And I've got the dandiest pork chops you've ever seen."

She went into the sleeping cuddy.

"Dan, haven't you brought in those blankets?"

"No."

"Maybe you and Fortune'd better get 'em right away. They'll get damped out in the dew."

"I'll get them," said Fortune.

Molly poked her head through the curtains while she buttoned on a work dress.

"What did Mr. Butterfield say?"

"He said the boat was mine. I'm to haul for him. We'll make the Watertown haul to-morrow morning early."

"It's our boat," she said.

"Yeanh."

"Dan, I've got you a kind of a present."

She held out a clay pipe. Dan took it and slowly turned it over.

"Thanks," he said; but there was tremor in his voice. He felt all at once very kind toward her.

"There's some tobacco in the basket," she said shyly. "I thought maybe you'd like it."

Friendly came bunting through the door, his arms stuffed full of blankets.

"Where'll I put 'em?"

Molly came out of the cuddy, flinging the curtain open.

"Stretch them on the bed," she said.

It was grown dark. While the chops were sputtering in the pan and Molly was setting the table, Dan, with his pipe lighted, went forward to feed the horses and hang out the night lantern. The old ex-preacher, sitting in the rocker, watched Molly moving about, his nostrils widening now and then to the fry-smell.

"How did you come to hire on with him, Molly? Through Lucy Cashdollar's?"

"No. I seen him first in Hennessy's."

"Oh, you did, eh?"

"Yes," she said, with a little nod.

"You made up your mind right then, I guess."

She nodded again, with a rather shy smile.

"Where's Klore?"

"I left him," she said, poking sharply at a chop. "I was sick of him."

"Did he take it kind?"

"No. He gave me a licking first."

"He'll lay for Dan. Do you think it's right by Dan?"

"He knows it," she said, turning on him.

"Then they'll have to fight it out," Fortune said. "Is Dan afraid of him?"

"I don't know," she said in a small voice. "But he's terrible strong."

"It ought to be a dinger," said the old man, his eyes gleaming.

"I hope Dan'll lick him. He's got the strength. I hope he'll lick him down."

The ex-preacher glanced at her sharply.

"Well," he said after a moment, "it's a good sign. Do you love him, Molly?"

She caught her breath, and made eyes at him without speaking.

"Lord," he said, "you've got pretty, Molly. Lord! If Klore saw you now he'd go crazy."

She smiled to herself.

"It generally happens once," said the ex-preacher. "I guess it's best for you both to go through with it this way; but the end of it's likely to be hard for you both, Molly. I got to thinking a little while ago that Dan wouldn't last on the canal. Getting this boat and all is good, but he don't look like a boater; he don't talk right; he's half asleep, Molly."

"Asleep!" she cried. "I know better!"

"He hasn't found out who he is; he hasn't shook hands with himself," said the ex-preacher moodily.

Molly turned, her hand holding the fork on her hip, a loose strand of her hair caught in her white teeth.

"Look at me, Fortune. Do you think he's going to go away without me?"

"No—hardly!"

"Well, then!"

The old man's smooth face became sober and wise as he looked at her.

"That's the hell of it—going in for it hard this way. It ain't natural and proper for you and me, Molly. We've just gone along rubbing elbows with folks, the way boaters do, and seeing things, and learning things; and they're so many they don't matter. But when a man like Dan wakes up to what he wants it's a hard thing. He's got the whole of everything inside of him. He doesn't move light enough to let them go out. That's the hell of it, Molly. You'll want to quit him."

She laughed, throwing up her chin.

"Lord!" said the old man.

"Yeanh? You don't know nothing, Fortune."

"I know you, Molly. I've taught you a lot. I've taught you what I think. And now you're busting right out against everything. But you're built like me. There's no profit doing things hard, Molly."

"Go along with such talk."

"You're in for it now; you couldn't get out if you tried. It's bright all over you."

"Why should I leave him?"

"I don't know," he said, feeling of his hands.

"He's big and he's strong, and sometimes he don't seem only a baby to me; and then again he scares me, just setting there looking at the wall with them eyes of his."

Fortune nodded his head.

"But he's handsome!"

"Yes," said Fortune. "He's about as fine-looking as they come."

She bent over and kissed him, and the loose strand of hair brushing along his cheek tickled him.

"Lord!"

"Fortune," she said, seriously, "can't you see I can't leave him? I wouldn't want to. Not him! Why I can't get him out of my sight!"

"You mean you love him."

"Yeanh. That's why I couldn't leave him. It wouldn't be right!"

"Of course, you couldn't," he echoed her. "It wouldn't be right."

"That's the hell of it," he said to himself, as he heard Dan's heavy tread on the deck above them.

A Mirror and a Pair of Shoes

"Are them the only shoes you've got?" Molly asked Fortune Friendly.

He was sitting facing the stove, his heels resting on the corner, his thin shanks sharply outlined through his trousers.

"They are. What's the matter with them?"

"Gracious me! Those won't hold out for more than two days. They're so thin you can do everything but see through them."

The old man cocked one eye whimsically.

"Well, I ain't got the cash just yet; but I'll get a pair when wages come."

"Dan," said Molly, "you take him up and get him a pair of boots. Go to Lerba's—you can get good ones there cheap. If you let him go alone, he'd go and get to playing cards. He's such an old rascal."

"Well, it's too bad to get Dan out so late. The stores'll probably be closed," said Fortune, with a sigh over his supper. "It's real comfortable here."

Molly flicked the top of his head with a dish towel.

"It's Saturday night. Go on, now, you won't have time in the morning."

"Yeanh," said Dan, getting up and stretching his arms out sideways.

The old man sighed.

"Well, I guess it's wiser."

He and Dan went out, leaving Molly at work on the dishes.

They walked slowly through the dark streets; there were few lights.

"Lord," said Fortune suddenly. "If I had any money on me, I'd hate to meet this Gentleman Joe on a night like this."

Dan turned on him, but it was too dark to see the old man's face.

"What do you know about him?"

"Two thousand dollars reward for information leading to the capture, dead or alive," replied Fortune. "I got a job yesterday tacking them bills up all over Rome. I could say the danged things backwards. I got one of them in my pocket."

"Who'd you do it for?"

"Sheriff Spinning. That's how I came to get into a game of euchre with him."

"Spinning's no good," said Dan.

"No. That's true enough. I'd like to get a chance after this Calash. He ought to be hanged up. He doesn't belong here on the canal."

That's right," said Dan. "Do you know where Lerba's store is?"

"Yes, it's down here."

Fortune turned off to the left down a narrow street, and stopped before some steps leading down to a cellar. A window letting above the level of the ground gave them a view of a little man hunched over a form, a short squat hammer in his hand. He looked up as they entered.

"Hullo," he said. "What can I do for you shents?"

Fortune sat down on a box and crossed one leg over the other.

"This young man brought me in to buy a pair of boots," he said, waving his hand at Dan.

"It is a good place to buy shoes, Lerba's," said the cobbler, packing a quid of nails into his cheek and laying down his hammer. "I will get out some boots, hey?"

"Heavy cowhide," said Dan. "Double sole."

"Here is some good ones," said the cobbler, bringing out a bunch of them. "Five dollars, with lacings."

Dan undid the knot of laces and selected a pair.

"Kind of stiff," he said.

"They work smooth," said the cobbler, disgorging a nail. "It is good leather in them boots—no scraps in Lerba's five dollars. Just the best all the time, like tenderloin to the butcher's, only cheap."

He smacked the nail in and rolled another off the end of his tongue.

"Try 'em on," said Dan.

Fortune took off his shoes and rolled his trousers up along his shanks. "It fits all right," he said, stamping his foot on the floor.

"Sure," said the cobbler through the rat-tat of his hammer.

"Try the other one," said Dan. "When you buy a team, you look at both horses."

"The young man is right," said the cobbler; "only at Lerba's you don't need to look at both—it is all tenderloin, not?"

The dim lamplight cast his shadow grotesquely against the leather stacked by the wall, where it did a pantomime of hammering, and the nails rolled down from a pendulous lip, larger than life. The whole little underground shop smelled strong of leather, with a sharp damp odor mixed in. There were traces of mould on the walls.

Fortune got up and walked round. The shoes squeaked protestingly.

"I said they was stiff. You'll get sore feet with them, I guess, Fortune."

"Noo," said the cobbler, laying down his hammer and disgorging a handful of nails over his tongue. "It is just the leather is so lively getting acquainted."

"I don't know . . ."

"It is good shoes," said the cobbler. "I give them away for four dollars and half."

"I guess they ought to be all right," said Fortune.

"Sure, the old shent wears them. He should know."

"All right," said Dan.

"It is good," said the cobbler, pushing his hands down his leather apron. "It is fine. I am an honest man and it is fine."

Fortune took them off.

"I go find some paper," said the cobbler.

His bent back disappeared through a door and they heard him creaking up some stairs and calling, "Rachel, come quick! There is paper for shoes sold."

"He's a funny old turkey," said Fortune. "Him and his wife sell furniture upstairs and take in a lodger once in a while."

"That is right," said the Jew from the top of the stairs. "Would you shents have furniture?"

"No," said Fortune.

"It is good furniture, bargains. There is bedroom crockery with pansies, and some good quiltings, and some mirrors . . ."

Dan started.

"Gol," he said. "I might get a mirror, at that."

"Sure," said the cobbler. "A pretty mirror very cheap."

"I guess I'll go and look at it."

"All right," said Fortune.

They felt their way up the narrow stairs, the cobbler looking over the rail at the top and guiding them with his voice.

"It cannot fall, them stairs. But don't step on the next one to the top one. It isn't."

Dan and Fortune found themselves in a fairly large first-floor room with two windows facing the street. The ceiling was high for so small a house. Chairs, beds, tables, wash-hand stands, were piled along the floor in complete disorder, with crooked spaces between through which a person could barely walk. Dishes and crockery sets "with pansies" were scattered over all objects with a horizontal surface. In the doorway stood a dark-haired woman in a loose brown dress which kept falling away from her right shoulder, showing a smooth pale skin. The lamp she held over her eyes swayed a little from side to side, so that there was a constant slow procession of shadows back and forth across the wall.

The cobbler held his apron tight to the sides of his legs and picked his way between two rocking-chairs.

"Here is the mirror, mister. See. It is pretty, with the carving on the wood all around."

"There's a chip off it," said Dan.

"Secondhanded goods has chips," said the cobbler stoutly. "That is why they are secondhanded goods. Such a mirror is four dollars at Lerba's. You take it with the shoes, it is eight dollars for the combination. Look, it is a good mirror. You can hang it two ways—up, so, or sideways, so. Whichever way you hang it, it makes the other way look not right. It is a good mirror."

One corner of the glass was freckled, but except for that, and for the chip, it looked very respectable to Dan. Broadways it would be just the thing to hang in the cabin. It would please Molly.

As it lay against the arms of the chair, Dan caught in it a glimpse of the ex-preacher staring nervously about him, and of Mrs. Lerba's thin hand holding the lamp.

"Hey, Lerba," asked Fortune in a friendly voice, "got any lodgers now?"

"No, no lodgers any more."

"I thought you always kept lodgers."

"No, mister, it was one kept, but not no more."

"That's funny," said Fortune. "I thought I heard somebody moving around upstairs."

The apron rattled in Lerba's hands and the lamp swayed, and suddenly beside and behind the reflection of it, looking over a stair rail outside, Dan saw the tall figure of a man peering in from under his wide hat brim. While Dan watched, the figure moved softly down, and he thought he heard a quick closing of the outer door.

Lerba cleared his throat loudly and said seriously to Fortune, "No, it is the Missis says there is a baby, so we put a nursery in the lodging room and don't paint it with paint this year. No. There is no lodger."

"Hey, there!" called a voice from the foot of the stairs up which Dan and Fortune had felt their way.

Again the lamp swayed suddenly.

"Make a light steady, Rachel," said the cobbler. "You will take this mirror?"

"Yeanh."

"All right, we take it back down with us."

"Hey there, Lerba!"

The voice had a cavernous echo, coming from the cellar shop.

"Yes, yes," cried the cobbler. "I make a hurry."

He caught up the mirror and picked his way quickly to the head of the stairs.

"Get paper, Rachel," he called to his wife, and then, to Dan and Fortune, "Make sure about the steps."

They came back into the shop. Henderson was sitting on the cobbler's stool, his fat short legs crossed, his hat on the back of his head, pulling at a big dead cigar.

"Hullo!" he said on seeing Dan. "You here?"

"Yeanh."

"The shents came to buy boots and a mirror—good ones, a bargain," explained the cobbler.

"I'll bet it was a bargain, all right," said Henderson.

Lerba nodded his head with a pleased smile.

Henderson nodded affably at Fortune Friendly.

"I just dropped in, Lerba," he explained. "Just a friendly visit."

"Sure," said the cobbler. "What is the name? Boots is cheap."

There was a sudden scratching and rustling down the stair treads. "It is paper," exclaimed the cobbler. "It is paper from Rachel."

He ducked out to get it.

"Got a lodger, Lerba?" asked Henderson when he came in.

"No, not no more at all."

"You used to have one."

"No more no lodger, not at all."

"Did he leave?"

"Yes, it is. There is a baby, Rachel tells—the shents say so. It makes a nursery."

"Well, I want to poke round the nursery," said Henderson.

"These shents tell . . ." protested the cobbler.

Henderson looked at the end of his cigar; then with his left hand he pulled his suspender through the armhole of his waistcoat.

"Sure," said the cobbler, at once. "Rachel, there is a shent wants to see the nursery. Show him with light."

Henderson got up and disappeared through the door, whistling "Walky-Talky-Jenny." They heard him climbing the stairs behind Rachel. Lerba went about wrapping the boots and mirror, using his teeth as a third hand in tying the string. By the time he had finished, Henderson was coming back.

"Well, well," he said pleasantly. "It'll be a nice nursery. When do you expect the new Lerba?"

The cobbler spread his hands.

"It is not my business; how should I tell? Rachel makes it."

"All right, Lerba. I won't bother you any more to-night. You gents walking back towards the canal?"

"Yeanh."

They went out.

"How's Samson?" Henderson asked Dan.

"He's dead."

"I guessed he would. He looked bad when I seen him that night. Who's got the boat?"

"Me."

"You have, eh?"

"I asked Mr. Butterfield about it. I'm hauling for him."

"Well, I guess it's right if he says so. Seen any more of Gentleman Joe?"

"No."

"I expected he might be lodging at Lerba's here. I guess he's cleared out. I know where he's gone, though. Who's this gent?"

"Fortune Friendly," said Dan. "Know Mr. Sam Henderson."

The ex-preacher shook hands.

"He's driving for me."

"Where are you bound for?"

"Carthage," said Dan.

"Well, you may run into me up that way. If you do, I'll probably have Calash with me."

He put his hands in his pockets and turned aside down a street.

"Who's that man?" Fortune asked.

"He's Department of Justice," said Dan. "He calculates he'll get Gentleman Joe."

Samson's Bank

"I'm tired," said Fortune Friendly, when they got back to the cabin of the Sarsey Sal. "I think I'll go to bed."

Molly glanced up from the toweling she was hemming.

"Did you get the boots?"

"Yeanh."

"They're regular bullhead boots," said Fortune.

He got himself a dipper of water from the water butt under the stairs and then went to the single bunk and drew the curtain. Dan sat down, re-filled his pipe, and lit up.

"Is it a good pipe?"

"Yeanh. It's breaking in real handy."

He stretched out his legs to the stove and tilted the chair back. Molly bit off her thread, close to the toweling, pressing the cloth tight against her cheek.

"I'm going to look at Fortune's boots."

She squatted down on the floor before the package, like a child.

"Let me have your knife, Dan."

He tossed it to her.

"Ugh," she exclaimed, pressing her upper teeth down on her under lip. "I can't open it. You open it, please."

He grinned and handed it back to her.

"They're good boots, I guess. My, they're heavy!"

"Yeanh," said Dan. "They'd ought to exercise him good."

"Poor old man," she said softly, "he ain't going to like driving for very long."

"I don't know. He seems to like you a lot, Molly. How'd you come to know him?"

"Pa used to let him travel a lot on his boat. He used to say old Fortune was a gentleman for all his ways at cards. Fortune never did a lick of work, but he'd used to sit on deck when I was a little girl with my hair in a ribbon, and he'd tell stories. And Pa would listen just as hard as me. He'd tell stories all about witches and such things, and Pa believed 'em as much as me. And when Pa died Fortune asked me did I want to stay on the canal. And then he took me down to Lucy Cashdollar's and told her to look out for me careful."

She pushed the boots to one side.

"What's in the other package?" she asked.

Dan pressed down the tobacco in the bowl of his pipe with his thumb.

"It's an article I bought to Lerba's."

"What is it?" she asked again, looking back at him over her shoulder, and squinting a little against the light.

"I got it for you," said Dan, awkwardly.

She flushed.

"Oh!" she exclaimed as she pulled away the paper. "Oh! Ain't it pretty? Ain't it big? Why, I think it's real pretty, Dan."

She stood up lithely, her eyes shining.

"Why, Dan."

Dan gave an inarticulate grunt and leaned forward to open the draft of the stove, his face red.

She caught him by the shoulders and held him down, shaking him.

"Why didn't you tell me right off?"

"You didn't ask."

"You old surl," she said, stooping to kiss him. Then she jumped away from his arm and picked up the mirror. "There's a wire on to it to hang it broadways, Dan. It'll just fit over the table."

She took down the little mirror that had been Samson Weaver's and hung the new one in its place.

"Now I can see to do my hair."

She took out the pins and shook it down over her shoulders. He stood behind her and gathered it into a handful and pulled her head back against his chest, grinning at her. She pushed his face away.

"Don't, Dan. Not now." She turned her eyes to the sleeping cuddy. Dan laughed. "Listen," he said.

Fortune Friendly's deep breathing purred suddenly, unmistakably.

"Let's look for Samson's money," Dan said. "It'll be our money when we find it."

She put a finger to her lips, and smiled behind it, a conspirator's gleam in her eyes.

"Fortune's a good enough body," she whispered. "But it's just as well he didn't know."

Dan nodded.

"Where'd the old boater say it was?" she asked.

Dan lowered his voice.

"He didn't say—only that it was in a beam, and that part of it lifted out."

Together they looked round the cabin from the middle of the floor. There was a beam across the middle of the ceiling, and one across each end, and a heavy beam sill jutting out of each rear corner. Dan began running his finger along the middle beam.

"It would be on the back side," Molly said. "The light wouldn't hit there."

They found no crack in the middle beam, and Dan began feeling along the end ones. Molly began to examine the corner sills. Suddenly she made a little crowing noise, and, looking round, Dan saw her hunkered down in the corner. She had lifted out a false front close to the floor and was holding out to Dan two limp rectangular packages wrapped in dirty brown paper.

Dan took them back under the lamp and sat down in the rocking-chair, and Molly perched herself on his knees. The packages were tied with red cord, a bowknot directly at the crossing, the ends corresponding exactly with the loops, as though old Samson had taken care and pleasure in wrapping them. The paper was thumb-marked and stained, and when Dan opened the first package some tobacco ashes slid down on the back of his hand.

Molly drew in her breath and looked down at him. There was a friendly feeling in the touch to Dan, and he held his hand close to his eyes. Spidery long ashes, made from Warnick and Brown, that Samson had smoked.

"He was a nice feller," Dan said seriously. "I think he was a good man, though he was bothered with Annie's running off."

Molly blew off the ashes suddenly. They rose in a burst, and scattered in an indiscernible fine powder. She leaned closer and kissed his hand.

"Let's count it, Dan."

He stared at her as he did not quite comprehend.

"Let's see how much there is," she whispered again.

He tossed both packages into her lap. She took out the bills and started laying them down one by one on her knee.

"You'll have to steady them," she told Dan.

He pressed his hand down on them and lifted it when she put down another bill. It became a kind of game for the two of them to play, like children stolen out of bed when the house is sleeping—a fugitive, trembling sort of game, requiring a touch of hands. Molly frowned and kept the tally with silently moving lips, heedless of Dan's watching gaze on the curve of her cheek and the soft mass of her hair.

Finally she stacked the bills together with firm little raps on her knee.

"Dan!" she exclaimed softly. "There's eight hundred and thirty-five dollars. Eight hundred and thirty-five dollars. My, that's a lot of money for a man to have!"

She caught Dan's left hand and brought it round her waist, and let herself lean back against his shoulder, her face close to his cheek.

But he was staring at the opposite wall. Eight hundred and thirty-five dollars—it was a lot of money. It represented many things. With it a man could start a farm, a small farm. As he sat there with Molly against him, he seemed to see again the hip-roofed barn, and himself behind a heavy team going out to plough long furrows in rich earth. He saw more than he had seen before; he saw Molly churning on a kitchen stoop. He heard the lowing of cows; and he saw himself and Molly moving from one to the other in the hay-smelling shadow to milk them.

"What're you going to do with it, Dan?"

He took hold of her hands with their strong long fingers. She watched him carefully, almost jealously, and cast a worried glance at the side of his lean head, tracing the curve of his ear. Beyond the curtain they heard Fortune Friendly's even, sure breathing, purring a little now and then at the end of the breath. The canal beyond the curtained windows was silent and dead.

The stillness was very close to them.

"What're you going to do with it, Dan?"

"It's a lot of money," Dan began uncertainly.

Suddenly, thin and faint, they heard the blast of a horn, blowing for the weighlock; and when the silence came again they were conscious of the ripple of the water. The horn sounded a second time—louder.

Molly sighed and stirred against Dan's shoulder, and he twisted his neck to look at her.

"I guess I'll buy a good team," he said. "A good heavy team. I'll want 'em in the spring for heavy hauling."

She drew a deep breath of relief.

The clock whirred and rapidly beat out ten strokes.

"Good land! Dan, it's time we went to bed."

They returned the money to Samson's bank and blew out the lamp; and when the east-coming boat passed they were asleep.

Ecclesiasticus

Five days later the Sarsey Sal was nosing along southward up the Black River behind a string of four boats. Leading the string, the sidewheel tugboat smacked the river with her paddles and belched a line of dark smoke in which hot wood cinders swirled. The northwest wind blowing on their backs carried the smoke free.

It was mid-afternoon. Small cold showers coming with the wind at intervals of an hour all day had washed the air clear under the tumbling grey sky. Once in a while a spot of sunshine running across the valley would cover the boats for an instant with a bright warmth; but the cloud-shadow swooping down after it immediately brought back the darkening chill.

"It feels quite a lot like snow," said Dan, who was steering.

"It does, at that," said Fortune Friendly. The old man was stamping up and down the deck beside the cabin windows, smoking at an alder pipe he had cut and baked himself. The wind had whipped a bright red into his cheeks and nose, and his sharp eyes glistened.

"This is the good part of boating," he said. "The walking ain't so bad now my boots are broke in,"—he glanced down at them,—"but I like riding the river this way, when all I've got to do is take a turn at steering."

They were almost opposite Lowville, now, on their way back from Carthage. To the west, the great hogback of Tug Hill began climbing over the bank-side trees. As they went on, the edges of the nearer hills crept up against it, until they were winding through a flat deep valley.

The hardwood was turning to sombre browns and yellows; even the maples were rusty; there was no brightness in the leaves. The poplars on the hilltops shook and leaped in the pitch of the wind; but the great pines on the valley floor stood straight, only their tops stirring with a slow lifting of arms. The entire land brooded before the solemn approach of winter; it appeared to be breathing the clear bite of the air; and on it, with the rolling sky above their heads, men and animals moved with circumspect minuteness. A woman stood in a yard, pumping glittering water; two dogs stalked a woodchuck taking his final meal of the year; two men spread manure, tossing forkfuls first on one side, then on the other. Back and forth across a slope a farmer moved behind a dappled team, uncovering dark threads with his plough.

"It's a fine land for farming," Dan said.

The old man knocked out his pipe and sat down on the cabin roof, clasping his knees with his smooth hands.

"I was born in this section," he said.

"Yeanh?" said Dan. "Was it good for dairying?"

"Sure, as good as any land. My folk were related to folks at Lyons Falls. We had a good farm. And then Pa come into money from some city kin, and Mother said I'd ought to be a minister. So I went to college."

"Yeanh," said Dan.

"I learned a lot it wasn't good for me to learn," said the old man. "But my pa had money, so it didn't do no real harm. But when I come back I didn't go to preaching, as I might have if I'd growed up here. I'd learned a lot to make a man afraid of preaching."

"Yeanh."

"I come back and said I'd settle down. I married and I lived on a farm my wife's kin owned by Lyons Falls. I built barns and I planted an orchard, and I dammed a brook and made a fishpond. I had three men working for me, and there was a maid in the house. And when my pa died and the money come to me I got a good dairy started and my wife was happy."

"Gol!" said Dan.

"But it was the same thing every year. First the winter, and then the summer; calves dropped, and growed and milked, and the crops sowed and harvested. And the field ploughed in the fall, when the ducks went south. I finicked with my orchard, and I raised some good horses. I was a regular farmer. And the second year Hester had a child. And she did the third year. It became a habit with her."

"Yeanh."

"Then one day, when the canal had been put through, I saw a girl on a boat. She had hair as black as a crow's, and she had an orange-colored dress on, and she waved her hand when she went by. And I went home that evening. It was in August, near the end, and the men were drawing oats. I saw nothing in it, just the bundles staggering up on the forks. So I said to my wife, 'Let's quit this country. There's no profit in just farming. We'll go to the city; I've got money enough. We'll live in New York.' And she said, 'Fortune, I wouldn't want to move the children.' "

"Yeanh."

"It don't count, farming, or anything else a man does. Where does he get to? He works his fields and gets crops and raises cattle and builds a house, and he says it's his. It's the same way in everything. There's nothing we've got under the sun. We haven't even got a hold on our selves. We're just a passing of time. So next morning I got up early and took a hundred dollars and cleared out, and that was twenty years ago. I've been on the canals, I've been out West, I've been on the sea and sailed in ships. And it's just the same as if men were asleep, making a dream with their business. And it don't get them anywhere, does it?"

"It's how you look at it, I guess," said Dan.

"They learn new names to call things," said the old man. "But they always call the new names by the same old one. They say progress is what they're making. But progress is like time. It's just the same from beginning to end, because it can't move. 'As it was in the beginning, is now, and ever shall be, world without end, Amen.' And that's true, Dan, no matter what you say it about. All we've got is the working of our own minds."

He refilled his pipe.

"I went down the canal, Dan, and when I was hungry I played at cards. A man I lived with at college had taught me the tricks of that. And once in a while when I needed money real bad I'd preach, which is another kind of game, only the preacher holds the trumps and the temptations are very strong. I saw people fold their hands round a prayer on Sundays, Dan, as if they were doing business; but there's a peculiar comfort in it for some people. And I've preached funeral sermons for people I never saw the face of, for a meal and five dollars. I did it once for an Oneida half-breed for a glass of liquor and a venison steak, and the men's kin were real pleased with what I told them. Only his wife went off in the woods when I was done and mourned. There ain't anything new under the sun, Dan."

Molly, who had been listening at the cabin door, came up on deck, and the wind caught hold of her dress and hair.

"Did you ever see the gal again with the black hair, Fortune?"

The old man looked at her, sombrely.

"No," he said. "I was telling Dan that."

He went down to smoke his pipe in the quiet of the cabin.

Molly sat down in his place, drawing the collar of Dan's shirt up about her ears.

"I was talking with a woman on one of the boats." She nodded ahead at the string. "We'd ought to get into Lyons Falls this evening."

The queue of boats followed the tug round a wide bend to the right. The brown-and-gold tints of the sunset merged into a pale green twilight, with copper edges to the lower clouds. The beat of the paddles slackened and the roar of falling water increased in volume. Still, through heavy mutter, Dan's ears caught the clear ring of cowbells, and looking away to the left he saw a great farm opening out through the pines, a long herd of cows tailing through a pasture, the pale light washing the white on their bodies to silver, and, against the faint glow of the eastern slope, the white skeleton of a rising barn.

"Look at them cows, Molly."

"They're pretty, Dan."

"That barn they're building there's the biggest barn I ever see."

"Why should anyone want so big a barn?"

He did not answer her.

Little figures of men in blue overalls were coming slowly down the ladders, backward, their faces turned on the work they had done.

"It's as big as a church," Molly said.

"It's bigger," said Dan.

Then the river straightened ahead of them, and the tug swung in by the side of the lock that let the canal into the river. A string of boats was forming to go down-river. Another tug, beside the pier, was spouting up columns of oily smoke, a white hiss now and then escaping the valve. Men were loading five-foot logs aboard for the fires.

Visitors

Down below, Molly got supper. When they came into Port Leyden in the darkness, Dan called to Friendly to tie up behind a squat white boat.

Just as they were finishing their meal, they heard footsteps on deck and a rapping on the cabin roof.

"Come in," Molly called.

Before Dan could go to the door, footsteps clattered on the stairs, and a hearty voice called, "My, my! Where's Dan Harrow?"

There was a familiar ring in the voice. The door was flung open and a little man wearing a cap, with the ear mufflers up, peered in.

"Dan Harrow aboard?"

"He ought to be if he ain't," said the hearty voice from behind. "It's the Sarsey Sal, ain't it?"

"Hullo," said Dan. "Hullo, Mr. Tinkle."

The little man beamed and stretched out his hand. Then he put his head back through the door and shouted, "Come on, Lucy!"

They heard her puffing down the stairs.

"She's getting awful fleshy," the little man confided. "Don't know but what she's getting wheezy."

"I ain't neither. Sol, that's a lie. I don't tell tales on to your rheumatiz, do I?"

The fat woman came breezing in, her hat a little on one side from bumping on the stairs.

"My stars, Dan, ain't this grand?"

She swept over to him and enveloped him in her arms.

"To think of you owning a boat, being a regular boater! I always let on to Sol you would be, but he'd shake his head, when the rheumatiz wasn't bothering him too much, and he'd say he guessed not. Mr. Butterfield told us about you. We're hauling for him now."

She stepped back and cast her bold eyes round the room.

"It's real comfortable and homey, ain't it? These old boats are nicer, I think. They've got a better feel into them. You don't feel so old in them. And it's clean, too. And curtains on the window. My! Ain't it a nice boat, Sol?"

The little man was holding his cap in both hands, the lamp shining on his bald head, a grin of pleasure puckering his face.

"Listen to him!" exclaimed Mrs. Gurget. "Just standing there and looking round as if he'd never been out of Stittville all his life. You'd hardly think but what he was a deef-and-dummer. Can't you talk, Sol?"

"Once in a while I edge in a word, Lucy."

"Fresh," said the fat woman, tossing her head. "Well, how be you, Dan? You look thriving. Don't he, folks? Introduce me, Dan. I always feel itchety till I know who folks are. Gives a person a handle for conversation."

She drew herself up with a smile.

"Now's your chance, Dan," said Solomon.

Mrs. Gurget tossed him a frown.

"This here's Fortune Friendly—he's driving for us. And this is Molly Larkins. Mrs. Gurget and Mr. Solomon Tinkle," said Dan, the blood bright in his cheeks.

Mrs. Gurget gave the old man a smile and beamed at Molly.

"I'd knowed there was a woman on board as soon as I laid eyes on them curtains, fresh ironed. A man alone might as well hang up a dishrag."

"Won't you set down?" said Molly, pushing forward the rocking-chair. Dan watched her with open admiration. She was very cool about it.

Mrs. Gurget sank down and threw back her red shawl to show the locket on her bosom.

"Well, it feels good to set down. I've been steering all day. We unloaded in Lyons Falls this afternoon and Sol said we'd ought to start right back. Mr. Butterfield asked us if we knowed you, Dan, and then he told us you'd got a boat. It gave us a start. I thought Sol'd spit right there in the office. So when we see your boat coming in a while ago Sol wanted to go right on board, but I told him to mind his manners and give you folks time to eat. That's the way men are," she said to Molly, patting her hand; "so long as they see smoke in a stovepipe, they think there ought to be food set right out to feed a circus. How do you like cooking for this man, dearie?"

Molly smiled.

"He's a real nice man to work for."

Mrs. Gurget gave her another pat.

"I think so myself. Dan's all right—yes, sir. Oh, me," she sighed, with a smile at Solomon, "we're all young once. Don't you find it so, Mr. Friendly?"

The ex-preacher leaned back on his stool, his hands clasped over one knee. He had been smiling ever since Mrs. Gurget entered the cabin.

"Well, some of us never lose it, Mrs. Gurget."

The fat woman laughed delightedly.

For a minute or two the conversation hinged on minor gossip, on the triplets borne by Mrs. Scroggins on the Pretty Fashion while the boat was going through Lockport,—a child for every other lock, as Solomon said, —and a new cure for consumption, and the "Rheumatic Amputator" Solomon had bought at a horse fair out of Syracuse from a traveling surgeon. He pulled up a trouser leg to show it to them, a thin lead band that fitted just above the calf of his leg. "Careful," Mrs. Gurget admonished. "We're in company." "It burns the rheumatiz right out," Sol explained. "See them little teeth on the inside? Well, you soak them in sour cider and that generates the beneficent electrical that balances the blood by getting it to proper temperature. It helps a lot. Why after I've wore it an hour I can feel the heat a-swarming in to beat the cars. Yes, sir."

"It only cost seventy-five cents," Mrs. Gurget said. "Ain't it wonderful the progress that science can make for the money?"

Fortune Friendly nodded gravely.

"It's as good as God."

"It's better for the rheumatiz," said Solomon.

"Hush, you," said Mrs. Gurget.

Molly smiled.

"You'd ought to get out that rum you got in Carthage, Dan. Unless you prefer cider, mam."

"No—no, thanks." The fat woman laughed. "Rum noggin's a healthy habit with me."

Molly got the glasses and Dan brought a small keg out of the sleeping cuddy.

"Here, Sol, get up and help Dan. He's a great hand at driving a bung, Dan. Sol's the handiest man at it I ever see. Let him do some work. Dearie, can't I help you with them glasses? Mr. Friendly, it's nice for old folks to be waited on, ain't it? I don't count Sol as only a child. There's times, seeing him with a bottle, I think he still ought to be sucking."

The kettle was purring full on the stove, and the sharp odor of lemon that Molly was cutting mingled with the smell of rum. Mrs. Gurget spread her nostrils over her glass.

"It's a regular party. Well, here we be. You're a lucky man, Dan, though I don't know if you know it."

She drank it down to "Dan and Molly and getting together."

"Now Lucy's got her belly warmed, she may soother down," said the little man. "Butterfield says he wants for you and me to get potatoes in Denley,—there's a load there,—and to Boonville, Dan; but while we're waiting here along you come; so here's how."

He drank, and broke into conversation with Fortune Friendly. Mrs. Gurget was occupied with Molly. The cabin looked very homey all at once to

Dan; and Molly, with a bright look on her face, bending toward the fat woman, was prettier than he had seen her. He felt a little nervous, but very happy, and Molly's collectedness gave him a sense of comfort. Now and then the two women glanced his way, as if they were talking about him, a sort of smile in their eyes. The kettle steaming, the warm light of the lamp, the scent of rum coming after the day in the cold air, brought an air of establishment to the Sarsey Sal. His guests, his boat. . . .

Solomon turned back, laying his hand on Dan's knee.

"I've been talking to Mr. Friendly, Dan," with a pert nod in the ex-preacher's direction, "and I've got an idea. All at once, like, there's been a lot of talk coming up about this feller Calash. I've kept my eyes looking out and my ears listening, Dan, and I reckon he's up here, especially after what Mr. Friendly's been saying about Henderson in Rome. I think he's up here."

"I guess that's right," said Dan.

With elaborate nicety, the little man tapped Dan's knee with the end of his forefinger.

"How would two thousand dollars, split three ways, go between us, Dan?"

Dan was uneasy.

"Why, I don't know."

"Two thousand dollars!" exclaimed the fat woman, glancing up. "Where's two thousand dollars?"

Solomon pointedly ignored her.

"This feller Henderson's up here, but he won't ever get him. He don't know where he is. But I'll bet I do. Why don't me and you and Mr. Friendly round him up, then?"

"Why, I don't know," repeated Dan. He felt suddenly uncomfortable and worried. It would mean seven hundred dollars to him, a lot of money. But he had a liking for the man, somehow; he did not know why. He had seen him once in Boonville when he came on the canal, and once on the haul to Rome, and twice in Rome; and the man had put him aboard his boat in Utica; and he had petted his horse, and the horse had liked him. It was a lot of money. He did not know why he liked him. There seemed to be a lot of things tied up in the man. . . .

"He's a criminal," said the little man. "He's wanted dead or alive. He ought to be caught afore he breaks loose here."

"My land!" exclaimed the fat woman, settling her hat straight. "He ought! It ain't safe with him roaming around like a bug on a hot night; there's no telling where he'll bump into. I get a start every time I hear a team on the towpath!"

Solomon Tinkle nodded approvingly.

"That's it; there's no telling what he'll do. We'd ought to go after him. It's a duty."

"That's right," said Mrs. Gurget. "It's a duty."

The ex-preacher nodded gravely.

Molly was regarding Dan with a queer questioning light in her eyes.

"I don't know," he said uneasily. "How'd you go about it, Sol?"

"I've figured out just about where he's liable to be. You know, down by Denley, where the road crosses to the river. There's an old brown house down there."

"Yeanh, it's the Riddle house," said the fat woman. "I know it. It's eight-sided."

"Yeanh," said Solomon, leaning forward, his glass clasped in both hands. "It's got eight sides. Old Riddle built it when he got off the canal. He was born in these parts, so he come back to build. Wanted to get away from folks, so he built him a house down in that God-sake hole. He was born deef, and they say from living alone that way he lost the power of speaking. Used to bring his order into the Denley store on Saturdays, wrote out on a paper. It's the dangdest house I ever see. He lived by himself, and two winters ago he died into it."

"He always liked chocolate cake," said Mrs. Gurget.

"I heard tell of it," said Molly. "They found him after a heavy blizzard. He was sitting dead in a chair."

"He was a funny old bezabor," Solomon continued. "Well I mind him on his boat in them canvas pants he used to wear, snarling his horn in his chin whiskers and blowing like they'd reëlected Jackson. They say he used to blow it some down to his house. Once in a while Murphy tells me they still hear it blow."

"I heard about him," said Fortune Friendly. "He had the horn in his hand when they found him."

"I've always wondered if the rooms was shaped like pieces of pie," said Mrs. Gurget. "Having eight sides to a house would make a person think so."

"I don't know," said Solomon. "I ain't never been inside. But I'll bet who is inside right now. It's a comfortable house and a good place for him to stay while he's up here. I reckon we three might edge in there to-morrow night and see."

"I don't see how we could handle him," Dan said.

"I'll take my revolver," said Solomon. "I'll hold that on him till you get your arms round him, Dan. Then we oughtn't to have no trouble. When you hold him, I'll knock him on the head."

"He's a menace," said Fortune. "If we can get him, it's our right duty to get him; and we'd ought to be able to collect the reward."

"Well—" Dan began; but they were all looking at him, Molly still with that queer worried expression. Maybe they thought he was scared.

"All right," he said.

He did not wish to go; but at the same time he felt an irresistible desire to see the man's face. . . .

Riddle's House

They hauled into Denley in the afternoon—a bit of a village with the store and post office in one building, and two houses, and a small cheese factory, all in a row facing the river valley. Lumber wagons loaded with potatoes from neighboring farms were waiting on the towpath. The boats tied up, and Solomon and Dan took their teams aboard for the night. By five o'clock the boats were loaded; by six they were all eating in the cabin of the Nancy. Mrs. Gurget had insisted on that, so that Molly could keep her company while the men were away. Solomon put his revolver in the pocket of his coat, where it made a heavy bulge, and he and Dan and

Fortune went on shore. The little man was white with suppressed excitement.

It was quite dark, and a rain was falling. There was no wind. Solomon carried a lighted lantern in his hand.

"We might as well stop in at Murphy's and have a sniff first," he said.

"Suits me," said Fortune.

They tramped down the towpath toward the square of light cast by the store window. Against it they could see the rain falling in grey streaks, and drops twisting down the glass. Inside, Murphy, the storekeeper and postmaster, sat on a stool before the round-bellied stove and smoked his pipe at a saturnine man, with black hair, a thin face, and bat ears.

"Hullo," he said, when the three entered.

"Evening," said Sol. "We just come down to get a glass of strap and see how you were making out."

"Pretty good," said Murphy. "I seen you loading your boats."

"Yeanh. We loaded 'em."

Fortune nodded to the bat-eared man.

"Evening," he said.

"Let me make you acquainted, gents. That's Reuben Doyle, gents. He drops in in an evening to make me some conversation."

Doyle returned his nose to his glass and grunted.

Murphy drew them glasses of strap and then leaned against the counter to make some exchanges on the weather. Fortune sat down on a wooden box and Dan lingered by the door, shaking the rain from his hat.

"I hear old Riddle's dead," Solomon remarked after a while.

Murphy started, his thin mouth opening with surprise.

"Why, yes, he's been dead two years, Solomon. I thought you knowed about it."

"Well, I'd heard a remark here and there," said Solomon. "But not enough to pick up and believe."

"He's been dead two years now. He died after a hard blizzard. Rube, here, found him."

"Stopped in to get the loan of a chew," said the bat-eared man.

"Yeanh, Rube found him sitting in his chair, holding his horn, and dead. Didn't you, Rube?"

"Hard as a post."

"He saw he was dead right off."

"Whiter'n cheese."

"So he come right along."

"Wasn't a chew in the house," explained the bat-eared man.

"It was awful cold that week," Murphy went on. "But we turned out and had a funeral and buried him. It was hard work digging his grave."

"Got up a sweat at twelve below," said the bat-eared man.

"Rube used the pick," said Murphy. "I can remember him down in the snow and the pick head coming up and glancing and going down. *Tunk!*"

"A handy tool," observed the bat-eared man.

"So we shoveled in the dirt and locked up the house."

"Been down there since?"

"Once," said Murphy, a little white. "Went down with Rube to borrow a chair my old lady'd took a fancy to. Just to borrow it against some of

Riddle's folks turning up. Just a loan it was to be. But when we turned into
the holler we heard a horn blow out loud. It was his horn and blew out
loud, didn't it, Rube?"

"Dismal," said the bat-eared man in a low voice.

"So we come away."

"How'd you know it was his'n?"

"Why we buried it with him. Who else's could it be?"

"Had it in his fist," said the bat-eared man.

"Heard it again?"

"Rube heard it last week."

"Fact."

"Anyone seen round the house?" asked Solomon.

"That's what give me such a start," said Murphy. "There was a man
here this afternoon, just afore you come in, wanted to know about the
house. Said he was going down to look it over. He said he was going to buy
it, maybe, off'n the estate."

The three boaters perked their ears.

"Yeanh. What did he look like?"

"Fat man. Had on a hard hat. Said his name was Henderson. He smoked
a cigar."

"Gol," said Dan.

Solomon swore.

"What's it all about?" asked Murphy.

"Nothing," Solomon said. "I used to know Riddle, the old bezabor."

"Well, it's all right by me," said Murphy.

"We'd ought to be getting along back," Fortune said.

"That's right. Lucy'll be getting nervous. Good night."

"Fifty cents will cover it," said Murphy.

They paid and went out.

"What do you know about that?" Solomon exclaimed, as they paused on
the stoop to turn up their collars. "The fat little twerk. No, sir. I wouldn't
have guessed it."

"We ought to go down and see if he's all right," said Fortune, "even if
we don't come in on the reward."

Solomon nodded sharply. He took the lead, carrying the lantern under
his coat to protect the chimney from the rain. A dim rim of light was
cast about his heavy shoes. Now and then it glistened on a puddle. It was
raining harder; the drops had begun to bounce on the water of the canal;
they could hear the heavy roar of it out of sight upon the hills.

Except for the little spot of lantern light that marked Solomon's feet,
squelching along the road and picking up great clouts of mud, the night
closed in on them, as black as tar. In intervals in which the rain appeared
to be catching its breath, they could hear the river, far down on their left,
muttering over the rapids.

The Sarsey Sal loomed up beside the towpath, its windows dark; but Dan
heard one of the bays grunting as it lay down in the stable. Then a little way
ahead the lights from the cabin of the Nancy poked out onto the towpath.
As they passed, Dan had a glimpse of Mrs. Gurget playing solitaire at the
table, and of Molly knitting beside the stove, a yellow glow on her brown

hair. She looked up, as he came abreast, but her eyes were on the wrong window to see him.

They turned down a road toward the river, the rain roaring on invisible trees to their right and left, and stirring a heavy smell of rotting leaves out of the ground. Dan's feet kept slipping in the mud; he followed the jerking patch of light blindly. The little man stepped sturdily on, as though he were well acquainted with the road, and Fortune, treading at his heels, made easy progress.

After a while Solomon stopped, scattering a rim of drops from his coat and holding up the lantern. The light picked out their faces redly, a-shine with wet, against the dim veil of rain. They looked at each other, counting noses.

"I'll bet he didn't go down," Solomon said.

"Maybe not," said the ex-preacher.

"He probably went back after help."

Dan did not feel so sure; he had a growing respect for the fat man—he had seen him so often on Gentleman Joe's heels.

"I don't want no share of the reward," he said suddenly.

Solomon stared up at his big bulk, then shifted his gaze to where a little channel of rain ran off his hat.

"What?"

"I don't want no share of the reward."

"You're coming with us, ain't you?"

"Yeanh."

Fortune's smooth face poked close to theirs.

"What do you know about that?" exclaimed the little man, snatching the trickle from the end of his long nose.

The ex-preacher grinned.

"It makes that much more for you and me, Tinkle."

A drop pinged against the glass, and Solomon hurriedly lowered the lantern.

"It ain't natural."

He took up the lead again, and for a while the others found it hard to follow the feeble light about his feet. The lantern had left a red glow in their eyes.

It was perhaps ten minutes later when Solomon stopped again, and again they stared at each other in the close light of the lantern.

"Riddle's road branches off on the right pretty quick," said Solomon. "You want to keep watching for it and let me know if you see it afore I do."

They pushed on. Dan became conscious of the weight of his hat and of the beat of rain upon it. The ex-preacher's trousers were soaked through and moulded close round his thin shanks. He walked with a long, lurching stride, his hands in his pockets. Now and then he chuckled as though he were enjoying himself. Dan's hands swung limply from the wrist, close to his legs. Solomon's feet, leading the way, went with a martial tread. Once in a while one stumbled, or slipped over a stone; and then the light would escape from his coat for an instant and shine on the twisted branches of the trees.

Suddenly Dan caught hold of Fortune's shoulder. The ex-preacher whirled round, and then laughed under his breath.

"Hey, Sol!" Dan called.

"Yeanh?"

"Ain't that the road?"

Solomon walked back.

"I don't see how it could be so soon."

He was disgruntled.

He swung the lantern up, and great shadows were evolved against the rain and fled away. He lifted the chimney and blew the flame off the wick. The darkness struck them, leaving an ache under their eyelids.

"It's all right. Take hold of my coat, and, Dan, you take hold of Friendly."

He began to move into the side road marked by two ridges of grass between the ruts and the horse tread. Fortune shuffled along at his heels, Dan behind him; the three bent over, moving stealthily in the invisible rain, like monkeys holding each other's tails.

For a hundred yards they went ahead at a fair speed, the road easy to their feet. Then Solomon stopped and they felt for each other and laid their heads close together.

"The ruts has stopped," the little man said in a low voice. "We must be in the yard."

Dan and Fortune lifted their heads, but saw nothing.

"It ought to be dead ahead," said Solomon.

"How're we going to do it?" Fortune asked.

The little man took hold of his long nose in the darkness. Dan kept his eyes searching for the shadow of the house.

"First," Solomon said, "we'll get up close to the house. If he's inside, he's asleep. If we don't hear nothing, we'll open the door if we can, and I'll sneak inside on my stummick with my revolver. I've got a-hold of it now."

To know that somehow comforted all of them.

"Don't be scared," said the little man. "I'm pretty good at using it. When we're inside, Dan goes left and Friendly goes right; and when I thump, you stop. There ain't any back door and the stairs comes down facing front. Then I'll light the candle I got in my pocket and we'll wait under the stairs for him to come down."

"What if we can't get in the door."

"We'll have to find another way."

"It sounds all right to me," said Fortune.

"All right."

Once more taking hold of each other, they crept ahead. The rain found the collars of their coats now, and ran down inside, but they did not notice it.

Then Solomon's outstretched fingers bumped against clapboards.

"We'll try left," he whispered. "Look out for the well. It's got boards on it, but I wouldn't trust a trained flea on to them."

Again they crept forward. Dan's ankle scraped against a board, and a loosened bit of wood struck water somewhere far down.

"Shhh!"

Solomon was crawling up the stoop steps to the vague grey blur of a white door. His hand reached up and found the latch. It lifted silently, and to their surprise the door swung gently open. Wriggling, Solomon crawled inside. After a moment Fortune followed him. Then Dan started.

Through the front door he turned to the left, keeping close to the wall. He came to a shallow corner and went on. Then there was another shallow corner, and he realized that the ground-floor room must be eight-sided, like the outside of the house. A little farther ahead his hand came against the belly of a stove. It was still warm, but the fire must have died down two or three hours before.

He crouched beside it as a thump on the board floor sounded back by the door. A plank creaked faintly as Fortune stopped opposite him. For an instant they all lay still in the darkness, listening. At first, through the monotonous drum of rain on the roof, the silence seemed breathless; then Dan became aware of a fourth person in the room. He was not sure of hearing anything. It was impossible to see. He could not be certain of the position of the fourth person; but he was convinced, suddenly, that it was not Gentleman Joe. For he smelled a faint, stale smell of burnt woolen.

A spit of blue fizzling burst out beside the door, turned into a cloud of greenish biting smoke, caught in a yellow flame upon the candlewick. The flame lowered, then climbed up, tremblingly. The candle balanced on the floor, stood upright, and Solomon Tinkle scurried to one side, his blinking eyes on the stairs.

Water filled Dan's eyes for a moment; he noticed Fortune staring foolishly at the lone candle in the door and the grey rain beyond, drumming on the mud of the yard; Fortune, with his back to the stairs, squatting, his hands on his knees, helpless if Gentleman Joe had been in the room. Only Solomon Tinkle was looking in the right direction, and his gun was wavering in his hand, and his staring eyes wept after the darkness.

"Jeepers!" he said.

Dan felt the blood in his face, and turned round from the door. In a rocking-chair against the wall beyond the stove sat Henderson. A revolver, in his hand, rested its muzzle on the floor. A fat cigar had caught in his lap, and the ashes were smudged all over his waistcoat. He was slumped down on the small of his back, his fat legs sprawled out in front of him. He seemed to be sleeping; his tight little nostrils stirred to an uneven breathing very faintly. His coat on the left side was wet and dark, and there was a small pool on the floor, spread out.

Fortune chuckled ridiculously.

"You shut up!"

Solomon moved forward to the stairs. Hunkering down, Dan watched his small bowlegs out of sight into the shadow. His feet trod forward over their heads, sending down a faint silt of dust through the board ceiling. Then he came down.

"I knowed he was gone," he said, pocketing his revolver. "I knowed it as soon as I saw that twerk. Is he dead?"

Fortune stepped forward and pushed his hand against Henderson's side.

"No. It's lucky it wasn't one of us. Calash could have nailed Dan and me and then knocked you on the head afore you could've seen him."

"Cripus!" snorted Solomon. "I'd have nailed him first. I'd have screwed the lid on him right there."

He pulled a red handkerchief out of his pocket and wiped his face. "What'll we do with him?" he asked, nodding his head at Henderson.

"He's hit pretty bad," Fortune said. "But he ain't bleeding now to speak of. We'd ought to carry him back."

"He's heavy."

"I guess I can shoulder him part of the way," Dan said. He felt relieved; he had not wanted to find Calash. Now that the man was safe away, he had nothing to worry about.

"We could go back and get a wagon. I'll go back," said Solomon, "and you could stay here."

"It would take too long," said Dan. He wanted to get back to the boats, to see Molly. An unexplainable enthusiasm took hold of him. "I can carry him all right."

"It's better than half a mile."

"Let him try," said Fortune, looking at Dan's big shoulders, "I'll bet he can."

Solomon went out for the lantern. When he had lit it, Dan picked Henderson up across his shoulders. The man's head swung sharply down and bumped against his cheek. They blew out the candle and closed the door. The house faded behind them, eight-sided in the rain.

It was easier walking with the lantern only partially shielded, but Dan's shoulders ached by the time they got to the towpath.

"Had we ought to take him on the boats?" Fortune asked.

"Why not?"

"It might scare the women."

"It'd take a fatter dead man than she's a woman to scare Lucy," Solomon said.

The women had heard them, for they came on deck.

"Lord, what rain!" Mrs. Gurget exclaimed. "That you, Sol?"

"Yeanh."

"Is that him?"

"No, it's the Department of Justice man. We're going to bring him on board."

"Say," she cried. "Spinning's down by the store. He'd got a letter from him to be here to-night. You'd better fetch him down there. I'll come along with some whiskey and a towel."

Dan carried Henderson on down the towpath to the store. A buckboard stood in the light, which also picked out the wet and glistening rumps of the team. The horses stood quietly, but they looked fresh.

"I'll bet he didn't founder 'em trying to get here," said Solomon.

They barged into the store. Spinning was standing straddle-legged, his back to the stove. The bat-eared man still regarded his glass, and Murphy was whittling a chew from a plug of Hammer Brand. All three started, and Murphy and the bat-eared man got to their feet.

"What in hell?" said Murphy.

"That's what I'd like to know," said the bat-eared man.

"It's Henderson," said Dan, easing him down on the counter and rolling him over on his back.

"We found him down in Riddle's house," said Solomon. "He must have gone down there alone. Calash shot him, I reckon."

"What in glory was he doing down there?" demanded Spinning, with a bluster in his voice. He bent forward, suddenly. "Why, it's the horse trader. What was he doing down there?"

"He got shot," said Fortune Friendly.

The bat-eared man bent over Henderson's stout stomach and poked his coat open to look at his waistcoat.

"It's the truth," he said solemnly.

Henderson's face was pasty white.

"Is he dead?" asked the sheriff.

"No."

"That's a blessing," said Murphy; "we won't have to dig a hole for him, anyhow."

"It's damned funny," said the sheriff, taking off his hat. "I got a letter from the Department of Justice man that was working on the job. He wanted me up here with a rig at eight to-night. I threw a tire coming into Boonville and it took three hours to get it on again. Gol! If it hadn't been for that we might have got him."

"Gol!" echoed Fortune. "I guess you might. There wasn't no other rig in town, I suppose."

Spinning flushed.

"Hold your jaw, old man. You're a bad character. I'll take you in with me if you don't shut up."

"Now, now!"

Mrs. Gurget came rushing in, the rain streaming down her cheeks. In one hand she carried a bottle of whiskey, in the other a towel wrapped round some strips of clean linen. Molly was at her heels, and Dan instinctively moved toward her. Her hair was soaked through, and dark, and tight curls were stuck to her forehead. She gave him a glance, and smiled to see how bright his eyes were. He was still panting from his heavy load and he kept stretching his shoulders to ease the stiffness out of them.

Mrs. Gurget bustled over to the wounded man.

"Heat some water, dearie," she said to Molly.

"I'll get some. The kettle's full."

Murphy disappeared into the kitchen.

"Shall I get the old woman?" he asked, as he came back with the kettle.

"No," said Mrs. Gurget, shaking a spray of drops from her hair. "I don't want to be hindered. You men go and set somewheres and leave him to me and Molly."

They took their seats round the stove, and Spinning transferred his attention from Molly to the inside of his hat.

"I got a letter from Jones, telling me to meet the Department of Justice man here at eight. Here it is." He pulled a damp envelope out from the sweatband. "I wonder who the hell he is and where he is now."

Dan pointed his thumb in the direction of the counter.

"That's him there."

Spinning swore.

"I don't believe it."

"It's him," Dan repeated.

"That's a fact," said Fortune.

"I don't believe it," said the sheriff, angrily. "Why, that feller's been along with me a dozen times. He's just a horse trader. I told him all about this Department man, and told him just what I thought about this Department man. He didn't say nothing. Calash had stole his horse. That's what he was after."

They looked back to the counter. Mrs. Gurget handled the fat man as if he were nothing at all. She had pulled off his waistcoat and shirt and was bathing the wound in his side. Then she rolled him on his back.

"Come out clean," she said. "It'll lay him up quite a spell, but I don't think it's done a lot of damage. He'd ought to see a doctor, though, as quick as I've bandaged him."

"I'll take him back," said the sheriff, "as soon as I've found this Department man."

"It's him."

Spinning glared angrily at Dan.

"My," Mrs. Gurget said to Molly who was helping her, "you're real handy bandaging a man. I got too many thumbs to do it proper. Get a dry shirt, Mr. Murphy. And don't tell Mrs. Murphy. She'd have a hollering fright. They always come easy to her."

She forced some more whiskey down the man's throat.

"There. Now you can see he's the man."

Dan pointed to a suspender strap that fell off the counter, swung, and bumped against it with a smart rap.

The sheriff took it in his hand and his face became crimson.

"The son of a bitch!"

"It's all right," Fortune said. "He can't hear you."

They bundled him up in blankets, put him in the wagon, and the sheriff, still swearing, drove rapidly off toward Boonville.

Potatoes for Rome

Next day the Sarsey Sal pulled out of Boonville, leaving the Nancy to go up the feeder after her load of potatoes. Even in those days Boonville potatoes were favorably known in the New York markets and fetched a high price.

The fat woman stood on the steersman's deck wrapped up in a great cloth coat, the collar turned up at the back of her neck. It was a man's coat, so that her bulges came all in the wrong places. The wind blew the tails down against her barrel-like legs; and when she lifted her arm to wave to the Sarsey Sal the back puckered between her shoulders and crept up into a small hump.

She had waked that morning in a panic, wondering if the dye in her hair would hold after the wetting it had got. But, once she saw it in her mirror as red as a carrot, her relief had expanded into uproarious humor. With Molly to keep her company, she had joked all the way to Boonville, old jokes that Molly could hardly follow. But just before they parted Mrs. Gurget said, "He's a good lad, Molly, dearie. Stick to him. It ain't often a girl gets such a fine-looking man."

Now, as she looked back at the Sarsey Sal drawing out of the basin, she let out a gusty sigh. "Young. Ain't they pretty? They go good together —same height, same color, a matched pair. He's heavier-built, but that ain't no more'n right."

She looked ahead to where Solomon walked behind his mules, pulling reflectively at his pipe, the smoke popping past his ears.

"Ain't you going to wave good-bye, Sol?" she called.

He turned round, took off his cap, and the sun glanced on his high bald poll. Mrs. Gurget smiled to herself.

"A matched pair," she repeated, to herself. Then she saw that the Sarsey Sal was drawing away out of sight round the hill, Molly and Dan standing together on the stern, and Molly waved, but her face was turned away to Dan's.

"Young," said Mrs. Gurget again, in a low voice; and then she snorted and began singing the weaver's song in her full hearty voice.

"They're real nice, I think," Molly was saying to Dan.

"Yeanh," said Dan. "They was good to me."

The bays had pulled clear of the docks with their sharp stride, and behind them Fortune Friendly was tramping along the towpath, the broad brim of his hat curling up behind. Now and then he threw a glance over his shoulder at the river valley they were leaving; but with a little shake he set it forward again, a grin on his smooth face.

"I'll be glad to be getting back," Molly said to Dan. "I don't like it up here."

He said nothing, but kept his eyes on the towline. She watched his big hands on the rudder sweep, and turned her eyes to the hard high line of his cheek—brick-red from the sun and wind. His blue eyes squinted against the sunlight on the water. But they were bright and eager. She thought he looked happy. Standing beside him, she swayed a little to let her shoulder touch his.

"Aren't you glad to be getting back?" she asked.

"Yeanh."

He glanced sidewise at her for an instant. The collar of his shirt rolled up against her face, and her hair, whipped forward by the wind, caught here and there on the rough blue wool.

They swung southward, heading for the Lansing Kill.

"I come onto the canal, to Boonville," he reminded her.

She slid a hand inside his arm. He was remembering his strangeness; she could see the half-timid look on his face.

"You belong on it now," she said.

"Yeanh."

"You've got a boat and team, and you've got quite a lot of money, Dan."

"Yeanh."

He was staring ahead along the towpath, Fortune treading in the shadows of the team. The trees were coming bare, only the beeches carrying their bright rust of leaves.

A boat was creeping up heavily against the current. The driver's whip cracked and hissed, the mules were lathered. Fortune slowed the bays and Dan swung the Sarsey Sal to the far side of the canal. The steersman of the other boat shot a squirt of tobacco juice through the reflection of a window and wiped the back of his hand across his mouth.

"Say!" he said. "Heard the news?"

"What is it?" Molly asked.

"This Calash laid out a marshal up to Denley. Just missed his lung. I seen him in Western. He looked bad."

"Yeanh."

"Funny you didn't hear about it. I guess Spinning took him out too fast. I'd seen the feller before, but I'd never guessed he was a marshal. Little fat feller. His head was rolling all over his shoulders like an old apple in a wind. He sure looked bad."

He got his jaw going and spat again.

"Seen anything of this Calash?"

"No," said Dan.

"Most likely not," agreed the other. "He's cleared out. They say he's back on the main ditch. They'd ought to get him. Folks is beginning to talk."

"That's right," said his driver. He stung the mules, and they lurched ahead into their collars. The boats drew apart.

"So he got away again," said Molly.

"Yeanh," said Dan. He was remembering now how he had first seen Calash on the Boonville docks, talking to Jotham Klore; and how he and Solomon and Hector Berry had had a glimpse of the man riding down the Lansing Kill. He would be riding ahead somewhere now.

"They won't get him this winter," said Molly. "It was that little fat man who could have caught him. I felt sorry for him lying there in the store. I really did. Now he's out of it, it'll be just luck to catch him."

"Yeanh."

"You're glad he got away."

He kept his eyes on the team, and Fortune walking with his hands in his pockets.

"Yeanh."

"Then I'm glad, too."

She stepped round in front of him, so that he had to look at her.

"I don't see why you like him. You don't have anything to do with him, do you, Dan?"

"No."

"I can't see why you like him, then. He's a bad man all through; he's got to be, or they wouldn't be after him."

Dan was silent.

"Everybody says so."

"Yeanh."

"Why do you like him, Dan?"

He avoided her eyes.

"Just because he helped you out in Hennessy's? He wanted you to help him, that's why he did it."

"Maybe," said Dan. "I don't know."

He let his eyes meet hers, with their bright frank look. To her he seemed a little bit ashamed.

"Why do you like him, Dan?"

"I don't know, Molly. I seen him there in Boonville talking with Klore, and then later. He done a couple of things for me. He put me back on my boat in Utica." Dan was breathing hard.

"Yes," she said.

"He's been all along the canal. I've seen him everywhere I've been to." He talked awkwardly. "He helped me out twice, like I tell you. You seen him fix Klore."

A slight frown wrinkled her forehead. Then she smiled.

"I don't care," she said. "If you like him, I'll like him. I won't say anything."

She turned and went below, leaving Dan puzzled and uncomfortable. How could he explain to her? Or to himself, for that matter? Why should he have to? He didn't see. It wasn't the man's clothes, or his fine way of talking. Anyway, Dan knew he was a criminal. There had been a lot of talk round the docks in Boonville. People were on the watch for him now. He would stand a small chance up in this country. Dan had seen him first on the Boonville docks,—Uberfrau's,—and he had made no move to stop him. He was a stranger; so was Gentleman Joe. He had never seen his face, even. Yet he felt a definite friendliness for him, as if in some way they were both involved together. . . . He could not explain. He wished he could see the man's face and talk to him. . . .

At Westernville a man came out of Han Yerry's Hotel and signaled them in to the dock.

"Sorry to stop you," he said. "We're looking over every down-boat." He pulled open his coat and showed a badge.

"Can't tell where to expect this Calash."

"He ain't here," said Molly.

The man gave her an admiring grin.

"I don't doubt it, girl. I'm acting on orders."

He went over the Sarsey Sal quickly but thoroughly. There were not many places to look.

"Where're you bound for?" he asked Dan.

"Potatoes for Rome. Hauling for Butterfield."

"All right. Sorry to bother. You've got a nice boat."

He gave Molly another admiring glance and went ashore.

On the dock Fortune was talking to an old man fishing for sunfish.

"Not any luck," the old man said, gumming a pinch of snuff. "It's getting too cold nights for fish to bite good. The worms is dozy. It's the winter coming. See there!"

Overhead, a line of geese pricked the sky.

Getting up a Party

It was Friday morning in Utica. The Sarsey Sal lay tied up beside the Wheaden dock, which was now, as Solomon called it, a Butterfield proposition.

"It'd be a good place for us to tie up at for the winter, Dan. Though I guess probably Lucy'll want to be farther downtown."

The little man was sitting on the side gang of the Sarsey Sal, his thin bow legs hanging into the pit.

"I guess we'll tie up here," Dan said. "Molly likes it all right, and I'll be stabling the teams in the barn back."

"Put your grease on upwards," Solomon said suddenly. "Then rub it down."

Dan glanced up from the trace he was greasing.

"I don't see why."

Solomon leaned backward to spit overside; then he poked the stem of his pipe in Dan's direction.

"There's a lot of things you don't know the why of in this world, but that ain't saying they ain't true."

Dan grunted and went on with the greasing. The headstalls and collars hung from spikes he had driven loosely into the wall of the pit, and the traces hung down from the hames.

"You going up to that fair?" Solomon asked, after a while.

"I guess so," said Dan.

"Aiming to buy horses?"

"I want a good team. I'll need two next summer."

"Well, I guess I'd ought to go along and see you don't get squeezed by one of these damn dealers. You're still kind of new on to the canal, Dan, and they're sharp-edged."

"I know what I want," Dan said, picking up the rubbing rag and watching the leather soften and come out black under his hand.

Solomon nodded.

"That's the hell of it. Once they know what you want, you ain't got a chance. They c'd set up a bar'l on four sticks with a brush broom for a tail and make you think it was Lexington himself. But when you got home with it you'd most likely find the contraption didn't even have no bung in it."

"I know a horse," said Dan.

The little man cocked his head and peered at Dan out of his bright blue eyes. For a moment he sucked some poison out of the clay stem of his pipe and sent it overside. He picked at it critically with a splinter and tried to look into the bowl.

"We could hire a rig," he said. "We could start early. They're going to hang Mary Runkle to-morrow morning."

"I don't know as I'd want to see that."

"No, but the crowd'll get there early. Nothing to see. They're doing it inside of the jail. Folks always come around if a woman's going to be hung. She strangled her husband."

"How'd they come to find it out?"

"A cigar peddler discovered it," said Solomon. "She strangled him in bed one night and told her daughter to come and hold his feet as her pa was having a fit. Then she let on he'd died of pneumonia. The cigar peddler'd sold him some cigars two days afore and he found the butt ends of four cigars in the ash pit of the stove. Made him suspicious. A sick man's got no pleasure in smoking."

It was a cold, clear day, but the sunlight in the sheltered pit of the boat was warm and pleasant.

"What come of Mr. Friendly?" Solomon asked.

"I paid him off," Dan said. "I guess he got tired of driving. He was headed down for Albany. Aimed to spend the winter there."

"He's a queer bezabor," said the little man.

Dan finished the harness, and then leaned back against the wall and lit his pipe. Solomon came down and sat beside him.

"Trade's falling off," said Solomon. "Some people already tying up for the winter. Line boats are going, though."

They listened to the horn of one coming down. The team tramped by above on the dock and the rope crossed over their heads against the sky, while its shadow crept along the pit, climbed to the stable, and vanished. They heard the low swish of water against the boat, and the ripple shoved the Sarsey Sal against the wharf, where it rubbed with a high-pitched squeak.

About noon they heard Mrs. Gurget's voice break out on deck over their heads.

"There they be, setting alongside of each other just like two toads."

Her bebonneted red-haired head was thrust out over the pit; and suddenly beside it appeared Molly's face, smiling, and a sharp, dried woman's face under a bristling hat, and the pompous round face of a man.

"Look what we run into, Sol," cried Mrs. Gurget. "Walking along as large as life."

She patted the man so forcibly on the shoulders that his hat bobbled forward over his eyes, and he clutched at it frantically. Solomon grinned.

"Hector Berry! Gol! And Mrs. Berry along with him. Looking younger every minute!"

Hector waved his hand in a magnificent greeting, and Mrs. Berry worked her wrinkled lips into a smile.

Solomon scrambled up the cleats on the stern wall of the pit and reached down to take the harness as Dan handed it up. In a minute they were all in the cabin, the womenfolk on one side, the men on the other.

"Dan and me have decided to go up to that horse fair tomorrow," Solomon announced.

"Where?" asked Hector, perking up.

"Whitesboro. Dan allows to buy a team."

"Is that right? Well, I guess maybe it would be a good thing if I was to go, too. I was calculating to, anyhow. It takes more'n one man to buy a team of horses. Bad time to buy, too."

"Yeanh?" said Dan.

"Yes, sir, they're trying to get the lumber-camp trade, and matched teams will fetch high."

"I'll buy single," said Dan. "I'll do my own matching."

"It's a good idee if you're any good at it," said Berry, leaning his chair back against the wall, hooking his legs through the rungs and his thumbs through his galluses. "Yes, that's right—match 'em yourself. But it takes judgment. I'm allowed a good hand at it. I'd better come along with you."

Dan dropped his eyes to the floor. He was nettled, for he wanted to do his trading by himself. But he could see no way out of it. He realized that he had already proved himself a fool by telling even Solomon he wanted to buy a team. Fortune Friendly had told him that. "A man's best friend'll see him cheated on a horse deal," he had said one morning. "Everybody in the world likes to see a man pay money for a horse." So Dan nodded.

"Well, well! My!" exclaimed Mrs. Gurget. "Listen to them boys talking, and not one thinking of asking the girls. Never mind, dearie, you and me and Nelly, here, we'll get up a shindig of our own. I know a grocerman."

"No, you won't," Solomon said quickly. "I got it all planned with Dan you're coming along with us. We'll hire a rig."

"So long as I can wear my new dress somewhere, it don't matter." The fat woman rolled up her eyes and passed her hands down over the front of her, smoothing her skirts. "It's real pretty, ain't it, Molly? You ought to see how it's going to hang—so. Right in style."

She posed herself on light feet, as though she were examining herself in a mirror, and turned slowly round before them, pointing out the merits of the new dress. It did not seem to matter that the material lay wrapped up in brown paper on the table.

"What you wearing, Nelly?"

"I don't know," said the wizened little woman sharply. "I don't bother over such light notions. Dressing pretty's just nothing to an honest woman."

She cast a supercilious glance at Molly, and Hector wiggled his hams uncomfortably on his chair.

"I don't know as I'll go, even," she said.

"Yes, you will," said Hector suddenly. "We're going to start in good time, too."

Solomon turned a questioning glance on him.

There was an unusual and determined gleam in Hector's eye, as he snapped a cigar into his small round mouth and cocked it towards his eye.

"I want her to be outside the jail when they're hanging that woman," he said in a low voice that the women could not hear. "I just want Nelly to be there for a while to think it over. That woman always bossed her husband."

The women would not have heard him, anyway. They were discussing what they would wear and what they would take to eat. Mrs. Gurget promised her new dress and sandwiches, Molly a cake, and Mrs. Berry a pie.

"Well, you're in luck, Dan," Berry said. "You're in luck all around. A good boat and a good cook. But don't let her get her chin up high. I'd heard about you out in Manlius. Ran across Jotham Klore; he was out there. He said some hard things about you. I'd look out for him, if I was you. He says you took his cook away from him, but he says he'll get her back. I never seen him act that way. He used to get riled easy, but he didn't look riled then. Seemed kind of steady and sour inside. He says when he finds you he'll give you the dangdest licking a man ever got."

"Shucks," said Solomon. "Molly cleared out on him of her own accord."

"He don't look at it that way. No man will," Hector said sententiously. "It ain't in nature."

Dan glanced across at Molly, sitting under the window with the light coming over her shoulder, and found her eyes on his. Her gaze was searching, and he felt uncomfortable. Then Mrs. Gurget swept her off on a point of dress.

"There ain't anything for you to worry about now," said Berry. "Klore's tied up out there for the fall and he's got a contract working his team on the railroad this winter."

"Yeanh."

"He's a regular bear for fighting," Berry said. "I've seen him three times. That time he licked O'Mory of Little Falls was the worst fight I ever see. I had five dollars on O'Mory."

"Cripus! When him and Dan hooks horns, I'll put my money on Dan. He's got the heft. It's a sure thing."

Berry raised his brows and made a silent whistle round his cigar.

Dan glanced up to see Molly looking at him again.

"I guess that's right," he said, suddenly. Her eyes brightened, and her head lifted with a sudden wildness, like the lift of a mare's head. Dan felt the blood in his hands. Outside a horn was blowing for the weighlock—a flat, harsh, ringing note, stirring him.

Mrs. Gurget got to her feet. "Come along," she said. "We've got to eat, Sol. And I've got to make me up that dress."

When they had all gone, Molly set about cooking dinner. Dan sat smoking, with his eyes upon her. She moved easily from table to stove, aware of his eyes, not noticing them. When she spoke her voice was low and full. She told him about Mrs. Gurget's shopping.

"My, she was funny, Dan. I declare I think she wrapped herself in twenty different colors for me to see how they matched her. She bought a yellow silk—it was pretty expensive, and she was awful fidgety coming back home. She was kind of pretty all flushed up."

She put the food on the table.

"What time are we going to start?"

"Sol says we'd ought to get going about eight. He's going to bring the rig around to the dock."

"You'd ought to get you some new clothes, Dan "

"Maybe I'd ought not wear 'em to-morrow. Not if I'm going to buy a team."

"It don't make any difference. You ought to have a new suit. You can afford it, Dan. I'm going to get you some shirts this afternoon. How does it pay a woman to keep looking pretty if the man she's going with don't dress up to take her? You're rich enough."

"I don't see any point in it."

"Sometimes a man can be too close with money," she said, giving him a steady look. "Then he finds it's all he's got."

Dan was silent.

"The others'll be wearing Sunday clothes," she said.

"I guess that's right," said Dan. "I don't know much about buying clothes."

"Then I'll go along," said Molly.

After they had finished their meal, Molly put on her hat again and the dark brown cape she wore on cold days, and they set out to a tailoring establishment, where, according to Molly, men's clothes could be bought at a fair price.

"Ready-cut?" asked the tailor's clerk.

"Yeanh," said Dan.

Now that they were at the point of buying, Molly seemed ill at ease, and Dan found that he would have to do the talking. The clerk wiped imaginary water from his hands and looked Dan over with an appraising eye.

"We don't run much of a stock of ready-cut," he said dubiously. "What would you want, a tail coat?"

"Nothing fancy—just a suit."

Through a door in the back they got a glimpse of an old man, wearing square spectacles, who was examining a piece of broadcloth with all the force and concentration of a preacher considering a text. His great brass-bolted shears were held open in his right hand, and now and then the points traced an imaginary pattern.

"What size, William?" he asked, without removing his attention from the cloth.

"Forty-four, p'r'aps," said the clerk.

"Show the brown suit made up for Mr. Potter."

"By jiminy, that might do."

The clerk disappeared headfirst into a wardrobe and came out again holding a dark brown homespun coat and trousers. He held up the coat.

"It ought to just about do," he said. "Try it on, mister."

Dan slipped into it. The clerk led him to the mirror, where he examined himself nervously.

"It's smoother'n honey. By jiminy, there's what I call a fit. Ain't it, mam?"

It did fit well. In his enthusiasm, the clerk began to praise the cloth.

"Hard as iron, wears like steel, and there's no chance for its getting a shine on it. Just the thing for you, I'd say. Quiet and sober and looks rich. It's a gentleman's coat. And the cloth is very especial. Imported out of England. Yes, sir. It goes elegant into a pant. We made some of it into pants especial. Right there, mister," holding up the trousers, "is an elegant pant. There isn't a pant in the store—or in the city, for that matter—to come up to it. You don't have to try 'em on to see they'll fit."

It was just about what Dan wanted. He liked the color. So did Molly. It was becoming to him.

The clerk went ostentatiously to one side to look for more coats.

"What do you think of the cloth?" Dan asked. "It seems all right to me. It's good and heavy."

Molly fingered it.

"Yes, I think it's good, Dan. It looks good on you, too."

"Yes, it's good cloth. Can't be beat," said the clerk, returning.

"How much?"

"Well, it's good cloth, but it's been made up. That would cut it down. Twenty-five is a cheap price. Your wife can see what good stuff it is, I'll bet."

Dan started slightly, but Molly, watching him closely, saw no change in his expression. After an instant of feeling the trousers, he said, "Got anything cheaper?"

She let out her breath slightly.

The clerk ran his hand down over his face.

"Well, I dunno. Maybe."

Through the door the tailor said, "Twenty-one we let it go for, William. No less."

The clerk stared over his shoulder and let out a low whistle.

"That is low," he said, as if to himself. "Well, Mr. Perkins is the boss."
"I don't know," said Dan, still fingering it. "What do you think, Molly?"
She had him step over to the window to get the light. It did look well on him.

"I'd take it," she said.

"All right," said Dan, relieved that it was over. Through the door the tailor was focusing hard on the broadcloth. As soon as Dan spoke, the difficult pattern must have appeared to him, for he began to cut.

The clerk wrapped up the suit and took the money, and Dan and Molly went on to a haberdasher's. She walked vigorously beside him, saying little, and whenever Dan glanced at her she was looking straight ahead. Now and then men turned to look at her as she passed, and he felt a glow of pride. It was a great credit to him to be walking with her.

They bought a couple of shirts, and Molly fussed over some ties until she found one that suited her taste, a dark green, flowing silk one.

"It'll make your eyes bluer," she said, holding it up to his chin. Dan flushed uncomfortably, and the clerk smiled.

"A woman always likes to buy her husband's neckties," he said.

This time they carried it off well; but once they were outside the store, they went nervously again, like conspirators. If Dan had asked her then to marry him, she probably would have said yes.

But, back on the Sarsey Sal once more, there seemed to be no point in the question. Dan said nothing.

Buying a Team

Dan and Molly had no more than finished clearing away breakfast than they heard the trotting of a light team coming along the dock. Then the horses stopped, and they heard Solomon calling to them to hurry; and all at once there was a burst of hearty laughter.

Dan slipped into his new coat while Molly pinned on her hat before the mirror; and they grabbed up the cake on a plate and ran up the steps, locking the door behind them.

Mrs. Gurget looked at their flushed faces and began laughing again good-naturedly. Hector, with his hands folded on his waistcoat and a new cigar upended in his mouth, said sententiously, "Spooning never made for spinning," which made their faces even redder, at which Mrs. Gurget started laughing again on the rear seat, while Mrs. Berry sniffed and pointed her sharp nose in the direction of the horses.

Solomon had scrambled down over the wheel, after passing the reins to Hector, and he was now rearranging the luncheon baskets under Mrs. Gurget's seat.

"Molly," he said, "seeing you're thinnest, I guess you'd better set here with Lucy. I had to put her in the back to bring her as close over the rear ax' as I could."

"That's a lie," the fat woman said with a broad smile; "he didn't want to talk to me. I made him shave."

The buckboard was a light three-seater, and the team looked uncommonly well for livery horses.

"I thought I might as well get a decent pair," Solomon said to Dan as they climbed into the front seat. He picked up the reins, took out the whip, pulled his hat down over his eyes, and looked over his shoulder at the others. Mrs. Berry was got up in a bombazine dress, beribboned and black, and Hector wore a pot hat on the back of his head. Behind them Molly, in her new hat, was talking to Mrs. Gurget. The fat woman felt Solomon's eye.

"Go on, Sol," she said.

The team, which had been lifting their forefeet nervously from time to time, started off with a lunge and broke into a smart trot.

"My gracious!" cried Mrs. Berry, clutching her bonnet. "Be they safe, Hector?"

"All right till we make the turn to the bridge," said Hector, swinging his cigar across his lip.

She braced her feet and sat back rigidly, her tense mouth bringing her chin up towards the end of her nose.

"You persuaded me, Hector," she said, and thereafter she preserved an ominous silence.

"It's all right, Nell," Solomon cried over his shoulder. "The hind wheels'll stay down, I guess."

"You shut up!" called Mrs. Gurget.

The rig rattled over the planks, and Solomon made a smart turn over the Genesee Street bridge. They turned west into Whitesboro Street, and the team settled into a flinging trot. There were several wagons on the road ahead of them.

"Getting out to see the execution," Solomon said. "Not that they'll see it; it's coming off in jail. I remember the Peters case in 1810. I was just a boy, but I remember it real clear. They hanged him on the hill west of the town. The sun come up just when he stopped kicking. It was a high gallus, and there was a drunken man kept a-wondering and a-wondering if Peters had seen it come up. He was ten feet higher than what we were. It's queer how people will go to see somebody hanged. But they do it in the jail now. It was a clever notion to have the fair there that day. A lot of folks that wouldn't have come to a fair'll stop to look at them horses; and looking at a horse is next to buying."

As they swung past the last houses of the city and saw fields beginning to appear, they felt the sun warm on their necks. Mrs. Gurget wiggled the shawl looser and straightened up on the rear seat, so that Molly had to grab the rail to keep from being jogged off.

"Your hat's real pretty," she said to Molly. "And don't Dan look nice?"

"I made him go out and get some clothes yesterday. He was getting ragged. I had an awful time arguing with him. He's kind of close with money."

Mrs. Gurget smiled, and let her eyes rove the road. She began commenting on the turnouts, on the women's clothes, pungent words popping out of her plump mouth, her face warming with laughter. Molly laughed with her and watched Mrs. Berry wincing whenever they passed another wagon. Dan was silent, but, as they slowed down behind a string of five horses which a gypsyish-looking man was leading from the back of a wagon, she saw his eyes on a big black horse with a white blaze and muzzle. Even when they turned out to pass the string, Dan kept his eye on the black horse.

The gypsyish man, who wore a red shirt and a heavy sheepskin waistcoat and sat with his legs hanging over the tailboard, grunted something to the man who was driving the wagon—a seedy, thin man, who wore a high-crowned hat and chewed tobacco with a speculative swaying of his jaw. At the other's grunt, he lifted a languid pair of eyes at Dan, nodded, spat, and went on chewing.

It became quite warm. By the time they entered the village of Whitesboro and turned out before the jail, Mrs. Gurget had taken off her shawl altogether. Molly herself felt warm, and even Mrs. Berry perked up and jerked her bonnet straight.

"I don't see why we come so early," she said to Hector, "and I don't see why we had to stop here. The fair's up behind the hill, ain't it?"

"Yeanh," said Hector, humbly. "But I ain't driving this rig, Nelly."

"What's all these wagons here for, and people got up so for?"

"That's right, Nelly. They do seem to be wearing Sunday clothes."

"What for?"

"Well, it's Mary Runkle," said Hector, managing to tip a wink at Solomon with his off eye.

"What about her?" demanded the little woman angrily. She scented a conspiracy.

"Nelly talks so she ain't had time to hear the news, I reckon," explained the fat woman kindly. "You see, Nelly, it was whiles you was up to Westernville, Mary Runkle killed her husband."

Berry produced his ponderous watch from his waistcoat pocket.

"That's it, Nelly, and in five minutes they're a-going to hang her. She had it coming, I guess. She used to bother her husband a lot, bossing him all the while, I've heard."

"That's right," said Mrs. Gurget.

The wizened little woman suddenly drew herself up, slapped Hector's face, jumped out of the wagon.

"You're mean, you're all nasty-mean, all of you!" she cried, and her voice choked and she ran away round the corner of the jail.

Berry stared after her with round eyes. He touched his cheek with the ends of his stubby fingers and drew in his breath.

"Well, damn me," he said. "Who'd have guessed it? It was your idee, Sol."

"Yeanh," said Mrs. Gurget, hedging herself a trifle. "You got it up, Sol. You'd better go after her, Hector."

But Hector had already jumped to the ground and run after his wife.

"Nell, Nell!" they heard him shout.

"I declare, Sol," said Mrs. Gurget. "What did you have such a notion for is beyond me. Right here in all these people. Why I can't hardly think how to look."

Solomon was the most amazed of them all.

"Why, Lucy, I didn't have no idee. I didn't say to do this."

He glanced at Dan for support, then pushed his hat over his eyes to scratch the back of his head. "I didn't have no idee."

Mrs. Gurget laughed suddenly.

"It got her sudden. And her nose was awful red to start with. I'll bet she's a sight. She's a good body for such a measly woman."

"I think she's nice," said Molly.

"Too nice," said Solomon. "She makes it awkward, being that way." He switched round and leaned to the left to get his watch out.

"It ought to be going on now."

The space in front of the jail was crowded with wagons. There must have been thirty or more, mostly farmers, who could take the morning off. They stared at the expressionless front of the jail with sombre eyes, talking now and then in low voices so that a breathing murmur seemed to hang under the bare branches of the elms. Some stood among the wagons, and a couple of old men sat with their backs to the trunk of a tree and drank out of a glass bottle and looked at their watches between drinks. Between 10 A.M. and 2 P.M. had been the judge's sentence; and Sheriff Jones would put it through as soon as he could.

Tied to a hitching post, the doctor's horse dozed in the shafts of his buggy, one hip slung for comfort. He looked like a fast trotter, but he had learned to take what rest he could when he could, no matter how fresh he was. A big farmer in a pepper-and-salt suit was driving a pair of colts in a surrey up and down the street. Every time they came opposite the old men sitting against the tree they shied and bolted, and it took the farmer two blocks to turn them and bring them back. He seemed to be afraid to take the time to unhitch them and leave them in a shed.

The bell in the schoolhouse clanked once to mark the end of an hour, and a complete hush fell upon the crowd. One of the old men against the tree untied the tobacco-pouch strings under his chin which held on his straw hat, so that he could take it off in an instant if it should prove to be the proper thing to do. And through the stillness they heard the farmer swearing at his colts when they started to bolt for the third time. He looked up as he passed and saw everyone's eyes on him and flushed deeply. Glancing back, Dan saw Mrs. Gurget obviously holding her breath, a dazed, awe-struck expression sucking dimples into her fat cheeks, and Molly looking white, her eyes dark. He took out his new handkerchief and wiped a cold damp from his neck.

A bit of blue flashed over the heads of the people, and, lighting on a branch, a blue jay began to squawk profanely at them. Instantly a red squirrel answered him angrily. And the people watched them. All at once the noise ceased, the attention of both squirrel and jay being caught by the opening of the jail door. The doctor came out, dressed in black, carrying his bag in his hand. He paused a moment to talk to the sheriff, who had come out after him.

"Good-bye, Sheriff," they heard him say. "I've got to get along. Man at Oriskany caught his hand in a loom belt."

"Bad?"

"Probably lose a finger."

"A thing like that's apt to be serious," said the sheriff.

He watched the doctor get into his buggy, wheel the horse, and go rattling up the valley. His jaw was set grimly. All at once he became aware of the people watching.

"Get out of here!" he shouted. "Get out! Do you think this's a circus?"

They grinned at him shamefacedly. One of them called, "Morning, Mr. Jones."

The sheriff raised his hand.

"Get out," he said again, and wheeled and went into the jail, banging the door after him.

Solomon shook the reins.

"We'll hurry to get a place in Finkel's shed," he said to Dan.

In the shed they found the Berrys waiting for them. Mrs. Berry looked very red about the nose and eyes, and Hector was wearing an embarrassed expression. For once he did not have a cigar in his mouth. Mrs. Berry gave Dan a conversational smile.

"So it's done, is it?"

"I guess so," Dan mumbled. A hearty man was lifting his daughter over the wheel of the buckboard next to theirs. He looked round.

"It's the first execution I ever got close to," he observed, "but for downright push and horror, give me the wind colic. Out there all you did was set and watch your watch."

Mrs. Berry was straightening Mrs. Gurget's shawl, while Molly was getting out the lunch basket.

"Coming to buy?" asked the hearty man.

"Yeanh," said Solomon.

"Well," he said, "it ain't much of a fair. No fancy stock, anyway. But we might poke around together. Jed Johnson might have some good teams. He generally has. What are you looking for?"

"Me?" asked Solomon. "I ain't looking for anything. It's my friend here." He pointed his thumb at Dan.

"Pleased to know you, gents," said the hearty man, shaking hands with Dan. "My name's Brackett—just Bill Brackett—a plain, honest man."

He gave himself a light pat on the chest and nodded his head at his daughter, a little girl with two braided pigtails of yellow hair, blue ribbons in each, blue serious eyes, and a very freckled nose. "Daughter Nancy. Likes to set on the back of the buckboard and lead home pa's horses. Can't leave her home."

The child dug her toe into the ground and stared upward from under her lids, blushing furiously. Suddenly she caught the fat woman's eye and smiled.

"Why don't we take her with us?" said Molly. "That will leave you men free."

Brackett took off his hat.

"That's downright kind of you. Since you offer, I accept. Maybe I can put you in the way of a good deal," he said to Dan.

The girl bashfully joined the three women, but when they came out of the shed she was holding Mrs. Gurget's hand.

"Me, I'm looking for a light horse," said Brackett, fishing a stout stick from under the seat of his wagon. "What are you after?"

"I want a pair," said Dan. "About thirty-three hundred."

"Matched pair, eh? Well I'll bet my friend Jed Johnson will have just about what you want. He always has three or four pairs of real handsome horses he brings up from the South. Suppose we go and see what he's got."

"I don't know as I'll buy a team outright. I guess I might match a pair."

"That's a good idea, young man. It's good if you know enough to do it. Buying from Johnson, you're sure of a good team, though."

They sallied out of the shed together, Brackett with his left hand on Dan's arm, his right swinging the stick. He wore a light brown homespun coat and black trousers and a scarlet tie, and stuck his legs out handsomely as he walked.

Solomon and Hector kept in the rear.

"How's Nell?" Solomon asked.

Hector let out a long sigh. Then he turned on Solomon with a shame-faced grin.

"Me and Nelly ain't talked the way we just did since we been married. She allowed she'd been mean, but that she hadn't meant anything by it; and then I said it wasn't right the way I'd treated her; and she said she'd stop naggin'. Can you beat that, Sol?"

"No!" said Sol. "Did she, though?"

"Yes, sir! She admitted it. But it was worse than that. It was worse than seeing an execution."

"Yeanh?"

"By Cripus, I'd got so wound up, I said I'd give up cigars."

Even to recall his promise petrified Hector's round face.

"That's too bad," said Solomon, judiciously. "You hadn't ought to have done that."

"Well, I done it. We was so loving all to once, I couldn't think of anything else to say. And when I said that, Nelly kissed me right in the shed with all them horses, and then made me say it over. She's been pert as a squirrel ever since."

They found that they had lost sight of Dan and Brackett, but on looking round they sighted the fat woman before a gypsy's tent, with the gypsy woman, her head covered with a red handkerchief, talking to her through the opening of the tent, one brown hand stretched out, palm up, gracefully. A little behind the fat woman stood Molly, with the little Brackett girl, who was carrying the lunch basket. Farther down the line of tents they saw Mrs. Berry, her small bonnet bobbing from right to left as she tried to fool a pea-and-thimble artist.

"She will try it," said Hector sadly, "and she's close-sighted too."

Shivers of superstitious delight were passing up and down the fat woman's back. Now she drew herself up with a shuddering breath as a keen deduction of the gypsy woman went home, and then she leaned over chuckling outrageously over some revelation for the future. All the time the black eyes of the gypsy kept glancing up from under her brows at the broad red face.

"Let's sneak up to the back side of the tent," Solomon whispered. "Maybe we'll get a gossip on to Lucy."

But, before they could start, the gypsy woman dropped the fat woman's hand and held out her own again, palm up. Mrs. Gurget giggled like a schoolgirl as she dropped a quarter into the hand.

"I sure got my money's worth," she chortled. "See what she says about you, Molly."

The two men saw the girl leave the child and step up to the gypsy. Her fresh, bright coloring made a vivid contrast with the gypsy's brown skin and black hair. The palmist let her bold eyes rove over Molly, trying to learn what she could from her general appearance. Then she took Molly's hand and slanted it to the sun. For an instant the two heads bent over it; Molly bending easily, the short tails of her jacket flaring upwards; the gypsy leaning forward from her seat, her black eyes glittering. Once in a long while a palmist sees a hand which makes clear sense according to the laws of the science, and which can be read without invention. She glanced up at Molly's face, said something in a low voice, then drew her shawled head back through the flap of the tent. To the amazement of the others, Molly followed her.

There were a dozen or so of tents set up opposite the hitch-racks and shed; and most of the people seemed to be interested in the attractions they offered. The gypsy fortune tellers and palmists were popular, and the Egyptian phrenologist, K. Kopulos, who was just starting a vogue in the Mohawk country; and the glass blowers, making magic with their breath and fingers—they could always be found at any such gathering. In this instance they were a Swiss family, who had found the fortune they sought in their old profession. Little white glass bucks and bluebirds could be found in half the corner cupboards of the river counties. At the end of the line a quack had set up a booth from which he hawked, in a thin, monotonous voice, rheumatic belts, stone water for gall stones, smallpox antitoxin, and the inevitable panacea for man and beast, claiming even that it stopped the roup in poultry. His tall, bony figure in the black pipe hat and black coat, the velvet collar of which had long since turned a rusty green, caught the eye and held it. He had an interested, kindly face and knew a cure for every ailment. Across the way the reputable agent for Dr. Brandreth's Pills, a jolly, healthy, stubby man, himself a product of the medicine he offered (according to his advertisement), writhed impotently as he watched the quack's sales. Even the famous *Symptom Diary, or Invalid's Almanac* he carried as a side line went poorly. He looked too healthy to be sympathetic.

Behind, under a long shed, or tied to a hitching rail outside, stood the horses, their manes and tails stirring on the slight north wind, some fidgety at the noise and bustle, some trotting round the rings behind a boy as the dealer stood beside the expected buyer, cracking his long-lashed whip and pointing out what virtues the purchaser might miss. Like a refrain to the rise of human voices came the stamp of hoofs and the rattling of halter rings.

The morning sun washed over the crowd, picking out here and there the bright red and green of gypsy dress, or the pearl grey of a gentleman's hat or the gloss of his tile. The old grass was a dull green underfoot, and at the entrance to the grounds and in the ring, where horses' hoofs had loosened the frost, the dark mud showed through.

For a minute, with all the bustle round them, Hector and Solomon watched the flap of the gypsy's tent. Then Solomon swore.

"She'd ought to have more sense than to do that."

They joined the fat woman and the little Brackett girl, who was eating her way into a pink nest of spun sugar.

"Well," Mrs. Gurget admitted, "it is queer, Sol. But I don't see as anything can rightly happen to her so long as we watch till she comes out."

"Guess I'll go round back," said Hector. "If there's any monkey business, it'll show there."

But a few minutes later Molly appeared in the door of the tent. Her face had lost some of its color, and her hair, escaping from under its bonnet as it always did, hung lifeless. Her shoulders slouched. For an instant she did not appear to see Mrs. Gurget and Solomon, but stood with dull eyes.

The fat woman drew a sharp breath.

"My gracious!" she said sharply. "Open your eyes, dearie."

Molly glanced at her and lazily pulled a wisp of hair from in front of her eyes. She smiled, but it was a lifeless smile.

"Shucks!" snorted the fat woman. "What's she been telling you?"

Molly looked down at her hand, then wiped it down over her hip.

"She said it was a true hand."

"You'd oughtn't to go believing an ugly witch like her," said the fat woman. "It's just a game for making money."

"She said it was true," repeated Molly. "She asked me first if I wanted to hear."

"What did she tell you?" asked Mrs. Gurget, drawing her out of earshot.

Suddenly Molly laughed.

"It don't matter—it's nonsense. You'd laugh to hear it. I ought to go back where I can do up my hair."

"All right," said Mrs. Gurget, patting her arm. "We'll go look for a place to eat, and leave the men find Dan. He's off buying horses."

"No," said Molly, suddenly. "Let's all go look for Dan."

"Surely," said the fat woman.

They picked up Mrs. Berry and Hector.

"What did she tell you, Molly?" Hector asked.

"Oh, nothing. It's all lies, that talk," said the fat woman, but she frowned aside at Hector and put her finger to her lips. He stared at her, then winked and said solemnly, "Sure, all lies. They told me I was going to marry a pretty, red-haired gal."

"Well, didn't you?" asked the fat woman.

"It was too white to tell when I did. But the temper was there."

"You shut up," said his wife, angrily.

The little Brackett girl had finished her sugar. Her eyes were shining and the corners of her mouth and the end of her freckled nose were grubby and sticky.

"Let's get some more," suggested the fat woman.

The child gave her a glance of mute admiration.

"Vi'let," she suggested in a small voice. . . .

Mr. Brackett had started to lead Dan down the line of horses before the shed. He walked slowly, swinging his stick with gusto.

"Jed has his horses at the bottom end of the shed," he explained. "We might as well head there first."

Dan said nothing, but kept running his eyes over the horses. Most of them were work teams, generally looking puffy as if they had been greased and heavily corned for a short while. He mistrusted all such horses.

Now and then Mr. Brackett would nod to a dealer. The dealer would nod back at him as though he were an old acquaintance.

"Got some good-lookers there," Brackett would say, and the dealer would nod and put a cigar in his mouth or a chew, according to his disposition, and cross one foot over the other in preparation for making a trade. But Brackett would pass on.

"Jed's reliable," he said to Dan. "Let's see what he's got. You've got to watch these fellers."

"Suits me," said Dan.

But then, just as Mr. Brackett was about to wave his hand to his friend Johnson, someone touched Dan's elbow.

"Looking for a horse?"

Dan saw the gypsy whom they had overtaken earlier in the morning driving his string to the fair. His eyes languidly surveyed Dan's waistcoat buttons, and a long straw drooped over the middle of his lower lip.

"Yeanh," said Dan.

Mr. Brackett turned an indignant gaze on the gypsy.

"Who are you?" he demanded.

"Who are you?" the man echoed in a mild voice.

"Brackett," said the farmer. "Just Bill Brackett. There's plenty to vouch for my character."

The gypsy raised his hat delicately by the crown half an inch off his head and let it drop back. Then he took his straw out of his mouth, examined the chewed end critically, and put in the unchewed end.

"Pleased to meet you."

"Get out," said Brackett. "My friend wants to buy a team."

"That's what I was asking him."

"He's going to deal with Mr. Jed Johnson, a reputable dealer," said Brackett, throwing out his chest. "I vouch for Jed Johnson's character."

"I don't want to show my character," said the gypsy. "I want to show this gent my horses."

"Sure," said Dan, "let's look them over."

Mr. Brackett grunted savagely and then strode behind them, a look of determination on his red face. The gypsy led them to a corner of the lot, where five horses were lined up under the care of the red-shirted man. Most of the horses were light, carriage weight. But Dan's eyes lighted again at the sight of the big black with the white blaze and muzzle. He was dirty and looked thin. Mr. Brackett let out a gust of air through his teeth.

"You ain't looking at that, be you, Harrow?"

"What?" asked Dan.

The red-shirted man winked, ostensibly at Dan, but including everybody within reach.

"Gent means a horse, probably. Don't know the name."

Brackett swore.

"Horse! That, eh? You ain't looking at that bald-snouted brush-harrow, be you?"

"Yeanh," said Dan. "I kind of like his looks. He's a bit high to match, though."

"Sure," said the owner, taking out his straw to point with. "But his shoulders is set on straight. He's short-backed. He's a fast walker. Sam, show him round."

The red-shirted man unhitched the halter rope and walked the horse up and down. He had a good stride.

"Trot him," said the dealer.

The red-shirted man jerked the rope and the horse threw up his head and trotted in a circle.

"Limber," remarked the dealer. "He's kind and sound. He's a good horse."

"How old is he?"

"Five."

Brackett snorted and said, "Five!"

"Why don't you look at his teeth?" suggested the dealer.

"I wouldn't get in reach of that animal's eye, let alone his teeth. He's vicious."

"Well, I wouldn't then. Sam, open the horse's mouth so the gent can look without getting breathed at."

The red-shirted man led the black over to them, caught his off ear in one hand to hold the head down, and pinched the lower jaw. The horse flared his nostrils, but his mouth opened.

"Twelve," observed Mr. Brackett. "Look at them rings."

"Sure," said the dealer. "Three on each."

Dan ran his hands down over the horse's legs. The horse stood easily. There was no sign of ringbone.

"Sound," remarked the dealer.

"Spavined," said Brackett. "I thought I'd noticed."

"No," said Dan.

"He's had a fall," said Brackett. "Ain't his nigh knee broke?"

"How much do you want for him?" Dan asked.

"Ninety-five, cheap."

"Yes, it is," said Dan. "Was he stolen?"

The gypsy let his languid eyes drift over the skyline.

"No," he said.

"Where was he raised?" asked Dan.

"Man I bought him off didn't mention."

"Where'd you buy him?"

"A pasture lot in Round Top."

"Where's that?"

"Tioga County, Pennsylvania."

"All right," said Dan. "Can you keep him here for a while? I want to match him up. When I get the horse I want, I'll fetch him and pay you."

"Option?"

"Five dollars?"

"Sure."

Mr. Brackett seized Dan's elbow.

"Boy, boy. You want to look out. Of course he was cheap. But them'll stick you, them gypsies."

"Yeanh?"

"You'll have a hard job matching him. But I heard Jed speaking about a grey roan he had might do."

"Might as well see," said Dan.

At the end of the line in the shed a puffy-looking man leaned against a hitch-post. He wore a long coat and high leather boots and had a dirty fawn-colored hat on his head. At sight of him, Brackett waved his arm.

"Hey there, Jed, how be you?"

Mr. Johnson uncrossed his legs, looked up, said "Hello" in a hoarse voice, and crossed his legs again. He was chewing tobacco, and Dan could see by the way he could spit through the hitching ring on the side of the shed that Mr. Johnson knew what was where.

"Jed, here's Mr. Harrow come to buy a horse."

Johnson ran his one eye over Dan, and then seemed to perk up a little. His heavy cheeks collapsed on the heels of a long spit and he wiped his mouth with the back of his hand.

"How big?" he asked hoarsely.

"Not over seventeen hundred, fourteen to fifteen and a half hand," said Dan.

"Not notional in color, be you?"

"No," said Dan. "But black would go best."

Mr. Brackett thought it was time to put in a good word.

"Granting you could find the ideal horse," he said in a confidential tone to Dan, "I bet your neck Jed will have it."

"I'll show you what I got, young man," said Jed.

He stowed his quid behind his nigh back teeth and put two fingers on his tongue. His cheeks filled like a balloon and he whistled.

"That was for my man," he said, when he had listened a moment. "He ain't going to answer. He never does. He's lazier'n a beef cake. Reckon he's sleeping off some likker. God damn him, anyway."

"Ain't sleeping, ain't drunk!" cried a high voice. "Ain't a cow cake, neither. Go to hell."

A skinny man with a grey beard and big hands drew himself out of the manger in front of the horses and looked them over owlishly.

"What's the trouble, Jed?"

"Gent wants to see a horse."

"Thar's seven," said the old man, pointing down a line of friendly snouts. "He can take his pick, can't he?"

"Get up," said Jed hoarsely. "Get up, will you?"

"Sure."

He clambered out, clouted a horse's shoulder for room, and joined them.

"What'll the gent see first?"

"Wants seventeen hundred, fifteen hand," said Johnson. "Black."

"Why, bless his brisket, we've got the picture of it right here."

"That's what I was thinking," said Johnson. "Lead her out, Jimmy."

While Jimmy was getting a big black out of the string, Johnson said, "Five-year-old mare, kind and honest. Real pretty. I'd call her better than seventeen hundred now, but she's in heavy flesh. She'll train down. There she is. Good head and neck, well set on, not a scar on her feet, heavy quarters—a good hauling horse."

Jimmy walked her round. The horse was loggy, Dan said to himself, stiff. Her size was right, but she was too long in the back. She wouldn't keep up with the other horse for more than a mile. She lost motion every step.

"Nice horse," he said. "How much is she?"

"Well, I'll tell you, Mr.—"

"Harrow," said Brackett, putting his hands in his pocket and striking a critical pose as he watched the mare.

Johnson spat and began again in his hoarse voice, "It's this way, Mr. Harrow. There's a five-year-old mare, broke double or single, active worker, handsome shape, if I say it myself. None of your Southern horses, not her. Raised on my farm to Canandaigua. I'll tell you about her. Her own sister was matched up with her, the neatest spitting picter they made. You couldn't tell one from the other, I'll swear it, except by the way they'd hold their tails in dropping. Fact, ain't it?" He turned to Jimmy. Jimmy halted the mare, looked round her and under her, said you could match hairs on them. "Sure," continued Johnson, "that's how they was. I aimed to sell 'em as a pair. But a gent came and offered me a hundred and fifty dollars for that other one. But I held out for two hundred and he was glad to pay. This one I'll sell for one-fifty, seeing it's late in the season and going single. I was to ask four hundred for the team. I was a fool to sell the other."

Dan went over to her and looked at her neck. Her mane was trimmed cleverly, but he had been right at first. Her neck was set too low on her shoulders. A week of heavy hauling and she'd have sores.

Out of the tail of his eye he kept watching a brown. The horse was thin and out of condition, but he liked its set. It stood easily in the line and kept its head up. It looked clever. Dan turned back to the mare.

"Let's see her trot."

Johnson uncoiled the lash of his whip and cracked it. Jimmy yanked on the lead. The mare lumbered heavily. Then she stumbled.

"First time she ever done that," said Jed.

"I ain't sure I like her," said Dan. "Got anything else?"

"There's a grey roan. Not so slick an article. But good. All my horses are. Take him out, Jimmy."

While the old man was bringing out the grey roan, Johnson ran through his catalogue of virtues, named one twenty-five for the price, and declared that the horse was seven years old. Dan decided that the horse was fourteen.

"You're making a mistake to look at this one," said Johnson. "That mare's what you want. Still, for a steady horse, this one'd do a man proud."

"First-rate horse," said Jimmy, with a grin in his beard. "He's a regular odacious clever one, he is. Name is Ponto."

Dan went over him carefully.

"He looks pretty good to me," he admitted. "What's wrong with his left eye?"

"Wrong?" asked Johnson hoarsely.

"Eye?" asked Brackett.

Jimmy grinned again.

"I ain't told Mr. Johnson," he said. "That's a most odacious clever horse. He's got the moon-eye."

"Moon-eye?" asked Dan.

"That speck you seen," explained Jimmy. "It grows along with the moon. In a couple of weeks you'll see it going down. It commences with the new moon. If it's rainy when the moon commences, you can look at his eye and see what the weather's going to be like. It shows like a new moon, wet or dry. You can make money betting on the new moon."

Johnson spat a long squirt.

"I've heard tell of the moon-eye," he said with hoarse frankness, "but I never seen one. Why didn't you tell me, Jimmy? I'd have put the price up."

Won't now, though. Jed Johnson never put a price up'ard on any deal he makes to offer."

"That's honest gospel," said Brackett. "I vouch for it."

"What's the good of the moon-eye?" Dan asked.

"Don't you know that?" Jimmy asked. "Gol! And you out to buy a horse?"

"A horse with moon-eye don't need no light for traveling," Johnson explained, winding the whiplash round his thumb. "He can see in the dark."

"Well, he looks good," said Dan, "but I ain't sure."

"I don't know as I've anything to offer that'd suit. You can look, though."

Dan went down the line. He had a chance to see the lean brown, and the horse looked good to him. He guessed he was not over seven, and he saw that he was healthy.

"I tell you," he said. "Let me go and get my other horse and see if the black or the grey goes best."

"Sure," said Johnson. He sat down on a bucket and took another chew, and began talking to Brackett.

"Well, Bill," he said, "I guess I'll owe you a commission for that one."

"I think so myself," said Brackett. "You'd ought to stick him high."

"I aim to," said Johnson.

Halfway back to the gypsy's string, Dan saw Solomon and Berry and the womenfolks coming down the line towards him. It had begun to get colder again, and the northwest wind was bringing clouds over the valley. Once in a while a horse would snort and rear over a swooping shadow. Molly saw him first and waved her hand. When he reached them, she put her hand inside his arm and walked along beside him. The wind, which fingered her loose hair, had brought a color up in her cheeks.

"What luck?" Solomon asked.

Dan told them about the black horse he was about to buy from the gypsy. Then he spoke of trying to match it, and Mr. Brackett's enthusiasm for Mr. Johnson's horses.

"I think Brackett and Johnson has a deal on between them for trade," Dan said. "They're trying to get me to buy a black mare that shows she's a cribber and broken-winded, and a fourteen-year-old grey with the moon-eye. I let on to like them. But they've got a brown horse in the string that'd match up with the black better'n any horse I've seen to-day. I didn't let on I seen him. I figger Brackett must get a piece of all trade he brings. I think he's foxy."

Brackett's small daughter pulled her freckled face out of the nest of spun violet sugar and wiped the stickiness off her lips. She smiled at them proudly.

"My pa's slicker'n polish," she said. "He says so himself."

They all started to grin, and Mrs. Gurget swept up the child, sugar and all, for an enormous hug which made her squeak with terror and pleasure.

"I'll bet he is," said the fat woman.

"I was thinking," Dan went on, "how it would be for Hector, maybe, to go down and buy that brown horse for himself. He's awful poor and Hector'd ought to get him cheap. Then I'll bring the black along to match with the grey."

"How much'd you want to pay?" asked Hector.

"Not over a hundred and twenty, with the poor flesh he's in."

"I'll pay for everything he costs over one hundred and ten," Berry promised.

"Hector!" exclaimed Mrs. Berry. "Ain't that betting?"

"Kind of." Berry grinned.

"Well, you ain't going to bet no money, see?"

"Why not?"

"I said so. You shouldn't ought to go betting our money that way."

"Well, I won't lose."

"Shut up. You heard what I said."

"Quit your nagging, Nelly."

"I won't quit. I won't have you betting our money. Why'd I ever marry a gambler," she wailed rhetorically.

"Didn't know no better. A sheltered honey like you wouldn't't," soothed Mrs. Gurget.

"Quit nagging," said Hector.

"I won't."

Hector gave a jubilant shout.

"She ain't going to stop nagging! You all heard her say it. Then I might as well smoke."

He poked a cigar between his lips, and the enlargement of his button mouth brought back a jolly good-humor to his face that had been lacking all morning.

"Now," he said to Dan, "I'll pay you every dollar that horse costs you over one hundred."

He strode off with pompous quick steps of his tubby legs, spouting great clouds of smoke down the wind ahead of him.

"Hector's a great hand to make a bargain," Solomon chuckled. "He can find more things wrong in a horse than there is in a horse to be wrong. I'm going down to the back side of that shed to listen to him talk."

"Come on," said Mrs. Gurget.

"I'll go with Dan," said Molly.

They went slowly, to give Berry plenty of time to drive his bargain, and Molly kept close to Dan.

"Is he a nice horse?"

"He's a dandy," Dan said. "Him and the brown'll look good on the tow-path hauling the old Sal."

She smiled and squeezed his arm. He looked down at her.

"What's the matter, Molly?"

"Nothing, Dan. I'm kind of tired, I guess."

"You oughtn't to be tired. Wait'll you see my team."

They found the gypsy and Dan paid him the money. The man took the money and then lifted his languid eyes and looked from Molly to Dan.

"That Brackett's slick," he said. "He gets trade for Johnson. Better watch out."

"Thanks," said Dan.

The red-shirted man gave him the lead rope.

"You won't have no bother with him. He stands easy. He's a clever article."

They went slowly back down the slope with the big black at their heels. When they came in sight of the end of the shed, they stopped in to see how

Berry was coming on with his bargaining. They could see Jimmy trotting the horse round. Dan nodded.

"He looks as if he'd match up proper."

"My, he's big," said Molly. "Look at his feet."

Just then the black head with a white muzzle was pushed between their shoulders and the black horse snuffed at Molly's bag for sugar. She started and looked up to see Dan grinning at her. "He's took a notion to you," Dan said. She smiled and put her hand on the horse's crest. He pricked his ears and swung his head gently closer to her.

"He's nice," she said. "What's his name?"

"You name him," said Dan.

"Let's call him Prince."

"I'd thought of it myself," Dan said admiringly.

Down ahead, they could see Berry running his hands over the legs of the big brown. At every joint he shook his head and counted on a finger. Brackett and Johnson were looking on gloomily, and Jimmy did not seem to take much interest in the proceeding. Then Berry started to walk off, his plump legs rigid with simulated disgust.

Johnson lifted his head and sent a long squirt ahead of him.

"Ninety dollars," Dan heard him say.

Berry turned back, fished out his wallet and paid out the money like a shot.

Then Dan and Molly came up. Behind the dealer they saw Solomon waving his arms and grinning ecstatically at the corner of the shed.

"Here's Mr. Harrow," said Brackett.

Johnson looked up.

"That the horse?"

"Yeanh," said Dan.

"Trot out the grey, Jimmy."

"How about that brown?" Dan said, pointing to the horse Berry had just bought.

"Sold," said Johnson.

"I'd like to try him with the black."

"Go ahead," Hector said affably. "Maybe there's a deal somewhere in it for us."

He slipped the lead rope through the halter ring of the black, and took both ropes in his hand. The horses walked off stride for stride. They were a good match.

"Trot 'em," said Dan.

Berry managed to run for a few yards and the team trotted without breaking stride, eyeing each other warily and keeping fairly well apart.

"If they make friends," Dan said, "they'd ought to make a good pair."

"Sure," said Berry.

A premonition of evil had sobered the faces of the dealer and Brackett, but Johnson managed to swear.

"Say," he said, "how about trying that grey?"

"I only want two horses," Dan said. "Mr. Berry, here, bought the brown one for me."

"Cheap, too," said Hector, proudly. "Ninety dollars."

"My God," said Jimmy. "I'm going to get some sleep."

He crawled back into the manger.

Brackett's jaw dropped.

"I don't think it's nice, Harrow. It wasn't honest."

"He's slick," said the little girl, looking at Dan admiringly.

"You're a swell man to get trade," Johnson said to Brackett.

"It amounts to the same thing," Brackett said. "The party bought the brown one. Where's my per cent?"

"It was another deal," said Johnson.

"The little fat man bought him for Harrow, and I brought Harrow here to you," Brackett maintained, his voice rising angrily.

"Go spit in the river," Johnson growled, and turned his back, and got out a fresh chew.

The rest moved off, Molly and Dan bringing up the rear with the two horses.

"Let's eat lunch now," Mrs. Gurget said. "I'm all hollowed out with hunger."

They ate in the shed, to escape the rising wind.

"They'll make a good team," Berry said.

The horses were looking each other over carefully; after a while the black lifted his muzzle to the other's ear, then they touched noses, and afterwards, when Dan grained them lightly, they ate contentedly side by side.

"What'll we call the brown one? We named the black one Prince."

"Call him Earl," Solomon suggested.

"Those are good names," Hector said nodding. "They'll make a good team."

"Well," said Mrs. Gurget, starting to open the second pickle jar. "Their bones look good."

6

THE WINTER TOGETHER

IT began to snow that afternoon; it snowed all night. The next morning it was still snowing, small flakes drifting lazily through a bright sun. It stopped at noon, but the temperature sank in the first cold spell of the year. In the afternoon, word was given out at the weighlock that the canal was shutting down. Dan and Molly noticed the dropping of the water that afternoon.

The old Sarsey Sal groaned during the night, waking them, at first, until they became used to the sound. A stiff wind was drawing down the valley, and a smart ripple slapped the hull. Dan went to sleep again with the sound of it in his ears.

But later he woke suddenly, stiff in the bunk, with a cold damp on his face. He lay quite still trying to determine what was wrong. The clock in the cabin whirred and struck rapidly, three notes. Then there was dead silence in the boat. Outside he could hear the shrill whistle of the wind.

He shifted slightly, and became aware that Molly was awake, as tense as he. For an instant neither of them spoke; then he asked, "What is it, Molly?"

She did not answer.

It occurred to him that someone must have come on board. But he felt sure that he would have heard the creak of the cabin stairs; and the wind would have rattled the door. But, with the idea, Jotham Klore's face, black-bearded, had come back into his mind, for the first time in many days.

He got up slowly, cautiously, letting his weight come gradually on each foot. Little by little he edged into the cabin. A faint moonlight, white and brittle as it was reflected from the new snow, lay in two bars across the room. In a moment he was able to pick out the familiar shapes, the chair, the stove now dead and cold, the mirror with an unreflecting pallor in it, his own hat and Molly's coat hanging side by side on the door.

"There ain't anyone aboard," he said in a low voice.

In the cabin he heard Molly stirring. Presently she came out quietly, about her shoulders a pink Mother Hubbard she had recently bought, mysteriously colorless in the stillness. Her face was vague, and her light hair had acquired shadows. Only her eyes, dark and large, seemed real to Dan.

There was an unreality in the world for both of them, as if they were ghosts—they made no sound, their voices were inarticulate whisperings, like the touch of flakes against the windowpanes. They stood facing each other in a silly, breathless hush.

Then Dan drew a deep breath; and the faint food smell in it, and the cold in his lungs, reassured him. He could hear Molly's even breathing. "What woke you up?" he asked her.

"I don't know."

Her voice, too, was low. He could catch her uneasiness in the sound of the words. Again he felt a terror overwhelming him. He would have welcomed a sight of Jotham Klore opening the door and standing there with his black beard and heavy fists.

"I don't know, Dan," she said again, almost plaintively.

She kept her eyes on the door as if she also expected someone to come in. He knew she was afraid of Klore. He did not know how badly. Ever since he had met her coming towards him with Mrs. Gurget, the Brackett girl, and the rest at the fair, she had been uneasy, paler than usual. She had smiled to watch him with his new team, and she had gone with him to see them stabled in Butterfield's barn back of the wharf. She had kept close to him the rest of the day. He had felt an insecurity in the old Sarsey Sal, which he dared not admit to himself.

As he stood opposite her there in the dim light, his flannel nightshirt rubbing on the backs of his ankles, he realized how pleasant she made living on the old boat. For the first time he took her into the personal account of his own life. Before, she had been a matter of course—essential to the Sarsey Sal as the rudder and the towline. Seeing her now with her deep broody eyes staring at him out of the paleness of her face, she became important to him; but it was hard to say how.

Things had come upon him since he had left the Tug Hill country. They had come by pieces, here and there, almost without his seeking; certainly without his knowing that he sought. And as each came he had a dim awareness that he had expected its arrival, as the jobs he had got, as the Sarsey Sal, as Molly Larkins. It was hard to see where they might all be fitted in.

Behind it all there had been the moving figure of Gentleman Joe, with a price upon his head, as strange to the canal as Dan himself, who seemed to keep tabs on Dan's journeying back and forth, and who yet was followed step by step by the fat marshal, Henderson. It almost seemed as though they traveled the same road. He could not see where it would bring them out, for Gentleman Joe had Henderson to reckon with, and Dan had Jotham Klore. But for the winter, by all accounts, Henderson was out of the picture, and by all accounts Klore was also. But Molly stood in front of him, between sleeping and waking. He was puzzled. He rubbed his hair back until it stood on end, tousled and ungainly. He did not know what had waked him; Molly had said she did not know.

Then she laughed and came over to him. There was a high note in her laughter, but even so it comforted him. She led him to a window on the canal side of the cabin and stretched on tiptoe beside him to look out. The wind was blowing swirls of snow off the roofs; a white moon glittered. It was silent but for the breath of the wind.

"See, Dan, that's why we woke up."

She pointed to the bed of the canal, where the low water should be lying, and he saw that it was still in the wind, with a dark unruffled lustre.

"It's frozen over, Dan."

"Yeanh."

He put his arm about her and felt her draw in close to him. She was laughing to herself; he could feel her shake. But when he lifted her chin to look at her, he saw her cheeks glistening.

Now that the stillness was explained, he felt it close about them both. It had a comforting touch. He put his haunting uneasiness behind him, for though he knew that he must make up his mind about where he was to take his stand in the path sometime, and choose his way, he knew that the winter lay before them. The canal had frozen in.

They woke next morning with the run of sleigh bells in their ears. The sound had a closeness and intimacy, coming and going quickly, with no echo, that caught Dan's ears.

"More snow coming," he said to himself.

Molly was already stirring in the kitchen, and the smell of coffee was coming in to him, with the humming of a little tune.

> "If you don't love me,
> Love who you please;
> Throw your arms round me,
> Give my heart ease."

There was plaintiveness under the light dance in the tune. Though he could not see her, the humming brought to Dan's mind Molly's face as he had noticed it at the horse fair—pale, anxious. And it brought back her face as he had seen it the night before, in the dark, with the winter coming in round the old boat. . . . Afraid—she was afraid. Jotham Klore was safely out of the way, working his team on the railroad between Rochester and Syracuse. When they had heard the news of him, Dan had covertly watched her face. He had noticed that she listened breathlessly; then she had dropped her eyes to something else. Her expression had made him think of her as he had seen her for the second time, just after she had run away from Klore, after Klore had given her her licking. He had felt, as he could feel it now, the same hot anger coming up in him, and he wanted the boater in reach of his hands. He had toughened during the fall; the easier winter would build him up. His shoulders had thickened through; he was putting on weight. Molly had noticed it in the mornings when he shaved, with his shirt hanging from his belt.

He got up and greeted her in the cabin, went up to wash. There was a grey film of cloud hanging over the roofs of the city; the morning smokes spread out under it mushroomwise. The air was quite still, but heavy to breathe. It seemed strange not to see boats stirring in the basin, not to hear horns blowing for the weighlock. Boats lay tied up to the docks, resting low down, like the Sarsey Sal, with just enough water to keep them off the bottom. Smoke came from the stovepipes of some, feebly against the grey air, and it hung low over the bed of the canal. The boats seemed sleeping—on the verge of death; and yet they were in the heart of the city, which was full of life, going about with its accustomed activity, on its morning chores. The sounds of wagons on the docks were muffled; there were few now, anyway. But across the canal Dan caught glimpses, between the warehouses, of city bucks racing their trotters in cutters up and down Canal Street. They went by with a flash of bright red and silver, and a jingling of bells that burst out and faded away all up and down beside the course of the canal. And a smell of more snow coming hung over the city.

As he shaved in the cabin, he caught glimpses of Molly out of the tail of his eye in the mirror. Once or twice he surprised her watching him with a speculative glance, doubtful; the same expression he had seen upon her at the fair. It worried him; he wondered what she was afraid of, with Klore out in Rochester.

The second time he caught the look on her face, he asked her flatly, "What's bothering you, Molly?"

And she said, "What would be bothering me?"

"I don't know," he said.

She brought up a smile for him.

"You hadn't ought to talk till you've had breakfast."

He looked at her awhile, till the bright color came up to her cheeks, and she busied herself with the dishes on the table. She was wearing a bright pink gingham with short sleeves and a low neck, and she needed color to set it off.

"Ain't you going to get harness for your team?"

"Yeanh," he said, buttoning his shirt. "Sol knows a man. I'll take them round with him."

"I like them," she said. "I like the black one with his big white nose."

"He's a good horse," Dan nodded. "But he's got an awful thin hide. I'd ought to have some hemlock syrup to rub his shoulders with till he gets hardened up."

"I'll make some to-day," she said.

His mind full of the team, he ate his breakfast quickly.

"When will you commence hauling up to Goldbrook?" Molly asked.

"First of the week, I expect. There ought to be good snow then."

The team went well. As soon as he had seen them making friends in the shed off the fair grounds, Dan had said to Molly, "I could take them just as they be and win a prize in a ploughing match." He could believe it himself, now, watching them walk. Their stride was so well matched that they kept step as a natural thing. They would, he felt sure, turn in two miles better than the bays in their trick on the towline, for all the others appeared to move faster.

The bays were ahead now, drawing Solomon's sleigh, and on the down grades they broke into a smart trot and drew away from Dan. But on the up grades the long, even-tracking stride of the big team caught up with them, and, looking round, Solomon would see their noses close to the tail of his sleigh.

They pulled without strain, though they were hauling by far the heavier load, close to two tons; they gave no evidence of the weight at all in their even stride; only the puckers in their haunches showed deep. Dan did not need to hold the lines. After the first mile he kept his hands inside his coat; and Solomon, watching them over his shoulder, called back, "See them keep a sight on where they're going. After a couple of trips you won't hardly need to be on the sled."

The little man had the horse blankets round his knees, and he wore a horsehide coat with the high collar turned up. Even when he turned round, all Dan could see of him was his thin nose, red as a strawberry, poked between the edges of the collar, with a white patch of frost under it, and his protuberant blue eyes, water-dimmed with cold.

Crouching behind the barrier of boxes and barrels he had constructed round his seat, Dan had nothing to do but watch the sky and the woods. The scrunch of the travois runners on the snow, the insistent, light jingle of the trace chains, the squeak as the bobs tracked round a turn, merged into an unheard monotone. As even as their stride, the breaths of the team spouted in four puffs ahead and whitened on their withers.

The road led them past farms, at first, and then into the woods round the base of Deerfield Hill. At times they tracked over corduroy stretches. And once they crossed a small brook on a high narrow bridge, from which the woods had drawn back, so that on a dark night it would almost be invisible.

It was slow going, and on windy days, with the temperature way down, Dan let the team drive themselves, and made it his business to keep warm. He had nothing to do but think of the warm comfortable evenings in the Sarsey Sal. Three nights a week he stayed in the camps, hauling out from Utica three days and three days hauling in. But three nights he spent aboard the boat and he had his Sundays off.

Those were pleasant evenings: he and Molly, sitting together in the cabin of the old boat, the fire roaring till the draft holes and the belly of the firebox reddened, the kettle purring on the stove and spouting its stream of steam. Behind them on its shelf, the clock ticked the minutes out and beat the hours rapidly.

Molly had fixed over the cabin until it seemed like a different place. It had taken on a clean, healthy smell; there was no dust. She had made new curtains for the sleeping cuddy, heavy green ones that kept out the light in the morning, so that he never woke till she had his breakfast ready.

Now and then Mrs. Gurget breezed in with Sol to pass an evening, or they went to the Nancy. More often they were alone, and then Dan sat in a sort of comfortable daze, listening to her voice and watching her; wondering in a vague way where they would be next winter. He never thought of that long; this winter was enough for him.

Once in a while they went out to dinner with Mrs. Gurget and Sol, to eat at Baggs's or some other place; and on Sundays they went to church —to different churches, for Molly liked the variety. She was interested in the clothes of the women; but she had real devoutness, and Dan enjoyed seeing her kneel beside him. He liked it also when people turned to look at her, to catch a friendly smile from an older woman; to listen to the sermon and to take the benediction, solemnly and seriously, with Molly; and then to walk out into the fresh air with the other people and slowly to take their way back to the Sarsey Sal, squatting low and ungainly beside the dock with the ice round about her and the snow drifted up toward the outer windows; to go aboard and start the fire in the stove, while Molly pinned an apron over her Sunday dress; to tend his horses in the barn and chat with the stableman on feeds and liniments and the price of oats in the dim, musty-smelling shadows by the hay chutes; to go inside the cabin and take off his coat and sit at ease, smelling the cooking food and listening to Molly dressing the sermon with observations on millinery. Lazy, comfortable days were Sundays, between the long drives up to the lumber camps in Goldbrook; something to look back at. . . .

In the lumber camp he and Solomon unloaded their sleighs at the storehouse and took their teams into the long log barns. Here in the woods the snow hardly melted during the days. The road leading in was feet about the earth, packed hard on its double tracks; and the snow had drifted up against the buildings till the windows on the northern walls had tunnels dug down to them to let the light in.

The stable had a line of long single stalls running down one side, and a space at the end for hay. It was dark inside, and the unfrozen earth just under the board beds of the stalls smelt fresh and strong. At night, with the teams all in, it was as warm as the bunk house, and the air was thick with steam, choking with the smell of sweat and sharp ammonia. It braced Dan like a tonic after the long cold ride.

Then he and Solomon sat in the cookhouse, with their backs to the great stove, where the cook worked in an undershirt and apron, his blacksmith's arms hot and red from baking, his quick stiff fingers white with flour. He could bake twenty pies at a time in the great oven; he had eighty men to feed all at once. It was a man's job. Yet all the time he gave them gossip over his shoulder and asked for news of Utica. And when the talk went low he told them how he lost his foot on a steamboat, when a connecting rod broke in a race down the Hudson; and how he had a wooden foot made in its place and took to cooking.

"I couldn't keep away from a fire. Feeding pies to jacks is just the same as raising steam in a boiler. It's harder work on your arms, but not so hard on the foot."

It clacked and banged on the planks as he moved back and forth.

"I had it carved in the shape of a shoe," he said. "So I only have to get one real shoe made to a time. And it don't squeak, nor does it need a shine—only once a year."

He pulled his moustache away from his mouth, leaving the end white with flour.

The men came in and lined at the tables, and the cook's helpers put the food in front of them. They did not talk as they ate; they were too tired. Now and then the cook made a snatch at conversation with Dan and Solomon in an effort at hospitality. After the meal he cleaned his skillets and pans, leaving the dishes to his helpers. The men went to sleep in the bunk house early, and Dan and Solomon went after them. A single lantern burned by the door, making a feeble glimmer in the long room with its double rack of bunks. Beyond it in the shadows the deep steady breathing and heavy snores mingled with a hum and drone like twelve-foot band saws ripping virgin pine. It was a heavy sound, beating upon Dan's ears, and it brought into his mind, each night he spent there, the quiet of the cabin on the Sarsey Sal. He turned in his sleep on the narrow mattress and fought the wall. Or he lay awake for a time, his eyes on the small square window at the far end, where the moonlight cut a slice through the darkness and showed a glimmer on the snow outside. Once he heard wolves running.

Then, next day when the lumbermen were at work in the woods once more, the cook made them up lunches and he and Solomon harnessed their teams and took the road back. All the long ride, his mind went ahead to the Sarsey Sal, where Molly would be getting his supper when he arrived, and where he would have his hours of ease, to stretch the stiffness from his back, to eat hot food that made him sleepy just to eat it; to have the deep quiet night of sleep.

The days and weeks went by like a dream; and he felt lazily contented. The routine absorbed his consciousness, with the nights on the boat and Sundays to keep track of and remember. Molly, in a print dress and fresh apron, at the cabin door to greet him and and look him over with her frank blue eyes. Sometimes she came out along the road on fine days to meet him, when he could be expected early; and they rode into the city together. The smoke rose up against the gathering darkness like a shelter from the snow. Molly, Sunday mornings combing her light brown hair in front of the mirror, with the sun against it, glowing on her shoulders; and he sitting there looking at her, pulling at his pipe now and then, taking pride in her while she made talk.

It snowed heavily in February; there were four feet on the level in the open valley; and in the woods, if a man jumped from his snowshoes, he went in up to his neck. The snow was piled higher than Molly's head along the sidewalks. The city went about its daily life with a curious hemmed-in feeling in the air.

Few minstrel shows traveled during the cold months. What entertainments there were had been got up by church workers. Generally they were given for special audiences. But even so Dan did not care to go to them, for they were apt to come on Saturday nights, and he was tired after his day on the sleigh. He preferred to sit in the Sarsey Sal, to listen to what Molly would tell him of her doings. Her accounts of marketing, of shopping for dress goods, of a hardware sale, of a walk in the streets, never seemed to him to be the same. It was enough to hear her voice.

When he talked, himself, he talked about the team.

"They're good, Molly. They couldn't be better-matched if they was own brothers."

"Yes," she would say, with her eyes on the cap she was crocheting.

"I'd like to see 'em working on a plough."

His eyes were fixed on the windows with a far-away glance when Molly looked up at him. She had seen him so more often lately. It was the time of year.

"I'll be glad when the canal opens," she said. "I can't hardly stand waiting for spring."

"Yeanh. Men'll be going over their seed potatoes soon."

They were silent.

"What've you been doing?" he asked.

"I've been working on a rug," she said, with a sudden lifting of her head. He caught the strain in her voice. "I got some odd pieces yesterday."

She got up to show them to him.

"They're pretty," he said, scraping the bowl of his pipe.

"Me and Mrs. Gurget went after some red flannel in the afternoon. We didn't get any. She couldn't find none with a yard and a half in a piece, and she needs all of it in a petticoat."

"Yeanh."

"Eggs have dropped two cents," she said.

"Pullets commencing to lay," he said. "I thought they'd be coming in about now."

They talked on, in odd sentences, Dan watching her out of the corner of his eye, and she him. When their glances met, they dropped them. She did not seem natural to him; ever since the fair she had acted queer. It was the wear of the winter, perhaps.

"What's the matter with you, Molly?" he asked, suddenly, when their silence had left the tick of the clock to itself for several minutes. His voice sounded harsh to his own ears.

She looked up swiftly, her eyes shining as he had never seen them. He thought she was going to cry; he hadn't meant to speak so roughly. He stared out of the window, waiting for her answer.

Suddenly she forced a laugh.

"There's nothing the matter with me. Is there?"

He did not look at her, for his ears had noticed the catch in her voice.

"Well," he said heavily, "I guess I'd ought to fix the team for the night."

He got up, put on his hat, and went out. On deck he paused, wondering to himself. Then he glanced in the windows. Between the curtains he could see her. She had broken down, crying. He wondered whether he should go back; then he decided she would not want him to see her. He grunted and went to the barn.

There he fussed with the team for a few minutes, slapping their bellies after he had taken up the blanket straps, and grinning when they humped themselves.

"Only a month and a half," he said to them, "and you'll be sweating on the towpath."

When he came out of the barn, he paused, glanced at the Sarsey Sal, and then went swiftly along the basin until he came to the Nancy. Mrs. Gurget told him cheerfully to come in. She was sitting in a rocking-chair, with her feet against the stove, her red hair in a thick braid round her head. She was alone.

"Hullo," she said. "Come in, Dan. Where's Molly?"

Dan took off his hat and sat down.

"She's on the Sarsey Sal."

Mrs. Gurget rocked jerkily back and forth. After a while she remarked: "Sol's gone up to Bentley's for a snort to soak his nose in.

"What's the trouble?" she asked.

"I don't know," Dan said. "Molly seems to act queer. She's crying now, to beat all. And there ain't anything to cry about I can see."

Mrs. Gurget watched her toes as she rocked. Then she said, "Reach me that pie on the table, Dan."

There was one piece left, and she held the knife over it with a firm hand.

"Have a piece?" she asked.

"No."

She sighed, picked it up deftly in her fingers, and began to nibble it. "I always did like cold pie," she remarked.

She watched her toes over the piece of pie as she rocked.

Dan said, "She's been queer off and on since she was to the fair. When I ask her what's the trouble, she don't say nothing."

Mrs. Gurget nodded her head and munched.

"I noticed that, Dan. I'll tell you. She had her fortune told there by a gypsy. It give her a turn, I think."

"She ain't been singing lately," said Dan.

"Don't get worried," said Mrs. Gurget, smiling at him and running her tongue along her lips. "She's young, and young gals is notional."

"What did the gypsy tell her?" Dan asked.

"She won't say. I've tried to edge it out of her a lot of times when she'd be aboard here to spend the day. She won't tell. I've told her all such ideas gypsies has is untrue nonsense. But she'll just set there, and then after a while she'll perk and laugh."

"I've noticed it," Dan nodded gloomily.

Mrs. Gurget studied him with a kind light in her eyes.

"Don't you worry, Dan. Gals is notional at times. There ain't anything you can do if she's getting notional. I'll bet when you go back you'll find her all perked up. She'll have rinsed herself all out."

Mrs. Gurget put the last of the pie into her mouth, munched it deliberately, swallowed it down. She sighed and licked each thumb.

"How long've you and Molly been living together?" she asked.

Dan reckoned up: "Four months."

Mrs. Gurget pulled her shawl up round her neck.

"That's just about time to get to know each other, ain't it?"

"Lord!" said Dan. "I know her all I need to know her. She's a good gal."

"Yes," said Mrs. Gurget. "I think she is."

Dan felt comforted. Then, mulling on her words, he was startled.

"You don't think there's another man she's took a notion to?"

Mrs. Gurget dodged the question momentarily.

"The gypsy's talk upset her, didn't it?"

"Seems so," Dan admitted.

Mrs. Gurget nodded.

"All gypsies has two lines of talk," she said. "If it's a gal they're a-reading for, they talk about a journey and sickness, or about a dark and a light man. You're light. I'll bet she's worrying about you. She'd ought to know better, but in the winter little odd notions get growing. But she's good to you, ain't she?"

"You ain't any idea," said Dan, earnestly. He was thinking: a dark man or a light man—a journey and sickness—a dark man and a light man. "You're light," Mrs. Gurget had said. Maybe he was. And Jotham Klore was the dark man.

"Well," said Mrs. Gurget, "you don't need to be worrying about anybody else only you two. Molly wouldn't hold to but one at a time. Should she change her mind, she'd leave like knocking a bung; all in one rap. Don't you worry, Dan. There ain't anything you can do."

"Do you think she'd want me to marry her?"

"Well . . ."

"I'd thought about it," Dan said.

"You can ask her," said Mrs. Gurget, "but I don't think it would help. And if you ask her, it's like saying—" the fat woman shied clear of her words. "Mostly there ain't anything wrong in not being married on the canal. As long as you're honest there ain't any real sense in it. It's different if you're going to get off the canal. Then you've got to act like other folks. But here living's just a working agreement, and if you want you can get a minister to lick the revenue stamp to seal it with; but it don't add a lot. And a gal's free to back out. Sometimes it makes it hard for her, but if she wants it that way, it ain't any bother of yours. Unless you want to take her off'n the canal. Be you going to stick at boating, Dan?"

"Yeanh," he said.

"Then don't you worry, Dan. I'll bet when you get back to the Sarsey Sal you'll find Molly's all chippered up."

The fat woman drew in her breath. Her deep bosom arched, and a little locket hanging there caught the light.

"I used to be young and pretty like her, and have notions," she said. Her fat fingers opened the locket and she turned it to the light.

Dan glanced at a crude pencil drawing that looked as if it had been taken from a lithograph. It was the head of a very pretty girl on a slim neck, with a gay upward curve to the chin. The fat woman chuckled somewhere deep down in herself.

"Ever see the face afore?"

"No," he said.

"Well," said Mrs. Gurget, "that's me. I was a notional gal and I turned down Sol, who wanted to marry me—such a wizzen of a man, I thought. I went West with another. But when I came back on the canal, looking like this, he was looking for a cook, and I took the job. Sometimes he asks what's in the locket and then I put him off and say he'd better not know, and he pesters, and I laugh. And nighttimes he talks about Nancy when he's sleeping. It knocked him bad to lose her."

Suddenly she laughed, and her voice rang true.

"It's funny my telling you, Dan," she said. "I never told anybody else but you, but you won't tell anybody. Sol's asked me to marry him; but I said no. It wouldn't be fair to him now; and there ain't any sense. We both have a good time, living along."

She laughed again, leaned over, and kissed him.

"Run on back, Dan. You'll find Molly's chippered up expecting you."

The light still burned in the cabin of the Sarsey Sal. Molly was not there, but when he opened the door she came out of the cuddy in her night clothes. He looked at her covertly; her face was fresh and clear again, and she smiled, and her eyes were tender as he had seen them when he first came aboard his boat. By secret consent, neither said a word, but when Dan sat down Molly sat on his lap, her feet curled up on his knees. He took them in his hand to keep them warm.

It was dead still, a quiet night. They kept silent with the march of the clock in their ears, the breathing of the kettle. Her hair, braided for bed, hung over her shoulder and swung back and forth against his waistcoat as she breathed; and he felt each touch against his heart.

Monday Sol and Dan pulled out from the city under a leaden sky. The low-hanging city smoke behind them looked white. Now and then the horses snorted and shivered their withers as they walked. The air was breathless, and Dan felt the skin on his neck tingling.

"It smells like a blizzard coming," Solomon said. And Dan agreed.

Before they reached the woods, snow began to fall; here and there a flake, drifting straight down. When one lit on his cheek, though the day was not cold, a chill touched him.

Behind them the great Mohawk valley dipped, then mounted to the sombre arch of the sky. There were no clouds, but an even darkening, out of which the flakes stole downward. The snow on the ground shone with a miasmic pallor. The runners of the bobs scraped on the snow with a hollow sound, and the clink of the trace chains was small, dull, and struck the air a close note that died instantly. There was no echo.

After his one remark, Solomon hunched down inside his coat and said nothing. For all the stillness, it required effort to speak; the air was heavy in the lungs, and words clung to the teeth. To try to make the voice carry, a man had to shout his words, as though he were battering a wall with them. His only refuge was inside himself.

A week had gone by for Dan since his talk with the fat woman, and the quiet night with Molly. The happy life had come back to them. But now, with the darkness closing in, he remembered Mrs. Gurget's words—a light man and a dark man. Untrue nonsense. But the words revolved in his mind, and he saw himself and Jotham Klore. Even at the beginning he had seen Jotham Klore; even the old peddler who had brought him down to the canal had warned him against the man. A big bully, in his last fight he had licked the Buffalo man, they had heard; he was cock on the canal. . . . A light man and a dark, and Molly in between. . . .

When the wind came, it came stealthily. A cold breath from the north, unnoticeable except for the drift of the snowflakes. Now and then they lifted just before they came to earth, and drifted southward a few feet before settling down.

So slowly did the wind take hold that before it found its strength the sleighs had entered the woods, tiny figures in the stillness, crawling along the winding track, with the snow feeling its way through the branches to light upon them. Gradually the loads whitened with a thin powder. The big flakes were thinning out.

With the new snow, the gleam went out of the ground; a dullness enveloped the world. Space closed in, distance became an illusion. Time was measured by the steady stride of the horses, the faint sound of trace chains clinking. Light spread through the flakes and thinned and died. Dan traced patterns in the falling snow. The cold crept closer.

As the wind grew, there came a sigh out of the trees. When they passed spruce clumps, Dan saw the upper branches lifting and falling in a monotonous ritualistic rhythm. Down on the road they could not feel it. They would hardly have known it was storming, had it not been for the mounting snow in the tracks. It lay soft and thick and powdery.

An hour passed. Then, with no warning, the sound of their passage was snuffed out. A great hand rocked the trees; the snow smothered the sound of the runners; the mounting roar of the wind, so gradual, had taken possession.

When they came into the first long clearing, the drive of the gale struck them. The tails of the horses before Dan whipped back straight at him like flung spears; it seemed that he could see the skin on their quarters pulled tight; their heads dropped as if they had been malleted. For a second they stopped, then lunged on the collars and fought ahead. The snow drove on them so fast that Dan could not say how it blew, up or down; there was a thick mist between him and the trees; and he felt the cold cutting past his coat into his stomach.

He had a glimpse of a group of ancient pines on the hill on his left. Their old stalwart trunks were bending; their great branches stretched southward, as if they had turned their backs to the wind.

Then once more the forest, and the roar of wind in the trees, and a lightening of the pressure on his breath. The teams picked up pace and forged ahead, eager for the camp. The snow deepened. The horses had to lift their feet.

Hour by hour, with no knowledge of the time. It was early afternoon when they entered the camp and saw dim lights behind the snow. Both teams were white with frost and snow; the sleighs were coated. Dan was so stiff he could hardly fight to his feet; he felt as if he must break to do it. Gradually he thawed in the kitchen; then went out again to rub his team down. Solomon sat by the fire, stretching out his hands as if he begged a precious thing, and the cook clogged back and forth with his wooden foot, making great kettles of coffee, for the men would be coming in early. "This ain't going to stop," he said. "It's got a tail hold on all the winds in time, and it's out to travel somewhere."

Wind gripped the roof of the cookhouse and shook it. It found the doors and beat upon them till they groaned like living things. When a man lifted the latch to open them, they were snatched from his hand and cracked against the wall so that a murmur broke out on the shelves of kettles. The man came in hunched over and fought the door to shut it. He was white over, though his red face sweated.

"Palery's hurt," he shouted to them, and he shook his fists, as if he thought they were not listening to him. "Him and Franks was cutting a four-foot spruce," he cried, "when the wind took hold afore they was more than half through. It buck-jumped right across his legs, right here." He smashed his fists across the front of his thighs. "He's a mess!" he shouted. "Can't you hear me? He's just a mess. They're fetching him in."

Six men broke through the door, carrying a man on a stretcher of poles and coats and put him on the table and looked at him and drank coffee. He was unconscious, his face a dead white like rotten snow. The manager came in ahead of more men. He looked him over.

"Don't take his pants off," cried a man shrilly. "Don't take 'em off, for God's sake."

The manager felt of the man's legs. "No use," he said. "He ain't bleeding, but we can't do anything. He'll have to see a doctor."

"You couldn't get him down through this," the cook said, passing out sugar.

"We've got no team knows the road enough," the manager said. "A man couldn't see."

He forced whiskey into the man's mouth. After a while they brought him to, and he screamed at them.

The manager turned to Dan. "Could your team make it?" he asked. "They know the way."

"They've had a hard haul," Dan said.

"They'll be going light."

"He'd freeze," said a man.

"We can rig him a tent back of some boards and put lanterns under the blankets."

Dan hesitated. His team was tired. The track was sheltered in the woods. If the snow was not drifted too high in the clearings, they might make it. He nodded. The black would smell out the track.

"One other man, to help in a drift," he said.

"I'll go," said Franks. "I was with him—I'll go."

He was a huge fellow, smooth-shaven, with a low forehead and dark sunken eyes that gleamed.

"All right," said Dan.

The hurt man heard them, for he began to curse them and beg them to let him stay.

In the barn, Dan harnessed his horses, talking to them in a low voice. The black nuzzled him inquiringly, but the big brown merely stared at the wall and shook the harness down comfortably. They had put on flesh since Dan had bought them.

"They're fine horses," said the manager. "I'd like them here."

At the entrance to the stable the black snorted, but the brown pushed out uncompromisingly, walking to the sleigh.

"Second link!" Dan shouted to the men who hitched them.

Palery had been loaded aboard under blankets. The lanterns under them were bringing out the smell of horses. Dan squatted down in the lea with the big man Franks at his side. "Ged-dup!" he shouted.

The team looked round, then lunged into the darkness, walking slow. At the edge of the woods they reared slightly to break the drift. Behind, the camp was swallowed from sight. Then they entered the woods and the wind passed over their heads, shaking the trees on either side, where branches shrieked as they fought against each other. There was a wild tumult in the storm, now, a hideous uplifting of voices as it beat the woods, and the old great pines groaned in the darkness. Only the road had comparative quiet, running under the uproar, like a tunnel of silence.

Once inside, the team broke into a trot before Dan's urging. He had never trotted them before, but he knew they must make their best speed to get into the city before the deepening snow stopped them altogether. Once stopped, there was no exit. The road would be a coffin and the wailing trees the mourners.

Once in a while, during the first hour, when the wind died down to let them listen, they could hear the hurt man jabber and shout. At first Dan feared he might throw the blankets off; but when he touched the blankets to see how the man was, Franks caught his arm in a great hand and shouted close to his ear.

"Leave him be! He's tied."

There was a gleam in the big man's eyes, a green glow in the dark, like an animal's, as he crouched beside Dan. Now and again he would lift his face at the wind and shake his fist. But the cold, striking his throat, would make him duck down again.

The rumps of the horses were snow-white. The deepening snow had slowed them to a walk, but they made good time. The cold came under the howl of the wind to freeze the sweat as it formed.

At the first clearing they stopped. Then they went ahead slowly. The snow was over their bellies and they gathered their hind legs up under them until their haunches sat on the snow, and then jumped like rabbits. Between each thrust, they stopped again, panting in racking gasps, and lowered their noses, as if they smelled for the track. Then they jumped again. Once in a while they seemed to dispute a turn and stood with their heads close together. When they moved next, they would lean against the snow at their chests and push their feet forward to select the track.

It took them fifteen minutes to buck the clearing of a hundred yards. In the shelter of the woods Dan stopped them and let them breathe a minute before he walked them ahead.

The feeling of night came over them with added cold, but no darkening beyond the snow. The power of sight had been taken from them; Dan and Franks glued their eyes to the rumps of the horses and trusted to them. The lines were frozen in Dan's mitten; the lids of his eyes had stiffened. He had to rub them to keep them open. But his companion sat glaring ahead from his sunken eyes, and now and then he appeared to laugh at the howling wind and the wild thrash of the trees.

The third clearing they were barely able to win through, and the horses shook and staggered as they burst into the shelter of the woods. From here each step was a task. Gouts of snow were snapped from the branches, building the road up in lumps, and the sleigh bucked over them in jerks and shunted from side to side.

They came to the edge of a ravine, and Dan shouted suddenly, "There's a bridge!"

But the fury of the storm was in the horses. They did not stop. The sleigh lurched drunkenly into the open, slipped sideways. Franks leaped to the far side and caught the tail end in his hands and drew on it with a gigantic heave; and then the team found the corduroy under their shoes and stamped as they crossed it. Franks leaped on again, his eyes gleaming, laughing and throwing his arms at the storm. He reached under the blankets and felt beside the hurt man and drew out a huge dinner bell which he swung back and forth over his head. The wind took the sound as it was born, but they could think of it rushing miles away across the valley. The team heard it, and pricked their ears.

"Three miles!" shouted Dan.

They struggled downhill through the drifts into the valley. On and on; it took an hour or more for each of those last three miles. But the team were roused and battled the snow with a steady strength. . . .

Windows lighted with warmth blossomed out of the snow beside them. In the street they heard the clamor of their bell; and the team shuddered and stopped and tried to shake themselves. Dan wrenched the lines apart in his hands and felt his mouth crack as he grinned at the bald face looking round and the great head of the brown stretched forward, waiting to be driven. Franks grabbed his arm in a monstrous mitten and rang his bell at the horses, and shouted in his ears, "The dirty sons of bitches, look at them stand there!" and he burst out crying, letting the tears freeze on his cheeks.

They drove to a doctor's and carried the man in. He was still alive.

"Come and get a drink," cried Franks, "on me, on the camp."

"I got to go home," said Dan. "I've got to mind the team."

They shook hands, and, still ringing his bell, Franks went lurching through the snow to Bentley's to get drunk. But no liquor could make him drunk now.

Dan drove the team to Butterfield's barn. He turned in by the Sarsey Sal and saw a faint light burning in the cabin windows. He unhitched the horses and led them to the barn and rubbed them down. He felt weak and staggery, and they were spent.

He pushed the cabin door open. The lamp had been turned low.

"Molly," he called.

He was weaving on his feet when she came out of the cuddy, but a light of achievement burned in his face. She stood looking at him, pale in her nightdress, feeling suddenly small before him. He had acquired stature.

Her eyes lighted.

"Dan!"

He sat down heavily, too tired to take off his clothes.

"Where'd you come from?"

He grinned, and said stiffly, "Goldbrook. There was a man had his legs broke. I brought him down with a man called Franks. I think he's crazy." She stood off a little way. Then she said, as if to herself, "It ain't possible."

Both of them listened to the wind, the menacing whisper of the snow on the frosted windowpanes audible in lulls of the wind. He looked at her seriously.

"If you'd see the horses now, you wouldn't think it was possible. It's a wonder they weren't killed. They're a team, Molly. They're the only team I know could have done it."

He let his head back with an infinite satisfaction and went to sleep. She stood looking down at him, pride suffusing her, as a mother might feel who sees her son grown up.

A knock sounded on the door, and Mrs. Gurget burst in.

"He's here!" she cried as she saw Dan. "A man came around from Bentley's to tell me. A man came in busting for drink a while back saying they'd come down through the blizzard. Folks wouldn't believe him till one of them went to the doctor. They can't hardly believe it now. My land! There must be twenty of them out there looking at them horses, late as it is."

She shed her wraps right and left.

"How is he?" she asked, her hearty voice sinking to a whisper.

Molly said, "He just come in. He went right to sleep there."

Mrs. Gurget stepped forward, put her hand on his forehead.

"I don't want to advise, dearie, but I'd get some blankets out and heat 'em and take his clothes off and wrap him up and feed him hot tea. And if you don't do it I'll do it myself."

Molly nodded, "It's the best."

They worked over him quickly, the fat woman puffing loudly through her broad nostrils. He only half woke to take a cup of tea, grinning at them foolishly.

"Now he's sweating you'd better put him to bed, dearie. He's all right— only played out. I'll stay with you."

They sat together before the stove.

"They must be a great team," said Mrs. Gurget. "It was a fine thing bringing that feller down, poor man. They say he'll live, but I don't doubt he'll be a cripple."

Molly nodded.

"He's a good boy, dearie," said Mrs. Gurget, after a time. "Don't you love him?"

Molly nodded again.

"You were a lucky gal," said Mrs. Gurget. "I love him myself."

Molly said a strange thing.

"I know how you mean."

The fat woman looked at her speculatively. "Such a pretty," she said to herself. Then she nodded. "Dan's a good boy."

"Yeanh," said Molly. "He's an awful good boy. Sometimes I think he don't know what he wants. He just sits there looking out the window seeing things to himself. He's so good-looking. The big shoulders and neck and them blue eyes of his'n. It scares me sometimes." She folded her arms round her knees and leaned her head back as if she were tired. The fat woman breathed hard.

"You started it," she said accusingly.

"I played up to him," Molly said. "I let it catch me."

"What're you going to do now?"

"I don't know. I love him. Honest, I do. If he wants me to stick, I will. It's only fair now. But I couldn't stand it off'n the canal."

The fat woman's broad face worked into a smile.

"Poor pretty," she said. "I don't blame you. When did you find out?"

"That gypsy told me partly. She didn't know very good herself, I think. I'd been wondering afore."

"That's how it was?" The fat woman mused. Then she sighed.

Molly spoke softly.

"He was so big and so nice. Right away I liked him. He didn't seem to know nothing, and I wanted to see him take hold. I thought I could make him."

"It's what you've got to do now. He don't know where he's standing," said the fat woman.

Molly nodded.

"He's thinking what he wants to do. When he knows, he'll do it."

"If he stays here on the canal, you've got to stay with him," said the fat woman grimly.

"I couldn't go with him anywheres else."

"If he sticks, he'll have to fight Klore."

Molly nodded.

"It'll be a big one. Dan's awful strong."

"Right now he'd want to dodge it," Molly said.

"Not now," said the fat woman. "He's commenced to wake up. I could see it on him sleeping there."

"If he fights Klore, he'll lick him."

"It would be a good job," said the fat woman.

Molly stared at the clock striking three. At times she felt as if she expected to see the horse start galloping.

"I tried to make him have a good winter," she said.

Mrs. Gurget patted her hand. "He's had it, dearie."

She cleared her throat.

"We've got our own lives we're born with," she observed. "Once in a while we reach outside of it, but there's only something that'll fit. It ain't in us really to pick and choose like men. When it comes to the finish afterwards, you've got to do the best you can with it. I've seen women fixed like that."

Molly drew in her breath.

"I do really love him."

"I know it," said the fat woman.

Toward the end of the month they began to get rains from the southeast and the roads became bad. Dan and Solomon traveled early every morning to take advantage of the frost. A thinly veiled excitement began to show in people's faces, and one morning the fat woman came bursting in to show Molly some cotton crêpe she had just bought for summer nightgowns.

That day, coming down from the camps, Solomon, who was leading, stopped the bays until Dan had caught up. Close beside them in a sugar bush a man was tapping maple trees and hanging buckets out.

"Look," said Solomon, pointing the stem of his clay pipe and loosing a ring of smoke.

Mist was hovering all along the riverbed, and it wavered with a delicate lifting motion. While they sat there with the red sunset glow on their faces, —Dan watching the mist, not knowing what to see, for he had not lived by a river,—the horses, all four of them, suddenly pricked their ears.

"I thought so," Solomon said, a tremble in his voice; and he took off his hat and wiped his high bald head with his red handkerchief. "Now look at it, Dan."

Gradually a motion became apparent in the mist, a pulling away up-stream. As the dusk settled and the violet shadows came into the valley with grey darkness on their heels, the mist stole off over the river, faster and faster, until they saw the last of it, a single streamer, vanishing.

The tapping of a man's hammer in the sugar bush ceased. He came out to the road.

"If it goes up three nights," Solomon said, "we'll have spring."

The man nodded.

That night Dan found a new excitement in Molly, a shine new in her eyes, in the place of the broodiness he had seen there all winter.

When they crossed the river in the morning on their way into the woods, they heard the water talking under the ice. Just below the bridge, where the wind had swept snow clear, they saw bubbles passing under.

The next afternoon they stopped again on the edge of the sugar bush. The farmer was collecting buckets with his two boys. They had worn hard trails in the snow going from tree to tree, and a small path came out to the road, from where they could see the valley. Now the man walked out, and he had to step over the top rail of the bordering snake fence.

"The snow's melting underneath," he said, and he sat down on Solomon's sleigh and took a chew.

"Did the mist go up again last night?" Solomon asked.

"Yeanh," said the man.

"Two nights," said Solomon.

"I've seen it lack the third in March many a year," the man said. "I ain't expecting it now."

"Let's wait and see," Solomon said.

Dan nodded.

The horses shook themselves with a jingling of traces, and the bald-faced black pawed at the snow and snuffed up deep breaths.

From where they sat the men could see the valley spread out below them, the city small and flat in the perspective, and the farmhouses dots upon the grey snow. The farmer licked his thumb and rubbed the edges of his nostrils and drew deep breaths.

"There's a sour smell to the snow."

"I'd noticed it already," Solomon said. "The tracks are running wild all through the woods."

"The river's been talkin' all day."

A deep silence brooded.

"I had my cows in the barnyard this morning," the man observed. "My wife'll turn them out soon for a spell."

Even as he spoke, out of sight beyond the woods on the right they heard a cowbell ringing. The sound brought a lump into Dan's chest and he stared as if he would pierce the trees to see the spotted figures.

Beyond the river the railroad tracks ran straight in a narrow black band. Along it a train swooped, the engine a bright glitter of blue and silver, spouting a trail of smoke. As it passed, it gave a long whistle, then two short; and the sound crept up to the two boaters until it seemed to lie at the feet of the horses. In all the scene the train was the only moving thing. The farmer pointed it out and gave a long spit of brown down the road toward the valley.

"They're going to kill the canal."

The little man snorted.

"Them dinkey wagons," he said.

"They make money in the winter," the farmer said. "In summer now they can cut their rates for competition. They go fast."

"Cripus!" said Solomon. "Let 'em try."

But it came to Dan that the farmer might be right. And the farmer said, "People like things to come quick. Mail, and freight, and money. It saves a bother of thinking."

As the sun set, the same soft colors they had seen before were evolved on the hills, shades of vermilion, and violet, and cobalt blue. A cloud of rolling masses of grey reared up in the south, with a warm look of rain in the depths of it. Far down on a farm, dull sappy chunks of sound broke out; a man was splitting firewood. His axe glittered in front of the shed, flashing a speck of gold.

All at once, in the snow round them, they heard a pulse begin to beat, a faint slow ticking, as if a clock, dusty and forgotten in an attic, had suddenly begun to run. Without warning a blotch of gold broke out in an open space beside the road, and spread upon the snow and began to move toward the river.

They stared at it unbelieving.

"I never knowed a brook ran there," Solomon said. "I'd never guessed it."

"Yeanh," said the farmer. "There's good fishing into it. My boy caught a trout weighing better than a pound last May."

Suddenly he pointed, his arm rigid.

"Look!"

The mist was being born upon the river. It spread rapidly. Feelers of it began to creep up from the valley, winding in and out among the balsams, bringing the perfume of the trees with it.

For a breath they watched it.

"It's moving up," Solomon said. "Look, you can see it down there against them elms."

"Yeanh," said the farmer.

He got to his feet.

"I've got to be getting back. I expect a heifer due tonight. She might be coming in early."

He went back into the sugar bush, calling his boys.

Dan and Solomon still lingered. "It's spring," the little man said. Each began to see in his mind's eye the canal coming to life, the long lines of boats moving east and west. The strokes of the axe sounded like the crack of whips. They heard a wail like a horn, and for an instant they were tense, looking for the boat. But it turned out to be a train of cars, running in from Albany, and the engine blew again on a flat whistle.

"Ged-dup," said Solomon.

The teams started on into the dusky valley. Both men felt the spring stirring, and the brook on their right went with them toward the river. They thought of the boats, and the sound of water, and Dan had a picture of the big teams pulling the Sarsey Sal, and Molly on deck in his old blue shirt, with the wind fingering her hair.

Then also he saw a picture of the farmer in the shadow of the barn, with his wife holding a lantern while he helped the heifer with his hands.

Word was given out from the weighlock next morning that the canal would open early the next week. In the basin a new life had entered the boats tied up. Men were oiling harness and going over their towlines foot by foot. A woman was putting a patch on a grey canvas pit-covering. A little man was painting his boat—a gay pink-salmon shade—while his wife looked on with a voluble friend and considered the color of the trim; and he brushed away with his hat over his eyes, his eyes furtively watching the docks for men who might guy him for his wife's artistic tastes.

On the Sarsey Sal, Molly gave Dan a letter from Butterfield. It ordered him to report to Rome as soon as the canal opened.

"It'll be good to get free," she said, her eyes dancing.

That evening she and Dan roamed here and there over the boat, trying the stable hatch and gazing at the heavy coil of the towline.

"I'll order feed to-morrow," he said.

"I wonder where we'll haul to first?" she said. "I'd like to go west again."

"We'd likely meet Klore out there, Molly."

She looked at him.

"We'll have to sometime," she said, her face brave.

He felt the spring growing in him.

"Yeanh."

He had beaten out the blizzard; he could take a chance at Klore.

He worked over the towline next morning.

A voice hailed him from the dock. He looked up to see a fat man in a dark suit and pot hat and high cowhide boots smoking a cigar.

"How be you?" asked the fat man.

"Good," said Dan. "How're you, Mr. Henderson?"

The Department of Justice man grinned.

"Fine. I'm back at work now. Say, I'd ought to thank you for fetching me out of that house to Denley. Spinning'd never have gone down that night."

"It's all right," said Dan, affably. At that time he could not help feeling a liking for the fat marshal. The sun was too warm in him.

"How'd you come to find me?"

Dan glanced down.

"A man I was hauling with figured Calash might be there," he said.

"I wish I'd knowed as much as you seem to."

"He just guessed," Dan said. "I didn't know he'd be there."

"I don't believe you did. But you're friendly for him, ain't you?"

Dan said nothing.

"I can see why," said the fat man. "But don't you get mixed up with him. I'm going to get him this time," he said grimly.

Then he smiled, taking his cigar out of his mouth to do it.

"I heard how you brought Palery down. It was a fine thing. I've been looking at your team. They must be extraordinary good ones."

"They be," said Dan.

"Well, good luck."

The fat man put his cigar back and waved his hand.

That night the Sarsey Sal began to groan. Now and then the ice cracked in the bed of the canal. Dan and Molly lay awake, listening, feeling the boat shift under them. Now and then the timbers squealed as she lifted.

"It's the water," Molly said. "They're letting it in, Dan."

Then there was quiet, until they began to hear a thin ripple washing the side of the old boat. They seemed to feel it themselves, a slow soothing touch, and their bodies relaxed, as if it were taking the winter from them.

On the planks over their heads a gentle sound increased to a whisper, a mutter, and they heard rain falling, loud drumming rain, grey rain washing the air.

Dan found Molly's hand in his.

"I wonder if Fortune'll be back in time," she said. . . .

But when they were eating breakfast in the early morning the old ex-preacher put his thin head through the door.

Molly jumped up with a cry of delight, and Dan pumped his hand. Fortune lifted his thin nose to the smell of the coffee.

"I guessed I'd get here before it got cold," he said. "I needed it. My luck's been bad at cards."

There was an affectionate pucker at the corners of his eyes as he looked at them.

"Bad at cards?" The fat woman's voice broke out beyond the door. "My land! I like to hear that. Mine's just dandy."

She bustled in, bringing a breath of spring air with her in the swirl of her skirts. Her laughter was gay and warm as the morning sunlight.

Solomon, in a new grey flannel shirt, stepped in behind her.

"I'm hauling for Rome in an hour," he said.

"So'm I," said Dan.

7

THE LAST HAUL

Open Canal

IT was a typical March sky; grey clouds on the rising edge of the valley to the south and east, with the sun breaking through in golden showers. There was a sweep of wind upon the hills, so fresh that it seemed to acquire visibility and color—a wind of silver in the morning.

It blew upon Dan and Molly on the stern of the Sarsey Sal, whipping her skirts toward him, until he felt them brushing his ankles. She had turned her shoulder to the wind; she had the sun and the wind in her hair; she had a warm light in her eyes, like the glow of the sun in the open sky; and the spring warmth brought the color to her cheeks, after winter's paleness.

The valley stretched westward under a still white carpet; but on the edges of the woods the balsam pitch had made the snow black; and they saw it black and old on the white feet of a hound trotting home after a night of chasing rabbits. It was old snow, dying, and it put its own peculiar sour smell on the wind; a tang like vinegar, urging the lungs to deeper breaths.

The valley had come to life overnight. The rain had swelled the brooks; they were bursting free on the slopes and eating out their channels to the river. They made bright gleams on the old snow; and when they reached the river ice they spread out eagerly in glittering pools.

As yet the river slept; but it was stirring. Where its course came close to the canal, they could hear it muttering, taking in sobbing breaths at the air holes, like an old man struggling to wake after a long night of sleep.

But the canal, in the midst of silent farms, led straight away westward with a blue darker than the skies. The boats had rushed to meet it that morning. At the weighlock they cleared as fast as the men could put them through; empty mostly, going after cargoes, of wood, of flour, or spring machinery. Some would leave Utica later in the day with loads. But the first boats traveled light on their first haul, as if their owners had sent them off merely to see them moving on the water.

They came behind the Sarsey Sal making a tumult in the valley; horns blowing when there was no need of horns, blown merely for the blowing; long wails that went ahead upon the wind to the far southern clouds to bring the rain; men and women laughing, jollying, red-faced after their warm breakfasts, turning their faces to the wind; children large-eyed, running in the tracks of the horses, shouting in the empty pits until the plank walls boomed. Some boats came out with bright new paint upon them, gleaming blues and yellows and colors more fantastic, nourished by the dark hours of winter and brought into the sun.

Even the horses partook of that first ungovernable flush of spirits, tossing their heads, bringing them down to snatch at the snow with vicious snaps of their brown teeth, wriggling their withers to settle the collars that later would bring sores. Solomon's old mules, opposite the stern of the Sarsey Sal, came along with nervous lifting feet. They had had an easy winter; they were fat as butter tubs; and they twirled their ears like three-year-olds. The little man walked behind them with a sprightly step, a wide, unmeaning grin on his thin mouth. Back on the Nancy, the fat woman in a flannel petticoat more red than her dyed hair cocked her head to listen to the blowing of the man behind, grinned, and put her own horn to her lips and mastered all sound in a wail that woke the hills. Her breast rebounded after the blast; she waved her fat arm over her head, brandishing the horn like Michael's sword, and blew again.

A flock of crows came flapping over the valley to see what had disturbed them. They lit in some poplars and watched the fat woman pass. She blew again on her horn, pointing it toward them, and they shrieked with pleasure, giving stiff-legged hops off the branches, swooping up, and turning over.

Up ahead, Fortune Friendly was walking behind the big team. They hauled on the boat as if they had done just that all their lives. They had started it easily with a handsome upward pull in the collars. The black kept looking round at first, to see what this odd wheelless vehicle might be. He pricked his ears to see Molly. But the brown kept his head forward. He had business to do. As Fortune had remarked, he took work the way a Quaker took religion.

The ex-preacher was glad to get back. His luck had held good for the first part of the winter, but with the new year had come a change for the worse. Eventually he had had to get a job on the docks—hard work. His cheeks were thin, a little hollow, as if he had had poor food, and the seat of his pants was worn through. Molly had been obliged to put a patch on them that morning. "A lucky thing," Mrs. Gurget said when she saw it. "It wouldn't have been polite for me to set here steering."

Sitting by the stove drinking coffee in the early morning, Fortune, with a blanket round his bare shanks, while Molly mended his trousers, had gossiped. He had seen Henderson a month before. The Department man had two deputies with him. A big man one of them was, with a down-South way of bringing out his words. You could tell him by his long light moustache. The other had a slight limp, and a bullet scar on his right temple. He slicked his hair down like a foreigner. "Regular pomatum by the smell of it," Fortune said; "but I'll bet it's lard with a drop of perfume thrown on after. Smells like violets."

Dan had gone out to get the team and uncoil the towline. The old ex-preacher had sat there smoking a pipe, his fine smooth-skinned face and twinkling eyes turned toward Molly. He had looked her over searchingly. She caught his gaze in glancing up when she stopped to bite off her thread.

"Did you have a good winter?" he asked.

"Yeanh."

"How was Dan?"

"He was good."

"Oh, I don't mean was he sick."

"Did you hear about him bringing that jack down through the blizzard, February?"

"No."

She told him.

"It was a fine thing to do," said Fortune. "There aren't many would have done it."

"No," she said, proudly.

The old man drew his ideas into himself for a minute. He sat there looking down at the blue socks on his feet. Molly thought he was handsome, with his white hair and red cheeks and black moustache.

After a while he raised his head.

"He's a good lad, Molly."

"Yeanh," she said with a smile.

"You've changed."

"Getting old already?"

"Don't nonsense," he said. "You're just as pretty. You will be."

"Fat?"

He looked at her again.

"Not a mite."

"No," she said.

"I'm like your pa," he said.

"That's what you always say when you been hungry."

"You've changed," he said. "He has, too."

She caught in her lower lip against her teeth.

"Oh, no, he still's keen after you. Not that way. He's catching on, that's all. He looks more like he knew what he was doing."

"Yeanh. He's been that way more since he come out through the blizzard."

"Molly, do you still love him like you did?"

Her stitches were careful, very neat.

"Did you have a good winter?" he asked when she did not answer.

"He was real good," she said in a low voice. "He was good to me, Fortune. He's a good boy."

His face was sober.

"Are you going to marry him?"

Her head lifted like a doe's and there was a sudden flight of amusement through her eyes.

"Gracious me! You ain't preaching!"

"No," he said, "I ain't preaching. I'm just asking."

"Why do you ask it?"

"I think he'll ask you to marry him."

"Land!" she said, and dropped her eyes.

"There ain't any hiding it in you," he muttered. "It isn't bright on you the way it was."

"No," she said, her eyes following her swift needle. "It ain't that I don't love him, Fortune. Only he's just a boy. He's handsome to see; I like to go out with him. But he don't talk. He's a farmer. He's close with money, not like—"

"No," said the ex-preacher.

"Maybe when we get to moving on the canal it'll come back."

She said it without hope.

The ex-preacher sighed.

"You're like me, Molly. You just want to move around. You'll never want to owe nothing to anybody."

"No," she said seriously. "It ain't that, Fortune. I'd as lief owe myself to a man. But I don't want it way off on a farm. I can see it coming in him. Last night he was late coming to supper, so I went to the stable and the man said Dan was to the granary. They'd been bagging seed oats and he was setting there by himself with a lantern just picking up handfuls and then letting 'em run out through his fingers. I could see it in the set of his shoulders."

"I don't think he'll get off the canal if you stick with him. I wouldn't if I was Dan—or any other man. By gadger, I wouldn't, not even if I was Fortune Friendly himself."

"Go on," she said with a slow smile. "Go put your pants on."

She handed them to him.

"Then what're you going to do, Molly?"

Her voice had a note of plaintiveness.

"I don't know, Fortune. I love him, that's the truth; but the burn's gone out of it."

"Yeanh. But no burn, less scorch. You might marry him, at that."

"Wouldn't he get tired then? It wouldn't be right for him."

"Maybe. What're you going to do? If he stays, he's bound to run foul of Klore. Then what?"

"He'll lick him. I've been hoping for him to do that. That was one reason I wanted him. He could have licked Klore to Hennessy's if he'd had a mind to. He's got it now."

"Molly, what're you thinking about Klore?"

Her lips sprang open, then changed to the square grin the old man was so fond of. She tilted her head and laughed. "Go put on your pants, Fortune."

Holding the blanket up with one hand, he had shuffled in to the cuddy. She had done it well, he said to himself. He peeped at her through the curtains. She had gotten herself into something beyond her strength of heart; getting out of it would leave a mark on her, he was afraid; and he was very fond of her.

She was braiding her hair and putting it in a coil round her head. . . .

Now, standing beside Dan on the stern deck, she drew deep breaths of the bright March wind. Her breast arched finely. The loose man's shirt could not hide the strength of her figure, but it made her seem more slender, brought out the suppleness of her hips. Above the up-turned collar the feminine lines of her face had a quaint softness, appealing to Dan. As he watched her breathing in the wind, her frank blue eyes on the far western notch of the valley, he felt himself older and stronger. For all the long winter together she had not been so intimately near to him as she was now, with the boats before and the boats behind, the rush of the coming spring in the air, the rising and falling notes of the horns. She breathed deeply through her nose, her lips equably closed, giving her an added appearance of vitality. It stirred him; he took the air in quietly and felt it in his lungs. It had a mysterious intoxicating quality that traveled to all parts of his body, until he felt it in his fingers, and his toes curled in his boots to grip the deck. There was no need of speech for him; it was enough to be out at last, with the blue water coming towards them, with the hurry in the sky, with the white banks passing on either side.

The boats wound on beside the towpath, one behind another. Sweat had come out upon the teams, as the morning grew, and the snow turned soft underfoot. The hoofs of the horses picked up great clots of it, which they kicked free. Seen from across the valley they appeared to the farm folk an orderly procession, creeping with the slowness of an ancient habit, as boats had passed, year in, year out, as long as they remembered. For now the boisterous blowing of the horns had begun to fade out.

But in the faces of the people the unpent joy of moving shone as freshly. Their own lives had been given to them again. Winter had died. For the farmers it still lay upon the fields; for the boaters it had gone. The canal had opened.

Haircut

In a day, life on the Sarsey Sal had reassumed the pleasant routine of the preceding autumn. All day long they were hauling now, alternating the two teams in three-hour shifts. The first night in Rome the big horses had been nervous about going aboard. The black, which Dan had taken first to the gangplank, hung back, distrusting its narrowness. So, after a minute, he had tried the brown. The big fellow was eager for his stall, and, once Dan had stood upon the planking, he set his own forefeet upon it, slipped them forward inch by inch, and then, with a deep, satisfied grunt, went aboard, turning round inside to face the hatch. The black had looked on anxiously, but, once the brown was inside, no living power could have kept him on the dock. When he crowded round he found the other already started on his supper. After that they needed no leading, and the black somehow managed always to be the first on board. He found that, if he was, he could snatch at least one mouthful from the brown's manger.

In the gorge of the Lansing Kill they came against shrill winds with a breath of ice out of the woods. The Kill roared in its course under the trees with a deep power that reverberated on the snow. The high falls at the head leaped far clear of the overhanging lip.

Old Ben, at the Five Combines, went about his duties with a subdued fury, swinging his long staff and shouting militant hymns over the gorge, where his deep voice met and mingled with the uproar of the falls. The cold days reddened his hands and brought blue chapped patches on his cheeks; but his long beard had a warmth in its whiteness against the blue shadows of the snow.

At the next lock Ethan Allen McCarthy came out, wearing mittens. He nodded his head toward the Five Combines and told them, "Ben thinks it's spring come when the boats commence to move. His religion's festered his mind all up. I tried to get him to wear a hat, but he told me to get out. The poor old rooster ain't even got room left in his head for a cold."

The Sarsey Sal went on down the gorge. The sound of Dan's horn was thin through the cry of the wind and the roar of the Kill. They stopped at Delta, late one afternoon, to get a load of ploughs from the factory.

The shipping superintendent gave Dan his orders. The ploughs were to go through to Buffalo. They tied up for the night at the Delta dock. Sleighs brought the ploughs in crates from the factory—a mile haul. The arm of the feeder had not yet been built to the village, so that all boats loaded here, which made good trade for Denslow's Delta House.

Fortune Friendly wheedled all through supper for an advance on his wages. A quack doctor, peddling gout removers and corn cure, had put up for the night. There was a chance for pinochle. Denslow had a great thirst for the game.

"But he never won nothing off me," Fortune said. "The doctor thinks he's a master hand, but he ain't never come up against me. Come on, Dan, don't be a tight-fist farmer."

Finally Dan let him have the money, and within five minutes the game was under way. Dan looked through the door after supper. Denslow was nursing his cards in both hands, frowning at the corners, his lips forming figures to himself; and by the look of him Dan judged that the figures were small ones. The quack leaned back in his chair. His high black hat stood bottom up beside his feet, and his face wore his customary encouraging smile. He played as if he had a faith in better things. The old ex-preacher sat between them, his thin nose drawn down, his manner sober; but when he looked up Dan saw a gleam of seraphic happiness in his eye. His luck was in.

Dan went back to the Sarsey Sal. The night was blustery, a cold wind under stars and no moon. The waves slapped sharp along the shore and chugged against the side of the boat. The teams were restless; he could hear one of them stamp.

Buffalo—he was hauling to Buffalo. Sooner or later he had known that he must stand up to Jotham Klore, if he was to hold Molly. It seemed that the time would be at hand. He wished, however, that it had not come so soon. He was not afraid, but he was not eager. Though Molly had been happier in the last few days than he had ever seen her, he had felt a change in her kindness for him. Her happiness lay in the breaking of winter, as if she were leaving it behind; and the winter had been the happiest time he had had. He felt a new strength in himself; but at the same time he was aware of an aloofness in Molly, not physical, for the spring was in her, but mental, as if she stood aside to watch the spring. It roused his hunger, but strangely it did not make him anxious to find Klore and settle her between them. It was as if he smelled defeat, as he could smell the old snow on the earth. He knew that there was one way in which the question could be settled.

When he went into the cabin, he found her drying her hands after finishing the dishes. Her face was flushed from bending over. As soon as he entered she read the question in his eyes, and a dread bordering on panic swept her down. But she rallied.

"Do we start early?" she asked.

"To-morrow morning first thing."

"Buffalo?"

"Yeanh."

The blood came into her cheeks again; her eyes were frank with pleasure.

"I always like going out there, Dan."

"I've never been," he said.

"Where's Fortune?"

"Pinochle."

He sat down and looked at her.

"Molly . . ."

She had turned to the mirror and was poking a wisp of her hair back into place. Now she wheeled round with the lithe motion he loved.

"You didn't get your hair cut, Dan, when we was in Rome. It looks awful. I declare I'd be ashamed to have a friend see it. What would Lucy Gurget say?"

He fingered the back of his neck and said seriously, "I guess it is kind of long. I didn't have no time."

"You won't have time going out, either, and when we get to Buffalo it'll be as long as Ben's."

He grinned sheepishly.

"I've got a mind to do it myself, Dan."

"Well, it couldn't look no worse."

"Don't sass."

She gave one of her small decisive nods.

"I will do it, too."

"All right."

She laughed.

"I've got a pair of scissors I keep for myself. Bring the chair under the lamp, Dan."

He did as she told him, and she covered him over with a pair of towels, tucking them into his shirt collar tight enough to choke him. She pulled her sleeves back over her round forearms; he could see the soft brown down on them in the light of the lamp; and then she tilted his head forward with a sharp push.

"Thank you, mister," she said, for all the world like a barber.

Her fingers were clever; she cut quickly.

"Molly," Dan said again. Now that she was occupied near him, she would find it difficult to turn a question.

"Yeanh."

She turned up the wick of the lamp. In the interval they both heard the wind and the water, and, as it often had before, that peculiar, almost suffocating sense of intimacy entered the old boat.

So close beside him, the feel of her arm touching his cheek, the swift clipping of the scissors in her fingers, her steady, gentle breathing, the warm lamplight over them both, he felt his question rising up in him without his control.

"I want to marry you, Molly."

He heard her breath catch, but, with her woman's instinct urging her hands, the scissoring went on. She had thought she could keep the question away from him.

He sat staring toward the window with the quiet preoccupation which she had learned to expect, but which always made her uneasy. Only now the stiff tilt into which she had forced his head made it foolish and somehow whimsical.

"When, Dan?"

Though she had dreaded the question, now that it had come she was pleased with it.

"Right away."

"But we've got to go out to Buffalo. There wouldn't be any chance." He considered this. They would not have time in any port.

"When we get back," he said, "I'll take time off."

She snipped up the back of his neck and followed the curve of the hair over his ear.

"I'm well fixed, Molly, you know that."

"Yes," she said. "Put your head over.—It's awful good of you, Dan. I want to thank you. But there isn't any call for your breaking your hauling. It don't bother me, our being this way."

He realized, as he felt her hand on his head, that she was taking the seriousness from his question.

"I want to," he said slowly.

Just to see the bend of her elbow made him want her.

"It isn't as if we needed it on the canal," she said.

"I'd feel better."

"Why? If I like it this way, why do you want to change, Dan?" He couldn't tell her that.

"Will you stay on the canal?" she asked. There was a challenge in her words which he could not accept honestly.

"I don't know," he mumbled. "I hadn't thought about it."

The scissors clicked sharply.

"You been thinking about it right along lately," she said. "I could see it on you."

He didn't answer.

"Will you stay in a city?"

"I don't know."

"No. You don't know. Do you like it, Dan?"

"Yeanh," he said, slowly.

"Then what're you worrying about?"

"I thought you'd like it if I asked you to."

She worked in silence for a while.

"I do like it, Dan."

He could feel her fingers running in the hair on the top of his head. She was not cutting; she was just letting her fingers run through his hair.

"I like it a lot, Dan. I don't think there's anybody I'd like better to hear say it."

She took up the job again, letting him ponder her words.

"I thought you loved me, Molly."

He did not say it accusingly; but he felt her fingers stiffen. Then, suddenly, she came round in front of him and pushed his head back, the heel of her right hand on his forehead. Her blue eyes were very kind.

"I do love you, Dan. Can you doubt it?"

Looking at her then, he could not doubt it. He saw her as he had seen her in the fall, when she had first come aboard, with all the familiar details of the stovepipe, and the ventilators, and his hat hanging on the door behind her. The clock whirred to strike nine. Involuntarily they both glanced at the proud little figure of the prancing horse.

"No," he said.

His quiet face, earnest now, and his steady blue-green eyes must have brought back the first days to her, days she had found sweet, when she could see him take what she had to give him and grow stronger for it. She felt her own weakness as the light brightened in his eyes, and she pushed his head down as he settled his feet to rise.

"Just a minute, Dan, don't get grabby. I ain't quite finished."

She brought his hair forward on his forehead and trimmed it back close in a rounded bang, letting the ends fall down on his eyes. Then, as he shook it off, she stepped back laughing, low and husky, as if she were feeling her way toward mirth. As he got to his feet they heard Fortune walking down the dock, whistling "Gamboleer's Pay."

They looked at each other silently, her laughter still on her lips. He kissed them and grabbed his hat and the night lantern.

"I want to rub some more hemlock syrup on Prince." He turned to the door as Fortune came in looking very guileless and satisfied.

"Well!" he exclaimed. "We've got a regular barber!"

Dan went forward to rub the black, to prod him with his elbow and slap him good-naturedly and call him all kinds of a loafer.

Fortune hung up his hat, smiling to see the kindness in her eyes.

"The cards liked me, Molly. All the queens kept coming right to me, and the kings came after them to see where they were." He chuckled.

"I reckon that medicine peddler's still scratchin' his head, wondering about the phenomenons of nature," he went on as she swept the floor. "You'd ought to've seen him. I wish that fat woman had been along. For all she's so lucky, she wouldn't have stood a show-in. You look pretty well happy yourself, girl. Has Dan been telling you things?"

She nodded, the glow still on her.

"Wants to marry you?" he asked, his shrewd black eyes twinkling. She nodded.

"What did you do?" he asked anxiously.

"I said we'd leave it be awhile. He's an awful good boy, Fortune. I almost thought I'd tell him I would. I don't know; maybe I will yet."

"He was looking happy, all right, when he went out," he said.

"Yeanh."

"But it's better to leave it be." He began counting his winnings. Then he looked up. "You certainly did a good job cutting his hair."

She smiled.

"He looks nice with it cut short that way, don't he?"

"He does. Where did you learn to cut it?"

Her body sagged and she leaned on the broom heavily.

"I learned it cutting Jotham's hair."

They stared at each other hopelessly. Then, mechanically she stooped to sweep the loose hair up in the dustpan. She slid it into the stove, where it fizzled a moment. The she put back the lid, hung up the dustpan and broom on their respective nails and went to bed.

"You poor fool," Fortune said to himself. "You old gibbering rooster. Oh, lord!"

He put his money back in his pocket.

Coming in later, Dan found the cabin empty and silent. He sat awhile, as if he expected Molly to come out. But she did not come, and when he went into the cuddy she was lying quiet on her side, as if she slept.

The Chase Westward

Cold winds still blew out of the north, reminding them that winter was still hard in the mountains.

The Sarsey Sal made good time westward. The big team were fast walkers, and the bays, getting a proper share of rest, kept the boat moving at a good pace when they were on the towline. Traveling beyond Rome, they found the towns sparser and smaller. Dan began to have a better idea of the greatness of the canal. Mile after mile, heading southwesterly, to Lenor, and then due west to Syracuse through sandstone country.

Dan took turns relieving Fortune on the towpath. He preferred the long stretches of walking. Since the long haul had started with that night at Delta, he had had a growing excitement. He had seen Molly roused again for a moment then, and though he had found her subdued the next morning, with that same haunting watchfulness in her eyes, he had felt that perhaps he might yet bring her back to him. At times she seemed closer to him than before, but she always kept some vital part of her just out of his reach. The exercise of walking helped to alleviate a growing urge in him for speed. He must get west and find Klore. For he was convinced that he and Klore must settle her between themselves before he and Molly could come together in the old vein.

Then, too, he had a feeling that he and Gentleman Joe would see each other again. It was a meeting that he looked forward to with a mingling of fear and excitement. Whenever he felt the spell of the canal, it was wound up for him in the figure of the mail robber. The man was so sure of himself, so able to preserve himself, that even the marshal, Henderson, who trailed him, gave him a grudging admiration. The more Dan found his own way muddled, the more he found himself regarding the image he created of the criminal riding the towpaths and roads on his fine grey horse. That he had never seen Calash's face added to the illusion. When he had seen it once, he felt that he would see his own way clear. Perhaps he would find a secret there of the man's strength. In his brooding way he tried to imagine the man's features, but he could find nothing in his mind to build them on. The man was associated with action, with Dan's first night on the wharf in Boonville, his first day on the canal, with his getting his own boat, in his very life with Molly. Even when he had bought a mirror for her, he had first seen the man's reflection in it. . . .

In the morning, when they had hauled out of Delta, the first word of the chase had reached them. The night before, Henderson had been seen in Rome, outside the jail, talking to Sheriff Spinning, while his two deputies had stood by the heads of their horses in the street. Then the three had mounted and ridden south out of town.

At a canal tavern in East Boston they had tied up for the night. Here Fortune Friendly, in the process of cards, learned that Henderson had been in the village the night before—"A little fat twerp chewing a cigar like honest-to-God tobaccer," the owner had described him. But this time he was alone. He had talked to the bank walker in his cabin, and the bank walker had refused to say anything about the interview, beyond telling them that the man was a Department man on the heels of Gentleman Joe. "Him a marshal!" the owner snorted, dealing the cards. "No wonder they can't catch the rat." Fortune remembered his very words because, when he picked up his hand, he had found double pinochle looking him in the eyes.

The canal was alive now with heavy trade. They had the familiar sight of boats hurrying ahead, passing during the night when they tied up. The relay stables on the towpath were a-scramble with teams going in and coming out. In the early morning when they went by they could hear the *siss* of men brushing down the mules like the whisper of bees.

The Sarsey Sal pushed on. They stopped in Syracuse next day for a little while to have one of the bays reshod. The blacksmith did a quick job, and while he worked he told Dan how he had made a shoe for a road horse. "A big grey," he said, "and the dandiest plate shoe I ever worked out. A tall feller brought him late in the afternoon just when I was shutting shop. But trade isn't so heavy just at this season, so I took the horse in."

"Yeanh," said Dan.

"I made a good penny out of it," said the blacksmith. "It was a special job," he added quickly. "I charge regular rates on work horses."

"When was that?" Dan asked.

"Day afore yesterday," said the blacksmith, sticking the hot shoe into the hogshead while a wisp of steam coiled out of the black water.

When Dan started to lead the bay out, he saw a man walking down the street leading a saddle horse. The man had a long yellow moustache, and Dan heard him say to the blacksmith that he wanted the nigh front shoe reset on his horse. He spoke with a gentle slur and drawl. Dan remembered the description Fortune had given them of Henderson's two deputies. He hadn't a doubt that this was one. He wondered what the blacksmith would say about the good penny he had made when he learned the tall man's identity.

They passed the vast Montezuma swamps, where the towpaths rose like dams on either side, and the canal ran like a waterproof trough in level country. Here and there patches of black water showed, and the only growth was alder brush and gaunt cat-tails, broken over by the winds, or occasionally thin tamaracks, or clumps of cedars, or the skeletons of ancient trees. Fortune told him that in the early days the highwaymen who covered the western roads hung out here safely. Only they knew the winding trails by which a horse could pass the bogs. Even the Doanes and Tomblesons had used it in their day. If the great swarms of mosquitoes made their stay miserable, at least they knew no man could get at them. It was a melancholy stretch of thirty-five miles to haul through; it wore an aspect of death. The broken flight of low-hung clouds served only to heighten the sombre spirit of stagnation; and the blue open water of the great canal, with its slowly moving boats and horses and bright-faced people, held the eye with a promise of escape.

They hauled on. Twelve miles out at Geddes, where the salt works were, they saw Henderson riding along the towpath. He kept opposite them for a short time; he was a poor rider, his fat body thumping his horse unmercifully. The pot hat on the back of his head seemed perpetually on the point of sliding off, but he paid no attention to it. His cigar stuck upward from the corner of his mouth as rigidly as if he were standing on a street corner. . . .

As they entered Weed's Basin, a man held them up to ask if they had seen anything of a man on a grey horse. The questioner had a scar on his temple, and when he took off his hat to Molly they saw that his hair was slicked down with some kind of grease and a smell of violets came to their nostrils. But they had no news for him. He stopped several other boats, and a little before dark he rode on westward.

"It's queer," Fortune said as they ate supper. "We keep seeing them all the while, here and there, but we don't never get a sight of Calash. Nobody appears to. It makes me feel I'm dreaming."

They came into Rochester, the Flour City, with the houses close to the towpaths and the roar of the high falls in their ears. At the Water Street turn two men stood talking, Henderson and the deputy with the long moustache. But the Sarsey Sal pushed on toward Buffalo with her load of ploughs, across the aqueduct, under the Exchange Street Bridge and the Main Street Bridge and on through the basin. . . .

John Durble's Story

Dan sat on the edge of a dock at Buffalo; the Sarsey Sal was to take pork back to Rochester and there pick up a load of flour for Rome; they would start back in the afternoon. It was warm and dry where he was sitting. The raw, growing city with its high wooden buildings, some of the houses carrying triple porches, lay at his back, with the hill rising behind. Before him the canal ran into the open lake. A schooner was coming in on a brisk wind, heeling over toward the curve of her great sails, like the bend of a woman's hip. But the bows caught snatches of diamond foam out of the water and shook them after her. Streaming out behind, and with thin cries to the wind, a flock of white gulls rose and dipped with the motions of the boat.

In the shelter of the warehouses, the sun had melted away the snow. A dry dusty summer smell rose out of the planks. Boats were coming and going at the far end of the basin. Teams worked back and forth along the wharves. Where Dan sat, it was quiet; he barely caught the hum of the city.

While he was watching the schooner drawing in, he became aware of a man standing within a few feet of his shoulder. He was sturdily built, with big, blunt-fingered hands, smooth-shaven but for a white goatee on his chin. Suddenly his brown eyes turned to Dan. His square face broke in a smile, and he came over and sat down beside Dan on the wharf.

"I like to see the gulls," he said; "they're the most beautiful fliers in the world."

"Yeanh, they be pretty to watch, but they don't fly as keen as a hawk does, mister."

The stranger took snuff from a square silver box.

"That's true," he said. "Maybe I like to see 'em because they hang round people."

"Yeanh."

"Do you work on the canal?"

"Yeanh. I work a boat."

The other glanced at Dan.

"You've done well to get a boat so soon."

"I was lucky," Dan said.

"The canal's the greatest thing this country has done; it's the greatest thing it ever will do."

"It must have been a big job," Dan agreed.

"I saw it finished," said the man. He sat with his hands on his knees, looking out to the west. "See there," he pointed to a lake boat up whose gangways immigrants were crowding. "They all come by the Erie Canal. They may go clear to Ioway, but what they grow will find its way back through the Erie."

"Yeanh."

"I saw it finished," said the man. "My name's John Durble."

"Mine's Dan Harrow."

They did not shake hands. There seemed to be no need of that.

"I was a carpenter, forty years ago, when I come to this country. I got work in New York and New Jersey. I made money fast. I was a master tradesman. I spent five years building houses for other people."

"I've never been to New York," Dan said.

"It was a growing city, but they say it's grown a lot faster since the canal went through."

"Yeanh."

"I worked at the carpenter trade. It was good pay, but it seemed I was getting tired of it. I wanted to settle down on a place of my own."

"Yeanh."

"One day I was working on the roof of a house on Abingdon Road— fifty three was the number. I'd been reshingling a patch; and I was coming down for the end of the day when I saw a girl no more than twenty coming out of the door. She was looking white, and she was carrying a bag in her hand. I was a likely-looking lad and she a girl, so I asked her what was wrong, and she told me she was looking for service, but hadn't been able to get any. Her money was running out, and she'd come over from England with her mother and her mother had died on the way, and there she was alone. So I said, 'Come along to Asa's,' where I had a little cubby room on the top floor, and where I knew she could get one for but a little, and so she did. When I'd left my tools and put on a coat and washed my hands, we had a meal in the back tap, cheese and beer and a slice of cold beef; and, watching her, I saw the color come back. She was a very pretty girl. So after supper we walked out Love Lane and down by Lepner's. It was a warm evening; there were a lot of couples out, but nobody paid no attention to us. Couples were never noticed in Love Lane. I told her how I was fixed; and I was proud about it, and had a right to be so, for, though I was a young lad, I was a master carpenter and earned my dollar with the best of them. Perhaps I said I had more money than I had, but that was only a natural thing, I got to liking her so. Her clothes was worn, but they were neatly sewed and I could see how clean she was.

"We sat in the meadows and watched the sun down over the river. So I told her how I had saved money and how I wanted to go up the state to the great Genesee Valley I'd heard of, where the land was so rich, and take to farming the way the folks had in England—Dorset; I remember the sheep, and the oil smell in the house at shearing. And I said I had planned to go before the month ended, but that a man settling a country alone did a poor job, because it took more than a man to settle. Still I said I didn't know but what I would go. She asked where I went to get there, so I told her by boat to Albany, but after that I was vague about it, only mentioning Rochester, which was that year only a village. But I didn't know that. In truth I had just only got the idea of being a farmer at all. Then she told me again how she was just alone and right at the end of everything, and we sat watching the sun down over the river and I as dumb as an owl at noon.

"But in the dusk we went round about back, all the way out to Kissing Bridge."

The old man paused, took the silver box from his pocket, had his snuff, and watched the boat and the gulls. His face never changed expression.

"I took her there, for she was strange to the city, but after all I think she had a better acquaintance with the bridge than I did. We got married the next morning, and a month later we managed to reach Rochester. It was not more than a thousand people big. I doubt there were more than fifty buildings, all in all, built all on the west side of the river, and no more than a light bridge thrown across. She'd stood the trip dandy, but when she saw what a little place we'd come to I think it closed her up a little. But I'd got the fever then for getting my own place. They said land was high in the Genesee Valley, and I'd got the urge for gettin' westward. We'd picked up a couple of cows in Rochester, and a pair of horses and a cart we'd got in Utica. I bought a plough and grain and flour, and we went on to the Tonawanda, where I'd been told there was good land much cheaper. It took a week nearly to get out, she driving and I bringing on the cows.

"We came in one night on the valley and we found a house there in meadows cut out and burnt by a settler. It was a log house, just one room and looking small in front of the woods, but there was a light in the window and I got a smell of pigs from a pen out back. A man came out wearing a coon cap and leaned on a gun and just looked at us. It was the only farm we'd seen in two days. Just someway it was neither of us spoke, and then his wife came out of the door and right away mine got down and the man shook hands with me. We spent the night there. There was a good fire and the woman gave us bacon and tea. The woman and my wife slept in the bed bunk and he and I slept on the floor."

The old man took snuff again. He looked over the lake as if he saw the cabin, and not the schooner, now so near they could make out the people on deck.

"Next morning," John Durble went on, "I told the man—his name was Cutler, James Cutler—that I was aiming to settle down here. I asked him if there was land. He didn't say anything. He just waved his hand right round. Then he said would I want to buy improved land. Pretty soon I figured out he wanted to sell his farm. I could see it was good soil, and I liked it being close to the Creek. Running water's a great help—just to see it and hear it. We made a deal. Then we went in to the women. My wife didn't say anything—but I think she was pleased to be living where there'd been other people living, as long as there weren't going to be any neighbors. But the woman's eyes sort of glassed—as if there was something curling shut inside of her. She looked older than her husband.

"He took me outside and we spent the morning walking the place—a hundred acres, and I could have more after I'd been settled there for a year or so; but now I had enough cleared meadow and all. I paid the man dollar-down for the land, for six hogs, two cows, and three sheep. There was a couple of chickens, too, but he throwed them in on the deal. We took two days off riding down to Black Rock and making the papers over, and then me and Ellen, my wife, settled in for the winter. There was wheat and oats to be got in, and still the firewood to cut for winter. I was busy. Ellen worked into the house and tended a bit of a garden the other woman had kept there. Just when she left, the other woman had dug up some daffodil bulbs; but she left us one to grow. That was all she done—she didn't speak about leaving. But my wife said she'd been on six different places since she had married. Her husband did that, cleared and sold improved land. He couldn't abide."

Nobody looking at Dan and John Durble would have guessed that the old man was talking, he spoke so quietly. Or, if they had known that, they would not have thought that Dan listened. Both men sat in the same position, backs to the wall, hands on knees, both looking out over the lake. The schooner had come in now, and the wharf hands began to unload her. She carried fur from the winter's trapping—

"The nearest person to us was eighteen miles down the creek toward Black Rock. In and about the creek was heavy timber. We didn't get the full smash of winds off the lakes. But I think it commenced to wear on Ellen, just the shadow of them and the wind-shriek in the branches. Our boy was born that summer. We were lucky. A man wagoning west had his wagon-reach break half a mile from the house, so him and his wife came in and I mended his wagon and the wife minded Ellen.

"But I'd become a farmer. I'd done well with crops and my sheep had lambed and I had three litters of pigs. We weren't troubled during the summer. But late in the fall the bears come after them.

"It's the second winter comes hardest; but Ellen had the boy to fuss with, and so did I. I'd built onto the barn that fall and put a storeroom on the cabin; but now I got to planning that when I'd got settled well, maybe in two years, I'd set right out to build a big house—that is, if there was a way I could get lumber. There wasn't no mill yet on the Creek. I'd even gone and spotted the place I'd build at. On a rise down the Creek, where a kind of flat land came in from the north. You could see quite a ways from there—pretty near to the lake. But it snowed heavier and heavier that winter—the worst I've seen. And I took sick, and my wife had to do the whole job. Lucky I'd got my wood in.

"But I'd generally had to go down about the January light-snow time to Black Rock for stores. This year I couldn't. Our tea give out. Worms got into the flour. I was getting bad, and I couldn't only lie on the bed bunk. My wife kept up pretty good. She always had a smile. And she still looked pretty in her eyes and hair; but the worry was making her thin. We knew we was in for a bad time.

"Then one day, when it was all-harry cold and the wind cracking the trees like rifles, somebody knocked on the door. My wife opened it and in come an old feller, brown as an Injun, with white hair. He had a long-eared hound dog with him. He set down on a bench and kind of looked us over, and my wife said 'Hello' to him and talked about the winter, watching his face close. He set there looking at us; he had a hooked nose and his eyes was so light they looked white alongside of his skin. After a while he grinned at my wife and he said, 'Don't you worry.' And right away she smiled at him. Then he come over to me. I hadn't been able to speak none at all. He sat down and took a-hold of my hand. I'd been figuring and figuring how to get to town, but I couldn't get no sleep for worrying. And right off, when he took hold of my hand, I went to sleep. When I come to, it was sun shining through the winder right across the blankets, and I thought I could feel the sun through them. My wife was cooking tea. I asked her where the old man was. She said he'd gone to town. I asked her where she got the tea, and she said he'd taught her to make it out of white-pine bark. It was good. I had a cup. Then I went to sleep. It had frozen solid, so he'd gone with the two horses down the Creek. Someway I knew he'd come back right enough.

"He did. After that he come round regular till I'd got well. Seems like he'd had a cabin back in the woods about four mile. He'd knowed all along we was there, but hadn't come till one day he'd been by and seen my wife going out to mind the barn. After that he come round again to make sure. Then he'd come in with some rabbits and a bird, and then gone off to get our flour. He was a trapper. All his life he'd been in the woods. He'd seen three wars come and go through these woods, but he hadn't mixed. He kept by himself off in the woods. There wasn't much trapping through these parts, but he done well enough for him. He couldn't read nor write, but he knew a lot of great men by the way of his talk. His name was Parchal Smith.

"But he never stayed long. Till I got well, he brought in game twice a week and stayed for a meal. After that he only came round once in a while. The winter dragged through. We'd see him once in a while in summer. He'd bring fish. He'd took a fancy to Ellen, I guess. But if there was anybody with us he'd leave the fish by the door, and we never knowed he was there till we went out and found him gone.

"That summer word come through that they was planning to start the canal. People talked about that like it was Judgment Day getting close. They'd commenced to dig in Rome. People said it would be fifty years by the time it got to Black Rock, and others said it would be three. We'd hear from time to time how it was getting along. The first year they did fifteen miles. The next year there was three thousand men working on the line, by all accounts. In '19 they turned the Mohawk water in at Rome and ran a boat to Utica. That was late in the fall. We heard about it a month later where we were.

"There had been two farmers moved in within walking distance of my place. I helped them build. My wife went over to help in their houses. She'd got a loom now and was handy at making cloth. In '19 a mill was built up above us on the Creek. The man that built it was looking forward to the canal. I did the work and hired a man to mind the farm. I made money, but I worked on half pay, meaning to take the rest out in lumber. I'd got it fixed I'd build a real house and barn. And after planting, next spring, I commenced the work. The rest come round and said I was building too big, but me and my wife knew now that we had to settle there for good or give up the country. It was a notion I had that that would be the last carpenter work I'd do. I wanted to build my own house. Ellen and me'd dreamed about that house, just how we wanted it—two stories with a peaked roof and dormers.

"It took me a year to build. It was right on the rise I told about, and I'd put a long stoop round the side facing out. There was more people going through. By this time the canal had opened beyond Syracuse, so there was less space for them to haul across in wagons. I made money selling them food and grain. My wife was handy making cheese. That sold well. Only now and then she'd go give a cheese away. Just when she saw a young wife that couldn't buy it. Them would look at the house I was building like it was the last they'd ever expect to see.

"Old Parchal Smith come round less. Three other families had moved in,—but none more,—but that was too much for him. He only come in the middle of winter or late at night in summer. He was getting restless. He'd leave his hound outside, and as soon as he'd hear the dog growl he'd go out. He didn't like the talk of the canal.

"It was easier for Ellen now, with three other women round. They'd hold parties 'mongst each other, and make us get dressed up to go. They'd send round letters by one of the children, when they could have walked as well themselves. They figured out a lot of manners that way. And they was particular about them.

"We'd talked about the canal. It didn't seem like it would ever get to us. They'd surveyed in '19, and the route would come close to my place. We knew it would be good for trade, and Winster, who had the mill, figured he would sell planks for boats.

"It was different with the women. They watched the news; they got it out of everybody that come along. They wanted the talk about it, I guess.

"I'd moved into my big house, though I hadn't enough to furnish it decent, and the neighbors had said I was foolish to build so big. But me and Ellen didn't care. We guessed they'd wished they'd builded that way to begin with. It was the finest house west of Rochester.

"Then, first thing we knowed, in '23, men commenced working on the route between Black Rock and Lockport. Black Rock figured they would be the port, and Buffalo figured they would. Once a month one of them would hold a celebration, according to the news. We'd hear the guns and fireworks clear to Tonawanda Creek. The men that worked was Irishers mostly, though we hired out teams.

"I remember, two springs after that, how me and Ellen sat on the big stoop in June. A warm afternoon. The word come the water would come in from Erie. And after a while we seen it come. Brown and muddy, very slow; so's not to rip the banks. It went by us in a little creek. We watched it rise all day. At night it was still getting up. Brown and muddy. Me and my wife just set there holding hands, and we dassn't try to speak. It seemed like the garden would have more flowers that year—there'd be people to look up and see them on the rise. Then she put the children to bed, and come

out again. We didn't have no supper. We didn't want it. We'd listen to the
water eddy down below all night. In the morning it had come off blue in the
sun—pretty near that color."

The old man pointed.

"We hadn't realized the water would come so close—but now it was
there we liked it. People said there would be noise, but we liked it. They
finished Lockport that fall. Tolls was taken on the first of October. It
had been a fine farming summer. I'd had more money in than I'd expected
for a single year. Then on the twenty-sixth the opening come."

He stopped again, his eyes far off, as if he listened.

"It was a masterful event. The leaves had turned late that year, and there
was still color to the woods. Wednesday night, me and my wife was waked
up by a knock, and, going down, there was Parchal. He'd heard. He'd
been down to the water of the canal. He had a pack on his back and his
long rifle in his hand. The dog looked gay. He knew he was going on a
hunt.

"They had put cannon—you know how—all along the canal and down the
Hudson. There was an old ten-pounder mounted on my rise of ground, its
snout pointing west, and there was one of McDonough's sailors—an old
horny man snoring upstairs in the best room—there to touch it off. The
neighbors came next morning early. Ellen and the women had gotten up
a big feast, and a lot of the Irishers had come in from Lockport, remembering us, to get the food. Old Parchal that night took us out and showed us
a doe deer, fat and prime, he'd brought for us. 'I had my eye on her all
summer,' he said. But his eyes was cold and kind of still.

"That next morning we got up and the women went to work. The men
sat on the porch, looking down the canal to the lake. I had some Jamaica
and Golden Medford for them—it was a brisk morning. Cool from frost at
night, but no wind at all. The smoke from our pipes hung under the roof.
The children played round—noisy. The cook smells came out to us. The
sailor, Benjy Wright, sat on the cannon's butt, patting her once in a while,
and telling us how he used to shoot her. Parchal stood off by himself on the
grass, leaning on his rifle, the hound dog sitting right in front of him.
Both their heads was still, but they both looked westward. And the hound
was working his nose. Some of the men laughed at the lean old feller and
his big dog, but when I told 'em how he'd fed me and my wife one winter,
they stopped.

"About nine o'clock Benjy cut him a hard plug with his sailor knife. He
had a tail of hair on his neck, and he'd oiled it that night, staining the
piller till my wife could have cried. He wore a red-and-white striped shirt
and had pressed his pants himself. They was wide pants. Now he petted the
butt of the old cannon and he says, 'Lilah, when it comes your turn to
talk, you talk out loud.' He lighted his match and we stood waiting. Then
a cannon sounded down by Buffalo. And Benjy touched the match to
the fuse and in a minute the old gun bucked and roared, and a glass broke
in the window of the parlor. The Irishers jumped up cheering, and the
little girls commenced to cry. And the women come out. They wasn't
crying, but they had wet eyes. Then we sat down and watched Benjy load
up the cannon. And an hour and forty minutes later there was a cannon
faint to eastward of us. And our gun bucked and shot again and we heard

a gun boom in Buffalo. But with that sound from the eastward of us we knowed that New York knowed. The sound of it told us that.

"All to once we knowed there was other people back east who knowed about us. We were in a country as big as half the world, but with that shot it all come closer together. We weren't alone.

"My wife," said John Durble, "come and sat in my lap and cried."

"Yeanh," said Dan.

For a while there was silence.

"Clinton's boat come along a while later when we were eating dinner. The food got burnt somehow. But we cheered him by and his four grey matched horses, and he waved to us. And we cheered the other boats. We finished eating. But it was only when my wife and I put the children to bed that night we noticed Parchal Smith was gone. When the shot sounded eastward he must have gone. Him and the hound both. I never heard of them again. But nights now me and my wife hear the boats once in a while—a horn, maybe—or, when it's still, the clink of a trace chain. Or we see the night lanterns. The railroads come in time. But here it didn't make so much difference. They come too easy and quick.

"The canal brought us money, and built great cities along the line—it's building this one. But it brought something better to me and my wife. I couldn't tell you, son. We hear the horns."

After a while he said, "I got to get home."

And he went away.

But that evening, as the Sarsey Sal moved eastward by the intake gates of Tonawanda Creek, Dan looked up and saw a house on the gentle rise of ground. A white house, peaceful, comfortable, two stories, with dormer windows on the peaked roof. He blew his horn, softly. It sounded gentle on the air. Molly, who was standing close beside him, asked, "Why did you blow it, Dan?"

Dan pointed to a lighted window. The shadows of two figures appeared standing together. Then one opened the window and leaned out, to follow with his eyes the light of the night lantern along the velvet water. The light caught a red glow in Dan's high cheeks and traced golden threads in Molly's hair as she combed it out and braided it there on the deck.

It was very still; it was spring. Tree toads lifted clear treble voices against the black sky; and the chirrup of tiny frogs along the canal went with the Sarsey Sal in a rising throaty song.

In Erlo's Boarding House

The horses had the rhythm of the long hauls. They went with a plodding stride, and Fortune went slowly behind them, head down and hands in his pockets.

It was a warm April morning, and the sun had just cleared the light mists from the meadows. Tendrils of it still lingered where the balsams shaded the canal. A flock of ducks scrambled out of a setback, leaving a white trail of foam over the water, and started out again on their northward journey. A little later Dan heard a distant murmur, a cry taken up by twenty voices, and thrown back and forth between them, singly and in a swelling chorus. Fortune, too, heard the honking and kept his eyes on the sky. Dan called Molly on deck. Soon they saw them in the liquid, early morning sky, high up, a line of geese rippling northward.

At Lockport they caught up to a long line of boats going down. Far below, the canal shot straight away, out under the high bridge. On their left the water thundered over falls. Boats, like tiny chips pulled by ants on a cobweb thread, moved out at measured intervals from the downward flight. All along the locks tenders worked quickly at the levers, their shirts soaked with sweat. Regularly, life-sized boats issued from the top lock of the upward flight and hauled past the waiting queue. Dan sat on deck by the rudder and watched them pass. The immigrant season had started. A line boat came by, bright yellow, one of the Michigan Six Day, with an old German smoking a porcelain pipe, his stocking feet straight out on the cabin roof in front of him, the soles turned to the sun. Women's voices rose from the cabin, and the sound of a fiddle wheedling at a tune. Steering was a tall upright old man with a long white beard.

"Ben!" Dan cried. "Ben Rae!"

The Jew turned his fine face toward the Sarsey Sal, a puzzled light in his eyes. Then he recognized Dan and waved his arm.

"Hullo, Dan. How be you?" He turned to the cabin door, his deep voice booming, "Hey, Julius! Julius! Here's Dan Harrow."

The lanky black-haired Wilson sprang out on deck.

"Hello, Dan. Glad to see you. Who're you boating for?"

"*My* boat," Dan said proudly.

"Say," said Wilson, "I met Berry back in Rochester. He said to tell you Jotham Klore was hauling east, working on the Boonville feeder. He said you'd want to know."

Fortune had turned to see who was talking. He recognized the Jew.

"Hey, there, how's pinochle?" he shouted.

"How's preaching?" cried the Jew.

Wilson laughed, shook his fist, and Fortune chuckled. The boat drew away. Line boats worked on schedule. Their crews could not stop to talk. Dan felt sad.

The Sarsey Sal sank down between the stone walls, and down again when the gates closed, until it came out once more on the smooth flow. The big team waited for it, with their heads turned round, and stepped out on the towpath of their own accord as Dan tossed the towrope to Fortune. They heaved and went on.

They kept the teams at a good pace that day, and late on the afternoon of the next they saw the roofs of the city ahead of them in the southeast. The windows were afire with the sunset, and, as the boat pulled forward, the red light moved from pane to pane along the entire city front. There was a slight haze of flour dust over the roofs of the mills. On their left the thunder of the swollen falls beat heavily.

There was an empty berth for the Sarsey Sal just under the Main Street Bridge. They ate in the cabin with the shadows stealing over the canal. Boats passed in each direction. But the shouts along the dock, where men had been loading, grew fainter, thinned out. The boats passing now were bound straight through.

After supper, in the cool of the evening, Dan sat awhile on deck, smoking his pipe, while Molly cleaned the dishes. It was a peaceful scene he looked out upon from under the rafters of the bridge. The boats lay still all along the banks in a double row; smoke and the smell of cooking rose from their cabins. A horse stamped in his stall, and sighed over his oats. Along the wharf a few men moved leisurely; and a couple loitered on the bridge over his head, their voices falling toward his hands in a soft murmur.

Fortune had gone off on his eternal pilgrimage to cards.

Molly came up after a while in her street dress with its tight-waisted jacket and flaunting hem. At the news of Klore's being on the Boonville canal, a worried expression had left her eyes. She had been quietly happy that day. Now she was smiling when she took Dan's arm.

"Let's walk around a little, Dan, if you ain't too tuckered."

They stepped to the towpath and made their way up to the bridge by a little flight of stairs set in against the wall. For a while they strolled up Plymouth Avenue and through the streets of the third ward, past the fine houses with their lawns under towering elms. There was a misty vagueness in the line of the trees against the twilight, and the dusk about their roots was deep.

They made their way down again toward the canal along Exchange Street, getting glimpses of the dark water of the river between the mills. The night had closed in. Lights came in windows on their left; roof lines were lost against the sky until the stars came out, when, gradually, they were born again.

They went down to the canal and walked out along the towpath on the aqueduct. They leaned on the parapet, looking downstream. Here and there were lights in the dives on Water Street, and the reflections of them seemed to be running on the river. The thunder of the falls below came to their ears in a steady muttering and made speech an intimate thing.

"I wonder where Gentleman Joe is," Dan said after a while.

Molly was standing close to him, her hand still in the bend of his arm. Now he felt her turn.

"If he was here, he'd be in one of them houses, I guess."

She pointed to the row of houses on their right, rising three stories high, their foundations licked by the river. Their clapboarded sides, even in that dim light, had a neglected look, and their odd, old-shingled roofs made an unkempt line against the stars. The nearest of the row, not twenty feet from where they stood, showed no lights; but a wisp of smoke floated upward from its chimney. The windows of its second story, close to the aqueduct, were not more than three feet above the parapet.

Dan and Molly, taking up their stroll again, moved under it. As they passed, they heard a guarded voice call to them.

"Say!"

They both looked up. There was no one visible in the window, and the voice seemed to come from above it.

"There's a dormer set back on the roof," Molly said suddenly. "I remember noticing it before."

Dan stepped back until he could see the dormer. He could barely make out a man's figure leaning out of it.

"Hello," he said quietly.

He caught a movement of the man's head.

"It's all right," he said. He had guessed who the man was. "It's me—Dan Harrow. There ain't anybody around."

He thought he caught a sound of sharply indrawn breath.

"Say," said the man, again.

"Yeanh?"

"Henderson's watching all along the street. The only way I can get out's by this window. Can you bring me up a line? They won't be keeping people out of the houses. It's people coming out they're watching for."

"All right," Dan said.

"Listen. Do you know where Jannard's stable is?"

Dan felt Molly at his side.

"I do," she whispered.

"Yeanh," he said.

"Then go there. I'll make it worth while for you. The horse's in the back box stall, saddle by the door. There's a line hanging from the hook next to it. I seen it yesterday. Bring the horse here and come into the house. The horse'll stand. It's straight up at the top—three flights."

"All right."

The man drew back. Dan turned to Molly. She was looking at him steadily. Then, as if she knew what she had read in his face, she took his arm. A block back across the river, down on Front Street, they found a small stable. A lantern burned dimly in the harness room. Dan took it. In a moment he had found the big grey, the saddle, and the coil of rope.

The grey snorted at the strange hand, but gave himself readily to the girth. Running his hands down the clean forelegs, Dan could feel the trembling of the horse.

"He knows what's up," he said softly.

He ought to by this time," Molly said.

The horse walked gently behind them. At the door Molly stopped.

"Wrap that line round under your coat," she said. Dan gazed at her a moment with admiration.

"Hurry up, Dan," she said. Now that she had made up her mind to help him, she thought clearly. He hadn't asked her to help him, she was doing it because she wanted to.

On the towpath again, she stopped.

"I'll stay here with the horse. You go down over the aqueduct. It's Erlo's boarding house. The door's on Water Street."

Dan went ahead alone. There were no lights in the dingy street, but he kept close to the walls. He thought he saw a movement three houses ahead of him, and he paused. But there was no further indication of a watcher. Relieved, he turned into the doorway by his left hand. It was pitch-dark in the narrow hall. In a room over his head he heard a man snoring. Then the creak of a bed. There was a sour smell of old carpet. In the back, a whisper of the river running by. He felt his way cautiously up the stairs.

On the landing he paused. He had heard no sound, but a cool breath of air told him that the street door had opened. He tried to reassure himself by thinking that he had failed to latch the door after him in his care to be silent. But he was sure he had latched it.

There was no sound, no creak of boards. He held his breath. But he heard nothing but the trip of his heart. Still he stood quiet. After a few moments he began to think that no one had come in. He was just putting out his foot for a step along the hall, when something made him stop. It was nothing he heard, nothing he could see. But up the stairs was stealing an odd perfume, a faint smell of violets.

At first he thought a woman had come in. Then before his mind's eye was flashed a picture of a man with a bullet scar on his temple and slicked black hair. The hair had smelled of violets.

Both men waited—an interminable time. The rush of the river was in the ears of both. The ticking of a clock back in the kitchen crept into the silence. The man in the bedroom snored on.

After a time, Dan heard a creak below him. Then again the breath of cool air came up to him. Again it was shut off. The man had left.

All over him Dan felt the sweat breaking out. But he went on now more confidently. In a moment he came to the door of the attic room and rapped gently. It swung open. All he could see was the pallid patch of the window. Something was poked into his back.

"It's me," he said quietly.

The pistol was taken away.

"Got the rope?" Calash asked.

Dan unwound it. They tied it to the knob of the door.

"Where's the horse?"

"My cook's got him at the other side," Dan said. "I didn't want to leave him alone."

"All right. You'd better come down after me. They'll stop you if you go out how you came in."

He put one leg over the sill and began to lower himself. Dan saw his tall thin silhouette sliding down. Then he stopped, his face against the shingles, lying breathlessly still. Round the bend in the towpath came the jingle of trace chains. They heard the breathing of mules harsh above the mutter of the distant falls. The boat went by with a ripple along its sides casting a bright patch on the water.

"Evening," they heard the driver say. Dan knew he must have seen Molly with the horse.

"You'd better hurry," he said.

The man slid down, his face turned away from the light. The rope tightened on the shingles and moved half an inch from one side to the other, with tiny squeaks. Then it jerked, and Dan went down slowly.

When he reached the towpath, he found Calash mounted. Molly was standing by the horse's head.

"It's lucky the driver didn't see that rope," Calash said.

He bowed over the horse's withers to Molly.

"It was mighty fine of you to bring the horse," he said to her.

She did not reply.

He leaned down to shake hands with Dan.

"I owe you a lot."

He put his hand in his pocket.

"No," said Molly suddenly, in a firm low voice.

"I wasn't going to," Dan said.

"Not money," Calash said. He put something in Dan's hands. "You can have this to remember by."

"Thanks," he said again, his voice odd, harsh.
Then the grey horse leaped forward.
Molly caught Dan's arm.
"They'll hear him," she said. "Come quick, Dan."
She hurried back across the aqueduct. Before Dan could move, two men came out of Front Street. They were mounted.
"Did you see a horse?" they shouted.
Dan waved his hand eastward.
"He turned off," he cried.
They dashed into the darkness.
Molly met him on the far side.
"If he crosses the canal beyond the Wide Water," she said, "he can lose his trail in the woods by Cobb's Hill."
Slowly they went back to the Sarsey Sal. In the cabin, with the lamps lighted, Dan sat down and opened his hand. Gentleman Joe had put a small pin into it, shaped like a running horse.
"I wonder if they're diamonds," he said.
Molly turned from brushing out her hair.
"It's pretty," she said. Then, "Dan, don't help him again. Keep clear of him."
"Why?"
"Did you ever see him?"
"Why, sure," he said. "I've seen him a lot of times."
"His face, I mean?"
"No," he said, "I never seen it. I'd like to."
It surprised him to have to say it. He knew perfectly well that he had never seen Gentleman Joe's face, but his impressions of the man were woven in so closely with his life on the canal, that to hear his admission in plain words was startling.
"I saw it against a window light," Molly said.
He did not hear her; he was looking at the horse again, shining on the callus on his palm; he was happy.

To Boonville

Henderson and his deputies had missed Calash in Rochester. After Dan's brief glimpse of them there, the chase vanished again, as completely as if they fled behind the moon.

The Sarsey Sal took up her appointed journeyings; back and forth between ports, from Albany to Buffalo. Life in the cabin ran smoothly. But once more Dan detected a cool aloofness stealing into Molly's kindness. His mind returned to Klore. They had heard of him. He was doing job hauls on the Boonville Canal. Sooner or later Butterfield would have to send the Sarsey Sal up the feeder, where she could not be missed.

Dan had grown heavier during the summer. His skin had taken on the warm brown shade the sun and wind give to light-haired people. He walked now, or stood beside the rudder, with a new erectness. He seldom had men dispute his place at a lock. Once in the night at Number 54, another boat had tried to overtake them and hold them from going through the lock.

Dan called to Molly to pole the boat in; the horses knew enough to wait at the upper end; and at the lower, in the light of the lock-tender's lantern, Dan and Fortune settled the other crew. Fortune returned breathing war and nursing a black eye with the palm of his hand, but Dan went merely to the team, hitched the towline on the evener while the big black looked over his shoulder, and took up the trail again.

Back and forth, back and forth, in hauls of varying length, the life which the boaters loved for its variety, the different places to tie up, the waterfronts of different ports, Dan began to find monotonous. After the first sight, the rush and hurry at the locks, the gush of waters, the lifted voices in the long basins, the line boats passing with their noisy immigrants, the crack of whips, were all the same to him. Yet he still held to the canal. For one thing, he liked to watch his big team overhaul another with their long stride. For another, he had Molly. For a third, the wail of the horns at night.

Then, one morning in August he hauled into Rome and went to the warehouse office for shipping orders. Mr. Butterfield was reading a letter at his desk. He merely nodded to Dan, pointing out a chair. Dan sat down, put his hat on the floor, and glanced round the cool room, then at Butterfield's handsome white head.

Mr. Butterfield had been kind to him. They liked each other.

After a minute the older man folded the letter with his clean fingers and rapped it gently on his desk.

"Harrow," he asked, "do you intend to keep to canawling right along?"

Dan glanced at him curiously.

"I ain't sure, Mr. Butterfield. I hadn't really thought."

The cool grey eyes looked across at him thoughtfully.

"Some like it," he said.

"Yeanh."

"I should think a man like you would get tired of it. Just hauling another man's goods back and forth between cities."

"Well, I do sometimes, Mr. Butterfield."

Mr. Butterfield continued gently tapping the letter on the desk.

"This letter's from a friend of mine," he said. "He wants to know if I know of a good man to take charge of his dairy. That is, really, he wants a superintendent for his place. Would a job like that interest you?"

"Where is it?"

"Lyons Falls. He has the finest farm in Lewis County. Maybe you saw the barn he was building last fall."

Dan remembered the ribs of the great structure rising on the meadows, as lovely to him as a cathedral.

"Yeanh."

"He has a fine herd," Mr. Butterfield continued.

"I saw it," Dan said.

"Have you had any experience?"

"Not with fine cattle," Dan said. "But I'm pretty good with cows. I admire good cows."

"He says he doesn't care for too experienced a man. He wants a young fellow willing to learn."

Dan remembered the wide meadows on the river bottom and the long herd winding in. Above all, he remembered the great barn rising. "You'll get three hundred a year to begin with, and keep. And if you work out right, the salary will go up."

"It sounds like a good proposition," Dan said, slowly, looking down at his hands.

"He wants a man in the fall, in time for fall ploughing."

It seemed to Dan that he could feel the plough helves on the heels of his palms.

"And he wants a single man," said Mr. Butterfield. "So right away I thought of you."

Dan looked up.

"That might sort of stop me taking it, Mr. Butterfield."

"Why?"

Dan was embarrassed.

"I'm sort of bound up here. I couldn't take it single."

"Do you think she'd go with you? She's nice for a canal cook, I know that; generally they won't leave. They've got a taste for travel in them."

"I'd like to talk it over with her," Dan said.

"All right. There's no particular hurry. I'll write Mr. Wilder and see what he says. I think it would be a good place for you, Harrow. And I think Mr. Wilder would find you a good man for him."

They turned to business abruptly. Dan was to take a load of corn to Boonville. . . .

That evening Dan told Molly and Fortune that they would be heading for Boonville in the morning. Her face paled slightly.

"Klore's up there," she said.

"Yeanh," said Dan.

"Well, it's got to come to a wrastle one way or another," Fortune said.

They started out of Rome in the grey before dawn, when the mist lay on the water and the air was still. Dan was steering. It was on such a morning that he had entered Rome the year before. Under his feet his own boat moved; his team went along the towpath; and his own cook worked in the cabin. He had all these. They would be worth fighting for. He knew that Klore stood between him and all his life on the canal.

Molly had said little during breakfast. She was having one of her moody days. Later she came on deck and stood beside him in the stillness, her eyes on the towline stretching into the mist; ahead the clink of the traces, and occasionally, as the mist swirled, a sight of the rumps of the team and Fortune's thin shanks walking. Drops formed on her hair and crept slowly over her cheeks.

Just as they cleared the basin they met a boat coming in. The other team stopped and the Sarsey Sal went over the tripped rope. As the rudders passed, a harsh voice hailed them.

"What boat's that?"

"The Sarsey Sal," Dan said.

The heavy voice swore a hard oath; and, as if the mist cleared before it, they had a glimpse of Jotham Klore, blackbearded, looking after them. He did not try to get ashore; he said nothing further; he just looked after them. He would be on the up trip before they could come down.

Then the mist closed in between him and Dan, and when Dan turned to Molly she had gone below.

When the mist burned off, they saw men reaping oats in the fields, men in a line, swinging the cradle scythes in beautiful rhythm, while women and boys walked after them tying bundles.

Molly came out again into the warmth of the sun and sat opposite Dan with her basket of sewing, mending the collar of one of his shirts.

For a while Dan said nothing, but he let his eyes roam over the meadows where the wind made waves in the grain and the corn lifted its leaves and whispered. Finally they came to rest on her, on the light hair at the nape of her neck, and the print dress tight over her bowed shoulders.

"Mr. Butterfield says there's a job for me up at Lyons Falls—superintendent of that big farm where we saw them building the barn."

She kept her head bent.

"It's three hundred a year, to start with, and keep."

"Yeanh?"

Her voice was toneless.

"Yeanh," he said. "It's a fine dairy."

A note of enthusiasm crept into the words.

"It's a fine job to start with."

"What did you say, Dan?"

He grew moody.

"They want a single man."

She looked up at him quickly.

"What did you say, Dan?" she asked again.

"I said I couldn't take it single."

"Yeanh."

"Mr. Butterfield said he'd write and see. I couldn't take it single. I couldn't leave you, Molly."

Her eyes were wet.

"Molly, will you come with me if they'll take us double?"

Her face bent toward her work again.

"Dan, why don't you want to stay on the canal?"

"What's the use? Just going back and forth—all places the same. There ain't any interest into it."

She drew a long breath.

"Will you come, Molly, if I get the job?"

She didn't answer.

He looked at her a long time.

"Will you marry me if I stay on the canal, Molly?"

She kept her eyes on her hands, but there was a slight heave in her shoulders, and when she finally looked up he saw that she was crying. Eventually she went below without having given him an answer.

He brooded as they went along, steering by instinct. He knew that even if Mr. Wilder offered the job to him, as a married man, he would have to say no. His eyes followed the reapers and rested on a wagon being loaded with bundles, jumping up on the underhand swing of the forks. He turned his head to get a last glimpse of them, as if he were saying good-bye. His emotion ran so deep that he could scarcely feel it. After all, he would have the boat and his two teams and Molly.

The hills closed in. They entered the Lansing Kill, and began the long slow climb through seventy locks. . . .

In Boonville they met the Nancy. The fat woman was in high good humor. She had learned a new recipe for cheese pie.

"It's good," Solomon said. "I don't deny it's good, but when you get it seven days in the week the boat smells so even the rats get out."

"Go along," said Mrs. Gurget.

"It troubles the digestion," Solomon said.

"Sol!" cried the fat woman.

"It's true," he said grimly. "It segashuates right—"

"You shut up!" she said. "Where's your manners?"

Fortune broke in tactfully.

"I wonder if we mightn't get a game of cards?"

Mrs. Gurget snatched her breath.

"My stars! Cards! Pinochle! I ain't played in a week."

She hitched her chair forward to the table.

"Show me a pack."

Dan looked questioningly at Molly.

"I've got a pack," said Fortune, "only they're kind of dirty."

"That's all right," said Mrs. Gurget in her hearty voice. "Sol ain't washed his hands. He says it spoils his luck, but he's a dirt-easy proposition anyways. How'll we play?"

"I'm no good at it," said Molly.

"Me neither," said Dan.

"It ain't right. One of you ought to play. Still," the fat woman comforted her conscience, "three-handed pinochle is a lot better game than four-handed. Ain't it, Mr. Friendly?"

"Yes, there's a kitty three-handed."

Molly cleared off the supper things, and the game started and went on while Dan helped her wash the dishes.

The fat woman played with gusto; one end of her shawl, trailing over the back of the chair, twitched like a third monstrous arm as she put her card on a trick. She would hesitate an instant, then put forth the card, snapping a corner down sharply, and whenever she took the trick she would break into her hearty laugh. As the playing progressed, her laughter became more frequent and good-humored. The melds she declared were extraordinary; four times she held a hundred aces, with an extra ace or two at that, and she seemed to be able to fill one hundred and fifty of trumps whenever she liked. Even double pinochle came to her hand; and the kitty always favored her.

"Some day she'll get a thousand aces," grunted Solomon; "and that will serve her right, too. There's three people I've heard tell about getting a thousand aces, and they all had their hearts stop."

"Mine wouldn't," chortled the fat woman. "I'd be too anxious to see it again to die."

Fortune Friendly said nothing. But he watched the fat woman's playing and followed her luck with eyes as rapt as Jacob's must have been in his dream. When he shuffled with his quick fingers, he got himself good hands, but all the other good cards went to the fat woman; and when she or Solomon dealt, her luck was monolithic.

Solomon was like the fly between the two irresistible forces.

Molly and Dan sat down on the far side of the cabin, listening to the click of the cards and the remarks of the players, and Solomon's intermittent groaning. Whenever the fat woman leaned back in laughing, the lamplight glittered on her locket and fell full on her broad red face. And Dan thought of the face in the locket, and looked at Solomon sitting across the table from her, his thin nose beaded with sweat as he concentrated on his cards. But then the fat woman would straighten up and settle her hat with both hands and go about the business of dealing.

Dan leaned back and drowsed with the sound of the playing in his ears. Content in each other's presence, he and Molly did not talk; but now and then she glanced up at him with a smile at one of Solomon's groans or Mrs. Gurget's delighted shrieks. They were all his friends, Dan thought, and it was pleasant to have them there together; and he forgot Jotham Klore coming up from Rome.

The fat woman's voice broke in upon him, as she made conversation in dealing.

"Do you know Mrs. Quackenbush?"

"The woman that pumped the canal dry three times?" Fortune asked.

Mrs. Gurget laughed.

"That's her. Nell Berry's sister. Well—" She was swept into a paroxysm of laughs, her sides lifted, her face reddened, and she clutched at her bosom with a fat hand. Solomon looked up from picking up his cards with an air of disgust.

"It's funny," he snorted. "Jeepers, it's the funniest story you ever heard."

The fat woman was not at all disturbed.

"Sol's right, at that. Mrs. Perkins up to Slab City gave Mrs. Quackenbush an order for a hat like hers last month. One of them strawy ones with decorated pansies onto it. But the old woman got to Utica and she couldn't recollect which woman had asked her. So she went off and bought a dozen just alike. She buys clothes for a lot of them women up there, so she knew the sizes. Then when she come up she sold each one of them twelve women a hat. They was pretty, and the women was anxious to buy them; and each one figured she'd be right up in the top of style and show up in church next Sunday with a new hat right before the rest, and show off on to the others. None of them said nothing: they wanted for it to be a surprise. I wasn't there, so I don't rightly know, but I hear tell that a bad time was had by all."

She bent over, slapping her knees, and let out a screech of laughter as she straightened up.

"What happened to Mrs. Quackenbush?" Fortune asked with a chuckle.

"Land! As quick as she'd sold them all she traveled out of there like all get out."

"Two-fifty," Solomon bid dryly.

The fat woman picked up her cards.

"Four hundred," she said. "Any dispute?"

The playing went on until about ten o'clock, when the fat woman got up to go.

"When are you traveling to Rome?" she asked Dan.

"To-morrow morning."

"So're we. The Berrys'll be coming through from Port Leyden. We might as well all go together. It'll be a regular party."

"Sure," said Dan. . . .

Next morning the three boats started down, the Sarsey Sal, the Nancy, Berry's boat, at the head of a line of nine.

On deck Dan stood with Molly close beside him.

"You ain't afeard, Dan?"

He did not answer. It was early morning; there was no up traffic yet. Behind him the boats wound silently under the sunrise; a sweet, cool day, with dew on the meadows, and the bells of cows sweet in the night pastures. Ahead of him, somewhere, Jotham Klore was coming up with his boat.

They wound down along the valley until the roar of the falls sounded ahead and the upper gate beams of the Five Combines stood out white against the trees. Dan sounded his horn, and the gorge took the echoes back and forth, down, down, below the line of sky.

Then, at the foot of the flight of locks, another horn broke out in three sharp blasts.

Molly's head sprang up, and she looked square at Dan.

"It's Jotham Klore."

Dan nodded. . . .

The Fight at the Five Combines

It was a morning of bright sunshine and swift white clouds. They scudded over the gorge on the breast of the wind. But in the meadows there was no feel of the wind, which passed high up, stroking the leaves of only the topmost trees.

The Lansing Kill and the overflow from the canal fell into the gorge within sixty feet of each other; and between them a diamond-shaped patch of grass made even footing for the fight. The crowd had taken up their places on two sides, so that the space of short grass resembled a square— on two sides people, on two sides the open gorge and the falling water, and the Kill seething into foam eighty feet below. The roar of it rose up, passing the ears of the crowd, until it seemed a wall against the open sky.

As their boats stopped at the lock, both Dan and Klore had gone to the lock-tender's shanty to wake the old man. The other boaters were too far back to hear what they said, and Ben was too deaf; but they stood opposite each other by the door until the old man came out, his trousers in his hand. Then, as they stepped together, he poked his staff between them.

"No one ain't going to fight in front of my house," he said. "There's a good patch of grass up by the Kill. If you're so all-fired eager, get up there."

"It don't matter to me," Klore said. "One place is as good as the next."

"I'm agreeable," said Dan.

"Then come along with me," said the old man.

He walked with a long stride, his red underwear bright against the grass, his bare feet gripping the earth, his staff swinging, his white head bent, like one of the prophets. Dan and Klore walked behind him, a little apart; and after them the boaters came sprinting from their boats as the word spread that Dan Harrow was to fight Jotham Klore. As they ran they made bets.

The fat woman came running down the towpath, one hand holding her bonnet down, the other holding up her skirts; but before she reached the locks she turned, sent Solomon scurrying back for a vinegar bottle and a sponge, and then came on more slowly. Hector Berry, hanging back among the others to put money on Klore, found himself suddenly face to face with Solomon, who was returning with the vinegar. The little man's thin nostrils were white with scorn.

"You're betting against Dan?"

Berry flushed and screwed a new cigar into his mouth and put his hands in his pockets and crossed one foot before the other, and managed to appear even more embarrassed.

"Why," he said. "I was asking how the odds was."

"What was they?"

"Two to one on Klore most people're giving."

Solomon set down his sponge and bottle carefully and yanked his wallet out.

"I wasn't going to lay no money against him," Hector said uneasily.

"Didn't I hear you ask for money on Dan?"

"Well . . ."

"How much?"

Berry hesitated. "Ten dollars," he said at length.

"All right," said Solomon.

He fished out five dollars, and they looked round for a stakeholder. Fortune Friendly was going by. He affably consented to hold the money.

"Sol!" cried Mrs. Gurget.

The little man snatched up the vinegar and ran across the meadow. The fat woman was standing close beside Molly in the front of the crowd, her face flushed, her eyes dancing.

"Take off your shirt," she said to Dan. "Here, put down your head."

She stripped the shirt over his head and then the undershirt and laid them across Molly's arm. Klore had taken off his shirt and waited in his undershirt. He stood now with his heavy legs spraddled, his thumbs hooked in his belt, and looked the crowd over. When his pale eyes came to Molly, he grinned slowly. She saw his teeth white through his beard.

She met his eyes squarely, and for a moment Mrs. Gurget's quick glance caught a faint flush in her pale cheeks. She rumbled faintly some remark to herself, then smiled as Molly, without changing her expression, turned to Dan. The girl's lips moved stiffly when she spoke; her voice was strained.

"Lick him, Dan. You've got to lick him."

Solomon bustled through the crowd behind them.

"Shucks," he exclaimed. "Dan'll lick the poison right out of his hide."

He reached up to rub Dan's shoulders, found the muscles loose and easy, and grinned.

"Watch him, Dan. Watch his right. Watch it all the time. Don't never let it get out of your sight."

Old Ben was putting on his trousers. Years ago he had fought in a ring.

"No gouging by Ben's lock," he said. "No tripping nor sabutting."

As he buttoned up his trousers, he pointed one hand to his stick.

"I'll lay out the first one that does. I'll douse him back of the ear."

Jotham Klore grinned.

"No bother. I can lick him without that."

"You'd better," said the old man. "I'll give the word, and then you can commence. Now I'll announce you and make it a regular occasion."

"Make it quick," said Klore, clenching his heavy hands and turning his pale eyes to Dan's.

Suddenly Dan's eyes lighted. He had caught sight of a white head over the crowd. Julius Wilson and Ben Rae came up to him, and shook his hand. "We're with you, Dan," said Julius. The Jew nodded. They stepped back.

"Say, what're you doing up this way?" a voice asked.

Fortune stepped up to them, shook hands, introduced them to Mrs. Gurget and Sol and Molly, and they all shook hands.

"We're taking a minister up to Lyons Falls. Reverend Williams—him and his family." Wilson chuckled. " 'What's the delay?' he says to Ben. And then he locks his family into the cabin and comes along to see."

He pointed to a black-clad dignified figure on the edge of the crowd, a man with a pale face, watching the proceedings out of timid eyes. The fat woman was impatient. Her whole soul was shining in her eyes, and her eyes were on Dan. "I could dang near say a prayer, dearie," she said to Molly.

Molly gave her a small smile. She stood stiff, trembling slightly, pale. Mrs. Gurget patted her shoulder.

"Cheer up, dearie. He'll win with half a chance."

Molly did not answer, and again Mrs. Gurget saw her eyes meet Klore's and a smile in the man's, confident, not only of Dan but of the girl. The fat woman read it as plain as print.

"Snake's eyes," she said to herself—it felt like a shriek inside of her. She grabbed Molly's arm and squeezed with all her might. "Look at Dan—he's looking at you. He's got to lick him, you hear me? That's what you took up with him for, ain't it? To make him lick Klore. You told me that yourself. Don't tell him in that measly voice. Look like you meant it."

She felt Molly wince.

"Remember how Klore licked you?"

She felt Molly's arm stiffen, and saw the hot flush come for a moment into her cheeks.

"Give him a smile," she said grimly.

She was watching Dan, now, and the fat woman thought she had never seen anything handsomer than when he grinned.

"If he's scared," she said to herself, "and I'll bet he is scared hollow, he don't show it."

She waved her arm and shouted to him.

"Watch his right! Watch his right and break his eyes. Blind him."

There was a little bitterness in her as she saw his eyes on Molly's. For a moment her hand caught at her fat breast. Then she threw up her head, took a deep breath through her nose, and roared, "We're all with you, Dan! Take off his pants and hang him over the edge for the flies to bite. Blind his eyes, Dan, blind his eyes."

Dan heard her and gave her part of his smile. Then his glance went to Klore and fixed in an unmoved stare. It had come at last and it was to be. He heard dimly, through the roar of water, the crowd's murmur still, and Ben's voice, "Dan Harrow versye Jotham Klore, unbeat Bully of the Big Ditch."

Ben's staff fell forward to meet its shadow on the grass; the old man's resonant voice lifted in a shout:—

"Fight!"

They met in the middle of the open square of grass, neither giving an inch, striking for the middle, landing. Then came the Jew's voice: "Block with your elbows, Dan."

But Dan knew no more of the science than did Klore. It became a question of which man could wear the other down. The fists of Jotham Klore came in against his belly, and he felt his own fists sink into Klore's undershirt, felt the leap of muscles under his knuckles.

Then the fat woman: "Blind his eyes!"

He raised his hands, felt a stunning smash on his ribs, and, as he slipped a little to the left, brought his right forward to Klore's eye. Klore snarled, shook his head, and the blood came down from the cut.

As they drew apart for an instant, measuring each other, the complete stillness of the crowd was broken by a rising mutter of voices.

"Did ye see thim belaboring?" exclaimed a red-headed driver. "Did ye ever see the loike?"

"It's a fight," said his captain, driving his wooden leg into the grass for a firmer stance. "The lad can stand up to him."

"What're they fighting for?" a man asked. He worked on a farm whose buildings stood scarce a hundred yards above the locks.

The Irishman whistled a bar of a jig.

"Phwat would they be fighting for? Sure for a girl, and there she is herself, her with the brown hair that's holding the young feller's shirt on her arm."

"I wonder how our passenger's doing?" Julius Wilson asked the Jew. The Jew grinned, and pointed.

The Reverend Mr. Williams was shinnying up the side of a boulder, a few yards back of the crowd. His black coattails fluttered over his thin hams in an agony of excited haste.

But Mrs. Gurget and Molly and Solomon never for a moment took their eyes from the two men before them. Solomon was down on one knee, leaning his forearms on the other out in front of him, and he kept saying, over and over, like a prayer, "Watch his right, Dan. Watch his right."

The fat woman stood with one hand on his shoulder and one on Molly's arm. She breathed as heavily as the two men, and her eyes glared at Klore's as if she would blister him. At every blow a little grunt escaped her, as if she had hit or been hit herself. As for Molly, the fat woman could make nothing of her, and once the fight began she tried to make nothing of her. She stood, as white as before, but a feverish shine was in her eyes and she clutched Dan's shirt in her arm.

The two were circling warily now, taking time between their blows.

"Keep him away, Dan, keep him away!" the Jew cried suddenly. "You've got the reach. Don't let him get close."

Jotham Klore came in slowly on Dan, his arms half raised. He stamped slightly as he put down his feet, digging his toes into the sod, as a bull steps to settle himself before a rush. His pale eyes, generally on Dan's, darted now and then to one part or another of him, as if he were selecting his point of attack. His grey undershirt clung to his back and wrinkled from one side to the other between his shoulder blades as he moved his arms. It was sweat-soaked in a darker stain round his neck, but the half-length sleeves left his massive forearms free, yellow-skinned and furred with close-curled black hair. As he moved his head, the hairs of his black beard caught on the undershirt and jumped free, like small released springs. Once in a while he snatched the blood from his right eye with the back of his hand.

Dan moved backward before him, with a lightness of tread that was almost delicate. Sweat glistened on his shoulders. His hard flat stomach was reddened, but he breathed easily. There was no readable expression on his face; it was almost vacant; but his greenish eyes kept steadily on Klore.

Suddenly Klore led with his left, and, as Dan's hands dropped, he brought his right over in a heavy swing. Dan heard Solomon's voice shrill; he ducked, and the blow took him on the top of his head. His back bent under the shock, and the people in front could see his heels sink into the sod.

"Watch his right!" Solomon cried.

And then again there was silence, except for the roar of the falls.

Klore rushed suddenly, head down, both fists driving from the shoulders, and, instead of dodging, Dan stepped in; his back jumped straight as a whip, and his fists found Klore's eyes. The boater's head snapped back, and when they drew apart the people saw the blood blinding one eye completely and the other getting brown.

Then he came in again, more slowly, more steadily, his hands high to guard his face. The two came together and the blows sank in.

"Go after his belly!" shrieked Solomon.

Again they stood close, trading massive, slow blows. The fight became an impersonal thing to the onlookers. The roar of the waters in their ears grew small and far away. They held their breaths and watched and heard the grunt of the man hit, and the sigh of the man striking. There was a deliberateness in both of them.

They saw the slow rage climbing in Klore, but he did not shout and growl as they had heard him in other fights. He kept his head down and a little to one side, to see better. As if he knew that he must wear Dan down before he could beat him, he went slowly, getting in a heavy blow at times, and taking one with a short shaking of his head.

The knees of both men held; there was no sign of a knockdown. It came to the crowd that the first man down would be the man licked.

The fight went on. The hot sun shining under the high cloud made a bright carpet of the square of grass on which the shadows of the men fought as they did, following each other here and there and hitting heavily. As the warmth increased, the people caught the hot smell of sweat when the fighters came in close to them; and a pair of bluebottle flies flew round their heads investigating.

The whole of Dan's chest and belly began to darken; but there was no mark to see on the bully, beyond his swollen eyes. He guarded them now like precious things. Dan's breathing had shortened. His hands were slower to meet a blow. Both men used their fists as though there were weights tied to them. . . .

The morning pared their shadows on the grass to little men. But the slow fight went on, the harsh breathing, the long thud of blows.

Even Solomon had fallen silent.

The roar of the water was forgotten; the passing of the day; the sun and the clouds. All the world came in upon the little square of bright green grass, on two sides the small figures of the boaters, on the others the forgotten chaos of the water.

The men fought with the persistence of the two flies buzzing.

All the world came in upon them in the hush, on the fighters, on the crowd, on the straight brown-haired figure of Molly Larkins.

More boats tied up, a long line either way, and the canawlers crossed the meadow to look on; but the silence remained, and the harsh breathing of the two men marked the time. . . .

"God!" cried Solomon. "It can't last no longer."

The two stood still again, facing each other, their hands hanging like lead balls.

Painfully they raised them. Old Ben, clutching his staff, his chin resting on his wrists, watched them with sombre eyes. The fat woman let the tears run into the corners of her mouth. There was a misery in the eyes of many people.

The bearded man's face was a mass of blood and raw flesh from which his beard grew. It had no shape, it flecked drops when he shook it. The nose was a lump over the hair raised on his swollen mouth, and one eye showed as a slit. He kept spitting, trying to stir the hair that cut into his mouth, and he made a blubbering sound when he did so that suggested the color of his face to the people on the outskirts of the crowd. Yet he came on, peering out of the corner of his partly open eye.

The younger man could scarcely lift his hands; his body was livid, in places the skin had broken; and his chest heaved and heaved, and yet he seemed to get no air. But his face had almost no mark, and his blue eyes were as calm as those of a farmer who harrows his meadow.

"It can't last no longer," said Solomon, and he found the fat woman's hand awkwardly trying to get into his.

Without a sound Klore rushed, his head down.

"He's going to butt!" someone shouted. "He can butt in a door."

Dan tried to dodge, was slow, turned his body slightly and took the glancing blow of Klore's head on one hip. They both went down. They struggled up together, and the movement seemed quick and light to the stiff watchers.

Dan had his back to the lip of the falls. He backed away slowly. All sense of direction had gone from both men. There was only one space in the world, and that lay between them.

Shrill cries rose warning Dan; but it was too late. He could not dodge to either side. And with a harsh, half-swallowed roar Klore rushed again, butting with his head. His short legs bowed; he leaped with a fumbling ungainliness; his hands swung.

The crowd saw Dan rigid, outlined against the sky, with the roar of water behind him. They saw his hand come up, gnarl to a fist, come down on the back of the black head—a heavy blow.

They heard no sound. They saw Dan standing with his hands at his sides. They saw Klore lying on the ground, his legs twitching, his shoulders still. They said nothing. It was the end.

Dan stood looking at the black head at his feet, the raw face hidden on the grass, looking down. He wavered a little on his feet, but he stood looking down. Then he felt someone beside him. Molly, slipping his shirt round his shoulders. She lifted his arm over her shoulder; and she looked down at Klore. Then he heard the fat woman sobbing and saying, "Dan, Dan, Dan," over and over. And Solomon had his hand. Then the Jew. But the others, like Dan, still stood looking down at Klore.

Then, all at once they heard a voice over their heads, and glancing up they saw the minister on the boulder, hands stretched upward, his timid eyes lost in the sky:—

"Praised be the Lord!"

A murmur grew among them; it swelled and swelled; it ended in a shout.

They went back to their boats slowly, by twos and threes, and Ben began locking them through.

Gentleman Joe Calash

Brown and squat upon the water, the old Sarsey Sal worked down through the locks of the gorge. The other downstream boats had gone ahead, the Nancy last of all, the fat woman waving her arm to Molly from the stern.

They had put Dan to bed in the cabin; he was sleeping there now; and Fortune walked behind the team. Solomon had relieved him of the stakes he had held on the fight—at the last minute, for Fortune had made himself as inconspicuous as possible.

Molly steered. Where they had a mile stretch ahead of them, she called Fortune on board, for the big team could be trusted to hold their steady pace. He sat down on the cabin, folding his hands round his knees, and looked at her with his keen black eyes.

"It was a great fight," he said after a while.

"Yeanh," but a shiver passed up her back and she set her teeth.

The ripple cuddled on the old bow and ran along the sides gently, and the team went steadily, faithfully on the towpath.

"I didn't think Jotham Klore had that much grit," Fortune said after a while.

"He's got a lot," Molly said quickly. "I'd thought Dan would do a quicker job."

The shiver ran up her back again. Both she and the ex-preacher saw the battered face in their mind's eye, and the squat legs bent, and the heavy hands raised as Klore kept heading in.

She brushed the hair back from her forehead and let her hand rest there. The same tired, white look that had been on her face all the while Dan was fighting still lay in her eyes.

Far ahead a horn wailed for a lock.

"Did Dan tell you he'd got a job offered him on a farm at Lyons Falls?"

"No," said Fortune.

"It's a fine job," she went on; "only they want a single man."

"What did he say?"

"He said he'd take it double. Mr. Butterfield's going to let him know about it when he gets to Rome."

"It's the kind of a job he wants. It's what he wants to do."

"That's right."

Her voice was tired.

"He ain't no boater. He won't stay long on the canal, no matter what."

The ex-preacher glanced at her with a worried, affectionate look.

"No," he said, in a little while.

"All he wants to do is farm—clean out a stable—watch his wife do chores."

"Maybe he don't look at it that way, Molly."

The sudden flush went down again.

"I know, Fortune. I hadn't ought to've said it. And he ought to take it."

"It would be a good thing," Fortune agreed. "Suppose you did marry him, Molly?"

"Suppose I did marry him," she repeated, turning her fine frank eyes to his. "Suppose I did. Supposing I could love him like I did. Would I help him any? Wouldn't it come around how I'd lived? Them are fine folk he's going to—they'd be notional having a canal cook living on their place, whatever she was then."

"They wouldn't have to find out," he suggested.

"There's people would know inside of a week. A man can keep secrets about himself and nobody mind particular. But a woman hasn't any show in a small town."

He nodded angrily.

"It wouldn't be right by Dan," she said. "And I can't love him like I did. I'd get tired and I wouldn't be happy. Then he wouldn't either. Even if he got his own farm, people would talk about me. It ain't as if I was even middling old."

"No," he said. "You're too pretty."

"He's a good boy. He's close with money. That ain't his fault—it's into him to be. But I couldn't stand it. I've got my wages now, so I don't mind. Alone on a farm, all the year . . ."

Fortune stared at her sympathetically.

"He's a good boy. He's done a great thing," she said proudly.

"Yeanh. He's licked Klore."

"Yeanh. He was afraid of him, and he licked him." Then she said, with almost a wail in her voice, "If he'd been licked, maybe it would've been easier for me."

The old man clucked his tongue on his teeth. For all she looked so pretty, she could not live with a strong man unless he made a slave of her. While she had thought of Dan as weak, and seen him afraid, she could love him. She must rule or be ruled.

"Molly," he said suddenly, "you ain't going back to Klore?"

She caught her lower lip with her teeth.

"No. I can't now, after being with Dan. I did love Dan, Fortune. I loved him hard. I couldn't go back."

He understood. She could not let a beaten man override her.

THREE STALWARTS

"What'll you do, then?"

"I don't know, yet. I'll go back to Lucy Cashdollar's a while, maybe. I don't want a job, but I could stay with her. Maybe if I could get a boat I'd go boating for myself. Mrs. Quackenbush does that."

He grinned suddenly.

"Want a driver?"

She smiled.

"Shucks. You? You'd be running off all the while to play pinochle." Her face sobered. "Anyway, it ain't possible."

"When'll you quit?" he asked.

"I don't know. Dan ought to have a free hand when he gets into Rome. He hadn't ought to stay on the canal."

"How is he?"

"Sleeping," she said. "It don't seem possible. But there ain't a single mark onto his face. You'd hardly know . . ."

She shivered, as poplar leaves shiver, at a touch.

On the next bend, Fortune jumped ashore. The black turned his bald nose round and gave the old man a glance.

"It don't seem right," Fortune said to the rumps of the horses. "Each one thought he was fighting for her. And neither one won."

Down the old Sarsey Sal sank in the walls of the locks. It grew colder. An old man sat on the dock at Han Yerry's fishing for sunfish.

"Frost to-night," he prophesied to Fortune.

Dan came stiffly on deck. His eyes fell first on the plank road where it ran into the gorge. There was a rope stretched across it, and two men sat under a tree, holding shotguns over their knees.

"What's up?" he asked the old man.

Without removing his eyes from his float, the fisherman gummed snuff.

"They swore in twelve men here in this town," he said. "They've closed all the roads. It's said Calash is headed this way. All them that hain't swore in is out watching for him. There's a reward onto him—two thousand dollars, dead or alive." He rolled the sum over his tongue.

The Sarsey Sal pushed on into a green twilight. The cold bit sharper. Twice they saw men posted near the towpath, their eyes roaming, as men watch for a fox.

Dan said little, standing beside Molly. Once again the chase for Calash was coming toward him on the edge of night.

"I wonder if they'll get him," Molly said.

He did not answer. Perhaps this time they would; but he did not think so. Always he had seen the man come, and go again; and he had never seen his face. Men were out after him, but they had never seen him. None of them had any record of the man's past; but they feared him and discussed him angrily among themselves and waited by the roads to kill him.

"I'd like to see him," Dan said.

He had a superstitious foreboding. The man had come into his sight always at the moment of some happening to Dan—when he first came on the canal; when he first saw Molly; when Samson Weaver died, to leave him the boat; and again before his fight with Jotham Klore.

"I'd like to look at him," he said again.

Under the flap of his shirt pocket, he carried the little diamond horse, and now he felt of it with his hand.

In a wide piece of water they tied up the old boat and brought the team aboard. Dan put light blankets on them. Fortune lit the night lantern and hung it out.

Their supper was very quiet. Dan moved awkwardly, his muscles aching. But his eyes, as he followed Molly's movements between the table and the stove, were steadily calm. Now and then a smile played over his mouth.

After supper Fortune went out. He said that he would walk on to the Delta House—it was but a mile down—and find a pinochle game. "My luck ought to be smart after to-day," he said. "I'll strip Davis dry. You can pick me off the towpath in the morning." He smiled at them, sitting at the table, with the lamplight on them. His face looked older and friendly to both of them. "So long," he said.

Dan dozed in his chair, his weariness still on him, while Molly cleared the supper things. She glanced at him from time to time and gave him a tender smile. Then she interrupted her work to get him his pipe, filling and lighting it for him. He puffed at the tight-wadded load for a while; but his lungs were still sore, and the effort of making the pipe draw was too hard on them. So he grinned and put it down. . . .

The striking of the clock made him open his eyes at the little prancing horse. "When it strikes I think he's crossed a bridge maybe." That was what Samson Weaver had said.

Molly was standing at his side. She stood very straight.

"Don't you think you'd ought to go to bed, Dan?"

He smiled at her.

"I guess that's right."

Then they both started. A horse was trotting swiftly along the towpath. They glanced at each other, seeing the same thing in each other's eyes.

She put her hand under his arm, helping him to get up.

"I'm going up, Molly."

She brought him his hat and sweater without speaking.

On deck they found a white moon shining. The smell of frost was on the air. It was very still. The light of the night lantern made a faint light on the old boards of the deck.

On the towpath stood a grey horse, dark with sweat, breathing in deep steady pants. But his head was up. The rider dismounted slowly.

"Henderson's pretty close after me," he said in a dry voice. "Can you put up this horse and hide us till he goes by?"

Dan felt Molly take his arm.

"No," she whispered.

He thought of the roads and the men watching.

"Yeanh."

The gang was still out. He saw Gentleman Joe stagger when he tried to walk.

"I'll take the brown horse out," he said. "You can take him into the pasture back of them bushes. I'll blanket your horse alongside of my black."

Calash tried to take down the bars of the pasture.

"I can't do it," he said. "One of them got my arm."

They noticed then that his left arm was tied up with two handkerchiefs.

"You do it," Dan said to Molly.

He took the grey in and put the blanket on over his saddle. In the far corner a man would have to look twice to see it. The horse was as tall as the brown and his grey legs might be mistaken for white stockings. The brown came out good-humoredly and went into the pasture with the fugitive.

It was still in the cabin again. Dan and Molly sat opposite each other before the stove without speaking. The clock ticked quickly.

After a minute or two their ears caught the murmur of running horses on the towpath. It grew swiftly, and beats made out a rhythm. Then the jingle of bits, the scrape of shoes, and the long hard breathing. Men spoke.

"Sarsey Sal," one read.

"Harrow's boat. Jeepers! He's the man beat Klore. I'd like to look at him."

Feet pounded on the deck. Henderson came in, fat, puffing slightly, a dead cigar tilted in the corner of his mouth. His red cheeks were smooth as ever, but there was a hot light in his brown eyes. As he pushed the pot hat back on his head, they could see that his mind was only on business.

"Seen Calash come this way?"

"Yeanh," said Dan. "He come on the towpath five minutes ago."

"That right?" Henderson jerked his question at Molly.

She nodded.

"Did he come aboard?"

"No," said Dan.

"Better look," Henderson grunted to the men peering curiously through the door. Dan saw the long pale moustaches of one of the deputies, and a stir of air brought him a smell of violets.

"How many horses?"

"Four," said Dan. "One a heavy team."

"Take the lantern," said Henderson.

The deputy was gone a minute.

"All right," he said when he came back.

"Come on," said Henderson. In a minute they were gone.

When Molly and Dan came out on deck again, Gentleman Joe was leading the brown horse out of the pasture. Dan brought the grey off the boat and took his own horse aboard. By the time he had the stable hatch closed down, Gentleman Joe was mounted.

"Thanks," he said. "I owe you a lot."

He sat staring up the towpath, a tired man. His coat hung limp against his horse's flanks, the brim of his hat slouched, and the words came past his lips with a drag, as if each one hurt him.

"Where're you going now?" Dan asked him.

"I guess I'll keep on back of them and try to slip through when they turn back at the Kill."

"Everybody's turned out there. I seen 'em when we come down."

"Maybe I can break through."

"There's a couple of men along the towpath waiting with shotguns."

The man sighed.

"I ought to have got out last winter. Damn Henderson. Who'd've thought a little fat man like him?"

"Whyn't you cut back?"

"No use. A water rat couldn't get by them."

"They'll be coming back this way," Dan said.

The man sighed again. Then he drew up his shoulders. The horse, feeling the movement, lifted his head and tested the ground under his hoofs.

"I tell you. I'll cut across to the Watertown road. The guard won't be so heavy. It's only a couple of miles cross-lots. The horse can jump."

"Yeanh."

"So long."

"Good-bye." And again Dan had not seen his face.

Calash turned his horse at the bars, and he cleared them from a standing jump. The tall figure atop him seemed to have lost its weariness. It sat straight as the horse went away at an easy lope.

Dan went back to the boat, but on deck he turned to look west to the Watertown road. Against the sky he could see the low hill it passed before taking the climb up Tug Hill. There was the place to watch. He sat down with his back to the cabin. Molly came out with a blanket and sat down beside him and spread it over both of them.

"I hope he gets away," Dan said.

"He's got a chance."

He felt drowsy in spite of the cold air, and a great content settled over him. At last the canal and Molly belonged to him. The tired figure of the highwayman hung in his mind; the same tired-looking body that he had himself. But he had seen the horse clear the fence, and Gentleman Joe headed for freedom. Only the man had had to go alone.

Affectionately he put his arm over Molly's shoulders and felt her draw in to him. They listened to the ripple against the boat and the small sounds of water washing the bankside grass.

"Dan."

The light of the night lantern came to them feebly, barely tracing her profile. Her eyes were dark to the moonlight.

"Yeanh, Molly."

He felt her straighten up under his arm. For a bit she was silent.

"We'll get into Rome to-morrow," he said. "You and me both, and then . . ."

He felt her hard warm palm in his.

"Dan, if Mr. Butterfield gets word you can take that job double, will you take it?"

He paused, feeling his way.

"No," he said. "No, I'm going to stay on the canal. You and me are going to stay together, now, ain't we?"

"It's a good job, Dan, isn't it?"

He drew a deep breath.

"Yes. It is a good job. Mr. Wilder has one of the best dairies in the county. Blooded cattle."

She caught the thrill in his voice; his hand moved in hers.

"I'm going to stay here," he said. "Boating's the thing for me, with you along. You ain't changed your mind? You wouldn't come with me?" he asked suddenly.

"No, Dan. I've not changed my mind. I'd hinder you to come. I wouldn't have no heart in it; and then, after a while, you'd lose yours."

"It's best staying here," he said gloomily.

"Sometimes it's best for two people to hurt each other, Dan."

"What do you mean? It don't mean us. We're going in to Rome to-morrow. It ain't like him—" he pointed to the low hill by the Watertown road. "I wonder will he get through."

"Sometimes it's best, Dan."

He scarcely heard her.

"You love me, Dan?"

"Yeanh," he said, turning to grin at her.

Her face lay in shadow against his shoulder.

"You won't forget it, Dan?"

Her low voice was husky.

"Forget it? Say, to-morrow I'm going to ask you again."

She seemed to draw comfort from that and pressed closer to him. . . .

Far away, against the low hill, points of light flashed. They heard the raps of rifle shots.

Neither spoke, but Dan felt suddenly tired as he went below. He could not sleep. For hours he heard the water by his head, running in a ripple on the planks. A rat splashed in the mud. . . .

Slow hoofs on the towpath; men's voices; a snatch of laughter; a voice hailing him—so they came back. They had come across lots, three of them on their horses, leading a horse, not a grey horse, but one which carried Gentleman Joe.

They laid him on the cabin roof and spread a blanket over him.

"We're tuckered out," they said. "Can we sleep in your cabin?"

"Yeanh," Dan said.

They threw themselves like logs on the floor—men he had never seen.

"Special depities," they introduced themselves. "Just farmers," they said proudly.

"Where'd you get him?" Dan asked.

"He come through the Watertown road. Henderson took us over there. He's gone to bring in his men now. He told us to take him into Rome. George, here, shot him."

"Yeanh," said an old man, with lean strong hands and bright eyes. "It was a running shot. He came right across from me in the shadow, and I feared I'd miss him. But I always was good with a rifle. Shot a running fox when I was eight."

"What was he wanted for?"

"How do we know?" the spokesman said. "Two thousand dollars—that's what for. George got him—it's his'n."

"Well, I won't forget the man that stood with me," said the old fellow. "I'm no undertaker."

"Something he did out West. One of them states. Train or something." The man yawned. "Me, I'm right tuckered."

Very weary, Dan went back to his bunk. . . .

He woke in the breath of dawn. He was still tired. Beyond the curtain, the men snored heavily. Now and then a boot scraped on the floor as one of them turned in his sleep. Molly had got up, but Dan saw his clothes neatly spread on the foot of the bunk ready for him. He heard a fire snapping in the stove. She must have been quiet not to wake the men.

He got up and dressed and went into the cabin. She was not there; but the room was warm with the fire, and the coffee kettle was beginning to boil. Dan went on deck to find her.

As he turned round at the head of the stairs, his eyes fell on a stiff, blanketed figure stretched out on the cabin roof. The dim light of daybreak washed it with a pale light, bringing out a shadow between the rigid legs and under the left arm. The blanket had settled during the night, till now it shaped him.

For a long time Dan stared at it, not moving. He thought of how he had seen him, in action, riding his grey horse. Whenever Dan felt the canal come close to him, he had seen this man. He had had grace, beside which the determination of the fat marshal was turned into something drab. Now he lay here on Dan's boat in the early morning. . . . Perhaps, after all, he had escaped . . .

Always Dan had seen him at night, with his face in darkness. Something to draw him on, it had been; something to know, like his first embarrassed interest in the canal folk themselves. At last he had only to lift the blanket from it.

Very slowly Dan reached forward and drew the blanket from the face. For a minute he looked down at it in the morning light as it grew stronger, little by little, as if it were afraid to come—and as he looked he felt the lean dawn wind on his cheeks.

It was dead grey. The skin was stretched on the cheeks and down each side of the broad nose. The bitter thin lips drew back from snuff-stained teeth. The eyes were open, rolled upward, but Dan caught an edge of the cold grey. It was ugly, cruel, mean.

Dan let the blanket fall back and stood looking over the meadows where the grey light followed the shadows.

He had seen Gentleman Joe. He had looked for him wherever he went, like the canal folk and the farmers who shot him for the reward he represented, without knowing really why. He had felt a secret kinship for him, and built it up. Only the fat marshal, who went round about his business with the methodicalness of a grocer weighing sugar, had known. Molly had once seen him. . . .

There was a dull ache in Dan's heart, and he looked round for Molly, wondering why she had not greeted him. But the boat was bare. He went to the stable, where the black horse scrambled to his feet, nickering gently. But the stable held only the two teams. He came on deck again and looked across the meadows. But the only things alive were the shadows. He went down the towpath, and there he found her narrow tracks.

He followed them down until he came to the landing before the Delta House. It stood gaunt and bare in the grey light, its windows curtained, a trace of smoke climbing its chimneys from the dying fires. The tracks ended on the wharf, but away ahead he heard the clink of trace chains. And then in the shadow of the steps he saw Fortune Friendly sitting, silent, his black eyes watching him, and he knew. . . .

"Set down, Dan," said the ex-preacher, quietly.

Dan sat down.

"She's gone."

"Yeanh," said Fortune. "She come down with her bag and went aboard the Nancy. I heard her waking Mrs. Gurget and pretty soon they put out."

"Did she tell you where she was going?"

"No. I was setting here. I'd never held such cards. I missed a thousand aces by one on the last hand; I couldn't sleep. So I was setting here. She just went aboard."

"I wonder where she'll go."

"Maybe back to Lucy Cashdollar's for a spell."

"Yeanh."

They sat side by side, hearing the water wash the dock.

"Where'll you go?"

"Why, I don't know for sure," Fortune said. "There was a Brandreth man and a peddler and old Davis, and I cleaned them out. Just now I'd be rich if I hadn't give Tinkle all of it."

"You done that?"

The old man grinned shamefacedly.

"It's time maybe I invested some. I thought I'd buy a boat, maybe. He's going to get me one in Rome if he can. Boats'll be cheap in fall."

"That's right, I guess."

Dan got slowly to his feet.

"Maybe we'd better get back," he said dully.

Fortune coughed.

"Them horses could get you into Rome without no driving, couldn't they?"

"I guess so."

"I thought maybe I ought to stay here and give those rascals another chance at their money, while my luck's in."

"All right."

"If you could let me have my wages."

"All right."

Dan paid him.

"Good-bye."

"Good luck," said the ex-preacher, shaking hands.

Dan walked back till he came to the old Sarsey Sal, rubbing heavily against the bank. He gazed at it, half seeing, and then he turned to look toward Rome. His lean brown face did not change. He was very still, and a muskrat slipped into the water and swam just to his feet before it saw him. It looked at him out of its sharp eyes for an instant, saw that it was not observed, and dove without a sound.

A little way off, cows in their pasture lifted their hind legs and got up with a jangle of a bell or two. Dan went aboard to find that the coffee had boiled over.

Rome Haul

The men caught their horses in a group of trees a hundred yards from the towpath and tied the body to the spare one. It was an awkward job, but at last it held.

They came aboard to thank Dan and shake his hand.

"I shot him," said George, "but you licked Jotham Klore. You don't get no reward. It's tough."

"Yeanh," said the spokesman. "That's how it is."

Dan harnessed the big team and took them to the towpath. The black looked round till he had heaved the gang aboard and taken the sweep in his hands. Then, perhaps, he said something, for they both started together.

It was a silent trip. They passed the Delta House, blind and asleep. Dan was glad Fortune was out of sight. Going alone, the heart seemed out of the boat. He kept his eyes on the team, once in a while meeting the glance of the black as he turned his head.

They slipped into the morning mist. All round Dan the sound of cows broke out, the distant song of their bells. The mist was cold and wet on his face; there was nothing left to see but the dip of the towline and occasionally the rumps of his big team pulling faithfully.

He heard the water life awakening—the splash of a rat, the dive of a frog; the sounds slipped quickly to his ears and were gone.

So they went on—the Sarsey Sal, the two horses, and Dan. When the sun rose, flooding the sky above the mist with color, they were close to Rome.

They came into the bustle of the great basin in the clear day, and the team took him to Butterfield's wharf. There they stopped, both waiting for him to take them aboard.

When they had been unharnessed, he went to Butterfield's office. Men about him were talking excitedly at the double news, the death of Calash and the defeat of Klore. Some looked at Dan as he went past, and some pointed him out, proud of knowing who he was.

Mr. Butterfield shook his hand.

"I heard about the fight," he said. "It must have been a great one. I'll get you to tell me about it later."

"There ain't much to tell," Dan said heavily.

Mr. Butterfield looked at him keenly. Then he came swiftly to business. It was soon settled.

"About that farm proposition, Harrow. I'm sorry to say Mr. Wilder writes that he can only take you on single."

"I'll take it."

Mr. Butterfield said nothing for a moment, but there was understanding kindness in his eyes that embarrassed Dan.

"I'm glad. It's a good job for you. You'll do well. You ought to go at once, if you can."

"I'd like to start to-day."

"What will you do with the boat?"

"I think I know a man that will buy it and the light team," Dan said. "They won't fetch much of a price."

"No, not now. But how about your fine team?"

"I was wondering about them," Dan said shyly. "I was wondering would you keep them for me awhile? They could earn their keep."

"Certainly. But I'd be glad to pay you a full price for them."

"I wouldn't want to sell them."

"I see."

They shook hands, and Dan went out.

8

THE ROAD AND THE PEDDLER

HE was walking along the Watertown road. A man driving a buggy had given him a lift as far as Ava. Now he was climbing the long slope of Tug Hill from the south.

As he went on, the stiffness began to run out of him; his back limbered and his breathing eased. He stopped to eat a sandwich under a tree beside a small spring. Close to him a pair of cows looked on affably. It had come out hot after the cold night; there was a dry dusty August gleam on everything.

The little cool pocket off the road, where the cows discussed the world together over their cuds, invited him. A little way off wasps whined about their nest; but they had no quarrel with the three at the spring.

The cows were thin, scrawny creatures, with matted coats and little pinched bags.

"Dinkeys," Dan said to himself; and he thought of the fine cattle he was to work among. Already he was looking forward.

It was only when he came to the great hill, where the road was no better than a track, that he stopped to look back toward the wide Mohawk Valley. He could see the thread of the canal and the white lines of bridges; and to his left, five miles away, he caught a glimpse of the Black River Canal, and a small boat on it. The boat was the merest speck of white in the rolling land of green. But it seemed to him that he could hear its horn, echo after echo, in the Lansing Kill. . . .

The imagined sound brought back to him a picture of the fat woman; she had come down to the Sarsey Sal that morning and had taken him into her arms. For some reason he had not been embarrassed, even when Solomon poked his bald head through the door and, after looking at them asked, "Can I come in?" The three had sat together without a word for several minutes.

Then Solomon had cleared his throat nervously and asked him what he would sell the boat for. "I'm not buying it for us, Dan." "You'd understand that," the fat woman had said. "It's Fortune"—and Dan told them how he had talked to Fortune at the Delta House. "He wouldn't buy a boat for himself," the fat woman said, and Solomon nodded—and then they had all three looked at each other, guessing whom he wished to buy it for. "How much did he give you?" Solomon had told him, "A hundred and fifty dollars." And Dan had given him the boat and the bays for that. "My land, it's giving it away!" said the fat woman; and she and Solomon had looked at each other.

Then Dan had told them his plans. Mr. Butterfield had offered to invest his money for him and had promised to keep the big team; but they, if Dan could have use for them, would be sent on in the late fall—"in time for fall ploughing," Dan said, and Solomon had nodded. For a young man, he was well off.

"I should think you'd farm it your own self," said the fat woman.

"I got to learn more about dairying," Dan said. "I didn't have only a few dinkeys on Pa's place. There's a lot of things to learn handling good land."

"I guess that's right," she said.

"Plain horse sense," said Solomon.

"Later I'll maybe get me my own farm," Dan said.

He got up and went forward to the stable. Solomon made a move with his feet; but Mrs. Gurget said, "Leave him be alone." And he went in by himself to thump the ribs of the brown and stroke the bald white nose of the black. The brown stared stolidly at the wall and rested his nigh hip; but the black nuzzled him for sugar and blew gentle breaths into the palm of his hand. They were a good team.

When he returned to the cabin, Mrs. Gurget and Solomon had helped him to pack his bag.

Then he gave her the clock—and the tears had jumped out on her cheeks. "My, my, I always did like that little pony, prancing and raring like he'd just been stung! Ain't he pretty, Sol?"

Dan had put an envelope in Solomon's hand. The couple could not say very much. The fat woman kissed him good bye and Solomon wrung his hand, muttering something about stopping off at Lyons Falls to see how he was. "If anything comes wrong, just write and we'll turn the old boat and come galloping," he promised. "Shucks," said Mrs. Gurget, "gallop them mules?" "I'll leave you on shore, then they can," he said. The fat woman kissed Dan again and whispered in his ear, "Don't remember her too hard, Dan."

They had waved to him till he turned the corner. He had had a last glimpse of the little bowlegged man and the great woman, with her high bonnet, her red hair, her scarlet petticoat, and the boats going by behind them.

Of all the people on the canal, they were his best friends. . . .

Then he turned himself.

For a minute he saw Molly before his eyes, as she had come aboard that night, flushed cheeks and blowzy hair, and he felt heavy and sad.

But the road led downward under his feet and he stepped ahead. The road would take him down past the barren farms to rich meadowland where fine cows grazed. He would feel them with his hands and milk them in the dusk of the great new barn.

As the shadows came in on the track, he made out the marks of wagon wheels, fresh in the dry road. From the first they seemed familiar. Then he remembered. They went from side to side of the road and stopped where the grass had been lush. There a horse had cropped it up.

Farther on, where the road ran up a short ridge, he saw where the old horse had lengthened his stride; and now he was certain that the old peddler was ahead of him, riding his wagon, wondering where the road would bring him out.

He would be reading a book.

Dan changed his bag to his left hand. Perhaps he would get a lift.

ERIE
WATER

For My Mother

One

THE WEDDING

1

"The captain said I was strong"

AN April morning in 1817, two passengers stood on the bows of the Greenbush Ferry.

"So you're heading west, hey?"

"Yes."

"Aiming to square off a piece of a section on your own hook? Well, you're young, and you look stout."

While the young man leaned his wrists on the ferryboat rail, his companion looked him over. His sharp, humorous eyes drooped kindly, as if a young man heading west appealed to him.

The young man was staring cross-river, at the shipping, the sloops at the dock, the New York packet getting up a head of steam, at the warehouses and stores, and behind them the houses of the city itself perched on the steep slope. Through the middle of the city, from the river to the green park before the Capitol Building on the summit, a white line went straight as a ferule.

"That's State Street, son." The man pushed back his tall Quakerish hat and pointed a long forefinger. "That's the way you pass through the city, whether you take the Great Western or the Mohawk Pike. For the first you keep right straight after your shadder. For the other, you branch right at the Capitol."

"That brown building with the white stripes on it?"

"Yes. But those stripes are pillars, better than four feet thick, and built of stone—Connecticut marble, I've heard tell."

But the young man was not interested in stone. His lean strong hands, tanned and calloused, took hold of each other. His brown eyes were earnest. The older man bent close to his shoulder and examined his profile.

The face was lean, like the hands, the nose strong, curved, with a hint of humor. The cheeks were slightly hollow, because of the high bones, but the jaw was set well. He was dressed in a worn homespun suit halfway between a grey and a brown, the trousers tucked into the boots, and the cloth bundle with shoulder straps lay between his feet.

"Albany's an almighty big city," he said now, turning to his companion.

"There's bigger, son. There's Boston, and Philadelphy, and New York. There's Baltimore, and I've heard Charlestown is a reputable city, too. But there's no denying Albany sets handsome against the river. Haven't you ever seen it before?"

"No."

"Where do you come from, son?"

"From Uniontown."

"Uniontown? Say, what's your name?"

"Jerry Fowler."

"Fowler! Not kin to Preston Fowler that farms the creek bottom along the mill road there?"

"He's my Pa."

"By draggit! I know your Pa. My name is Bennet. Maybe you've heard him use it?"

The young man turned.

"You ain't Issachar Bennet? The Shaker missioner?"

"I'm called so, son."

"I've heard Pa speak about you."

The skin about the Shaker's eyes puckered.

"What did he say?"

"He said you was the only man that ever tied him in a horse deal."

"Spoke kind of sharp?"

"He said it was the most vicious piece of business but one he'd ever been a party to. But this time *he* got the horse."

The Shaker tilted his hatchet head. Innumerable wrinkles appeared in his face. His laughter rang over the water.

Behind him the ears of the two brown horses hitched to his wagon pricked forward.

"That was a handsome deal, son, even if it was against your Pa."

He pulled forward his hat again, and leaned his arms upon the rail. Now and then a chuckle rose in his long throat and his shoulders quivered. "Ain't nothing like a horse deal," he muttered. "One way or the other, there ain't nothing like it."

The ferry tilted under their feet as the last wagon rolled aboard. Jerry looked behind him at the boat. The skipper was casting off the ropes, and the horse boy had picked up his short whip.

"All right, there, Joey!" bawled the skipper, and the boy yelled, "Whoa!"

The ferry horses, which wore collar and traces, had been dozing in their places inside the wheel housings, the one on the right facing the stern, the one on the left the bow. When the driver boy yelled "Whoa!" they lifted their heads and started walking, and Jerry saw that the channel they trod in was no more than the rim of a gigantic wheel under the ferry deck. He heard the creaking of wooden gears and the splash of paddles against the water, and the flat-bottomed old ferryboat began to edge out into the river. The skipper caught up a rudder stick and fastened it into the post aft.

The ferry made slow progress. It was loaded to capacity. Besides the Shaker's outfit, there were two movers' wagons; an old couple in the one, and a young married pair, obviously their son and daughter-in-law, in the other. At the rear, an oxcart, piled high with seasoned spruce boarding, leaned down on a yoke of somnolent red-and-white oxen, and the Dutch farmer who drove them braced his back against the outturned rump of the nigh beast and dozed himself.

Jerry turned back to face the river.

"That's quite a notion of Mason Jakes's," observed the Shaker. "He trains his ferry horses backwards. Starts them with a whoa. A lot of horses coming on board the first time is nervous, and if you said 'giddap' as gentle as a meadow mouse they'd hop right over the rail."

He looked sidewise at Jerry.

"Where do you aim to look for your land? Ohio? Illinois? Or do you figure to go out into Injun country?"

The boy shook his head.

"Not that far. I don't hanker for prairie land. It's my idea to get to the Holland Purchase. Have you seen it?"

"I've passed through the south bend of it once or twice—Batavia way. But I've never seen the northern half, which they say is best. It's marshy ground, full of the ague when it's opened up. But I hear there's a fine depth of soil."

"Which way is the best to get there, the Western or the Mohawk?"

"It depends," said Issachar Bennet. "They both join together out in Manlius. If you had a horse, I'd say take the Great Western. But if you're footing it, you'd better go by the river pike. There's more taverns and farms. Beyond Cherry Valley, the Western's scarce of settlements, unless you follow the southern companies through Otsego to the border."

"I'm footing it," said Jerry.

"It 'pears to me, son, that you ain't taking much of an outfit."

"I've got nothing to hinder me."

"Still, a man needs an outfit. Next spring you'll need oxen or a team, and a plough. Have you got any money?"

"Yes. I've got ninety dollars. I aim to use fifty for a down payment on fifty acres and take out articles to pay the other two hundred. They say you have eight years' time from the Company."

"That's true. They're good folks to deal with."

The young man stared across at the city. The ferry had made enough of the distance to let him see the men swarming on the docks. Everywhere he looked he saw sloops tied up. On one, men were deviling black bags onto their backs.

"That's a coal boat," said Issachar Bennet. "Wood's coming high in Albany and coal comes from New Jersey. I've heard the Corporation's offered a thousand dollars to any man that finds a mine of coal in five miles of the river."

The sun was hot in the blue sky. The river sparkled to a warm breeze drawing up from the south. White soft spring clouds were floating over the valley. Under the continual swoop of light after shadow, the city seemed to move. Jerry saw a flock of pigeons sweep over the warehouse roofs and flutter down on the docks. Their wings glanced with a bright ripple of blue and white.

He could hear the shouts of the dock hands faintly over the water. Men were loading a sloop with wheat sacks, man after man, carrying bags on their shoulders. Behind them all manner of wagons passed, oxcarts and lumber wagons. The teams moved slowly, or drowsed between slack traces.

To the right he saw a Pennsylvania wagon under its stained grey hood swing out of a by-street behind its six-horse team and halt before the largest warehouse in sight. A moment later a second had drawn up beside it; and in another moment still a third. A swarm of men, some carrying great scoops and others bags, had invested them.

His eye roved.

"It's kind of exciting," the Shaker said sympathetically. "Every time I see it, it gives me a flip in my insides. It wasn't so long ago Albany wasn't no more than a trading post with a couple of Dutchmen practising on the Injuns." He paused. "There's the New York packet."

Jerry turned downstream. Cutting a great roll out of the river with its sharp bows, he saw the packet boat. Her towering stack was belching black tumultuous rolls of smoke that the breeze snatched and carried forward. While he looked, a tuft of white, like a bursting milkweed pod, sprang out against the side of the stack. The harsh, half-human scream of steam shot up the river.

At the sound, the skipper shouted to the driver boy.

"Giddap," cried the boy, and the ferry horses stopped their treading. The wheels and the creaking gears fell silent, and the boat drifted.

The packet loomed over them with incredible swiftness. Jerry saw passengers thronging the upper deck. In the bridge house a man leaned from a window, the white beaver on his head precariously cocked. One hand inside the window toyed with the spokes of a wheel. The packet veered and slid past.

Jerry heard a panting in her, like the panting of a horse after a long run. He saw the walking beam above the decks tilt up and down and the boil of white foam breaking away from her paddles. On the huge wheel housing, scrolled in gold, he read the packet's name—*Olive Branch*.

The ferry skipper swung his flat hulk to meet the wash, and the ferry lifted and dipped, slapping her bottom on the water.

A terrific jangling of bells broke out in the steamboat. The paddles ceased their beating of the river, and with a majestic quiet she slid into her landing.

When the ferry quieted, the horses took up their endless progress. She was past midstream now, with her slip yawning plainly before her at the lower end of South Market. Jerry was once more leaning over the rail with the water sliding smoothly towards him.

"That's a queer-looking bunch of people."

Issachar Bennet looked where he pointed.

A sloop was tied up at the dock. In the bow a couple of hands sat idly kicking their heels. On the stern deck a group of people made a knot, like a knot of herded cattle. There was a kind of bewilderment on their faces; they stood over bundles and bags, or held them in their hands.

"Why don't they land?" asked the young man. "I've seen them since we started."

A man in a blue pea-jacket and a varnished black straw hat was standing on the dock beside the sloop, talking to a knot of townsfolk. His face shone a brilliant burned red over his sandy square beard, and when he took a few steps he moved with a rolling gait.

"Looks like Henry Fearon," said Bennet. "He's master of a brig. They look like a load of redemptioners. Wait a minute."

He fished in his coat pocket.

"Here's yesterday's *Gazette*."

He turned the small pages, his sharp eyes running down the lines of fine print.

"That's what they are all right, son. Here's the advertisement, if you want to read it."

The young man took the paper. On the second page he found, under the lottery advertisement, the following paragraph:

FROM THE BRIG, BUBONA—LIVERPOOL TO HUDSON

The Passengers

At the sloop dock, April 15, 1817, at half after eleven, who are willing to defray the expense of their passage by engaging themselves for a limited time, consist of persons of the following occupations, besides women and children; viz:—13 farmers, 1 baker, 1 butcher, 1 whitesmith, 2 shoemakers, 1 brewer, 1 wheelwright, 2 barbers, 1 cabinetmaker, 1 stockingweaver, 1 coalburner, 2 coopers.

Apply on board Honeyman's sloop, *Lady*. Henry Fearon, master *Bubona*, present at that time.

Issachar Bennet watched the young man's lips carefully framing the words. Jerry's color heightened as he read. He returned the paper without comment, and the Shaker pocketed it.

"Poor things," he said. "I feel sorry for them. It's not so bad for the men. It's the women and children. The young ones. They don't know what's in for them and they can't choose. Fearon signs them on to any that meets his price, and if there's a difficulty about the pounds and dollars in it, he just whacks on extra time to make it up."

Jerry kept silent. A cloud shadow that had been passing the docks drew suddenly up the hill, and the sunlight, like a moving thing, supplanted it.

Among the redemptioners his eyes were caught by a coppery gleam. It flashed sharply before the brown warehouse walls, the dun city. In all those sea-pale faces it shone like a flower blooming, and he shifted along the rail to see it better.

A young woman was standing behind the others at the very rear of the sloop deck. A couple of bundles lay at her feet, but she stood straight. She had a mass of coppery hair carried round her head in two tight braids. Her chin was up; but as the ferry nosed in towards its slip he saw the rapid rise and fall of her breast and her grey eyes moving over the docks, the redemptioners in front of her, the captain's jaunty figure, the city with its noon hour smokes whipping northward. She wore a brown wool dress with a dark blue shawl over her shoulders and a small black scarf, like mourning, round her throat. And he saw that she was afraid.

"It don't seem right," the Shaker was saying in his ear. "Up there in the Capitol they've passed a bill this spring to free the slaves; and they'll tell you redemptioning is legal."

His long sharp face grew serious.

"I'm not exactly a good man, son. But it riles me. And I'm a good preacher. And I'd like to preach a sermon against men like Fearon. He's what his church calls an uncommon good man, goes regular on Sundays and collects money to missionate the heathen with, but I'd like to preach a sermon against him just the same, just if I knew every word of it would come true."

"Easy, there," the driver boy shouted behind them to his horses. "Slow."

"We're almost in," said Bennet.

"What time is it?" asked Jerry.

"Fifteen after eleven, I should judge, son."

He glanced at the boy.

"Don't let it rankle you, son. There's nothing you can do about it." He paused. "Well," he said, "I guess we won't see each other in a minute. I've got some dealings here and in Schenectady afore I cut south."

"South?" echoed Jerry, mechanically.

"Yes, I'm on a mission trip to Kentucky. We're making a start there in the mountains. There's one thing I'd like to know, boy. How'd you manage to get past your Pa?"

A small grin stretched the young man's lips.

"Pa said I was crazy. But I'd served out my twenty-one years to him, and last winter I worked out for hire. So I said I was bent. And he gave me twenty-five dollars and said he was shut of me."

The Shaker chuckled.

"I envy you, son. I mind my first trip westward on my own. There's nothing like it in the world. Good luck to you." His lean fingers gripped Jerry's hard palm with surprising strength.

"Maybe we'll meet again, some day. I'm apt to wander most anywheres."

The boat bumped into the slip and the skipper ran forward to set the gang. Jerry picked up his bundle and stepped aside for the Shaker's team. The skinny old man was on the wagon seat, his knees bent sharply towards his chin. He flourished his whip to Jerry and pushed the brown team into a trot. The iron tires spun on the cobbles, and as he swung into South Market Street Jerry caught a last wave of his thin hand.

Jerry stood where he was while the movers' wagons filed off. They were followed by a couple of amiable cows who confronted the city with staring eyes. But a small dog yapping at their heels and the stick in the younger man's hand urged them forward. The boat tilted as they passed onto the dock, and the oxen had to draw their cart up a grade.

The horse boy reversed the position of the two horses and the captain sat down on a box and mopped his face.

"I'm a Dutchman," he remarked to Jerry. "Yes, sir, I'm a blasted Dutchman if this ain't the hottest April day in my remembrance. Winters ain't what I recollect as a boy."

ERIE WATER   601

"It's real hot," Jerry agreed.

Just up the dock he saw the sloop load of redemptioners. He had a clear view of the girl in the blue shawl now. Some of the spirit had slipped out of her attitude. Her shoulders were drooping a little. Her eyes had ceased their restless wandering and were bent down-river with a passive, hopeless stare.

Her profile was half turned to him, so that he saw the curve of her cheek and the moulding of her chin. Most of her companions were older people, making her seem younger than she probably was. Her grey eyes were large, set rather wide, and her short straight nose rather broad between them. She had a full chin, with suggestion of a dimple. The others talked among themselves, now and then pointing out buildings or people to each other. One man, who in his pink plumpness could only be the baker, cracked a joke that made his neighbors laugh. For the most part, though, they were merely accepting their situation. It meant nothing to them; for a while they would have to work without pay—that was all.

But the girl was afraid. She did not talk to the others; she kept to herself. A sailor, rolling down the dock, spied her and hailed her. The sloop hands laughed. And the girl, with a swift lift of her head, noticed him, her color deepened, and she bit her lips and moved indefinably closer to the others, as if she meant to conceal herself. As she stared round, her eyes met Jerry's.

For an instant he felt like waving to her; but he was conscious of the ferry captain's scrutiny, and turned his head.

"How do I get to the Mohawk Pike?" he asked.

The captain was stuffing a chew into his jaw. He spat phlegmatically into the river and wiped his lips with the back of his hand.

"That's South Market Street. Go along that to State Street and turn up the hill. When you get to the Capitol, if you ask, somebody's bound to know."

Jerry looked back at the sloop. The girl was standing in her former attitude, staring down-river. Issachar Bennet was right. There was nothing he could do about it. He picked up his bundle.

"Thanks," he said.

But the captain was talking to himself. "I'm a Dutchman if it ain't hot. Not that I'd hold out against a Dutchman, but they make an honest man sick for a steady diet."

Jerry turned away. The hot breeze, the slap of the ripple against the piles, were behind him. He was his own man, for a fact. And that, the Shaker had said, was the finest thing in the world. For years he had looked forward to this day. Having crossed the river, he felt that he had entered western territory, with Albany but a step for him to pass. He thought of the land he would square off. He would pick his piece with good timber, lowland for deep soil, with a brook, if he could find one, running through.

He entered the street, right foot first for luck. His lean face grinned.

It seemed to him that he had never seen so many people, so many horses and wagons, or heard such a noise in his life before. People kept coming out of stores, and entering them, and even inside the dusky interiors he heard the hum of their voices. A light dust that littered the street, unlike country dust, rose at every puff of wind; and even in calm moments he could see it creeping in the cracks between the cobbles. It had a dry choking smell that made him wonder how the myriad sparrows could get down in it and sort its particles.

A tavern stood on the corner, with windows on three sides facing the river and street. Through the wide glass panes he saw a couple of sloop hands at the bar, and the barmaid, with a broad red Dutch face, resting her hands on her hips and tilting her chin to laugh.

Jerry's mouth drew down in distaste, and instinctively he turned his face back to the docks. He saw no more of the redemption girl than her bright hair, but his memory drew her frightened eyes as clearly as if they looked to him.

He swore under his breath and continued his walk. He couldn't act like a fool the first day he was his own man. He must get on.

Across the street an old woman, sitting in a narrow shop door under a sign which read MRS. MACHARG, THREADNEEDLE STORE, noted his bright flush and waved to him. The tips of her fingers shone like ivory above the black knitted mitt. Jerry waved back, and she ducked her thinly haired old head and her face puckered smilingly.

For a block he stepped out resolutely, his eyes watching the eddy and flow in the street. Another Pennsylvania wagon turned in from State Street, its high drill hood topping all other vehicles. Its pointed front rose over the wheel team's rumps like the bow of a boat. Six bells above the wheelers' hames beat lazily to their long strides. The teamster, who walked beside them with the dust of miles and miles stiffening his boots and trousers, paid no heed to anything but his horses. He carried his fifteen-foot whip coiled round his right wrist, and now and then his hard mouth opened stiffly to speak a gentle word at his beasts.

A carriage spun past behind a light pair of matched bays, and Jerry caught a glimpse of two ladies in straw bonnets with silk muffs on their knees.

As the freight wagon drew up-wind the smell of raw wheat was blown to him. His step quickened. Some day one of these wagons would be drawing his wheat into Albany—a two-hundred-mile haul. He saw himself in the spring, helping the teamster load the wagon—perhaps on the floor of his log barn; and when it was loaded he would take the teamster into his house and call for a glass of whiskey to send him off. And suddenly, instead of the teamster, his eyes made a picture of the girl he had seen on the sloop, barelegged, her work dress open at the throat, green sunlight on her breast.

For a while he walked mechanically, not seeing, not hearing, conscious only of his heartbeats. But he would have to square off his farm and raise his house and burn black salts to buy oxen with. He had just money enough for the land and his first winter's food. He shook his head to clear his eyes.

But his stride slackened, and he began to loiter.

A thin man, like a clerk, with heavy spectacles over his eyes, sat in a little stall against the blank wall of a building. Through the rubble of street sounds his nasal voice was monotonously lifted. Prints; penny ballads; new ballad sheets; *Fratricide, or the Evil Case of John Tuhi, by Drink, Damnation, and Hanging, in the Town of Whitestown;* the *Harbeck-Tragedy,* engraved in copper, in eighteen verses; *Highland Mary;* the *Emigrant's Guide to the New West;* the *Mechanic's Handbook;* parsing books, grammars, and scholars' arithmetics; novels, fashionable and religious; notes on the Gospels. . . . His voice made a drone in the mutter of passing feet. And Jerry stood still on the footwalk while the people eddied round him. Carts rumbled from the docks, loaded with stove wood. A Yankee farmer's wagon drew up before him. A woman with a thin face held the reins and cradled a bundle. Jerry could see nothing of the baby's head; the bundle made no movement; but all at once the woman bent her face and he saw in an opening the baby's starlike hand.

Through all the noise he heard the woman humming,—

> "There was a frog lived in a spring,
> *Sing-song paddy woncha ky-me-o* . . ."

The man behind Jerry said in a drawling nasal voice, *"Emigrant's Guide."*

"Two-and-six."

The woman's eyes lifted. There was an aspect of pain that made the corners dim. She spoke to the horses. They stirred reluctantly. The man followed, grasping the cow's tail in his left hand, while with his right he held an open book before his eyes. One of the wagon's wheels needed greasing. Jerry wondered if there were something the matter with the baby.

The clerk-like vendor continued to intone his wares. Prints; penny ballads; *Arson in the Jail, or Elisha Green Cremated.* . . .

Jerry hesitated, took a step past the booth, turned, and walked up to the old man. He was reading a book—*Waverley* it said on the back; but his lips continued their meaningless expositon of the human mind. *Universalism, Explained, Argued, and Condemned; Cookery of Wild Herbs; Gazetteer to the Western Counties; Natural History of the Far West;* Bradwhite's *Medicinal Herbs, Their Habits and Approximate Situation.* . . .

"What's the price generally asked for a redemptioner, mister?"

"Eh, eh? *Redemption of Sally Neal,* six pennies."

He peered up through his glasses, his eyes bulging pale blue spots in a sea of swimming water.

"What did you say, sir?"

"What's the price of a redemption girl?"

"Oh? Eh? I'm hard of hearing, mister. Kind of hard of hearing. Just you write it down."

He handed out a tablet and pen.

Jerry slowly wrote his question. The vendor read it, holding the sheet close to his nose.

"I don't know. I don't know. I've heard forty dollars. But I'm not sure. You'd better ask. I wouldn't say, sir."

He dipped back into his book, his hands shaking as if he had been seriously disturbed. Jerry turned away.

Forty dollars was a lot of money. Forty dollars was the best part of his farm. His first day as his own man he couldn't make a fool of himself.

That was it, he was his own man.

"I don't owe a thing to nobody," he said aloud.

A messenger carrying a bag jostled his shoulder, and a hand at the edge of the roadway steadied him.

"Careful, my boy. This ain't a village. Wagons roll fast in Albany."

A carriage with flashing green spokes went spanking down the cobbles. A gentleman inside sat with his hands resting on a stick, his beaver hat immaculately set on his white forehead.

"There goes Martin Van Buren. Wonder how things are going in the Senate?"

"Thanks," said Jerry.

All at once he found himself retracing his steps. He would take another look, he said to himself, and if the girl were gone, that would settle it. He felt like a fool, but he was his own man to do as he liked.

He turned down a by-street to the docks along a row of shops with here and there a carriage waiting at a door. Inside he caught glimpses of the shop people measuring cloth or serving customers. A butcher with a fresh red face whistled through his teeth as he steeled his knife. The strokes made a shivery sound. A tailor's prentice, sitting cross-legged in a window, winked at him and adjusted his black horn thimble. Strange foreign smells mingled with the city dust, herbs and spices, calico bales, smoked fish and outland leather. The footwalk was shadowed; but ahead the sun beat down on the spars of sloops and transformed their rigging into shimmering threads like wire.

Turning down the docks, Jerry threaded his way between the wheels of carts and under the noses of dozing horses. Dock hands grunted against the heft of bales and hauled on tackle ropes. A long row of barrels gave forth a strong sickly sweet smell of wine. A shipment of Jamaica chickens kept up an amazed chattering. Men shouted above the turmoil. A flock of pigeons with fluttering wings flipped out of the roadway, dipped over the roofs in a solid phalanx, circled, and by ones and twos came fluttering back.

An old crone shuffled out of a snuff shop, fumbling with her trembling fingers in a little bag, and rubbed the brown dust across her shrunken gums. She watched Jerry striding past and turned to follow his progress, niddering to herself. Her weak eyes peered with an almost malignant curiosity.

A hundred yards down the quay a sea captain took off his varnished hat and confronted a little group of townspeople. The old woman watched Jerry walk into the group and stand still. His thin face had to her worn eyes an untouched look; he was eager, he was alive, he was reckless. She tasted the snuff. He was looking for something; she peered close; a girl, she saw, with a coppery glint in her hair. The old woman's hand snatched out a wisp of her own hair and stuffed it back under the shrunk knot. The wind drew across the people, swept the dock, and flapped the crone's skirts about her bare ankles.

A hawk, that had been cutting high circles over the Capitol, stooped like a bolt for the riverside. With wings snapping like taut silk, the pigeons exploded from the wagonway and whistled into the open windows of a rope loft; and the hawk towered, screaming, unheard above the city noise. But the tip of his wing cut across the sun and caught Jerry's eye. His tilted eager face watched the bird soaring. When he looked down again, Captain Fearon was saying, ". . . gave me no trouble. A first-rate lot. Them as reach agreement will meet me here and sign papers."

He stepped to one side, turning his back, and stroking his sandy beard. He had the detached air of a farmer offering poultry at a fair.

Jerry crowded onto the sloop with the other prospective buyers. Only a couple of ladies under French parasols remained on the dock. One of them spoke to a green-liveried negro manservant, pointing out a girl or two, while her companion fished in her reticule for an almond.

Jerry walked over to the outside rail of the sloop to give himself a last moment of reflection. Then he faced about. The girl was standing just to his left; and she was looking at him. As they exchanged a silent glance, the negro in green livery stepped up to her.

"You engaged?" he asked in a husky voice.

His brown eyes with flecked yellow whites went over her slowly and arrogantly. Even standing still he seemed to strut. But the girl appeared not to heed him. Her grey eyes did not shift from Jerry's; she had a wide low forehead; her skin was creamy white, unburned by the sea glare, a faint suggestion of freckles giving it warmth. She had drawn herself up and, with the wind touching her, she gave Jerry an impression of freshness and strength.

"You engaged, you guhl?" demanded the negro sharply.

Jerry's heart began to race—he paid no heed to the negro, but took a step forward to cut off his talk.

"Hey, you!"

As the negro shouldered him, he wheeled suddenly. His thin face was tight and keen, and his brown eyes narrowed.

"Get out!"

The negro's breath spread his broad nostrils. For a moment he hesitated, pomposity swelling every seam of his elegant livery; then, meeting Jerry's eyes, his pursed liver-colored lips lost their assurance.

"Yassuh."

Jerry turned back to the girl. His hands were shaking. He said, "I'm going to buy your papers."

For answer, with a curiously passive gesture, she swung up the two bundles at her feet and lowered her eyes.

"Do you know what your price is?"

"Forty dollars."

"That's a good deal," he thought; but he thought also, "I'll have to hire out a winter and make it up."

The color had flooded her cheeks. It seemed to come and go with her breathing. She had lost her erectness. Her shoulders drooped submissively. And Jerry felt himself suddenly go cold.

"What's your name?"

"Mary Goodhill."

Her voice was tentative, pitched very low.

"All right. Come along."

He walked to the dock with set face, as if he were conscious of the curious stare of the sloop hands. The captain eyed him noncommittally. This was plain business to him: dollars and cents.

"Agreed, mister?"

"Yes," said Jerry.

He set down his bundle on the crate that served the captain for a desk and undid the corners. Inside a rolled flannel shirt he found a piece of oil-cloth from which he took a sheaf of bills. Forty dollars he counted out.

The captain lifted his sandy brows and made a small noise in his whiskers.

"Just a minute, my boy." He drew a notebook from his jacket pocket and riffled the pages. "Mary Goodhill?" he asked the girl. She drew up slowly beside Jerry and nodded. "There's a mistake then. This girl's valued at eighty dollars."

Jerry swung a questioning glance at the girl. Her eyes were enlarged as she stared at the captain. He noticed that her mouth was white and trembling. His jaw set.

"You said forty dollars," he said to the captain.

"My book's eighty. You can see it yourself."

He held out the notebook. Jerry ignored it.

"Eighty dollars ain't a fair price, for one."

He spoke quietly, his lips stiffly framing the words.

"Oh, I see," said the captain. "Just a mistake. She didn't say her mother died in passage?"

The girl shook her head.

"What's that got to do with it?" Jerry demanded.

The captain smiled guilelessly.

"It's business, young man. The old lady died in sight of Sandy Hook. As near a complete passage as a plain mortal can make of it. And it's fair this girl should reimburse me. I don't want you to lose, though. The eighty dollars stands for two years. It's on the papers. Sorry if you can't make it. But there's a couple of others. There's a nice little dark girl. Welsh. Welsh are thrifty. Think it over."

Jerry looked at Mary Goodhill. She was standing listlessly, as if all hope had been drained out of her. Then he saw over her shoulder the waiting face of the black man.

"It don't seem right for her," he said.

The captain shrugged. He started to turn away, then thought better.

"I'll make it seventy," he said suddenly. "And I'll surprise you in the papers. That's a cut price if I ever made one. She's strong. She looks honest and a hard worker. And she's nice-looking. It's an offer."

Jerry flushed. The bills in his hands fluttered. He had not meant to bargain, but he felt the girl's eyes on him. Without a word he counted out thirty more dollars. It left him a pitifully flimsy sheaf.

"You've made a bargain, young man."

The captain was bent over the papers, sorting them. He selected a duplicate pair and weighted down the others with a copper spike. Then, taking out a quill pen from a pocket, he dipped it into an inkhorn fastened to his belt and drew a line through a phrase. He wrote there, "Two and a half years." ". . . from the above date," finished the sentence.

"Sign here," he said.

Without speaking, Jerry bent over the papers and twice slowly and carefully signed his name.

"Can you write?" the captain asked the girl.

She shook her head.

"All right, I'll write your name for you and you can make X's."

While she bent over the crate, Jerry looked away. There was a sick empty feeling in his insides. His first day on his own, and he had spent practically all his money. "I mind my first trip westward on my own. There ain't nothing like it in the world." His eyes roved. He saw the Greenbush Ferry crossing east, almost at the far side of the river, the horses patiently treading in their channels. The steamboat lay quiescent at her wharf, no trace of smoke from her empty furnaces, only the watchman aboard and he with his heels hanging over the lower deck while he fished the river. His glance passed on, over the city, tracing the white line of State Street mounting westward to the Capitol, and just behind the massive building a tufted white cloud. The sun was a little past noon and edges of shadow marked the eastern eaves.

A man with flour dust on his trousers was leading another man off the sloop. The air was bright on their faces.

The girl bent up from the crate stiffly. She regarded Jerry quietly a moment. The captain handed over the papers. He blew a drip of ink from the point of the quill and wiped it on his trousers, gave Jerry a brief grin, turned to the baker.

"Agreed, mister?"

Jerry tied up the papers in his bundle.

"Come on," he said to the girl.

For the second time that morning, Jerry Fowler turned into South Market Street. The wind still blew on his shoulders, and the sunlight filled the street; but his attention was not on the people or the roadway.

He eyed the girl at his side, walking slowly with her head bent down. She had grown unaccountably white; she moved listlessly; her shoulders bowed to the heavy bundles. He stopped for a moment.

"Here, you take my bundle,—it's light,—and let me have yours."

For an instant she seemed reluctant, but he took the bundles away roughly, and then she meekly accepted his.

"We'll go up to the park," he said. "I want to talk to you, but I can't here."

He shouldered her two bundles and led the way forward, wondering at what he had done and what he was to do. He held his face turned resolutely from her, but all the time something kept singing in his head— that he had set her free, but that if he chose to keep her, legally she was his.

He became aware after a moment that she was no longer beside him, and, looking back, he saw her following a few feet in his wake. He halted for her to catch up. She walked painfully slowly. A greenish tinge had touched her forehead, and beads of sweat formed over her eyebrows. He said nothing, but when they went on he matched his pace to hers.

They turned the corner into State Street and began laboriously to mount the grade. Here the high buildings shouldered off the wind and the sun beat on them fiercely. The Dutch aspect of the city was giving way to more modern buildings. Ahead, beyond the little park, loomed the brown front of the Capitol.

The noon hour blanketed the city with a kind of hush. The wagons in view were for the most part motionless beside the curb. In a parallel street, the rattle of wheels made an uncanny uproar. Only the sparrows, taking advantage of the stillness, bustled here and there among the cobbles.

As they climbed, Jerry and the girl passed through occasional zones of air laden with the sound of voices and crockery and the smell of cooking. The doors were open on the street, and through them he caught glimpses of their smoke-filled Dutch interiors, with city men sitting at the tables, their beer mugs between them. Their voices rolled forth into the street in a dim, meaningless uproar.

In one of these streams of talk and cookery, Jerry halted to ask the girl if she were hungry.

She shook her head. Though she seemed glad of the stop, she moved away from the door into the thin strip of shadow beside the eating-house wall. She held his bundle in front of her knees and wearily straightened her back. He saw that she was breathing in deep breaths, that her lips were tight closed and her eyes dull.

"Do you feel sick?" he asked kindly.

Her lips moved stiffly.

"A little."

"Catch your wind, then. Wait here and I'll get something for us to eat. It'll make you feel better."

Without waiting for her denial, he dropped the bundles at her feet and entered the eating house. Two gentlemen in black coats sitting at a window table eyed him momentarily under raised brows before resuming their controversy. Jerry felt nervous and out of place. Some serving men kept coming and going through the tobacco smoke, breaking it into waves with the speed of their passage. Gouts of foam flipped from the tankards they carried and slapped on the broad board floors. Somewhere in the dim interior sounded a continual rattle of dishes, and at minute intervals voices bawled unintelligible countersigns. The din was terrific in Jerry's country-bred ears; yet the men at the tables talked in lowered voices, easily.

"*Three beef, eight.*"

And the echo, nasal and shrill, "*Three beef.*"

"Still sitting?" a neighboring diner asked his companion.

"Yes, sir."

"*One plum tart, two.*"

"*One plum,*" came the echo.

"It's all straight through the Assembly. But the Senate is holding its horses."

"A good thing, too. It would be better for us if they threw the whole damned bill out."

"They won't. Clinton's got the back country pretty solid behind him. They're scared."

"The southern tier's solid."

"Tammany!"

"What of it?"

"They want their finger in the pie. They don't see it's the only thing to save New York. Population dropping there, and lands falling off in price. They've voted solid against the bill at every ballot. That's what's got our backs up, and it's what will pass the bill."

"Not in the Senate."

"Even Van Buren's for it."

"*Three beer! One lobo pale sherry, all fourteen.*"

"It will be a great thing for Albany."

"Surely will. Eight million dollars is a great thing. It's worth twice that, money being so tight. People are scared."

"They ought to be. Land speculation, and they never stopped to consider how to develop their investments. They sink a hundred dollars at a cast and sit back and expect a fortune!"

"Well, the canal ought to mean dollars in *my* pocket," said a dapper little man, leaning over. "I've got a hundred yards of river frontage right where the basin's going to be."

"If they dig it, mister, if they dig it."

Jerry dove desperately for a passing waiter.

"Yes, sir."

He halted, recklessly tilting his tray over his shoulder.

"Can you get me a loaf of white bread, a quarter wedge of cheese?"

"Table, sir?"

"Table."

"Number of your table?" The waiter had wide-open eyes.

"Oh," said Jerry. "I want to take it with me."

"This here's a coffeehouse, young man. Try the cheap store round the corner in South Pearl."

He darted off. Jerry flushed and turned back to the door. The girl was still standing where he had left her. There was something pathetic to Jerry in her passive indifference. He felt protective towards her.

"Do you like buttermilk?"

She nodded.

"I'll be back in a minute."

A row of shops extended along Pearl Street, showing their signs above the walk.

FLOUR AND FEED STORE
MRS. WIDGET'S CAKE AND BAKERY
LEATHER AND FINDING
J. TROMPER, UNCURRENT NOTES BOUGHT

A little shop with a single window bore in plain lettering:—

CHEAP STORE

Jerry turned in. It was no more than a stall, smelling pleasantly of butter and cream. A yellow kitten uncurled itself on a table top, opened its blue eyes, and yawned at him.

While he waited he scratched its chin, and it squinted up at him lazily and purred. Then a fat old woman came through a narrow door in the rear.

"Yes, mister?"

"I want a loaf of bread. . . ."

"White or black? Coarse or fine?"

"White—a penny loaf. And a half pound of cheese. And have you any buttermilk?"

"Yes. Got a jug?"

"No."

"Two cents for a quart jug."

"All right."

The girl was still where he had left her. As he came round the corner, she stooped for their three bundles. She seemed better for her rest, but her underlids were reddened as if she had been crying. He handed her the jug and food and took all their bundles, and side by side they continued their ascent to the park.

The grounds looked new and neat, with small trees set out in an orderly fashion, and shrubs staked up. They found a bench under a somewhat larger maple whose small leaves filtered the sunlight. There were no people in the park, though the gates stood open; and they opened their bread and cheese with a comforting sense of privacy.

"We've got nothing to drink with," said Jerry. "I didn't think of that."

For answer the girl bent over one of her bundles and fished in it with her hand. She drew out a small earthenware mug with a picture in red on its side of a castle amid trees, and in the foreground a man sleeping while his dog watched two small sheep.

Jerry examined the picture.

"It's pretty. Where is it? Don't you know?" as she shook her head. "It's a queer-looking house."

She took the mug from his hand and tilted up the bottom. Under the glaze her name was written, and a date, "14 June 1798."

"It's your name cup?"

She nodded. He thought, "1798 from 1817: nineteen years." And he looked at her more closely. She had seemed older than that.

"Do you feel like drinking a little? It's cool."

"Yes."

Her voice was stronger. It had an appealing husky note that was saved from harshness by instinctive modulation.

"Here."

While she held the mug he poured out the white drink with its swimming golden flecks.

"No, you first." He watched her while she sipped, and then cut the bread and passed her a piece of cheese between two thick slices. She nibbled at it tentatively. But as the food entered her she gained confidence. Her color rose quickly, and after a few moments she ate as heartily as he. The bread was fresh, with a clean rich wheaty taste and a hard brown crust. They ate in silence.

When they had finished and shaken the crumbs off for the sparrows, Jerry thriftily bound the remnant of cheese and bread in his bundle and, holding it on his knees, leaned back contentedly. All of Albany was spread out under his eyes: the grey roofs going down to the river in steps; the hills southward broken by the steep ravines; the blue belt of water, with the sparkling masts; a white sail carrying forward a sloop; and the sun shining like fire on the glass dome of the Albany Bank at the bottom of State Street. The breeze reached the two in the park and made them cool; and at its touch on his cheeks Jerry put out of his mind the thought that he had done a foolish thing. He turned suddenly to find the girl's eyes examining his face.

Her eyes had lost their look of worry; the dark grey had deepened still further, almost with a tinge of blue. They were tender to Jerry and full of a meaning that he could not read. But he felt more and more acutely the coolness of the breeze and the fire in the sunlight; and he became aware of his hands, the stiffness of the palms and the thickness of the finger joints. They were slow in following his will; they shook as he reached them into his pocket; and they fumbled the papers awkwardly. And all the time he felt the wind blowing.

"Here are your papers," he said. "You're free now."

He saw a question coming into her eyes.

"You can go anywhere you want to, now."

A puzzled crease came down between the girl's brows. He had turned away from her. He was speaking softly; as if he listened for something over his own voice. Her eyes wandered over his old clothes, noting the dust on his boots thickening the oil, and the fact that a button would need tightening, and that if she wove homespun in with a needle on the knee of the trousers within a day or two, she could ward off a hole. She glanced at his face—he was looking away at the river—and she thought that he had small flat ears, and that, though his nose was large, it was well shaped. And then she looked away, resting her chin on her hands, and drew a deep breath, for these things she had been thinking were none of her business. She tried to answer him; but she found no answer. And as they sat, both staring at the river, the wind, blowing across them, kept them aware of each other.

After a while, Jerry asked, "Didn't you have any plans?"

She shook her head.

"Didn't your mother know anybody in this country?"

"She never told me that."

"What are you going to do?"

"I don't know."

She had a slightly foreign twist to her way of speaking that broadened the vowels.

"I can't take you with me."

She glanced at his bent head. And he looked up to meet her eyes, and for a moment he thought that she was secretly amused, and he flushed.

"I can't keep you."

She made no comment.

"I haven't got but twenty dollars and a few cents. I know a trade, but I don't know where I'll find work. Mr. Faggis gave me a recommend as millwright and carpenter after I worked a winter for him."

The sloop on the river had passed Albany. As it ran against the waterside meadows of the Rensselaer land, he saw that it was pointing for Bath.

"I was going out to the Purchase to buy me some land."

She said, "Purchase?"

"It's a westward territory in this state. Then I saw you. If it hadn't been for Bennet, I'd have gone on. Now I can't buy. They wouldn't sell me twenty acres—they sell no lots under forty. I'll have to work a spell. You see I can't keep you."

It was now the girl who looked away; so that he could examine her undisturbed by her grey eyes. She had a strong chin and the line of her throat was youthfully clear. Nineteen. The wind was feathering the hair at the curve of her cheeks, making a spray like spun copper.

"I'm sorry," she said. "I didn't know."

"No blame to you. I wanted to. I don't know why."

"I'm grateful."

He leaned his wrists upon his knees and stared between his feet.

She said in her low voice, "Perhaps you can find someone to buy my papers."

He was silent. Then he said, arrogantly, "I didn't buy them for that."

She still averted her eyes.

"You oughtn't to lose your money. I'm sorry. But if you'll let me go along with you, I'll find work where you work until I've paid off the papers. And I'll work for you."

"But I can't pay for coach fare."

"I can walk." She met his eyes at last. Her cheeks were pink. "The captain said I was strong."

"It wouldn't be right for you to go along with me."

"Why not?"

"You know why."

He tried to stare her down; but she met his eyes quietly, until he turned his head. Then her lids fluttered and suddenly drooped, and she colored deeply.

"I don't mind. It's legal, isn't it?"

He seemed to be putting himself a question that he could find no answer for. And all the time he was aware of the wind and the sun. A great bird as white as glass was flying up the river, a gull searching the banks. And while he tried to think, the city came to life. A trickle of men, of all sorts, men who looked like tradesmen, like farmers in their unaccustomed tweed suits, gentlemen with high hats, began to filter through the park towards the Capitol. In twos and threes they mounted the broad steps and disappeared into the great doors behind the marble pillars. The Senate was going back into session on the Canal Bill.

"I couldn't hardly expect work here," Jerry said. "It might be better out westward." He thought of the conversation he had overheard in the coffeehouse. If the bill passed there would be work for him, maybe, on this canal.

"Have you any money?" he asked the girl.

She shook her head.

"I used up what we had—it was only a little. My mother had to have medicine. It cost a lot on the sea."

"Then we'll have to save mine as much as we can. We ought to sleep out if we can't get free lodging."

"I don't mind."

He saw the shadows of clouds sweeping down the Berkshires, and he felt the lift of the wind against his eyes.

"All right," he said. "We'll go by the Mohawk route. The country's better settled."

Her answer was to stoop for her bundles.

"I'll carry them," he said. "You take mine and the jug. We can eat what's left for supper."

They faced each other. His face was red and set; hers quiet, but her eyes were bright and the color remained in her cheeks.

"Come on, Mary."

He turned for the northern gate of the park.

2

"You've got something money don't usually buy"

WHEN at last Jerry stopped beside the road, Albany lay seven miles behind them.

"Let's sit down for a while."

He had been following the teamsters' footpath off the shoulder of the pike, but inside the row of Lombardy poplars. The slender, pointed trees bent to the wind, swaying like dancers from their hips, while the dry upper branches rattled sharp as castanets. As far as they could see the road ran straight and flat through the barren land. They had been walking for three hours; but not once had they seen a thriving farm. The apple orchards had a shrunk, parched look; the endless forests of pine were stunted. Jerry had heard of the Schenectady upland, and now that he was passing through it he felt a fine contempt for the soil and the man who was fool enough to settle there.

"How are you feeling?" he asked the girl.

She had kept up with him well, but when she stopped, the vigor went out of her and her back drooped a little. But she smiled at him.

"I'm feeling all right. I've lost the use of walking since being on the sea."

"You're doing fine."

He sat down beside her with his back to the same tree. Her hands were folded in the lap of her brown skirt, and she leaned back with perfect relaxation. She had loosened the shawl, and inside the square yoke of her dress he saw her breast rising and falling evenly.

The white sandy dust that carpeted the pike lifted from time to time in eddies of wind. When a wagon passed, it was thrown back in a great cloud that the wind spread upon the grass, dulling the new green. There were few farms, and fewer taverns. Now and then, at the doors of the latter, idlers had watched them past; and Jerry had felt them speculating behind his back, and wondered if they could guess.

He turned his thoughts to his home. If he had stayed he would now be putting in his plough for the final furrow in the four-acre piece they were sowing to barley. His eyes would be on the white house between the broad roan rumps. His mother would be out beside the woodshed hanging the clothes on the line, her dark head lifted, her skirt rising at the sides of her boots. The furrow would be coming back to his feet; and he would leave the plough standing at the end, unhook the team, and go on to the buildings. And he would go into the kitchen with its smell of hanging hams, of pumpkin fillets hanging from the beams, and steaming corn mush, for a drink of milk. And then he would join the team at the barn door, unharness and water them, and bring in the cows for the milking. He would milk in the grey twilight of the barn, resting his head against a red flank while his eyes watched the ducks parading up from the creek. . . .

Far down the road they heard the afternoon stage driver's horn. In a moment the team came into view under the cloud of dust, four brown horses trotting roundly. The driver was alone on the box. He held the reins and the whip in his left hand, and his windburned face was tilted behind the long brass horn. He caught sight of them and offered them an extra trill. The sun made a highlight on his cheek stuffed out by an enormous chew.

The coach spun past to a rattle of spokes and a squeak of leather. The curtains were rolled up. Inside sat a couple of ladies and a small boy and a gentleman in sober clothes. The luggage-flap at the back was swollen, for all the world like the pouch of a laying hen, and it wobbled right and left to the inequalities of the road.

They followed the stage's course. Far ahead, in a break in the poplar lines, a white gate stretched over the ruts. They saw the coach dwindle and stop. In a moment the gate rose. Faintly against the wind came a single toot of the horn, and the gate sank down. And for a while the road was empty, and they listened to the blowing of the wind.

"Ain't you afraid to come this way with me?" Jerry asked suddenly.

The girl slowly turned her face.

"No. Why?"

"You're all alone," he said foolishly, and turned the conversation. "Where do you come from?"

"Wiltshire."

"Where's that?"

"In England."

"Yes, I know. Why did you and your mother come over?"

"Father was younger than my mother. He went away with someone else, and then he brought her back, and Mother wouldn't stay. We came away together."

Her face became moody.

"Was it hard on sea?" he asked curiously. "Did you mind the ship?"

"I didn't mind it. I'm strong. But it was hard on her. Being on deck all the time, even at night, and not sleeping for fear of being taken by waves. Mother minded the cold, but she wasn't taken till we got into fog."

"Couldn't you take her into shelter?"

"No. We had to stay on deck. The cabin was full. They gave us a little stove to cook at—that was all. You couldn't keep warm by it, because they put it out when you were done eating, for fear of fire."

"Was it nice country, where your farm was?"

"Yes, it was pretty. There were the hills north, but our farm was low down."

"Did you have a dairy?"

"We had a cow."

"One?"

"Yes. I used to milk her."

"How many horses did you have?"

"One."

"Just one?"

"Yes, it was a nice farm."

"Our farm had eight cows and three horses," Jerry said.

"Yes? Why did you want so many?"

"To make money," he said, looking at her.

"Oh."

He could not understand what she meant.

"Gran'pa, he cleared the farm. He was a settler," he explained. "We come from Connecticut as a family. Gran'pa come by himself with ten dollars in his pocket. Now Pa's well off. He's a justice of the peace."

"Then why did you leave there?"

"My brother will get the farm. I want my own. I didn't want to work for other people all my life. I want to get rich."

She made no answer. But her hands picked up two pieces of dry grass and began idly to plait them. He watched her strong fingers, wondering at their deftness.

"Can you spin and weave, Mary?"

"Yes."

"I'll buy you a wheel, some day."

She gave him another of those slow questioning glances that he was beginning to expect, and his face flushed; and he looked at the sun.

"There's no use trying to get to Schenectady to-night, I expect. How are you feeling?"

"I'm rested a lot."

"That's good. We'll wait a little longer."

He could see little lines indrawn to the corners of her mouth.

Up the road they heard a voice crying commands.

"Get along there. Bring them back, Jody. Fetch them in. Go on. Get along, will ye?"

A dry patter of hoofs came along the road, and presently they made out the faces of sheep, in a foolish cluster, from which a little stream sprang suddenly, running for a way, and then halting as if the road were dammed. Then the voice was uplifted and a dog would bark, and the process was repeated.

The sheep passed them with big lacklustre eyes in their white faces,—the road dust stiffening the points of their wool,—and presently a small brown collie dog brought up some stragglers and sat down on its tail to wait for the old man who plodded a hundred yards in the rear.

He walked bent over, leaning heavily on a long stick. When he saw that the sheep had stopped again, his left hand clawed open his grey beard and his cracked voice shouted, "Get on, blast ye! Can't you keep them moving, Jody?"

The little dog sucked in his tongue and barked.

"Hey!" Jerry hailed the old man.

"Eh?" He turned rheumy, red-lidded eyes.

"Can you tell me how far it is to Schenectady from here?"

"Schenectady, you say?"

"Yes."

"Beginning from the toll gate,"—he wheeled slowly and lifted the stick in a trembling hand,—"there's some calls it eight miles and some calls it six."

"About seven?"

"I calculate," the old man said. "I calculate it's seven."

"Thanks."

"No bother," said the old man. "Get on, blast ye!"

Jerry turned to the girl.

"Let's get through the gate, anyway."

He swung up her bundles and led the way along the footpath.

The gate seemed to creep towards them at an infinitesimal pace. A low yellow house flanked one paling; the other stretched to the opposite poplars. The gatekeeper, smoking a rank pipe, stood by the windlass in his shirt sleeves.

He pulled the pipe out of his lips and emptied his lungs of smoke.

"Howdy," he said. "It's a fine day."

He had a square red face, the jowls pronounced; and his eyelids had a way of trembling downward, so that he kept snapping them up.

"Hello," said Jerry. "How far do you make it to Schenectady?"

" 'Bout eight miles. You a-heading there?"

"Where else does the road go?"

"That's a question! Why, young feller, it's the beginning of all roads west." He put his pipe back in his mouth and sucked a moment. "There's all the river towns—you can turn off at Canajoharie for the Great Western at Cherry Valley. You can follow our Pike into Little Falls, Herkimer, and Utica and Manlius, where the Fifth Company Western Pike joins in. And when you get to Manlius, you've got the whole western territory in front of your toes. You a-heading for Schenectady?"

"Heading through," said Jerry with a grin. He stepped to the foot passenger's wicket in the great gate.

"Head away," said the gatekeeper, his eyes roving over Mary. "But it's going to cost you sixpence for the two of you. You ain't a doctor, by your cut, nor is it Sunday, so you ain't going to church neither." He put his pipe back in his mouth and took another look at Mary. His protuberant blue eyes expressed admiration. Jerry fished out his purse.

"Here you are."

The man leisurely moved away from the winch, and, as he began to walk, Jerry saw that his back was crooked.

"Have a drink?" he asked as he let them through and took the six pennies. "No."

"Water, then? There's a good well."

With a glance at Jerry, Mary accepted.

"Wife?" asked the gatekeeper, staring after her.

"No."

"Don't get stuffy, son. I ain't meaning harm." One of his eyes drooped almost shut. "All the world goes past me here and I learn to see a sight of things. Whatever she is, strikes me you picked good company."

Jerry did not answer.

"Ain't a redemptioner, is she?" asked the gatekeeper.

"What business is that of yours?"

"Why, depends on how you look at it. Seems queer now, considering she's a redemptioner, that she'd be traveling along of a lad of your cut, don't it? There's some that buys them," his eye drooped again, "and there's some that borrows, in a way of speaking. Us gatekeepers get advertisements."

He leaned himself against the winch again.

"Don't get bothered, son. She ain't advertised. It's funny you come to buy her, though. You must have paid pretty high for a man of your pocket. You ain't willing to deal on her?" he asked casually.

Jerry flushed.

"No."

"All right, all right. Easy. It's just I could use a good girl round my house. I'd be willing for one like her to cover the price with a bill or two."

"She carries her own papers," said Jerry.

"Then there's no objection if I make her an offer?"

"Yes, there is!"

The gatekeeper eyed Jerry coolly.

"It's a hot day," he observed. "You wouldn't consider a little beer at a fip for a tumbler?"

Jerry did not answer.

"Hottest day I ever see," said the man, raising his voice. "Real unseasonable weather. But I read there's a storm coming. Seems a pity a handsome girl should have to tromp along a road on a day like this. Oh, there you are, missy. Did you get your drink?"

She was smiling, her red lips freshened and glistening with the water.

"It's a good well," she said. "Thank you."

The gatekeeper's eyes rested on her face. Jerry noticed that he was hiding his twisted back from her.

"You wouldn't want to take a job with a gatekeeper? Easy housekeeping and steady pay? Serve drinks to the gents and fetch water to lady passengers, now?"

She smiled at him.

"No," she said, but Jerry read her estimation of him, and wondered if he had been a sound man whether she would have agreed. He kept stiff and silent. "No," she said. "I'm bonded to this man."

"Oh, you are? I offered him the price of his papers, but he said you wasn't bonded."

She turned suddenly to Jerry, and her eyes shone.

"Did he?" she said over her shoulder; but she was looking at him, and he wondered what she was thinking that had so brightened her.

"Come along, Mary," he said stiffly.

She bent meekly for her bundles, but her lips did not lose their curve. And as they walked away, she kept at his side.

"That was a bad-looking man," he said, as soon as they were out of earshot. "I wonder you could talk with him so."

She eyed him sidelong for a few paces.

"But you were there. It was all right, wasn't it?"

His chin lifted, and she noted his set jaw, and she saw that she had pleased him. So she kept her face forward, and walked in silence.

"I wish, Mary, you'd call me by my name. It might save talk."

"I will if you want me to."

"Then do."

"But I don't know what your name is."

He remembered that she was unable to write her own name; therefore she could not have read his. It embarrassed him to tell her.

"My name's Jeremiah Fowler. But I'm called Jerry."

"All right, Jerry."

Her stride was easy, her legs swung freely from her hips. She did not bend forward like most women, but kept herself erect. He wondered what could have freshened her so.

"That water felt so good," she said after a time. "I washed my face in the bucket and did up my hair again. I feel I could walk all day, now."

He did not answer.

"Did you mind my taking so long, Jerry?"

"No."

After a moment, she asked, "Would you have let me go to that man?"

He shot a swift look at her, but she was keeping her eyes to the road.

"Why do you ask that?"

"I was wondering."

Her voice was small. He felt his thoughts blur. He tried to think, and he did not answer her. But she drew in her breath slowly and smiled to herself. And he gave up thinking, and they went on until they heard hoofs trotting behind them, and suddenly a voice cried, "Boil me if it ain't young Jerry Fowler!"

The Shaker missioner reined in his spanking pair and stared down at them from shrewdly twinkling eyes, and his long face grinned through a network of wrinkles.

"I expected I might catch you up," he said, "but not so soon as this. Climb in."

"Thanks," said Jerry. He crossed the roadside ditch and heaved up his two bundles.

"Stick them in the back," directed the Shaker. "Who's the lady?"

Jerry stammered.

"Mary Goodhill. This is Mr. Bennet."

The Shaker lifted his high hat and gave her a smile.

"Pleased to meet you, miss. Issachar Bennet's my name. I made Jerry's acquaintance this morning. We crossed on the same ferry. Now under that oilcloth there's a feather mattress I'm taking outwards for the elder Meachem in Kentucky. I'll warrant it soft. You lay down on it, missy, and, Jerry, you climb up alongside of me."

As soon as they were aboard, he clucked to his horses and shook them into a trot.

"It's uncomfortable hot for foot travel," he said. "When did you leave Albany?"

"Past one," said Jerry. "The sun was a good piece past noon when we got to the Snipe Street Gate."

"I thought I might come up with you," said the Shaker. "Dudley, back there, who tends the halfway gate, told me about you. I reckoned it was you, Jerry; and I guessed it my own way."

"How?"

"You'd never know so I might as well tell you. He kept talking about missy's hair."

He glanced backward at the girl.

"What do you think of our country, missy?"

"I haven't seen much of it." She was resting against a bundle, facing forward. "It seems flat here, and a long way between places."

"This is a dull stretch of road. You'll like it better when you come to the Mohawk. How do you like this young man?"

She flushed up and made no reply. Bennet chuckled delightedly and surreptitiously drove his elbow into Jerry's side. He seemed in a bubbling humor; all at once he shot a quid out of his lips, drew his hand across his mouth, and started humming. Jerry shifted uncomfortably at the tune and fixed his eyes between the horse's back-pricked ears.

> *"A roguish youth asked me to woo,*
> *Heigho! The buds were blowing.*
> *And I was puzzled what to do,*
> *Heigho! The buds were blowing. . . ."*

From a swift-rolling wagon, the road wore a different aspect. The ruts showed plainly, the narrow marks of dearborns and chaises, the broad tracks of the Pennsylvania wagons, the ruffled spots of the footprints of herded cattle. It ran straight as an arrow, and the horses trotted it back with their hoofs, as though they were running a treadmill, and the shadows of the poplars, as the sun declined, made bars across the road, that flashed sunlight and shadow past the wagon in a continual bright glittering. The hoofs of the horses thudded a pleasant tattoo, and the axles rattled in the hubs and the spokes clattered and the harness slapped against the horses' ribs, working out edges of lather, filling the air with a comfortable horsy smell, and the dust trickled down the fellies of the wheels and rolled out behind in a white cloud.

The Shaker spoke in a lowered voice.

"So you went and did it?"

Jerry nodded.

Ahead of them on the road he saw a line of grey hoods appearing, another wheat train.

"I saw it bothering you," said the Shaker, with his bubbling chuckle. "Young man, going west. I told you there was nothing like it in this world. But now where's your farm?"

Jerry made no answer.

"I'll bet a girl like her comes high off Henry Fearon's boat. . . . Didn't she?" he asked after a few rods.

Jerry nodded. He could not meet the Shaker's quizzical eyes.

"Seventy dollars," he said. "She's signed for two and a half years to meet it."

"What are you going to do with her, eh?"

"I don't know. I gave her back her papers."

The old man shifted his feet after a jounce.

"Riding all right back there?" he called over his shoulder.

"Fine." She was smiling. Her face was tilted to see over the edge of the wagon box, and the breeze was plucking out wisps of hair from her neat braids.

"And she come along?" said the Shaker.

Jerry nodded. "She hadn't nowhere else to go to."

"So what are you going to do about that, Jerry?"

"I haven't thought. I can't buy my farm. I'll have to work for a year."

The Shaker looked at him squarely. "Sorry you did it?"

Jerry lifted his face. "No."

"Good boy." He broke into his humming.

"*The roguish youth asked me to kiss,*
Heigho! The buds were blowing!"
I frown'd to show I took 't amiss,
Heigho! The buds were blowing!

"She's a right pretty young girl, son. I think you're lucky at that. What do you want with a farm? Get yourself work. There's going to be big doings in this state from now on, whatever you do. Listen, when I left Albany it was a good while after you, and word was round the city. I heard it in the Planters' Bar. They've passed the Canal Bill."

"Have they?"

"They surely have. You living in Uniontown, you haven't no idea what it's going to mean. Clinton preaches about the farmers—that's sensible—he needs the vote. But the cities are going to feel it, too. For why? Take Albany. Every ounce of grain that comes from the west will pass through there. Every bit that goes to the farmers will pass through there. Same for New York. Tammany Hall will be neck-deep in money in a dozen years. Trade that's going to Philadelphy will come here. There ain't no one else can compete. Damn my blinkers if I don't think the best thing that ever happened to you was catching sight of missy's hair, boy. You've got to keep where the money is."

Jerry's face brightened. He did not answer.

"Outside of the fact that it was a damn handsome thing for you to do. By crinkus, shake hands."

He stretched out his lean fingers. They were rolling down on the wheat train. They heard the notes of Pennsylvania Bells. The horses were bending to their long stride, the teamsters walking in the footpath, whips in hand. The hoods and the boat-shaped boxes were filmed with dust. The wheels were caked with grey dried mud. Under the axles swung the leather water buckets and the grease pails. They also showed gobbets of grey dirt. The Shaker pointed.

"Heavy hauling westward of here. Them are the wagons that'll be put out of business. Those tough bezabors don't think so, but it's so. We'll have a new idea of haulage in a dozen years. A hundred tons at a lick, maybe, and night travel. I wish I was in your boots, Jerry, heading into the midst of it with a girl along."

His face sobered, his eyes drooped sadly for a while. Then he cheered up.

"I had my turn at it in my time, and there's still some hell in me. Watch out, boy, or I may chuck you against the head and drive off with your girl."

He chuckled.

"What'll I do with her?" Jerry asked.

"Been bothering you?"

"Yes."

The Shaker laughed aloud.

"It wouldn't have bothered me! Just now she thinks you're the handsomest article in pants she ever came across. Just look at her if you don't believe it. I'll bet you a York shilling against a kiss from her that she's studying the back of your head and wishing you had a hair-cut."

"Fair enough," said Jerry.

They turned around together, confronting her, the Shaker grinning like an amiable old devil, Jerry puzzled and bright-faced.

"I win," said the Shaker, and he poked Jerry's ribs, while the girl wondered what they had been saying about her. She heard his voice singing the tune he had hummed, but she couldn't catch the words, because they were pitched for Jerry's ear. But something in the tune must have touched a nerve, for she appeared to draw into herself and muse.

"Heigho!" sang the old Shaker.

> *"The roguish youth asked me to wed,*
>   *Heigho! The buds were blowing!*
> *I looked wise and shook my head,*
>   *Heigho! The buds were blowing!*
> *My confidence grew less and less,*
> *He so determined was to press,*
> *Though I meant No,—I cried O* YES!
>   *Heigho! The buds were blowing!"*

The sun was going down behind a burning cloud; the wind was dropping. A bite of coldness had crept across the sky. Far on his right, Jerry saw the twilight reaching up like a curtain from the east.

"You'd better get right at it!" said the Shaker. "Or else you're a better boy than I was at your age!"

He chuckled and slapped his horses with the reins. A mile ahead they saw the dip of the valley and a dark blot near the river. Schenectady.

The end gate stood at the edge of the slope, and the horses slid to a stop with their noses against the palings.

"Hey, Ike!" The stout keeper greeted Bennet with a knowing wink. "Two fips, you old bezabor."

The Shaker tossed out two coins of six cents' value.

"Wind up your gate, Ted. Wind it. Work the lard off your middle. My off horse smells a wedding."

The keeper laughed and turned his crank with his red hands, and the gate slid silently up in its channels and they passed through.

"They know me out westward," said Bennet.

He drove a half mile silently.

"You must think I'm a queer preacher. But I'm just Ike Bennet. I was born with the gift of exhortation, but the Lord never touched me." There was a strange solemnity in his tone. "And I went west like any young man —but I wasn't a farmer. I had to keep moving. So I took to preaching, boy. I'm right good at any kind of preaching, Baptist, or Church of England, or Methody. But I always travel as a Shaker in these parts. It's all right for a Shaker to have his pint. And they outfit me handsome back in Lebanon."

He cocked his head to estimate the daylight.

"I'm an unrighteous man by all accounts; but I reckon I didn't do no particular harm to anybody. And I can preach! Some day maybe you'll hear me!"

"I've got nothing against you," said Jerry.

"Being an unrighteous man," said Bennet, "I know how to advise a human being."

He glanced over his shoulder.

"Boy," he said, "you've lost a farm this morning, but you've got something money don't usually buy. If I was you, I'd just put that transaction right out of my head. Owning her's the only bad thing I see for you. It wouldn't hurt her, but it's bad for a man."

"It don't seem right."

"To hell with it," said the preacher. "There's Schenectady, the Dutchest damned town in this country, and the only place I was ever squeaked in a horse deal. No wonder the college boys riot them! I'm spending the night here. How about you?"

"We've had a good ride in your wagon. I think we'll get across the bridge."

"Tromping all night?"

"There's an hour's walking light."

"Just about. Well, it won't hurt you, you're both stout. Where are you heading for?"

"I'll stop where there's work. Utica maybe."

"Utica's a good city. They'll start the canal near there. I wouldn't stop short of it. And now, I guess I'll take you on to the bridge."

The horses' hoofs slapped on cobbles. The wagon box vibrated dizzily and the girl looked about her.

"Schenectady, missy," said the preacher. "Over there's the college buildings. I'm taking you to the bridge."

He swung the horses down a straight, sloping street, carried them half a dozen blocks, and drew up the wagon to the footwalk. He jumped over the wheel and helped Jerry unload their bundles. Then he took off his hat, and held out his hand to the girl.

She took it and jumped to the ground, and he cocked his eye at Jerry.

"Missy, you owe me a kiss," he said seriously.

"Do I?" she opened her eyes wide.

He chuckled.

"It's a bet your man made with me, missy. An honest bet."

She put on complete submissiveness and held up her mouth. He kissed her squarely, wheeled, shook Jerry by the hand, and jumped onto his wagon.

"You're a lucky young man, Jerry, blast you!" He put on his hat and took up the reins.

"If you want to know what the bet was about, missy, ask Jerry. And ask him afore he forgets."

The horses jerked against the collars, the wheels spun, and in the next instant Issachar Bennet had vanished round a dusky corner.

The girl turned to Jerry questioningly.

"I'll tell you later. Let's get across the bridge. Shelter's cheaper out of town."

Giving her no time to speak, he took up the bundles and started for the bridge.

3

"A grass piece against woods"

THE quiet of early evening hushed the town behind them, and when Jerry turned on the ramp of the bridge to look back, darkness was creeping through the streets, blurring the doorways with their quaint high-backed benches on either side, leaving only the high gables that fronted the street visible against the sky. But as the darkness gained, the lights in the windows began to brighten, until, up and down the river, Jerry could trace the courses of the streets, like an illuminated map.

Somewhere beyond the outskirts of the city, wagon bells were chiming. And Jerry turned again and looked westward along the line of the river, that gleamed like a sheet of strange green metal. As far as he could see, the banks were dark; trees lifted out of the blackness in black silhouettes. The sky held a nebulous, shimmering piece of the twilight at the end of the river, and even as he watched it he saw it fading downward, as though the river were drinking it; and then the river began to grow dim; the blackness stole out upon the water from each shore; the light shrank until it was a thread, then a thread that was broken into little pieces; and the night swept over them like the wings of a bird, with a soundless stirring of air. Jerry saw the stars coming out, and the starlight tracing the outline of the girl's face.

Only when he felt the chill of dew did he realize how long he had stood there. An indefinable feeling of loneliness stole upon him, a sense of separation from the world, as if the lighted windows and the bridge and the westward valley and even the girl, patient at his side, were as remote from his touch as the stars. He shook his head to clear his eyes of the image, and his hands, holding the bundles over his shoulder, changed their grip. His voice was thick as he said, "Come along."

The bridge made an inky tunnel through the darkness, but at the head of the ramp a faint light shone on the plank way and edged the upright palings of the gate. On the left side the pedestrians' wicket gave upon a footwalk. Jerry cleared his throat.

"Hey, there!"

He saw now that a small house had been grafted into the bridge timbers on the north side; and the light slanted through a window from a small, low-ceilinged room. Through the panes he had a glimpse of a low stove burning redly, and a man with a hairless head smoking a stone pipe. He did not move at Jerry's hail; he might never have heard it; but a coil of smoke backfired from the broad bowl of the pipe.

Suddenly a door swung open, and Jerry was confronted by the hairiest man he had ever seen. His reddish beard was streaked unevenly with grey, but the light coming over his shoulders seemed to edge it with fire. He stooped a little to peer under his bushy eyebrows.

"Aye?"

"Two foot-passage," said Jerry.

The man slowly reached behind him for a thornwood stick as gnarly as his broad hand.

"It's late for foot passengers," he remarked, bringing forward a lantern and a great brass key. His voice was sharply pitched, the words bitten short, as if it were an effort to him to get speech past his whiskers. He held the lantern up to Jerry's face and then turned it slowly on the girl. It made bright spots in his own blue eyes.

"Where you bound?" he asked.

"West."

"West? They're all going west, boy." He lifted his beard. "Uncle!"

A deep voice rumbled through the door.

"Yeanh? Vat iss?"

"Boy about twenty, dark, thin-faced, about two inches under six feet?"

"No."

Jerry saw the pipe come out of the mouth of the bald-headed man for the word, and then pop back.

"A girl?" said the bearded man. "Hair reddish. About similarly tall. Similar age. Got grey eyes."

"No."

The bearded man extended a furry paw.

"Four cents, young mister."

Jerry paid him the toll, and when he had pocketed the pennies the keeper opened the wicket.

"It's all right, mister. We just look out for runaways. There's been a lot lately, and sometimes we collect a re-ward. Uncle, he remembers them for me. You heading far to-night?"

"No," said Jerry.

"Have you et?"

"Not yet."

"You can eat with me and Uncle, if you like."

"No, thanks."

"What's your name, mister?"

"Jerry Fowler. This is Mary Goodhill."

The bearded man made a knuckle at his forehead.

"I ask," he explained, "because I keep me a di'ry. I built this bridge. My name is David Hearsay. It's the biggest bridge this side the ocean. You've heard that, no doubt?"

"Yes." Jerry was anxious to be gone.

"I built it under Theodore Burr. Eight years ago, mister. And I seen it was a good job, and the best I would ever do, and I couldn't keep away from it, so they let me take the toll job. Me and Uncle Stoeffel lives here now. And I like to keep a di'ry of who goes acrosst."

"Yes."

The bearded man peered out into the long reach.

"It's quite a bridge, mister. Notice the beams. You'd better keep to the footwalk. A person sometimes get confounded when a wagon comes against him there. It's the noise. Good night. Good luck."

He stood a moment watching their figures dwindle beyond the scope of his lantern. Then he slowly reëntered his house and closed the door.

As the light was shut off behind them, Jerry's eyes began to pick out the wooden structure of the bridge. All of it was covered over, but here and there, through small windows in the sides, they saw the river running. The boards beneath their feet gave an impression of vast strength. Under a window starlight dimly etched the two-inch planks of Norway pine, bolted together into four-foot beams. There was a smell in the tunnel of all the things of travel, of horses, of wheat dust, of cattle droppings, of men and women, as if the bridge enclosed an atmosphere of its own and were a world in itself. The sound of their boots on the planks echoed hollowly under the roof, and overhead a restless whisper was aroused. They heard the twittering of small birds and a pungent, unearthly smell of bats was loosened, and suddenly they felt the stirring of naked wings; and black specks crossed the window, and little voices were uplifted.

Jerry felt the girl coming closer to him.

"It's a long bridge, Mary," he said, and found himself whispering.

She made no answer, but he felt her shoulder touching his, and indescribably it comforted him. He could not see her. There was just the touch. And then, as he passed a window, he smelled her hair. He became aware of his hands; he knew that night had fallen; the west seemed a far place, and their passage to it, as their passage of this bridge, a thing that might last forever. The words of the old Shaker occurred to him—"You've got something money don't usually buy."

He said to himself that at the next window he would ask her; the window slid past them uncannily soon, and he marked a third for his question. He shifted his bundles so that he carried them both with one hand, and as they came to the window he reached out the other, and as if her hand knew its way in darkness it came against his. He couldn't take it, but as it suddenly touched his again, he knew that the Shaker was right. He turned his head to her, to see her against the next window they passed; and at that moment they felt the cold night air in their faces.

Jerry looked up.

He saw the shape of the bridge roof against the stars. When he looked down he was just able to make out the beginning of the ramp.

"Stop," he said.

She halted at his side.

"Mary. . . . What were you thinking all across the bridge?"

She drew in her breath.

"I was wondering what the old man's bet was with you."

Jerry said slowly:

"He bet you were looking at me."

"And was I?"

"Yes."

"That's a funny thing to bet about."

"What he meant was you'd marry me if I asked it."

He set down the bundles gently. They felt the night air drawing across from the west. Far away, at what seemed an infinite depth below, they heard small frogs piping along the water's edge.

"Will you, Mary?"

"You don't have to ask me."

"Forget the boat, Mary. Forget the papers. Here, where are they?"

"In my bundle."

"Give them to me."

He was aware of her bending down; he heard her hands fumbling; papers rustled crisply. He took them from her, held them between his hands, and tore them across. He tore them again and again until they were small bits, and then he scattered them over the river.

"Now, it's your own country, Mary. You're as free as I am. Did Mr. Bennet win his bet?"

She still said nothing.

"You don't have to say yes. You can come with me and I'll take care of you till you want to go somewhere else, only . . ."

"Only?"

In the silence once more the frogs' piping gained clarity. The notes traveled in waves, rising and falling.

"If you want me to," she said.

He tried to see her, but she was only a shadow in the bridge mouth. She made no move, and he wondered if she were waiting. As he stood before her, the voices along the river rang in his head, and a strong rhythm crept into the song. But as he put out his hands, he heard a murmur in the great timbers. A dog barked far away, and in an instant a great beast was roaring at their very ears; hoofs thudded in the darkness, and a moment later ponderous feet trod against their faces. Wheels rumbled, reëchoing. There was thunder all about them. He felt her hand thrusting for his and he took it.

"Come on, Mary. There's a wagon train on the bridge."

A cow lowed as they stepped into the night air hand in hand; and Jerry breathed deep. The farm was a thing he had dreamt about, something that had no connection with him. He went eagerly, for he held reality in his hand.

As they drew away from the bridge they heard the echoes thundering at the entrance, and now more clearly approaching them the actual sounds of the movers' progress. They had gone but a hundred yards when the two sounds mingled, and, looking back, they saw the lantern that swung in the front bow of a lumber wagon shining down on the heads of a four-horse team, and on a stout woman in a yellow shawl and red petticoats who sat on the seat and held the reins in her hands.

Though Jerry set a brisk pace, the wagons slowly overhauled them; as if the teams were aware that camp would soon be made. The wheels rolled over the gravel road, linchpins creaked, voices of the drivers were flung back and forth. Looking over his shoulder, Jerry saw the ears of the leading team pricked towards him, and between them the driver peering beyond the edge of lantern light.

"Hello there!" her voice rang heartily.

Jerry halted at the roadside for the wagon to come up. Behind its tailboard the lights of three more wagons were strung along the road; and behind the last wagon a small flock of sheep was followed by a knot of cows, all shepherded by four anxious dogs whose black shapes darted back and forth across the road, appearing and disappearing through the clouds of dust to which the lanterns gave a kind of incandescence.

At the very rear a man astride a small mule carried a lantern on a slender pole four feet over his head; and as it swung with the beast's stride the light was spread alternately over the roadside ditches to the rail fences.

"Hello," repeated the fat woman who led the train.

"Hello," said Jerry.

"Do you know a likely spot for camping?" She had pulled up her team, and behind her the other wagons came to rest and the dogs swung the driven beasts into a tight group. A couple of men came striding along the road.

Jerry looked up at the woman's full red cheeks and snapping black eyes.

"No, ma'am, I don't. I'm strange to this road."

"You going west too, young man?"

"Yes."

"Well, that ain't no help to us. But you're footing it, ain't you?"

"Yes."

"Then toss your bags on here, if you've a mind to. And let your girl ride with me," she added kindly. "If you'd like to camp along of us."

Jerry glanced at Mary. It would solve their sleeping for the trip out, if they stayed with this train.

"Thank you, ma'am. We'd be obliged."

"All right, then. Hand us in your bags." She stuffed them back under the hood of the wagon and held out a fat hand to Mary. "We'll go till we find water. Come on."

She helped Mary up over the wheel with one strong pull and shook out the reins. Jerry stood by the road until the wagon had passed. The two men walked up to him. They were lean, tall men, thin-faced, farmers; they looked like brothers. One held out his hand.

"Me, I'm George Halleck. This is my brother, Joe."

Jerry shook hands.

The wagon lanterns passed over them and the dust rose in their faces. The dogs were barking again. Joe Halleck lifted a whip made of a five-foot birch wand with a leather thong bound to the end.

"Go on. Git, you." He cracked over the backs of the sheep, starting a flurry of hoofs. The nearest dog yapped excitedly, and threw himself at the rear end of a lagging ewe.

"The beasts are getting fractious. We've come from beyond of Lansingburg to-day."

"That's a long pull with driven cattle."

The cows passed slowly, turning their faces right and left. The lead cow wore a bell which clinked dully, as though it were half choked. Two more men, their dust-laden cheeks streaked with sweat, followed the cows. George Halleck named them to Jerry.

"Abel Marcy and Abijah Judson."

The men merely grunted. Abel Marcy rubbed his reddened eyes. Their tempers were on edge with their long walk and the task of keeping the cattle to one side of the road. As soon as they had passed, the dust cloud covered them; but their hoarse voices broke out from time to time, and Joe Halleck's long whip, still farther ahead, snapped waspishly.

George Halleck and Jerry fell in behind to watch for stragglers. George's long body sagged as he walked.

"I never argued for wet travel before this," he said, "but now I'm minded for a week's rain. My skin's parched."

Once in a while he tilted his head to look back at the rider.

"He gets to mooning," he explained to Jerry. "He's likely to ride clean off'n the road if his hinny takes the notion. It wouldn't differ to me only he's carrying a lantern of Ma's."

"Who is he?"

"Damned if I know. We picked him up in Lansingburg this morning about sunrise. He thought he was traveling west. He was reading a book. And he never knowed he was heading straight for Canady. Ma talked to him, and now we've got him along. Hello! Ma's stopped again. Maybe she's spied water."

He lengthened his stride. As they came up with the restless cattle once more, they heard the stout woman shouting for George. Over the settling dust they made out her red face peering round the side of the hood.

"Yes, Ma. I'm coming."

"George. There's a creek here."

The cows lowed behind them as they scented the water. Jerry heard a rushing brook. A bit ahead the road crossed a low bridge.

"George, just you step over that fence. Look if there's camping ground. Here, take a light with you."

As she reached over her head for the lantern, Jerry looked up at Mary. She met his eyes for an instant, and then looked away. A smile tugged at the corners of her mouth.

"I'll come with you," he told George, his voice strong.

"The ditch is easy here," said George, crossing it in a stride of his long legs. The snake fence zigzagged in front of them. They swung over. "Looks like pasture ground. No, it ain't. It's just a grass piece against woods. It would do fine, don't you think so?"

"There's plenty of room," Jerry said.

George lifted his light.

"No bogland," he said. "The bank's dry to the crick." He lifted his voice. "All right, Ma. We'll take down a part of the fence."

It took the two of them only a minute to remove one angle of the fence, and at Jerry's suggestion they laid the rails in the bottom of the ditch to take the yank off the wagon reaches as the wheels came down. He held up the lantern beside the gap.

The fat woman spoke to her team. As they took up the roll, she swung them expertly.

"Jim! Hup! Hup, you Prince!"

The collars bucked up from their withers, slapped down as the traces snapped the weight, and they scrambled up the farther side. The lantern in Jerry's hand found cups of light in their thrusting quarters. The top of the wagon swayed, lurched down and up; and the stout woman wheeled the team round to face the gap.

One by one the other wagons crossed, the women driving them handily. Then Joe Halleck came running forward to guard the road against breakaways. His whiplash writhed and snapped in the dust, and he kept yelling,

"Hey, hey, hey!" The two men behind the critters began to shout; the dogs made a bedlam of barking; and the sheep poured through among the wagons. The cows followed. The old lead cow paused on the edge of the ditch, as if she fingered it with her front hoofs; then she crossed clumsily with her udder bumping between her legs. As soon as they were all through, the stout woman drove her wagon across the gap, closing it.

"Don't appear there's no farm near," she said. "We won't make trouble, anyways."

She swung over the wheel with surprising agility, striking the ground lightly, almost bouncing.

Jerry waited at the crossing for the pole-bearer to come up. He carried the pole like a cross, his eyes lifted to the stars. As he rode, his lips moved silently in time to the twitch of the hinny's ears.

"Hey?" cried Jerry. "We're spending night here, mister."

The man's lips ceased their silent speech, his eyes were lowered and vaguely sought out Jerry in the earthly night.

"Eh? Stopping here, you say? It's late, isn't it?"

His voice was pleasantly modulated. He turned his face to the wagons, drawn up now in a line behind the stout woman's. Under the lantern he bore, Jerry had a good look at his face. A fine straight nose, a forehead impractically high, and that gentle mouth.

He did not touch the reins, but the little mule scented rest and water and pasturage. She began twirling her right ear. Briskly she went down into the ditch, crossed the fence rails on nimble feet, and edged round the stout woman's wagon-pole. Jerry followed, swung the pole to close the entrance tightly, and set his lantern on the eveners. The camp gathering was complete.

The movers followed a system that established their camp swiftly. The four men had unhitched the teams, and now were giving them a brisk rub-down. The women divided their labors. One went to the creek with the dogs to keep an eye on the sheep. Another was filling the feed troughs with grain for the horses. A third had got out a brass pail and milking stool and disappeared among the cows. And the fat woman herself was properly engaged in building a fire and managing supper. She had a lantern on the ground, a little way from her wagon, a faggot of dry sticks beside it. Jerry saw Mary crouched down watching her.

"I always gather me a faggot in the morning," explained the fat woman; "then I'm ready for supper."

She began laying the sticks of the faggot in a small open pile. Then she opened her lantern, dipped another stick in the oil, and touched it to the flame. It made her a small torch, which she placed carefully under the pile and shielded from the breeze with her broad hands. The flame began to climb.

"Where's that boy of yourn, dearie?"

He stood still in the shadow watching Mary's eyes roam the camp ground. The flicker of the growing fire animated her face and put coppery lights in her hair. Her eyes passed his, lingered a moment, and returned. They were secret with a strange bashfulness.

"Here I am, ma'am," Jerry said, stepping towards them.

The stout woman turned on her heels. She blew out her round cheeks and grinned.

"My name's Betsey Halleck, boy. Everybody here calls me Ma."

He grinned at her.

"All right, Ma Halleck."

"All right, Jerry. If you want to make yourself useful, get an axe out of my box and get me some good wood. I'm partial to birch, but most anything will suit me, seeing it's dry."

She turned back to Mary.

"There's a stew pot and kettle along with the axe, dearie. Would you fill them for me by the crick?"

Mary rose without a word and followed Jerry to the wagon. They leaned in over the tailboard side by side. Their hands encountered each other in the darkness and stole away.

Suddenly Ma Halleck chuckled behind them and, as she lifted the lantern, surprised their hands with light.

"You'd do easier with a light," she said, and saw them off on their tasks. She herself fished out a firkin and returned to her fire, humming to herself. Presently the ringing strokes of Jerry's axe sounded in the woods. She saw his light glimmering in the trees. And then Mary returned with the filled pot and kettle.

"He's a nice boy, dearie. Young for his years. But he's a nice boy."

Mary said, "Yes," in a low voice. Ma Halleck eyed her sidelong. She made a kind of sigh high in her broad nose. She said nothing as she went about the details of sorting the materials of her stew and setting the iron crane.

Supper was her chief business; and from the firm closing of her plump lips Mary deduced a devotion to good cookery. She watched Ma Halleck closely, gathering knowledge for herself.

From the firkin, as the water heated, Ma Halleck took cuts of meat. "Spring lamb, dearie. A measly little boy lamb. He didn't look equal to travel, so I had him for this journey. I wish hogweed was growing. There ain't nothing like a hogweed stew. But I'll use some kept turnips for to-night."

As the pot started simmering she dropped in the turnips and a savor began to creep among the wagons. Mary saw Joe Halleck pause in his tethering of a horse and lift his face.

"You might set the tea to boiling, dearie."

She shoved over a packet and Mary, calculating, quickly sifted tea leaves into the kettle and hung it in its place.

"Where do you come from, dearie?" Ma Halleck was paring off slivers of cheese and adding them to the meat stew.

"I'm from England."

"I don't know that land. We're all from Rutland County. That's Vermont. Wallingford way. Been in this state long?"

"I landed to-day."

"To-day, now? Gracious me!" She lifted her shining round face, but her black eyes were kindly. "You're right strange then. I'd not have guessed it, dearie. Was you from Albany?"

Mary nodded.

"How'd you meet up with him?"

Mary's voice trembled.

"He was passing through when we were at the dock. And he saw me."

"You all alone?"

Mary nodded. "I was a redemptioner. He bought my papers."

"Him? Why, he ain't but a boy."

"He was heading west. He'd saved up his money. He wanted to buy him land in the west, he told me. But he seen me, and it took about all his money."

"Just like that." Mary's eyes lifted timidly. Ma Halleck was smiling.

"Tell me all about it, dearie."

"I didn't have nowhere to go when he handed me my papers."

"He handed them to you?"

"Yes," said Mary softly. "He did. And then we met up with a funny old man that gave us a ride in his wagon and that knew him. He brought us to Schenectady. We crossed the bridge just ahead of you."

Ma Halleck nodded.

"And what are you going to do, dearie?"

"Just afore you come along, he took my papers off me again."

"Did he?" There was a new note in the stout woman's voice.

"Yes. He tore them up and threw them away, and then he asked me to marry him."

Ma Halleck sucked an audible breath through her teeth. She glanced a moment at the bowed head of the girl, and her plump lips smiled softly.

"And you said yes," she said gently. "All on short notice, both ways. Well, I don't wonder. When are you a-going to do it?"

"Jerry ain't said."

"Do you love him, dearie?" Mary lifted her eyes. They looked at each other. "Yes, yes. You'd go anywhere for him, wouldn't you? You'll labor for him." She jerked her head. "I'd thought he was a swelled-up boy. But he's done a good thing, I guess. For himself anyways."

She stirred the pot with a horn spoon. Clouds of pungent vapor enveloped her shining face, and a kind of distillation of it seemed to bead the red skin.

"I'm glad we come acrosst you," she said as she replaced the lid, "for I do love a wedden." She appeared to ruminate. "I had two in my time. I done well with the first, George and Joe, and Angy and Esther, and their two men with them now are all right. And George's girl is a nice little chit. She's going to have a baby come fall. Then I married a man named Wilson Goudger. Seemed like I couldn't stand it single. He took most of my money off'n me and yankeed out west. Used a partial of it on a section in the Purchase, and most of it on my hired girl. He come back repentant home and died. So now we're going out to my land. But I'm my own woman now and aim to remain. So, seeing my children is all Hallecks, I think I'll stay one myself. I never did feel proper wedded to Wilson. But I do love a wedden." She cut a square of maple sugar. "That's Vermont sugar, dearie. Made by me. Just drop it in the kettle for a sweeten."

The milker returned with the pail brimming.

"Not so much, to-night, Ma. Just the one pail."

"It's the travel," said Ma Halleck. "Angy, this is Mary Goodhill. Angy's Judson's wife." As the other two women approached, she introduced them:

"Esther, her name's now Marcy, wedded in March. And this is George's Prue."

They seated themselves beside Ma Halleck and Mary. The two daughters resembled their mother, cheerful-faced, plump if not so stout, strong-looking girls. George's Prue was a slip of a thing. The child already showed under her brown wool dress and she opened the laces for comfort as she sat down. Alone of the four women, her eyes questioned the night.

The men came up and sat down at the other side of the fire. Except for George's "How's for eating?" they said nothing.

"I wish that Jerry boy would come along."

They saw him then with an armful of good sticks.

"Birch for you, Ma," he said, and flung down the load like an offering before her. "I had to hunt it some."

"It's wild wood," said the fat woman, bending for a stick and laughing. "This stick'll make me the last bubbles. I do like birch. It's cooking wood."

She laid the stick, and all their faces watched the oily sputtering run over the curled bark. Ma Halleck arranged a stack of bowls in front of her knees. Her nostrils spread as she lifted the lid, and her lips moved gently.

"There's cups for tea," she said to Mary; and began to serve. "Where's the minister?"

Jerry cast her a quick glance.

"Yes, boy. He's a minister traveling to the Black River Country. Sent out by Hartford City in Connecticut. He got lost and we're bringing him as far as Utica. Mr. Atterbury!" Her hearty voice reëchoed from the wall of woodland.

The minister came slowly from the creek. His face was shining from his wash. His mild eyes benignly surveyed them.

"Set down, Mr. Atterbury, and say us grace."

He sat down in the gap between the men and women, folded his hands, and lowered his eyes before the fire. His shadow reached far behind him to the hood of the wagon in the gap. The light rippled on his fine silver hair.

"God bless us, and guide us. Make us thankful for this good food, and give us grace to appreciate Thy blessings. Amen."

His gentle eyes lifted and his hands went out automatically for his bowl. As they ate silently, a sheen lighted the sky in the east over the wagon tops.

"The moon's lifting," said George, pointing with his spoon.

They ate and drank comfortably, warm in the firelight. Their faces relaxed as their weariness slowly faded. George's Prue kept her eyes on the eastward moon. There was a queer mysteriousness in the tilt of her face, as if she dreamed, and were afraid to dream. Jerry turned from her to Mary, and he saw that she too had been watching George's Prue.

And Ma Halleck looked from one to the other, and then she turned her eyes on her children, one by one, as if she counted them.

She leaned over to the minister, and touched his knee.

"I do love a wedden, don't you, Mr. Atterbury?"

"Eh, madam?"

The minister's vague eyes were startled.

"I do love a wedden," said Ma Halleck, her black eyes glancing in the

firelight. "And a man's got to pay for his keep. So you owe me a wedden."
The minister smiled vaguely.

"Gladly, madam," he said politely. "Who can I wed?"
Something moved in Jerry's being.

"Me," he said strongly. "Me to Mary Goodhill."

But when he looked boldly across at her, she was looking down. And he flushed at the open smiles of the others. All but George's Prue were looking at him. But she had heard nothing. She was humming to herself, and now she began to sing the words.

> *"Awake, awake, you drowsy sleeper,*
> *Awake and listen unto me,*
> *There's someone at your bedroom window,*
> *A-weeping there, most bitterly."*

Her small voice was clear. Silver gently lighted her face from the rising moon. As if a magic had touched them they lowered their eyes, all but George, who silently shifted his lean frame to sit close to his wife.

Jerry felt his skin prickling round his eyes. And then a new voice softly joined the singer's, clear as her own, but with a quiet strength.

> *"Mary raised her head from her drowsy pillow,*
> *To see who calling her might be,*
> *Whom did she spy but her own true lover,*
> *A-weeping there most bitterly."*

Angy and Esther joined in in a faint humming undertone to the plaintive tune:—

> *"He said, 'Mary, dear, go ask your father,*
> *If you my wedded bride may be . . .'"*

The cows ceased chewing their cuds, the sheep stood still. One of the dogs that had drawn up to the circle of firelight lay down, trembling on its paws, and whined in its nostrils. Along the creek peepers sang.

The moon rose through the fleece of clouds and soared over them. In the quiet Ma Halleck rose from the fire, gathered the dishes, and went down to the creek. She made no sound at her washing, but when she returned, she said, "You can share with Joe to-night, Jerry. Mary, you come into my wagon with me. Mr. Atterbury can have blankets under my wagon. We'll start early to-morrow—if there's to be a wedden in the evening, we'll want to stop early."

4

"I won't need no remembrance"

"LORDY me," said Ma Halleck for the fiftieth time, "how I do love a wedden!"

She stood beside the wheel of her wagon, her black eyes staring across the flat land towards the river.

"Seems how the rain was a good thing, dearie," she remarked over her shoulder to Mary; "seems like the land lays brighter for it."

The wagons had hauled off the road again; but this time with an hour yet to spend before sunset. They were drawn up in a triangular strip of pasture, harboring a sugar bush of old trees, so tall that the Mohawk Nation in its time might have held tribal powwows in their shade. The rough trunks glistened, wide apart. Round their roots the ground was beaten hard. It was a dry spot to find after an all-day rain.

"Get back of the flaps," said Ma Halleck sharply. "Now, Jerry, what call have you got to be nosing around this wagon?" Her tone was severe, but her black eyes danced. "You go unhitch from Prue's wagon, and send George up to mine—if you're so minded to unhitch."

"George ain't here. He stopped back behind us when we came by Failings'."

"Now what do you suppose he's doing there?" asked Ma Halleck, smoothing her skirts over her broad hips. " 'Pears to me that's a queer way to act when there's a wedden planned! Well, then, you send Joe up here."

She watched Jerry turn sheepishly back to George's wagon, heard Joe's guffaw, and saw her sons-in-law wink at each other. A delighted grin spread her plump lips.

"That's the way men are," she said over her shoulder. "They take a wedden lightsome. Seems as how they don't feel nothing into it and all they think about is something to drink out the fire with. It's different to us. Seems like it comes into a woman's nature. It's like spinning on a wheel, or drawing thread across a loom—only it's different, too." Her voice lifted to a brighter note as her bouncing humor reasserted itself. "Now, dearie. Here's your chance to make the sugar bush while your man's busied up with the horses. Tend yourself and come along back by the fence. It don't do for a man to meet his woman 'fore the rightsome time."

She watched closely for signs of insurrection from the men, her ears conscious of Mary's swift flight into the shadows of the old trees.

Mary's face was calm, but her shoulders drooped as if they felt the burden of an old acknowledgment of her sex. Before the sun, the old trees seemed to bow down their shade upon her through the washed evening air, and cover and guard her.

Across the rail fence, Ma Halleck watched a man ploughing. His furrow lay close to the fence, and his team were bringing him towards the wagons.

The wet earth was shattered into crude lumps by the share; and down the field crows, prospecting for worms, hopped stiff-legged like boys on stilts and shouted through the stillness. Ma Halleck was glad of the rain, for it had garbed the valley with a scent of spring. She went lightly down to the fence, where the water that had attracted them welled up, and leaned upon the railings.

"Evening, mister," she greeted the ploughman.

He stopped his team at the end of the furrow, took off his hat, and mopped his face with his sleeve.

"Evening," he said. The blue eyes in the square German head were kindly.

"Heavy ploughing," remarked Ma.

"That is so."

"Do you mind if we camp in your pasture?"

"*Nein.* Mine cows along the river are. You going west?"

"Yes, I'm heading my family for the Purchase."

"So. You stop early to-night?"

"Yes. We're going to have a wedden."

"*Ja?*" His eyes slowly passed over the wagons while his gnarled fingers sorted some sweat from his beard. "Which is it?"

"There's the boy. The girl's in the sugar bush. Mister, do you know where I could get some wood for a big fire?"

The German turned round to lean his back against the crosspiece of the helves.

"None near. I tell you, though. This corner post is bad in the fence. I was laying two new sections next week. You burn them rails." He turned his eyes on her, as she thanked him, and asked, "Yours the boy?"

"No. Neither one of 'em mine. They're going along with our train as far as Utica." She looked at him closely, and her voice bubbled up, "But I do love a wedden, mister."

He opened his mouth and laughed.

"Me also. I'm Heinrich Hartmann."

"Betsey Halleck."

She bobbed a comic curtsey. And he smiled.

"Give good luck to the young ones. Me, I must plough."

"What are you planting?"

"Parley." He waved his hand. "I like to see it from mine house, a parley field."

From where she stood, Ma Halleck saw his frame barn, bright red, and the white house beyond; a prosperous farm. The flat land was rich land.

He spoke to his horses and they dragged the plough round to the homeward furrow. He did not return.

Jerry Fowler, with a red face, was rubbing down the last horse when Ma Halleck passed him. She showed him the rails the German had donated.

"You and Joe can bring them up. Me, I've got to get supper."

She was back at her wagon again in time to guide Mary across the clearing.

"Inside with you, dearie. I'll have the girls with you soon." She sought out the minister. "Now, Mr. Atterbury, where are you heading for?"

"I thought I'd just wander down to the river awhile. I like to have time to myself before a wedding, or a burial."

"I like a short service," said Ma. "Don't you think they're the best?" He regarded her mildly. And suddenly his eyes clouded. He made a wide gesture with his white hand.

"Yes, yes. Here. That could almost wed them. I don't know." His eyes were struggling with some kind of puzzlement. "There's a strange feeling in this place—in all this valley." And he lifted his eyes to the sky, and saw the sun like a red chariot wheeling across the clouds. Watching his retreating back, Ma Halleck gave herself a brief shake. There was work to do.

But Esther was coming in with the milk from the cows which had found browse beyond the spring, and Angy was carrying up two buckets of fresh water.

"You, Angy and Esther, you tend on Mary. Her and Jerry will have my wagon for their wedding night," she directed as Prue came towards them. A smile fluttered her lips as she added, "No maids for the bride— you'll have to do; and Esther's but just turned the corner." Esther giggled. "But Prue's a woman finding her time. She'll help me."

Prue's small face was wistful; but it had put on the wedding smile. "We're going to make a feast, Prue."

And Mrs. Halleck sprang into activity. . . .

Down by the last wagon the men had finished their work, and now Joe cornered Jerry and sat him on a bucket, and with his two brothers-in-law hopped up on the tailboard, looking down.

"There he is," said Joe, working his lean face into becoming solemnity. "Jerry Fowler, we want to question you on your fitness for the wedded state."

Jerry kept his eyes along the reach of the wagon, but the blood had reddened even his ears.

"Jerry Fowler, was you brought up in Christian Faith?"

Jerry gave them a short glance. They squatted like three foolish frogs a-row.

"That's a serious question," said Abijah Judson, stroking his pale moustache. "Difficult for a young man to answer. But we got to report to the Reverend—Fowler."

Jerry's face was burning. Over and over, above the thumping of his heart he kept seeing the end of the Mohawk Bridge in darkness, the shadow of her face; he heard the peepers, and her voice; and the scent of her hair was in his nostrils. And these grinning frogs, to ask him questions.

"He's all bebuzzed in his head. Not a clear-thinking boy."

"No," said Joe, in his nasal Vermonter's voice. "Hardly thought on the troubles of the wedded state. Answer our question."

"Yes," said Jerry, desperately.

"Do you shave mornings?"

"No."

"He shaves of nights. That's mark of a lightsome fellow. I knew a man that shaved of nights. He never was married, but he calculated fifteen children round the county to be hisn. His name was Jerry, too. Jerry Parson was his name. A rampant man."

The tailboard quivered under their hams.

"Well, he's passed on the faith, I guess. Just squeaked by. Now we come to the practical business of marriage. You, Jerry Fowler, answer these questions. When a man goes home does he blow out the lantern?"

"He don't seem very knowing. But he's young."

"Does he turn it down, then?"

"If he don't turn it down, does he turn anything down?"

"By crinkus, this lad's a mortal strange man for a mortal!"

"He don't appear very learned, that's the honest fact of it."

"Don't know what a girl's going to do, if she meets up with him."

"Do you take off your shoes in the kitchen?"

"He ain't very good."

"Shucks! He comes from York State. Near by where the Shakers are."

"That's the trouble. They're big shakes at shucking. Don't give Christians room for tillage."

"How do you measure property?"

Jerry lifted badgered eyes.

"By the acre," he said at last. . . .

Up by the fire, Ma Halleck, putting corn dough to bake in a pan, looked over at Prue. "Now what are them roosters roaring at?"

Prue shook her head.

"There's George coming at last," and her voice was clearer.

"Makes you homesick, honey," Ma Halleck said understandingly, "all this doing, withouten your rightful man?"

But Prue did not answer. Her eyes were for her husband, coming with long strides. He circled Ma's wagon and thrust a bottle under her apron.

"It's the best they had, Ma. A wedden gift to drink them with."

Prue smiled into his eyes, and a sudden answering hunger in his face paled her cheeks. Then she crimsoned, and he said, "Lordy, Prue!" and tumbled her dark hair. . . .

Inside Ma Halleck's wagon the three girls knelt on a feather tick and looked through Mary's two bundles.

"I fancy seeing you wear that reddish dress," Angy said. "It's a real pretty piece of wearing. I'd like to see you wear it with that white wool shawl."

"That was my mother's," Mary said.

"I'm partial for that, too," said Esther. "And that bit of blue ribbon braided in your hair. I'd like it. I had white in my hair when I was wedded."

Mary sat back while the two young women poked through her small belongings.

"There's a pretty silver chain," Angy exclaimed, undoing a wrap of linen. "My, and there's a ring, too."

"Are you going to be wedded with a ring?" asked Esther. "Abel wedded me with a ring."

And she held up her hand for Mary to see the slim silver band.

"It comforts a girl to look at a ring—just to feel it on her hand."

Angy nodded soberly.

"It's a comforten thing," she agreed. "Maybe Jerry ain't got one with him. Seems as how he couldn't have." And suddenly the two giggled. They looked sidelong at Mary, and then exchanged glances. "Would you like for to be married with your mother's ring?"

Mary suddenly shook her head.

"Don't give it to Jerry!"

"Why not?"

"A man marries a girl with his own mother's ring, maybe. But he don't wed her with a ring she gives him," said Angy.

"But this one's gold!" cried Esther. "Think of being wedded with a gold ring!"

Mary hardly heard them. It was stuffy under the wagon hood; and the space was crowded. All the back end was piled high with household things: spinning wheels, the large for wool, the small for flax; a heavy bedstead; a trammel and a stack of pots; a chest strong with sage that might be housing linens; another chest, mouse-proof, for seeds; a dasher churn—these and many other things Mary could identify in the close-packed space. There was just enough room left for the feather tick; and standing room behind the seat.

Angy was peeking round the flaps.

"The sun sets low," she said. "George is back again. Him and Joe are bringing up some fence rails for the fire. Ma's a-baking and a-bending round the fire. Abijah's getting out the likker keg. Men will need likker for a celebration, always."

"Where's Jerry? I do notion to see a man's face afore he's wedded. I mind peeking down the loft stair at Abel. He was setting there and saying *yes* and *no* and feeling of his hands. He's got powerful big hands. I mind me how I skittered looking down on them-there hands of hisn."

"You was shameless and hussyfied a girl as ever was wedded," said her sister dryly. "Reckon you was wedded just about in time."

Esther tossed her head and giggled.

"Some wedding women thinks of other things," said Angy, pursing her mouth. And she nodded at Mary.

"Where's Mr. Atterbury?" demanded Esther, craning past her sister.

"He went down by the river, by himself alone."

"My! Supposing he was to fall in? Supposing the water caught and drowned him? An awful thing!"

"It isn't you that has to fear, praised be!"

"There's a little boy coming up along the fence. Staring his eyes to see all! What's fetching him this way?"

"He's a funny-looking little boy, ain't he?"

"Maybe he's the farmer's boy."

"Look, he's clomb the fence. He's carrying in his hand. What's he carrying, Esther?"

"He's got a string of fish. Lordy, ain't they large ones? I wonder do the fish grow bigger out this westward."

"He's handing them to Ma. Shush you, Esther. Leave us listen."

Ma Halleck got to her feet laboriously.

"Hello, young mister."

"Hello," said the towheaded boy, examining her out of staring blue eyes. "Them are handsome fish you've got."

"Pa said I was to fetch them for the wedding."

"My! Ain't they handsome? Look, Joe, did you ever see such trout?"

"No. I'd like to catch some. Did you fish them, son?"

"Yeanh." The boy placed one bare foot over the other and rocked himself. He put his hands in his pockets and looked scornful. "I fished them this afternoon. I know where they rest. I ain't telling, though."

"Were they all so big?" asked Ma.

"No. But Pa said I was to fetch the biggest. But I kept out the very biggest, though. And then there was a monster trout that got away."

"He must have been a mammoth fish, judging by these here."

"Well, I guess that's likely."

"Tell your pa my thanks. And thank you, too."

"It's all right. I get them all the while. Bigger'n them. Are you the wedded lady?"

"No. Do you want to see the lady that is wedded? You can stay if you do."

"No, I ain't got time for weddens."

"Do you like maple sugar?"

"I don't mind eating of it."

Ma Halleck giggled as she gave him a chunk. He bit off some, and chewed it, and looked up.

"Thanks."

Staring right and left, he walked slowly back to the fence. He paused astride the top rail and bit off another mouthful. "It's pretty good sugar," he called, and then ducked down for home.

"My, ain't they daisies, though? Look at the red in them!" Ma Halleck held the trout up. "I'll wrap them in corn and fry them fresh. They'll just make our edibles complete."

And she bent over vigorously. . . .

"I can see the Reverend acrosst the meadowland," said Esther. "It's time you was dressing, Mary. The sun's setting deep down, now."

Far away the barking of a dog, taking a herd out, echoed faintly. A cowbell tinkled.

Mary stood up.

"We shouldn't rightfully touch you, being married women," said Angy. She and her sister hoisted themselves on the seat, and the flap closed over Mary.

All alone in the stuffy wagon, she stood still a moment. Then her hands went slowly to the laces of her dress. Slowly, she undid them, and slowly let the dress down about her feet. Slowly, as if it hurt her, she took off her petticoats and let them fall. She bent again, and her undershift of rough wool slid down her knees. She straightened her back as if a pain were there. And she stood alone with herself, white and still.

The sisters had left the bucket accessible under the seat. Mary went about her washing with a quiet stealth. Scarcely breathing outside the flaps, they yet could not hear her. Their faces sobered, even Esther's, and suddenly they looked away.

There was a hush in the air that even the twitter of roosting small birds did not break. Only a wagon rumbling far down the road made an undertone in the silence, as though the earth had begun to breathe.

Mary heard it as she plaited the blue ribbon through her hair. Her hands stopped in the task, and she stood with white arms uplifted. In the dusk of the wagon her skin shone dimly with the beauty of her approaching time; and her eyes, half fearful, veiled themselves with lids grown heavy. "Reverend's coming. He's crossing over the ploughed land now"—Esther's voice. And the voice farther off of George hailing Mr. Atterbury, and his voice coming near and replying, and the two of them fixing the spot for the wedding. Jerry being called, and the low mutter of the minister talking to him. Rumbling of the wagon wheels approaching down the pike, growing louder. Scents of cookery, and the hush in Ma Halleck's chatter. Angy's whisper: "Near time, Mary. Are you ready?"

Mary stooped her head through the gathered red-brown dress, settled it over her body with half-dead hands that trembled. She put the shawl across her shoulders and the silver chain round her throat. She stood up, and as Angy parted the flaps her eyes became still.

They helped her down over the wheel, adjuring her softly not to falter. Their plump faces were sober now, and they walked with a stiffness in their knees.

Dimly, down the slope of ground, past the fire, as she walked, Mary saw the movers; beyond them, Jerry, red-faced, set-lipped, his dark eyes on hers; and her blood began to stir. She saw the white head of the minister, his blue benign eyes, his gentle mouth to say the everlasting words. Two dead mullein stalks rose up, one either side of him, against the fence rails; and she wondered if the legend were true that bees drowsed out the winters in the dark, hollow rods. Beyond lay the ploughed land, broken, brown, and heavy, making its preparation for the seed. She tried to see it as it would be in its abundance—gentle with grain, swaying to the touch of heaven.

She was aware of the girls halting stiffly behind her; and now she advanced alone. She felt Jerry's strong, lean hand in hers, and hers in his. But she did not see anything but the vision of barley, and she felt only the breath-taking life in her heart. . . .

The minister talked softly. He had been by the river, and he had seen on the high banks the painted pictures of the Indians, older than the remembrance of the oldest settler, and a little of the mystery of earth clouded his soft voice. . . .

But Jerry woke to the singing blood, and he took out the ring he had fashioned from a horseshoe nail, and put it upon her finger, and he bent forward to kiss her, with the minister's eye upon him, and her lips were cool, and living.

A flock of crows that straggled across the sky hushed their vaunting bedlam at the uncommon sight. The stillness of evening mantled the valley, and the first planet made a spot against the afterglow.

And then Mrs. Halleck cried, "Oh, I do love a wedden!"

She swooped down the alleyway between her children and gave the wedded pair great hearty smacks of kisses, and the others clapped, and all at once the late afternoon stage went whirling by for Albany. The driver cried and tootled his horn, and handkerchiefs were waved, and laughter came back to them.

The lid lifted on the kettle and Ma gave a shriek, and in the midst of the others Mary and Jerry were ushered up to the fire. They were sat down side by side and given plates piled high. The minister was served.

Tea was offered for the womenfolks, but Joe passed out glasses of whiskey for the men. As the daylight drew downwards into the west, the firelight sought out their faces, George with his arm round his wife's waist, the two other couples paired off.

"Come, Ma," said Joe. "It's you must take a bachelor man, if the Reverend won't have you."

His mother slapped his cheeks.

"Don't be naughty, Joey." But the minister had not heard. And Ma's stout face beamed in spite of herself, and she edged against his output arm and dipped her corn cake in Joe's whiskey glass and giggled as she ate it down.

"'Pears to me that married couple over there ain't eating hearty."

"Married pairs ain't given to food, I've noticed. Not new-married." Jerry grinned.

"Food's for to comfort," he said. "And I've been comforted already."

Abijah laughed and clapped his calloused hands.

"By the Lord, I wisht there was a floor for dancing. Every time I look at those two married-person faces I feel my feet get lightsome."

"Your feet lightsome!" Esther laughed. "Seems my ears still ring with your feet stomping down below at my own wedden."

"Abijah's a great dancing man," Angy said pridefully.

"Wish we had music. I like weddens with some music. I wish there was a fiddler hereabouts. I'd walk a mile to hear some fiddling."

"Joe," said George, "where's your harp?"

Joe grinned up from beside his mother.

"Right in my pants' pocket, George. Do you calculate on a tune?" George nodded.

"Now we've finished eating. First, though, we'll drink this couple with some wine."

Ma Halleck was gathering the whiskey glasses, rinsing them in the water pail. Now George took out the yellow-sealed bottle.

"Don't break the shield!" cried Ma, as he started to break it. "Maybe Mary will want to keep it for a remembrance. It's so pretty."

Mary, who had sat quiet, chin on hands, spoke gently.

"I won't need no remembrance."

Jerry eyed her sidelong. Beauty was in her eyes. He had seen Joe glancing at her again and again, had seen the eyes of the other men admiring, had seen Angy's eyes with a touch of envy. His own face felt stiff and circumspect to himself. But he felt that he had done well. He was proud of her. It made him strong and masterful. He was his own man now, a masterful man.

And then he looked again at Mary, and reading the quiet in her eyes he was jolted back into the intimacy of the present, and he became aware of the overarching shadows of the old grove, of the grey vague rain-stained shapes of the wagon hoods and the ritualistic coils of flame. For a brief space his brain saw clearly. He was conscious of his own unease, a sense of darkness between himself and the fire, and, as he sought to struggle through it, all he could see was Mary's face,—himself a shadow,—and from her self-containment, like a little boy, he drew assurance.

It seemed to him that he was growing in that flitting time: he remembered himself in the pantry of his father's house in Uniontown, stealing from the sweet-pickle jar, and his nose was alive to the remembered smells, the cream and butter smell, the dry odor of ageing hams and flitches, the mixed scent of tansy, and tarragon, and camomile, and may-weed, and boneset; the woodshed was clear in his brain with its scent of chips, and he heard his father's stern words and the swish of the strap, but he did not feel; and a voice was saying, "Love apples are for birds," and he remembered being sick; and he saw himself going to school under old Jeptha Harris; and he remembered his agony as he stole behind the sleeping old pedagogue and tied the tail of his wig to the chair back, and he saw the red stolid faces of the schoolroom regarding him dispassionately under the old man's voice; he saw himself later walking through the pine woods with Nancy Van Tripp, the miller's daughter; he saw the miller's threatening face; and then his father was saying, "Critters behave in spring, but a man makes his own way," and yet his father had withstood his seeking his own future; he saw himself going away, his brother waving after him, his mother walking to the gate at his side; his own man at last—he heard the Shaker preacher's voice, "Money don't usually buy"; and his strength returned. But the sense of time in him was divided into three parts, and now he listened in the past, and he looked in the future, and he felt the blood in his body, and the time was near.

He stood up to thank them and they cried to him and to Mary to drink glasses together. Mary rose at his side, slowly, without awkwardness. They drank to each other, for it was a thing of instinct, in which they had no need of speech. He was aware of the others clapping, and the twanging of the jew's-harp as Joe's hand began to fan. Abel Marcy raised his hoarse voice in the courting song:—

> " 'Hi,' said the blackbird, sitting on a chair,
> 'Once I courted a lady fair;
> She proved fickle and turned her back;
> And ever since then I've dressed in black.' "

The jew's-harp caught up a beat:—

> *Towdy-owdy, dil-do-dum,*
> *Towdy-owdy, dil-do-day,*
> *Towdy-owdy, dil-do-dum*
> *Tol-lol-liddy, dil-do-day.*

George's voice, sonorous and true:—

> " 'Hi!' said the little leather-winged bat,
> 'I will tell you the reason that,
> The reason that I fly by night
> Is because I've lost my heart's delight!' "

And the harp:—

> *Towdy-owdy, dil-do-dum. . . .*

Angy and Esther and Prue and Ma Halleck had stolen away to Ma's wagon. Jerry saw the hood bulge as they moved here and there. They were fixing.

Stroking aside his pale moustache, Abijah Judson tilted his head:—

" 'Hi!' said the little mourning dove,
'I'll tell you how to regain her love.
Court her night and court her day,
Never give her time to say, O Nay!' "

What were songs when the land was ploughing and the dew fell and spring was just beyond the southward hills?

Tol-lol-liddy, dil-do-day.

Jerry stood close to her, his eyes saw her eyes drooping, the bend of her neck, the ripple of the fire through her hair. The skin in the notch of her shawl was creamy and warm. The past was fading, for the time was coming. And all he brought with him out of the past was a remembrance of bloom in the spring. He saw the firelight through darkness and heard the whisper of cows over their cuds. Mist was on the river and starlight on the mist.

Ma Halleck was coming back with the girls; now she was sitting down. Her voice in her stout throat bubbled over:—

" 'Hi!' said the woodpecker, sitting on a fence,
'Once I courted a handsome wench;
She got scary and from me fled,
And ever since then my head's been red.' "

The girls were round about Mary. She was going away to the wagon. Her head was bent, and her shoulders curved. Quietness and lowliness were in her walk; and beside her the girls' faces wore a strange abashment of mirth that struggled with the time, as if they dared not let it loose. But Jerry's head lifted; and left alone he became aware of himself: how his hands moved on the wrist joints; how his heart beat against his ribs and his lungs swelled with breathing; and his feet were light on the ground.

Tol-lol-liddy, dil-do-day.

Now the girls were coming back, and the men were standing up. He felt them beside him, leading him, and the night was growing still. But ahead of him was stillness beyond the world, and the wagon was sleeping against it. They were taking him round to the far side of the wagon. They were unlacing his boots, removing his coat. Now they were leaving him. And he was alone. He did not hear, he did not see. Prue's voice singing softly to herself by the fire was beyond his scope, for the past was behind him, and his being was his own.

With a swift arrogance he poised himself before the flaps. And now his ears could hear the littlest sounds and his eyes see the smallest things.

He could hear a trout rise far away in still water, and see a spider laying an anchor thread from the hub of the wheel to a dried clover stalk; he could feel the dew; and the breathing of darkness was in his ears; and only the wagon was still.

And then, as his hands reached for the flaps, he felt them tremble with the uprising of his being. But he hesitated no longer, for the time was now.

5

"A northwest wind means clearing"

IN all his life, Jerry had never suspected there could be a road like the Mohawk Turnpike. It seemed to him that all the world was moving on it. He was standing in the middle of the roadway on top of a rise of ground. It was afternoon, and Mary had come back from Ma Halleck's wagon to walk with him. There was no wind that day; the night had been cold, carrying a hard frost; but the sun now shone full on them, filling the world with a bright glitter so that even the new green of the meadows glanced against one's eyes and the river shone like blue fire.

"We'd better be getting after the wagons," he said.

The road led them downward toward the flat land that stretched out ahead as far as they could see. The hills drew back from the river here, their slopes more gentle, and the river itself began meandering back and forth across the valley. The road seemed closer to the land, and the travel on it less rapid.

Marigolds were blooming in the wet spots, skunk cabbage was unfolding its bright green leaves. In strips of drier pasture, quaker-lady flowers were sifted through the grass like a pale fine bluish snow. The trees were coming into leaf, the maples hazy pink and lilac in the wood lots, the elms a soft golden olive, like tapestry trees.

Jerry caught some of the peacefulness, and, as they were alone in the road, he reached shyly for Mary's hand. His eyes shone with a light of possessive pride. And her grave glance was tender. They did not notice the man harrowing beyond the fence; they did not see him stop and grin at them; but when he started his team once more he whistled a tune.

"Mary," Jerry asked suddenly, "what would you like to have best in all the world?"

Her brows puckered and for a long time she was silent.

"I don't know. I hadn't thought," she said at length.

His voice was slightly impatient.

"What would you like most to have me be?"

She said, "I hadn't thought, Jerry."

"You're a queer girl."

"Am I?" She lifted her face with an effort. "I'd like a farm. I'd like a small farm, maybe, with a brook beside it and a spring house. I'm a fair hand at dairying."

"Are you? But you're a queer girl for a man to marry. Wanting a small thing always. I can't figure it out." His keen eyes, restless again, went roaming.

"It's a funny thing, Mary. But since I got onto this road, and since I got wedded to you, I've kind of lost my hankering to farm. Money comes slow in farming. Everything's bound in acres. I'd rather have money. I want to be rich. I'd like to make you rich, with hired girls to help you in the house."

She smiled behind her eyes.

"I don't need helping, Jerry. I'm willing to work."

"I guess you'll have to for a while, Mary. But on this road I've got to feeling something different will come. I feel as if I could lick the world."

Her eyes lost their self-contentment; the lids drooped submissively. Her voice became husky.

"I'm not very good at things, Jerry. But I'll help you all I can."

Jerry put out his hand with a swift gesture and caught hers.

"It don't seem I could get it out of my head that we are wedded."

His face was set straight forward as he walked, his cheeks reddened.

"I wisht I could have give you a better ring. I couldn't think of anything else to fashion it with. But when I get rich I'll buy you a gold one."

"No, no."

He looked at her in amazement.

"Wouldn't you like a gold ring better?"

"I like this one."

"But, Mary . . ."

Her mouth and eyes became firm.

"No. I'll always want this one."

He walked ahead a pace, his eyes downcast and troubled. Then, as she caught up, he said, "I'll have it plated with gold, then."

She drew a quiet breath, and he said, "You like it because I fashioned it?"

She nodded.

"That's nice," he said warmly. "That's nice."

He was happy once more.

The road swung round a curve, and at the end of the next straight stretch they saw a tollgate, and a village beyond. The gate had a house beside it, and a bridge upon the near side led up to the upraised grating across a wide creek. The slats of the gate glistened white against the sun, and their shadows made blue bars upon the backs of the Hallecks' driven beasts. They saw George standing under the gate, pointing back at them, and a blowzy woman nodding her head.

As they approached she went about her business of winding down the grating, and then she sat down under the signboard of her little taproom, and folded her hands on her skirt of scarlet calico. She was smiling broadly.

"You're of that party?" she greeted them, and Jerry nodded.

"New-wedded folks will linger. Ain't you tired a-walking?" she asked Mary.

"No, ma'am."

"New-wedded folks don't get tired, I calculate it. Will you come in for a sup to fresh you with, mister?"

"No, thanks."

"I've got a cozy tap. I offer good trade," she nodded at the sign above her head; "but you're new-wedded."

Jerry read the sign, and flushed. It showed a beehive in yellow on a green ground, and underneath a jingle in red letters.

> Sugar is sweet
> And so is honey
> Here's the place
> To spend your money.

ISABELLA HUNEY, PROPRIETOR

"That's me, mister. But I reckon you're well chosen."

She began elaborately plaiting a wisp of her red hair, and made staring eyes at Jerry. He looked uncomfortably at her red mouth; and he noticed lines coming down from her nostrils.

"Can we get through?" he asked stiffly.

She gave a silent nod, and he and Mary went through the picket. They did not speak any more. The blood was up in his face. But once he surprised Mary's glance as if she had found something new in him, and in a way it made him proud.

A hundred yards farther on they overtook George Halleck trudging in the dust and reading from a book. Jerry missed something in the line, and for a moment he did not realize that it was the minister who had gone.

"Where's Mr. Atterbury?"

George closed the book, but kept his finger in his place.

"So you've caught up," he grinned at them. "I don't know what's happened to the Reverend. I guess he just drifted off. He's a strangely-minded man. Seems his preaching must have disconnected him somewhere."

Jerry wondered if the hinny mule had spied some tempting pasturage. He could well imagine the little creature browsing while the black-clad Reverend on her back closed his vague eyes to his vague thoughts.

He looked down at the book that George was carrying and asked, "What have you got in that book?"

George held it up.

"It's kind of a guide," he said. "I bought it off Mrs. Huney at the gate. An outright woman, ain't she—she and her sign together right on the road?"

Mary had gone round the sheep to overtake Ma's wagon, and he grinned as he watched her quick walking.

"Did she try to persuade you to tarry, Jerry?"

"Yes."

George laughed.

"She did me, too. Brassy, right there in sight of wagons. But you —new-wedded! I'd told her, too!" He poked Jerry's ribs. "I reckon you've a kind of bait for women, Jerry!"

Jerry didn't answer the grin, and George lifted the book once more as if he had just remembered it.

"I was just looking up where we were. Right ahead to northward's Herkimer Village. A post town. It says there's a gristmill up the creek back there—West Canada by name. And a sawmill up above it. That-there stone church you see was fortified against the Indians in the Revolution war. South of the river lies the German Flats. Rich land. You can tell that by the farms. It's plain to see where we are—fifteen miles from Utica."

He traced the words on the page, then closed the book and grinned at Jerry again.

"Ma wants to talk to you and Mary. . . ."

"Did you have a nice time walking with your man, dearie?"

Ma Halleck's red face wore a friendly grin as Mary adroitly swung herself onto the moving wagon. She nodded as she took her place on the high seat.

"I believe we'd better camp soon. We've had a fine spell of weather, but there's rain coming. I read it in my almanac and I expect it to-night. I like to get my dinner cooked afore it rains."

She shook the lines and bawled at the slacking leader.

"Git, Joe! Lord, I'd like to leather you. He's been slacking back all day, dearie. He always was a lazy. Git, you!"

The leader for the moment bent industriously into his collar and Ma turned to Mary.

"How does it feel being a woman four days wedded?"

Mary smiled against the sun. To the southward dark clouds were piling up, their bellies beginning to catch fire. Mary watched them with unseeing eyes, and suddenly the fat woman put her hand over the girl's wrist.

"Come rich or poor," she said, "God wish you children, dearie."

Her eyes softened as she watched the tranquil face. If she were a man, she thought, she would read the wealth in the girl, wealth to steady a man and make him comfortable; but she sighed—men did not see the things a woman saw. They valued even dollars differently. She eyed the face again, and tried to see it with a man's eyes. The bloom in the skin—it had a clarity and freshness that younger girls in this land seemed to lack; she noted the curve of the ear and jaw, and the throat line sweet as a filly's; the grey eyes nearly blue; and the quiet mouth with its awakening curves. Any man could see those things; and a wise man could read deeper.

"Are you happy, dearie?"

As she met the grave, level glance, she sighed.

"No need to ask," she said, lifting her voice a note. "I mind me of my own wedden morning. I wasn't then so stout—more Esther's build—but wilder than she. I felt let loose. I felt like a filly in spring pasture. I was bold then—I wasn't ever a timorous woman—but them days I would cock up my heels at a man, skitterful." Her glance became abstracted and one stout hand was lost under her breast. "My Halleck was an oldish man, sober in years. I was wild loving him. Nonsensical, I mind me. Not a sober girl like you, dearie. Aye-oh! but I was young!"

Suddenly her big body sagged.

"I hate to think of parting from you two. I've got fond of you, dearie. And Jerry's so young. You're both young. I'd like to keep my eyes onto you both."

"Jerry can look out for me," said Mary softly.

"So he can, I make no doubt. It's me I'm thinking of, missing you."

At that moment, Jerry's voice called up from the road, "Hey, there! Can I have a ride?" and in spite of herself Ma grinned. For a breath she imagined herself young and skitterful again.

"It's loading my horses shameful, but if so be you're tired walking."

He jumped over the wheel, stepped over the seat, and leaned forward between them.

"George said you wanted to talk to me and Mary, Ma."

Ma Halleck gave the reins another shake. Her round cheeks grew even redder and she fixed her eyes on the off leader's ears. Her voice, when she found utterance for her words, was offish in its tone.

"Well, here it is. I'll out with it straight and you can take it or leave it as you're minded. My land's lot ten, township fifteen, in range two. I've got the papers here,"—she pointed over her shoulder to the wooden chest, —"but I don't know what it's like, beyond it's wooded and holds fourteen acres of swampy ground. It means hard clearing, and it ain't noways settled round it. That's how the boys are figuring to take land close by. But I ain't got but Joey to work my land. So I'm offering you, Jerry, a job at working for me. And 'stead of wages you can work for an interest in my farm. That's what it is."

She expelled a gusty breath, as if her stout being had been eased; and for the first time since she had started speaking she turned her eyes to see how Jerry might consider her proposition.

She could see that he was pleased—Mary, too. And suddenly a kind of giggle forced itself out of her mouth.

"Think of me!" she cried. "Getting halfway westward afore I ever considered my farm help!"

Jerry said softly, "Thank you, Ma. But you've got Joey."

"That roosterish brat-boy! He ain't no more reliable than hen's peckings. Like as not, the first spring, he'll take a notion for a girl and sashay out to prairie country. No, there's no dependence in Joey."

Jerry said nothing. He was looking out ahead of the horses' ears.

"It would be a good thing for you, and for Mary," continued Ma, warming to her own idea. "You don't know a single body out this westward. It'll be hard getting started. And you could come out with us, and if it didn't suit you in a year, why, you could move off."

Jerry dropped his eyes to his hands, that were folding themselves carefully.

"If it's the boys you're thinking about, or Angy and Esther, you can put it right out of your mind. They're well fixed. They'll be all the gladder not to have to work for me. I've talked with them about it, Jerry."

Jerry said, "It's nice. It's a nice idea. I was figuring, though, on stopping off in Utica a spell."

Ma Halleck turned to Mary, to persuade her over Jerry; but she changed her mind. Mary was looking at her husband, and her face was utterly tranquil. Ma Halleck twitched her shoulders. It wasn't right a boy his age should have a complete say.

"You don't need to answer right this minute," she said.

"It's tempting to me," Jerry said. "And I'm real grateful, Ma."

"You don't need to feel that way. It's business to me. Come on, now. Say you're going to close." She hesitated, seeing his face making up to answer; and then she added diffidently, "You know, Jerry, we all feel fine to you. And you're hard put against it, having used your money."

Jerry looked up swiftly.

"I've got plenty, Ma."

But his eyes swung from her to Mary and back. His jaw set, and for the first time Ma Halleck noticed the bones in his face.

"I've thought, Ma." His voice was slow. "Me and Mary are real grateful to you, but we're stopping off in Utica." And suddenly, as her fat face fell, he added, "I don't know how we would have got along if you hadn't been so good to us. I don't, really."

Ma turned and grinned at him, but her glance was for the girl. There was no readable expression in her face. She was slightly flushed and her eyes were downcast as though she had read some disapproval in Jerry's face.

"Well, I'm sorry, Jerry. I've got a hankering for you two."

She spoke to the horses again, sharply, and eyed the roadside.

"Wouldn't that look like a likely spot for unhitching?"

Jerry looked.

"It appears a good place. Them trees would break a south wind rain. And there's room this side the fence."

Ma lifted her voice.

"We're camping, George."

The sun was going down sullenly, its fire damped in the clouds. The cattle were taken in and tethered to the fence and the men used the wagons and lengths of rope to make a kind of yard for the sheep.

Ma worked industriously at the supper. She made no comment on Jerry's decision, even while she and Mary were alone; but she talked of her house back in Vermont. "Halleck was the youngest son," she said. "We had a hillside farm and it was giving out. But I liked the house. I had an oven there could golden a loaf like none you ever seen." And she talked about homey things her mother had taught her.

It was twilight when they had finished eating, and the rain was a visible shadow across the river. They could see the pucker coming into the quiet surface, the first drops, and the wind, and then the rain itself. A drop struck Ma's stout cheek. She said, as she wiped the last dish, "I feel real lonesome, sort of. To-morrow night we won't have these new-wedded folks along."

George looked at her understandingly.

He said, "I'm sorry, too."

Jerry—who had been silent all through the evening—looked down.

"You've been real good to us."

"Shucks," said George, as he shooed Prue to her wagon. His lean face offered no comment. And before the heavy rain had reached them, the people were in their beds.

Jerry listened to it, drumming on the wagon hood above their heads. Outside a horse was crunching the grass. He could hear the small sharp sound of tearing roots.

"Mary."

"Yes, Jerry."

"Did you tell Ma about us?"

"I'm sorry."

"Why did you tell her that?"

There was a long silence.

"Why?" he said again.

She spoke brokenly, as if the words wrenched her.

"I couldn't help it. Seems as if I had to tell somebody about you and me."
He lay a long while, stiff on his back. He had an idea that she was crying;
but she was so quiet in all the things she did, he did not know.
"I don't blame you. Only, I wouldn't like for you to tell anyone else."
"I won't again."
Her voice was very low.
"Of course, with Ma and them it doesn't matter so. In Utica nobody will
know about it."
She said nothing more, but he could hear her making her breath even.
Far away, thunder rolled into the valley. . . .

The movers went silently about their morning chores. Rain still was
falling; and the sunrise was no more than a dim spot behind them in the
notch of hills. It was cold, with the wind veering to the northwest. Through
the drizzle, harder showers spat slantingly. Sight of the country was shut
off. Other wagons, starting their morning's haulage, appeared inexplicably
in the murk and passed with a sludge of horse-hoofs. The surface of the
road became a kind of paste that opened under the tires and closed its
lips behind them, leaving no trace.

Jerry walked with Abijah Judson. The man's pale moustaches dripped
rain against his chin; he had turned up the collar of his shirt to protect
his throat, round which Angy had tied a strip of black silk half an inch
wide to guard against the quinsy. Vermonters, he informed Jerry, were
inclined to get the quinsy when they traveled out of their valleys, and for
a strong man he himself had always been extraordinarily partial to disease.

Jerry did not answer. His hat brim sagged with wet. His close-buttoned
coat was stained with seeping rain; and he could feel sorry for the sheep
whose thick fleeces dragged them down like sopping mops. The dogs
splashed in the ruts, their tempers savage. It was a dreary day for a man
who was arriving westward.

He now felt doubtful of his wisdom in refusing Ma Halleck's proposition. Last night she had conveyed an impression of hurt feelings. With
George it didn't matter; he could take yes or no and let it go at that.
But women were queer in their business; and he wondered if Mary had
been crying in the night.

She looked fresh and bright as she sat beside Ma Halleck on the high
seat. She had a gift for keeping her clothes from looking draggled. Beside her every morning, Angy and Esther were frowzy creatures; and even
Prue was wan. Travel didn't agree with George's wife; she kept turning
eastward, Jerry noticed. At each halt she looked backward even if George
was with her on her wagon; and at nights, as they sat at supper, she always
seated herself to face the road they had traveled during the day. She seemed
to fear the westward prospect. She was a frail little woman, with small
hands, lost in her own transplanted being.

At eight o'clock they came to Sterling's gate; and there they had to draw
up while two teamsters hauled through. The bells over the wheelers rang
with a choked note; and as soon as they were past, a gust of wind swallowed
the sound of their going. Up ahead, George paid out the toll, and Sterling,
in unlaced boots, a little man with a crooked back and twisted face, threw
back his wet black hair with one hand while he ran over the silver in the

other palm. Banging crazily over his head, the signboard of his bar shed sprays of wet. On the eastward side it had a picture of a teamster walking on a snowy road, with his team at his shoulder; and underneath were the words,—

TEAMSTER'S TRAVEL

And on the other side the same teamster was depicted before a red-hot stove. A couple danced behind him on one side, and on the other a black man fiddled, and the teamster held on his right knee a tankard of blue earthenware, and on the left a bouncing hussy in a yellow dress with bright green ribbons in her hair. And underneath this picture the artist had painted,—

TEAMSTER'S REST

The wind grew in power as the first wagon rolled hollowly under the uplifted palings. Its top was shuddered with rain. And Jerry and Abijah herded the sheep closer for Sterling to check his count.

While they stood there the rain barrel at the corner filled suddenly, and the sound of rain from the pouring eaves' troughs was choked off and then a new gush of the overflow began to spatter into the stone gutterway beside the road. "Nasty weather," said the little man, as he backed into the shelter of his open door.

Neither Jerry nor Abijah answered him. They had a glimpse inside of a woman bending down in front of a stove and a girl with a blank, sleepy face coming in with spring water in a pail. A smell of stale liquor floating out unsettled Jerry's stomach. Behind him Sterling let the gate thud into the mud and reëntered his house. The door slammed dully.

Then the road was curving southward over flat land and the full blast of the wind came sidewise at them. The old lead cow shook her white ears and bellowed. She would have balked but for the dog snapping her hoels.

"I don't blame you wanting to stay in a town," shouted Abijah.

"Hey?"

"I don't blame you wanting to stay in Utica. This eternal travel."

"I can't hear." Jerry moved across the road.

"To hell with it!" said Abijah, and he drew some water from one side of his moustache.

The land was level, but the fields were lost in rain. Once they passed pastured cows, tails turned to the wind; and once they saw a farmer in his barn door staring helplessly at the sky. . . .

Up on the leading wagon Ma Halleck was valiantly recovering her spirits.

"Rain afore seven," she quoted to Mary. "And a northwest wind means clearing, though I calculate on colder weather. Brisk for traveling."

Mary was eyeing across the flat land under wetted lashes.

"How far do you think Utica is, Ma?"

"Too near by half. I reckon on its being only four miles more. I'm going to miss you, dearie, after all these days."

Mary smiled.

"We've come a long way. How far have we come, Ma?"

"From Albany?"

"Yes."

"Ninety miles or so."

"It seems far."

"It seems far to usn, coming from Rutland County. It can't seem but a piece to you, all the way you've traveled."

"I expected the ocean travel to seem long. But this seems such a big land we've been across."

Ma patted her with a damp hand.

"Do you feel lonesome for your own land, dearie?"

"In a way. There's so much happened to me, Ma."

She became quiet, and Ma went on aimlessly patting her.

"There's just one thing, dearie. After all this suddenness. If you ever need a place to come, just you recollect of your friend Betsey Halleck. I'll always have place for you."

She seemed to consider.

"You'll find me out westward in the Purchase. There ain't no town name to it yet, but you can get to Rochester. That's a post village. And then you can inquire. Range two and town fifteen. If I ain't knowed about that close to home, it'll be because I'm dead, I guess."

Mary was looking forward.

"As a matter of fact," said Ma, "maybe you'd better write it down."

"I can't write."

"Can't write? Didn't you go to school?"

Mary shook her head.

"Well, I never!" exclaimed Ma. "I wasn't no real scholar, as maybe you could tell. But I learned writing, and reading to get along with print. Maybe I'd better write it for you."

"I won't forget it."

"Sure?"

"I'm long at remembering things."

"Maybe it's best. Jerry might not like it. I feel somehow Jerry don't like me now."

"Yes, he does."

"No, he feels different. What done it? Was it my speaking about how you and him got connected?"

Mary made no answer and Ma nodded to herself. Suddenly she lifted her shoulders and blew out a blast through her nose. . . .

With the mysterious swiftness of northwest weather, the clouds were cut apart. Suddenly the movers felt a warmth upon their backs, and the horses raised their heads and shook rain from their ears. They saw the road, with long thin puddles of shining water, the meadows green again, and cattle here and there, and ploughed land, and fences every way a person looked. Farm buildings on their right and left and a windmill just opposite them spinning its vanes; the river a winding, leaden-colored sheet with blue flashes gaining distance. And beyond the river, rising to a gentle slope, the brown roofs of houses.

Smoke was whipping from the chimneys; weather vanes made glittering spots on the higher roofs; and over all a steeple rose, sharp, clean, and white, with the sunlight full upon it and the blue sky beyond racing with clouds.

Each member of the Halleck train, whether man or beast, walked with uplifted face; for, though the wind was cold, the sun brought a scent of spring from the soaking land. The horses put themselves willingly into the collars, the cattle gazed right or left upon the pastured herds, the sheep made sporadic attempts at breaking away and jiggled their tails as the dogs brought them back, and the dogs, all four in turn, left cards upon a milestone.

George and Joe, walking in the van, began a story that called for laughter; Ma scrimped up her shawl round her fat throat and spruced her skirts and roved the land with her black eyes, calling Mary's attention to those curtains, or this spring house, or the early spinach dock or rhubarb knubbles; Mary rested chin on hands and stared with a shine in her eyes at the city roofs, while her ear caught up the noise of their travel, the sudden clear squeak of the kingbolt over a stone, the sound of feet in mud, and Angy's shrill voice reminding Esther of Mrs. Percy Pennel back in Wallingford, who always claimed she best enjoyed the rainy weather; Prue sat silent and alone, holding the reins in her small hands, and letting the sunlight fall upon her back as her body gave sluggishly to the jolts of the road; and Abel Marcy called a cow "old lady" as he caught hold of her tail and marched along, as it were, holding hands. Abijah pointed to him, laughing, and said he was as foolish as the rooster who claimed the egg; and Jerry grinned. But alone of all of them his face was seriously set; and like Mary he kept eyeing the town and marveling at the size of its buildings, the big hotel at the river edge, the church, the new houses visible along a westward street.

The wagons were rolling down the slope to a kind of square, where elms grew against the buildings and a covered pump stood just off the crossroads. On the left-hand side a huge, four-storied building of brick and stone cast a shadow towards them. A couple of brown dogs were walking on stiff toes towards the Halleck dogs.

Ma leaned down from her seat.

"It's Utica, Jerry." Her stout cheeks were sober now. Beside her Mary was silently fishing the bundles out of the wagon. Jerry took them one by one. They made a small pile on the sidewalk.

"We're hauling straight through, Jerry. We're going to miss you."

Jerry found it hard to speak.

"Thanks for all you've done, Ma. You and the others."

"It's all right, Jerry. You won't change your mind?"

He shook his head. Mary climbed slowly down. As she perched on the hub, Ma Halleck flung fat arms about her.

"Good-bye, dearie." She kissed Mary heartily. "I'd kiss that Jerry boy, only he wouldn't like it."

Jerry tried to grin.

George came up with Joe and shook their hands. Then Esther and Angy came from their wagons to kiss Mary. Prue said, "Excuse me staying here; it's hard for me to climb," but she blew a kiss. Abijah and Abel waved farewells as they struggled with the sheep at the crossroads. Mary moved closer to Jerry, and they stood together behind their bundles staring up the slow slope of the westward street as the wagons mounted. One of the dogs looked back at them and waved its tail.

And suddenly Jerry was sorry he had not accepted Ma Halleck's proposition. Even then he might have overtaken them. But as Prue's wagon top just started to sink beyond the rise a voice said at his ear, "Morning, young mister. You settling here in Utica?"

6

"A considerable piece of work"

JERRY turned on his heel. Standing with his back against the half-dead trunk of an elm, a mild-faced man regarded him over the bowl of a large pipe. He was very short, with wavy brown hair growing straight back from a phenomenally high, sloping forehead. His face was pale, and his nose large, broad-nostriled, with a faintly humorous cock to the tip. With his left hand he kept batting a floppy hat at an inquisitive blue fly.

Jerry said, "Yes, sir."

"Well, I don't see exactly why you should want to stop here. But that's your business. Ever been here before?"

"No."

"Ever heard of Utica before?"

"Yes."

The little man grinned. His teeth were oddly spaced under his broad lips and showed yellow snuff stains.

"Well, you're worse off than most movers. Most of them never heard the name of this city and don't seem even to see it. They pass right through. You've got connections?"

"Connections?"

"People to stay with," explained the little man politely. "You've got a job?"

"No," said Jerry, "I've got neither."

"I'd better introduce myself." He stepped away from the tree to make a stiff little bow. "I'm Lester Charley."

Jerry said, "My name's Jerry Fowler. This is my wife, Mary."

Lester Charley made a lower bow to Mary.

"I'm honored. Let me welcome you to Utica, Mrs. Fowler."

His eyes puckered and his yellow teeth reappeared. He batted again at the fly, then put his hat on his head. It had a brim so wide that under it he appeared like the stem of a mushroom. He tilted his head and peered out at Mary.

"You've come a long way?"

"Albany," said Jerry for her.

"You must be tired."

"Oh no," Mary said. "We've only come a short way this morning."

The fly zoomed under the little man's nostrils, but he did not appear to notice.

"Well, well," he said. "Let me place myself at your disposal. Perhaps you're looking for lodgings?"

"I'd been considering it."

"I don't want to thrust myself upon you, Mr. Fowler, but the truth is that I have a loft room, comfortable bedstead, unlimited pump in the back yard, and a window with a handsome view of Genesee Street, over my establishment."

"We can't pay very high rent," said Jerry.

"Dear, dear. A few cents one way or the other. I'm not trying to persuade you, mister. But the truth is my wife sent me out this morning. The room's empty and she told me to go down and intercept any likely newcomers to this town. You're likely, I guess. The board and all comes to two dollars a week."

Jerry hesitated.

"You'll be following the footsteps of many of our best citizens," said Lester Charley. "Lots of them spend a week with me. They move on. Why?" He shrugged his narrow shoulders. "Seven children. Seven little Charleys. I feel I should mention them. They are included with the pump and bedstead."

Jerry turned to Mary.

"What do you think?"

She said, "We might look."

"Fine!" exclaimed the little man. "If I bring you to the door, Mrs. Charley will manage the rest. She can ask no more than that. If I might make a suggestion, we had better get along. It's time I opened the store. Here, let me have one of your bundles."

Smiling, he bent down for the smallest bundle, and then with quick steps led them up the street. Little pops of smoke from his pipe blew back in their faces with strong, pungent breaths.

"I run a bookstore," he said over his shoulder. "It does as well as could be expected. Naturally, now that Utica is a town with its own corporation, I expect improved business. Things are going to boom. Yes sir, boom is the word Mr. Cozier used to me yesterday. You'll find that when anything happens in this western country it happens with a boom."

A bell in the white steeple bonged lethargically for nine o'clock. Jerry saw women coming down the street towards the public market to the right of the hotel. Inside, a butcher in a new apron was sharpening his knives. The dry-goods store with DEVEREUX painted over the door already showed customers at the counter. Down the street that led to Rome rumbled a heavy wagon loaded with casks. A farmer was driving in from Deerfield, the eight legs of two slaughtered hogs topping his load; and the sun shone indecently on their shaven whiteness.

Lester Charley swung suddenly in to a small house with a frame front; but Jerry caught a glimpse of the log walls in the back and a small garden patch with a well sweep protruding from a peaked roof. The house was set a little back from the roadway, giving a drowsy sense of quiet behind its two slender locust trees. But the quiet at the moment of their entrance was broken by the smack of a stick and shrill wailing.

"Henderson!" cried a sharp voice.

A small red-headed boy raced round the corner clutching a firkin to his middle with one hand while with the other he fished frantically for green pickles and stuffed them into his mouth. The vinegar syrup slopped at each step he took. His shirt front was soaked with it. As he confronted his father he stopped so suddenly that a wave sloshed forward onto the pathway.

At that moment an active little woman with sharp, bare elbows and an upraised butter paddle raced round the corner. Her mouth was tight closed and she breathed hard through her nose as if she had made up her mind to a long chase. When she saw Lester Charley she stopped, but not before she had caught the boy's collar and whacked his head lustily with the paddle. He roared and broke away, resigning the firkin; but as soon as he reached the street his roaring slid into an Indian whoop. Two more boys of nearly his own age and size scudded up to him and he passed out booty from his dripping fingers. Eating elaborately, they strolled out of sight.

"A fine thing you've made him—that boy of yours . . ." the little woman began shrilly.

Lester Charley lifted a hand. His face was sober.

"Alice!"

For the first time she seemed aware of Jerry and Mary. With a quick gesture she put the paddle into the firkin, set them down on a stone, and wiped her hands on a rumpled apron. Her thin freckled face assumed a smile.

"Mr. and Mrs. Fowler, Mrs. Charley," said Lester with something of an air. "They seemed interested, my dear. I thought I'd bring them up for you to show them the room to. I regret that I can't go with you. I must open my store."

Something like a snort vibrated the tip of Mrs. Charley's nose. But she said, "Come in."

Gathering up the firkin, she led the way round to the kitchen door.

"I wouldn't wish to bring you round the back, but seeing as we've met so near it, it's handier. And I've got a pot in the fire to look at."

The kitchen was a long room running the width of the back of the house. The wall had been sealed in pine, but the log rafters, long since bare of bark, crossed the ceiling. The oven was of brick; the fireplace, large enough to roast a lamb, bristled with spits and trammel and crane. Dishes used and unused cluttered the washboard; odds and ends of clothing hung on pegs; it smelled clean enough, but it was as disordered as a magpie's nest.

Mrs. Charley paused to lift the lid of an iron pot that was simmering in a bed of coals; she whipped off her apron, and tossed it on the table.

"The room's this way," she said. "We can't rent but the one."

She led them forward through a narrow passage. Jerry had a glimpse of two bedrooms with tousled bedclothes on four beds. A ladder stairway led upward to a hole in the hall ceiling; and up this Mrs. Charley scampered as briskly as a squirrel.

"This is the room," she said. "It's under the roof, but it's well aired and it keeps warm in winter from the kitchen."

She pointed to a small trap set directly over the hearth.

"When you open this you get a powerful rise of heat."

She moved over to a back window and drew aside a faded calico curtain. At the inflow of light, Jerry and Mary looked round. Set as far to one side as the slope of the roof permitted, a huge double bedstead was covered with half a dozen old blankets. Mrs. Charley went over to it.

"It's a comfortable bed. We slept in it ten years after we was married. My six oldest was born in it. It's comfortable for sleeping." She leaned a hand on the blankets. The cords creaked.

"That's a good feather tick, Mrs. Fowler. Real deep. My mother made it. Nothing but white goose. You can't find many like it nowadays. It's a wide bed."

She went over to the front window and drew aside the somewhat brighter curtains that screened it. A chest of drawers propped up by some old almanacs to make up the want of one leg, a wash-hand-stand with a cracked basin and a brass water pail, and two chairs made up the rest of the furniture.

"Them trunks," said Mrs. Charley, "you can move them out of sight most anywheres—I never use them."

She swung round on them, holding her hands.

"The lady's free to use my washtubs Wednesdays. I give one six-inch candle every week. Bedding can be aired to suit the fancy. We've got three meals, et with family. Breakfast at seven, dinner at noon, and supper at half past five. I don't know if my husband thought to tell you, but the board and bed comes to two dollars for two people."

She sniffed suddenly.

Jerry glanced embarrassedly at Mary.

"Could we think it over a minute?"

"Surely." She went quickly to the stair. "I'll be in the kitchen," she called up from below.

Jerry turned to Mary.

"What do you think?"

Mary was lifting the blankets, a slight wrinkling of her forehead her only comment.

"It's cheap," said Jerry. "It would give me a chance to look around, and then when I got work we could move."

She turned to him slowly, read his anxious eyes, and smiled.

"It will do fine. I'll air it out and air the bedding. I'll get some sage, though I don't think there are bugs."

"I wish it was a nicer place."

"It'll be fine."

"Those children are going to raise an awful row all day. It'll be hard on you."

"I don't mind them, Jerry. And I like the little man."

"I don't know what to make of him. I don't exactly like him myself."

"I do. We can try it."

Jerry moved away to the front window.

"It ain't the kind of start I'd hoped we'd be making, Mary. Maybe it's going to be hard to find work."

"Well, you've got something, to last us a while."

"*We* have, Mary."

"You're awfully good to me. Jerry?"

"Yes?"

"When I've settled this room and all, I'd like to work, too."

"No."

"But I don't see why not. I want to help. I won't have anything to do here."

"I don't want you to. I can keep us both."

"But I could use the money to put into our own house when the time came."

"No."

She looked down, but her lips set gently against each other. He gave her a covert glance, and his heart rose to see her sitting there on the bed with her head bent and her shoulders acquiescent.

"I'm going out," he said. "Shall I tell Mrs. Charley we'll stay?"

"Why not?"

"Well, it isn't a very nice room."

His voice was troubled.

Mary looked up. She smiled quietly.

"I'm going to like it, I think. A person can feel all alone up here under the roof."

She raised her head.

"Shh, Jerry."

Light feet walked just above their heads, and suddenly a pigeon began cooing and they heard the flutter of wings.

Jerry stooped over and kissed her tilted face.

"I'll go out," he said.

He left her sitting on the bed, staring at their three bundles in a row before her feet.

Jerry went first to the kitchen. The smell of steaming linen made the air pungent. A couple of hot irons stood on end over the coals and an ironing board had been laid across two chairs.

There was a sound of heavy breathing.

"Hold still, Tom. By the gracious! I don't mind if it is in your eyes! They ought to smart. Putting your head in a 'lasses barrel for two minutes just to win a penny bet. Where's that penny, anyway? Spent? I'll be bound it's spent. On licorice rope most likely!"

Mrs. Charley's voice floated through the sunny window. She was holding another small son by the scruff of the neck as she lathered his head with a handful of homemade soap.

Beside the hearth a small red baby was squalling in a dishpan. It had dropped a spoon out of sight in the suds and was now leaning forward to fish between its feet. Just as Jerry entered, it collapsed with a gurgling yawp. Mrs. Charley let go of Tom to rush in for the baby, which by this time was emitting bubbles. Tom fled. As she looked up from rescuing the child, which now, for some reason, strangely resembled Mr. Charley, Mrs. Charley smiled apologetically.

"I declare if little Alice ain't helpless as Lester," she said. Her narrow shoulders sagged. "I might know the only girl I had would look like him, but I didn't expect she'd act like him at five months."

"She's a nice-looking baby," Jerry said, averting his eyes. The baby had stored up enough water in her mouth to make a handsome splutter.

"Did you make agreement on the room, Mr. Fowler?"

"Yes, we decided to take it a week anyway. Shall I pay Mr. Charley?"

"No! You pay me—if you're minded to pay in advance. He talks about business in his store, but I never see no signs of it. You pay me. Thank you. That's real nice of you. I hope you'll like it."

She pinned the bill into her dress and carried the silver to a cupboard. She took out a jar, and dropped the change into a dark liquid.

"Vinegar," she explained. "It's the only place them young thieves wouldn't look for it—or Lester neither."

In a moment she was back at the pan, fishing out a towel from a mess of other things on her way. As he went through the door, Jerry heard her talking sharply to the baby.

Lingering for a moment in front of the house, Jerry looked up and down the street. On his right he heard the whine of a small metal saw, then the tapping of a light hammer. Through the window he saw a gunsmith working at his bench.

He didn't know where to turn. Back in Uniontown, where one knew everybody, getting work was a different proposition; but here a man didn't feel just like stopping anybody on the street, like a beggar, to ask him for work. Jerry had eighteen dollars in his pocket; and if they stayed at Charley's that would keep them nine more weeks—barring sickness or accident. He shuffled his feet in the white dust and looked through the windows of Mr. Todd's cigar store. Behind him on the street a gentleman rode by on a big spanking bay while a hound dog followed, threading the trees along the sidewalk.

Attracted by the sight of a good horse, Jerry walked slowly down Genesee Street. The wind was dying and the heat of the sun was gaining strength. Women returning from market, laden with baskets, or carrying a bucket of well water, stopped in the narrow strips of shade for brief gossips. Jerry only half caught their discreet voices; but as he went on, wondering what to do, he began to feel more at home. For all its size, Utica was a country village: these people were country people, like the people back in Uniontown. It occurred to him that a good place for him to go would be the blacksmith's. In Uniontown that was the gathering place for men towards noon.

He halted a Quaker couple coming towards him in their drab clothes. The man lifted his sloping high hat.

"Thee wants a blacksmith, young man?"

"Yes."

"Thee is a stranger here in Utica?"

"I got in this morning."

"Then thee might try John Jones's beyond Bellinger's. It's opposite the harness maker's, Mr. Dana's, on Whitesboro Street."

"Thanks, I know that street."

The man touched his hat again, and the woman soothed the head of a white duck that protruded from her basket.

Jerry continued his way to the square at which the Hallecks had dropped them. All along the sidewalk, tied to hitching posts, drowsed horses. A pair of bullocks hauled a load of limestone on their creaking cart. Coming up from the stage house, Jerry encountered the largest Pennsylvania wagon he had ever seen. Nine horses were harnessed in the team, and the driver carried an eighteen-foot whip, such as only a heavy-muscled man could handle. A second man sat on the seat with a shotgun across his knees; and as the great wheels rumbled round the turn for Genesee Street, Jerry saw a third holding a rifle between the rear flaps.

Other pedestrians stopped beside Jerry to watch the wagon take its slow way out of the town.

"They're a tough-bitted looking pair of guards," said a voice.

"They have to be, I guess. Sleeping out with that wagon in these western counties."

"Last time they come east they raised a rumpus down in Bellinger's. Weren't nobody could handle them to throw them out."

"Well, they're sober enough heading west."

"Where are they hauling now?"

"Erie Bank in Pennsylvany. Carrying specie."

"I wouldn't want to tie up with them. Hank's a noted gouger in the western counties."

"Nobody to bother them, I guess. Time's gone since the Doanes and Tomblesons was at it."

The bells made small notes in the sun. The wagon top drew a circular spot of shadow in behind it. Down Main Street Jerry saw a hostler bringing out the four-horse team for the north-country stage. The driver was leaning against the nigh front wheel chewing tobacco with a lank jaw. He spat a fly from the tire and brandished his whip at a hired girl in one of the hotel windows. She giggled, cried out, "Go on!" and slammed the sash down.

Whitesboro Street was cooler. The stores were not as pretentiously fronted. The houses were smaller. A little ahead, Jerry saw a signboard hanging over the walk, and BELLINGER'S TAVERN painted on it. Behind the tavern a low, log-walled barn made one side of a yard. It looked like a farm that had been captured and fenced in with houses. Somewhere in the loft an excitable hen was announcing the arrival of an egg.

"It does beat all," said a man in the street, "how surprised a hen can be."

Jerry grinned and looked over at a red, sweating face under a broad grey hat.

"That's right," he said. "It seems like even an egg could tickle a hen."

The man lifted his face and guffawed. He was wearing a prodigiously fuzzy brown homespun coat and black pants stuffed into cowhide boots, and his shirt was a bright green flannel. The horse he was leading by a halter rope caught Jerry's eye. It was a brown horse, black-pointed, with good legs, a small head. Jerry took one look at the crest and front and moved round behind.

"Like him?" asked the fat man.

"I'd have bet he was a stallion," Jerry said. "But he ain't."

The man stepped round with Jerry, his paunch jerking tubbily to his short steps. He bent over at the end of the rope and breathed loudly.

"The man I bought him off in Cooperstown had come up from south. He said he was gelded to his knowledge two years back. Claimed he was three years old. I bought him last week—but all I've been able to figure out about the brute is that he ain't a mare, anyway."

Jerry grinned.

"Maybe he's a ridgeling. No gelding ever growed a neck like that."

The fat man looked doubtful as he straightened up. He tilted his hat forward over his round nose to scratch the back of his head.

"I ain't much of a man with horses. But I got him pretty cheap and I've been looking out for a horse could drag me around a lot these coming years and not get tired. It takes a good piece of flesh to drag me, mister."

Jerry eyed the horse.

"He ought to do that."

The horse stood still in the street, disdainfully moving his ears above their heads. He was deep-barreled. The ribs were set high and deep-sprung. His short legs were clean, with small, neat, round hoofs.

"I'm going to get him shod," said the owner.

Jerry said, "He don't look to me as if he ever wore iron. He's a strange-looking animal, but I notion his looks."

"I calculated he might be Morgan," said the fat man.

Jerry shook his head.

"He ain't Morgan. He's too big, too square across the quarters. I'd like to take a look at his mouth."

"Go ahead. I ain't got up the nerve myself, and if I did I wouldn't know nothing."

Jerry took the lead rope and laid his right hand under the horse's jaw. He pinched easily and caught the lip.

"You wasn't cheated on age," he said. "The rings are sharp. Here, you!" as the horse jerked back. The fat man snatched the rope, and planted his feet.

"By God, I couldn't stand that brute's running away on me again. Not up Genesee Street."

The horse recognized an unbudgeable weight on the end of the lead rope and haughtily resigned himself.

"I'll just take him into Jones's. Then it's up to him."

"I was just going there," said Jerry. "I'd like to see him shoe that horse."

"You a stranger?" asked the fat man, as they proceeded.

"Yes," said Jerry.

"I thought you looked new to Utica. My name's Caleb Hammil."

Jerry introduced himself, and the fat man extended a monstrous paw. Behind them the hen tripped through the barn doors and viewed the world. She was still cackling; but suddenly she squalled. They wheeled to see her feathers ruffling as she turned tail and scudded round the corner. A moment later a rooster went by leveled out from bill to tail. His pale yellow, spurred legs glistened through the puffs of dust, and he had a purposeful eye.

"That looks like one of the old Bellinger cocks," said Hammil. "You like cockfighting?"

"Never seen a good one."

"It's pretty good sport," said Hammil. "I used to go in for it, but every cock I ever owned seemed to put on flesh too quick to make more of than meat." He scratched his head. "It's a funny thing. I never could figure it out."

Beyond the tavern hitch-rail, the footpath was crossed by a horse walk, leading up a slight incline to the smithy. Old catkins from the two maples flanking the doorway still furred the planking. From inside came the whirring of the forge fan and the clang of a hammer against iron and the mutter of desultory voices. A dog gave a sharp bark as the horse's hoofs struck on the plank, and the hammer clanked and was still.

"It's Hammil with his new horse."

"Hello, Caleb. When did you get back?"

"Yesterday, John. Morning, Francis. Morning, Ed."

"Morning," they said, as the two men entered. The horse stopped still in the door. His ears were pricked and his nostrils suddenly blossomed at the fire.

The smith, a short black-bearded man with long arms thickly haired, cropped a chunk of soft coal on the fire and came forward out of the shadow. A small smooth-coated black dog sprang down from somewhere and trotted up beside him. They took a stand in front of the horse.

"Here he is," said Hammil, handing over the halter rope.

The smith took it and continued his examination of the horse. He did not move a hair. The two loafers, who had been sitting with their backs against the iron-bench, scented an unusual thing and got up creakily. They were a senile pair—one with staring lazy eyes half blank, half sharp; the other a thin unwhiskered old man in leggings, who had a wheeze in his speech. They lined up beside Jones.

"Where'd you get him?" asked the smith.

Hammil repeated his tale of the southern man. "This young chap, Jerry Fowler, said he looked like a stallion. Myself, I don't know."

The smith continued his scrutiny in silence. But Francis let out a wheeze, and said, "He 'pears uncommon to me."

He bent down and took hold of his moustaches with both hands.

"Reckon I can tell a stallion when I look," he said, with an air of maintaining it against the world. "That ain't no stallion."

"Might be a ridgeling," Hammil said. "That's Fowler's idea."

The two men gowked at Jerry. Then as one man they turned back to the horse. They shook their heads. Francis whistled between his teeth.

Hammil was leaning his back against the wall with all the defensive indifference of the man who has brought back a new horse. Jerry felt a moment's sympathy, but his attention was on the smith.

John Jones casually put the halter rope under his arm and fished under the tail of his apron. He brought out a rope of twist and poked it into his beard and gnawed off a chew. The muscles in his temples went in and out to the clamp of his jaws. His forge-red face and his blue eyes were calm.

"It's twenty years since I come across the water," he said at last. "I've never seen the like of this animal since then. He don't exactly resemble a cob, Hammil, but he's pretty like it. If he's got the blood of it in him, you've made a buy."

Suddenly his hands shook under his apron and his eyes blazed. He looked the horse straight in the eye, and said an outlandish word. The horse looked back steadily, his feet neatly braced, his pointed small ears unmoving. The smith swore under his breath. "If he was brought over he'd remember Gaelic." He jerked the lead rope.

The horse hesitated.

"Come up!" Jones said harshly.

The horse entered, nostrils a-flutter at the smell of fire and old hoof. The two loafers returned to their boxes against the iron-bench and Hammil joined them. Jerry remained in the doorway. Jones hitched the animal to a ring in one of the upright cedar trunks that braced the loft, and said, "I doubt if he's been shod. I want room."

Hammil grinned.

"That's what Fowler said. I wish you luck, John."

The smith looked over at Jerry.

"What do you know about horses?"

Jerry's cheeks flushed.

"Just a little."

"Well, I calculate you're right. And I believe he's a ridgeling myself. It was a dirty trick to spoil a horse as good as that, but I guess it was the Irish blood in him held up on the bloody devil that done it."

He went about among his tools and then proceeded to the iron-bench. He turned there to speculate on the hoofs once more.

"Want plates, Caleb? Or a bar shoe? Or light caulks?"

"Whatever you say, John."

"Road work?"

"Yes."

"If it wasn't for their macadaming so much lately I'd say leave him as he is. Those hoofs ain't going lame in dirt, not with hocks as dainty as his."

"I'd consider him too let down," said Francis, round a wheeze.

"That's because you never knowed anything about a horse," said the smith gruffly, picking up bars. "Blow—Rip!"

The little dog cocked an ear and sprang onto a small treadmill set up to the left of the forge. His tan feet began to fly. His stump of a tail jerked and bobbed. In a moment his tongue slipped out of his mouth and little bobs of froth flecked his cheeks. Inside the forge sounded the whirr of the fan. Jones stepped over and raked together the coal the blast had opened up, and a minute later the fire bloomed red.

Over by the bench in the sunny window, Hammil and the two old men began to talk. But the smith paid them no heed.

"We'll have to gentle the brute," he said to Jerry, as to a man who could understand; and Jerry watched admiringly as his big hands stroked the nervous muscles and firmly handled the front hoofs. While the iron heated, the smith walked round and round the horse, putting his shoulder against its belly, lifting its hoofs, sniffing them, letting them go, and watching their set upon the floor. The horse was distinctly on guard, but the sure strong hands quelled with their knowledge any disposition to violence before the horse himself had felt it. It was an artist at work that Jerry watched, cutting out the hoofs and framing them. The rasp cut level without fraying.

"Clean hoofs," said Jones. "Did ye ever smell a real sound hoof?"

Jerry nodded.

"There's no smell like it," said the smith, and he dropped the last hoof, stroking the inside of the hind leg, apparently oblivious of the horse's turned head and watchful eye. He went over to the forge and thrust in the iron.

"Hye, Rip! That's the boy."

The little dog slapped a yap out over his flying tongue and ran with his eyes on the smith's hand. After a moment the smith raised it, and Rip sat down. The whirr of the fan died away. The tongs grasped the iron and in a moment the sparks were fountained by the hammer's nose and the anvil roused its voice and the cooling smell of moulding iron filled the smithy.

Jerry began to listen to the voices of the other three through the rhythmic din.

"What did you see in Albany, Caleb?"

"I went to Troy first," said the fat man, leaning back to ease his stomach. His hat was on one knee and his red face was drying off. "I put an order into the nail factory with Hanley. They've got in two new stampers and a new roller."

"Is that right?" said Ed. "It must be quite a factory. I mind ten years ago when they was starting out."

"Yes, it's considerable of a business. They can shape up a thousand tons of iron now to a season."

Francis wheezed, "Seems hard on Devlin."

Hammil laughed easily.

"I talked it over with Devlin. His store couldn't rightfully expect to handle an order that big."

"Big?" said Ed curiously.

"Sure. Three tons of fours." Hammil stretched his stubby legs. "There's no harm saying now. I got the contract on the middle section locks, the timberwork."

Ed opened his mouth.

"I've heard telling the bill's through."

Caleb nodded importantly.

"I got the contract. Timber foundations for locks and aqueducts, a seventeen-thousand-dollar contract. I seen the Commissioners in Albany. Thought I'd be right on the spot; and put it up to Myron Holley. I had letters off Kip, Walker, and Stocking from the bank."

His jovial eye rolled round the room. Jerry was looking at him with a close attention. It made the contractor proud to see admiration in the young man's face. But the smith was shaping the shoe, working with never an eye for the hoof, but with a sure touch in his hand that told even Hammil that the shoe would fit when he had it done.

Ed leaned back and lifted a knee to clasp it. He spat at a knothole. "There's a lot of worry in a contract like that. You'll have a lot of traveling. Where do these-here locks come?"

"They begin at Cossett's swamp and run out to Montezuma. That's what I need a good horse for. My wife wouldn't rest if I didn't get home once in a week. She's tender-bred that way," Hammil said proudly.

"What does a lock look like?" demanded Francis.

"Well, I'm a contractor and no mechanic. I've never seen one. But they've got them down in Massachusetts, so I guess we can build them. Anyway, I've got a book about it. And hell, what's engineers for anyway?"

He lifted his hat to slap it back on his knee. The smith, bending over a fore hoof, raised angry eyes.

"Keep that hat quiet," he said passionately. "I'm shoeing a green horse.

You, Fowler, just stand by his head and gentle him when I lay this iron on. You've got hands."

Jerry stepped over to the horse's head and laid his hand under the throat against the off cheek. The horse tilted his head against the hand. The iron hissed on the hoof, and a pungent scent came out with the steam. The smith studied the mark while his off hand swung the shoe. He lifted the hoof a mite for Jerry to see, but he made no comment. None was needed.

Then he slapped the horse gently.

"That's a knowing brute, if he don't talk Gaelic. It's a pity a fat fool like Caleb is to have his handling."

Hammil grinned amiably.

"So long as he don't kill me, he can do as he pleases," he said.

"That's the trouble," said the smith, going back to the fire and calling up the dog. "I could shoe him backwards and you'd never notice so long as it didn't make the horse go backwards too."

"I never put much stock in this canal," said Ed.

"What's locks for? What have they got to do with a canal?" demanded Francis.

"Well," said Hammil, grinning aside in Jerry's direction. "There's locks in a bank, ain't there, Francis?"

Francis thought it over before he committed himself to a nod and "I guess that's right."

"Well," said Hammil, "ain't there banks to a canal?"

Ed, who had nodded, but wisely said nothing, whooped at Francis, and the wheezing man looked down huffily at the toe of his boot. The smith said, "Quit that squeaking or I'll fix you two bezabors with a hot shoe in your pants." But he was grinning through his black beard.

"What I don't see," said Ed, after a while, "is where they're going to put the blasted thing."

"Right through the upper end of Utica," said Hammil.

"No! What do they run it that far up for? 'Pears like water would run better alongside the river—or into it, maybe."

Caleb said, "They've got to keep it level."

"I don't understand it, I guess," said Francis, making an effort.

The smith went about the shoeing and the horse was quiet under Jerry's hands. Hammil kept eyeing him from time to time. When, at noon, the horse was shod completely and the little dog lay panting on the treadmill and the smith had pocketed his money and now looked openly with a just pride at his work, the fat man suggested to Jerry, "Walk along with me a ways. I'd like to proposition you."

"You lead the brute," said Hammil, handing Jerry the rope. "He makes me feel chancy when he gets to looking over traffic."

Jerry took a short hold and walked along with the cob's head over his shoulder. He had always admired horses.

As they turned into Genesee Street, an acquaintance hailed Hammil from the seat of a passing rig.

"Hey, Caleb! Glad to see you. That's a likely horse. Yours?"

Caleb raised a fat hand and chortled.

"Yeanh. Fifty dollars."

He was at ease again.

"Look here," Hammil said, "I want to talk to you. But we can't talk in the road. We'll put the horse up in my barn. And you stay to dinner. Mrs. Hammil's out."

"Surely," said Jerry.

They turned left off Genesee Street into Bleecker and passed down between two rows of comfortable houses; but a little way along, the right-hand row gave way to pasture land. The roadway, here, was merely dirt, but it was well ridged in the middle and already dried after the night's rain. Trees stretched their limbs across the house roofs, and on a corner grew a towering hemlock, perhaps four feet through the butt. It was like a monument to the woods, standing alone at a corner in a rail fence. Jerry looked up against its glistening mass of needles. It was so old and high that the winds had stripped the dead twigs from its branches, and he could see the top stirring to the wind which in the street he could not feel.

"Here we are," said Hammil.

A little two-story house, painted a bright blue with a white trim, was set back in a garden.

In the rear, beyond the kitchen yard, with its well house, was a little barn, also painted blue; and the inside, when Hammil swung back the door, was the neatest Jerry had ever seen. There were not even cobwebs on the sealed walls. In the middle of the floor stood a light dearborn. Hammil said with an air of pride, "I got it into Albany a year ago. You'll notice the springs," and, without waiting for comment, went on to the stable door.

Jerry found two stalls, one used, in which he tied the cob.

"Water?" asked Hammil. "That bucket's got some. I drawed it fresh just afore I took the horse down-town."

The horse dipped his nose and dribbled water. He kept lifting his hoofs and setting them down restlessly. Seeing Hammil eyeing the new shoes, Jerry said, "He's just not used to them. They're well hung. He won't go lame."

Hammil nodded.

"I guess John knows his trade. What had I ought to feed him? I kicked out Stanley—he worked here—this morning. The Missus couldn't stand his chewing. You don't chew?"

"No."

"Well, she don't mind smoking in the office. But outside of there tobacco's barred. Seems all right to me, too. A woman has to live in a house all the while."

"Yes, it does," Jerry said politely.

Hammil seemed relieved.

"There's oats in here."

Jerry took up a measure and judged a meal. He grained the horse while Hammil wrestled down a fork of hay.

"Now," said the fat man, "let's go eat."

He led Jerry to the back door, where on a shelf a basin and pitcher and a bar of white soap stood ready for washing. They took turns.

Inside the kitchen, which to Jerry's eyes was as neatly fixed as a parlor, Hammil said to the middle-aged, homely hired girl, "Mr. Fowler's having dinner with me."

"It's been ready ten minutes," said the girl shortly.

Hammil preceded Jerry to a small dining room and showed him a place at a dark, polished table.

"It's a nice little house, if I do say it," he said, watching Jerry's admiring gaze. "My wife had a little money of her own. She comes of good family. Her name was Kip afore she married me. But I've paid for all this." He looked round contentedly and tucked a napkin into his shirt collar. "Sometimes I think she distastes my business, but she can't deny it brings in money. I've built half the buildings in this city, church and Academy and houses; and I've laid the streets. Utica's a rising town, Jerry. Now, with this canal contract, I aim to be a rich man."

The hired girl served them with a steak of fresh pork, kidney beans, and bacon, brandy, bread, butter, cheese, and apple pie. When she had laid the things, she brought her own plate and sat down at the bottom of the table. She had nothing to say, but ate noisily.

After dinner, when Hammil had led the way to his office,—a small room in a wing, with an iron cash chest on the floor, a copper spittoon, two comfortable rocking-chairs, and a broad plain desk,—the fat man stretched himself comfortably. He put his feet on the desk and offered Jerry a cigar, and when Jerry declined lit himself one and for a few moments contented himself with breathing out long streams of smoke.

"Truth is," he said, "I'd like that house a damned sight better if Mabel didn't hang onto that old girl. She worked for her when we got married, and it might have been included in our contract for all the chance I've got of getting rid of her. All the while she's got her eye upon a person; and when she's not eyeing, she's scenting with that limber nose of hern."

He sighed and examined the ash of the stogy. Then he screwed it into his round mouth and hooked his thumbs into the armholes of his waistcoat.

"Let's talk business."

Jerry nodded.

"Do you want work?"

"Yes."

"Where do you come from?"

"Uniontown."

"Married or single?"

"Married."

"Wife here?"

"Yes."

"How old are you?"

"Twenty-two."

"Well," said Hammil, relaxing behind a long puff of rank smoke. "The fact is, I like your looks. I'm going to make you a proposition. But first I'd like to know what you're doing here in Utica."

Jerry hesitated. The fat man had surprised him with his rapid-fire questions. He felt a new respect for Hammil under the jovial, easy-going exterior. He did not think of his admonition to Mary until he had finished his story. But the fat man seemed to understand.

"All right, boy. You needn't worry. I won't tell anybody. It doesn't make you sound like a man for business, but then I haven't seen the girl. Have you got your recommend with you?"

Jerry brought a piece of heavy folded white paper from his coat pocket. Prying his cigar to the far corner of his mouth, Hammil took the paper and opened it. His fat face was expressionless, his chin lost in flesh.

"It's a good recommend as far as it goes. But it don't say anything about mechanics. You understand mill work, though. Can you read? Yes. Well, none of us know anything about locks, I guess, and you can learn. Can you follow a plan?"

"I never tried."

Hammil nodded.

"Don't say you can do a thing if you ain't done it afore. But don't say you can't do a thing—that's worse."

He handed over the recommend and then leaned back again in his chair.

"Jerry, here's what I was going to offer you. Drive me and mind my horse when I'm traveling for timber. Three dollars a week and your keep, when we're traveling. But, now, if you get the hang of buying and show you can spot timber, I may send you out alone; and give you five dollars. If you make a hand at building when we get to the active work, I'll put you up to seven dollars."

He looked across the desk shrewdly.

"That's my proposition."

"I'll take it."

"Good. I'm glad." He held out his hand, and for the second time that day Jerry shook it.

For a moment Hammil grinned at him. Then he popped the cigar back in his mouth and leaned over the desk.

"Look here," he said, "I'll show you a plan drawed of a lock."

He opened a drawer in the desk and took out a roll of stiff grey paper.

"Hitch around next to me," he said, unrolling it.

The sheet was headed at the top with fancy printing in a scroll.

GEN! PLAN FOR LOCKS

For No. 1

on the Erie Canal

(3 miles east of Cossett's in Onondaga Co.)

And underneath the draftsman had made a picture of the completed lock with a boat entering the lower gate. Across the centre of the sheet were the ground plans of the timbering, with sections cut away. Hammil pointed these out with the wet end of the stogy.

"This is our job, the foundation work and gates. Considerable of it will have to be piled. This plan calls for four-foot piling. But Holley claims the locks are all located in clean gravel and mud to made a solid bottom. They're all sunk two feet under water-bottom to allow coverage for the cills."

Jerry nodded. That was easy to follow. Double cribs upon the piling and a foundation of twelve-inch hewn beams set solid.

"Is that bottom layer of plank to be matched?" he asked.

"Single-jointed." Hammil nodded delightedly. "Them three-inchers cover the whole foundation."

"Then the two-inch planking's just inside the stone."

"That's right. They're water-jointed."

"I don't know that country at all," said Jerry. "Have they got good mills out there?"

"That's the trouble. There ain't any nearer than Hannibal. Joshua Forman has a grist and saw mill there and guarantees my sawing, but the roads are bad. We'll have to do considerable roading for ourselves."

"Do they aim to use hemlock for the bottom?"

"Maybe for the timbers. I'd recommend it. There ain't any wood to beat it under water. Mostly, though, they're talking spruce and cedar for the gateposts."

"We don't bother with the stones," said Jerry.

"No. Masonry and cutting is going to be let out to different hands. But Holley said he wanted somebody reliable to do the foundations." Hammil looked up and his fat face tried comically to conceal his pride. "Of course, they ain't given me the written contract; but they've promised it."

Jerry bent over to read the minute figures along the arrows.

"Ninety feet," he read aloud, "and that's just between the gates; and fifteen foot across between the lock-walls. The change in water level's eight feet. How big a boat do they plan to run on this canal?"

"Sixty feet by seven, drawing three and a half. It figures up to thirty tons."

"How many horses draw it?"

"Two. Though one could, I guess. They say one horse on water hauling can outhaul sixty on a wagon."

"Lord!" said Jerry. "That alters hauling, don't it?"

Hammil looked up.

"Say," he said, pointing his dead cigar, "do you realize, boy, just what it means? It means that freight is going to be hauled more than two-thirds cheaper. A hundred dollars a ton they figure will cost less than thirty when this ditch is dug between Albany and Buffalo. To-day a farmer gets thirty cents for wheat when the market's up in the Genesee Valley. He'll get better than a dollar in bad years. Do you think that ain't going to make a difference? Ohio trade's coming this way now. We'll take the whole works right out of Pennsylvany's hand. Look here, I've traced a map."

He shoved the plans aside and fished from his drawer a copy of Eddy's Map of New York.

"I don't draw very good," he apologized as he opened it. "But I've marked out the line it's going to follow. Here's Utica,"—he made a smudge with the end of his cigar,—"now follow left or west and here is Rome. That's where they commence."

"It seems queer commencing in the middle," Jerry said.

"Don't it? But it's pretty cute. Look, the south counties have voted solid against the canal from the beginning. Tammany don't see the sense of spending money they can't get their fingers into. Well, supposing we commence at Albany? It's the hardest part of the digging, and they'll say it don't pay. But up here's a long level. Working east, it goes to Frankfort. Going west, it reaches into Cossett's swamp (they've marked it 'Salina' here). The whole of it's close to seventy miles. Now you see, commencing here, the progress is immediate. There's money spent and a lot to show. That'll hurt Tammany's feelings. But they won't let us stop till we reach Albany, so's they can get the benefit. But here's the idea. We work both ways to oncet. They wouldn't let us start at Buffalo, so we'll have to work out that way backwards. It'll be a long time afore we see Erie water reaching into Montezuma; but we ain't going to put Mohawk in the Hudson until we've done just that."

He spoke as if he had been a party to the whole scheme.

"There's plenty of times I've seen Mr. Wright riding down the Mohawk sighting out the lay of land. I've seen him and young White and Broadhead laying levels, with some of our college boys to hold the markers, working for nothing. I went along with Judge Geddes part of the way beyond Montezuma—that's going to be tough digging, Jerry. But I do believe I never did suppose we'd get to the actual point of digging."

He leaned back.

"I come here when I was a lad, Jerry. Just a lad, younger than you. Utica was a young village then. Just a crossroad without even a school. I built the first one. That was my first job. I don't know how I come to settle here. I guess I'd have moved on after I made my first money if I didn't light my eyes on Mabel Kip. Right then I said, even if my father was a carter back in Catskill and died in prison for the price of a horse, I'd marry her. But I didn't let on until I'd got five hundred dollars put away, and then I went to the old man. It took me four more years, but we got wedded. And I've gone right ahead. And once I stayed here I commenced to see that Utica was a coming place. Better than Canandaigua, where I'd planned on going. Right now there's more money here. I built the market. Yes sir, but I remember when we used to get out to the Oneida Castle for to buy our peaches off the Indians every fall for pickling."

He looked across at Jerry.

"Utica's a good place for you, boy. And I'm going to help you start. You stick with Caleb Hammil. By God!" Suddenly his mind caught something out of his enthusiasm. "You handled them plans and read them out most as quick as me. I hadn't thought of it."

Jerry flushed. Hammil leaned forward to pat him on the shoulder.

"You read them like a real mechanic. You're going to make a good man for me. I guess we can build as good a lock as Mr. Weston himself or any seven-thousand-dollar engineer from England—when a man not even a mechanic can see the whole of it as good as you."

He bent forward over Eddy's map.

"Look here, Jerry. Here's where the locks is going to be. Here's number one, like I showed you. Two comes a mile beyond of it. Three's eastward of Camillus at Owasco outlet. Four's direct in Jordan. Five comes here, just westward of Port Byron. Six and seven let you down to Montezuma and the marshes. Seven locks. I'm going to do foundation work on aqueducts, but there ain't been no plans passed on. I'm glad we're going to work in reasonably settled country. . . . Well, Jerry, what do you think of it?"

Jerry hesitated.

"It looks like a considerable piece of work. How far is the whole of it, Mr. Hammil?"

"The Erie's three hundred and sixty-three miles as drawn. And that leaves out the Champlain Canal. I don't thing the Champlain's worth for much but lumber trade."

"That's a long way to dig."

"Oh, the digging don't count for so much. It's just a matter of time. It's the locks and aqueducts that count. Take the Genesee! That river's more than twice the size of ours and yet we've got to cross it. I don't know who's tackling that, but I'd hate to have it contracted up with me."

"How long do they think it's going to take?"

"Five years. Perhaps a year more. They've done a thorough scout, but you can't ever tell what you're going to come across underneath the ground. Marl would make slow digging. But marl is worth something. And gypsum. They might get coal in some of them westward counties. Coal enough to pay the whole expense."

His eyes glistened as he sat back once more.

Behind him, through the window, Jerry noticed the shadows lengthening from the trees and daffodils. Some hornets, nosing the swelling plum buds, sparked like jewels. He had never heard any discussion of the canal before. But now he realized that it was a job about to be tackled; and the magnitude of its conception thrilled him. Here he had taken better than a week to come this far west, and yet he was less than a third the length of the canal. He had walked. Other men would have to dig that distance. Dig a ditch for water, forty feet across, and four feet deep.

Outside along the pathway quick steps disturbed the gravel. Looking forth together, they saw a woman in a print silk dress, full-skirted and high-bodiced, with a shawl drawn over her shoulders and across her breast. The fringed point at the small of her back fluttered to her walking.

"There's Mrs. Hammil," said the fat man with an air of pride.

She looked much more at home in her surroundings than did Hammil. From the small fingers protruding from her crocheted mitts of silk to her small oval face with the dark hair and eyes and composed mouth, she was daintily made. She walked as if the world were hers; and when she mounted the stoop and paused at the door, her figure was poised and graceful.

"There's something for a man to work for," said Hammil. "Well, Jerry, we'll have to be stopping. I didn't notice it was late. I'm busy to-morrow. You mind the horse. Next day I'm driving westward, and I'll want you with me."

He got up and again they shook hands. As Jerry came round the house to the street, he heard the woman's silvery voice greeting her stout husband through the open door.

"I've just hired a young man," he heard Hammil say. "A clever boy. He looks ambitious."

Ambitious. Jerry stepped out. His chance lay clear before him. Hammil had succeeded in an earlier day; but a greater day was coming. And he, also, had something to work for. As he went along, he thought of Mary and how he would tell her his good news.

Walking back towards Genesee Street, Jerry heard beyond the city limits the bells of cows coming in from pasture. The streets were quiet in the late afternoon. Down Genesee Street he saw the storekeepers in their doorways taking a look at the weather or talking back and forth across the roadway. A party of movers were coming up the hill. They were poor-looking folk. The men's faces were sullen; the women's dull. A troop of children of all ages padded barefoot in the dust. They eyed the sights of the town with half-wild eyes.

Watching them pass, Jerry's senses again reacted to the ceaseless travel of this road. But he saw it now with new eyes, a choked thoroughfare, carrying in driblets but a portion of its natural trade. Eastward, towards Deerfield corners, where the afternoon sun was brightening the great hill, he heard the sound of Pennsylvania Bells. There had been scarcely an hour, he realized, since he had left Albany that he had not heard that chime. He saw the hood gleaming white far down below in the valley where it crept along the causeway; and the distance made it a small thing.

As he went down Genesee Street, people nodded to him. He nodded back; but his pace quickened. Time was getting on for supper, and he wanted to tell Mary. And at the same moment it occurred to him that, poor as their room might be, this was the first time in his life that he was coming back to his own home.

He saw the shop ahead of him, a trail of violet smoke ascending from the kitchen chimney. As he came abreast he had a glimpse of wash hanging out upon the line behind the house. At the corner of the gunsmith's a small boy, obviously one of the Charleys, was having a parting word with a companion. They eyed Jerry cautiously when they saw him turning towards the door, and he was aware of their making comments.

"Hello," said Mr. Charley from the dusk of his store. "We didn't see you for dinner. Did you have any luck?"

"Some," said Jerry, as he went by towards the stairs. He mounted them two at a time and swung himself through the trapdoor. It was shadowy in the narrow loft. A breeze was drawing through the south window.

"Mary," he said softly.

There was no answer.

He walked the length of the room to the window, where a chair had been drawn up to get the light. Beside it on the floor his bundle lay open, and on top of it one of his shirts. He saw that she had been sewing, for the threaded needle was stuck through the eye of a new horn button.

Suddenly he sat down and took up the shirt. It was one of his old work shirts, badly worn; and as he turned it over in his hands he saw how she had been reënforcing the elbows with new scraps of flannel. He sat quite still, holding the shirt in his hands, and his eyes slowly roved the room.

All the musty smell was gone. The boards gleamed clean with a faint scent of lye soap. The bed had been moved farther into a corner and the old trunks that belonged to the Charleys dragged out of sight beyond the trap. A piece of calico had been tacked to the rafters halfway down one side. He got up slowly and went over to it. His hand fumbled as he lifted it. From more nails driven in the rafters hung her wedding dress and clothes. And next to them his own meagre stock—side by side.

He came back to the bureau. Her name mug was set out to hold a little bunch of Mayflowers. He wondered where she had found them. He noticed that the water bucket was filled and a clean towel hung on either side of the wash-hand-stand. And he sat down again, realizing the privacy she had created with the stamp of her own cleanness. Overhead he heard a flutter of wings, and then the soft voice of the cock pigeon.

He heard her feet in the hall below. He knew they were hers at the instant they stepped out of the kitchen. She was mounting the stairs. Her head shone with a faint coppery lustre as it came up through the trap. Then she was in the room, her arms stuffed out with bedding, her cheeks pink with the ascent.

"Jerry!"

Her grey eyes were blue, and her voice was glad. But she dropped the blankets on the bed and started quietly to make it up.

"When you didn't come back to dinner, I thought I might have time to get the room all ready."

He watched the efficiency of her hands. In giving her back her papers he had given her more than her freedom; he knew it now, and he was not sorry. When she had finished she sat down on the bed and let her hands rest in her lap. She had asked him no questions. But as she regarded him now, her eyes were confident; and he found it difficult to tell her.

"It looks as if you'd been busy all day."

She smiled.

"It looks nicer, doesn't it? It was pretty dirty."

"It's real nice."

"I wanted it all done for you to come back to."

"It's nice, Mary."

She got up slowly and came forward to his chair. Her eyes were happy, but her face wore the quiet, submissive look that he had seen there ever since their wedding day. He felt that in another moment he would have to shout. As she bent down to pick up the unfinished shirt he put his arms round her waist and drew her down on his lap.

He tried to mask his voice.

"Tell me all you've been doing all day, Mary."

She gave without objection to his arms, but her head she kept bent over the shirt. Her fingers drew the needle from the cloth and began stitching.

"First," she said in a low voice, "I cleaned the roof, after I'd hung out the bedding, and then I cleaned all the floor and moved the trunks. I didn't get done till nearly dinner time."

"How was dinner?" he asked when she paused. He was intensely curious now to find out how she occupied her time.

The twilight in the loft, with the muffled quiet of the street outside and the spring-scented breeze drawing across them, made the day mysterious.

"It was all right. Mrs. Charley isn't a cook like Ma Halleck, I guess, and she appears all the time to be distracted."

"What did you have to eat?"

"We had some corned mutton and samp cake. Mrs. Charley hadn't ever heard of capers."

"Were the children too bad?"

"Just noisy. Mrs. Charley tried to make them wash, but it didn't do much good. Mr. Charley brought in a book and read out of it, but I didn't understand much of it. And anyway he read to himself most of the time. Mrs. Charley talked about people that live here and complained that flour cost so much."

"What did you do afterwards?"

"Henderson said he knew where there were some Mayflowers and asked if I would like some. I said I didn't know what they looked like, but I would like some very much. He said he knew there were some near, so we went to get them. Don't they smell sweet? He picked a bunch more and took them to the lady Mrs. Charley washes for to sell them."

She twisted the thread round the button and bit it off close. Her eyes met his sidewise. She bent for another button, put it in place, and anchored it.

"Then I finished cleaning and made us a place for our clothes, and then later I sat down here in the window to sew and look out."

"Were you watching for me?" he asked.

"Yes." She turned over the shirt and sewed from the back, by touch.

"Stop sewing," he said. "Throw the damned thing away." He snatched it from her and tossed it across the room. He heard her sharp breath and saw her quick glance at her thumb. A spot of blood domed slowly where the needle had caught.

Jerry's dark face bent over it, flushed and excited.

"Let me have it."

He sucked the blood away, and inside of himself he was glad. His arms tightened.

"Did you miss me?"

"Yes. But I kept busy."

"Kiss me, Mary."

She bent her face obediently and as he drew her closer a wave of tremulousness passed over her. Her eyelids quivered as they closed. And yet when he let her go she seemed as usual to withdraw into herself.

"You haven't even asked me one question," he said accusingly.

Her eyes opened wide, and the faint pucker came between her brows.

"Didn't you care, Mary?"

"I was afraid you mightn't have found anything."

He loosened his hold and looked across at the distant window. The arms of the old maple in the yard beyond were just visible. Mrs. Charley's voice was shrilling.

"Alva, wash your feet. My land, where have you been treading?"

"I don't know, Ma. Honestly. I just went down by the mud flat and then me and Josey Wood was playing Castle King behind Bellinger's barn."

But the voices were removed from their quiet room. Jerry did not turn his head. His words came slowly, as if he found speech difficult.

"I happened into luck, Mary. I met a man that's got a contract for all the locks on this part of the canal they're going to build."

"Yes."

"It's the Grand Canal. It was being passed by the Senate when we came through Albany. Do you remember, when I left you on the corner to go get food?"

"I remember that," she said in a hushed voice.

"I heard them talking about it then in the coffeehouse. It will run from Albany to Buffalo, three hundred and sixty-three miles!"

"Yes, Jerry."

"I don't suppose you know what that is—locks, and things. But this man —his name is Caleb Hammil—is going to give me three dollars a week to start with, and then five if things are all right."

"That's fine, Jerry."

"It's going to mean I'll be away a lot of the time. We'll have to scout

for timber. And when the work begins I'll be out west a lot—the first lock's
fifty miles from here. Will you mind being alone?"

"No, Jerry."

"But you'll miss me, won't you?"

"Yes, of course."

Here and there through the town they heard hand bells rung for supper,
and under them there was a sudden noise of feet—Mr. Charley coming
out of his store, Mrs. Charley shrieking to Henderson to tell the Fowlers
supper was on the table, and the bare soles of the boy's feet as he crept
up the stairs, and his head poked over the floor.

"Ma says supper's ready."

Mary had sprung up, and now Jerry hurried to wash.

The Charley family were assembled when they reached the kitchen.
Mary's and Jerry's chairs were together on Mr. Charley's right. The little
bookseller was helping large slices of corned mutton, over which he poured
a vinegary syrup from a small pitcher. Mrs. Charley helped the plates to
boiled potatoes. There was a glass of beer at Jerry's place—which a neighboring small Charley eyed curiously. His smutted cheeks kept puffing with a
hidden breath, as if he were barely able to keep himself from scudding off
the froth. For those that wanted it, Mrs. Charley poured tea into deep
brown saucers.

In the presence of a new male boarder, the boys were unaccountably
quiet. Mr. Charley helped himself and said, "Well, young man, did you
find any work?"

Jerry nodded. Two tallow candles in their individual basins lighted the
kitchen. He could see the remnant of clothes in a basket half hidden in a
corner. The baby's cradle was out of sight beside Mrs. Charley, conveniently placed for her foot to rock it if the child should waken. But noise
meant nothing to the baby, and it snuffled away as placidly as a well-fed
little pig.

"Who're you working for?"

"Caleb Hammil."

"The contractor. What's he going to do now?"

"He's got a contract on the canal. Locks and aqueducts."

"Greek to me," said Lester Charley. "But it sounds like a lot of work."

"It's a big thing to tackle," Jerry said, accepting a buttered slab of
bread from young Henderson.

"What are you getting?"

Jerry told him.

"That's good pay. Well, I had an idea you'd have luck, young man."
He raised his eyes to meet Mrs. Charley's expected comment.

"Luck!" she said sniffing. "When did you ever make three dollars a
week? He went to look for it, that's how."

Lester Charley grinned to himself.

"Alice," he said soberly, "you know if I went out for a job like that you'd
lose half your pleasure in life. There's nothing you like better than working
to keep me comfortable, and then complaining about me to everybody."

She sniffed.

"A person has to say something."

"I suppose so," said the bookseller, with a sigh. "Apple pudding? That's nice of you, my dear. It's a difficult dish to make. Next time I'd recommend more cinnamon."

"It's awful expensive nowadays, Lester," she said apologetically. "But if you want a little extry to sprinkle on I'll get it."

"Thank you, I would."

He grinned sardonically at Jerry, but his eyes twinkled at his wife while she sprinkled on the cinnamon.

"I suppose you'll be away a lot with Caleb," he said to Jerry.

"Quite a lot."

"I can't reduce the rent," Mrs. Charley said defensively.

"It doesn't matter now."

She sighed with relief.

"Alva, you get me some wood for to-morrow morning."

Alva lowered.

"Me and Robert was going fishing for bullheads."

"It won't take you long to get in the wood."

"Bullheads are chancy, Ma."

"Alva," said Mr. Charley, "if you don't get it I shall have to."

"Do as you're a mind to," said his mother, "but if the wood ain't in to-morrow morning, you'll get a trimming."

"Ain't it time Purly was getting it in? He's big enough," suggested Alva.

"No."

Alva resigned himself.

The rest finished their supper to the sounds of the boy's groaning in the woodshed. He came staggering in with a small armful that would not have disturbed a boy of half his size.

"Now I'm all of a sweat," he grumbled. "And if I get the ague in the cold, I guess you won't be sorry."

Nobody paid him any attention, and a moment later they heard his voice whooping down the street for Robert.

"Catching bullheads must be very fascinating to Alva," observed Mr. Charley. "I never liked them as fish."

He got up to go out for his evening session at Bellinger's, pausing to light his pipe at the kitchen fire. Jerry declined his invitation.

He had not looked at Mary all evening. But now he met her glance in the smoky tallow light. She lowered her eyes. His hands were trembling. He waited for her at the trapdoor and watched her through and closed it. It was quite dark in the room. Beyond the window he saw the stars down the long reach of the valley. Peepers in the swamp filled the air with a continual rhythm. A whippoorwill was singing in the middle of Genesee Street. He undressed slowly, feeling the breeze on his bare body. The bed strings creaked under Mary's weight.

"Mary," he whispered. "Don't you love me?"

He put out his hands. And as he touched her he knew that all evening he had been aware of her excitement. She moved into his arms and the feather tick surrounded them. She was alive and strong. He saw again the drop of blood and tasted it again between his lips. Far away, from Herkimer, he heard approaching the bells of a teamster's wagon hauling west.

7

"Bourbon"

"WE turn right, here," directed Hammil.

Jerry turned the horse. The great cob had brought them six good miles an hour since seven o'clock that morning. They had had breakfast in Mother Carey's inn at Westmoreland, waited on by one of her pretty daughters. There were seven of them, whispered Caleb, each one lovely as a waxwork, and some gentlemen travelers called them Mother Carey's Chickens. He'd heard tell they were a bird, like a kind of plover, that lived on the ocean and brought dreams to sailors. The inn was a small, low-ceilinged house, with windows giving on the road; and they had had the dining room and a brisk fire to themselves. Only when they were coming out did the night stage from Batavia draw up and the sleepy travelers unbundle stiffly. Caleb had had ale and steak, and Jerry eggs and ham and apple pie. The inn had a peculiar deadness in that early hour; even the girl's light footfalls echoed.

But the sunlight had flowed over the land as they drove on; and Jerry had received his first impression of the western country. The road rolled over low, round hills, straight as a man could lay it. In the valleys they had been lapped in the cool of dawn, with the spring creeks frothing down through knots of balsam trees and alder. And from the next hilltop they had seen the sunlight cresting the land, for mile upon mile, as far as sight could stretch. Fields were neatly squared off and ploughed to the fences. One herd of cattle showed a clear strain of Hereford. They came in from pasture with their white faces dew-washed from the sunrise browse and their horns glistening like silver. The farmyards were awakening: the strenuous crowing of roosters; the blat of sheep; the trundle of the pump-wheel; and the children on the front stoop staring with murky morning eyes.

But the cob traveled past with the sweep of dawn in his reaching stride. His shoulders worked smoothly with the levelness of flowing water. His square quarters thrusting back the pike, he held his head high; and his ears were pricked as he breasted the land. The wheels racketed over stony patches, and the wagon kept up a steady mutter against the road.

Hammil said, "He's a masterful horse. I'd ought to give him a name."

He settled himself comfortably on the seat and drew forth a stogy. From time to time, almost with the mileposts, he suggested names and again discarded them. Duke, he said, and Earl, and Prince—good horse names; and then he decided that they didn't suit the land the horse was bringing them through. John and Elisha and Nimrod were good Bible names. Nebuchadnezzar, but that was too long. He had thought to call a boy Joab, if he ever had one, but maybe his wife wouldn't like it in a horse. What were some Irish names, if the brute was Irish, as John Jones supposed? All the good ones he could think of had a "Mc" between the thills. Balboa was a Span-

iard, and the Spanish were a rotten people—half Mexican, he made no
doubt. He took the task seriously, his fat red face absorbed. Indians had
high-sounding names, but, excepting the Oneidas, they were a treach-
erous race, and the Oneidas were sottish people now, over-thirsty, lazy.
Look at their lands there on the left. Babies running naked like young pigs.
There was a man drunk, and noon only half-risen. Skenandoa was an eloquent man, and a powerful one in the Rebellion—he'd stood by the settlers
handsomely against the Mohawks. You could see his red house off the
road beside the creek—there in the peach trees. Oneida Creek would
need an aqueduct where the canal was going to cross it. Skenandoa was a
good name for a horse. Skenandoa, even if he was an Indian. You could
see LeFevrier's house, if you looked. He'd married an Indian woman—
a thing that came queer in a white man, but the French were an impartial
race that way, so long as it was a woman and she had a dowry; he'd sent
his sons to college—Amherst, Hammil thought—on the money his brown
wife had brought him. Indians could live up to a white man,—the women,
in their early time,—but when they got old they went back to Indian ways.
The Madame chewed snuff and lost her teeth, they said, so the Colonel
kept her out back of the house and gave her snuff and whiskey. A foreigner's trick. Lafayette was the only foreign man that ever amounted to
shucks. Lafayette was a good name for a horse; but Lafayette was a little
man, and look at that brute leg it for the hill! Breakneck Hill, they called it.
Jerry had better hold him in going down. There was a turn halfway, and
teamsters always cramped across a turn. They didn't care if a wagon banged
itself, the lousy bullies.

He'd have to think of a name out of their own country, maybe. Washington wouldn't do. A great man, but he didn't belong to New York. Now
Andrew Jackson was more to a man's liking. He was a man, all right.
He was a comer, and just getting up his steam. Reckon the British got a
dose off him. There was talk about his being President. Hammil would
like to vote for him some day. No hanky-panky gentleman farmer with a
black man to blow his nose between the Senate and the House, like Madi-
son, who vetoed the surplus bill for state improvement and signed the Lord
knows how many thousand dollars into his own Virginia's reticule to
build her Cumberland road with. To hell with them all! Von Steuben was
a foreigner, but Hammil couldn't forget how his uncle looked after drilling
under the old German beer-swizzler. Drill, drill, right, left. My God! It
made him scant right where he sat to think of it. Hammils always had
been fleshy fellows. Perry—he was a good man; McDonald, that was the
Irish of it—you couldn't get away from the Mc's. Weren't there names in
history books? Darius? Cyrus? Didn't mean a thing.

He knew a man had named a horse after a drink. Now that was an idea!
Take the wines. Ports didn't have good names, but the sherries had Lobo,
and Amber. Sherry didn't go with a horse like this one, though. Nor did
Madeira, even if Kirby was a good name and a good drink too. Governor
Kirby's Old Original. Hammil smacked his lips. There was Calcutta (good
for a filly some day) and Holloway and Bobby Lennox. Rum was more
in the line of it. Jamaicy, Barbados, or Medford. Cheap names. Whiskey?
Whiskey was a man's drink. By God, he had it!

"Bourbon!"

"It's a good name," said Jerry.

Bourbon! There was a name. What if it was furrin? Queens and kings was named it over there across the ocean, but here in North America it stood for whiskey—the primest in the world.

"Git you, Bourbon!" shouted Hammil. And the cob laid back his ears and shook out half an inch of the reins and laid his belly to the road.

"He's recognized it," cried the fat man, clapping Jerry's shoulder. "By God, I'll give him a drink of it at noon!"

And he did just that. In Canaseraga Hollow they put up at Webb's. They came down Quality Hill to the tavern ahead of a rush of dust. A stage was standing beside the door and the driver gave them a toot; and, as they drew up under Jerry's neat driving, he got down off his seat, and while the passengers waited impatiently, he went all over the horse.

"Hye, Caleb," he greeted them. "Where'd you happen onto this?"

Caleb narrated the purchase, and this time mentioned the price with confidence.

"You've got a bargain," said Apollos Smith, the driver. "I never seen a double for him, but I know an original horse. When did you leave town?"

"At seven o'clock."

The driver fished in his pockets for a chew, then put it back.

"If I got a chew working, I'd lose it sure in my horn. That's a horse. He ain't even hard-breathed. Look at his eye, will you! Well, my freight is getting anxious." He stepped deftly round the corner of the inn to kiss a chambermaid and came back stroking his moustache. His lank figure slouched to his seat. An inside passenger eyed him indignantly, snapping her shawl into place, folding her hands and setting her lips pursily. Perhaps she had seen the chambermaid's petticoats. The stage rumbled up the hill on its red wheels.

They ate in a half-filled dining room.

"I'm scouting for timber," Hammil explained to Mr. Webb. "Me and Jerry Fowler, here."

"Is it right the canal's going through?"

"Sure as shooting," said Hammil, mouthing down some turkey and reaching for the salt. "It's going to cut into your business, Webb."

"Time enough for me to worry when it's built," said Mr. Webb, showing his teeth in an elegant smile. He was a curiosity of the westward counties. He took a fashion magazine and dressed himself according to London. To-day he was got up in skin-fitting fawn-colored trousers that were strapped under his Russia leather shoes. His linen was daintily fine; his blue coat, high-waisted and roll-collared, fitted his elegant figure as a silk stocking might snug a lady's ankle; and he wore white buckskin gloves on his hands with a gold ring over the leather on his little finger. He walked back and forth among the tables, elegantly on his pointed toes. But his board was one of the best on the Pike.

"You don't happen to want to sell your horse?" he inquired.

"Bourbon?" Hammil flourished the name. "I wouldn't dicker horse meat with you, Webb, not even if I was a Jew. Bring me a pint of your best Bourbon."

And when it was brought Hammil led a small procession round the yard to the stables and poured from the bottle onto Bourbon's corn. The horse scented it daintily and then ate with lifted lips. When they started out after dinner again he was rolling his bits like a charger.

"I wouldn't do it again," said Jerry.

"All right."

"I'll drive him easy for a few miles, till he gets his hang again."

"All right, but I didn't give him the whole of it. Just enough to baptize him. Here."

"No, thanks."

"A swaller."

"Just a swallow." Jerry tilted the bottle.

"I'll down some," said Hammil, "and we'll nurse the rest. Cossett has poison only."

But his method of nursing consisted of ticking off the milestones with the bottle. He grew eloquent as he called Jerry's attention to landmarks and described the people who lived on places familiar to him. His impressions were slightly blurred, but abounding with color. It was only in the nick of time that he recognized Chittenango village and pointed out to Jerry the turn-off for the Orville road. . . .

The sun was waning westward and drawing long shadows over the rolling country. Houses and farms were scarcer. This was no turnpike they were traveling, but a local track, with here and there corduroy bridges and long stretches of scant, brushy woodland. They met only one wagon between Chittenango and Fayetteville and that was a farmer's bolster carrying rails for the spring fence-work.

Bourbon had found his wind again and bowled them along steadily. His shod hoofs were muffled by the dirt surface. His withers were streaked with sweat and the light traces had edged themselves with lather; but his stride was as unfaltering as ever. Jerry saw that he was an honest traveler, who held to the pace selected. In a race he would not take the first five-mile heat from three horses, but he would place second in the third, and finish the last two in the lead.

The wheels went quietly, with a faint mutter inside the boxes, and a continual whisper of dust back from the felloes. The road was following higher ground, a low ridge, apparently, and to the right Jerry caught glimpses of flat country.

Hammil, rousing himself, caught the direction of Jerry's glance and stared with a kind of owlishness.

"That's the beginning of the swamps," he pronounced. "They'll bring the ditch in there from northeastward."

He relapsed into solemn silence, eyeing the mouth of the bottle held upright between his hands.

Suddenly he jerked himself from another doze.

"By crinkus! You're a carpenter, Jerry!"

"Am I?" Jerry grinned.

"Sure-ly. You're a carpenter."

After a while he added, "I'm a carpenter."

He eyed the horse for a moment.

"Bourbon's a carpenter," he announced. His voice rose. "We're the whole of us carpenters. And by thunder we're all three of us a-going to build Clinton his canal!"

"Sure," said Jerry, keeping an eye on the lurching fat body.

Hammil was serious. He looked down over the dashboard, his neck arched. Suddenly his chin emerged from its folds and a tremendous bubble of air escaped him. He smacked his lips to sing, and Jerry smelled the Bourbon.

> "The world it is a *bag of nails,*
> And some are very queer ones,
> And some are *flats* and some are *sharps,*
> And some are very dear ones."

Hammil's voice had a surprising depth and resonance, but, being still a little mixed, he had adopted the refined nasal interpretation that a churchgoer would give his hymns.

> "We've *sprigs,* and *spikes,* and *sparables,*
> Some *little, great,* and *small,* sir.
> Some folks love *nails* and *monstrous heads,*
> And some love none at all, sir."

A snore punctuated the stanza, and, in a friendly way, the fat man leaned himself on Jerry's shoulder. Jerry might have been alone now, except for the weight of the sleeping Hammil, and his thin face grinned as he thought to himself that he understood why Hammil might like to have a man to drive him. Probably in Utica the fat man didn't dare get drunk. He had a reputation there that he had to maintain. Mrs. Hammil looked like one of those dainty, sweet women that stood for no nonsense. Most likely she had no inkling of Hammil's overflowing pride and joy in this contract; she would have no conception of the magnitude of the work he had undertaken. It had seemed to Jerry extraordinary that, in a town like Utica, through which the great canal was bound to pass, there was not more talk about it.

"Come along, Bourbon."

The cob switched his tail affably. He had made a monumental journey that day and he was leaning a trifle against the bit; but he still put out his front hoofs courageously. It was stirring to watch him all day long. A runner was a handsome thing to see, but a fine trotter was beyond all other things eye-filling to a horseman.

Evening was coming after them from the east. In the Mohawk Valley you could see it taking form between the hills; but here in this vast rolling country it came more gradually, like a cool breath behind the sun, giving the traveler a notion of the earth's rotation.

Jerry tried to make a picture of what Mary would be doing now. He saw her moving about the room, quietly preparing the order for night, and he wondered if it seemed empty to her, and if she sat down, perhaps, at the window, to think of him.

They passed through Orville, which was no more than four houses, one a kind of general store with a grindstone and a table lamp in the window; and then the woods dwindled out on either side of the road, and Jerry had his first view of the flat country. On the left, a hubbly pasture extended behind a snake fence, showing moss through the grass, and bits of bogland with tamaracks growing beside them. Way ahead a small farm made a cluster of a log barn and house and a tool-shed. But to the right, the land sloped northward into a tremendous growth of marsh grass. Where it stood unbent by snow, Jerry had never seen grass so tall, and it looked old, as if its roots were bedded by layer upon layer of matted dead blades. Unbelievably great swarms of blackbirds kept lifting into the sunlight, their red shoulders sparkling like gems, their voices making a continual drone, as if they were a kind of monstrous swarming insect. When they perched, they lit only momentarily sidewise upon cat-tails. Jerry saw some crows cutting through the sunset from the southwest, and he noticed as they approached the swamp they were lifting steadily. It was no safe place for a crow or hawk or any predatory bird. Once the blackbirds were roused they would batter a crow to earth by sheer force of numbers.

As they neared the farm, Jerry saw a man coming in behind two cows. He waved to the wagon and Jerry pulled up the horse.

"Hello," said the farmer.

"Hello," said Jerry. "Can you tell me how far to Cossett's?"

"Mile and a half, or thereabouts. Say, who's that with you?"

"Caleb Hammil."

"Thought I recognized the fat bezabor. I'm Bob Melville."

At his name, Caleb roused himself. He blinked his eyes, spotted the farmer's image, and said, " 'Evening, Bob."

"What you doing this way? It's good to see you. Why don't you light down to-night? Dorothy'd be glad to have you."

After his nap, Caleb seemed more able to collect himself.

"Thanks, Bob. We're going in to Cossett's. I've got talk for him from Holley. This here's Jerry Fowler, working with me. We're out scouting timber for the canal."

Melville blew his long nose. His brown eyes stared steadily at the two men on the wagon.

"Canal, Caleb?"

"Canal!" said Caleb. "Sure. Clinton's Canal."

He twisted himself on the seat, causing the wagon to creak down on the left, and stared out over the marsh.

"I got the contract on this section locks. Look at right over there, beyond them cacktails where that cedar stub pokes up." He pointed his thick arm. "That's where number one will be. You see the drop of ground, Jerry, at the commencement of this marsh? Right there."

They stared at him instead.

"I been through here," said Caleb. "I seen Wright mark that spot. You'd see the stakes but for the grass being high."

Melville was staring still. The humorousness that had invested his long-nosed face was gone. His Adam's apple was bobbling in his throat and he spat once before his voice came out.

"Dorothy!" he called. *"Dorothy!"*

The door of the log cabin swung open on its squeaky straps. A tall, square-shouldered woman stepped out. Man's boots were on her feet. When she caught sight of the wagon, her arm raised itself in greeting and a merry welcome broke over her large face. But her husband cried, "Dorothy!"

She came forward quickly, then, her eyes on her husband, and stood beside him at the fence.

"It's going through," he said. His voice was choky. They looked at each other, as if the two men and the horse and wagon were not there.

"It's going through," repeated Melville.

"Actual?" she said. Her deep voice spoke softly, vibrantly.

He nodded.

Jerry stared down at them, wondering what it all meant.

Then, suddenly, the woman laughed.

"Light down," she invited. "I'm using our last buckwheat flour for cakes for supper. And I'll mix a punkin flip."

Caleb shook his head.

"We can't. We're going in to Cossett's."

But she did not heed. She and her husband still looked at each other laughing. And suddenly they looked away, and as the man's face turned Jerry saw his eyes swim, and the woman suddenly sniffled, comically, for one who looked so strong and humorous.

Melville spoke.

"I've seen Wright going through, surveying, and I didn't think nothing. I've seen Geddes here way back eight years ago. He said then it was just somebody's idea. Not his, not Colden's, not Dewitt's. But they both of them stayed here, them and their levelers and rodsmen and axemen, and often me and Dorothy have thought about it. We used to tell each other how we'd put a porch onto the house and set here looking at boats go past. There ain't a thing travels this road, you know, and it gets lonesome, not having even any children. And last year they went through boring holes down into the marsh, scaring ructions out of all the birds that live there. But we didn't think nothing after—it's been so long a time. And now you come along, sleeping like a fat old drunken ground hog, and if I hadn't stopped you I wouldn't have knowed."

He looked embarrassed at his burst of speech. Jerry turned his eyes. Caleb seemed uncomfortable.

"Say, Bob, we've got to get along. It's getting on towards dark."

They didn't protest. They just waved good-bye; but when Jerry looked back he saw them still leaning on the fence together, eyeing the marsh.

Caleb made a poke at laughter.

"It took them kind of hard," he said, "Bob's had a hard time farming here. Crops was bad, too, last winter. I'll tell Holley to ask him to take a contract hauling stone or maybe I'll give him one on timber."

Jerry said, "It's a lonely place."

He was thinking of Dorothy Melville's eyes.

And Caleb said, "Yes. It's a funny thing she never had no children. Her built so strong."

"Yes," said Jerry. "It must be lonesome for her."

"She works along with him. Two years ago I come through this road, and their steer had died, and her and him was pulling on the plough along with the ox, taking turns. She's powerful strong, for a woman. I didn't think to see her take on so."

Dusk was settling on the marsh, a warm, still evening. Sounds of frogs in the rushes echoed heavily across the level grass. The road skirted the wet land carefully. Bourbon kept his nostrils working, as if he distrusted the smell of it. Through the rising haze, they saw a light born over the grass, and the road turned towards it, and at the same time Bourbon's hoofs thumped on corduroy.

"There's Cossett's," said Hammil. "I'd like better to be with Melvilles, but I've got to see this brute; and them two looked as if they'd like to set alone just holding hands."

As Caleb said, the wonder about Cossett's tavern was that it had ever been built. And the wonder about Cossett was that when you saw him you couldn't imagine how a woman had ever consented to live with him, and when you saw Mrs. Cossett it seemed impossible that any man had ever considered her a proposition.

The tavern stood right in the middle of the marsh. There was one way up to it, and one way out beyond. Nearest was Melville's, and on the other side it was two miles to the salt works at Salina. A small frame building, once a mustard yellow, its scabrous clapboards were now the color of dead marsh grass. It had no trees to shade it, there was no sign of shrubs or flowers. A little weedy garden patch behind the kitchen stoop seemed to cower at the encroachment of the marsh.

The earth had a peculiar feeling underfoot. It made Bourbon uneasy and, in spite of his long travel, obviously impatient to be gone.

Caleb's roaring hails, batting back from the walls, were lost against the marsh mist. The door opened and a little man with a twisted shoulder and a permanent cock to his head came out with a lantern.

"What do you want?"

"It's me, Hammil," said Caleb. "I want a room for to-night."

"Single or double?" said the man, eyeing Jerry.

"Don't talk that way," Caleb said. "You know there ain't a body in the house outside of you and Missus."

The man grumbled.

"Want to stable the horse, I s'pose."

"Fowler can do that," said Hammil. "Give him the light. Say, Jerry, fix Bourbon, will you? And don't use tavern oats. They all go sprouty here. Use ourn."

Jerry took the lantern from Cossett and led Bourbon round the tavern corner. Built against the end wall was a small stable. He unhitched Bourbon outside and led him through the door. The barn smelled sour and damp. The lantern showed him cobwebs on the walls, black with sticky dust. There were three stalls; and in one a mangy mule turned flat, gleaming eyes, and laid her ears back.

Jerry shook his head. It was a poor spot to night a horse after a long trip. He spent half an hour rubbing him down dry, rubbing him till the lather was gone and the skin was loosened under his bare hand. Then he scraped the stall out and found some comparatively dry dead marsh grass and made a deep bedding. He gave Bourbon only a smack of water, for he distrusted its smell. Just enough to cool his mouth.

"I'll fetch you out some brandy to take the disease out of it and give you a real drink."

Bourbon pointed his small ears, and nuzzled Jerry's shoulder. He snuffled eagerly when he heard him taking out the grain bag.

Jerry left him uneasily. It was no fit place to night a horse in, he told himself again. And when he entered the inn he told himself that it was no better place to night a man.

There was just one room for public use downstairs. A bedroom and storeroom opened off it. Upstairs, he judged, were public bedrooms. The whole house was musty with the marsh air, but stale also with the smell of years of liquor and tobacco. The only fresh thing, barring a few new cobwebs, was the fire. Caleb sat close on one side of the fireplace with Cossett standing beside him. Across the hearth, a mountain of shawls, a woman snuffled upon a low stool. The eyes of all three were bent upon the cook. She was a negro girl, with the sinuous lank back of her race and the peculiar stiffness of the shoulders, neck, and arms. Her coal-black skin and frizzled brush of hair gave her a strange air of lowliness even in this marsh night where all life seemed to live at crawling. She looked wild— like a creature trapped in from the bogland and broken to human service.

As Jerry entered, all but the woman on the stool turned their heads. Caleb, solemn, puffing his pipe and drinking whiskey, asked about the horse.

"It's a damp barn. A poor place for a horse," said Jerry.

Cossett grinned, showing misplaced yellow teeth. His small eyes glittered. "Damp? Ain't it natural? What do you expect, young cock?"

The negress's eyes showed white at the outside edges.

"Get back to work," said Cossett.

Something in her glance made Jerry look at her more carefully. He noticed the dull sheen of her bare, black, narrow arms. But as he took a stool close to her, her scent came to him, pungent and overwhelming. He saw that the shawled woman was regarding him from sardonic eyes. She said nothing. All that long evening, even while she ate, she made no sound except to wrestle with her breathing. And all evening Jerry knew that if he looked at her he would find the eyes open, staring at him. Cossett and Caleb talked snatches about stone. Myron Holley had commissioned Hammil to ask. Cossett knew the stone hereabouts. He would deliver it if Holley gave him a contract when he came up in June. Gumaer would haul. Who was doing mason work? Hammil didn't know that. Mr. Hayward Lewis, maybe, who lived in Onondaga. Cossett grunted. He didn't know about mason's work; but he could cut stone. His wry lips unfolded from his yellow teeth. A funny thing. Before he had left England he'd been prenticed to a stonecutter making burial stones. Years ago, that was. Now his trade was coming handy. Cutting stone for locks. A funny thing.

The nostrils of the woman on the stool made a sudden buzzing noise. They looked across at her. She was looking at the negro girl, who was finishing her cookery.

The negro girl rose to her feet. She bent stiff-kneed from her hips to pick up the pan of bullheads and bacon. She stooped again for an iron skillet that had been hidden under ashes. She took the teapot from the crane. She set them on the table and dragged it closer to the fire. She put another candle in a bottle neck and lit it and brought brown plates of earthenware. She stood around behind them, and Jerry saw that she was barefoot and noticed the long, flat heels and ankles. She waited on them, rolling her brown eyes in the yellow whites.

The food was incongruously good to eat. The skillet contained a soft, golden pone—a dish neither Hammil nor Jerry had tasted. The woman hitched her stool along the floor and ate. The food seemed to disappear among her shawls.

Through the end wall of the tap, Jerry heard Bourbon munching his oats. Outside, in the night, the restless silence seemed alive with creeping. There was a small wind somewhere, stirring the grass, that whispered and whispered. The naked feet of rats scurried overhead between the walls. Far away a frog kept croaking hoarsely, and the night smell of the marsh stole through the windows.

Cossett watched his face.

"You'll be working out there," he said. "Wright and his engineer boys think it's easy digging ground. They don't know marsh ground."

He looked round him.

"Me, I've lived here now for fifteen years. I found this crossing from an Indian. Some of St. Leger's Indians went across here. I built a house because I wouldn't have no man to bother me here. But there's things here Wright ain't thought about."

He swabbed his plate with a mess of pone and paddled it onto his knife.

"He ain't thought about the August fever," he said, his head cocked queerly. "He ain't listened to this marsh working. It's old, older than all the land there is about it. It's got things living deep down under. Why does it shake to a man's walk? Why can a man dig up ocean clams, fresh and living, if he knows where? Why is the water bracky when on the solid ground like here I've got a well of living fresh?"

He drew the back of his hand across his mouth and got up and hunched himself through a door. He returned with a thin bottle.

"Brandy," he said; and then he lifted his voice by the shawled woman's ear and shouted, "Brandy!"

She moved her eyes and suddenly her nostrils buzzed.

"Get glasses," he ordered the negress.

The black girl came back with four thick glasses clamped in the thin fingers of one hand.

"You can eat now," Cossett told her, and the others moved back to the fire, the woman hitching along on her stool. The negro girl sat down at the table and began scraping the dishes.

Jerry said, "I'd like a tumblerful of brandy to sweeten Bourbon's water."

"The well water's all right," said Cossett, "if you draw it new."

Hammil nodded.

"That's right, Jerry."

"Annabel can take him a bucket," said Cossett. "She's got to tend the mule."

Jerry looked at the negress.

Her face was drawn, but she left her eating silently, at Cossett's stare, and went out to water the beasts. They heard her drawing up the bucket in the dark outside.

"Where'd she come from?" asked Hammil.

"Runaway. She'd used up what she had when she got here. I kept her. She's feared to fainting of the marsh—she dassn't run away in the dark."

He cuddled the brandy glass and drank. Presently the girl came in again and set about cleaning the dishes. They sat together awhile and then Jerry and Hammil were taken to their rooms.

"You'd best lock your door," Hammil said, holding a candle against Jerry's face. "Cossett won't do harm to us, but he might steal."

He went away to his room and Jerry listened to him fitting the back of a chair under the latch. He looked round his own room, a cubby near the stairs, with a damp board bed and a mattress of marsh grass. Rats chattered near the head of it. He blew out the candle and looked out through the window. The mist lay level with the sill, and there was starlight on it. Jerry saw nothing else.

He went to his bed and lay down gingerly in his clothes. He could not sleep for a long time, thinking of Mary and the sweet, cool scent of their room, the pleasant sounds of the sleeping town, and her clean warmth. Then he thought how it would be to work out here for weeks without sight of her, and he resolved to bring her out and maybe let her board with Melvilles, so that he could get back nights. And that contented him, for already he felt her nearer.

As he drowsed down, he dimly heard Cossett bolting doors and the wheezing and creaking the fat woman made moving to her room. He heard the bare feet of the negro girl, like a rat's feet, slithering up the stairs, and a while later Cossett, hunching himself along the wall and following to her room. The house became very still. But even in his sleep he seemed to feel the marsh mist pushing against his window.

The sun came in with a white light, and they left early, feeling cramped and stiff from their night's sleeping. Bourbon went eagerly across the marsh. All round them under the mist was the harsh mutter of blackbirds, but the mist clung to earth until they had emerged from the dead grass and were once more on solid road.

That morning they passed the wooden vats of the salt works in Salina, and Hammil told him how they made the water evaporate by leading hot air in pipes through the troughs, but in other works they let the sun do it, and in Geddes they boiled the water off in enormous cauldrons.

They followed a road along the river into Hannibal, where Hammil spent a half day discussing lumber with Ashel Pritchard, who ran the mill for Esquire Forman. There were fine spruce growths south of the town, Pritchard said; and the next morning Jerry and Hammil drove from farm to farm contracting the hewed beams.

For the first time Jerry saw land in process of clearing. The little log houses that came so close to the finished farms on the edge of timber, the women hoeing in between the stumps to ready their garden patches; the burnt pieces; the trees in other places being felled in windrows for the fall burning and the gathering of black salts which were traded at the stores as a man used money; the acres of trees standing girdled. It seemed to him that the land was spoiled and stark and dreadful, without shape and without promise; and he had to wait again until he saw a pasture, or a field of wheat, smooth with green, before he regained his confidence in the promise of the earth.

Hammil went about his dickering with tremendous gusto. It was astonishing how many people recognized him. He knew the women, who had ready smiles for him, and seemed somehow to remember all the children's names. He would walk out with the man of the place to inspect the timber and sit down on a log and quote him prices, spending often a good hour bringing down the man to his own figure.

"If I give you a dollar fifty more a thousand," he would say, "what am I going to tell Jonas Whitbeck? He lives half a mile from here and his timber's just as sound and grows freer. He's stacking his beams, hewed, in wagon reach of the road. And taking my price, too. I've got to haul, remember that. And I pay cash money as the timber leaves your fences."

The man would cut himself a toothpick out of pine and whittle it to suit and talk about the price of wheat and how the cattle got the split-hoof, and ask Caleb if he knew the story that was going round about McNeiland's daughter. So Hammil would gather in that story and cap it and air his patriotic pride in this great canal he was going to build.

"My work's got to be sound. That's why I come down here for timber, Haskins. I could buy spruce up over by Marcellus, but that wet land's sour, and there's a touch of red heart."

"This canal ain't going to do me no good."

"Why not?"

"It's too far off. All they're going to do is to tax me for it. Don't I pay high enough anyways? Here's my wife needing a new wheel and we're trying to get round to hire a schoolmaster now."

"That timber would pay all of that twice over. And listen, Haskins. You talk about the canal being far off from you. Don't you see what it amounts to? Every farmer will be just as close to Albany market as he is to the canal. Your wheat now fetches you but twenty-nine cents. Why? You've got to have it hauled—the miller does, I mean—close to two hundred miles. Now the canal is just about fifteen. It's going to mean a dollar to the bushel to you."

"You show me that dollar," said the farmer, "and I'll show you my bushel. Wheat's getting blighted hereabouts, anyways."

But in the end he would come round, and Hammil and Jerry would turn Bourbon towards the next farm.

The fat man seemed to know his roads and turnings as if he had been born in this far county. And when at last they struck south on the Onondaga road, he had his timbers all lined out.

"Daggit!" he said that morning. "It's going to be good getting home. It's good enough for a man like me to sleep in log-house bough-beds or be an edible to bugs, but I do like my own bed to home."

He grinned.

"When I got married," he said, "I had a bed made just to suit me. It makes our hired girl complain on wash-days—but"—he chuckled—"I ain't to home on wash-days."

Now that his business was done, he seemed able to put every trace of it out of his mind. He had a hundred anecdotes to tell, and his loud laughter echoed in the taverns. When Bourbon put his forehoofs on the turnpike, he, too, seemed to understand that they were bound for home. He struck his eight-mile trot and went mile after mile without a falter.

The immigrants were crowding the road. At Manlius, where the Cherry Valley turnpike entered, there was a bawling knot of cattle and wagons that it seemed could never be straightened into line. It took Jerry half an hour to thread his way through the village.

They nighted at The Purple Whale in Lennox, and it was growing on into the afternoon next day when Bourbon brought them into the Oriskany Valley and Jerry recognized ahead the rise of Paris Hill and knew that Utica was just an hour's drive.

Hammil laid his hand upon Jerry's knee.

"Anxious for your girl, boy?"

Jerry did not answer.

Hammil talked half to himself.

"I wonder," he said, with his eye on Jerry's profile, "if you didn't do better than I did? Marrying young. You and her starting off together right from the mark. I got my wife for working—and I'm not sorry, either. But you make or lose together and your heart won't need to burn you. I used to be that scared sometimes. I mind well the night my timber got afire for the last job afore I wedded. That had me scared."

For a moment he was silent.

"I wonder what there'll be for supper," he said.

And then, as they came into sight of Utica and saw Genesee Street sloping down and all the houses lifting supper smokes, he said, "I think we had a good trip, Jerry. I like you fine. There ain't going to be so much for us to do till we get to active working. . . . You ain't a talkative cuss, anyway."

"I liked it," Jerry managed to say.

Caleb fished out his purse.

"Here's your first pay. Now you hop off here. I reckon that I won't kill Bourbon tending him for one night. Kiss your girl from me and say I'm coming round to see her."

Jerry tried to protest, but the fat hand fairly pushed him out. He stood an instant before the store watching the fat figure turning into Bleecker. Then he looked down into his hand. There were four dollar bills. He had got his first raise his first week. He flushed. He had not earned it.

There was a shrill whooping at the back of the store.

Henderson was shouting, "Mary! Mary! Where's Mary! Mr. Fowler's back home!"

At first it seemed to Jerry that the evening would never end; but as Mr. Charley questioned him over his pipe and beer, his heart warmed.

"It seems queer," he said. "You traveling fifty miles along the pike and then when you bend northward coming on the line of this canal. You say it's going to be forty feet across?"

"Yes," said Jerry. "The prism's forty feet at top and twenty-eight at bottom, and it's four feet deep."

"That's like a river," said Mr. Charley. "All the time I thought, while you were away, how it would be to travel." He made an ambulatory gesture with his pipe. They were sitting in the bookstore with a brisk fire roaring in the stove. "Look at this. I don't do any business; and all the time I've got to talk to the same people. My brain gets ruts. What's the matter with it?"

Jerry said, "You might clean out this room and put the books on shelves."

Lester Charley drew a hand across a pained forehead.

"I might. It might be a success. But what good would that do *me?* Just so much extra bother. No. I've been thinking, why couldn't I get a boat and do my business on it? I could circulate a library that way; and the only taxes would be toll. They say it won't amount to much."

"I don't know about that," Jerry said. His ears were for the kitchen, where Mary could be heard helping Mrs. Charley.

"Your wife," said Mr. Charley, "has turned out right helpful. She's a nice girl."

Jerry had a thought that they were paying good money for rent and board, but remembering Mrs. Charley's gratitude voluminously expressed to Mary after supper, he saw that it was a decent thing to do.

"Shucks," said Mr. Charley, reading his thoughts. "Women hanker for that kind of thing. Here, I'll even it up to you with another glass of beer."

He filled Jerry's glass from the jug, and Jerry thought he might be right. A woman wanted occupation. So he leaned back comfortably, aware of the four boys listening on the stairs in unnatural quiet, and told about their trip. He held up Bourbon to the bookseller's admiration, and told about Melvilles and the queer place Cossett's was. He became so enthralled in the land he had visited that he hardly noticed Mary stealing in and sitting on a pile of books before the window. Her face was quiet, as it had been since he had come home. She folded her hands in her lap, but when he turned towards her, her eyes dropped down.

Mr. Charley turned down the lamp and listened gravely to all he had to say. Now and then his big mouth grinned at some remark of Caleb's and now and then he threw a glance at Mary. He must have read in her the impatience Jerry could not see, for at last he took pity and said that it was time they went to bed.

It was only then that Jerry's impatience reawoke from the sound of his own voice. He looked at Mary sheepishly, and followed her upstairs.

The dim-lit loft was quiet. As he came through the trap, Mary was setting down the candle. She took a step towards him, and then dropped her hands and bent her head. She did not move. . . .

The travel still in Jerry's nerves awoke him early. Dawn had yet to come. Beside him Mary slept on; and he lay quiet not to wake her.

It seemed to him that the most wonderful thing that had ever happened to him was that moment in the loft. They had not talked; and yet Mary had told him all the things he wanted to know.

Overhead he could hear a night rain falling on the roof, and through the windows the damp air brought a scent of lilacs. Mid-May in Utica had opened the lilacs in his absence.

It was so clean; the scent was so sweet. She had put new curtains at the windows. He could see the order in the room; their clothes hung where they should be; the end of her comb just sticking over the top of the bureau. He was glad she was a quiet, unspoken girl. He slept again, this time with a delicious sense of laziness, as if his whole body were drinking rest from the bed. . . .

When he woke the second time she was awake.

Jerry took her hand, and now he told her of Hammil's saying that they would have less traveling for a while. Her fingers closed the least bit and were still. She was glad he was back; she had missed him. He told her of his raise in pay and his hand waited. But, instead, she used spoken words to tell him that was fine; and all at once a rooster crowed somewhere behind Charley's yard, and Jerry sprang out of bed.

Downstairs Mrs. Charley's feet were slapping into the kitchen. Henderson was complaining over the weight of the loaded bucket as he hauled down the well-sweep. In the street a wagon rattled by to a horse's spanking trot.

After breakfast Hammil appeared at the shop.

"No, I don't want books, Charley; I wouldn't have time to read them. Where's Jerry?"

"He just came in a while ago from fixing your horse."

"Would he be upstairs?"

"Most likely."

Hammil's feet clumped up the stairs. He poked his bare red head through the loft in time to see Mary finishing the bed while Jerry watched her.

"Good morning," he said. "Is this Mrs. Fowler?"

Jerry introduced him, and Hammil shook her hand while he puffed from climbing the stairs.

"I'm real glad to know you, Mrs. Fowler. Your husband's told me all about you. Jerry, I think you're a pretty good hand for business after all. How do you like Utica, Mrs. Fowler?"

Ill at ease himself, Jerry wondered at her calmness in bringing Hammil a chair and answering, "It's a nice town, Mr. Hammil. Jerry and I've been lucky."

"It's a good town. But I don't know how you've been lucky."

"Here," she said. "The Charleys are good to me, and Jerry was lucky meeting you."

Hammil sat down and placed a hand on each knee, and looked at some spot between their heads.

"Lucky," he snorted. " 'Tain't luck. I took a fancy to him and he seems to be all right, that's all."

He looked very sheepish.

Mary smiled, quietly.

"I've got work to do downstairs," she said, "if you'll excuse me, Mr. Hammil."

"I don't see how I can," said Hammil, heaving himself to his feet and standing while she went down. "But I'll do the best I'm able."

Jerry felt proud, even when Hammil stepped quickly up to him to poke him with a broad thumb.

"You never told me a single thing about her, Jerry. You're a sly one. Utica may be a lucky place, but you're the luckiest man I've seen in some time."

He sat down again immediately to talk business. He said that he had had a letter waiting for him from Myron Holley. Work on the locks probably would not start till autumn; but Holley wanted one built before winter. That would be number one at Cossett's. The canal wasn't going to be started till July Fourth, Independence Day. In the meantime he would finish up a few small jobs he had on hand in Utica. His carpenter was in charge there and Hammil thought it would be a good thing for Jerry to work with him, mostly roofing work. He himself would have to take another trip to Albany. He wanted specifications for the iron strapping and sluice gates and quoin points for the locks. They would be cast in Utica and Rome. And he thought he might still hunt a few extra contracts for fencing —yes, the whole canal would have to be fenced on both sides—and odd work, just for pin money for Mrs. Hammil. If Jerry was minded so, they could walk up to the Devereux house where the carpenter was and Jerry could be introduced. While Hammil was away, Jerry could mind Bourbon, feed and exercise him. Mrs. Hammil would make no call on his time—that was understood.

Jerry got his hat and followed Hammil down. In the hall, the contractor halted and said, "You'd better take time to tell Mrs. Fowler. It's a good thing, when able, to tell your wife where you're going to, Jerry."

Lester Charley called through the open door, "It's damned sight better, Caleb, to tell her when you're not able."

Caleb chuckled.

Jerry found Mary in the yard, helping Mrs. Charley hang clothes on a line. Her hands were stretched above her head, the line of her back arched slightly from the hips, and her hair was straggled from wrestling with the heavy linen. When she turned at his voice she had a clothespin in her teeth. She snatched it out to smile, and her cheeks flushed bright against the white sheet.

Jerry told her what Hammil had said.

"Ain't that fine?" said Mrs. Charley, ducking under a sheet. "My, it will be nice for Mary to have you home."

Jerry thought that it was strange for Mary to help Mrs. Charley with her washing. He could see that those sheets were not used in the house. But there was no time to ask.

Hammil led him down Genesee Street into a side street to a large house. A ladder leaned up against the eaves, and on the top a man was nailing shingles. The thump of his hammer made a din along the roadway.

"Hey, Rogers!"

The man unbent his back and cautiously approached the eaves. He poked over a lugubrious face.

"Yeanh?"

"Come on down," bawled Hammil.

A pink-cheeked servant girl looked out through an open window and grinned impudently at Hammil, but when she saw Jerry's upturned face she drew back behind the curtain coyly.

Rogers backed slowly down the ladder. When he stood in front of them he sighed and rubbed his hands over his buttocks.

Hammil performed the introduction and explained the circumstances.

"Yeanh," said Rogers. "It don't make odds to me."

He turned back for the ladder.

"What's your hurry?"

"I've got to climb back up there, don't I?"

He spoke all round a mouthful of shingle nails; he looked like a man who had been martyred so often that suffering was just a habit. He laid

a slow hand on a rung and began to climb. As he reached the upstairs
window, the servant girl shook out a mop.

"Say!" bawled Rogers, and the nails tumbled out of his slack mouth.
The girl looked up in pretty dismay.

"Oh, I'm *sorry*, Mr. Rogers! I didn't see you coming."

Hammil guffawed, and the maid slanted an eye at Jerry and slid back.
They heard her tittering.

"Self Rogers is a good worker. He's suffering from dyspepsy and toothache, one thing or another, pretty near continual. Well, you start work
this afternoon, Jerry. Now I've got to get along."

That was the last he saw of Hammil for two weeks.

Jerry first went to Nailer Devlin for a hammer, saw, and shingle hatchet
which he charged to Caleb's account. The Nailer was a hearty man, with
hands that smelled of iron. "It's a fine morning," he said, and offered
Jerry some hammers for heft. Jerry chose deliberately.

"Here's a bender saw," said the merchant. "Ready set. You wanted a
cross-cut, didn't you?"

"Yes."

Jerry bent the saw against his knee and then tapped it for the temper.

"Working hereabouts?" asked Nailer Devlin. "You are? Hammil, hey?
He's a good customer. Surely. I'll charge it to him."

Jerry took his tools and went outside. A man with a misanthropic face
and an axe on his shoulder stopped to look at him.

"Morning, mister."

"Morning," said Jerry.

"I couldn't interest you in a town lot, could I?"

"I don't know as you could."

"Utica is a hell of a town," said the man. He pulled a snuff-stick from
his pocket. Little bits of bark and dust had furred it over, but he bit off a
nibble and worked it over his gums with his tongue.

"Me, I was an early settler hereabouts. I aimed to farm it. Look at it now.
If a cow strays, she don't stand hardly no show at all. If the movers don't
snatch her, a teamster carves him out some tenderloin."

His mouth delivered itself of the excess juice.

"So I'm selling my land. Three dollars the acre, cleared. I got a nice
lot west of Bagg's."

"Whereabouts?"

"Over there." The man pointed. "I've left a elm a-growing. See the top
to it. Over the Northern Hotel there."

Jerry considered. He had a half hour yet to lunch time and Rogers
didn't expect him till afternoon. And he had in his pockets two week's
wages in advance, against Hammil's trip to Albany.

"It ain't but three minutes' walking," said the man. "My name is Charlie
Green. It's a well-dreened piece."

"All right," said Jerry. "I'll look at it."

Charles Green turned himself round to lead the way at a shambling
walk. There was a kind of subdued eagerness in his face.

Back of the Northern Hotel, which was the teamster's stopping place,
was a long barn and shed. In the yard an aged stable hand was sitting on
a bucket, plaiting his summer hat from stable straw. A Pennsylvania wagon

stood in the noon glare, and from under its hood came a strong smell of barreled whiskey. One of the kegs was leaking, a drop at a time, and the hat maker had placed a broken teacup on a brick to catch the drip.

Beyond the stable, Jerry saw the acre, backing on the town, a mass of spiræa bushes and old dead goldenrod. The corpses of a dozen trees lay here and there over the ground.

Charlie Green pointed.

"Next wet," he said, "I'll burn it over for ye."

Jerry walked the length of it. At the far end, where the ground rose to the town's slope, a pair of red stakes forty feet apart were driven. To the right, the line they marked ended in an open street.

Green spied them.

"Blast," he said. "They're always sticking in them sticks. There was a big bezabor told me not to pull them out. I guess I can, on my own land. I guess I ain't going to let no canal come spoiling of my land."

He stopped, eyed Jerry shrewdly.

" 'Course it ain't but just talk. There's a couple or so of cranky cusses hereabouts that spend their time a-planting of these-here sticks. It don't mean nothing."

But Jerry caught his breath. Canal-side land was bound to rise.

"I'd have to have a deed," he said quietly.

"I'm full of deeds," said Green. "It's all I got. Deeds and this blasted ground. I got nigh onto a dozen acres, and yesterday I said, 'I'll just rid of it and mosey me out west.' You're the first man I spoke, having just cleared this first acre."

He fished a paper from inside his shirt.

"Just come with me down to the bank. It won't take half a minute there for Mr. Kip to deed you."

"All right," said Jerry. "I want to start me a bank account anyways."

He concealed his own excitement under a casualness as apparent as the older man's. They returned to the square and entered the bank. Green loudly asked for Mr. Kip, and, as if they had known him for some time, the bank people humored him.

"I know Green's title's good," said Mr. Kip. "Where've you been all this time, Charlie? I thought I might buy a piece of your holding, myself."

"If you'll buy the rest of them eleven acres," said Green, "I'll offer you a straight figger for thirty dollars."

"Just wait till we've finished with Mr. Fowler. You're working with Hammil, aren't you, Fowler?"

"Yes. I want to open an account."

"All right. We'll soon fix that."

Mr. Kip passed the deed to a clerk and brought a bill of sale for both of them to sign. Charlie Green signed with a cross and Mr. Kip wrote his name for him. Then he handed Jerry over to the cashier and Jerry deposited the remnant of his two weeks' earnings. He felt embarrassed to put in seven dollars among all these gentlemen, but they seemed to take it as important business, and called him Mister; and when he was headed for home again he felt that he had made a distinct step forward. He decided that he wouldn't tell a soul. It seemed a foolish thing to sink most of a week's pay in land; he wouldn't really have considered it if he hadn't caught sight of those red stakes. It was a lucky stroke. . . .

During the rest of May and most of June, he worked at odd jobs with Self Rogers.

The weather continued warm and dry. Working on a roof, Jerry could see out over the town to the fields that were becoming green. A haze hung over the valley. Under it the travel of the road was indistinct. At times a fierce impatience uprose in him.

After work hours, he hitched Bourbon to the rig to exercise him, and he and Mary took long drives together. They would head out with a supper in a bag and sometimes cover fifteen miles. Mary was quiet on these drives, as she was always, watching the land, admiring Bourbon when Jerry called her attention to the horse. She seemed in her placid way to have accepted her new life. Her eyes had completely lost their look of fear, and Jerry had less and less often that memory of her standing among the other redemptioners on the sloop deck by the Greenbush Ferry dock.

Sometimes they took the Charleys with them—Bourbon made nothing of the extra load—and Mrs. Charley would dress herself in her Sunday clothes, regardless of the appearance her family made at her back. Mr. Charley would direct them out to Clinton to examine the college, or they would drive out to Paris Hill, where a few carrier pigeons still nested, and Mr. Charley would tell about the great flocks he could remember as a boy.

An era of prosperity had started for the Charleys. Mrs. Charley was getting a reputation for washing linen. Jerry had erected new poles for her in the yard. Once he had remonstrated with Mary for helping her, but Mary said that she needed something to occupy her and she only helped occasionally.

July came hot, and on the evening of the third, Hammil, who had returned the week before, said, "We're going out to Rome to-morrow morning—making an early start, Jerry. I want you to hitch Bourbon up at two o'clock."

8

"That's Clinton"

JERRY had borrowed a clock from Mr. Charley, a queer little brass affair with a noisy tick, and placed it on a chair beside the bed. He had left the glass open so that he could feel of the hands in the darkness. And now when he woke again and touched them the minute hand pointed to six, and the hour hand was a little way off twelve. He lifted the bedding to slide out; and, from the dark, Mary whispered, "Is it time?"

"It's thirty minutes after one," he whispered back.

She slid out on the other side like a conspirator to help him dress. She had pressed out his homespun coat after supper and washed and ironed his best shirt. The little Charley boys had stood around to watch him oil his boots. Fine people, the papers said, were going to attend the breaking ground of Mr. Clinton's Canal. It would be a ceremony with cannon and speech-making; all the northern country would turn out. Jerry had gone down to Samuel Stocking's in the afternoon to buy himself a hat—six shillings, a dark-grey felt, flat-crowned. It hung on the back of his chair where all the family could admire it.

Mr. Charley had drunk his beer and read out excerpts from the paper. In its last two numbers the *Columbian Gazette* had given considerable notice to the canal project, and people in Utica had begun to talk about the possible effect of a canal on the town, should such a canal ever be completed.

"Mr. Clinton is going to make a speech, and maybe Simeon DeWitt. A regular party, by the sound of it."

And Mrs. Charley had sniffed a little as she said, "If you was half a man you'd be there, too."

"Nobody asked me, my dear," said Mr. Charley calmly. "And anyway I never did like the noise of cannon. . . ."

Jerry felt a shiver as he put his shirt over his head.

"It's cold, Mary," he whispered. "You'd better get back to bed."

She was standing in her nightgown, barefooted, holding out his coat. "I'm not cold."

He held back his arms for the sleeves and she drew the coat onto his shoulders. He took his hat from the bedpost and put it on and looked a moment at the white blur of her face. In the window beyond, the stars were dim.

"Good-bye."

He kissed her and left her standing there. The ladder steps creaked under his weight. No sound came from Mr. Charley's room, but one of the boys was snoring in his sleep.

Outside the door, Jerry took a deep breath. The town was absolutely still. He began to run, keeping to the road, to deaden the thud of his boots.

Bourbon scrambled up as he opened the stable door. He blew a shuddering blast to open his nostrils. Jerry's hands trembled in buckling the bridle latch. As he led the horse into the yard, Hammil's back door opened and the fat contractor sneaked out.

"Shhh! Mabel's sleeping sound. How be you, Jerry?"

The wagon squeaked as he climbed over the wheel. Neither of them spoke until they had turned into Genesee Street.

The windows of Bagg's Hotel were dark. In the faint light the high brick walls were insubstantial. Out across the river, mist covered the alders, and the causeway seemed to float upon it. Somewhere underneath, a cow was floundering in swampy ground.

Caleb still whispered.

"It's going to be fine, praise glory!"

He was rubbing his hands together. Jerry shortened the left rein and turned the horse into Whitesboro Street.

"Unloosen him," cried Hammil. "We're late, Jerry. Let's see what he can do! By daggit, I'm notioned now to see him race!"

The sound of his voice set the cob flying. In a moment they had whirled by Jones's smithy, with its old hoof smell strong in the dewy air, and were heading for the open country just ahead.

"Do you feel kind of queer, Jerry?"

"Sort of."

"Me, too. It's starting things for us."

"Yes."

Jerry found it hard to speak. For a moment they were both absorbed in the hard dry thuds of Bourbon's slashing hoofs and the rattle of the spinning wheels.

"It's fifteen miles," said Hammil. "Do you reckon we've allowed time enough?"

"I guess so."

"I've got to get there. Sunrise is a queer time. More special if a man has got to travel to it. Me, I've got to stand alongside Esquire Forman—right in back of Mr. Clinton!"

Bourbon had laid himself down in his trot. The hind wheels of the wagon were weaving slightly on the road-crown. It seemed strange to Jerry that there were not more rigs on the road.

Their flying passage reëchoed from the Court House wall in Whitesboro; in a flash the village lay behind; and they were out again in farming land with the mist over the flat valley rolling uneasily above the fences.

All of a sudden, Hammil cheered up. He began to laugh over nothing at all, that Jerry could see.

"By daggit, Jerry, it's like going to a party. It makes me feel like a young lad sparking. . . ."

He leaned out to peer along the horse's side.

"Ain't that a couple of rigs up there, Jerry? I seen a tailboard just skittle round that bend."

Ahead of them as they took the bend in their turn, a couple of wagons were scudding through the duskiness. Bourbon pricked his ears and laid himself down. Foot by foot he gained. Hammil roared with laughter.

"It's the Bagg boys racing Dr. Sweet."

Jerry saw them now.

"Every time those rascals get a new horse off their pa they lay around to race the doctor. They've never beat him yet. Nor will they while he drives them chestnuts."

The Bagg boys were driving a pure-white stallion with a long, combed mane. Jerry saw them draw abreast, but the doctor was coolly holding his course just off the middle of the road and the boys lost nerve.

"He ain't put on real steam," said Hammil. "Jerry, do you dasst race the doctor?"

"Sure."

Jerry felt his heart beat time to Bourbon's hoofs.

"He gives a man fair road room, but not an inch extry," Hammil said. "Bourbon ain't a sprinter, you say, but what can he do in five miles?"

"Let's try it out!" cried Jerry.

"I've got money on it then," bellowed Hammil. "Bring me up in hearing distance."

Jerry did not speak to Bourbon. There was no need. Something had infected the cob that morning. He was really racing. No flash of blinding speed, but little by little he was adding to his stride. It was still dark. An angry dog barked at their passing. As Jerry let the reins creep in his fingers, he felt the dew in his face and a rising breath of wind.

He lifted the whip from the socket and just touched Bourbon's flank. And Bourbon understood. His head dropped a trifle. There was no visible addition to his effort, but the wheels began whining in their boxes.

"I didn't think a horse of his build could do this," shouted Hammil. "Boy! Did I do a deal on him?"

Bourbon's head and tail were joined by his back in a straight line. He began to rock a little to his stride. He went up and up; and the wind thrust against Jerry's teeth, and all at once he noticed that Hammil was holding on with his hands between his legs, standing in an effort to spring his weight from dead to live by the bend of his knees. The rig seemed stationary now, and the road a streaming ribbon, ash-grey in the dusk. Then the Bagg boys became aware of them—but it was too late. Jerry had stolen in on the off side and put Bourbon's nose against the doctor's tailboard. The white stallion broke stride and Jerry swung Bourbon across and caught the key position beside the doctor's nigh hind wheel, and the Bagg boys were shut out for good.

"That's driving, Jerry boy," howled Caleb. He was rocking with excitement, springing his knees where there was no call for it.

The little doctor heard him and looked back. He had been sitting back with an evident sense of his reputation being comfortably in his hands. Now Jerry saw him eye the new horse, eye the flared nostrils and the splendid forward thrust of the front hoofs, with their steady rhythm, as easy as flowing water.

"Free road, Doc!" Caleb bawled. "Free to the river bridge! First over for five dollars!"

The doctor nodded, faced his horses, and began to drive.

Almost at once he opened the road.

"That gives you five miles, Jerry—four and a half maybe. Can you do it?"

"Let's try," said Jerry again. He ate back an inch of reins with his hands and steadied Bourbon down. But even so the doctor had to whip it. "They've been racing quite a ways."

Bourbon chose the pace, settled himself, and went like a machine. He was behind, but he was setting the pace. The doctor didn't dare let him up again. And yet, between applications of the whip, he saw Bourbon's sharp ears steal up against his eye. He grinned in his small trimmed beard and drew away again.

Caleb laughed. Way back somewhere the Bagg boys with their white stallion were eating dust. Old Bagg probably paid a hundred dollars for that horseflesh.

The doctor was holding his side of the road. His hub-tips reached just to the middle. For two miles the seesawing of the chestnuts against the cob continued, but now their bursts carried them less and less to the front. And Jerry began to ease the reins once more.

There was a faint light behind them when Jerry made out the dew-wet back of a barn ahead.

"The bridge is round back. You make a slow turn," bawled Caleb.

Jerry nodded. He paid out leather and Bourbon took the wagon out from under them. Hammil sat back hard.

"Set down!" roared Jerry. He was running this race. At that instant, he wouldn't have minded Caleb's pitching over the wheel. Two hundred pounds of extra weight.

The doctor went to the whip, but too late. Bourbon had looked the nigh chestnut in the eye, and the horse faltered. Jerry's nigh wheel went way down to the ditch; Bourbon lunged left and right, and snapped the wagon back onto the crown, and they had the open road ahead. Behind them the doctor was hauling in. The bridge was a single track and he was fairly beaten. Jerry felt rather than heard the thunder of the planks; and he caught a glimpse of water. The doctor pulled up beside them and the wagons rocked to the panting of the horses. The little man leaned over, passing bills into Hammil's red paw.

"I'd been racing those Bagg boys, Caleb, but you were carrying double. What would you take for that horse?"

Hammil chuckled.

"Free road and no favors."

The doctor sighed and pulled out a handkerchief to wipe his spectacles.

"I don't blame you, Caleb. That means I've got to nose around for something faster. I can't have the second-fastest horse in Utica. Who's your driver?"

"Jerry Fowler, Doc. He's working with me on this canal contract."

"You're a good driver, young man," the doctor said with a crisp little bow. "Hammil couldn't have managed it."

Jerry flushed and grinned.

"I'll repeat it," said Hammil heartily. "Gospel truth. Did you see him nip the Bagg boys, Doc?"

"No."

Hammil succulently described the manœuvre and the doctor raised his pointed beard and broke out into peals of laughter.

"That's worth the five dollars, Caleb! Lord, they must have been surprised at being nosed out by a cob. They fancied that pacer."

They started on, the doctor leading the way at an easy trot. To their left the morning mist was lifting from the river. A heron broke from the bank and flopped ponderously aloft. As it topped the mist they saw the light from the yet invisible sun glinting on its crest.

"There's Rome." The doctor gestured with his whip. "We're in good time."

The village on their right was just stirring to daybreak. In a moment they were trotting along the southern edge of it. A moment more and they had come to James Street and turned left.

Wagons were crowding the short stretch of road, and Bourbon had to slow down.

"Come on," cried the doctor. "I'll clear for you, Caleb. You've got to be up front. Stick to my tail, Fowler."

In one last smart burst they swung to the outside, and, crowding the wagons over, made for the Arsenal, whose cream-colored brick walls were faintly washed with pink.

The sun was rising through the eastern notch of the valley—placid, large, and red.

"You tend to Bourbon, Jerry."

Caleb sprang out and trotted heavily for the little knot of men who stood together in the swale grass.

One of them was speaking, a man with collected eyes and an unconquerable squareness of shoulder. Jerry caught some of his words over the heads of the other listeners.

"Canal . . . as to the countries it will connect . . . as to the consequences it will produce . . . without a parallel in the history of mankind."

There was a disturbance in the gathering of onlookers. Heads turned angrily and people split apart and Jerry caught a glimpse of Caleb's gleaming black straw hat. Then the people closed behind it like water behind a boat, and Caleb's fat face, triumphant as the sun, solemnly composed itself behind the speaker's back.

Another speaker addressed them.

"We have assembled to commence the excavation of the Erie Canal. . . ."

He held a shovel in his hand. Now he passed it over to the first speaker; and once more Jerry was impressed by the man's square shoulders, and strong, still eyes.

"That's Clinton," said the doctor.

The man with the square shoulders was setting the point of the shovel in the sod. He stood back, leaving the shovel upright. An older man stepped from Hammil's side. "That's Judge Forman," said the doctor. He put his shoe upon the shovel's edge, he grasped the handle with a laborer's hand. As he paused a moment, looking eastward, Jerry caught another glimpse of Hammil, grinning, and still blowing, and wiping off the sweat with a gorgeous handkerchief in red and yellow.

The shadows of the men were born suddenly upon the grass. The outline was defined. They reached westward through the crowd, and the crowd's shadows stretched westward over them. The sun was up.

Judge Forman leaned upon the shovel with his heel, lifted it loaded with black muck. Water dribbled from the point. He tossed the load aside. It was lost in the grass.

From the Arsenal wall a cannon boomed. The muscles jerked in Bourbon's loins; his head sprang up. The doctor's pair no more than lifted their slim heads. A flock of crows flapped out of a meadow with raucous indignation. The Baggs' white pacing stallion reared, whirled, and set out for home. The mist rose and the heat of the sun struck on them all.

Standing on the wagon, Jerry looked out over the heads of the people, —perhaps a hundred men and women in their Sunday clothes,—and his hands made fists; for east and west, as far as he could see, the red marking stakes stood perpendicular upon their shadows. And the little knot of men grouped about the tiny shovel hole were shaking hands.

Interlude

"Just this one passway"

The Shanty

ADELPHUS BURNS left off cradling his wheat. The scythe rested upright on the cradles, the snathe curving its back like a snake. The wheat-piece fence enclosed eight acres; there was a morning's mowing left to do along the south boundary. The farmer stretched his stiff arms overhead, and then let go his muscles and looked down upon his farm—a double log house near him, and a new frame barn built into the hillside. The shorn meadows wore a fresh green; there was a rank grass smell in the still air; and all day he had found the ripe wheat pliable before the scythe edge.

His grown daughter came up behind him and her shadow fell back as she bent to bind the last armful of wheat. Adelphus Burns did not look around. His burned Yankee face was turned, with its grey eyes, to where two men were hammering in the last sheath of a bark roof on a building forty feet by twenty wide. The bark was lovely silver grey, but the new planks shone yellow in the evening sun.

Behind him his daughter bent up stiffly and eased her loins. At the new building, one of the men climbed down and went inside. Presently, through the roof hole, a smoke pipe was stuck up and the man remaining steadied it.

The farmer said, "They've got it finished."

"Yes."

She moved slowly to his side. Her height matched his to a hair. She had the same lean face, the same still passion in the eyes, but there was a strong repression in her mouth.

"Ralph's gone after the cows," said the farmer.

"Yes."

"Me, I'm going down to see it."

"I'll start supper afore milking."

"I wish somehow your ma had lived to see it."

She was silent.

"Right where them stakes run."

He picked up his cradle, but his left arm pointed. Both traced the triple line of red stakes westward through their fields—past the house, three at the yard fence, three beyond the barn, then on through the potato piece, the cornfield where the corn was rustling torrid sabre-leaves, past the hillside where the land leveled into the tamaracks.

"They've done it quick," said Adelphus Burns. "A week, maybe."

"Yes." Her lips compressed. "A week, last Monday."

She had brown hair, the color of crisp leaves. She stood straight, broad-shouldered as Adelphus; but under the linsey dress her bare legs showed a woman's ankles, and the curves of her hips and breast surged strongly.

"I'll miss them both—even the old one," said Adelphus, pushing back his hat. He let out his breath. "Well, after harvest I'll go into Fayette and look me up a gang. Then we'll have more company a spell. They say two years afore the water comes."

She said nothing, but walked at his side until the time came for her to branch off to the house.

Adelphus leaned his scythe against the wall of the new building and went inside. In the kitchen, he found Jerry and Self Rogers inspecting the box-iron stove.

"Hello, boys," Adelphus said. "It's all complete. You've done it fast."

He sat down on the cook's bunk and looked the shanty over. The stove was set halfway into the partition so that the heat could lend some warmth to the men's sleeping room. He could see into that through the open door, the three tiers of bunks, the long table and board benches, a single sash and an outside door.

"Yes," said Self Rogers, pulling out his thin moustache. "It's another one of these damned chicken boxes knocked together."

Adelphus grinned at Jerry, who grinned back.

"Self gets kind of disgusted sticking up these shanties," Jerry said. "You may have noticed."

"Thirteen of them," said Self. "Thirteen. It's got to be a habit with me. It comes natural now, like spitting out a chew." He cupped a full cheek in one hand.

"Thirteen?" Adelphus looked round. "That's how you laid it up so quick. 'Tain't a bad job, neither. Not that I aim to sleep into it. Not with my own bed over there. No, sir. Built for forty men? It ain't too bad for eighty dollars. Sound boarding. Maybe when I've dug my length of this-here ditch I'll seal it up inside and make a store to sell to boats with. I'll use a part of it for poultry maybe."

"Pullets!" ejaculated the carpenter. "Them bunks would make good nesting boxes!" He spat. "I signed a contract up with Hammil to build him nine more. Contract! Now I'm caught, legal. I never seen nothing like this contracting that everybody's doing. You've got one?"

"Yes," said Adelphus. "A B-contract for digging out a mile. There ain't no grubbing. I done all that when I come here ten years ago. I get twelve and a half cents the yard of dirt. It makes a twenty-five-hundred-dollar contract. I have good credit, so they give me a hundred dollars to buy tools with and I paid Hammil for this shack myself."

He turned to look through the open door at his clean fields.

"Do you suppose there will be heavy boating past this place?"

They didn't know.

Bending over his tool chest, Jerry wrapped his tools in greasy rags.

"It's been nice working here. We had some bad times back in the Rome swamps—no farms—no decent food, and rain all the while."

"You're moving on to-morrow?"

"Yes."

"Me and Dencey's going to miss you."

"It's been nice for us, ain't it, Self?"

"I ain't had the toothache, anyway," said Self. "A good thing, too. Out here a man can't get no ether-paint upon his cheek to drink the misery out. I'm caught here with a contract. Afore this damned canal a man just said he'd work. Now he signs a paper. A man is captured and held legal."

He bent to his tools. The farmer stared out. Beyond the door, a red stake showed its shadow like an hourglass upon the trodden sod.

"I settled here on Limestone crick ten years ago. It was quite a piece off the pike, but then I didn't want my fields broke in with movers, or my rail fence lifted all the while by teamsters prizing out their wagons in the wet, and disremembering to put them back. I picked this land to build a barn—there's nothing like a sidehill barn to winter beasts in. You could have knocked me double Injun when them surveyors come along and sighted their levels right against the barn. I've got to move it, even though I'm paid. It's going to save a little digging, though."

"When do you commence your digging?" Jerry asked.

"After harvest I'll hire a gang. Eighty cents a day I figure for a digger's pay."

"Well," said Self, strapping up his tool box, "I'm glad it's done. Caleb's due to fetch us out to-morrow."

"You boys have been going it quite a while."

"I ain't been home since July sixth," said Jerry.

Dencey

Jerry milked for Dencey. She had picked blueberries on Sunday; so she made him a blueberry pie to pay for his kindness. Now they had a clear evening, with the sun gone down beyond the red stakes, and a full moon rising. Self had gone to bed. The boys were fishing in the creek, and her father was sitting up alone reading out the paper, the *Christian Visitant*, that came once a month when they had time to ride four miles to Fayetteville to get it. There was a story that he fancied, "Little Annie's Sparrow" —a pretty story. She had read it two days ago.

Down by the shanty, she found Jerry in the moonlight sitting on the dewless grass. She sat beside him. There was a little wind that drew across the flat of the meadowland.

Jerry turned his head in the darkness.

"Do you mind if I come down and visit with you, Jerry?"

"No."

"I brought my crochet along."

"What are you making, Dencey?"

He saw that she had put on shoes and stockings—low-heeled black shoes, and stockings of white cotton.

Her head was bent.

"Oh, I'm crocheting."

"Can you see to do it in the dark?"

"Finely."

"It's a wonderful thing the way a woman can crochet out of light."

"A woman gets able to do it after a while."

He looked away. The hillside sloped against the sky.

"It's pretty down here to-night. The bugs are all after Pa, where the light is."

"Yes, I come down away from the buzzing of them," said Jerry. "Back home in Uniontown we don't have flies so thick."

"Is that where your girl is?"

Dencey spoke with a soft huskiness, a slurring of her words, as if a pulse were beating in her throat.

"No. That's where I was born. No. My girl's in Utica. We're wedded, Dencey."

Dencey's strong hands plied the needle.

"Is she pretty?"

"Yes," said Jerry. "She's pretty." He stopped.

"Don't fear to tell a girl." Dencey's voice was low.

"Yes," he said. "Yes."

"How tall is she?"

"Not tall."

"Not so big as me?"

"No. She's not small, neither."

"Not so big as me," repeated Dencey. "I'm big. I look most like a man." Her bitterness hushed them both.

Jerry stirred uneasily. She was giving him something to read, under the bitterness, and the kindness.

He saw her chin against the western luminance. The world was still. Crickets were fingering the harvest strings.

"I'm going to miss you, Jerry. It's been pleasurable here lately. More pleasurable than I can remember, but I guess you'll be anxious to get back home."

"Yes."

Dencey was still.

"Jerry, hear that bird? What do you name it?"

"It's a thrush."

"Thrush. That's a pretty name. Out here, we call it 'brown-bird.' "

"That's pretty, too, Dencey."

"I hear it nights this autumn time of year. Did you ever listen to it, Jerry? Didn't it make you have thoughts in yourself? A kind of pain?"

"No. Not pain."

"Plain people have got pain more easily, I guess."

Jerry looked down to the dark trees.

"What do you think about, Jerry?"

"I'm thinking I would get back home inside the month, maybe."

"And then?" Her voice was resigned now, muted, slow.

"Then I'm building a lock for Caleb out by Cossett's. Maybe."

"All alone again?"

"Maybe."

"I'm going to miss you, Jerry."

Silence: the tick of insects in the grass; the stars beyond the hill-back; the girl still, her face bent, her hands working.

Jerry sat there, with his thoughts on Mary, fingering grass. The night stirred him, and Dencey's voice in the sultry hush. He raised his shoulders. To-morrow he would be going on. He asked her, "Dencey?"

"Yes." Her hands were quiet and her face was turned. Between them in the little space each heard the other breathing.

"You ain't told me what your crochet was."

She laughed; close, hard laughter.

"Just a pretty. Just a private pretty."

Suddenly she bundled up the work in her hand and rose strongly to her feet.

"Nighttime for sleeping, Jerry."

He got up with her. They started for the one lighted window of the house. A cowbell clanked.

"What for?"

"Just for myself. A little dainty, Jerry. It gives a girl an ease to make her one."

"It's a wonder," Jerry said. "A crochet in the dark's a wonder to me."

"It's easy enough with practising, Jerry."

They came to the house. Dencey went to bed. By the light of her own candle she looked down at the hopeless snarl of white cotton thread.

Lock-site

They stood together in the swamp. A haze was low over the grass. October smells of woods fires somewhere made it heavy. The young engineer shook Jerry's hand.

"When you get started next week, I'll come along from time to time. But it seems to me you know about as much as I do in this line. I'm just beyond my prentice surveying days myself."

"I read those plans," said Jerry. "I've got them memorized."

"None of us know anything about locks or aqueducts. Till Canvass White gets back from England, I guess we'll have to work them out as we go along. All I can do is see the work is done honestly."

"You've got quite a lot of ground to cover, Mr. Roberts."

"I don't have to worry about your and Caleb's work anyway."

He looked down at the trodden grass. Split-wands marked off the space for the well. Ninety feet by fifteen. And east and west, ghostly in the haze, the red stakes marked the line.

"It seems funny, doesn't it? Digging a lock here all by itself. Setting up the gates and all. And no water possible for over a year. But we've got to practise."

"Is there much work back east?"

"I came straight out from Rome, Jerry. Three sections are half dug. It's awful slow-seeming work. I don't think us Yankees are much good at shoveling. The English and Irish and even the Dutch dig better. They don't wear themselves. But one man is using a horse scoop. That's going to work. And the grubbing goes fast. Getting out the roots. But every time I pass a section it seems so small a way, I feel afraid."

Jerry nodded.

"If we had machines to get rid of the stumps," said Roberts. "We can't afford to blast them. Powder's high. You never know anyway how it will work on a stump."

His face, bareheaded, touseled hair, looked boyish.

"I'd like to get back home," said Jerry.

Roberts gave a sympathetic smile.

"Yes. I don't wonder. Caleb told me about you. Just married, weren't you? And he's had to keep you way out here. He says you're the only man he has to trust."

Jerry flushed.

"If you like I'll go around and see your girl," said Roberts, "and let her know how you are."

"I'd like that."

"I'm coming back in two weeks' time."

"I'll be glad to see you."

Jerry looked out at the tall lines of grass. Here and there a dead cedar or a small tamarack poked up pathetically.

"I've got to stay to weigh the stone." He looked at the scales beside the space marked off for the lock. Already a tier of stone, grey, squarely cut in eighteen-inch blocks, was piled there like a wall. Behind them a shanty, like all the ones that he and Self had built, raised its new walls in the haze.

They walked round to the shed, where Robert's little sandy pony dozed under her saddle. Roberts loosened the bridle reins and led her out.

"She's getting to know the route as well as I do."

He mounted.

Something he saw in Jerry's face made him linger.

"Why don't you bring your wife out here?"

"I've been thinking of it. Maybe she could board at Melvilles."

"I'd do it."

The pony trotted off.

Dorothy Melville

Dorothy Melville, with her wispy hair knotted tight behind her homely face, greeted them cheerfully.

"I've milked early. Dumple didn't like it. But I wanted supper cooked for you two traveling men and time enough afterwards to get to fixings."

In the corner of the kitchen was the extra bed, the frame boards leaned against the Melvilles' own. Jerry took his seat at table and glanced round. This log-house kitchen always made him comfortable.

Like many large women, Dorothy had a leaning to frills. She had frills on the gingham curtains—bird's-eye blue—and ruffles tacked to the cupboard shelves. Her own bed had a quilt of brilliant patches and a spread in blue and white—a pattern from down south, she said, where she had come from; "Wind in the Valley" was its name. There was an old Welsh dresser to the right of the clay-and-stick fireplace, an open-hearth fireplace with the clay back, and the chimney resting on an over-jut, like a French hood. It had the biggest trammel Jerry had ever seen; and there were copper kettles, many of them, for copper shone like glass in Dorothy's strong hands. The two wheels stood in the corner with the spinning stools like terriers crouched down on guard. The bark-clad beams that braced the loft bristled like hedgehogs with iron hooks, and the orange pumpkin discs hung up for drying, the hams, the bunches of gathered herbs—coltsfoot, wintergreen and senna, camomile, euphorbia, pleurisy and blood roots—all made a spice in the air.

"Set you down, you two travelers, and eat strong, for I'm going to work you after."

Melville came back from stabling his horse and sat down at the table. The top was made of cherry planks, but rubbed and polished from long use to a mellow shine. The tea was simmering in the black lustre pot. The mush of green corn and milk in the yellow bowls was sweet. The long twist-loaf cut through like silver fluff.

"Do you reckon Mary will keep warm enough up there in winter?"

"Shucks-a-daisy, Bob! Most time she'll be down here with me. At nights we'll quilt her up like a March duckling. She'll nest herself."

Jerry's face warmed. Something was tickling his inside at Dorothy's words. "She'll nest herself." It made a picture.

"Look at him, Bob. Poor boy, it's hard a-waiting, ain't it?"

Jerry nodded. These were like his own people, and to-night it seemed he loved them more.

Dorothy emptied her bowl and leaned against her chair-back. She looked fondly at her husband's long nose. It always quirked her lips to see it —ever since she could remember.

"Hard a-waiting! Honey, don't I know? Hard for you, Jerry-boy. But harder for a girl. It tickles a girl to have a man await her, but when she is awaiting him, it stretches things inside of her. Especially me, that had my *Yes* all ready long afore poor Bob had even any idea."

"You don't know half of it!" Melville pushed back his bowl, and fished out his tobacco. His eyes were bright. "I was plumb terrified to ask a pretty girl."

"Oh, lordy! A pretty girl!"

"Still are." He nodded, tamping down his pipe. "I see with my own eye, Jerry. Can you see it, too?" His large mouth was agrin.

Jerry, looking, could see. For a trace of flutter in her eyelids and a flush in her hard, tanned cheeks still made Dorothy young. She laughed uneasily, within herself.

"To think I got that bed out! Years and years we've had it; ain't we, Bob? I never thought to see it used, when we first come here, with the land so wild. There was a bobcat lingered in the buttonwood to catch our piglets."

Melville nodded, balancing the hot coal on his pipe.

"He come at night. I placed the moon behind the tree and got him."

"That 'stead's a plain thing, but the cords are easy. And this noon I sorted out the feathering of the bed. It used to be my Uncle Henry's when he lived in Williamsport. It'll be warm for Mary—a nest for her and maybe for a little girl, some day. I'd like to live and see that."

Something passed between the two that Jerry saw was not for him.

They took the bed upstairs and placed it in the loft. Dorothy held the candle to superintend. It was clean, and the smell of herbs rose sweetly. The candle flame was pooled in four glass panes set in the gable end.

"You've made a window for her," Jerry said.

Melville smiled. Dorothy said, "There was a chink. It was as easy to enlarge as stuff it."

They went down again and sat before the fire. One of the sticks burned bluely.

"Won't you night it with us?"

"No, thanks," said Jerry. Speech came hard to him.

Melville nodded.

"It's been a long time."

"Since July sixth."

Dorothy said, "A long time."

Outside the moon was shining dimly over the marsh mist. Jerry took the new-made track for the new-made shanty.

Mortar

"My name's Lewis, Hayward Lewis. Pleased to know you, Fowler. I'm masoning this lock. I come around to have a see at this-here stone."

"That's all that's come."

"There's time enough to get the rest afore the lock is dug and timber laid. I wanted to see was Cossett cutting it even. It's good cutting. I didn't know the old bezabor could so fashion stone."

"It's clean," said Jerry.

"Don't take any course under nine inches. There's a weight of water to stand off. But stone has got to be heavier than that to handle frost. Measure it, mister. Measure it every doubtful course, will you?"

"I've got my eye on it."

"You don't have to take what's thin. Do you know what the boring brought up?"

"Hard pan at eighteen feet."

Lewis, a grey man, bent-backed, sat down on some of the new timbers.

"They haven't bored for the wood foundation, then. I hope you don't strike nothing underneath. These are flaw-free-looking beams."

He folded his hands upon a knee.

"I'm troubled over mortar. English plaster costs too high. And quick-lime mortar ain't designed for water. It won't hard itself except when dry, and there'll be leaching in this swamp."

"Ain't they trying something new in Utica?"

The mason nodded.

"I've heard tell Canvass White's got hold of something back in New Hartford. They're trying it out in a cistern there. But he ain't no mason. I won't trust it till I've got my own trowel into it. And anyway I don't believe we'll get it in time for this-here lock."

He leaned back, rocking himself.

"I don't know much about canals; but laying stone is something I can do. There ain't anything to beat finishing a job of laid stone. It's a thing a man can see and put his hand against and think it's going to last a time. Most of any job, it depends on the commencement. You lay me square foundations, boy, and I'll lay you up two walls that won't come down like Jericho's."

He stared away across the swamp. A hawk, swinging low, pounced and came up with something furry. He lit on a dead cedar to open up his catch.

"A water rat, I reckon."

"I reckon so," said Jerry.

Lewis got to his feet.

"I must mosey. A man gets curious thinking about his job. I thought I'd come and see it, Fowler. Pleased to know you."

They shook hands.

The Teamster

The oxcart had creaked off an hour before, and Melville had waved from the woods. A new course of stone was beginning. Jerry was adding up the figures in his tally book. He had his luncheon frying on the stove. Now, he closed the book and brought his food into the main room to eat.

As he finished, he heard a sound he had not heard for many days. Pennsylvania Bells. He set down his teacup.

Melville had said at parting, "Caleb's due to-day. Maybe you'll be visiting a girl in our house after dark."

He sat there in the beam the sunlight threw across the room. It was a clear day on the marsh; a northwest wind was combing out the marsh grass, drawing whispers from it as it dried, bending it down in waves of olive grey. In the sky the clouds were tumbling like blown bees. He could feel the wind against the shanty wall, a steady pressure, making the flies uneasy.

He put his dishes in the kitchen and went to the door. He passed through it, walking slowly down to the piled stone, and sat himself there. Now the wind hummed a din of grasses in his ears, but he could hear the bells more plainly. And after a while he saw the first team turn out of the cedar scrub into the marsh. He saw the teamster's head and shoulders, and his small brown hat with the goose feather in its band, and his cracking whip. And last, lumbering and pitching, the high white hood rolled forth on its wide wheels.

The leaders were matched blacks; but one had a white blaze. He heard the clink of their heavy trace chains.

"Morning," said the teamster. "You're Jerry Fowler, I should say."

"Good morning. Yes."

"My name is Roger Hunter. I've brought a wagonload of edibles for Caleb's men."

"There's solid ground around that shanty."

"Good. I'll draw up alongside the kitchen end."

He spoke to his horses. "Hup! Come on, Nate, Joe." The team took up the load, the wagon lifted to the slight rise of ground, the five-inch tires squeezed out water from the sod and left damp snails' tracks.

"Come on inside," invited Jerry. "Have a cup of tea."

"No, thanks. I had my breakfast back a ways. I'll just blanket up the team." He was reaching through the tail flaps and now he slung a pack of oilcloth blankets on the ground. Jerry helped him spread the stiff grey cloths over the horses' backs.

"Have a stogy?" asked the teamster. He had opened up his tool chest and taken forth a small cedarwood box.

"No, thanks."

Selecting a seven-inch stogy, the teamster came into the kitchen to find a light. Then they sat down in the bunk room, and he filled the sunbeam with blue coils.

The teamster's cheeks were drawn thin, the bones showed in his face, and the weather in his eyes. As he puffed the cigar, his lean-fingered hands kept plying the supple lash of the long whip that lay coiled before him on the table. In the sunlight it smelled strong of tar, and it gleamed with a semi-lustrous oiliness like an actual snake.

"This is the hardest place I've had to haul through," he said. "Ox-carts always bite a road."

"It's pretty bad," said Jerry. "Have you seen Caleb?"

"He ought to be pretty close behind me. He stopped a while at the farm back there." Hunter glanced at Jerry's eager face. "He dropped a girl there."

"Did he?"

"Yes, he did," said Hunter, grinning. "A right pretty girl. She's hair the color of my sorrel wheeler."

He said it with the manner of a man who could judge women. Jerry flushed. A fly bungled against the sash.

"Where do you come from, Hunter?"

"Rochester."

"Where is that? I never heard of that town."

"That's likely. It's a brand-new town. I settled there and have been drawing wheat. It's on the Genesee."

"I've heard of Genesee wheat. A valley for it. That's where Wadsworth farms are, ain't it?"

"I draw his wheat. But he's mostly going in for sheep. He's practising with merino lines. Like the Friends out by Crooked Lake—Jerusalem. I own six wagons now and I've been doing pretty well. But this big ditch by all accounts is going to spoil my trade."

"I guess that's right."

"I've thought I might go into boating. I'll look for a likely partner to do building of them, and myself to manage hauling."

He looked straight out through the door as if he saw his laden boats.

"With wagoning a man most generally loses money hauling west. But when this ditch is dug there's going to be a land opened up beyond a natural dimension—and it's going to have just this one passway, as I see it. There'll be more traffic westward then than there is eastward now."

He stretched his legs.

"I wonder when that blasted cook will get along to empty out my wagon?"

"Cook?"

"Yes. Your diggers weren't only a little piece behind me. Aaron's brass! They're coming now."

They had not heard the two big bolster wagons bumping in from Orville.

But now voices rose by the lock-site, and a pompous man was standing in the doorway.

"My name is Edwin Brown."

"Are you the cook?" demanded Hunter.

"I have engaged my services to Mr. Hammil."

"Well, engage them for me and unload that wagon out there."

Edwin Brown drew up his thin shoulders.

"Sir?"

"Yes!" Hunter reached for his whip and began idly to manipulate the lash. "Where I come from, Brown, we don't use these on horses. We use them there to scarify a man, mostly cooks."

"Yes, sir," said Edwin Brown. "I'll get my helper. Tom! Tom!"

He went out through the door, his voice yodeling over the marsh. They saw him single out a fuddled-looking old fellow, completely whiskered, with mismated eyes. A moment after, he was standing behind them in the kitchen, shouting out directions while the helper groaned and wrestled with the barrels.

Hunter grinned. "Here come your diggers," he said.

A big, stoop-shouldered fellow stood in the doorway, fumbling a hat in his hands.

"My name's Plute Sowersby, mister. There's forty of us here."

He was thrust aside by a diminutive fellow, incredibly long-armed, with popping blue eyes and a drawn, frog-like mouth.

"Introduce me, Plute."

"This here's the gang-boss. He's my partner, Mr. Fowler. Name of Turbe."

The little man grinned amiably at Jerry, but Hunter started.

"Not Cosmo Turbe, the rough-and-tumbler?"

Turbe's frog's mouth stretched fatuously. He sidled up to Plute and cocked his ear.

"Identical," said the big man. "Celebrated in Kentucky, on the 'Hio river, and anywhere along the Zane Trace."

"What are you doing back here?" asked Hunter.

"He's aiming after a little money. Him and me. And actual liquor. He wants to find a man worth marking."

Jerry stared. He had heard tall stories of the rough-and-tumble fighters in the territories.

"Mark?" he asked.

For answer, Cosmo Turbe sprang up on the table just in front of Jerry's hands. His boot heels flashed silver in the sun. He dropped himself flat on his back, his heels just over the marks the nails had left.

The nails had dug a pattern in the new wood, a star traversed by a jagged line.

"A star," explained Plute, "and a bar of lightnin'. For a marker. They match." He pointed to the nails. Cosmo Turbe swung off the table and sat quietly on a bench.

Just then a wagon clattered to the door. Jerry saw Bourbon's head and restive forefeet. He ran outside.

The fat contractor jumped over the wheel, and the whole wagon rocked.

"Jerry—boy! How be you? Gol! I thought I'd never get here."

He shook hands heartily.

"We're ready to commence. We've got to hustle, boy. Martin's grubbers will be working in from east in no time."

But Jerry did not look at him, for on the seat sat Mary. They did not speak; but he had an impression of the wind against their faces.

Caleb thumped him on the back.

"Get out of here. You ain't no use to me. Take Bourbon back to Melvilles. You're fired."

Jerry turned slowly round.

Caleb was grinning, tipping winks at Cosmo Turbe and Hunter, and they were grinning back.

"Show up to-morrow morning and maybe I'll hire you on for foreman at ten dollars to the week. Get out. I can't have my lock all fluttered up with married people."

Two

MARY

1

"Being wishful makes a woman look for signs"

"Co' BOSS! Co' boss!"

Mary tried to make her voice ring nasally like Melville's. When he called, it was amusing to see Dumple and the heifer turn obediently from their browse. But her clear voice never fooled them. They would look up to see if they had been seen, and then placidly pursue their way until she overtook them and turned them for the barn.

"Co' boss!"

She braced herself against the wind and felt the thrust of it on her breast. Moulded tight across her thighs, her heavy woolen skirt fluttered behind her. Loose ends of her hair were snarled. Her cheeks were brilliant and her eyes shone as deep blue as the open spaces in the clouds. She had to turn her cheek to the wind to call, "Co' boss!"

For a month the wind had leaned upon the land. In the morning, Melville would stand in the kitchen doorway, his long nose pointed westward, reading the clouds for snow.

"It's strange," he would say. "It smells of snow, but it don't come. Maybe it's going to be an open winter. That's bad for hauling."

"Why is it bad?" Mary wanted to know.

"The snow would fill up all the sink holes. We could haul on runners twice the stone and timber we are hauling now."

He would go out and she would hear the clink of Dumple's bell in the barn, comfortably muffled by the heavy walls. She would help Dorothy with the cookery for breakfast.

The board was very cheap, for, with Melville hauling, Mary helped Dorothy to mind the farm. They had threshed together, laying the boards behind the cow stall and beating out sheaf after sheaf with flails. Dorothy handled a flail like a man, as if she took pleasure in it.

Except for Sundays, Jerry spent all his time at the lock. Some days Mary and Dorothy had walked out along the corduroy to see it. It always seemed like going down under water when they entered the marsh grass. The farm would be shut off, the trees; they would walk in the dry rustling alley with the wind unfelt above their heads. Birds, frightened by their passing, would let loose their perches and toss up in the wind and be snatched. The wet muck had a crust of frost, with splinter-like crystals interwoven that held their feet, but crumpled under cart wheels.

At the lock-site they would look into the black rectangular hole sinking steadily to the men's shoveling. Jerry would leave off his work on the mitre-cills. He would show them the cills, triangular frames of wood, braced with V's, and explain how the gates would fit. Mary listened to his voice without hearing the words.

The men looked small and sweat-soaked and muck-booted digging. She heard their names while she was there, but they seldom spoke in her presence. Only the cook at the shanty was talkative. He had a grievance.

"Just my luck to be settled here in this damned swale."

Sometimes, when he saw them coming, he would hurry out to his clothesline to bring in his underwear. He told Mary that he put his pay every week into the literature lottery. He had never held a lucky ticket. But some day he would win the prize—ten thousand dollars; and would he get out of here promptly? Words, he said, were feeble things.

Mary felt sorry for the aged helper with his mismated eyes that took her in in turn.

"Me," he said, "I'm a poor man. I put my money in the bank. I've got maybe fifty dollars saved up there. But Edwin's going to get ten thousand."

"Don't heed him, Mrs. Fowler. He's twirly, but he don't mean harm."

Later the gang moved on half a mile to the second lock-site and only a handful remained with Jerry to set in the cribbing—huge, heavy timbers resting on the hard pan. . . .

Mary came out on a rise of ground from which she looked for miles across the land. The wind enveloped her and drank her breath. Her body was young, poised there; it bent pliably with a curve like the deep-rooted grass. She knew the spot from many searches; of all the places she had ever been, in this she seemed most alone.

Yet she had no loneliness like that she suffered from in Utica, where, when Jerry had gone, the Charley family seemed to throng around her, and close out all her senses with their ceaseless bickers. Instead, the wind encompassed her, uniting her mind and body, and she could know herself.

She smiled again as she leaned into the wind, and called, "Co' boss!"

Dumple and the red heifer were standing side by side regarding her from beyond a patch of alders. They had their rumps to the northwest and their tails were pressed tight against their bags.

Mary laughed down at their undisturbed white faces. She walked down the slope and turned them homeward.

But as she walked the wind still filled her with its living. She felt it pushing at her back, unraveling her hair and netting it over her lips. It made her laugh.

Overhead, a line of geese cut like a knife blade through the tumbling clouds.

Mary hitched the stool further forward till her shoulder rested under the boat-like curve of Dumple's belly and her forehead leaned against the soft flank. She could feel a distant muscle working to the cow's chewing of her cud. The teats, which were old, long, and scarred from briers and sharp marsh grass, filled her cold hands and, as the milk came, warmed them.

The log walls had no windows; chinks left open under the mow served for ventilation and the open door for light. But now it was dark outside; only a green sheen lingered westward under the lines of clouds. Mary could see, past the ratty tail of the old cow, the waving marsh grass beyond the yard fence.

As night came, the wind blew fitfully, leaving long intervals of quiet when the sound of milking was articulate. Then the heifer stirred uneasily, for her bag grew heavy from the suggestive sound. She eased herself, and dropped her muzzle.

Dorothy swung through the door, her heavy boots thumping on the planks. The horse nickered gently.

"How are you, dearie? Tired of milking?"

"Oh no."

Dorothy paused a moment, her homely face down-bent. Her eyes quietly searched Mary's flushed face, turned sidewise towards her against the cow's flank. The hair across the level forehead was curled with damp.

"It's nice and warm in here," said Dorothy. "It is, even with the door held open."

Mary smiled. "You mustn't work at this if it gets you tired, dearie."

"It's resting."

"You were a long time finding them."

"I took my time."

"Does walking in the wind bother you?"

"No," said Mary. "Why?"

"It does some people."

Dorothy looked ill at ease. She bulked like a man as she leaned against the post.

"It doesn't me, any more, Dorothy. I like it."

"I've got to like it myself except in winter. In March, when the spring seems long a-coming."

"I feel as if it let me loose."

Dorothy nodded. "I'll feed Squirrel."

She left the lantern while she tended the horse. Between Mary's knees the milk was mounting the side of the pail. She could see it white with a head of froth; its warm odor wrapped her face. The bag had lost its life and the teats their spring in her hands. Dumple was breathing out long sighs.

As Dorothy returned from feeding and watering the horse, Mary kicked back her stool and set the pail down by her feet.

"She milked well to-night, Dorothy."

"She's milked close to a pint better since you had her."

Dorothy reached down for the pail with her strong hand.

"Three quarters full. I'll make extra into a curd cheese and we'll have pie for Jerry, eh?"

Mary smiled.

"It bothers me the last two days, Dorothy."

"What bothers you?"

"Lifting the pail."

"You ain't felt very likely, have you, dearie?"

"Mornings only. Sometimes I feel dizzy in my head. This morning I was sick, Dorothy."

"You was?"

"Yes."

She lifted her face to Dorothy's eyes and saw an unexpected tenderness there.

"It's queer, isn't it, Dorothy?"

"Maybe not queer, dearie."

The strong mouth worked as if the older woman found speech hard to hold. Suddenly Mary smiled.

"I think I'm going to have a baby, Dorothy."

Then Dorothy laughed. "Lord bless you, dearie! I've known it four weeks past."

"You have?"

Dorothy nodded. "I've seen it in your eyes, Mary. There's a way to tell."

"How do you know?"

"I guess being wishful makes a woman look for signs. Oh, I'm glad."

Suddenly turning away, she stamped about the stable, making ready for night. She held the door open for Mary and then closed it. Inside the dark stable there was an instant's silence, then the heifer moaned softly.

The two women crossed the yard together. They did not speak as they got their slight supper by the hearth, but Dorothy set out a larger pewter full of milk for Mary. Mary smiled.

"I'm not sure yet."

"You've not told Jerry?"

"No. Not yet."

"When will you?"

"Not until I'm positive."

"Me and Robert have been talking of it these past days, Mary. I hope you ain't going to mind that. He's most as excited as me."

She was waxing the tops of the apple preserves she had made that day. Indian apples, she called them, though they had come with the white man.

"Why don't you get to spinning? Spinning's good for a body, Mary."

"What do you want done?"

"Can you weave?"

"Yes."

"There's flax. Me, I'm spinning woolen. Why don't you spin you loose-thread and made a coverlet for it? There's time enough to fashion necessaries."

Mary smiled. "All right. But you must let us pay for flax."

Dorothy got out the wheel. "Time enough to argue, too."

She placed the wheel beside the hearth and the stool handy to the treadle. She brought flax in a basket; and she stood for a while as Mary seated herself and sorted the things in readiness.

"I'll finish up my crocks," said Dorothy, "and then I'll join you with the big one."

The sharp, high whirr broke out. Dorothy kept her face to her task until she had finished it. But when she rose at last, Mary saw that her eyes were wet.

"Do you feel lonesome up there when Jerry's not here, dearie?"

"Oh no."

"We could move you down. It wouldn't be no trouble. There's room on the wall end. You could have a curtain for your privates."

"I don't feel lonely. I like being alone up there. You've made it nice for me."

Dorothy bent down to take her boots off. She thrust her feet in moccasins and padded heavily to the corner for her wheel. She set it down on the other side of the hearth, so that the fire flowed over the floor between them. Presently the deep hum joined the little whirr. A sound like music came to life, drawing the log walls closer. Dorothy sat bolt upright on the stool, her foot beating the treadle as if she were a sergeant beating time. For a long while neither spoke.

When Dorothy at last found words, her voice was strong with the deep tones of her wheel.

"It's the feeling that gets into a woman's body makes the wheel a comfort in a house. Seems as though it eased her body. Seems as though it gave her time to remember all the things she's forgot."

Mary nodded. Dorothy saw the sweet submissive bend of her neck. Her hands and her foot were flying, but her body swayed gently and her eyes were still. In the quiet of the cabin the thread was like life in her hands.

"I remember," said Dorothy, still in her deep voice. "I mind me how I was a little girl. My father had a farm. I had four brothers and three sisters. There was a creek branch by the house. We had a room with pictures in it, set in frames; I mind my mother setting there and spinning. There was a picture of a church that had a high white steeple."

"Were you a little girl then?"

"I was a long-legged coltish thing, I recollect. More like a boy. Lissa, and Prue, and Lavvy were more girl-like, like my mother. I was the oldest-born. I ran like a wild colt in the fields. It seemed I never could get onto spinning and I never learned to weave. It didn't seem I ever would take comfort spinning. I even played at boy with other girls."

"Didn't any boys come after you?"

"No. Never one. I wasn't made for boys to play with. I could throw a boy in wrestling. It didn't seem I ever would have a man. I didn't want it. Not till I saw Robert. It's a queer thing, Mary, what stirs a woman so."

Mary was quiet.

"I didn't care that he was poor. I didn't mind what Pa told me of it. Not that he didn't like Robert. But it didn't make no difference to me. It never has. But then I wanted a girl baby in the house. It didn't seem I hankered after boys. But we never had one."

The solemn deep tones of her wheel rose unfaltering.
"Where did you meet Jerry, Mary?"
"In Albany, Dorothy."
"Did you just meet?"
"Yes. I'd just landed."
"He's done well."
"Yes, he's done well."
"He'll make you a fine place some day, I've no doubt."
"I'd like a little place some day that was my own."
"He'll make you one, I have no doubt. Do you think he wants a girl-child or a boy-child?"
"I don't know."
"Which do you?"
"It doesn't seem to matter to me."
"I'd think he'd want a boy-child. Most men do—young men, that is."
"He's never said. Sometimes it seems he doesn't think of nothing excepting his work only."
"This canal."
"Yes."
"It's a great thing. It's taking a long time. I think of seeing boats maybe. Esquire Forman has been telling Robert maybe he'll lay out a town where Cossett's is. He owns that land."
"Does he?"
"Yes. We'd be right close to town then. Think of it! A village close. I wonder what he'd name it?"
"Has he said?"
"He told Robert he might call such a village Syracuse. A strange name. A book-name he said it was."
"I never heard of it."
"Me neither."
The wheels spun steadily. The two women's faces remained calm, as if their spirits had absorbed the comfort of the ordered birth of thread.
"Where will you be planning for your child to come, Mary?"
"I ain't thought, Dorothy."
"December, January, February, March," the deep wheel hummed and the thread in Mary's plastic fingers grew. "April, May, June," Dorothy's voice was hushed; "July and August. An August baby. They'll have finished nigh to four locks, then. Out westward."
"Maybe I'll stay here. I think Jerry wouldn't want hampering with me and a baby."
Dorothy's voice trembled.
"That would make us glad. I'd take care of you, dearie. I'd do everything a body could. I'd labor for you, all I could."
"I'd like having it here—where now I've got a friend."
"Oh, I'd be so glad, Mary."
"How would Robert?"
"Robert too."
"Jerry's working so hard," Mary said. "Maybe he'd feel easier if I was here."

"They say Dr. Earl in Onondaga is well liked. He'd come, I have no doubt."

"Does he come this far?"

"Oh yes. He's a nice man—a youngish man. He's gentle, they do say. Women like a younger man, I've heard. Me, I don't know. I don't know anything. But I'll make comfort for you, Mary."

"I'll be all right, I guess. I'm healthy."

"It doesn't frighten you?"

"It doesn't seem to frighten me. To think of it displaces things. As though everything I'd knowed was past."

Dorothy nodded.

"You'd best tell Jerry."

"I've thought of it. Is it bad not to?"

"I don't know, Mary. Some say and some say not. Mostly some say not. I believe, though, it is a woman's feelings make the difference."

"I feel as though—I feel that something's past of both of us sometimes. We've got no right."

"Perhaps it's so."

"And then I feel I'm debted so to Jerry that it must be right to ease him."

"He'd understand."

"He thinks about his working. When he visits, then I feel he's finding something. Sometimes he don't seem happy when he comes, and when he goes he seems as though he'd relished something. Then he's tender to me. I try to see out of his eyes, but I don't understand."

"A man builds on it. But with us it's different."

"Sometimes I'm afraid he'll go off tired of me."

"That he couldn't, dearie. Don't you fear. I mark him when he comes. His face is burning after hunger. He loves you."

"You mustn't ever tell. He took me with him because I had no place to go. It may be he was sorry for me. I was a redemptioner, Dorothy."

"Poor dearie. Did he buy your papers?"

"Yes."

"And brought you with him?"

"Yes."

Dorothy was not shocked.

"He gave me back my papers and he married me. A minister married us. Jerry fashioned out this ring himself."

She turned her wrist to show the horseshoe nail.

"He'd used up all the money that he'd saved to buy a place, and bought my papers."

Dorothy's face was glowing.

"He wouldn't let me work to earn him back his money. He has a pride of it. But I worked in Utica and saved some money. I did washing. Thirty dollars I have saved from it. But I wouldn't dare to pay it to him. I thought I'd save it till we had a place and then I'd buy with it. As if I had brought money to my wedden."

"Poor dearie, don't you worry over notions."

"Maybe he'll like my having him his child. That would bring him something."

"Do you love him mightily?"

"Yes." Mary's voice was lost in the wheel.

Dorothy was silent.

"I love him so that if he should forget me I'd creep off from him to leave him free."

"Don't talk so," Dorothy said sharply. "Those are notions some women get at your time. You mustn't think of those things. They are bad. Like bearing out of wedlock. Nurse-wives tell you that."

Mary sighed and let her hands fall.

"I've spun and spun. I'm tired now."

Dorothy rose awkwardly, went over to Mary as she left her stool, and put her arms about her.

"You must rest you, dearie. I'll tend you. And I'll try not to pester you, though, because I am so glad of it."

She bent down to kiss Mary. The hair, curling over the forehead, was still damp. She felt the body in her arms shake suddenly with sobs.

"Don't be afraid, Mary. Don't be afraid. I'm tending of you."

2

"There isn't any smell of men"

ONCE a week the teamster, Roger Hunter, hauled in from Manlius, his great Pennsylvania wagon rolling in the snow on silent wheels, and the bells of his team crystal-clear with frost. His hands and face kept their summer brown, showing no winter change. He did not seem to feel the cold; his hand that cracked the fifteen-foot whip was unmittened.

He spent one night at Melvilles, coming back from the lock with Jerry. Melville was away, but Mary and Dorothy cooked them a special supper. Cheese pie, and a haunch of venison that Melville had been given by a woodsman, potatoes roasted with the meat, and winter squash. Dorothy brought out pumpkin flip to drink and the two men lingered, talking while the women spun.

"Is there any snow in Utica?" asked Dorothy.

Hunter said, "No. I wish there was. I wish it would do one thing or the other. Every haul I make I am uneasy."

His face was still as he listened to the wind.

"A southward change would bring snow or rain. It's a bad thing, getting caught with a heavy wagon by a snowstorm. Four years ago I undertook a trip in December and got snowed up halfway out of Jerusalem. I had to walk back with the horses. You couldn't move that wagon. It stayed where it was till April."

"Jerusalem?"

"Yes, on Crooked Lake. It's where the Universal Friends have settled. That she-preacher, Jemima Wilkinson, brought them there. I was a young man then and fell in love with her." He grinned and sipped his flip. "Most men did. She was a strange woman, way past middle years, and there was I, who'd been by no means good, in love with her. All the men was."

"I've heard tell of her," said Dorothy. "Wasn't there a law-court case a while ago?"

"Yes. She claimed all the land in Jerusalem was hers. All that her people had done was hers. She was a thrifty woman. And she had queer ideas. Half the time she dressed for a man. She did not hold with swearing, war, or weddens—the three curses of women she used to call them. But just the same there was plenty of children round about. It's said she died when she was eighteen years old and her body it got repossessed of by a Jesus. She was a pretty girl in her time and men took fancies to her. She did well. It's a queer thing." He shook his head. "But she did preach beautifully, too. After she'd won her case in court she preached on the blessings of the faithful."

"How did you come to win free of her?" Jerry asked curiously.

"I got interested in her niece. She called the girl her niece. A black-haired girl, Eliza. And right away Jemima put me out and married the girl to one of the old men there."

He shook his head again.

"A queer thing, too. I went back for the girl, but she acted as if she hadn't ever seen me."

Dorothy began to hum under her breath to the humming of her wheel. The men's voices dropped lower. From time to time, Mary turned her eyes on Jerry. He was leaning his elbows on the table, his jaw set in his hands, his dark eyes bright. His hair was long on his neck, in need of cutting. He was saying, "The grubbers have come in sight of Number One. Martin's gang."

"They've done considerable work west of Rome," said Melville. "Sixteen miles. Three miles completed. It's a strange thing to see. The banks all shaped and the towpath waiting for the horses."

"They're making quicker progress, Roberts says. Martin's gang have got a plough—thin-edged and set back like a coulter—cutting the roots. They use a double of oxen. And they've got a contraption now that hauls down trees—a winch upon two wheels. They hitch a rope halfway up the trunk and chock the wheels and crank it down. One man cranks down a ten-inch tree."

Hunter had put the whip on a peg beside the hearth. His eye was on it now.

"It marks the end of six-team hauling. Jerry, I've been thinking. I'm going out to see Colonel Rochester when hauling stops. If he will put up money, I've been wondering would you come in with me? To build my boats. We could be partners in a business."

The hands of the women continued their absorption in the spinning, but their ears were alert.

Jerry looked into the fire. He spoke slowly. "I'd thought about it, too. I'd like to, maybe. But I've got yet a year to work for Caleb."

Hunter nodded. "Caleb wants you to stay with him. He's told me so."

"It ain't Caleb," Jerry said. "I'd like to see this shebang finished."

"There's time enough. Boating won't commence till water's flowing. It will be some time when it gets west to Rochester."

"What kind of a place is Rochester?" demanded Dorothy.

"It's just a village, ma'am. But it's on the finest water power in the westward country. There's four mills there already and there's room for fifty. It's going to be a city some day."

Dorothy's lips compressed. She looked at Mary.

Jerry said, "I've planned to settle in a city when I've saved up money."

Hunter laughed.

"When you get out to us, we'll have the city started."

Jerry nodded seriously.

"I want money. I want to have a house as fine as any man's."

"There'll be money in boating."

"I've got one hundred dollars in the bank, in Utica."

The men were silent.

"There's time enough," said Dorothy. "There's other things can happen to a man."

She got up suddenly and brought a jar of pickled gooseberries. The men went on with their talk.

Then Hunter stretched himself.

"I haven't had so nice an evening for three years." He smiled at Mary. "Some day I hope to see you living out in Rochester, Mrs. Fowler. If I can persuade your husband."

Mary returned the smile. Dorothy was silent. In a moment he had said good-night. Jerry went out to see him to his bed made in the barn loft.

"You ain't told Jerry yet," said Dorothy. "Isn't it time you should?"

Mary seemed preoccupied as she replaced the small wheel in the corner.

"There's no doubt to you now, is there?"

"No," said Mary.

"He should know, I think, before he goes on making plans."

Mary said, "I'll tell him soon."

She went to bed in the still warmth of the loft. She left her candle burning on the stool. Her heart was tremulous to-night. She could trace Jerry's movement entering the house; his boots crunching through the light, frosty snow, the opening of the door, its closing causing a flicker in the candle flame, his low voice and Dorothy's as they banked the fire together, and their soft good-nights. He came quietly upstairs.

She watched his head come through the opening, the candle pooling in his eyes. Beyond, on the windowpanes, frost was drawing fern leaves.

"It's getting cold," he whispered.

She watched him take his stand beside the chair and undress swiftly. He always stripped as if it were a business to do, like work, quickly and thoroughly. He tossed the clean nightshirt over his head, and stood a moment, luxuriating.

In the past months his dark, pointed face had gained a confidence—it had changed mightily from that of the self-conscious boy who bought her papers, even the eager boy who wedded her. She wondered if her own change showed to him.

He was whispering, "It smells sweet here. There isn't any smell of men. It's funny how men living together smell different from a man that lives with a woman. A queer thing."

His eyes brightened suddenly; and in the instant he stooped to blow the candle out.

Mary always felt the birth of darkness in the loft in a way that she had never felt it before. She knew that wherever time might take her with her husband, darkness would be a different thing. Here it was warm with the fire and sweet with herbs; it came upon her like a downy quilt —comforting, protective, rich in quiet. Here it was full of happiness, where her being had first been opened to her. She had awakened in this darkness from a sleep that all her life had lain like a mist upon her senses.

Jerry was a part of it. The stealth of his opening the blankets; the stir of feathers under her back; the rush of air past her face bearing her own scent; his movement stretching out beside her and searching for the channel underneath her shoulders; and the slow settling down of blankets, like soft hands, on her breast, her knees, her thighs, her ankles, round her neck, until she was completely wrapped and his face came into the hollow on her shoulder.

Outside, the frost was settling on the shingle roof; in the marsh the powdery afternoon snow was fluffed with crystals and the feet of moving shrews made ladder tracks. The new moon was going down, and from it, on their velvet cloth, the facets of the stars caught pricks of light. The strange green northern lights would breathe.

Jerry said, "Do you like Hunter?"

She heard her body saying, "Yes. He's got an honest face." But her heart was dwelling deep inside of her, and her real hearing was turned inward.

"It would be better, beginning in a new town, Mary. A man like me would go much farther, I should think."

"I wouldn't know."

"It seems more likely."

"Maybe."

"Mary, you seem a more unspoken girl all the more I see you. Do you love me?"

"Yes."

"Really?"

"Yes, Jerry."

"Sometimes, lately, it seems there's something on your mind. Is there something?"

"Something, Jerry?"

Now the stillness.

"What is it, Mary?"

"Yes. I'll tell you, soon."

"You aren't unhappy?"

"No."

She wondered why he couldn't see, or feel? There must be difference for a hand to trace, she felt so changed.

He leaned on his elbow to kiss her. His face lingered. She felt his breath steal down her face and throat and rest upon her breast.

"Sometimes when I kiss you, Mary, your mouth tastes of milk. That's a queer thing, isn't it?"

He stayed half raised, thinking this queer thought. And Mary felt herself sink down in humbleness, and then her body surged and filled and her hands and her breasts and her legs were charged with life. She held her breath.

But he was saying, "Lewis is setting the cap tier to-morrow. One side's done and I have got the gates built. Caleb's bringing up the casted wastegates in the morning."

She felt his breathing close against her side.

He tried to laugh.

"I've got this thing in my head, I guess. I can't get it out. If I couldn't come down here to you, every week, I don't know what would come of me."

She said nothing.

"You remind me of different things. Of late, I keep remembering the barley field where we got wedded. Do you mind, he was ploughing it for barley? And that little boy fetching us trout? Some way, the minister looked troubled to me."

His voice was whispering.

"When I go back in the morning the work seems smaller to me. Lifting is an easy thing. And the westward end don't seem so great a way to reach."

His hands were trembling. Her outside self became aware of his quest and she knew that she was empowered to fulfill it. But her being was still inward. This was the darkness; and she could not bear to lift it.

The rattle of wheels woke the farmhouse early the next morning. Jerry slid out of bed. The loft had the chill night smell of a sleeping house. Beyond the sash, Mary saw a faint greyness beginning in the east.

Jerry stood still, listening to the sharp slap of the horse's hoofs.

"That's Bourbon," he said suddenly. "Caleb's come with the castings." He reached for his clothes.

"You stay abed, Mary. He'll want to get right out to the lock. Now he's got up here at last, he'll be impatient to get out there. I could have used them castings six days back."

As he threw his shirt over his head, the wagon rattled into the yard and stopped. There was a complete silence. Then they heard the wheels squeaking slightly as the wagon jerked to the deep breathing of the horse.

"He's wondering if I'm here," said Jerry.

Downstairs Dorothy was getting up. At the first sound of her boots across the puncheons a mighty knocking shook the door. Dorothy crossed to the window. Laughter shook her voice.

"Just a minute, Mr. Hammil, while I decent myself a little. Robert's out."

"Is Jerry Fowler inside there?" bawled the contractor's voice.

"Yes. He's getting up."

"Tell him to hurry up. Slug-a-bedding this way, and a whole lock to be completed! It's terrible cold out here, Mrs. Melville. Can't you let me in? I won't look nowhere."

"Just a minute, Mr. Hammil. I'll just hike on a petticoat." She opened the door. "There, come in. You do look cold. I'll boil you up some tea."

"Can't wait, thank you." He blew out a tremendous breath. "That cold has got me breathing like a bellows, Mrs. Melville. Just point me at your fire and I'll have it blazing up in no time."

"I'll do it."

"Jerry up?"

"Yes. I hear him moving."

Caleb sat down before the hearth and raked open the bedded coals. Mrs. Melville dropped a stick upon them.

"By daggit! When a man like me gets cold there's a lot of him to feel it." Jerry came back to the bed.

"I'm going. He's left Bourbon unblanketed out there. Why don't you come out to the lock this afternoon if it grows warmer? You've not seen it now in quite some time."

"I will, maybe."

She was glad to be left. She felt miserable again this morning. The cold grey dawns seemed always clutching at her. She lay still, heard Caleb's greeting, boisterous, full of simulated anger, the door closing in the face of Dorothy's protests, Caleb saying, in what he took to be a whisper, "Well, if I was you, and you was me, you'd have to wait a danged sight longer, boy."

Inside Dorothy chuckled.

"The old he-sheep! He considers that he's lusty."

The wagon sped away.

When she went down a little later, Mary met Hunter coming from the barn.

His hands and face were ruddy from the icy washing, his leather clothes smelled strong of hay.

"Good morning, Mrs. Fowler."

"Good morning, Mr. Hunter. It's a cold morning."

"It's snappy."

She saw his knowing eyes upon her face drop swiftly. In spite of her sickness she colored. He looked away, and let her go in peace; but when she came into the kitchen again, his eyes greeted her with half a smile.

He did not talk much, but, on leaving, his thanks touched the two women. They watched him striding off beside his chunky horses, his boot heels raising clods from the road. The bells twinkled in the sunlight and the notes were clear.

Dorothy said, "He noticed you this morning. He asked me. I told him."

"Oh," said Mary.

"Shucks-a-daisy, dearie. You couldn't hide nothing in that line from that man. He'd notice things a boy like Jerry'd miss. He must have had his own high times."

"He doesn't look like that."

"Why should he? He's an honest man, and he's handsome. There's plenty of girls would visit with him by a fence, I reckon. Withouten even asking. Why shouldn't he?"

Mary said nothing; and she and Dorothy began their morning tasks.

The sun shone bright all morning; all the swamp was glittering white. A few pinched clouds were hanging in the piercing blue of the sky. After noon, Mary said that she was going to walk out to the lock.

"Do you feel equal to it, dearie?"

Dorothy's homely face was bent solicitously.

"It's cold, you know. And I could go out with you, if you're bound to do it."

Mary laughed.

"I'm bound. And I feel fine now."

"Dress warm."

Dorothy superintended dressing. She stuffed a pair of Melville's boots with swamp grass dried before the fire and pulled on over Mary's feet an extra pair of woolen socks. She had forced her to dress in one of Jerry's heaviest red suits of underwear, both of them giggling at the figure Mary made.

"Good land!" cried Dorothy. "You're image to a boy! You've got no business getting big. It's scarcely decent."

Mary laughed.

"I expect it will look queer."

But now she was bundled up from the top of her head to her small toes nesting in the grass in Melville's boots. She had a sheepskin coat over all and a heavy flannel skirt of dark red-brown, and a deep-blue woolen shawl upon her head, pinned close beneath her chin.

Her face was pink. The shadows under her eyes brought out their depth of grey.

"She's going to tell Jerry," Dorothy said to herself. "It's troubling her."

She watched Mary along the road to the beginning of the corduroy. The stuffed boots made her shuffle and the erect figure moved very slowly. Her short shadow, flickering along the ruts, was vivid blue.

Mary took her time. She thought that if she arrived when they were nearly finished at the lock, Jerry would let her wait and come back with her.

The sun had peeled the snow from long stretches of the corduroy, leaving the scarred logs bare. Where the snow lingered, she could make out Bourbon's tracks, blurred by the slight noon thawing. She looked about her as she walked. The cold lacked fierceness and the air was clean to breathe. From time to time she stopped to view her shadow.

In half an hour she came into view of the shanty. A thin smoke from the stovepipe vanished just above the roof, as if in the cold air it could no longer live. A few of the men had been living on there of late, and yet the shanty wore a look of utter desolation. Then she saw that no more dish towels hung on the wash-line, and that the kitchen window had been boarded over. That meant one thing: to-night the rest of the men were going to move on down to Number Two, and Jerry would come home with her.

Two week-day nights together, she would have him. Suddenly she felt the cold. She shivered, and for an instant she felt ill. Then she turned to the lock. She could see it now; there were two walls of grey stone rising side by side. The mason was working at one end of the near wall. Caleb knelt upon the other shouting down directions. She heard Jerry's voice answering. Then the odd little man, whose name was Cosmo Turbe, bawled loudly for helpers. In a moment half a dozen men were lifting up a great square frame of planks. They had a pulley on a tripod to let it slowly down, and Cosmo's sleepy helper was gripping the rope in monstrous red chapped hands. Their figures were all tense, their voices brittle with excitement.

Mary stayed where she was to watch. Left and right she saw a line cut through the marsh grass, alders rooted up and dragged aside—a broad avenue, like the commencement work up on a turnpike. But the red marking stakes stood just where they had been. As far as she could see, the ground lay open, torn and uneven, black with frost, ready for the bite of shovels. It was like a wound from a gigantic ragged knife, and the marsh was white and deathly. But the men's voices, their red sweaty faces, dripped with life. . . .

"There," said Lewis, cutting the mortar cannily along the outside corner of the capstone. "You can dog that gate in now."

His pointed trowel tinkled where he dropped it. He fished in his pockets for tobacco and slowly stuffed a pipeful.

"That mortar's all set solid. She'll hold frost. I'd like to have the water cement, but even so them walls will not fall down like Jericho's."

Jerry, walking the board floor of the pit, moved to the southwest corner. On either side the light-grey walls of stone rose twice his height. The edges fitted true, each stone had settled neatly; a monument could be no smoother.

One of the men shouted.

"Here comes Roberts! There's a feller with him."

"Never mind them," said Caleb. "Put that gate in. Heave her up." He signaled with one hand. "Way up. Easy now. A little more." The gate shut out the sunlight over Jerry's head. The end beams rubbed off splinters on the stone. There was a squeak of wood on stone. Then the lower edge tilted down. He put up his hands to guide it. "Lower, easy," Caleb cried. The iron socket in the base of the hingepost slowly swung to meet the upright quoin point. Suddenly it clanged and the rope in Plute's red hands went slack.

Hammil was on the gate in one squat spring.

"Hold her!" he roared. "I've got to get that anchor strap screwed on."

He passed a three-inch iron strap over the top of the hinge-post and rammed the threaded ends through the sockets in the tie-straps grouted into the stone wall. His fat fingers twirled the heavy nuts.

"Where in hell's the wrench?"

Cosmo came running with it. Caleb heaved the long handle till the nuts bit solid.

"Ease off."

Plute sighed and let the rope go. The timbers groaned as the gate settled.

Jerry stood for a moment in the pit. All four gates were open, and he looked eastward. The mounting courses of stone gave meaning to the floor he had laid in so many days ago. They showed the step down at the head that made the lock's descent, their wings stretched wide as if they waited for the water. He turned to west. Again there were wings, pointing the full width of the canal, showing the track of the grubbers.

It was his work that he had done with his own hands. Sunk in the sprawling marshland, its exactitude was beautiful. He stood quite still, till Caleb cried, "Climb out, Jerry! Here's the Chief Engineer."

Jerry climbed the ladder, slowly. Roberts greeted him. Standing beside

Roberts was an elderly man, with a wise, strong face. He was shaking Caleb's hand, but his eyes were staring into the lock-well. Jerry saw them noting everything.

"Roberts tells me it's solid work, Hammil. He ought to know. But I can see from here the work is right. It's fine, square workmanship."

Caleb beamed.

"It's honest, every inch. I can vouch for it. I know the man that built it under me is right."

He gestured.

Mr. Wright looked up at Jerry, smiled, held out his hand.

"It's good work, Fowler. Roberts has told me about you." He turned back to Caleb. "The commissioners aren't quite so eager to come inspecting at this time of year. But I'm glad I came. We've got three completed sections finished west of Rome, but this is the first stone work. The whole canal will rest on the stone and timber work."

Caleb swelled with pride as Mr. Wright added, "I hope it all will look as well as this does."

A little later, the men turned away. Caleb was beaming.

"Let's try the gates!"

Cosmo Turbe yelled and ran across the beams, his nailed heels leaving marks at every step. They manned the gates together, eight men, six wondering how they worked while Caleb explained to them.

"She's at high level for a boat from Rome." His stout voice bellowed. "There comes the mules. Stand back, you dumb bezabor. Do you want to get kicked by a hinny mule?" A tall man ducked aside, so vivid was the sudden picture. Plute guffawed, and clapped his hand upon his mouth. "Whoa!" shouted Hammil, red cheeks all a-sweat. "Easy on that boat there. Do you want to knock her bow in? Here she comes. Right in. Sixty feet of her, loaded to draw three feet with Devereux whiskey bound for O-hio. Now we close the upper gates. You work that one, Cosmo. The water's at high level. Open up the sluice-leaves in the lower." They ran in two groups down along the lock walls. Only the mason continued sitting on his stone. He had laid up walls that wouldn't come down like Jericho's. Hammil cranked the sluice-leaf open on his side. "The water's running out. You can hear the overflow from east commence upon the tumble bay. The boat's going down. See her! She's eight foot, ten foot, lower than she was. There she is at bottom level. Push round that beam, there, Cosmo!" The lower gates swung open. "Git, you hinny! Git, you mules! There she's easing out. See her. She's bound for Buffalo. Maybe the boater passes me a quart drawed from a keg in fair exchange for water."

With staring eyes the men followed his pointing finger along the black muck track the grubbers left. They saw the marsh, and the shadow of a cloud slowly moving.

Suddenly Caleb laughed and tossed his hands apart.

"By gravy, boys! We've finished Number One!"

Jerry looked up, and he became aware of Mary, standing off a little way, the slight wind riffling the edge of her shawl, a still figure against the snow. . . .

Caleb said, "I'm closing up this shanty, now. Will you two ride along with me?"

The men had moved on down to Number Two.

Lewis had gone with his mule and his helper. The marsh was empty but for the three of them and Bourbon standing at the shanty door. The shadows had drawn out. The evening cold was stealing in.

"I'd like to walk," said Mary. "Thank you, Mr. Hammil."

She looked at Jerry. Jerry nodded.

"All right, then. I'm going back to Utica, Jerry. I'll deposit for you, shall I?"

"Yes."

"All right. I've sold this shanty as she stands to the man that's got the digging contracts. A good sell. I didn't lose a penny. Jerry, you'll go down to Cossett's lock and finish up the boarding. Maybe Lewis can lay stone for two weeks more if the frost don't bear down too heavy. I'll come up in two weeks if the roads are passable."

He poked the latchstring in.

"Good-bye, you both."

He climbed over the wheel. Bourbon set himself to start. Jerry suddenly broke his silence.

"Don't leave Bourbon stand outside unblanketed."

Caleb looked down. He seemed to estimate the tone. His fat face was set seriously. Then he grinned.

"I'm not a complete fool."

He waved his hand and rattled off.

Mary touched Jerry's arm.

"What's the matter, Jerry?"

"There's no matter."

"I thought the way you said that, that you and Caleb might have quarreled."

"No," he said. His face stared sombrely at his toes in the snow. He walked slowly to the lock and took a last look at it. "I'm glad you wanted to walk. I wouldn't want to ride with him just now."

Mary was concerned.

"But why?"

"Oh, he acts as if he'd built the lock himself. It's funny, Mary. When he hired me and showed me that-there plan, I thought he knew a lot. He don't. Self knows more than him. It's me that did the work."

"But he put up the money. He's responsible."

"Just the same, they think he did it."

Mary stole a sidewise glance.

"They know your work. Caleb said so. Mr. Roberts must have said so to Mr. Wright, from what Mr. Wright said. I'd judge so anyway."

He looked down.

"Anyway it's good work, Mary. Lewis does fine work in his masonry. The gates fit tight. Look how easy they handle."

He swung one of them.

"You could do it. Try against it."

Smiling, Mary tried. It was surprising how easily the gate swung.

"I built them," Jerry said. "Just from plans."

His eyes were moody. He did not seem to want to leave his work.

After a while, though, Mary said, "I take so long to walk in all these bundlings. Hadn't we better start?"

He looked up quickly at her.

"Yes. Let's go. It's cold." He started out beside her. But as they came to the bend in the corduroy, he turned for a last look at the lock.

"Eight weeks we've been there. Maybe I'll never take another look at it. But it's a good job."

Mary looked at his face, turned in profile. She could see a little muscle quivering behind his jaw bone. It seemed so silly to have an affection for a thing of stone that you yourself would never handle. He looked unkempt, but she loved him so.

Beyond him, the sun was setting—a flat reddish disc, without warmth, giving no color to the sky, but touching the clouds with bronze. The horizon rose no higher than his shoulders, the marshland lay flat beneath his hand. Down by Number Two she saw a light gleam in the shanty window. Far away under the sun was Cossett's tavern. It showed no light, only a line of smoke to northward of the sun. Everywhere between, the skeleton grass lifted broken leaves.

He loomed before her, larger and larger as she saw these things, and the dim, half-felt sorrow that stilled his face also made it beautiful. He let out a steamy breath, and turned to her.

"Why, Mary, what's the matter? What are you crying for?"

She sniffled up her sob.

"It's nothing, Jerry."

He put his arm across her shoulders. She could hardly feel it through the thickness of her wraps, but the weight of it lay on her.

"What is it? I know something's been troubling you."

"I want to tell you, but I can't." She tried to laugh. "It's funny, ain't it, Jerry?"

"Tell me what you were thinking of, looking out over there."

"It looked so lonesome, Jerry."

"It does look lonely," he said. "I never liked it just as land."

He shivered.

"I'd hate to be that lock-tender."

"Esquire Forman plans a town here, Dorothy says."

"A town?" He laughed, his laughter making clouds. "I do believe a lot will happen, but not that."

He stared westward.

"A town 'twixt here and Cossett's!" His arm tightened round her shoulders. "Mary, it makes me glad to be wedded to you, you coming along with me this way. It wasn't just the lonesomeness that made you cry?"

"I'm not crying now."

"No. But what was it?"

"Jerry, why don't we get land now that you've saved up money? We've got enough to start. I'll work hard. I'm strong. I'll make it comfortable. I want to work along with you." Her voice grew lower; she spoke hurriedly, her eyes fixed straight ahead. "Now you're just bringing me along, just as if I was a fancy—"

She bit her lip.

Jerry's arm almost fell away. He was examining her with wide eyes.

"Why, Mary. What made you think of that?" His face grew set and his eyes cold. "You know I never thought of no such thing."

"I don't care. It makes me feel that way."

"Can't you forget those papers?"

"No. I never can. Jerry, I feel just like a satchel property."

"I'm sorry," he said quietly.

She raised her eyes, and suddenly the tears broke out.

"I didn't mean it, Jerry. Honestly. I'll go anywhere. I don't feel so—only it seems you are way off from me. Back there in Utica."

"It was just as bad for me," he said grimly. "Maybe worse." He thought of Dencey.

"Oh, but you were working, doing things. But it don't matter, and I'm lucky now to be along and live with Dorothy. She's been so good."

He kept walking as if he marched, steadily, left, right, left, right, as if there were no corduroy to slip on.

"I'm happy, Jerry, I'm happy. Honest. You mustn't mind what I said. There's time enough. Only I do get lonesome."

Her contrition was as breathless as her burst of discontent. She eyed him as she walked. And seeing him thinking, her eyes suddenly grew shy.

Before he turned she had stopped, but he stepped back swiftly to her, took her shoulders in his hands, and shook her gently. He was grinning.

"Tell me just what's wrong, Mary. Don't put it off."

"I'm going to have a baby, Jerry."

She opened the throat of his coat with her hands and hid her face inside. Her shoulders heaved. She felt him stiffening.

"I didn't know," he said. "I just knew something, but I never thought." His hands kept fumbling with her shoulders. "How long have you known it, Mary?"

She said, her voice muffled almost to extinction, "Almost a month, now."

"You might have told me sooner."

"I didn't want to tell you till you had the lock done. You was so excited." He patted her.

"You weren't scared to tell me?"

She could not speak for sobbing, but he felt her face jerk up and down.

"For God's sake, why?"

"It seems as though I'm just a drag hitched to you. Always costing money."

"We can afford it. I guess there ain't a better way to spend it. A doctor, I've heard tell, will cost you round about two dollars. We can get a woman in to help you. I wouldn't care if it was twice as much. Why, Mary, soon I'll be earning more. You ain't scared for yourself?"

Her sobs were easing. She shook her head.

"Not much. A little sometimes. Way out here."

With a bent forefinger he fished for her chin.

"Think of it." He laughed a little. "Three of us. Right here."

She smiled. Her eyes were wet and drops were stiffening the lashes. He bent his head and kissed her.

"It's time we hurried. You mustn't take a risk of cold."

He held her close to his side.

She asked him, "Jerry, would it be all right for me to stay at Dorothy's to have it? It seems homey, somehow."

"Surely. Let's see, when will it?" He counted.

"August, maybe," said Mary.

He counted again.

"By then I will be working out in Jordan Lock. I'll come back when your time is due. You mustn't be scared, Mary."

She put her hand in his. They walked silent through the silence. The twilight came in, pale green and wavery. The night rose up in the east, a steely curtain cut for stars. They heard the frost rustling the grass.

Jerry kept his glance ahead, and Mary looked up at his face. She traced his ear under the fringe of hair, the set of his jaw, until her eyes ached. He must be thinking of the lock to build in Jordan, she thought. And then she thought with pride that it would be a fine lock. She felt very proud, now, of his work. Caleb had praised it. Mr. Wright. They spoke to him as to a man of equal station. It made her humble to feel proud, and she did not mind his thinking of his work. But when she asked him what he thought about he answered promptly.

"I was just revolving names. I'd thought of Richard for a name. Or Francis. I like Francis, don't you, Mary?"

She lifted her face.

A mischievous quirk bent her lips.

"Yes, but suppose it is a girl."

"I never thought!"

He felt something inside his arm that made him pause. They were just on the verge of the farm. They saw the lighted window and Dorothy's face anxiously peering forth.

"For such an unspoken girl it seems to me you've said a lot."

3

"As if they minded cold"

WHEN the winter came at last, it settled an icy grip upon the farm. Christmas Eve began with thawing; the roofs dripped rhythmically all the morning; but as the day wore on, the dripping slowed. When Melville went out at dusk to measure the icicles hanging from the kitchen eaves, he found one four feet long.

"Four feet of snow," he reported. "It don't seem possible."

"Four feet deep upon the ground?" Mary was incredulous.

The end of Melville's long nose bent humorously.

"I guess the snow don't fall like that in England."

"No," she said, and Jerry remembered a winter when the snow was six feet deep in Uniontown and the ground-floor windows had up-slanting tunnels dug down to them to bring in light. Then Melville told tall stories of the drifts. A minister had been entrapped in Pompey meetinghouse one Sunday morning by a blizzard. The congregation never could dig in to him, or he dig out. They found him frozen stiff next spring,—it was so cold,—but he had preached a sermon for them. The whole sermon was frozen stiff. They brought the words out one by one into the warm air and listened to them thawing. A fearful tale. Only the deacon was an unread man, and mixed the words.

"Shush, shush, you Robert," Dorothy said. "Such tales before a girl!"

He looked embarrassed, with a sidelong glance at Mary. Jerry hushed. Mary smiled at her spinning. She knew that time was showing in her, but it was comforting to be so guarded.

One week later the snow began in earnest. The sun had lost itself at noon, and all the day long the wind veered slowly through the north to eastward. At sunset time, without a warning, it snapped back again to west and the snow started.

After dark she listened to it, working crisply on the shingles overhead, the wind a steady drone like hiving bees; and the cold stole into the house and the log walls shrank and groaned. When morning came, a stillness hushed the world. Melville's stockinged feet thumped loud as guns when he got up and opened up the door.

"She's snowed all right," she heard him telling Dorothy. "My Lord! I'll bet two feet has fallen."

His voice was loud, as if he took pride in this elemental demonstration. "Dry snow," he said. "It's drifting powerful."

"You'll have to dig us out a passage to the barn," said Dorothy. "Mary hadn't ought to flounder out in snowshoes. Early-morning sweats are bad at her time."

Jerry woke up with a startling catch of breath, and sprang from bed. "It's surely snowed for fair."

He looked round the loft.

"Funny," he said, "how snow will creep in places you think chinked."

He laughed and bent to gather a handful from the floor. His face was bright. Laughing again, he showed it to her in his fist. Suddenly he jerked his nightshirt off and rubbed himself all over till his skin was red. He kept on laughing through his chattering teeth.

Melville bawled up through the opening.

"No more carpenteering now for you, Jerry, for a spell."

"It don't look so."

"Even hauling won't be possible for a piece."

"I've got my flooring ready hauled for Number Two," said Jerry. "That's all I care about."

That day they did not even attempt to break the roads. They kept a trench shoveled to the barn and spent their time in splitting wood. Mary watched them through the window, red-faced, their clothes all fresh with color against the sky and snow, their axes rising and swooping, their voices talking between the stroke-sounds.

At dusk the snow began again.

That evening she started to weave her coverlet on a frame that Dorothy had stored somewhere. The two women discussed the pattern. Neither knew a design for so small a spread and so they made it up. A star set in the middle with little stars for borders, red and white. Dorothy had dyed the red. She made the tint in peachwood-brew.

From time to time the men would walk across and look on, making knowing suggestions. Mary and Dorothy would accept these silently and then go on with their own plans.

Every day, no matter how bright the morning was, it seemed to Mary that the snow began again at dusk. At first it fascinated her, the endless gentle downward drift of flakes, or the wild skirling westward winds that smothered everything with the very excess of their breath and fired icy flakes like birdshot from the racing clouds. There was a comfort in feeling herself shut in, herself and Dorothy completing the household duties early and spending their long hours inventing new flavors for their simple food or indulging in their fill of spinning, weaving, and sewing.

She milked at evening when the barn was warm and cosy, the air invigorating with ammonia. The heifer calved and made a fuss about her calf, and they had a week of fun in teaching the awkward thing to dip its muzzle in a pail.

There was excitement, too, in seeing Melville take the ox-sled out to break the roads, the white curving horns dimly shining through the flakes as the oxen bent their necks and buffeted the drift with crooked knees. He had a contract to keep the road open; for one contractor was still digging in the marsh. It had been found that in the wettest stretch the men made better progress when the muck was frozen—even though they had to shovel out the snow each morning.

Their food was brought in once a week on three horse-sleds. Each sled could carry little, for the perishables had to be wadded thick with straw.

Dorothy would look out when she heard jingling of bells along the Orville road. Her homely face worked.

"From December into March, me and Robert never saw a person but our own two selves, and now they come past close to every week."

Strange faces had no interest for Mary. Jerry was off again, now that the crust was formed, buying and hauling timber to the other lock-sites. She liked to sit at her sewing or weaving, close to the hearth, watching the big day-log disintegrate and calling Dorothy when the time had come to pry another foot of it into the coals. She could see the flakes through the window, drifting down, and her eyes traced patterns in their fall that brought strange meanings to her.

Icicles sprouted on the eaves and broke away according to the fluctuations of the weather.

One still clear night it got so cold that Mary woke half numb. It seemed to her for a long time that only the child inside of her kept her alive. She thought she could feel it taking on the forms of life, breathing, turning over to rest its side from its long dormance. The cold was all in her legs and arms and face; her chest felt shriveled with it. She knew she should get up and find additional warmth, and she tried to steel herself to movement. But her muscles remained unwilled. She thought, "I'll die, surely." Downstairs it was as still as death. The Melvilles had each other for their warmth. She wondered where Jerry might be, where he was that minute, if he thought of her or if he slept. Her thoughts swam into one another, confusing her, and she only knew she was cold.

Outside the cabin the brittle whisper of the snow put life into the stillness. It had a sinister low note. Without looking at the window, she knew that there was moonlight.

Then a queer, sharp, living voice came to her ears. At first she thought a dog was barking, but it was querulous, half human. The sound of it frightened her, and she had a sense at once of the snow pushing against her, smothering her like a blanket so large that she could find no edge. The voice was like the voice of snow. She lay still, shivering.

Next morning, she described it to Melville.

"Foxes," he said. "It's been a poor season for small animals. They must be in the marshes hunting mice."

Dorothy nodded.

"I heard them last night, too. As if they minded cold."

"We used to hear wolves sometimes when we first came here," said Melville, pouring cream into the churn—they planned on butter for a treat. "I knowed they couldn't harm us, but I was always fearful when I heard them. They would come down over the lake, perhaps from Canady. A pack. You'd hear them miles away and heading for you. Then they would go by some place far off."

"I saw one once," said Dorothy. "A fearsome sight. It used to be easy to have children in on time for dark. They were afraid of wolves. But now the youngest ones will come in when they're minded. Wolves don't 'fraid them any more."

Mary shivered. Foxes, she said, were bad enough for her.

"You wouldn't have minded," Dorothy said. "Only that baby in you frightened you."

"I was so cold. But after I had heard them he moved once. Real hard. I wasn't feared of them then. I got up and put on socks and a shirt of Jerry's. I was real warm after."

But the cabin had grown smaller since that night. She began to move with a sense of care, deliberately measuring off the little spaces between the hearth and the table, the table and the dresser, the wheels and the side of the Melvilles' bed. Outside, the barn seemed farther from the house and the snow walls to the path much higher; but, oddly, the sky had limited the land—the world looked small.

Yet in the evening Mary would listen to the singing kettle or the slow drip of the roast into its pan or the steady beat of the dasher in the churn, and the sight of Dorothy's strong, manlike hands would comfort her. Then she would sing softly, conscious of the harmony these things made with her own feeling.

"Shining Dagger" pleased her. She would hum it at first, but gradually the words would steal into the antique melody:—

> "It is no use to ask my mother;
> She too intends to set us free.
> So go, my dear, and court some other,
> And I no more will trouble thee."

The walls seemed to stand more sturdily against the snow. The fire would burn more evenly. The kettle would lull its note more hollowly in its round belly.

"Oh, I can climb the tallest tree, love,
And I can reach the highest nest,
And I can pluck the sweetest rose, love,
But not the heart that I love best."

Jerry would seem not so far away; and the winter a shorter space. The warm air of the cabin would grow brighter with the candlelight.

Sometimes, shyly, Melville would ask her for some other tune. He liked the old tunes, and it pleased Mary to be asked. It reminded her of her girlhood, when she sang for her mother. She would smile at him and Dorothy; their homely faces became kind in her eyes. Perhaps she would sing them "Daily Growing" or "Warranty Deed," or a newer song, like "Highland Mary," or one of Tom Moore's, or a little thing she had once heard and remembered for its tune:—

"Love, lady, love!
There's always joy in loving,
But sigh not when you find
That man is fond of roving.
For when the summer bee
Takes wing through beauty's bower,
He knows not which to choose
Among the many flowers."

March changed. There was a thaw, when all the snow seemed sinking on the marsh and the taller heads of grass showed their broken backs. But then the snow came again. The wind was boisterous, the cabin shook to its pummeling. At dusk the barn would be full of chaff-dust and the lantern flame would quiver. The beasts stirred uneasily. Their eyes kept swinging. Now and then the heifer would lift her muzzle and bawl, and the sound of her voice would be deafening in the narrow space. Mary felt her head swim, and her knees quiver on the overburdened pail.

The days grew longer. They ate supper before twilight; but the snow lay as heavily against the walls, the top fresh as before from the night's downdrifting; and the rotting that was going on underneath it was concealed.

Mary felt a desperation growing in her. They had not heard from Jerry for two months. At times, at night, she was afraid. She would begin to wonder whom he might be staying with. She made pictures of him to herself meeting imaginary girls. The fitfulness of the wind would shake her, and while she slept she dreamed.

But little by little, as the time drew on, her being became calmer. As the snow went each day, she grew more aware of the possession of her that the child was taking. She united little events with their significance to herself. Spring, she felt, would not stir her as it was beginning already to stir the Melvilles; for time became centred in her consciousness with the end of summer.

4

"Some men work hard; they haven't understanding"

BUT the spring came with a suddenness that captured Mary after all. One dawn she woke with a sense of freshness in the loft. There was no sound of wind, but the wind was blowing. She could feel it on her face, a warm draft from the window; the curtains were lifting gently; and on the roof was a sound she had forgotten.

Steady, gentle, it seemed to draw her being out. She felt herself relaxing on the bed, as if her brain let go one by one of all her nerves, and they were soothed and sleepy. She could feel it in the air. The snow had turned to rain. . . .

All the world was enveloped in the greyness—no sunset showed, and there would be no moon, no stars. She was alone. Behind her in the black gulf of the barn door she heard one of the oxen snuffle softly.

Then her senses jerked. . . .

He was coming from Onondaga way. She had recognized his step the moment she heard it. She strained her eyes against the misty darkness. The feet sludged towards her steadily. Sometimes the sound was faint, then it came loud and close and she made her voice ready; and then again it faded out, almost to nothing. And suddenly, when she was sure she had a minute yet to wait, she saw a swirl in the darkness and his figure standing there while he peered for the cabin lights.

"Jerry."

She could make out the turning of his head.

"Jerry," she called.

"Mary!"

He had discovered her. Her heart swelled to see the life reëntering his stride. He came close. She smelled him now, hot, his clothes steaming. He put his arms round her and bent down to kiss her. His face, like hers, was wet with mist.

"How did you know I was coming?"

"I heard you back by the barn."

"How are you, Mary?"

"Fine."

Her hands felt of his hard body through the wet clothes.

"I'm glad to come back. It didn't seem that spring would ever come."

"You're soaking wet."

He laughed.

"I doubt if you could get a horse through from Onondaga. But when I got there before noon I couldn't stop."

He took her arm and together they threshed back to the kitchen door and Jerry lifted Mary's pail.

"Hello, there," he said. "I've just come in from milking."

"Well, by dog!"

Melville jumped up from his sprouting. . . .

All that night and all next day, the rain sluiced over the roof. They talked and talked. They made Jerry tell them every last small thing that he had seen.

"I bought and hauled in timber for four locks. . . .

"They're ready waiting now at Geddes, and Camillus, and Jordan, and Port Byron. . . .

"Caleb will buy for Montezuma locks. I came out that way. . . .

"It's quite a town, two churches, thirty houses, nearly. . . .

"The Cayuga River's lifting. It floods back near six miles, they say. Bad digging. . . .

"I had the intermittent fever. . . ."

"And I wasn't by," thought Mary. But he looked well. His face was thinner and in some way he seemed to have grown taller. His eyes had a shine in them when he looked at her. She could tell his gladness. She felt a ripeness growing in herself, as if her being were at work in sorting out her feelings.

They had a special dinner. Dorothy cooked a smoked-beef pie and brought out pickled currants.

"Work will start next week if wagoning will open," Jerry said. "As soon as maybe Caleb will send up the men. . . ."

Melville was sanding his plough that afternoon. Sun was shining in a watery sky and the marsh beyond the windows stretched out grey and hubbly, as if the old clumps of grass were thrusting shoulders up against it.

"I saw Hunter in Marcellus. He was hauling in to Utica. He'll haul for Caleb again this year. He had a load of merino bales for Oriskany milling. He tells me Rochester's a growing town. . . ."

Dorothy smiled and smiled. From time to time her eyes would swing to Mary.

"Haven't we cared for her fine?" she would ask proudly. "Don't she look handsome to you, Jerry?"

Jerry grinned and laid his hand on Mary's.

"She does, surely."

Dorothy would walk away about some job or other, still smiling to herself.

In the evening they had to show Jerry what they had made that winter. There was the coverlet completed. He felt it with his hand. "Real pretty. Look at those red stars. You might have drawed them." There was bedding made, a flannel blanket. "They look small," said Jerry.

"It's time you made a cradle, I should say. You've been an unproviding man as ever lived, I'd think."

Jerry grinned.

"Have you got boards?" he asked Melville.

"I've got a piece of half-inch pine," said Melville.

After supper, then, there was a sound of sawing as Jerry made the cradle. A simple box to fit the blanket. He whittled out the rockers with a knife. Next morning he floundered out to the wood patch and came home an hour later, red-faced, hot, and dripping, with birch wands. He peeled them carefully and worked them into bows and set them into the sides of the box.

"For a hood," he explained.

He hung the bows against the chimney to dry and stiffen into shape.

"Like a regular Pennsylvany wagon," Melville said. "I'd never have thought of that myself."

They all admired it—Dorothy, Melville, and Jerry. Mary smiled to see them tentatively poke it with their feet as they sat talking. Its rockers made a little sound. . . .

Over the marsh the snow seemed to collapse. It fell in in broken dish-like holes, and the grass showed through. Ponds of yellow water spread out overnight. Plover flew over it through the mist, calling. Their voices came at dawn and sunset, marking the day. . . .

The road opened suddenly. On the day after, Jerry said that he would have to go down to Number Two to see that everything was ready for the men. Dorothy suggested that he take the horse and drive himself down. Mary could ride with him and drive back. So they harnessed the old horse and set out towards Cossett's.

The sky had cleared. It was pale blue, for April, full of sunlight and unaccustomed warmth. The old horse wiggled his mulish ears and took his own route and pace; for the road was like a long, thin pudding, clutching the wheels, and treacherously rutted with ribbon-like gleaming pools.

Number Two was an exact replica of Number One in its early stages. The shanty was identical with all the others along the line. It made Jerry grin to see it and think of old Self Rogers. He told Mary about the old man, traveling the route and setting up these shanties against his conscience.

The well of the lock was two feet deep in water.

"We'll have to drain it," Jerry said. He examined all sides carefully. "There's too much water to have just drained in. I think we will need piles."

But there was nothing he could do and he and Mary walked round to the shanty and the horse-shed. In the shed, they found fresh droppings and the marks of hoofs. After studying them a while, Jerry said, "That's Roberts's pony. I wonder what he was doing here."

Together they took the boards off the shanty sashes and opened the doors. The shanty was full of the odor of winter. They stood to one side while the dampness drew past them, mouldy and dank, like fleeing ghosts that one could nearly see. Then they lit a roaring fire in the stove and sat together to eat their put-up luncheon.

"It makes me think of being back in Utica," said Mary. "Do you remember how we picnicked out with Bourbon, Jerry?"

He smiled at her over his bread and butter.

"Yes, I do. We were new-wedded folks then, weren't we? It seems a long time ago. And it's less than a year. I wasn't earning but three dollars a week, those days."

"It does seem long ago, Jerry." She eased her tired body on the hard bench; but her face was serene with remembered sweetness. The sunlight shone in upon her, putting copper on her hair. She had let her bonnet back upon her shoulders, and the bow nestled close under her chin.

"I'm anxious to get back to work," said Jerry. "I wonder what Roberts was doing here."

He had his answer almost immediately. Over the road they had come by sounded bells. The notes were slow in the lazy sunshine.

At the door, Jerry cried, "It's Hunter's team."

Mary joined him. She moved heavily and leaned herself against the door-jamb. Before she gazed out over the marsh she took a look at Jerry. There was a slight mist in her eyes; they were soft grey to-day. She thought, "The work has caught him again." Her breast rose softly. She had had him for so short a while. Then she turned her eyes to follow his.

It was Hunter, sure enough. She recognized his black leaders and the rain-streaked swaying top of his great wagon. He himself was striding in the mud beside the sorrel wheeler. The ringing bells sparkled faintly. Cataracts of muddy water ran back from the wheels, and on either side of the road the stagnant water trembled, shivering the reeds. In clearer places a reflection was born, first the horses two by two, then Hunter, then the wagon's box, a grey blue in the bright blue of the sky.

Behind, two more wagons lumbered. Men like monkeys clustered on the loads. She could make out Edwin Brown, the cook, and the funny, froglike figure of Cosmo Turbe crouched down beside his inseparable big friend.

Hunter stopped his team beside the well. The other wagons drew past it to the shanty. The men jumped down. Those that had worked before came forward to greet Jerry. Hunter and the cook took off their hats to Mary; but the others stayed where they were, eyeing distastefully the flooded hole.

Hunter said to Jerry, "I've brought you up a new contraption. Roberts says there's quicksand underneath the lock. You will need piling. Caleb said to tell you he was sending in the piles to-morrow. So I brought the engine for driving them and here's the man that works it."

From the rear of the Pennsylvania wagon strutted a small, fussy man with a bowler hat on his head and a quarter-inch black velvet ribbon round his neck against the quinsy.

"Name is Bemis," he introduced himself. He peered into the lock. "I've drove piles in everything but quicksand, but they ought to go down easy."

Mary had gone back to Melville's wagon. From the seat she watched Jerry taking hold, ordering the unloading. Edwin Brown was yelling for his helper. The other men, under the direction of Bemis, were hauling out heavy timbers from Hunter's wagon and setting them in line upon the ground. Mary spoke to the horse and turned him homeward. No one noticed her going.

An insufferable loneliness pressed her down. . . .

But on the afternoon of the following day, Hunter came back past Melville's farm. He stopped in a moment.

"They've set up Bemis's engine," he said. "They're about ready to use it."

While he loitered, they heard it begin, a heavy thump. Then there was silence for a while, and then again the thump. All the rest of the afternoon, long after Hunter had left them, Mary and Dorothy heard that dull thumping going on. It was a small sound at that distance, but even so they felt the weight of the blow.

"It's like a bittern," Dorothy said, "only it comes too slow."

For four days it went on steadily. Thump—and then the interval in which she heard the life upon the farm, the noise of the blackbirds returning to their nesting, Melville's voice talking to the oxen in the far lot, the dithery sound of Dorothy's hoe in the garden patch. It was like a clock with an irregular tick, marking the long minutes. Her nerves were growing sensitive to time. She felt each blow, bringing her back into the world to listen again, and then the slow resurgence of herself, while her inner ears were stretched.

On the fifth day, the engine stopped; moved onward, it was reported, to the lock and aqueduct at the Otisco outlet. For a long time Mary was oppressed by silence, and time stood still for her. . . .

Almost daily now, men or wagons were going past into the marsh. Digging moved at a fast pace. All through the swamp the sections were occupied with men, teams, and shovels. Loads of hay went past for the horses, lumbering heavily along the corduroy, the wagon reaches squeaking; edible-wagons for the men; loads of tools sent in by the contractors; wheelbarrows made of iron to hold mud, root-cutting spades shaped like the marks on playing cards; sharp ploughs and scoops. New things, new horses, new men every day. But the novelty wore off. One morning, when she heard Dorothy's voice shrill with excitement, she was slow in getting up. She would have missed the sight entirely if the young man bringing it had not unhitched his team to ask for water for them.

What she saw standing in the road was an enormous pair of twelve-foot wheels, connected by an axle eight feet long, made of a tree-trunk. The spokes of a third wheel were fixed into this axle and bore on their ends a monstrous grooved tire coiled with rope. While he watered his horses the young man explained that it was an engine he had invented for pulling stumps. The big wheels were chocked on either side of the stump, a chain was fastened to it and the axle. Then he hitched the horses to the rope that wound around the inner wheel; a simple piece of leverage, he said. The stump came up like pie and the big wheels trundled it off the line.

"Thank you, ma'am," he said to Mary, "I do like buttermilk."

He took the jug from her hands and drank directly from the lip. His grey eyes surveyed her shyly. Reading their admiration, she smiled back; but she felt no emotion, and in a little while he went along, behind his monstrous wheels, whistling "The Waterman's Song."

Dorothy laughed after him.

"A likely boy, Mary. He had an eye at you." And then she said, "To think of a young man like him inventing anything so large."

Dorothy was perpetually overcome by the wonderful things men did. . . .

May came with a growth of green. The pastures bore their grass, and the cows, with the calf tailing them in a kind of wonderment, went out to browse. At night Dorothy put a raw leek beside each place to eat before a person drank, for the taste of the wild onions was strong in the milk. Melville sowed his barley, buckwheat, and corn, and all three spent a day in putting in potatoes.

Mary worked steadily with them. Her senses were close to the earth, and her weariness each night offered her release. Less and less as time went on she seemed to miss Jerry. Some Sundays now he did not return at all, for he was several miles westward, working at Geddes.

The June heat brought fogs out of the marsh; and Dorothy would not allow her to go for the cows any more in the evening, for the mist carried ague.

On one of the latter days of June, Dorothy had said, "It's nearly time for Mr. Falk to come around."

"Mr. Falk?" Mary asked listlessly.

"Yes. Harley Falk. He's shoemaker for us. He generally comes about this time."

When Mary heard the creak of the wheel out on the summery road, she remembered this. Melville and Dorothy had gone to Fayetteville for buying things long needed at the farm; and Melville considered investing a part of his last year's earnings in some western land company. Mary had preferred to stay behind; for it was a hot day, without a breath of wind, and dry weather during June had covered the road deep in dust. So she was alone in the cabin. The curtains were drawn across the open windows, dimming the drone of bees in the buttercups and making the cabin cool. But from her stool beside the hearth she could see out through the open door, over the square of sweltering grass, to the road.

At length, through the mullein stalks along the fence, she saw the white ears of a horse, flopping like a mule's to his shambling walk. He carried his head low. And following after she saw the man upon the wagon seat. He seemed to be drowsing, hunched over his wrists, which rested on his knees. She could see nothing of his face. He wore a wide black hat dusted from the road to a silvery grey, and the shoulders of his old black coat were whitened. She remembered that Dorothy had said of the cobbler, "He's a queer-appearing man. Robert don't like him much, I fancy, and he makes me, too, uneasy. And yet he's real obliging."

When he came to the end of the fence, Mary had a clear view of the horse, a thin white animal; his uncurried coat was dull and ragged. He walked incredibly slow, with a stiff-kneed step and his muzzle dipping continually close to the road. She could see his nostrils pink as he snuffed of the way. Then he stopped, raised his head, and turned it towards the door; and Mary saw that his eyes were as white as his coat. The horse was blind with cataracts.

The driver raised his head abruptly, glanced at the cabin, and turned in his rig. Once more the wheel emitted tedious creaking; and before Mary had had a chance properly to see the man he had passed out of sight towards the barn. She heard the wheel creak past the house into the farmyard; and when it stopped again, the silence seemed to rise out of the earth like an incredible plant.

But Mary could not move. The white eyes in the white face of the horse seemed to stare at her; with a haunting power, as if somewhere, she could not remember when, she had seen them long ago. While she waited, she heard above the bee-sounds how the man was unhitching. The shafts rattled loosely as the horse stepped out of them; she heard the feet of man and horse treading on the plank walk in the barn; and after a while the man came out and drew a bucket at the well. Then the place was silent for a long time. She listened breathlessly for his footfalls across the yard; but still she could not move.

"Hello inside? Is anybody here to home?"

Mary turned slowly on her stool. She did not move her hands from her lap, but the color rose in her cheeks.

"Good afternoon."

Her own voice startled her. She had not heard him come, but there he was standing in the door.

"Melvilles are away this afternoon," she said.

The man had taken off his hat. In the open door he made against the shivering heat a still black silhouette.

"May I come in then?"

He had a pack on one shoulder.

"Are you Mr. Falk?"

He nodded.

"Then you'd better come in," said Mary. "Both of them have work for you."

"I will come in."

He stepped across the sill and closed the door, and in the renewed cool dusk inside the cabin he moved quickly past her to the far side of the hearth and swung his pack down, as if that were an accustomed corner.

She watched him unemotionally. A big man, obviously—he had tremendous shoulders, long arms, and ponderous hands—a strange-appearing man to cobble shoes. When he undid the rawhides binding his pack, a scent of tanned leather was breathed forth. Mary's nostrils quivered; her cheeks ripened suddenly; she felt a faint stir fingering her.

Falk said, "I'll just go out and get my last and bench and then I'll be complete."

Returning after a moment, he put the last down beside the sack, sat himself upon the bench that held the iron upright, and pulled out his drawer of nails and tools. Then he looked across at Mary.

He saw her face high-colored, her grey eyes wide and fixed on his. There was no fire in the hearth; and the ashes, bluish-white, lay unruffled. A spot of sunshine down the chimney lighted the clay back of the fireplace, put a bright spot on a copper kettle, and covered Mary with a gentle sheen.

She was dressed loosely in cool gingham, a bird's-eye blue, that draped her sympathetically.

He asked, "When did Melvilles go?"

"Quite a while before noon."

She could not tell his age. Hunched upon his stool, he made a powerful figure; but his head was small. His cheeks were smooth, as if he had just shaved. His long upper lip nearly overlapped his lower. His nose was straight and pointed; his forehead high and almost transparently white—a strange face for a man. His eyes were brown of an indeterminate sort; when they met the light inside the chimney they showed a green tinge.

Save for the drone of bees beyond the curtains, the cabin harbored utter stillness.

Suddenly he asked, "You don't know what kind of shoes either one of them would want, do you?"

Mary shook her head. Her eyes were fixed on his; following their wandering up and down her figure; meeting them whenever they found hers.

He said, "That's too bad. If I knew that, I could begin cutting." His broad fingers dipped into a drawer and pulled out a knife. The blade looked tiny in his fist; it was curved, whetted along the inside edge.

"What's your name?" he asked.

"Mary Fowler."

"Mary Fowler," he repeated it after her, his long upper lip caressing the syllables. "Are you a kin of Melvilles?"

"I'm boarding here."

She felt his eyes reading her body.

"Your husband's working on the canal?"

"Yes. He's a foreman for Caleb Hammil."

"On the locks, then?"

"Yes."

"He is away?"

"Yes, he's away." Her voice was oddly toneless.

"He's been away for long?"

"For a long time."

"He ought to be back before so long."

"I don't know."

Suddenly the man smiled. His teeth, catching the light, were small, even, and white.

"You get lonesome."

"Sometimes."

"I've noticed women do. It's too bad. Some men work hard; they haven't understanding—well men haven't."

Mary was silent. But in her heart a little prick of gratitude was stirred. Little by little her attention was absorbed by his face, gentle and sympathetic. He had turned his eyes away from hers and was staring through the open door. A strange man, she thought—and she felt queerly sorry for him, with his face and body so mismated.

"Have you always been a cobbler, Mr. Falk?"

He started.

"No."

He bit the word off short.

She said, "Myself, I need a new pair of boots. Would you care to make me one?"

As she turned she saw eagerness in his eyes. They had a peculiar humility, like the dog of a dishonest man.

"I'd be glad to. What kind of a boot, Mrs. Fowler?"

"A regular boot. Not too high. One to use in housework or for walking."

"I've got some especial calfskin. Not too heavy." He bent over the sack. In a moment his big hands had found the leather he was seeking and he brought it to her.

It was cool in her hands, extraordinarily pliable, and the tanned scent breathed out from it seemed to weight her eyelids.

"It's nice," said Mary.

"It's fine leather. It will wear, and it will shape to meet your foot."

He bent down before her on one knee and took her foot in his hand. Then his big fingers unlaced the old boot, with its wear, its thin sole, all the voyage from England in it and the miles westward she had traveled. His hands were caressing as he handled it, drawing it off and taking her foot; it followed her ankle downward, cupping the heel and feeling of the arch.

"High arches."

She shivered distantly, and only by an effort kept her open eyes upon his hand.

"So seldom are there arches built like yours. Not out here. The women's feet are coarse from working inside heavy boots. They let them down." His hand held the arch, but suddenly the other hand was taking her toes. Mary was breathless. Against her arch she felt a steady pulse, whether hers or his she did not know, but there was a mounting rhythm in the beat. Yet, when he continued, his voice was steady. "A long second toe is a thing many Albany belles would crave. It makes the natural foot. It is a beauty for a woman."

He slowly raised his face.

What she saw Mary did not choose to read beyond the humility.

"Can I see it bare?" he asked her. "It isn't often."

Mary's hands obeyed. She swung herself a little to one side and reached inside her skirt. She pulled the stocking to her knee. "Shameless," she thought; but she was shameless.

He took the rolled edge of brown cotton and slowly bared the leg. She felt the coolness of the cabin strike against the skin, his soft palms and the calloused finger-tips made rough by tack-points. The shivering again possessed her. Her color came into her cheeks; her lips were full, her eyes still. Then he looked at her, and all at once, in the cabin dusk, she felt a chill, and she saw not his eyes but the white, sightless eyes that she remembered in the horse. This was a thing she had not willed to do; her will was not her own. There was an impulse in her like the wind; and she put her hands in her lap to hide them, feeling them like leaves.

But the cobbler was quietly examining the foot. After a while he slipped the stocking on, and to Mary's ears the dim droning of the bees returned. She saw the mullein stalks beyond the road-fence, the sky burnished blue, with small hot clouds in it.

He finished lacing up the shoe.

It seemed to Mary that the incident was a thing long past. She watched him now impersonally, cutting the leather from memory, bending it in his big hands. He laid out his needle, waxed his threads. The needle caught a bit of light, moving it up and down like quicksilver.

As he worked, they talked.

He said he had been born back east. He did not say why he had left New England, but he told her all the places he had seen.

"It's as if I had a beast inside me gnawing. I get restless. I haven't worked a district more than five years ever."

"Have you worked many?"

"Eight, I mind."

"You wouldn't look that old."

"Generally I don't dwell five years on one."

"Oh."

"I'm not yet forty-five, if you would want to know."

"How did you come to cobbling, Mr. Falk?"

"It was a way to make a living, when I went out into new country."

"Oh."

"People don't always like me," he explained. "I don't know why. The men don't and some women are afeared."

He said it quietly. But she caught the sadness and felt sorry for him. He said he had been eastward.

"They've had some trouble with the diggers. Irish and niggers don't mix. Any man can get a job. There've been riots. They pay them part in whiskey. Men together fashion strange ideas."

She watched his leather taking shape under his big skilled fingers. It was magical. When the Melvilles returned before sunset, old Squirrel dragging the wagon tiredly, Falk's hammer was tapping. The cabin had grown darker as the light crept up the chimney out to westward. And Mary was quiet with a strange sense of an inner freedom, talking to this man. He listened well, waiting to catch her roundabout allusions; and his understanding eyes would veil themselves at her voice and when she was silent look deeply into her.

"So soon as I heard that hammer," Dorothy cried, "I said to Robert, 'Mr. Falk has come.' I'm glad to see you. Both of us need boots."

The cobbler smiled over the shoes he made for Mary.

Dorothy stripped off her straw bonnet. Her wispy grey hair looked tight as ever behind her homely face. She turned her eyes searchingly on Mary and made a mouth to herself. Then she looked at the shoes.

"My, aren't they pretty ones! Alike as alike, and shaped like city kid." She laughed at Falk. "You never made a pair of shoes like that for me."

He raised his face to hers.

"Oh, don't deny!" she said. "I know why. The reason's there."

She stretched her own long foot out underneath her skirt. Dust was on the old boot. Falk examined it with his eyes, then raised them to her face.

"It's worn well," he said; but Mary saw that Dorothy drew back, and her face became cold.

That evening, as Falk completed his work, she and Robert sat quietly watching him. But his eyes were discreet. He hardly spoke from supper onwards.

Only when Mary tried on the shoes and felt his hands lacing them, and the leather like a caress through the stocking against her skin, did she feel a return of the release of spirits that had so stirred her that afternoon. She noticed afterwards, for the two days he worked at the farm, that Melville kept himself occupied not far from home; and twice she came upon him exchanging low talk with Dorothy, which they turned awkwardly into an open channel.

But once as she milked at twilight Falk came into the barn, where his things were and where he slept, and leaned for a moment against the post. She felt his eyes on her bent shoulders, where the collar of her dress gaped loosely up.

She did not speak, but her hands became more conscious of the milk.

At length he said, "I'm through to-morrow. I won't forget our afternoon together."

He passed her quietly, going out again.

But after he had gone, when she wore the new shoes on a Sunday, she became aware of a strange unholiness in her thoughts which she tried to put away; and the white eyes of Harley Falk's white horse would enter her dreams as if through them the man himself watched her secret thinking.

5

"In some old countries women kneel"

MARY had dispossessed the Melvilles of their bed. She lay straight out upon her back, her feet against the footboard, her wrists in leather loops. One of Squirrel's reins had been passed round the footboard and under the bedding with loops stitched in the ends for her to grasp. But now she had a respite; her senses were released from their inward fury and fled out on dusky paths. . . .

Between two rafters dwelt a spider. She wondered how many days ago he had set up his web. She had seen him when they first had put her in the bed; he was connecting a new brace, his hands marvelously deft in spreading the sheaf of threads he spun. But, from the time that Mrs. Hovey first brought the lamp to the bedside, the spider had been troubled. Mary had seen him hiding himself inside his web, as if he would have closed his lidless eyes; and now when the quiet returned he had made up his mind —he was reeling in skein after skein in readiness for moving.

She watched him till he had unfastened the last thin, silken anchor. He lingered a moment as if to take one farewell look. Then he put out his hands and began his scuttling travel. Choosing the shadow of a rafter, he ran the whole length of the ceiling. Mary saw his body five times lift to cross a rafter upside down before he scrambled down the wall and ducked out through the door. . . .

In the big bed her body felt indescribably small. The wide spread of sheets was like the ocean she remembered crossing—years and years the crossing seemed, years before she had seen Jerry, years before she had come westward to her stay in Utica, and years again before she had moved on to Melvilles, where she and Jerry had united time. Time was in her back; time absorbed her being. They had taken time together to fashion it; and now time was seeking freedom.

Immediately she heard a stool-leg gently bump and Mrs. Hovey was bending over the pillow.

"Well, dearie."

Mary opened her eyes. It was the first time she had taken a coherent look at Mrs. Hovey. "Ma Hovey," Dorothy named her; for it was said that she had helped at half the births in Onondaga County. She had arrived with Melville early in the afternoon, a jouncing figure crowding him halfway off the wagon seat. Squirrel dripped lather to his stifles; but Ma Hovey had no eye for him. Directly, she had scrambled down and waddled into the cabin, and before her shawl was off she had taken the command from Dorothy.

"She'll use this bed right now. Later we'll ready the table for her when it's time."

Mary had not noticed her face, but she had felt the hands upon her body.

"There'll be time and time," Mary had heard her voice. "How is it, dearie? Pretty bad?"

She had not expected an answer: Mary felt that her hands would tell her whatever might be needful. She heard her saying to Dorothy, "A fine girl for bearing. I'm not troubled. And she's healthy. I should estimate a girl by place and action. Light a fire."

Now Mary saw her face—round-cheeked, with a small, serious mouth, and unworn eyes. Her skin was freshly pink and white—a strange thing in so old a woman living westward; only her hands were toil-scarred.

Ma Hovey brought a pitcher of cool water and a rag and pressed the hair back from Mary's forehead.

"Does that feel better, dearie?"

Mary nodded.

"Rest yourself, then, all you can."

For a moment the unworn eyes, clear blue, looked down into Mary's wide grey shadowed ones. It was like seeing an immeasurable distance upward; she was soothed as if white clouds touched her with dry soft coolness.

Mary obediently closed her eyes, but when she heard Ma Hovey's broad feet turn away she opened them and looked at the grizzled curly hair caught neatly in its crocheted purple basket.

There was a distinct spring in the old woman's step. Bringing a woman through childbirth was the stuff of life to her; when she put her hands upon a laboring body, she put her own years out of sight. She sat down softly on her stool, and Mary heard her laying down laws upon laws to Dorothy.

Dorothy's voice was humble. To the last moment, her homely face had kept its determined cheerfulness. She had made little jokes with Jerry. Had he thought of twins, for instance? Would he like it four in family? But when Ma Hovey came, she had relapsed into a frightened creature who held Mary dear.

But Mary had not cared; these things were all like wind at night—unseen, but dimly listened to.

Ma Hovey had said, "You might as well fetch Dr. Earl."

Both men had said that they would go. He was expecting; he would be ready; he had promised, at a word.

"One of you two had ought to stay."

Dorothy sounded panicked.

Ma Hovey grunted.

"No, let them both get out. They're no use, their dreary faces."

But Robert had gone alone.

"I'd feel ashamed," said Jerry.

Mary wondered where he was. She did not want to see him. She resented the fright in his eyes that infected her in her still moments. But she listened now. Would he be by the well, perhaps, getting himself a drink of cool? Or would he be out in the barn? Or maybe listening by the back window, where the cockscomb lifted shriveled tufts?

What she could see her eyes found tiresome. The smell of steaming water on the hearth was stifling in her nostrils; her skin identified the lamp heat, and the fire warmth; and she lay dully at the mercy of the things that made a man and woman.

A little breath of night air stole through the slightly opened door. She seemed to feel it coming long before it came to her. She was aware of it creeping past the ankles of the seated women; it flickered the fire gently; it stole on across the floor to the foot of the bed and tried to lift itself. She lay deathly still, unable to help it, seeking to will it upwards. Then it did rise across the sheet; it stole upon her body with its cooling finger-tips; she felt it in her nostrils, damp and sweet with meadow smells. It eased her eyelids, and touched the stiff skin on her forehead, chilling the bubbles of sweat. For a precious breathless instant, it carried her senses through the cabin walls.

How was it that she could hear through the dry, piled logs the beat in the night outside: the ticking of the crickets; the throb of greenbugs in the grass; the indefinable stir of the small creeping things underground and on the ground—the moles, the grubs, the worms; the wet sly inching of the marsh slugs; the ants awake in sandy palaces; the spiders casting their dew-pearled threads; the gnats that hatch in darkness, troubling the still pools; the unseen midget things that make the pulse and keep the earth alive?

She had not been born in these wide sprawling lands, she had not grown where one burnt acre stood for the first work of a man against the wilderness; yet her senses were alive to them, as if the soft hollow in her hardened palms could feel the whole world sleeping.

And then through it her stretched ears caught the steady crunch of boots upon the road. They trod stiffly back from Onondaga way, and she remembered that night before the spring came, so long ago, when Jerry walked to her out of the mist. She knew his step. He stopped at the turn-in to the cabin. She could imagine his thin face staring at the window light. But her heart hardened in her. He had turned away. The dismal burden of his boots crunched out the precious little sounds. The burden entered her, her eyelids were made heavy, and her heart bent down. . . .

"He's young," Ma Hovey was saying just above the gentle beating of the fire. "But he's been civil to me and I do allow that he does well. A young doctor, but minded to learn from those that know his business better. He doesn't hold with cotton swathe or cricket mark or twice around the basket, but he's young. Young people don't believe—Hark! There's the boy. Poor boy. I feel a pity for him. Hush. . . .

"Yes, dearie, coming on? Let them. Old Ma's tending of you. Carry them through, stronger. But not too strong. You've got a long ways to travel, dearie, but you're fine. Here's water for your forehead. Yes, be easier. My, that was a dandy big one! That's the kind that counts. Yes, I know it. Yes, but that's the kind. It's like an extra horse hitched to a wagon. Guarantees you through the bog holes. But don't think of it. Don't think of anything, dearie. That's a fine girl. That's a good one, too. You've got a good long ways to travel, but Ma Hovey's riding with you. . . .

"Yes, Mrs. Melville. Still some time; but just the same, that young man of a doctor might as well turn up or else I'll have to get him a surprise to greet him. . . .

"No, now don't look worried, Mrs. Melville. Land to goodness, Ma Hovey's brought a basketful of babies free with her own self. You needn't be a-worrit. Give the young feller his two dollars, get a medical blessing if you like, and leave him stay to home—that's what I'd say. But this boy's like them all. He's earning money and thinks he's bound to spend it. Like a funeral, too. What good's a coffin? Oh, I've laid them out, poor things. Three that I helped to being born. The same very hands, identical, these here. It's funny. . . .

"Yes, I've helped my lot of babies. I always call them mine, Mrs. Melville. And why not? A good percentage of them wouldn't be at all except for me. I mind the first. The doctor couldn't make it in his sleigh with two fat horses. Couldn't venture it. Those horses got floundered down in snow, he said, and he was troubled with deep rheumatism, making him lame. But I walked in on Indian snowshoes. I went out that afternoon, I mind, and bought them for a dollar and a half, a yard of India cloth. I wasn't troubled by a pair of horses. Yes, it was Tremaster's boy. She was a little thing, no more than a curled leaf to handle, and the baby ranting in her like a scalping redskin. The man's no better than a howling baby himself. I saw that just at once I got inside the door and stamped the snow off'n the shoes. So I told him, 'Wipe your nose and boil some water.' He done it, but he never liked me after. I showed him how to hold her hands, and I did everything. At least the baby did, a ranting boy; I never knew one lust so hard for air. He'd got the cord around his neck and was choked blue. I do declare he swore in French when I had cut him free. And do you know there wasn't thread in all that house? Poor little pretty, out there striving in those woods without a blessed notion. She had a woolen skirt of English weave and I unraveled a thread. Yes, Mrs. Melville. And there wasn't any harm, and the boy's a man now down in Albany, making speeches in Assembly, no doubt about canals. Oh, well, Tremaster never really liked me, I suppose. And that was how I started in, so don't you fret yourself. . . .

"Yes, dearie, if you want a sip. Now take a good hold of them straps. Drive yourself if you're so minded. There's hills and rivers, but there's time. I'll cool you, Dearie. . . .

"Yes, Mrs. Melville. He better had turn up. You and me might just as well arrange the table. Yes, it's hard; but that's all right. There's nothing comfortabler than a good stout table, all concerned. The places I've seen babies born in! In some old countries women kneel. I saw a Swedish girl that did it that way. Her man just held her there, between his knees. They were moving westward; it came on sudden; and there wasn't chance to bring her to a house. Twins, I tell you, for a fact. Under a beech tree with the curiousest little chipmunk. That's it—just stretch it that way.

"Now, Mrs. Melville, let's us set down and wait a minute, comfortable. My feet get tiresome to me sometimes and if I don't set down I get all wearied. If you had a wet of cordial, and you might cook up a little tea to give her after. Not too strong and without sugar. Bohea tea's the best, though I don't gainsay a cup of hyson, and the city people fancy souchong. Yes, I am slightly partial to peach cordial. It's a pleasant drink for surely.

It settles flutters in a woman. Good for you, too, Mr. Melville. Don't you worrit. Drink it slow—and you might just companionate what I've got left here with a small drop more. I make mine in a burnt-oak keg, but this is very tasty. There! There's the doctor. Yes, he's coming fast. That quiet boy has stopped him. Asking how his wife is, probably. And the doctor says she's dandy. Oh, well, you might as well set back those glasses, Mrs. Melville. I'd rather he had nothing till we're finished. Out of sight is out of thinking. . . .

"Yes, Dr. Earl. We're doing nicely. . . ."

Mary no longer cared to ravel out the messages her twisted senses carried to her. She tried to fetch a smile forth for the doctor; she saw his face bent over her, the lamplight on the tightened skin beside his eyes, the slow contraction of his pupils after his dark night ride. It was the face of a young man under thirty, with shaven cheeks and a gently optimistic mouth that smiled back at her.

"How are they, Mrs. Fowler? Pretty bad?"

She nodded.

His clothes smelled strong of horse-sweat and tobacco. He had curling hair, cropped short, bright brown in color.

"Everything's fine," she heard Ma Hovey telling him; and his voice, "Good." And Ma Hovey, a bit sniffily, "I expect you'll want to see for yourself."

Their faces with their voices swam backward.

When they returned, the doctor was speaking. "You're quite right, as usual, Mrs. Hovey—though I think you underestimate the time."

Ma Hovey's voice was pleased.

"She's one of them that gets determined on it, Doctor."

"Maybe so. I'll wash my hands now."

Dorothy bustled for a basin and a clean towel for him, but Ma Hovey lingered by the bed, tending Mary with a proprietary bending

"You're doing finely, pretty. Finely. Oh, ease down your back! Does it feel better when I put my arm down under it?"

The doctor seated himself beside the hearth and pulled his pipe out. He whittled off tobacco in his palm and stuffed the bowl. The rich blue coils of smoke were tapered out and whisked into the chimney.

"The road surprised me," he said to Dorothy. "I expected it much rougher with all the heavy travel passing over it."

"You didn't have no trouble finding here?"

"No, no. Not a bit. I'd been up to the corners less than a week ago. A man got knifed in the gang that's working next to Cossett's tavern. Whiskey brawling, I expect. They got me Sunday morning. So all I had to do was turn right, there, instead of left, and yours is the first house."

He wiped the crumpled leavings of the whittled plug off on his trouser knees.

"Come in, Mr. Fowler," he invited.

"No, thanks," said Jerry.

"Want to see me?"

Jerry was wordless, but the doctor read his eyes. He stepped through the doorway with him, his arm on Jerry's shoulder.

"Everything looks right enough. Don't worry."

Ma Hovey returned to the hearth.

"A nice young man, I think," said Dorothy, her voice stiff and thin. Ma Hovey grunted in her short, round nose.

The doctor was gone for several minutes. Once in an interval Mary heard his footsteps matching Jerry's in the front yard. The beat was methodical, heavy, a little out of stride. What right had Jerry to keep the doctor outside? She wanted to see him again. She was pinning her faith on his optimistic face. She must see it. She shut her teeth together, closing sound.

Dorothy looked timidly over the bed. There were little bulges just beside the corners of her homely mouth. She glanced at Mary's eyes, and her own were frightened. Mary fretfully tossed her head. Then Ma Hovey's clear blue eyes swam up beside Dorothy's head.

Her hand came out to rest on the set forehead.

"What is it now, dearie?"

Mary's lips were calm in their deliberate speaking. Her voice was surprisingly clear. She heard herself:—

"I think it's beginning to happen."

Ma Hovey had ducked down with questing hands. Mary heard Dorothy mumbling something. Words were slurred. "I never knowed there was such power in a body."

"Go get in that doctor," Ma said shortly.

Then Mary's sensations boiled out like a flume. She heard Dorothy: "Come inside, Dr. Earl." The doctor's quick heavy steps. Her own distortion. Her lips opening. Jerry's footfalls halting at the door, stock-still. The silence. Then the lamp swam down and round and she was on a harder bed. The firelight was red, red, red. She saw herself upon a road. Her legs ached. Her feet were stumbling and her eyes looked down and saw not even pebbles. A wheel kept creaking, way off somewhere. It approached irregularly from behind. Voices kept talking, sharp hard-breathed snatches. The creak came on. She made a desperate effort, but the revolution of the earth held back her feet. There was a darkness not far off, a black lid above the light that someone was putting down. The creak came clearer. She dared not look around. That sound. It creaked again. She shut her teeth and did not hear it. But the blackness was inexorable. There was but the thinnest ray of light. A knife edge at the edge of the world. It entered. She had not heard the wheel that turned; but now it came again beside her ear. She saw a white face, she saw the bones under the skin, and the white sightless eyes. And in each eye a mirrored face. . . .

Time had been. . . .

She heard the doctor laugh. He held a little squirmy thing above her face. Ma Hovey said, "Her's a lovely." She was bustling. Somebody was weeping. "Here, you hold her, Mrs. Melville." The evolution had caught up with her and passed, and she was free.

She closed her eyes.

Heat that was deathly all day long, sweltering marsh-side heat that shimmered in lazy waves over the still, high grass, that killed the sounds of passing wagons, that dulled men's voices; in the wood lot south of the barn the locusts made an all-day sawing.

But the log walls of the cabin enclosed coolness born of the living, unsunned earth on which the puncheons rested. It lapped round Mary, cradling her. It stilled Jerry's eyes when he sat at the bedside, holding her hand in quiet. It put a change on Melville whenever he came in from reaping, and when he went forth again the clack of the whetstone on the scythe fell through the torrid shrieks of the cicadas like drops of water.

In the quiet, Dorothy moved in softness. She made little dainties out of the food she had, fresh beans and young potatoes; squash, too, were forming; for supper she went out for the fresh wheat and ground it in a small burnt-oak mortar by the kitchen door and made milk mush of the milky grains. As regular as time, she came into the kitchen, her long face red with sunlight, to watch Ma Hovey emptying the cradle and moving softly for the bed.

Those were the moments that marked Mary's being for her now. She would see Ma Hovey with the corner of her eye and hear her movements making ready. Outside, Melville's scythe would shear through wheat stalks, swinging as if it walked. But inside, the stillness would be great with waiting. Then a cry would break forth, a thin parody of human utterance, but blatant as life itself. There would be a breath in the air as Ma Hovey came forward towards the bed. Dorothy would stand by the footboard, looking down, her face all swollen with her childless heart. But then Mary would turn on her side and look away from her, straining her eyes to see as Ma Hovey turned back the blanket and put inside the short, wrapped bundle. Ma Hovey would unwrap the band that barely seemed to hold the milk in check. Sometimes when the breast was free, before the small red lips could make their ring upon the nipple, the milk would pour forth.

Then Ma Hovey laughed.

"There's life in there to drink a bucketful. My, my."

And she would direct the mouth to its holding. Her pink face would grow pinker yet with sentiment.

"See the little pretty drink it! Ain't she the hungry girl? A little guzzler. Hark, how she puffles, squashing in her nose. She'll take it all to-night, I'll guarantee."

Even Dorothy at the bed-foot could hear the anxious breathing. She would steal round the corner, boots a-creak, and fill her eyes.

But Mary did not notice them then. However her back ached by evening, in that twilight time she felt her life uprise in the full breast. ("There's no thing like it," said Ma Hovey, "to ease a woman's troubles.") It was outpouring from the instant that the ring was formed by the child's lips; it seemed to rise from untouched wells; it carried forth the mark of time, making her body young; it took strength from her in a flood that seemed to have no end; and it left strength in its place, to heal and grow; it was rich with warmth; it had a scent of its own, stronger than the milk of beasts—a sweet, rich scent that made a perfume in the baby's skin. In all the world, she felt, no spring uprose from earth that came more freely, and she felt proud to hear Ma Hovey saying, "I never did see such a mass of milk in living woman. She should be rearing twins at very least. Look at the baby, ain't she the pretty? Look at her bulging midwards, will you,

Mrs. Melville? Such a little guzzler for a girl!" "Drink," thought Mary, "drink. There's more, and more, and more. There will be always more." The baby would begin to sigh and loiter in her sucking. Her round cheeks would redden over the new inward warmth. The flush would spread in a recognized progression. The ears, the eyelids, forehead, even the skin between the tiny, separate hairs that made her eyebrows, would grow hot. A distillation, silvery as a night sheen on red clover heads, would come forth upon the skin. Only the button nose stayed white from its own pressure. Yet even while the baby drowsed and woke, suckled and drowsed in always longer spells, Mary was conscious of her inexhaustible outpouring. Even at last, when it slept in surfeit, rocking its head like a honey-drunken bee, a few last drops would ooze forth on its lazy mouth.

Then the feet of the two women would move softly here and there. Mary would lie quiet, with the still ease of new being. So the evening stole in, and she herself dozed in the sound of firelight.

She did not listen to their quiet going-off to bed: Dorothy and Melville looking down; Melville's eyes embarrassed, Dorothy's bright; Jerry's good-night, the three days he stayed after the child came, when Ma Hovey went outside for nightfall and they were alone.

Jerry sat close to the bed; the low stool brought his head just level with the pillow.

"I've got to be leaving soon, Mary."

She would hush him with her hand. His dark thin face was still. His hair made a shade against the light. It was a wonder to her that the baby had fair hair.

"I'd want to name it, now, before I go."

"What do you want to name it, Jerry?"

He found it hard to meet her eyes.

"I'd like to name it Mary. I would. Do you remember when you told me, after we finished the first lock? I said boys' names. And you said what if it was a girl? And you were right."

She smiled. It made her happy. Then he kissed her and stole out to his bed in the barn. She heard his good-night voice to old Ma Hovey; and Ma Hovey came in and helped her make ready for sleep. They were alone, then, like two women at a mystery, when the night was breathing just beyond the window. And she wished this time might never end.

6

"He said the woman had a baby"

MARY sat in the cabin doorway sewing patches on a shirt of Jerry's. It was the first time in many days that she had thought of him to mend his clothes; and all she could find for her penitence was this tattered shirt he had left behind two months ago. Dorothy said that the shirt was not worth mending: "I wouldn't touch no shirt of Robert's was so disconnected."

The elbows were completely raveled out; and a piece of the tail had been cut off and sewed for an extra pocket on the breast. The small, uneven, manlike stitches made her face sober.

October was coming in. Down beside the marsh the maple which stood with half its roots in water was touched on the northward side with pinkish red. The marsh grass was acquiring yellow, and the meadow had turned a duller green. The blackbirds flew in mammoth flocks, higher than in summer; and when they settled, the grass was jarred with their unceasing bickers. The arch of the sky was untouched blue; and the sun shone strongly.

Mary had the baby in the cradle on the doorstone. She was sleeping now; and from time to time Mary touched the cradle with her foot to hear the rockers mutter on the uneven sill. Then she looked up and out across the marsh. Many of the diggers had passed on. One shanty smoke with which she had been long familiar rose no more; and Melville said that the contractor had his section finished. You could see his section shaped, the prism for the water, and the towpath wide enough for horses, and on the other side the narrow berm. But here and there for miles both east and west the little knots of men were digging slowly. To Mary it was all a dream. She thought of it now, vaguely, for the shirt in her lap and the needle in her fingers. The needle needed threading. Mary stared westward.

Far away she saw a dust cloud traveling along the fence. It approached her with an unwavering swiftness that even to her eye carried a familiar gait. After a little she saw the horse's head, held high, with the small ears freshly pointed, and then on the seat of the wagon a figure she recognized immediately.

She made herself ready to wave; for he was traveling at such a pace that she supposed he wished to reach Utica at nightfall in the very least. His head was bared to the sun and his fat red cheeks were wind-burned. He grasped the reins in a fat hand and Mary saw the mouth of the racing horse half opened by his weight of wrist. There was no mistaking Caleb Hammil.

As he came to the corner of Melville's first field he spied Mary seated in the cabin door. He waved his hat, yanked the right rein—and Bourbon took the turn-in skillfully, lifting the inside wheel and snapping the rear ones into line. He braced his feet and slid to stop.

Never heeding him, Hammil threw the reins over the dashboard and hopped off. His fat face beamed.

"Hello there," he said. "How are you now?"

Mary smiled.

"Just finely," she said, looking down.

The fat man followed her gaze, and instantly dropped his voice to a whisper.

"So that's the baby. A girl, I've heard tell; a pretty one. Can I look at her?"

"Yes. She's sleeping now."

"Just to see her face. Don't wake her, Mrs. Fowler. I'll bend down."

He knelt before the cradle's foot and with infinite pains stretched one fat hand forth to lift the blanket's edge. His breath whistled from the effort of kneeling.

"It's a pretty baby. Takes after you, I judge," he whispered. "I'm real glad it came out well."

He let the blanket fall back into place and carefully got to his feet. "Can I set down and visit a little spell?"

"Yes, please. But let's go in. Can't I get you something?"

"No. I've ate an hour since."

"Some milk—a piece of pie?"

They moved softly into the cabin.

"What kind of pie?"

Mary smiled. The contractor always made her think of an eager little boy. He had no consciousness of self.

"Fresh currant, Mr. Hammil."

"Well, a little piece."

She fetched it. He had seated himself at table with his hat between his outstretched hands. She sat down opposite and watched him eat a quarter piece of pie and drink his milk. Now and then he would look shyly at her.

Finally he wiped his lips and said, "Mrs. Fowler, you know I'm fond of Jerry."

Mary said nothing.

"He's a good boy. But his ambitiousness is likely to do him harm some day."

"What is it?" she asked quietly.

"We're going to split. When he does Byron lock, his contract with me's finished. That's going to be next month. I made a special trip to see him about staying with me."

"Yes, Mr. Hammil?"

"Yes. I wanted him to work for me. I've been paying him well and I offered him some more. But he said it wasn't enough. He was talking kind of high and mighty. I didn't pay no attention to that, for I was a young lad myself. But I showed him I couldn't pay him any more and make a proper profit under my contracts." His face was sober. "Where are the Melvilles?"

Mary said, "They're out back in the lot, digging the potatoes."

Hammil nodded.

"I just didn't want to have them break in onto us." He looked down at his fists, which made a gathering gesture. "I don't know what it is. But Jerry appears changed to me. I noticed it back when we completed Number One. And all the way home from Jordan I thought I'd drop in to ask if you knew what it was on his mind." He turned his face embarrassedly to the window. "That's why I took this road instead of the Pike."

Mary too looked from the window. She didn't want to hurt him by telling him that Jerry was jealous. Jerry, she saw, had no right to be.

"I don't know."

"I thought he might have told you it." Hammil sighed. "That's why I determined to stop by."

Mary felt a kind of hush steal into her.

"What happened?"

Hammil said, "I guess I lost my temper. I told him I had brought him out of nothing and that he owed me gratitude. I'm sorry I said it, because he's earned his earnings. I haven't had to be out here at all. He's done the locks about a third again as fast as what I had expected. He's a fine workman and knows twice as much about lock-building as I'll ever get into my noodle. That's one main reason that I hate to see him go. I've got other men working on my culvert contracts, but not one capable of making locks. But it ain't all that. I'd thought that maybe soon I'd make him partner with me. Only he's too young and too unsettled just a while yet. Good land, ma'am, it took me ten years to get ahead the way he's done in one. He don't realize he's made his progress because I had my money back of him. But then he's more able than I was. I don't deny. Roberts and Mr. Wright, the both of them, say he's doing the best timber work they have on this-here section."

His face was a comical mixture of injured pride and real affection. Mary felt her heart lean towards him.

"What do you want me to do?"

"I thought, when you saw him, and found him favorable, you might just say that Hammil would consider partnership right now. He's getting on"—Hammil glanced at the cradle sunning in the doorway—"and he ought to get established. Do you know what his ideas are?"

Mary said, "He wants to work westward with the canal, I think—And then him and Roger Hunter talk of starting a boat business."

"That would take money. He's earning fast and saving nearly all. But he can't put money all in boats and start a home for you two."

"I know," said Mary. She hesitated, testing words for meanings. "Since the baby there got born, I've been thinking. It seems someways Jerry's younger than I am. He's got a kind of feeling after this canal. It ain't just money to him."

Hammil snorted angrily.

"I thought he had some fool idea. He'd better stick with me. Of course it's money. That's the whole notion of it. I don't expect him to skimp work and wood—he knows that, for I told him. But I thought he wanted money."

"Yes, he does."

"Yes. But what in nation does he want besides? It does beat all."

"Yes. It does. I guess we can't understand."

"He raises my bile. He needs a lesson." Suddenly the fat man caught Mary's sympathetic eye. He looked confounded. Then they laughed together. "Just the same," he said, "what I told you goes. Ungrateful or uppish or the Lord knows what, I've got a fondness for him. I have for both of you," he grinned again winningly and slapped his leg, "for the whole three of you."

Mary said, smiling, "I don't think Jerry is ungrateful. And I'll always remember you kindly, you and Mrs. Hammil."

Caleb waved his hand.

"Oh, that work was nothing. My wife said she never had such laundering and makes a moan about it now you're gone." His face grew tender. "Once Jerry told me how you and him met up. I guess that's what got me fond of you. But I promised never to tell anyone. You see he's proud."

Mary nodded.

"That's it," cried Caleb. "He's proud—proud as the black devil."

"Yes," said Mary. "Sometimes it makes him worry."

Caleb looked as if everything were settled.

"Hell!" he said. "I'm proud myself! I never thought of that. You'll tell Jerry, won't you?"

"I won't see him for some time, most probably."

In the act of getting up to go, Caleb's jaw struck open.

"I'd almost forgot! He asked me to tell you to come out and meet with him in Montezuma."

"Move?"

"Yes."

"But how?" Mary was astonished.

"Hunter's going through next month. I'm to tell him to stop for you."

"Yes."

"I'd best get along. You won't forget." His fat bulk loomed over her.

"No."

"He says he'll have a place ready for you in the village there."

"Yes."

Hammil looked right and left. His mouth framed words. But he did not seem able to speak.

"I'd better get to going," he said at last. "Good-bye."

Mary watched him roll out of the door. He went elaborately on tiptoe past the cradle, turned the horse, and bellowed, "Get up, Bourbon."

The wheels rattled through the yard and down the road. The dust they raised came floating back. Mary sat still at the table. To have to move, when she felt just established! She saw that she could not make a home of the Melvilles' house forever, but it pained her to leave them now. She had a thought of herself, packing up and moving all her life, following Jerry westward. Suddenly the corners of her mouth bent down in a little bitter smile. There was little enough to pack. She looked out through the door. Then she sprang to her feet. The baby had worked loose her blanket. She went out. One thing at least had been established in her life. As she bent over, she talked softly.

Across the marsh, by Cossett's, a shanty cook was beating his wagon-tire gong. The flatulent notes were harsh. Blackbirds swarmed aloft, alive with jibbered protest. Mary's breasts grew heavy. She brought the baby in and made ready for its supper. Her head bent over its small face, her hair touching its cheek. The springs were rising in her, and a little haunting tune sang in her head:—

> "Awake, awake, you drowsy sleeper,
> Awake and listen unto me."

When the potato wagon trundled into the yard behind old Squirrel, she was calm again. She told Dorothy as they got supper. Dorothy's long face reddened; her lips compressed. "It ain't no time to move you. Hasn't he any consideration?"

"I couldn't stay here with you forever, Dorothy."

"Ain't we been good to you?"

"Yes, Dorothy. I think my own mother couldn't have tended me better."

Dorothy's face softened. Tears came into her eyes.

"But then—but, Mary, I'd like to keep you here till I died. And think of you staying on after."

Mary kissed her. Tall, and gaunt, and wordless, Dorothy hugged her close. Her eyes stared over Mary's head. Her lips silently framed, "That Jerry!"

Mary said quietly:

"You'd follow after Robert, wouldn't you, Dorothy?"

"I suppose I would." Dorothy tried to laugh.

"Then you mustn't blame Jerry."

But Mary felt that she must steel herself.

Mary had a letter: the mail had left it in Orville and a man brought it up as a favor. It was marked *important* on the address side. The carrier was a young man.

"Set down, mister. . . ."

He flushed.

"Elverta Judkins."

Looking at his stodgy face, the smallish eyes ill at ease, yet bound, as she supposed, to discover the contents of the important letter, Dorothy almost giggled. She avoided Mary's eye as she invited him to sit down.

"It was real kind in you, Mr. Judkins."

" 'Tweren't neither," said Elverta. "My uncle's storekeeper."

"Oh yes—Mr. Diderick. Yes, surely."

"Well, he looked that letter over, and him and Pa considered it. And Pa said, seeing as how it was Sunday, and the Lord's day, I might as well straddle the colt and come along."

Dorothy bubbled with fun.

"Who do you expect it is, Mary?"—though they knew it must be from Hunter.

Mary said, "It's an expensive-appearing letter."

"One sheet," said Judkins, peering over. "Uncle says it. Twenty-five cents postage wrote in the corner. That's one sheet and seventy-five miles travel—less maybe, but not more. By postage law."

Mary opened it deliberately. Then she passed it over to Dorothy.

"Doesn't seem as though I could make to read it. You do, Dorothy."

Dorothy mouthed the spelling.

"Yes, it is from Roger Hunter—signs himself *your servant*, Mary. Says Caleb told him to pick you up for Montezuma. Good land!" Dorothy forgot her game. "Says he's coming Wednesday—early. Getting here by sunrise—my, that's seven o'clock."

Dorothy and Mary stared silently at each other. The tall woman's face was tragically expressionless. "So soon," she muttered. Neither of them thought of the boy until he asked, "That's all there is in to it?"

"Yes," said Dorothy bitterly, "every bit."

"Well, then, I might as well be going home."

He sounded disappointed.

"It was real kind of you to fetch it, Mr. Judkins," Mary said.

" 'Tweren't neither."

"I take it kind," she repeated fully.

His hands kept twisting his limp hat.

"No, 'tweren't," he said again, stubbing his toe against a puncheon.

Then he turned and ran out. They heard him vault onto the colt, heard his heels thwack the ribs, and the colt's spirited scrabble in the yard and thudding hoofs along the road.

Dorothy looked across.

"Well, dearie."

Her voice was old and sad. . . .

Long before the wagon came, they heard the Pennsylvania Bells. The haunting rhythm of the long-walking horse was in their notes that came like silver beads, evenly slid along a silver wire.

The baby whimpered fretfully.

"She's not used," said Dorothy, holding her. "So early."

"It'll be something maybe for her to tell some day, that she rode in a Pennsylvany wagon," Melville said, his long face honestly lugubrious.

Mary looked anxiously over her bundles. One for herself. Inside were her clothes and the baby's extra bedding and some gifts from the Melvilles —a lustre teapot for herself, and a little pewter cup for the baby when the time came for her to drink from it. Holding her now, Dorothy wondered if she would ever see her drink from it. Beside the big bundle was the baby's own little one, wrapped in a piece of scarlet calico, the four ends knotted. And next to that was the cradle. Three things to remember.

"You've got your money?"

"Yes. It's in the teapot," Mary said.

They remained silent, while the bells approached. A premonition of the dawn faintly lighted the cabin. The air was cold. The first burst of flaming in the hearth had subsided, and the coals glowed mellowly. Mary did not look at them. She kept her eyes on the window till she saw the horses and the great hood of the wagon. Then she picked up the baby's bundle and stepped out. Dorothy came after with the baby. Hushed, Melville brought the other things.

The team did not turn in. It took too long to turn a wagon of that size in a small farmyard. But Hunter walked up to meet them. "Sorry to be so early. We must get through by dark. It's thirty-three miles and heavy going since the rain."

His brown face was friendly, and he said tactfully little. It was but a moment before he had hoisted Mary to the high seat. Dorothy reached the baby up on quivering arms. Her lips were shaking.

While Melville and Hunter stowed the big bundle and the cradle in the back of the wagon, the two women looked into each other's faces. It was a time when women spoke without words, their understanding clear between them; but when the men came forward Dorothy said, "Good-bye, dearie. Good-bye, both," stiffly, as if it were a foreign speech. Melville bared his head.

"Good-bye, both," said Mary.

Hunter looked at them, then mercifully uncoiled his whip. It cracked. The horses' heads went down, as though they made obeisance to the road, and Mary felt the wheels stir under her, and the great wagon come to life. It rolled. She leaned round the hood and waved her hand. Then she faced front. . . .

She sat still on the high seat, the circular opening of the hood framing her red-shawled head. The bundle, in which the baby now had gone to sleep, lay over her knees, and the crook of her left elbow felt the hard spot through the wadding that marked the baby's head. She lifted the face flaps just to see if she was fast asleep and looked a moment at the short, dark lashes bent against the round of cheek. Then she closed the flaps against the morning marsh mist, and stared forth along the road.

From her high place she looked directly down on the six broad backs. The leaders alone were matched in color, coal black. Their long-walking stride was mated so perfectly that they moved like a machine. Mary could see no slack trace in all the twelve. Almost within touch of her feet the arches over the wheelers' withers carried the six silver bells.

By bending forward she could see Hunter walking, his stride matched to his horses', just beside the shoulder of the off-wheeler. His whip was coiled about his wrist. His hat was tilted back from his face and his eyes were on the road ahead.

Under her she felt a rolling from the wheels. The seat jutted far forward beyond the front axle, even over the wheelers' rumps, so that when the wheels went into a sink hole she herself seemed already to have passed it, and she felt only a sudden swooping forward and a slow rise afterwards, without a jar. It seemed to her as if she rode in the bows of a boat, and the marshland were water, and now and then she lifted to a long low roller.

There was no sound of wagon-moving. The wheels turned silently in their greased boxes, the balance of the great body prevented squeaks and rattles; only occasionally the drill top shuddered slightly with a noise like shaking sails.

The top was carried upon six birch hoops. Inside, when she looked back, the wagon was like a dusky cave with a small hole of light at the far end. It was piled with boxes and gave forth smells of loading, whether of this load or of earlier ones she could not say.

The movement lulled her, and the baby slept as peacefully as if she were snugged in her cradle. The bells, so near, seemed to ring no louder than the bells of wagons she had heard in passage during night.

The wagon moved through mist. Mary could look down upon a floating whiteness level with her feet, in which the horses and the teamster moved like half-dreamed animals beneath the sea. Even the marsh grass was hidden. Now and then she made out groves of trees, lifting a darker grey in cut-out patterns. She saw them as floating shapes that drifted backward. There seemed to be two layers of the mist—the one upon the ground to hide the horses, and another, higher, resting on the tops of trees; and she and the grey drill wagon-hood moved on a sacred level above the one and under the other.

Plover were flying south. Their voices, slung back and forth high up, were filtered slowly down to mingle with the bells. She heard a flock of ducks break from a marsh pool, their nasal uproar shattering the mist and starting eddies, their shapes like bullets fired at the sun.

The horses raised their heads and pricked small ears. Hunter looked up. "Mallards," he said. His brown face was like an Indian's.

Mary rode as a person on the verge of waking—that still moment when the senses are alive but the mind is lulled and only half perceives. And

Hunter, glancing up at her from time to time, read her still face, and let her be. . . .

The horses strode at three miles to the hour. A steady pace, at first glance it seemed slow; but they were bred to hold it, fourteen hours to the day, days on end.

When the sun had cleared the mist, and the marshes lay open to view, the wagon had got past the Onondaga crossing and headed westward on the Geddes road. Cossett's tavern lay behind them, a brown square shape, like a marsh growth in the grass. A barrack lifted its grey bark back a little way beyond it; and Mary saw the men coming forth from the door, hiking their trousers after breakfast, and straggling down in twos and threes for the raw black furrow through the grass. Two teams with scoops were drawing up the bank, stamping their feet to hold in mud while the handle-man bore down to lift the edge and then, on top of the embankment, heaved; and the scoop turned over, leaving its dump, an oozing mound. She could see the furrow winding off northwesterly, deep in the still brown grass, and she smelled the stagnant water that crept out of the banks to puddle in it.

But the road to Geddes went straight away west; and in a little while the canal had disappeared and they were rolling up on higher ground and farm lands began to show their fences here and there, houses and log barns, like the Melvilles', cattle coming forth from milking, a boy slapping cow hocks with a strap, a barking dog, stilling suddenly to lift his leg against the gatepost, and a woman, who might have been herself, carrying two loaded buckets back across the yard.

The sun shone warmly. The wet road showed its ruts in narrow, gleaming lakes; but the earth smelled wholesome again. With the warmth, the color began to rise in Mary's cheeks. She raised her head and saw white clouds in a blue sky. The bells under her feet picked up a clearer tune and the horses shook their withers. Hunter caught up a pace on them so that he walked where he could look at her over his shoulder. He heard the baby snuffle and gasp.

He laughed.

"Comfortable?"

"Yes, thanks."

She opened the flap over the baby's face and shifted the round head to lie under her breast. She smiled at Hunter.

"It's more comfortable than any riding I have had."

He laughed again.

"I seldom ever ride. It makes a man too tired, all day long."

He looked as if he could go on walking until his horses put their forefeet in the sea.

"But it's an easy-riding wagon."

He seemed never to glance at his horses. Even when they met an ox-cart with two children popping round eyes at them over the box edge and had to take the off edge of the road, he merely said, "Gee, Edward," quietly and watched the off front wheel. When it had touched the shoulder, "Up!" he said, and the three teams straightened one by one. The oxcart had to look out for itself. A Pennsylvania team had right of way. It gave what it could, and if that was not enough the other vehicle must get into the ditch.

There were no stages on this road. It was back-country—a few farms here and there just taking on establishment. Geddes, when they reached it, was no more than a hamlet, round a tiny store that bore a sign, Post Office. . . .

By noon they had passed Camillus, a larger village with a small frame church and schoolhouse. Mary saw the children coming forth to eat their lunch, and the teacher, an oldish man in sober black, eating his bread and cheese upon the doorstep. Half a mile beyond the village the tolling of the bell for afternoon caught up with them. A brassy noise, unmusical, yet it rang as if the master unloosed his pride in it.

For their own lunch they stopped beside a moss-bedded brook as cold as ice. The horses came down in pairs to drink from it, careful with their forehoofs not to muddy it, dipping their muzzles to the eyes. Mary watched the gulps traveling up the arching throats. The horses lingered for an instant to let the water dribble from their nostrils, then turned back to the wagon, where Hunter had fastened their feed box to the rigid pole. They took their orderly stations before their own compartments. He stayed until all were eating. "That grey's kind of a thief," he explained. "He don't go actually for to steal, but to play a joke; but when a horse is hauling, a joke like that comes heavy on him."

He made a small fire and sank in crotched sticks on either side of the flames, put another over them, and hung an iron kettle floating tea leaves. Then he brought out collops of lean pork.

"You'll have one, Mrs. Fowler?"

"If you'll share my pie and cheese."

"That's fine."

While he cooked the sizzling meat on pointed sticks, Mary nodded her dress. She had already changed the baby's cloths, rinsed the used in the spring, and spread them on a bush. But now a fly had waked the baby to a sense of famishment. It batted its hands against the breast and laid hold eagerly. And again, as she had felt in the beginning days, the wonder of her strength was waked in Mary and she bent far over the child. To-day it looked to her like Jerry. Its eyes, she thought, would not be grey like hers, but dark as his. A dark-eyed girl, she thought, with yellow hair.

As the milk flowed, she straightened her back. Across the fire she met the teamster's frank eyes. He was smiling at her.

"I've never seen her, Mrs. Fowler. Can I now?"

Mary nodded. He came forward to bend down by the suckling baby. He touched its cheek with a tar-stained thumb.

"Pretty," he said softly. His thumb, in drawing off, just brushed the breast. But Mary was untouched by it; her being was absorbed as it had always been, and Hunter's brown face smiled as he returned to his fire.

The baby fell asleep when it had finished, and they ate together side by side upon a log. They did not talk, but when they were done Hunter lighted a cigar and puffed awhile, and then rose up and hitched his team.

He helped Mary to her seat and handed up the baby. He took a last look at the spring.

"If some teamsters had seen me there with linens all spread out they would have laughed."

But Mary did not hear. Her eyes were for the road beyond the leaders' ears.

"Will we meet Jerry on the road?"

"I don't know. I'm hauling in to Montezuma. If he's working still at Jordan, likely not. We go on to Brutus before we turn north."

She scarcely was aware of the start, the wagon rolled so smoothly. They passed through miles of woodland, sweet with balsam, where she saw rabbits under ferns. Hunter pointed out a partridge eating berries, but before she saw it the bird had thundered off into the trees.

Elbridge, a little village, met them in the woods, and then at a little after three they came to Brutus. Here the westward road ended in a tavern against which a horse-shed leaned, and they turned north away from the Auburn road. They now traveled in the thickest woods that Mary had ever seen. The branches bent down to scrape the wagon-hood, and the box swayed and pitched over corduroy. The bells were a muffled, close sound which she could almost touch.

Without warning they rolled out in a clearing. The road ran on to dry ground at a corners where a cabin stood. Burnt land showed stumps and the charred bodies of trees. A man and woman were working, between them dragging a hand brush-harrow over lumpy ground. And inexplicably the raw ditch of the half-dug canal stretched out of the trees from the right and went away to west beside a raw new road.

Hunter stopped the team and walked across to the young couple.

"Hello," he said.

The man took in the whip and the great wagon and the panting team. His eyes hardened; and the woman drew close to his side.

"Hello," he said.

Hunter smiled friendlily, but the man's eyes were unchanged.

"You ain't seen a man named Fowler round about here?"

"Fowler?" asked the man, stiffly. He turned to the woman. Labor had hollowed her oval face. She spoke in an edged voice.

"He's the one that left the letter?"

"Maybe him. I disremember names. These diggers are all alike. They answer only to a gun."

He looked at Hunter, then slowly to the wagon. Both he and his woman then saw Mary.

"Is it her expects a letter?"

"It might be her or me."

"He left a letter for his wife."

"Suppose you let us see it."

"How'll we know? A letter ain't a thing for everybody," said the man. The woman added, "I have got it hid. You can't have it."

It might have been their meagre stock of coins they talked about.

Hunter said, "You could let me read it. If it's not for us we'll hand it back."

The two looked at each other.

"Maybe that's so," said the man. "Fetch it, Anna."

The woman tiredly entered the house. The man followed her. He came forth with a rifle in his hand. Then the woman brought a folded square of paper. It was not sealed. Hunter looked at the address.

"It's for you, Mrs. Fowler."

He made to hand it up to Mary.

"I won't let you hand it up," the man said suddenly.

Mary's heart had fallen.

"Read it there. I don't want to get down, disturbing the baby."

"You've a baby?" demanded the woman.

"Yes."

"He said the woman had a baby—was his wife. George, you recollect."

The man nodded.

"Could I see the baby?"

Dully, Mary opened the blanket flap. The sight of the small red face comforted her. But the woman had sprung up on the eveners and was peering in with avid eyes.

Suddenly the eyes filled, and she whispered up to Mary proudly, "I'm expecting my own self. In February."

Mary looked round the small clearing. She thought of the woods road and snow.

"I'm glad," she said, and the woman smiled and nodded.

"I guess it's all right, George," she said over her shoulder.

Hunter was reading the letter. He said, "Jerry's sorry he can't come to meet you. He's hired you a little house in Montezuma, belonging to a Mrs. Peck. It's ready for you. There's firewood and she has got in edibles. He's coming down next week."

The woman smiled at Mary.

"A hired house," she said; but Mary thought, "He wouldn't come to meet us. Yes. A hired house."

Port Byron stood in fields. And from Port Byron the broad wheels rolled on a better road. The horses tossed their bits as if their collars had been cured of pain. At sunset they saw a town below them. Beyond, a river gleamed in a meandering channel, making islands. A great marsh was spread out, as far as the eye could see. The grass was bending in a wind like waves of dim grey water. Mary had never seen such grass; it rose, out of water, ten feet high.

The village street followed the higher bank of the river. There were buildings on each side. A tannery ran a long shed beside the road and gave out green hide smells. A church had a small square tower. There was a tavern with a yard, and a man brushing down a sweated horse.

Across the river, two long barracks stood on little hillocks, and in the sunset sheen men were digging to their waists in muck. A boat coming across the river carried three men wrapped in blankets. As Hunter's wagon passed the landing, one of the two rowers jumped out and made fast to the planks. He looked at Hunter, spat into the water, said, "Just three more fevers."

"Much of it?" Hunter asked.

"Not much now. They had three hundred sick last August."

The wagon rolled down the street.

Hunter asked a man, "Where's Mrs. Peck live?"

The man pointed a thumb.

"That frame house at the end of the street. A widow-woman. Her husband owned the tannery; she's rich. That house—with the first cabin back of it."

Mary followed the thumb's pointing. The man was staring up at her. But she did not look at him. She saw the cabin. It was lifeless.

Hunter wheeled the team round the frame house. A weedy garden patch was back of it. He helped Mary down at the cabin door, and carried in her bundles for her. He said, "I'll light you a fire before I go on."

There was wood behind, which he brought in. He started a roaring blaze. The cabin was dank with mould. The baby cried.

A voice said, "What are you doing in my house?"

A shawled, bent, hook-nosed woman leaned on a stick in the door.

"This is Mrs. Fowler," Hunter said.

"Oh, her?" She stood a moment eyeing Mary with sharp grey eyes. Her hooked nose seemed to draw down as if she smelled the whiskey on her lips. "I hope you're comfortable, Mrs. Fowler."

She turned herself slowly round.

"I won't drop in until you're settled."

Hunter said, "Is there a well?"

"A good one," said the woman. "In the garden."

She went off.

Hunter drew a bucket for Mary and then went out to his team.

"I'll stop in before I leave to-morrow," he said. Then he smiled at her weary face. "It won't look so bad in the morning. All it needs is the fire. Log walls dry fast."

Mary thanked him, watched him go. Then she looked around the cabin. It had glass windows, two of them. There was a bed in the corner, but the blankets hung from the rafters were damp-smelling. She got them down and spread them over the table. There were two splint-seated chairs beside the table and a few dishes on a shelf. A chest held flour and bacon and some eggs, butter, and a jar of milk.

Mary looked down at them. Then the baby cried, again. She turned, picked it up, drew a chair to the fire, and sat down. She opened her dress, and, feeding the baby, comforted herself. But her eyes kept wandering. She thought again, "A hired house."

Interlude

"Spit on your hands and dig"

Independenceville

ON a Sunday morning, the Mayor came walking down the main street of the city. He wore an old three-cornered hat upon his head; the black rolled felt shone dimly green. His old blue army coat with the buff facings had been brushed threadbare; and his buff waistcoat showed no single spot, "because," as the Mayor would tell a person, "for thirty year I've took it off to eat my Sunday dinner." But instead of breeches and black gaiters he wore homespun pants stuffed into cowhide boots.

"A-1." Mayor Barley leaned upon his stick to contemplate the shoes. "A new cobbler made them for me back in March. He bought out Willie Bender's circuit here. A man I wouldn't notion towards for a citizen to live into my city, but handy as a cobbler. Name of Harley Falk, he drives a blind white horse."

"I've heard of him," said Jerry. "He made my wife a pair of shoes."

"You're married, are you, boy?"

"Yes."

"Look here!" The Mayor turned on him. His little sky-blue eyes swam sentimentally. "Why don't you bring the Missus here and settle? Here's the rising city of the west. I tell you what. I've took a notion to you. And the copriation will make out a lot to you for nothing. Just toss your eye around, boy, and see where you are standing. There's Jackson Avenue a-coming into Main Street where we stand, with Steuben Alley running into it. (I give Steuben an alley for remembrance of his everlasting present arms.) Now here, real handy, is the public market. Look over there—what do you see?"

Jerry looked. He saw a dead skunk cabbage beside an aphised alder clump.

"A handsome site. That's the Constitution Opera House. A handsome building. Across the way is the Washington Hotel, or Lafayette Bar, I disremember. The lettering's wore off."

Jerry walked over to a painted signboard tilted halfway over.

"It's got the mark of a P, and there's an R a little way along."

"God damn!" Mayor Barley struck his stick deep into the mud. "Elkanah's got them mixed again. The idea of a livery stable setting in amongst an oprey house! Paul Revere Livery. No sir—it's the bar. I'll show it to you on my map. Then if you're minded, as you say, to build you boats on this canal, I'll let you have a yard on the main basin. Elkanah's digging of it in the spring. I had to make him alderman to do it. He's the common council now for putting up these buildings, besides being swamper in my bar."

The sun glanced brilliantly on his red nose.

"Ain't it handy?" he demanded, proudly.

"It's a handsome layout," Jerry said.

"I take it I've been kind of cute in naming of the streets. I've got it close to near completion, only for the schoolhouse. And I've got a bell to put in that."

"I don't believe I'll settle down just yet," said Jerry.

"Well, it makes me sorry. But I'm glad to have you living in my bar. It's going to do me good to see some part of this canal get done. By dog it! I've set on my porch and watched those poor bezabors heeling down in muck and getting nowhere. All the while they get the fever. Even whiskey don't do any good. You'll mark I laid this town out on high ground. I've lived here twenty year and never had a touch of ague. Yes sir!" He touched Jerry's elbow with his stick.

"Let's just turn in to Clintonia Street, right here. It takes up by the town hall into the park where Linas Barley's is. A good place for a drink!" The Mayor stuck in a word of advertisement for his tavern. "Good liquor and a bug-free bed to follow."

They walked along over the hummocky ground marked off with myriad signboards. The streets had no relation to pedestrian comforts. They clambered over logs or circled tamarack trees and crossed a sluggish creek on one frail board.

"Some day I'll trace that crick back," said Linas Barley. "It ought to flow from salt or maybe coal, I ain't made up my mind."

They circled the park, where an aged cow was brooding over clover dreams and chewing a cud of buffalo grass, and came out of the sparse woodland on the edge of the marshes.

There a large log house, of two full stories with a lean-to kitchen in the back and a porch on cedar piles in front, faced eastward. The air was clear of haze. Jerry could see as far as Montezuma, nine miles off. The marsh grass was a maze of grey netted with blue, meandering threads, and through the middle of it, straight away, ran the line of the canal. It showed not as a ditch but as a ribbon of roiled water. There were no diggers on a Sunday, but the eye could sight the thin lines of stone laid down on either side, waiting for puddling.

"You've tackled a hard job to lay foundation for that lock. One contractor has gone bust on it. I don't know why young Dancer Borden bought him out. But he won't never muddy his Russian boots in any mud. He told me just the other day he'd found a man to make it—meaning you, I've got no doubt."

He stamped up the porch and into the tap. Jerry followed. At the table sat his helpers, Plute Sowersby and Cosmo Turbe.

Plute grinned to see him.

"Do we get a driver for the piles, Mr. Fowler?"

"We'll need one," Jerry said.

"Cosmo has been hankering to put his hand on one of them contraptions."

The little frog-mouthed man grinned blandly. He poised his hand above a sugar-colicked fly that lay kicking just in front of him. His left hand made a motion of cranking and the right hand was raised slowly. Then he knocked an imaginary paul and the right hand came down like lead. Plute shuddered ostentatiously.

Cosmo Turbe turned his hand over. Underneath, the fly still kicked with colic. He had cupped his palm. He grinned and whistled in his teeth. Slowly he cranked up his hammer. Once more the palm came down. When Plute looked back, there was no fly.

"Now what you gone and done to it?" demanded Plute.

Cosmo put his eye level with the table and ostentatiously blew some dust.

Linas Barley was taking off his coat and waistcoat. He hung them on a peg, came forward to a chair beside the iron stove, and sat down comfortably. He had a pipe in his hand and tobacco in a brass box. The sunlight, shining on his shoulder, touched his leathery old cheek.

"Yes sir," he said, "she's quite a city."

Plute looked at him under his shaggy brows.

"Me and Cosmo has been looking at the map of it." He pointed with his thumb at the wall behind him. "It's going to be a handsome place, Mr. Barley. But ain't there going to be no church?"

Barley lit his pipe; he put out little puffs.

"I didn't bother to set them down," he said. "I figgered they'd just come themselves. They always do."

Jerry went to his small sleeping room. The tavern was strangely clean. Upstairs the walls were papered with old news-print. The window of his room had colored paper curtains—blue and orange; they crackled faintly in the breeze. His bundle lay on the foot of the bed, ready for unpacking. With one ear alert for the dinner bell, he set to work to put away his things. Below, he could hear Linas Barley holding forth to Cosmo Turbe.

"I got these lands by the Pension Law of '83. They wasn't good for farming, so I just settled down here and built me a bar. The Durham boaters come in sometimes. And lately I got word of this canal. Right then I got my notion for a city. There she is."

The dinner bell clanged brassily.

"Six hundred acres for a sergeant. Elkanah, he come with me. Now I've got me a black woman for a cook and things are comfortable and the diggers make me trade. I've sent in copriation papers into Albany, but they don't answer. Not that it makes a lot of difference. If a man intends to have the finest city of the westward land, who's got the right to stop him?"

They ate at the long table along the taproom wall. Elkanah Kew was a cadaverous image built of skin and bone. His eyes were bleary and his nose bothered him in breathing.

"Elkanah ain't got much enthusiasm for this canal. He don't exactly fancy digging out the basin, do you, hey?"

Kew did not raise his head.

"Wait till you get stuck, waist-down in that-there muck," he said to Cosmo. "Hell! A little wart like you will be chin-deep."

Cosmo rolled his eyes.

An ample black woman wearing a bright green kerchief served them with fried bass and buckwheat fritters. Elkanah stabbed in heavy mouthfuls. A bone in his jaw kept knocking as he chewed. His monotonous words came round the food.

"Last summer half the gangs was sick with fever. Every time they shoveled out the muck, some more ran in. There's niggers working now, and they get sick with colds."

"It's a fact," said Barley soberly. "They've dug a year at it and only got a mile to show. The muck, it wets right in."

Dancer Borden

Mr. Dancer Borden's residence overlooked the marshes from the south shore of Mud Creek in the southwest corner of the town of Galen. It was a white frame building, handsomely fronted with pilasters that merged into arches over the second-story windows. A grove of young elms gave it delicate shade.

Mr. Borden lived alone. He had a dozen negroes on the place to work his orchards and tend his blooded cattle; but no sight of them was visible from the house itself. The barns, the oast-house, and the deerhound kennels were all concealed by skillful hemlock planting.

"Mistuh Bo'den is expecting of you, suh."

The sly-eyed, slim mulatto girl gave Jerry a knowing glance. She seemed to giggle underneath her skin to see his sturdy shoes slicked up with grease, his homespun coat that wrinkled on the shoulders; even his freshly laundered flannel shirt amused her.

She left him in a drawing-room whose windows overlooked the slope down to the creek. The sun was setting westward. A mile away Jerry could see Linas Barley's tavern and the site of Independenceville. In the marsh itself the black-gnat specks of negroes waded in the muck. On the very edge of the marsh he saw the site of the lock and the web-like beams of the pile driver waiting to be hauled away.

The river gleamed with a steady change of sunset color. Far away towards Montezuma, an active pile driver was thudding piles to hold the causeway towpath.

But the windows revealed these things as interesting pictures that a man could put out of sight by a mere drawing of brocaded curtains. A flowered carpet made comfortable the floor, and silken-covered chairs invited elegant meditation. There were small tables of foreign makes; one, carved in dull black wood, attracted Jerry. Some day, perhaps, when he had his own house, he would buy such a table.

"How are you, Fowler?"

In the door stood Dancer Borden; an indolent, slim figure, oval-faced, with black, possessive eyes. He held his hand out.

"Evening, Mr. Borden."

Jerry was conscious of the hat held in his hand. Mr. Borden made a tiny gesture, and the mulatto servant stole in and gently removed it to the hall. She passed her master with a demure bending of her head; and he ignored her.

"Dinner," he said, "is waiting."

A pointed finger-tip on Jerry's elbow guided him along the hall; his thick-soled boots raised clatters from the tiling. The dining room was walled with a French paper on which pink shepherdesses disported with pink swains. The furniture was pale Domingo, suggesting, in its slimness, the elegance of the master of the house.

He seated Jerry on his right and took his own place. He left his napkin folded on his knees. There was an odor in this house that puzzled Jerry, a fine perfume he thought might come from antique wood. He had smelled nothing like it in his life. It made it hard for him to speak; and he was glad that there was only Dancer Borden to confront him.

They ate a creamy pinkish soup—tomatoes; then fish, broiled collops of a western sturgeon, liberally sauced with a flavor Jerry was unable to identify; then quail, split upon a kind of toast, with a glass of wine; and wine again to go with the roast of lamb; and another wine to follow venison; and then a strange fluffy dish on which Dancer Borden sent out his compliments to the kitchen. He called it a soufflé. Always, after that evening, Jerry would think of Dancer Borden by that outlandish dish that looked so frail, like fluff between one's teeth, and had a virile taste of foreign cheese. It grew upon one after it was gone.

Two new maids waited on them, both mulattoes, in caps and dark brown dresses. They moved silently, with trained, averted eyes. In all the houses Jerry had eaten in the waiting girl sat down at table, but these two were like shadows, of which he only seemed aware.

Borden talked with charm. There was no unmanly posture in his speech. He talked about his hounds. He hunted deer with them, on horseback, like a western gentleman. One carried a rifle and followed the hound's voice as close as the horse could take one through the woods, striving to head off the deer at a clearing. It made for chancy shooting. He asked Jerry's advice on boring worms in apple trees, and Jerry spoke of the potash ring they used in Uniontown, and Borden made a little note of that in a little book with a silver-capped small crayon.

After dinner, when they had gone into his library, a maid brought brandy in a small glass bottle. Borden explained that it was old French his father had brought back from Quebec, when he was a prisoner there ("Seigneur's Brandy"). And only then did he ask about the progress on the lock.

"My job's done except for the gates," Jerry said. "Your mason's putting in the tiers."

"That's fine. I knew when I laid eyes on you that you would do the trick."

"I've had experience by now."

The firelight beat on the still, pale face of Dancer Borden like small hands. His profile, turned to Jerry, offered clear-cut lines. His dark eyes had grown velvety, woman-like, Jerry thought. Though here was no woman-like creature; but a man who could mark his buck at forty paces from a galloping horse.

The brandy grew in Jerry, blossomed inward, and turned his thoughts from digging. Through the curtained windows, where the night was still and cool and clean on the neat lawn, he looked back to Montezuma. Mary would be in her cabin. She seemed happier now. It was a counterfeit of the small home she hungered after. She would have put the baby to bed by this time, and would be spinning, maybe, or sewing at his worn-out clothes, or making herself a dress out of the stuff they had bought together at the store. This summer she had worked a little garden patch. She had had daffodils in spring, and planted rhubarb. She moved about her daily round with a placidity that sometimes Jerry longed to break, but could not move against.

And all at once he tried to think why this strange gentleman had invited him to dinner; for he had caught some of the same restlessness, half reckless, and half bitter, like a distillation from all these beautiful luxuries. But when Jerry looked up to meet the dark, cool eyes, Dancer Borden laughed. "Go lightly," his laughter seemed to say. "Look about you, see, and have. But do go lightly."

"I was thinking," Dancer Borden said, "that we've been digging through that swamp for twenty months. And there hasn't been any real progress. One Galen and three Mentz contractors have been broken by it. What was done was done in winter. It's not the men's fault. They're pretty faithful, but the fever weakens them. Poor devils." He laughed lightly. "I suppose I'm a fool, but I've taken up the contracts."

Jerry stared.

"I see you agree, Fowler. But you know the marsh involves just one thing. That's human toughness. Now they've tried our local peasantry that ought to be inured to ague and the intermittent fever. They went down south for Pennsylvania Dutch, strong shovelers, but the fever pole-axed them. Just about every race under the sun was tried except the yellow men from China—where that table came from that you were admiring, by the way. Then I got interested. My own niggers have kept healthy. So I sent down into Virginia for a hundred negroes. I bought them. When they got up here I set them free under the recent act, but put them under contract to work for me two years. They still work like slaves under that big buck, Jay-Jay. You've seen him. The fellow with the earrings. But they're chilled; they can't stand that wet muck. It seeps right through their black hides."

He made a little gesture with his hand.

"Two months ago when I was in Albany I fell to talking with a sailing master. I put the problem up to him. And he said right away there was one race to dig it—the Irish bog-trotters. I commissioned him to get a shipload of them. They ought to land at Hudson before long. We'll have them here next month."

Jerry said nothing. He wondered vaguely what a bog-trotter would look like; but he felt no interest. The brandy blurred his senses, and Dancer Borden's face hung like a medallion beyond his mazy stream of thought. . . .

Rough-and-Tumble

"She's done," said Plute. Nodding his head, Cosmo Turbe swung a gate back and forth. Jerry looked out over the marsh. Work was where it had been, for all that an eye could see. The cook came forth from the first barrack to clang his gong for supper. The three lock builders gathered their tools.

"Cosmo," said Plute, "she's done, and me, I'm going to get drunk."

The little man examined his partner, with popping eyes.

"How about it, Cosmo? How do you feel?"

"Real active, Plute."

They trudged together up the hill, along the Canal Boulevard of Linas Barley's Independenceville. Jerry remained to pack his chest. He heard the dinner bell ringing in the tavern. A fine rain was sifting through the dusk.

As he walked up the hill, half an hour later, he saw a group on the tavern porch. Old Linas Barley in his tricorn hat stood right between two men, like a master at a ceremonial.

The others were mostly strange to Jerry. Another gang, he supposed, to try their luck with fever. Or else they had come from the marsh, it being Saturday. As he drew closer he supposed they had come from the marshes. Their eyes were angry, their faces tightly drawn. Then he saw that one of the two men between whom Linas Barley stood was Cosmo Turbe. His squat figure was quite still. He looked like a man ready to sleep. Only his eyes were staring at the other.

"What's doing?" Jerry asked.

"That timber-beast squashed Henry," said Plute.

"What for?"

"He beat his own bug in a race."

Cosmo had a cockroach that he used to race against all comers; or if there was no racing competition, the bug was used to play roulette with. Cosmo called it Henry.

Plute took Jerry's arm.

"You can see him if you are a-mind to, in the bar."

Jerry stared at the other man. He stood close to six feet. In front of him, Cosmo was a little boy. The man's eyes glittered. He had put his week's pay in a lump on his own bug; he had no drinking money left.

"Stand back, Mr. Fowler," Linas Barley said. He addressed the two men. "It's rough-and-tumble to a finish, open all. I introduce you Cosmo Turbe, the runtish man, and Noble Eddy out of Pompey."

"Wait," said Jerry.

Plute whispered, "Leave him be. Cosmo is an active man."

Hung from the doorpost a lantern threw a gleam out against the sifting rain. The eaves were dripping slow big drops. The faces of the two men stood out like masks. And as Barley stepped back, and said confidentially to Jerry, "I ain't seen a rough-and-tumble wrassel in nine years," Jerry saw Cosmo's flat mouth grin and his long tongue lip his mouth.

The other men were breathing hoarsely. Marsh digging roughened a man's breath.

Then all at once the big man moved; and Cosmo ducked; and the porch shook under their feet. They slid in and out so quickly that in the dim light Jerry's eyes were dazed. He heard a blur of voices, "A French lip. . . . Gouge him. . . . There's a Buffalo-roll, by God . . . the little feller's neat. Four shillings to a fip on Noble . . . a butt . . . I'll cover them four shilling." The last was Plute's voice, confident, ready to laugh. Jerry could see no mark on either man; but their boots stamped; the porch shook as one fell to dodge a groin kick. . . . Then, as quickly as it had begun, the thing was over.

Cosmo had missed a thrust at Noble's nose, to catch the nostrils with hooked fingers. He rolled over the other's upthrust knee, and kept on rolling over the boards. Noble pounced with a hoarse roar. But as he would have landed, Cosmo seemed to rise on his stiff elbows, head and shoulders on the floor, and his heels flashed their nails in the lantern, and Noble Eddy crumpled like a rotten stick. He lay still on his face, his hands under it, making no sound. Cosmo got up and turned him over.

Blood was oozing through Noble's fingers, but Cosmo took his hand away. One boot had caught the mouth, opening the lips raggedly. In the misplaced bloody hole, Jerry saw a yellowish tooth. The other heel had sunk into the cheek. Cosmo touched the marking with his fingers. A star with a jagged line. He shrugged his shoulders.

Jerry felt sick. He went inside. He heard Plute collecting his four shillings. "Champion of the trace. An active man. His name is Cosmo Turbe."

Jerry ordered a glass of Devereux whiskey. As he sat down at table with it the men came trooping in. They were silent, sullen-eyed, and they did not look at Cosmo.

On the table was a squashed brown cockroach.

Irondequot

Bates was a matter-of-fact sort of man.

"Fowler, Mr. Bouck."

The commissioner shook hands with Jerry.

They sat down together on the steps of Linas Barley's porch. Bates, the assistant engineer, opened the conversation.

"Mr. Bouck and I've been out along the line to Rochester. Most of the way the digging will look easy when we get this marsh done."

Mr. Bouck nodded.

"It looks pretty hopeless. If there was some way to drain them."

"Well, it's Dancer Borden's worry."

"He doesn't care. He's got money to spend, as much as he wants. It's a game to him."

"That's it," said Bates. "He takes it as a sporting proposition, and he'll finish it."

"Well, maybe. But here it is in late September. Back at Rome they'll soon let Mohawk water into the Utica section. Next spring boats will be moving out to Montezuma. But here we haven't a thing to show yet. Digging all the way to Erie won't help things if we can't dig out across that marsh. We've got the stones laid for the trunk, but if we can't empty out the muck and puddle it with clay, next high water will wash in what little we have dug. It did before."

"Leave it to Borden," Bates said. "What we wanted, Fowler, is to see you about Irondequot. Do you know that place?"

"No."

"Out there Irondequot Brook cuts through the Rochester level. There's high land on each side. We can't lock down to the creek because there isn't water to make another high level between there and here. We've got to open a straight flow for Erie water to these marshes. See it?"

Jerry nodded.

"How deep is the creek under level?"

"Eighty feet," said Mr. Bouck.

"There's just one place to get across," said Bates. "Geddes found it on his first survey in 1809. The creek loops a small round hill there, then there's another cut it must have dug in Indian times, but dry now. That's easy to fill. We've got to trunk across the top of that round hill, and luckily its top is wide enough. But the creek crossing is another pullet. What do you think? Could you make an aqueduct of wood that high?"

"How long?"

"Five hundred feet."

"There's too much weight of water," Jerry said.

"Geddes thought so," said Mr. Bouck. "I think so myself and so does Bates. But back in Albany, the Tammany delegates are getting nervous of the money we've been spending. Every time a thing crops up they tell us to try it in wood."

"If we make an earth embankment," Bates said, "we'll need a culvert for the creek. What we want to know is whether you'll be free next spring."

"I guess so."

"Will you hire on to the state to build that culvert floor? We don't dare contract it out. It's too ticklish. One waving pile would start the whole embankment washing."

"What does the state pay?"

"What do you get from Dancer Borden?"

"A hundred shillings flat a week."

"Will you take that for this job?"

"Yes."

Wild Irish

Edwin Brown had cooked the breakfast for the new gang. In the main room he heard them stirring in their bunks. O'Mory, the boss, with his thick black beard stuffed inside his shirt to drink his tea, was asking for more bacon. Crazy Tom was scuttling in and out. But Edwin Brown was not worrying. This morning marked an era.

It seemed to him that, like the wandering Jew, his life moved under a curse. He had tried every lottery available in these two years, but never yet had he found the lucky number. And here he was stuck down at his old job, in a marsh ten times as big as any he had worked in yet. He hated the cold, he hated the getting up on a morning to cook for heavy-smelling men. And he had come into a fever-ridden shanty, just in time to see a weary gang go out and these new brown horrible outlandish men come in with their jabber of strange talk. Gaelic, the big boss said it was; himself was New York Irish.

But this morning things looked better to Edwin Brown. For in the interval between the old gang's going out and the coming in of these queer creatures with their lathelike arms and legs he had provided himself with a winter comfort. From the timber leavings of the marsh lock he had been given by Mr. Fowler, he had constructed himself a privy. He had laid it up himself. Three by five, and six feet high, it had a sloping roof. As he surveyed it yesterday evening, he thought that he had seldom seen a better-constructed piece of work. The fit of the door was just as good as any carpenter could have made it. The inside walls were papered to keep out the wind. It would be cold, of course, in winter, but the wind was what he had minded most these two years past.

Luxuriously he emptied the last drop of tea from his own cup. In the main room, the men were talking softly. Now and then he caught an English word, ignorantly mispronounced, as one or other of the men attempted conversation with the boss. He supposed he ought to take a look at them to see if crazy Tom had done his job, but he wasn't going to spoil the gentle ecstasy of this initial morning. He put his cup down.

Slowly he got to his feet and took his stiff hat from its peg. He rolled his sleeves down and took off his apron. Then he worked his arms into his coat.

He moved softly to the door. But just there he remembered something. He returned to the sink and got the latest newspaper. It had the lottery drawings which he had read in misery two days ago. A little smile spread his small mouth. He put the paper in his pocket and stepped out. It was a misty morning. Down the line for the river, the driver, piling on the causeway, had begun its work. The thuds came to him in a kind of muffled drum-beat for a fine slow march.

Edwin Brown followed the path through the wet, silvered muck. He saw the structure sitting there with a sublime aloofness. It was as he had left it, door closed, the latchstring hanging forth. That, he considered, had been his consummating inspiration. A privy with an actual latch.

He paused a moment to take in the lines with all the pride of real achievement. Then, smiling half modestly, half bashfully, he pulled the string, opened the door, and stepped inside.

For a moment the scene was one of utter quietude. The marsh mist lifted silently to the sun's drinking. The morning was brought in with peacefulness.

Then, in the thinning mists, some shapes began to move. They were men, walking in bare feet, single file behind their leader. The damp was pearled in his black beard. His shirt was open to the waist, showing his bright red undershirt.

"Hogan."

His voice whispered incredibly soft and hoarse, but a little bat-eared fellow with jouncy steps moved up beside him, and cocked his face to get his orders.

"Yis?"

"Ye've got the hammer and the big spike wid ye?"

"Yis, O'Mory."

"Then it's you for nailing the door."

Hogan grinned. As he began stealing for the door, O'Mory motioned up his cohorts. The rush-men carried two fifteen-foot poles.

"As soon as Hogan dhrives his spike, you bhoys rush up and belabor on thim two-by-fowers."

He moved with them cautiously. The latchstring was drawn in. From the inside of the privy no sound came, and outside the Irish crept with an unholy stealth.

Suddenly Hogan's hammer banged. It banged again—the sound of a heavy spike being rammed in. And then as the mist swirled under the sun, the marsh was made alive with shrieking. A dozen men nailed on the two-by-fours. Along behind them came the stamp of running feet. They screamed with laughter, but the privy remained as still as death.

O'Mory roared above them all. His teeth glistened like porcelain through the black hairs of his beard.

"Lift it up, me bhoys. It's in an unconvaniant place. Just bring it round until I've found it out a dacent spot."

A dozen men put shoulders under the bars. The privy swung aloft. It teetered as they took their first step forward. Then a dark-faced boy named Peter started singing. He sang in Gaelic, a hero's song, how his most faithful soldiers carried him to his bier. The others caught the tune. Their faces lighted with a kind of melancholy joy. Their feet moved into time, and like a palanquin of a queen they bore the privy towards the shanty. The other shanties had been built on reasonably dry ground farther along the marsh. Singing still, they started down the berm. Half of them went before and half followed after. From the peg over his bunk O'Mory had brought forth the fire helmet he had worn to fires with his company back in New York. Bright red, its varnish sparkled in the rising sun. He marched before the palanquin with the strut of a queen's bed-master.

A quarter of a mile they bore it down, and at each shanty other Irishmen lit up their eyes and joined them till they had a hundred strong. And they all sang.

They turned about, and slowly came back along the marsh. At Independenceville, old Linas Barley in his tricorn hat first heard them. He called for Jerry.

Bates and Jerry caught the wild swirling of voices. The singing was like nothing human they had heard. Without music, it had music in its heart; it had no beauty, but it was sad with a desire. They forgot, in hearing it, the letter from Utica that Bates had just begun to read, and they came out with Linas and looked down on the brown procession winding serpentwise along the berm.

O'Mory came marching up to them. He stopped beside the wall of the finished lock. He spied there two eighteen-foot planks left over from the gate planks. He lifted them up alone and cast them over the well. Then, motioning his men, he had them inch the privy out so that it stood in the middle of the lock, ten feet over the bottom flooring, with the door flush with the outside edge of the front plank.

He raised his hand for silence.

"Here's a place, me bhoys."

In the sudden hush of those wild men, a frantic hammering sounded from inside the privy. O'Mory's jaw fell open.

"God deliver me, there's someone in it!"

"Hey!" came the muffled voice. "Hey! Hey! Let me out."

"Oh God," wailed the jouncy little Hogan—"I think it's Mister Brown."

"Why didn't annybody tell me he was in it?" roared O'Mory.

Every face was hangdog.

"Don't stand shtupiding! Let the poor man out! You, Hogan, you're handy with a hammer."

The little jouncy man jumped on a plank. He reached around the corner with his hammer and clawed forth the spike. The iron squeaked through the wood. And Jerry and Bates, with laughter grasping them, managed to look soberly at the door. An instant there was silence. The door swung wide, and in the privy they saw Edwin Brown, doing up the buckle of his belt. He took one dizzy step and then shrank back.

The faces of the Irish were very sad. They looked embarrassed.

And then O'Mory said, "We beg yer pardon, Misther Brown. We didn't know it was a private privy. The bhoys is very sorry. Shall we carry you back?"

Edwin Brown had his great moment then.

"No thanks, O'Mory. I think I'll walk. It's time I had my morning constitutional."

They carried off the privy. Handsomely, Edwin Brown stepped out. Without a word he started walking back to the shanty, and behind him half a dozen men, like naughty children, bore his privy for him.

"Wait a minute, O'Mory," Bates said. "It's pretty funny in a way. But it's time you had your gang at work."

"We didn't intend no harm, sor. We wouldn't never have done it if we'd known that Misther Brown was in it."

"Oh, I know that," Bates's voice was sober as the Irishman's. "But this isn't play you boys have tackled. I've just had a letter that I want to read you. It will show you that this is a great thing that you're working at."

He fished the letter from his pocket.

"This canal," he said, "used to be a dream of a few men. But now there's water in it. It's up to you to carry it west through this marsh." He opened the letter. "It's from a gentleman I know in Utica. He says he thinks I'd like a comment not official. This is what he writes:—

> "On Friday afternoon I walked to the head of the grand canal, the eastern extremity of which now reaches within a very short distance of this village, and from one of the airy bridges which crossed it I had a sight that could not but elevate and exhilarate the mind. The waters were rushing in from the westward and coming down their untried channel to the sea. Their course, owing to the absorption of the new banks of the canal and the distance they had to run from where the stream entered it, was much slower than I had anticipated. It was dark before they reached the eastern extremity, but at sunrise next morning they were on a level two and a half feet deep throughout the whole distance of thirteen miles. The interest manifested by the whole country, as this new internal river rolled its first wave through the state, cannot be described. You might see the people running across the fields, climbing on trees and fences, and crowding the bank of the canal to gaze upon the welcome sight. A boat had been prepared at Rome, as you probably knew, and as the waters came down the canal you might mark their progress by that of this new Argo which floated triumphantly along the Hellespont of the West, accompanied by shouts and having on her deck a military band. At nine the next morning, the bells began a merry peal, and the commissioners, in carriages, proceeded from Bagg's Hotel to the landing."

Mr. Bates looked up from his reading. He saw the clustered faces watching his lips with a polite absence of expression. His voice faltered. He had moved himself tremendously, but all at once he remembered that these men spoke very little English.

"O'Mory," he said.

"Yes sor."

"You might explain it to them."

"Yes sor."

O'Mory turned on his men. His black beard bristled as he drew a mighty breath. He roared in Gaelic:—

"The gent's been reading at you unlearned devils, from a letter from the governor ginral of this-here nation. He says in it for me to paste the first wan of you that disobeys me ordhers. Ye see that stretch of bogland? Well, he wants it dhug by spring. It's wet in there, me bhoys. Git back to it. Take off yer pants. There's brand-new shovels and tin barrows for yez. Spit on your hands and dig."

Three

NORAH

1

"The wood lots have a shape"

"SHE doesn't really look like either one of us."

Jerry was sitting beside the hearth of the small cabin. It had become a comfortable place under Mary's hand. The curtains at the window were a warm red woolen, heavy enough to shut out darkness. She had made closets with soft yellow cloth, and a quilt of dyed yellow for the bed. She liked the warmer, softer colors. It was a wonder to Jerry how she had made this cabin over, stamping it with herself.

Mary looked up quietly from the dough her hands were kneading. Flour had dusted her wrists. Her sleeves had been tucked up and she was kneeling on the hearth. Her quiet eyes turned back into the room where the child sat banging the head of her wooden doll upon the floor.

"I don't know, Jerry. I keep thinking she takes after you."

"Not with that coloring. Fowlers are always dark-complected."

"She's got the same-shaped head."

"Maybe."

He didn't really care about it. It was talk. His eyes were for his wife. When he came into the cabin and smelled the sweet, free smell she brought into the place, his mind was carried back inevitably to that morning on the Albany docks, the sunlight and the river, and the taut snapping of pigeons' wings. He had paid for her papers, owning her; and yet, since he had married her, he had never felt that she was actually his.

He had been home for three days. April was nearly over. It was time that he moved on to Irondequot. They were going to tackle it at last. Bates had gone out two days ago. He had to tell her that now.

He said, "Those Irishmen have surely dug a great strip out of the marsh."

Mary said, "They're wild-appearing men. The people here are frightened every Saturday for fear they'll visit in the village."

"They haven't done any actual harm, have they?"

"No. They fight amongst themselves. But they don't look bad to me—just strange, and I like to hear them singing. Polly was in the garden patch the other day. I'd left her on a blanket in the sun. One of them picked her up and took her down to the tap, and I didn't miss her until three of them brought her back again. She was laughing fit for all and pulling at the big one's beard."

"O'Mory," Jerry said.

"Maybe it was. There was a little man with pointed ears beside him and a boy with dark and sad-appearing eyes."

"Jouncy Hogan."

"They were all three drunk, but real polite. They took their hats off and went off on tiptoe. I don't know why they went off on tiptoe. Perhaps not to frighten us." Mary smiled.

The knocking of the doll's head came as steadily as the beating-out of time. The baby made a funny little crooning sound. Then she laid the doll down and spat on it carefully.

"What does she do that for?"

"She does it to anything that's lovely—in her notioning at least."

"It's a queer thing to do, even for a baby."

"It would seem strange unless you knew her. She's quite a stranger to you, Jerry. Isn't she?"

Jerry checked himself from looking at Mary. After a moment she said, "I'm getting that way, too. Ain't I?"

"What do you say that for?"

His voice had become brittle.

"It's true, isn't it?"

He thought, "It's true. It's not my fault. She doesn't see I have to work. It's she's grown different." He did not answer out loud. Instead he picked the doll up.

"It doesn't look pretty to my eyes, I must say."

"Maybe it doesn't."

"Where'd you get it? You didn't carve it out yourself?"

Mary shaped the loaf and carefully tucked its edges into the baking iron. As she thrust the iron in the ashes and raked on the coals she said, "Oh no. Harley Falk made it for her. They're real good friends."

"Does he come here often?"

"He stops in most generally, when he goes through."

"I've heard queer things said of him."

"So have I. I don't believe them, though. Have you ever seen him, Jerry?"

"I saw him once, riding by. He was going to the Irish shanties. But even then I didn't like his face. It looks wrong somehow to me."

"I don't see that it does. I feel sorry for him."

"I wish he didn't come around here."

"What do you want me to do? Close the door on him?"

"I didn't mean that."

"It's nice to know somebody may come in to see me."

Jerry was quiet for a moment. Then he said, "I'd want to shoot a horse like that."

"Poor thing. I suppose Mr. Falk has got a friendly feeling to it."

She got composedly to her feet and wiped the flour from her hands. "Why do you feel so short, Jerry?"

"I don't feel short."

She gave her head a little shake, drew up a chair, and resigned herself to sewing.

"What are you making?"

"Overalls."

"For Polly? For a girl?"

"Yes, why not? They keep her clean."

"Boys' clothes on a girl."

"What's wrong with it?" She bit a thread.

"Nothing."

She gave him again that odd, searching glance. He stirred uncomfortably.

"Is everything all right here?"

"Yes."

"You don't have any trouble with Mrs. Peck?"

"Oh no. She's a sinful drinker for a woman; but she's kind enough." Mary laughed lightly. "Lately she's taken to dressing like a woman under thirty. She sent down to Albany for a yellow wig. She told me she was forty actually. And I've been told she has passed seventy for a fact."

"I've got to see her."

"About rent?"

"Yes. When would she be found?"

"Most any time."

"I think I'll just go over and see her now."

Jerry's voice was muffled. He got up suddenly and stepped outside. The baby looked round at the inflow of cool air. Mary continued her sewing.

Jerry crossed the yard in a few strides. The path brought him to the kitchen door. He knocked.

While he waited for an answer he looked out across the river flats. It was still, with the half-grey of evening. On the banks he could see a snipe loop down. Beyond, the traces of the digging showed along the causeway towpath. The Irish were still working. Since they had come not one had fallen sick. Fever and ague never troubled them. They were too tough. A minister had preached against them in the church.

The high water had not flooded over the berms this year. Even if it came now, it was evident that the Irish would dig through by fall.

Jerry knocked again.

The door opened silently, and Mrs. Peck confronted him. She looked at him closely past the sides of her hooked nose. A girlish dress hung loosely from her old bent shoulders.

"Well!" Her voice was hoarse. "It's the wandering husband come back to home."

"Mrs. Peck?"

"You've seen me before, ain't you?" Suddenly she chuckled. "But not to look like this, I guess." She put an effort at coquetry into her words. "Step inside if you want to see me."

She drew the door wide open and stood aside for him. He passed through a dim pantry into a kitchen. Behind him her stick scraped across the boards. "There's a chair, young man. Set down."

Muttering to herself, she bent slowly backward into a rocker. A sigh escaped her. She pushed back her gorgeous yellow hair to show thin grey bristles underneath, and wiped aside some sweat with a hard-veined hand.

On the corner of the table stood a bottle and a glass.

"Have a little joyful?" she suggested.

"No, thanks."

"Well, I will then, if you'll pardon me."

The bottle neck knocked against the tumbler rim. She smacked her lips, and her old teeth started niddering. As she lifted her chin to drink, Jerry saw her neck in the shawl, thin, weazened, corded like an old hen-turkey's.

He said, "I just dropped in to tell you I'd like to pay for the cabin for three months' advance."

"That's all right with me."

She peered at him sharply.

"Going to be away a spell?"

"That long, maybe," Jerry said stiffly.

"I'm just a curious old woman. People say I'm evilly inclined. I drink too much." She chuckled. "But I was an honest woman up to now. 'Tisn't every woman was honest to a tanner for a husband. What are you up to?"

"There's work out at Irondequot."

"Thought of taking her along?"

"I don't know what it's like out there."

"Well, I don't, either."

She bent her head to her glass, then lifted her chin again to swallow. The illusion of the drinking old hen-turkey was renewed.

"Told your wife about it?"

Jerry said, "If you're willing, I might as well pay you now."

"You don't like to listen to an old woman. Nobody does that's young. I'm not so old, my boy. I know a thing or two. I'm not so old. Not by a half so old." She chuckled. In the midst of the pleasant kitchen, Jerry thought of her there alone, growing gradually insensible—chuckling to herself.

He pulled the money from his pocket.

"I see that you ain't told her. Well, you'd better. She was ailing all through January. There! Bite on that if you won't have my whiskey."

"What do you mean?"

She grinned.

"Well, she's a healthy girl. And you came home three days in January from your gallivanting. It looks to me it'd happened once already."

Jerry stared at her.

She winked one thin, lashless eyelid.

"Maybe you want to reconsider now?"

"I can't take her along."

"Oh no."

She watched him slyly.

"I'll look after her. She's all right with me, young gallanter. You step off."

Her skinny hand at last accepted his money. He thought suddenly that she would wait, listen and wait, until she was sure she was alone before she hid it. People said she never banked her money.

He went quickly out.

It had grown darker in the yard. He stopped for a moment. He had not heard a thing. After waiting awhile he heard a wagon coming along the road. His eyes dimly made out a white horse. He thought, "It's not my business," and went on to the cabin. Mary had lit a lamp there. He entered. He had business there.

She had put Polly into her cradle and was shoving it back in its dark corner. The child was already sound asleep. Jerry looked down over Mary's shoulder at the blond, curled knot of hair.

"Mary."

"Shh! Don't talk so loud."

He waited till they were both seated by the hearth.

"Mary, how have you been?"

"Finely, thanks."

"Mary, don't talk that way."

Her eyes met his accusingly.

"Mrs. Peck's been talking."

He nodded.

"Why didn't you tell me?"

But his voice was contrite.

"I didn't know you wished to know."

"Mary!"

She softened to him.

"Jerry, I'm a bad, cross woman. I guess it just gets me so. You mustn't mind."

She said again, "Being without her husband makes a woman strange maybe."

After another time she said, "I'm grateful to you, Jerry. I love you, for a fact."

Then she said, almost laughing at them both, "I guess you can tell me now, Jerry. You needn't look at your boots no longer."

His face reddened.

"Yes," said Mary. "You have got to go off again for a long spell. I'll be good."

He nodded once more; but he said, "Mary, you seem so strange from what you used to be."

"I guess we both are."

"You've changed to me."

Her level forehead puckered slightly. When she looked up her eyes were bright with honesty.

"Jerry, I don't believe it. But yet, being so much alone hurts a pride in me. I brighten me all up when you're to come back. But all the time I've got it working in me to make you stay outside. As if I was a vengeful person, though I'm not truly so."

"I don't see."

"I guess we're different that way."

"I thought this cabin would be like what you wanted. I'd think after two years it would seem like yours. You said you wanted a little place."

"Yes, I did. But I saw us both in it, Jerry."

"Here we are." He laughed a little. "And yet I feel outside of there." His eyes were on the door.

"Yes. You often seem so to me. Even when you've held to me, I see your thoughts outside of there."

"I don't plan it so."

They looked at each other.

Again, with the firelight across her eyes, Jerry caught the ripple of the Hudson River. He heard the dock sounds. He saw her head against the Greenbush bank, all alone among those other redemptioners.

"Mary," he said.

"Yes, Jerry."

"Maybe this is the last time I've got to go away from you. The very last. Let's pretend so. Let's us pretend we are beginning right at the beginning. The way it was in Albany and this time is like the time we went along the road. When Issachar Bennet picked us up. Do you recall him?"

She said, seriously, "Yes. I'll try. But then we were together. I think it's being left so much alone this second time."

As he watched her eyes he felt as if he saw a mantle closing down in them. He felt himself grow thin. He had no strength. There was a time in Uniontown when he put bacon in the smokehouse and the door blew shut behind him, enclosing him in fearful darkness. He beat upon the door with fists. They were so feeble against the heavy boards that no one heard him. It took him a long time to notice the smoke-hole. It made a spot of light upon the floor. When his family finally discovered him, he was sitting in that spot of light.

"I've got to leave first thing to-morrow morning."

"I'll make your travel dinner now," said Mary.

He watched her set about the work; efficient, quick, she made good lunches. In the corner of the cabin he noticed a new coverlet that she was weaving.

"That?" she said in answer. "Oh, I have to have something to do. It's easing to me, weaving is."

He drew a kind of comfort from her voice. He did not know how, nor see why. He felt himself like the little boy hammering at the smokehouse door. They spent the night in quiet.

Just at dawn they rose together and Jerry dressed.

It was a fine clear sunrise. Already the Irish were at work across the river; he could see them clearly, armpit deep in the cold, watery muck. The skin on one's bare buttocks was silver as a fish's.

"Good-bye." Her kiss was cool. He could tell by her eyes that she had not slept.

"Good-bye, Jerry."

"Hye! Hello there, young man."

Jerry looked up. He was a mile or so out of Lyons Village, and the time was a little before noon.

He saw a bolster wagon, hooded, coming along behind four fine fat mares. They looked fresh and sleek, in spite of the hot sun, and their trace chains made a jingling. The driver who had hailed him was a plain-faced fellow; but he had a ringing voice.

"Morning," Jerry said.

The man drew up his team.

"You seem to be passing my way, young man. Would you ride?"

"Surely," Jerry grinned.

"Stand on, then. I'm aiming to get on a good piece before sundown." As Jerry jumped over the wheel and sat on the broad seat, the driver whistled to his mares. Out in front of Jerry's feet their backs looked fat as suet puddings. They had fancy harness, with dyed feather tufts and red horsehair tassels. He took another look at the driver.

"Yes, sir," he turned on Jerry suddenly. "I'm calculated a medium kind of a man—height, heft, and coloring. Meet me, mister—Merwin Gandy."

When he talked his mouth shaped out each word with extraordinary largeness. Jerry could see his teeth, and his tongue, and if he chose he thought he might have looked all the way down to hardpan.

"Jerry Fowler, eh?" continued Mr. Gandy. "Fowler's a good name. Shocks up well with Gandy." He arched a judicious spit between the off mare's legs. "You don't meet up with them too often. Where are you heading? Me, I'm out for beyond Palmyra. Got my order four days back. Rounded up four beeves, killed and slaughtered, peeled and loaded them, and dug right out. I come from Oaks Old-Stand, that's in Vienna township. Greatest beeving meadows in this country. Fat? There ain't no beeves in these United States a man can sink an arm in farther than our cattle. Gandy beeves. I'm not a boasting man, myself, but look along those mares. There ain't one single straight line in the four of them. By God, they even bend their traces. That means horseflesh, young man. Same way with my hogs. You ought to see my hogs. That's why I get prime prices. Folks call me talkative, but that ain't so. Git, Lizabella. (Named for my first daughter— a pretty mare, but devilish when she smells a stallion.) Yes, we run to stoutness as a family, barring me. I'm kind of medium only. But you've got to leave off somewhere. Even the Lord, He had to borrow a rib, by God! Where did you say that you was headed?"

They were rolling along at a brisk trot, and a bit of lather was rubbed out between the plump thighs of the wheel mares. The sweat smelled fat and strong.

"That's what I would call coincidental. Me, a medium man with four stout mares, and you a youngish fellow, pretty tall. Now, if that ain't the strangest thing. Here, us two in this wide world; why should we set out that way and meet up at this very place? Why should I say, neighborly inclined (back in Vienna township they call a Gandy neighborly), why should I say, 'Stand on', to you? Because you was a likely-looking youngster? No, that ain't what it is. The whole thing's a coincidence. That's what the world turns on, seems as how. I told my wife that, when she announced me she was cornered. She said I was a twig. 'Merwin Gandy, if you ain't a twig!' she says. And I told her that was what she said to me the morning after she was brided. Mostly in Vienna township womenfolks will call all Gandys twigs. Not that I hold with nigger-pipple, bundling boys with girls, or topsy-turvy notions. I'm a churchman, deacon, too, and just a pure and simple man."

Jerry had been brooding all along the road, but now he could not help but smile. He asked, "Have you got quite a family, Mr. Gandy?"

Gandy arched another spit; under his beard his cheeks collapsed like pricked balloons. He wiped his mouth with his medium hand.

"My old girl piles them up on me for fair. Four girls, at this date instant, three boys, and something in the wind."

Jerry said, "I'm not much of a family man myself. I've got one girl; but my wife is expecting something soon."

"The month?" demanded Merwin Gandy.

"I'd put it down as sometime in October."

"October!" Gandy bugled. "Didn't I say coincidence? I ask you. My wife's planning on her bedding for October! By God, Fowler, let me shake your hand. All along, since you got on this wagon, I've been thinking. 'This here is coincidence.' Most men would think of it as offering a lad a lift. But not me. No, not Merwin Gandy. Come on here, Anna May! (Named for my aunt of the same name.) Well, sir. There's the coincidence complete. I wonder what it means for us. You here, me there. At Palmyra, now, I set you down. You here, me there. Maybe we'll never see again or hear of hide nor hair of one another. That's part of the coincidence. I get to thinking of these things and wonder what there's into it. Now what do you think of this canal, hey?"

"It seems all right to me."

Gandy drew a breath and launched himself. The trace chains jingled through his voice. "It is. But it is changing this whole land. Look at Lyons—springing up like fountain water. We're heading for Palmyra—she's growing stout. Time was when these-here lands was pretty well wooded. My Grampa used to carry a shotgun when he herded to Niagara and take along a dozen boys. For why? Because the Doanes and Tomblesons was scouting out the cattle money. Well, they're gone. Roads did it, and the canal that's coming is going to do it more. We used to see land-clearer's smoke all round of us. They've moved. The wood lots have a shape now. Why, you'd hardly see a log house round Oaks Old-Stand now. And them along this road are mostly shingled. Trappers they have moved out westward. Most of them have even left the Purchase, as I hear tell. You'd oome upon their shanties handy to most every beaverfly. But now they've fallen in. I know just one. It sets a way off'n this identical road. A feller, name of Lager, a most curious old coot, he used to trap it then. There wasn't any road—this-here is new, you see. Lager's logs, we called it. I wouldn't house a Chester boar in such a place myself. But he hid out there. It's got a butternut down in the ditch along the road. Not far from where you're going, too. He moved out when he seen Geddes coming through the first time. Said the woods had smelled of men too strong for foxes. There's coincidence again. Just last week I told a man about it. He preached in our meetinghouse. We fixed the price. He told me he made two deliveries. A dollar for a plain good sermon, and fifty cents was extra for a spray of hell-fire. Well, I paid him and he earned it. He had each last one of us sweating there for fair, and when you make a Gandy sweat, you're getting somewhere. Well, I told him what I have been telling you; and the queer thing was I ended up the same way."

Gandy turned his medium eye.

Jerry bit: "Kind of a coincidence, wasn't it?"

"Boy," said Mr. Gandy, "boy, you are a twig."

It was a little after two when he released Jerry a mile beyond Palmyra. His last words were, "It's got me going, our coincidence. I wonder what is into it. But I'm a wondering man. Back in Vienna . . ." But his mares wheeled him forward out of hearing. Jerry looked back. The road had crossed the course of the canal, again—it veered in a long curve to north-ward; but the road went straight west through a rolling land, well wooded with low oak trees. And only for a little way he heard the work of diggers going forward: the shouts of men shoveling, the stamp of horses drag-ging scoops, the shriek of the wooden chain-drum of a stump-lifter, or the muffled thud of blasting powder where some poor devil of a contractor had come upon a ledge of stone. Half the line from the marsh to Rochester had been contracted; and work was well in hand. It would be finished by the time the marshes were dug through.

In the bright sunlight, between him and the village, he saw the sites of locks eight and nine. A local carpenter was scratching his head over the fit of an iron casting in his timbers; his helper chewed a languid cud; and a mason was laying stone.

Then Jerry turned into the woods, and their shadow passed over him. The road stretched forward through a dimness; what light there was shut in between the levels of the tree leaves and the top of the scrub growth.

2

"A man is caught by beauty"

IT was quiet along the new post road. No tracks turned off to hidden farms. Though he had walked for an hour, he had met no travelers, nor heard any wheels. The fresh tire marks of a wagon that had passed on before him gave the only evidence that anyone besides himself had traveled the road this day. Even the woods were hushed. The mood that had clouded his face before Merwin Gandy overtook him now returned. He walked with his eyes upon the track, heedless of what he passed, unconscious even of the change that was taking place above the treetops.

The hot green light that filtered through the new leaves began perceptibly to whiten, then grow cool. There was no sound of wind; and if a leaf had stirred it would have startled him. His feet made the only sound, a steady thud, muffled by the light dust of the road.

Then, all at once, he felt the sweat upon his face growing cold. He raised his eyes. Breathing had become difficult—as if in the lifeless sky a vacuum had been created and was drawing the air up through the trees. The light was dying and in the south a shadow pressed down on the woods. And then he saw that it was sweeping towards him through the trees. Far off, he heard muttering thunder; and still farther off the whisper of rain.

He came suddenly to himself.

Oak woods offer scant shelter against rain. Nowhere within sight was any sign of evergreens. He saw no fallen trees large enough to shield him. But a little way ahead the darkening road turned downward in a curve. He quickened his step.

The woods were thicker here. In the growing darkness, a few beeches made a silver twilight. He glanced up once at a roll of cloud, black, high-piled, with a hungry forward licking of small tongues frayed out by the swollen wind it carried. The forest shook with the ominous low thunder that comes with hard rain.

Beside the road he saw a tree lying in the ditch. A short, thick tree, its branches were lopped off along the sides. The axeman's heavy blade had left clean cuts like shining faces. A tree like that would offer shelter underneath it if it were not in a ditch. But he ran for it, anyway.

As he bent down to look under the stem, his eyes fell on the bark.

"That's a butternut," he said aloud.

Butternut, he thought; there was something to remember about a butternut; and then he grinned as he recalled Merwin Gandy. "It's got a butternut down in the ditch along the road. . . . Lager's logs." A Gandy wouldn't keep a Chester boar in it, maybe, but for Jerry Fowler it would offer better shelter than a fallen tree.

Jerry looked along the road edge. He saw a little way forward where the fresh wagon tracks had halted, then turned over the ditch and up a slope of ground. A spring came down between round stones to meet the ditch. There had been an old track there in other years. It was choked up with undergrowth, but the wagon had managed to draw through. Here and there a slim stem showed a scrape of bark. Jerry pressed forward.

The cloud had rolled across the woods and the thunder in its heart was gathering frequency. The first shadow of blackness was passing on. Torn fragments of bluish-white cloud were racing under it. A grey wet light was being born, and far to south Jerry heard the rain take hold of the woods.

The path was easy to sight out; it carried straight up the slope to level ground and then wound in among the larger trees. Jerry began to run. He came suddenly into what had once been a small clearing. Along the woods' edge the trees bent down, and then as their arms lifted again he saw the trees on the other side heel away. Great heavy drops struck into the dry earth and seemed to bounce. They left their marks in hollow rings. The wind was on the world. Lightning pitchforked over the clearing; thunder swallowed the hot strike; and in the echoes a tree crashed down.

In the far corner of the clearing, a small cabin lifted scabrous walls. Beside the door there stood a wagon. Jerry shouted and ran for it.

When he left the trees the wind pounced on his back. Behind him the woods roared with rain. Before he was halfway over, the sluices were unloosed upon his shoulders, and as he ran he heard the rain pass on across the world.

The door was closed. Already rain was pouring from the roof of broken bark-sheathes. He pushed against the door. Its old latch was closed and there was no string. He knocked. Immediately it opened. A tall man held it as Jerry rushed in; then leaned against it heavily. But the wind was like a foot thrust over the sill, and Jerry had to help him. The door went shut with a dull bang, and dust came powdering down.

Jerry looked at the man. Seen once, a man could not forget the hatchet face, the humorous eyes enmeshed in wrinkles. He held his hand out.

"Mr. Bennet! Do you remember me?"

Issachar Bennet wiped the rain from his face.

"You do put me in mind of someone."

"Three years back," suggested Jerry. "About this season. You won a bet off me."

"Now I recollect." The thin face wrinkled up to smile. "I recollect the name—it's Fowler. Jerry Fowler. I made a bet with you about a girl."

"That's right," said Jerry.

"How did it turn out?"

Jerry said, "We did get married. We've a girl. They're living in Montezuma while I come out here to Irondequot."

Bennet beamed; then he turned suddenly.

"I'd heard of this place from a talkative man in Oaks Old-Stand. I smelled the storm a-coming."

"Merwin Gandy. He told me this morning."

But the lean face had grown serious.

"I found it out all right. But look what I found in it."

Jerry looked into the cabin. Scarce ten by ten, the floor was rubbled with the trash of years of desolation. The stick and clay chimney was crumbling. Even as Jerry looked, a chunk gave way under the rain. The rain and wind beat in the single window, fluttering the broken edges that had once been paper panes.

Bennet had brought his horse inside, a small, black, flashy mare. She was standing close against the front wall, her rump to the open window and her tail tight tucked in under the wind. But her head was bent as if she understood the preacher's words, and, as she eyed the corner in the shadow of the hearth, her sensitive ears kept pricking and falling back and pricking again.

Old Lager, or whoever had last used the cabin, had made a bed of hemlock tips in the corner. They were dried out now and dusty; but as Jerry stepped forward to see better, he made out a woman huddled on them.

"She's in bad shape," Bennet whispered. "She was stunned when I came onto her. She's been mishandled."

He had moved up behind Jerry's shoulder; and his voice spoke with a deep resonance that made Jerry turn. The amused eyes had grown sombre.

"When a man travels round the way I do he sees a lot of queer things. But this is one of the queerest things I ever come across." He stroked his mouth with long fingers. "Look there by her feet!" He pointed suddenly. In the dustlike needles, Jerry made out rawhide thongs. He looked round at the Shaker.

The old man nodded.

"Some man has beaten her. All over. Yes—" a remnant of a twinkle fluttered his eyelids at Jerry's expression. "I took her clothes off to see if anything was bad with her. She hadn't any wounds, just marks of withes. Whoever it was he tied her up and left her—whether he wanted her to die, or whether he's a-coming back, I couldn't tell. Most like he wanted her to die."

"Why?"

"Well, she was here all last night anyway."

"How do you know?"

"There on the edge of her skirt. Where it ain't tossed. A cob-spider used it for one corner of his web. Cob-spiders spin at night."

He paused, his face bent down in thought. A fine dust came drifting down through the murk in the single room, bringing a smell of dry-rot. The mare's black coat had lost its sheen. Jerry became aware of the thunder again; it was rolling off to north of them. Through the stripped window he saw a silvery wet line rising over the trees. The straggling ends of the rain were passing them with fitful gusts. The air smelled leafy.

"You know, Jerry," Bennet was saying, "if that talkative man hadn't felt obliged to tell me everything he knew in this world I'd have driven through that storm, and she'd have still been tied here." His hand again caressed his chin. "A thing like that makes even me consider Providence."

He bent down suddenly beside the woman.

"She's just a girl," he said gently.

Jerry bent forward. Bennet had a bowl on the edge of the hearth.

"Water and brandy," he said.

His dry old hand crept with sensitive fingers under her cheek and turned up her face. He dipped his handkerchief in the bowl and began bathing the forehead. As Jerry watched, his cheeks grew slowly red.

From her left temple across her nose and down her right cheek to the barely visible angle of her jaw, a welt showed purple. She was small-featured. Her nose was short and slightly arching; her chin was close and round, with greater breadth than length; her small lips, fully rounded, were curved as if she slept. She had black hair; not the blue-black of an Indian's hair, but inky as a crow's wing.

"Pretty hair." Old Issachar pressed it back from the forehead. It was tight-curled there, damp. His free hand reached behind her shoulder and drew it forward like a rope. The ends were tangled from being lain on, rough with hemlock needles, with here and there a hairpin loosely skewering them.

"Fine hair," said Issachar. "It would fall down real easy."

He draped it over her shoulder and laid her back upon her side. Getting to his knees stiffly, he kicked his feet out and walked over to the window.

"It would be a torture to her now to put her in a wagon," he said. "We can't leave her here alone. We've got to stay. Or I ought, anyways. How about you, are you due anywhere to-night?"

"Not 'specially. I'm going to Irondequot."

"That isn't above an hour's walking. You can get in there to-morrow."

"I'll stay with you."

"The point is one of us has got to wrestle up some wood."

"I'll go."

"That ain't it. There isn't any handy to the cabin here. We've got no axe. And anyway she ought to have some milk in a little while. One of us has got to get provisions—for ourselves as well as her. There ain't sense in our going hungry."

"All right, I'll get them." Jerry stepped to the mare. But Issachar Bennet stretched out his hand. When Jerry turned he kept his eyes averted.

"I was thinking, Jerry, suppose the warrior that did this-here to her comes back. I'm an oldish man." He looked comically at Jerry and began a feeble grin. "I'd be plumb scared to death. I never was any good in a rough-and-tumble."

"Don't you carry a pistol?"

"Yes, I do. But I've never had a load for it. I'd be frightened to let it off. That's actual fact. . . ." He looked down along his lanky legs. "Now I guess you know the kind of man Ike Bennet is.

"Waiting here in dark," he muttered.

The sky had cleared, but the sun was already going down.

"I'll stay, then," Jerry said. "But she ought to have a fire." He cast round the cabin. A couple of rafters had fallen in at the back end. He broke them off. The remnant of bunk made planks of good dry wood. He rested them across the sill-log and jumped on them until he had convenient pieces. It took a minute only to start the shavings he made with his knife. The smoke bent and doubled before the chimney sucked the draught.

"Thank the Lord it's rained," said Jerry. "It wouldn't take much to start that chimney burning, with the clay so loose."

The Shaker had observed all his proceedings with vastly relieved eyes.

"I'll be getting along," he said. He caught the mare's bridle. "Come on, Daisy."

Jerry went out with him to help him hitch. As he started to climb in the wagon, he said, "Oh, Jerry. I've got some snake-oil salve laid up in bear fat." He fished in a pack behind the seat. "I'm peddling cures along the side for them that can't pay me for religion." The good humor in his voice was restored. He brought out a small earthenware jar. "But this stuff's good. I paid a shilling to a squaw near Buffalo for it for myself. Rub it in light, and keep on rubbing till the skin feels loose."

"Me rub it on her?"

"Surely. Better you than me. Ain't you a married man?"

He chuckled, clucked up his mare, and turned her for the road.

Jerry watched him go.

The sun had set, and looking into the west, he saw the afterglow like cool green water floating lilac clouds. A steamy breath of soaked leaves lifted through the woods. Somewhere a thrush was calling.

He touched the fire up. Hearing its crackle, he could forget the cob-webbed wall. He thrust two sticks into the ground and draped the old blanket Issachar had left across them to get warm. Then he closed the door and dropped the latch in place.

For an instant he stood facing the warped boards, his ears alert. He could hear no breathing over his own. He went slowly to the hearth and looked down. Her eyes were closed. The arched brows were smooth and the thick, straight lashes brushed the cheeks. Her skin was without red; but it had a velvety texture in the firelight. Seen in sleep her face was almost like a child's. He glanced at the jar in his hand for a moment, distaste-fully, then looked back at her.

Her eyes were open.

Her eyes were black, like her hair, with a faint lustre, very large. As she looked at his embarrassed face, a little painful smile touched her mouth with a hint of coquetry. Then as she tried to move her head, her lower lip snapped in against her teeth, and Jerry heard her indrawn breath.

He said, kneeling down beside her, "I'm going to rub your back with salve. It's going to ease a lot. Do you mind?"

She smiled a little.

He spread the blanket on the hearth in double thickness. Then as carefully as he could he lifted her. His hands could feel the pain in her body. But she was wordless, like some small hurt animal. He put her down upon the blanket on her face, and awkwardly bent over her.

She said, "My dress is laced in front."

Her voice was barely above a whisper. He helped her onto her side, and her eyes looked up at him. They were looking into his with a total absence of abashment.

"I don't mind."

She said it almost bubblingly, as if she found drollery even in pain.

His fingers seemed stiff with large blunt ends, and their very carefulness was clumsy. She lay motionless under his touch, and sick though she was, her body gave him a sense of life. She was young, but she was no child. She was not beautiful by the points that he judged beauty by, but her duskiness was lovely. He kept his eyes resolutely on his hands, but in spite of him his sight would stray.

At last he got the dress unlaced and rolled her forward on her face. She shivered as he drew the dress back from her shoulders, worked her arms out of the sleeves and bared her slim back.

"Who did this to you?"

She did not answer; she had laid her cheek against the blanket. He felt the nerves spring under the skin as he spread on the salve. It reeked strongly in the heat, but it sank in as if the skin were hungry for it, and he thought under his hand he could feel the welts lie down.

She made no sound till he was done; but after a while her lids closed over her eyes, and she sighed.

"It makes me feel so much easier, mister."

"My name's Jerry Fowler."

She was silent for a minute; then she said, "Mine's Norah Sharon."

"Who did this?" he asked again.

"I'm very grateful." Her voice was low, upon the edge of drowsing. He gave up the question.

She asked after a while, "Who's the old man that was here and gave me brandy?"

"His name's Issachar Bennet. He's gone for milk and things. So you can eat."

"I'd like to drink a little milk."

"That's fine. Feeling any better?"

"Lots better."

"Do you want me to move you back?"

"No, it's nice here."

"Is there anything I could do to make you feel better?"

"If you could find a comb I'd like my hair combed."

He had a carved bone comb of his own in his pocket and he fished it out. She was like a cat under the touch of it. Her head moved imperceptibly to meet a stroke in some spot that she cherished. It made her drowsy. By the time Jerry had untangled the ends and tied the rope with a thread, she was fast asleep.

He sat still, letting the firelight wash over her against his knees, hearing his own heart beating, watching her quiet sleep. He could not keep his eyes from her; they kept questing for her face. She was not beautiful, he told himself again. She was too small for beauty.

The night became a still, clear time for thinking. But Jerry could not sort his thoughts. Whenever his eye fell on the sleeping figure, his brain became disturbed. He saw the curve of a shoulder into the small ribbed back, and he wondered how she came to be there, what man had brought her to this cabin, what his right over her had been. He felt his own heart thud against his chest. He saw the sweep of the black lashes on her cheek. The warmth of the fire brought her color back; a clear bright red —it almost startled him to see it. He put one hand lightly against her cheek to see if she was fevered, and her left hand stirred in her sleep, creeping up to brush his fingers, and he snatched away his hand. He looked at his hand a while. Long ago his mother said he had the gift of handling things; it was a gift in a man, like preaching or making money in the law. He wondered in his brain how the hand might be that had put those marks upon her back.

So he heard, long afterwards when his firewood was getting low, the thresh of a wagon on the brushy trail. He went outside to meet it. Issachar Bennet's mare was threading over the clearing.

The Shaker shook himself when he climbed down.

"It is the dreariest-looking place I ever saw, by moonlight. How is she, Jerry?"

"She's sleeping now."

Bennet reached into his wagon.

"Here's milk." He handed over a cool jar. "If it ain't buttered by the jouncing. Here's a smoked ham, small, the joint end. Here's corn meal and sugar and tea. It ought to last us out."

He unhitched the mare.

"I'll bring her in. She's used to sleeping with me outside of a barn and will act quiet."

The mare was dainty with her hoofs. She seemed to know a sleeper should not be disturbed. While Jerry unharnessed her, Bennet went over to the girl.

"She does look better. She ain't really badly hurt. Just sore. She'll get righted quickly."

He came back to feed the mare, and then the two of them sat down on the floor at the girl's feet. With their knives they whittled off ham to eat while waiting for a tin of tea to brew.

"Did she come round, when I was gone?"

"Yes."

"She didn't tell you nothing?"

"No. She wouldn't answer who did it."

The Shaker examined her sleeping face.

"It's a peculiar strange thing. Finding her so. Most likely she won't ever tell."

Jerry said, "I've been wondering how it come that Merwin Gandy should tell us both about this place."

Issachar Bennet looked up. His eyes twinkled like little bits of glass.

"Do you think he done that? Then you ought to see his wife. That man's hen-ridden for a rooster, Jerry. No, he told us of this place because it's one of the few little things he knows about. I stayed with him. Give him half a day and that man just begins repeating. It is a wonder to him to speak out like a man."

He shook his head.

"Merwin Gandy can graft fat on animals. But he couldn't do that thing."

The tin of tea put out a fragrance.

"I'll lace it with a thread of brandy," Bennet said, "then we can talk a while."

Under the brandy the cabin seemed to close in with comfort. Bennet had brought an armful of split oak that burned with quiet evenness. And Jerry told him what he had been doing. The old man had no interest in his work; he wished to know of Mary, and the baby.

"It makes me feel I started things. Adam you and Eve for her. I ought to make a garden."

Jerry said, "Where did you get that mare?"

"Oh, I got kind of tired of them bays I had. I drove a roan a while. I traded him for her one night down in Ohio. I don't know whether she's Ohio bred. I never saw the man to ask him."

He had been wandering for three years, covering eight states and a territory.

"I haven't been back in New Lebanon. The more I wander round, the less I consider being of a sect. I never took it serious. It is a pity, for I've got the gift for preaching. Sometimes it makes me fearful." He sighed. "All they want is to be told how sinful this world is. And I know that. I tell them all about me, only the way their minds consider such things."

He stared a while at the fire.

"It's a peculiar thing, Jerry. You travel through the west and you see people settling down. At first they're far apart. They're neighborly and stand together. The Indian was a great thing for them. Now the Indian's gone and they have to look for devils. It's queer."

He sipped his tea.

"As soon as they get money they set up a school. Later a church. But always the school first. It seems these people want to get to being gentry-fied. Learning is a splendid thing if you can take it just for knowledge. But to them it means money, setting up above your neighbors. One year a man will go to help his neighbor, Joe, nine miles off. Next year that same man's in a town, incorporated under statute, and he says, 'That Joe must be a backward man. He's still living under logs.' And his wife says, 'I do feel sorry for Joe's womenfolks, to have to work in darkness under paper windows. Why, she hasn't had a petticoat in these three years.' They feel sorry for them and they leave them be."

He nodded at the sleeping girl.

"Now I don't feel sorry for that girl, beyond the pain she's in. Most likely she's just caught herself in her own spinning."

Jerry said, "In an incorporated town the way you say, it couldn't happen to her."

"No. Maybe not. But she could raise a powerful harm against some other person. This way she just got caught. The man did it, and he's gone. He won't be even hanged."

"He ought to be."

"No doubt. But suppose he come back and you should rise up and kill him. That would be all right, too, I suppose. At least you wouldn't have a lot of people all aroused to kill him with you. You've never seen a public hanging, Jerry."

Jerry brooded. He felt the firelight against his hands. He thought it would have been a better thing if he had walked the storm out. Better for him, better for Mary.

"Suppose," said Bennet, stroking his thin chin, "suppose now you should get caught by her. I wouldn't blame you. Supposing you to think yourself in love with her. If I was younger I might be myself. She's got a sense to rouse a man. It is a natural thing. A man is caught by beauty, some man by a peach tree, some man by a horse, and some by women. That's what the Lord, supposing it is God, put into us. But it takes different ways. The pity is until we are too old for it, we generally don't know what we're after—Jerry, if you ever see it, you dig in and grab it."

His eye fell on the mare again and he laughed softly.

"I wonder if the man that owned that mare saw any beauty in that hammer-headed roan I left him? But he's a better traveler than she'll ever be. And anyway the next time I feel called upon to deal, the next man will have her. She's dainty, isn't she?"

As he spoke, the girl woke up. She stirred, turned over, and her eyes were swimming with her drowse.

"What did you say, mister?"

Bennet smiled.

"Just a word. How are you feeling, missy?"

"Ever so much more easier."

"Would you like some milk?"

"Yes."

He warmed her a cup of it. Jerry watched the girl's eyes take the old preacher in. A strange man for a preacher. Then her glance came round to him. She gave him a long look. There was slyness in it, estimate, and the same strange sense of invitation.

"Thank you, mister," she was saying to Bennet.

"What's your name, missy?"

"Norah Sharon."

"That's a pretty name," he said. "It seems to suit."

She was drinking her milk. When he spoke, she took her lips from the cup and looked aside at Jerry. Jerry was just aware of her. He saw her tongue come out and lick aside a drop. She lowered her glance to the cup, and as her lips met the rim she smiled a little.

The wrinkles at the corners of the preacher's eyes were gathered up in nets. He rubbed his hands with a small, dry, whispering sound.

"Have you got any friends out here?"

She shook her head.

"Nowhere to go, no money?"

"No, mister."

Jerry's heart began to beat. But he kept his eyes away.

Bennet said, "I'm on a preaching circuit. I wish I could help you. But strange people are close-questioning about their preachers."

He appeared to think.

"Nowhere you could go back to?"

She said, "I left my home. I couldn't stand it."

"What'll we do with you?"

"Never mind me," she said to Bennet.

She spoke sturdily, but Jerry felt his pity for her rise.

"What do you say, Jerry? We can't just turn her loose."

Jerry spoke thickly. His face was sweating and he was ashamed of his utterance.

"I'll board her, if she needs it."

"You can't stick her in a working camp."

"Maybe Mann's Mill. I've heard Mr. Bates say it was handy."

"You can't have a girl like her so close to workers." Bennet clasped his knees. "Corbal's up the creek. He runs a little gristmill. He's an oldish man. He might board her.

"You'd rather be alone a spell, wouldn't you?" he asked Norah.

She nodded.

"I'd feel scared of him finding me again."

"Who is he?" Jerry demanded for the third time.

"I don't know his name."

Bennet looked over her head at Jerry and shrugged.

"You'll never find that out," he seemed to say.

But she was undisturbed. She seemed content to take whatever came her way. Finishing her milk, she lay back again and closed her eyes.

Bennet said, "We might as well all of us get some sleep."

He and Jerry took the dusty bed of needles. The girl was already sleeping. Jerry lay still. The firelight kept flowing over the recumbent figure of the girl within reach of his hand. Her head was towards him. In the corner the mare drowsed with hanging nose.

After a while, Bennet began to snore, and Jerry eased himself into a more comfortable position. He watched the girl. She stirred a little, and then her hand stole out and came upon his hand. The touch was warm and very dry; and the blood stiffened in his veins. The mare turned her head, her eyes dull coals against the firelight.

He could not sleep. The mare lay down carefully and quietly. Bennet snored on, and the fire died. Outside the cabin a barred owl hooted mournfully. But he had a feeling that a loneliness that he had lived with many months was lifting, that the hand in his had touched a nerve, and that it was not right he should feel glad. . . .

In the morning, the girl said that she was able to ride. Her face was brighter. She was very quiet, between them on the seat; and both of them were speechless in the early morning.

The mare, stepping briskly, pitched her ears at roadside clumps, and tossed her bits. The wheels rolled smoothly down the road. Bennet drew up at the corner of a side track.

"This way turns up to Corbal's. Mann's is just beyond the woods. Listen. You can hear the men."

They could hear voices.

"You'll want to get in this morning, Jerry?"

"Maybe I'd better."

"Then if you'll pass the girl a couple of dollars, I'll take her up. I'll tell Corbal she's my niece and I'm boarding her while I'm on my circuit. He knows who I am—or thinks he does."

The girl smiled down at Jerry. Her eyes were soft.

Bennet said, "I'll tell Corbal you're a relative and keeping an eye on her. Maybe you can visit with her sometimes."

"Yes."

The old man chuckled. He spoke to the mare. The wheels spun.

The girl looked back. Her eyes were speaking for her. Jerry watched till she was out of sight. She was not pretty by the way he had always judged a girl: she was too small.

When Jerry came forth from the woods, he found the Irondequot Valley sloping downward from his feet. On the left of the road, Mann's mill-dam stuck out of a sheer hillside; it backed up water in a narrow lake along the edge of the hill. On the north shore was lower land. The mill itself was next to the wheel housing on the north end of the dam: a big overshot wheel of eight-foot radius. The mill was built half in stone and half in wood.

Jerry could not make out how far the pond extended. The dam, constructed of cribs and broken rock and earth, had a lift of twenty feet, so the pond must reach much farther than his eye could carry.

Leaving the road before he reached the bridge, he climbed the hill. It was heavily scrubbed with maple, birch, and hemlock; but near the top the shrubbery thinned out; and suddenly, in an open space, he came upon red stakes, three in a row. A little way ahead, to mark the beginning of a northward curve, he saw another set. He followed them. As he went on, the ground rose on his right; it was bushed over lightly there with blueberries and buffalo sod. He mounted with it, and in a little while he saw, standing on the apex of the hill, Bates and Myron Holley, the commissioner.

At Jerry's shout Bates turned round. He waved his hand and his face lit up. He touched the commissioner's elbow. Myron Holley turned. Together they waited on Jerry's approach.

As he came up, his eye took in the course of the crossing; instantly he felt a wave of admiration for Geddes, who, alone with one axeman and one rodsman back in 1809, had had the vision to find out this place.

Bates shook his hand.

"I'm glad to see you, Fowler. I thought you might come yesterday."

"I nighted in the woods."

"It was a heavy storm," Myron Holley said. He had a quiet, cultured voice, and calm brown eyes. It was the first time Jerry had met him face to face; but next to Clinton, Wright, and Geddes, he admired this man's work. With a single driver he had to cover over a hundred miles of digging, paying off the contractors, making judgments for farm damage, settling fifty-cent accounts to axemen, rodsmen, ploughmen, hearing the troubles of a man who laid a culvert and making out his advance, or spotting misappropriation of state funds and bringing in the magistrates. He nighted where night found him, in shanties, in a tent he carried on his wagon, making out his day's accounts by candlelight, with a smoke pot on the table to ward off the bugs, accounts that ran from a ten-thousand-dollar digger's contract down to a fourteen-cent spike-lifter. Three years after, the legislature would rise up in wrath because he could not tell them where thirty thousand dollars had gone; truly, during seven years of service, he had had to handle over two million dollars in cash, of varying state currencies in shillings, fips, silver half-dollars, and local factory bills from seventy-five cents upwards; but couldn't a man keep ledgers, they demanded? He told them that for two months in the spring he traveled on foot —carrying his cash in his hand satchel, with one man to bring his clothes and tent and able to keep only rough notes of expenditures; but that, they said, was not the point: an honest man who handled public funds kept books. . . . But now Jerry saw a man already tired in his body.

He said, "I consider this the biggest work the whole line will show. Bates has been arguing me out of wood, Mr. Fowler. I don't need much convincing."

Bates, in his dry, matter-of-fact voice, said, "Yes, Jerry. Look here. Look over there. You're not an engineer, but you can tell how much wood will do for us. Can you build us a trough to carry forty feet by four of water over there?"

Jerry looked down upon the crossing as if he looked down on a map. "The hill looks ninety feet to me," he said.

It dropped off sheer from his feet. Now he could see the course the canal would follow. The hill stuck out into the horseshoe pond like a lizard's tongue. To west the ground sloped up again, almost to the hill's level.

"We're standing on a hundred feet," said Bates. "But the bottom of the ditch is seventy-six feet over the pond level. Eighty feet in all. And west, there, the ground mounts up again to this level in twelve hundred feet. Near a quarter mile."

"How wide's the pond water there?"

"Four chains and seven links from edge to edge."

Jerry thought.

He said, "Water that length and height would have an awful outward thrust against the braces. Myself, I wouldn't undertake to make it hold— whoever drew me plans."

Holley sighed.

"I think the same. But I have got to convince them back in Albany. They passed over my head in ordering timbers."

Bates said, "We can use them other places. Now they've spent that money for economy they may feel better towards us. They've showed their will."

"What am I to do?" Jerry asked Bates.

"Mann's done all his spring sawing. We've had to rent the mill for summer to let down the water. We're going to build a stone culvert.

After that, we'll tell them. Then if they want wood they can send someone out to build it. They won't get any engineer."

"And me?" said Jerry.

"You're to lay a flooring, boy. You've got to set in piles. I've figured out embankment slope for that height. The floor has got to be 245 feet long. Twenty-six across will handle all the water if we make the arch full Roman. The piles are all stacked down there."

Next to the monumental stacks of gleaming, brand-new timbers, Jerry saw a great black heap of piling.

"Most of them are twenty foot," said Bates. "You've got to pile in quicksand and I've figured on eight hundred piles. But there are two hundred more in case it's bad." He faced east. "Mann's opened up his sluice."

Jerry and Myron Holley looked down across the treetops. Mann's dam made just a thread beyond the deep-blue pond, and his mill was a tiny box to look at. But below the dam a surge of coffee-colored water boiled away.

"It will take two days, to get it down," said Bates.

"You've got a piler?"

"Bemis. Roger Hunter has brought him in."

Jerry looked back at the culvert-site. Behind a clump of hemlocks stood a shanty, and beside the shanty he saw a small grey spot that marked a wagon-hood. He made out Hunter's odd-colored horses grazing alongside.

"We might as well go down," said Bates. "I've got a boat to row across with."

Holley said good-bye.

"My driver's down at Mann's. I've got to get back to pay up with Dancer Borden by to-morrow night."

He went away.

Jerry looked out before he followed Bates. Miles and miles west he could see across the level upland. Rochester lay that way, the Genesee, and miles beyond was Erie. But he turned quickly south. There lay the end of Mann's pond, and the creek coming in through flags. His eyes followed the course southward through a soft-wood forest. There was a clearing a half mile beyond, and in it he saw a little gristmill. Eastward the view was closed to him. . . .

In the shanty, Hunter was polishing his bells. He rose up eagerly as Jerry entered.

"Jerry Fowler—man, I'm glad to see you." He shook hands powerfully. "When I got in last night I seen your tool box in the corner. And I thought I'd wait."

His hard face shone, and he sat down again and occupied his strong hands with vigorous polishing.

"I haven't seen you for a long time."

"That's right, I guess. We've been right occupied in Rochester. They're trying to make stone stick in the Genesee above the falls. And I've been hauling it for them. Jerry, when do you plan to come out there?"

Jerry smiled.

"There's time enough."

"Not too much. Water will be in Montezuma soon. In two years more water will be in Albany, and long before that time boats will have hauled clear in to Rochester."

"That's time enough."

"Listen here," said Hunter. "I used to think a pity in it that I couldn't roll my Pennsylvania wagon any more when this got finished. Now I am pernickety as a filly brought to stud awaiting its completion. I've spoke to Colonel Rochester, and he will back us up in a transportation company. Say, will you join in with me?" He looked across. "There's no one I'd like better."

Jerry could not think of things ahead; something in him was stirred; a new nerve ripened.

He said, "I've got this place to set up first."

"Well, you'll have company for it. A suckish little runt. Bemis, you remember him? But Jerry, I'll hold out for you till next spring. Can you let me know then?"

"I'll let you know then."

He felt Hunter eyeing him shrewdly.

"If I'd not known you was a married man, I'd think you were girl-piney. Maybe you are at that. I wouldn't blame you, knowing your wife."

The door slammed open.

Bemis swaggered in under his bowler hat.

He passed Jerry an unfilled receipt for haulage of a piler.

"Here," he said. "Will you sign this?"

"I'll do my best," said Jerry.

"Thanks," said Bemis.

Jerry filled the receipt and passed it over to Hunter.

"What's news back eastward?" he asked.

"They're making progress," Bemis said. "Them southern delegates don't know how us Americans can dig. You remember Weston?"

"The English engineer?"

"Yes, him. He said it would take two whole years to blast the rocks around Cohoes. We've done it in eighty days."

Hunter gave Jerry a wink at Bemis's "we." But he said, "An Englishman's all right. The only trouble with him is he hasn't ever considered an Irishman. You put an Irishman against a stone mountain and give him plenty of blasting powder and he'll go through. An Englishman would do it scientific, but an Irishman would just bust loose."

He had fought himself to keep away; but to-day with a south wind tossing out the trilliums up the bank, he would go.

The track for the hammer was bolted together and was being raised on its angle braces. It squatted knee-deep in the slimy muck from which the water had drawn down, its sledges buried; and Cosmo Turbe on his spiked boots climbed the steep of the track with the rope to carry the weight. He passed it over the pulley. Plute Sowersby, boot-deep in mud, caught the end and guided it round the winch-drum, turned the right-hand crank until the driver's weight was taken up and its wheels caught on the iron tracks. Dripping wet upon the bank, his plump, smooth face mud-smeared, Bemis rubbed his hands together and stuffed himself with pride.

"She's my own idea. I done her new this winter. A take-down piler especially built for this big ditch. I've got a patent onto her," he added warningly for Jerry's benefit.

But Jerry was thinking with the wind against his face, "I'd ought to go and see if she's all right. I'm responsible for her. I'd have gone up sooner but for starting things. I will go up to-night."

Plute was patting the crank.

"I've always hankered to get my fists on this. You and me will have a picnic, Cosmo."

The little man slid down the tracks, leaped off, and landed in the mud. He came up squeezing fistfuls of black slime. He held them out to Plute.

"You poor bezabor, what do you think you have got there?"

Grinning widely, Cosmo opened his slimy hands.

"What do you think you've got, you poor dumb frog?"

"Picnic hands," said Cosmo seriously.

"Picnic hands? My God, what are you talking of?"

"Well," and Cosmo bashfully dropped his eyes, "the girls would have to wear white stockings."

Bates was casting the sight for the two corner-piles. His rodsman steadied a striped stake on the upward line upon the hill.

With his monster all complete, Bemis forgot his importance. He was hungry to feed it. He laid his bowler hat face down upon a tuft of grass and sprang into the muck. He floundered out to his vast engine, an impish figure, his pants moulded tightly over his solid little buttocks.

Four gangs laid hold of corner ropes and dragged the engine to face north. She crept forward inch by inch to where Plute now held the up-ended pile; his great hands flattened like red lichens on the wood; his shoulders bent and his mouth breathing audible prayers for speed. They inched the engine forward until the angle of the track came flush with the top of the pile, and Cosmo set on the angle cap that transferred the slam of the hammer into a vertical thrust against the pile-crown. He leaped into the well and took the left-hand crank. Another man laid hold of the right. They turned. The paul tickled and the hammer climbed. Bemis with a mallet knocked up the paul. The hammer moved; the rope slid faster than the eye could follow; the drum gears roared; there was a heavy thud and Plute was looking down at his crooked arms and the blisters on his palms.

"By dog," he whispered, "she went down three foot."

"She's set her tooth. Wind up them winches."

The gears began to rattle and the paul danced lightly. Once more Bemis tapped it up. The hammer fell like a bolt. This time the men holding the corner ropes felt the thud in the muck against their boot-soles; and the driver automatically lifted over the blow and squatted down again a good foot backward.

Plute took Cosmo's place at the left winch. They sank her in a dozen drives.

Two men held up the new pile on the line that Bates was calling. The driver sludged her way ahead. Her beetle jaws took hold of the pile; she seemed to take it with an appetite for hemlock. Cosmo patted her timbers.

"Bite her, Josey."

Josey bit.

But Jerry, passing Bates's orders and figuring the cribbing, thought, "I'd better not go up. I dassn't trust it." And as the pile-driver thudded down, he seemed to hear old Issachar say, "I wouldn't blame you."

Bates said, "That's old grass muck. It smells like ague."

3

"I take the candle"

CORBAL'S MILL was a tiny shack housing a single set of stones. A nameless brook running west into the Irondequoit supplied power for its ten-foot wheel; and a woods track of a quarter mile connected it with the Victor road.

Jerry came upon it all at once. A turn round a balsam opened the tiny valley. A meadow full of swale grass bordered the brook with cowslips and the clean-edged blades of blue flag. The stream slid over a bed of moss and cress; when he lay down, the sod was cool and springy against his chest, and the water he sucked up was cold as snow.

He splashed his face with water, and a trout sprang off as if some finger had released a trigger in it.

Down the glade he heard the mutter of the running mill; and when he had followed the road a little way, he saw its roof against the tamaracks, shaking over the drive of the trundle. The race was drinking; just beyond it the buckets of the wheel caught frothy cupfuls.

Jerry stood at the edge of the dam to listen to the noise of milling the rush of the spillway, the sloshy creak of the wheel, the rumble of the trundle, and the mouthing roar of stones.

His eyes swept over the clearing. There was a smoke in the house chimney. The door was open, letting a finger of sunlight into the kitchen, but he could see no moving dress. Behind the tamaracks a fretful dog was barking; the sound came faintly over the mill din. Corbal, he thought, must keep a cow. But nowhere could his eyes find what they searched for. So he stepped down over the shoulder of the dam to the mill door.

Inside, a mist was powdering from the hopper. The upright timbers shook like trees in wind. The miller bent over the millspout to let the flour dribble through his fingers. Now and then he rubbed it in his palms and blew upon it. Then his left hand touched the brayer lever. He did not hear Jerry's entrance; no sound could live in the running mill but that made by the feasting stones. But when Jerry put his hand on the man's elbow, he turned slowly.

"My name is Jerry Fowler," shouted Jerry.

In all his face the miller's still blue eyes alone had color. His cheeks were dusted, his beard was coated white on every hair.

His beard opened to say, "Hey?"

He was without surprise.

Jerry repeated his name. "Can you say if Norah Sharon's in the house?"

The miller looked at him a moment, shook his head, and slowly moved to the other side of the trough. His grey boot kicked the trundle lever.

There came an instant diminution in the thunder of the mill. The dust rose thinner; the trundle clacked emptily on its ratchet; the timbers shook more easily; only the wheel outside, relieved from work, began to gain a revolution. Silence beat in upon them, harder for Jerry to speak against than mill sounds.

"Eh?" roared the miller. "I'm kind of hard of hearing. Speak out louder, mister."

Jerry bawled his question once more, conscious of the miller's eyes on his strained mouth. The stones were falling off from their full-throated roar. The note rose up for a dramatic instant, then whimpered down.

"You want to see the girl?" shouted the miller.

"Yes."

"You needn't get so hot about it." The miller beat his sleeves out. "Most likely she's down to the creek. A person, there, can hear that engine beating where they're making the canal."

"Thanks."

"You're Bennet's nephewy?"

"Yes."

"You needn't look so hot. My name is Nathan Corbal. I was a boy myself once, queer as you may think it. So I ain't surprised. Stay back for supper."

"Thanks," Jerry said again.

Corbal kicked the trundle lever over and the water laid its hand upon the mill, and the silence that had seemed so mastering a breath before was battered forth.

The miller hoisted a sack and cast its contents into the hopper with a practised fling of his shoulder. He caught the flour from the spout.

"This wheat smells colicsome to me," he shouted.

But Jerry had gone out.

A footpath meandered along the brook bank; and the grass that Jerry walked through reached halfway to his knees. The sun was warm against his face, and the air perfect in its stillness; and the sunset flush reached itself upward, and floated a misty veil over the small valley.

The stream crept under the overhanging grass banks, occasionally offering reflection in the corner of a bend; its current was like glass. It curved round the tamaracks and suddenly entered the dark water of the Irondequot; and here the footpath turned north, mounting into the woods.

Jerry came upon her in an open patch of fine pale woods-grass where honeysuckle and rue unfolded darker leaves. She was looking down at the running water of the creek. On the far bank, flags raised a palisade along the water, and gazing back at the girl a heron stood on tiptoe. They looked as if they had not moved for hours. But when Jerry stepped forth, the heron tilted forward. He lost his grace; his wings became lugubrious, heavy, pulsing oars, and his reflection in the water, which had been so clear when he stood still, now broke across the eddies of the central current.

The girl lifted her head to watch the heron go. For an instant Jerry saw her profile, clear-cut against the leaves, the small arched nose, the dark eye absorbed in the bird's flight. She was wearing the same dress, fitting her slim arms closely as she leaned back upon them with her hands in grass.

He could find no words.

Then she turned slowly to face him. Her lips bent quietly. The heavy, deep-fringed lids sank slightly over her dark eyes, and her head bent.

He sat down awkwardly beside her.

"I couldn't come up sooner," he said at last. "I hope you've been all right."

She lifted her eyes to his.

"Mr. Corbal has been nice, and his wife too."

Her answer subtly conveyed a different meaning.

"It must have been lonesome to you."

"A person feels quiet here. A person feels safe."

"Just the same, it must have been lonesome to you."

Her glance was slow, time-taking; her voice half toneless.

"Down here I heard where you were working."

"That was the piler."

"It sounded powerful. Like a bittern. But it came all day long."

Jerry's hands twitched on his knees.

"It does get into one."

Her eyes dropped down before him.

"Yes. It must be a powerful piece of work," her voice went on. "And the queer old man that brought me here said you had charge of it."

"I'm just building the culvert flooring. There's stonework to do after, and then the embankment."

"I would mightily like to see it sometime."

"There's nothing to see now, except a lot of men working in muck mud."

"What do you do?"

"Drive piles."

He felt a little prick of pleasure at her interest. But as he looked at her, his instinct veered away from work. Now, by an ironic twist, he saw that he would rather be away, lost in a new land; and without thinking of it he saw his life as Mary had desired. Himself alone, performing his own tillage, coming home.

"Drive piles," he repeated. "That's all. Then nail on wood. People will look at it after and say how fine the engineering is."

He listened to the creek.

Norah said, "I haven't told you thanks for what you've done, Mr. Fowler." Her eyes swept up from her hands to his face. And again she lowered the lids with that odd conveyance of humility and invitation. "I'm very grateful to you. There aren't many men, I guess, would take such care of a strange girl. I take it very kind."

Jerry's hands plucked strongly at the grass. He felt a power in his fingers' ends. An impulse stirred him to tell her she might always count on him.

"Sometimes," he said, "I get tired of working on the same thing."

Her voice came quietly.

"It must be hard upon a married man, so far away."

"Who told you I was married?"

"Mr. Bennet said so."

"Well, I am. I've got my wife in Montezuma and a baby."

Her hand made a little flutter through the grass. The fingers were pale, slender as new grass leaves.

"I'd feel sorry for a married man."

Jerry found his voice. He looked away for speaking.

"You could be a comfort for me—if you didn't mind my coming here sometimes to see you."

"I'd be glad to have you come. It seems I'm grateful to you."

He watched the shadows growing under the flags, the purpling of the stream. A tanager, like a spark flung from the sunset, darted past their faces. The water sucked hungrily against the banks. The night stole coolly inward.

To Jerry in the darkness came some understanding of the man who had bound up the girl in Lager's cabin. And it made him afraid; for she was not afraid, but sat there waiting in her silence. She was not beautiful in the way he thought of beauty—she was so small; but she put keenness in his senses to read her strength. In her slim body was a spark to start the forces moving—fires uniting on a single stick, the eddy joining separate streams, the thrust of wind beneath the snow.

He was afraid.

He said, "The dew's begun to form itself."

"I like the feeling of it on me."

In the gathered dusk, her face was like an orchid petal. Her dark eyes were large, and the lashes were shadows; and as she looked at him he felt as if he looked into a well at night, his eyes swimming with the darkness, until he saw the reflection of stars on the water, but so far away he could not tell whether he looked up or down. He felt his hands grow large upon his knees. His voice was thick.

"We'd best go back to Corbal's."

She made no answer. But when she rose to her feet, her body was light in lifting. Her hands fluttered against his sleeves like pale moths; but when they touched his hands he felt them warm and dry, and the strength in them.

Corbal's wife was placing supper on the table. A squat little woman, with brown, wrinkled features. She did not speak to them; it was as if she had not been aware of them at all. But the miller, with his hands red from washing, greeted them heartily.

"Come and set, boy. Kin to Ike Bennet is always welcome here, be they he or she. There's lobbered milk for ye and cinnamon for sprinkling and corn pancake for sopping it. Lobbered milk is easy to a dusty throat."

He squared his elbows and ate noisily, breathing upon each mouthful.

The girl occupied her place becomingly. She kept her eyes veiled. Mrs. Corbal sat next to the miller. Her appetite was frugal. Watching her stolid brown face, Jerry wondered whether she carried Indian blood.

It was a strange meal, taken so in utter silence. But the slovenly kept kitchen was cool and dry, and the door was tight against mosquitoes.

When he was done, Corbal sighed and pushed himself away from table.

"That wheat I ground to-day smelled colicsome. Bottom-land growing.

I argued against Dan Ledyard many's the time." He shook his head. "He'll have an ailing family this winter."

He made the remark at his wife as if he expected no answer. He stroked his beard, patting out small clouds of mill dust. He did not look at either of them.

"Any time you're wishful to come visiting, boy, you're welcome."

He stamped through a door. They heard his bed strings creak, his boots thud on the floor. A wooden clock ticked steadily. The woman gathered up the dishes, took a pan from the fire, and dumped them in. She washed them stolidly.

When she was done she looked at them. Her eyes were black and lustreless against the light.

She said, "Good night," with surprising clearness; then she followed her husband.

They had gone so suddenly that Jerry had had no decent chance to take his leave. He stared across at Norah.

She was sitting at the table still, her hands folded in her lap. Her face was calm, her cheeks smooth, pink and white; the blackness of her hair was almost stormy.

Then she raised her eyes. Her small mouth smiled.

"Just like that every night. First him, then her."

Jerry said, "She's strange-appearing."

"Yes."

The frankness of her eyes on his disturbed him.

"But I've gotten used to it. I suppose now it is my turn. I take the candle and go through that door. The stairs are built against the wall."

Jerry felt his hands upon the table. Outside the spilling water hushed and roared. Looking at him, she laughed softly. "Good night, Mr. Fowler. Come again sometime."

She left him seated in the darkness.

He sat there like a fool, staring at the dark space of the open door. He watched the candlelight creep after her up the stair wall. He saw the cracks in the plaster fade away. He heard her feet move overhead; he heard them in her shoes; and then he heard them bare. He swore at himself.

Then he got up. He hesitated. His hands felt hot as they groped for his hat. "Mocking of me. Let her stay there." His hand encountered his hat brim. He fumbled for the door. He tried to go quietly that she might not hear him. "Leave out of here, you fool. Leave her be. She doesn't know." The cool was against his face. He closed the door behind him. The latch clacked in its notch and he pushed in the string.

There was no candlelight upstairs. He strode out savagely. "Get back, you, Jerry Fowler, and don't come back or you will be the Lord's own fool."

He walked away.

"You hold to be a decent man. Leave out of her. Blast her, if she mocked you."

The mill was quiet as an empty church; the dew was heavy on the grass.

"Go now, and don't consider coming back."

He would go now; but he knew too that he was only serving time. He was afraid.

Day after day, the men at the crossing drove their piles. They had to sink a staging to work on, for the piler broke the mud crust and a man would lose his boots in quicksand. They drove two hundred piles. In June they drove two hundred more. The crowns stuck up through the muck like cobble-heads. The sun hung high in the blue sky over them, or they had rains. A dank, outpouring stench followed the rain and made miasmatic shimmers in the men's eyes. They ate into the great stack of piles, dragging them one by one to the edge of what had been the pond with an old, chest-foundered horse whose lungs rattled in the heat; they dragged the piles out from solid ground by hand, rolling them through the muck with peavies, and staggered them up to feed to Josey's beetle jaws. For days on end they seemed forgotten of the world. Mann had left to spend the summer in Canandaigua on the strength of the state's rental of his mill. Even Bates had had to leave them.

They had three cases of fever in the barrack; and as the men did not get better, they used a Saturday and Sunday to set up a shanty on the brow of the hill where the men could lie looking down at the driving in the muck. They built the shanty out of the lighter timbers that had been stacked to build the ordered wooden aqueduct. A solid structure, it might serve some day to house a watchman for the earth embankment.

The provision wagon came in once a week. But the driver always was anxious to get back again. Sometimes, though, he brought a paper in which they read that boats had come to Montezuma. They read about that for three weeks—it had made a deep impression on the editor. The first boats bore the canal commissioners and gentlemen and ladies, and a brass band in blue uniforms. As Bemis read it out to them, they watched the fireflies weaving patterns over the mud flats that had been the mill pond. Water-logged tree trunks and stumps, from whose roots the mud had shrunk in drying, sprawled in monstrous shapes that waited only for a devil's word to rise and walk. A brass band! Gentlemen and ladies!

When they came in at evening, they left their shoes outside the door and put their socks in a common tub to soak the mud out. Now and then one of them would make a fuss at mending clothes, for the cook had an oldish needle he would lend. One of the men knew barbering and shaved their heads to make them easier to wash. They saw the shapes of each other's heads as ivory images; and all the shapes seemed wrong. There was no tavern in four miles; so each man kept wage-whiskey in his leather bottle or Hessian wood flask hung on the wall above his bunk, and drank it lying there while Bemis read the paper. A brass band, gentlemen and ladies!

To amuse himself the cook put in a dozen hills of potatoes; they sprouted quickly. Every day the cook would go out to see how much his potatoes had come up overnight. There was a patch of mallow just beyond the potatoes; but he never saw the mallow bloom. A blister beetle came one morning out of nowhere to eat the potato vines; and he brought it in to drown it. But Plute declared that only the most unmissionated cannibal would boil a living beetle in a pot; he saved its life and kept it under a tumbler next the salt dish on the table. For a while they played roulette with it. They whittled lines like sunbeams from the tumbler rim, and Plute with a watch kept time while they laid money on the lines. Whichever heap the beetle pointed to at the tenth minute took the pot. It was a slow game, drawn out like their nerves. . . . They fed the beetle on green leaves— until he began ailing. Cosmo Turbe slipped out while the cook was snoring and cut leaves from the potatoes, and for a while it lived on them. But in the end it died.

Bugs came overland to infest their bedding. Bedbugs traveled an unconscionable way through wilderness. They got rides on animals; but they always dropped off at the smell of human meat. Jerry ordered sage because he could find none growing round about, but it took two weeks to get it. The other men hunted out their bugs and passed them on to Bemis's bed one evening while he tarred the piler. Bemis made easy pickings for a bug.

Sometimes they wondered how the boss found energy to take long nightly walks.

"Visiting somewheres, maybe."

"Where's a man to visit here, I'd like to know?"

"He's not a drinking man."

"Not enough to walk eight miles for plain corn liquor."

"We've got better here, anyway."

"A girl, most likely."

"Where's a girl, I'd like to know?"

"Sometime, maybe, when I have got the time, I'll find that out."

They pricked their ears.

"It ain't possible round here."

"A girl."

Cosmo and Plute exchanged glances.

"You're dumb crazy, Andrews. Fowler's married."

"What else would he sashay out that way for?"

"His wife's a handsome article, I tell you."

"She's two days' walk away unless he rides. He can't get back to her. And he's been here three months."

"What's that got to do with it?"

"It's hard upon a married man."

The speaker bent his thumbs back, each in turn, and snapped them forward. He had large hands; in the palm of one an R was burned. It was an old scar, hardly visible, dull grey; but when he used hot water for his washing, it stood out lividly. He was a runaway redemptioner; in westward land few people questioned such.

He got up slowly, sat him on his bunk, unlaced his boots.

"Christ! It was better breaking stone on the Cumberland. A man could find him a plantation nigger if he could dodge the dogs."

He pulled his shirt off. His red undershirt had stains under the arms, the color of logwood dye. His forearms bulged under their straight black hairing. He stretched himself and yawned. . . .

All day long Jerry would find his thoughts veering away to Corbal's. There it seemed like a different earth to him, as if when he put down his tools he had cast loose the anchors. Once, he remembered, before he found his manhood, a camp-meeting had been held near Uniontown. As he walked, the fireflies brought back the scene to him: the torches redly waving, spewing their resinous smoke into the air; the narrow redemption aisle that led to the exhorter's pulpit—four empty rum kegs from his father's farm for pillars. The men stood to the right, their faces lean, their hands half closed, their breathing like a steady wind when there was silence. It made a deep impression on a little boy to find men he had seen bending easily to many toils suddenly grown so wooden that their bodies stood like trees. Across the aisle the women's figures were pliable as grass before the wind of the exhorter's words; and under the torches their eyes shone with the unfed fervor of their souls. Jerry remembered little of the afterspell, when the feelings were unleashed to the storms of preachment. Rather he recalled the quiet beginning; the white hair of the exhorter, his hollow cheeks, the fine mobility of his eloquential mouth. He had said that the soul of every man or woman was like a boat with sails, and life was like the sea to sail it on, with a wind that blew away from Heaven. The strong soul rowed against the wind, but the weak soul sailed with it. The exhorter's hands performed a period; the meeting sighed in expectation of the agonies to come. Then he lifted his face to the sky; his lean chest swelled; with all his might he shouted, "Ain't it so, Peter?" The woods were breathless; and from somewhere in the upper branches they heard the deep voice of Peter answering, "Yes, Brother Thompson, you have put it well." Then the exhorter would begin again to work on their emotions; and again, at the tantalizing instant, he withdrew his fervor, calling upon a saint: "What do you say to that, Paul?" or "Come now, John, speak up and tell us." Preacher Thompson had a speaking acquaintance with the saints. There was no question of it; a person could see that he saw them—the gift was in his face. As he stole away, Jerry observed Saint Luke wetting his whistle with a bottle; Saint Luke was in a tree, straddling a branch, and hugging the trunk to his breast, and Jerry thought that his buttocks stuck through his coat tails uncommonly like the buttocks of Preacher Thompson's lay companion, Arnold Jones. But the picture the old exhorter had drawn of his soul remained with Jerry; and now as he walked through Corbal's meadow he felt it as a boat with sails.

He entered the mill and touched the miller's elbow; and Corbal kicked out the trundle, shook his hand, and shouted against the silence, "Pleased to see you, boy. She said she would be down the meadow"; or, "She's gone, I take it, gathering berries in the pasture"; or, again, "I reckon you'll find her by the creek. She likes it there." He beat the dust from his loose sleeves and said, "Stay back for supper with us."

Jerry went forth as he had been directed, to find her waiting for him. As he sat and talked to her, the thought occurred to him that she was still awaiting. Her face was calm; but the blood that moved so close under the dark skin was always ready at a word to blossom. Sometimes she seemed to him like earth too rich for the sowing of plain seed; and again, her eyes were sad, as if she kept a secret self and it were hungry.

She looked so fragile then that he felt that if he could take her in his hands she would bruise like a leaf of maidenhair; the thought would leave him unprepared for her veering back into her mocking vein, when her small body became vibrantly provocative and her dark eyes tantalized him with a kind of dance. Yet even then she seemed to him like an over-gifted child. . . .

"Where were you born, Norah?" he asked her one day. She had been gathering late strawberries along the woods edge of the pasture.

"I don't know, Jerry, for a fact; but I expect it was in the tavern on Wood Creek."

"Wood Creek? The one that passes Rome and runs into Oneida?"

She nodded.

"Yes, it was a wild place. Just the tavern. The sign said Jackson's Tavern. But my father's name was Ferris."

"I've heard of Jackson's Tavern on Wood Creek."

"There's only one, I guess. It tended to the Durham boaters."

Jerry nodded.

"That must have been when the Inland Navigation Company was running its locks."

"I don't know. Ma was terribly fearful of the Durham boaters."

"What was she like, Norah?"

"I guess she was a lot like me." She took a strawberry from her basket and bit the end off. A drop of red juice formed on her lower lip. She sucked it in, smiled, and offered Jerry the bite from the hull.

"She hardly ever spoke. She never chided me for running in the woods. But when a Durham boat came up the creek, she'd holler for me, if Ferris wasn't there, and hide me in a closet. She served them with a shotgun. She was fearful of them. I don't know why."

"I've heard they were a chancy lot," said Jerry.

Norah shook her head to free her mouth of a bonnet ribbon curled up by the wind.

"Some of them looked so, I guess. But some were young."

She munched her berries thoughtfully.

"Ferris could never like me somehow. Maybe it was because I was afraid of him. It makes a man cruel if a woman's scared of him, I guess. He used to strop me sometimes. For being late, or little things—however it fancied him. When I was thirteen and he once caught me bad for fair, though, it didn't seem to make a difference to him."

"What was your mother like, Norah?"

"She never talked to anybody much. Not even me. She was a silent person, Jerry."

"Where was she born?"

"I don't know. I've never heard it."

"It must have been a dreary place."

"It did get dull when the turnpikes opened up and boats got few. I used to be so scared when the boats came through. Ma hid me in under the roof; but there was a knothole looking into the tap. I remember crawling out and watching boaters drink. It made me fearful to see Ma so fearful and I'd hold my breath. But I was curious to see what they would look like. Once one looked up and met my eye. He was young and looked away. I remember him. He came back after."

She sorted over the berries in her lap.

"I mind when I was just a little girl a boat came down from Rome with gentry in it. One of them had a uniform, and one was very young and

stood up straight. Ma talked to him a little. His name was Mr. Clinton, or
something like it. They didn't sleep inside, but had a fire down beside the
creek."

"When did you run away, Norah?"

"Oh, I don't know. Some time ago. It was in spring and I had been out
fishing in the woods. It seemed to me it was a shame to go back home.
When I looked up and seen the tavern in the dark and Ferris in the tap
awaiting for me, I just took his skiff and lit out down the creek. Then I
landed and got out and walked south through the woods. I came out on a
farm. There was a young surveyor there; and since then I've been here or
there."

Her eyes looked slantwise toward him. "Now I'm here," they seemed to
tell him. Jerry fingered a loose callus in his hand. She sighed a little.

"It scarcely seems as if I'd been brought up. It seems there's only just
one thing I know to do. And sometimes I feel sad."

Jerry's heart hammered.

"What do you like the most in all the world, Norah?"

She gave him her little tingling smile; but suddenly her eyes darkened;
she put her bonnet back from her head and let the evening wind blow on
her face.

"I'd like to hear a sermon. There're no camp-meetings round about here,
are there, Jerry?"

"I don't know."

"I'd like sometime to hear a meeting and an exhortation. The exhortation
is the best there is to hear." Her voice became abstract. "When there's
a powerful exhorter I can feel a push in me, as if I lifted on my toes. It's
like what I suppose deliverance is to a woman."

Her voice broke down.

"I've never been gifted to confess myself. Jerry, have you ever confessed
in public meeting?"

Her mouth was trembling and her eyelids uncertain: she looked ready
to cry.

"I always go if I'm opportuned to it. Hoping. But it never comes. Jerry,
I think if you could take me sometime, maybe I could. You've been so
good to me. You're a good man, Jerry. I have never felt so good toward
anyone before. Maybe I could."

She put her hands on his knees.

"Jerry, if one should hold hereabouts, would you take me to it?"

"Surely, Norah. If you want it."

He saw her black eyes melting.

The wind was drawing from the south. It had a cool touch on the hot,
dry meadow; it combed the grass to lift the bee from the black-eyed Susan
and shake the bells of columbines. It brought no clouds, but it was soft
with rain. . . .

4

"You had a key in your hand"

SHE had strange ways. He never knew how next she would approach him. One day she asked him, "Jerry, what's the most beautiful thing you ever saw?"

He tried to think as they walked together along the creek. But she had ceased seeking his answer.

She said: "The most beautiful thing I ever saw was when I ran away from home. I landed on the south shore of the creek at night, and walked all night till I was tired. I slept under a pine tree—and in the morning the sun woke me by heat upon my eyelids. I opened them and saw an apple tree blooming in the middle of the woods."

He said: "That must have been beautiful."

She was walking with bent head and her voice was soft.

She said: "Lately I've remembered it, Jerry. When I'm out here by myself, listening to your piler striking down the valley, it comes back to me. It was so still that morning that you could hardly trace a petal's falling. Why do you suppose I think of it?"

He said: "I don't know, Norah."

For a while she walked with her eyes lost. Then she lifted her face to his. She had to lift her chin to see his face.

She said: "Can you think why, Jerry?"

He said: "No."

"But I know why, Jerry. I thought of it just now."

Her eyes were glad, like a child's.

"But I'm not going to tell you, so don't ask me, please."

"I won't ask it if you don't wish it, Norah."

Her voice grew tender.

"Thank you, Jerry. Very much. Because if you were set and minded to find out, I couldn't keep my secret, and it seems it's the first thing of my own I've ever had. . . ."

She was a strange girl, because she could not bear to be touched; when they walked, even if they were out of sight of Corbal's, she would not let him take her hand. But she would play around him with her words.

"Jerry, how do you love me best?"

He flushed, as she stood off, tilting her face up at him.

"You won't say, will you, Jerry?"

"Why do you want to know?"

She seemed to bubble at him, but her eyes were sly.

"Do you want to know how I love you the best, Jerry?"

"How?"

She shook her head.

"It's not a decent time to tell you. You're too slow. Why were you so slow with me, Jerry?"

He made no answer.

"You looked at your two hands, Jerry, rightful and wrongful. But you couldn't help it. Tell me that."

She shook her head again: "No, you've told me by your face."

She came stealing up to him, standing quite close, on tiptoe.

"Am I mean to pester you, Jerry? Does it matter? Us alone? We have found some comfort. It's not wrong."

He said harshly: "Have you ever seen a mare, Norah?"

"Yes. She is afraid of being beautiful. She trembles."

"Yes. Did you ever see a doe who's heard an answer?"

"Yes, I've seen a doe. . . . She is a humble thing. . . . It makes her meek."

"Or a vixen, all sleek, and knowing all there is?"

"No. I've never seen a vixen, Jerry."

"Even the vixen doesn't turn her head."

Her laughter pealed through the leaves.

"Am I the one thing with no modesty, Jerry, because I look at you?"

She looked into his lean, dark face. She saw his eyes grow harder. Her laughter softened, and she touched his hand.

"Is it unbecoming, Jerry?" . . .

It surprised him to hear her sing. Her voice lost clearness when she sang; it was husky then, and had unexpected depth.

One day he found her alone. He had come up to Corbal's on a Saturday afternoon when the piler needed greasing and the gang had struck off early. Corbals were away in Victor, and she was alone in the kitchen carding whole wool for the miller's wife. He heard her voice when he came past the dam.

> "Why is red the rose's dye
> That it may seem thy blushes' hue?
> All that's fair by love's decree
> Has been made resembling thee."

The comb was idle in her hand, the fleece like a billowed cloud to rest her feet.

> "Why is falling snow so white
> But to be like thy bosom fair?
> All that's fair . . ."

After that she sometimes sang for him. She liked soft songs that required a small range for her voice.

> "Just like love is yonder rose,
> Heavenly fragrance round it throws,
> Yet tears its dewy leaves disclose,
> And in the midst of briers it blows."

She was singing it to him.

"And when rude hands the twin buds sever
They die and they shall blossom never.
Yet the thorns are sharp as ever,
Yet the thorns are sharp as ever."

She let the carding comb drop into the fleece. Her wet eyes lifted to his. Sometimes she cried easily; and at such times it seemed to him that he could trace more plainly where the welt had been laid on across her face. But to-day it had nearly vanished; and when she said, "Jerry, don't you know that that's what's going to happen to us—you a married man, and me?" a queer little piece of instinct in him asked, "Why does she want to stay here? She's got along the way she wished without money up to this time. Why does she want to stay?"

But she said, "I feel like a different person here, Jerry. I feel so good that I feel bad. It's you make me feel different, I guess, because I never felt the same before."

He said, gruffly, "There's no need for feeling different."

"I do. I do, now, when you say that but won't look at me."

She took up the comb again and began idly carding.

"Is it a sin? It is; but it's a comfort to you. Is it a sin for me, then? To repay you with comforting? Haven't I brought you what you never had?"

Her little hands became savage on the fleece.

"Answer me, Jerry. Answer me, I tell you."

"Yes, Norah."

"Then why?"

"I don't know. I wish I did. It don't seem rightful."

"It's you," she said. "It's in you."

She pointed her finger.

"Stop it!" he shouted. "Shut that everlasting clap, can't you? I can't stand it. What difference does it make to you? It never has."

She seemed to withdraw upon her stool. He got up and walked out of the door. He put his hands in his pockets and walked resolutely.

"Jerry."

He would not look round.

"Please, Jerry." Breathlessly. Her feet were running after him along the grassy track. He would not hurry, nor would he slow.

"Jerry, what've I been saying? It don't count. There's me, isn't there? Here. All of me, Jerry."

She was not beautiful, the way he had thought to look at beauty. She stood close under his chin with her head bent, her hands hanging, the palms of her hands stiff, like a child's, ready to beat her skirt. The hair grew high on the back of her neck, from a little point, and the ends curled like grapevine tendrils. . . .

Corbal looked back again at Norah. His stiff, square beard had been brushed free of flour for his trip to town. He wore his madder-yellow linsey shirt with the green worsted scarf for a belt; and now he was downing his malt brew. They had had a stew of bass for their supper, done with leeks and pork and sour milk—a dish his wife knew.

"No," said Corbal. "I don't know if there ever was a camp-meeting here—

abouts." He squared his elbow to the table and lifted his pewter. "I don't hold with public prayer. Religion is bad for a man; it turbulates his blood, making it too hot for him; it's like running stones too long without no wheat for them to bite on. If a man becomes interested in religion, pretty soon he gets to running out of wheat. Or else it thins the blood in him like ague or the intermittent fever. There are such, but I can't stand for them. They feel the need of wheat like any stone, and look around for other people's. No, I don't know that there is going to be camp-meeting hereabouts."

He looked at the girl not unkindly.

"Of course," he said, "I wouldn't set myself against a preacher-wedden. Not that I regard it's necessary. Me and my old lady there got joined without no minister. I just laid out some dollars in a pair of breeches for her pa, a length of French calico to suit her ma's complexion, a Sutherland muskit, and a barrel of prime Devereux. We've got along right good."

His wife was clearing up the supper table, her short, stolid figure heedless as a deaf woman's.

"With women, now, perhaps it's different. I'm not a man to lay down laws regarding women's needs. I wouldn't say."

He got up for his nightly passage to his room. He closed the door, sat on his bed, and threw his boots on the floor. The bed strings creaked.

Coming up behind Norah, Mrs. Corbal touched her shoulder. It was so unexpected that Jerry as well as Norah jumped. Mrs. Corbal's face was smiling down at them. She had an air of secret pride. She put her thumb against her breast and nodded at them.

"Me—Christian woman."

"Oh," said Norah.

"Yes." She nodded. "Camp-meeting comes next month."

Norah's face lit up.

"Where?"

The woman lowered her voice.

"Corbal doesn't like it. I go every year. Beyond Pittsford. This side Rochester. By Little Stone Brook crossing. In Henslow's woods."

She smiled at them. Her broad, high cheek-bones made her face look moonish.

"I go," she said. "Oh, yes. Confess."

Looking back from her bedroom door, her dark red-brown eyes were mystic.

Norah said: "Oh, Jerry! Can I go?"

"Why, yes."

"Will you take me?"

He said, "I don't know how the work will be then. We are getting on. I'm laying the flooring on the southward end."

"Promise me it will be done so you can go."

He smiled into her eyes.

"I will if I can get away."

"I wouldn't want to take you off the work, if you didn't want to come, Jerry. But I want to go. Oh, I want to go. I feel it in me. As if I had a string to pull me. I can feel it even now. Already."

"We'll go."

"Oh, Jerry, you're so good."

She moved over to the miller's stool to sit beside him. For once her hand crept into his unasked. She sat quite still; but Jerry felt as if the palm in his were singing.

"Jerry." She whispered. "To me it's like your work for you."

"It looks as if it meant a lot more to you than my work does to me."

"It's similar. I feel it. As if I could do things if once I could confess. Maybe with you along I could."

He was glad to see her happy, but in himself he felt a staleness.

"It's funny, Norah. But since I've come here my work don't stand for much with me. It seems I'm sick of it. It doesn't matter."

"It does. You will be rich by it. Men will look up at you. Men will say, when everything is done, He did that crossing. He made that lock."

"It doesn't seem to matter any more. And I don't make it. I just do what I'm told. Norah, I feel as if I'm looking somewhere for something. Something in me is unloosed and questing. It seems as if I heard littler things, as if I could smell new smells. But I don't care for working any more. I used to take a joy for feeling a hammer in my hand."

"You've never shown me your work, Jerry."

"I'll take you down on Monday if you want to see it."

"Monday afternoon."

"In the evening when the men are inside the shanty."

"I want to see it. I want to know every last thing you do, Jerry. . . ."

"Jerry, when you are that way, I feel as if my hands had turned to vines. Have you ever cut a grapevine and seen the sap come out of it? My fingers feel like every one a broken vine."

"It's time I went back now."

"It's early yet. Jerry, I couldn't bear for us to part now. Rightful or wrongful, I couldn't bear it."

"We don't have to."

"We will soon. I can feel it. Jerry, to-night I thought you wouldn't ever come. I felt as if I walked in a strange town. And the watch found me and put me in the jail for vagranting. My body felt like vagranting. And they put me in the mill to make me humble and the jail matron beat me till I trod it."

"You were dreaming, Norah."

"Yes, it was a dream. I dreamed it. And then they took me out when I had trod the necessary hours. And my feet were sore. They put me into a cell, on the floor, and left me there. And I felt the time in my feet, the time of waiting. In the soles of my feet. I felt it mounting in me and I was like the jail itself without air and light. But I didn't feel humble, for I heard you coming. And you opened the jail with a key, Jerry. You had a key in your hand and you turned it in the door and I smelled apple blossoms."

"It's time I went."

"Do you ever smell the apple tree?"

"It doesn't seem so."

"Jerry, did you ever lie in grass upon your back and watch clouds go over your head with the sunlight in the wind behind them?"

"Corbal will be getting up."

"Not yet, Jerry. Lie still."

"He will be wakening now."

"He never hears. His head is like grinding millstones."

"Mrs. Corbal, then."

"She doesn't care."

"Norah, I've got to go. I've got a two-mile walk for work."

"There's time, Jerry. Lie back. Did a person ever tell you you looked beautiful at sunrise?"

Jerry laughed.

"No, not anyone at sunrise."

"I don't mean that. With the sleep all white on your skin."

He forced himself to go.

"Jerry. . . ."

5

"The sun sets in the lap of God"

"YOU must speak soft, Norah."

"Is that where you live?"

"Yes. In the barrack. The kitchen's on this end."

"And that's where the men sleep?"

"Yes. You can see them through the window. Now let's go down, if you want to look at the work."

"What are those, Jerry?"

"Those? Oh, the piles. We've drove eight hundred of them now. The driving's nearly done. That's the engine."

"That big thing?"

"Yes."

Their shapes stole softly out on the plank floor of the crossing. Norah laid her hand against a beam.

"Oh." She snatched it back and sniffed her fingers. He heard her breath thin and shivery. "What's on it? It's all over it."

"Tar oil. We have to keep the tracks greased or there'd be fire."

"It smells awful."

"I'm sorry. I should have told you."

"I'd like to see it work. I'd like to see it driving down a pile."

Her voice was vibrant. She touched it again with her finger-tips.

"It's in me, the sound of it. Driving all day long. I'd like to see it piling on a log. Driving it down."

"It's not much to see."

"The sound of it is hurtful."

"Stand back in the shadow, Norah."

"Why?"

"Quick. Unless you want to get found."

"What would happen?"

"Stand there. Don't talk."

She was obedient under his hand, but his grip tightened, till he felt her wince.

A bar of light was put forth from the shanty as the door opened. A gust of voices came forward with it. One of the men was singing.

> "The dogs began to bark,
> And I peeped out to see,
> A handsome young man a-hunting;
> But he was not hunting me."

They could not see who sang. But Jerry recognized the two figures in the doorway.

"That's Andrews," he whispered. "He's a redemptioner—runaway, I guess."

The two men stepped out into the edge of night and were lost.

Norah was very still.

Then she whispered, "Who's the other one?"

"He's a cobbler. His name is Harley Falk. He made a pair of shoes for Cosmo Turbe."

"Oh."

"What are you shivering for?"

"It's the damp. It must be hard to work in the damp. To smell the mud."

"We do get sick of it."

"Shh. They're coming back. The cobbler's going away. See his white horse."

"Do you know him?"

"Shh. Softer, Jerry. No."

"What are you feared of? You were bold enough two minutes past."

The voice of the man who was singing carried tonelessly towards them. He sang as if even his song made no difference.

"Do you know that cobbler?" Jerry asked suddenly.

"No."

"Then what are you frightened of?"

"The head of the horse, Jerry. When he crossed the door. Did you see it? The light in his eyes?"

"He's a blind white horse."

"Yes. White!"

Her hand fluttered in his. They were still. Falk was in his wagon and he now drove it down the road beyond the barrack. Andrews walked beside the wheel. They stopped out of hearing of the barrack, just opposite the piler. Their low voices came in snatches.

"Find out, then," said Falk. "I'd like to know what he's doing."

"I've already found out pretty well. There's a girl at Corbal's."

"Oh. What about her?"

"That's to ask. It's pretty plain, I'd say. But I aim to get the particulars."

"Well, I'm glad to know. You can have the particulars."

"Where are you going now?"

"Back to Montezuma."

"Well, it's your own business."

The wagon moved off down the road. One of its wheels needed greasing. Norah and Jerry by the piler, Andrews by the corner of the barrack, listened to its going. For a long time it seemed to make no progress through the darkness. Then the sound of it went out.

Andrews moved slowly to the door. He lingered there. They could see his eyes staring towards them. They held their breaths. But at last a voice shouted:—

"Shut that door, can't you? You've let in half the bugs in Monroe County."

He went in.

"Let's go back," Norah whispered. "Quick, Jerry."

"He's gone in. It's all right now."

"Jerry, come quick."

She urged him with her hands; she was like a moth in the darkness beating him with hands for wings.

"Jerry, please."

He humored her; but as they walked along the road, the warm summer air became bleak in his face. What was Harley Falk talking about? There was something wrong with that man. He'd scarcely noticed him round the barrack these last three days; he never talked to him. "What does he want to know about me for?" he thought. And then he remembered how he had warned Mary that he didn't like the cobbler. It bothered a person, being spied on. He tried to puzzle it; but the road kept swimming up to meet him.

"You acted just as if you knew him."

"I didn't. Honestly. I was afeared."

"But you weren't afraid when we went down."

"I was afeared when I saw his horse. The white eyes. They looked right at me. Jerry, I felt all naked in that horse's eyes."

He laughed shortly.

"Well, you're all right now."

They were coming out in Corbal's meadow. The mill roof was frosted with a silver dew, the pond a looking-glass for stars. She drew a long breath.

"Yes. I feel safer here. With you along, Jerry."

She kept the path beside him, pressing against him. She turned her face below his shoulder and looked up. Her face was pointed by the starlight, her eyes dark.

"What's the matter, Jerry? You're troubled."

"You troubled me, Norah."

"I'm sorry."

"Was he the man that left you in the cabin?"

He thought he could see even in the dimness the line across her face.

"No. No." She laughed. "I must have had a silly on me. And you are silly to mind it. Look. Corbals are asleep."

"No. I'm going back."

"No, don't. It's unhealthy there."

"I'm going back."

"You act so strange."

"I feel queer."

"Oh, please come in. Come in and see me upstairs through the dark."

"No."

She pleaded silently.

"Go on in, Norah."

She gave a little sigh.

"Jerry, you're not mad with me? You'll still take me down to Henslow's woods?"

"Yes, yes, yes. Anything. But go to bed."

She stole away.

He waited while she closed the door. He heard her light steps slowly mount to her room. Then he started back along the path.

It was dark in the woods. The lights in the shanty were out when he came into the Irondequot Valley. He waited a moment beside the crossing frame, for he felt very tired.

"Hello, Mr. Fowler."

A man moved out from the shadow of the kitchen end.

"What are you doing up so late, Andrews?"

"Calomel night—against the ague." He chuckled softly. "You look as if you'd better have some."

"I've not caught it."

"It's a fine night out, ain't it? When it gets late the bugs fly back into the woods. A man can take his comfort."

"It's a nice night."

Men were snoring in the barrack. A wave of human scent drew past Jerry. He stole across to his bunk and stretched himself out on it. In the darkness he saw Cosmo Turbe rise up on his elbow, watch Andrews enter, and nudge Plute. They whispered. Jerry thought, "Everyone talks secret here." But he didn't care.

"Mr. Bates, I want to get away. Can't you get someone else to finish here?"

"What's the matter, Fowler? You'll finish up next month."

"I'm sick of it."

Mr. Bates looked at him dryly.

"I guess we all get sick of it in spells. Four years of mauling through this country makes anybody sick. You're no worse off than the rest of us."

"My wife's expecting," Jerry said lamely.

"I didn't know that, Jerry. When?"

Jerry hung his head.

"October."

Bates laughed shortly.

"That's time enough. It's your second, isn't it?"

"Yes, but . . ."

"We've all got buts, Jerry. It's not long. A month at most. Hang on. Look here, boy. I could stay here if I had to, but that would keep me off the rest of my line. It would mean a month redoubled in time lost. Just because you got panicky. This thing is too damned ticklish for us to do that. They're feeling very chancy down in Albany. Especially now, because we've got their agreement for an earth embankment. Stone's ordered already. The southern tier of noodles are just waiting for a chance to stop us, now, God damn them!"

"Who's going to lay it up?"

"That perks you up, eh?"

"Who?"

"I don't know. One man has given better figures than any we've had. He's coming up here soon. If we've got the flooring done it will encourage him. I think he's some friend of Dancer Borden's down in Galen."

"I'd like to go away," repeated Jerry.

"Listen. You think you're getting a hard deal here. Think of old Geddes tramping through this country ten years ago. Wild woods most of it. But he cleared every foot of it for his level-sights. He wore a bucket on his back with a smudge in it to keep off the bugs. He didn't even have a tent. And you complain. Fowler, if you quit on me, I'll spread it all around."

"Go ahead. What's to prevent me walking right out any time?"

"Not a thing. Go on. Get out."

Jerry stared at the flooring he was laying. His arms felt dead. His wrists were overthick. His forehead bothered him as if his hatband had been cast in lead. His fists were like balls. But on the piler winch, Cosmo Turbe was bawling, "Active, Plute! Real active!" And Bemis stood with his hammer ready to tip up the paul. He made the knock. The hammer roared and hammered home. The shock came through the flooring against Jerry's feet and jarred him to his teeth. But Bemis rubbed his hands and judged the inches. "Just a little way, boys." They let the hammer fall a short one. "Dainty," said Plute. "It's leveled dainty, Mr. Bemis." And Bemis said with a kind of modest twitch of his important buttocks, "Shucks. I could drive a feather with her, without bend or break."

"I'll stay, Mr. Bates."

"Good boy. . . ."

"I've been away a considerable, ain't I, Jerry?"

Issachar Bennet grinned at him.

"You haven't changed horses anyway," said Jerry.

"No. I've got fond of Daisy. Say, you don't look very well."

"I feel queer," Jerry admitted.

"Well, come on up to Corbal's to-night."

"Yes, I was coming anyways."

"Been often? How is she?"

"I've been there right along. Too often, maybe."

Bennet sympathetically clacked his tongue.

"She's fine, though."

Bennet looked out over the work. His hatchet face was wrinkled with distaste.

"It's quite a job by the look of it, Jerry."

"I'm sick to death of it."

"I don't wonder. I couldn't stand working in one place. I had to quit on my last congregation. Baptists. It's hard being Baptist—keeping dry." His eyes twinkled in the tiny wrinkles. "But I done so good I didn't think they'd let me go until I promised to preachify at the camp-meeting."

"You're going?"

"Well, I've passed my word. The rest lies in the Lord."

"Norah is possessed to go. I said I'd go along with her."

"We might travel down together."

"Yes."

"It's going to be a mighty time." He gathered up the reins. "Well, I'll push on, and you come up to-night."

Jerry quit work at sundown. The last pile was in and the cribbing lacked but a few timbers. It was good, stout workmanship. Old Josey had been hauled up on the bank with tackles, and now she lay collapsed; as though with her last blow her soul had given out.

He carried his tools to the barrack. The cook brought out his basin of hot water. He stripped himself and washed by the sunny doorway. The men were sprawling on the ground, waiting for supper.

"How much longer are we going to be here, Mr. Fowler?"

"Only a few days more."

Jerry lathered himself with the yellow bar and scrubbed his hands and face. He rubbed himself all over with a coarse towel. His skin felt dry and full of tiny pricks.

"Plute?"

Plute looked up from the manicure he was performing with a copper nail.

"I'm going to be away over the Sunday. I put you in charge. Some of the men are going to get restless."

Plute grinned.

"A couple of them might. Can I have Cosmo for my leftenant?"

"Anyone you like."

He smiled at Cosmo's flat frog's grin. He was getting fond of these two men.

"What do you want us to do, Mr. Fowler?"

"There'll be Josey to load on for Bemis. I don't know where he's going with it, but he leaves to-morrow. Then stack the other piles. And after that you can dig out the earth on either side of the flooring. Level it flush with the floor level. You won't strike quicksand."

"Sure," said Plute. "The boys hate digging. But we'll get it done in no time, won't we, Cosmo?"

Cosmo nodded.

"Real active."

Jerry dressed himself in his homespun coat and pants, combed back his hair, and put his razor in his pocket. The men still sprawled before the door.

"Oh, Plute, if Bates brings orders to move on the gang, you can let 'em go. Don't argue with him. But you two might as well stay."

He walked along the track. An unearthly stillness in the evening woods bore down upon him. The cicadas had cut off their shrilling a little while ago; but his ears still buzzed with them. He tried to clear his head of dizziness. As he walked, all his senses stretched before him for the coolness of Corbal's quiet valley. This was the kind of evening on which, if she felt kind, Norah would soothe and comfort him. He longed to get to her, but he could not hurry. And he wondered if Bennet's being there would bother her. He felt himself that nothing in the world could bother him. He wondered if she would come to meet him as she sometimes did.

When he rounded the corner that turned down for the meadow, he lifted his eyes to see if she was sitting on the beech-tree stump. He saw her there. But she was not sitting. Small and birdlike she stood upon the stump, and two gentlemen on horseback were talking down at her. They had their hats in their hands.

Jerry's eyes took in the horses. They were blooded beasts, one bay, one black. They tossed their double bits and moved their forefeet lightly; and the low slanting sunlight dappled their shining hides with leaf-marks.

Jerry looked up at the men's faces. One he had never seen; but he who talked to Norah sat his beast with indolent grace. And in his oval face and possessive eyes Jerry's tired head found something familiar.

Then the man laughed clearly, so that his horse moved under him and had to be reined back with a wrist of dovelike steel. But Jerry placed the laugh. "Go lightly," it seemed to say. "Look about you, see, and have. But do go lightly." He felt the blood in his face resenting Norah's answering mirth. She laughed with a clear, light passion of excitement; her small red lips opened; her body seemed to lift and sway; and Jerry saw the faintest flush in Dancer Borden's olive cheek as he made a bow.

Borden's companion was a square-faced man with a rusty beard trimmed close. His cold discerning eyes spied Jerry first. His horse slid imperceptibly sidewise and he touched Borden's elbow with a gloved forefinger.

Dancer Borden and Norah turned together. Her face was flushed bright pink; her mouth still quivered half demurely; but her eyes were flashing black.

"Oh, Jerry, I was waiting for you."

"I'm a little late," he said in a dull voice. But he looked at Dancer Borden.

Borden's eyes traveled from him to Norah and returned to him. He reached down to hold out a slim, gloved hand.

"It's the carpenter. I remember you—you came to dinner. How are you, Fowler?"

Half the greeting seemed an explanation for his companion. Jerry looked over to the cold eyes and was surprised to find them understanding.

"I've seen your work." He did not offer to shake hands. "It's good work."

That was all he said, but his eyes twitched toward Norah.

Norah stood at Jerry's side, and Dancer Borden gracefully curved his mount to face them both.

"We were talking as we came along," he explained. "And our horses chose this path before we noticed. This lady has been setting us right." He made a bow.

"Thank you." He spoke to his companion. "We ought to move along, if you're going to meet Bates there to-night."

Both men doffed their hats again. Their little spurs stabbed at their horses. They cantered off—straight-backed; one wore blue and one wore green. The dust rose up from the dainty shoe-plates of their horses. The sun flecked gold and green upon their flanks.

Jerry felt Norah's hand upon his wrist.

"Oh, I'm glad you've come."

Her small face was lifted towards him. Her cheeks were glowing. Her eyes looked longer; and the lids half veiled them.

Her voice was vibrant.

"I waited and waited and I thought you'd never come, Jerry."

"Has Issachar Bennet got here?" he asked heavily.

"Yes. He came a little while past noon. He's been talking with Corbal. He's a nice old man, I think. He's fond of you, Jerry."

"Did he tell you of the camp-meeting?"

"Yes. He said he was going down. He said he'd take us."

She put her hands together before her dress, and her eyes sparkled. She had strange ways, he thought.

"Oh, Jerry. I'm so glad."

They walked together slowly towards the mill.

"Do you feel tired, Jerry?"

Her voice was kind. His heart lifted a little. She would be kind.

"Yes, I feel tired to-night."

"Let's sit a while, here on the bridge. It's cool here and I like to sit close to the water when it's still this way. Look, Jerry, you can see the lizards swimming in the weeds. That red one, and there's one with spots like little gold currencies all over him. I've heard that trout get spots from eating lizards."

The pond was glass-like. It did not feel the lightest wind. . . . But the arrowheads along the shallows quivered in the water's motion.

"Are you awfully tired, Jerry?"

He mumbled, "I'm kind of tired."

"Here, put your arm across my shoulders. It gives you something to lean upon, small if it is. Jerry, I've been thinking how good you were to me. I've been so happy here."

Underneath his arms, against his ribs, he could feel her shivering.

"What are you trembling about?"

"Nothing, Jerry. I'm not trembling."

"Yes, you are."

"Silly." She slid her hand between their sides. "It's your own heart beating."

"It isn't me."

He felt again the small ecstatic shivering under his arm.

"Why do you do it, Norah?"

She laughed softly, hanging her head and looking at the water.

"I'm excited. I keep thinking of camp-meeting, Jerry. You and me. Oh, it would please me so to be gifted with confession. Jerry, I can feel it pulling in me. Like a string I'm led by."

She looked straight over the water to the west. The lower edge of a dull red sun was dented upon a cloud. Her face was rapt, and her whole being seemed to listen. Jerry held his breath.

"When will we start, Jerry?"

"In the morning, Norah."

"Will Mr. Bennet be one of the exhorters?"

"I believe so."

"I'd like to hear him exhort a meeting."

"He says he's got the gift of eloquence."

"I'll believe it. Will we go past the crossing?"

"No. The road takes you past Mann's Mill."

"Oh, that's where the gentleman said he was bound for when he lost his way."

"I thought he said you told him the way. How did you know it?"

"I didn't. I just said the road was plain ahead where they turned off beyond the hemlock."

She plucked a switch of marsh grass to dabble in the pond.

"He talked as if he knew you, Jerry. He said you came to dinner."

"I did. An evening dinner," Jerry said.

"Was it a fine house?"

"Yes. It was a very fine house. I couldn't feel quite easy eating there. The food was funny." He could taste the soufflé now as plainly as if he had just finished eating. "The house was full of girls—mulatto girls. The chairs had silk."

Her eyes half closed. She hung upon his words. Then, suddenly, she turned to him.

"Jerry, I love you so."

She put her hands upon his arms and buried her face in his shirt. He looked down at the curling hairs upon her neck. His hands patted her clumsily. He could feel happy again, for the face of Dancer Borden faded out.

Smoke was rising out of the cabin chimney. They heard Bennet's voice calling Corbal, and the mill wheel ceased its turning. Norah sighed.

"We've got to go, I guess." She sprang lightly to her feet, casting a fleeting glance at the woods, and helped him up. "Poor Jerry. You do look tuckered out. Mr. Bennet's sleeping in the room back of Corbal's. You come up to-night."

They started walking just in time to see the head of the Shaker rising up over the dam; and as he rose his long black figure took its image in the pond.

Corbal was a long-suffering man.

"Every year," he said, "about this time Anna sneaks off on me. She don't say a word. She just lights out. She bakes me up a lot of beans. She fixes me a ham. She puts a bunch of bread into that cupboard." He waved his pewter at the article referred to. "You can look at it now. There's food in there to last a man a week. She had this supper all laid out for fair. But yet she's gone." He shook his beard, sprinkling a dust of flour on the table. "If she was Christian I would think it was camp-meeting. But she ain't no Christian. Wedded me Injun fashion for a muskit, whiskey, breeches for her pa, and calico."

Bennet's eyes twinkled. He hunched himself forward over a large tankard. From time to time he dipped his nose.

"Women are queer, Nathan." He smiled aside at Norah. Norah bubbled at him. But Corbal did not look at them; he was beset with the peculiarities he had wedded.

"That's a certain fact, Ike Bennet. They do the dangedest things. Now there's Anna. The first time she done it I lambasted her when she got back. It didn't do no good, though I kept it up three years on principle. Then when I seen her getting uneasy again, I took away her clothes. Injuns are sensitive to shame. But she wasn't bothered. No, sir, when I come in one night she had cleared out. She'd took my two best shirts and made herself a skirt outen them. Then I took to locking her up. I locked her up in the smokehouse; but blessed if she hadn't put a shovel in there first. She dug a hole out under." He shook his head. "There ought to be Scripture about a woman like that."

" 'A woman shall compass a man,' " Bennet quoted.

"Is that Scripture?"

"It's out of Jeremiah, the prophet."

"Well he was a danged good prophet all right. How long ago did he say that thing, Ike?"

"A long time ago, Nathan. Three thousand years, maybe."

"To think of that! Him way back in the Jerusalem-land, seeing me here. Me, Nathan Corbal, in the town of Victor, Monroe County, York State, in America." He rubbed a dusty cloud out of his head. "He was a prophet all right. Now if he was in a camp-meeting, maybe I'd go to it."

"They don't come like that nowadays, Nathan."

"Well, he didn't say nothing about Anna, did he? What she goes a-hunting after?"

"Not that I know of, Nathan."

"Well, that's it. For four days now, I've got to eat cold vittles. I don't mind that. It's cleaning of the dishes wears a man down, though. It puts a frailty in me just to consider."

He sighed, got up, and made his nightly passage to his room.

Bennet grinned at them.

"It's just as well he never got to camp-meeting to hear his wife confess."

"Does she?" asked Norah.

"Oh, yes. She's got the gift. If I could exhort as powerful as she confesses, I'd not be traipsing backwoods circuits. I'd be setting in my coach in Albany or Philadelphia or even in Boston."

"I've never been gifted to confess," said Norah, earnestly.

"It's a kind of habit once it starts. I wouldn't worry now if I was you. It seems to me a person will have to do it all over again once he's dead." He grinned. "But Anna she'll confess the most remarkable things. She will confess how she has lived in sin with Corbal. Things that would make him die to hear. Things that never got into his deaf head. She'll get the holy rolls; she'll shake; she'll swound and then get up and scream she's been bedfellow of the Devil. One time she did confess to murdering Nathan. That was so remarkable, we kept an eye on her and sent someone back here. He found Nathan crying here because he was lonesome for her. Of course we didn't let on. Exhorters get her now to lead the way."

His birdlike chuckle filled the room.

"Norah."

He spoke softly. He would not wake her if she was asleep. A breeze drew through the tiny windows, filling the low-ceilinged room with the damp, cool breath of sifting rain. The eaves dripped slowly. He heard drops falling on the kitchen doorstone. First one drop; then a pause; then two in close succession. *Drip—drip, drip.* Over and over. The sound of the spillway lulled him. In the rain it was inarticulate, gentle, hushed.

"Norah."

He had never thought before how easily his lips shaped her name. Norah Sharon. Lying there, he could see faintly the curve the ceiling made to meet the eaves. In Uniontown the room he and his older brother used to share had such a ceiling, bending down to the window-tops, so that the night air flowed in like a stream, level with one's sleeping body.

"Norah."

It seemed to Jerry that a scent of roses stole through the rain; but there were no roses in Corbal's valley. A wild rose likes light soil. He had seen them cover the cinder heaps beside blast furnaces. There were no roses anywhere near Corbal's, but the scent was sweet.

Thought of her was like a fragrance in his being. He could hardly stir for fear the fragrance would be gone. In all the weeks they had known each other, he had not felt so deeply moved as he was now. She had had the excitement of the afternoon to offer him.

"Norah."

He could not bear to be alone. He lay still, stretching his ears to hear her breathing.

Drip—drip, drip.

There was no wind; there was no sound of rain upon the roof.

Drip—drip, drip.

Gradually he woke to a perception of the world asleep. He could not hear her breathing. He turned suddenly in the bed and put his hand between the blanket and the tick. Her place was empty.

Drip—drip, drip.

He felt of the tick, his finger-tips grown sensitive. It was still warm, and bit by bit he traced the shape her body had left in the feathers.

"Norah."

He waited for her to return. He seemed to doze and wake and doze.

Then, in a period when his senses were alert, he became aware that the fragrance of roses was a thing he must have dreamed. The room was empty and her place was growing cold. There was no sound in the house. No sound outside the window but the drip of the eaves' drops on the kitchen stone.

He put his bare feet on the floor. In the darkness he groped for his trousers and slid them on. His shirt felt damp and cool upon his back; his shoes were stiff to his feet.

He went down softly to the kitchen, stepped over the board that creaked, and listened. Through their closed doors he heard Corbal and the preacher sleeping evenly. But the kitchen door was open and the drops struck on the stone with little barbs of sound.

"Norah," he whispered.

He was afraid. His heart was empty. His skull felt thin as paper from the pain inside his head.

The rain was drifting on the valley. It made no earthly sound. It did not fall. It seemed to hang like a veil that he could put his hand against, that he could strike with his fist, that was too light to break.

The water at the mill slid down with a hushed frail sound like laughter. "Do go lightly." The filled buckets on the wheel caused it to sway and it creaked faintly on the spindle.

"Norah!"

The rain wrapped its veil round his voice. It muffled his lips. Jerry began to run.

His feet should know the track. He thought as he ran, "I've traveled it often enough by dark to know it now." He walked when he thought the corduroy was due; and at the first stride it was there. It made him bitter.

She couldn't leave him now. It was not possible. She had been so set on going to camp-meeting. She wanted to confess. The urge was in her; she said it pulled her like a string. She'd said that if he went she thought she could confess. And he was going. He had promised her to go. She would not have run off; it was not possible. Why, Dancer Borden could not have spoken half a dozen words to her before his friend. It was not possible. Something had happened to her.

Sometimes she had gone outside at night to walk. Sometimes he had gone with her. She had just walked along the track to the Victor road, and then she had come back. To-night, with the spirit of confession strong within her, she had wanted her time alone. She had walked down to the Victor road. But it was raining and she hated rain. Dew she loved; but rain she could not bear. She would be cold to him when he came upon her. She would not speak as they walked back to Corbal's. She would seem small, and chilled, and her being would be withdrawn where his blundering could not reach it.

But his feet took him doggedly ahead. He must know. They sludged upward to the Victor road. He stood still there, listening. The rain drifted through the leaves. Its drip was hushed between the roots. There was no sound but the dry labor of his heart.

A stick broke behind him. He whirled to meet two outthrust arms.

Jerry smelled the man's strong scent. The muck odor in his clothes was unmistakable.

"I guessed you'd be coming back."

The arms drew him in. The hands slipped up upon his shoulders.

"Leave go," said Jerry.

The man swore.

He dropped his hands and stepped back.

"Who are you?"

The man spoke up surly.

"What difference?"

"Andrews, aren't you?"

"What if I be?"

"What are you doing here?"

"What difference?"

"Tell me, blast you."

The man stepped forward. Jerry could see him looming in the rain.

"Listen, cocky. I don't take no more orders from you. I came here to meet a girl, see? I've had my eyes on her some time."

The rain stuck Jerry's shirt against his shoulders.

"Did you see her?" he asked quietly.

Andrews laughed shortly.

"Not exactly to see her. She skun out of my hands. I don't exactly know. I caught my toe on a God-damned root. I took out after her, but

I couldn't make up. My ankle smarted me. So I come back. I thought she'd come back sometime."

"Which way did she go?"

"One way or another—how'd I know?"

"Which way?" Jerry's voice rose.

"How could I tell. My nose was in the dirt."

"Which way?"

Andrews laughed.

"You go back home, cocky. She'll come back. I'll fetch her to you."

"Which way?"

"Go wipe yourself."

The white blur of his face reached over Jerry. Jerry knew that the face was grinning. As he stared up at it, his eyes drew in the features, the bright, small eyes and widening nostrils, the short brown beard. His fist closed in the darkness at his side. He struck at the face in the dark rain.

The tingling in his knuckles was real. He felt the jaw snap back from them and the squelch of the man's boot heels.

"Which way?"

He heard Andrews stroke his jaw and his breathing go deep.

"I've always wanted to trim you, cocky. I've always aimed to give it to you sometime."

"Which way?"

"This way."

He saw the face come over him again and felt the hands reach out. Stepping back, he struck again, his right against the jaw, his left low down as he stepped in. He felt the man wince, and his elbow was struck up by a rising knee. He glanced aside; his shoes slewed in the muddy road, skidding him round.

Andrews laughed.

"A spiteful little cocky, ain't you?"

The sludge of boots came at him, slowly, carefully. The man limped a trifle from the twist he had had. But Jerry watched for the white blur of the face. He glanced upward under his brows to show his own as little as might be. His head was very clear.

He missed the jaw, but found the throat, and Andrews fell back gasping. Jerry stepped in. He sank two blows as low as he could guess, and as Andrews lunged he threw himself down and stretched his foot out. Andrews fell, and Jerry sprang up and kicked with all his might. His boot found solid flesh. Andrews made no sound. He got up slowly in the dark, but his breath rasped through his beard. He launched himself low down, his head catching Jerry's thigh and spinning him off. The pain came dully, stiffening his leg. But Andrews was hampered by his weight in the slippery mud. Jerry did not jump on him as he kneeled. He slipped behind him, and as the man rose on his feet he said, "Which way?"

Andrews turned oxlike in his slow surprise to meet the blow with his mouth. Jerry could feel the hair over the lips, the lips themselves, and the teeth under them. He stepped back as Andrews spat.

The woods were still. The rain came through the leaves as still as ghosts. It wetted their faces. It stuck their shirts against their steaming skin.

"Which way?"

It gave him pleasure to cut in at the blurred face. He could not see what he was doing; he could only launch his fists. His head sang from the hammering inside his ribs; his head felt light above his feet, and the cold of the rain upon his skin was remote. The only sounds were their breathing and the slip and squelch of their shoes in the muddy road.

"Which way?"

The only words he knew. His voice was cold, like another person's voice. It kept asking questions over his head. It asked where he had stood a moment since and Andrews charged it like a thundering bull. The redemptioner had lost all sense of cunning. His fury carried him in. He did not try to strike. But he began to whisper over and over, as if he prayed, "Just let me get my hands on him."

He was too slow to cope with Jerry. In daylight, if he could have seen, it might have been a different matter. Now he was like a beef to carve.

Jerry felt the flesh of the blurred face grow loose under his knuckles. A sticky warmth sprang out upon his hand and crawled into the notches his clenched fingers made. He felt so light. He felt his head as clear as water in a wineglass. His body took on joy.

"Which way?"

Andrews drew back and took a shuddering breath in through his lips.

"Mann's Mill."

Without a word, Jerry turned on his heel along the road. And then, with the ugly swiftness of a bear, the redemptioner was on his back. From chin to toes his body struck the road. The great hands on his shoulders twisted the fingers in. The knees climbed up upon his back and the man lifted himself on his hands and hurled himself down on Jerry's back.

He forced Jerry's face into the mud.

"I got my hands on him." There was wonderment in his voice. He stretched himself flat on Jerry, suffocating him with his rank odor, and whispered in his ear, "Eat it, cocky. Eat some mud. Eat it. Eat it."

The lightness had gone from Jerry. His head was stonelike in the man's hands. He could not move with the weight pressing him down. A little fountain made of fire seemed to play in the back of his head and the spray from it came out before his eyes in specks of all the colors in the world.

Suddenly Andrews got up.

He stood over him a moment.

"Get up. I won't hurt you any more. It's just a taste of a man's fighting." He laughed harshly to himself, caressing his jaw.

"Go after your girl if you like. . . . She'll consider you a pretty little cocky to make love to. Get along. I'm done with both of you."

Lying in the road, Jerry listened to his broad feet treading back. He seemed to feel the blows they made in the mud against his cheek. His back was aching in slow waves of pain that began at his heels and rose and rose until they lapped his neck, and then went down. And the going down hurt more than the rising.

His head was like a stone. He tried to lift it; but his neck had lost strength to bear the load. He let it fall again to draw his breath. He tried again. This time he got his hands beneath him, thrust his knees forward. He swayed on hands and knees trying to lift his head. At last he got up.

He began to walk. At first it was hard for him to keep the road. But as he went on, his feet walked for him. His head kept saying, "Mann's Mill." And something further back said, "Two miles. . . ."

A light had been left burning in the miller's house. He opened the door and leaned against the post.

"Good God in Heaven!"

Mr. Bates and the man who had ridden in with Borden sat at the kitchen table with a pile of papers between them. A lamp burned on the table, and a moth with rosy splotches on his wings was fluttering round and round the pricked brass shade. The pricks made spattered patterns on their staring faces.

"Where's Dancer Borden?"

"Dancer!" Mr. Bates looked blank.

"Where's Dancer Borden?"

"What happened to you, boy?"

"Where's Dancer Borden?"

The second man looked annoyed.

"He lit out. He said he wanted to get back to Victor. He lit out at ten o'clock."

"Wait a minute!"

Mr. Bates came to the door. He blinked his eyes against the falling rain.

He said: "What happened to him?"

"He's had a fight," said the dry voice. "I'd say he got licked."

"I've got to get him back."

"Come inside. We've got to settle up the yards of earth."

"To hell with your embankment!"

But Jerry had vanished in the rain.

He struck into a path to keep away from Bates. He heard him pass along the road. His voice came thickly through the rain. He waited until he had gone back. Then he himself went on.

He took the backward road. The rain kept falling. It came now more heavily and drops were things to feel. He lost the road awhile and moved along through underbrush. His face was whipped by twigs. Sickness began to grow in his stomach. It crept up in him.

The dawn was pallid in the rain. Along the road he began to meet wagons. The men were driving with set faces. They had their women on the seat at their sides and their children back of them in the boxes.

"Which way?" he asked.

"You're heading wrong, young man," the man said. "Henslow's woods lie west."

"Dan, look at his face."

The man swore under his breath.

"Hey, wait a minute."

A man came riding on a leggy bay with slatted ribs. The rain ran off the brim of his tall hat and spattered on the white hands folded on the horse's withers.

"Which way?"

The exhorter lifted wet grey eyes that showed red half-moons for the underlids.

"At Henslow's. West of Pittsford."

"Which way?"

"Set your face to the path of the sun. The sun sets in the lap of God."

His eyes did not observe, but he made a blessing in the air.

A tinker drove by clattering his pots. His woman was clad in rags and snatches of bright colors.

Jerry struggled to think.

"Which way?"

The woman looked at him.

"Stop a minute, Rafe. The boy's been hurted."

The man yanked at his pony.

"What are you looking for, boy?"

"A girl." He said it stiffly. "A man on a black horse."

The woman looked at the tinker. The tinker laughed.

"The both of them on one black horse? We've seen them, boy. We seen them afore sunrise riding out of Victor. She rode behind him on a blanket pillion with her arms around his middle. She looked at us—and laughed because his horse shied at our rattling load."

He seemed to take pleasure in the telling. Then he spoke to his pony. But the woman grabbed the reins.

"Where do you live, pet?"

Jerry stared stupidly at her. His tongue was thick between his teeth. It filled his jaws when he tried to answer.

The woman said, "We'd better take him with us."

The tinker cursed.

"You've gotten me eight miles off my route to tend camp-meeting. What do you want now?"

"He needs tending, Rafe."

She jumped over the wheel. Her legs flashed bare. They were round and hard. She came back to Jerry and took his swaying shoulders in hard hands.

"You're sick, pet. Come get into Rafe's wagon."

Rafe grumbled.

"The pony's overloaded as it is."

"I'll walk, then."

Rafe cursed.

"Where'll we take him to? We can't turn up at camp-meeting fetching anything like him."

"We're not going to camp-meeting. The boy's got fever. We'll stop him at the first house along the road."

"There ain't no houses on this road."

"We've got to get him shelter from the rain."

Rafe grumbled.

He got down slowly.

"You are the damnedest bitch at altering things."

He helped her shove Jerry into the box. She spread a blanket over him. Rafe climbed aboard and cut the pony viciously.

"*You* needn't change your mind. Get on."

He hunched himself against the rain. The woman bent over Jerry. The rain was running in her hair, down her brown cheeks. She had brown, slanting eyes and a long nose with curving nostrils. Her clothes smelled of leaves and stables, and her skin gave out a musky, overpowering, sweet scent.

She said to the tinker, "If you're sick of me, you can go on to meeting. I've got no trouble finding me a man."

The man croaked raucously.

"There, pet," she said to Jerry. Her voice was high-pitched when it grew gentle.

The little pony trotted doggedly. The rain slanted down on Jerry's face like grey, blunt-headed arrows. The boles of the trees showed black sides to the rain. Their branches drooped with the weight of rain. But the woods were alive with traveling people.

Wagons came up behind the tinker's rattling cart and passed with a whisper of wheels along the muddy road. The people in their bright best huddled under the rain, but their faces looked straight ahead to where the sun would set in the lap of God. Some were excited; and their words tossed over Jerry like bright-colored birds.

"Preacher Eddy's coming up from Cincinnatus to exhort."

"He is a powerful exhorter."

"He uses his hands powerful in exhorting. Seems like he puts his hands upon the Devil's tail to twist him out of my breast. He lays right hold of the Devil in everyone that hears him, causing the Devil to howl, Preacher Eddy does. . . ."

"I listened to a minister in Oaks Old-Stand. Deacon Gandy hired him. A notable breather this man is. He breathes into a person's eyes to clear them for the sight of God."

"He breathed into my sister's eyes. She said she saw the Jesus crucified, and angels on a ladder, climbing up to God like painters, only for buckets each one carried a Commandment set in gold."

"That's right, I guess. She said she heard the Israelitish trumpets clear as Pennsylvany Bells."

"It's going to be a powerful endeavoring against old Satan. Fifteen exhorters will be there."

"Captaining against the Devil."

"I feel my soul get heavy with the Devil now."

"Exhorter Marcy will deliver you, sister. I put store in Marcy. He's got acquaintance with the saints."

They passed on and the pony trotted his jingling load in silence. The rain gained force. The tinker swore.

"You are the most bedeviling bitch I ever ditched with, Besy. I won't go on no more."

"All right, then. Then I'm done with you, Rafe."

"I wasn't going to turn you off. There's a cabin used to stand here—a trapper's cabin. I'll turn up to it."

"Has it a roof left?"

"How do I know? It used to have."

The pots clashed together as the wagon tilted over the ditch. The pony's hoofs, pastern deep in loam, struck into a steep grade. Bushes scraped under the box.

"An old man named Lager. I mended him a fry-pan once. He aimed to start out west. He headed out to Mackinaw, he said, endeavoring to join the Pacific Company."

"It's a dismal-looking place, Rafe."

"Feared of ghosts again? For a lusty bitch you have got strange fearings."

"Who said I was feared?"

Rafe pulled the pony up beside the door.

"Who in hell is here?"

"What are you seeing, Rafe?"

"There's a horse behind the cabin. Hear him?"

"There is, Rafe."

"Hey, there!"

"Rafe, there's another wagon coming up from the road."

"Hell's perdition! You've got me into this . . ."

"Put up your sticker, Rafe. These ain't no sheriffs."

"Hey, mister?" The tinker's voice was surlily polite. "We've picked a young lad up, bad hurted, and brought him here as nearest shelter."

"What's happened to him?"

Rafe shrugged and spread his hands.

Somebody lifted Jerry. He could not open his eyes, but he heard them talking.

"Easy, you tinker. Don't knock in his head against that door. There's an old bed in the corner. Lay him there."

He smelled dusty needles, felt them sticking against his wet clothes. A fire was roaring near by. The woman was stripping him. He opened his eyes.

The man said, "Here's somebody else. Who're you, mister?"

A dark-clad figure loomed over Jerry. A hatchet face looked down.

"Jerry! I've been looking for you all night and day."

His eyes swam.

The gypsy woman looked up.

"He's fainted. He's got the fever. Who's Mary?"

"Mary's his wife," Bennet said.

"Do you know him?" asked the tinker.

"Yes."

"Come along, Besy. There's no call for you now."

"All he needs is tending, mister. He's healthy. Read your hand, mister? Read the born hand for a fip; the both, for past and future, for a shilling?"

"No, thanks. Here's a shilling for tending the boy. You're a kind-hearted woman."

"Get moving, Besy. We'll be late for meeting."

6

"So long as her eyes light on you"

AUGUST was nearly spent when Anna came home from the camp-meeting. She waited on her husband with a blank but attentive eye. To Jerry she was peculiarly kind, in her stolid fashion; two or three times a day she might have been seen going into the woods to seek him herbs. She brought them in in a little basket, jealously covered with fern leaves to keep them fresh, and she brewed them in a stone pot—a crudely shaped thing that she told Jerry had come down through her family. She used it exclusively for medicines.

The fever had left him thin and taken the color from under his burn. But six days after she told him that his blood was sweet again, Bennet had announced that he was heading eastward.

"I'm taking the Victor road to join the pike at Waterloo. If you want to get back to Montezuma, you could ride along with me to the east end of the Cayuga Bridge."

Jerry accepted gratefully. He was not yet fit for all-day walking, but he wanted to get home.

Anna came stolidly to the door and handed them up a luncheon.

" 'Bye."

They stopped at the mill to shake hands with Corbal. He hardly noticed them. Daker had sowed some Russian wheat and he was absorbed in the flour.

"I think it ought to have a finer grind than my stones can give."

He took a pinch.

"Look here."

He put some in their hands.

"What's that?" He cupped a hand behind one ear. "Oh, you're going? Come again sometime. Now this here wheat . . ."

Before they had got out again to Daisy, Corbal had kicked in the trundle and the mill was roaring. As they drove through the woods their ears still sang from the stones. Bennet laughed.

"He leads a good life for a man, I think. His deafness shuts him in and he doesn't give an earthly dang for anything in the world but wheat. You ought to see him grinding buckwheat. Dumps it in and drags it out. Coarse or fine, whichever way the stones are set. But wheat's a misery on his soul. He's always figuring about wheat."

He eyed Jerry aslant and chattered on.

"All foreign seed comes bad here in three years. The German's been no good at all. I was talking to Mr. Clinton about it, and he's interested. North of Rome two years ago it seems he's discovered some native growing. Whether from foreign seed originally or a native article he didn't know. But he took seed and he's trying it. Tall straw he says, and a crisp beard, and

short kernels. If it's a blight-free wheat it will be the greatest thing that
ever happened to our farmers."

Jerry, he saw, was not listening. It didn't matter to Issachar. He talked
that Jerry could think out his thoughts in peace. Himself, he didn't care a
hang for wheat. His long face was kindly. He clucked at Daisy.

Daisy stepped high. She was frisky with the valley grass; and to-day was
cool for an August afternoon. A brisk northerly wind was shivering the
poplars, and drawing chords from the oaks and balsams. The road was
hard from the dry weather; the clear sun patterned it with leaves; and as she
trotted, light and shade passed over her sleek back, making her seem to trot
the faster.

From Victor the land opened up in farms, and men were cradling grain
while their women and the children followed them to bind the sheaves and
shock them. The wind bowed the grain before their scythes, and cloud
shadows swept on them endlessly.

As they came into Manchester, Bennet said, "It's high time I was getting
back to Lebanon. They'll be wondering what's become of me and the letters
I'm to bring them. I guess between here and Albany I'll have to invent
me an excuse." He expelled a humorous sigh. "But traveling with a story on
your mind makes a long trip. I'll just forget about it till I reach Schenectady.
That's a town the sight of which always brings me back to sober fact."

He glanced again at Jerry.

Jerry was slouched upon the seat. He was still pale. His eyes looked un-
seeingly at Daisy's ears.

Bennet touched his knee.

"What's bothering you, boy? You haven't said three words since we left
Corbal's."

Jerry looked miserably round at him.

"I'm thinking what a blasted fool I've been."

"Is that all?" asked the preacher.

"Isn't it enough? I'm wondering how I'm going to go back to Mary."

"Devil it, boy! Walk in on her. She ought to be so glad to see you she
won't think of one thing else. Once she's shown how glad she is a man can
always ride out a woman after."

"I can't just walk in on her."

"Why not?"

"You don't know how she is. She's unspoken for a girl. She's quiet.
But she looks at me sometimes. Seems as if I could see her looking at me
now, this minute."

Issachar rubbed his nose.

"Well, I'm blessed if I can see what else there is for you to do. It seems
kind of late to take yourself with qualms."

Jerry did not answer.

"If you can't just walk in, then tell her the whole business and ask her
to forgive you. It's awful hard for a good woman to hold out against for-
giving someone she is fond of."

"But how am I going to tell her? It doesn't seem to make no sense when
I look back at it. All the time now, it seems I was just wanting to get back

838 THREE STALWARTS

to her. This last time before I came out here she'd kept herself so secret from me. . . ."

"Don't say nothing about that," said Bennet sharply. "Don't do that, boy."

His eyebrows drew together in perplexity.

"I think," he said slowly,—"and you'll recollect I only seen her once, Jerry,—but I think the way she was looking at you that one time, she wouldn't say no to you, no matter what you did, so long as her eyes lit on you."

"Do you think so?"

Some of the haggardness seemed drawn from Jerry's eyes.

"I do for a fact," said Bennet, solemnly.

It seemed that the thud of Daisy's hoofs grew dimmer for a while; and the mile markers on the roadside fences came back to Jerry with insufferable slowness.

He said aloud, for Bennet to hear in witness:—

"I'll move her out to Rochester this fall, and I'll build her the kind of house she's wanted so bad, for her own, not too close to town. I've got the money now to do it. And enough left over to take in business with me joining Roger Hunter. I will do it."

Issachar solemnly nodded his head.

"A good thing to do, Jerry. It seems to me you might owe her that much."

They drove along in comfort for a little way. But as the afternoon drew on and they passed Manchester and the Geneva crossroad, Jerry felt his head growing lighter. He was still weak from the long bout with fever.

Yet the Shaker's kind voice had planted a little seed of gladness in his brain. "So long as her eyes lit on you." That was what he had to do—get back to her, to see her, and to hear her speak. The time he had been away became one long silence she had imposed against him. He thought, "I'll quit the canal for good. I'll live along with her from now on." He remembered things between them—things that made him blush to think of. Once he had promised to buy her a spinning wheel. Now he would make that right. As soon as they got to Rochester, he would take her to a store and let her pick the one she fancied—never mind the cost.

The sun went down at their backs before they reached Waterloo; but Bennet pressed the mare forward through the village. It was supper time along the street. People were inside eating, or if they had finished they were out on the stoops to watch the road in their comfort. Daisy's hoofs tossed beats against the walls and brought back echoes. The rattle of the wheels was duplicated by the high brick courthouse with its new, white, staring windows.

"What do you say, Jerry? Shall we night it here or get along a ways?"

"You're driving."

"You look tired. But four miles on, there's the White Bear—kept by Rube Sammons. It's a good enough place. What do you say?"

Jerry's whole soul responded.

"Let's get along."

"There's light enough for a ways."

Bennet smiled towards the dusk.

The pike stretched straight away, and Jerry saw the night rising up like a steel sheath. The sky was domed. Faint stars hung here and there.

The mare trotted gamely. As she snuffed the coolness her nostrils bloomed and she shook her head.

"She's a good little beast," Bennet said affectionately. "Willing for all there is."

Jerry was thinking that if they had Hammil's horse, the cob, Bourbon, in the thills, they could go on all night. But the mare was an honest lady who deserved her rest.

Once the steel had reached the zenith, the night made swiftly. The stars gained brilliance as the wind died. A little beyond the northern ditch Jerry saw the fire of some movers. Their wagons were circled round it and he saw the flames and the seated figures through the wheels. The sight brought back their wedding. Now he remembered how he had been ashamed of the ring he had fashioned for Mary out of a horseshoe nail; and he told himself that it was an uneven work, half done, but that if she would still wear it he would never again suggest a gold one.

The rising notes of a teamster's bells swam over them. He had not noticed their approach. He would not have heard them or seen the high front of the wagon had the teamster not cracked his whip.

"Good girl, Daisy. Half a mile."

It seemed a long time before they spun into the tavern yard and Issachar sprang out. Jerry's knees wobbled under him, and though he was ashamed to take the preacher's hand, he knew that he could not have clambered down himself.

The light from the open door blurred before his eyes as Bennet helped him through. He heard him whisper to the keeper, "Just got over fever."

"A little beer?"

But the keeper's wife came bustling up.

"Would you murder the lad, Rube? Beer! Some buttermilk is the proper fancy. Come, lad, sit over here not too close the stove. A glass of buttermilk fresh from the spring-floor."

A couple of farmers were talking to a peddler in the tap. Their voices surged and swam. Local court was over and there were things to tell.

The tavern keeper leaned over their chairs.

"How's business been, Rube?"

"I can't complain. To-night's a good night, filling beds with singles—you and the cobbler and this boy."

Jerry was able to walk up to his room alone. He threw his shoes off and flung himself on his bed. Bennet, looking in later, covered him. He scarcely slept at all before Bennet was back waking him. While they ate their breakfast in the sun-filled tap, Mrs. Sammons sowed the floor with gleaming new sand. She was a talkative woman.

Jerry did not listen. He was fretful to get started. The flies in the windows droned. The clattering of the ducks across the yard was deafening. It seemed an hour before Bennet was ready to leave the table.

But at last the hostler brought out Daisy.

"A dainty mare you've got, mister. It's pleasing to me to tend her—what with that blind white brute in the stable that would as soon step on a baby's foot as eat an oat."

Bennet grinned with pleasure. He stood off to admire Daisy with the hostler. Jerry could hold himself no longer.

"Let's get going," he cried.

Issachar Bennet carried a bulbous silver watch. He said that he could always tell when he was beginning to get fleshy by the difficulty he had getting it out of his pocket. He checked the pointing of its plump hands with the slant of the sun.

"Ten o'clock, Jerry. We'll be sighting Bridgeport pretty fast."

He stuck the watch away and shook the reins. Daisy picked up pace and the tires hummed on the crushed stone. They came out on the edge of a grade with the pike sloping down easily between two rows of maples. At the far end a glint of blue shone beside the track; and over the heads of the trees they saw the lake stretching out to southward. The little mare snorted with joy and went kiting down the grade full tilt. The wheels began to sing in their boxes; and the end of the wagon whipsawed dizzily.

Bennet laughed.

"She never lets the breeching catch her if she can help it. Well, no harm. The grade's easy."

They met the Batavia stage toiling up towards them. The horses were walking. The curtains were rolled up, showing a full load of passengers, some taking after-breakfast naps, others fuming at the length of time required to mount from the lake. The driver sat placidly on his seat, a broken straw suspended from his underlip. But when he caught sight of them his eyes brightened and he gave the mare a fancy toot on his horn and waved his whip.

Then they were past. Glancing back, Jerry saw their dust covering the stage and rolling upon the road two hundred yards behind them.

"Here's Bridgeport. Thank the Lord the tollgate's in Cayuga or Daisy'd take it along with her onto the bridge."

They flashed through a hamlet which had a tiny sloop dock and thudded out on the bridge. For over a mile it stretched before them, a causeway built on piles, the track wavering up and down. The unnailed planks lifted and banged under the wheels. Way on the other side they saw a small white speck that marked a wagon.

Bennet slowed Daisy to a walk.

"I always go slow across here. It's the one dust-free passage on the Seneca pike. There's always a breeze here, and a person can see out."

The lake lay between its low shores one sheet of blue. A light breeze sparkled it with sunlight. They could see farms along the banks south of them, cattle grazing and sheep like veils on the hilltops. On the Bridgeport shore a man was working in a vineyard.

"I hate leaving you so soon, Jerry."

"You've been real good to me, Mr. Bennet."

"Some people would call you a fool, Jerry. But I don't think it's done you harm. Just so long as her eyes light on you it will be all right."

Jerry swallowed a lump in his throat.

"Give her my love." Bennet gazed beyond the ears of his mare. His long face was momentarily sad. "I've kicked around all my life. It seemed to me I was more unhampered doing that. But bad as you think you are off, Jerry, I believe now I'd change shoes with you if I could. I'm getting old, I guess."

His eyes crinkled nearly shut. In a moment he was grinning.

"Just you walk in," he said. "Just you walk in, Jerry. It seems to me the Lord isn't so much interested in religion for His own part. But it seems to me He likes young people."

Daisy did not fancy the bridge. She lifted her hoofs with care and set them down precisely. She was fidgety when Bennet drew her over to the edge to let the movers by. A woman drove a pair of horses on the wagon, and a couple of children brought along some cows. But the man of the family was having the devil's own business to keep the two pigs moving. Daisy blew out her nostrils at the hog scent, and, as soon as she was past, broke into a thundering trot. In three minutes she was standing before the tollgate on the Cayuga shore.

The gatekeeper accepted a York shilling for his toll and wound the gate up. They drove ahead to the crossing road that ran between Aurora and Montezuma. Bennet drew up at the corner.

"Good-bye, Jerry."

His lean hand gave Jerry a sense of confidence.

"Good-bye, Mr. Bennet. And thanks."

"Shucks, boy. Get along home."

He handed Jerry down his bag and tool chest, touched the mare. The wagon spun away, and for a moment Jerry had a sight of his narrow shoulders topped by the Quakerish hat between the houses. Then an oxcart loaded with hemlock bark for the tannery cut in behind him. The lump rose again in Jerry's throat. He hefted the tool chest, thought a moment. An inn stood across the road. He would leave the chest there, for he and Mary would be coming back this way so soon. . . .

He was tired from walking; he had come ten miles; and the two miles left to cover seemed a long way.

The afternoon was breathless. The clear sunshine of the morning had faded to a flat brown light that turned the river on Jerry's left to a leaden sheet. Beyond the farther bank the grass of the Montezuma marshes stood still as death. Not a blade moved. In the sky tumultuous clouds were rising up, slate-grey, white-violet, and a blue so deep that it looked black. Far beyond them the sky appeared to have been laid on in paint. There was no feeling of air. But the clouds continued to build, mounting, gaining distance over the earth, their dark hearts revolving lightning.

The voice of roadside crickets made little brittle cries; chickens in farmyards lifted their faces sidewise and scanned the portents; in an elder bush, laced over with its parasols of green berries, Jerry heard the cheeping of a young sparrow.

He pressed on. The gathering clouds intoxicated him with a sense of haste. He must get home before the storm. He mustn't be stopped to shelter from it. "So long as her eyes lit on you."

"You'd best stop in, young man," a woman cried from her porch. "That storm's a dinger. It's been making for three days. Stop in and welcome."

Her face was lifted apprehensively at the sky.

"No, thanks," said Jerry.

Perhaps she was afraid of thunder. Some people dreaded thunder. Perhaps her man was out at work. But he was afraid of more than thunder.

The clouds had wind in them. High up, where the denizens of earth could not feel it, wind was blowing. It tore off wisps from the thunderheads and spread them across the dim brown light. But the clouds made themselves new shapes and continued their brooding.

He could see ahead as far as the village. The houses stood out from the green grass. They and the trees that gave them shade were cut clear, as if a child had set them up in paper. The steeple of the church pierced the tree-tops and caught a wavering sheen on its white paint.

Strung out above the marsh, a flock of crows were winging towards him. The young birds cried from time to time, but the older members plied their wings in silence. They were flying low, turning their heads this way and that to spy a cover.

Jerry pressed on. He had stopped feeling tired. But his head lifted above his shoulders at each step, and settled down again with a jolt of pain.

The great cloud in the southwest seemed to rear its full height upward, showing its black belly. The tissues churned in it, and behind unexpected transparency Jerry saw lightning forking.

He pressed on. For all his dread, he experienced a kind of gladness. He was coming home. In another fifteen minutes he would be in the village street; he would be turning in to the little cabin. Already he saw the stark, square walls of Mrs. Peck's frame house. An apple tree cut off the view of the cabin behind it; but at every step he saw more of the yard, the pump shed, the garden patch Mary had made.

He scarcely cast a glance at the swamp. He did not notice the rope across the river to the beginning lock and the causeway towpath. His ears took no heed of the shouts of the diggers, to make his eyes turn again to the brown, puddled berms shutting the marsh grass from the ditch. He kept his face ahead as he pressed on, for he was nearly home.

As his foot fell over the line where the road widened into the street, his ears were startled. A little to eastward of the tannery a flat, long-carrying "*trahn-ahn-ahn-ahn*" cut through the houses. The strangeness diverted his eyes from their first view of the cabin. He walked with his eyes along the street. It came again: *trahn-ahn-ahn-ahn*.

A man was entering his house. Jerry hailed him.

"What's that racket, mister?"

The man turned lacklustre eyes towards him, looked him up and down.

"Didn't you never hear a boat horn for a lock?" He tilted his head at the sky. "Rain," he said, "is likely to be wet. You'd better get under a roof, young feller."

The flat surface of the river was suddenly disturbed. Big drops struck it, studding it with nail-heads. But Jerry stood stock-still. A basin had been cut into the main street, and a white-railed bridge arched over the canal. As he looked, he saw two mules walk under the bridge. Little by little a towline crept across the street, and a man walked beside the rope with a whip trailing behind him in the dust. Then the boat slid by. It was painted a bold red, and the windows had yellow shutters. On the rear deck a man leaned indolently against the tiller. He didn't even look where he was going, but watched the storm with calculating eyes. As Jerry watched he lifted a long brass horn to his mouth and again the *trahn-ahn* carried towards him down the street.

"Now," said the man in the door of the house, "you've seen a boat—a canal boat on the big ditch. If you stay here you'll hear that racket a dozen times a day." He spat. "Myself, it makes me sick. There ought to be a law against them horns."

The rain, falling in the river, spread itself eastward under the stately march of the clouds. Thunder rolled again. Jerry recollected where he was. He could hear the rain now in the marsh. He had one glimpse of the eight-foot blades bending under the weight of falling water. A roar like all destruction swept up out of the southwest. Pops of dust were whipped out of the street. The man slammed his door. The banging of closing windows resounded through the village. A gust of cool air fell across Jerry's shoulders like a whip. He hitched up his bag and ran.

The chimney showed no smoke. The door was closed, but the latchstring was out. He yanked it. "Mary!" He burst in as the wind took hold of the village. "Mary!" He looked round him. It was cool in the cabin. There was no fire in the hearth. It was bitter to find her out the very minute he came home. But he called, "Mary!" again and waited. No one came. He would have to wait by himself in the rain. But he would have a fire for them if they came in wet.

He let his bag fall and went to the wood-box. It was nearly empty, but enough sticks remained for a small fire. He took them to the hearth and raked the ashes open. There were no coals. He took some ashes in his fingers. They were dead. They had been dead for a day at least. He couldn't be fooled as to that.

He got up slowly, dusting his hands. The cabin had a peculiar look. The closet curtains hung blankly. He went over to them and lifted them. There was nothing on the hooks. He looked round again. Now he knew. The bedstead had no blankets. It was like a joke. He could have laughed.

"Mary!" he called. Then he smiled a little. "Polly!"

He stood still with strained ears, his mouth awry.

His legs washed out under him. He sat down. The storm rolled on the village, shaking the cabin with its thunder and wind, sluicing the roofs, filling the air with the cool scent of water. Squeaking crazily upon its strap hinges, the door creaked and banged. A branch tore off the apple tree and crashed. Jerry sat still.

At last the storm passed on, leaving an empty freshness in its wake that human sounds crept into with a pitiful smallness. A stick poked the door wide and a voice cried harshly, "What are you doing in my cabin?"

Jerry looked up. It was hard for him to see.

"Why, it's the young gallanter come back home!"

Mrs. Peck leaned on her stick in the doorway. Her beautiful gold wig was pushed back from her forehead. Her eyes peered closely at him round her hooked nose.

"High time, too," she said unctuously. "High time. High time."

As she put out her chin to laugh, she reminded him more than ever of a weazened old hen-turkey.

"The rent's all paid. You settled when you left. I guess you might as well set there, if you're minded to." She cocked her head at him, "Eh?"

"Where's my wife?"

"Where's his wife? Oh, my God! Where's his wife?"

Her shoulders heaved.

"I don't know, gallanter. How should I know?" She switched to anger suddenly as a cat. "You go off gallanting, leaving the poor child here, and ask me that. Oh, oh! What a clever question!" She laughed again.

Jerry stared stupidly at her.

"A quiet girl. She set here by her lone most of the time. Weaving. A fine weaver. She's wove lots of spreads and made good money, too. 'When's Mr. Fowler coming back, honey?' I'd ask her. And she'd say, 'I haven't heard from him lately. Pretty soon, maybe.' She's always said those same words, month after month." Suddenly the old woman raised her stick. "Gallanting's all right, mister. But you can't go off that long."

In her silence, Jerry said, "She must have left some word."

"Word? Word? What word would she leave for you? You traipsing round with a fancy gal, gallanting fit to bust a pig for three whole months. Flesh and blood won't stand it."

She struck her stick on the floor, came a little forward, and swallowed noisily.

"You needn't flush up so, gallanter. We know the whole of it. Mr. Falk told the whole of it to me, after he told her. They went away two days ago."

"Falk? Harley Falk? What was he doing?"

"Falk?" she mimicked him. "Yes, Harley Falk. He's been out where you was. He told what was going on. And she got kind of still to hear it. Not mad nor nothing. Just still. She didn't shed a tear. She talked with Mr. Falk, and next morning they hauled out, her with one baby on her lap and another inside of her. I watched them down the street. I could hear the wagon squeaking after that. 'Good-bye, Mrs. Peck,' she said to me. That was all she said. Not mad nor nothing."

Mrs. Peck wiped her eyes with clawlike knuckles.

"Didn't she leave any word for me?" Jerry asked hopelessly.

"Word?" said the old crone again. "Word? I don't know. She left a parcel for you, if that's what you mean."

"For God's sake give it to me."

"Why, if that's what you want, come along." She leaned heavily upon her stick. "Now don't go hurrying me too much. I ain't nearly spry as I used to be. It don't do no good to hurry me. I can't go just so fast. My stars! How did I know it was the parcel you was after? Give me time, mister. And leave go my arm. Leave go or I'll lambaste you. You can't get it without me. So just hold your check. I'm coming along."

She fumbled at her kitchen door, led him into her kitchen. She shuffled over to a cupboard and fished in a sugar crock. Her skinny hand withdrew in tantalizing slowness a folded piece of paper sealed with tallow.

"There 'tis," she said breathlessly and let herself down in her rocker. She rocked jerkily, fighting for her breath.

"My stars! I've not scampered this way in a good ten years."

Jerry shook off the grains of sugar. He broke the flap and put his hands inside.

"What's into it, gallanter? Let me see."

In a panic he ruffled the contents. There was no word, no letter. Mary couldn't write. There was not even any sign.

"Speak up, boy. It's money, ain't it?" Her eyes gleamed avidly. "Count it, mister. That's what a sane body generally does when he gets money."

Jerry could not think. Mechanically he took the money to the table. All in papers. They were sorted. Most were on the Canandaigua bank, but there were bills for Oriskany Mills, Devereux, and the Utica banks, fifty and seventy-five cent bills, a dollar and two dollars. While he counted, he heard the quick, light rocking of Mrs. Peck's chair. She edged for the table and reached out to take a half-filled glass. She began to sip it; her swallows made little rattles in her throat.

Forty dollars, forty-five, fifty, fifty-two, fifty-two seventy-five, fifty-three twenty-five, fifty-four. . . . The little bills made slower counting.

"Seventy dollars, if you want to know," he said at last.

Slowly he patted the bills into a sheaf, folded them into the paper, and buttoned it into his inside pocket.

"Well," said Mrs. Peck. "That's quite a word!"

"Yes."

"My land, boy, you look sick."

"I've had the fever," he said politely.

He could only think of her riding off with Harley Falk. He seemed to see the white eyes of the horse in the white face. Even if she wouldn't have him he must find her before she came to harm.

"Seventy dollars," said Mrs. Peck. "It's quite a word."

"Yes."

Interlude

"Buy land and build a house"

The Driver

HE had caught the Pioneer stage for Rochester in Cayuga village; and he sat next the driver, for the stage was traveling light.

"You was quite a surprise to me," the driver said, skillfully passing the whip to his rein hand and fishing for a flat bottle in his pocket. "The Pioneer line don't go very good. I can't see how Aristarchus Chapman can make money on it. People won't take a stage line that stops all travel Sunday."

He pulled the stopper with his teeth and drank through the side of his mouth—the way he himself would drench a horse.

"But then he's just as crazy as Josiah Bissel. People won't stand for it. They've run pieces in the paper against the line. 'Shall we become slaves to an order of men that style themselves Presbyterians?' Have a drink? It's cold this morning. It wouldn't hurt you to be a Presbyterian for a minute."

Jerry had a nip from the flat bottle. The driver slapped the stopper in, put away the bottle, took back the whip, and snapped the nine-foot, yellow rawhide lash.

"Yes, sir, you surprised me. Just stepping on beyond the station. 'Can I get on?' says you. 'Sure,' says I. 'How far?' says I; and you says, 'To the

White Bear this side of Waterloo.' Why wouldn't I be surprised? You paying stage fare for a trip you could walk inside four hours."

"I'm in a hurry," Jerry said shortly.

"Well, that's your business, mister. Though why a man would be in a hurry to get to the White Bear is a peculiar thought. Well, here we are on top the grade, and if you are in a hurry I'll drive you, mister."

His whip snapped. A clever thing to see, the green bow on the lash-end became a green wasp stinging the four sleek horses. The off right cheek of the off leader, the nigh of the nigh. They caught the stage like a feather and broke into a hard canter. The driver eyed them speculatively as the stage careened in a rut.

"One thing I'll say for Aristarchus. He don't feed his drivers no crow-bait."

Jerry had to grip the outside rail as they swung round a freight wagon. The outside wheel just trembled on the shoulder and the rear wheel spun for an instant. But the driver squinted between his horses and continued the easy mastication of his quid.

"A shave," he remarked. "I'm pretty cute to shave the road shoulder. I *was* a mite slow," he admitted. "If I'd had them running proper you wouldn't have felt a feather. It's my idee that if you're going fast enough you can most generally track a stage past anything."

He watched the sweat break out upon the horses.

"Well, I guess I might as well let them out a while."

His whip snarled through the air and the horses laid down their ears and backs. The stage under Jerry felt lighter than the dust the wheels rolled back. The wind was in his teeth.

The driver took one look at his face and chuckled. Here was a man who wanted fast driving. He wasn't even looking at the road. By dog it! Maybe he was in a hurry. Well, if he wanted speed, Russ Cooper was the man to offer it.

And he did. It seemed scarcely five minutes before he swung his lathered team into the yard of the White Bear.

Jerry sprang out.

"Thank you, driver; that was a rapid twist. What's your charge?"

The driver turned away his eyes with pleasure at the praise.

"Oh, shucks! I guess the company can stand the loss of that fare."

"Thanks."

"Luck," said the driver, turned his leaders, and drew off down the road.

Mrs. Sammons

Jerry heard a stir behind the closed door of the tavern. The night latch was still drawn in. He knocked. The stirring hushed. He knocked louder. Over his head, the white bear looked out from his signboard in an icy calm. He used his fist on the door.

It swung open.

Mrs. Sammons stood there with her hands adjusting her morning dust-cap.

"Listen here, young smarty. What do you mean by hammering my door that way? At five o'clock in morning, too."

"Mrs. Sammons?"

"Yes. I'm Mrs. Sammons. What's your business? Breakfast? Then you'll have to wait till my fire draws, that's all I can say. And be polite about it, or I'll have Rube in upon you." Her hands dropped down to tie her apron strings. "My land of heaven, such a howdy-do I never heard."

"Mrs. Sammons, I want to ask you something."

Her snapping eyes fell on his face. He had taken off his hat; the dawn made his skin pale; and he had dark circles under his eyes. She thought from the set of his mouth that he would cry if she gave him a chance.

"Good gracious, boy. Maybe I've been kind of flustered. That dratted fire! Come inside and tell me what you want."

Jerry followed her into the tap. She paused to poke the new fire in the stove and led the way into her kitchen. There, on the broad hearth, flames crackled briskly under a simmering kettle and a pan was laid ready with its pale slices of bacon.

"Do you remember me, Mrs. Sammons? Two nights ago I was here with Issachar Bennet."

"The boy that Rube wanted to give beer! And I got buttermilk for. Why, yes indeed, now I look at you. What's the matter?"

"Was there a cobbler nighting here? A blind white horse? With a woman and a little girl?"

Mrs. Sammons fluttered.

"I said she was a lovely person. I remember telling it myself. So pretty, too. Her hair all red-like. Yes indeed."

"Do you know where they were heading for?"

Mrs. Sammons gave him a shrewd look.

"What's she to you?"

"My wife."

Mrs. Sammons finished her examination.

"I believe you. Poor boy, is she leaving of you?"

Jerry nodded.

"Poor boy." Mrs. Sammons's sympathies had been instantly enlisted. "You do look miserable. And you never set eyes on her. Oh, dear! I feel so sorry. You thinking of getting home, and she here all the while. Poor boy!"

"It's my fault."

"Yes, naturally. But you do look so sorry, I declare she would forgive you. She looked so kind of sad herself. It grieved me so I took up water for her. If I'd just made her fetch her own, you might have seen her. Oh, dear!"

"I've got to find her."

"Yes, yes. I wished I knowed."

"Didn't she tell you anything?"

"I did lay out a hint for her to answer. . . . But she didn't let on anything. And she looked so sad, I just left her be. Oh, dear!"

A vision of the reconciliation that might have taken place beneath her roof watered Mrs. Sammons's romantic eyes.

But Jerry sat as if he had been crushed. He did not hear her voice run on asking him to think of it. "So long as her eyes light on you." It was like a gospel that he had been repeating these past three days. She was gone.

"You've got to find her," Mrs. Sammons ended her rambling with finality. "I didn't like the look of that cobbler at all. He made me afraid to look at him. Not that he wasn't polite to her. But his horse and the way he looked . . ." She shivered.

"That's it," said Jerry, heavily.

"Of course it is. That's just it. So I've been thinking every minute. I said to Rube last night, 'That's it,' I said. She's so confiding for a person."

"Which way did she go?"

"Let me see. They came in from Bridgeport. I remember that real plain. I was out collecting my eggs when they drove up with that noisy wagon. Yes, now I recollect, of course. They went on toward Waterloo."

"West."

"Naturally, Waterloo is west of here," she said with a spice of tartness. "Everybody knows that. Let's see: they might have took the Geneva route, holding the pike for Canandaigua, but they might have turned south at Lima instead of following on to Batavia; or they could have turned off —for Manchester—on the north road." For the moment even Mrs. Sammons looked blank. "Good gracious! . . . They could have gone most anyways . . . but they did start west. . . . I'm positive of that. . . . That's something anyways."

Jerry got heavily to his feet.

"Now what are you up to?"

"I'm going on."

"Not without breakfast, you ain't. No, sir. I'll call Rube if you do; and Rube will handle you like paper. A powerful man with his hands, Rube is. Bacon, and tea and bread and a fresh egg. My gracious, boy, you'll make the time up in the first two miles."

The Forks

At Waterloo, in the tavern yard, a hostler was polishing the silver trimmings of a harness. He was leaning back against the whiffletree of a high wheeled cart whose hood was folded back, and as he rubbed he sang in a liquorish voice.

> "Bound prentice to waterman, I learned a bit to row,
> But bless your heart I always was so gay,
> That to treat a little water nymph that took my heart in tow
> I runned myself in debt a bit, and then I runned away."

"Well, mister, how does that shine in your eye?"

"Very bright."

"It's got to be bright or I lose my job."

"You've made it shine."

"Haven't I, though? A man might trim his whiskers in that blinker monnygram, considering he had whiskers."

"Yes, he could."

"Mr. Van Buren's friend ain't got whiskers, but he's out raising votes for his Bucktail party. Well, he'll raise a few tails this way, maybe."

"Do you think so?"

The hostler winked and rubbed his freckled nose with the polishing rag.

"Oh yes, though I don't guarantee he'll find a vote under them."

He gathered the harness over his shoulder and stepped into the barn. He hung it over the hook.

"Would you like a look at John Quincy Adams?"

"Yes," said Jerry, humoring him.

"There he is," said the hostler. He pointed to a raw-boned, powerful horse with a canny eye. "That's what he calls him. A good joke, says he, and gives a penny for beer to the hostler and drives off. Well, to my mind he looks a danged sight more like Andrew Jackson."

He leaned himself against the stable door.

"What are you after, mister?"

"I'm trying to find someone."

"Oh, you are? And you want me to tell you where she is, is it? Well, now, what time ought I to have seen the lady?"

He looked waggishly at Jerry for a moment. Then he grinned.

"I didn't hit you, mister. Come on now, I'll do the best I can. But it's dusty work, as I can tell by your boots. So just remember."

"He'd have been through here yesterday round ten o'clock."

"Morning?"

"Yes. He has a wagon that squeaks and he drives a white horse, with white-blind eyes. He had a woman with him and a little girl."

The hostler popped a short whistle.

"It so happens I saw him. I saw the horse go by. Look out under the tunnel into the square. He walked right through that piece of sun. And he turned his face this way. But, mister, the wheel was greased."

"Thanks. What time?"

"Nearer eleven. I judge it by the cook getting the lard off the back stoop."

"You didn't see where they went?"

"No, they were headed for the forks. You might ask there, though it's unlikely. Women commencing dinner. Men working. It's unlikely. It's all right, mister. Dusty, though. Dusty work."

He half reached out his hand.

"Thanks," said Jerry. "I'm no Bucktail like Van Buren's friend, though."

The hostler swore. Then, as he took in Jerry's light satchel and work clothes, he grinned.

"One for you, mister. Welcome, too."

As Jerry went out of the yard he heard the hostler's whistle traipse into the barn.

"I was born on a day when my mother was out. . . ."

A chestnut tree spread a broad shade over the forks. Against its bole an iron horse trough was mounted on a block. The ground between forks rose into a knoll, that gave back on a wood lot. A spring welled in the slope above the trough, and a grooved puncheon had been laid to conduct the water. Jerry bent over to drink the trickle as it fell clear. The water was cold enough to start his teeth aching. It seeped all through him, livening his nerves and easing the parch the sun had wrought in his skin.

To the left the turnpike stretched straight as a cord, meadows on either hand, with fine rail fencing. To the right, the Manchester road came down from the woods. Turnpike or road, left or right. Both west. He looked round him. There were no houses from which a person might readily observe the choice of a driver. But sitting against the bole of the chestnut an old man was niddering on a stick of licorice. His sharp eyes met Jerry's. He said with an asthmatic roar:—

"I was wondering when you'd take (*herrr-rop*) notice of me."

"Morning. It's a hot day."

The old fellow nodded.

"It's a nice place for a man to set," said Jerry. "Do you generally set here?"

"Mostly."

"Were you here yesterday?"

"Was."

"Round noon?"

"About."

Jerry asked his question: "Did a cobbler go by?"

The old man took a suck.

"A cobbler? A cold-faced son of a stamp? (*Herrrr-rop.*) There's plenty such. They go through all the time. Passing me out westward. Driving a white horse? White horses (*herrrr-rop*) ain't uncommon. A light wagon? A young woman with him? Well, couples are most frequent, mister. A man sees plenty setting here. The horse is blind, white-blind, you say. (*Herrrr-rop.*) Now we're getting somewheres."

He stabbed the licorice into his mouth.

"*Herrr-rop,*" he gasped. "I'll tell you how it is. Each one of all them things don't mean a two-foot spit on a dusty road. But when you pile them up, then by—*herrr-rop*—you make out an idee."

"Which way did they go? Pike or road?"

"Now, now," he said. "I ain't said I seed them mister, did I? I reckon I was asleep."

Palmyra Woods

Jerry was following a tote road made by a farmer to get out some scantling timbers from his pine lot. The track he had followed made no sense. For a month he had wandered. He had followed the pike from Waterloo to Geneva, but no one he asked had any word to tell him of the cobbler and his white-blind horse.

Then he had returned to Waterloo to find the old man sleeping by the trough. This time the old man told him he wasn't sure, but he thought he must have been asleep.

"Why do you think so?" Jerry asked.

"Because when I woke up there was two shillin' in my fist."

For two shillings more, he averred that he had had a dream of a white-blind horse that took the road to Manchester. By then the track was stale, but Jerry doggedly followed it. He asked every man and woman, every child along the road. Before he came to Manchester word had gone out ahead of him. Sometimes a wag invented a monstrous tale, but more often information was at hand. At Manchester, he learned that they had continued on towards Victor. But Victor offered a dead end. They hadn't passed, to anybody's knowledge. Jerry back-tracked. The south side of the road was the better-farmed. But on the north side a road ran into the woods, a corduroy, narrow and twisting. He tried it because there was nothing else to try. It led him farther and farther, without visible reason, towards the northeast. It was too dry for tracks; but in a swamp the corduroy had broken recently. There were signs of a man's feet in the stiff muck.

Then the road dwindled out in oak woods and Jerry struck out blindly. It was his second day in the woods and he had discovered nothing. He had not had food for twenty-four hours; he was lost; and his heart sickened in him.

His strength had returned with the miles of tramping, but his mind felt dead. At nights he was given to dreaming. He dreamed of himself as hunting sometimes in the woods, sometimes in cities; and the birds took up a noise of mourning; and somewhere a dark shape flitted, laughing with Norah's voice. He had the dream again and again.

Now he was lost, and he decided to sit down where he was to wait for the stars to come. When he saw the dipper he'd head north. Heading north, he was bound to strike the canal.

He waited for the night to darken under the trees, and he looked for the stars. Before the dipper came, he saw a light shining far off among the oaks.

The light turned out to be a fire burning between two trees. A young man, with round, smooth, red cheeks, was stretched on his stomach on the ground. He had a piece of clay in his hand on which he was marking signs with a stick.

"Evening."

The young man started. He turned his face. His eyes regarded Jerry with a stupid sort of cunning.

"Hello."

"Can you tell me which way Palmyra lies? Or Victor? Or Manchester, for that matter? I've got lost."

"There's Palmyra, two miles off. The others are there and there, but a longer ways. What was you after to get lost?"

"I'm hunting a man with a white-blind horse, a white horse."

The man sat up. His shifty eyes sparkled.

"Kind of like the Apocalypse horse, to hear you."

Jerry stared. Under his eyes the man turned surly.

"Well, I ain't seen them nohow."

"I hardly expected it," Jerry said hopelessly. "Mind if I sit down a while?"

"No, I don't. Set over there."

"What are you making?"

"I'm writing what I thought of this afternoon. Did you ever read the Bible, mister?"

"Not much."

"But did you ever stop to think of the easy money in the Bible?"

"No."

"Nobody has but me, I guess. Back home they want me to hoe potatoes or corn, or reap, or milk. Why should I? I've got a better idea to make money—without working."

"How?"

"That's my idea." He turned his eyes slyly.

"Are you writing on that clay?"

"I don't write. But that don't matter. This is practise. I've got to figger something nobody but me can read. Then I'll have something on people. Something they've got to come to me to get." He grinned. "Did you ever think of all the things you'd like to have, mister?"

"Not all at once."

"But that's what I'm a-doing now. Everything. Money, land, servants, girls." He licked his red lips. "Every last little thing."

"Can you tell me how to find Palmyra?"

"Go down that slope to the crick. There's a path. If you meet a girl a-coming, just tell her Joe Smith's up on the rise a ways."

He grinned.

"Just tell her Joe's got the Holy Ghost right handy if she gets here quick enough."

Jerry left quickly, for the man made him queasy. He found the creek, but he did not meet the girl.

As the inn in Palmyra was closed, he slept in the barn, and next morning went his round of questions. But the trail was too cold, now. Nobody remembered the white-blind horse.

It made no sense: their starting west, then doubling back towards the east. She wanted to lose him, or Falk did, and they had vanished. He tried to think where they had gone. One chance occurred to him. He would go to Utica, trying at Melvilles on the way.

Hammil

Caleb Hammil regarded him with genuine regret.

"I'm sorry you won't stay with me, Jerry. There's my partnership ready for you."

"I'm promised to Hunter."

The fat man nodded.

"Work's what you need. Work ahead, Jerry. Do everything you planned to do if she was there—that's what I'd do myself. You've had hard luck. But if you keep going, it's my idea something will turn up."

"I will."

"I wish, though, you could have seen the bank I laid along the Mohawk down by Herkimer. We've got the canal running half on the hill and half where the water was. It's a sight to look at. More especially when a boat runs by. Lord, how those packets travel!"

"I'm going straight out to Rochester."

"Some day I'll come out to see you, when I've time."

"I wish you would."

"How are you fixed for money?"

"Good enough. But, Mr. Hammil, I'd like to sell that lot of mine."

"Charlie Green's old lot?" The fat man rubbed his chin. "Colonel Tyler was speaking to me about it two days ago. Wanted to know if I could tell where you was. He said he'd offer to pay a hundred dollars for that lot."

"A hundred!" Jerry looked blank.

Hammil chuckled.

"What was it you paid for it?"

"Three dollars."

"Well," said the fat man with a shrewd look, "why don't you sell it —if you're willing—and use the money to buy you a plot in Rochester and build a house?"

"I was thinking that."

"A good frame house, two stories and a full attic, costs less than fifteen hundred dollars. You could build, yourself, when you had the time. The lumber wouldn't come to nothing, then."

Jerry said nothing. But he thought, "I'll do it. I'll save this money towards my land, and I'll build a house."

Hammil was rubbing his hands together.

"Now Colonel Tyler's offered to pay a hundred. I should guess you could get two hundred out of him. Say, why don't you let me handle it? We can trot down to the bank and you can make out an agreement for me to be your agent in the business. Tyler's told me all his troubles. It's the only decent canal-side plot for a packet landing left. He's got to have it for his Erie Navigation line of packets. I'll guarantee two hundred dollars."

He caught up his hat.

"You'll have time enough. The packets are stopping under the bridge now, and the *Montezuma* don't haul out till ten."

As they walked along Jerry asked about his friends. Hammil had all the news. Lester Charley had run off—nobody knew where; but Mrs. Charley was taking hold of the store. "She don't know nothing about books, but she's making the store pay. She handles books like shoes, or dresses—it's the best way. Decorates her shop and has a lot of picters. Want to stop in?"

"No, thanks." He'd rather not see the place now, having to answer questions. Hammil nodded. His eyes were bright with understanding.

"Self Rogers," he changed the flow of Jerry's thoughts, "come back from the west considerably ganted. He marched in and swore he'd never build another shanty for me. That was all. The last I see of him that day he was in the pothecary's. Watson told me afterwards that the old fellow'd got himself gone over thoroughly. He had an ether paint for toothache, a dose of calomel, snake oil on his legs for rheumatism, and Pholadelphis for the gout. Then he went down to Bellinger's and got insensible on whiskey and when he woke up he come right back to me and asked for a new job. We signed papers and I sent him down beyond Little Falls—on a shanty contract."

He chattered on. Bourbon was out at pasture; he needed a week's rest from the summer traveling. Jerry was sorry not to see the horse. Except for the north-country hauling, one didn't see the same number of freight wagons any more. The town was changing. Growing fast. The boats surprised one with their numerousness. Already they were hauling east of Little Falls. Little Falls to Montezuma—quite a stretch.

At the bank they made out papers for the sale of the lot. Jerry found that his balance had grown with interest. There was two years' work with Hammil.

"You're pretty well off for a young man," Hammil said. "You've got enough to make a handsome start. Fifteen hundred dollars would be a handy sum for any man."

They were walking up Genesee Street now. Under the bridge, the Navigation Company had a booth for the passenger agent. Jerry paid four dollars for passage money. It entitled him to the use of a berth and his meals on the forty-eight-hour trip.

The fat man stood uneasily on the dock while Jerry's bag was put aboard. "I ain't been onto one myself." He laughed nervously. "Truth is," he added "two phrenologists has told me that I'll get my death of water. So I just don't chance it."

He put his hands in his pockets and leaned against a bridge timber. His face saddened.

"Jerry, I hate to see you going. I'm glad we don't feel hard against each other. I did a while when you got through and went west on me. But I'm over it. I'm real glad to see you again."

"Something was into me, I guess," said Jerry.

They both stared at the packet in their embarrassment. The other passengers were all aboard. The captain stood beside the steersman with his watch out, and looked up the canal towards Liberty Street, where the company stable was. Then they saw the driver boy coming down with his team. They were hitched tandem and the boy rode the rear horse. The captain tooted his bugle a warning blast.

Hammil shook Jerry's hand.

"Good-bye, Jerry." The small mouth was serious in the fat face. "Seems I'll always remember you outside of Bellinger's hearing that hen announce her egg. I took a fancy to you then. Good luck."

He wrenched his hand away and turned. He stumbled on the steps to the street level. Jerry stared after him. He himself was heading west to Rochester now; he was well off to make his start; but the world seemed lifeless. The agent touched his elbow.

"Best get on."

Jerry climbed the gang to the deck. The steersman heaved it in and leaned it in its clamps against the cabin wall. The horses were hitched to the towrope; the captain blew an ornate call upon the bugle. The team took up the rope and a couple of loafers on the dock helped shove the boat out. They did it carelessly, as if they did it every day.

The Packet Boat

The *Montezuma*, like her sister boat, the *Chief Engineer*, was seventy feet by thirteen. Loaded, she drafted thirteen inches.

As Jerry stood beside the steersman he was surprised at the ease with which the tow horses slid her through the water, as they walked her out through the basin.

"We'll get to going pretty quick," said the steersman.

The town had changed. From the bridge westward, the canal ran through a line of brand-new docks and warehouses. But already the scent of traffic lay about them. In the still September heat, Jerry smelled meal and grain, potatoes, pork and pickled salmon, iron smells from new ploughs greased for shipment, and stoves, green lumber, gypsum, hay in bales. The docks were crowded with men handling barrels, scooping grain. Most of the newest warehouses had their second stories jutting over the plankway, and let down tackles through trapdoors to swing up crates and slings of kegs. Men shouted back and forth, gave orders, checked on tallies. The horses dozed with slung hips, letting the clamor pass their drooping ears. Pigeons and sparrows cluttered the road and found bonanzas in the dust, and small boys scampered on and off the waiting boats.

He eyed them like a carpenter, judging the curve of the bows, the height of siding, the space between the ribs, the construction of the stable, and the way the cabin stairs let down from the deck. They were of all colors, mostly built by men along the canal, some obvious experiments. No two were alike and all seemed very short for their beam. Soon he would build his own; but not one under sixty feet or to carry less than thirty tons.

"When the ditch is opened up both ends," the steersman said, "I reckon there'll be a danged sight more of them. They're a terrible nuisance to us already. By law they've got to give us way. But now and then you strike a Yankee and he's cussed as all git."

Jerry nodded.

"There'll be ten to twenty most any time to see here. Utica's well disposed for traffic. Every month it seems to me I see a new boat. That *John Van Ness Yates* is a Little Falls boat, came on last month. She's hauling water lime for the lower aqueducts. And the *Western Trader*'s also new. She's one of the first built, but a farmer made her out of green pine timbers and he didn't get a hundred yards before she sank. They couldn't keep her caulked. So they took her out and let her weather and she's just lately back. I class her new for that."

Jerry nodded.

"I guess I'll go inside."

"I hope you like us," said the steersman, affably.

The men's cabin extended two thirds of the boat's length. The walls were painted yellow; and there were two long tables side by side. Along the walls the berths were folded up. They consisted of iron frames on hinges with a yard of canvas stretched across them. Jerry identified his berth by his bag.

He sat down opposite it and stared round. There were some fourteen men and three women. The women were sitting in a little library under the steersman's deck. The rest of the travelers were already splitting into little groups. Some elected cards. A couple of farmers talked of crops. Three merchants bewailed Albany prices. Their voices blended into a drone, like the drone of flies against the windows, hushed but ceaseless. It was so quiet in the cabin that if Jerry had not looked through the windows he would never have known that they were moving. And he marveled at the casualness of the passengers, who seemed to take it all for granted.

A talkative man in a grey hat, whom everybody else edged off from, caught sight of him. Jerry rose hastily. He didn't want to talk, or listen to talk. He went on deck again.

There it was peaceful and still. The sun fell straight down, putting light on the blue line of the canal. The steersman nodded.

"It's nice up here. Why don't you go to the front deck? Most likely you won't be bothered there."

Jerry went forward, past the kitchen window, which exuded a scent of carrots and fall cabbage and beef, and the windows of the ladies' cabin. The deck offered a ten-foot space. And till dinner time he was alone watching the play of the towrope against its cleat, eyeing the new banks, already healed with grass, and hearing the ripple of water washing past the bow.

They passed through Whitesboro at a trot, changed horses short of Rome, drew into Rome at two. He could see the Arsenal's straight cream walls, and the town beyond it on his right. A passenger got on at the dock; and two others disembarked—a man and his wife, evidently, for there was a carriage waiting for them.

And just beyond the dock Jerry thought he could identify the place where Governor Clinton had pricked the sod at dawn of July fourth. It seemed a long time ago. Time enough for all this ditch to be dug, to fill with water, and for grass to seed itself and grow. Time enough for him to build seven locks, to lay a culvert bottom. Time enough to have a baby, to be a fool, to lose his wife. He tried not to think of Mary; but even here, in placid travel, while two strong horses pulled him in a tandem hitch, he seemed to see her driving on some road, with his daughter on her lap, behind a white-blind horse. "Not mad nor nothing."

The dinner bugle tootled and he went below.

The Talkative Man

But in the afternoon the talkative man found Jerry out. He was a little man, with grey hair nearly white, a sharp face, and rather close-set, patriotic eyes.

"Hello there, my boy," he said. "I wondered what had become of you all day. Mind if I sit down?"

Moving over, Jerry made room for him, in the spot of shade. The gentleman sat down, easing his fashionably tight trousers, and parting the skirts of his coat. He pulled a cigar from a morocco case, and said, "My name's Vanderbilt Blue." He put his hand out and eyed Jerry knowingly. "People call me a naturalist, or an explorer, or even a savant—titles I don't deserve. Citizen of Utica is more my style. Where do you come from, my boy?"

"Nowhere in particular," said Jerry.

"Come, come," Mr. Blue essayed a smile, "you must have been born, you know."

"I've heard so."

"Well, your name, then?"

"Fowler. I was born in Uniontown," Jerry relented; then saw too late his error. A gleam rose up in Mr. Blue's eyes.

"I've been through there—a pretty village. . . ." But he managed to imply that Utica was something more than that. "A very pretty little village. Is this your first voyage on our Grand Canal?"

"Yes," said Jerry.

Mr. Blue put his cigar between his lips and rubbed his hands. He had the kind of thin mouth that shapes itself all over a cigar.

"Doesn't it give you a thrill, my boy? Not very? Well, it ought to. If you were as curious as me, you'd get more interest out of life. I'm always asking questions. I want to know. I look for data. I was, to take an instance, along with Alexander Wilson when he routed the theory that the swallow dives under the river in the fall and winters in the mud. We turned a creek aside and shoveled up the muck together. There wasn't a sign of a swallow. Yes, I waded in like any Johnny. I tell you that,"—he gestured modestly,—"just to show the way my mind goes after things. But next to learning,"—and his eyes swung round,—"I like to impart knowledge. I regard it as a duty. Now, as long as we're on this canal, and it's your first trip, maybe I'd best begin on that."

He spat overside, folded hands on his knees, and looked ahead. His chest swelled. He spoke.

"Now, riding along in all the comfort of an elegant hotel, with all the peacefulness of a well-ordered home, you'd never guess the trouble that went into the creation of this for you—for me—for all the world. I suppose you know it's going to be the longest canal in all the world?"

"I've heard it mentioned," Jerry said.

"It's an interesting fact that most of the men concerned with this great work have come from Utica. Or environs. Isaac Briggs, for instance. Canvass White, who went to England and discovered in New Hartford waterproof lime. It isn't so much to say that without lime this work would be impossible. I can claim Geddes as a sort of neighbor. Wright. My boy, it makes me proud. Caleb Hammil set up all the locks. And these men —do you realize it?—had nothing but their wits to work with. No books, no experience. By gad, it's wonderful."

"Ain't it?"

"When I think of the way they traveled through here in the wilderness, in rain and snow, and you and me now riding in a palace on the distillation, as it were, of all those honest brains, I can't but feel an urge to seize even a humble spade."

"I should think the diggers had the hardest job."

"Diggers! My boy, they hadn't anything to do but dig!"

"That's it, it seems to me."

"My boy, think of the vision. The responsibility!"

"Yes," said Jerry humbly.

"The young don't stop to consider those things," Mr. Blue said kindly. "I think of Elkanah Watson planning this all out on his first journey, even to some of the locks. You ought to hear him speak. He's a friend of mine.

We've much in common. Washington, too, immortal George. He had an idea of it. Geddes! It's the greatest thing in the world."

Jerry looked out beyond the horses. They were traveling the curves of the swamp section west of Rome. He saw a workman's shanty half grown over by the woods. He thought of Self Rogers groaning over his toothache.

But Mr. Blue was following his gaze.

"Isn't it amazing? There's that work barrack set up by a carpenter, and half destroyed by woods. But here's this mighty work right by it, clear and strong, untouched."

He rambled on. He showed Jerry sights he ought to notice.

"We're coming into Limestone Creek. Let's get up on top deck and view the aqueduct. It's small, but well constructed. My boy, you ought to show more interest. Some day you'll tell your child, 'I was an early traveler on the Grand Canal.' "

He urged Jerry up.

"You don't want to look at that farm, nice as it is. That's not the wonder. The wonder is the canal that made this farm to prosper.—Look." His voice burbled louder than the creek. But Jerry saw the barn. A sidehill barn, it had been moved. A store stood on the towpath and a woman off a boat was buying eggs. He saw her through the door. He heard a strong, clear voice asking happy questions.

Dencey Burns. It seemed a miracle to him that a thrush in the balsams should begin to sing so early in the afternoon. . . .

"Wait till we get to Syracuse," continued Blue. "Then you're going to see a lock. That's the most wonderful thing, in my estimation, in the whole tremendous structure. Harnessing the power of water to lift a whole great boat upward or to set it downward, gently as a boy might float a leaf."

But Jerry was not listening. His eyes were on a sight by the bank. The horses were coming into Oneida Creek, and as the boat slid up to the easy curve, he saw a red-faced man with a bald and sweaty head who stood on the deck of the half-painted, brand-new boat. The boat was up on land, showing its belly clear, and the man, who had finished his painting for the day, was striding back and forth across the steersman's deck.

Mr. Blue observed the sight with a little laugh.

"A quaint old fellow. The whole idea's very quaint, isn't it?"

"What idea?"

"Why, he was a salt-water sailor who got impressed in 1812. He wouldn't work for a British boat, so they stuck him into Dartmoor Prison. That's the story I've heard of him. His name, by the way, is Hank McNab." Mr. Blue rolled his cigar between his lips. "An ignorant man, he wouldn't go to sea any more after he was released in fourteen. But he came up here—why, I can't imagine—and built himself that house in what was wilderness then. He married a half-breed Indian woman. He didn't farm. They say he used to just sit in the door all day long, smoking, looking at nothing —a perfect picture of the sotted peasant. He wouldn't speak to a living soul. He never even noticed the surveyors. The diggers meant nothing to him. All day long he used to sit there like a sot. Even when the water was let through I've heard he would not go down to the bank. He never budged until one day a neighbor, going by, heard him yelling for his spyglass. He had an old brass one. His wife brought it and he fixed it on the eastern view. He'd seen a boat. The neighbor waited to see what he would do. He got up and walked down to the canal and watched the boat pass —the longest walk he'd had in seven years. He said 'Good evening' to his neighbor—the first word he'd ever addressed to him. Next day the neighbor saw him in the mill selecting seasoned timber. Since then he's been building the boat. They say it's all fitted out with fine wood, and really very well made. I'd like to see inside it, though. It must be comical."

Jerry did not join his laughter.

But when the sailor waved his arm and shouted, "Ahoy, *Montezuma!*" he joined the steersman's answer with a wave.

"A loutish face, isn't it?" said Mr. Blue.

"Yes, very."

The self-styled savant turned at the tone of Jerry's voice. His eyebrows were scornfully arched.

"Fowler, I believe you've scarcely listened to my conversation."

"You're right about that, anyway, Mr. Blue."

"What do you mean? 'About that, anyway'?"

"I worked on this line of the canal," said Jerry. "As a matter of fact, I was the man who built the locks."

Mr. Blue drew a deep breath. His cheeks slowly crimsoned. His eyes grew blank as tapioca. Then he rallied.

"By George," he said, "I've always wanted to know the man that built those locks!"

But Jerry had turned his back; and by the tiller the steersman choked a good guffaw.

Night Travel

They ate supper as they traveled, and after supper Jerry went on deck again. He wanted to see his locks in action. At dusk the captain hung a lantern in the bow. And along the line of the canal now and then they saw other lights gliding like unwinking fireflies. At the change stables, the hostlers had the new team ready so that the boat never lost its way. A new driver came with each team.

The land spread out again in farms, but the houses showed as lighted windows. The barns were shapes in blackness. Unseen cowbells sounded in the back pastures. A dog barked at the passing lantern. The crickets shrilled in the woods, the bullfrogs roared their autumn choruses. The sounds mingled in a great wave, before them and behind, but the boat itself seemed to be traveling in a well of silence.

They came to Number One at last, and Jerry saw the level ready for them, and the tender in his nightshirt; and the captain's bugle call hung behind them in the darkness. Jerry felt still and cold as the upper gates closed and the water gushed in the sluices and the sound of the tumble bay ceased. He saw the lock walls rise past them, he saw bats crossing the lanterns, he saw the lower gates open and the sheen of the canal mirror-like ahead. The team drew out.

"Pretty neat, ain't it?" asked the steersman. "Reckon it looks different from the way you knowed it."

Jerry just nodded. He was thinking of the timbers out of sight under the water, of Hayward Lewis dubious over mortar, of Nathan Roberts on his pony, and of Mary coming up in time to see Hammil and Cosmo work the empty gates. He heard her say again, "I'm not crying now."

Behind them the water crept round the tumble bay again; but the sound gradually faded. A hundred feet ahead, the horses made scarcely any sound. A muskrat slithered in the mud; the dry marsh grass rattled its blades, though there was no wind; and the moon was small. He watched the banks slide into the light and pass. He heard the sleeping passengers stir on their hard beds. A boat came by, its team drawn over to one side and its towrope rasping along the packet's bottom. A child in the cabin cried, a thin wailing among the night sounds. A woman moved in the cabin and a light went on. As they slid forward Jerry heard her voice singing low:—

"The trees they are tall and the leaves they are green,
And many a time my true love I've seen.
Oh, many an hour I've passed all alone—
My bonnie lad's a long time a-growing."

"That the *Montezuma?*"

"Yeanh. Night shift now. How's the boy, Jake?"

"Fine. Fine. Getting a tooth, that's all."

"By docket, is he?"

"Yeanh. Upper. . . ."

The voices swam farther and farther apart.

Another lock, a light on the right beyond: Cossett's. Then Jerry saw shapes of new houses. A canal opened north.

"Salina side cut," said the steersman. "Since your time, I expect. There's a salt boat now."

More houses and a warehouse. All dark. Time for a man to sleep. But Jerry stayed out in the warm stillness. He wouldn't have to dream to-night.

"Next year this time," the steersman volunteered, "we'll be giving you a ride as far as Irondequot. Maybe into Rochester if they get the embankment laid up."

"That will take another year," Jerry said. "We only laid the culvert this summer."

"That so?"

The steersman leaned against the stick. He seemed to steer by instinct. His narrow face was hard-cut in the faint light.

"Jake's got a handsome boy."

Jerry said nothing.

"I only just got married myself, mister. But I reckon I'll be cutting teeth afore long, too."

They went on, and on, meeting a boat now and then, with the night against their eyes, moving with a silence as earthless as the wheel of the stars over their heads. . . .

Boat-builder

Roger Hunter looked keenly at Jerry.

"Colonel Rochester took a shine to you."

"He's a fine-looking old man."

"Yes, he is. As fine as they come. It's a great thing for Rochester. We won't be held back the way Rome was by Lynch. But it was handsome of him letting us have the land for our yard on such an easy mortgage."

The silver-haired, keen old gentleman had given Jerry an understanding look. "We old fellows have laid out this town," he said. "But it's you young ones who'll make a city of it. Good luck to you."

"What are we going to do now?" Jerry asked.

"What we want to do is get the jump. We want two boats ready anyway by the time they open the Feeder and the Embankment. It seems to me you'd better get after the plans and models. I've collected a few. Order timber. John Biden's ready to give us good prices. You'll have to set up your cradles."

Jerry grinned.

"What'll you do, Roger?"

Hunter laughed.

"Sounds kind of one-sided, don't it?"

They were standing on the lot of ground the Colonel had assigned to them. At their feet the wide-dug channel for Hill's Basin showed a surface of baked mud interlaced with cracks. Eastward the diggers had left the shape of the canal in their wake.

"I've got to get ready for business. I've seen Ely—we can handle his flour if we have the boats ready. But I've got my Pennsylvania horses. And I'm trying to do a dicker with the Navigation Company to share their barns. They'll have a chain from Rochester to Albany. They haven't planned on further west yet."

Behind them the river roared towards its falls. The first attempt at an aqueduct had been washed downstream. Brittin had died, and Hovey had taken over the contract. The state had offered him convict labor at a nominal price and Nathan Roberts was the engineer in charge.

Jerry looked back at the town. A low site, a cluster of frame buildings, its one beauty the river with its falls; and even these were obscured by the gaunt sides of the mills. A perpetual thunder lay over the town, mingled of the falling water and the grind of wheels. But it conveyed a sense of excitement, of a power for growth completely disproportionate with its newness.

"Rochester'll never be a town in the right sense," Hunter said. "To-day she's an overgrown village and to-morrow she'll be a city."

Townsmen spoke of their village as a city already. "Give us a bank and a city charter—that's all we need."

The sun was setting beyond the river. It had passed down the line of the serpentine hill; but as it vanished long arms of crimson began to spread across the sky. As they reached up they began to open, fanwise, until from north to south the whole sky was made vibrant.

As Jerry looked at it, his heart shook off its deadness. He saw it as an omen. In the time of waiting, he would work.

"I'll have the boats for you, Roger. But along with it there's something else I want to do."

"What's that?"

"Buy land and build a house."

Four
ERIE WATER

1

"To build the double flight"

An easterly breeze was springing up, bending the smokes of the village away westward after the setting sun. Storekeepers were shutting up their stores. Along the river, the mills were slowing down; the race mouths ceased to froth; the wheels clacked slower and slower over their ratchets. A slight evening mist was playing over the swift slide of the river, and the roar of the falls was gaining strength.

On the aqueduct sounded the chisel and hammer as the grey-clad knot of workers placed the last post for the iron guard rail. The engineer and the contractor were walking back and forth over the length of the empty trunk. The sunset brought out the pink sandstone, coloring it like blood. Solid stone, ten arches, nine of fifty feet, one of thirty, set twelve inches in the solid rock to stand the worst the Genesee could do against it: their two faces were quiet and their eyes expressed a kind of wonder at the massive creature they had wrought.

Over in Hill's Basin, Roger Hunter asked the yard foreman, "Where's Fowler gone, Self?"

Self Rogers leaned himself against the hull of the last new boat.

"I guess he's gone back to his house."

He took hold of the helves of his long moustache and looked sad.

"He clears out every evening about four. Leaves me a list, he does, for the completion of the day. *He* ain't bothered with no toothache. All he thinks about is finishing that house."

"Have you seen it?"

"Me? Well, just the outside. It ain't a bad piece of work. But he won't let me touch so much as a one-inch board inside of it. Why, Mr. Hunter, 'tweren't so long ago I was his boss. What does he know about building?"

Hunter looked serious.

"You know what I'd do if I was you, Self?"

"No. What would you do if you was me, Mr. Hunter?"

"I'd have my teeth pulled out."

Self Rogers stroked his jaw.

"Well, Mr. Hunter, that ain't a bad idea at all. But it's only got one trouble with it. You ain't me."

Hunter grinned.

"That's so." He stepped back a moment to look the boat over. "She's a nice boat. I'm glad we picked on white with grey for the line colors. It makes a boat look speedier."

"Well, white or grey or red or yeller all look pretty much identical once one of them dock wallopers gets to dragging barrels over it." But Self Rogers took a look himself.

The boat rested on her carriage, ready to slide into the filled basin. For a month now, the canal had been open over the Irondequot. The two sister boats of the new Rochester six-day line were somewhere east, one traveling for Schenectady, the other probably in Utica waiting for a load of beer, whiskey, and cloth, a pick-up haul.

"This boat," said Hunter, "is going to be the first to travel west. I'm picking up a load of cattle in Brockport, Self, and taking them down to Albany. We'll be the farthest western boat into Albany when they open it up next month. It ought to make them take some notice of us down there."

"Oh, they're going to open up down there, be they?" Self Rogers slapped the hull. "Well, it's all the same to me. It just means I'll have to build another. It's just about as bad as raising shanties."

But the old man's eyes were proud. The boat was a good job. Sixty-one feet by seven and a half, to draw three and a half feet when she was loaded up to thirty tons, she had the general lines of a packet. But the cabin took up only twenty feet of her. The rest was cargo space.

She had two windows on each side of her cabin, and sliding doors and a top-hatch for loading freight.

"She's a dandy. I consider you and Fowler turn out the best freights on the canal, Self."

"I guess that's right," old Self said modestly. He gathered up his tools.

Hunter grinned.

"Good night, Self."

The old man did not answer, and Hunter strode off. He crossed the river by the Exchange Street bridge and then turned up Spring Street. This was the newer section of the town. The house foundations wore a bare, earth look; the roadway still was roughly crowned in dirt; and the footwalk was a path that wound where the going was easiest.

A robin in a maple called for rain, over and over, showering the stillness with his liquid notes. A couple of dogs were getting together for a night's philandering. Two little boys stopped by a hitching post to feel each other's shirts.

"How's the water to-day?" Hunter asked them as he passed. They started guiltily, paled, then grinned.

"Not so bad, mister."

"Warm enough for a fast swimmer," said the other.

As he crossed Fitzhugh Street he heard the brass band playing on the

Corners to advertise Mr. Bishop's latest waxwork. It had been announced that morning. A lively presentation of the notorious Love Duel between Commodore Barron and Decatur, complete with seconds. The brasses of the band came in strong to the tune of "John Bull Caught a Tartar," and Hunter hummed as he went along. Crossing Sophia Street, he saw Jerry's house ahead on the corner of Eagle. He had chosen the lot because the slant in Spring Street gave him an uninterrupted view straight west.

It was a two-story house, rather small, with a dormered roof, and well shaded by the maples. A spring welled out of some rocks behind the house, and on such a still afternoon the tinkle of water came plainly to the street. Hunter vaulted the fence, strode up to the kitchen door, and let himself in.

"Jerry?"

"That you, Roger?"

There was no sound of work, nor any sign of it in the shed or kitchen. He passed out into the small front hall with its staircase of pine and black walnut. The parlor opened on his right.

"Hello, Roger."

"All through working for to-night?"

"It's all done." Jerry drew a deep breath. He had been watching the play of light through the western windows. "I set up the stove a minute ago. There's nothing left to do to it."

Hunter, hands in pockets, stared round him.

"It's a dandy little house, Jerry. But it looks to me as if it needed inside painting and papering."

"It's not going to get it," Jerry said.

"I thought you was."

"I'd planned on it," Jerry admitted after a while. "But to-night I got thinking that it would be better to leave it as it is. If she comes back, then she can choose to suit her fancy. I even got to wondering whether I hadn't ought to have waited for that before I built the house."

Hunter forced a laugh.

"Good Lord! She couldn't help but like the house!"

For a moment Jerry's face brightened.

"It kept me off of thinking about it. It sort of seemed that if I did it all complete I'd hear something about her when I got it done."

"You haven't heard anything?"

"Nothing." His eyes went round the bare, clean-swept floor. "I'd been hoping she'd see my piece in the paper. But there's nothing come into Mr. Weed's hands either. Nothing at all. So we've dropped it."

Hunter's quick, affectionate glance took in his partner's moody eyes. The lean face had lost its keenness; the shoulders, which had grown heavier in the past four years, were rounded; there was a touch of grey over his temples. He looked very different from the young man he had met back at Number One on the edge of Cossett's swamp.

"You hadn't ought to let it eat into you this way, Jerry."

"I suppose not."

"How long's the advertisement been running?"

"Half a year."

Hunter stared out of the window.

He said, "You've been acting worse and worse about it. When you come here you seemed to take it pretty well; but lately you've let it eat you. Go on with your house. If there's anything she don't like you can change it."

Jerry raised his eyes.

"You don't understand it, Roger. For four years I dragged her round— making her put up with anything that came handy. She never had anything of her own. Never a thing. And all I thought about was working and getting ahead. It seems to me in that time I missed what was under my nose. I used to feel sorry for myself not seeing it. Now, if I ever get her back, we're going to start even."

"But aren't you going to buy any furniture?"

"No."

"You ain't going to live here?"

"No. When I go out to-night I'll lock up all around. I won't come into it again until I come with her."

"But that's just plain foolish."

"Maybe so."

"Then you'll stay on with me?"

"If you can stand it?" Jerry's eyes conveyed a grin.

"I guess I'll have to. Come along, Jerry. We ought to be getting down to supper. I'll help you shut up."

Jerry answered by moving to the window. He closed the blinds. The last rays of the afterglow slanting through the cracks streaked his face with red. He closed the window. One by one they closed the blinds—upstairs as well as down—and then bolted the front door and padlocked the rear. Dusk was shrouding the maples, stealing along the street. Jerry did not look behind him.

"Let's not go back to Mrs. Frey's," Hunter said suddenly. "Let's have a change."

"All right. Where do you want to go?"

"Let's go down to the Summer Garden."

Over on Exchange and Main Streets the brass band was adjourning to the Eagle Tavern for a drink. But as they passed up State, Jerry heard the parrots in the museum shrieking.

The Summer Garden was a place to eat and drink. Sometimes a fiddler strayed there and one could hear tunes. It stood below Christopher's on Carroll Street and was advertised by a sign on which three apple trees were painted. A notice on the door announced:—

> NO LADY IS PERMITTED UNLESS A GENT ACCOMPANIES
> SAME. OR THERE IS A FAMILY OF CHILDREN

The garden was enclosed by a high wood fence; it had been planted for an orchard once; a long time ago, for the trees were well grown. One of the wives of Indian Allen might have set them out, the white woman perhaps. It was a quiet place now, though, with rough tables under the tree and paper lanterns strung from the branches.

Hunter and Jerry nodded to their acquaintances as they made their way across to a corner table; but they found it occupied. The engineer, Nathan Roberts, was alone.

"Good evening, Hunter. Evening, Jerry. I took your pet table, didn't I?" He smiled at them. "I hoped you might be coming down to-night."

Hunter sat down and stretched his legs out under the table.

"I didn't plan on it myself. But Jerry's in need of beer. Ma Frey won't serve intoxicating drinks to her boarders—only brandy."

One of the Crabble girls came up to them with a bright smile.

"Evening, Mr. Fowler," she said. "The regular?"

Hunter grinned at her.

"Yes, darling."

"Oh, Mr. Hunter!"

She flounced her skirts out as she turned.

Hunter said, "There they are always eyeing him and he doesn't care a dang. What good it was for me to be a teamster I don't see."

"You don't want to try anything on the Crabble girls. They're pure ornamental," Roberts said.

"Like the waxworks in the museum. I wonder who they model those waxwork ladies after. The Albany Belle I've heard was taken from Juliana Yates in Pompey. But she's nowhere near Ophelia being stabbed by the darkey." He sighed comically. "Well, I'm a respectable citizen now, and these things don't interest me any more."

Roberts smiled.

"I'm glad you two turned up. It's my last evening in Rochester."

Jerry looked up.

"Where are you going now?"

"They've picked me out to build the double flight at Lockport and superintend the stonework in the deep cut. The work's moving too slowly. The first line is only half dug and they can't handle the rocks."

"We're going to miss you beering here," said Hunter.

Roberts grinned boyishly.

Jerry said, "I didn't know you were so near done."

"We set the guard rail this afternoon. It's ready for travel now, and I've given orders. They'll let the water through next week." He looked up quickly. "It's funny that I've moved away from every job I've finished before the water came through. I've seen it afterwards of course, but I've never seen the water rising in the canal."

"You're going to be resident engineer in Lockport?"

"Yes. It's a promotion. I get full salary now. Fifteen hundred. And I'm glad to be away from this aqueduct. There wasn't anything to interest me here once we got the piers down solid. At Lockport it's going to be different. Rock to blast and lift. The walls will be thirty feet, and the deepest cut is over a mile long. The locks are a double flight five high—the only double flight there is on the whole line. Jerry, I wanted to see you to-night to ask if you'd come out and build my timberwork."

Jerry looked up from his hands. Old Crabble was lighting the candles in his lanterns and colored spots of light began to bloom like strange big flowers in the trees. The girl slid up with their bowls of steaming samp, sweetened by syrup.

Roberts went on, "You and I started the first lock. In 1817—six years ago. It occurred to me it would be fun to build the last on the line."

Jerry looked across at Hunter. The teamster was looking back at him. The keen eyes in the hard brown face belied the sarcastic grin.

"Why not?" said Roberts. "You could get away a year. Your company's doing well."

"That's it," Jerry said. "I've got to be on hand now. We're getting outside orders for boats."

Hunter broke in.

"Jerry, you might as well get out. Self can handle the other boats. You ought to have a change, and do some actual work for once. He's getting soft, Roberts. And he thinks the Six-Day couldn't get along without him." He swung round facing the engineer. "He goes round looking gloomier than Self without his toothache. I'm sick of him; and I wish you'd drag him off."

"Who's offering the contract?" demanded Jerry.

"State job."

"The regular thing?"

"I don't know the allowance. But with the water into Brockport, hauling timber won't cost much. Honestly, I wish you'd come, Jerry."

Jerry looked over at Hunter.

"There's no earthly reason for staying here," Hunter said seriously. "The company will give you leave of absence. You deserve a rest."

Jerry saw that these two had cooked this up between them.

"When do you start?"

Roberts said, "To-morrow morning."

"When do you want me?"

"In a day or two. The pits are dug in solid stone. Timberwork's going to be simple."

For a moment Jerry hesitated. But Hunter said, "Look here, Jerry. I know what's on your mind. If anything turns up I promise you you'll get it within a day."

"I'll go, then."

Jerry was walking by himself. The town was fast asleep, no lights in the streets, only the moon breasting a wrack of cloud. The roar of the falls came upstream in a muffled drone.

As he passed the museum, Mr. Bishop let himself out.

"Evening, Fowler," said the old man.

"Evening," Jerry said.

"I hear you're leaving out of here to-morrow?"

"Yes, going out to Lockport."

The old man rubbed his hands.

"The last barrier." He talked in a literary way. Since he had become proprietor of the waxworks he had adopted a literary style.

"How's business?"

"Fine." His rubbing hands whispered in the darkness. Then he said soberly, "Do you know where I could get a hand for model?"

"I'd let you have mine if I wasn't leaving. What do you want it for?"

"To turn Lord Nelson into Tell."

"You could get one in any canal house for a drink."

"That's an idea. Good night."

"Good night."

The mill walls shook to the thunder of the river. Jerry leaned on the towpath guard rail of the aqueduct. He could see the moon in the water sliding under him. The new stone gleamed. The water in the trunk held another moon, placid and round.

"Evening, mister."

A man leaned on the rail beside him. He wore a plain grey worsted shirt and worsted pants.

"Evening."

They leaned silently together. After a moment the man asked:—

"You got any ideas for a speech, mister?"

"Speech?"

"Maybe you ain't seen the paper?"

"Not yet."

"To-morrow they're going to open up the akeduck. Speechifying and a packet. Into the paper it says one of the workers is going to make a speech. I'm it."

"Oh? How'd you get leave to come out?"

"I'm paroled for to-night. I told the warden, 'I've got to get idees to speech about. Maybe I could get it on the akeduck.' 'All right, Storey,' he says. And here I be. But I ain't had no idee. I've never broke parole, but maybe I will. When they ditched me for popping out that nigger's gizzard I wasn't half so turbulated."

"How'd they pick on you?"

"We had an election. I was boss convict. I was a mason in my better days, you see, mister. So they elected me. Just like president. The bastards always hated me because I made them work."

"I'm no man to think of speeches."

"That's it. All I can think of is going back to jail. 'Hell,' I says to the warden, 'I won't speech worth a dang!' 'Where's your patriotism?' he says. Me, I'm not patriotic. 'What'll they do if I don't?' I asks him. 'Put you in the mill,' he says. Ain't it hell?"

Jerry leaned on his wrists. In the river the moon stretched, leaped an eddy, spun, and came to rights again.

"Why don't you tell them how hard you worked? How you were glad to do it? Because you got a patriotic feeling, even as a jailbird. Say how the noble feeling of building something solid is a great inducement to the man that sees the errors of his ways. Lay it on like mortar."

"A serious kind of joke, you mean?"

"Yes, a joke for you and your gang, but serious to them townsfolks."

"Mister, there's an idee! I'll just up and moan how noble it all is. How we've enjoyed sweating in the river and grouting stone. I'll tell about how we thought of our little chillern doing it, hoping some day their daddies would be remembranced by their work. God, I wonder where my chillern are this minute. Trooping around after that fiddler Madge was fancy for, I guess."

He went away, turning heavy phrases on his tongue.

"Say," called Jerry. "Would you sell me your paper?"

The convict came back.

"Mister, to you it's a gift."

"Good night."

"Good night."

He put the paper in his pocket and wandered round to his house. Its walls shone faintly in the moon. He identified the rooms by the shuttered windows. He swallowed hard. He started walking again.

This time to-morrow he'd be up at Lockport. He was catching a boat that would slide through the sleeping town while nobody saw or heard. And to-morrow they would hold their celebration for the first boat over the aqueduct. Storey would make his speech. He would like to hear that speech, but he was glad to miss the rest.

He wandered on down Exchange Street and out on the bridge.

Rochester was a wild town, nowadays. The *Telegraph,* a week ago, had claimed that there was more riffraff to the honest man than in any other American city. Talk was up of organizing vigilantes. The town watch wasn't capable of handling the canallers.

Down the boardwalk of South St. Paul Street he heard them coming. The lanterns gleamed against their legs. They spied him on the bridge and hailed him.

"Hey, you!"

"Evening."

"What you doing?"

"Killing time waiting for a boat."

"Oh, it's Mr. Fowler. Evening, Mr. Fowler. We didn't make you out so clear. Nice night, ain't it?"

The three rather apprehensive pairs of eyes relaxed. Edwin Avery put back his horse pistol. William Wilbur cut a chew. Newton Rose frankly wiped his forehead.

"Any places open?" Jerry asked.

"Billy Lusk's, I guess. We ordered him to shut up shop. We had an argument. But he agreed to do it in half an hour. There was a passel of canawllers in there. Me, I personally preferred this city afore they opened up the ditch."

"I think I'll drop down there."

"If it ain't dark, Mr. Fowler, will you tell him that if it ain't dark when you get there I intend to summons him?"

"Surely."

"Good night."

"Good night all."

Billy Lusk's showed lights. It stood on the northern bottle neck of Hill's Basin. Jerry walked in.

A few boaters still hung out in the tap, seedy with sleep. It was an orderly place to-night.

"Evening, Mr. Fowler."

"Evening, Billy. Bring me a strap and a candle. I've got to kill time. Oh, Newton Rose said he'd summons you if I found you lighted."

Billy Lusk grinned toothlessly. A boater guffawed.

"Jem Pine," he said, "was ordered out by them watches. They said, 'If you don't get out we'll throw you out.' 'All right,' says Jem, 'I'm going.' But he threw them out ahead of him."

Jerry opened his paper and sipped the sweet, thick drink.

"Jamaica, and good Boston 'lasses," Lusk said proudly, swobbing aimlessly with a rag. "I ought to know. I was a steward for a Shippen boat out of Boston oncet."

Jerry's eyes ran down the paper. News of the city. Canal data. An editorial in favor of Mr. Adams—Thurlow Weed was an Adams man. "Swims naked in the Potomac, I've heard," said Lusk. An article on the aqueduct —the greatest single work on the canal. It should be named for Clinton. Here were the advertisements. Parson Brent's cow strayed or stolen. Two boys run away. A shilling for their return. Anna Knapp keeps plain bonnets for Friends. Books at Pecks, *History of Greece, St. Ronan's Well.* North Road Stages Leave Auburn at 5 A.M., Arr. Rochester at 6 P.M. The Six-Day line for swift and economical forwarding. "The Sternatory Fashionable," Havana snuff for Doctors, Lawyers, Divines, and ladies. Charles Lalliet opens a school for dancing. Married: Jonathan Jacket, son of Red Jacket, to Yee-ha-wee at Buffalo Reservation. Burrel Reed, *Tonsor* and *Friseur,* will seize occasion by the forelock and attend both sexes in their homes. Silver's Pulmonic Syrup. Inventory of the Bonaparts. Bingham, the Tailor, for the military and also civilians. West's Potash Kettles warranted to endure. Buy Halleck maple sugar, made the Vermont way. . . .

Jerry looked up from his paper.

Halleck. He remembered the fat woman and her family. After he had come to Rochester he had met George Halleck one day in the street. They were doing well. He hadn't had much to say, and Jerry had not felt like talking.

His hand dropped the paper. He saw again a maple grove, and Mary's figure stealing into it. He was not supposed to have seen her then; he had not let on to the boys. But that scene kept rising up before him—as if even then, before their wedding, she had tried to flee. The bar stank suddenly in his nostrils. He did not say good night; but he went out. Walking again. Walking.

He found himself in the boat yard and walked round the new boat. The moon silvered the grey sides. It traced the broad white name clearly for him to read. *Western Lion.*

Eastward beyond the basin a boat horn sounded.

He stood still in the shadow of his boat. The light was born beyond the elm woods. It came stealing towards him. Suddenly he looked at his watch. They'd be coming into town in fifteen minutes. And he had to jump the boat—there were no orders for them to pick up. They were bringing the bog-trotters to cut out the rock in Lockport. They had licked the Montezuma marshes into shape and hired themselves for Lockport. There were no workers like them. It would be like old times to hear them shouting. And Roberts thought that working against the black boys they'd make time, for there was a feud between the gangs.

He walked swiftly back to the aqueduct, up the Exchange Street Basin to Mrs. Frey's. His bag and tool chest lay inside the door. When he came back again to the canal the boat was sliding over the aqueduct.

He hailed it.

"Hey?"

The horses toiled by him. The boat came up with a slight rippling against the piles.

The driver said, "What do you want?"

"I'm riding with you into Brockport. Commission orders. My name's Fowler."

"Fowler?" cried the steersman.

"Yes."

"Hop on."

The boat slid deftly up to the wharf, barely touching its side. Jerry sprang on. The steersman leaned against the rudder stick to turn them out again. "Go slow, Chris," he called to the driver. "This is new channel and I've got to see."

Jerry looked at the broad face, white in the moonlight.

"Lester Charley!"

A birdlike chuckle answered him.

"I'm a boater now, Jerry. How are you?"

The ex-bookseller shook hands.

"I skipped the family. Bought this boat on shares. I'm making money. I send Alice pin money now and then."

He chuckled.

"I think you got me started."

"Me?"

"Yes, you. After you'd left Utica I got to reading about the ditch in the papers. Pretty soon I got to wanting to see the places they wrote up about. And the rest just happened."

"Do you like it?"

"It's the life for me, Jerry. I used to sit around my store reading books and wondering about places. Now I ride along with not a blessed thing to bother my head. I stop in in the towns and get a good stiff drinking. I've got a tough enough driver, so we make a good average getting through the locks ahead of other boats. And now when I read a book it's got a meaning for me."

His eyes looked black as marbles.

"Are you going to haul a boat all your life?"

"Why not? I'm a misfit doing anything else. I'm one here; but on the ditch nobody notices it. And I do just as I please. Back home Alice makes money with the store. The children are learning manners, and when I come home I serve a moral lesson."

They were turning north by Broad Street. The houses slid away behind them. Trees beside the towpath cast deep shadows. Under their feet in the freight hold snored the Irishers.

"I've got them loaded like cordwood," said Mr. Charley. "Even on deck, a hundred of them."

Jerry dimly made out their blanketed shapes. As he looked, one of them reared on an elbow to stare forward. His bat ears were pink against the bow lantern. Jouncy Hogan. O'Mory would be somewhere near.

"Tell me about yourself," said Lester Charley.

"Nothing to tell. I'm going out to Lockport."

"How's Mary? How's the baby?"

"Fine," said Jerry.

2

"Heavy—down!"

"WA-A-AY up!"

Jerry heard jouncy little Hogan's voice at the front of the toiling gang. "Heavy . . . down!" The clap of the sledge upon the drill re-echoed flatly.

Jerry paused on the newly completed section of the towpath. Here, in the cut, the stone felt hot against his boot-soles. His eyes felt bare against the shimmer. The shape of the canal was carved in living rock. No men were working here, and only half a mile of the three and a half of deep cutting remained to finish.

Up ahead he heard the little Irishman's voice: "Wa-a-ay up!" It rose through all the clatter of men nibbling at the indurated clay and gravel that blasting powder would not loosen. "Down!" It came again; and the neat clap of the sledge thrust after it.

Jerry looked down from the towpath. The water trunk was a smooth cut, nineteen feet on the bottom, twenty-seven on the top, to carry a five-foot depth. Rising sheer from the towpath side, a retaining wall of carved blocks made a six-foot horseway; and from that level and the equal level of the opposite berm, the rock sloped up at a forty-five-degree angle into clay, into gravel, into earth. The sky—the limit of the laborer's view—blistered the earth with its blue glare twenty-five feet above their heads.

Jerry walked south until he overtook the mason. Two men with two-wheeled barrows fed the mason mortar, two more mixed it with hoes in a wooden trough, and four stood ready to lay down the stones. The pulley shrieked in the tripod and the grey block settled in the mortar. The mason tapped it with the butt of the trowel and stroked the blade across the joint.

"Morning, Hamlet."

The mason looked up. His face was the color of half-cooked beef, his eyes carried blood from the reflected sunlight. One cheek bulged to his chew. He spat and wiped his ragged beard.

"Morning, Mr. Fowler."

His voice was stupid with heat. The helpers leaned themselves gratefully here and there and took long breaths.

"Do you know where Roberts is?"

Hamlet Aimsley squinted back along the line of stone. Beautiful masonry, and he knew it. It ran as straight as a man could rule a line on paper. Engineers had drawn that line on paper; visitors to the work would speak their names in awe when they saw it; but Jerry knew, and Hamlet knew that he knew, that he had set those blocks without so much as a plumb string, with only his quid to balance his eye.

"I don't know where Roberts is. God damn you lousy crumbs, feed me some mortar."

He stretched out his trowel and his men shifted lazily to his low voice. Jerry grinned. Up ahead jouncy little Hogan's voice sang flatly. "Wa-a-ay up!" And in a moment the sledge clapped for the everlasting encore.

Jerry went on towards the sound of drilling. The men were working almost as deep as the finished cut at the mouth of the mountain ridge, but beyond them the bottom narrowed and sloped upwards into the burning sky. Fringing the lips southward, hand-worked cranes lifted up baskets of broken stone that the Irish had blasted, and returned the baskets empty. Cranes, the men called them. They moved their necks like cranes; and Orange Dibble had taken that name for his invention.

The two-foot shoulder that Hamlet Aimsley had yet to convert to a towpath made uneven footing. But Jerry followed it to look down on the Irish. Sweat blotched their undershirts; it stung their eyes when they looked up. Those who noticed him grinned, the long upper lips tightening comically. Jerry waved back. Fifty of them were drilling, but the sledge of the boss gave them time, and Jouncy Hogan's voice compelled them.

"Wa-a-ay up!" O'Mory, his black beard thrusting out, swung the sledge behind his right calf. His long back hollowed as the swing continued in a circle upward behind him. "Heavy," chanted Hogan, and the sledge poised shoulder high. "Down!" The hammer met the drill head; white dust, like smoke, sprang out of the clay and gravel indurated solid as stone; and the clap of it cut through the rattle of the other drilling like a stallion shouting down the whinnies of his herd.

Squatting on his hams, Jouncy Hogan shifted the drill cunningly and O'Mory drew breath and began again the rhythm, effortless to see, but pouring the sweat out on his throat and shoulders. To watch the grey iron sledge traveling its circle made Jerry forget the sweat stench, the reek of stagnant water lying in the rubble, the blaring heat of the sky. Jouncy Hogan cocked his bloodshot eye, squinting upward to spy Jerry. He grinned as he cried, "Way up!" O'Mory caught the grin, but his eye was fastened to the drill head. His back hollowed, the arms lifted on bent elbows, his back arched, burying the beard against his chest, and the clap drew smoke from the drill point. "Wan more for luck," he growled to Hogan.

Hogan's cry dinned into Jerry's blood with the bite of the sun; his ears rang with it. For a year he had listened to it, creeping farther and farther south through the cut. He woke up with it at night in his ears.

O'Mory let the sledge stand upon its head and wiped the sweat from his eyes. The black hair, drawn flat by sweat, won free as his chest rose and fell.

"How are ye, Misther Fowler?"

His teeth were white in the black beard. Jerry grinned. Seeing O'Mory stop, all the rest of the gang were taking a drop of ease.

"Have you seen Roberts this morning?"

O'Mory turned to Hogan.

"Have ye, Hogan?"

The little man cradled the drill in his leathered palms.

"I seen him passing by a while back, Misther Fowler."

"He seen him passing a while back," said O'Mory. "Myself, all I see is that drill head. It's dancing in me eyes this minnit. Wance I thought I was going to crack Hogan's head, I seen the drill so plain against it. There's no wan else can set for me."

Hogan's hands became affectionate with the drill.

"Who would ever think so small a man would have the hands like his own?"

Even Hogan looked at his hands in wonder.

"Which way was Roberts going?"

"South," said Hogan.

O'Mory nodded.

"South."

"Then I think I'll move on. How's the work going?"

O'Mory grinned.

"Foine. We've a hundred yards' lead on the black bhoys, and we're houlding it now. But they're right along themselves." His shoulders twitched as the sun burned off the sweat; he felt the salt. "We've put a mark up to work to, to finish up against this fall. I've always claimed with Jay-Jay that his bhoys was second best to mine. I'll show him when I come to the mark." He grinned delightedly. "And then I'll prove it to him."

His fist reached for the sledge-helve. But at that moment the air of the cut pushed suddenly against them. A dull thunder echoed past, stone crashed.

O'Mory's jaw fell open.

"The divil!" he said. "They're back in solid rock again and using powdher!" His eyes took in his idling gang.

"Blast yez!" His roar fell on them. They jumped to their drills and sledges. "Wa-a-ay up!" Hogan's voice slid into his and the sledge seemed to swing itself in his hands.

The embryonic towpath stretched its narrow way along to where the local men were hollowing down to the solid rock. They moved slowly, wearily, leaving behind them a jagged path to be shaped and leveled. In the blistering cut only the black gang and the Irishers could stand up under hand labor.

Jerry found Roberts watching the shapes the morning blasts had left. His face was drawn.

"We'll never get through in September," he said. "October maybe."

"But you'll finish this fall?"

"Yes." They watched two men crank up a basket; when it reached the block, the spruce saplings cleated in a V, turned on their wheel table, swinging the load out of sight.

"Yes," Roberts repeated. "October at the latest. O'Mory and the negroes are working like all possessed. It's a funny thing, neither gang knows what it's all about. They're working against each other. I had to get O'Mory and Jay-Jay in and make them promise to keep their boys in their own camps until the work was finished. Then they can maul each other as much as they want to."

He shivered slightly from the heat.

"I'll be glad when it's done."

He seemed to see Jerry for the first time.

"Looking for me, Jerry?"

"I came to tell you I was all through."

Roberts stretched up his hand for a lift onto the towpath.

"All done? Let's go back and look at them."

He started walking back along the shoulder. As they passed the Irishers, Jerry caught Hogan's wink. Beyond the mason, Roberts paused to let Jerry come up beside him. He was staring north to the end of the cutting.

"When the first section was shaped, I was discouraged, Jerry, because it seemed such a small bit. Even when we got through the second section it didn't seem possible we could ever burrow through this ridge to a level with Lake Erie. Why, it took me hardly a minute to walk it every morning. But now it's a long way from here to your lock gates."

They looked along the steep trench. The sunlight poured straight down on the tilted arms of the gates. Beyond was the everlasting sky—nowhere a tree or a bit of green to quiet the eye; only raw stone, raw wood, and the raw sky.

"Come along, Nathan. It's nearly noon."

They trod their shadows under their feet to the end of the cut. The sweat poured out upon their faces; but when they came to the locks a western breeze drew across the mouth to cool them as they looked down on the stair-like locks.

"All done," Roberts said again, as if he couldn't believe it.

He sat down suddenly, looking down. "Lord, I'm tired."

Jerry sat down with him.

There was no change to see beyond their morning inspection. The locks went down in two sets, the lower gates of one forming the upper gates of the next. They were separated by a flight of stairs. The planking gleamed white as fresh-gnawed bone. But since morning the balance weights had been hung from the beams and the sluice gate worms set in.

"Neat," said Roberts. "If you've got the water, it's the only way to build locks. Here we've got all Lake Erie behind us." He laughed. "Just as much as Niagara has."

Jerry gave him a queer look.

"Don't worry now, Jerry. My brains aren't cracked. But sometimes I laugh. Except for you and your helper, young Collins, there, and Thomas or Bates when they come around, there's no one that realizes what's going to happen. Erie water carried in a new channel—all the way to Montezuma. 'Is it a brook, then?' Hogan asked the other day."

He leaned back against the lock beams.

"Thank God for a bit of cool." His face seemed slowly to clear. He turned to Jerry. "It's been a longer job for you than I anticipated. I couldn't spare you the men to cut your wells. You've not lost by it though, have you?"

"No."

They watched young Collins putting away tools in the new lock-tender's house.

"Hamlet's applied for the job of tending locks," Roberts said suddenly. "I've worked it for him. A good man."

Over by Eseck Brown's Tavern the waitress beat her dinner gong, and in a moment the shanty cook came out to hammer on the wagon tire at the edge of the cut. The strokes boomed south along the cut.

"Dinner," Roberts said mechanically. "What are you going to do now?"

"I guess I'll go back to Rochester," Jerry said.

"How's the Six-Day coming along?"

"Hunter says we're making money already. He's made a first payment on our yard to Colonel Rochester."

"That's fine."

"He wrote me the other day that Self asked him when I was coming back to work. We've got orders for more boats than we can handle."

"You're going to be a rich man some day, Jerry."

Jerry nodded.

"I've always had the feeling. But it took a long time to get started. Now, when it don't seem to matter, it comes almost of itself."

"It has been a long time, hasn't it?" Roberts leaned forward on his knees. "The papers all say how cheap the canal really was built. So does the legislature. Only eight years, they say. Only eight years. Jerry, that's a long time for men as young as we are."

"It does seem long."

"Well, I suppose you'll be going to-morrow. I don't know how I can hold on here without you to talk to at night. Are you taking Collins back with you?"

"I've made him an offer. He's a good carpenter. But he doesn't seem very enthusiastic. I think he's got a girl somewhere."

Roberts nodded.

"I know." It was surprising how much he knew about his men. "She's a farmer's girl four miles down. A black-haired little thing. Looks Irish. O'Mory's sweet on her, too."

"O'Mory?"

"Yes. But, Jerry, I'd like to keep Collins on hand here till we're done. There's no telling what might spring up. Do you mind?"

"No. It's only three months or so."

"Do you think he would?"

"If he's got a girl round about I shouldn't think there'd be much doubt."

"I'll ask him to-night."

They did not heed the second bell from Brown's, nor the Irishers trooping past them to their dinner.

Lockport Village, brand-new, created by the Deep Cut, straggled out along the bluff that made the ridge between the Erie and Ontario Levels. The location of this line for the canal was another tribute to Geddes's indefatigable industry. He had worked it out when there was not a cabin between Buffalo and Brockport. Now there was a town—Eseck Brown's the first tavern, built to accommodate the workers; Tucker's store; the Mansion House erected two years ago. First there had been a contractors' corduroy laid through the woods from the Ridge Road; now there was a ditched and shouldered thoroughfare, thirty feet across.

"We'll need a bridge over the cut some day," said Roberts.

Jerry was not listening. He looked down at the locks. For him these finished the canal. A long time ago since he left Uniontown with ninety dollars in his bag and a recommend from carpenter Faggis. It made him smile to think of his high hopes that early morning: he had not thought ever to use that recommend. But once across Albany River, things had worked out strangely. Instead of farming, here he was a business man becoming rich. Money, the thing he had dreamed about, lay waiting to be gathered—how much only a few people had any inkling of. All because he had caught sight of a head of reddish hair among a sloop-load of redemptioners. And now he had his original dream and had lost Mary. But he smiled as he thought of the lean young man with his bag over his shoulder.

"Did I ever show you my recommend for serving prentice, Nathan?"

"No. I'd like to see it."

Jerry took a rumpled paper from his pocket. "I got it out this morning, just to look at."

Roberts unfolded the stiff paper:—

CERTIFIED BY ME TOM FAGGIS MASTER CARPENTER

At Uniontown, Renselaer County, York State,
April five in 1817:
THAT this day Jeremiah Fowler finished with me per contracto—
He is a good carpenter. Can build a house. Has done some millwork. Is equal to scarfing, joining. He knows his ratios and is a moderate mechanic. Is sober, is hardworking, is honest so far as I know.
SIGNED AS ABOVE, *Tom Faggis.*
WITNESSED: *Adam Lucas*
            Henry Witmuller

Roberts chuckled.

"He seems to know his classics, Jerry."

"He was partial to Latin. He considered himself a gifted man."

"What does he mean about your knowing your ratios?"

"I guess that's figuring out the horsepower for diameter of a wheel and fall of water."

Jerry took back the paper.

The maid at Brown's came out again and beat her gong with viciousness.

"I suppose we ought to go in, Jerry."

But Roberts did not move. He pulled a pipe from his pocket, loaded and lit it, and smoked it through in silence.

"Yes," Jerry said, "I've come quite a way. I'm going to be rich, Nathan."

"I shouldn't wonder. And I'll be a poor engineer."

"Things change. You're happier than me."

Roberts rose suddenly.

"Cheer up." He clapped Jerry on the back. "Things will come right. I think you've got a lucky star."

Jerry got slowly to his feet. The Irishers had eaten and were trailing back into the deep cut. As he crossed the locks he heard jouncy little Hogan's voice uplift.

"Wa-a-ay up!"

It carried the same wild sadness he had heard the morning the Irish had arrived in Montezuma to devil Edwin Brown. Their joy in sorrow.

"Heavy . . . down!"

The sledge clapped on the drill.

3

"You'll see a barn"

H<small>E</small> had heard that a Pratt and Meech boat was waiting in Newport for some overland cargo from Buffalo. They would probably give him a ride back to Rochester. But he was near enough to the village to take it easy now.

He stopped on the Oak Orchard Embankment to look down at the creek; a high crossing, with the embankment divided in the middle by an aqueduct of solid stone. Over on his left, the Oak Orchard feeder, that supplied the Brockport to Rochester level until they could tap Erie water, flowed into the main line with a steady purring through its splash gate.

The creek slid past the piers. A pale twilight filtered into the tree-tops, which were level with Jerry's eyes so that he could see mysteriously deep among the leaves. He watched the dart of squirrels to their holes and the ruffling of birds that settled themselves for night. Far off a woodpecker was driving solid blows rapidly into a dead tree.

Jerry looked down at his folded hands.

He thought, "I'm getting old. Showing Nathan that recommend—I never looked back that way before." His heart was sore; but the night sounds, the peace of creatures coming home, brought him a kind of resignation: as if after the broiling din of long days in the deep cut the coolness were a hand laid on his forehead.

His figure gave no indication of his thoughts. It was like a shadow against the stone. "Work's what you need," Hammil had said. "It's my idea if you keep going something will turn up." "Going?" He had gone at it hard as any man. He wondered if this new peacefulness that stole over him might be what Hammil had in mind.

The slide of the water was placid as glass. Farther back in the woods, however, stones broke it; and as the dusk gained darkness and the trees became still, Jerry heard the chatter of a small rapid.

"Not mad nor nothing." A wedded man, a widower,—self-made in a fashion,—a successful man likely to be rich in time; what was left?

"Evening, mister."

A ragged man in undershirt, his pants rolled up to show bare feet, leaned on the coping at his side. He wore a home-woven hat of straw that had lost its crown, but carried a crow's feather in a string. He too looked at the water.

"Evening," said Jerry.

They stood together, feeling the silence, silent themselves as if to share its fullness.

After a while the man said, "Traveling?"

"In to Newport."

"That right?"

Jerry did not answer.

The man asked, "Getting a boat?"

"Yes."

"There's a Washington Line boat there."

"Pratt and Meech? That's the one. I heard she'd haul some time to-night."

The man spat over the coping.

"Not her. Wagon's got broked back up near Johnson's. Hell of a thing to have to haul, cannon be."

"Cannon?"

"Yeah. Cannon. All kinds. Commydore Perry left them up in Presque Isle and they're spreading them out all along the ditch. What for I don't know, unless it is the way they tell me."

"How's that?"

"Why, they're a-going to stick 'em all along the line, ten to fifteen miles apart. They've put a thirty-two pounder up in Buffalo, they say. And these others they're taking along down. They'll put them all the way down to New York City. Then when the water is all let in, they'll fire the first one. The noise of it will travel that way, from one gun to the next, right out to the ocean. People out there will notice that Mr. Clinton has got started."

He scratched his head.

"Quite a lot of work involved to make a noise, it seems to me. But it is coming to Clinton, the way I think. What with the Bucktails knocking him off the Commission and all. Yes, it's coming to him. I'll be listening for it. You come from Lockport way? How soon do you figger, mister?"

"Better say October."

"That's quite a time. But it don't seem long to me, mister."

Jerry said, "Well it's time I moved along."

"What's your hurry, mister? The boat ain't going to haul till morning at the soonest. Come back to my house and have some supper."

"Thanks. Where do you live?"

"Right handy."

Down the canal Jerry saw that a light had been lit in a window.

"You live here?"

"Yes, I'm tender to the feeder gate. They built me that house to live in. Come back with me, mister."

"I will, and thanks."

They walked a hundred yards to the end of the embankment. A small house, painted salmon pink, stood next to the towpath. A lamp on a table poured light through the open door.

"My name is Birdnut, mister."

Jerry took his diffident hand.

"Mine's Fowler."

Birdnut dropped his hand and stepped into the house.

"Kind of a small house," he said apologetically. "But as they was building it for me, I felt no call to complain. And it's comfortable for a man alone."

"You're alone?"

"Yes. I'm by myself. You set there, mister, and I'll dish out my pork, and tea. Ain't much of a supper, mister; but I wasn't counting on no visit."

Jerry sat at the table.

"Ain't much of a house," said Birdnut again. "But it's comfortable for me. I like it all right."

There was a single room with a window on each side, and the door with its tiny stoop in front. In back, another door led to a woodshed and a privy.

"Ain't much of a privy," said the tender. "I built it for myself. They said they couldn't build a privy for me—the legislature wouldn't vote expenses for Oak Orchard privy so I built it. But I don't complain."

There was a solid bunk in one corner and a cookstove opposite. Shelves over the cookstove held pans and dishes. A table and a chair and a rocker, in which Jerry sat, filled the front of the room. In the ceiling a trapdoor opened into an attic.

"Ain't much of an attic, the way it's fixed," Birdnut apologized. "I'm a man alone so they didn't give no ladder for it. They had to build the attic because the legislature voted an upstairs room on Oak Orchard. Voted me that room, but not no privy, but I don't complain."

Jerry watched him. He was a thin, stooped man, smooth-shaven, raggedly but cleanly dressed. He had long-haired, curving eyebrows that shaded dark eyes singularly still. He moved as slowly as he spoke.

He dished out pork and potatoes into two plates.

"This one has got a crack into it, so I'll use it, mister. Here's your tea. Ain't much of a cup, being chipped. But it don't burn your mouth like metal."

It was utterly still in the cabin. They could not hear the rapids at that distance, and the water just outside the door flowed quietly.

"What do you do all day?" asked Jerry.

"Why, I clean my house in mornings, and do some fishing maybe. Ain't much fish in the canal yet. Maybe when Erie water comes along I'll get some bass. They're big fish in Lake Erie, I've heard tell. A body of water that is."

"That's all you have to do?"

"Why, no. I've got to read the level on the guard lock. If it's too high I get up to the creek lock and shut down. Too low, I go up there and open up. 'Tain't hard, mister."

"Going to stay here through the winter?"

"Maybe. There's a muskrat bounty. Maybe I'll trap rats."

"How did you happen to get this job?"

Birdnut dropped his eyes.

"Why, mister, I guess I thought I wanted it. I was a settler back there in the Purchase." He nodded his head at the open door. "Came west, I did, for fame and fortune as the books say. Yes, I bought a parcel and cleared and burned it and made ashes. Then the first winter I went east and got my girl. Her mother didn't want for her to come, but I persuaded of her and she was willing."

His eyes faded, and he reached for a black pipe. He put back the table cover and slowly whittled the load off the plug. He seemed to want to talk.

"I got her in the woods with me and seemed she pined somewhat. She was right young, I guess, mister; I guess as how she missed the sight of neighbors. She couldn't stand to see a bear." He looked down at his hands. "I labored hard, and she did too, but she pined. But we made a place of it with likelihood of good farming. I couldn't stand her being lonesome. Seems it made me short with her. I'd laugh. I told her it was better being in the woods. One day we got word they was surveying for this canal. I didn't believe it. But it perked her up some little. She used to talk about it. When would it come? Where would they put it? But it took years, I guess, to get things going. I can't remember how long it was. I got right sick of hearing her talk about it. I didn't believe in it myself. But she was always running over to our neighbors for the paper. Every month she would run over. It got so I shut her in the cabin."

He looked down at his hands.

"Yes, I shut her up sometimes. I was right fond of her, but it seems I couldn't stand to hear her talk. Our farming wasn't so good. We didn't have no boys coming along to help me. Wheat dropped down and my land was just against the swamp."

"Tonawanda?"

"Yes. Seen it? It's big; thirty miles from end to end. There's some marsh timber, but mostly flags a-growing round in islands, cacktails and such. Birds nested into it all summer." His eyes stared against the wall. "People got unneighborly towards us. Seems now as if maybe I was afraid to quit and just hung on there while she pined. I don't know. Maybe, I guess. She got the fever two years past. Word come then they was letting a feeder ditch into the swamp from Tonawanda creek on the other side. The swamp dreens through a rock cleft into Oak Orchard here. But when I was told that it made me laugh. I didn't hardly believe it until one day I heard her crying. I hadn't noticed nothing except that some of the birds was stirred and moving. But a little after she hollered there was a terrible noise in the swamp. Seemed like all the birds in all the world was there in all the sky. Screeching and hollering, rising up and dropping down. She said they'd let the water in. But I wouldn't believe it till I saw it rising in the grass that night. It had covered up the nests."

He stopped and looked down.

"Then I went inside and told her, 'I guess they have built it and you was right all along.' She said she was glad. Seems something in me gave out then. She said we'd best go home. I said it was all right, we would. She died on me a week later. So I come out. My farm, it was half covered over."

"Didn't you file for damages?"

"Damages? I don't know. I didn't appear to consider anything. But I come out here to notice the canal. I seen them starting this-here house. I asked them what for, and then I got the job."

A rat slopped into the water.

They sat silent.

The man looked over at Jerry's plate.

"Ain't much of a supper," he said. "I don't usually have visits. Sometimes the cobbler drops in. Generally folks go by. But when I seen you, I thought maybe I'd ask you."

"Cobbler?" Jerry asked. "A friend of yours?"

"Kind of a friend, mister, by the way I look at it. He's a lonesome man. He's got a girl, but she won't marry him."

"He don't come by often?"

"No, not often. But once in a while he drops in. He was by here last week. He was going up to Lockport, but he come back the same day. Seems like he'd scarcely gone afore I heard his wagon squeaking back along the towpath and looked out and seen his horse."

The night, for Jerry, became very still. His hands lifted slowly until they grasped the table edge. He felt his heart beating and the blood rising against his ears. His lips were stiff, but he framed the words distinctly.

"A white-blind horse?"

The tender lifted his slow eyes.

"Yeanh. He drives a white-blind horse. Do you know him?"

"What's his name?"

"Falk, he calls himself, I guess, mister. I never asked him."

"Harley Falk?"

"I'm not positive. But I wouldn't say it wasn't, neither."

Jerry forced his voice to be casual.

"Does he circuit hereabouts?"

"Here and there, I guess. I never asked him. Once in a while he would drop in."

"Did he ever talk about this girl?"

"Sometimes he would, mister. Not often. Sometimes he'd talk about her. Told me she was beautiful. Told me how she was beautiful, he did. One night over and over. Seemed to me he was going to cry on me. But I didn't say nothing. I don't say nothing when a man gets that way. No, not any more."

"Did he ever say her name?"

"Seems to me, he might have said her name. I wasn't listening. Once in a while he would drop by and visit with me."

"Tell me," said Jerry. "I've got to know. Did he say where she was staying?"

Birdnut passed his hand over his eyes.

"Seems to me you're curious about him,—or her, maybe,—mister?"

"Yes. I am."

"Well, I've felt kind of partial to you, mister. But it's hard for me to recollect things. Seems as how she was staying down south of Newport, maybe, with some folks. Folks of hers? No, I don't recall. Not their names. He said it was a big farm, mister. Four farms together. Whereabouts I wouldn't dasst to say. I though he was going to cry on me, so I didn't ask him nothing. I felt kind of sorry for him. Loving her so long. He took her away from a man misused her, but she didn't love him, he said; she wouldn't go off with him. Women, he said, was feared of him. He said I was his only friend. Sometimes it made him riley. It gave him misery, sometimes."

Jerry waited. He held his breath. The tender was regarding him with a queer, sidewise glance.

"Mister, you ain't the man misused her, are you?"

"Yes."

"Was you her husband?"

"Yes."

"I guess that's why I felt partial, then." He dropped his eyes to his hands. "Mister, I can't recall names or places very good. But I recollect he said she lived in Range two. Queer to remember. Range two. There's a list to the post office in Newport. Maybe they'd have some idea."

He looked up again.

"Feeling sickly, mister?"

"No. Not that way. I've got to go. Thank you for supper. If you ever need anything let me know in Rochester. Jerry Fowler, of the Six-Day."

"Grey boats. They're nice-looking, mister. No. I won't be bothering you, I expect. Good night, and welcome, mister."

A dog was scratching for fleas on the porch. His leg thumped steadily. Then he lay down on his side and closed his eyes and sighed. In the store, Philetus Bumpus measured off some calico. He had a yard mark painted on his counter, and his practised fingers stripped the cloth.

"It'll make you a nice Sunday apron, Mrs. Jordan. It's a new pattern and will show up well in meeting."

Mrs. Jordan dabbled in her purse.

"Seventy-five cents a yard, Mr. Bumpus? Three yards. Dear me. Figures do twitter a person."

The storekeeper took a chalk from behind his ear. Stooping forward, he made figures on the counter.

$$\begin{array}{r} 75 \\ \times 3 \\ \hline 225 \end{array}$$

"Multiplying, carry your dots straight down. That makes two dollars and a quarter, federal money."

"I didn't know it was so high. How multiplying does mount up in figures! Three separate seventy-fives wouldn't look half so large."

But she nodded and smiled and bustled out.

Groaning as he rose, the dog turned his other side, and began scratching again. His leg bumped on the floor.

"Well, mister, what can I do for you?"

"I came in to see if you had a lot map of Range two."

Mr. Bumpus pushed his spectacles up.

"Well, mister. It's likely I have. You moving in to buy?"

"No."

"Well, if you ain't intending to move in, I don't see what you want to look at a map for."

Little knots of muscle bulged along Jerry's jawbone.

"What's it to you if I want to see the map?"

Mr. Bumpus scratched the back of his neck. It was stuffy and dark in the store; the door made a blinding spot of sunlight framing the scratching dog.

"Well," said Mr. Bumpus, "it's a walk back to my house if you got to see that map, and it's a hot day, and I wasn't intending to go back till noon. Now, if you was to wait till noon, I'd take you up and glad to do it."

"I can't wait that long."

Mr. Bumpus ran a finger round the inside of his shirt band. He took a cotton handkerchief from his pocket, looked at it, wiped his forehead, blew his right nostril. The dog stopped scratching to eye a rooster on the bridge that carried the Oak Orchard road over the canal. A woman came in to trade some butter for cotton backing for a quilt. Mr. Bumpus wiped his nose and said apologetically to Jerry, "Well, I guess it will be handier if I just match this up for Mrs. Losey, and then we can get back to talking."

Jerry seethed as he watched the interminable yes-and-noing going on at the counter over the shades of thread needed to match the backing. A wagon rattled away over the bridge. An oxcart loaded with white-wood boarding lumbered up to a waiting boat. The boatman and the driver of the cart started a chain from cart to boat, and the boards went up and down between their hands, like inchworms walking. The dog roused himself with a kind of moan in his nose and began to scratch, thumping his leg endlessly.

Mrs. Losey satisfied herself she had the right shade.

"For God's sake," Jerry cried as she went out, "let me see that map, before she comes back again."

"Now don't get worried," said Mr. Bumpus tolerantly. "You're going to look at that map, mister. But while I was helping Mrs. Losey match up I was thinking." He rubbed his sandy hair upward on the back of his head. "Yes sir. I was thinking that if you told me your business maybe it would save me the trip back to my house. And anyways," he added contentedly, "I don't see as how I could get up there afore noon—with nobody tending the store for me."

Jerry cursed.

"It's too bad," said Mr. Bumpus. "But I figger we can be comfortable here a-talking things over until noon."

The dog's thumping picked up a beat; then they heard him groan as if hope were lost. He sighed as he lay down. Jerry felt sorry for that dog; he knew how he felt.

Mr. Bumpus took a seat in a rocker that had one leg too short; but he rocked it just the same and fanned his face with an old turkey wing. "Reckon it's hot out. Makes a man feel kind of dozy right in here." He pulled his spectacles down and eased his pants where they needed easing and looked across at Jerry. "If you don't intend to buy and you want to look at that map, it 'pears to me you must be looking for somebody."

"You've got it exactly right, Mr. Bumpus."

"Oh shucks. If a man has time to think. . . . But that being so, why didn't you tell me just who you wanted to see?"

"That's the trouble," Jerry said. "I don't know."

Mr. Bumpus rocked his chair, *squeak* as it went forward, *bump* when it came back. He fixed his eyes on the door. He had the short, round nose, a little swollen, of the man who deals with small ideas in a large way. In the door the dog sprang up joyfully to try under his chin. His leg thumped.

"If you don't know the folks you're looking for, mister, I don't see as how looking at a map is going to help."

Jerry said patiently, "I don't know it will help. But I've been thinking that if I could see the names, maybe I'd have some idea."

Mr. Bumpus sighed. "I guess maybe then you've got to look at that map, eh?"

"That's the idea."

"But look here." The rocker stopped in the middle of a squeak. "Why don't you ask me the names? I know everybody."

"Everybody?"

"Yes sir." The rocker continued. "Just as good as a map myself. Who do you want to know first?"

"I don't know. Wait a minute. Is there any especially big farm?"

"Lansing's is big, but that's mostly on the corner of Range three. Let's see, Range two. Why, there's Halleck's."

"Halleck's! Four farms. Of course. I've been a complete damned fool, Mr. Bumpus."

"Oh, I wouldn't go so far as to say that, mister."

"A damned fool—for three years."

"Why . . ."

"I never asked George Halleck, and he didn't tell me nothing." Jerry grabbed his hat. "Whereabouts do Hallecks live?"

"Why, their land lies mostly in township fifteen, mister. They've got a pile of land to wheat, and the old woman sells fancies, sugar and such things. I sold her a wagonload of butter firkins myself last spring. Don't get impatient, mister. I'm coming round, all right, and if you use up to-day you've always got to-morrow. Well, let's see. You might take the canal footpath, but I guess you'd do better by the road. Yes, you take the Oak Orchard road. Cross that bridge there and keep a-going. When you come to the swamp causeway you'll see a road off your right. Take that, mister, and keep right on straight as your nose until you come to a big frame barn and a couple of houses. That's Halleck's."

"A red barn?"

"Yes, no, I think it's white. Funny to paint a barn white, but Mrs. Halleck's notional, they say. Leastways it's the first barn you come to."

"Thanks, Mr. Bumpus."

"No trouble."

The dog got over to give Jerry free passage. He sat down to watch him across the bridge. It was hot beyond the porch steps. Inside the store Mr. Bumpus watched too. Then a strained look settled in the dog's eyes. He began scratching.

But Jerry went quickly.

"I'll walk fast," he told himself. "I won't stop to think. I'll just walk right there. I'll say, *Where's Mary?* and they'll tell me and I'll just go up to her, and she'll say, *Jerry!* and I'll say . . ." Wheat stubble covered the land with golden bristles. It showed the shape of the land with its even trim, the little curves and hollows that the eye would never trace in grass; and in itself it showed the sweeps of the sower's hand, sweeps like the curve of the scythe blade where the seed had fallen, taken root, made milk and grain, been reaped—a cycle for the eye to grasp in a single glimpse. "Walk fast, Jerry Fowler. Three years is a long time. Walk fast. They'll say she's in the cow barn watering the calves. They'll look queer at me. Maybe they'll stand off; but who cares for that? So long as her eyes light on me. *Mary, I've been sorry. For three years I've been sorry. It was my fault, Mary.* And she'll say . . ." Fox grapes showing their clusters, the hard green softening with blue; the crinkled leaves lifting their whitening edges, and the tendrils like silver springs. The dust lifted behind his feet. The roadside shrubs were dusty. The chokecherries wore a film of it. "I'll just go in if they're at dinner. *Mary,* I'll say, and they'll look up at me. Her eyes will light on me. . . ." The road ran through a point of the old oak forest that gave it its name; and then it turned a little west through broad country. To the left the causeway stretched into the swamp. In places it rose up on islands; in places it floated on the water. Tamaracks showed ashy green. Way off a sycamore lifted immense white limbs, like the living ghost of a tree. But there was a road branch on the right that turned back into the rolling wheat stubble. It led behind low oaks. "Maybe I turn here." . . .

A wagon rumbled over the causeway. Four horses dragging early threshed wheat to Ingersoll's warehouse, the driver said.

"Does this road lead past Halleck's farm?"

"Yes, it does. Betsey Halleck. And her children and her grandchildren. Settled down in a tract like Jemima Wilkinson and her Universal Friends. But these Hallecks are proper Christians. They're a tribe to see. A half mile, mister, and you'll see a white barn on your right."

"Thanks."

"Welcome to you, mister. Hot day for foot travel or hauling wheat. But it's been a good season."

"It's been a fine season."

"Never knew a better myself."

"Nor I."

"Git there, Trip. 'Bye to you, mister."

"Good-bye."

4

"A man that cuts his own pie"

WITH almost painful clearness he saw the farm. One mighty barn dominated the wheat and cornfields. Its sheer white walls, unpierced with windows, stood square to the four compass-points. Just off the road was a large house with a great brick chimney; next to it the log cabin it had supplanted; between them and the barn, wagon-sheds, tool-sheds, corncribs, a poultry house, and smokehouse made the square complete. Jerry could see hens dusting themselves in the yard. The herd-run leading back to pasture was laced deep in cowpaths. Two old horses dozed against the paddock rails. Pigs were grunting lazily somewhere out of sight. It was still with the midday stillness.

The sun struck full on Jerry. His trousers were white with dust, his boots powdered and caked. Sweat from his hard walk had soaked through his shirt and made brown stains under his coat sleeves. But as he stood there a smile came over his face, half shy, half fearful. He wiped his face with a handkerchief and pushed his dark hair back beneath his hat. His back straightened. Then, drawing a deep breath, he started down the slope.

The door letting out on the back stoop opened. A stout figure, suddenly familiar for its light, quick step, came down into the yard. Even at that distance, Jerry saw the shine of cookery on the round red cheeks.

Ma Halleck walked over to where a bell was hung between two cedar posts. Her red hands laid hold of the rope. Her fat arms pulled down. The heavy bell lifted its mouth. The clapper caught a spark out of the sun. Ma Halleck's arms straightened to let the rope slide up, and the bell swung. Deep-toned, ample, brassy, the bell's voice might have been her own. She swung it lustily, sending the notes over the wheatfields and the marsh, distributing to the four corners of four hundred acres her call to come and eat. Echoes came back from the barn wall, from the woodland, from the very heaven itself. Even when she had stopped, the overtones clung to the air in imitation of the passing clangor.

Dinner was in the act of passing from fire to table. The bell was its servant to announce its passage.

Ma Halleck stepped back into the house after pausing for a last look over her farm. A small, dark figure took her place. That would be George's Prue. She was waiting for something. Then Jerry heard shouting, and a parcel of children streamed round the corner of the barn. One was holding up a fish on a hooked stick—a boy, as dark as Prue herself. While he walked his eyes took in Prue's pantomime, bending to greet the children, hefting the fish with admiration. There was a bright golden head at the last, leading a little boy. He came stumbling and laughing, reaching up to hold the girl's hand; and his hair had a copper shine in the sun. Jerry stopped a moment, waiting.

Prue was calling over her shoulder, and in a moment Mary came out upon the stoop. Her cheeks were flushed from the kitchen warmth, her hair mussed. She ran down the stoop and over to the little boy, swooping him up in her arms. She paused for a moment beside Prue, and Jerry caught her laugh before she carried the child back through the door.

For a minute his feet were rooted to the road; he could not move. Her care-free attitude dismayed him. She might have made a joke, for Prue was laughing after her. But Prue went in again and Angy took her place. There was no mistaking Angy Judson, fussing with the children to make them wash their feet in the pump-tub. Laughing loudly, her sister joined her, but she was careless with the children as her eyes roved for her husband.

As he watched Esther, Jerry's smile came back to him and he resumed his slow walk down the long slope to the farm. Now he became aware of the men coming in from different ways and keeping pace with him in answer to the bell. They were like a congregation converging on a house of worship where Ma Halleck was the preacher. Out of a woods road Abijah trotted, sitting sidewise on a galumphing bay mare. He held an axe and crowbar balanced on her rump, and the chisel blade and mallet in his apron pocket showed that he had been mending fence. There came the two Hal-

leck brothers, long, rangy men, their lean faces unchanged, walking beside
a wagon piled high with ears of early corn. Glints of the golden kernels
showed through the dry green husks. Over a slope walked Abel Marcy, the
arch of the scythe snathe over his shoulders, and his two arms outstretched.

The children had passed in ahead of Angy. Esther was reaching out
to Abel, smacking his cheek with her plump mouth and being kissed square
on it for her pains. Her high laugh echoed against the barn wall, and Abel
with a sheepish look was drawing his hand across his mouth. The two
Hallecks drove their wagon under a shed, their horses to the barn. Jerry's
stride loitered as he saw the horses pause to drink at the trough, dribbling
diamond water from their bits. The brothers took them through the doors,
came out, and walked over to the well. Judson turned loose his mare and
joined them.

Now the men were taking turns hauling up the well bucket. They
lathered their hands and faces and the backs of their necks with brown
bar soap and sluiced each other's heads with bucketfuls. The water poured
on them a glittering jet, broke into silver spray, and left them glistening.
Jerry could hear their voices as they dried themselves, men's crop-voices,
low and steady.

The road pitched down suddenly for the yard. He felt the thud of his
heart against his ribs. Though he was almost on them, none of them had
noticed his approach. He could hear their voices clearly now. George asking Judson about the back-lot fence, and Judson stroking his pale moustache
and saying how he never had liked maple for a fence post.

Ma Halleck came to the door. Her ringing voice admonished them:—
"Ain't you boys never coming in to eat? A roasted loin with young
potaties and our new carrots. Melon pickle, and a huckleberry pie."

Joe lifted his lean face to grin.

"Ma's with me like Esther is with Abel. Can't abide to see me stay
outside."

"Shush you, Joey!" She made a flounce upon the stoop, snapping her
stiff skirts in her hands. "Some day a girl is going to capture you, and then
you'll remember your fat Ma, I reckon. . . . Good land of gracious!
What's Ginger see?"

Out of the shadow of the bushes by the cellar wall two dogs darted. They
crouched low down over their forepaws.

"Here you, Ginger! Toby! Come back here!"

The dogs stopped at the gate.

"Who is it, walking in a-foot?"

"Hello, there, mister. Them dogs won't bother you."

Jerry unlatched the gate, opened it, stepped through, latched it again.
His breath was short and his heart felt high in his chest. He wanted to
smile, but his lips were trembling. He turned full on them and took off his
hat.

"Hello, Ma Halleck."

The fat woman started. She clapped a red hand hard under one breast.

"Hello, George. Hello, Joe . . ." He was walking towards them with a
dog snuffing at each heel. "Hello, Abel. Hello, 'Bijah."

There was a close, set look on the mouths of the four men. Their eyes
stared hard at him, but he did not mind.

"I reckon you've forgotten me, Ma."

Her bold stare took him in. Her mouth opened.

"Jerry Fowler!"

Her voice carried throughout the house. There was a scurry for the door. His eyes switched to it. Angy, Esther, and Prue stepped out beside the fat woman, and the children clustered behind them.

Then in the doorway he saw Mary. She stood quite still. The shadow of the door-jamb slanted just across her throat; her eyes were shadowed by it, and quiet in their surprise. As he looked at her he lost awareness of the others, but he remembered old Issachar's voice, "So long as her eyes light on you," and he waited.

They were all so still that when a hen dusted herself behind them the dry ruffle of her feathers was like the clap of hands. Ma drew a deep breath and bent her middle over the rail.

"Jerry! So you've turned up at last."

The welcome in her voice was tinged with stiffness.

"You're just in time for dinner. Come in and eat with us."

She turned round, shooing the children through the door, crowding Mary back into the kitchen. Her daughters followed her like two stout ewes, but Prue lingered a moment, giving him a little smile. His hands felt empty at his sides, and he turned dully to face the men.

Abijah was stroking his moustache, Abel chewed a stick. They seemed uneasy with him there in front of the hens. George's face was troubled. But he and Joe came up together, holding out their hands.

"I'm glad to see you back with us," said Joe. "It's been a real long time since we came out along the Pike together."

George found it hard to meet his eyes. But he said, "Me, too, Jerry. I'm glad you've come here." He seemed relieved when Jerry took his hand. "I couldn't rightly tell you then. I didn't know what Mary wanted. And you didn't ask about her."

"It's all right now," Jerry said.

Abijah and Abel followed the brothers' example quietly. They stood around a moment, shifting feet, hiking their trousers up.

"I guess we'd better be moving inside," Abel said.

Their shoes thumped heavily up the steps.

Joe laughed and put his hand on Jerry's shoulder.

"You look as though you needed rinsing, Jerry. Come over to the well and I'll draw you up a bucketful."

George followed them.

"You've come quite a ways? By the look of you, you've been walking."

"I walked in from Newport this morning. I was on my way back from Lockport."

He stripped off his coat, unbuttoned his shirt and slid it over his shoulders. Joe dropped the bucket down the well and seized the dangling rope.

"It's cold water," he said. "Ten feet deep. It never changes level, summer or winter."

Down in the well the bucket teetered, gulped, and sank. Joe's hands bore down and brought it up brimming. Jerry caught a little in his hands to lather the soap and scrubbed himself.

"Put down your head."

The icy water sloshed upon his head. The cold sank into his skull. When he bent up again the barnyard reeled before his eyes.

"You're looking good," said George, while Jerry dried himself.

"You too," said Jerry. "You've got a handsome farm."

"It's good land. And we've been lucky. We built that barn last year. We're notional about that barn. I'll show you the inside of it this afternoon."

Joe said, "There's a comb and a piece of mirror alongside the door."

Jerry combed the water from his hair, put on his shirt and coat. From the kitchen Ma called, "Dinner's getting cold."

They trooped in together.

With the sunlight full on her shoulders Ma faced them at the end of the long table. On her left the fireplace and oven lifted a dull-red mass of brick straight to the ceiling timbers. An enormous pickle cauldron, that hung on the crane, was bubbling softly, lifting its crust of foam in different places, and filling the room with a warm, vinegary smell.

"You set here, Jerry."

Jerry saw that all the grown folks were paired off; man and wife sat side by side. On Ma's right, next to Mary, was an empty chair. George moved over to Prue on Ma's left, and Joe slid into an odd chair next the children.

"Maybe you'd ought to meet your children," Ma said. "There's Polly, growed to quite a girl. And next to her is Jerry—we call him Jed."

Jerry looked down at his children: Polly eyeing him shyly as a stranger; Jed putting his sturdy legs apart and giving him a frank, appraising scrutiny. He could not speak. She had run off from him—and yet she had given the boy his name. "Not mad nor nothing." He raised his eyes from their wondering stare and looked across the table. Mary was looking back at him. Her forehead was cool, her eyes steady.

But Ma said, "Come and set down here."

She had carved a double chop from the loin and put it on his plate. Now from the steaming row of dishes she was heaping it with new potatoes boiled in their thin jackets, mashed carrots from an orange mountain running butter down its sides, stewed cabbage shot through with cheese, and strips of melon pickle. To finish it she loaded a knife blade with butter and scraped it off on the edge of the plate.

"You must be hungry after walking. Prue, cut him off a slice of bread. A man needs food."

Mary sat at his side, eating quietly, and, when she had finished, letting her hands rest in her lap. He dropped his eyes to see them, and found them trembling. He dared not look at her face. She was wearing a lavender calico, a color that brought out the red in her hair, and her apron was blue checked gingham.

He found it hard to eat.

Ma said, "It's a bit better meal than I used to give you on the turnpike, Jerry."

"I can't remember any better than those were, Ma."

He smiled at her. But she said, "This is an actual dinner. Those was stewpot messes."

Down the table, Joe said, "Ma likes to see a lot of dishes handy to her.

She likes to eat and eat and know she'll have enough left over to stay her stummick with if it gets qualmish before supper time."

"Joey!"

Ma gave a shriek.

"It ain't true, is it, Mary? It's only that I like the taste of real good food. Look, I've only had one help. Ain't that a fact, Abijah?"

Abijah Judson stroked his pale moustache.

"It's always seemed to me," he pronounced heavily, "the person giving helps don't have no call to help herself a second time."

From the foot of the table where the children stood before their plates, a titter rose. Ma bent a frown upon them, but Joe laughed out loud.

Jerry passed Joe's grinning wink to steal a look at Mary, but she was quiet. And suddenly Norah's face rose up in his mind's eye for him to put beside it, and he wondered how he had ever thought Norah beautiful. She had no strength, no quiet in her being. And seeing the strength in Mary's face, he was afraid because of it.

Ma said, "You don't seem hungry, Jerry. Don't you like my dinner?"

"All people wasn't born a Halleck, Ma," George said.

Jerry looked gratefully over to him, meeting a smile from Prue, and saw her hand steal into George's lap. But Angy sniffed as she reached across his shoulder to take out his half-empty plate.

Ma bent herself to conversation and the carving of the huckleberry pies. Their wide crusts shone brown with butter, and when she withdrew her knife the blade bled purple drops.

"What have you been doing these three years, Jerry? You seem like quite a stranger to me, and I want to know."

He felt their eyes turn on him as he watched Ma's deliberate cutting.

"I've been in Rochester, Ma. My partner, Roger Hunter, and I've been building boats and starting a freight company."

"I believe a man can make good money in that business," Abel said.

"We're doing well enough to make a payment on the mortgage of our boatyard."

"What do you call your company?"

"The Six-Day Line."

"That's a good name—six days to the 'Hio country, I expect."

"What else have you been up to?" Ma demanded.

From the corner of his eye, Jerry saw Mary draw a breath and her cheeks flush up. But the fat woman was unabashed: she merely eased the yoke of her dress on her swelling bosom and bent herself to pie.

"I've spent a year building the Lockport locks." Jerry ignored the caustic implication in Ma's tone. "It was coming back from there I heard that you lived here. A crossing-tender by Oak Orchard had been seeing Harley Falk, and I thought Mary might have come here, even though George hadn't told me of it back in Rochester. But I put an advertisement in the paper for six months for Mary."

The men's eyes dropped before his; but Angy snuffled in her nose as she pleated her napkin. Ma Halleck stopped her eating. But Jerry looked at Mary; for her eyes were large and looking directly into his.

And her flush deepened.

"I never was able to read, Jerry."

"I remember that. But I thought whoever you might live with would read it to you."

Mary looked round the table; then her eyes met Ma's.

"Did you see it, Ma?"

Ma's bold eyes showed no uneasiness.

"Yes, I seen it. I told the rest not to say nothing of it."

"I think that was my business, Ma."

"Perhaps it was, dearie. But sometimes other folks understand a person's business better than their own selves."

Mary's voice was strained.

"I'd ought to be the judge of that."

Ma shrugged her shoulders.

"A man that cuts his own pie gets what's coming to him, seems to me."

Abijah had already tramped off with Abel for the buckwheat field.

George said:—

"Ma's acting touchy because the butter didn't make this morning. That's what they're working at right now."

He was taking a final pull of his pipe on the kitchen stoop, and watching the barn doors for Joe's emergence with the team. His eyes were troubled.

"It don't seem friendly, us leaving you this way. But I'm afraid of early frost."

He glanced aside at Jerry.

"Of course you'll stay with us a spell?"

Jerry looked up from his hands.

"I ought to be getting back to Rochester. I've been away from the yard for quite a while, now."

George tapped his pipe out.

"I'd like to see you stay awhile." His eyes followed the mincing arrogance of two young cockerels. "I'll come in early this afternoon. I reckon you don't feel like picking corn after your walk."

"No thanks, George."

The brown faces of the team appeared in the door. Their traces jingled as they walked to the shed. Joe hooked them to the eveners. George got to his feet. He stood a moment with his back to Jerry, clearing his throat. Then he said, "Maybe she felt jolted seeing you walk in the way you did. I'd give her time."

He slowly strode over the yard, joined Joe upon the seat. The team rolled them round the corner of the barn. Jerry sat still, watching the motions of the poultry.

It seemed to him that he was more lonely than he had been in all the years since she had left him. He had had no chance to speak to her—a few words after lunch, that was all; and she was cool and quiet, meeting his eyes with a glance that told him nothing. Then Ma had hinted her strongly to the pantry and Jerry had joined the men upon the stoop. The children had long ago dispersed. There was nothing for him to see, nothing to hear except the steady thump of the dashers in the churns beyond the kitchen, where Mary and Ma were wrestling with the cream, and the clatter the others made in clearing up the dinner. Out of sight in the bushes one of the dogs was chewing on a bone.

He got up slowly, for he couldn't bear to sit by himself any longer. He walked over to the barn. Inside the doors, the long rows of wooden stanchions ran down either side, with the horse stalls at the back and pens for the young stock and the bull. The runs smelled clean with straw, reminding him of Melville's barn, a little place—eight of them could be put inside of Halleck's barn entire.

In the pen the bull rubbed up against the timbers to snuff his alien scent. The tight-curled forehead pressed against a crack, and, stooping down, Jerry met the dim glare of the eyes. The bull moaned softly as if he had caught Jerry's restlessness.

At the back of the barn a set of steps led up to the wagon-well between the mows. There were no windows up above, but cracks left under the eaves for the escape of winter heat of cattle put a dim, sun-fused luminance against the rafters. The store of hay eaved over the mow wall level with his eyes and swelled upwards as a grey-green hill. The smaller mow gaped in its readiness for wheat and buckwheat straw, and there was no smell in the dusty air but the aromatic pungency of clover.

He sat down on a loose forkful on the floor with his back to the wall of the empty mow that he might look up at the hay and lose his thoughts against the rooftree. Here there was peace. The walls encompassed the quiet of fulfilled harvest. The high doors had been closed to a crack which allowed a spear of sunlight to lean against one corner of the hay; and in the light he heard the small sounds of the small things of the farm—the stir of hens, the leathery slap of ducks' feet returning from a marsh excursion, and distant voices from the house.

He felt himself remote. But as the quiet sifted through his beat of thoughts, his ears became aware of other lives imprisoned with the hay. He heard the rustle a grasshopper makes in drawing up its legs to spring, the chirp of crickets finding themselves dark burial places, and high on a rafter a cicada turned its grindstone feebly.

Through the crack in the doors he heard steps coming out on the kitchen stoop; then voices crossing the yard: Angy and Esther and Prue were going out to the buckwheat field to bind and shock the cradling Abel and Abijah had left upon the stubble. He saw the colored glint their bonnets made in passing the crack—rose, lavender, and blue. For a moment their voices gave actualness. He caught a word: "I wouldn't myself if I was her"; and Esther's voice replying, "I couldn't stand to be away from Abel no matter what there was." The voices dimmed. The mow resumed its quiet.

Out of the stair door a cat came quietly. She paused for a sinuous breath, her tail just shivering its tip. A wave of metallic lustre crossed her eyes as she turned her head to see him. She stared at him with complete impersonality. Then she moved forward daintily over the hay. With no forewarning she bounded against the mow wall. Her claws hooked into the rough boards, her tail sheered up like a sword as she gained the crest of hay; she gave a low, guttural call, and dimly from a far corner kittens were breaking their long silence. Somewhere, the hay rustled. He heard a long-drawn breath, and he realized that he was not alone in the barn. Then the whispers of children came to him. He could not hear what they were saying; he had no way of knowing which they were; but with a queer sense of anticipation he began to watch the head of the ladder that reached up against the hay.

After a while they came towards him. They were still talking of their discovery, and one voice was adjuring the other to keep their secret. There had been some talk of drowning kittens, but the voice declared that only baby kittens were drowned. If they did not give away the hideout of the old cat, the kittens would grow up enough for them to keep them all.

Polly's head appeared at the top of the ladder, and she was staring down, her eyes made round with consternation. It had been easy enough to get her little brother up ahead of her to lie in wait for the cat; she had not considered getting him down until this minute.

Her eyes roved down the ladder and round the floor. She did not see Jerry till he got quietly to his feet.

"Stay there, Polly. I'll come up and get Jed and then you can come down."

For an instant his unfamiliarity frightened her; but when he put his head above the ladder-top, she was sitting in the hay with a tight hand on her brother's belt. He smiled at them and sat down on the edge of the ladder.

"Did you find the kittens?"

"Yes."

His glance passed over her to his son. Jed, completely untroubled with the problem of descent, was examining him with a fresh interest.

"Where did you find them?"

Polly nodded her bright head. "Back there. This side of the hay chute."

Jed nodded and pointed. "Right back there."

"How many were there?"

"Four. Three of them have got spots."

"Yes. One of them is all black."

Jed drew a deep breath and put his fists upon his knees, impressed with his own observation.

Jerry grinned. "Maybe I'd better take you down now. We can talk on the floor."

He had Jed put his arms round his neck and he crooked his left arm round the boy's legs and backed down the ladder. The boy's hard little body was perfectly relaxed. Then as they reached bottom and he looked up to watch Polly's descent, Jed said, "Ain't you going to set me down?"

Jerry obeyed; and Jed looked up at his sister.

"I got down first," he said.

Jerry sat down in his former position, and the two children hunkered in front of him. Now that he was confronted by their eyes, he found it hard to think of anything to say.

Polly examined him gravely.

"You won't tell on us, will you?"

He said, "No. But don't take Jed up again, will you?"

She shook her head—shaking her two bright braids across her shoulders.

"I won't," she promised. "But it was so easy going up."

"I can climb up," said Jed.

Where they sat, the bar of sunlight put a shine upon their skin, making it seem transparent. Both of them had their mother's fair complexion; he thought they were more Mary's children than his own.

"Where are the others?" he asked, to make conversation.

"I don't know. We don't play with them always."

"Won't they let you?"

"Oh yes, sometimes. But sometimes we'd rather not."

"Why?"

"We aren't family the way they are. Generally they make us it in games we play."

"You're my Pa," Jed said with complete suddenness.

"Yes," said Jerry. "You're named after me."

He looked at them gravely.

"Would you hate to leave here?"

"Are we going to?"

"I don't know yet."

His eyes dropped before their wondering stares. Then Polly looked away.

"Yesterday, Mr. Falk was here. He wanted Ma to go away with him. Are we going away with him?"

"No, not with him—maybe with me."

"I don't want to go away with him," Polly said.

"Me neither," Jed said, stoutly.

It made a period for conversation, and Jerry was still.

"Does Mr. Falk come here often?" he asked Polly after a while.

She shook her head.

"Not very. Uncle George don't like him much, I guess. He makes us shoes. But mostly he sits where Ma is."

"Does she like him?"

"Yes. I guess so. She sits with him after supper, generally, when she's weaving."

"Does she weave much?"

"Yes, a lot. She's a handsome weaver, Uncle Joe says. He sells her weaving for a price."

Jerry thought, "She's earned her keep and made herself money." He leaned his hands upon his knees.

"What are you looking at?" demanded Jed.

"Nothing," he said.

Polly said, "Mr. Falk said he might come back to-night."

"Did he?"

"Yes." She looked at him honestly. "I don't like him. Do you like him?"

He did not answer. Instead, he asked:—

"Would you like to come away with me, if your Ma came too?"

"Yes, maybe."

"Wouldn't you miss living here?" he asked again.

Again their eyes were puzzled.

"I live in Rochester," he said. "I've got a brand-new house there. I built it myself for your mother and you. It isn't as big as Ma Halleck's house, but it would seem big with just us in it."

"Has it got two stories?"

"Yes, it has. It's got some trees around it and a living spring. And a place for a garden."

They stared at him.

"I've made the kitchen facing east for morning sun and to be cool in afternoon. There are dormer windows in the roof. It stands on the edge of the town, on Eagle Street."

"I saw an eagle last fall," Jed said with a flicker of interest. "Uncle George showed it to us."

"Did he?" Jerry looked down at his hands again.

After a space of silence, Jed got up boredly and moved to the stairs.

"I want to find the hen's nest. It's downstairs somewhere. I want to capture her eggs."

Polly followed him slowly. At the door she paused. Her eyes looking back gravely at him made him think of Mary's. There was the same faint crease between the brows.

"You won't tell on me, will you?"

He shook his head. . . .

Sitting alone once more, Jerry listened to the search below him for the stolen nest. The children's hushed voices called back and forth to each other; their hands rustled in straw; and their feet thudded softly over the planks. Suddenly they were gone. The silence of the barn was renewed with a cricket's chirping. . . . He could sit still no longer.

The bull was uneasy in his pen. As Jerry looked through the upper bars, he saw the great roan beast brooding with his forehead against the timbers. He was completely unaware of Jerry. But he rocked gently over his crooked knees, and the light thump of his skull against the boards made the upright shudder under Jerry's hand. Then, with no warning sound, he reared against the wall. His ears were pricked; his thick, short horns shone in the upper shadows dim as ivory.

Jerry went out quietly.

He stood for a moment in the doors to blink the dazzle from his eyes. Except for the dog, who still got flavor from his antiquated bone, the yard was empty. No sound came from the house; there was no sign of Ma or Mary.

The dog gave him a brief glance, and whipped some dust with his tail; but Jerry continued round the kitchen stoop, round the corner of the house, until he came to the pantry wall. Inside he heard the steady thumping of the churn. He stood beside some shrubs and looked through the open door. Mary was sitting on a stool, the churn between her knees. Her hands rhythmically followed the dasher up and down; but her eyes were turned to the window. He could not see her face clearly, for the light did not fall on it, but he thought that she was crying. Her shoulders sagged; from time to time she braced them with a conscious effort.

But before he could move, he heard Ma Halleck coming through the kitchen. He could not see her, but her cheerful voice reached him clearly.

"Ain't it made yet? There must be a witch in that churn. What's the matter, dearie?"

"Nothing, Ma. I'm tired."

"It's been a long wrestle. You let me have that dasher. I do think I hear it coming."

The beat of the churn became stronger, and Jerry thought he also detected a heavier splashing.

"It's a-coming," cried Ma. "I'll have it in a minute."

By leaning forward he could see her standing over the churn, her broad hands in place of Mary's on the stick. Her dress bounced on her shoulders in tune to the thrust of her hands. Mary had turned upon her stool to ease her back. Now she stood up.

"I'll fetch the working bowls."

In a moment she had set two shallow wooden bowls upon the table. The butter in the churn was quickly gaining weight.

Ma said, "I'll help you work it. You set still a while."

"Where's Jerry, Ma?"

"I don't know. I ain't seen him since dinner time. Traipsing around, I guess."

Mary sat down again.

She said in an even voice, "When we get done, I want to talk to him. By myself."

"Made up your mind?"

Mary gave no answer, and Ma snorted.

Jerry drew back. As he returned to the yard, his eyes fell on the woodshed. An axe was driven deep into a block, and cooking wood, waiting for splitting, was piled beside it—work for his uneasy hands. He hung his coat on a nail and laid hold of the axe, and the helve met his palms coolly. With a light drive of the bit, he hooked up a chunk and set it ready against the block. His wrists absorbed the rap as the twisting edge rebounded. As he swung again he felt himself take hold of life. The log split and he leaned one half upon its face to quarter it.

In the pantry, Ma Halleck rested her hands to hear the strokes of the axe. She nodded to Mary.

"There he is, dearie." Mary was listening to the steady blows as though they had some message for her. "In the woodshed," Ma went on, "splitting wood."

She chugged away at the dasher once more. The sound of butter was plain enough now for anyone. In a moment she stooped to draw the vent plug and let out the air. Then she removed the lid and stared inside.

"A twelve-pound mess, or thereabouts." She edged a bucket forward with her toe to drain the buttermilk into. As she bent down to tilt the churn a seam gave way somewhere among her clothes. She crouched there, looking up at Mary. Her fat red face grew serious.

"Dearie." Her voice was throaty all at once. "If you wanted to go back with him, you know I wouldn't stand in your way. It's just I couldn't bear to see you cheated for a second time."

Mary half smiled.

"I know it, Ma."

Ma went on, "When I heard that wheel of that old wagon coming up the road that night, I was awake in my bed. I had been thinking of you and Jerry and wondering would we ever see you any more. But I didn't know who it was, and I hollered over to George to get up and see. The dogs was fussing so."

"I remember, they did rush out barking long before we got into the yard."

"It was that wheel. Then I looked out my window and heard Falk answering George, and George lifted up his lantern on your face. And I felt it was your ghost. Ghosts mostly come after a person thinks about their bodies. George didn't recognize you just at first. But I did—just as if you was my own daughter. I just put on my coat and come on down—and when I saw you there, sitting alongside Falk and Polly asleep between you and Jed showing plain right under your dress, I knowed what had happened to you. I was glad to have you, dearie; but I felt set hard against Jerry. You looked so peaked."

Ma drew her breath and let the churn sit up. She took both paddles and reached her bare arms in for the butter. She lifted it expertly and held it up.

"I do like bright-colored butter. White butter always makes me think of fish. Dead fish."

She dropped it in a bowl and spread it out, halved it, and gave the second half to Mary. She took a handful of coarse salt and sprinkled the butter, folded it, and began to work it over with the paddle. Mary took the other bowl upon her lap.

"You've always got a home here, dearie. I took good care of you, didn't I, when Jed was coming? Not but what he was an easy baby borning." She paused a moment. "It's just that if you went away I'd feel much better not to ever think you might be coming back that way again." She reached one hand up to pull her apron strap back on her shoulder. "Perhaps you feel the need of a man around again. I'd used to think of Joe, maybe. He needs a steadying girl. But I've seen you'd never fancy him."

"I like Joe," Mary said.

"All girls do. But I expect Joe won't ever marry. He's a kind of twig. Right since he was born I've never planned for Joe to marry. No, I've always thought of him staying to home with me."

"I believe he will."

"You never can tell, dearie. But, dearie, you've got to think. A man that goes off once is apt to get head-free again. I don't deny Jerry looks older. And he's a handsome man, now he's got his heft. And seems he's done well, too. But leaving of you for a slut. Oh, Falk's told me all about it. I never could abide Harley Falk, I think, but for the way he looked after you."

"He was good to me," Mary said. "I feel sorry for him. He's said to me the whole world was against him. I was the only person that had ever been nice to him."

"I wouldn't trust him myself, though," said Ma. "The way he goes after you with his eyes. It riles George, too."

"If he's happy visiting me, I don't mind."

"Didn't you say he was coming back to-day?"

"Yes. He wanted me to go away with him. He's wanted to marry me, I guess. All along. He's said I could get justice before law for being deserted. But Jerry hasn't really, Ma. I went off from him. I've just remembered that this afternoon."

Ma glanced at her. Her voice softened unexpectedly.

"Dearie, I've made one or two mistakes before. Maybe I did in hiding those pieces in the paper from you. There's just one thing, though, I would say if a girl was fixed the way you are."

Her hand dipped in the salt crock.

"If you do make up your mind to have him back, don't never remember
what has happened—not in talk."

Her hand sprinkled the salt, but her head was raised. She was listening
through the door.

"Speaking about ghosts," she said. "Hear that!"

Mary listened too.

Unexpectedly close they heard the laborious, slow squeaking of a wheel.
It was coming down the slope for the yard.

"It's Harley Falk," cried Ma. "I must have been hearing it right along,
but thought it was a locust or a screeching bird. Why don't he ever grease
it?"

She stepped to the door.

"It's him. The horse looks as if he's traveled quite a ways. He's tired."

Mary's face wore a white, stricken look.

"What'll I say to him, Ma?"

"Him? What does that matter? What'll you say to Jerry?"

"I feel so sorry for him. It seems I understand him better just this
minute."

"Shall I go out and talk to him for you?"

"No, Ma. I'd ought to do that myself."

But she sat still in spite of herself. The wheel wound down slowly. It
turned into the yard. Each squeak cut knifelike through the quiet. Then it
stopped.

"Good land!" cried Ma. "I wonder how much salt I've worked into this
butter!"

Mary set down the bowl.

"I'm going out, Ma."

Watching her quiet figure through the door, Ma's eyes grew wet. She
picked up Mary's bowl and tasted her butter on a thumbnail.

"Thank gracious! She's forgot to put in any salt at all."

She threw the two workings together and her strong wrists worked the
paddle through the doubled mess as if they were the makings of a man
for whom she felt considerable distaste.

Jerry heard the squeaking wheel turn into the yard. He looked up in
time to see the old white horse start for the barn trough as though, even
in blindness, he was familiar with the way. He drove the axe into the block
and slowly walked out from the shed.

Harley Falk was getting down over the wheel. He caught the reins in
the whip socket and turned.

His face was burned red from the long driving through the heat; but
Jerry saw under the burn the face set slowly. The man's eyes fastened on
him; and his hands went to his breeches' pockets. He stepped back and
leaned against his wagon wheel.

He said, "It's pretty hot to-day."

"Yes," said Jerry.

"You been here long?"

"I got here this morning."

Falk took his right hand from his pocket and pulled gently at his lips.

"I stopped to water my horse," he said. "Got any objections?"

"It's not my farm."

Jerry did not move. Under the red skin he saw the man's face getting white. His eyes were losing brightness. He said, "I thought I'd see how Mrs. Fowler was."

"She's all right."

The dog, Toby, passed between them, went over to the horse, sniffed at his weary pasterns, and fixed a wheel.

Neither of them noticed him. The yard was dead with the full heat of mid-afternoon. Even the hens had moved from the dust to the strip of shade beside the barn foundation. It was so still that the two men plainly heard the footfalls coming through the kitchen from the pantry; but though both recognized the step, their eyes held each other.

Mary came quietly between them. She held a bonnet by the strings. Her eyes were grave, and as she looked at Harley Falk her lips trembled and smiled.

The cobbler took his hat off. His eyes, swinging to Jerry, were sardonic. He understood her smile, and for an instant amusement at Jerry's face conquered his self-pity.

At his glance, Mary's color waved in her cheeks. But before she could speak, the cobbler put his hat back on his head.

"I was just passing through to the Birdnut cabin. I stopped to water the horse, and when I saw Mr. Fowler was here I just lit down to pay respects."

"Stay here to-night," Mary said.

"No, I guess not. The cabin's dry and the barn's all right for the horse. I'm only going to camp a little while, and I've got food along." His eyes swung back to Mary, and Jerry saw her color rise again. His hands clenched, and suddenly he felt his heart beating heavily.

Falk's voice went on, "It's been an unseasonable hot day. Driving makes me dry. I'll just have a drink afore I go." He stooped down beside his horse and sucked some water up. He wiped his mouth slowly.

"I might as well be getting on."

"Good-bye," said Mary. She moved quickly forward and held out her hand. Falk shook it, let it drop. His glance passed over her head to Jerry.

"Good-bye."

He lifted the reins and started the old horse. The white, sightless stare of the animal crossed them both. The wheel squeaked lethargically. A little dust half lifted and fell back in its place. The wagon tracked between the woodshed and the barn and out along the meadow road.

They watched it through the grass; the horse's head low to the track, the man leaning his elbow on his knees. Jerry turned slowly to Mary.

She still looked after the wagon and her hands were pleating the ribands of her bonnet. He too looked after the wagon once more. The road was leading the cobbler round the edge of the marsh towards a line of small oaks.

"Jerry."

"Yes, Mary."

"Let's go away from the yard, down there. It's quiet there."

He turned back to her.

Her eyes were on him.

They stood together on the edge of the great meadow that grew clover heavy enough in two cuttings to winter a herd of forty cows. The dog, Toby, who had joined them on their walking, eyed them for a moment with comical disgust, then bounded off to find a woodchuck hole. At their feet clear water of the flooded marsh land reached to the edge of meadow grass.

Mary was facing the water. Her breast rose sharply over her quickened breathing. Her eyes were grey and her cheeks had paled in the bright sunlight. She had put her bonnet on when they left the yard, but now it hung on her back, the knotted ribands close under her chin; and her hands were joined, straight down before her, pressed tight, as if she felt a pain.

"Mary, I've been a terrible damned fool."

She seemed so near him; she stood so still; he could have touched her by a turning of his wrist.

"I looked for you everywhere I could think of, Mary. I thought you had gone east somewhere."

She was holding their life together between her palms. But she did not stir.

"I've been sorry. Ever since. Three years. A long time, to me."

"It's been a long time to me, too, Jerry."

His eyes followed hers along the blue curve of the marsh. He could not remember the thing he had wanted to tell her. His voice was dead in his throat. He said, "I came to ask you to come back with me, Mary."

She did not breathe; but her hands twitched suddenly, and the sun caught on her wedding ring. He reached out slowly to touch it. His voice shook.

"When I fashioned that nail, I was ashamed of it. But I've thought since it was the one best thing I ever did."

Her hand rose under his and she turned to face him.

He could not meet her eyes.

"Will you forgive me, Mary? Will you come back?"

She said, quietly, "Yes, I'll come back."

He said, "I'll try to make it up to you."

Her eyes looked into his as if she were remembering things.

"I've got a house waiting for us. It's your house. There isn't any mortgage on it. I built it myself."

She smiled a little.

"I'll like that."

"I've made it nice." He looked back at the farm. "I've told Jed and Polly of it." His mouth smiled wryly. "They said they'd come."

"It will be nice for them. I've been thinking of them. Out here they seem half Hallecks' and half mine."

"They'll be our own in Rochester."

"Yes."

He felt the sun upon them, entering them both. Fifty yards away, the dog was exchanging insults with the woodchuck, up and down the hole, but their voices were muffled by the earth and grass.

He said, "I'm making money now. You can have anything you want."

He flushed suddenly when she was quiet.

"I mean we won't have to move around any more. My work's in Rochester, and the canal is nearly done. I've finished the last locks at Lockport. I won't have to go off any more."

Her face was grave. If she thought that his hair was grey above the ears and that his eyes looked tired, she did not show it. She stood quite still with the close-leaved clover touching the hem of her skirt.

Watching her, his eyes renewed for him the curve of her cheek and throat, the curl of hair above the ears, her strong, straight back. He was afraid to touch her, for she stood so still.

A breath of wind was ruffling the marsh water, setting the reeds bending. . . . It started a shivering in the tops of the sycamores. It came over the meadow—combing the clover in short waves to show a gleam of silver underneath the leaves—and blew upon their faces.

Mary turned her face to it.

"When will you come back, Mary?"

She smiled a little.

"I'll go back when you do, Jerry."

His voice was tentative.

"I've been away so long from Rochester, I ought to go soon. It's not fair to Hunter, staying away so long."

She said, "I think it will be best to start back soon."

"You'll have things to pack up, and to say good-bye to all of them."

"It won't take long to pack."

"It will be hard to go away from them," he said. "Ma's been good to you."

"Ma has. She didn't want to let me pay her for our keep. But I didn't want for us to owe her anything that way. I've helped her in the house, and I've made money weaving, too."

He caught her meaning. She was an independent person, coming back to him of her own free will.

He said humbly, "Maybe George will take us down to Newport. We can find a boat there maybe."

"Yes."

"If we could get a boat starting early in the morning it would get us home that night."

He glanced at her.

"Or maybe a night boat would be better."

"Either one."

"There won't be much for us to carry."

She said almost shyly, "Jerry, I'd like to take along my weaving loom, if I could."

"Why, yes. We'd take that along surely. Only you won't have to weave any more unless you want to."

"It's been a comfort, weaving."

"Yes, surely. On a boat it won't take up much room."

"It would be nice to have it."

"We'll take anything you'd like."

"There isn't any other thing—only our clothes."

"I'll ask George if he knows of any boats."

"Maybe he'd know."

"It would be nice if one of our own boats was hauling up this way—

to go back on it. In Rochester they fetch the best price of any boats made there. They're allowed to be good boats anywhere along the Erie."

He saw her smile.

"I've never seen a canal boat, Jerry."

"Ours are grey boats with white trimming."

"I'd like to see one."

"I'll find out if one is here. It's longer than by wagon, but it's nice to travel on them."

In the farmyard a shrill whistle sounded. Toby backed out of his woodchuck hole, cocked his ears, and bounded off across the meadow.

"Joe is whistling him to get the cows," Mary said.

They watched him dash into the yard. The big team was turning the wagon up to the corncrib. Joe jumped over the wheel and the two dogs waved their tails in front of him.

"Maybe we'd better be going back."

"Maybe," said Jerry. He hesitated. "Mary, if there's a boat to-morrow, shall we go on it?"

"Yes. Whenever there's one."

The sun was westering; it threw their shadows forward side by side upon the clover. The white walls of the barn gleamed golden. They saw Ma Halleck passing the shed to the spring house with a butter firkin cradle on her hip. Her dress made a vivid splash of scarlet over the green, and as they drew near she spied them and waved her hand.

"I'll tell her," Mary said.

He watched her move away to intercept the fat woman. She had not changed. Himself, he went to seek out George.

5

"Bless and prosper"

THE men's eyes were embarrassed to see Ma Halleck press against the wheel.

"I can't bear to let you take them off me, Jerry."

Her round red face looked almost woebegone.

"Shucks, Ma. Ain't you got enough ones left?" Joe kicked the dust with his boot. "Here's me, to begin with; there's George and Prue; and Abijah and Angy; and Abel and Esther; and the young ones that I'll name, if you've forgot. . . ."

Ma whirled.

"Fresh! There isn't enough for me in all the world. And anyway she's growed my fav'rite child—so there!"

But she had begun to smile again.

"Good-bye, dearies. I'm coming down to look at you real often now."

George shook hands.

"Leave Prince in the Eagle barns, Jerry. I'll boat down with my season's shearing and drive him back."

George had laughed at the idea of their taking a boat. "You'd not get in till late, and Prince can take you down by dark."

Jerry said, "We'll keep him in our own barn."

"Use him all you want, then."

Halleck faces thronged the yard. At the rise they looked back to see them waving. Then the ground rose up behind the wheels and shut them off.

The two children, on a straw bedding in the back, were tied to the loom. Jed prattled contentedly at things they passed; and Polly looked forth with eyes entranced at the thought of this long journey. Jerry stared past the trim head of the little Morgan, his thoughts already reaching ahead to Rochester.

"We're going home at last," he said.

The Hallecks had insisted that they spend another day at the farm; to Jerry it seemed the longest day he had ever spent. The women monopolized Mary every hour; the men had left off work to sit and talk interminably with him. It might have been a second wedding that they were arranging. "When we're alone," he thought, "it will be easier. It's all them watching her that makes her act this way." But now, driving the Morgan at a spanking trot, he thought, "When we get home."

They had made an early start, and the sun was fresh against their eyes, drawing mist from the streams and putting jewels in the dew.

"Yes," said Mary.

Her face was turned to the road, with its familiar lift of the chin. The sight of it carried him back to Albany, to the post road and themselves sitting under the poplars, when for all her silence she had seemed so ready to meet his thoughts. A flush crept under his tan, and he dropped his left hand to the seat between them.

"Do you remember, Mary, how I said once that some day I'd buy you a wheel?"

"Yes, I remember that."

He spoke quietly.

"I've not bought it, but I've left the money with Mr. Burr so you can pick out any one he has." He did not look at her. "You won't need to do any spinning now if you don't want to; but I'd be pleased to see you buy one."

He found an unaccountable sadness in her voice; but she met his eyes with a smile.

"I'll buy one, Jerry. I've always wanted one of my own."

He put his eyes back to the road, and in a little way his hand returned to the reins. Prince jogged them rapidly through Newport and on to the Ridge Road, where he swung right.

To the left a line of pines lifted their crests. Suddenly from the highest top a crow cawed. Raucously he cast his call over the grove; the cry stole down upon the fields, over and over, the same note. And as if to answer him, the pines stirred—one shape after another hopped free and spread its wings, and the branches in the still air rocked from their black disburdenment. The sky was filled with milling crows, cawing, wheeling, lighting, vaulting off against the risen sun. Then, as one bird, the flock beat their wings, and in a thin line headed south.

As they rode on, they saw the farmyards cleaning up for Sunday, the herds gone forth, and men easing themselves upon their stoops, and watching the rig go past with incurious eyes.

Jerry said, "It was my fault, Mary."

She held her silence for a long while. A milepost passed. When she spoke, it was gently.

"I don't know whose fault it was. When such a thing happens, I think now that you can't say this person or that person was to blame. I'd rather we forgot it."

He could not touch her.

The little Morgan maintained a handsome gait. He held his head high and pricked his ears. He eyed a maple stub as if he had never seen a maple stub before in all his life. He shook his head when the breeze fluttered his mane; and when he saw a wagon of churchgoers on the road ahead he seemed to take delight in spanking past and raising all the dust he knew.

But people were in a good humor and hailed the passing wagon cheerfully. Jed had learned to wave a handkerchief, and he waved back to them. He waved at everything, at pastured cows, at horses, at the people. When a man got out his best bandanna in return, he shrieked at his mother to look.

"We'll get into town early this afternoon. We'll go straight home."

"Yes."

He drew his breath. Looking at him, she saw a ludicrous dismay come over his face.

"What is it?"

"There's nothing in the house. Not so much as a dipper to drink from, Mary."

"Never mind," she said. "I guess we can hire a room for one night anyway."

He apologized abjectly.

"I didn't get anything to put in the house. I'd planned for it to be your house—the way you wanted it."

She did not laugh.

"I'll like it better for your having thought of that."

She drew a deep breath. She too was thinking of coming home. She had not planned it so, but her thoughts went forward as they spun along the road. It was enough for now to watch the pale blue sky.

As they rolled down on Clarkson Village, they saw rigs hitched along the street. The meetinghouse was a plain frame building with a double door. Jerry slowed down, not to disturb the horses, and they took the crossing at a walk.

Through the open windows the exhorter's voice came to them profoundly nasal in the closing prayer, and as they went by the door Jerry looked in.

The upright figure of the preacher, garbed in black—the white hand outstretched above the bowing people—the closed eyes in the lifted face with the sunlight full upon them—the voice, sonorous down the tilted nose, came out to the passing wagon: ". . . bless and prosper . . ." They carried the words with them. . . .

They passed through Parma after lunch, through Ogden Village; and then they dipped off the ridge and turned southeast. For a way they ran along the canal, overtaking a line boat. Jed, who had waked after a long nap, got out his handkerchief, and the steersman answered with a shattering blast of his horn; and Jed was so surprised that he made no other move or word throughout the afternoon.

Jerry reached into his pocket and pulled out a fold of paper and handed it to her. "We're nearly there," he said, "and I want you to take this before we get back home." Puzzled, she opened it. She did not need to look at the sheaf of paper money.

She held it for a long time in her lap, watching the houses growing nearer.

"Jerry," she said at last, "I can't take it back."

"I can't either, Mary."

"It doesn't belong to either one of us," she said.

Jerry was silent.

"Shall I throw it away, then? But it wouldn't be right to throw that money away."

"I won't keep it. Not any more."

She tapped the edge against her thumb-nail.

"I'll keep it, then. But I'll keep it for Polly and Jed. It belongs to them in a way—more than either of us."

He nodded. He had not touched her yet, but she was closer. ". . . bless and prosper . . ." Given time.

6

"It's the water coming through"

AT Lockport, in the long barrack set up to house the Irish gang, jouncy little Hogan was darning the toe of his sock. He was sitting tailorwise on his bunk behind the central stove, his right foot propped against his left knee, his flat mouth pursed. At every stitch his hands trembled; they were extraordinarily calloused hands—the palms worked stiffly as rhinoceros hide. Drilling hands, O'Mory had said, as soon as he laid eyes on them.

The gang sprawled desultorily in their bunks along the forty-foot walls, except for two groups playing filch and blackjack at one of the two long tables; and a few were gathered close to Hogan to watch his machinations with the needle. It was an interesting process when a man darned with the sock on his foot.

"Reach me down me old Hissian, Peter," he said at last.

A dark-faced, lanky boy unhooked the wooden flask from its nail and gave it to the little man.

Hogan had broken off the wool. He took the Hessian in both hands and sucked a mouthful of corn whiskey, rinsing it about his uneven teeth. His lips flattened behind the swallow and he sighed and handed back the flask.

"Hang her up again, Peter, will yez?"

He stretched out his foot and admired his toe artistically. The darn was yellow on a grey foundation. Sighing, he lay back upon the bunk and closed his eyes. As if the room had kept silent from a nice appreciation of the delicacy of his operation, voices now loudly broke out.

"I wisht I was home again," said the young lad, Peter.

"What do you wish that for, Peter?"

"I do," said Peter.

Hogan raised himself on one elbow. His bright blue eyes examined the boy.

"Did ye ever come by such good money annywhere in the owld counthry?"

"No."

"Did ye ever foind betther whiskey?"

"Just as good," said Peter surlily.

"Did ye ever find more, now?" Hogan pointed a thick finger. "Did ye ever have whiskey come with yer pay, and over and above it, too?"

"No."

A one-eyed man with grizzled hair, who had watched the whole darning of the sock without a word, spat into the sandbox and said, "Is it the priest ye hone afther?"

The boy said seriously, "Well, there ain't anny, is there?"

"Pho!" said Hogan. "What would ye say to the Father was he here?"

"Nothing," Peter admitted gloomily.

"That's what's bothering the boy!" Hogan exclaimed. "He misses the girrels! Oh, Peter! Ye're right enough. There isn't even anny timptation in these lands. But, Peter, now the labor's done and ye've got time to think, are you going back whome?"

"I haven't anny money."

"What have ye done with all yer pay?"

"It come in whiskey and money," said the boy. "But it all come to the same thing."

Hogan yawned.

"The trouble with you is ye're too comfortable."

"That's a fact," said the one-eyed laborer. "If he was unhappy, he could feel real comfortable."

"What are we waiting for?" cried a man down the room. He wore a small, pointed hat on the top of his head and a dirty bandage on his left foot; and between the two he was naked.

"Put on yer pants, McCarthy," said Hogan. "Ye're no dacent sight."

"Well, what am I going to do next?"

"Whatever you like."

"I don't know what I like."

"Maybe I'll go out to Ohio," said another man. "They're digging a ditch out there, they say."

"That's an uncivilized counthry."

"They're digging another in Delaware."

"They've seen yez dig," said Hogan, "so they flatther yez and come over yez. But digging ain't the nat'ral state for anny wan of us. Me, I'm going to wait till O'Mory gets whome."

"Where's O'Mory, annyway?" asked a new voice.

"At a wedding?"

"Yis," said Hogan. "At young Collins's wedding. The young lad who helped Misther Fowler on the lock-gates."

Silence fell over the long room. But all at once Peter asked, "And was she the one O'Mory went round with in the spring? Her that had black hair?"

"Herself the same," said Hogan.

"I thought he had his own hone for her."

"He did so," said Hogan. "But I wouldn't remind him of it whin he gets whome."

"Then I don't undherstand."

"Maybe the girrel asked him over. I guess she did, and what is one girrel the more or less to him?"

"What is?" asked a skeptical voice.

"That's what I said," said Hogan, unruffled. "What is?"

"To be sure," said the skeptical voice.

Hogan asked for his Hessian and the boy handed it down. It was made like a very shallow barrel with a strap round the drum and a spigot to draw from. Hogan sucked noisily. He wiped his mouth.

"All the blather," he said. "Annyway we beat the black bhoys to the mark, didn't we? And the work's done, ain't it? Well, me, I'm going to wait until O'Mory gets back. I am. And if me Hessian gets empty with waiting, I'll just fill it."

"What will O'Mory know about what we're to do?"

"He knows the counthry," said Hogan, and he pointed overhead. O'Mory's bunk was over his own, and, hung from a nail, his red fireman's helmet, with the golden *Phoenix, No. 22,* glistened like an outrageous jewel. All their eyes turned to it, and the trouble went out of their faces.

"I wonder will Jay-Jay come over?" said McCarthy, the naked man.

"Let him come," said Hogan. "He hasn't the numbers we have."

"We've been laid off three days," said somebody. "What are we waiting for?"

Silence fell on the room. Through it they could hear the stoves, the clatter of the metal ware as the cooks washed up. Hogan got up and with a bored face went over to the door. When he opened it a cold draft swept in.

They could all see him against the night sky. The stars were white and the young moon silver with frost. The barrack stood on the lip of the ridge just west of the locks, and the new timbers in the gates shone white as bone. In the cleft of the rock they saw the dipper low down.

"To catch the wather if it comes," said a man.

"When is it coming?" asked Peter.

"Anny time," said Hogan over his shoulder. He stepped through the door.

As the little man breathed the cold air and stared across the miles of wilderness, broken only by the line of the canal and the lights in the few buildings of this new village, it came upon him that that was what they were waiting for. They wanted to see the completion of their work, the water from Lake Erie filling the lock-wells. Not one of them had seen Lake Erie. Roberts had told him it lay to the southwest, a body of water endless as the sea, where real ships sailed. Behind him he heard the boy Peter say, "What do they want this canal for annyway?"

It was the first time they had ever asked such a question. He had never asked it himself. It had been enough for him to shovel, to devil boulders, to feel the blister of the hot drill in his palms. To beat the work of the other gangs. They had licked them all, even the niggers.

The door swung to; and he went out on the bridgehead over the top lock. From there he could see the canal bed behind him in the deep-cloven rock, four miles in length, thirty-six feet deep. The cranes had been taken away. There was just the clay, the black gleaming stone, the trickle of leakage in the bottom, the straight wall of the towpath.

He turned his back on it to lean on the rail and looked over the lower level to where the canal channel turned due east. Water came to the lock-gates. One boat was tied up, the boat that had brought in their last provisions. It was lovely to look at, the still boat sleeping on the water, like a chip caught by a grass blade, in the shade of the forest.

The stars could almost talk. On the height to left and right clustered the village lights. That upper lamp in Eseck Brown's came from Mr. Roberts's room. He was still making out his accounts. He did not know what the real work felt like; there was no ache in his hands. Hogan's palms tingled.

He leaned over the rail to spit from his quid and listened for the fall on the plank bed of the lock. It came. At the same instant his wide ears caught along the Deep Cut the scrape of boots, and, peering into the darkness, he saw the shapes of men strung out along the towpath.

"That's Jay-Jay," he said under his breath. "I wish O'Mory was whome."

He cast another look down the canal. The bhoys were no good in a shindig without O'Mory's voice to compel them. Then his heart lifted. From the other direction, low down under his eyes, another man was coming. There was no mistaking the swift length of that stride. Without a sound, Hogan turned and ran for the barrack. The Irishers lay round the room as he had left them.

"Bhoys!" They looked up. "Jay-Jay's coming."

Instantly their faces brightened.

"Give me me pants," cried McCarthy. A man laughed.

"What'll we do with them?"

"I wisht O'Mory was whome," said Peter.

Hogan said, "He's just coming round the bend. He won't be here for five minutes or more. But just set round nat'ral and easy, like ye'd expected them in for a pot of tay."

Round the room the men disposed themselves easily. Conversation broke out on the weather, on whiskey, on girls. Their troubling was forgotten. A couple in the corner by the kitchen door started a song:—

"Rory's scowlding wife is dead,
    'Heigho!' cries Rory.
'Me dearest duck's defunct in bed;
'The devil's cabbaged her; she's fled!
'With her roly, poly, gammon, and spinnage,
    'Heigho!' says Rory."

Hogan started to laugh. He laughed at the boy Peter, winking at him, making faces. And then, still laughing, he turned round to the door and wiped his eyes.

"Good evening, Misther Jay-Jay," he said. "Shtep into me poor house and meet me bhoys. Is it very cold to-night?"

Through the door stepped Jay-Jay. He was not very tall, but he was built with tremendous weight. His barrel chest showed through his thin shirt as plainly as if it were naked. It arched from his collarbone to his high, thick stomach. His arms were smooth, showing the muscle by their shape. His legs were thin and flat, and for all his weight he moved lightly. His thick lips, his brown eyes with the yellow whites, his kinked, close hair, his tight-set ears, and his broad, flattened nostrils had an almost aboriginal cast. His neck appeared to bulge outward from the base of his ears. With his shining black skin and the flexing of his nostrils, he appeared among the slender Irish like some tremendous stallion. But when he returned Hogan's greeting, his voice was gentle and husky: "Evenin', Mistah Hogan. Mistah O'Mory heah?"

"He is not," said Hogan. "But he's coming. Shtep inside."

"Brought along some mah boys, Mistah Hogan, if it ain't no bothah to yo'."

Hogan licked his lips. He giggled suddenly again. "No trouble at all, Jay-Jay."

Thirty negroes trooped through the door. Most of them were black as Jay-Jay, and they brought with them an outlandish, tropic odor. Hogan indicated tables and benches.

"Set down," he invited them. "We was just talking about you black bhoys when you came to the door."

"Was yo'?" said Jay-Jay, rolling his eyes round at the little man. "What was yo' sayin', Mistah Hogan?"

"We was just saying we kind of expected yez. Here we've been waiting all this time for yez to finish up back there and it was getting lonesome. It must have been hard," said Hogan pityingly, "but maybe it was the wet. Ye never could stand the wet."

"Say so?" said Jay-Jay, folding his thick hands.

McCarthy, buckling his pants, took the wink from Hogan.

"It was the lizyards," he said. "Back the first day in Montezuma, whin I jumped into the mud, a pair of thim came up against me belly. I could feel thim niddling their mouths against me stummick. They niddled up and niddled down and then one of them got to me pip. 'Hello, Alice,' he says as plain as me father in Gaelic. 'This don't look right. There's no milk in this bhoy.' Then I seen Alice sticking her eye out of the mud be me arm and having a look. 'No, Michael,' she says. 'This bhoy's got a white skin. Come along, maybe we can find a nigger.'"

The Irish stamped and roared.

Some of the negroes looked up hotly, turning from the Irishmen to their leader. But Jay-Jay was sitting with perfect calm, staring at the liver-colored nails in his folded hands. Hogan tossed a look at the door and came forward with his Hessian and two glasses.

"Have a dhrink, Jay-Jay?"

"No, suh."

But Hogan's heart patted his ribs.

"Then I will," said a voice behind them. O'Mory in his Sunday suit was closing the door. His boots were muddy from his long walk, his bright eyes dry, his mouth soberly closed in his black beard; but Hogan could tell by the way his hands took hold of the insides of his pants pockets that his friend had been drunk and had brought the devil back with him.

He walked forward easily and reached a hand over the negro's shoulder for the full glass.

"Well," he said, "if nobody else will drink, bedevil, I will annyway. Here I come back from putting a boy to bed with his girrel and find ye all glooming like crows come home to a clean roost."

He held the glass to the light as if measuring his swallow. "I seen Misther Fowler in Newport and he tells me the wather's coming through to-night. Peter, me lad, run out and take a look at it."

Peter went forth reluctantly. O'Mory turned to the negro. His eyes glittered.

"Here's spit in yer eye, Jay-Jay," he offered for a toast. "I believe it's a custom of yer counthry."

Hogan started. Something was eating the man. It was the wedding, of course: O'Mory had been bottled up the two whole days and he wanted to rouse the negro.

But Jay-Jay continued to sit silently, and the smacking of O'Mory's lips was like breaking sticks in the long room. His mocking eyes roved over the black faces.

Jay-Jay at last looked up. When he spoke his voice was full.

"Brought mah bes' boys, O'Mory, to lick your bes'. But they ain't no sense in them fightin'. They'd on'y spoil it fo' us. Goin' lick yo', instead."

O'Mory's savage grin grew almost friendly.

"Me bhoy, it's time ye said something. I need the exercise." His eye took in the black, massive torso. "Maybe I'll get it."

"Mebbe yo' will," said the negro, calmly, eyeing the Irishman. In his own way, O'Mory was something to see. He was built leanly. His long arms were muscled hard as whips; under the skin on his forearms the cords moved like strings as he stretched his hand out to grasp Hogan's Hessian.

"Here's a glass to ye, Jay-Jay. You and yer men wasn't much in the marshes, but perhaps you can fight."

The negro brushed the glass aside. His loose lips pursed and he spat full into O'Mory's beard.

"*Is* a custom of mah counthry," he said softly. And suddenly his brown eyes were lively.

O'Mory roared. He opened his hand, drew back, and struck the negro a tremendous swat upon the cheek. The sound echoed behind the stove, and the negro's head snapped back. His neck stiffened. He got up from the bench slowly and said, "Try it again."

"Annything to oblige," said O'Mory, and he struck again.

The negro took the blow without a sign; but the crack sounded like a blacksnake whip on hide.

The door opened and the lad, Peter, came in.

"I couldn't tell was the wather anny deeper. It's too dark."

He stopped. Nobody had heard him. And as he stopped, the negro knocked O'Mory down.

There was a roar from the men that made a wind to shake the lantern flames. Tongues of smoke leaped out.

O'Mory jumped to his feet.

"Get them tables out of the way. Hogan, hold me shirt."

The stamp of feet filled the room, the scrape of table legs upon the puncheon floor. But the Irishers were watching Jay-Jay with a new light in their eyes. No one had ever knocked O'Mory down.

The negro had drawn back a pace before his men. His great closed fists swung by his sides in little jerks. His feet were flat on the ground, his knees slightly sprung, but his back was straight, and his barrel chest heaved with a quick easy breathing and his nostrils went in and out like the flutter of a stallion's.

O'Mory's shirt was off and his chest shone a lively white through the black mane upon it. The structure of the man showed beneath the skin. His breathing eased again.

When the room was cleared, he said, "Whichever one of us two beats the other, lave the black bhoys be." He turned to Jay-Jay, "Come on, me bhoy."

He sprang.

His arms cracked in. The two blows were lightning, striking like bolts, a flat, hard crack to the head, and a dull thud to the belly. The negro met them like a rock, and then he was in motion. So quickly, so lightly, did he move that he seemed scarcely to change his place. His feet did not step high and briskly like the Irishman's, but they moved, instead, flat and close to the floor, with a faint shuffling sound, putting him here and there with ugly swiftness.

His round smooth black arms were like the pistons of a steamboat's engine. And when his fists struck, they thundered on the Irishman's chest. And when they came away, the others saw that they had left their color on the skin, as if the white could breed to black, octoroon, quadroon, mulatto, black.

O'Mory's body whipped before the blows and his teeth showed in his beard. He seemed far quicker than the negro, with his lithe strides, the grace of his arms, and the snakelike lashes of his fists.

Hogan screamed, "Go afther him, O'Mory! Bhoy! Bhoy! Don't let him grasp ye!"

"Watch his feet!" cried the one-eyed man.

"Look out he doesn't grasp yer lip!"

"Mind yer eyes, O'Mory!"

A roar of voices swelled. The Irishers were all upon their bunks. The negroes were lining the wall by the doors. They were silent. Their dusky faces made a line of intensity against the yellow of the planks. Suddenly one jabbered in an outlandish tongue, as the two men came together.

"O God!" shrieked Hogan. "Stand off from him!"

Each had his chin on the other's right shoulder, and out of sight between them their hands interlocked like antlers.

There was not a breath of movement.

Suddenly the Irishman's left hand shot round the black man's waist, slipped down behind his thigh, and his foot slid forward. He strained heavily, his muscles crackling. The negro lifted; the flat feet shuffled suddenly in air; and then slowly they came back to the floor and the two men snapped apart. The negro had broken the hold; but he spun as he came free and went against the table. With a roar O'Mory was on him and bent him back upon the board. The Irishman's knees pressed into the negro's crotch, keeping his legs vertical, while, with both hands reached under the black man's armpits, he caught his chin and forced the neck back. . . . The eyes in the black face swelled. The whites became bloodshot. A strange moaning broke from the negroes, and jouncy little Hogan began to jibber with delight. "O'Mory, O'Mory, O'Mory, ye darlin'!"

And then the negro's hands drew back and his foot lifted. The blow seemed futile from that angle, but it found the Irishman's chin. The black hand was lost in the black beard, the head snapped back, and the white hands broke from the black chin like limp straps. At the instant, the negro's feet found room and kicked the Irishman away.

O'Mory reeled. The walls swam in front of him, a dizzy line of faces. He heard a shout of warning. He heard a weird, high-pitched kind of moan. "He's butting!" He heard the pad of feet. It seemed to be behind him. He tried to whirl, but the black head caught him on the thigh and he spun away and fell.

As he fell he heard the crash the negro made. He had been hurt, he knew he had been hurt, but he could not feel it. But it was a hurt that gave something into his hands. He wasn't lonely any more. The wedding was out of his mind now and he was a man, and he found that he loved Jay-Jay, loved him as a precious object for his hands to destroy. A grin broke his lips apart. His hands found the planks and he was on his feet.

As the negro faced him, O'Mory knew that he also was hurt, and he put back his head and laughed with pure joy. Nathan Roberts, who had come to the door when the hullabaloo broke loose, with the clerk and the cooks, and the axemen and rodsman, understood why someone had called this gang the Devil's Angels. For the rest of them had caught O'Mory's laughter and laughed with him, and the long room heaved with roaring.

But the negro had become a travesty of the human thing. The purpose of the human brain was behind him now, but the face was bestial.

They came together.

"Stand off from him!" cried Hogan.

But, as though they had agreed to it, they abandoned themselves to their fists.

O'Mory saw the black face before him, the one thing in the world, and his love for it filled his heart with the desire to feel it breaking under his hands.

They traded great blows. They had no notion of defense. They broke each other as they would have broken stone, with the instinct of three long years in the Deep Cut to compel their arms and shoulders.

O'Mory felt the pain growing in his body like grass. He felt the blades like arrows in his chest and the roots fingering his vitals. But his brain sang as he saw that the negro's blood was red. He swung without moving his feet, again and again and again, until his arms had acquired a rhythm. And through the room, which had once more grown silent, he heard the voice of Hogan catching it for him, giving his hands truth. "Wa-a-ay up! . . . Heavy . . . Down! Wa-a-ay up! . . . Heavy . . . Down!" Over and over. And the sting in his forearms was like the taste of the sledge. But he was hammering rock that would not break. He knew that it would never break and his heart sang with laughter and he was glad.

He saw in Jay-Jay's face a change coming slowly, as if his understanding had been lighted from the same fire. All at once the broken lips of both men grinned covertly at each other. For a few blows they continued from the pure joy of it. Then, as at a word, they held back their arms, stepped together, and shook hands.

Jouncy little Hogan laughed. He came leaping down on his bowlegs with his old Hessian high over his head. He baptized them both with stinging whiskey and gave them the drum to drink from, first the negro, then the Irishman. As the two drank, there was silence. And in the silence all men heard a different sound.

It came from the open door, from the frosted night, from the spot where the Great Dipper was suspended over the cleft in the mountain ridge. It was the sound of water. It was the sound of a small trickle of water finding its way down the tumble bay beside the double flight of locks.

But for a moment the Irishmen and the negroes did not understand what it could be. It was not until Roberts, the engineer who had given their labor form, cried suddenly, "It's the water coming through!" that they knew.

But they stood still. They heard his feet pounding down to the bridge-head, they heard the broken note in his voice, they saw the rodsman and the axemen and the cooks running after him, but they stood still, with a queer wonder in their eyes.

Some smiled, some simply stood with open mouths. O'Mory put his arm across Jay-Jay's shoulders and grinned at jouncy little Hogan.

He knew.

It meant the end of their long initiation. Roberts wanted to see it because of the shape it would have, the form for the picture he had seen in his mind's eye; the rodsman and the axemen because it meant the end of their stay in this piece of wilderness; the cooks because it meant that they would no longer have to wash the plates of Irishmen and negroes. To the contractors it would mean profit or loss. To the farmers in Ohio it would mean a decent price for wheat. To the merchants in the east it would mean cheap transportation. Even in New York City it would mean money in the hope chest of Tammany Hall.

His face lengthened.

But to himself and to these wild Irishers, who had chopped at stumps, who had shoveled where half of each shovelful ran back at their toes, who had wheeled barrows, who had had the sun on their backs, the frost in their feet, the cold wet against their bellies, the ague and fever in their lungs, who had had stumps to pull, and piles to drive in quicksand, limestone to blast, and rock to devil which no force but their own could loosen, this water meant the sweat they had dropped in labor; it meant the blood of life in their veins; it meant the end of the job.

He looked round on them. They were staring at him hopelessly. Even jouncy little Hogan was staring at him like a miserable lost dog.

He said to them, "It's finished, bhoys."

The one-eyed man asked over his quid hoarsely, "What'll we do now, O'Mory?"

And he said, "In Newport at the wedding Misther Fowler said that freight boats now are wanting crews. They'll hire ye on." He laughed. "What more do ye want? Ye've built the thing. It's whome to ye. I've had me offer already. I'm a captain as I stand. Hogan, will ye be a crewman? Ye're short. Ye won't have to duck for bridges."

Hogan's flat mouth opened, stretched, and grinned.

"Have a pull at me old Hissian, O'Mory, Captain, sir."

O'Mory felt a stiffness in the shoulders under his arm. He felt sorry for the black men now. They were sons of toil. It was the tradition in their blood.

"Niver mind, Jay-Jay," he said. "You can lick anny man but me. Let's go on out and see the thing."

They walked down to the Deep Cut, and they saw that the canal was more than half full. Coming slowly for the new banks, the water had made small impression till the lock gates dammed it. Then it had risen quickly. It made a dark, straight track along the towpath wall, stretching back into the still blackness of the stone. But even in that blackness it held reflections of the stars.

The moon was directly overhead. At their feet it swam upon the water. And all at once, in the white pool, the men saw a long, black shape.

"What's that?"

"It's a fish!" cried Hogan.

"It's too big a fish to be one."

"And I saw it, I'm telling you. I saw the tail of it,—and the fins of it,—and the mouth of it,—and the round eye as great as a whale."

The rodsman bent over. He was a man from Buffalo. As he looked, the long shape swam across the light again.

"It's a muskallonge," he said. "I've seen plenty since I came out here. They're handsome fish and grow to forty pounds."

"No!"

"Isn't he telling you?"

"How big is this one, would ye say, Misther Roberts?"

Roberts, who had drawn off to be by himself, came back. He too knew the fish.

"It's a muskallonge all right. I'd call it over thirty-five pounds."

"What do you suppose he's afther, now?"

The fish had approached the tumble bay. They could just make him out, estimating the water, and finning backward from it.

"I'll tell you," cried Roberts. "I'll work him through the locks, if he wants to go. O'Mory, you get over on that other gate. Take that lever and pull up; that opens the sluice."

He opened the gate on his side of the western flight.

The water sluiced through with a loud, thirsty swish, tumbled over the upper sill. In a moment the new plank of the floor had lost its gleam. The level began to rise in the inner chamber of the well. The men watched it silently. For the time they had forgotten the fish. They saw the water fingering the walls, they saw the stars borne upon the surface. A pool was made to float a boat, higher, higher, until it rose above the cill, to the level in the Deep Cut.

Roberts leaned on the balance beam of the nearest gate, and O'Mory, with Jay-Jay to help him, opened the other. They swung silently through the water and the moon floated in between, and under the moon went the fish. The men cheered. The gates were closed.

"He knows a thing or two," cried Hogan, delightedly, peering over.

Moving slowly, the men followed the water down, and through each lock the fish swam composedly eastward, and at the very end he slid out on the Rochester level. He hung for a moment at the bottom of the tumble bay, over which the waste water was already gaining considerable volume. Then he wheeled with a smooth eddy and disappeared. The silent men watched him go.

O'Mory heard a man crying softly behind him. He turned. It was the boy, Peter. He understood.

He laid his hand upon the boy's shoulder.

"I'll be needing another hand on me boat besides Hogan. Will ye sign on, Peter, lad?"

The boy nodded, and the growing roar of the water on the tumble bay mastered all other sounds.

7

"There has been a fine young man"

THE sun was going down into a blazing pile of clouds.

In Rochester, little knots of people came out on the streets, and converged slowly on the four corners. Little by little, they moved on down Exchange Street, past Child's Basin, to the end of the aqueduct, mounted the arched bridge over the canal, and looked down on the manœuvrings of the packet boat, *Young Lion of the West.*

The four matched blacks that the United States Mail Line had furnished for the occasion were hauling the boat out from the dock. On the bow, a gentleman in a tailed coat and high black stock and dove-colored waistcoat raised his arm as if to hail a boat.

"Who comes there?" he cried.

There was no one coming, but at his words the eight companies of

militia lining the canal raised rifles. No shot was fired. And the gentleman
on the boat dropped his arm futilely.

Someone on the bridge asked his neighbor, "Is that Mr. Child?"

"I take it for Levi Ward."

"Can't be. He ain't tall enough, mister. It's Jesse Hawley, I believe."

The sun was in their eyes. Due west of them the canal ran between lines
of brand-new warehouses, broken by the Presbyterian house and an occasional back garden wall. Here and there freight boats were tied up;
from a few, smoke issued white against the deepening shadows. The boater
of one was putting a pair of horses aboard the bow. On another a woman
in a blue calico dress was gathering in a line of wash, stuffing her arms
with red and white. The eastern wind at their backs was drawing the scent
of the flour mills across the river.

"What are they doing with that-there boat?" asked a wondering farmer.

"To-morrow they're going to welcome Clinton's boats from Buffalo.
They're practising."

"What for?"

"My Lord! Don't you know that the canal's been opened past Lockport?
Clinton's on the way."

"I heard a powerful lot of cannon-shooting this morning," said the farmer,
reminiscently picking in his ear. "Then in about two hours I heard a powerful lot more. I calculated some kind of a party was getting up."

He got his jaws working again on his tobacco. Behind him a woman
tittered.

"Mamie," she whispered, "that man don't know the canal's been
opened."

"No!"

"Can you credit it?"

Titters again. The farmer leaned his overboned wrists comfortably on the
rail.

"Now they're bringing the boat back to the edge," he announced. "Appears to me they ain't doing nothing."

"They're practising for to-morrow."

"What for?" he repeated.

"It's the celebration. The canal's finished, you see." The speaker was
elaborately patient and polite for the sake of the tittering behind him.

"Well, I don't see what they got to celebrate for. It's done, ain't it?" He
let out a deep breath. After a moment he spat in the canal. A frog by the
dock gulped and dove. When he came up, he swam cautiously with only
his eyes out of water. "Me," said the farmer, "I've got milking to get home
to."

He moved slowly away. One of the young women pulled her jacket
collar up over her neck,—a provocative small collar that served no useful
purpose,—and took the farmer's place. The man who had answered him
stole a glance sidewise at pinked cheeks. The crowd jostled them. When
the crowd moved back his arm was through hers. The hair under the
shawled bonnet was golden and smelled of Rose Cardine.

"So long, Mamie." The other girl moved down the bridge.

Jerry, come back from the wedding of his assistant, Collins, turned for
home. The sun was down behind the western hill. Shadows were moving

towards the Exchange Street bridge, shadows of boats, of the other bridges; they were clear-cut enough to show the peeled white maple stick with which a skinny old tatterdemalion fished aimlessly from the butment of the Sophia bridge.

"Hello, Mr. Fowler," he said as Jerry came abreast.

Jerry grinned at the impudent old face.

"Evening, Randy. Caught anything?"

The old man twitched his improvised rod, and eyed the cork bobbet halfway down the cotton twine.

"Not exactly," he said.

Jerry sat down beside him.

"I don't see what you expect to catch here, Randy."

"It ain't so much what I expect as what I might catch."

He eyed the cork sagaciously.

"Of course, you know there's sunfish, Mr. Fowler. And I've heard tell of perch. It ain't exactly that, though. They tell me the canal's been opened up to Erie. There's fish in them lakes—muskallonge and catfish—big around as a man's leg. One of them might want to take a trip this way."

"What are you using for bait?"

The old man drew up his line. There was a yard of it below the bobbet, then a hook, and tied to the hook with a piece of thread a monstrous whiteheaded beetle.

"That's a funny thing to use for bait," Jerry said.

"Fishing's like getting wedded. It ain't so much what a man uses fishing; it's how the things go together."

He tossed the beetle back into the water, laid down the rod, and looked round. His sharp old eyes twinkled.

"You look kind of bothered. How's business these days?"

"More than we can handle. Right now I've got three boats building."

"Any packets?"

"No. Hunter and I've decided to stick to freight. Two of these new ones are for us."

"Where's Hunter these days?" asked the old man. "I ain't seen him around the town for quite a spell."

"He's in Troy. He's making connections for our line. It's our idea to carry through-transportation—nothing else."

Randy slapped his skinny knee.

"You're right, by grummit! That's what I'd do was I in the business. Thank God I ain't. A man in business ain't got time to think."

He touched his pole again with sensitive fingers.

"Now I calculate, Mr. Fowler, you don't never get no time for fishing, do you?"

Jerry grinned.

"I guess you don't get any time for work, do you, Randy?"

Randy cackled.

"No. Never did. Never had the knack for it anyway."

Jerry's face sobered. He stared down the canal. The color was fading on the water. At the mouth of the aqueduct he saw the *Young Lion of the West* tied by for the night. The riflemen were filing off. Over the river the pale green light was dying out of the sky as if it were being sucked through an invisible flue in the zenith, and a purple shadow was slowly mounting.

The old man followed his gaze.

"They've gone home to supper." He hawked a spit into the canal. "Here they go making a noise and taking off their hats, just in practise! It makes me sick. Even if there was a fish here, what chance would a man have with it?" He paused.

"I don't deny it's a great work; but I wish they wouldn't keep a-hammering it against a man's ear-leather. I'm getting so's I can't digest my food. Every time I get me a meal I come outside and somebody says it's the longest canal in the world, or it's got the most locks. A man says the pyramids don't compare to it. Hell—it ain't what a man makes counts; it's how he uses what he's made."

The *Montezuma,* packet, coming in from Schenectady, swung into the basin on the left, and the swirl of its rudder caught a final gleam from the sunset.

Randy said, "You going to be in on this-here celebration, now? You done a lot towards this-here ditch, that ain't even got fish into it."

Jerry looked at his hands. The palms were calloused, the fingers hooked from gripping tools.

"I'm not going."

"I'll bet they never asked you," grumbled the old man.

"They did, though, Randy."

"Did they? Well!" The old man stared incredulously at Jerry. "And you sit here and mean to tell me you don't want to go to it? By grummit! You're a queer one. Nobody would have to ask *me* twicet. Shaking celebrated people by the hand. Getting into the paper. And you say, No!"

He lifted his pole and slapped it down again.

"Why not?" he demanded.

"I don't know," said Jerry. "I didn't feel like it. It didn't seem to count."

He looked at the little old man, but the back was turned to him, rigid with disgust.

"I've stayed too long." Jerry smiled. "I want to get home. Good night, Randy."

"Good night," said Randy. "Guess I'll stay here a spell. I might as well drowned this beetle anyways."

As Jerry walked slowly through the shadow, he lifted his face to the west, where the afterglow was rising in its curious fan. His face wore a strange sadness—the work was over, all done. He was doing his own work now.

As he passed a boat beside the towpath, he heard a woman humming a tune, and he peered through the cabin windows. The woman was sitting before the little stove, her head bent under the yellow light of the lamp. Though her face was hidden, he could see that she was young. She was all alone. He paused a moment to watch her, and the tune floated out to him, old and wistful in this new town.

> "O Missis Mouse, are you within?
> *Sing-song paddy woncha ky-me-o!*
> O yes, kind sir, I sit and spin. . . ."

She shifted her right shoulder enough for him to see the baby on her lap, the small pink legs entirely naked, froglike, drawing up at her touch. She was changing its cloths. In spite of himself, Jerry lingered.

She finished putting on the clean cloths, and with her left hand unfastened her dress. Her face bent lower as she lifted the child. Her shoulders seemed to stiffen. Then they relaxed. Her head came up, and her lips opened, and she sang with closed eyes.

> "There has been a fine young man.
> *Sing-song paddy woncha ky-me-o.*"

She had a broad, homely face, strong with youth. Her shoulder jerked as the child wrenched the nipple; but her voice gained fullness.

> "And I will have him if I can."

Her lids lifted heavily and her eyes met Jerry's. He started to draw back, but her face was so placid that he realized she had not seen him. The cabin was impregnable, and she saw his face without knowing what it was. And then she smiled, and her head bent down, and she shifted the burden against her breast, and he saw the thin black hair of the baby's head.

He drew carefully back and tiptoed on his way. He had finished his work on the canal, but people were living on it already. People were being born on it. They did not notice his work, any more than he noticed the culverts under the streets. Aqueducts, marsh-trunks, they took for granted. Traffic had taken possession of his building. He felt tired, and yet vaguely comforted. He was going home.

When he climbed the steps from the towpath to the Washington Street bridge, he looked back. The boat was invisible against the dock, for the curtains were drawn over the outside windows; the only mark of its existence were the two faint gleams of light upon the towpath planking. The woman was alone there, with her child, the man and the driver no doubt had gone off for a night's carouse in Parthy's house or Billy Lusk's saloon. The business was done, and yet the business was just beginning; but it was what he had worked towards.

He ought to be getting home. It was late. The children would be asleep, and Mary must have been saving supper for him for two hours. Two months had passed since he had brought her home from Halleck's; two months of uneventful living. He had not been away from home one single evening till last night of dancing at Young Collins's wedding. He drew a long breath. Time he was home.

He turned down the street. House lights on Spring Street shone dimly behind curtains. At the corner of Eagle, he saw his own house through the trees. A lamp was burning in the kitchen window. As his heels rang against the new boardwalk, the kitchen door opened. Mary was looking out. She knew his step.

His hand on the fence railing trembled under his weight as he vaulted over. The light was a guide to him across the lot.

"The boat was late, Mary."

"I've saved supper," she said quietly.

They went in silently. While he washed at the sink she put the food upon the table. They sat down together. The kitchen seemed quiet and peaceful to him after the last night's dancing. He watched her face as she ate with him.

"Was it a nice wedding, Jerry?"

"Yes. A nice girl. I wished you could have come."

"The house seemed lonely."

Her voice trembled.

He pushed his plate back on the table.

"What did you do all yesterday?"

"I went down town."

"Yes?"

"To Mr. Burr's."

She looked at him.

"I bought something. Have you finished, Jerry?"

"Yes. I've finished."

"I'll show you what I bought."

He rose slowly. She took his hand to lead him into the little parlor. She had left a candle lighted there, and as he looked at the new spinning wheel he felt her fingers stir on his palm.

He turned to her then. The color came up in her cheeks. Her lips curved, the upper trembling a little.

"It's a fine wheel, isn't it, Jerry? It was hard to pick it out, but Mr. Burr was pleasant, helping me get the very one I wanted."

He could not speak, but he felt her draw close.

"Jerry, I never told you. But back in Albany that day I saw you long before you saw me. I saw you clean across the river, getting on the ferry. I saw you talking with Mr. Bennet. It seemed yours was the only face I saw I wasn't feared of. And when you looked at me, I felt my heart rise up. And all the time you stood near by with the ferryman, I held my breath for hope. Hoping you would buy my papers, Jerry. And when you went away I wanted to cry. And when you came back along the dock, I didn't dare to look at you. . . ." His hand squeezed hers, but the hurt gladdened her.